The Norton Anthology of English Literature

SEVENTH EDITION
VOLUME 2B
THE VICTORIAN AGE

THE MIDDLE AGES
David / Donaldson

THE SIXTEENTH CENTURY
Logan / Greenblatt

THE EARLY SEVENTEENTH CENTURY
Lewalski / Adams

THE RESTORATION AND THE EIGHTEENTH CENTURY
Lipking / Monk

THE ROMANTIC PERIOD
Abrams / Stillinger

THE VICTORIAN AGE
Christ / Ford

THE TWENTIETH CENTURY
Stallworthy / Daiches

The Norton Anthology of English Literature

SEVENTH EDITION
VOLUME 2B
THE VICTORIAN AGE

Carol T. Christ

PROFESSOR OF ENGLISH AND EXECUTIVE VICE CHANCELLOR AND PROVOST,
UNIVERSITY OF CALIFORNIA AT BERKELEY

M. H. Abrams, *General Editor*

CLASS OF 1916 PROFESSOR OF ENGLISH EMERITUS,
CORNELL UNIVERSITY

Stephen Greenblatt, *Associate General Editor*

HARRY LEVIN PROFESSOR OF LITERATURE,
HARVARD UNIVERSITY

W • W • NORTON & COMPANY • *New York* • *London*

Copyright © 2000, 1993, 1990, 1986, 1979, 1974, 1968, 1962
by W. W. Norton & Company, Inc.

Since this page cannot legibly accommodate all the copyright notices, page A-64
constitutes an extension of the copyright page.

The text of this book is composed in Fairfield Medium
with the display set in Bernhard Modern.
Composition by Binghamton Valley Composition.
Manufacturing by R. R. Donnelley & Sons, Inc.
Cover illustration: William Holman Hunt, *The Lady of Shalott* (detail). Wadsworth
Atheneum, Hartford, The Ella Gallup Sumner and Mary Catlin Sumner Collection Fund.

Editor: Julia Reidhead
Developmental Editor/Associate Managing Editor: Marian Johnson
Production Manager: Diane O'Connor
Manuscript and Project Editors: Candace Levy, Barry Katzen, David Hawkins,
Ann Tappert, Will Rigby
Editorial Assistant: Christa Grenawalt
Permissions Manager: Kristin Sheerin
Cover and Text Design: Antonina Krass
Art Research: Neil Ryder Hoos

Library of Congress Cataloging-in-Publication Data

The Norton anthology of English literature / M. H. Abrams, general
editor : Stephen Greenblatt, associate general editor. — 7th ed.
p.   cm.
Includes bibliographical references and index.

ISBN 0-393-97486-3 (v. 1). — ISBN 0-393-97487-1 (pbk.: v. 1).
ISBN 0-393-97490-1 (v. 2). — ISBN 0-393-97491-X (pbk.: v. 2).

1. English literature.   2. Great Britain—Literary collections.
I. Abrams, M. H. (Meyer Howard), 1912–   .   II. Greenblatt, Stephen, 1943–   .
III.   Title: Anthology of English literature.
PR1109.A2   1999
820.8—dc21   99-43298
CIP

Volume 2B, The Victorian Age:
ISBN 0-393-97569-X (pbk.)

W. W. Norton & Company, Inc., 500 Fifth Avenue, New York, N.Y. 10110
www.wwnorton.com

W. W. Norton & Company Ltd., 10 Coptic Street, London WC1A 1PU

2 3 4 5 6 7 8 9 0

Contents

Preface to the Seventh Edition

The outpouring of English literature overflows all boundaries, including the capacious boundaries of *The Norton Anthology of English Literature*. But these pages manage to contain many of the most remarkable works written in English during centuries of restless creative effort. We have included epic poems and short lyrics; love songs and satires; tragedies and comedies written for performance on the commercial stage and private meditations meant to be perused in silence; prayers, popular ballads, prophecies, ecstatic visions, erotic fantasies, sermons, short stories, letters in verse and prose, critical essays, polemical tracts, several entire novels, and a great deal more. Such works generally form the core of courses that are designed to introduce students to the history of English literature, a history not only of gradual development, continuity, and dense internal echoes, but also of radical contingency, sudden change, and startling innovation.

One of the joys of literature in English is its spectacular abundance. Even from within the geographical confines of Great Britain and Ireland, where the majority of texts brought together in this collection originated, there are more than enough distinguished and exciting works to fill the pages of this anthology many times over. The abundance is all the greater if one takes, as the editors of these volumes do, a broad understanding of the term *literature*. The meaning of the term has in the course of several centuries shifted from the whole body of writing produced in a particular language to a subset of that writing consisting of works that claim special attention because of their formal beauty or expressive power. But any individual text's claim to attention is subject to constant debate and revision; established texts are jostled both by new arrivals and by previously neglected claimants; and the boundaries between the literary and whatever is thought to be "non-literary" are constantly challenged and redrawn. The heart of this collection consists of poems, plays, and prose fiction, but these categories are themselves products of ongoing historical transformations, and we have included many texts that call into question any conception of literature as denoting only a limited set of particular kinds of writing.

The designation "English" provides some obvious limits to the unwieldy, unstable, constantly shifting field of literature, but these limits are themselves in constant flux, due in part to the complexity of the territory evoked by the term (as explained in our appendix on "Geographical Nomenclature") and in part to the multinational, multicultural, and hugely expansive character of the language. As Geoffrey Nunberg's informative essay "The Persistence of English," commissioned for this Seventh Edition, makes clear, the variations in the forms of the spoken language that all go by the name of

English are so great as to call into question the very notion of a single tongue, and the complex history and diffusion of the language have helped ensure that its literature is enormous. In the momentous process that transformed England into Great Britain and eventually into the center of a huge empire, more and more writers from outside England, beginning with the strong Irish and Scottish presence in the eighteenth century and gradually fanning out into the colonies, were absorbed into "English literature." Moreover, English has constantly interacted with other languages and has been transformed by this interaction. The scope of the cross-currents may be gauged by our medieval section, which includes selections in Old Irish and Middle Welsh, along with works by Bede, Geoffrey of Monmouth, Wace, and Marie de France—all of them authors living in the British Isles writing in languages other than English. Their works are important in themselves and also provide cultural contexts for understanding aspects of what we have come to think of as "English literature." Certain literary texts—many of them included in these volumes—have achieved sufficient prominence to serve as widespread models for other writers and as objects of enduring admiration, and thus to constitute a loose-boundaried canon. But just as there have never been academies in English-speaking countries established to regulate the use of language, so too there have never been firm and settled guidelines for canonizing particular texts. English literature as a field arouses not a sense of order but what the poet Yeats calls "the emotion of multitude."

The term "English Literature" in our title designates two different things. First, it refers to all the literary productions of a particular part of the world: the great preponderance of the works we include were written by authors living in England, Scotland, Wales, and Ireland. Second, it refers to literary works in the English language, a language that has extended far beyond the boundaries of its point of origin. Following the lead of most college courses, we have separated off, for purposes of this anthology, English literature from American literature, but in the selections for the latter half of the twentieth century we have incorporated a substantial number of texts by authors from other countries.

The linguistic mobility and cultural intertwining reflected in these twentieth-century texts are not new. It is fitting that among the first works in this anthology is *Beowulf*, a powerful epic written in the Germanic language known as Old English about a singularly restless Scandinavian hero, an epic newly translated for this edition by the Irish poet Seamus Heaney. Heaney, who was awarded the Nobel Prize for Literature in 1995, is one of the contemporary masters of English literature, but it would be potentially misleading to call him an "English poet," for he was born in Northern Ireland and is not in fact English. It would be still more misleading to call him a "British poet," as if his having been born in a country that was part of the British Empire were the most salient fact about the language he speaks and writes or the culture by which he was shaped. What does matter is that the language in which Heaney writes is English, and this fact links him powerfully with the authors assembled in these volumes, a linguistic community that stubbornly refuses to fit comfortably within any firm geographical or ethnic or national boundaries. So too, to glance at authors and writings included in the anthology, in the sixteenth century William Tyndale, in exile in the Low Countries and inspired by German religious reformers, translated the New

Testament from Greek and thereby changed the course of the English language; in the seventeenth century Aphra Behn touched her readers with a story that moves from Africa, where its hero is born, to South America, where she may have witnessed some of the tragic events she describes; and early in the twentieth century Joseph Conrad, born in Ukraine of Polish parents, wrote in eloquent English a celebrated novella whose vision of European empire was trenchantly challenged at the century's end by the Nigerian-born writer in English, Chinua Achebe.

A vital literary culture is always on the move. The Seventh Edition of *The Norton Anthology of English Literature* has retained the body of works that have traditionally been taught as the principal glories of English literature, but many of our new selections reflect the fact that the *national* conception of literary history, the conception by which English Literature meant the literature of England or at most of Great Britain, has begun to give way to something else. Writers like William Butler Yeats (born in Dublin), Hugh MacDiarmid (born in Dumfriesshire, Scotland), Virginia Woolf (born in London), and Dylan Thomas (born in Swansea, Wales) are now being taught, and are here anthologized, alongside such writers as Nadine Gordimer (born in the Transvaal, South Africa), Alice Munro (born in Wingham, Ontario), Derek Walcott (born on Saint Lucia in the West Indies), Chinua Achebe (born in Ogidi, Nigeria), and Salman Rushdie (born in Bombay, India). English literature, like so many other collective enterprises in our century, has ceased to be principally the product of the identity of a single nation; it is a global phenomenon.

A central feature of *The Norton Anthology of English Literature*, established by its original editors, was a commitment to provide periodic revisions in order to take advantage of newly recovered or better-edited texts, reflect scholarly discoveries and the shifting interests of readers, and keep the anthology in touch with contemporary critical and intellectual concerns. To help us honor this commitment we have, as in past years, profited from a remarkable flow of voluntary corrections and suggestions proposed by students, as well as teachers, who view the anthology with a loyal but critical eye. Moreover, we have again solicited and received detailed information on the works actually assigned, proposals for deletions and additions, and suggestions for improving the editorial matter, from over two hundred reviewers from around the world, almost all of them teachers who use the books in a course. In its evolution, then, this anthology has been the product of an ongoing collaboration among its editors, teachers, and students.

The active participation of an engaged community of readers has been crucial as the editors grapple with the challenging task of retaining (and indeed strengthening) the selection of more traditional texts even while adding many texts that reflect the transformation and expansion of the field of English studies. The challenge is heightened by the wish to keep each volume manageable, in size and weight, so that students will actually carry the book to class. The final decisions on what to include were made by the editors, but we were immeasurably assisted, especially in borderline cases, by the practical experience and the detailed opinions of teachers and scholars.

In addition to the new translation of *Beowulf* and to the greatly augmented global approach to twentieth-century literature in English, several other features of this Seventh Edition merit special mention. We have greatly expanded the selection of writing by women in all of the historical periods. The extraordinary work of scholars in recent years has recovered dozens of significant authors who had been marginalized or neglected by a male-dominated literary tradition and has deepened our understanding of those women writers who had managed, against considerable odds, to claim a place in that tradition. The First Edition of the *Norton Anthology* was ahead of its time in including six women writers; this Seventh Edition includes sixty, of whom twenty-one are newly added and twenty are reselected or expanded. Poets and prose writers whose names were scarcely mentioned even in the specialized literary histories of earlier generations—Isabella Whitney, Aemilia Lanyer, Lady Mary Wroth, Elizabeth Cary, Margaret Cavendish, Mary Leapor, Anna Letitia Barbauld, Charlotte Smith, Letitia Elizabeth Landon, and many others—now appear in the company of their male contemporaries. There are in addition three complete long prose works by women: Aphra Behn's *Oroonoko,* Mary Shelley's *Frankenstein,* and Virginia Woolf's *A Room of One's Own.*

The novel is, of course, a stumbling block for an anthology. The length of many great novels defies their incorporation in any volume that hopes to include a broad spectrum of literature. At the same time it is difficult to excerpt representative passages from narratives whose power often depends upon amplitude or upon the slow development of character or upon the on-rushing urgency of the story. Therefore, better to represent the remarkable achievements of novelists, the publisher is making available, in inexpensive and well-edited Norton Anthology Editions, a range of novels, including Jane Austen's *Pride and Prejudice,* Charles Dickens's *Hard Times,* Charlotte Brontë's *Jane Eyre,* and Emily Brontë's *Wuthering Heights.*

A further innovation in the Seventh Edition is our inclusion of new and expanded clusters of texts that resonate with one another culturally and thematically. Using the "Victorian Issues" section long featured in *The Norton Anthology of English Literature* as our model, we devised for each period groupings that serve to suggest some ways in which the pervasive concepts, images, and key terms that haunt major literary works can often be found in other written traces of a culture. Hence, for example, the adventures of Edmund Spenser's wandering knights resonate with the excerpts from Elizabethan travel accounts brought together in "The Wider World": Frobisher's violent encounters with the Eskimos of Baffin Island, Drake's attempt to lay claim to California, Amadas and Barlowe's idealizing vision of the Indians as the inhabitants of the Golden Age, and Hariot's subtle attempt to analyze and manipulate native beliefs. Similarly, the millenarian expectations voiced in the texts grouped in "The French Revolution and the 'Spirit of the Age' " helped shape the major writings of poets from William Blake to Percy Bysshe Shelley, while the historical struggles reflected in texts by Jawaharlal Nehru and others in "The Rise and Fall of Empire" echo in the fiction of Chinua Achebe, V. S. Naipaul, and J. M. Coetzee. We supplement the clusters for each period with several more topical groupings of texts and copious illustrations on the *Norton Anthology* Web site.

Period-by-Period Revisions

The scope of the revisions we have undertaken, the most extensive in the long publishing history of *The Norton Anthology of English Literature,* can be conveyed more fully by a list of some of the principal additions.

The Middle Ages. Better to represent the complex multilingual situation of the period, the section has been reorganized and divided into three parts: Anglo-Saxon England, Anglo-Norman England, and Middle English Literature of the Fourteenth and Fifteenth Centuries. Nearly fifteen years in the making, Seamus Heaney's translation of *Beowulf* comes closer to conveying the full power of the Anglo-Saxon epic than any existing rendering and will be of major interest as well to students of modern poetry. The selection of Anglo-Saxon poems has also been augmented by *The Wife's Lament.* We have added a new section, Anglo-Norman England, which provides a key bridge between the Anglo-Saxon period and the time of Chaucer, highlighting a cluster of texts that trace the origins of Arthurian romance. This section includes selections from the chronicle account of the Norman conquest; legendary histories by Geoffrey of Monmouth, Wace, and Layamon; Marie de France's *Lanval* (a Breton lay about King Arthur's court, here in a new verse translation by Alfred David), along with two of her fables; a selection from the *Ancrene Riwle* (Rule for Anchoresses); and two Celtic narratives: the Irish *Exile of the Sons of Uisliu* and the Welsh *Lludd and Lleuelys.* To Chaucer's works we have added *The Man of Law's Epilogue* and *Troilus's Song;* we have added to the grouping of Late Middle English lyrics and strengthened the already considerable selection from the revelations of the visionary anchoress Julian of Norwich; and we have included for the first time a work by Robert Henryson, *The Cock and the Fox.*

The Sixteenth Century. Shakespeare's magnificent comedy of cross-dressing and cross-purposes, *Twelfth Night,* is for the first time included in the *Norton Anthology,* providing a powerful contrast with his bleakest tragedy, *King Lear.* The raucous *Tunning of Elinour Rumming* has been added to Skelton's poems and the somber *Stand whoso list* to Wyatt's, while Gascoigne is now represented by his poem *Woodmanship.* Additions in poetry and prose works have similarly been made to Roger Ascham, Henry Howard, Earl of Surrey, Sir Walter Ralegh, Fulke Greville, Samuel Daniel, Thomas Campion, and Thomas Nashe. Along with the grouping of travel texts described above, another new cluster, "Literature of the Sacred," brings together contrasting Bible translations; writings by William Tyndale and Richard Hooker; Anne Askew's account, smuggled from the Tower, of her interrogation and torture, along with the martyrologist John Foxe's account of her execution; selections from the Book of Common Prayer and the Book of Homilies; and an Elizabethan translation of John Calvin's influential account of predestination. In addition to Anne Askew, another Elizabethan woman writer, Isabella Whitney, makes her appearance in the *Norton Anthology,* along with a new selection of texts by Mary Herbert and a newly added speech and letters by Queen Elizabeth.

The Early Seventeenth Century. In response to widespread demand and to our own sense of the work's commanding importance, both in its own time and in the history of English literature, we have for the first time included the whole of Milton's *Paradise Lost.* Other substantial works that newly appear in this section include Ben Jonson's *Masque of Blackness* and Andrew Marvell's *Upon Appleton House,* extensive selections from Elizabeth Cary's *Tragedy of Mariam,* and poetry and prose by Aemilia Lanyer and Margaret Cavendish. Additions have been made to the works of John Donne, Jonson, Lady Mary Wroth, George Herbert, Henry Vaughan, Richard Crashaw, Robert Herrick, and John Suckling. The "Voices of the War" cluster, introduced in the last edition, now includes Anna Trapnel's narrative of her eventful voyage from London to Cornwall; and a new cluster, "The Science of Self and World," brings together meditative texts, poems, and essays by Francis Bacon, Martha Moulsworth, Robert Burton, Rachel Speght, Sir Thomas Browne, Izaak Walton, and Thomas Hobbes.

The Restoration and the Eighteenth Century. John Gay's *The Beggar's Opera*—familiar to modern audiences as the source of Bertolt Brecht's *Threepenny Opera*—makes its appearance in the *Norton Anthology,* along with William Hogarth's illustration of a scene from the play. Hogarth's "literary" graphic art is represented by his satiric *Marriage A-la-Mode.* Two new clusters of texts enable readers to engage more fully with key controversies in the period. "Debating Women: Arguments in Verse" presents the war between the sexes in spirited poems by Jonathan Swift, Lady Mary Wortley Montagu, Alexander Pope, Anne Finch, Anne Ingram, and Mary Leapor. The period's sexual politics is illuminated as well in added texts by Samuel Pepys, John Wilmot, Second Earl of Rochester, and Aphra Behn. "Slavery and Freedom" brings together the disquieting exchange on the enslavement of African peoples between Ignatius Sancho and Laurence Sterne, along with Olaudah Equiano's ground-breaking history of his own enslavement. The narrative gifts of Frances Burney, whose long career spans this period and the next, are newly presented by six texts, including her famous, harrowing account of her mastectomy.

The Romantic Period. The principal changes here center on the greatly increased representation of women writers in the period: Mary Robinson and Letitia Elizabeth Landon are included for the first time, and there are substantially increased selections by Anna Letitia Barbauld, Charlotte Smith, Joanna Baillie, Dorothy Wordsworth, and Felicia Hemans; to Mary Wollstonecraft's epochal *Vindication of the Rights of Women,* we have now added a selection from her *Letters Written in Sweden.* Conjoined with Mary Shelley's *Frankenstein,* presented here in its entirety, these texts restore women writers, once marginalized in literary histories of the period, to the significant place they in fact occupied. A new thematic cluster focusing on the period's cataclysmic event, the French Revolution, brings together texts in prose and verse by Richard Price, Edmund Burke, Mary Wollstonecraft, Thomas Paine, Elhanan Winchester, Joseph Priestley, William Black, Robert Southey, William Wordsworth, Samuel Taylor Coleridge, and Percy Bysshe Shelley. The selection of poems by the peasant poet John Clare has been expanded and is printed in a new text prepared for this edition. We have also added to Sir Walter Scott the introductory chapter of his *Heart of Midlothian,* and to William Wordsworth his long and moving lyrical ballad *The Thorn.*

The Victorian Age. The important novelist, short story writer, and biographer Elizabeth Gaskell makes her appearance in the *Norton Anthology,* along with two late-nineteenth-century poets, Michael Field and Mary Elizabeth Coleridge. Rudyard Kipling's powerful story *The Man Who Would Be King* is a significant new addition, as is the selection from Oscar Wilde's prison writings, *De Profundis*. Dickens's somber reflection *A Visit to Newgate* has been added. There are new texts in the selections of many authors as well, including John Henry Cardinal Newman, Elizabeth Barrett Browning, Alfred, Lord Tennyson, Elizabeth Gaskell, George Eliot, Dante Gabriel Rossetti, William Morris, and Gerard Manley Hopkins. Bernard Shaw's play *Mrs. Warren's Profession* has been moved to its chronological place in this section. New texts have also been added to the "Victorian Issues" clusters on evolution, industrialism, and the debate about gender.

The Twentieth Century. The principal addition here, in length and in symbolic significance, is Chinua Achebe's celebrated novel *Things Fall Apart,* presented in its entirety, and, with Joseph Conrad's *Heart of Darkness* and Virginia Woolf's *A Room of One's Own,* the third complete prose work in this section. But there are many other changes as well, in keeping with a thoroughgoing rethinking of this century's literary history. We begin with Thomas Hardy (now shown as fiction writer as well as poet) and Joseph Conrad, both liminal figures poised between two distinct cultural worlds. These are followed by groupings of texts that articulate some of the forces that helped pull these worlds asunder. A cluster on "The Rise and Fall of Empire" brings together John Ruskin, John Hobson, the Easter Proclamation of the Irish Republic, Richard Mulcahy, James Morris, Jawaharlal Nehru, and Chinua Achebe, and these texts of geo-political crisis in turn resonate with "Voices from World War I" and "Voices from World War II," both sections newly strengthened by prose texts. We have added selections to E. M. Forster, James Joyce, and T. S. Eliot, among others, and for the first time present the work of the West Indian writer Jean Rhys and the Irish poet Paul Muldoon. Samuel Beckett is now represented by the complete text of his masterful tragicomedy, *Endgame.* Above all, the explosion of writing in English in "postcolonial" countries around the world shapes our revision of this section, not only in our inclusion of Achebe but also in new texts by Derek Walcott, V. S. Naipaul, Anita Desai, Les Murray, J. M. Coetzee, Eavan Boland, Alice Munro, and Salman Rushdie. Seamus Heaney's works, to which another poem has been added, provide the occasion to look back again to the beginning of these volumes with Heaney's new translation of *Beowulf.* This translation is a reminder that the history of literature is not a straightforward sequence, that the most recent works can double back upon the distant past, and that the words set down by men and women who have crumbled into dust can speak to us with astonishing directness.

Editorial Procedures

The scope of revisions to the editorial apparatus in the Seventh Edition is the most extensive ever undertaken in *The Norton Anthology of English Literature.* As in past editions, period introductions, headnotes, and annotation are designed to give students the information needed, without imposing an interpretation. The aim of these editorial materials is to make the anthology self-sufficient, so that it can be read anywhere—in a coffeehouse, on a bus, or under a tree. In this edition, this apparatus has been thoroughly revised in response to new scholarship. The period introductions and many headnotes have been either entirely or substantially rewritten to be more helpful to students, and all the Selected Bibliographies have been thoroughly updated.

Several new features reflect the broadened scope of the selections in the anthology. The new essay, "The Persistence of English" by Geoffrey Nunberg, Stanford University and Xerox Palo Alto Research Center, explores the emergence and spread of English and its apparent present-day "triumph" as a world language. It provides a lively point of departure for the study of literature in English. The endpaper maps have been reconceived and redrawn. New timelines following each period introduction help students place their reading in historical and cultural context. So that students can explore literature as a visual medium, the anthology introduces visual materials from several periods—Hogarth's *Marriage A-la-Mode*, engravings by Blake, and Dante Gabriel Rossetti's illustrations for poems by Tennyson, Christina Rossetti, and Rossetti himself. These illustrations can be supplemented by the hundreds of images available on Norton Topics Online, the Web companion to the *Norton Anthology*.

Each volume of the anthology includes an appendix, "Poems in Process," which reproduces from manuscripts and printed texts the genesis and evolution of a number of poems whose final form is printed in that volume. Each volume contains a useful section on "Poetic Forms and Literary Terminology," much revised in the Seventh Edition, as well as brief appendices on the intricacies of English money, the baronage, and religions. A new appendix, "Geographic Nomenclature," has been added to clarify the shifting place-names applied to regions of the British Isles.

Students, no less than scholars, deserve the most accurate texts available; in keeping with this policy, we continue to introduce improved versions of the selections where available. In this edition, for example, in addition to Seamus Heaney's new verse translation of *Beowulf*, we introduce Alfred David's new verse translation of Marie de France's *Lanval*, the Norton/Oxford text of *Twelfth Night*; and Jack Stillinger's newly edited texts of the poems of John Clare. To ease a student's access, we have normalized spelling and capitalization in texts up to and including the Victorian period to follow the conventions of modern English; we leave unaltered, however, texts in which modernizing would change semantic or metrical qualities and those texts for which we use specially edited versions (identified in a headnote or footnote); these include Wollstonecraft's *Vindication,* William Wordsworth's *Ruined Cottage* and *Prelude,* Dorothy Wordsworth's *Journals,* the verse and prose of P. B. Shelley and Keats, and Mary Shelley's *Frankenstein.* In The Twentieth Century, we have restored original spelling and punctuation to selections retained from the previous edition in the belief that the authors' choices, when they pose no difficulties for student readers, should be respected.

We continue other editorial procedures that have proved useful in the past. After each work, we cite (when known) the date of composition on the left and the date of first publication on the right; in some instances, the latter is followed by the date of a revised edition for which the author was responsible. We have used square brackets to indicate titles supplied by the editors for the convenience of readers. Whenever a portion of a text has been omitted, we have indicated that omission with three asterisks. If the omitted portion is important for following the plot or argument, we have provided a brief summary within the text or in a footnote. We have extended our longstanding practice of providing marginal glossing of single words and short phrases from medieval and dialect poets (such as Robert Burns) to all the poets in the anthology. Finally, we have adopted a bolder typeface and redesigned the page, so as to make the text more readable.

The Course Guide to Accompany "The Norton Anthology of English Literature," by Katherine Eggert and Kelly Hurley, University of Colorado at Boulder, based on an earlier version by Alfred David, Indiana University, has been thoroughly revised and expanded; it contains detailed syllabi for a variety of approaches to the course, teaching notes on individual authors, periods, and works, study and essay questions, and suggested ways to integrate the printed texts with material on the Norton Web site. A copy of the *Guide* may be obtained on request from the publisher.

Two cardinal innovations, one print and one electronic, greatly increase the anthology's flexibility: The book is now available in both the traditional two-volume format, in both clothbound and paperback versions, and in a new six-volume paperback version comprised of volume 1A, *The Middle Ages*, volume 1B, *The Sixteenth Century / The Early Seventeenth Century*, volume 1C, *The Restoration and the Eighteenth Century*, volume 2A, *The Romantic Period*, volume 2B, *The Victorian Age*, and volume 2C, *The Twentieth Century*. By maintaining the same pagination as in the original two volumes, the six-volume format offers a more portable option for students in survey courses, while the individual volumes can be used in courses dealing with periods of English literature.

Extending beyond the printed page, the Norton Topics Online Web Site (*www.wwnorton.com/nael*) augments the anthology's already broad representation of the sweep of English literature, and greatly enlarges the representation of graphic materials that are relevant to literary studies. For students who wish to extend their exploration of literary and cultural contexts, the Web site offers a huge range of related texts, prepared by the anthology editors, and by Myron Tuman, University of Alabama, and Philip Schwyzer, University of California, Berkeley. An ongoing venture, the Web site currently offers twenty-one thematic clusters—three per period—of texts and visual images, cross-referenced to the anthology, together with overviews, study explorations, and annotated links to related sites. The site also includes an electronic archive of over 185 texts to supplement the anthology. In addition, the Audio Companion to *The Norton Anthology of English Literature* is available without charge upon request by teachers who adopt the anthology. It consists of two compact discs of readings by the authors of the works represented in the anthology, readings of poems in Old and Middle English and in English dialects, and performances of poems that were written to be set to music.

The editors are deeply grateful to the hundreds of teachers worldwide who have helped us to improve *The Norton Anthology of English Literature*. A list of the advisors who prepared in-depth reviews and of the instructors who replied to a detailed questionnaire follows on a separate page, under Acknowledgments. The editors would like to express appreciation for their assistance to Tiffany Beechy (Harvard University), Mitch Cohen (Wissenschaftskolleg zu Berlin), Sandie Byrne (Oxford University), Sarah Cole

(Columbia University), Dianne Ferriss (Cornell University), Robert Folken-flik (University of California, Irvine), Robert D. Fulk (Indiana University), Andrew Gurr (The University of Reading), Wendy Hyman (Harvard University), Elissa Linke (Wissenschaftskolleg zu Berlin), Joanna Lipking (Northwestern University), Linda O'Riordan (Wissenschaftskolleg zu Berlin), Ruth Perry (M.I.T.), Leah Price (Harvard University), Ramie Targoff (Yale University), and Douglas Trevor (Harvard University). The editors give special thanks to Paul Leopold, who drafted the appendix on Geographic Nomenclature and revised the appendix on Religions in England, and to Philip Schwyzer (University of California, Berkeley), whose wide-ranging contributions include preparing texts and study materials for the Web site, assisting with the revision of numerous headnotes, and updating appendices on the British baronage and British money. We also thank the many people at Norton who contributed to the Seventh Edition: Julia Reidhead, who served not only as the inhouse supervisor but also as an unfailingly wise and effective collaborator in every aspect of planning and accomplishing this Seventh Edition; Marian Johnson, developmental editor, who kept the project moving forward with a remarkable blend of focused energy, intelligence, and common sense; Candace Levy, Ann Tappert, Barry Katzen, David Hawkins, and Will Rigby, project and manuscript editors; Anna Karvellas and Kirsten Miller, Web site editors; Diane O'Connor, production manager; Kristin Sheerin, permissions manager; Toni Krass, designer; Neil Ryder Hoos, art researcher; and Christa Grenawalt, editorial assistant and map coordinator. All these friends provided the editors with indispensable help in meeting the challenge of representing the unparalleled range and variety of English literature.

M. H. ABRAMS
STEPHEN GREENBLATT

Acknowledgments

Among our many critics, advisors, and friends, the following were of especial help toward the preparation of the Seventh Edition, either with advice or by providing critiques of particular periods of the anthology: Judith H. Anderson (Indiana University), Paula Backsheider (Auburn University), Elleke Boehmer (Leeds University), Rebecca Brackmann (University of Illinois), James Chandler (University of Chicago), Valentine Cunningham (Oxford University), Lennard Davis (SUNY Binghamton), Katherine Eggert (University of Colorado), P. J. C. Field (University of Wales), Vincent Gillespie (Oxford University), Roland Greene (University of Oregon), A. C. Hamilton (Queen's University), Emrys Jones (Oxford University), Laura King (Yale University), Noel Kinnamon (Mars Hill College), John Leonard (University of Western Ontario), William T. Liston (Ball State University), F. P. Lock (Queen's University), Lee Patterson (Yale University), Jahan Ramazani (University of Virginia), John Regan (Oxford University), John Rogers (Yale University), Herbert Tucker (University of Virginia), Mel Wiebe (Queen's University).

The editors would like to express appreciation and thanks to the hundreds of teachers who provided reviews: Porter Abbott (University of California, Santa Barbara), Robert Aguirre (University of California, Los Angeles), Alan Ainsworth (Houston Community College Central), Jesse T. Airaudi (Baylor University), Edward Alexander (University of Washington), Michael Alexander (University of St. Andrews), Gilbert Allen (Furman University), Jill Angelino (George Washington University), Linda M. Austin (Oklahoma State University), Sonja S. Baghy (State University of West Georgia), Vern D. Bailey (Carleton College), William Barker (Fitchburg State University), Carol Barret (Northridge Campus, Austin Community College), Mary Barron (University of North Florida), Jackson Barry (University of Maryland), Dean Bevan (Baker University), Carol Beran (St. Mary's College), James Biester (Loyola University, Chicago), Nancy B. Black (Brooklyn College), Alan Blackstock (Wharton Community Junior College), Alfred F. Boe (San Diego State University), Cheryl D. Bohde (McLennan Community College), Karin Boklund-Lagopoulou (Aristotle University of Thessaloniki), Scott Boltwood (Emory and Henry College), Troy Boone (University of California, Santa Cruz), James L. Boren (University of Oregon), Ellen Brinks (Princeton University), Douglas Bruster (University of Texas, San Antonio), John Bugge (Emory University), Maria Bullon-Fernandez (Seattle University), John J. Burke (University of Alabama), Deborah G. Burks (Ohio State University), James Byer (Western Carlonia University), Gregory Castle (Arizona State University), Paul William Child (Sam Houston State University), Joe R. Christopher (Tarleton State University), A. E. B. Coldiron (Towson State University), John Constable (University of Leeds), C. Abbott Conway (McGill University), Patrick Creevy (Mississippi State University), Thomas M. Curley (Bridgewater State College), Clifford Davidson (Western Michigan University), Craig R. Davis (Smith College), Frank Day (Clemson University), Marliss Desens (Texas Tech University), Jerome Donnelly (University of Central Florida), Terrance Doody (Rice University), Max Dorsinville (McGill University), David Duff (University of Aberdeen), Alexander Dunlop (Auburn University), Richard J. DuRocher (St. Olaf College), Dwight Eddins (University of Alabama), Caroline L. Eisner (George Washington University), Andrew Elfenbein (University of Minnesota), Doris Williams Elliott (University of Kansas), Nancy S. Ellis (Mississippi State University), Kevin Eubanks (University of Tennessee), Gareth Euridge (Denison University), Deanna Evans (Bemidji State University), Julia A. Fesmire (Middle Tennessee State University), Michael Field (Bemidji State University), Judith L. Fisher (Trinity University), Graham Forst (Capilano College), Marilyn Francus (West Virginia University), Susan S. Frisbie (Santa Clara University), Shearle Furnish (West Texas A&M University), Arthur Ganz (City College of CUNY; The New School), Stephanie Gauper (Western Michigan University), Donna A. Gessell (North Georgia College and State University), Reid Gilbert (Capilano College), Jonathan C. Glance (Mercer University), I. Gopnik (McGill University), William Gorski (Northwestern State University of Louisiana), Roy Gottfried (Vanderbilt University), Timothy Gray (University of California, Santa Barbara), Patsy Griffin (Georgia Southern University), M. J. Gross (Southwest Texas State University), Gillian Hanson (University of Houston), Linda Hatchel (McLennan Community College), James Heldman (Western Kentucky University), Stephen Hemenway (Hope College), Michael Hennessy (Southwest Texas State University), Peter C. Herman (San Diego State University), James Hirsh (Georgia State University), Diane Long Hoeveler (Marquette University), Jerrold E. Hogle (University of Arizona), Brian Holloway (College of West Virginia), David Honick (Bentley College), Catherine E. Howard (University of Houston), David Hudson (Augsburg College), Steve Hudson (Portland Community College), Clark Hulse (University of Illinois, Chicago), Jefferson Hunter (Smith College), Vernon Ingraham (University of Massachusetts, Dartmouth), Thomas Jemielity (University of Notre Dame), R. Jothiprakash (Wiley College), John M. Kandl (Walsh University), David Kay (University of Illinois, Urbana-Champaign), Richard Kelly (University of Tennessee), Elizabeth Keyser (Hollins College), Gail Kienitz (Wheaton College), Richard Knowles (University of Wisconsin, Madison), Deborah Knuth (Colgate University), Albert Koinm (Sam Houston State University), Jack Kolb (University of California, Los Angeles), Valerie Krishna (City College, CUNY), Richard Kroll (University of California, Irvine), Jameela Lares (University of Southern Mississippi), Beth Lau (California State University, Long Beach), James Livingston (Northern Michigan University), Christine Loflin (Grinnell College), W. J. Lohman Jr. (University of Tampa), Suzanne H. MacRae (University of Arkansas, Fayettesville), Julia Maia (West Valley College), Sarah R. Marino (Ohio Northern University), Louis Martin (Elizabethtown College), Irene Martyniuk (Fitchburg State College), Frank T. Mason (University of South Florida), Mary Massirer (Baylor University), J. C. C. Mays (University College, Dublin), James McCord (Union College), Brian McCrea (University of Florida), Claie McEachern (University of California, Los Angeles), Joseph McGowan (University of San Diego), Alexander Menocal (University of North Florida), John Mercer (Northeastern State University),

Teresa Michals (George Mason University), Michael Allen Mikolajezak (University of St. Thomas), Jonathan Middlebrook (San Francisco State University), Sal Miroglotta (John Carroll University), James H. Morey (Emory University), Maryclaire Moroney (John Carroll University), William E. Morris (University of South Florida), Charlotte C. Morse (Virginia Commonwealth University), Alan H. Nelson (University of California, Berkeley), Jeff Nelson (University of Alabama, Huntsville), Richard Newhauser (Trinity University), Ashton Nichols (Dickinson College), Noreen O'Connor (George Washington University), Peter Okun (Davis and Elkins College), Nora M. Olivares (San Antonio College), Harold Orel (University of Kansas), Sue Owen (University of Sheffield), Diane Parkin-Speer (Southwest Texas State University), C. Patton (Texas Tech University), Paulus Pimoma (Central Washington University), John F. Plummer (Vanderbilt University), Alan Powers (Bristol Community College), William Powers (Michigan Technological University), Nicholas Radel (Furman University), Martha Rainbolt (DePauw University), Robert L. Reid (Emory and Henry College), Luke Reinsina (Seattle Pacific University), Cedric D. Reverand II (University of Wyoming), Mary E. Robbins (Georgia State University), Mark Rollins (Ohio University, Athens), Charles Ross (Purdue University), Donelle R. Ruwe (Fitchburg State College), John Schell (University of Central Florida), Walter Scheps (SUNY Stony Brook), Michael Schoenfeldt (University of Michigan), Robert Scotto (Baruch College), Asha Sen (University of Wisconsin, Eau Claire), Lavina Shankar (Bates College), Michael Shea (Southern Connecticut State University), R. Allen Shoaf (University of Florida), Michael N. Stanton (University of Vermont), Massie C. Stinson Jr. (Longwood College), Andrea St. John (University of Miami), Donald R. Stoddard (Anne Arundel Community College), Joyce Ann Sutphen (Gustavas Adolphus College), Max K. Sutton (University of Kansas), Margaret Thomas (Wilberforce University), John M. Thompson (U.S. Naval Academy), Dinny Thorold (University of Westminster), James B. Twitchell (University of Florida), J. K. Van Dover (Lincoln University), Karen Van Eman (Wayne State University), Paul V. Voss (Georgia State University), Leon Waldoff (University of Illinois, Urbana-Champaign), Donald J. Weinstock (California State University, Long Beach), Susan Wells (Temple University), Winthrop Wetherbee (Cornell University), Thomas Willard (University of Arizona), J. D. Williams (Hunter College), Charles Workman (Stanford University), Margaret Enright Wye (Rockhurst College), R. O. Wyly (University of Southern Florida), James J. Yoch (University of Oklahoma), Marvin R. Zirker (Indiana University, Bloomington).

The Persistence of English

If you measure the success of a language in purely quantitative terms, English is entering the twenty-first century at the moment of its greatest triumph. It has between 400 and 450 million native speakers, perhaps 300 million more who speak it as a second language—well enough, that is, to use it in their daily lives—and somewhere between 500 and 750 million who speak it as a foreign language with various degrees of fluency. The resulting total of between 1.2 billion and 1.5 billion speakers, or roughly a quarter of the world's population, gives English more speakers than any other language (though Chinese has more native speakers). Then, too, English is spoken over a much wider geographical area than any other language and is the predominant lingua franca of most fields of international activity, such as diplomacy, business, travel, science, and technology.

But figures like these can obscure a basic question: what exactly do we mean when we talk about the "English language" in the first place? There is, after all, an enormous range of variation in the forms of speech that go by the name of English in the various parts of the world—or often, even within the speech of a single nation—and it is not obvious why we should think of all of these as belonging to a single language. Indeed, there are some linguists who prefer to talk about "world Englishes," in the plural, with the implication that these varieties may not have much more to unite them than a single name and a common historical origin.

To the general public, these reservations may be hard to understand; people usually assume that languages are natural kinds like botanical species, whose boundaries are matters of scientific fact. But as linguists observe, there is nothing in the forms of English themselves that tells us that it is a single language. It may be that the varieties called "English" have a great deal of vocabulary and structure in common and that English-speakers can usually manage to make themselves understood to one another, more or less (though films produced in one part of the English-speaking world often have to be dubbed or subtitled to make them intelligible to audiences in another). But there are many cases where we find linguistic varieties that are mutually intelligible and grammatically similar, but where speakers nonetheless identify separate languages—for example, Danish and Norwegian, Czech and Slovak, or Dutch and Afrikaans. And on the other hand, there are cases where speakers identify varieties as belonging to a single language even though they are linguistically quite distant from one another: the various "dialects" of Chinese are more different from one another than the Latin offshoots that we identify now as French, Italian, Spanish, and so forth.

Philosophers sometimes compare languages to games, and the analogy is apt here, as well. Trying to determine whether American English and British English or Dutch and Afrikaans are "the same language" is like trying to determine whether baseball and softball are "the same game"—it is not something you can find out just by looking at their rules. It is not surprising, then, that linguists should throw up their hands when someone asks them to determine on linguistic grounds alone whether two varieties belong to a single language. That, they answer, is a political or social determination, not a linguistic one, and they usually go on to cite a well-known quip: "a language is just a dialect with an army and a navy."

There is something to this remark. Since the eighteenth century, it has been widely believed that every nation deserved to have its own language, and declarations of political independence have often been followed by declarations of linguistic independence. Until recently, for example, the collection of similar language varieties that were spoken in most of central Yugoslavia was regarded as a single language, Serbo-Croatian, but once the various regions became independent, their inhabitants began to speak of Croatian, Serbian, and Bosnian as separate languages, even though they are mutually comprehensible and grammatically almost identical.

The English language has avoided this fate (though on occasion it has come closer to breaking up than most people realize). But the unity of a language is never a foregone conclusion. In any speech-community, there are forces always at work to create new differences and varieties: the geographic and social separation of speech-communities, their distinct cultural and practical interests, their contact with other cultures and other languages, and, no less important, a universal fondness for novelty for its own sake, and a desire to speak differently from one's parents or the people in the next town. Left to function on their own, these centrifugal pressures can rapidly lead to the linguistic fragmentation of the speech-community. That is what happened, for example, to the vulgar (that is, "popular") Latin of the late Roman Empire, which devolved into hundreds or thousands of separate dialects (the emergence of the eight or ten standard varieties that we now think of as the Romance languages was a much later development).

Maintaining the unity of a language over an extended time and space, then, requires a more or less conscious determination by its speakers that they have certain communicative interests in common that make it worthwhile to try to curb or modulate the natural tendency to fragmentation and isolation. This determination can be realized in a number of ways. The speakers of a language may decide to use a common spelling system even when dialects become phonetically distinct, to defer to the same set of literary models, to adopt a common format for their dictionaries and grammars, or to make instruction in the standard language a part of the general school curriculum, all of which the English-speaking world has done to some degree. Or in some other places, the nations of the linguistic community may establish academies or other state institutions charged with regulating the use of the language, and even go so far as to publish lists of words that are unacceptable for use in the press or in official publications, as the French government has done in recent years. Most important, the continuity of the language rests on speakers' willingness to absorb the linguistic and cultural influences of other parts of the linguistic community.

THE EMERGENCE OF THE ENGLISH LANGUAGE

To recount the history of a language, then, is not simply to trace the development of its various sounds, words, and constructions. Seen from that exclusively linguistic point of view, there would be nothing to distinguish the evolution of Anglo-Saxon into the varieties of modern English from the evolution of Latin into modern French, Italian, and so forth—we would not be able to tell, that is, why English continued to be considered a single language while the Romance languages did not. We also have to follow the play of centrifugal and centripetal forces that kept the language always more or less a unity—the continual process of creation of new dialects and varieties, the countervailing rise of new standards and of mechanisms aimed at maintaining the linguistic center of gravity.

Histories of the English language usually put its origin in the middle of the fifth century, when several Germanic peoples first landed in the place we now call England and began to displace the local inhabitants, the Celts. There is no inherent linguistic reason why we should locate the beginning of the language at this time, rather than with the Norman Conquest of 1066 or in the fourteenth century, say, and in fact the determination that English began with the Anglo-Saxon period was not generally accepted until the nineteenth century. But this point of view has been to a certain extent self-justifying, if only because it has led to the addition of Anglo-Saxon works to the canon of English literature, where they remain. Languages are constructions over time as well as over space.

Wherever we place the beginnings of English, though, there was never a time when the language was not diverse. The Germanic peoples who began to arrive in England in the fifth century belonged to a number of distinct tribes, each with its own dialect, and tended to settle in different parts of the country—the Saxons in the southwest, the Angles in the east and north, the Jutes (and perhaps some Franks) in Kent. These differences were the first source of the distinct dialects of the language we now refer to as Anglo-Saxon or Old English. As time went by, the linguistic divisions were reinforced by geography and by the political fragmentation of the country, and later, through contact with the Vikings who had settled the eastern and northern parts of England in the eighth through eleventh centuries.

Throughout this period, though, there were also forces operating to consolidate the language of England. Over the centuries, cultural and political dominance passed from Northumbria in the north to Mercia in the center and then to Wessex in the southwest, where a literary standard emerged in the ninth century, owing in part to the unification of the kingdom and in part to the singular efforts of Alfred the Great (849–899), who encouraged literary production in English and himself translated Latin works into the language. The influence of these standards and the frequent communication between the regions worked to level many of the dialect differences. There is a striking example of the process in the hundreds of everyday words derived from the language of the Scandinavian settlers, which include *dirt*, *lift*, *sky*, *skin*, *die*, *birth*, *weak*, *seat*, and *want*. All of these spread to general usage from the northern and eastern dialects in which they were first introduced, an indication of how frequent and ordinary were the contacts among the

Anglo-Saxons of various parts of the country—and initially, between the Anglo-Saxons and the Scandinavians themselves. (By contrast, the Celtic peoples that the Anglo-Saxons had displaced made relatively few contributions to the language, apart from place-names like *Thames, Avon,* and *Dover.*)

The Anglo-Saxon period came to an abrupt end with the Norman Conquest of 1066. With the introduction of a French-speaking ruling class, the written use of English was greatly reduced for 150 years. English did not reappear extensively in written records until the beginning of the thirteenth century, and even then it was only one of the languages of a multilingual community: French was widely used for another two hundred years or so (Parliament was conducted in French until 1362), and Latin was the predominant language of scholarship until the Renaissance. The English language that re-emerged in this period was considerably changed from the language of Alfred's period. Its grammar was simplified, continuing a process already under way before the Conquest, and its vocabulary was enriched by thousands of French loan words. Not surprisingly, given the preeminent role of French among the elite, these included the language of government (*majesty, state, rebel*); of religion (*pastor, ordain, temptation*); of fashion and social life (*button, adorn, dinner*); and of art, literature, and medicine (*painting, chapter, paper, physician*). But the breadth of French influence was not limited to those domains; it also provided simple words like *move, aim, join, solid, chief, clear, air,* and *very*. All of this left the language sufficiently different from Old English to warrant describing it with the name of Middle English, though we should bear in mind that language change is always gradual and that the division of English into neat periods is chiefly a matter of scholarly convenience.

Middle English was as varied a language as Old English was: Chaucer wrote in *Troilus and Criseyde* that "ther is so gret diversite in Englissh" that he was fearful that the text would be misread in other parts of the country. It was only in the fifteenth century or so that anything like a standard language began to emerge, based in the speech of the East Midlands and in particular of London, which reflected the increased centralization of political and economic power in that region. Even then, though, dialect differences remained strong; the scholar John Palsgrave complained in 1540 that the speech of university students was tainted by "the rude language used in their native countries [i.e., counties]," which left them unable to express themselves in their "vulgar tongue."

The language itself continued to change as it moved into what scholars describe as the Early Modern English period, which for convenience's sake we can date from the year 1500. Around this time, it began to undergo the Great Vowel Shift, as the long vowels engaged in an intricate dance that left them with new phonetic values. (In Chaucer's time, the word *bite* had been pronounced roughly as "beet," *beet* as "bate," *name* as "nahm," and so forth.) The grammar was changing as well; for example, the pronoun *thee* began to disappear, as did the verbal suffix-*eth*, and the modern form of questions began to emerge: in place of "See you that house?" people began to say "Do you see that house?" Most significantly, at least so far as contemporary observers were concerned, the Elizabethans and their successors coined thousands of new words based on Latin and Greek in an effort to make English an adequate replacement for Latin in the writing of philosophy, science, and literature. Many of these words now seem quite ordinary to us—for example, *accommodation, frugal, obscene, premeditated,* and *submerge,* all of which are recorded for the first time in Shakespeare's works. A large proportion of these linguistic experiments, though, never gained a foothold in the language—for example, *illecebrous* for "delicate," *deruncinate* for "to weed," *obtestate* for "call on," or Shakespeare's *disquantity* to mean "diminish." Indeed, some contemporaries ridiculed the pretension and obscurity of these "inkhorn words" in terms that sound very like modern criticisms of bureaucratic and corporate jargon—the rhetorician Thomas Wilson wrote in 1540 of the writers who affected "outlandish English" such that "if some of their mothers were alive, they were not able to tell what they say." But this effect was inevitable: The additions to the standard language that made it a suitable vehicle for art and scholarship could only increase the linguistic distance between the written language used by the educated classes and the spoken language used by other groups.

DICTIONARIES AND RULES

These were essentially growing pains for the standard language, which continued to gain ground in the sixteenth and seventeenth centuries, abetted by a number of developments: the ever-increasing dominance of London and the Southeast, the growth in social and geographic mobility, and in particular the introduction and spread of print, which led both to higher levels of literacy and schooling and to the gradual standardization of English spelling. But even as this process was going on, other developments were both creating new distinctions and investing existing ones with a new importance. For one thing, people were starting to pay more attention to accents based on social class, rather than region, an understandable preoccupation as social mobility increased and speech became a more important indicator of social background. Not surprisingly, the often imperfect efforts of the emerging middle class to speak and dress like their social superiors occasioned some ridicule; Thomas Gainsford wrote in 1616 of the "foppish mockery" of commoners who tried to imitate gentlemen by altering "habit, manner of life, conversation, and even their phrase of speech." Yet even the upper classes were paying more attention to speech as a social indicator than they had in previous ages; as one writer put it, "it is a pitty when a Noble man is better distinguished from a Clowne by his golden laces, than by his good language." (Shakespeare plays on this theme in *1 Henry IV* [3.1.250, 257–58] when he has Hotspur tease his wife for swearing too daintily, which makes her sound like "a comfitmaker's wife," rather than "like a lady as thou art," who swears with "a good mouth-filling oath.")

Over the course of the seventeenth and eighteenth centuries, print began to exercise a paradoxical effect on the perception of the language: even as it was serving to codify the standard, it was also making people more aware of variation and more anxious about its consequences. This was largely the result of the growing importance of print, as periodicals, novels, and other new forms became increasingly influential in shaping public opinion, together with the perception that the contributors to the print discourse were drawn from a wider range of backgrounds than in previous periods. As Samuel Johnson wrote: "The present age . . . may be styled, with great propriety, the Age of Authors; for, perhaps, there was never a time when men of all degrees of ability, of every kind of education, of every profession and employment were posting with ardor so general to the press. . . . "

This anxiety about the language was behind the frequent eighteenth-century lamentations that English was "unruled," "barbarous," or, as Johnson put it, "copious without order, and energetick without rule." Some writers looked for a remedy in public institutions modeled on the French Academy. This idea was advocated by John Dryden, Daniel Defoe, Joseph Addison, and most notably by Jonathan Swift, in a 1712 pamphlet called *A Proposal for Correcting, Improving, and Ascertaining* [i.e., "fixing"] *the English Tongue*, which did receive some official attention from the Tory government. But the idea was dropped as a Tory scheme when the Whigs came to power two years later, and by the middle of the eighteenth century, there was wide agreement among all parties that an academy would be an unwarranted intervention in the free conduct of public discourse. Samuel Johnson wrote in the Preface to his *Dictionary* of 1775 that he hoped that "the spirit of English liberty will hinder or destroy" any attempt to set up an academy; and the scientist and radical Joseph Priestly called such an institution "unsuitable to the genius of a *free nation*."

The rejection of the idea of an academy was to be important in the subsequent development of the language. From that time forward, it was clear that the state was not to play a major role in regulating and reforming the language, whether in England or in the other nations of the language community—a characteristic that makes English different from many other languages. (In languages like French and German, for example, spelling reforms can be introduced by official commissions charged with drawing up rules which are then adopted in all textbooks and official publications, a procedure that would be unthinkable in any of the nations of the English-speaking world.) Instead, the task of determining standards was left to private citizens, whose authority rested on their ability to gain general public acceptance.

The eighteenth century saw an enormous growth in the number of grammars and handbooks, which formulated most of the principles of correct English that, for better or worse, are still with us today—the rules for using *who* and *whom*, for example, the injunction against constructions like "very unique," and the curious prejudice against the split infinitive. Even more important was the development of the modern English dictionary. Before 1700, English speakers had to make do with alphabetical lists of "hardwords," a bit like the vocabulary improvement books that are still frequent today; it was only in the early 1700s that scholars began to produce anything like a comprehensive dictionary in the modern sense, a process that culminated in the publication of Samuel Johnson's magisterial *Dictionary* of 1755. It would be hard to argue that these dictionaries did much in fact to reduce variation or to arrest the process of linguistic change (among the words that Johnson objected to, for example, were *belabor, budge, cajole, coax, doff, gambler,* and *job,* all of which have since become part of the standard language). But they did serve to ease the sense of linguistic crisis, by providing a structure for describing the language and points of reference for resolving disputes about grammar and meaning. And while both the understanding of language and the craft of lexicography have made a great deal of progress since Johnson's time, the form of the English-language dictionary is still pretty much as he laid it down. (In this regard, Johnson's *Dictionary* is likely to present a much more familiar appearance to a modern reader than his poetry or periodical essays.)

THE DIFFUSION OF ENGLISH

The Modern English period saw the rise of another sort of variation, as well, as English began to spread over an increasingly larger area. By Shakespeare's time, English was displacing the Celtic languages in Wales, Cornwall, and Scotland, and then in Ireland, where the use of Irish was brutally repressed on the assumption—in retrospect a remarkably obtuse one—that people who were forced to become English in tongue would soon become English in loyalty as well. People in these new parts of the English-speaking world—a term we can begin to use in this period, for English was no longer the language of a single country—naturally used the language in accordance with their own idiom and habits of thought and mixed it with words drawn from the Celtic languages, a number of which eventually entered the speech of the larger linguistic community, for example, *baffle, bun, clan, crag, drab, galore, hubbub, pet, slob, slogan,* and *trousers.*

The development of the language in the New World followed the same process of differentiation. English settlers in North America rapidly developed their own characteristic forms of speech. They retained a number of words that had fallen into disuse in England (*din, clod, trash,* and *fall* for *autumn*) and gave old words new senses (like *corn,* which in England meant simply "grain," or *creek,* originally "an arm of the sea"). They borrowed freely from the other languages they came in contact with. By the time of the American Revolution, the colonists had already taken *chowder, cache, prairie,* and *bureau* from French; *noodle* and *pretzel* from German; *cookie, boss,* and *scow* and *yankee* from the Dutch; and *moose, skunk, chipmunk, succotash, toboggan,* and *tomahawk* from various Indian languages. And they coined new words with abandon. Some of these answered to their specific needs and interests—for example, *squatter, clearing, foothill, watershed, congressional, sidewalk*—but there were thousands of others that had no close connection to the American experience as such, many of which were ultimately adopted by the other varieties of English. *Belittle, influential, reliable, comeback, lengthy, turn down, make good*—all of these were originally American creations; they and other words like them indicate how independently the language was developing in the New World.

This process was repeated wherever English took root—in India, Africa, the Far East, the Caribbean, and Australia and New Zealand; by the late nineteenth century, English bore thousands of souvenirs of its extensive travels. From Africa (sometimes via Dutch) came words like *banana, boorish, palaver, gorilla,* and *guinea;* from the aboriginal languages of Australia came *wombat* and *kangaroo;* from the Caribbean languages came *cannibal, hammock, potato,* and *canoe;* and from the languages of India came *bangle, bungalow, chintz, cot, dinghy, jungle, loot, pariah, pundit,* and *thug.* And even lists like these are misleading, since they include only words that worked their way into the general English vocabulary and don't give a sense of the thousands of borrowings and coinages that were used only locally. Nor do they touch on the variation in grammar from one variety to the next. This kind of variation occurs everywhere, but it is particularly marked in regions like the Caribbean and Africa, where the local varieties of English are heavily influenced by English-based creoles—that is, language varieties that use English-based vocabulary with grammars largely derived from spoken—in this case, African—languages. This is the source, for example, of a number of the distinctive syntactic features of the variety used by many inner-city African Americans, like the "invariant *be*" of sentences like *We be living in Chicago*, which signals a state of affairs that holds for an extended period. (Some linguists have suggested that Middle English, in fact, could be thought of as a kind of creolized French.)

The growing importance of these new forms of English, particularly in America, presented a new challenge to the unity of the language. Until the eighteenth century, English was still thought of as essentially a national language. It might be spoken in various other nations and colonies under English control, but it was nonetheless rooted in the speech of England and subject to a single standard. Not surprisingly, Americans came to find this picture uncongenial, and when the United States first declared its independence from Britain, there was a strong sentiment for declaring that "American," too, should be recognized as a separate language. This was the view held by John Adams, Thomas Jefferson, and above all by America's first and greatest lexicographer, Noah Webster, who argued that American culture would naturally come to take a distinct form in the soil of the New World, free from what he described as "the old feudal and hierarchical establishments of England." And if a language was naturally the product and reflection of a national culture, then Americans could scarcely continue to speak "English." As Webster wrote in 1789: "Culture, habits, and language, as well as government should be national. America should have her own distinct from the rest of the world. . . ." It was in the interest of symbolically distinguishing American from English that Webster introduced a variety of spelling changes, such as *honor* and *favor* for *honour* and *favour*, *theater* for *theatre*, *traveled* for *travelled*, and so forth—a procedure that new nations often adopt when they want to make their variety of a language look different from its parent tongue.

In fact Webster's was by no means an outlandish suggestion. Even at the time of American independence, the linguistic differences between America and Britain were as great as those that separate many languages today, and the differences would have become much more salient if Americans had systematically adopted all of the spelling reforms that Webster at one time proposed, such as *wurd, reezon, tung, iz*, and so forth, which would ultimately have left English and American looking superficially no more similar than German and Dutch. Left to develop on their own, English and American might soon have gone their separate ways, perhaps paving the way for the separation of the varieties of English used in other parts of the world.

In the end, of course, the Americans and British decided that neither their linguistic nor their cultural and political differences warranted recognizing distinct languages. Webster himself conceded the point in 1828, when he entitled his magnum opus *An American Dictionary of the English Language*. And by 1862 the English novelist Anthony Trollope could write:

An American will perhaps consider himself to be as little like an Englishman as he is like a Frenchman. But he reads Shakespeare through the medium of his own vernacular, and has to undergo the penance of a foreign tongue before he can understand Molière. He separates himself from England in politics and perhaps in affection; but he cannot separate himself from England in mental culture.

ENGLISH AND ENGLISHNESS

This was a crucial point of transition, which set the English language on a very different course from most of the European languages, where the association of language and national culture was being made more strongly than ever before. But the detachment of English from Englishness did not take place overnight. For Trollope and his Victorian contemporaries, the "mental culture" of the English-speaking world was still a creation of England, the embodiment of English social and political values. "The English language," said G. C. Swayne in 1862, "is like the English constitution . . . and perhaps also the English Church, full of inconsistencies and anomalies, yet flourishing in defiance of theory." The monumental *Oxford English Dictionary* that the Victorians undertook was conceived in this patriotic spirit. In the words of Archbishop Richard Chevenix Trench, one of the guiding spirits of the OED project:

> We could scarcely have a lesson on the growth of our English tongue, we could scarcely follow upon one of its significant words, without having unawares a lesson in English history as well, without not merely falling upon some curious fact illustrative of our national life, but learning also how the great heart which is beating at the centre of that life, was being gradually shaped and moulded.

It was this conception of the significance of the language that led, too, to the insistence that the origin of the English language should properly be located in Anglo-Saxon, rather than in the thirteenth or fourteenth century, as scholars argued that contemporary English laws and institutions could be traced to a primordial "Anglo-Saxon spirit" in an almost racial line of descent, and that the Anglo-Saxon language was "immediately connected with the original introduction and establishment of their present language and their laws, their liberty, and their religion."

This view of English as the repository of "Anglo-Saxon" political ideals had its appeal in America, as well, particularly in the first decades of the twentieth century, when the crusade to "Americanize" recent immigrants led a number of states to impose severe restrictions on the use of other languages in schools, newspapers, and public meetings, a course that was often justified on the grounds that only speakers of English were in a position to fully appreciate the nuances of democratic thought. As a delegate to a New York State constitutional convention in 1916 put the point: "You have got to learn our language because that is the vehicle of the thought that has been handed down from the men in whose breasts first burned the fire of freedom at the signing of the Magna Carta."

But this view of the language is untenable on both linguistic and historical grounds. It is true that the nations of the English-speaking world have a common political heritage that makes itself known in similar legal systems and an (occasionally shaky) predilection for democratic forms of government. But while there is no doubt that the possession of a common language has helped to reinforce some of these connections, it is not responsible for them. Languages do work to create a common worldview, but not at such a specific level. Words like *democracy* move easily from one language to the next, along with the concepts they name—a good thing for the English-speaking world, since a great many of those ideals of "English democracy," as the writer calls it, owe no small debt to thinkers in Greece, Italy, France, Germany, and a number of other places, and those ideals have been established in many nations that speak languages other than English. (Thirteenth-century England was one of them. We should bear in mind that the Magna Carta that people sometimes like to mention in this context was a Latin document issued by a French-speaking king to French-speaking barons.) For that matter, there are English-speaking nations where democratic institutions have not taken root—nor should we take their continuing health for granted even in the core nations of the English-speaking world.

In the end, the view of English as the repository of Englishness has the effect of marginalizing or disenfranchising large parts of the English-speaking world, particularly those who do not count the political and cultural imposition of Englishness as an unmixed blessing. In most of the places where English has been planted, after all, it has had the British flag flying above it. And for many nations, it has been hard to slough off the sense of English as a colonial language. There is a famous passage in James Joyce's *Portrait of the Artist as a Young Man,* for example, where Stephen Daedelus says of the speech of an English-born dean, "The language in which we are speaking is his not mine," and there are still many people in Ireland and other parts of the English-speaking world who have mixed feelings about the English language: they may use and even love English, but they resent it, too.

Today the view of English as an essentially English creation is impossible to sustain even on purely linguistic grounds; the influences of the rest of the English-speaking world have simply been too great. Already in Trollope's time there were vociferous complaints in England about the growing use of Americanisms, a sign that the linguistic balance of payments between the two communities was tipping westward, and a present-day English writer would have a hard time producing a single paragraph that contained no words that originated in other parts of the linguistic community. Nor, what is more important, could you find a modern British or North American writer whose work was not heavily influenced, directly or indirectly, by the literature of the rest of the linguistic community, particularly after the extraordinary twentieth-century efflorescence of the English-language literatures of other parts of the world. Trying to imagine modern English literature without the contributions of writers like Yeats, Shaw, Joyce, Beckett, Heaney, Walcott, Lessing, Gordimer, Rushdie, Achebe, and Naipaul (to take only some of the writers who are included in this collection) is like trying to imagine an "English" cuisine that made no use of potatoes, tomatoes, corn, noodles, eggplant, olive oil, almonds, bay leaf, curry, or pepper.

THE FEATURES OF "STANDARD ENGLISH"

Where should we look, then, for the common "mental culture" that English-speakers share? This is always a difficult question to answer, partly because the understanding of the language changes from one place and time to the next, and partly because it is hard to say just what sorts of things languages are in the abstract. For all that we may want to think of the English-speaking world as a single community united by a common worldview, it is not a social group comparable to a tribe or people or nation—the sorts of groups that can easily evoke the first-person plural pronoun *we*. (Americans and Australians do not travel around saying "We gave the world Shakespeare," even though one might think that as paid-up members of the English-speaking community they would be entirely within their rights to do so.)

But we can get some sense of the ties that connect the members of the English-speaking community by starting with the language itself—not just in its forms and rules, but in the centripetal forces spoken of earlier. Forces like these are operating in every language community, it's true, but what gives each language its unique character is the way they are realized, the particular institutions and cultural commonalties which work to smooth differences and create a basis for continued communication—which ensure, in short, that English will continue as a single language, rather than break up into a collection of dialects that are free to wander wherever they will.

People often refer to this basis for communication as "Standard English," but that term is misleading. There are many linguistic communities that do have a genuine standard variety, a fixed and invariant form of the language that is used for certain kinds of communication. But that notion of the standard would be unsuitable to a language like English, which recognizes no single cultural center and has to allow for a great deal of variation even in the language of published texts. (It is rare to find a single page of an English-language novel or newspaper that does not reveal what nation it was written in.) What English does have, rather, is a collection of standard features—of spelling, of grammar, and of word use—which taken together ensure that certain kinds of communication will be more or less comprehensible in any part of the language community.

The standard features of English are as notable for what they don't contain as for what they do. One characteristic of English, for example, is that it has no standard pronunciation. People pronounce the language according to whatever their regional practice happens to be, and while certain pronunciations may be counted as "good" or "bad" according to local standards, there are no general rules about this, the way there are in French or Italian. (Some New Yorkers may be stigmatized for pronouncing words like *car* and *bard* as 'kah' and 'bahd', but roughly the same *r*-less pronunciation is standard in parts of the American South and in England, South Africa, Australia, and New Zealand.) In this sense, "standard English" exists only as a written language. Of course there is some variation in the rules of written English, as well, such as the American spellings that Webster introduced, but these are relatively minor and tend to date from earlier periods. A particular speech-community can pronounce the words *half* or *car* however it likes, but it can't unilaterally change the way the words are spelled. Indeed, this is one of the unappreciated advantages of the notoriously irregular English spelling system—it is so plainly *un*phonetic that there's no temptation to take it as codifying any particular spoken variety. When you want to define a written standard in a linguistic community that embraces no one standard accent, it's useful to have a spelling system that doesn't tip its hand.

The primacy of the written language is evident in the standard English vocabulary, too, if only indirectly. The fact is that English as such does not give us a complete vocabulary for talking about the world, but only for certain kinds of topics. If you want to talk about vegetables in English, for example, you have to choose among the usages common in one or another region: Depending on where you do your shopping, you will talk about *rutabagas*, *scallions*, and *string beans* or *Swedes*, *spring onions*, and *French beans*. That is, you can only talk about vegetables in your capacity as an American, an Englishman, or whatever, not in your capacity as an English-speaker in general. And similarly for fashion (*sweater* vs. *jumper*, *bobby pin* vs. *hair grip*, *vest* vs. *waistcoat*), for car parts (*hood* vs. *bonnet*, *trunk* vs. *boot*), and for food, sport, transport, and furniture, among many other things.

The English-language vocabulary is much more standardized, though, in other areas of the lexicon. We have a large common vocabulary for talking about aspects of our social and moral life—*blatant*, *vanity*, *smug*, *indifferent*, and the like. We have a common repertory of grammatical constructions and "signpost" expressions—for example, adverbs like *arguably*, *literally*, and *of course*—which we use to organize our discourse and tell readers how to interpret it. And there is a large number of common words for talking about the language itself—for example, *slang*, *usage*, *jargon*, *succinct*, and *literate*. (It is striking how many of these words are particular to English. No other language has an exact synonym for *slang*, for example, or a single word that covers the territory that *literate* covers in English, from "able to read and write" to "knowledgeable or educated.")

The common "core vocabulary" of English is not limited to these notions, of course—for example, it includes as well the thousands of technical and scientific terms that are in use throughout the English-speaking world, like *global warming* and *penicillin*, which for obvious reasons are not particularly susceptible to cultural variation. Nor would it be accurate to say that the core vocabulary includes all the words we use to refer to our language or to our social and moral life, many of which have a purely local character. But the existence of a core vocabulary of common English words, as fuzzy as it may prove to be, is an indication of the source of our cultural commonalities. What is notable about words like *blatant*, *arguably*, and *succinct* is that their meanings are defined by reference to our common literature, and in particular to the usage of what the eighteenth-century philosopher George Campbell described as "authors of reputation"—writers whose authority is determined by "the esteem of the public." We would not take the usage of Ezra Pound or Bernard Shaw as authoritative in deciding what words like *sweater* or *rutabaga* mean—they could easily have been wrong about either— but their precedents carry a lot of weight when we come to talking about the meaning of *blatant* and *succinct*. In fact the body of English-language "authors of reputation" *couldn't* be wrong about the meanings of words like these, since it is their usage by these authors that collectively determines what these words mean. And for purposes of defining these words it does not matter where a writer is from. The *American Heritage Dictionary*, for example, uses citations from the Irish writer Samuel Beckett to illustrate the meanings of *exasperate* and *impulsion*, from the Persian-born Doris Lessing, raised in southern Africa, to illustrate the meaning of *efface*, and from the Englishman E. M. Forster to illustrate the meaning of *solitude*; and dictionaries from other communities feel equally free to draw on the whole of English literature to illustrate the meanings of the words of the common vocabulary.

It is this strong connection between our common language and our common literature that gives both the language and the linguistic community their essential unity. Late in the eighteenth century, Samuel Johnson said that Britain had become "a nation of readers," by which he meant not just that people were reading more than ever before, but that participation in the written discourse of English had become in some sense constitutive of the national identity. And while the English-speaking world and its ongoing conversation can no longer be identified with a single nation, that world is still very much a community of readers in this sense. Historically, at least, we use the language in the same way because we read and talk about the same books—not *all* the same books, of course, but a loose and shifting group of works that figure as points of reference for our use of language.

This sense of the core vocabulary based on a common literature is intimately connected to the linguistic culture that English-speakers share—the standards, beliefs, and institutions that keep the various written dialects of the language from flying apart. The English dictionary is a good example. It is true that each part of the linguistic community requires its own dictionaries, given the variation in vocabulary and occasionally in spelling and the rest, but they are all formed on more or less the same model, which is very different from that of the French or the Germans. They all organize their entries in the same way, use the same form of definitions, include the same kind of information, and so on, to the point where we often speak of "*the* dictionary," as if the book were a single, invariant text like "the periodic table." By the same token, the schools in every English-speaking nation generally teach the same principles of good usage, a large number of which date from the grammarians of the eighteenth century. There are a few notable exceptions to this generality (Americans and most other communities outside England abandoned some time ago the effort to keep *shall* and *will* straight and seem to be none the worse off for it), but even in these cases grammarians justify their prescriptions using the same terminology and forms of argument.

THE CONTINUITY OF ENGLISH

To be sure, our collective agreement on standards of language and literature is never more than approximate and is always undergoing redefinition and change. Things could hardly be otherwise, given the varied constitution of the English-speaking community, the changing social background, and the insistence of English-speakers that they must be left to decide these matters on their own, without the intervention of official commissions or academies. It is not surprising that the reference points that we depend on to maintain the continuity of the language should often be controversial, even within a single community, and even less so that different national communities should have different ideas as to who counts as authority or what kinds of texts should be relevant to defining the common core of English words. The most we can ask of our common linguistic heritage is that it give us a general format for adapting the language to new needs and for reinterpreting its significance from one time and place to another.

This is the challenge posed by the triumph of English. Granted, there is no threat to the hegemony of English as a worldwide medium for practical communication. It is a certainty that the nations of the English-speaking community will continue to use the various forms of English to communicate with each other, as well as with the hundreds of millions of people who speak English as a second language (and who in fact outnumber the native speakers of the language by a factor of two or three to one). And with the growth of travel and trade and of media like the Internet, the number of English-speakers is sure to continue to increase.

But none of this guarantees the continuing unity of English as a means of cultural expression. What is striking about the accelerating spread of English over the past two centuries is not so much the number of speakers that the language has acquired, but the remarkable variety of the cultures and communities who use it. The heterogeneity of the linguistic community is evident not just in the emergence of the rich new literatures of Africa, Asia, and the Caribbean, but also in the literatures of what linguists sometimes call the "inner circle" of the English-speaking world—nations like Britain, the United States, Australia, and Canada—where the language is being asked to describe a much wider range of experience than ever before, particularly on behalf of groups who until recently have been largely excluded or marginalized from the collective conversation of the English-speaking world.

Not surprisingly, the speakers of the "new Englishes" use the language with different voices and different rhythms and bring to it different linguistic and cultural backgrounds. The language of a writer like Chinua Achebe reflects the influence not just of Shakespeare and Wordsworth but of proverbs and other forms of discourse drawn from West African oral traditions. Indian writers like R. K. Narayan and Salman Rushdie ground their works not just in the traditional English-language canon but in Sanskrit classics like the epic *Rāmāyana*. The continuing sense that all English-speakers are engaged in a common discourse depends on the linguistic community's being able to accommodate and absorb these new linguistic and literary influences, as it has been able to do in the past.

In all parts of the linguistic community, moreover, there are questions posed by the new media of discourse. Over the past hundred years, the primacy of print has been challenged first by the growth of film, recordings, and the broadcast media, and more recently by the remarkable growth of the Internet, each of which has had its effects on the language. With film and the rest, we have begun to see the emergence of spoken standards that co-exist with the written standard of print, not in the form of a standardized English pronunciation—if anything, pronunciation differences among the communities of the English-speaking world have become more marked over the course of the century—but rather in the use of words, expressions, and rhythms that are particular to speech (there is no better example of this than the universal adoption of the particle *okay*). And the Internet has had the effect of projecting what were previously private forms of written communication, like the personal letter, into something more like models of public discourse, but with a language that is much more informal than the traditional discourse of the novel or newspaper.

It is a mistake to think that any of these new forms of discourse will wholly replace the discourse of print (the Internet, in particular, has shown itself to be an important vehicle for marketing and diffusing print works with much greater efficiency than has ever been possible before). It seems reasonable to assume that a hundred years from now the English-speaking world will still be at heart a community of readers—and of readers of books, among other things. And it is likely, too, that the English language will still be at heart a means of written expression, not just for setting down air schedules and trade statistics, but for doing the kind of cultural work that we have looked for literature to do for us in the past; a medium, that is, for poetry, criticism, history, and fiction. But only time will tell if English will remain a single language—if in the midst of all the diversity, cultural and communicative, people will still be able to discern a single "English literature" and a characteristic English-language frame of mind.

GEOFFREY NUNBERG
Stanford University and Xerox Palo Alto Research Center

The Norton Anthology
of English Literature

SEVENTH EDITION

VOLUME 2B

THE VICTORIAN AGE

The Victorian Age
1830–1901

1832:	The First Reform Bill
1837:	Victoria becomes queen
1846:	The Corn Laws repealed
1850:	Tennyson succeeds Wordsworth as Poet Laureate
1851:	The Great Exhibition in London
1859:	Charles Darwin's *Origin of Species* published
1870–71:	Franco-Prussian War
1901:	Death of Victoria

In 1897 Mark Twain was visiting London during the Diamond Jubilee celebrations honoring the sixtieth anniversary of Queen Victoria's coming to the throne. "British history is two thousand years old," Twain observed, "and yet in a good many ways the world has moved farther ahead since the Queen was born than it moved in all the rest of the two thousand put together." And if the whole world had "moved" during that long lifetime and reign of Victoria's, it was in her own country itself that the change was most marked and dramatic, a change that brought England to its highest point of development as a world power.

In the eighteenth century the pivotal city of Western civilization had been Paris; by the second half of the nineteenth century this center of influence had shifted to London, a city that expanded from about two million inhabitants when Victoria came to the throne to six and a half million at the time of her death. The rapid growth of London is one of the many indications of the most important development of the age: the shift from a way of life based on the ownership of land to a modern urban economy based on trade and manufacturing. "We have been living, as it were, the life of three hundred years in thirty" was the impression formed by Dr. Thomas Arnold during the early stages of England's industrialization. By the end of the century—after the resources of steam power had been more fully exploited for fast railways and iron ships, for looms, printing presses, and farmers' combines, and after the introduction of the telegraph, intercontinental cable, photography, anesthetics, and universal compulsory education—a late Victorian could look back with astonishment on these developments during his or her lifetime. Walter Besant, one of these late Victorians, observed that so completely transformed were "the mind and habits of the ordinary Englishman" by 1897, "that he would not, could he see him, recognize his own grandfather."

Because England was the first country to become industrialized, its transformation was an especially painful one: it experienced a host of social and economic problems consequent to rapid and unregulated industrialization. England also experienced an enormous increase in wealth. An early start enabled England to capture markets all over the globe. Cotton and other manufactured products were exported in English ships, a merchant fleet whose size was without parallel in other countries. The profits gained from trade led also to extensive capital investments in all continents. After England had become the world's workshop, London became, from 1870 on, the world's banker. England gained particular profit from the development of its own colonies, which, by 1890, comprised more than a quarter of all the territory on the surface of the earth; one in four people was a subject of Queen Victoria. By the end of the century England was the world's foremost imperial power.

The reactions of Victorian writers to the fast-paced expansion of England were various. Thomas Babington Macaulay (1800–1859) relished the spectacle with strenuous enthusiasm. During the prosperous 1850s Macaulay's essays and histories, with their recitations of the statistics of industrial growth, constituted a Hymn to Progress as well as a celebration of the superior qualities of the English people—"the greatest and most highly civilized people that ever the world saw." Other writers felt that leadership in commerce and industry was being paid for at a terrible price in human happiness, that a so-called progress had been gained only by abandoning traditional rhythms of life and traditional patterns of human relationships. The melancholy poetry of Matthew Arnold often strikes this note:

> For what wears out the life of mortal men?
>   'Tis that from change to change their being rolls;
>   'Tis that repeated shocks, again, again,
> Exhaust the energy of strongest souls.

Although many Victorians shared a sense of satisfaction in the industrial and political preeminence of England during the period, they also suffered from an anxious sense of something lost, a sense too of being displaced persons in a world made alien by technological changes that had been exploited too quickly for the adaptive powers of the human psyche.

QUEEN VICTORIA AND THE VICTORIAN TEMPER

Queen Victoria's long reign, from 1837 to 1901, defines the historical period that bears her name. The question naturally arises whether the distinctive character of those years justifies the adjective *Victorian*. In part Victoria herself encouraged her own identification with the qualities we associate with the adjective—earnestness, moral responsibility, domestic propriety. As a young wife, as the mother of nine children, and as the black-garbed Widow of Windsor in the forty years after her husband's death in 1861, Victoria represented the domestic fidelities her citizens embraced. After her death Henry James wrote, "I mourn the safe and motherly old middle-class queen, who held the nation warm under the fold of her big, hideous Scotch-plaid shawl." Changes in the reproduction of visual images aided in making her the icon she became. She is the first British monarch of whom we have photographs. These pictures, and the ease and cheapness with which they were reproduced, facilitated her representing her country's sense of itself during her reign.

Victoria came to the throne in a decade that does seem to mark a different historical consciousness among Britain's writers. In 1831 John Stuart Mill asserts, "we are living in an age of transition." In the same year Thomas Carlyle writes, "The Old has passed away, but alas, the New appears not in its stead; the Time is still in pangs of travail with the New." Although the historical changes that created the England of the 1830s had been in progress for many decades, writers of the thirties shared a sharp new sense of modernity, of a break with the past, of historical self-consciousness. They responded to their sense of the historical moment with a strenuous call to action that they self-consciously distinguished from the attitude of the previous generation.

In 1834 Carlyle urged his contemporaries, "Close thy *Byron*; open thy *Goethe*." He was saying, in effect, to abandon the introspection of the Romantics and to turn to the higher moral purpose that he found in Goethe. The popular novelist Edward Bulwer-Lytton (1803–1873) in his *England and the English* made a similar judgment. "When Byron passed away," he wrote, " . . . we turned to the actual and practical career of life: we awoke from the morbid, the dreaming, 'the moonlight and dimness of the mind,' and by a natural reaction addressed ourselves to the active and daily objects which lay before us." This sense of historical self-consciousness, of strenuous social enterprise, and of growing national achievement led writers as early as the 1850s and 1860s to define their age as Victorian. The very fact that Victoria reigned for so long sustained the concept of a distinctive historical period that writers defined even as they lived it.

When Queen Victoria died, a reaction developed against many of the achievements of the previous century; this reinforced the sense that the Victorian age was a distinct period. In the earlier decades of the twentieth century, writers took pains to separate themselves from the Victorians. It was then the fashion for most literary critics to treat their Victorian predecessors as somewhat absurd creatures, stuffily complacent prigs with whose way of life they had little in common. Writers of the Georgian period (1911–36) took great delight in puncturing overinflated Victorian balloons, as Lytton Strachey, a member of Virginia Woolf's circle, did in *Eminent Victorians* (1918). A subtler example occurs in Woolf's *Orlando*, a fictionalized survey of English literature from Elizabethan times to 1928, in which the Victorians are presented in terms of dampness, rain, and proliferating vegetation:

> Ivy grew in unparalleled profusion. Houses that had been of bare stone were smothered in greenery. . . . And just as the ivy and the evergreen rioted in the damp earth outside, so did the same fertility show itself within. The life of the average woman was a succession of childbirths. . . . Giant cauliflowers towered deck above deck till they rivaled . . . the elm trees themselves. Hens laid incessantly eggs of no special tint. . . . The whole sky itself as it spread wide above the British Isles was nothing but a vast feather bed.

This witty description not only identifies a distinguishing quality of Victorian life and literature—a superabundant energy—but reveals the author's distaste for its smothering profusion. Woolf was the daughter of Sir Leslie Stephen (1832–1904), himself an eminent Victorian. In her later life, when assessing her father's powerful personality, Woolf recorded in her diary that she herself could never have become a writer if he had not died when he did. Growing up under such towering shadows, she and her generation mocked their predecessors to make them less intimidating. In his reminiscences *Portraits from Life*, the novelist Ford Madox Ford (1873–1939) recalled his feelings of terror when he confronted the works of Carlyle and Ruskin, which he likened to an overpowering range of high mountains. The mid-Victorians, he wrote, were "a childish nightmare to me."

The Georgian reaction against the Victorians is now only a matter of the history of taste, but its aftereffects still sometimes crop up when the term *Victorian* is employed in an exclusively pejorative sense, as prudish or old-fashioned. Contemporary historians and critics now find the Victorian period a richly complex example of a society struggling with the issues and problems we identify with modernism. But to give the period the single designation *Victorian* reduces its complexity. For a period almost seventy years in length, we can hardly expect generalizations to be uniformly applicable. It is, therefore, helpful to subdivide the age into three phases: Early Victorian (1830–48), Mid-Victorian (1848–70), and Late Victorian (1870–1901). It is also helpful to consider the final decade, the nineties, as a bridge between two centuries.

THE EARLY PERIOD (1830–48): A TIME OF TROUBLES

In the early 1830s, two historical events occurred of momentous consequence for England. In 1830 the Liverpool and Manchester Railway opened, becoming the first steam-powered, public railway line in the world. A burst of railway construction followed. By 1850, 6,621 miles of railway line connected all of England's major cities. By 1900, England had 15,195 lines of track and an underground railway system beneath London. The train transformed England's landscape, supported the growth of its commerce, and shrank the distances between its cities. The opening of England's first railway coincided with the opening of the country's Reform Parliament. The railway had increased the pressure for parliamentary reform. "Parliamentary reform must follow soon after the opening of this road," a Manchester man observed in 1830, when the railway opened. "A million of persons will pass over it in the course of this year, and see that hitherto unseen village of Newton; and they must be convinced of the absurdity of its sending two members to Parliament while Manchester sends none." Despite the growth of manufacturing cities consequent to the Industrial Revolution, England was still governed by an archaic electoral system whereby some of the new industrial cities were unrepresented in Parliament while "rotten boroughs" (communities that had become depopulated) elected the nominees of the local squire to Parliament.

By 1830 a time of economic distress had brought England close to revolution. Manufacturing interests, who refused to tolerate their exclusion from the political process any longer, led working men in agitating for reform. Fearing the kind of revolution it had seen in Europe, Parliament passed a Reform Bill in 1832 that transformed England's class structure. The Reform Bill of 1832 extended the right to vote to all males owning property worth £10 or more in annual rent. In effect the voting public thereafter included the lower middle classes but not the working classes, who did not obtain the vote until 1867, when a second reform bill was passed. Even more important than the extension of the franchise was the virtual abolition of the rotten boroughs and the redistribution of parliamentary representation. Because it broke up the monopoly of power that the conservative landowners had so long enjoyed (the Tory party had been in office almost continuously from 1783 to 1830), the Reform Bill represents the beginning of a new age, in which middle-class economic interests gained increasing power.

Yet even the newly constituted Parliament was unable to find legislative solutions to the problems facing the nation. The economic and social difficulties attendant on industrialization were so severe that the 1830s and 1840s became known as the Time of Troubles. After a period of prosperity from 1832 to 1836, a crash in 1837, followed by a series of bad harvests, produced a period of unemployment, desperate poverty, and rioting. Conditions in the new industrial and coal-mining areas were terrible. Workers and their families in the slums of such cities as Manchester lived in horribly crowded, unsanitary housing; and the conditions under which women and children toiled in mines and factories were unimaginably brutal. Elizabeth Barrett's poem *The Cry of the Children* (1843) expresses her horrified response to an official report on child labor, describing five-year-olds dragging heavy tubs of coal through low-ceilinged mine passages for sixteen hours a day.

The owners of mines and factories regarded themselves as innocent of blame for such conditions, for they were wedded to an economic theory of laissez-faire, which assumed that unregulated working conditions would ultimately benefit everyone. A sense of the seemingly hopeless complexity of the situation during the Hungry 1840s is provided by an entry for 1842 in the diary of the statesman Charles Greville, an entry written at the same time that Carlyle was making his contribution to the "Condition of England Question," *Past and Present*. Conditions in the north of England, Greville reports, were "appalling."

> There is an immense and continually increasing population, no adequate demand for labor, . . . no confidence, but a universal alarm, disquietude, and discontent. Nobody can sell anything. . . . Certainly I have never seen . . . so serious a state of things as that which now stares us in the face; and this after thirty years of uninterrupted peace, and the most ample scope afforded for the development of all our resources. . . . One remarkable feature in the present condition of affairs is that nobody can account for it, and nobody pretends to be able to point out any remedy.

In reality many remedies were proposed. One of the most striking was put forward by the Chartists, a large organization of workers. In 1838 the organization drew up a "People's Charter" advocating the extension of the right to vote, the use of secret balloting, and other legislative reforms. For ten years the Chartist leaders engaged in agitation to have their program adopted by Parliament. Their fiery speeches, delivered at conventions designed to collect signatures for petitions to Parliament, created fears of revolution. In *Locksley Hall* Tennyson seems to have had the Chartist demonstrations in mind when he wrote: "Slowly comes a hungry people, as a lion, creeping nigher, / Glares at one that nods and winks behind a slowly-dying fire." Although the Chartist movement had fallen apart by 1848, it succeeded in creating an atmosphere open to reform. One of the most important reforms was the abolition of the high tariffs on imported grains, tariffs known as the Corn Laws (the word *corn* in England refers to wheat and other grains). These high tariffs had been established to protect English farm products from having to compete with low-priced products imported from abroad. Landowners and farmers fought to keep these tariffs in force so that high prices for their wheat would be ensured; but the rest of the population suffered severely from the exorbitant price of bread or, in years of bad crops, from scarcity of food. In 1845 serious crop failures in England and the outbreak of potato blight in Ireland convinced Sir Robert Peel, the Tory prime minister, that traditional protectionism must be abandoned. In 1846 the Corn Laws were repealed by Parliament, and the way was paved for the introduction of a system of Free Trade whereby goods could be imported with the payment of only minimal tariff duties. Although Free Trade did not eradicate the slums of Manchester, it worked well for many years and helped relieve the major crisis of the Victorian economy. In 1848, when revolutions were breaking out all over Europe, England was relatively unaffected. A large Chartist demonstration in London seemed to threaten revolution, but it came to nothing. The next two decades were relatively calm and prosperous.

This Time of Troubles left its mark on some early Victorian literature. "Insurrection is a most sad necessity," Carlyle writes in his *Past and Present*, "and governors who wait for that to instruct them are surely getting into the fatalest courses." A similar refrain runs through Carlyle's history *The French Revolution* (1837). Memories of the French Reign of Terror lasted longer than memories of Trafalgar and Waterloo, memories freshened by later outbreaks of civil strife, "the red fool-fury of the Seine" as Tennyson described one of the violent overturnings of government in France. It is the novelists of the 1840s and early 1850s, however, who show the most marked response to the industrial and political scene. Vivid records of these conditions are to be found in the fiction of Charles Kingsley (1819–1875); Elizabeth Gaskell (1810–1865); and Benjamin Disraeli (1804–1881), a novelist who became prime minister. For his novel *Sybil* (1845) Disraeli chose an appropriate subtitle, *The Two Nations*—a phrase that pointed out the line dividing the England of the rich from the other nation, the England of the poor.

THE MID-VICTORIAN PERIOD (1848–70): ECONOMIC PROSPERITY, THE GROWTH OF EMPIRE, AND RELIGIOUS CONTROVERSY

In the decades following the Time of Troubles some Victorian writers, such as Dickens, continued to make critical attacks on the shortcomings of the Victorian social scene. Even more critical and indignant than Dickens was John Ruskin, who turned from a purely moral and aesthetic criticism of art during this period to denounce the evils of Victorian industry, as in his *The Stones of Venice* (1853), which combines a history of architecture with stern prophecies about the doom of technological culture, or in his attacks on laissez-faire economics in *Unto This Last* (1862). Generally speaking, however, the realistic novels of Anthony Trollope (1815–1882), with their comfortable tolerance and equanimity, are a more characteristic reflection of the mid-Victorian attitude toward the social and political scene than are Ruskin's lamentations. Overall, this second phase of the Victorian period had many harassing problems, but it was a time of prosperity. On the whole its institutions worked well. Even the badly bungled war against Russia in the Crimea (1854–56) did not seriously affect the growing sense of satisfaction that the challenging difficulties of the 1840s had been solved or would be solved by English wisdom and energy. The monarchy was proving its worth in a modern setting. The queen and her husband, Prince Albert, were themselves models of middle-class domesticity and devotion to duty. The aristocracy was discovering that Free Trade was enriching rather than impoverishing their estates; agriculture flourished together with trade and industry. And through a succession of Factory Acts in Parliament, which restricted child labor and limited hours of employment, the condition of the working classes was also being gradually improved. When we speak of Victorian complacency or stability or optimism, we are usually referring to this mid-Victorian phase—"The Age of Improvement," as the historian Asa Briggs has called it. "Of all the decades in our history," writes G. M. Young, "a wise man would choose the eighteen-fifties to be young in."

In 1851 Prince Albert opened the Great Exhibition in Hyde Park, where a gigantic glass greenhouse, the Crystal Palace, had been erected to display the exhibits of modern industry and science. The Crystal Palace was one of the first buildings constructed according to modern architectural principles in which materials such as glass and iron are employed for purely functional ends (much late Victorian furniture, on the other hand, with its fantastic and irrelevant ornamentation, was constructed according to the opposite principle). The building itself, as well as the exhibits, symbolized the triumphant feats of Victorian technology. As Benjamin Disraeli wrote to a friend in 1862: "It is a privilege to live in this age of rapid and brilliant events. What an error to consider it a utilitarian age. It is one of infinite romance."

England's technological progress, together with its prosperity, led to an enormous expansion of its influence throughout the globe. Its annual export of goods nearly trebled in value between 1850 and 1870. Not only the export of goods but that of people and capital increased. Between 1853 and 1880, 2,466,000 emigrants left Britain, many bound for British colonies. By 1870, British capitalists had invested £800 million abroad; in 1850, the total had been only £300 million. This investment, of people, money, and technology, created the British Empire. Important building blocks of the empire were put in place in the mid-Victorian period. In the 1850s and 1860s there was large-scale immigration to Australia; in 1867, Parliament unified the Canadian provinces into the Dominion of Canada. In 1857, Parliament took over the government of India from the private East India Company, which had controlled the country, and started to put in place its civil service government. In 1876, Queen Victoria was named empress of India. Although the competitive scramble for African colonies did not take place until the final decades of the century, the model of empire was created earlier, made possible by technological revolution in communication and transportation. Much as Rome had built roads through Europe in the years of the Roman Empire, Britain built railways and strung telegraph wires. It also put in place a framework for education and government that preserves British influence in former colonies even today. Britain's motives, in creating its empire, were many. It sought wealth, markets for manufactured goods, sources for raw materials, and world power and influence. Many English people also saw the expansion of empire as a moral responsibility, what Kipling termed "the White Man's burden." Queen Victoria herself stated that the imperial mission was "to protect the poor natives and advance civilization." Missionary societies flourished, spreading Christianity in India, Asia, and Africa.

At the same time that the British missionary enterprise was expanding, there was increasing debate about religious belief. By the mid-Victorian period, the Church of England had evolved into three major divisions: Evangelical, or Low Church, Broad Church, and High Church. The Evangelicals emphasized spiritual transformation of the individual by conversion and a strictly moral Christian life. Zealously dedicated to good causes (they were responsible for the emancipation of all slaves in the British Empire as early as 1833), advocates of a strict Puritan code of morality, and righteously censorious of worldliness in others, the Evangelicals became a powerful and active minority in the early part of the nineteenth century. Much of the power of the Evangelicals depended on the fact that their view of life and religion was virtually identical with that of a much larger group external to the Church of England, the Nonconformists, or Dissenters—that is, Baptists, Methodists, Congregationalists, and other Protestant denominations. The High Church was also associated with a group external to the Church of England; it was the "Catholic" side of the church, emphasizing the importance of tradition, ritual, and authority. In the 1830s, a High Church movement took shape, known both as "the Oxford movement," because it originated at Oxford University, and as "Tractarianism," because its leaders developed their arguments in a series of pamphlets or tracts. Led by John Henry Newman, who later converted to Roman Catholicism, Tractarians argued that the Church could maintain its power and authority only by resisting liberal tendencies and holding to its original traditions. The Broad Church resisted the doctrinal and ecclesiastical controversies that separated the High Church and Evangelical divisions. Open to modern advances in thought, its adherents emphasized the broadly inclusive nature of the church.

Some rationalist challenges to religious belief that developed before the Victorian period maintained their influence. The most significant was Utilitarianism, also known as Benthamism or Philosophical Radicalism. Utilitarianism derived from the thought of Jeremy Bentham (1748–1832) and his disciple James Mill (1773–1836), the father of John Stuart Mill. Bentham believed that all human beings seek to maximize pleasure and minimize pain. The criterion by which we should judge a morally correct action, therefore, is the extent to which it provides the greatest pleasure to the greatest number. Measuring religion by this moral arithmetic, Benthamites concluded that it was an outmoded superstition; it did not meet the rationalist test of value. Utilitarianism was widely influential in providing a philosophical basis for political reform, but it aroused considerable opposition on the part of those who felt it failed to recognize people's spiritual needs. Raised according to strict utilitarian principles by his father, John Stuart Mill came to be critical of them. In the mental and spiritual crisis portrayed in his *Autobiography,* Mill describes his realization that his utilitarian upbringing had left him no power to feel. In *Sartor Resartus,* Carlyle describes a similar spiritual crisis in which he struggles to rediscover the springs of religious feeling in the face of his despair at the specter of a universe governed only by utilitarian principles. Later both Dickens, in his portrayal of Thomas Gradgrind in *Hard Times*, "a man of facts and calculations," "ready to weigh and measure any parcel of human nature," and John Ruskin, in his *Unto This Last*, attack utilitarianism.

In mid-Victorian England, however, the challenge to religious belief gradually shifted from the Utilitarians to some of the leaders of science, in particular to Thomas Henry Huxley, who popularized the theories of Charles Darwin. Although many English scientists were themselves individuals of strong religious convictions, the impact of their scientific discoveries seemed consistently damaging to established faiths. Complaining in 1851 about the "flimsiness" of his own religious faith, Ruskin exclaimed: "If only the Geologists would let me alone, I could do very well, but those dreadful hammers! I hear the clink of them at the end of every cadence of the Bible verses."

The damage lamented by Ruskin was effected in two ways. First the scientific attitude of mind was applied toward a study of the Bible itself. This kind of investigation, developed especially in Germany, was known as the "Higher Criticism." Instead of treating the Bible as a sacredly infallible document, scientifically minded scholars examined it as a mere text of history and presented evidence about its composition that believers, especially in Protestant countries, found disconcerting, to say the least. A noteworthy example of such Higher Criticism studies was David Friedrich Strauss's *Das Leben Jesu*, which was translated by George Eliot in 1846 as *The Life of Jesus*. The second kind of damage was effected by the view of humanity implicit in the discoveries of geology and astronomy, the new and "Terrible Muses" of literature, as Tennyson called them in a late poem. Geology, by extending the history of the earth backward millions of years, reduced the stature of the human species in time. John Tyndall, an eminent physicist, said in an address at Belfast in 1874 that in the eighteenth century people had an "unwavering trust" in the "chronology of the Old Testament" but in Victorian times they had to become accustomed to

> the idea that not for six thousand, nor for sixty thousand, nor for six thousand thousand, but for aeons embracing untold millions of years, this earth has been the theater of life and death. The riddle of the rocks has been read by the geologist and paleontologist, from sub-Cambrian depths to the deposits thickening over the sea bottoms of today. And upon the leaves of that stone book are . . . stamped the characters, plainer and surer than those formed by the ink of history, which carry the mind back into abysses of past time.

The discoveries of astronomers, by extending a knowledge of stellar distances to dizzying expanses, were likewise disconcerting. Carlyle's friend John Sterling remarked in a letter of 1837 how geology "gives one the same sort of bewildering view of the abysmal extent of Time that Astronomy does of Space." To Tennyson's speaker in *Maud* (1855) the stars are "innumerable" tyrants of "iron skies." They are "Cold fires, yet with power to burn and brand / His nothingness into man."

In the mid-Victorian period, biology reduced humankind even further into "nothingness." Darwin's great treatise *The Origin of Species* (1859) was interpreted by the nonscientific public in a variety of ways. Some chose to assume that evolution was synonymous with progress, but most readers recognized that Darwin's theory of natural selection conflicted not only with the concept of creation derived from the Bible but also with long-established assumptions of the values attached to humanity's special role in the world. Darwin's later treatise *The Descent of Man* (1871) raised more explicitly the haunting question of our identification with the animal kingdom. If the principle of survival of the fittest was accepted as the key to conduct, there remained the inquiry: fittest for what? As John Fowles writes in his 1968 novel about Victorian England, *The French Lieutenant's Woman,* Darwin's theories made the Victorians feel "infinitely isolated." "By the 1860s the great iron structures of their philosophies, religions, and social stratifications were already beginning to look dangerously corroded to the more perspicacious."

Disputes about evolutionary science, like the disputes about religion, are a reminder that beneath the placidly prosperous surface of the mid-Victorian age there were serious conflicts and anxieties. In the same year as the Great Exhibition, with its celebration of the triumphs of trade and industry, Charles Kingsley wrote, "The young men and women of our day are fast parting from their parents and each other; the more thoughtful are wandering either towards Rome, towards sheer materialism, or towards an unchristian and unphilosophic spiritualism."

THE LATE PERIOD (1870–1901): DECAY OF VICTORIAN VALUES

The third phase of the Victorian age is more difficult to categorize. At first glance its point of view seems merely an extension of mid-Victorianism, whose golden glow lingered on through the Jubilee years of 1887 and 1897 (years celebrating the fiftieth and sixtieth anniversaries of the queen's accession) down to 1914. For many Victorians, this final phase of the century was a time of serenity and security, the age of house parties and long weekends in the country. In the amber of Henry James's prose is immortalized a sense of the comfortable pace of these pleasant, well-fed gatherings. Life in London, too, was for many an exhilarating heyday. In *My Life and Loves* the Irish-American Frank Harris (1854–1931), often a severe critic of the English scene, records his recollections of the gaiety of London in the 1880s: "London: who would give even an idea of its varied delights: London, the center of civilization, the queen city of the world without a peer in the multitude of its attractions, as superior to Paris as Paris is to New York." The exhilarating sense of London's delights reflects in part the proliferation of things: commodities, inventions, products that were changing the texture of modern life. England had become a country committed not only to continuing technological change but also to a culture of consumerism, generating new products for sale.

The wealth of England's empire provided the foundation on which its economy was built. The final decades of the century saw the apex of British imperialism, yet the cost of the empire became increasingly apparent in rebellions, massacres, and bungled wars, such as the Indian Mutiny in 1857; the Jamaica Rebellion in 1865; the massacre of General Gordon and his troops at Khartoum, in the Sudan, in 1885, where he had been sent to evacuate the British in the face of a religiously inspired revolt; and the Boer War, at the end of the century, in which England engaged in a long, bloody, and unpopular struggle to annex two independent republics in the south of Africa controlled by Dutch settlers called Boers. In addition, the "Irish Question," as it was called, became especially divisive in the 1880s when Home Rule for Ireland became a topic of heated debate—a proposed reform that was unsuccessfully advocated by Prime Minister Gladstone and other leaders. And outside of the British Empire, other developments challenged Victorian stability and security. The sudden emergence of Bismarck's Germany after the defeat of France in 1871 was progressively to confront England with powerful threats to its naval and military position and also to its preeminence in trade and industry. The recovery of the United States after the Civil War likewise provided new and serious competition not only in industry but also in agriculture. As the westward expansion of railroads in the United States and Canada opened up the vast, grain-rich prairies, the typical English farmer had to confront lower grain prices and a dramatically different scale of productivity, which England could not match. In 1873 and 1874 such severe economic depressions occurred that the rate of emigration rose to an alarming degree. Another change in the mid-Victorian balance of power was the growth of labor as a political and economic force. In 1867, under Disraeli's guidance, a second Reform Bill had been passed that extended the right to vote to sections of the working classes; and this, together with the subsequent development of trade unions, made labor a powerful political force that included a wide variety of kinds of socialism. Some labor leaders were disciples of the Tory-socialism of John Ruskin and shared his idealistic conviction that the middle-class economic and political system, with its distrust of state interference, was irresponsible and immoral. Other labor leaders had been influenced instead by the revolutionary theories of Karl Marx and Friedrich Engels as expounded in their *Communist Manifesto* of 1847 and in Marx's *Das Kapital* (1867, 1885, 1895). The first English author of note to embrace Marxism was the poet and painter William Morris, who shared with Marx a conviction that utopia could be achieved only after the working classes had, by revolution, taken control of government and industry.

In much of the literature of this final phase of Victorianism we can sense an overall change of attitudes. Some of the late Victorian writers expressed the change openly by simply attacking the major mid-Victorian idols. Samuel Butler (1835–1902), for example, set about demolishing Darwin, Tennyson, and Prime Minister Gladstone, figures whose aura of authority reminded him of his own father. For the more worldly and casual-mannered Prime Minister Disraeli, on the other hand, Butler could express considerable admiration: "Earnestness was his greatest danger, but if he did not quite overcome it (as who indeed can? it is the last enemy that shall be subdued), he managed to veil it with a fair amount of success." In his novel *The Way of All Flesh*, much of which was written in the 1870s, Butler satirized family life, in particular the tyrannical self-righteousness of a Victorian father, his own father (a clergyman) serving as his model. In a different vein Walter Pater and his followers concluded that the striving of their predecessors was ultimately pointless, that the answers to our problems are not to be found, and that our role is to enjoy the fleeting moments of beauty in "this short day of frost and sun." It is symptomatic of this shift in point of view that Edward FitzGerald's beautiful translation of the *Rubáiyát of Omar Khayyám* (1859), with its melancholy theme that life's problems are insoluble, went virtually unnoticed in the 1860s but became a popular favorite in subsequent decades.

THE NINETIES

The changes in attitude that had begun cropping up in the 1870s became much more conspicuous in the final decade of the century and give the nineties a special aura of notoriety. Of course the changes were not in evidence everywhere. Throughout the empire at its outposts in India and Africa, the English were building railways and administering governments with the same strenuous energy as in the mid-Victorian period. The stories of Kipling and Conrad variously record the struggles of such people. Also embodying the task of sustaining an empire were the soldiers and sailors who fought in various colonial wars, most notably in the war against the Boers in South Africa (1899–1902). But back in England, Victorian standards were breaking down on several fronts. One colorful embodiment of changing values was Victoria's son and heir, Edward, Prince of Wales, who was entering his fiftieth year as the nineties began. A pleasure-seeking, easygoing person, Edward was the antithesis of his father, Prince Albert, an earnest-minded intellectual who had devoted his life to hard work and to administrative responsibilities. Edward's carryings-on were a favorite topic for newspaper articles, one of which noted how this father of five children "openly maintained scandalous relations with ballet dancers and chorus singers."

Much of the writing of the decade illustrates a breakdown of a different sort. Melancholy, not gaiety, is characteristic of its spirit. Artists of the nineties, representing the Aesthetic movement, were very much aware of living at the end of a great century and often cultivated a deliberately fin de siècle ("end-of-century") pose. A studied languor, a weary sophistication, a search for new ways of titillating jaded palates can be found in both the poetry and the prose of the period. *The Yellow Book*, a periodical that ran from 1894 to 1897, is generally taken to represent the aestheticism of the nineties. The startling black-and-white drawings and designs of its art editor, Aubrey Beardsley (1872–1898), the prose of George Moore and Max Beerbohm, and the poetry of Ernest Dowson illustrate different aspects of the movement. In 1893 the Austrian critic Max Nordau summed up what seemed to him to be happening, in a book that was as sensational as its title: *Degeneration*.

From the perspective of the twentieth century, however, it is easy to see in the nineties the beginning of the modernist movement in literature; a number of the great writers of the twentieth century—Yeats, Hardy, Conrad, Shaw—were already publishing.

In Dickens's *David Copperfield* (1850) the hero affirms: "I have always been thoroughly in earnest." Forty-five years later Oscar Wilde's comedy *The Importance of Being Earnest* turns this typical mid-Victorian word *earnest* into a pun, a key joke in this comic spectacle of earlier Victorian values being turned upside down. As Richard Le Gallienne (a novelist of the nineties) remarked in *The Romantic Nineties* (1926): "Wilde made dying Victorianism laugh at itself, and it may be said to have died of the laughter."

THE ROLE OF WOMEN

Political and legal reforms in the course of the Victorian period had given citizens many rights. In 1844 Friedrich Engels observed: "England is unquestionably the freest—that is the least unfree—country in the world, North America not excepted." England had indeed done much to extend its citizens' liberties, but women did not share in these freedoms. They could not vote or hold political office. (Although petitions to Parliament advocating women's suffrage were introduced as early as the 1840s, women did not get the vote until 1918.) Until the passage of the Married Women's Property Acts (1870–1908), married women could not own or handle their own property. Although men could divorce their wives for adultery, wives could divorce their husbands only if adultery were combined with cruelty, bigamy, incest, or bestiality. Educational and employment opportunities for women were limited. These inequities stimulated a spirited debate about women's roles known as the "Woman Question." Arguments for women's rights were based on the libertarian principles that had formed the basis of extended rights for men. In Hardy's last novel, *Jude the Obscure* (1895), his heroine justifies leaving her husband by quoting a passage from Mill's *On Liberty*. She might have quoted another work by Mill, *The Subjection of Women*, which, like Mary Wollstonecraft's *A Vindication of the Rights of Women* (1792), challenges long-established assumptions about women's role in society.

The changing conditions of women's work created by the Industrial Revolution posed an equally strong challenge to traditional views of women's roles. The explosive growth of the textile industries brought hundreds of thousands of lower-class women into factory jobs with grueling working conditions, and the need for coal to fuel England's industrial development brought women into the mines. The Factory Acts (1802–78) introduced increasing regulation of the conditions of labor in mines and factories, including reduction of the sixteen-hour day. Other changes in legislation extended women's rights. The Custody Act of 1839 gave a mother the right to petition the court for access to her minor children and custody of children under seven (raised to sixteen in 1878). The Divorce and Matrimonial Causes Act of 1857 established a civil divorce court (divorce previously could be granted only by an ecclesiastical court) and provided a deserted wife the right to apply for a protection order that would allow her rights to her property. Although divorce remained so expensive as to be available only to the rich, these changes in marriage and divorce laws, together with the Married Women's Property Acts, began to establish a basis for the rights of women in marriage.

In addition to pressuring Parliament for legal reform, feminists worked to enlarge educational opportunities for women. In 1837 none of England's three universities was open to women. Tennyson's long poem *The Princess* (1847), with its fantasy of a women's college from whose precincts all males are excluded, was inspired by contemporary discussions of the need for women to obtain an education more advanced than that provided by the popular finishing schools such as Miss Pinkerton's Academy in Thackeray's *Vanity Fair*. Although by the end of the poem, Princess Ida has repented of her Amazonian scheme, she and the prince look forward to a future in which man will be "more of woman, she of man." The poem reflects a climate of opinion that led in 1848 to the establishment of the first women's college in London, an example later recommended by Thomas Henry Huxley, a strong advocate of advanced education for women. By the end of Victoria's reign, women could take degrees at twelve universities or university colleges and could study, although not earn a degree, at Oxford and Cambridge.

There was also agitation for improved employment opportunities for women. Writers as diverse as Charlotte Brontë, Elizabeth Barrett Browning, and Florence Nightingale complained that middle-class women were taught trivial accomplishments to fill up days in which there was nothing important to do. The problem of nothing to do was acute in quite a different way for what contemporary journalists called "surplus" or "redundant" women, that is, the women in the population who remained unmarried because of the imbalance in numbers between the sexes. Such women (of whom there were approximately half a million in mid-Victorian England) had few employment opportunities, none of them attractive or profitable. Emigration was frequently proposed as a solution to the problem, but the number of single female emigrants was never high enough to affect significantly the population imbalance. Bad working conditions and underemployment drove thousands of women into prostitution, which became increasingly professionalized in the nineteenth century. The only occupation at which an unmarried middle-class woman could earn a living and maintain some claim to gentility was that of a governess, but a governess could expect no security of employment, only minimal wages, and an ambiguous status, somewhere between servant and family member, that isolated her within the household. Perhaps because the governess so clearly indicated the precariousness of the unmarried middle-class woman's status in Victorian England, the governess novel, of which the most famous examples are *Jane Eyre* and *Vanity Fair*, became a popular genre through which to explore women's roles in society.

As such novels indicate, Victorian society was preoccupied not only with legal and economic limitations on women's lives but with the very nature of woman. In *The Subjection of Women* John Stuart Mill argues that "what is now called the nature of women is eminently an artificial thing—the result of forced repression in some directions, unnatural stimulation in others." In Tennyson's *The Princess* the king voices a more traditional view of woman's role:

> Man for the field and woman for the hearth:
> Man for the sword and for the needle she:
> Man with the head and woman with the heart:
> Man to command and woman to obey.

The king's relegation of women to the hearth and heart reflects an ideology that claimed that woman had a special nature peculiarly fit for her domestic role. Most aptly epitomized by the title of Coventry Patmore's immensely popular poem *The Angel in the House* (1854–62), this concept of womanhood stressed woman's purity and selflessness. Protected and enshrined within the home, her role was to create a place of peace where man could take refuge from the difficulties of modern life. In *Of Queen's Gardens* John Ruskin writes:

> This is the true nature of home—it is the place of Peace; the shelter, not only from all injury, but from all terror, doubt, and division. In so far as it is not this, it is not home; so far as the anxieties of the outer life penetrate into it, and the inconsistently-minded, unknown, unloved, or hostile society of the outer world is allowed either by husband or wife to cross the threshold, it ceases to be home; it is then only a part of that outer world which you have roofed over, and lighted fire in. But so far as it is a sacred place, a vestal temple, a temple of the hearth watched over by Household Gods, . . . so far it vindicates the name, and fulfills the praise, of home.

Such an exalted conception of home placed great pressure on the woman who ran it to be, in Ruskin's words, "enduringly, incorruptibly good; instinctively, infallibly wise—wise, not for self-development, but for self-renunciation." It is easy to recognize the oppressive aspects of this ideology. Paradoxically, however, it was used not only by antifeminists, eager to keep woman in her place, but by some feminists as well, in justifying the special contribution that woman could make to public life.

In his preface to *The Portrait of a Lady* (1881) Henry James writes: "Millions of presumptuous girls, intelligent or not intelligent, daily affront their destiny, and what is it open to their destiny to *be*, at the most, that we should make an ado about it?" Every major Victorian novelist makes the "ado" that James describes in addressing the question of woman's vocation. Ultimately, as Victorian novels illustrate, the basic problem was not only political, economic, and educational. It was how women were regarded, and regarded themselves, as members of a society.

LITERACY, PUBLICATION, AND READING

Literacy increased significantly during the Victorian period, although precise figures are difficult to calculate. In 1837 about half of the adult male population could read and write to some extent; by the end of the century, basic literacy was almost universal, the product in part of compulsory national education, required by 1880 to the age of ten. There was also an explosion of things to read. Because of technological changes in printing—presses powered by steam, paper made from wood pulp rather than rags, and, toward the end of the century, typesetting machines—publishers could bring out more printed material more cheaply than ever before. The number of newspapers, periodicals, and books increased exponentially during the Victorian period. Books remained fairly expensive, and most readers borrowed them from commercial lending libraries. (There were few public libraries until the final decades of the century.) After the repeal of the stamp tax and duties on advertisements just after midcentury, an extensive popular press developed.

The most significant development in publishing from the point of view of literary culture was the growth of the periodical. In the first thirty years of the Victorian period, 170 new periodicals were started in London alone.

There were magazines for every taste: cheap and popular magazines that published sensational tales; religious monthlys; weekly newspapers; satiric periodicals noted for their political cartoons (the most famous of these was *Punch*); women's magazines; monthly miscellanies publishing fiction, poetry, and articles on current affairs; and reviews and quarterlies, ostensibly reviewing new books but using the reviews, which were always unsigned, as occasions for essays on the subjects in question. The chief reviews and monthly magazines had a great deal of power and influence; they defined issues in public affairs, and they made and broke literary reputations. They also published the major writers of the period: the fiction of Dickens, Thackeray, Eliot, Trollope, and Gaskell; the essays of Carlyle, Mill, Arnold, and Ruskin; the poetry of Tennyson and the Brownings all appeared in monthly magazines.

The circumstances of periodical publication exerted a shaping force on literature. Novels and long works of nonfiction prose were published in serial form. Although serial publication of works began in the late eighteenth century, it was the publication of Dickens's *Pickwick Papers* (1836–37) in individual numbers that established its popularity. All of Dickens's novels and many of those of his contemporaries were published in serial form. Readers therefore read these works in relatively short, discrete installments over a period that could extend more than a year, with time for reflection and interpretation in between. Serial publication encouraged a certain kind of plotting and pacing and allowed writers to take account of their readers' reactions as they constructed subsequent installments. Writers created a continuing world, punctuated by the ends of installments, which served to stimulate the curiosity that would keep readers buying subsequent issues. Serial publication also created a distinctive sense of a community of readers, a sense encouraged by the practice of reading aloud in family gatherings.

As the family reading of novels suggests, the middle-class reading public enjoyed a common reading culture. Poets such as Tennyson and Elizabeth Barrett Browning appealed to a large body of readers; prose writers like Carlyle, Arnold, and Ruskin achieved a status as sages; and the major Victorian novelists were popular writers. Readers shared the expectation that literature would not only delight but instruct, that it would be continuous with the lived world, and that it would illuminate social problems. "Tennyson," one of his college friends warned him, "we cannot live in art." These expectations weighed more heavily on some writers than others. Tennyson wore his public mantle with considerable ambivalence; Arnold abandoned the private mode of lyric poetry in order to speak about public issues in lectures and essays.

By the 1870s the sense of a broad readership, with a shared set of social concerns, had begun to dissolve. Writers had begun to define themselves in opposition to a general public; poets like the Pre-Raphaelites pursued art for art's sake, doing exactly what Tennyson's friend had warned against; mass publication included less and less serious literature. By the end of Victoria's reign, writers could no longer assume a unified reading public.

THE NOVEL

The novel was the dominant form in Victorian literature. Initially published, for the most part, in serial form, novels subsequently appeared in three-volume editions, or "three-deckers." "Large loose baggy monsters," Henry James called them, reflecting his dissatisfaction with their sprawling, panoramic expanse. As their size suggests, Victorian novels seek to represent a large and comprehensive social world, with the variety of classes and social settings that constitute a community. They contain a multitude of characters and a number of plots, setting in motion the kinds of patterns that reveal the author's vision of the deep structures of the social world—how, in George Eliot's words, "the mysterious mixture behaves under the varying experiments of Time." They presents themselves as realistic, that is, as representing a social world that shares the features of the one we inhabit. The French novelist Stendhal (1783–1842) called the novel "a mirror wandering down a road," but the metaphor of the mirror is somewhat deceptive, since it implies that writers exert no shaping force on their material. It would be more accurate to speak not of realism but of realisms, since each novelist presents a specific vision of reality whose representational force he or she seeks to persuade us to acknowledge through a variety of techniques and conventions. The worlds of Dickens, of Trollope, of Eliot, of the Brontës hardly seem continuous with each other, but their authors share the attempt to convince us that the characters and events they imagine resemble those we experience in actual life.

The experience that Victorian novelists most frequently depict is the set of social relationships in the middle-class society developing around them. It is a society where the material conditions of life indicate social position, where money defines opportunity, where social class enforces a powerful sense of stratification, yet where chances for class mobility exist. Pip can aspire to the great expectations that provide the title for Dickens's novel; Jane Eyre can marry her employer, a landed gentleman. Most Victorian novels focus on a protagonist whose effort to define his or her place in society is the main concern of the plot. The novel thus constructs a tension between surrounding social conditions and the aspiration of the hero or heroine, whether it be for love, social position, or a life adequate to his or her imagination. This tension makes the novel the natural form to use in portraying woman's struggle for self-realization in the context of the constraints imposed upon her. For both men and women writers, the heroine is often, therefore, the representative protagonist whose search for fulfillment emblematizes the human condition. The great heroines of Victorian fiction—Jane Eyre, Maggie Tulliver, Dorothea Brooke, Isabel Archer, Tess of the d'Urbervilles, even Becky Sharp—all seem in some way to illustrate George Eliot's judgment, voiced in the Prelude to *Middlemarch*, of "a certain spiritual grandeur ill-matched with meanness of opportunity."

The novel was not only a fertile medium for the portrayal of women; women writers were, for the first time, not figures on the margins but major authors. Jane Austen, the Brontës, Elizabeth Gaskell, George Eliot—all helped define the genre. When Charlotte Brontë screwed up her courage to write to the poet laureate, Robert Southey, to ask his advice about a career as a writer, he warned her, "Literature cannot be the business of a woman's life, and it ought not to be." Charlotte Brontë put this letter, with one other from Southey, in an envelope, with the inscription "Southey's advice to be kept forever. My twenty-first birthday." Brontë's ability ultimately to depart from Southey's advice derived in part from how amenable the novel was to women writers. It concerned the domestic life that women knew well—

courtship, family relationships, marriage. It was a popular form whose market women could enter easily. It did not carry the burden of an august tradition as poetry did, nor did it build on the learning of a university education. In his essay *The Lady Novelists*, George Henry Lewes declared, "The advent of female literature promises woman's view of life, woman's experience." His common-law wife, George Eliot, together with many of her sister novelists, fulfilled his prophecy.

Whether written by women or men, the Victorian novel was extraordinarily various. It encompassed a wealth of styles and genres from the extravagant comedy of Dickens to the Gothic romances of the Brontë sisters, from the satire of Thackeray to the probing psychological fiction of Eliot, from the social and political realism of Trollope to the sensation novels of Wilkie Collins. Later in the century, a number of popular genres developed—crime, mystery, and horror novels, science fiction, detective stories. For the Victorians, the novel was both a principal form of entertainment and a spur to social sympathy. There was not a social topic that the novel did not address. Dickens, Gaskell, and many lesser novelists tried to stimulate efforts for social reform through their depiction of social problems. Writing at the beginning of the twentieth century, Joseph Conrad defined the novel in a way that could speak for the Victorians: "What is a novel if not a conviction of our fellow-men's existence strong enough to take upon itself a form of imagined life clearer than reality and whose accumulated verisimilitude of selected episodes puts to shame the pride of documentary history?"

POETRY

Victorian poetry developed in the context of the novel. As the novel emerged as the dominant form of literature, poets sought new ways of telling stories in verse; examples include Tennyson's *Maud*, Elizabeth Barrett Browning's *Aurora Leigh*, Robert Browning's *The Ring and the Book*, and Arthur Hugh Clough's *Amours de Voyage*. Poets and critics debated what the appropriate subjects of such long narrative poems should be. Some, like Matthew Arnold, held that poets should use the heroic materials of the past; others, like Elizabeth Barrett Browning, felt that poets should represent "their age, not Charlemagne's." Poets also experimented with character and perspective. *Amours de Voyage* is a long epistolary poem that tells the story of a failed romance through letters written by its various characters; *The Ring and the Book* presents its plot—an old Italian murder story—through ten different perspectives.

Victorian poetry also developed in the shadow of Romanticism. By 1837, when Victoria ascended the throne, all of the major Romantic poets, save Wordsworth, were dead, but they had died young, and many readers consequently still regarded them as their contemporaries. Not even twenty years separated the birth dates of Tennyson and Browning from that of Keats, but they lived more than three times as long as he did. All of the Victorian poets show the strong influence of the Romantics, but they cannot sustain the confidence that the Romantics felt in the power of the imagination. The Victorians often rewrite Romantic poems with a sense of belatedness and distance. When, in his poem *Resignation*, Arnold addresses his sister upon revisiting a landscape, much as Wordsworth had addressed his sister in *Tin-*

tern Abbey, he tells her the rocks and sky "seem to bear rather than rejoice." Tennyson frequently represents his muse as an embowered woman, cut off from the world and doomed to death. The speakers of Browning's poems who embrace the visions that their imaginations present are madmen. When Hardy writes *The Darkling Thrush* in December 1900, Keats's nightingale has become "an aged thrush, frail, gaunt, and small."

Victorian poets build upon this sense of belated Romanticism in a number of different ways. Some poets writing in the second half of the century, like Rossetti and Swinburne, embrace an attenuated Romanticism, art pursued for its own sake. Reacting against what he sees as the insufficiency of an allegory of the state of one's own mind as the basis of poetry, Arnold seeks an objective basis for poetic emotion and finally gives up writing poems altogether when he decides that the present age lacks the culture necessary to support great poetry. The more fruitful reaction to the subjectivity of Romantic poetry, however, was not Arnold's but Browning's. Turning from the mode of his early poetry, modeled on Shelley, Browning began writing dramatic monologues, poems, he said, which are "Lyric in expression" but "Dramatic in principle, and so many utterances of so many imaginary persons, not mine." Tennyson simultaneously developed a more lyric form of the dramatic monologue. The idea of creating a lyric poem in the voice of a speaker ironically distinct from the poet is the great achievement of Victorian poetry, one developed extensively in the twentieth century. In *Poetry and the Age* (1953), the modernist poet and critic Randall Jarrell acknowledges this fact: "The dramatic monologue, which once had depended for its effect upon being a departure from the norm of poetry, now became in one form or other the norm."

The formal experimentation of Victorian poetry, both in long narrative and in the dramatic monologue, may make it seem eclectic, but Victorian poetry shares a number of characteristics. It tends to be pictorial, to use detail to construct visual images that represent the emotion or situation the poem concerns. In his review of Tennyson's first volume of poetry, Arthur Henry Hallam defines this kind of poetry as "picturesque," as combining visual impressions in such a way that they create a picture that carries the dominant emotion of the poem. This aesthetic brings poets and painters close together. Contemporary artists frequently illustrated Victorian poems, and poems themselves often present paintings. Victorian poetry also uses sound in a distinctive way. Whether it be the mellifluousness of Tennyson or Swinburne, with its emphasis on beautiful cadences, alliteration, and vowel sounds, or the roughness of Browning or Hopkins, a roughness adopted in part in reaction against Tennyson, the sound of Victorian poetry reflects an attempt to use poetry as a medium with a presence almost independent of sense. The resulting style can become so syntactically elaborate that it is easy to parody, as in Hopkins's description of Browning as a man "bouncing up from table with his mouth full of bread and cheese" or T. S. Eliot's criticism of Swinburne's poetry, where "meaning is merely the hallucination of meaning." Yet it is important to recognize that these poets use sound to convey meaning, to quote Hallam's review of Tennyson once more, "where words would not." "The tone becomes the sign of the feeling." In all of these developments—the experimentation with narrative and perspective, the dramatic monologue, the use of visual detail and sound—Victorian poets seek to represent psychology in a different way. Their most distinctive achievement is a poetry of mood and character. They therefore sat in uneasy relationship to the public expectation that poets be sages with something to teach. Tennyson, Browning, and Arnold showed varying discomfort with this public role; poets beginning to write in the second half of the century distanced themselves from their public by embracing an identity as bohemian rebels. Women poets encountered a different set of difficulties in developing their poetic voice. When, in Barrett Browning's epic about the growth of a woman poet, Aurora Leigh's cousin Romney discourages her poetic ambitions by telling her that women are "weak for art" but "strong for life and duty," he articulates the prejudice of an age. Women poets view their vocation in the context of the constraints and expectations upon their sex. Perhaps because of this, their poems are less complicated by the experiments in perspective than those of their male contemporaries.

VICTORIAN PROSE

Although Victorian poets felt ambivalent about the didactic mission the public expected of the man of letters, writers of nonfiction prose aimed specifically to instruct. Although the term *nonfictional prose* is clumsy and not quite exact (the Victorians themselves did not use the term but instead referred to history, biography, theology, criticism), it has its uses not only to distinguish these prose writers from the novelists but to indicate the centrality of argument and persuasion to Victorian intellectual life. The growth of the periodical press, described earlier, provided the vehicle and marketplace for nonfictional prose. It reflects a vigorous sense of shared intellectual life and the public urgency of social and moral issues. On a wide range of controversial topics—religious, political, and aesthetic—writers seek to convince their readers to share their convictions and values. Such writers seem at times almost secular priests. Indeed, in the fifth lecture of *On Heroes and Hero Worship*, Carlyle defines the writer precisely in these terms: "Men of Letters are a perpetual Priesthood, from age to age, teaching all Men that God is still present in their life. . . . In the true Literary Man, there is thus ever, acknowledged or not by the world, a sacredness." The modern man of letters, Carlyle argues, differs from his earlier counterpart in that he writes for money. "Never, till about a hundred years ago, was there seen any figure of a Great Soul living apart in that anomalous manner; endeavouring to speak forth the inspiration that was in him by Printed Books, and find place and subsistence by what the world would please him for doing that." This combination, of a new market position for nonfictional writing and an exalted sense of the didactic function of the writer, produces the genre we call Victorian prose.

On behalf of nonfictional prose, Walter Pater argued in his essay *Style* (1889) that it was "the special and opportune art of the modern world." He believed not that it was superior to verse but that it more readily conveys the "chaotic variety and complexity" of modern life, the "incalculable" intellectual diversity of the "master currents of the present time." Pater's characterization of prose helps us understand what its writers were attempting to do. Despite the diversity of styles and subjects, Victorian prose writers were engaged in shaping belief in a bewilderingly complex and changing world. Their modes of persuasion differ. Mill and Huxley rely on clear reasoning, logical argument, and the kind of lucid style favored by essayists of the eighteenth century. Carlyle and Ruskin write a prose that is more Romantic in character, that seeks to move readers as well as convince them. Whatever the differences in their rhetorical techniques, however, they share an urgency of exposition. Not only by what they said but by how they said it, Victorian prose writers were claiming a place for literature in a scientific and materialistic culture. Arnold and Pater share this as an explicit aim. Each in his own way argues that culture—the intensely serious appreciation of great works of literature—provides the kind of immanence and meaning that people once found in religion. For Arnold, this is an intensely moral experience; for Pater it is aesthetic. Together they develop the basis for the claims of modern literary criticism.

VICTORIAN DRAMA AND THEATER

If the Victorian age can lay claim to greatness for its poetry, its prose, and its novels, it would be difficult to make such a high claim for its plays, at least until the final decade of the century. Here we must distinguish between play writing on the one hand and theatrical activity on the other. For the theater itself, throughout the period, was a flourishing and popular institution, in which were performed not merely conventional dramas but a rich variety of theatrical entertainments, many with lavish spectacular effects—burlesques, extravaganzas, highly scenic and altered versions of Shakespeare's plays, melodramas, pantomimes, and musicals. Robert Corrigan gives figures that suggest the extent of the popularity of such entertainment: "In the decade between 1850 and 1860 the number of theaters built throughout the country was doubled, and in the middle of the sixties, in London alone, 150,000 would be attending the theater on any given day. Only when we realize that the theatre was to Victorian England what television is to us today will we be able to comprehend both its wide appeal and its limited artistic achievement." The popularity of theatrical entertainment made theater a powerful influence in other genres. Dickens was devoted to the theater and composed many of the scenes of his novels with theatrical techniques. Thackeray represents himself as the puppetmaster of his characters in *Vanity Fair* and employs the stock gestures and expressions of melodramatic acting in his illustrations for the novel. Tennyson, Browning, and Henry James all tried their hands at writing plays, though with no commercial success. Successful plays on stage were written by the lesser lights of literature such as Dion Boucicault (1820–1890), the period's most prolific and popular dramatist. The comic operas of W. S. Gilbert and Arthur Sullivan prove the exception to this judgment. Their satire of Victorian values and institutions, what Gilbert called their "topsyturvydom," and their grave and quasi-respectful treatment of the ridiculous not only make them delightful in themselves but anticipate the techniques of Shaw and Wilde. Around 1890, when the socially controversial plays of the Norwegian dramatist Henrik Ibsen (1828–1906) became known in England, Arthur Pinero (1855–1934) and Bernard Shaw began writing "problem plays" that addressed difficult social issues. In the 1890s Shaw and Oscar Wilde transformed British theater with their comic masterpieces. Although they did not like each other's work, they both created a kind of comedy that took aim at Victorian pretense and hypocrisy.

THE VICTORIAN AGE

TEXTS	CONTEXTS
1830 Alfred Lord Tennyson, *Poems, Chiefly Lyrical*	1830 Opening of Liverpool and Manchester Railway
1832 Sir Charles Lyell, *Principles of Geology*	1832 First Reform Bill
1833 Thomas Carlyle, *Sartor Resartus*	1833 Factory Act. Beginning of Oxford Movement
1836 Charles Dickens, *Pickwick Papers*	1836 First train in London
1837 Carlyle, *The French Revolution*	1837 Victoria becomes queen
	1838 "People's Charter" issued by Chartist Movement
	1840 Queen marries Prince Albert
1842 Tennyson, *Poems*. Robert Browning, *Dramatic Lyrics*	1842 Chartist Riots. Copyright Act. Mudie's Circulating Library
1843 John Ruskin, *Modern Painters* (vol. 1)	
	1845–46 Potato famine in Ireland. Mass emigration to North America
1846 George Eliot, *The Life of Jesus* (translation)	1846 Repeal of Corn Laws. Browning marries Elizabeth Barrett
1847 Charlotte Brontë, *Jane Eyre*. Emily Brontë, *Wuthering Heights*	1847 Ten Hours Factory Act
1848 Elizabeth Gaskell, *Mary Barton*. William Makepeace Thackeray, *Vanity Fair*	1848 Revolution on the Continent. Second Republic established in France. Founding of Pre-Raphaelite Brotherhood
1850 Tennyson, *In Memoriam*	1850 Tennyson succeeds Wordsworth as Poet Laureate
1851 Ruskin, *Stones of Venice*	1851 Great Exhibition of science and industry at the Crystal Palace
1853 Matthew Arnold, *Poems*	
1854 Dickens, *Hard Times*	1854 Crimean War. Florence Nightingale organizes nurses to care for sick and wounded
1855 R. Browning, *Men and Women*	
1857 Elizabeth Barrett Browning, *Aurora Leigh*	1857 Indian Mutiny. Matrimonial Causes Act
1859 Charles Darwin, *The Origin of Species*. John Stuart Mill, *On Liberty*. Tennyson, *Idylls of the King* (books 1–4)	
1860 Dickens, *Great Expectations*. Eliot, *The Mill on the Floss*	1860 Italian unification
	1861 Death of Prince Albert
	1861–65 American Civil War
1862 Christina Rossetti, *Goblin Market*	
1864 R. Browning, *Dramatis Personae*	

TEXTS	CONTEXTS
1865 Lewis Carroll, *Alice's Adventures in Wonderland*	1865 Jamaica Rebellion
1866 Algernon Charles Swinburne, *Poems and Ballads*	
1867 Karl Marx, *Das Kapital*	1867 Second Reform Bill
	1868 Opening of Suez Canal
1869 Arnold, *Culture and Anarchy*. Mill, *The Subjection of Women*	
	1870 Married Women's Property Act. Victory in Franco-Prussian War makes Germany a world power
1871 Darwin, *Descent of Man*	1871 Newnham College (first women's college) founded at Cambridge
1872 Eliot, *Middlemarch*	
1873 Walter Pater, *Studies in the Renaissance*	
	1877 Queen Victoria made empress of India. Gerard Manley Hopkins joins Jesuit order
	1878 Electric street lighting in London
	1882 Married Women's Property Act
1885 Gilbert and Sullivan, *The Mikado*	1885 Massacre of General Gordon and his forces and fall of Khartoum
1886 Robert Louis Stevenson, *Doctor Jekyll and Mr. Hyde*	
1888 Rudyard Kipling, *Plain Tales from the Hills*	
1889 William Butler Yeats, *Crossways*	
	1890 First subway line in London
1891 Thomas Hardy, *Tess of the D'Urbervilles*. Bernard Shaw, *The Quintessence of Ibsenism*. Oscar Wilde, *The Picture of Dorian Grey*. Arthur Conan Doyle, *Adventures of Sherlock Holmes*	1891 Free elementary education
1893 Shaw, *Mrs. Warren's Profession*	1893 Independent Labour Party
1895 Wilde, *The Importance of Being Earnest*. Hardy, *Jude the Obscure*	1895 Oscar Wilde arrested and imprisoned for homosexuality
1896 A. E. Housman, *A Shropshire Lad*	
1898 Hardy, *Wessex Poems*	1898 Discovery of radium
	1899 Irish Literary Theater founded in Dublin
	1899–1902 Boer War
1900 Joseph Conrad, *Lord Jim*	
	1901 Death of Queen Victoria; succession of Edward VII

THOMAS CARLYLE
1795–1881

W. B. Yeats once asked William Morris which writers had inspired the socialist movement of the 1880s, and Morris replied: "Oh, Ruskin and Carlyle, but somebody should have been beside Carlyle and punched his head every five minutes." Morris's mixed feelings of admiration and exasperation are typical of the response Thomas Carlyle evokes in many readers. Anyone approaching his prose for the first time should expect to be sometimes bewildered. Like Bernard Shaw, Carlyle discovered, early in life, that exaggeration can be a highly effective way of gaining the attention of an audience. But it can also be a way of distracting an audience unfamiliar with the idiosyncrasies of his rhetoric and unprepared for the distinctive enjoyments his writings can provide.

One of the idiosyncrasies of his prose is that it is meant to be read aloud. "His paragraphs," as Emerson observes, "are all a sort of splendid conversation." As a talker Carlyle was as famous in his day as Samuel Johnson in his. Charles Darwin testified that he was "the best worth listening to of any man I know." No Boswell has adequately recorded this talk, but no Boswell was needed, for Carlyle has contrived to get the sound of his own spoken voice into his writings. It is a noisy and emphatic voice, startling on first acquaintance. To become familiar with its unusual sounds and rhythms, one can best begin by reading aloud from some of Carlyle's portraits of his contemporaries that are included in the selections printed here. Many of these colorful portraits are from his letters, and it becomes evident that the mannerisms of the author were simply the mannerisms of the man and were congenial and appropriate for the author's purposes. Writing to thank Carlyle for some letters, a friend remarked that they, "unlike other people's, have the writer's signature in every word as well as the end."

Carlyle was forty-one years old when Victoria became queen of England. He had been born in the same year as Keats, yet he is rarely grouped with his contemporaries among the Romantic writers. Instead his name is linked with younger men such as Dickens, Browning, and Ruskin, the early generation of Victorian writers, for whom he became (according to Elizabeth Barrett Browning) "the great teacher of the age." The classification is fitting, for it was Carlyle's role to foresee the problems that were to preoccupy the Victorians and early to report on his experiences in confronting these problems. After 1837 his loud voice began to attract an audience; and he soon became one of the most influential figures of the age, affecting the attitudes of scientists, statesmen, and especially of writers. His wife once complained that Ralph Waldo Emerson had no ideas (except mad ones) that he had not derived from Carlyle. " 'But pray, Mrs. Carlyle,' replied a friend, 'who has?' "

Carlyle was born in Ecclefechan, a village in Scotland, the eldest child of a large family. His mother, at the time of her marriage, was illiterate. His father, James Carlyle, a stonemason and later a farmer, was proudly characterized by his son as a peasant. The key to the character of James Carlyle was the Scottish Calvinism that he instilled into the members of his household. Frugality, hard work, a tender but undemonstrative family loyalty, and a peculiar blend of self-denial and self-righteousness were characteristic features of Carlyle's childhood home.

With his father's aid the young Carlyle was educated at Annan Academy and at Edinburgh University, the subject of his special interest being mathematics; he left without taking a degree. It was his parents' hope that their son would become a clergyman, but in this respect Thomas made a severe break with his ancestry. He was a prodigious reader; and his exposure to such skeptical writers as Hume, Voltaire, and Gibbon had undermined his faith. Gibbon's *Decline and Fall of the Roman*

Empire, he told Emerson, was "the splendid bridge from the old world to the new." By the time he was twenty-three Carlyle had crossed the bridge and had abandoned his Christian faith and his proposed career as a clergyman. During the period in which he was thinking through his religious position, he supported himself by teaching school in Scotland and, later, by tutoring private pupils; but from 1824 to the end of his life he relied exclusively on his writings for his livelihood. His early writings consisted of translations, biographies, and critical studies of Goethe and other German authors, to whose view of life he was deeply attracted. The German Romantics (loosely grouped by Carlyle under the label "Mystics") were the second most important influence on his life and character, exceeded only by his early family experiences. Aided by the writings of these German poets and philosophers, he arrived finally at a faith in life that served as a substitute for the Christian faith he had lost.

His most significant early essay, *Characteristics*, appeared in *The Edinburgh Review* in 1831. A year earlier he had begun writing *Sartor Resartus*, an account of the life and opinions of an imaginary philosopher, Professor Diogenes Teufelsdröckh, a work that he had great difficulty in persuading anyone to publish. In book form *Sartor* first appeared in America in 1836, where Carlyle's follower Emerson had prepared an enthusiastic audience for this unusual work. His American following (which was later to become a vast one) did little at first, however, to relieve the poverty in which he still found himself after fifteen years of writing. In 1837 the tide at last turned when he published *The French Revolution*. "O it has been a great success, dear," his wife assured him; but her husband, embittered by the long struggle, was incredulous that the sought-for recognition had at last come to him.

It was in character for his wife, Jane Welsh Carlyle, to be less surprised by his success than he was. That Thomas Carlyle was a genius had been an article of faith to her from her first meeting with him in 1821. A witty, intelligent, and intellectually ambitious young woman, the daughter of a doctor of good family, Jane Welsh had many suitors. When in 1826 she finally accepted Carlyle, her family and friends were shocked. This peasant's son, of no fixed employment, seemed a fantastic choice. Subsequent events seemed to confirm her family's verdict. Not long after marriage, Carlyle insisted on their retiring to a remote farm at Craigenputtock where for six years (1828–34) this sociable woman was obliged to live in isolation and loneliness. After they moved to London in 1834 and settled in a house on Cheyne Walk in Chelsea, Jane Carlyle was considerably happier and enjoyed her role at the center of the intellectual and artistic circle that surrounded her husband. Her husband, however, remained a difficult man to live with. His stomach ailments, irascible nerves, and preoccupation with his writings, as well as the lionizing to which he was subjected, left him with little inclination for domestic amenities or for encouraging his wife's considerable intellectual talents. As a young girl she had wanted to be a writer; her letters, some of the most remarkable of the century, show that she had considerable literary talent.

This marriage of the Carlyles has aroused almost as much interest as that of the Brownings. Their friend the Reverend W. H. Brookfield (whose marriage was an unhappy one) once said cynically that marrying is "dipping into a pitcher of snakes for the chance of an eel," and some biographers have argued that Jane Welsh Carlyle drew a snake instead of an eel. Yet if we study her letters, it is evident that she wanted to marry a man of genius who would change the world. Despite the years she endured of comparative poverty, ill health, and loneliness, she had the satisfaction of recognizing her husband's triumph when the peasant's son she had chosen returned to Scotland to deliver his inaugural address as lord rector of Edinburgh University. While he was away, to Carlyle's great grief, she died.

During the first thirty years of Carlyle's residence in London he wrote extensive historical works and many pamphlets concerning contemporary issues. After *The French Revolution* he edited, in 1845, the *Letters and Speeches of Oliver Cromwell*, a Puritan leader of heroic dimensions in Carlyle's eyes, and later wrote a full-length biography, *The History of Friedrich II of Prussia, Called Frederick the Great* (1858–65). Carlyle's pamphleteering is seen at its best in *Past and Present* (1843) and in its most violent phase in his *Latter-Day Pamphlets* (1850). Following the death of his wife, he wrote very little. For the remaining fifteen years of his life he confined himself to reading or to talking to the stream of visitors who called at Cheyne Walk to listen to the "Sage of Chelsea," as he came to be called. In 1874 he accepted the Prussian Order of Merit from Bismarck but declined an English baronetcy offered by Disraeli. In 1881 he died and was buried near his family in Ecclefechan churchyard.

To understand Carlyle's role as historian, biographer, and social critic, it is essential to understand his attitude toward religion. Like many Victorians, Carlyle underwent a crisis of religious belief. By the time he was twenty-three, he had been shorn of his faith in Christianity. At this stage, as Carlyle observed with dismay, many people seemed content simply to stop. A Utilitarian such as James Mill or some of his commonsensical professors at the University of Edinburgh regarded society and the universe itself as machines. To such thinkers the machines might sometimes seem complex, but they were not mysterious, for machines are subject to humankind's control and understanding through reason and observation. To Carlyle, and to many others, life without a sense of the divine was a meaningless nightmare. In the first part of *The Everlasting No,* a chapter of *Sartor Resartus,* he gives a memorable picture of the horrors of such a soulless world that drove him in 1822 to thoughts of suicide. The eighteenth-century Enlightenment had left him not in light but in darkness.

In developing his views of religion, Carlyle used the metaphor of the "Clothes Philosophy." The naked individual seeks clothing for protection. One solution, represented by Coleridge and his followers, was to repudiate the skepticism of Voltaire and Hume and to return to the protective beliefs and rituals of the Christian Church. To Carlyle such a return was pointless. The traditional Christian coverings were worn out—"Hebrew Old Clothes" he called them. His own solution, described in *The Everlasting Yea,* was to tailor a new suit of beliefs from German philosophy, shreds of Scottish Calvinism, and his own observations. The following summarizes his basic religious attitude: "Gods die with the men who have conceived them. But the godstuff roars eternally, like the sea. . . . Even the gods must be born again. We must be born again." Although this passage is from *The Plumed Serpent* (1926) by D. H. Lawrence (a writer who resembles Carlyle at many points), it might have come from any one of Carlyle's own books—most especially from *Sartor Resartus,* in which he describes his being born again—his "Fire-baptism"—into a new secular faith.

The most appropriate term to describe this faith is *vitalism.* The presence of energy in the world was, in itself, for him a sign of the godhead. Carlyle, therefore, judges everything in terms of the presence or absence of some vital spark. The minds of people, books, societies, churches, or even landscapes, are rated as alive or dead, dynamic or merely mechanical. The government of Louis XVI, for example, was obviously moribund, doomed to be swept away by the dynamic forces of the French Revolution. The government of Victorian England seemed likewise to be doomed unless infused with vital energies of leadership and an awareness of the real needs of humankind. When an editor complained that his essay *Characteristics* was "inscrutable," Carlyle remarked: "My own fear was that it might be too *scrutable;* for it indicates decisively enough that Society (in my view) is utterly condemned to destruction, and even now beginning its long travail-throes of Newbirth."

In his inquiry into the principles of government and social order, Carlyle, like many of his contemporaries, is seeking to understand a world of great social unrest and historical change. This preoccupation with revolution and the destruction of the old orders suggests that Carlyle's politics were radical, but his position is bewilderingly difficult to classify. During the Hungry 1840s he was one of the most outspoken critics of middle-class bunglings and of the economic theory of laissez-faire that, in his opinion, was ultimately responsible for these bunglings. On behalf of the millions of people suffering from the miseries attendant on a major breakdown of industry and agriculture he did strenuous work. At other times, because of his insistence on strong and heroic leadership, Carlyle appears to be a violent conservative or, as some have argued, virtually a fascist. He had no confidence that democratic institutions could work efficiently. A few individuals in every age are, in his view, leaders; the rest are followers and are happy only as followers. Society should be organized so that these gifted leaders can have scope to govern effectively. Such leaders are, for Carlyle, heroes. Bernard Shaw, who learned much from Carlyle, would call them "supermen." Liberals and democrats, however, might call them dictators. Although Carlyle was aware that the Western world was committed to a faith in a system of balloting and of legislative debate, he was confident that the system would eventually break down. The democratic assumption that all voters are equally capable of choice and the assumption that people value liberty more than they value order seemed to him nonsense. Carlyle's authoritarianism intensified as he grew older. When the governor of Jamaica violently repressed a rebellion of black plantation workers, Carlyle served as chair of his defense fund, arguing that England owed the governor honor and thanks for his defense of civilization.

Carlyle's prose style reflects the intensity of his views. At the time he began to write, the essayists of the eighteenth century, Samuel Johnson in particular, were the models of good prose. Carlyle recognized that their style, however admirable an instrument for reasoning, analysis, and generalized exposition, did not suit his purposes. Like a poet, he wanted to convey the sense of experience itself. Like a preacher or prophet, he wanted to exhort or inspire his readers rather than to develop a chain of logical argument. Like a psychoanalyst, he wanted to explore the unconscious and irrational levels of human life, the hidden nine-tenths of the iceberg rather than the conscious and rational fraction above the surface. To this end he developed his highly individual manner of writing, with its vivid imagery of fire and barnyard and zoo, its mixture of biblical rhythms and explosive talk, and its inverted and unorthodox syntax. Classicists may complain, as Landor did, that the result is not English. Carlyle would reply that it is not eighteenth-century English, but that his style was appropriate for a Victorian who reports of revolutions in society and in thought. In reply to a friend who had protested about his stylistic experiments Carlyle exclaimed: "Do you reckon this really a time for Purism of Style? I do not: with whole ragged battalions of Scott's Novel Scotch, with Irish, German, French, and even Newspaper Cockney . . . storming in on us, and the whole structure of our Johnsonian English breaking up from its foundations—revolution *there* as visible as anywhere else?" Carlyle's defense of his style can be tested by his history *The French Revolution*. One may agree or disagree with the historian's explanations of how the fire started or how it was extinguished. But the fire itself is unquestionably there before us, roaring, palpable, giving off a heat of its own.

George Eliot wrote (in an essay of 1855) that Carlyle was "more of an artist than a philosopher." As she said: "No novelist has made his creations live for us more thoroughly." Carlyle is best regarded, that is, as a man of letters, the inventor of a distinctive and extremely effective prose medium that can bring to life for us the very texture of events in scenes such as when a king confronts a guillotine, a young agnostic confronts the devil, a talker such as Coleridge stupefies an audience of admiring disciples, or a man like himself struggles to create a new spiritual and political philosophy adequate to the age in which he finds himself.

[Carlyle's Portraits of His Contemporaries][1]

[QUEEN VICTORIA AT EIGHTEEN]

Yesterday, going through one of the Parks, I saw the poor little Queen. She was in an open carriage, preceded by three or four swift red-coated troopers; all off for Windsor just as I happened to pass. Another carriage or carriages followed with maids-of-honour, etc.: the whole drove very fast. It seemed to me the poor little Queen was a bit modest, nice sonsy[2] little lassie; blue eyes, light hair, fine white skin; of extremely small stature: she looked timid, anxious, almost frightened; for the people looked at her in perfect silence; one old liveryman alone touched his hat to her: I was heartily sorry for the poor bairn,—tho' perhaps she might have said as Parson Swan did, "*Greet*[3] not for me brethren; for verily, yea verily, I greet not for mysel'." It is a strange thing to look at the fashion of this world!

[From a letter to his mother, April 12, 1838]

[SAMUEL TAYLOR COLERIDGE AT FIFTY-THREE][4]

Coleridge sat on the brow of Highgate Hill, in those years, looking down on London and its smoke-tumult, like a sage escaped from the inanity of life's battle; attracting towards him the thoughts of innumerable brave souls still engaged there. His express contributions to poetry, philosophy, or any specific province of human literature or enlightenment, had been small and sadly intermittent; but he had, especially among young inquiring men, a higher than literary, a kind of prophetic or magician character. He was thought to hold, he alone in England, the key of German and other Transcendentalisms; knew the sublime secret of believing by "the reason" what "the understanding" had been obliged to fling out as incredible; and could still, after Hume and Voltaire had done their best and worst with him, profess himself an orthodox Christian, and say and print to the Church of England, with its singular old rubrics and surplices at Allhallowtide, *Esto perpetua*.[5] A sublime man; who, alone in those dark days, had saved his crown of spiritual

---

1. Carlyle once said that "human Portraits, faithfully drawn, are of all pictures the welcomest on human walls." With his pen, rather than with brush, he himself has created a strikingly colorful gallery of his contemporaries.
   A few of the selections printed here (all of them excerpted by the present editors) were written for publication, in particular the elaborate portrait of Coleridge; the majority of them, however, are sketches from his letters, sometimes in the vein of caricature. As Charles Sanders notes, all of them—like most of the portraits by Chaucer, Robert Browning, and Yeats—are "appraisal portraits." Carlyle has been called the Victorian Rembrandt. But with his sharp eye for absurdities, he is often the Victorian Daumier or Rowlandson. This element of caricature can be partly explained in terms of difference of age. It will be noted that most of the celebrities described were older than Carlyle, and he had the customary determination of youth to make fun of the pretensions of an older and established generation. In Carlyle's case, there was

the additional urge to be irreverent in that he was a provincial in a great metropolis with the provincial's need to assert his independence of judgment.
   The portraits are not presented chronologically. The first one is a sketch of royalty; the others are of English writers. Titles for each portrait have been assigned by the editors.
2. Sweet (Scottish).
3. Weep.
4. In 1816 Coleridge moved to a London suburb as a permanent guest in the home of James Gillman. Here he received visits from admirers of his philosophy such as Carlyle's friend John Sterling, from whose biography, by Carlyle, this selection has been taken. Carlyle's visits were made during his first residence in London in 1824–25.
5. Be thou everlasting (Latin)—the last words of Paolo Sarpi (1552–1623), theologian and historian, addressed to the city of Venice. "Allhallowtide": November 1, a festival in honor of all the saints, celebrated by the Roman Catholic and Anglican churches.

manhood; escaping from the black materialisms, and revolutionary deluges, with "God, Freedom, Immortality" still his: a king of men. The practical intellects of the world did not much heed him, or carelessly reckoned him a metaphysical dreamer: but to the rising spirits of the young generation he had this dusky sublime character; and sat there as a kind of *Magus,* girt in mystery and enigma; his Dodona[6] oak-grove (Mr. Gillman's house at Highgate) whispering strange things, uncertain whether oracles or jargon.

The Gillmans did not encourage much company, or excitation of any sort, round their sage; nevertheless access to him, if a youth did reverently wish it, was not difficult. He would stroll about the pleasant garden with you, sit in the pleasant rooms of the place,—perhaps take you to his own peculiar room, high up, with a rearward view, which was the chief view of all. A really charming outlook, in fine weather. Close at hand, wide sweep of flowery leafy gardens, their few houses mostly hidden, the very chimney-pots veiled under blossomy umbrage, flowed gloriously down hill, gloriously issuing in wide-tufted undulating plain-country, rich in all charms of field and town. Waving blooming country of the brightest green; dotted all over with handsome villas, handsome groves; crossed by roads and human traffic, here inaudible or heard only as a musical hum: and behind all swam, under olive-tinted haze, the illimitable limitary ocean of London, with its domes and steeples definite in the sun, big Paul's and the many memories attached to it hanging high over all. Nowhere, of its kind, could you see a grander prospect on a bright summer day, with the set of the air going southward,—southward, and so draping with the city-smoke not *you* but the city. Here for hours would Coleridge talk, concerning all conceivable or inconceivable things; and liked nothing better than to have an intelligent, or failing that, even a silent and patient human listener. He distinguished himself to all that ever heard him as at least the most surprising talker extant in this world,—and to some small minority, by no means to all, as the most excellent.

The good man, he was now getting old, towards sixty perhaps; and gave you the idea of a life that had been full of sufferings; a life heavy-laden, half-vanquished, still swimming painfully in seas of manifold physical and other bewilderment. Brow and head were round, and of massive weight, but the face was flabby and irresolute. The deep eyes, of a light hazel, were as full of sorrow as of inspiration; confused pain looked mildly from them, as in a kind of mild astonishment. The whole figure and air, good and amiable otherwise, might be called flabby and irresolute; expressive of weakness under possibility of strength. He hung loosely on his limbs, with knees bent, and stooping attitude; in walking, he rather shuffled than decisively stept; and a lady once remarked, he never could fix which side of the garden walk would suit him best, but continually shifted, in corkscrew fashion, and kept trying both. A heavy-laden, high-aspiring and surely much-suffering man. His voice, naturally soft and good, had contracted itself into a plaintive snuffle and singsong; he spoke as if preaching,—you would have said, preaching earnestly and also hopelessly the weightiest things. I still recollect his "object" and "subject," terms of continual recurrence in the Kantean province; and how he sang and snuffled them into "om-m-mject" and "sum-m-

---

6. An oracle in Greece. Prophecies were voiced by priests who interpreted the rustling sounds made by oak leaves stirred by the wind. "*Magus*": an Asian magician or sorcerer.

mject," with a kind of solemn shake or quaver, as he rolled along. No talk, in his century or in any other, could be more surprising.

* * * Nothing could be more copious than his talk; and furthermore it was always, virtually or literally, of the nature of a monologue; suffering no interruption, however reverent; hastily putting aside all foreign additions, annotations, or most ingenuous desires for elucidation, as well-meant superfluities which would never do. Besides, it was talk not flowing anywhither like a river, but spreading everywhither in inextricable currents and regurgitations like a lake or sea; terribly deficient in definite goal or aim, nay often in logical intelligibility; what you were to believe or do, on any earthly or heavenly thing, obstinately refusing to appear from it. So that, most times, you felt logically lost; swamped near to drowning in this tide of ingenious vocables, spreading out boundless as if to submerge the world.

To sit as a passive bucket and be pumped into, whether you consent or not, can in the long-run be exhilarating to no creature; how eloquent soever the flood of utterance that is descending. But if it be withal a confused unintelligible flood of utterance, threatening to submerge all known landmarks of thought, and drown the world and you!—I have heard Coleridge talk, with eager musical energy, two stricken hours, his face radiant and moist, and communicate no meaning whatsoever to any individual of his hearers,—certain of whom, I for one, still kept eagerly listening in hope; the most had long before given up, and formed (if the room were large enough) secondary humming groups of their own. He began anywhere: you put some question to him, made some suggestive observation; instead of answering this, or decidedly setting out towards answer of it, he would accumulate formidable apparatus, logical swim-bladders, transcendental life-preservers and other precautionary and vehiculatory gear, for setting out; perhaps did at last get under way,—but was swiftly solicited, turned aside by the glance of some radiant new game on this hand or that, into new courses; and ever into new; and before long into all the Universe, where it was uncertain what game you would catch, or whether any.

His talk, alas, was distinguished, like himself, by irresolution: it disliked to be troubled with conditions, abstinences, definite fulfilments;—loved to wander at its own sweet will, and make its auditor and his claims and humble wishes a mere passive bucket for itself! He had knowledge about many things and topics, much curious reading; but generally all topics led him, after a pass or two, into the high seas of theosophic philosophy, the hazy infinitude of Kantean transcendentalism, with its "sum-m-mjects" and "om-m-mjects." Sad enough; for with such indolent impatience of the claims and ignorances of others, he had not the least talent for explaining this or anything unknown to them; and you swam and fluttered in the mistiest wide unintelligible deluge of things, for most part in a rather profitless uncomfortable manner.

Glorious islets, too, I have seen rise out of the haze; but they were few, and soon swallowed in the general element again. Balmy sunny islets, islets of the blest and the intelligible:—on which occasions those secondary humming groups would all cease humming, and hang breathless upon the eloquent words; till once your islet got wrapt in the mist again, and they could recommence humming. . . . Coleridge was not without what talkers call wit, and there were touches of prickly sarcasm in him, contemptuous enough of the world and its idols and popular dignitaries; he had traits even of poetic humour: but in general he seemed deficient in laughter; or indeed in sympathy for concrete human things either on the sunny or on the stormy side. One right peal of concrete laughter at some convicted flesh-and-blood absurdity, one burst of noble indignation at some injustice or depravity, rubbing elbows with us on this solid Earth, how strange would it have been in that Kantean haze-world, and how infinitely cheering amid its vacant air-castles and dim-melting ghosts and shadows! None such ever came. His life had been an abstract thinking and dreaming, idealistic, passed amid the ghosts of defunct bodies and of unborn ones. The meaning singsong of that theosophico-metaphysical monotony left on you, at last, a very dreary feeling.

* * *

But indeed, to the young ardent mind, instinct with pious nobleness, yet driven to the grim deserts of Radicalism for a faith, his speculations had a charm much more than literary, a charm almost religious and prophetic. The constant gist of his discourse was lamentation over the sunk condition of the world; which he recognised to be given-up to Atheism and Materialism, full of mere sordid misbeliefs, mispursuits and misresults. All Science had become mechanical; the science not of men, but of a kind of human beavers. Churches themselves had died away into a godless mechanical condition; and stood there as mere Cases of Articles, mere Forms of Churches; like the dried carcasses of once-swift camels, which you find left withering in the thirst of the universal desert,—ghastly portents for the present, beneficent ships of the desert no more. Men's souls were blinded, hebetated,[7] and sunk under the influence of Atheism and Materialism, and Hume and Voltaire: the world for the present was as an extinct world, deserted of God, and incapable of welldoing till it changed its heart and spirit. This, expressed I think with less of indignation and with more of long-drawn querulousness, was always recognisable as the ground-tone:—in which truly a pious young heart, driven into Radicalism and the opposition party, could not but recognise a too sorrowful truth; and ask of the Oracle, with all earnestness, What remedy, then?

The remedy, though Coleridge himself professed to see it as in sunbeams, could not, except by processes unspeakably difficult, be described to you at all. On the whole, those dead Churches, this dead English Church especially, must be brought to life again. Why not? It was not dead; the soul of it, in this parched-up body, was tragically asleep only. Atheistic Philosophy was true on its side, and Hume and Voltaire could on their own ground speak irrefragably for themselves against any Church: but lift the Church and them into a higher sphere of argument, *they* died into inanition, the Church revivified itself into pristine florid vigour,—became once more a living ship of the desert, and invincibly bore you over stock and stone. But how, but how! By attending to the "reason" of man, said Coleridge, and duly chaining-up the "understanding" of man: the *Vernunft* (Reason) and *Verstand* (Understanding) of the Germans, it all turned upon these, if you could well understand them,—which you couldn't. For the rest, Mr. Coleridge had on the anvil various Books, especially was about to write one grand Book *On the Logos,* which would help to bridge the chasm for us. So much appeared, however:

7. Dulled.

Churches, though proved false (as you had imagined), were still true (as you were to imagine): here was an Artist who could burn you up an old Church, root and branch; and then as the Alchymists professed to do with organic substances in general, distil you an "Astral Spirit" from the ashes, which was the very image of the old burnt article, its airdrawn counterpart,—this you still had, or might get, and draw uses from, if you could. Wait till the Book on the Logos were done;—alas, till your own terrene eyes, blind with conceit and the dust of logic, were purged, subtilised and spiritualised into the sharpness of vision requisite for discerning such an "om-m-mject."—The ingenuous young English head, of those days, stood strangely puzzled by such revelations; uncertain whether it were getting inspired, or getting infatuated into flat imbecility; and strange effulgence, of new day or else of deeper meteoric night, coloured the horizon of the future for it.

[From *Life of John Sterling*, 1851]

[WILLIAM WORDSWORTH IN HIS SEVENTIES]

On a summer morning (let us call it 1840 then) I was apprised by Taylor[8] that Wordsworth had come to town, and would meet a small party of us at a certain tavern in St. James's Street, at breakfast, to which I was invited for the given day and hour. We had a pretty little room, quiet though looking streetward (tavern's name is quite lost to me); the morning sun was pleasantly tinting the opposite houses, a balmy, calm and sunlight morning. Wordsworth, I think, arrived just along with me; we had still five minutes of sauntering and miscellaneous talking before the whole were assembled. I do not positively remember any of them, except that James Spedding[9] was there, and that the others, not above five or six in whole, were polite intelligent quiet persons, and, except Taylor and Wordsworth, not of any special distinction in the world. Breakfast was pleasant, fairly beyond the common of such things. Wordsworth seemed in good tone, and, much to Taylor's satisfaction, talked a great deal; about "poetic" correspondents of his own (i.e. correspondents for the sake of his poetry; especially one such who had sent him, from Canton, an excellent chest of tea; correspondent grinningly applauded by us all); then about ruralties and miscellanies. * * * These were the first topics. Then finally about literature, literary laws, practices, observances, at considerable length, and turning wholly on the mechanical part, including even a good deal of shallow enough etymology, from me and others, which was well received. On all this Wordsworth enlarged with evident satisfaction, and was joyfully reverent of the "wells of English undefiled";[1] though stone dumb as to the deeper rules and wells of Eternal Truth and Harmony, which you were to try and set forth by said undefiled wells of English or what other speech you had! To me a little disappointing, but not much; though it would have given me pleasure had the robust veteran man emerged a little out of vocables into things, now and then, as he never once chanced to do. For the rest, he talked well in his way; with veracity, easy brevity and force, as a wise tradesman would of his tools and workshop,—and as no unwise one could. His voice was good, frank and sonorous, though practically clear distinct and forcible rather than melodious; the tone of him

---

8. Henry Taylor, contemporary playwright.
9. Editor of the works of Francis Bacon.

1. Spenser, *Faerie Queene* 4.2.32, referring to Chaucer.

businesslike, sedately confident; no discourtesy, yet no anxiety about being courteous. A fine wholesome rusticity, fresh as his mountain breezes, sat well on the stalwart veteran, and on all he said and did. You would have said he was a usually taciturn man; glad to unlock himself to audience sympathetic and intelligent, when such offered itself. His face bore marks of much, not always peaceful, meditation; the look of it not bland or benevolent so much as close impregnable and hard: a man *multa tacere loquive paratus*,[2] in a world where he had experienced no lack of contradictions as he strode along! The eyes were not very brilliant, but they had a quiet clearness; there was enough of brow and well shaped; rather too much of cheek ("horse face" I have heard satirists say); face of squarish shape and decidedly longish, as I think the head itself was (its "length" going horizontal); he was large-boned, lean, but still firm-knit tall and strong-looking when he stood, a right good old steel-grey figure, with rustic simplicity and dignity about him, and a vivacious strength looking through him which might have suited one of those old steel-grey markgrafs; whom Henry the Fowler set up to ward the "marches"[3] and do battle with the intrusive heathen in a stalwart and judicious manner.

On this and other occasional visits of his, I saw Wordsworth a number of times, at dinner, in evening parties; and we grew a little more familiar, but without much increase of real intimacy or affection springing up between us. He was willing to talk with me in a corner, in noisy extensive circles, having weak eyes, and little loving the general babble current in such places. One evening, probably about this time, I got him upon the subject of great poets, who I thought might be admirable equally to us both; but was rather mistaken, as I gradually found. Pope's partial failure I was prepared for; less for the narrowish limits visible in Milton and others. I tried him with Burns, of whom he had sung tender recognition; but Burns also turned out to be a limited inferior creature, any genius he had a theme for one's pathos rather; even Shakespeare himself had his blind sides, his limitations; gradually it became apparent to me that of transcendent unlimited there was, to this critic, probably but one specimen known, Wordsworth himself! He by no means said so, or hinted so, in words; but on the whole it was all I gathered from him in this considerable *tête-à-tête*[4] of ours; and it was not an agreeable conquest. New notion as to poetry or poet I had not in the smallest degree got; but my insight into the depths of Wordsworth's pride in himself had considerably augmented; and it did not increase my love of him; though I did not in the least hate it either, so quiet was it, so fixed, unappealing, like a dim old lichened crag on the wayside, the private meaning of which, in contrast with any public meaning it had, you recognised with a kind of not wholly melancholy grin.

* * *

During the last seven or ten years of his life, Wordsworth felt himself to be a recognised lion, in certain considerable London circles, and was in the habit of coming up to town with his wife for a month or two every season, to enjoy his quiet triumph and collect his bits of tribute *tales quales*.[5] * * *

---

2. Prepared to speak out or to pass over much in silence (Latin).
3. Borders. "Markgrafs": governors appointed by Henry I of Germany, "the Fowler" (876–936), to guard the borders of his kingdom.
4. Private conversation between two people.
5. Of such a sort (Latin).

Wordsworth took his bit of lionism very quietly, with a smile sardonic rather that triumphant, and certainly got no harm by it, if he got or expected little good. His wife, a small, withered, puckered, winking lady, who never spoke, seemed to be more in earnest about the affair, and was visibly and sometimes ridiculously assiduous to secure her proper place of precedence at table. * * * The light was always afflictive to his eyes; he carried in his pocket something like a skeleton brass candlestick, in which, setting it on the dinner-table, between him and the most afflictive or nearest of the chief lights, he touched a little spring, and there flirted out, at the top of his brass implement, a small vertical green circle which prettily enough threw his eyes into shade, and screened him from that sorrow. In proof of his equanimity as lion I remember, in connection with this green shade, one little glimpse. * * * Dinner was large, luminous, sumptuous; I sat a long way from Wordsworth; dessert I think had come in, and certainly there reigned in all quarters a cackle as of Babel (only politer perhaps), which far up in Wordsworth's quarter (who was leftward on my side of the table) seemed to have taken a sententious, rather louder, logical and quasi-scientific turn, heartily unimportant to gods and men, so far as I could judge of it and of the other babble reigning. I looked upwards, leftwards, the coast being luckily for a moment clear; there, far off, beautifully screened in the shadow of his vertical green circle, which was on the farther side of him, sate Wordsworth, silent, slowly but steadily gnawing some portion of what I judged to be raisins, with his eye and attention placidly fixed on these and these alone. The sight of whom, and of his rock-like indifference to the babble, quasi-scientific and other, with attention turned on the small practical alone, was comfortable and amusing to me, who felt like him but could not eat raisins. This little glimpse I could still paint, so clear and bright is it, and this shall be symbolical of all.

In a few years, I forget in how many and when, these Wordsworth appearances in London ceased; we heard, not of ill-health perhaps, but of increasing love of rest; at length of the long sleep's coming; and never saw Wordsworth more. One felt his death as the extinction of a public light, but not otherwise.

[From *Reminiscences*, 1867, 1881]

[ALFRED TENNYSON AT THIRTY-FOUR]

Alfred is one of the few British or Foreign Figures (a not increasing number I think!) who are and remain beautiful to me;—a true human soul, or some authentic approximation thereto, to whom your own soul can say, Brother!— However, I doubt he will not come; he often skips me, in these brief visits to Town; skips everybody indeed; being a man solitary and sad, as certain men are, dwelling in an element of gloom,—carrying a bit of Chaos about him, in short, which he is manufacturing into Cosmos!

Alfred is the son of a Lincolnshire Gentleman Farmer, I think; indeed, you see in his verses that he is a native of "moated granges," and green, fat pastures, not of mountains and their torrents and storms. He had his breeding at Cambridge, as if for the Law or Church; being master of a small annuity on his Father's decease, he preferred clubbing with his Mother and some Sisters, to live unpromoted and write Poems. In this way he lives still, now here, now there; the family always within reach of London, never in it; he himself making rare and brief visits, lodging in some old comrade's rooms. I think he must be under forty, not much under it. One of the finest-looking men in the world. A great shock of rough dusty-dark hair; bright-laughing hazel eyes; massive aquiline face, most massive yet most delicate; of sallow-brown complexion, almost Indian-looking; clothes cynically loose, free-and-easy;—smokes infinite tobacco. His voice is musical metallic,—fit for loud laughter and piercing wail, and all that may lie between; speech and speculation free and plenteous: I do not meet, in these late decades, such company over a pipe!—We shall see what he will grow to. He is often unwell; very chaotic,—his way is through Chaos and the Bottomless and Pathless; not handy for making out many miles upon.

[From a letter to Emerson, August 5, 1844]

Sartor Resartus *Sartor Resartus* is a combination of novel, autobiography, and essay. To present some of his own experiences, Carlyle invented a hero, Professor Diogenes Teufelsdröckh of Germany, whose name itself (meaning "God-Begotten Devil's Dung") suggests the grotesque and fantastic humor that Carlyle used to expound a serious treatise. Teufelsdröckh tells the story of his unhappiness in love and of his difficulties in religion. He also airs his opinions on a variety of subjects. Interspersed between the professor's words (which are in quotation marks) are the remarks of an editor, also imaginary, who has the task of putting together the story from assorted documents written by Teufelsdröckh. The title, meaning "The Tailor Retailored," refers to the editor's role of patching the story together. The title also refers to Carlyle's so-called Clothes Philosophy, which is expounded by the hero in many chapters of *Sartor*. In effect, this Clothes Philosophy is an attempt to demonstrate the difference between the appearances of things and their reality. The appearance of an individual depends on the costume he or she wears; the reality of that individual is the body underneath the costume. By analogy, Carlyle suggests that institutions, such as churches or governments, are like clothes. They may be useful "visible emblems" of the spiritual forces that they cover, but they wear out and have to be replaced by new clothes. The Christian Church, for example, which once expressed humanity's permanent religious desires, is, in Carlyle's terms, worn out and must be discarded. But the underlying religious spirit must be recognized and kept alive at all costs. Carlyle also uses the clothes analogy to describe the relationship between the material and spiritual worlds. Clothes hide the body just as the world of nature cloaks the reality of God and as the body itself cloaks the reality of the soul. The discovery of these realities behind the appearances is, for Carlyle and for his hero, the initial stage of a solution to the dilemmas of life.

Teufelsdröckh's religious development, as described in the following chapters, may be contrasted with J. S. Mill's account of his own crisis of spirit in his *Autobiography* (p. 1166). The first three selections are chapters 7 to 9 of book 2.

From Sartor Resartus

The Everlasting No

Under the strange nebulous envelopment, wherein our Professor has now shrouded himself, no doubt but his spiritual nature is nevertheless progressive, and growing: for how can the "Son of Time," in any case, stand still? We behold him, through those dim years, in a state of crisis, of transition: his mad Pilgrimings, and general solution into aimless Discontinuity, what is all this but a mad Fermentation; wherefrom, the fiercer it is, the clearer product will one day evolve itself?

Such transitions are ever full of pain: thus the Eagle when he moults is sickly; and, to attain his new beak, must harshly dash-off the old one upon rocks. What Stoicism soever our Wanderer, in his individual acts and motions, may affect, it is clear that there is a hot fever of anarchy and misery raging within; coruscations of which flash out: as, indeed, how could there be other? Have we not seen him disappointed, bemocked of Destiny, through long years? All that the young heart might desire and pray for has been denied; nay, as in the last worst instance, offered and then snatched away. Ever an "excellent Passivity"; but of useful, reasonable Activity, essential to the former as Food to Hunger, nothing granted: till at length, in this wild Pilgrimage, he must forcibly seize for himself an Activity, though useless, unreasonable. Alas, his cup of bitterness, which had been filling drop by drop, ever since that first "ruddy morning" in the Hinterschlag Gymnasium, was at the very lip; and then with that poison-drop, of the Towgood-and-Blumine[1] business, it runs over, and even hisses over in a deluge of foam.

He himself says once, with more justice than originality: "Man is, properly speaking, based upon Hope, he has no other possession but Hope; this world of his is emphatically the Place of Hope." What, then, was our Professor's possession? We see him, for the present, quite shut-out from Hope; looking not into the golden orient, but vaguely all round into a dim copper firmament, pregnant with earthquake and tornado.

Alas, shut-out from Hope, in a deeper sense than we yet dream of! For, as he wanders wearisomely through this world, he has now lost all tidings of another and higher. Full of religion, or at least of religiosity, as our Friend has since exhibited himself, he hides not that, in those days, he was wholly irreligious: "Doubt had darkened into Unbelief," says he; "shade after shade goes grimly over your soul, till you have the fixed, starless, Tartarean black." To such readers as have reflected, what can be called reflecting, on man's life, and happily discovered, in contradiction to much Profit-and-loss Philosophy, speculative and practical, that Soul is *not* synonymous with Stomach; who understand, therefore, in our Friend's words, "that, for man's well-being, Faith is properly the one thing needful; how, with it, Martyrs, otherwise weak, can cheerfully endure the shame and the cross; and without it, Worldlings puke-up their sick existence, by suicide, in the midst of luxury": to such it will be clear that, for a pure moral nature, the loss of his religious Belief was the loss of everything. Unhappy young man! All wounds, the crush of long-continued Destitution, the stab of false Friendship and of false Love, all wounds in thy so genial heart, would have healed again, had not its life-warmth been withdrawn. Well might he exclaim, in his wild way: "Is there no God, then; but at best an absentee God, sitting idle, ever since the first Sabbath, at the outside of his Universe, and *seeing* it go? Has the word Duty no meaning; is what we call Duty no divine Messenger and Guide, but a

---

1. A woman loved by Teufelsdröckh who married his friend Towgood. His distress is pictured in the preceding chapter, titled "Sorrows of Teufels-dröckh." "Hinterschlag Gymnasium": smite-behind grammar school (German).

false earthly Fantasm, made-up of Desire and Fear, of emanations from the Gallows and from Dr. Graham's Celestial-Bed?[2] Happiness of an approving Conscience! Did not Paul of Tarsus, whom admiring men have since named Saint, feel that *he* was 'the chief of sinners';[3] and Nero of Rome, jocund in spirit (*wohlgemuth*), spend much of his time in fiddling? Foolish Word-monger and Motive-grinder, who in thy Logic-mill hast an earthly mechanism for the Godlike itself, and wouldst fain grind me out Virtue from the husks of Pleasure,—I tell thee, Nay! To the unregenerate Prometheus Vinctus[4] of a man, it is ever the bitterest aggravation of his wretchedness that he is conscious of Virtue, that he feels himself the victim not of suffering only, but of injustice. What then? Is the heroic inspiration we name Virtue but some Passion; some bubble of the blood, bubbling in the direction others *profit* by? I know not; only this I know, If what thou namest Happiness be our true aim, then are we all astray. With Stupidity and sound Digestion man may front much. But what, in these dull unimaginative days, are the terrors of Conscience to the diseases of the Liver! Not on Morality, but on Cookery, let us build our stronghold: there brandishing our frying-pan, as censer, let us offer sweet incense to the Devil, and live at ease on the fat things *he* has provided for his Elect!"

Thus has the bewildered Wanderer to stand, as so many have done, shouting question after question into the Sibyl-cave of Destiny,[5] and receive no Answer but an Echo. It is all a grim Desert, this once-fair world of his; wherein is heard only the howling of wild-beasts, or the shrieks of despairing, hate-filled men; and no Pillar of Cloud by day, and no Pillar of Fire by night,[6] any longer guides the Pilgrim. To such length has the spirit of Inquiry carried him. "But what boots it (*was thut's*)?" cries he: "it is but the common lot in this era. Not having come to spiritual majority prior to the *Siècle de Louis Quinze*,[7] and not being born purely a Loghead (*Dummkopf*), thou hast no other outlook. The whole world is, like thee, sold to Unbelief, their old Temples of the Godhead, which for long have not been rainproof, crumble down; and men ask now: Where is the Godhead; our eyes never saw him?"

Pitiful enough were it, for all these wild utterances, to call our Diogenes wicked. Unprofitable servants as we all are, perhaps at no era of his life was he more decisively the Servant of Goodness, the Servant of God, than even now when doubting God's existence. "One circumstance I note," says he: "after all the nameless woe that Inquiry, which for me, what it is not always, was genuine Love of Truth, had wrought me, I nevertheless still loved Truth, and would bate no jot of my allegiance to her. 'Truth!' I cried, 'though the Heavens crush me for following her: no Falsehood! though a whole celestial Lubberland[8] were the price of Apostasy.' In conduct it was the same. Had a divine Messenger from the clouds, or miraculous Handwriting on the wall, convincingly proclaimed to me *This thou shalt do*, with what passionate readiness, as I often thought, would I have done it, had it been leaping into the

2. James Graham (1745–1794), a quack doctor, had invented an elaborate bed that was supposed to cure sterility in couples using it. In this passage, the bed is apparently a symbol of sexual desires.
3. Paraphrase of 1 Timothy 1.15.
4. I.e., Prometheus Bound; this is also the title of a play by Aeschylus depicting the sufferings of a hero who defied Zeus.

5. An allusion to Virgil's *Aeneid* 6.36ff., where Aeneas questions the Cumaean sibyl.
6. Exodus 13.21.
7. The Century of Louis XV (French), allusion to *Précis du Siècle de Louis* XV, Voltaire's history of the skeptical and enquiring spirit of 18th-century France during the reign of Louis XV (1715–74).
8. Land of Plenty.

infernal Fire. Thus, in spite of all Motive-grinders, and Mechanical Profit-and-Loss Philosophies, with the sick ophthalmia and hallucination they had brought on, was the Infinite nature of Duty still dimly present to me: living without God in the world, of God's light I was not utterly bereft; if my as yet sealed eyes, with their unspeakable longing, could nowhere see Him, nevertheless in my heart He was present, and His heaven-written Law still stood legible and sacred there."

Meanwhile, under all these tribulations, and temporal and spiritual destitutions, what must the Wanderer, in his silent soul, have endured! "The painfullest feeling," writes he, "is that of your own Feebleness (*Unkraft*); ever, as the English Milton says, to be weak is the true misery.[9] And yet of your Strength there is and can be no clear feeling, save by what you have prospered in, by what you have done. Between vague wavering Capability and fixed indubitable Performance, what a difference! A certain inarticulate Self-consciousness dwells dimly in us; which only our Works can render articulate and decisively discernible. Our Works are the mirror wherein the spirit first sees its natural lineaments. Hence, too, the folly of that impossible Precept, *Know thyself;*[1] till it be translated into this partially possible one, *Know what thou canst work at.*

"But for me, so strangely unprosperous had I been, the net-result of my Workings amounted as yet simply to—Nothing. How then could I believe in my Strength, when there was as yet no mirror to see it in? Ever did this agitating, yet, as I now perceive, quite frivolous question, remain to me insoluble: Hast thou a certain Faculty, a certain Worth, such even as the most have not; or art thou the completest Dullard of these modern times? Alas! the fearful Unbelief is unbelief in yourself; and how could I believe? Had not my first, last Faith in myself, when even to me the Heavens seemed laid open, and I dared to love, been all-too cruelly belied? The speculative Mystery of Life grew ever more mysterious to me: neither in the practical Mystery[2] had I made the slightest progress, but been everywhere buffeted, foiled, and contemptuously cast-out. A feeble unit in the middle of a threatening Infinitude, I seemed to have nothing given me but eyes, whereby to discern my own wretchedness. Invisible yet impenetrable walls, as of Enchantment, divided me from all living: was there, in the wide world, any true bosom I could press trustfully to mine? O Heaven, No, there was none! I kept a lock upon my lips: why should I speak much with that shifting variety of so-called Friends, in whose withered, vain and too-hungry souls Friendship was but an incredible tradition? In such cases, your resource is to talk little, and that little mostly from the Newspapers. Now when I look back, it was a strange isolation I then lived in. The men and women around me, even speaking with me, were but Figures; I had, practically, forgotten that they were alive, that they were not merely automatic. In midst of their crowded streets and assemblages, I walked solitary; and (except as it was my own heart, not another's, that I kept devouring) savage also, as the tiger in his jungle. Some comfort it would have been, could I, like a Faust,[3] have fancied myself tempted and tormented of the Devil; for a Hell, as I imagine, without Life, though only

---

9. *Paradise Lost* 1.157: "Fallen cherub, to be weak is miserable."
1. This maxim was inscribed in gold letters over the portico of the temple at Delphi.

2. A profession or practical occupation.
3. Both Christopher Marlowe and Goethe wrote plays about the temptations of Faust.

diabolic Life, were more frightful: but in our age of Down-pulling and Dis-belief, the very Devil has been pulled down, you cannot so much as believe in a Devil. To me the Universe was all void of Life, of Purpose, of Volition, even of Hostility: it was one huge, dead, immeasurable Steam-engine, rolling on, in its dead indifference, to grind me limb from limb. O, the vast, gloomy, solitary Golgotha,[4] and Mill of Death! Why was the Living banished thither companionless, conscious? Why, if there is no Devil; nay, unless the Devil is your God?"

A prey incessantly to such corrosions, might not, moreover, as the worst aggravation to them, the iron constitution even of a Teufelsdröckh threaten to fail? We conjecture that he has known sickness; and, in spite of his loco-motive habits, perhaps sickness of the chronic sort. Hear this, for example: "How beautiful to die of broken-heart, on Paper! Quite another thing in practice; every window of your Feeling, even of your Intellect, as it were, begrimed and mud-bespattered, so that no pure ray can enter; a whole Drug-shop in your inwards; the fordone soul drowning slowly in quagmires of Disgust!"

Putting all which external and internal miseries together, may we not find in the following sentences, quite in our Professor's still vein, significance enough? "From Suicide a certain aftershine (*Nachschein*) of Christianity withheld me: perhaps also a certain indolence of character; for, was not that a remedy I had at any time within reach? Often, however, was there a ques-tion present to me: Should some one now, at the turning of that corner, blow thee suddenly out of Space, into the other World, or other No-World, by pistol-shot,—how were it? On which ground, too, I have often, in sea-storms and sieged cities and other death-scenes, exhibited an imperturbability, which passed, falsely enough, for courage.

"So had it lasted," concludes the Wanderer, "so had it lasted, as in bitter pro-tracted Death-agony, through long years. The heart within me, unvisited by any heavenly dewdrop, was smouldering in sulphurous, slow-consuming fire. Almost since earliest memory I had shed no tear; or once only when I, mur-muring half-audibly, recited Faust's Deathsong, that wild *Selig der den er im Siegesglanze findet* (Happy whom *he* finds in Battle's splendour),[5] and thought that of this last Friend even I was not forsaken, that Destiny itself could not doom me not to die. Having no hope, neither had I any definite fear, were it of Man or of Devil: nay, I often felt as if it might be solacing, could the Arch-Devil himself, though in Tartarean terrors, but rise to me, that I might tell him a little of my mind. And yet, strangely enough, I lived in a continual, indefinite, pining fear; tremulous, pusillanimous, apprehensive of I knew not what: it seemed as if all things in the Heavens above and the Earth beneath would hurt me; as if the Heavens and the Earth were but boundless jaws of a devouring monster, wherein I, palpitating, waited to be devoured.

"Full of such humour, and perhaps the miserablest man in the whole French Capital or Suburbs, was I, one sultry Dogday, after much per-ambulation, toiling along the dirty little *Rue Saint-Thomas de l'Enfer*,[6] among

---

4. Calvary, the place where Christ was crucified.
5. Adapted from Goethe's *Faust* 1.4.1573–76.
6. St. Thomas-of-Hell Street (French). In later life Carlyle admitted that this incident was based on his own experience during a walk in Edinburgh (rather than in Paris). "Dogday": a hot and unwholesome summer period, coinciding with the prominence of Sirius, the Dog Star, is called the season of the dog days.

civic rubbish enough, in a close atmosphere, and over pavements hot as Nebuchadnezzar's Furnace; whereby doubtless my spirits were little cheered; when, all at once, there rose a Thought in me, and I asked myself: 'What *art* thou afraid of? Wherefore, like a coward, dost thou forever pip and whimper, and go cowering and trembling? Despicable biped! what is the sum-total of the worst that lies before thee? Death? Well, Death; and say the pangs of Tophet[7] too, and all that the Devil and Man may, will or can do against thee! Hast thou not a heart; canst thou not suffer whatsoever it be; and, as a Child of Freedom, though outcast, trample Tophet itself under thy feet, while it consumes thee? Let it come, then; I will meet it and defy it!' And as I so thought, there rushed like a stream of fire over my whole soul; and I shook base Fear away from me forever. I was strong, of unknown strength; a spirit, almost a god. Ever from that time, the temper of my misery was changed: not Fear or whining Sorrow was it, but Indignation and grim fire-eyed Defiance.

"Thus had the EVERLASTING NO[8] (*das ewige Nein*) pealed authoritatively through all the recesses of my Being, of my ME; and then was it that my whole ME stood up, in native God-created majesty, and with emphasis recorded its Protest. Such a Protest, the most important transaction in Life, may that same Indignation and Defiance, in a psychological point of view, be fitly called. The Everlasting No had said: 'Behold, thou art fatherless, outcast, and the Universe is mine (the Devil's)'; to which my whole Me now made answer: '*I* am not thine, but Free, and forever hate thee!'

"It is from this hour that I incline to date my Spiritual Newbirth, or Baphometic Fire-baptism,[9] perhaps I directly thereupon began to be a Man."

Centre of Indifference

Though, after this "Baphometic Fire-baptism" of his, our Wanderer signifies that his Unrest was but increased; as indeed, "Indignation and Defiance," especially against things in general, are not the most peaceable inmates; yet can the Psychologist surmise that it was no longer a quite hopeless Unrest; that henceforth it had at least a fixed centre to revolve round. For the fire-baptised soul, long so scathed and thunder-riven, here feels its own Freedom, which feeling is its Baphometic Baptism: the citadel of its whole kingdom it has thus gained by assault, and will keep inexpugnable; outwards from which the remaining dominions, not indeed without hard battling, will doubtless by degrees be conquered and pacificated. Under another figure, we might say, if in that great moment, in the *Rue Saint-Thomas de l'Enfer,* the old inward Satanic School was not yet thrown out of doors, it received peremptory judicial notice to quit;—whereby, for the rest, its howl-chantings, Ernulphus-cursings,[1] and rebellious gnashings of teeth, might, in the meanwhile, become only the more tumultuous, and difficult to keep secret.

---

7. Hell.
8. This phrase does not signify the hero's protest; it represents the sum of all the forces that had denied meaning to life. These negative forces, which had hitherto held the hero in bondage, are repudiated by his saying no to the "Everlasting No."
9. A transformation by a flash of spiritual illumination. The term may derive from Baphomet, an idol that inspired such spiritual experiences.
1. Curse devised by Ernulf (1040–1124), bishop of Rochester, when sentencing persons to excommunication. "Satanic School": term coined by Robert Southey (1774–1843) to characterize the self-assertive and rebellious temper of the poetry of Byron and Shelley.

Accordingly, if we scrutinise these Pilgrimings well, there is perhaps discernible henceforth a certain incipient method in their madness. Not wholly as a Spectre does Teufelsdröckh now storm through the world; at worst as a spectre-fighting Man, nay who will one day be a Spectre-queller. If pilgriming restlessly to so many "Saints' Wells,"[2] and ever without quenching of his thirst, he nevertheless finds little secular wells, whereby from time to time some alleviation is ministered. In a word, he is now, if not ceasing, yet intermitting to "eat his own heart"; and clutches round him outwardly on the NOT-ME for wholesomer food. Does not the following glimpse exhibit him in a much more natural state?

"Towns also and Cities, especially the ancient, I failed not to look upon with interest. How beautiful to see thereby, as through a long vista, into the remote Time; to have as it were, an actual section of almost the earliest Past brought safe into the Present, and set before your eyes! There, in that old City, was a live ember of Culinary Fire put down, say only two-thousand years ago; and there, burning more or less triumphantly, with such fuel as the region yielded, it has burnt, and still burns, and thou thyself seest the very smoke thereof. Ah! and the far more mysterious live ember of Vital Fire was then also put down there; and still miraculously burns and spreads; and the smoke and ashes thereof (in these Judgment-Halls and Churchyards), and its bellows-engines (in these Churches), thou still seest; and its flame, looking out from every kind countenance, and every hateful one, still warms thee or scorches thee.

"Of Man's Activity and Attainment the chief results are aeriform, mystic, and preserved in Tradition only: such are his Forms of Government, with the Authority they rest on; his Customs, or Fashions both of Cloth-habits and of Soul-habits; much more his collective stock of Handicrafts, the whole Faculty he has acquired of manipulating Nature: all these things, as indispensable and priceless as they are, cannot in any way be fixed under lock and key, but must flit, spirit-like, on impalpable vehicles, from Father to Son; if you demand sight of them, they are nowhere to be met with. Visible Plowmen and Hammermen there have been, ever from Cain and Tubalcain[3] downwards: but where does your accumulated Agricultural, Metallurgic, and other Manufacturing SKILL lie warehoused? It transmits itself on the atmospheric air, on the sun's rays (by Hearing and by Vision); it is a thing aeriform, impalpable, of quite spiritual sort. In like manner, ask me not. Where are the LAWS; where is the GOVERNMENT? In vain wilt thou go to Schönbrunn, to Downing Street, to the Palais Bourbon:[4] thou findest nothing there but brick or stone houses, and some bundles of Papers tied with tape. Where, then, is that same cunningly-devised almighty GOVERNMENT of theirs to be laid hands on? Everywhere, yet nowhere: seen only in its works, this too is a thing aeriform, invisible; or if you will, mystic and miraculous. So spiritual (*geistig*) is our whole daily Life: all that we do springs out of Mystery, Spirit, invisible Force; only like a little Cloud-image, or Armida's Palace,[5] air-built, does the Actual body itself forth from the great mystic Deep.

"Visible and tangible products of the Past, again, I reckon-up to the extent of three. Cities, with their Cabinets and Arsenals; then tilled Fields, to either

---

2. Holy fountains or wells, the waters of which were reputed to restore health.
3. Descendant of Cain, son of Adam and Eve (Genesis 4.1–22).
4. Headquarters of government in Vienna, London, and Paris, respectively.
5. The magic palace of a beautiful enchantress in Torquato Tasso's *Jerusalem Delivered*.

or to both of which divisions Roads with their Bridges, may belong; and thirdly—Books. In which third truly, the last invented, lies a worth far surpassing that of the two others. Wondrous indeed is the virtue of a true Book. Not like a dead city of stones, yearly crumbling, yearly needing repair; more like a tilled field, but then a spiritual field: like a spiritual tree, let me rather say, it stands from year to year, and from age to age (we have Books that already number some hundred-and-fifty human ages); and yearly comes its new produce of leaves (Commentaries, Deductions, Philosophical, Political Systems; or were it only Sermons, Pamphlets, Journalistic Essays), every one of which is talismanic and thaumaturgic,[6] for it can persuade men. O thou who art able to write a Book, which once in the two centuries or oftener there is a man gifted to do, envy not him whom they name City-builder, and inexpressibly pity him whom they name Conqueror or City-burner! Thou too art a Conqueror and Victor; but of the true sort, namely over the Devil: thou too hast built what will outlast all marble and metal, and be a wonder-bringing City of the Mind, a Temple and Seminary and Prophetic Mount, whereto all kindreds of the Earth will pilgrim.—Fool! why journeyest thou wearisomely, in thy antiquarian fervour, to gaze on the stone pyramids of Geeza, or the clay ones of Sacchara?[7] These stand there, as I can tell thee, idle and inert, looking over the Desert, foolishly enough, for the last three-thousand years: but canst thou not open thy Hebrew BIBLE, then, or even Luther's Version thereof?"

No less satisfactory is his sudden appearance not in Battle, yet on some Battle-field; which, we soon gather, must be that of Wagram;[8] so that here, for once, is a certain approximation to distinctiveness of date. Omitting much, let us impart what follows:

"Horrible enough! A whole Marchfeld[9] strewed with shell-splinters, cannon-shot, ruined tumbrils, and dead men and horses; stragglers still remaining not so much as buried. And those red mould heaps: ay, there lie the Shells of Men, out of which all the Life and Virtue has been blown; and now are they swept together, and crammed-down out of sight, like blown Egg-shells!—Did Nature, when she bade the Donau bring down his mould-cargoes from the Carinthian and Carpathian Heights, and spread them out here into the softest, richest level,—intend thee, O Marchfeld, for a corn-bearing Nursery, whereon her children might be nursed; or for a Cockpit, wherein they might the more commodiously be throttled and tattered? Were thy three broad Highways, meeting here from the ends of Europe, made for Ammunition-wagons, then? Were thy Wagrams and Stillfrieds[1] but so many ready-built Casemates, wherein the house of Hapsburg might batter with artillery, and with artillery be battered? König Ottokar, amid yonder hill-ocks, dies under Rodolf's truncheon; here Kaiser Franz falls a-swoon under Napoleon's: within which five centuries, to omit the others, how has thy breast, fair Plain, been defaced and defiled! The greensward is torn-up and trampled-down; man's fond care of it, his fruit-trees, hedge-rows, and pleas-

6. Miracle-working.
7. I.e., Giza and Saqqara near Cairo.
8. A village in Austria; site of Napoleon's victory over the Austrians, July 1809.
9. A fertile plain in Austria whose soil (according to Teufelsdröckh) was brought down from the Carpathian Mountains by the Danube ("Donau")

River.
1. Fortified chambers. Stillfried was the site of a battle in which Ottokar, king ("König") of Bohemia, was killed by the forces of Rudolph of Hapsburg in 1278. In 1809 the Hapsburg armies, under Emperor Francis ("Franz") I, were defeated by Napoleon at nearby Wagram.

ant dwellings, blown away with gunpowder; and the kind seedfield lies a desolate, hideous Place of Sculls.—Nevertheless, Nature is at work; neither shall these Powder-Devilkins with their utmost devilry gainsay her: but all that gore and carnage will be shrouded-in, absorbed into manure; and next year the Marchfeld will be green, nay greener. Thrifty unwearied Nature, ever out of our great waste educing some little profit of thy own,—how dost thou, from the very carcass of the Killer, bring Life for the Living!

"What, speaking in quite unofficial language, is the net-purport and upshot of war? To my own knowledge, for example, there dwell and toil, in the British village of Dumdrudge, usually some five-hundred souls. From these, by certain 'Natural Enemies'[2] of the French, there are successively selected, during the French war, say thirty able-bodied men: Dumdrudge, at her own expense, has suckled and nursed them: she has, not without difficulty and sorrow, fed them up to manhood, and even trained them to crafts, so that one can weave, another build, another hammer, and the weakest can stand under thirty stone avoirdupois. Nevertheless, amid much weeping and swearing, they are selected; all dressed in red; and shipped away, at the public charges, some two-thousand miles, or say only to the south of Spain;[3] and fed there till wanted. And now to that same spot, in the south of Spain, are thirty similar French artisans, from a French Dumdrudge, in like manner wending: till at length, after infinite effort, the two parties come into actual juxtaposition; and Thirty stands fronting Thirty, each with a gun in his hand. Straightway the word 'Fire!' is given: and they blow the souls out of one another; and in place of sixty brisk useful craftsmen, the world has sixty dead carcasses, which it must bury, and anew shed tears for. Had these men any quarrel? Busy as the Devil is, not the smallest! They lived far enough apart; were the entirest strangers; nay, in so wide a Universe, there was even, unconsciously, by Commerce, some mutual helpfulness between them. How then? Simpleton! their Governors had fallen-out; and, instead of shooting one another, had the cunning to make these poor blockheads shoot.—Alas, so is it in Deutschland, and hitherto in all other lands; still as of old, 'what devilry soever Kings do, the Greeks must pay the piper!'[4]—In that fiction of the English Smollett,[5] it is true, the final Cessation of War is perhaps prophetically shadowed forth; where the two Natural Enemies, in person, take each a Tobacco-pipe, filled with Brimstone; light the same, and smoke in one another's faces, till the weaker gives in: but from such predicted Peace-Era, what blood-filled trenches, and contentious centuries, may still divide us!"

Thus can the Professor, at least in lucid intervals, look away from his own sorrows, over the many-coloured world, and pertinently enough note what is passing there. We may remark, indeed, that for the matter of spiritual culture, if for nothing else, perhaps few periods of his life were richer than this. Internally, there is the most momentous instructive Course of Practical Philosophy, with Experiments, going on; towards the right comprehension of which his Peripatetic[6] habits, favourable to Meditation, might help him

---

2. Term often used in English newspapers to account for the frequency of wars between the English and French.
3. Where British armies fought against Napoleon (1808–14).
4. Horace's *Epistles* 1.2.14.

5. Tobias Smollett (1721–1771), *The Adventures of Ferdinand Count Fathom*, chap. 41.
6. Walking about, after the manner of Aristotle who delivered his lectures while walking in the Lyceum.

rather than hinder. Externally, again, as he wanders to and fro, there are, if for the longing heart little substance, yet for the seeing eye sights enough: in these so boundless Travels of his, granting that the Satanic School was even partially kept down, what an incredible knowledge of our Planet, and its Inhabitants and their Works, that is to say, of all knowable things, might not Teufelsdröckh acquire!

"I have read in most Public Libraries," says he, "including those of Constantinople and Samarcand: in most Colleges, except the Chinese Mandarin ones, I have studied, or seen that there was no studying. Unknown Languages have I oftenest gathered from their natural repertory, the Air, by my organ of Hearing; Statistics, Geographics, Topographics came, through the Eye, almost of their own accord. The ways of Man, how he seeks food, and warmth, and protection for himself, in most regions, are ocularly known to me. Like the great Hadrian, I meted-out much of the terraqueous Globe with a pair of Compasses[7] that belonged to myself only.

"Of great Scenes why speak? Three summer days, I lingered reflecting, and even composing (*dichtete*), by the Pine-chasms of Vaucluse; and in that clear Lakelet[8] moistened my bread. I have sat under the Palm-trees of Tadmor;[9] smoked a pipe among the ruins of Babylon. The great Wall of China I have seen; and can testify that it is of gray brick, coped and covered with granite, and shows only second-rate masonry.—Great Events, also, have not I witnessed? Kings sweated-down (*ausgemergelt*) into Berlin-and-Milan Customhouse-Officers;[1] the World well won, and the World well lost oftener than once a hundred-thousand individuals shot (by each other) in one day. All kindreds and peoples and nations dashed together, and shifted and shovelled into heaps, that they might ferment there, and in time unite. The birth-pangs of Democracy,[2] wherewith convulsed Europe was groaning in cries that reached Heaven, could not escape me.

"For great Men I have ever had the warmest predilection; and can perhaps boast that few such in this era have wholly escaped me. Great Men are the inspired (speaking and acting) Texts of that divine BOOK OF REVELATION, whereof a Chapter is completed from epoch to epoch, and by some named HISTORY; to which inspired Texts your numerous talented men, and your innumerable untalented men, are the better or worse exegetic Commentaries, and wagonload of too-stupid, heretical or orthodox, weekly Sermons. For my study, the inspired Texts themselves! Thus did not I, in very early days, having disguised me as tavern-waiter, stand behind the field-chairs, under that shady Tree at Treisnitz by the Jena Highway;[3] waiting upon the great Schiller and greater Goethe; and hearing what I have not forgotten. For—"

—But at this point the Editor recalls his principle of caution, some time ago laid down, and must suppress much. Let not the sacredness of Laurelled, still more, of Crowned Heads, be tampered with. Should we, at a future day, find circumstances altered, and the time come for Publication, then may these glimpses into the privacy of the Illustrious be conceded; which for the present were little better than treacherous, perhaps traitorous Eaves-

7. Legs. Hadrian (76–138), Roman emperor, who traveled extensively throughout his empire.
8. A pool at the base of a mountain in Vaucluse in southern France, one of Petrarch's favorite haunts.
9. Palmyra in Syria.
1. Napoleon reduced some of Europe's kings to

the status of mere tax collectors for his regime.
2. As manifested in the revolutionary outbreaks in France (1789 and 1830) and in the agitations in England preceding the Reform Bill of 1832.
3. Where Goethe and Schiller met during the 1790s when they were collaborating on their writings.

droppings. Of Lord Byron, therefore, of Pope Pius, Emperor Tarakwang, and the "White Water-roses"[4] (Chinese Carbonari) with their mysteries, no notice here! Of Napoleon himself we shall only, glancing from afar, remark that Teufelsdröckh's relation to him seems to have been of very varied character. At first we find our poor Professor on the point of being shot as a spy; then taken into private conversation, even pinched on the ear, yet presented with no money; at last indignantly dismissed, almost thrown out of doors, as an "Ideologist." "He himself," says the Professor, "was among the completest Ideologists, at least Ideopraxists:[5] in the Idea (*in der Idee*) he lived, moved and fought. The man was a Divine Missionary, though unconscious of it; and preached, through the cannon's throat, that great doctrine, *La carrière ouverte aux talens* (The Tools to him that can handle them), which is our ultimate Political Evangel, wherein alone can liberty lie. Madly enough he preached, it is true, as Enthusiasts[6] and first Missionaries are wont, with imperfect utterance, amid much frothy rant; yet as articulately perhaps as the case admitted. Or call him, if you will, an American Backwoodsman, who had to fell unpenetrated forests, and battle with innumerable wolves, and did not entirely forbear strong liquor, rioting, and even theft; whom, notwithstanding, the peaceful Sower will follow, and, as he cuts the boundless harvest, bless."

More legitimate and decisively authentic is Teufelsdröckh's appearance and emergence (we know not well whence) in the solitude of the North Cape, on that June Midnight. He has a "light-blue Spanish cloak" hanging round him, as his "most commodious, principal, indeed sole upper-garment"; and stands there, on the World-promontory, looking over the infinite Brine, like a little blue Belfry (as we figure), now motionless indeed, yet ready, if stirred, to ring quaintest changes.

"Silence as of death," writes he; "for Midnight, even in the Arctic latitudes, has its character: nothing but the granite cliffs ruddy-tinged, the peaceable gurgle of that slow-heaving Polar Ocean, over which in the utmost North the great Sun hangs low and lazy, as if he too were slumbering. Yet is his cloud-couch wrought of crimson and cloth-of-gold; yet does his light stream over the mirror of waters, like a tremulous fire-pillar, shooting downwards to the abyss, and hide itself under my feet. In such moments, Solitude also is invaluable; for who would speak, or be looked on, when behind him lies all Europe and Africa, fast asleep, except the watchmen; and before him the silent Immensity, and Palace of the Eternal, whereof our Sun is but a porchlamp?

"Nevertheless, in this solemn moment comes a man, or monster, scrambling from among the rock-hollows; and, shaggy, huge as the Hyperborean[7] Bear, hails me in Russian speech: most probably, therefore, a Russian Smuggler. With courteous brevity, I signify my indifference to contraband trade, my humane intentions, yet strong wish to be private. In vain: the monster, counting doubtless on his superior stature, and minded to make sport for himself, or perhaps profit, were it with murder, continues to advance; ever assailing me with his importunate train-oil[8] breath; and now has advanced, till we stand both on the verge of the rock, the deep Sea rippling greedily

---

4. Like the Carbonari in Italy, a secret revolutionary society in China during the regime of Emperor Tarakwang (Tao Kuang, 1821–50).
5. Those who put ideas into practice.

6. Religious fanatics.
7. From the far North.
8. Whale oil.

down below. What argument will avail? On the thick Hyperborean, cherubic reasoning, seraphic eloquence were lost. Prepared for such extremity, I, deftly enough, whisk aside one step; draw out, from my interior reservoirs, a sufficient Birmingham Horse-pistol, and say, 'Be so obliging as retire, Friend (*Er ziehe sich zurück, Freund*), and with promptitude!' This logic even the Hyperborean understands: fast enough, with apologetic, petitionary growl, he sidles off; and, except for suicidal as well as homicidal purposes, need not return.

"Such I hold to be the genuine use of Gunpowder: that it makes all men alike tall. Nay, if thou be cooler, cleverer than I, if thou have more *Mind,* though all but no *Body* whatever, then canst thou kill me first, and are the taller. Hereby, at last, is the Goliath powerless, and the David resistless; savage Animalism is nothing, inventive Spiritualism is all.

"With respect to Duels, indeed, I have my own ideas. Few things, in this so surprising world, strike me with more surprise. Two little visual Spectra of men, hovering with insecure enough cohesion in the midst of the Un-FATHOMABLE, and to dissolve therein, at any rate, very soon,—make pause at the distance of twelve paces asunder; whirl round; and, simultaneously by the cunningest mechanism, explode one another into Dissolution; and off-hand become Air, and Nonextant! Deuce on it (*verdammt*), the little spit-fires!—Nay, I think with old Hugo von Trimberg:[9] 'God must needs laugh outright, could such a thing be, to see his wondrous Manikins here below.' "

But amid these specialties, let us not forget the great generality, which is our Chief guest here: How prospered the inner man of Teufelsdröckh under so much outward shifting? Does Legion[1] still lurk in him, though repressed; or has he exorcised that Devil's Brood? We can answer that the symptoms continue promising. Experience is the grand spiritual Doctor; and with him Teufelsdröckh has been long a patient, swallowing many a bitter bolus.[2] Unless our poor Friend belong to the numerous class of Incurables, which seems not likely, some cure will doubtless be effected. We should rather say that Legion, or the Satanic School, was now pretty well extirpated and cast out, but next to nothing introduced in its room; whereby the heart remains, for the while, in a quiet but no comfortable state.

"At length, after so much roasting," thus writes our Autobiographer, "I was what you might name calcined. Pray only that it be not rather, as is the more frequent issue, reduced to a *caputmortuum*![3] But in any case, by mere dint of practice, I had grown familiar with many things. Wretchedness was still wretched; but I could now partly see through it, and despise it. Which highest mortal, in this inane Existence, had I not found a Shadow-hunter, or Shadow-hunted; and, when I looked through his brave garnitures, miserable enough? Thy wishes have all been sniffed aside, thought I: but what, had they ever been all granted! Did not the Boy Alexander weep because he had not two Planets to conquer; or a whole Solar System; or after that, a whole Universe? *Ach Gott,* when I gazed into these Stars, have they not looked-down on me as if with pity, from their serene spaces; like Eyes glistening with heavenly tears over the little lot of man! Thousands of human genera-tions, all as noisy as our own, have been swallowed-up of Time, and there

9. Medieval poet (1260–1309).
1. Unclean spirits (Mark 5.9).

2. Large pill.
3. Death's head (Latin).

remains no wreck of them any more; and Arcturus and Orion and Sirius and the Pleiades are still shining in their courses, clear and young, as when the Shepherd first noted them in the plain of Shinar.[4] Pshaw! what is this paltry little Dog-cage[5] of an Earth; what art thou that sittest whining there? Thou art still Nothing, Nobody: true; but who, then, is Something, Somebody? For thee the Family of Man has no use; it rejects thee; thou art wholly as a dissevered limb: so be it; perhaps it is better so!"

Too-heavy-laden Teufelsdröckh! Yet surely his bands are loosening: one day he will hurl the burden far from him, and bound forth free and with a second youth.

The Everlasting Yea

"Temptations in the Wilderness!"[6] exclaims Teufelsdröckh: "Have we not all to be tried with such? Not so easily can the old Adam, lodged in us by birth, be dispossessed. Our Life is compassed round with Necessity; yet is the meaning of Life itself no other than Freedom, than Voluntary Force: thus have we a warfare; in the beginning, especially, a hard-fought battle. For the God-given mandate, *Work thou in Welldoing*, lies mysteriously written, in Promethean[7] Prophetic Characters, in our hearts; and leaves us no rest, night or day, till it be deciphered and obeyed; till it burn forth, in our conduct, a visible, acted Gospel of Freedom. And as the clay-given mandate, *Eat thou and be filled*, at the same time persuasively proclaims itself through every nerve,—must not there be a confusion, a contest, before the better Influence can become the upper?

"To me nothing seems more natural than that the Son of Man, when such God-given mandate first prophetically stirs within him, and the Clay must now be vanquished, or vanquish,—should be carried of the spirit into grim Solitudes, and there fronting the Tempter do grimmest battle with him; defiantly setting him at naught, till he yield and fly. Name it as we choose: with or without visible Devil, whether in the natural Desert of rocks and sands, or in the populous moral Desert of selfishness and baseness,—to such Temptation are we all called. Unhappy if we are not! Unhappy if we are but Half-men, in whom that divine handwriting has never blazed forth, all-subduing, in true sun-splendour; but quivers dubiously amid meaner lights: or smoulders, in dull pain, in darkness, under earthly vapours!—Our Wilderness is the wide World in an Atheistic Century; our Forty Days are long years of suffering and fasting: nevertheless, to these also comes an end. Yes, to me also was given, if not Victory, yet the consciousness of Battle, and the resolve to persevere therein while life or faculty is left. To me also, entangled in the enchanted forests, demon-peopled, doleful of sight and of sound, it was given, after weariest wanderings, to work out my way into the higher sunlit slopes—of that Mountain which has no summit, or whose summit is in Heaven only!"

He says elsewhere, under a less ambitious figure; as figures are, once for

4. A plain in the Sumerian region (now in Iraq). "Shepherd": probably Abraham, who was commanded by the Lord to "tell the stars, if thou be able to number them" (Genesis 15.5).
5. A drum-shaped cage that turns when a dog runs inside the cylinder. This dog-powered device, attached to a kitchen spit, was used for turning joints of meat during roasting.
6. Paraphrase of Matthew 4.1.
7. Fiery or fiery-spirited, an allusion to Prometheus, the defiant Titan who brought the secret of fire making to humanity.

all, natural to him: "Has not thy Life been that of most sufficient men (*tüch-tigen Männer*) thou hast known in this generation? An outflush of foolish young Enthusiasm, like the first fallow-crop, wherein are as many weeds as valuable herbs: this all parched away, under the Droughts of practical and spiritual Unbelief, as Disappointment, in thought and act, often-repeated gave rise to Doubt, and Doubt gradually settled into Denial! If I have had a second-crop, and now see the perennial greensward, and sit under umbra-geous[8] cedars, which defy all Drought (and Doubt); herein too, be the Heavens praised, I am not without examples, and even exemplars."

So that, for Teufelsdröckh also, there has been a "glorious revolution":[9] these mad shadow-hunting and shadow-hunted Pilgrimings of his were but some purifying "Temptation in the Wilderness," before his Apostolic work (such as it was) could begin; which Temptation is now happily over, and the Devil once more worsted! Was "that high moment in the *Rue de l'Enfer*," then, properly the turning-point of the battle; when the Fiend said, *Worship me or be torn in shreds*; and was answered valiantly with an *Apage Satana*?[1]— Singular Teufelsdröckh, would thou hadst told thy singular story in plain words! But it is fruitless to look there, in those Paper-bags,[2] for such. Nothing but innuendoes, figurative crotchets: a typical Shadow, fitfully wavering, prophetico-satiric; no clear logical Picture. "How paint to the sensual eye," asks he once, "what passes in the Holy-of-Holies of Man's Soul; in what words, known to these profane times, speak even afar-off of the unspeakable?" We ask in turn: Why perplex these times, profane as they are, with needless obscurity, by omission and by commission? Not mystical only is our Professor, but whimsical; and involves himself, now more than ever, in eye-bewildering *chiaroscuro*.[3] Successive glimpses, here faithfully imparted, our more gifted readers must endeavour to combine for their own behoof.

He says: "The hot Harmattan wind[4] had raged itself out; its howl went silent within me; and the long-deafened soul could now hear. I paused in my wild wanderings; and sat me down to wait, and consider; for it was as if the hour of change drew nigh. I seemed to surrender, to renounce utterly, and say: Fly, then, false shadows of Hope; I will chase you no more, I will believe you no more. And ye too, haggard spectres of Fear, I care not for you; ye too are all shadows and a lie. Let me rest here: for I am way-weary and life-weary; I will rest here, were it but to die: to die or to live is alike to me; alike insignificant."—And again: "Here, then, as I lay in that CENTRE of INDIFFERENCE; cast, doubtless by benignant upper Influence, into a healing sleep, the heavy dreams rolled gradually away, and I awoke to a new Heaven and a new Earth.[5] The first preliminary moral Act, Annihilation of Self (*Selbsttödtung*), had been happily accomplished; and my mind's eyes were now unsealed, and its hands ungyved."[6]

Might we not also conjecture that the following passage refers to his Locality, during this same "healing sleep"; that his Pilgrim-staff lies cast aside here, on "the high table-land"; and indeed that the repose is already taking wholesome effect on him? If it were not that the tone, in some parts, has more of riancy,[7] even of levity, than we could have expected! However, in

8. Shady.
9. The overthrow of James II of England in 1688.
1. Get thee hence, Satan (Italian; Matthew 4.8–10).
2. Bags containing documents and writings by Teufelsdröckh.

3. Light and shade (Italian).
4. A hot and dry wind in Africa.
5. Revelation 21.1.
6. Unfettered.
7. Gaiety.

Teufelsdröckh, there is always the strangest Dualism: light dancing, with guitar-music, will be going on in the fore-court, while by fits from within comes the faint whimpering of woe and wail. We transcribe the piece entire:

"Beautiful it was to sit there, as in my skyey Tent, musing and meditating; on the high table-land, in front of the Mountains; over me, as roof, the azure Dome, and around me, for walls, four azure-flowing curtains,—namely, of the Four azure winds, on whose bottom-fringes also I have seen gilding. And then to fancy the fair Castles that stood sheltered in these Mountain hollows; with their green flower-lawns, and white dames and damosels, lovely enough: or better still, the straw-roofed Cottages, wherein stood many a Mother baking bread, with her children round her:—all hidden and protectingly folded-up in the valley-folds; yet there and alive, as sure as if I beheld them. Or to see, as well as fancy, the nine Towns and Villages, that lay round my mountain-seat, which, in still weather, were wont to speak to me (by their steeple-bells) with metal tongue; and, in almost all weather, proclaimed their vitality by repeated Smoke-clouds; whereon, as on a culinary horologe,[8] I might read the hour of the day. For it was the smoke of cookery, as kind housewives at morning, midday, eventide, were boiling their husband's kettles; and ever a blue pillar rose up into the air, successively or simultaneously, from each of the nine, saying, as plainly as smoke could say: Such and such a meal is getting ready here. Not uninteresting! For you have the whole Borough, with all its love-makings and scandal-mongeries, contentions and contentments, as in miniature, and could cover it all with your hat.—If, in my wide Wayfarings, I had learned to look into the business of the World in its details, here perhaps was the place for combining it into general propositions, and deducing inferences therefrom.

"Often also could I see the black Tempest marching in anger through the Distance: round some Schreckhorn,[9] as yet grim-blue, would the eddying vapour gather, and there tumultuously eddy, and flow down like a mad witch's hair; till, after a space, it vanished, and, in the clear sunbeam, your Schreckhorn stood smiling grim-white, for the vapour had held snow. How thou fermentest and elaboratest, in thy great fermenting-vat and laboratory of an Atmosphere, of a World, O Nature!—Or what is Nature? Ha! why do I not name thee GOD? Art not thou the 'Living Garment of God'? O Heavens, is it, in very deed, HE, then, that ever speaks through thee; that lives and loves in thee, that lives and loves in me?

"Fore-shadows, call them rather fore-splendours, of that Truth, and Beginning of Truths, fell mysteriously over my soul. Sweeter than Dayspring to the Shipwrecked in Nova Zembla;[1] ah, like the mother's voice to her little child that strays bewildered, weeping, in unknown tumults; like soft streamings of celestial music to my too-exasperated heart, came that Evangel. The Universe is not dead and demoniacal, a charnel-house with spectres; but godlike, and my Father's!

"With other eyes, too, could I now look upon my fellow man; with an infinite Love, an infinite Pity. Poor, wandering, wayward man! Art thou not tired, and beaten with stripes, even as I am? Ever, whether thou bear the royal mantle or the beggar's gabardine, art thou not so weary, so heavy-laden;

8. Clock.
9. Peak of Terror (German); a mountain in Switzerland.
1. A Dutch sea captain, whose ship was wrecked off the island of Nova Zembla in the Arctic in 1596, recorded in his journal his thankfulness at the coming of daylight.

and thy Bed of Rest is but a Grave. O my Brother, my Brother, why cannot I shelter thee in my bosom, and wipe away all tears from thy eyes! Truly, the din of many-voiced Life, which, in this solitude, with the mind's organ, I could hear, was no longer a maddening discord, but a melting one; like inarticulate cries, and sobbings of a dumb creature, which in the ear of Heaven are prayers. The poor Earth, with her poor joys, was now my needy Mother, not my cruel Stepdame; man, with his so mad Wants and so mean Endeavours, had become the dearer to me; and even for his sufferings and his sins, I now first named him Brother. Thus I was standing in the porch of that 'Sanctuary of Sorrow';[2] by strange, steep ways had I too been guided thither; and ere long its sacred gates would open, and the 'Divine Depth of Sorrow' lie disclosed to me."

The Professor says, he here first got eye on the Knot that had been strangling him, and straightway could unfasten it, and was free. "A vain interminable controversy," writes he, "touching what is at present called Origin of Evil, or some such thing, arises in every soul, since the beginning of the world; and in every soul, that would pass from idle Suffering into actual Endeavouring, must first be put an end to. The most, in our time, have to go content with a simple, incomplete enough Suppression of this controversy; to a few some Solution of it is indispensable. In every new era, too, such Solution comes-out in different terms; and ever the Solution of the last era has become obsolete, and is found unserviceable. For it is man's nature to change his Dialect from century to century; he cannot help it though he would. The authentic Church-Catechism of our present century has not yet fallen into my hands: meanwhile, for my own private behoof, I attempt to elucidate the matter so. Man's Unhappiness, as I construe, comes of his Greatness; it is because there is an Infinite in him, which with all his cunning he cannot quite bury under the Finite. Will the whole Finance Ministers and Upholsterers and Confections of modern Europe undertake, in joint-stock company, to make one Shoeblack HAPPY? They cannot accomplish it, above an hour or two; for the Shoeblack also has a Soul quite other than his Stomach; and would require, if you consider it, for his permanent satisfaction and saturation, simply this allotment, no more, and no less: God's infinite Universe altogether to himself, therein to enjoy infinitely, and fill every wish as fast as it rose. Oceans of Hochheimer, a Throat like that of Ophiuchus:[3] speak not of them; to the infinite Shoeblack they are as nothing. No sooner is your ocean filled, than he grumbles that it might have been of better vintage. Try him with half of a Universe, of an Omnipotence, he sets to quarrelling with the proprietor of the other half, and declares himself the most maltreated of men.—Always there is a black spot in our sunshine: it is even as I said, the Shadow of Ourselves.

"But the whim we have of Happiness is somewhat thus. By certain valuations, and averages, of our own striking, we come upon some sort of average terrestrial lot; this we fancy belongs to us by nature, and of indefeasible right. It is simple payment of our wages, of our deserts; requires neither thanks nor complaint; only such overplus as there may be do we account Happiness; any deficit again is Misery. Now consider that we have the valuation of our

---

2. Adapted from Goethe's Wilhelm Meister.
3. The serpent in the constellation Serpentarius.

"Hochheimer": Rhine wine or hock from Hochheim.

own deserts ourselves, and what a fund of Self-conceit there is in each of us,—do you wonder that the balance should so often dip the wrong way, and many a Blockhead cry: See there, what a payment; was ever worthy gentleman so used!—I tell thee, Blockhead, it all comes of thy Vanity; of what thou *fanciest* those same deserts of thine to be. Fancy that thou deservest to be hanged (as is most likely), thou wilt feel it happiness to be only shot: fancy that thou deservest to be hanged in a hair-halter, it will be a luxury to die in hemp.

"So true is it, what I then say, that *the Fraction of Life can be increased in value not so much by increasing your Numerator as by lessening your Denominator*. Nay, unless my Algebra deceive me, *Unity* itself divided by *Zero* will give *Infinity*. Make thy claim of wages a zero, then; thou hast the world under thy feet. Well did the Wisest of our time write: 'It is only with Renunciation (*Entsagen*) that Life, properly speaking, can be said to begin.'[4]

"I asked myself: What is this that, ever since earliest years, thou hast been fretting and fuming, and lamenting and self-tormenting, on account of? Say it in a word: it is not because thou art not HAPPY? Because the THOU (sweet gentleman) is not sufficiently honoured, nourished, soft-bedded, and lovingly cared for? Foolish soul! What Act of Legislature was there that *thou* shouldst be Happy? A little while ago thou hadst no right to *be* at all. What if thou wert born and predestined not to be Happy, but to be Unhappy! Art thou nothing other than a Vulture, then, that fliest through the Universe seeking after somewhat to *eat*; and shrieking dolefully because carrion enough is not given thee? Close thy *Byron*; open thy *Goethe*."

"*Es leuchtet mir ein*,[5] I see a glimpse of it!" cries he elsewhere: "there is in man a HIGHER than Love of Happiness: he can do without Happiness, and instead thereof find Blessedness! Was it not to preach-forth this same HIGHER that sages and martyrs, the Poet and the Priest, in all times, have spoken and suffered; bearing testimony, through life and through death, of the Godlike that is in Man, and how in the Godlike only has he Strength and Freedom? Which God-inspired Doctrine art thou also honoured to be taught; O Heavens! and broken with manifold merciful Afflictions, even till thou become contrite, and learn it! O, thank thy Destiny for these; thankfully bear what yet remain: thou hadst need of them; the Self in thee needed to be annihilated. By benignant fever-paroxysms is Life rooting out the deep-seated chronic Diseases, and triumphs over Death. On the roaring billows of Time, thou art not engulfed, but borne aloft into the azure of Eternity. Love not Pleasure; love God.[6] This is the EVERLASTING YEA wherein all contradiction is solved: wherein whoso walks and works, it is well with him."

And again: "Small is it that thou canst trample the Earth with its injuries under thy feet, as old Greek Zeno[7] trained thee: thou canst love the Earth while it injures thee, and even because it injures thee; for this a Greater than Zeno was needed, and he too was sent. Knowest thou that '*Worship of Sorrow*'?[8] the Temple thereof, founded some eighteen centuries ago, now lies in ruins, overgrown with jungle, the habitation of doleful creatures: never-

---

4. Adapted from *Wilhelm Meister* by Goethe ("wisest of our time").
5. An exclamation of Wilhelm Meister's (German).
6. Adapted from 2 Timothy 3.4.
7. Stoic philosopher (3rd century B.C.E.) who,

after being injured in a fall, is reputed to have struck the earth with his hand as if the earth were responsible for his injury. Afterward he committed suicide. Hence he is said to "trample the Earth."
8. Christianity.

theless, venture forward; in a low crypt, arched out of falling fragments, thou findest the Altar still there, and its sacred Lamp perennially burning."

Without pretending to comment on which strange utterances, the Editor will only remark, that there lies beside them much of a still more question-able character; unsuited to the general apprehension; nay wherein he himself does not see his way. Nebulous disquisitions on Religion, yet not without bursts of splendour; on the "perennial continuance of Inspiration"; on Proph-ecy; that there are "true Priests, as well as Baal-Priests,[9] in our own day": with more of the like sort. We select some fractions, by way of finish to this farrago.

"Cease, my much-respected Herr von Voltaire," thus apostrophises the Professor: "shut thy sweet voice; for the task appointed thee seems finished. Sufficiently has thou demonstrated this proposition, considerable or other-wise: That the Mythus of the the Christian Religion looks not in the eigh-teenth century as it did in the eighth. Alas, were thy six-and-thirty quartos, and the six-and-thirty thousand other quartos and folios, and flying sheets or reams, printed before and since on the same subject, all needed to con-vince us of so little! But what next? Wilt thou help us to embody the divine Spirit of that Religion in a new Mythus, in a new vehicle and vesture, that our Souls, otherwise too like perishing, may live? What! thou hast no faculty in that kind? Only a torch for burning, no hammer for building? Take our thanks, then, and—thyself away.

"Meanwhile what are antiquated Mythuses to me? Or is the God present, felt in my own heart, a thing which Herr von Voltaire will dispute out of me; or dispute into me? To the 'Worship of Sorrow' ascribe what origin and gen-esis thou pleasest, *has* not that Worship originated, and been generated; is it not *here*? Feel it in thy heart, and then say whether it is of God! This is Belief; all else is Opinion,—for which latter whoso will let him worry and be worried."

"Neither," observes he elsewhere, "shall ye tear-out one another's eyes, struggling over 'Plenary Inspiration,'[1] and suchlike: try rather to get a little even Partial Inspiration, each of you for himself. One BIBLE I know, of whose Plenary Inspiration doubt is not so much as possible; nay with my own eyes I saw God's-Hand writing it: thereof all other Bibles are but leaves,—say, in Picture-Writing to assist the weaker faculty."

Or, to give the wearied reader relief, and bring it to an end, let him take the following perhaps more intelligible passage:

"To me, in this our life," says the Professor, "which is an internecine war-fare with the Time-spirit, other warfare seems questionable. Hast thou in any way a Contention with thy brother, I advise thee, think well what the meaning thereof is. If thou gauge it to the bottom, it is simply this: 'Fellow, see! thou art taking more than thy share of Happiness in the world, some-thing from *my* share: which, by the Heavens, thou shalt not; nay I will fight thee rather.'—Alas, and the whole lot to be divided is such a beggarly matter, truly a 'feast of shells,'[2] for the substance has been spilled out: not enough to quench one Appetite; and the collective human species clutching at them!—Can we not, in all such cases, rather say: 'Take it, thou too-ravenous

---

9. False priests, mentioned in 1 Kings 18.17–40.
1. Doctrine that all statements in the Bible are supernaturally inspired and authoritative. Voltaire

had sought to demonstrate that this doctrine was absurd.
2. Empty eggshells.

individual; take that pitiful additional fraction of a share, which I reckoned mine, but which thou so wantest; take it with a blessing: would to Heaven I had enough for thee!'—If Fichte's *Wissenschaftslehre*[3] be, 'to a certain extent, Applied Christianity,' surely to a still greater extent, so is this. We have here not a Whole Duty of Man,[4] yet a Half Duty, namely the Passive half: could we but do it, as we can demonstrate it!

"But indeed Conviction, were it never so excellent, is worthless till it convert itself into Conduct. Nay properly Conviction is not possible till then; inasmuch as all Speculation is by nature endless, formless, a vortex amid vortices: only by a felt indubitable certainty of Experience does it find any centre to revolve round, and so fashion itself into a system. Most true is it, as a wise man teaches us, that 'Doubt of any sort cannot be removed except by Action.' On which ground, too, let him who gropes painfully in darkness or uncertain light, and prays vehemently that the dawn may ripen into day, lay this other precept well to heart, which to me was of invaluable service: '*Do the Duty which lies nearest thee,*'[5] which thou knowest to be a Duty! Thy second Duty will already have become clearer.

"May we not say, however, that the hour of Spiritual Enfranchisement is even this: When your Ideal World, wherein the whole man has been dimly struggling and inexpressibly languishing to work, becomes revealed, and thrown open; and you discover, with amazement enough, like the Lothario in *Wilhelm Meister,* that your 'America is here or nowhere'? The Situation that has not its Duty, its Ideal, was never yet occupied by man. Yes here, in this poor, miserable, hampered, despicable Actual, wherein thou even now standest, here or nowhere is thy Ideal: work it out therefrom; and working, believe, live, be free. Fool! the Ideal is in thyself, the impediment too is in thyself: thy Condition is but the stuff thou art to shape that same Ideal out of: what matters whether such stuff be of this sort or that, so the Form thou give it be heroic, be poetic? O thou that pinest in the imprisonment of the Actual, and criest bitterly to the gods for a kingdom wherein to rule and create, know this of a truth: the thing thou seekest is already with thee, 'here or nowhere,' couldst thou only see!

"But it is with man's Soul as it was with Nature: the beginning of Creation is—Light.[6] Till the eye have vision, the whole members are in bonds.[7] Divine moment, when over the tempest-tost Soul, as once over the wild-weltering Chaos, it is spoken: Let there be Light! Ever to the greatest that has felt such moment, is it not miraculous and God-announcing; even as, under simpler figures, to the simplest and least. The mad primeval Discord is hushed; the rudely-jumbled conflicting elements bind themselves into separate Firmaments: deep silent rock-foundations are built beneath; and the skyey vault with its everlasting Luminaries above: instead of a dark wasteful Chaos, we have a blooming, fertile, heaven-encompassed World.

"I too could now say to myself: Be no longer a Chaos, but a World, or even Worldkin. Produce! Produce! Were it but the pitifullest infinitesimal fraction of a Product, produce it, in God's name! 'Tis the utmost thou hast in thee: out

---

3. The doctrine of knowledge (German); by Johann Gottlieb Fichte (1762–1814), German philosopher.
4. Title of an anonymous book of religious instruction first published in 1659.

5. This and the previous quotation are from Goethe's *Wilhelm Meister.*
6. Cf. Genesis 1.3.
7. Cf. Matthew 6.22–23.

with it, then. Up, up! Whatsoever thy hand findeth to do, do it with thy whole might. Work while it is called Today; for the Night cometh, wherein no man can work."[8]

Natural Supernaturalism[9]

It is in his stupendous Section, headed *Natural Supernaturalism*, that the Professor first becomes a Seer; and, after long effort, such as we have witnessed, finally subdues under his feet this refractory Clothes-Philosophy, and takes victorious possession thereof. Phantasms enough he has had to struggle with; "Cloth-webs and Cobwebs," of Imperial Mantles, Superannuated Symbols, and what not: yet still did he courageously pierce through. Nay, worst of all, two quite mysterious, world-embracing Phantasms, TIME and SPACE, have ever hovered round him, perplexing and bewildering: but with these also he now resolutely grapples, these also he victoriously rends asunder. In a word, he has looked fixedly on Existence, till one after the other, its earthly hulls and garnitures have all melted away; and now, to his rapt vision, the interior celestial Holy of Holies lies disclosed.

Here, therefore, properly it is that the Philosophy of Clothes attains to Transcendentalism; this last leap, can we but clear it, takes us safe into the promised land, where *Palingenesia*,[1] in all senses, may be considered as beginning. "Courage, then!" may our Diogenes exclaim, with better right than Diogenes the First[2] once did. This stupendous Section we, after long painful meditation, have found not to be unintelligible; but, on the contrary, to grow clear, nay radiant, and all-illuminating. Let the reader, turning on it what utmost force of speculative intellect is in him, do his part; as we, by judicious selection and adjustment, shall study to do ours:

"Deep has been, and is, the significance of Miracles," thus quietly begins the Professor; "far deeper perhaps than we imagine. Meanwhile, the question of questions were: What specially is a Miracle? To that Dutch King of Siam, an icicle had been a miracle; whoso had carried with him an air-pump, and vial of vitriolic ether, might have worked a miracle.[3] To my Horse, again, who unhappily is still more unscientific, do not I work a miracle, and magical

---

8. Adapted from Ecclesiastes 9.10 and John 9.4.
9. Book 3, chap. 8. The characteristically paradoxical title of this chapter can best be understood by reference to the chapter on miracles in David Hume's *An Enquiry Concerning Human Understanding* (1748), to which Carlyle makes several direct and indirect allusions in his own exposition of the nature of the miraculous. In his skeptical analysis of miracles (Christian miracles in particular), Hume asserts: "A miracle is a violation of the laws of nature. . . . It is no miracle that a man, seemingly in good health, should die on a sudden. . . . But it is a miracle that a dead man should come to life, because that has never been observed in any age or country." The young Carlyle seems to have been impressed by Hume's arguments, as he had also been impressed (and depressed) by Gibbon's relentless exposure of traditional Christianity in *The Decline and Fall of the Roman Empire*. In his later resolution of his dilemma, he bypassed

Hume's arguments. Instead of arguing whether miracles in the traditional sense (such as the resurrection of Christ) have occurred, he contends that *everything* in our experience is a miracle of a supernatural and inexplicable order, hence an appropriate cause for wonder and joy. The natural *is* supernatural.
1. Rebirth. "Transcendentalism": a term loosely used here to refer to any philosophy that opposes materialism or empiricism and that asserts the domination of the intuitive or spiritual over the material [C. F. Harrold].
2. A philosopher of the Cynic school; near the end of a dull lecture he called out to his fellow listeners: "Courage, friends! I see land."
3. In his chapter on miracles, Hume cites an incident of an Indian prince refusing to believe that water can be turned into ice. Carlyle notes that anybody could do so by treating a flask of vitriolic ether with an air pump.

'*Open sesame!*'[4] every time I please to pay twopence, and open for him an impassable *Schlagbaum,* or shut Turnpike?

" 'But is not a real Miracle simply a violation of the Laws of Nature?' ask several. Whom I answer by this new question: What are the Laws of Nature? To me perhaps the rising of one from the dead were no violation of these Laws, but a confirmation; were some far deeper Law, now first penetrated into, and by Spiritual Force, even as the rest have all been, brought to bear on us with its Material Force.

"Here too may some inquire, not without astonishment: On what ground shall one, that can make Iron swim,[5] come and declare that therefore he can teach Religion? To us, truly, of the Nineteenth Century, such declaration were inept enough; which nevertheless to our fathers, of the First Century, was full of meaning.

" 'But is it not the deepest Law of Nature that she be constant?' cries an illuminated class: 'Is not the Machine of the Universe fixed to move by unalterable rules?' Probable enough, good friends: nay I, too, must believe that the God, whom ancient inspired men assert to be 'without variableness or shadow of turning,'[6] does indeed never change; that Nature, that the Universe, which no one whom it so pleases can be prevented from calling a Machine, does move by the most unalterable rules. And now of you, too, I make the old inquiry: What those same unalterable rules, forming the complete Statute-Book of Nature, may possibly be?

"They stand written in our Works of Science, say you; in the accumulated records of Man's Experience?—Was Man with his Experience present at the Creation, then, to see how it all went on? Have any deepest scientific individuals yet dived down to the foundations of the Universe, and gauged everything there? Did the Maker take them into His counsel; that they read His ground-plan of the incomprehensible All; and can say, This stands marked therein, and no more than this? Alas, not in anywise! These scientific individuals have been nowhere but where we also are; have seen some handbreadths deeper than we see into the Deep that is infinite, without bottom as without shore.

"Laplace's[7] Book on the Stars, wherein he exhibits that certain Planets, with their Satellites, gyrate round our worthy Sun, at a rate and in a course, which, by greatest good fortune, he and the like of him have succeeded in detecting,—is to me as precious as to another. But is this what thou namest 'Mechanism of the Heavens,' and 'System of the World'; this, wherein Sirius and the Pleiades, and all Herschel's Fifteen-thousand Suns per minute, being left out, some paltry handful of Moons, and inert Balls, had been—looked at, nicknamed, and marked in the Zodiacal Way-bill;[8] so that we can now prate of their Whereabout; their How, their Why, their What, being hid from us, as in the signless Inane?

"System of Nature! To the wisest man, wide as is his vision, Nature remains of quite *infinite* depth, of quite infinite expansion; and all Experience

---

4. The magic password for opening a door in the cavern in the story *Ali Baba and the Forty Thieves,* in *The Arabian Nights.*
5. Elisha's miracle of causing an ax head to float in water (2 Kings 6.6).
6. Paraphrase of James 1.17.
7. Pierre Laplace (1749–1827); author of *A Trea-*tise on Celestial Mechanics (1799–1825) and other astronomical studies.
8. A document issued with freight shipments, providing complete information about contents and routes. Sir William Herschel (1738–1822), astronomer credited with discovering thousands of stars and other celestial bodies.

thereof limits itself to some few computed centuries and measured square-miles. The course of Nature's phases, on this our little fraction of a Planet, is partially known to us: but who knows what deeper courses these depend on; what infinitely larger Cycle (of causes) our little Epicycle[9] revolves on? To the Minnow every cranny and pebble, and quality and accident, of its little native Creek may have become familiar: but does the Minnow understand the Ocean Tides and periodic Currents, the Tradewinds, and Monsoons, and Moon's Eclipses; by all which the condition of its little Creek is regulated, and may, from time to time (*un*miraculously enough), be quite overset and reversed? Such a minnow is Man; his Creek this Planet Earth; his Ocean the immeasurable All; his Monsoons and periodic Currents the mysterious Course of Providence through Aeons of Aeons.

"We speak of the Volume of Nature: and truly a Volume it is,—whose Author and Writer is God. To read it! Dost thou, does man, so much as well know the Alphabet thereof? With its Words, Sentences, and grand descriptive Pages, poetical and philosophical, spread out through Solar Systems, and Thousands of Years, we shall not try thee. It is a Volume written in celestial hieroglyphs, in the true Sacred-writing; of which even Prophets are happy that they can read here a line and there a line. As for your Institutes, and Academies of Science, they strive bravely; and, from amid the thick-crowded, inextricably intertwisted hieroglyphic writing, pick out, by dextrous combination, some Letters in the vulgar Character, and therefrom put together this and the other economic Recipe,[1] of high avail in Practice. That Nature is more than some boundless Volume of such Recipes, or huge, well-nigh inexhaustible Domestic-Cookery Book, of which the whole secret will in this manner one day evolve itself, the fewest dream.

"Custom," continues the Professor, "doth make dotards of us all.[2] Consider well, thou wilt find that Custom is the greatest of Weavers; and weaves air raiment for all the Spirits of the Universe; whereby indeed these dwell with us visibly, as ministering servants, in our houses and workshops; but their spiritual nature becomes, to the most, forever hidden. Philosophy complains that Custom has hoodwinked us, from the first; that we do everything by Custom, even Believe by it; that our very Axioms, let us boast of Free-thinking as we may, are oftenest simply such Beliefs as we have never heard questioned. Nay, what is Philosophy throughout but a continual battle against Custom; an ever-renewed effort to *transcend* the sphere of blind Custom, and so become Transcendental?

"Innumerable are the illusions and legerdemain-tricks of Custom: but of all these, perhaps the cleverest is her knack of persuading us that the Miraculous, by simple repetition, ceases to be Miraculous. True, it is by this means we live; for man must work as well as wonder: and herein is Custom so far a kind nurse, guiding him to his true benefit. But she is a fond foolish nurse, or rather we are false foolish nurselings, when, in our resting and reflecting hours, we prolong the same deception. Am I to view the Stupendous with stupid indifference, because I have seen it twice, or two-hundred, or two-million times? There is no reason in Nature or in Art why I should: unless,

9. In Ptolemaic astronomy, a circle in which a planet moves, the center of this circle being carried round on the circumference of a larger circle (the "infinitely larger Cycle").

1. I.e., a law in economics, such as the law of supply and demand.
2. Cf. Shakespeare's *Hamlet* 1.3.83: "Thus conscience does make cowards of us all."

indeed, I am a mere Work-Machine, for whom the divine gift of Thought were no other than the terrestrial gift of Steam is to the Steam-engine; a power whereby cotton might be spun, and money and money's worth realised.

"Notable enough too, here as elsewhere, wilt thou find the potency of Names; which indeed are but one kind of such customwoven, wonder-hiding Garments. Witchcraft, and all manner of Spectre-work, and Demonology, we have now named Madness and Diseases of the Nerves. Seldom reflecting that still the new question comes upon us: What is Madness, what are Nerves? Ever, as before, does Madness remain a mysterious-terrific, altogether *infernal* boiling-up of the Nether Chaotic Deep, through this fairpainted Vision of Creation, which swims thereon, which we name the Real. Was Luther's Picture of the Devil[3] less a Reality, whether it were formed within the bodily eye, or without it? In every the wisest Soul lies a whole world of internal Madness, an authentic Demon-Empire; out of which, indeed, his world of Wisdom has been creatively built together, and now rests there, as on its dark foundations does a habitable flowery Earth-rind.

"But deepest of all illusory Appearances, for hiding Wonder, as for many other ends, are your two grand fundamental world-enveloping Appearances, SPACE and TIME. These, as spun and woven for us from before Birth itself, to clothe our celestial ME for dwelling here, and yet to blind it,—lie allembracing, as the universal canvas, or warp and woof, whereby all minor Illusions, in this Phantasm Existence, weave and paint themselves. In vain, while here on Earth, shall you endeavour to strip them off; you can, at best, but rend them asunder for moments, and look through.

"Fortunatus had a wishing Hat, which when he put on, and wished himself Anywhere, behold he was There.[4] By this means had Fortunatus triumphed over Space, he had annihilated Space; for him there was no Where, but all was Here. Were a Hatter to establish himself, in the Wahngasse of Weissnichtwo, and make felts of this sort for all mankind, what a world we should have of it! Still stranger, should, on the opposite side of the street, another Hatter establish himself; and, as his fellow-craftsman made Space annihilating Hats, make Time-annihilating! Of both would I purchase, were it with my last groschen;[5] but chiefly of this latter. To clap-on your felt, and, simply by wishing that you were Any*where*, straightway to be *There*! Next to clapon your other felt, and, simply by wishing that you were Any*when*, straightway to be *Then*! This were indeed the grander: shooting at will from the Fire-Creation of the World to its Fire-Consummation; here historically present in the First Century, conversing face to face with Paul and Seneca;[6] there prophetically in the Thirty-first, conversing also face to face with other Pauls and Senecas, who as yet stand hidden in the depth of that late Time!

"Or thinkest thou it were impossible, unimaginable? Is the Past annihilated, then, or only past; is the Future non-extant, or only future? Those mystic faculties of thine, Memory and Hope, already answer: already through

---

3. Martin Luther (1483–1546), German Reformation leader, threw his inkstand at an apparition of the devil that visited his study when he was translating the Psalms.
4. In the legend on which Thomas Dekker based his play *Old Fortunatus* (1600), a magic hat ena-

bled the owner instantaneously to be anywhere he wished.
5. Small German coin.
6. Roman philosopher (4 B.C.E.–65 C.E.) who, according to legend, conversed with St. Paul.

those mystic avenues, thou the Earth-blinded summonest both Past and Future, and communest with them, though as yet darkly, and with mute beckonings. The curtains of Yesterday drop down, the curtains of Tomorrow roll up; but Yesterday and Tomorrow both *are*. Pierce through the Time-element, glance into the Eternal. Believe what thou findest written in the sanctuaries of Man's Soul, even as all Thinkers, in all ages, have devoutly read it there: that Time and Space are not God, but creations of God; that with God as it is a universal HERE, so is it an everlasting Now.

"And seest thou therein any glimpse of IMMORTALITY?—O Heaven! Is the white Tomb of our Loved One, who died from our arms, and had to be left behind us there, which rises in the distance, like a pale, mournfully receding Milestone, to tell how many toilsome uncheered miles we have journeyed on alone,—but a pale spectral Illusion! Is the lost Friend still mysteriously Here, even as we are Here mysteriously, with God!—Know of a truth that only the Time-shadows have perished, or are perishable; that the real Being of whatever was, and whatever is, and whatever will be, *is* even now and forever. This, should it unhappily seem new, thou mayest ponder at thy leisure; for the next twenty years, or the next twenty centuries: believe it thou must; understand it thou canst not.

"That the Thought-forms, Space and Time, wherein, once for all, we are sent into this Earth to live, should condition and determine our whole Practical reasonings, conceptions, and imagings or imaginings, seems altogether fit, just, and unavoidable. But that they should, furthermore, usurp such sway over pure spiritual Meditation, and blind us to the wonder everywhere lying close on us, seems nowise so. Admit Space and Time to their due rank as Forms of Thought;[7] nay even, if thou wilt, to their quite undue rank of Realities: and consider, then, with thyself how their thin disguises hide from us the brightest God-effulgences! Thus, were it not miraculous, could I stretch forth my hand and clutch the Sun? Yet thou seest me daily stretch forth my hand and therewith clutch many a thing, and swing it hither and thither. Art thou a grown baby, then, to fancy that the Miracle lies in miles of distance, or in pounds avoirdupois of weight; and not to see that the true inexplicable God-revealing Miracle lies in this, that I can stretch forth my hand at all; that I have free Force to clutch aught therewith? Innumerable other of this sort are the deceptions, and wonder-hiding stupefactions, which Space practices on us.

"Still worse is it with regard to Time. Your grand antimagician, and universal wonder-hider, is this same lying Time. Had we but the Time-annihilating Hat, to put on for once only, we should see ourselves in a World of Miracles, wherein all fabled or authentic Thaumaturgy,[8] and feats of Magic, were outdone. But unhappily we have not such a Hat; and man, poor fool that he is, can seldom and scantily help himself without one.

"Were it not wonderful, for instance, had Orpheus, or Amphion,[9] built the walls of Thebes by the mere sound of his Lyre? Yet tell me, Who built these

---

7. The idea that time and space are modes of perception rather than realities is derived from the philosophy of Immanuel Kant (1724–1804), author of *A Critique of Pure Reason* (1781).
8. The working of miracles and magical occurrences.

9. Legendary musicians who effected miracles. Orpheus, with his lyre, could spellbind wild beasts. Amphion's playing, during the building of Thebes, caused the stones for the walls to be drawn into place.

walls of Weissnichtwo; summoning out all the sandstone rocks, to dance along from the *Steinbruch* (now a huge Troglodyte Chasm,[1] with frightful green-mantled pools), and shape themselves into Doric and Ionic pillars, squared ashlar houses[2] and noble streets? Was it not the still higher Orpheus, or Orpheuses, who, in past centuries, by the divine Music of Wisdom, succeeded in civilising Man? Our highest Orpheus walked in Judea, eighteen-hundred years ago: his sphere-melody, flowing in wild native tones, took captive the ravished souls of men; and, being of a true sphere-melody, still flows and sounds, though now with thousandfold accompaniments, and rich symphonies, through all our hearts; and modulates, and divinely leads them. Is that a wonder, which happens in two hours; and does it cease to be wonderful if happening in two million? Not only was Thebes built by the music of an Orpheus; but without the music of some inspired Orpheus was no city ever built, no work that man glories in ever done.

"Sweep away the Illusion of Time; glance, if thou have eyes, from the near moving-cause to its far-distant Mover: The stroke that came transmitted through a whole galaxy of elastic balls, was it less a stroke than if the last ball only had been struck, and sent flying? O, could I (with the Time-annihilating Hat) transport thee direct from the Beginnings to the Endings, how were thy eyesight unsealed, and thy heart set flaming in the Light-sea of celestial wonder! Then sawest thou that this fair Universe, were it in the meanest province thereof, is in very deed the star-domed City of God,[3] that through every star, through every grass-blade, and most through every Living Soul, the glory of a present God still beams. But Nature, which is the Time-vesture of God, and reveals Him to the wise, hides Him from the foolish.

"Again, could anything be more miraculous than an actual authentic Ghost? The English Johnson longed, all his life, to see one; but could not, though he went to Cock Lane,[4] and thence to the church-vaults, and tapped on coffins. Foolish Doctor! Did he never, with the mind's eye as well as with the body's, look round him into that full tide of human Life he so loved; did he never so much as look into Himself? The good Doctor was a Ghost, as actual and authentic as heart could wish; well-nigh a million of Ghosts were travelling the streets by his side. Once more I say, sweep away the illusion of Time; compress the threescore years into three minutes: what else was he, what else are we? Are we not Spirits, that are shaped into a body, into an Appearance; and that fade away again into air and Invisibility? This is no metaphor, it is a simple scientific *fact*; we start out of Nothingness, take figure, and are Apparitions; round us, as round the veriest spectre, is Eternity; and to Eternity minutes are as years and aeons. Come there not tones of Love and Faith, as from celestial harp-strings, like the Song of beatified Souls? And again, do not we squeak and jibber (in our discordant, screech-owlish debatings and recriminatings); and glide bodeful, and feeble, and fearful; or uproad (*poltern*), and revel in our mad Dance of the Dead,—till the scent of the morning air[5] summons us to our still Home; and dreamy

---

1. The emptied stone quarry of *Steinbruch* looks now like the site of primitive cave dwellers ("Troglodytes").
2. Houses made of squared blocks of hewn stone.
3. Title of St. Augustine's famous work.

4. The Cock Lane ghost in London, which proved to be a fraud, was investigated by Samuel Johnson (see Boswell for the year 1763).
5. Cf. Shakespeare's *Hamlet* 1.1.148–56 and 5.58.

Night becomes awake and Day? Where now is Alexander of Macedon: does the steel Host, that yelled in fierce battle-shouts at Issus and Arbela,[6] remain behind him; or have they all vanished utterly, even as perturbed Goblins must? Napoleon too, and his Moscow Retreats and Austerlitz Campaigns! Was it all other than the veriest Spectre-hunt; which has now, with its howling tumult that made Night hideous, flitted away?—Ghosts! There are nigh a thousand-million walking the Earth openly at noontide; some half-hundred have vanished from it, some half-hundred have arisen in it, ere thy watch ticks once.

"O Heaven, it is mysterious, it is awful to consider that we not only carry each a future Ghost within Him; but are, in very deed, Ghosts! These Limbs, whence had we them; this stormy Force; this life-blood with its burning Passion? They are dust and shadow, a Shadow-system gathered round our Me; wherein, through some moments or years, the Divine Essence is to be revealed in the Flesh. That warrior on his strong war-horse, fire flashes through his eyes; force dwells in his arm and heart: but warrior and war-horse are a vision; a revealed Force, nothing more. Stately they tread the Earth, as if it were a firm substance: fool! the Earth is but a film; it cracks in twain, and warrior and war-horse sink beyond plummet's sounding.[7] Plummet's? Fantasy herself will not follow them. A little while ago, they were not; a little while, and they are not, their very ashes are not.

"So has it been from the beginning, so will it be to the end. Generation after generation takes to itself the Form of a Body; and forth-issuing from Cimmerian[8] Night, on Heaven's mission APPEARS. What Force and Fire is in each he expends: one grinding in the mill of Industry; one hunter-like climbing the giddy Alpine heights of Science; one madly dashed in pieces on the rocks of Strife, in war with his fellow:—and then the Heaven-sent is recalled; his earthly Vesture falls away, and soon even to sense becomes a vanished Shadow. Thus, like some wild-flaming, wild-thundering train of Heaven's Artillery, does this mysterious MANKIND thunder and flame, in long-drawn, quick-succeeding grandeur, through the unknown Deep. Thus, like a God-created, fire-breathing Spirit-host, we emerge from the Inane;[9] haste stormfully across the astonished Earth; then plunge again into the Inane. Earth's mountains are levelled, and her seas filled up, in our passage: can the Earth, which is but dead and a vision, resist Spirits which have reality and are alive? On the hardest adamant some footprint of us is stamped-in; the last Rear of the host will read traces of the earliest Van. But whence?—O Heaven, whither? Sense knows not; Faith knows not; only that it is through Mystery to Mystery, from God and to God.

> We *are such stuff*
> As dreams are made of, and our little Life
> Is rounded with a sleep!"[1]

1830–31   1833–34

---

6. Sites of two victories won by the army of Alexander the Great against the Persians under Darius (333–31 B.C.E.).
7. Shakespeare's *The Tempest* 5.1.56. "Plummet": a weight at the end of a line used to sound the depth of water under a ship.

8. A people living in perpetual darkness (cf. *Odyssey* 11.14).
9. The formless void of infinite space [NED].
1. *The Tempest* 4.1.156–58, a favorite passage for Carlyle, here slightly misquoted (Shakespeare wrote: "dreams are made on").

From The French Revolution[1]

September in Paris[2]

The tocsin is pealing its loudest, the clocks inaudibly striking *Three*, when poor Abbé Sicard, with some thirty other Nonjurant Priests,[3] in six carriages, fare along the streets, from their preliminary House of Detention at the Townhall, westward towards the Prison of the Abbaye. Carriages enough stand deserted on the streets; these six move on,—through angry multitudes, cursing as they move. Accursed Aristocrat Tartuffes,[4] this is the pass ye have brought us to! And now ye will break the Prisons, and set Capet Veto[5] on horseback to ride over us? Out upon you, Priests of Beelzebub and Moloch; of Tartuffery, Mammon and the Prussian Gallows,—which ye name Mother-Church and God!—Such reproaches have the poor Nonjurants to endure, and worse; spoken in on them by frantic Patriots, who mount even on the carriage-steps; the very Guards hardly refraining. Pull up your carriage-blinds?—No! answers Patriotism, clapping its horny paw on the carriage-blind, and crushing it down again. Patience in oppression has limits: we are close on the Abbaye, it has lasted long: a poor Nonjurant, of quicker temper, smites the horny paw with his cane; nay, finding solacement in it, smites the unkempt head, sharply and again more sharply, twice over,—seen clearly of us and of the world. It is the last that we see clearly. Alas, next moment, the carriages are locked and blocked in endless raging tumults; in yells deaf to the cry for mercy, which answer the cry for mercy with sabre-thrusts through the heart. The thirty Priests are torn out, are massacred about the Prison-Gate, one after one,—only the poor Abbé Sicard, whom one Moton a watch-maker, knowing him, heroically tried to save and secrete in the Prison, escapes to tell;—and it is Night and Orcus,[6] and Murder's snaky-sparkling head *has* risen in the murk!—

From Sunday afternoon (exclusive of intervals and pauses not final) till Thursday evening, there follow consecutively a Hundred Hours. Which hundred hours are to be reckoned with the hours of the Bartholomew Butchery, of the Armagnac Massacres, Sicilian Vespers, or whatsoever is savagest in the annals of this world. Horrible the hour when man's soul, in its paroxysm,

---

1. In telling the story of the French Revolution Carlyle composes the history as if in the midst of the action. This method of day-to-day eyewitnessing of events contributes to the effect of immediacy that Carlyle sought in what he himself called his "wild savage Book, itself a kind of French Revolution."

A second feature of his method is the device of weaving into the narrative a number of direct quotations from the sources he had consulted during the three years devoted to writing the history. Although later historians have been able to point out inaccuracies in *The French Revolution*, Carlyle did base his account on extensive research. G. M. Trevelyan has said of him that he was not only a great writer but also "in his own strange way, a great historian." Perhaps the most satisfactory comment on *The French Revolution* is J. S. Mill's statement in his 1837 review: "This is not so much a history as an epic poem, and notwithstanding . . . the truest of histories."

2. Part 3, book 1, chap. 4. In September 1792 the revolutionary party under George-Jacques Danton and Jean-Paul Marat urged desperate measures to defend Paris from the invading armies of Austria and Prussia. Hysterical fears of a counterrevolutionary "fifth column" in Paris led to the so-called September Massacres, in which fourteen hundred political prisoners were slaughtered in four days.

3. Priests who had refused to swear allegiance to the new church constitution established by the National Assembly in 1791. Sicard (d. 1822), head of a school for the deaf and dumb in Paris.

4. Hypocrites (from the title of Molière's play).

5. I.e., the king (Louis XVI). The Nonjurant Priests were accused of favoring the restoration to the king of his power to veto legislation, a power he had lost after August 10, 1792. At the same time he had been stripped of his royal titles and was thereafter referred to simply as Louis Capet, the family name of an early dynasty of French kings (Louis XVI was a Bourbon).

6. Hades, the underworld of the dead.

spurns asunder the barriers and rules; and shows what dens and depths are in it! For Night and Orcus, as we say, as was long prophesied, have burst forth, here in this Paris, from their subterranean imprisonment: hideous, dim-confused; which it is painful to look on; and yet which cannot, and indeed which should not, be forgotten.

The Reader, who looks earnestly through this dim Phantasmagory of the Pit, will discern few fixed certain objects; and yet still a few. He will observe, in this Abbaye Prison, the sudden massacre of the Priests being once over, a strange Court of Justice, or call it Court of Revenge and Wild-Justice, swiftly fashion itself, and take seat round a table, with the Prison-Registers spread before it;—Stanislas Maillard, Bastille-hero, famed Leader of the Menads,[7] presiding. O Stanislas, one hoped to meet thee elsewhere than here; thou shifty Riding-Usher, with an inkling of Law! This work also thou hadst to do; and then—to depart for ever from our eyes. At *La Force*, at the *Châtelet*, the *Conciergerie*, the like Court forms itself, with the like accompaniments: the thing that one man does, other men can do. There are some Seven Prisons in Paris, full of Aristocrats with conspiracies;—nay not even *Bicêtre* and *Salpêtrière* shall escape, with their Forgers of Assignats:[8] and there are seventy times seven hundred Patriot hearts in a state of frenzy. Scoundrel hearts also there are; as perfect, say, as the Earth holds,—if such are needed. To whom, in this mood, law is as no-law; and killing, by what name soever called, is but work to be done.

So sit these sudden Courts of Wild-Justice, with the Prison-Registers before them; unwonted wild tumult howling all round; the Prisoners in dread expectancy within. Swift: a name is called; bolts jingle, a Prisoner is there. A few questions are put; swiftly this sudden Jury decides: Royalist Plotter or not? Clearly not; in that case, Let the Prisoner be enlarged with *Vive la Nation*. Probably yea; then still, Let the Prisoner be enlarged, but without *Vive la Nation*; or else it may run. Let the Prisoner be conducted to La Force. At La Force again their formula is, Let the Prisoner be conducted to the Abbaye.—"To La Force then!" Volunteer bailiffs seize the doomed man; he is at the outer gate; "enlarged," or "conducted," not into La Force, but into a howling sea; forth, under an arch of wild sabres, axes and pikes; and sinks, hewn asunder. And another sinks, and another; and there forms itself a piled heap of corpses, and the kennels begin to run red. Fancy the yells of these men, their faces of sweat and blood; the crueller shrieks of these women, for there are women too; and a fellow-mortal hurled naked into it all! Jourgniac de Saint-Méard has seen battle, has seen an effervescent Regiment du Roi in mutiny; but the bravest heart may quail at this. The Swiss Prisoners, remnants of the Tenth of August,[9] "clasped each other spasmodically, and hung back; grey veterans crying: 'Mercy, Messieuers; ah, mercy!' But there was no mercy. Suddenly, however, one of these men steps forward. He had on a blue frock coat; he seemed about thirty, his stature was above common, his look noble and martial. 'I go first,' said he, 'since it must be so: adieu!' Then dashing his hat sharply behind him: 'Which way?' cried he to the Brig-

---

7. Frenzied women of Greece, followers of Dionysus. Maillard had led a mob of women in the march to Versailles in October 1789.
8. Paper money issued by the French revolutionary government. Royalists accused of forging such

currency were imprisoned.
9. The Swiss Guard, most of whom had been massacred on August 10, 1792, when defending the king's palace from a mob.

ands: 'Show it me, then.' They open the folding gate; he is announced to the multitude. He stands a moment motionless; then plunges forth among the pikes, and dies of a thousand wounds."

Man after man is cut down; the sabres need sharpening, the killers refresh themselves from wine-jugs. Onward and onward goes the butchery; the loud yells wearying down into bass growls. A sombre-faced shifting multitude looks on; in dull approval, or dull disapproval; in dull recognition that it is Necessity. "An *Anglais* in drab greatcoat" was seen, or seemed to be seen, serving liquor from his own drambottle;—for what purpose, "if not set on by Pitt," Satan and himself know best! Witty Dr. Moore grew sick on approaching, and turned into another street.—Quick enough goes this Jury-Court; and rigorous. The brave are not spared, nor the beautiful, nor the weak. Old M. de Montmorin, the Minister's Brother, was acquitted by the Tribunal of the Seventeenth; and conducted back, elbowed by howling galleries; but is not acquitted here. Princess de Lamballe[1] has lain down on bed: "Madame, you are to be removed to the Abbaye." "I do not wish to remove; I am well enough here." There is a need-be for removing. She will arrange her dress a little, then; rude voices answer, "You have not far to go." She too is led to the hell-gate; a manifest Queen's-Friend. She shivers back, at the sight of bloody sabres; but there is no return: Onwards! That fair hind head is cleft with the axe; the neck is severed. That fair body is cut in fragments; with indignities, and obscene horrors of moustachio *grand-lèvres*,[2] which human nature would fain find incredible,—which shall be read in the original language only. She was beautiful, she was good, she had known no happiness. Young hearts, generation after generation, will think with themselves: O worthy of worship, thou king-descended, god-descended, and poor sister-woman! why was not I there; and some Sword Balmung[3] or Thor's Hammer in my hand? Her head is fixed on a pike; paraded under the windows of the Temple; that a still more hated, a Marie Antoinette, may see. One Municipal, in the Temple with the Royal Prisoners at the moment, said, "Look out." Another eagerly whispered, "Do not look." The circuit of the Temple is guarded, in these hours, by a long stretched tricolor riband: terror enters, and the clangour of infinite tumult; hitherto not regicide, though that too may come.

But it is more edifying to note what thrillings of affection, what fragments of wild virtues turn up in this shaking asunder of man's existence; for of these too there is a proportion. Note old Marquis Cazotte: he is doomed to die; but his young Daughter clasps him in her arms, with an inspiration of eloquence, with a love which is stronger than very death: the heart of the killers themselves is touched by it; the old man is spared. Yet he was guilty, if plotting for his King is guilt: in ten days more, a Court of Law condemned him, and he had to die elsewhere; bequeathing his Daughter a lock of his old grey hair. Or note old M. de Sombreuil, who also had a Daughter:—My Father is not an Aristocrat: O good gentlemen, I will swear it, and testify it, and in all ways prove it; we are not; we hate Aristocrats! "Wilt thou drink Aristocrats' blood?" The man lifts blood (if universal Rumour can be cred-

---

1. Great-granddaughter of the king of Sardinia. She had married a Bourbon; was early widowed; and later became a close friend of Queen Marie Antoinette, with whom she had been imprisoned.

2. Thick lips (French); here a figure of speech to characterize the mob.
3. The sharp sword of Siegfried, hero of the *Nibelungenlied*.

ited); the poor maiden does drink. "This Sombreuil is innocent then!" Yes, indeed,—and now note, most of all, how the bloody pikes, at this news, do rattle to the ground; and the tiger-yells become bursts of jubilee over a brother saved; and the old man and his daughter are clasped to bloody bosoms, with hot tears; and borne home in triumph of *Vive la Nation*, the killers refusing even money! Does it seem strange, this temper of theirs? It seems very certain, well proved by Royalist testimony in other instances; and very significant.

Place de la Révolution[4]

To this conclusion, then, hast thou come, O hapless Louis! The Son of Sixty Kings is to die on the Scaffold by form of Law. Under Sixty Kings this same form of Law, form of Society, has been fashioning itself together, these thousand years; and has become, one way and other, a most strange Machine. Surely, if needful, it is also frightful, this Machine; dead, blind; not what it should be; which, with swift stroke, or by cold slow torture, has wasted the lives and souls of innumerable men. And behold now a King himself, or say rather Kinghood in his person, is to expire here in cruel tortures;—like a Phalaris[5] shut in the belly of his own red-heated Brazen Bull! It is ever so; and thou shouldst know it, O haughty tyrannous man: injustice breeds injustice; curses and falsehoods do verily return "always *home*," wide as they may wander. Innocent Louis bears the sins of many generations: he too experiences that man's tribunal is not in this Earth; that if he had no Higher one, it were not well with him.

A King dying by such violence appeals impressively to the imagination; as the like must do, and ought to do. And yet at bottom it is not the King dying, but the man! Kingship is a coat: the grand loss is of the skin. The man from whom you take his Life, to him can the whole combined world do *more*? Lally[6] went on his hurdle; his mouth filled with a gag. Miserablest mortals, doomed for picking pockets, have a whole five-act Tragedy in them, in that dumb pain, as they go to the gallows, unregarded; they consume the cup of trembling down to the lees. For Kings and for Beggars, for the justly doomed and the unjustly, it is a hard thing to die. Pity them all: thy utmost pity, with all aids and appliances and throne-and-scaffold contrasts, how far short is it of the thing pitied!

A Confessor has come; Abbé Edgeworth, of Irish extraction, whom the King knew by good report, has come promptly on this solemn mission. Leave the Earth alone, then, thou hapless King; it with its malice will go its way, thou also canst go thine. A hard scene yet remains: the parting with our loved ones. Kind hearts, environed in the same grim peril with us; to be left *here*! Let the Reader look with the eyes of Valet Cléry,[7] through these glass-doors, where also the Municipality watches; and see the cruellest of scenes:

"At half-past eight, the door of the ante-room opened: the Queen appeared

---

4. Part 3, book 2, chap. 8. On January 20, 1793, by a small majority, the Convention of Delegates in Paris had voted for the death of the king.
5. Sicilian tyrant whose victims were roasted alive by being confined inside the brass figure of a bull under which a fire was lit.

6. French general who was accused unjustly of treachery and executed in 1766. He was gagged, presumably to prevent his protesting his innocence.
7. He attended the king during his imprisonment and later published a journal.

first, leading her Son by the hand; then Madame Royale and Madame Elizabeth:[8] they all flung themselves into the arms of the King. Silence reigned for some minutes; interrupted only by sobs. The Queen made a movement to lead his Majesty towards the inner room, where M. Edgeworth was waiting unknown to them: 'No,' said the King, 'let us go into the dining-room, it is there only that I can see you.' They entered there; I shut the door of it, which was of glass. The King sat down, the Queen on his left hand, Madame Elizabeth on his right, Madame Royale almost in front; the young Prince remained standing between his Father's legs. They all leaned towards him, and often held him embraced. This scene of woe lasted an hour and three quarters; during which we could hear nothing; we could see only that always when the King spoke, the sobbings of the Princesses redoubled, continued for some minutes; and that then the King began again to speak."—And so our meetings and our partings do now end! The sorrows we gave each other; the poor joys we faithfully shared, and all our lovings and our sufferings, and confused toilings under the earthly Sun, are over. Thou good soul, I shall never, never through all ages of Time, see thee any more!—NEVER! O Reader, knowest thou that hard word?

For nearly two hours this agony lasts; then they tear themselves asunder. "Promise that you will see us on the morrow." He promises:—Ah yes, yes; yet once; and go now, ye loved ones; cry to God for yourselves and me!—It was a hard scene, but it is over. He will not see them on the morrow. The Queen, in passing through the ante-room, glanced at the Cerberus Municipals; and, with woman's vehemence, said through her tears, "*Vous êtes tous des scélérats.*"[9]

King Louis slept sound, till five in the morning, when Cléry, as he had been ordered, awoke him. Cléry dressed his hair: while this went forward, Louis took a ring from his watch, and kept trying it on his finger; it was his wedding-ring, which he is now to return to the Queen as a mute farewell. At half-past six, he took the Sacrament; and continued in devotion, and conference with Abbé Edgeworth. He will not see his Family: it were too hard to bear.

At eight, the Municipals enter: the King gives them his Will, and messages and effects; which they, at first, brutally refuse to take charge of: he gives them a roll of gold pieces, a hundred and twenty-five louis; these are to be returned to Malesherbes,[1] who had lent them. At nine, Santerre[2] says the hour is come. The King begs yet to retire for three minutes. At the end of three minutes, Santerre again says the hour is come. "Stamping on the ground with his right foot, Louis answers: '*Partons*, Let us go.' "—How the rolling of those drums comes in, through the Temple bastions and bulwarks, on the heart of a queenly wife; soon to be a widow! He is gone, then, and has not seen us? A Queen weeps bitterly; a King's Sister and Children. Over all these Four does Death also hover: all shall perish miserably save one; she, as Duchesse d'Angoulême, will live,—not happily.

---

8. The king's sister, guillotined a year later. Madame Royale (1778–1851), the king's daughter, duchesse d'Angoulême.
9. You are all scoundrels (French). "Cerberus Municipals": local officers, likened to Cerberus, the three-headed dog that guarded the entrance to Hades.
1. A delegate who had defended the king. He was guillotined a year later.
2. Jacobin leader who commanded the troops in Paris.

At the Temple Gate were some faint cries, perhaps from voices of Pitiful women: "*Grâce!*[3] *Grâce!*" Through the rest of the streets there is silence as of the grave. No man not armed is allowed to be there: the armed, did any even pity, dare not express it, each man overawed by all his neighbors. All windows are down, none seem looking through them. All shops are shut. No wheel-carriage rolls, this morning, in these streets but one only. Eighty-thousand armed men stand ranked, like armed statues of men; cannons bristle, cannoneers with match burning, but no word or movement: it is as a city enchanted into silence and stone: one carriage with its escort, slowly rumbling, is the only sound. Louis reads, in his Book of Devotion, the Prayers of the Dying: clatter of this death-march falls sharp on the ear, in the great silence; but the thought would fain struggle heavenward, and forget the Earth.

As the clocks strike ten, behold the Place de la Révolution, once Place de Louis Quinze: the Guillotine, mounted near the old Pedestal where once stood the Statue of that Louis! Far round, all bristles with cannons and armed men: spectators crowding in the rear; D'Orléans Égalité[4] there in cabriolet. Swift messengers, *hoquetons,* speed to the Townhall, every three minutes: near by is the Convention sitting,—vengeful for Lepelletier.[5] Heedless of all, Louis reads his Prayers of the Dying; not till five minutes yet has he finished; then the Carriage opens. What temper he is in? Ten different witnesses will give ten different accounts of it. He is in the collision of all tempers; arrived now at the black Mahlstrom and descent of Death: in sorrow, in indignation, in resignation struggling to be resigned. "Take care of M. Edgeworth," he straitly charges the Lieutenant who is sitting with them: then they two descend.

The drums are beating: "*Taisez-vous,* Silence!" he cries "in a terrible voice, *d'une voix terrible.*" He mounts the scaffold, not without delay; he is in puce[6] coat, breeches of grey, white stockings. He strips off the coat; stands disclosed in a sleeve-waistcoat of white flannel. The Executioners approach to bind him: he spurns, resists; Abbé Edgeworth has to remind him how the Saviour, in whom men trust, submitted to be bound. His hands are tied, his head bare; the fatal moment is come. He advances to the edge of the Scaffold, "his face very red," and says: "Frenchmen, I die innocent: it is from the Scaffold and near appearing before God that I tell you so. I pardon my enemies; I desire that France——" A General on horseback, Santerre or another, prances out, with uplifted hand: "*Tambours!*" The drums drown the voice. "Executioners, do your duty!" The Executioners, desperate lest themselves be murdered (for Santerre and his Armed Ranks will strike, if they do not), seize the hapless Louis: six of them desperate, him singly desperate, struggling there; and bind him to their plank. Abbé Edgeworth, stooping, bespeaks him: "Son of Saint Louis,[7] ascend to Heaven." The Axe clanks down; a King's Life is shorn away. It is Monday the 21st of January 1793. He was aged Thirty-eight years four months and twenty-eight days.

Executioner Samson shows the Head: fierce shout of *Vive la République*

---

3. Mercy! (French).
4. Equality (French); here the duc d'Orléans, a Royalist who had become a revolutionary leader. Despite his having voted for the king's death, he was himself executed in 1793.

5. A delegate who had voted for the king's death and was killed by a Royalist sympathizer.
6. Dull red.
7. Louis IX, king of France (reigned 1226–70).

rises, and swells; caps raised on bayonets, hats waving: students of the College of Four Nations take it up, on the far Quais; fling it over Paris. D'Orléans drives off in his cabriolet: the Townhall Councillors rub their hands, saying, "It is done, It is done." There is dipping of handkerchiefs, of pike-points in the blood. Headsman Samson, though he afterwards denied it, sells locks of the hair: fractions of the puce coat are long after worn in rings.—And so, in some half-hour it is done; and the multitude has all departed. Pastry-cooks, coffee-sellers, milkmen sing out their trivial quotidian cries: the world wags on, as if this were a common day. In the coffee-houses that evening, says Prudhomme, Patriot shook hands with Patriot in a more cordial manner than usual. Not till some days after, according to Mercier, did public men see what a grave thing it was.

From *Cause and Effect*[8]

Yes, Reader, here is the miracle. Out of that putrescent rubbish of Scepticism, Sensualism, Sentimentalism, hollow Machiavelism, such a Faith has verily risen; flaming in the heart of a People. A whole People, awakening as it were to consciousness in deep misery, believes that it is within reach of a Fraternal Heaven-on-Earth. With longing arms, it struggles to embrace the Unspeakable; cannot embrace it, owing to certain causes.—Seldom do we find that a whole People can be said to have any Faith at all; except in things which it can eat and handle. Whensoever it gets any Faith, its history becomes spirit-stirring, noteworthy. But since the time when steel Europe shook itself simultaneously at the word of Hermit Peter,[9] and rushed towards the Sepulchre where God had lain, there was no universal impulse of Faith that one could note. Since Protestantism went silent, no Luther's voice, no Zisca's drum any longer proclaiming that God's truth was *not* the Devil's Lie; and the Last of the Cameronians[1] (Renwick was the name of him; honour to the name of the brave!) sank, shot, on the Castle-hill of Edinburgh, there was no parital impulse of Faith among Nations. Till now, behold, once more, this French Nation believes! Herein, we say, in that astonishing Faith of theirs, lies the miracle.It is a Faith undoubtedly of the more prodigious sort, even among Faiths; and will embody itself in prodigies. It is the soul of that world-prodigy named French Revolution; whereat the world still gazes and shudders.

But, for the rest, let no man ask History to explain by cause and effect how the business proceeded henceforth. This battle of Mountain and Gironde,[2] and what follows, is the battle of Fanaticisms and Miracles; unsuitable for cause and effect. The sound of it, to the mind, is as a hubbub of voices in distraction; little of articulate is to be gathered by long listening

8. Part 3, book 3, chap. 1. Between the execution of the king and the advent of Napoleon, the revolutionary movement in France suffered from dissension and counterrevolutionary outbreaks that led to the Reign of Terror (1793–94). During this period most of the political leaders and thousands of their followers lost their lives. Before recommencing his narrative, Carlyle pauses, in this chapter, to consider some of the forces underlying these developments.
9. A leader of the First Crusade to Palestine in the late 11th century.
1. A 17th-century Scottish sect. Zisca (ca. 1360–1424), successful general and leader of the Hussites, a religious sect in Bohemia.
2. The Girondists were a party of moderate revolutionaries, often of middle-class backgrounds. They were overthrown by their opponents, the Jacobins, who were more adept in controlling the populace. Because the Jacobin delegates in the National Assembly sat in the most elevated place, the party was sometimes called the Mountain.

and studying; only battle-tumult, shouts of triumph, shrieks of despair. The Mountain has left no Memoirs; the Girondins have left Memoirs, which are too often little other than long-drawn Interjections, of *Woe is me,* and *Cursed be ye.* So soon as History can philosophically delineate the conflagration of a kindled Fireship,[3] she may try this other task. Here lay the bitumen-stratum, there the brimstone one; so ran the vein of gunpowder, of nitre, terebinth[4] and foul grease: this, were she inquisitive enough, History might partly know. But how they acted and reacted below decks, one fire-stratum playing into the other, by its nature and the art of man, now when all hands ran raging, and the flames lashed high over shrouds and topmast: this let not History attempt.

The Fireship is old France, the old French Form of Life; her crew a Generation of men. Wild are their cries and their ragings there, like spirits tormented in that flame. But, on the whole, are they not *gone,* O Reader? Their Fireship and they, frightening the world, have sailed away; its flames and its thunders quite away, into the Deep of Time. One thing therefore History will do: pity them all; for it went hard with them all. Not even the seagreen Incorruptible[5] but shall have some pity, some human love, though it takes an effort. And now, so much once thoroughly attained, the rest will become easier. To the eye of equal brotherly pity, innumerable perversions dissipate themselves; exaggerations and execrations fall off, of their own accord. Standing wistfully on the safe shore, we will look, and see, what is of interest to us, what is adapted to us.

1834–37   1837

From Past and Present[1]

From *Democracy*

If the Serene Highnesses and Majesties do not take note of that,[2] then, as I perceive, *that* will take note of itself! The time for levity, insincerity, and idle babble and play-acting, in all kinds, is gone by; it is a serious, grave time. Old long-vexed questions, not yet solved in logical words or parliamentary laws, are fast solving themselves in facts, somewhat unblessed to behold! This largest of questions, this question of Work and Wages, which ought, had we heeded Heaven's voice, to have begun two generations ago or more,

3. A ship filled with combustibles (such as gunpowder and brimstone) that is set adrift among enemy ships to create havoc.
4. Turpentine.
5. Maximilien Robespierre (the Incorruptible), chief of the Jacobin Party and principal instigator of the Reign of Terror.
1. In 1845 there were reputedly one and a half million unemployed in England (out of a population of eighteen million). The closing of factories and the reduction of wages led to severe rioting in the manufacturing districts. Bread-hungry mobs (as well as the Chartist mobs who demanded political reforms) caused many observers to dread that a large-scale revolution was imminent. Carlyle was himself so appalled by the plight of the industrial workers that he postponed his research into the life and times of Cromwell to air his views on the contemporary crisis. *Past and Present,* a book written in seven weeks, was a call for heroic leadership.

Cromwell and other historic leaders are cited, but the principal example from the past is Abbot Samson, a medieval monk who established order in the monasteries under his charge. Carlyle hoped that the "Captains of Industry" might provide a comparable leadership in 1843. He was aware that the spread of democracy was inevitable, but he had little confidence in it as a method of producing leaders. Nor did he have any confidence, at this time, in the landed aristocracy, who seemed to him preoccupied with fox hunting, preserving their game, and upholding the tariffs on grain (Corn Laws). In place of a "Do nothing Aristocracy" there was need for a "Working Aristocracy." This first selection is from book 3, chap. 13.
2. The previous chapter, *Reward,* had urged that English manufacturers needed the help of everyone and that Parliament should remove the tariffs (Corn Laws) restricting the growth of trade and industry.

cannot be delayed longer without hearing Earth's voice. "Labour" will verily need to be somewhat "organized," as they say,—God knows with what difficulty. Man will actually need to have his debts and earnings a little better paid by man; which, let Parliaments speak of them, or be silent of them, are eternally his due from man, and cannot, without penalty and at length not without death-penalty,[3] be withheld. How much ought to cease among us straightway; how much ought to begin straightway, while the hours yet are!

Truly they are strange results to which this of leaving all to "Cash"; of quietly shutting up the God's Temple, and gradually opening wide-open the Mammon's Temple, with "Laissez-faire, and Every man for himself,"—have led us in these days! We have Upper, speaking Classes, who indeed do "speak" as never man spake before; the withered flimsiness, godless baseness and barrenness of whose Speech might of itself indicate what kind of Doing and practical Governing went on under it! For Speech is the gaseous element out of which most kinds of Practice and Performance, especially all kinds of moral Performance, condense themselves, and take shape; as the one is, so will the other be. Descending, accordingly, into the Dumb Class in its Stockport Cellars and Poor-Law Bastilles,[4] have we not to announce that they are hitherto unexampled in the History of Adam's Posterity?

Life was never a May-game for men: in all times the lot of the dumb millions born to toil was defaced with manifold sufferings, injustices, heavy burdens, avoidable and unavoidable; not play at all, but hard work that made the sinews sore and the heart sore. As bond-slaves, *villani, bordarii, sochemanni,* nay indeed as dukes, earls and kings, men were oftentimes made weary of their life; and had to say, in the sweat of their brow and of their soul, Behold, it is not sport, it is grim earnest, and our back can bear no more! Who knows not what massacrings and harryings there have been; grinding, long-continuing, unbearable injustices,—till the heart had to rise in madness, and some *"Eu Sachsen, nimith euer sachses,* You Saxons, out with your gully-knives, then!" You Saxons, some "arrestment," partial "arrestment of the Knaves and Dastards" has become indispensable!—The page of Dryasdust[5] is heavy with such details.

And yet I well venture to believe that in no time, since the beginnings of Society, was the lot of those same dumb millions of toilers so entirely unbearable as it is even in the days now passing over us. It is not to die, or even to die of hunger, that makes a man wretched; many men have died; all men must die,—the last exit of us all is in a Fire-Chariot of Pain.[6] But it is to live miserable we know not why; to work sore and yet gain nothing; to be heartworn, weary, yet isolated, unrelated, girt-in with a cold universal Laissezfaire: it is to die slowly all our life long, imprisoned in a deaf, dead, Infinite Injustice, as in the accursed iron belly of a Phalaris' Bull![7] This is and remains for ever intolerable to all men whom God has made. Do we wonder at French Revolutions, Chartisms, Revolts of Three Days? The times, if we will consider them, are really unexampled.

Never before did I hear of an Irish Widow reduced to "prove her sisterhood

---

3. I.e., by the outbreak of a revolution, as in France.
4. I.e., workhouse for the unemployed. "Stockport Cellars": in a cellar in the slum district of Stockport, an industrial town near Manchester, three children were poisoned by their starving parents, who wanted to collect insurance benefits from a

burial society.
5. An imaginary author of dull histories.
6. 2 Kings 2.11.
7. Phalaris was a Sicilian tyrant whose victims were roasted alive by being confined inside the brass figure of a bull under which a fire was lit.

by dying of typhus-fever and infecting seventeen persons,"—saying in such undeniable way, "You *see*, I was your sister!"[8] Sisterhood, brotherhood, was often forgotten; but not till the rise of these ultimate Mammon and Shotbelt Gospels[9] did I ever see it so expressly denied. If no pious Lord or *Law-ward* would remember it, always some pious Lady (*"Hlaf-dig,"* Benefactress, *"Loaf-giveress,"* they say she is,—blessings on her beautiful heart!) was there, with mild mother-voice and hand, to remember it; some pious thoughtful *Elder*, what we now call "Prester," *Presbyter* or "Priest," was there to put all men in mind of it, in the name of the God who had made all.

Not even in Black Dahomey was it ever, I think, forgotten to the typhus-fever length. Mungo Park,[1] resourceless, had sunk down to die under the Negro Village-Tree, a horrible White object in the eyes of all. But in the poor Black Woman, and her daughter who stood aghast at him, whose earthly wealth and funded capital consisted of one small calabash of rice, there lived a heart richer than *"Laissez-faire"*: they, with a royal munificence, boiled their rice for him; they sang all night to him, spinning assiduous on their cotton distaffs, as he lay to sleep: "Let us pity the poor white man; no mother has he to fetch him milk, no sister to grind him corn!" Thou poor black Noble One,—thou *Lady* too: did not a God make thee too; was there not in thee too something of a God!—

Gurth,[2] born thrall of Cedric the Saxon, has been greatly pitied by Dryasdust and others. Gurth, with the brass collar round his neck, tending Cedric's pigs in the glades of the wood, is not what I call an exemplar of human felicity: but Gurth, with the sky above him, with the free air and tinted boscage and umbrage round him, and in him at least the certainty of supper and social lodging when he came home; Gurth to me seems happy, in comparison with many a Lancashire and Buckinghamshire man, of these days, not born thrall of anybody! Gurth's brass collar did not gall him: Cedric *deserved* to be his Master. The pigs were Cedric's, but Gurth too would get his parings of them. Gurth had the inexpressible satisfaction of feeling himself related indissolubly, though in a rude brass-collar way, to his fellow-mortals in this Earth. He had superiors, inferiors, equals.—Gurth is now "emancipated" long since; has what we call "Liberty." Liberty, I am told, is a Divine thing. Liberty when it becomes the "Liberty to die by starvation" is not so divine!

Liberty? The true liberty of a man, you would say, consisted in his finding out, or being forced to find out, the right path, and to walk thereon. To learn, or to be taught, what work he actually was able for; and then by permission, persuasion, and even compulsion, to set about doing of the same! That is his true blessedness, honour, "liberty" and maximum of wellbeing: if liberty be not that, I for one have small care about liberty. You do not allow a palpable madman to leap over precipices; you violate his liberty, you that are wise; and keep him, were it in strait-waistcoats, away from the precipices! Every

---

8. An incident referred to several times in *Past and Present*. Dickens in *Bleak House* also showed how indifference to the lack of sanitation in London slums led to the spread of disease to other parts of the city.
9. The attitudes of land-owning aristocracy who were committed to preserving their exclusive right to shoot game birds and animals. "Mammon [gos-

pel]": the pursuit of wealth according to the economic code of laissez-faire, whereby no one took the responsibility of caring for the starving widow.
1. Explorer and author of *Travels in the Interior of Africa* (1799); in 1806, he was killed by Africans. "Black Dahomey": a state in west Africa where human sacrifice and cannibalism persisted.
2. A swineherd described in Scott's *Ivanhoe*.

stupid, every cowardly and foolish man is but a less palpable madman: his true liberty were that a wiser man, that any and every wiser man, could, by brass collars, or in whatever milder or sharper way, lay hold of him when he was going wrong, and order and compel him to go a little righter. O, if thou really art my *Senior,* Seigneur, my *Elder,* Presbyter or Priest,—if thou art in very deed my *Wiser,* may a beneficent instinct lead and impel thee to "conquer" me, to command me! If thou do know better than I what is good and right, I conjure thee in the name of God, force me to do it; were it by never such brass collars, whips and handcuffs, leave me not to walk over precipices! That I have been called, by all the Newspapers, a "free man" will avail me little, if my pilgrimage have ended in death and wreck. O that the Newspapers had called me slave, coward, fool, or what it pleased their sweet voices to name me, and I had attained not death, but life!—Liberty requires new definitions.

A conscious abhorrence and intolerance of Folly, of Baseness, Stupidity, Poltroonery and all that brood of things, dwells deep in some men: still deeper in others an *un*conscious abhorrence and intolerance, clothed moreover by the beneficent Supreme Powers in what stout appetites, energies, egoisms so-called, are suitable to it;—these latter are your Conquerors, Romans, Normans, Russians, Indo-English; Founders of what we call Aristocracies. Which indeed have they not the most "divine right" to found;—being themselves very truly *Aristoi,* BRAVEST, BEST; and conquering generally a confused rabble of WORST, or at lowest, clearly enough, of WORSE? I think their divine right, tried, with affirmatory verdict, in the greatest Law-Court known to me, was good! A class of men who are dreadfully exclaimed against by Dryasdust; of whom nevertheless beneficent Nature has oftentimes had need; and may, alas, again have need.

When, across the hundredfold poor scepticisms, trivialisms, and constitutional cobwebberies of Dryasdust, you catch any glimpse of a William the Conqueror, a Tancred of Hauteville[3] or such like,—do you not discern veritably some rude outline of a true God-made King; whom not the Champion of England[4] cased in tin, but all Nature and the Universe were calling to the throne? It is absolutely necessary that he get thither. Nature does not mean her poor Saxon children to perish, of obesity, stupor or other malady, as yet: a stern Ruler and Line of Rulers therefore is called in,—a stern but most beneficent *perpetual House-Surgeon* is by Nature herself called in, and even the appropriate *fees* are provided for him! Dryasdust talks lamentably about Hereward and the Fen Counties; fate of earl Waltheof;[5] Yorkshire and the North reduced to ashes; all of which is undoubtedly lamentable. But even Dryasdust apprises me of one fact: "A child, in this William's reign, might have carried a purse of gold from end to end of England." My erudite friend,

---

3. Norman hero of the First Crusade. King William I of England (reigned 1066–87), surnamed *the Conqueror* after the Battle of Hastings in 1066. Being an illegitimate son, he also bore the surname of William the Bastard. Although some historians condemn William as a ruthless ruler, he is ranked by Carlyle as a hero because of his strong and efficient government. William fulfilled the requirements of the kingly hero described by Carlyle in his lectures *On Heroes:* a man fittest "to *command* over us . . . to tell us what we are to *do.*"

4. An official who goes through a formality, at coronation ceremonies, of demanding whether anyone challenges the right of the monarch to ascend the throne. He wears full armor ("cased in tin"). A symbol of outworn feudal customs.
5. His execution in 1075, on a supposedly trumped-up charge, is cited as a blot on William's record as king. Hereward the Wake, an outlaw whose exploits against William the Conqueror made him seem a romantic figure like Robin Hood.

it is a fact which outweighs a thousand! Sweep away thy constitutional, sentimental, and other cobwebberies; look eye to eye, if thou still have any eye, in the face of this big burly William Bastard: thou wilt see a fellow of most flashing discernment, of most strong lion-heart;—in whom, as it were, within a frame of oak and iron, the gods have planted the soul of "a man of genius"! Dost thou call that nothing? I call it an immense thing!—Rage enough was in this Willelmus Conquaestor, rage enough for his occasions;—and yet the essential element of him, as of all such men, is not scorching *fire*, but shining illuminative *light*. Fire and light are strangely interchangeable; nay, at bottom, I have found them different forms of the same most godlike "elementary substance" in our world: a thing worth stating in these days. The essential element of this Conquaestor is, first of all, the most sun-eyed perception of what *is* really what on this God's-Earth;—which, thou wilt find, does mean at bottom "Justice," and "Virtues" not a few: *Conformity* to what the Maker has seen good to make; that, I suppose, will mean Justice and a Virtue or two?—

Dost thou think Willelmus Conquaestor would have tolerated ten years' jargon, one hour's jargon, on the propriety of killing Cotton-manufactures by partridge Corn-Laws?[6] I fancy, this was not the man to knock out of his night's-rest with nothing but a noisy bedlamism in your mouth! "Assist us still better to bush the partridges; strangle Plugson who spins the shirts?"— *"Par la Splendeur de Dieu!"*[7]—Dost thou think Willelmus Conquaestor, in this new time, with Steam-engine Captains of Industry on one hand of him, and Joe-Manton Captains of Idleness[8] on the other, would have doubted which *was* really the BEST; which did deserve strangling, and which not?

I have a certain indestructible regard for Willelmus Conquaestor. A resident House-Surgeon, provided by Nature for her beloved English People, and even furnished with the requisite fees, as I said; for he by no means felt himself doing Nature's work, this Willelmus, but his own work exclusively! And his own work withal it was; informed *"par la Splendeur de Dieu."*—I say, it is necessary to get the work out of such a man, however harsh that be! When a world, not yet doomed for death, is rushing down to ever-deeper Baseness and Confusion, it is a dire necessity of Nature's to bring in her ARISTOCRACIES, her BEST, even by forcible methods. When their descendants or representatives cease entirely to *be* the Best, Nature's poor world will very soon rush down again to Baseness; and it becomes a dire necessity of Nature's to cast them out. Hence French Revolutions, Five-point Charters, Democracies, and a mournful list of *Etceteras*, in these our afflicted times.

* * *

Democracy, the chase of Liberty in that direction, shall go its full course; unrestrained by him of Pferdefuss-Quacksalber,[9] or any of *his* household. The Toiling Millions of Mankind, in most vital need and passionate instinctive desire of Guidance, shall cast away False-Guidance; and hope, for an

---

6. See n. 1, p. 1110.
7. By the splendor of God! (French): one of William's oaths. Plugson of Undershot was Carlyle's term to describe the new class of industrial leaders.
8. The idle aristocracy who wasted time shooting partridges with guns made by Joseph Manton, a London gunsmith. This speech sums up the pleas

of the High Tariff lobby in Parliament. "Keep the Corn Laws intact so that the aristocratic landlords may continue to enjoy shooting partridges on their estates; subdue the manufacturing leaders by preventing trade."
9. Horse foot quack doctor.

hour, that No-Guidance will suffice them: but it can be for an hour only. The smallest item of human Slavery is the oppression of man by his Mock-Superiors; the palpablest, but I say at bottom the smallest. Let him shake off such oppression, trample it indignantly under his feet; I blame him not, I pity and commend him. But oppression by your Mock-Superiors well shaken off, the grand problem yet remains to solve: That of finding government by your Real-Superiors! Alas, how shall we ever learn the solution of that, benighted, bewildered, sniffing, sneering, godforgetting unfortunates as we are? It is a work for centuries; to be taught us by tribulations, confusions, insurrections, obstructions; who knows if not by conflagration and despair! It is a lesson inclusive of all other lessons; the hardest of all lessons to learn.

Captains of Industry[1]

If I believed that Mammonism with its adjuncts was to continue henceforth the one serious principle of our existence, I should reckon it idle to solicit remedial measures from any Government, the disease being insusceptible of remedy. Government can do much, but it can in no wise do all. Government, as the most conspicuous object in Society, is called upon to give signal of what shall be done; and, in many ways, to preside over further, and command the doing of it. But the Government cannot do, by all its signalling and commanding, what the Society is radically indisposed to do. In the long-run every Government is the exact symbol of its People, with their wisdom and unwisdom; we have to say, Like People like Government.— The main substance of this immense Problem of Organizing Labour, and first of all of Managing the Working Classes, will, it is very clear, have to be solved by those who stand practically in the middle of it; by those who themselves work and preside over work. Of all that can be enacted by any Parliament in regard to it, the germs must already lie potentially extant in those two Classes, who are to obey such enactment. A Human Chaos *in* which there is no light, you vainly attempt to irradiate by light shed *on* it: order never can arise there.

But it is my firm conviction that the "Hell of England" will *cease* to be that of "not making money"; that we shall get a nobler Hell and a nobler Heaven! I anticipate light *in* the Human Chaos, glimmering, shining more and more; under manifold true signals from without That light shall shine. Our deity no longer being Mammon,—O Heavens, each man will then say to himself: "Why such deadly haste to make money? I shall not go to Hell, even if I do not make money! There is another Hell, I am told!" Competition, at railway-speed, in all branches of commerce and work will then abate:—good felt-hats for the head, in every sense, instead of seven-feet lath-and-plaster hats on wheels,[2] will then be discoverable! Bubble-periods,[3] with their panics and commercial crises, will again become infrequent; steady modest industry will take the place of gambling speculation. To be a noble Master, among noble Workers, will again be the first ambition with some few; to be a rich Master only the second. How the Inventive Genius of England, with the whirr of its bobbins and billy-rollers[4] shoved somewhat into the backgrounds of the

1. From book 4, chap. 4.
2. A London hatter's mode of advertising.
3. Periods of violent fluctuation in the stock market caused by unsound speculating.
4. Machines used to prepare cotton or wool for spinning.

brain, will contrive and devise, not cheaper produce exclusively, but fairer distribution of the produce at its present cheapness! By degrees, we shall again have a Society with something of Heroism in it, something of Heaven's Blessing on it; we shall again have, as my German friend[5] asserts, "instead of Mammon-Feudalism with unsold cotton-shirts and Preservation of the Game, noble just Industrialism and Government by the Wisest!"

It is with the hope of awakening here and there a British man to know himself for a man and divine soul, that a few words of parting admonition, to all persons to whom the Heavenly Powers have lent power of any kind in this land, may now be addressed. And first to those same Master-Workers, Leaders of Industry; who stand nearest, and in fact powerfullest, though not most prominent, being as yet in too many senses a Virtuality rather than an Actuality.

The Leaders of Industry, if Industry is ever to be led, are virtually the Captains of the World; if there be no nobleness in them, there will never be an Aristocracy more. But let the Captains of Industry consider: once again, are they born of other clay than the old Captains of Slaughter; doomed for ever to be not Chivalry, but a mere gold-plated *Doggery*,—what the French well name *Canaille*, "Doggery" with more or less gold carrion at its disposal? Captains of Industry are the true Fighters, henceforth recognizable as the only true ones: Fighters against Chaos, Necessity and the Devils and Jötuns;[6] and lead on Mankind in that great, and alone true, and universal warfare; the stars in their courses fighting for them, and all Heaven and all Earth saying audibly, Well done! Let the Captains of Industry retire into their own hearts, and ask solemnly, If there is nothing but vulturous hunger for fine wines, valet reputation and gilt carriages, discoverable there? Of hearts made by the Almighty God I will not believe such a thing. Deep-hidden under wretchedest god-forgetting Cants, Epicurisms, Dead-Sea Apisms;[7] forgotten as under foullest fat Lethe mud and weeds, there is yet, in all hearts born into this God's-World, a spark of the Godlike slumbering. Awake, O nightmare sleepers; awake, arise, or be for ever fallen! This is not playhouse poetry; it is sober fact. Our England, our world cannot live as it is. It will connect itself with a God again, or go down with nameless throes and fire-consummation to the Devils. Thou who feelest aught of such a Godlike stirring in thee, any faintest intimation of it as through heavy-laden dreams, follow *it,* I conjure thee. Arise, save thyself, be one of those that save thy country.

Bucaniers,[8] Chactaw Indians, whose supreme aim in fighting is that they may get the scalps, the money, that they may amass scalps and money; out of such came no Chivalry, and never will! Out of such came only gore and wreck, infernal rage and misery; desperation quenched in annihilation. Behold it, I bid thee, behold there, and consider! What is it that thou have a hundred thousand-pound bills laid up in thy strong-room, a hundred scalps hung up in thy wigwam? I value not them or thee. Thy scalps and thy thousand-pound bills are as yet nothing, if no nobleness from within irradiate

5. Teufelsdröckh, the hero of *Sartor Resartus.*
6. Giants of Scandinavian mythology.
7. A reference to a Muslim story in which a tribe living near the Dead Sea was transformed into apes

because the people had ignored the prophecies of Moses.
8. Buccaneers.

them; if no Chivalry, in action, or in embryo ever struggling towards birth and action, be there.

Love of men cannot be bought by cash-payment; and without love, men cannot endure to be together. You cannot lead a Fighting World without having it regimented, chivalried: the thing, in a day, becomes impossible; all men in it, the highest at first, the very lowest at last, discern consciously, or by a noble instinct, this necessity. And can you any more continue to lead a Working World unregimented, anarchic? I answer, and the Heavens and Earth are now answering, No! The thing becomes not "in a day" impossible; but in some two generations it does. Yes, when fathers and mothers, in Stockport hunger-cellars, begin to eat their children, and Irish widows have to prove their relationship by dying of typhus-fever; and amid Governing "Corporations of the Best and Bravest," busy to preserve their game by "bushing," dark millions of God's human creatures start up in mad Chartisms, impracticable Sacred-Months, and Manchester Insurrections;[9]—and there is a virtual Industrial Aristocracy as yet only half-alive, spell-bound amid money-bags and ledgers; and an actual Idle Aristocracy seemingly near dead in somnolent delusions, in trespasses and double-barrels,[1] "sliding," as on inclined-planes, which every new year they *soap* with new Hansard's-jargon[2] under God's sky, and so are "sliding" ever faster, towards a "scale" and balance-scale whereon is written *Thou art found Wanting;*——in such days, after a generation or two, I say, it does become, even to the low and simple, very palpably impossible! No Working World, any more than a Fighting World, can be led on without a noble Chivalry of Work, and laws and fixed rules which follow out of that,—far nobler than any Chivalry of Fighting was. As an anarchic multitude on mere Supply-and-demand, it is becoming inevitable that we dwindle in horrid suicidal convulsion, and self-abrasion, frightful to the imagination, into *Chactaw* Workers. With wigwams and scalps,—with palaces and thousand-pound bills; with savagery, depopulation, chaotic desolation! Good Heavens, will not one French Revolution and Reign of Terror suffice us, but must there be two? There will be two if needed; there will be twenty if needed; there will be precisely as many as needed. The Laws of Nature will have themselves fulfilled. That is a thing certain to me.

Your gallant battle-hosts and work-hosts, as the others did, will need to be made loyally yours; they must and will be regulated, methodically secured in their just share of conquest under you;—joined with you in veritable brotherhood, sonhood, by quite other and deeper ties than those of temporary day's wages! How would mere redcoated regiments, to say nothing of chivalries, fight for you, if you could discharge them on the evening of the battle, on payment of the stipulated shillings,—and they discharge you on the morning of it! Chelsea Hospitals,[3] pensions, promotions, rigorous lasting covenant on the one side and on the other, are indispensable even for a hired fighter. The Feudal Baron, much more,—how could he subsist with mere temporary mercenaries round him, at sixpence a day; ready to go over to the other side,

9. In 1819 a large open-air labor meeting in Manchester was broken up by charging cavalry. Thirteen men and women were massacred, and many others were wounded.
1. I.e., the only concern of the landed aristocrats is to keep trespassers off their game preserves and reserve shooting rights to themselves.
2. Parliamentary oratory, as in Hansard's printed record of debates in the House of Commons.
3. Home for disabled veterans.

if sevenpence were offered? He could not have subsisted;—and his noble instinct saved him from the necessity of even trying! The Feudal Baron had a Man's Soul in him; to which anarchy, mutiny, and the other fruits of temporary mercenaries, were intolerable: he had never been a Baron otherwise, but had continued a Chactaw and Bucanier. He felt it precious, and at last it became habitual, and his fruitful enlarged existence included it as a necessity, to have men round him who in heart loved him; whose life he watched over with rigour yet with love; who were prepared to give their life for him, if need came. It was beautiful; it was human! Man lives not otherwise, nor can live contented, anywhere or anywhen. Isolation is the sum-total of wretchedness to man. To be cut off, to be left solitary: to have a world alien, not your world; all a hostile camp for you; not a home at all, of hearts and faces who are yours, whose you are! It is the frightfullest enchantment; too truly a work of the Evil One. To have neither superior, nor inferior, nor equal, united manlike to you. Without father, without child, without brother. Man knows no sadder destiny. "How is each of us," exclaims Jean Paul,[4] "so lonely in the wide bosom of the All!" Encased each as in his transparent "ice-palace"; our brother visible in his, making signals and gesticulations to us;—visible, but for ever unattainable: on his bosom we shall never rest, nor he on ours. It was not a God that did this; no!

Awake, ye noble Workers, warriors in the one true war: all this must be remedied. It is you who are already half-alive, whom I will welcome into life; whom I will conjure in God's name to shake off your enchanted sleep, and live wholly! Cease to count scalps, goldpurses; not in these lies your or our salvation. Even these, if you count only these, will not be left. Let bucaniering be put far from you; alter, speedily abrogate all laws of the bucaniers, if you would gain any victory that shall endure. Let God's justice, let pity, nobleness and manly valour, with more gold-purses or with fewer, testify themselves in this your brief Life-transit to all the Eternities, the Gods and Silences. It is to you I call; for ye are not dead, ye are already half-alive: there is in you a sleepless dauntless energy, the prime-matter of all nobleness in man. Honour to you in your kind. It is to you I call: ye know at least this, That the mandate of God to His creature man is: Work! The future Epic of the World rests not with those that are near dead, but with those that are alive, and those that are coming into life.

Look around you. Your world-hosts are all in mutiny, in confusion, destitution; on the eve of fiery wreck and madness! They will not march farther for you, on the sixpence a day and supply-and-demand principle; they will not; nor ought they, nor can they. Ye shall reduce them to order, begin reducing them. To order, to just subordination; noble loyalty in return for noble guidance. Their souls are driven nigh mad; let yours be sane and ever saner. Not as a bewildered bewildering mob; but as a firm regimented mass, with real captains over them, will these men march any more. All human interests, combined human endeavours, and social growths in this world, have, at a certain stage of their development, required organizing: and Work, the grandest of human interests, does now require it.

God knows, the task will be hard: but no noble task was ever easy. This task will wear away your lives, and the lives of your sons and grandsons: but

---

4. Jean Paul Richter (1763–1825), German humorist.

for what purpose, if not for tasks like this, were lives given to men? Ye shall cease to count your thousand-pound scalps, the noble of you shall cease! Nay, the very scalps, as I say, will not long be left if you count on these. Ye shall cease wholly to be barbarous vulturous Chactaws, and become noble European Nineteenth-Century Men. Ye shall know that Mammon, in never such gigs[5] and flunkey "respectabilities," is not the alone God; that of himself he is but a Devil, and even a Brute-god.

Difficult? Yes, it will be difficult. The short-fibre cotton; that too was difficult. The waste cotton-shrub, long useless, disobedient, as the thistle by the wayside,—have ye not conquered it; made it into beautiful bandana webs; white woven shirts for men; bright-tinted air-garments wherein flit goddesses? Ye have shivered mountains asunder, made the hard iron pliant to you as soft putty: the Forest-giants, Marsh-jötuns bear sheaves of golden grain; Aegir the Seademon[6] himself stretches his back for a sleek highway to you, and on Firehorses and Windhorses ye career. Ye are most strong. Thor red-bearded, with his blue sun-eyes, with his cheery heart and strong thunder-hammer, he and you have prevailed. Ye are most strong, ye Sons of the icy North, of the far East,—far marching from your rugged Eastern Wildernesses, hitherward from the grey Dawn of Time! Ye are Sons of the *Jötunland*; the land of Difficulties Conquered. Difficult? You must try this thing. Once try it with the understanding that it will and shall have to be done. Try it as ye try the paltrier thing, making of money! I will bet on you once more, against all Jötuns, Tailor-gods,[7] Double-barrelled Law-wards, and Denizens of Chaos whatsoever.

1843   1843

---

5. Light carriages; to own one was a sign of respectable status comparable with owning certain kinds of automobiles today.

6. From Scandinavian mythology.
7. False gods.

JOHN HENRY CARDINAL NEWMAN
1801–1890

Like Carlyle, John Henry Newman powerfully affected the thinking of his contemporaries, whether they agreed or disagreed with him. Even today, according to Martin Svaglic, Newman attracts both "apotheosizers" and "calumniators" who praise or blame him "as an unusually compelling spokesman for what some consider eternal verities and others regressive myths." During his long lifetime, Newman frequently found himself at the center of some of the most intense disputes that stirred Victorian England, disputes in which he himself emerged as a controversialist of great skill—engagingly persuasive in defense of his position and devastatingly effective in disposing of opponents. Thomas Hardy, whose position was at the opposite extreme from Newman's, paid him a high compliment when he noted in his diary: "Worked at J. H. Newman's *Apologia* which we have all been talking about lately. . . . Style charming and his logic really human, being based not on syllogisms but on converging probabilities. Only—and here comes the fatal catastrophe—there is no first link to his excellent chain of reasoning, and down you come headlong."

Newman was born in London, the son (like Browning) of a banker. In his spiritual autobiography, *Apologia Pro Vita Sua* (in effect, his vindication of his life), he traces the principal stages of his religious development from the strongly Protestant period of his youth to his conversion to Roman Catholicism in 1845. Along the way, after being elected to a fellowship at Oriel College in Oxford and becoming an Anglican clergyman, he was attracted briefly into the orbit of religious liberalism. Gradually coming to realize, however, that liberalism, with its reliance on human reason, would be powerless to defend traditional religion from attack, Newman shifted over into the new High Church wing of the Anglican Church and soon was recognized as the leading figure of what was known as the Oxford movement. During the 1830s he built up a large and influential following by his sermons at Oxford and also by his writing of tracts—that is, appeals, in pamphlet form, on behalf of a cause. In these publications he developed arguments about the powers of church versus state and other issues of deep concern to his High Church colleagues—or Tractarians, as they were also called. Newman's own efforts to demonstrate the true catholicity of the Church of England provoked increasing opposition as his position grew closer to Roman Catholicism. Distressed by constant denunciations, he withdrew into isolation and silence. After much reflection, he took the final step. At the age of forty-four he entered the Roman Catholic priesthood and moved to Birmingham, where he spent the rest of his life. In 1879 he was created cardinal. In 1991, at the instigation of Pope John Paul II, his title became The Venerable John Henry Cardinal Newman, indicating the first of three stages toward sainthood.

In view of this development, Newman's response to a woman who had spoken of him as a saint is touching. In some distress he wrote to her: "Saints are not literary men, they do not love the classics, they do not write Tales."

Although the story of Newman's development seems to emphasize change, certain features remain constant. His sense of God's guidance is especially evident. Characteristic is a poem written in Italy in 1834, following a severe illness, which opens with the line "Lead, kindly light" and concludes with this stanza:

> So long Thy power hath blest me, sure it still
>   Will lead me on,
> O'er moor and fen, o'er crag and torrent, till
>   The night is gone;
> And with the morn those angel faces smile
> Which I have loved long since, and lost awhile.

Set to music, Newman's poem became one of the most popular hymns ever written.

The writing of verse, however, was a subordinate task for Newman; most of his writings are prose, and it is noteworthy that despite his mastery of prose style, Newman found the act of composition to be even more painfully difficult than most of us do. During his years at Birmingham, he was nevertheless prompted to write several books, including works of religious poetry and fiction. Most celebrated is the series of articles, published as his *Apologia* in 1864, in which he replied to an attack on his intellectual honesty made by the Reverend Charles Kingsley (1819–1875), an adherent of the Broad Church and also a popular novelist. Although parts of the *Apologia*, being devoted to fine points of theological doctrine and church history, are difficult for the ordinary reader to follow, the main argument is clearly and persuasively developed. The dignity and candor with which Newman reviewed the stages of his religious development, the repeated appeals to his fellow citizens' sense of honesty and fair play, the unobtrusively beautiful prose style, gained for his masterpiece a sympathetic audience even among those who had been least disposed to listen to his side of the dispute with Kingsley.

Seemingly less controversial than the *Apologia* are Newman's lectures on the aims of education, which were delivered in Dublin at the newly founded Catholic University of Ireland, a university of which he was for a few years the rector. These lectures, published in 1852 and later titled *The Idea of a University,* are a classic statement of the value of "the disciplined intellect" that can be developed by a liberal education rather than by a technical training. Like the later lectures of Matthew Arnold and T. H. Huxley, *The Idea of a University* shows the Victorian engagement with the role of education in society.

It should be noted that Newman's view of a liberal education is largely independent of his religious position. Such an education, he said, could form the minds of profligates and anticlericals as well as of saints and priests of the Church. In considerable measure, his view reflects his admiration for the kind of intellectual enlargement he had himself enjoyed as an undergraduate at Trinity College, Oxford. One of the most moving passages in the *Apologia* is Newman's account of his farewell to an Oxford friend, in February 1846, as he was preparing his final departure from the precincts of the university he loved:

> In him I took leave of my first College, Trinity, which was so dear to me. . . . There used to be much snapdragon growing on the walls opposite my freshman's rooms there, and I had taken it as the emblem of my perpetual residence even unto death in my University.
>
> On the morning of the 23rd I left the Observatory. I have never seen Oxford since, excepting its spires, as they are seen from the railway.

From The Idea of a University

From *Discourse 5. Knowledge Its Own End*

6

Now bear with me, Gentlemen, if what I am about to say has at first sight a fanciful appearance. Philosophy, then, or Science, is related to Knowledge in this way: Knowledge is called by the name of Science or Philosophy, when it is acted upon, informed, or if I may use a strong figure, impregnated by Reason. Reason is the principle of that intrinsic fecundity of Knowledge, which, to those who possess it, is its especial value, and which dispenses with the necessity of their looking abroad for any end to rest upon external to itself. Knowledge, indeed, when thus exalted into a scientific form, is also power; not only is it excellent in itself, but whatever such excellence may be, it is something more, it has a result beyond itself. Doubtless; but that is a further consideration, with which I am not concerned. I only say that, prior to its being a power, it is a good; that it is, not only an instrument, but an end. I know well it may resolve itself into an art, and terminate in a mechanical process, and in tangible fruit; but it also may fall back upon that Reason which informs it, and resolve itself into Philosophy. In one case it is called Useful Knowledge, in the other Liberal. The same person may cultivate it in both ways at once; but this again is a matter foreign to my subject; here I do but say that there are two ways of using Knowledge, and in matter of fact those who use it in one way are not likely to use it in the other, or at least in a very limited measure. You see, then, here are two methods of Education; the end of the one is to be philosophical, of the other to be mechanical; the one rises towards general ideas, the other is exhausted upon what is particular and external. Let me not be thought to deny the necessity, or to decry the benefit, of such attention to what is particular and practical, as belongs to the useful or mechanical arts; life could not go on without them; we owe our daily welfare to them; their exercise is the duty of the many, and we owe to the many a debt of gratitude for fulfilling that duty. I only say that Knowledge, in proportion as it tends more and more to be particular, ceases to be Knowledge. It is a question whether Knowledge can in any proper sense be predicated of the brute creation; without pretending to metaphysical exactness of phraseology, which would be unsuitable to an occasion like this, I say, it seems to me improper to call that passive sensation, or perception of things, which brutes seem to possess, by the name of Knowledge. When I speak of Knowledge, I mean something intellectual, something which grasps what it perceives through the senses; something which takes a view of things; which sees more than the senses convey; which reasons upon what it sees, and while it sees; which invests it with an idea. It expresses itself, not in a mere enunciation, but by an enthymeme:[1] it is of the nature of science from the first, and in this consists its dignity. The principle of real dignity in Knowledge, its worth, its desirableness, considered irrespectively of its results, is this germ within it of a scientific or a philosophical process. This is how it comes to be an end in itself; this is why it admits of being called Liberal. Not to know the relative disposition of things is the state of slaves or children; to have mapped out the Universe is the boast, or at least the ambition, of Philosophy.

Moreover, such knowledge is not a mere extrinsic or accidental advantage, which is ours today and another's tomorrow, which may be got up from a book, and easily forgotten again, which we can command or communicate at our pleasure, which we can borrow for the occasion, carry about in our hand, and take into the market; it is an acquired illumination, it is a habit, a personal possession, and an inward endowment. And this is the reason why it is more correct, as well as more usual, to speak of a University as a place of education than of instruction, though, when knowledge is concerned, instruction would at first sight have seemed the more appropriate work. We are instructed, for instance, in manual exercises, in the fine and useful arts, in trades, and in ways of business; for these are methods, which have little or no effect upon the mind itself, are contained in rules committed to memory, to tradition, or to use, and bear upon an end external to themselves. But education is a higher word; it implies an action upon our mental nature, and the formation of a character; it is something individual and permanent, and is commonly spoken of in connection with religion and virtue. When, then, we speak of the communication of Knowledge as being Education, we thereby really imply that that Knowledge is a state or condition of mind; and since cultivation of mind is surely worth seeking for its own sake, we are thus brought once more to the conclusion, which the word "Liberal" and the word "Philosophy" have already suggested, that there is a Knowledge, which is desirable, though nothing come of it, as being of itself a treasure, and a sufficient remuneration of years of labor.

---

1. A syllogism in which one of the premises is understood but not stated.

From *Discourse 7. Knowledge Viewed in Relation
to Professional Skill*

1

I have been insisting, in my two preceding Discourses, first, on the cultivation of the intellect, as an end which may reasonably be pursued for its own sake; and next, on the nature of that cultivation, or what that cultivation consists in. Truth of whatever kind is the proper object of the intellect; its cultivation then lies in fitting it to apprehend and contemplate truth. Now the intellect in its present state, with exceptions which need not here be specified, does not discern truth intuitively, or as a whole. We know, not by a direct and simple vision, not at a glance, but, as it were, by piecemeal and accumulation, by a mental process, by going round an object, by the comparison, the combination, the mutual correction, the continual adaptation, of many partial notions, by the employment, concentration, and joint action of many faculties and exercises of mind. Such a union and concert of the intellectual powers, such an enlargement and development, such a comprehensiveness, is necessarily a matter of training. And again, such a training is a matter of rule; it is not mere application, however exemplary, which introduces the mind to truth, nor the reading many books, nor the getting up many subjects, nor the witnessing many experiments, nor the attending many lectures. All this is short of enough; a man may have done it all, yet be lingering in the vestibule of knowledge: he may not realize what his mouth utters; he may not see with his mental eye what confronts him; he may have no grasp of things as they are; or at least he may have no power at all of advancing one step forward of himself, in consequence of what he has already acquired, no power of discriminating between truth and falsehood, of sifting out the grains of truth from the mass, of arranging things according to their real value, and, if I may use the phrase, of building up ideas. Such a power is the result of a scientific formation of mind; it is an acquired faculty of judgment, of clearsightedness, of sagacity, of wisdom, of philosophical reach of mind, and of intellectual self-possession and repose—qualities which do not come of mere acquirement. The bodily eye, the organ for apprehending material objects, is provided by nature; the eye of the mind, of which the object is truth, is the work of discipline and habit.

This process of training, by which the intellect, instead of being formed or sacrificed to some particular or accidental purpose, some specific trade or profession, or study or science, is disciplined for its own sake, for the perception of its own proper object, and for its own highest culture, is called Liberal Education; and though there is no one in whom it is carried as far as is conceivable, or whose intellect would be a pattern of what intellects should be made, yet there is scarcely anyone but may gain an idea of what real training is, and at least look towards it, and make its true scope and result, not something else, his standard of excellence; and numbers there are who may submit themselves to it, and secure it to themselves in good measure. And to set forth the right standard, and to train according to it, and to help forward all students toward it according to their various capacities, this I conceive to be the business of a University.

2

Now this is what some great men are very slow to allow; they insist that Education should be confined to some particular and narrow end, and should issue in some definite work, which can be weighed and measured. They argue as if every thing, as well as every person, had its price; and that where there has been a great outlay, they have a right to expect a return in kind. This they call making Education and Instruction "useful," and "Utility" becomes their watchword. With a fundamental principle of this nature, they very naturally go on to ask what there is to show for the expense of a University; what is the real worth in the market of the article called "a Liberal Education," on the supposition that it does not teach us definitely how to advance our manufactures, or to improve our lands, or to better our civil economy; or again, if it does not at once make this man a lawyer, that an engineer, and that a surgeon; or at least if it does not lead to discoveries in chemistry, astronomy, geology, magnetism, and science of every kind.

* * *

5

* * *

This is the obvious answer which may be made to those who urge upon us the claims of Utility in our plans of Education;[2] but I am not going to leave the subject here: I mean to take a wider view of it. Let us take "useful," as Locke[3] takes it, in its proper and popular sense, and then we enter upon a large field of thought, to which I cannot do justice in one Discourse, though today's is all the space that I can give to it. I say, let us take "useful" to mean, not what is simply good, but what *tends* to good, or is the *instrument* of good; and in this sense also, Gentlemen, I will show you how a liberal education is truly and fully a useful, though it be not a professional, education. "Good" indeed means one thing, and "useful" means another; but I lay it down as a principle, which will save us a great deal of anxiety, that, though the useful is not always good, the good is always useful. Good is not only good, but reproductive of good; this is one of its attributes; nothing is excellent, beautiful, perfect, desirable for its own sake, but it overflows, and spreads the likeness of itself all around it. Good is prolific; it is not only good to the eye, but to the taste; it not only attracts us, but it communicates itself; it excites first our admiration and love, then our desire and our gratitude, and that, in proportion to its intenseness and fullness in particular instances. A great good will impart great good. If then the intellect is so excellent a portion of us, and its cultivation so excellent, it is not only beautiful, perfect, admirable, and noble in itself, but in a true and high sense it must be useful to the possessor and to all around him; not useful in any low, mechanical, mercantile sense, but as diffusing good, or as a blessing, or a gift, or power, or a

<hr>

2. The Utilitarians argued that a useful education would be one that trained the mind in the "habit of pushing things up to their first principles." Newman had earlier pointed out that a liberal educa-

tion does exactly that and is hence useful.
3. John Locke (1632–1704), whose treatise *Of Education* advocated a utilitarian concept of education.

treasure, first to the owner, then through him to the world. I say then, if a liberal education be good, it must necessarily be useful too.

6

You will see what I mean by the parallel of bodily health. Health is a good in itself, though nothing came of it, and is especially worth seeking and cherishing; yet, after all, the blessings which attend its presence are so great, while they are so close to it and so redound back upon it and encircle it, that we never think of it except as useful as well as good, and praise and prize it for what it does, as well as for what it is, though at the same time we cannot point out any definite and distinct work or production which it can be said to effect. And so as regards intellectual culture, I am far from denying utility in this large sense as the end of Education, when I lay it down that the culture of the intellect is a good in itself and its own end; I do not exclude from the idea of intellectual culture what it cannot but be, from the very nature of things; I only deny that we must be able to point out, before we have any right to call it useful, some art, or business, or profession, or trade, or work, as resulting from it, and as its real and complete end. The parallel is exact: As the body may be sacrificed to some manual or other toil, whether moderate or oppressive, so may the intellect be devoted to some specific profession; and I do not call *this* the culture of the intellect. Again, as some member or organ of the body may be inordinately used and developed, so may memory, or imagination, or the reasoning faculty; and *this* again is not intellectual culture. On the other hand, as the body may be tended, cherished, and exercised with a simple view to its general health, so may the intellect also be generally exercised in order to its perfect state; and this *is* its cultivation.

Again, as health ought to precede labor of the body, and as a man in health can do what an unhealthy man cannot do, and as of this health the properties are strength, energy, agility, graceful carriage and action, manual dexterity, and endurance of fatigue, so in like manner general culture of mind is the best aid to professional and scientific study, and educated men can do what illiterate cannot; and the man who has learned to think and to reason and to compare and to discriminate and to analyze, who has refined his taste, and formed his judgment, and sharpened his mental vision, will not indeed at once be a lawyer, or a pleader, or an orator, or a statesman, or a physician, or a good landlord, or a man of business, or a soldier, or an engineer, or a chemist, or a geologist, or an antiquarian, but he will be placed in that state of intellect in which he can take up any one of the sciences or callings I have referred to, or any other for which he has a taste or special talent, with an ease, a grace, a versatility, and a success, to which another is a stranger. In this sense then, and as yet I have said but a very few words on a large subject, mental culture is emphatically *useful*.

If then I am arguing, and shall argue, against Professional or Scientific knowledge as the sufficient end of a University Education, let me not be supposed, Gentlemen, to be disrespectful towards particular studies, or arts, or vocations, and those who are engaged in them. In saying that Law or Medicine is not the end of a University course, I do not mean to imply that the University does not teach Law or Medicine. What indeed can it teach at all, if it does not teach something particular? It teaches *all* knowledge by teaching all *branches* of knowledge, and in no other way. I do but say that there will be this distinction as regards a Professor of Law, or of Medicine, or of Geology, or of Political Economy, in a University and out of it, that out of a University he is in danger of being absorbed and narrowed by his pursuit, and of giving Lectures which are the Lectures of nothing more than a lawyer, physician, geologist, or political economist; whereas in a University he will just know where he and his science stand, he has come to it, as it were, from a height, he has taken a survey of all knowledge, he is kept from extravagance by the very rivalry of other studies, he has gained from them a special illumination and largeness of mind and freedom and self-possession, and he treats his own in consequence with a philosophy and a resource, which belongs not to the study itself, but to his liberal education.

This then is how I should solve the fallacy, for so I must call it, by which Locke and his disciples would frighten us from cultivating the intellect, under the notion that no education is useful which does not teach us some temporal calling, or some mechanical art, or some physical secret. I say that a cultivated intellect, because it is a good in itself, brings with it a power and a grace to every work and occupation which it undertakes, and enables us to be more useful, and to a greater number. There is a duty we owe to human society as such, to the state to which we belong, to the sphere in which we move, to the individuals towards whom we are variously related, and whom we successively encounter in life; and that philosophical or liberal education, as I have called it, which is the proper function of a University, if it refuses the foremost place to professional interest, does but postpone them to the formation of the citizen, and, while it subserves the larger interests of philanthropy, prepares also for the successful prosecution of those merely personal objects which at first sight it seems to disparage.

* * *

10

But I must bring these extracts[4] to an end. Today I have confined myself to saying that that training of the intellect, which is best for the individual himself, best enables him to discharge his duties to society. The Philosopher, indeed, and the man of the world differ in their very notion, but the methods, by which they are respectively formed, are pretty much the same. The Philosopher has the same command of matters of thought, which the true citizen and gentleman has of matters of business and conduct. If then a practical end must be assigned to a University course, I say it is that of training good members of society. Its art is the art of social life, and its end is fitness for the world. It neither confines its views to particular professions on the one hand, nor creates heroes or inspires genius on the other. Works indeed of genius fall under no art; heroic minds come under no rule; a University is not a birthplace of poets or of immortal authors, of founders of schools, leaders of colonies, or conquerors of nations. It does not promise a generation of Aristotles or Newtons, of Napoleons or Washingtons, or Raphaels or Shakespeares, though such miracles of nature it has before now contained

4. Quotations cited from other authorities on education.

within its precincts. Nor is it content on the other hand with forming the critic or the experimentalist, the economist or the engineer, though such too it includes within its scope. But a University training is the great ordinary means to a great but ordinary end; it aims at raising the intellectual tone of society, at cultivating the public mind, at purifying the national taste, at supplying true principles to popular enthusiasm and fixed aims to popular aspiration, at giving enlargement and sobriety to the ideas of the age, at facilitating the exercise of political power, and refining the intercourse of private life. It is the education which gives a man a clear conscious view of his own opinions and judgments, a truth in developing them, an eloquence in expressing them, and a force in urging them. It teaches him to see things as they are, to go right to the point, to disentangle a skein of thought, to detect what is sophistical, and to discard what is irrelevant. It prepares him to fill any post with credit, and to master any subject with facility. It shows him how to accommodate himself to others, how to throw himself into their state of mind, how to bring before them his own, how to influence them, how to come to an understanding with them, how to bear with them. He is at home in any society, he has common ground with every class; he knows when to speak and when to be silent; he is able to converse, he is able to listen; he can ask a question pertinently, and gain a lesson seasonably, when he has nothing to impart himself; he is ever ready, yet never in the way; he is a pleasant companion, and a comrade you can depend upon; he knows when to be serious and when to trifle, and he has a sure tact which enables him to trifle with gracefulness and to be serious with effect. He has the repose of a mind which lives in itself, while it lives in the world, and which has resources for its happiness at home when it cannot go abroad. He has a gift which serves him in public, and supports him in retirement,[5] without which good fortune is but vulgar, and with which failure and disappointment have a charm. The art which tends to make a man all this is in the object which it pursues as useful as the art of wealth or the art of health, though it is less susceptible of method, and less tangible, less certain, less complete in its result.

1852, 1873

---

5. In a later work, *The Grammar of Assent* (1870), Newman enlarges on this aspect of his subject in a passage describing the impact that classical literature may have on us at different ages of our lives, a passage admired by James Joyce. "Let us consider, too, how differently young and old are affected by the words of some classic author, such as Homer or Horace. Passages, which to a boy are but rhetorical commonplaces, neither better nor worse than a hundred others which any clever writer might supply, which he gets by heart and thinks very fine, and imitates, as he thinks, successfully, in his own flowing versification, at length come home to him, when long years have passed, and he has had experience of life, and pierce him, as if he had never before known them, with their sad earnestness and vivid exactness. Then he comes to understand how it is that lines, the birth of some chance morning or evening at an Ionian festival, or among the Sabine hills, have lasted generation after generation, for thousands of years, with a power over the mind, and a charm, which the current literature of his own day, with all its obvious advantages, is utterly unable to rival. Perhaps this is the reason of the medieval opinion about Virgil, as if a prophet or magician; his single words and phrases, his pathetic half lines, giving utterance, as the voice of Nature herself, to that pain and weariness, yet hope of better things, which is the experience of her children in every time."

From Apologia Pro Vita Sua

From *Chapter 1. History of My Religious Opinions to the Year 1833*

It may easily be conceived how great a trial it is to me to write the following history of myself; but I must not shrink from the task. The words, "Secretum meum mihi,"[1] keep ringing in my ears; but as men draw towards their end, they care less for disclosures. Nor is it the least part of my trial, to anticipate that, upon first reading what I have written, my friends may consider much in it irrelevant to my purpose; yet I cannot help thinking that, viewed as a whole, it will effect what I propose to myself in giving it to the public.

I was brought up from a child to take great delight in reading the Bible; but I had no formed religious convictions till I was fifteen. Of course I had a perfect knowledge of my Catechism.

After I was grown up, I put on paper my recollections of the thoughts and feelings on religious subjects, which I had at the time that I was a child and a boy,—such as had remained on my mind with sufficient prominence to make me then consider them worth recording. Out of these, written in the Long Vacation of 1820, and transcribed with additions in 1823, I select two, which are at once the most definite among them, and also have a bearing on my later convictions.

1. "I used to wish the Arabian Tales were true: my imagination ran on unknown influences, on magical powers, and talismans. . . . .I thought life might be a dream, or I an Angel, and all this world a deception, my fellow-angels by a playful device concealing themselves from me, and deceiving me with the semblance of a material world."

Again: "Reading in the Spring of 1816 a sentence from [Dr. Watt's] 'Remnants of Time,'[2] entitled 'the Saints unknown to the world,' to the effect, that 'there is nothing in their figure or countenance to distinguish them,' &c., &c., I supposed he spoke of Angels who lived in the world, as it were disguised."

2. The other remark is this: "I was very superstitious, and for some time previous to my conversion" [when I was fifteen] "used constantly to cross myself on going into the dark."

Of course I must have got this practice from some external source or other; but I can make no sort of conjecture whence; and certainly no one had ever spoken to me on the subject of the Catholic religion, which I only knew by name. The French master was an *émigré* Priest, but he was simply made a butt, as French masters too commonly were in that day, and spoke English very imperfectly. There was a Catholic family in the village, old maiden ladies we used to think; but I knew nothing about them. I have of late years heard that there were one or two Catholic boys in the school; but either we were carefully kept from knowing this, or the knowledge of it made simply no impression on our minds. My brother will bear witness how free the school was from Catholic ideas.

---

1. My secret is my own (Latin).
2. *The Improvement of the Mind, with a discourse on Education, and the Remnants of Time, employed*

in prose and verse, by Isaac Watts (1674–1748), a Nonconformist clergyman. All text in brackets was added by Newman.

I had once been into Warwick Street Chapel, with my father, who, I believe, wanted to hear some piece of music; all that I bore away from it was the recollection of a pulpit and a preacher, and a boy swinging a censer.

When I was at Littlemore,[3] I was looking over old copybooks of my school days, and I found among them my first Latin verse-book; and in the first page of it there was a device which almost took my breath away with surprise. I have the book before me now, and have just been showing it to others. I have written in the first page, in my school-boy hand, "John H. Newman, February 11th, 1811, Verse Book;" then follow my first Verses. Between "Verse" and "Book" I have drawn the figure of a solid cross upright, and next to it is, what may indeed be meant for a necklace, but what I cannot make out to be any thing else than a set of beads suspended, with a little cross attached. At this time I was not quite ten years old. I suppose I got these ideas from some romance, Mrs. Radcliffe's or Miss Porter's;[4] or from some religious picture; but the strange thing is, how, among the thousand objects which meet a boy's eyes, these in particular should so have fixed themselves in my mind, that I made them thus practically my own. I am certain there was nothing in the churches I attended, or the prayer books I read, to suggest them. It must be recollected that Anglican churches and prayer books were not decorated in those days as I believe they are now.

When I was fourteen, I read Paine's Tracts against the Old Testament,[5] and found pleasure in thinking of the objections which were contained in them. Also, I read some of Hume's[6] Essays; and perhaps that on Miracles. So at least I gave my Father to understand; but perhaps it was a brag. Also, I recollect copying out some French verses, perhaps Voltaire's,[7] in denial of the immortality of the soul, and saying to myself something like "How dreadful, but how plausible!"

When I was fifteen, (in the autumn of 1816,) a great change of thought took place in me. I fell under the influences of a definite Creed, and received into my intellect impressions of dogma, which, through God's mercy, have never been effaced or obscured. Above and beyond the conversations and sermons of the excellent man, long dead, the Rev. Walter Mayers, of Pembroke College, Oxford, who was the human means of this beginning of divine faith in me, was the effect of the books which he put into my hands, all of the school of Calvin.[8] One of the first books I read was a work of Romaine's;[9] I neither recollect the title nor the contents, except one doctrine, which of course I do not include among those which I believe to have come from a divine source, viz. the doctrine of final perseverance.[1] I received it at once, and believed that the inward conversion of which I was conscious, (and of which I still am more certain than that I have hands and feet,) would last into the next life, and that I was elected to eternal glory. I have no consciousness that this belief had any tendency whatever to lead me to be careless about pleasing God. I retained it till the age of twenty-one, when it

3. A village near Oxford, whose parish was under Newman's care.
4. Ann Radcliffe (1764–1823) and Jane Porter (1776–1850), writers of romances.
5. Probably *The Age of Reason* by Thomas Paine (1737–1809), an attack on Christianity and the Bible from a Deist point of view.
6. David Hume (1711–1776), Scottish philosopher.

7. French satirist and philosopher (1694–1778).
8. John Calvin (1509–1564), Protestant reformer who stressed predestination, the sinfulness of humankind, and the power of grace. Mayers was one of Newman's schoolmasters.
9. William Romaine (1714–1795), Anglican clergyman and writer, of the Calvinist school.
1. The Calvinist view that God will not let His chosen fall away from Him.

gradually faded away; but I believe that it had some influence on my opinions, in the direction of those childish imaginations which I have already mentioned, viz. in isolating me from the objects which surrounded me, in confirming me in my mistrust of the reality of material phenomena, and making me rest in the thought of two and two only absolute and luminously self-evident beings, myself and my Creator;—for while I considered myself predestined to salvation, my mind did not dwell upon others, as fancying them simply passed over, not predestined to eternal death. I only thought of the mercy to myself.

*   *   *

There is one remaining source of my opinions to be mentioned, and that far from the least important. In proportion as I moved out of the shadow of that liberalism which had hung over my course, my early devotion towards the Fathers returned; and in the Long Vacation of 1828 I set about to read them chronologically, beginning with St. Ignatius and St. Justin.[2] About 1830 a proposal was made to me by Mr. Hugh Rose, who with Mr. Lyall[3] (afterwards Dean of Canterbury) was providing writers for a Theological Library, to furnish them with a History of the Principal Councils. I accepted it, and at once set to work on the Council of Nicæa.[4] It was to launch myself on an ocean with currents innumerable; and I was drifted back first to the ante-Nicene history, and then to the Church of Alexandria. The work at last appeared under the title of "The Arians of the Fourth Century;" and of its 422 pages, the first 117 consisted of introductory matter, and the Council of Nicæa did not appear till the 254th, and then occupied at most twenty pages.

I do not know when I first learnt to consider that Antiquity was the true exponent of the doctrines of Christianity and the basis of the Church of England; but I take it for granted that the works of Bishop Bull,[5] which at this time I read, were my chief introduction to this principle. The course of reading, which I pursued in the composition of my volume, was directly adapted to develop it in my mind. What principally attracted me in the ante-Nicene period was the great Church of Alexandria, the historical center of teaching in those times. Of Rome for some centuries comparatively little is known. The battle of Arianism was first fought in Alexandria; Athanasius, the champion of the truth, was Bishop of Alexandria; and in his writings he refers to the great religious names of an earlier date, to Origen, Dionysius,[6] and others, who were the glory of its see, or of its school. The broad philosophy of Clement[7] and Origen carried me away; the philosophy, not the theological doctrine; and I have drawn out some features of it in my volume, with the zeal and freshness, but with the partiality, of a neophyte. Some portions of their teaching, magnificent in themselves, came like music to my inward ear, as if the response to ideas, which, with little external to encourage

2. St. Ignatius of Antioch (ca. 35–ca. 107) and St. Justin Martyr (ca. 100–ca. 165), fathers of the church and early theological writers whose authority on doctrinal matters carried special weight.
3. Hugh James Rose (1795–1838) and William Rowe Lyall (1788–1857), contemporary theologians.
4. Convened by the emperor Constantine in 325 to deal with Arianism, a heresy that denied the full divinity of Christ. The Church of Alexandria was a center of Christian thought in the 3rd–5th centuries.
5. George Bull (1634–1710), Anglican theologian.
6. Alexandrian theologians of the 1st and 2nd centuries. St. Athanasius (ca. 296–373), an anti-Arian leader at the Council of Nicaea.
7. Another early Alexandrian theologian.

them, I had cherished so long. These were based on the mystical or sacramental principle, and spoke of the various Economies or Dispensations of the Eternal. I understood these passages to mean that the exterior world, physical and historical, was but the manifestation to our senses of realities greater than itself.[8] Nature was a parable: Scripture was an allegory: pagan literature, philosophy, and mythology, properly understood, were but a preparation for the Gospel. The Greek poets and sages were in a certain sense prophets; for "thoughts beyond their thought to those high bards were given."[9] There had been a directly divine dispensation granted to the Jews; but there had been in some sense a dispensation carried on in favour of the Gentiles. He who had taken the seed of Jacob for His elect people had not therefore cast the rest of mankind out of His sight. In the fulness of time both Judaism and Paganism had come to nought; the outward framework, which concealed yet suggested the Living Truth, had never been intended to last, and it was dissolving under the beams of the Sun of Justice which shone behind it and through it. The process of change had been slow; it had been done not rashly, but by rule and measure, "at sundry times and in divers manners,"[1] first one disclosure and then another, till the whole evangelical doctrine was brought into full manifestation. And thus room was made for the anticipation of further and deeper disclosures, of truths still under the veil of the letter, and in their season to be revealed. The visible world still remains without its divine interpretation; Holy Church in her sacraments and her hierarchical appointments, will remain, even to the end of the world, after all but a symbol of those heavenly facts which fill eternity. Her mysteries are but the expressions in human language of truths to which the human mind is unequal. It is evident how much there was in all this in correspondence with the thoughts which had attracted me when I was young, and with the doctrine which I have already associated with the Analogy and the Christian Year.[2]

It was, I suppose, to the Alexandrian school and to the early Church, that I owe in particular what I definitely held about the Angels. I viewed them, not only as the ministers employed by the Creator in the Jewish and Christian dispensations, as we find on the face of Scripture, but as carrying on, as Scripture also implies, the Economy of the Visible World. I considered them as the real causes of motion, light, and life, and of those elementary principles of the physical universe, which, when offered in their developments to our senses, suggest to us the notion of cause and effect, and of what are called the laws of nature. This doctrine I have drawn out in my Sermon for Michaelmas day, written in 1831. I say of the Angels, "Every breath of air and ray of light and heat, every beautiful prospect, is, as it were, the skirts of their garments, the waving of the robes of those whose faces see God." Again, I ask what would be the thoughts of a man who, "when examining a flower, or a herb, or a pebble, or a ray of light, which he treats as something so beneath him in the scale of existence, suddenly discovered that he was in the presence of some powerful being who was hidden behind the visible

8. Cf. Carlyle's Clothes Philosophy in *Sartor Resartus* (p. 1077).
9. John Keble's *The Christian Year* (1827), a collection of poems for the Christian calendar.
1. Hebrews 1.1.

2. Joseph Butler's *The Analogy of Religion* (1736), a theological work, and Keble's *The Christian Year*. Newman had previously discussed the influence both works had on him.

things he was inspecting,—who, though concealing his wise hand, was giving them their beauty, grace, and perfection, as being God's instrument for the purpose,—nay, whose robe and ornaments those objects were, which he was so eager to analyze?" and I therefore remark that "we may say with grateful and simple hearts with the Three Holy Children, 'O all ye works of the Lord, &c., &c., bless ye the Lord, praise Him, and magnify Him for ever.' "

* * *

While I was engaged in writing my work upon the Arians, great events were happening at home and abroad, which brought out into form and passionate expression the various beliefs which had so gradually been winning their way into my mind. Shortly before, there had been a Revolution in France;[3] the Bourbons had been dismissed: and I held that it was unchristian for nations to cast off their governors, and, much more, sovereigns who had the divine right of inheritance. Again, the great Reform Agitation was going on around me as I wrote. The Whigs had come into power; Lord Grey[4] had told the Bishops to set their house in order, and some of the Prelates had been insulted and threatened in the streets of London. The vital question was, how were we to keep the Church from being liberalized? there was such apathy on the subject in some quarters, such imbecile alarm in others; the true principles of Churchmanship seemed so radically decayed, and there was such distraction in the councils of the Clergy. Blomfield,[5] the Bishop of London of the day, an active and open-hearted man, had been for years engaged in diluting the high orthodoxy of the Church by the introduction of members of the Evangelical body into places of influence and trust. He had deeply offended men who agreed in opinion with myself, by an off-hand saying (as it was reported) to the effect that belief in the Apostolical succession had gone out with the Non-jurors.[6] "We can count you," he said to some of the gravest and most venerated persons of the old school. And the Evangelical party itself, with their late successes, seemed to have lost that simplicity and unworldliness which I admired so much in Milner and Scott.[7] It was not that I did not venerate such men as Ryder,[8] the then Bishop of Lichfield, and others of similar sentiments, who were not yet promoted out of the ranks of the Clergy, but I thought little of the Evangelicals as a class. I thought they played into the hands of the Liberals. With the Establishment thus divided and threatened, thus ignorant of its true strength, I compared that fresh vigorous Power of which I was reading in the first centuries. In her triumphant zeal on behalf of that Primeval Mystery, to which I had had so great a devotion from my youth, I recognized the movement of my Spiritual Mother. "Incessu patuit Dea."[9] The self-conquest of her Ascetics, the patience of her Martyrs, the irresistible determination of her Bishops, the joyous swing of her advance, both exalted and abashed me. I said to myself,

3. The July Revolution of 1830.
4. Earl Grey (1764–1845), prime minister (1830–34) during the "Agitation" leading to the passage of the Reform Bill of 1832. There were also growing demands for reform of ecclesiastical abuses.
5. Charles James Blomfield (1786–1857).
6. English and Scottish clergymen who refused to take the oath of allegiance to William and Mary when they succeeded James II. "Apostolical suc-

cession": the doctrine whereby the ministry of the Church is understood to be derived from the apostles by continuous succession.
7. Joseph Milner (1744–1797) and Thomas Scott (1747–1821), Evangelical theologians.
8. Henry Ryder (1777–1836), a prominent Evangelical.
9. The goddess stood revealed by her walk (Latin; *Aeneid* 1.405).

"Look on this picture and on that;"[1] I felt affection for my own Church, but not tenderness; I felt dismay at her prospects, anger and scorn at her do-nothing perplexity. I thought that if Liberalism once got a footing within her, it was sure of the victory in the event. I saw that Reformation principles were powerless to rescue her. As to leaving her, the thought never crossed my imagination; still I ever kept before me that there was something greater than the Established Church, and that that was the Church Catholic and Apostolic, set up from the beginning, of which she was but the local presence and the organ. She was nothing, unless she was this. She must be dealt with strongly, or she would be lost. There was need of a second reformation.

At this time I was disengaged from College duties, and my health had suffered from the labour involved in the composition of my Volume. It was ready for the Press in July, 1832, though not published till the end of 1833. I was easily persuaded to join Hurrell Froude[2] and his Father, who were going to the south of Europe for the health of the former.

We set out in December, 1832. It was during this expedition that my Verses which are in the Lyra Apostolica were written;—a few indeed before it, but not more than one or two of them after it. Exchanging, as I was, definite Tutorial work, and the literary quiet and pleasant friendships of the last six years, for foreign countries and an unknown future, I naturally was led to think that some inward changes, as well as some larger course of action, were coming upon me. At Whitchurch, while waiting for the down mail to Falmouth, I wrote the verses about my Guardian Angel, which begin with these words: "Are these the tracks of some unearthly Friend?" and which go on to speak of "the vision" which haunted me:—that vision is more or less brought out in the whole series of these compositions.

I went to various coasts of the Mediterranean; parted with my friends at Rome; went down for the second time to Sicily without companion, at the end of April; and got back to England by Palermo in the early part of July. The strangeness of foreign life threw me back into myself; I found pleasure in historical sites and beautiful scenes, not in men and manners. We kept clear of Catholics throughout our tour. I had a conversation with the Dean of Malta, a most pleasant man, lately dead; but it was about the Fathers, and the Library of the great church. I knew the Abbate Santini, at Rome, who did no more than copy for me the Gregorian tones. Froude and I made two calls upon Monsignore (now Cardinal) Wiseman[3] at the Collegio Inglese, shortly before we left Rome. Once we heard him preach at a church in the Corso. I do not recollect being in a room with any other ecclesiastics, except a Priest at Castro-Giovanni in Sicily, who called on me when I was ill, and with whom I wished to hold a controversy. As to Church Services, we attended the Tenebræ, at the Sestine, for the sake of the Miserere;[4] and that was all. My general feeling was, "All, save the spirit of man, is divine." I saw nothing but what was external; of the hidden life of Catholics I knew nothing. I was still more driven back into myself, and felt my isolation. England was in my thoughts solely, and the news from England came rarely and imper-

---

1. Hamlet's words, when he compares the picture of his father to that of his uncle (Shakespeare's *Hamlet* 3.4.53).
2. Richard Hurrell Froude (1803–1836), close friend of Newman's and fellow Tractarian.

3. Nicholas Patrick Stephen Wiseman (1802–1865), who did much to advance Roman Catholicism in England.
4. Psalm 51, part of the "Tenebrae" service, which is for the last three days of Holy Week.

fectly. The Bill for the Suppression of the Irish Sees[5] was in progress, and filled my mind. I had fierce thoughts against the Liberals.

It was the success of the Liberal cause which fretted me inwardly. I became fierce against its instruments and its manifestations. A French vessel was at Algiers; I would not even look at the tricolour.[6] On my return, though forced to stop twenty-four hours at Paris, I kept indoors the whole time, and all that I saw of that beautiful city was what I saw from the Diligence.[7] The Bishop of London had already sounded me as to my filling one of the White-hall preacherships, which he had just then put on a new footing; but I was indignant at the line which he was taking, and from my Steamer I had sent home a letter declining the appointment by anticipation, should it be offered to me. At this time I was specially annoyed with Dr. Arnold,[8] though it did not last into later years. Some one, I think, asked, in conversation at Rome, whether a certain interpretation of Scripture was Christian? it was answered that Dr. Arnold took it; I interposed, "But is *he* a Christian?" The subject went out of my head at once; when afterwards I was taxed with it, I could say no more in explanation, than (what I believe was the fact) that I must have had in mind some free views of Dr. Arnold about the Old Testament:—I thought I must have meant, "Arnold answers for the interpretation, but who is to answer for Arnold?" It was at Rome, too, that we began the Lyra Apostolica which appeared monthly in the British Magazine. The motto shows the feeling of both Froude and myself at the time: we borrowed from M. Bunsen a Homer, and Froude chose the words in which Achilles, on returning to the battle, says, "You shall know the difference, now that I am back again."[9]

Especially when I was left by myself, the thought came upon me that deliverance is wrought, not by the many but by the few, not by bodies but by persons. Now it was, I think, that I repeated to myself the words, which had ever been dear to me from my school days, "Exoriare aliquis!"[1]—now too, that Southey's beautiful poem of Thalaba,[2] for which I had an immense liking, came forcibly to my mind. I began to think that I had a mission. There are sentences of my letters to my friends to this effect, if they are not destroyed. When we took leave of Monsignore Wiseman, he had courteously expressed a wish that we might make a second visit to Rome; I said with great gravity, "We have a work to do in England." I went down at once to Sicily, and the presentiment grew stronger. I struck into the middle of the island, and fell ill of a fever at Leonforte. My servant thought that I was dying, and begged for my last directions. I gave them, as he wished; but I said, "I shall not die." I repeated, "I shall not die, for I have not sinned against light, I have not sinned against light." I never have been able quite to make out what I meant.

I got to Castro-Giovanni, and was laid up there for nearly three weeks. Towards the end of May I left for Palermo, taking three days for the journey. Before starting from my inn in the morning of May 26th or 27th, I sat down

5. For suppressing ten of the twenty-two bishoprics of the Church of Ireland, introduced in 1833.
6. The French flag.
7. The stagecoach.
8. Thomas Arnold (1795–1842), an educational and religious reformer of liberal views; father of Matthew Arnold.

9. *Iliad* 18.125. C. J. K. Bunsen (1791–1860), Prussian minister to the Vatican.
1. May someone arise! (Latin; *Aeneid* 4.265).
2. Robert Southey's 1801 poem tells the story of a young Arab, appointed to destroy a race of sorcerers.

on my bed, and began to sob violently. My servant, who had acted as my nurse, asked what ailed me. I could only answer him, "I have a work to do in England."

I was aching to get home; yet for want of a vessel I was kept at Palermo for three weeks. I began to visit the Churches, and they calmed my impatience, though I did not attend any services. I knew nothing of the Presence of the Blessed Sacrament there. At last I got off in an orange boat, bound for Marseilles. Then it was that I wrote the lines, "Lead, kindly light," which have since become well known. We were becalmed a whole week in the Straits of Bonifacio. I was writing verses the whole time of my passage. At length I got to Marseilles, and set off for England. The fatigue of travelling was too much for me, and I was laid up for several days at Lyons. At last I got off again, and did not stop night or day, (except a compulsory delay at Paris,) till I reached England, and my mother's house. My brother had arrived from Persia only a few hours before. This was on the Tuesday. The following Sunday, July 14th, Mr. Keble preached the Assize Sermon[3] in the University Pulpit. It was published under the title of "National Apostasy." I have ever considered and kept the day, as the start of the religious movement of 1833.

*   *   *

From *Liberalism*

I have been asked to explain more fully what it is I mean by "Liberalism," because merely to call it the Antidogmatic Principle is to tell very little about it.

*   *   *

Now by Liberalism I mean false liberty of thought, or the exercise of thought upon matters, in which, from the constitution of the human mind, thought cannot be brought to any successful issue, and therefore is out of place. Among such matters are first principles of whatever kind; and of these the most sacred and momentous are especially to be reckoned the truths of Revelation. Liberalism then is the mistake of subjecting to human judgment those revealed doctrines which are in their nature beyond and independent of it, and of claiming to determine on intrinsic grounds the truth and value of propositions which rest for their reception simply on the external authority of the Divine Word.

*   *   *

I conclude this notice of Liberalism in Oxford, and the party which was antagonistic to it,[4] with some propositions in detail, which, as a member of the latter, and together with the High Church, I earnestly denounced and abjured.

1. No religious tenet is important, unless reason shows it to be so.

Therefore, e.g., the doctrine of the Athanasian Creed[5] is not to be insisted on, unless it tends to convert the soul; and the doctrine of the Atonement is to be insisted on, if it does convert the soul.

---

3. In which Keble used the doctrine of apostolic succession to condemn the bill to suppress the Irish bishops as an apostasy.

4. I.e., the Tractarians.
5. Belief in the Trinity.

2. No one can believe what he does not understand.

Therefore, e.g., there are no mysteries in true religion.

3. No theological doctrine is anything more than an opinion which happens to be held by bodies of men.

Therefore, e.g., no creed, as such, is necessary for salvation.

4. It is dishonest in a man to make an act of faith in what he has not had brought home to him by actual proof.

Therefore, e.g., the mass of men ought not absolutely to believe in the divine authority of the Bible.

5. It is immoral in a man to believe more than he can spontaneously receive as being congenial to his moral and mental nature.

Therefore, e.g., a given individual is not bound to believe in eternal punishment.

6. No revealed doctrines or precepts may reasonably stand in the way of scientific conclusions.

Therefore, e.g., Political Economy may reverse our Lord's declarations about poverty and riches, or a system of Ethics may teach that the highest condition of body is ordinarily essential to the highest state of mind.

7. Christianity is necessarily modified by the growth of civilization, and the exigencies of times.

Therefore, e.g., the Catholic priesthood, though necessary in the Middle Ages, may be superseded now.

8. There is a system of religion more simply true than Christianity as it has ever been received.

Therefore, e.g., we may advance that Christianity is the "corn of wheat" which has been dead for 1800 years, but at length will bear fruit; and that Mahometanism is the manly religion, and existing Christianity the womanish.

9. There is a right of Private Judgment: that is, there is no existing authority on earth competent to interfere with the liberty of individuals in reasoning and judging for themselves about the Bible and its contents, as they severally please.

Therefore, e.g., religious establishments requiring subscription are Antichristian.

10. There are rights of conscience such that everyone may lawfully advance a claim to profess and teach what is false and wrong in matters, religious, social, and moral, provided that to his private conscience it seems absolutely true and right.

Therefore, e.g., individuals have a right to preach and practice fornication and polygamy.

11. There is no such thing as a national or state conscience.

Therefore, e.g., no judgments can fall upon a sinful or infidel nation.

12. The civil power has no positive duty, in a normal state of things, to maintain religious truth.

Therefore, e.g., blasphemy and sabbath-breaking are not rightly punishable by law.

13. Utility and expedience are the measure of political duty.

Therefore, e.g., no punishment may be enacted, on the ground that God commands it: e.g., on the text, "Whoso sheddeth man's blood, by man shall his blood be shed."[6]

6. Genesis 9.6.

14. The Civil Power may dispose of Church property without sacrilege.
Therefore, e.g., Henry VIII committed no sin in his spoliations.[7]

15. The Civil Power has the right of ecclesiastical jurisdiction and administration.
Therefore, e.g., Parliament may impose articles of faith on the Church or suppress Dioceses.[8]

16. It is lawful to rise in arms against legitimate princes.
Therefore, e.g., the Puritans in the seventeenth century, and the French in the eighteenth, were justified in their Rebellion and Revolution respectively.

17. The people are the legitimate source of power.
Therefore, e.g., Universal Suffrage is among the natural rights of man.

18. Virtue is the child of knowledge, and vice of ignorance.
Therefore, e.g., education, periodical literature, railroad traveling, ventilation, drainage, and the arts of life, when fully carried out, serve to make a population moral and happy.

All of these propositions, and many others too, were familiar to me thirty years ago, as in the number of the tenets of Liberalism, and, while I gave in to none of them except No. 12, and perhaps No. 11, and partly No. 1, before I began to publish, so afterwards I wrote against most of them in some part or other of my Anglican works.

* * *

I need hardly say that the above Note is mainly historical. How far the Liberal party of 1830–40 really held the above eighteen Theses, which I attributed to them, and how far and in what sense I should oppose those Theses now, could scarcely be explained without a separate Dissertation.

1864–65

7. The dissolution of the monasteries by Henry VIII.
8. An allusion to the abolishing of ten Irish bishoprics by liberal reformers in Parliament in 1833. This instance of interference by the state in affairs of the Church had prompted Newman and his associates into organizing what became the Oxford movement.

JOHN STUART MILL
1806–1873

In many American colleges the writings of J. S. Mill are studied in courses in government or in philosophy, and it may therefore be asked why they should also have a place in the study of literature. It may seem that Mill is less literary than other Victorian prose writers. His analytic mind, preoccupied with abstractions rather than with the concrete details that are the concern of the more typical writer; his self-effacing manner and his relatively transparent style are the marks of an author whose value lies in generalizations from personal experience rather than in the rendering of particular experiences for their own sake. Yet a knowledge of Mill's writings is essential to our understanding of Victorian literature. He is one of the leading figures in the intellectual history of his century, a thinker whose honest grappling with the political and religious problems of his age was to have a profound influence on writers as diverse as Arnold, Swinburne, and Hardy.

Mill was educated at home in London under the direction of his father, James Mill, a leader of the Utilitarians. James Mill believed that ordinary schooling fails to develop our intellectual capacities early enough, and he demonstrated his point by the extraordinary results he achieved in training his son. As a child, John Stuart Mill read Greek and Latin; and as a boy, he could carry on intelligent discussions of problems in mathematics, philosophy, and economics. By the time he was fourteen, as he reports in his *Autobiography,* his intensive education enabled him to start his career "with an advantage of a quarter of a century" over his contemporaries.

Mill worked in the office of the East India Company for many years and also served a term in Parliament in the 1860s; but his principal energies were devoted to his writings on such subjects as logic and philosophy, political principles, and economics. He began as a disciple of the Utilitarian theories of his father and of Jeremy Bentham but became gradually dissatisfied with the narrowness of their conception of human motives. His honesty and open-mindedness enabled him to appreciate the values of such anti-Utilitarians as Coleridge and Carlyle and, whenever possible, to incorporate some of these values into the Utilitarian system. In part, this sympathy was gained by the lesson he learned through experiencing a nervous breakdown during his early twenties. This painful event, described in a chapter of his *Autobiography,* taught him that the lack of concern for people's affections and emotions characteristic of the Utilitarian system of thought (and typified by his own education) was a fatal flaw in that system. His tribute to the therapeutic value of art (because of its effect on human emotions), both in his *Autobiography* and in his early essay *What Is Poetry?* would have astonished Mill's master, Bentham, who had equated poetry with pushpin, a trifling game.

Mill's emotional life was also broadened by his love for Harriet Taylor, a married woman who shared his intellectual interests and eventually became his wife, in 1851, after the death of her husband. Mill later described her as "the inspirer, and in part the author, of all that is best in my writings." They shared a commitment to the cause of female emancipation, one of several unpopular movements to which Mill was dedicated. Throughout human history, as he saw it, the role of a husband has always been legally that of a tyrant, and the object of his far-seeing essay *The Subjection of Women* (1869) was to change law and public opinion so that half the human race might be liberated from slavery into the status of individuals. The subjection of women was, however, only one aspect of the tyranny against which he fought. His fundamental concern was to prevent the subjection of individuals in a democracy. His classic treatise *On Liberty* (1859) is not a traditional liberal attack against tyrannical kings or dictators; it is an attack against tyrannical majorities. Mill foresaw that in democracies such as the United States the pressure toward conformity might crush all individualists (intellectual individualists in particular) to the level of what he called a "collective mediocrity." Throughout all of his writings, even in his discussions of the advantages of socialism, Mill is concerned with demonstrating that the individual is more important than institutions such as church or state. In *On Liberty* we find a characteristic example of the process of his reasoning; but here, where the theme of individualism is central, his logic is charged with eloquence.

A similar eloquence is evident in a passage from his *Principles of Political Economy* (1848), a prophetic comment on the fate of the individual in an overpopulated world:

> There is room in the world, no doubt, and even in old countries, for a great increase of population, supposing the arts of life go on improving, and capital to increase. But even if innocuous, I confess I see very little reason for desiring it. . . . It is not good for a man to be kept perforce at all times in the presence of his species. A world from which solitude is extirpated, is a very poor ideal. Solitude, in the sense of being often alone, is essential to any depth of meditation

or of character: and solitude in the presence of natural beauty and grandeur, is the cradle of thoughts and aspirations which are not only good for the individual, but which society could ill do without. Nor is there much satisfaction in contemplating the world with nothing left to the spontaneous activity of nature; with every rood of land brought into cultivation, which is capable of growing food for human beings; every flowery waste or natural pasture ploughed up, all quadrupeds or birds which are not domesticated for man's use exterminated as his rivals for food, every hedgerow or superfluous tree rooted out, and scarcely a place left where a wild shrub or flower could grow without being eradicated as a weed in the name of improved agriculture. If the earth must lose that great portion of its pleasantness which it owes to things that the unlimited increase of wealth and population would extirpate from it, for the mere purpose of enabling it to support a larger, but not a better or happier population, I sincerely hope, for the sake of posterity, that they will be content to be stationary, long before necessity compels them to it.

What Is Poetry?

It has often been asked, What Is Poetry? And many and various are the answers which have been returned. The vulgarest of all—one with which no person possessed of the faculties to which poetry addresses itself can ever have been satisfied—is that which confounds poetry with metrical composition; yet to this wretched mockery of a definition many have been led back by the failure of all their attempts to find any other that would distinguish what they have been accustomed to call poetry from much which they have known only under other names.

That, however, the word "poetry" imports something quite peculiar in its nature; something which may exist in what is called prose as well as in verse; something which does not even require the instrument of words, but can speak through the other audible symbols called musical sounds, and even through the visible ones which are the language of sculpture, painting, and architecture—all this, we believe, is and must be felt, though perhaps indistinctly, by all upon whom poetry in any of its shapes produces any impression beyond that of tickling the ear. The distinction between poetry and what is not poetry, whether explained or not, is felt to be fundamental; and, where every one feels a difference, a difference there must be. All other appearances may be fallacious; but the appearance of a difference is a real difference. Appearances too, like other things, must have a cause; and that which can cause anything, even an illusion, must be a reality. And hence, while a half-philosophy disdains the classifications and distinctions indicated by popular language, philosophy carried to its highest point frames new ones, but rarely sets aside the old, content with correcting and regularizing them. It cuts fresh channels for thought, but does not fill up such as it finds ready-made: it traces, on the contrary, more deeply, broadly, and distinctly, those into which the current has spontaneously flowed.

Let us then attempt, in the way of modest inquiry, not to coerce and confine Nature within the bounds of an arbitrary definition, but rather to find the boundaries which she herself has set, and erect a barrier round them; not calling mankind to account for having misapplied the word "poetry," but attempting to clear up the conception which they already attach to it, and to bring forward as a distinct principle that which, as a vague feeling, has really guided them in their employment of the term.

The object of poetry is confessedly to act upon the emotions; and therein is poetry sufficiently distinguished from what Wordsworth affirms to be its logical opposite;[1] namely, not prose but matter of fact, or science. The one addresses itself to the belief; the other, to the feelings. The one does its work by convincing or persuading; the other, by moving. The one acts by presenting a proposition to the understanding; the other, by offering interesting objects of contemplation to the sensibilities.

This, however, leaves us very far from a definition of poetry. This distinguishes it from one thing; but we are bound to distinguish it from everything. To bring thoughts or images before the mind, for the purpose of acting upon the emotions, does not belong to poetry alone. It is equally the province (for example) of the novelist: and yet the faculty of the poet and that of the novelist are as distinct as any other two faculties; as the faculties of the novelist and of the orator, or of the poet and the metaphysician. The two characters may be united, as characters the most disparate may; but they have no natural connection.

Many of the greatest poems are in the form of fictitious narratives; and, in almost all good serious fictions, there is true poetry. But there is a radical distinction between the interest felt in a story as such, and the interest excited by poetry; for the one is derived from incident, the other from the representation of feeling. In one, the source of the emotion excited is the exhibition of a state or states of human sensibility; in the other, of a series of states of mere outward circumstances. Now, all minds are capable of being affected more or less by representations of the latter kind, and all, or almost all, by those of the former; yet the two sources of interest correspond to two distinct and (as respects their greatest development) mutually exclusive characters of mind.

At what age is the passion for a story, for almost any kind of story, merely as a story, the most intense? In childhood. But that also is the age at which poetry, even of the simplest description, is least relished and least understood; because the feelings with which it is especially conversant are yet undeveloped, and, not having been even in the slightest degree experienced, cannot be sympathized with. In what stage of the progress of society, again, is storytelling most valued, and the storyteller in greatest request and honor? In a rude state like that of the Tartars and Arabs at this day, and of almost all nations in the earliest ages. But, in this state of society, there is little poetry except ballads, which are mostly narrative—that is, essentially stories—and derive their principal interest from the incidents. Considered as poetry, they are of the lowest and most elementary kind: the feelings depicted, or rather indicated, are the simplest our nature has; such joys and griefs as the immediate pressure of some outward event excites in rude minds, which live wholly immersed in outward things, and have never, either from choice or a force they could not resist, turned themselves to the contemplation of the world within. Passing now from childhood, and from the childhood of society, to the grown-up men and women of this most grown-up and unchildlike age, the minds and hearts of greatest depth and elevation

1. In his "Preface" to *Lyrical Ballads.*

are commonly those which take greatest delight in poetry: the shallowest and emptiest, on the contrary, are, at all events, not those least addicted to novel-reading. This accords, too, with all analogous experience of human nature. The sort of persons whom not merely in books, but in their lives, we find perpetually engaged in hunting for excitement from without, are invariably those who do not possess, either in the vigor of their intellectual powers or in the depth of their sensibilities, that which would enable them to find ample excitement nearer home. The most idle and frivolous persons take a natural delight in fictitious narrative: the excitement it affords is of the kind which comes from without. Such persons are rarely lovers of poetry, though they may fancy themselves so because they relish novels in verse. But poetry, which is the delineation of the deeper and more secret workings of human emotion, is interesting only to those to whom it recalls what they have felt, or whose imagination it stirs up to conceive what they could feel, or what they might have been able to feel, had their outward circumstances been different.

Poetry, when it is really such, is truth; and fiction also, if it is good for anything, is truth: but they are different truths. The truth of poetry is to paint the human soul truly: the truth of fiction is to give a true picture of life. The two kinds of knowledge are different, and come by different ways, come mostly to different persons. Great poets are often proverbially ignorant of life. What they know has come by observation of themselves: they have found within them one highly delicate and sensitive specimen of human nature, on which the laws of emotion are written in large characters, such as can be read off without much study. Other knowledge of mankind, such as comes to men of the world by outward experience, is not indispensable to them as poets: but, to the novelist, such knowledge is all in all; he has to describe outward things, not the inward man; actions and events, not feelings; and it will not do for him to be numbered among those, who, as Madame Roland said of Brissot,[2] know man, but not *men*.

All this is no bar to the possibility of combining both elements, poetry and narrative or incident, in the same work, and calling it either a novel or a poem; but so may red and white combine on the same human features or on the same canvas. There is one order of composition which requires the union of poetry and incident, each in its highest kind—the dramatic. Even there, the two elements are perfectly distinguishable, and may exist of unequal quality and in the most various proportion. The incidents of a dramatic poem may be scanty and ineffective, though the delineation of passion and char-acter may be of the highest order, as in Goethe's admirable "Torquato Tasso"; or, again, the story as a mere story may be well got up for effect, as is the case with some of the most trashy productions of the Minerva Press:[3] it may even be, what those are not, a coherent and probable series of events, though there be scarcely a feeling exhibited which is not represented falsely, or in a manner absolutely commonplace. The combination of the two excellences is what renders Shakespeare so generally acceptable, each sort of readers finding in him what is suitable to their faculties. To the many, he is great as a storyteller; to the few, as a poet.

In limiting poetry to the delineation of states of feeling, and denying the

---

2. Jacques-Pierre Brissot (1754–1793), a leading reformer during the French Revolution, is char-acterized in the *Mémoires* of Jeanne-Manon

Roland (1754–1793).
3. An early-19th-century publishing house that fostered the production of sentimental novels.

name where nothing is delineated but outward objects, we may be thought to have done what we promised to avoid—to have not found, but made, a definition in opposition to the usage of language, since it is established by common consent that there is a poetry called descriptive. We deny the charge. Description is not poetry because there is descriptive poetry, no more than science is poetry because there is such a thing as a didactic poem. But an object which admits of being described, or a truth which may fill a place in a scientific treatise, may also furnish an occasion for the generation of poetry, which we thereupon choose to call descriptive or didactic. The poetry is not in the object itself, nor in the scientific truth itself, but in the state of mind in which the one and the other may be contemplated. The mere delineation of the dimensions and colors of external objects is not poetry, no more than a geometrical ground-plan of St. Peter's or Westminster Abbey is painting. Descriptive poetry consists, no doubt, in description, but in description of things as they appear, not as they are; and it paints them, not in their bare and natural lineaments, but seen through the medium and arrayed in the colors of the imagination set in action by the feelings. If a poet describes a lion, he does not describe him as a naturalist would, nor even as a traveler would, who was intent upon stating the truth, the whole truth, and nothing but the truth. He describes him by imagery, that is, by suggesting the most striking likenesses and contrasts which might occur to a mind contemplating a lion, in the state of awe, wonder, or terror, which the spectacle naturally excites, or is, on the occasion, supposed to excite. Now, this is describing the lion professedly, but the state of excitement of the spectator really. The lion may be described falsely or with exaggeration and the poetry be all the better: but, if the human emotion be not painted with scrupulous truth, the poetry is bad poetry, i.e., is not poetry at all, but a failure.

Thus far, our progress towards a clear view of the essentials of poetry has brought us very close to the last two attempts at a definition of poetry which we happen to have seen in print, both of them by poets, and men of genius. The one is by Ebenezer Elliott, the author of "Corn-law Rhymes," and other poems of still greater merit. "Poetry," says he, "is impassioned truth."[4] The other is by a writer in "Blackwood's Magazine," and comes, we think, still nearer the mark. He defines poetry, "man's thoughts tinged by his feelings." There is in either definition a near approximation to what we are in search of. Every truth which a human being can enunciate, every thought, even every outward impression, which can enter into his consciousness, may become poetry, when shown through any impassioned medium; when invested with the coloring of joy, or grief, or pity, or affection, or admiration, or reverence, or awe, or even hatred or terror; and, unless so colored, nothing, be it as interesting as it may, is poetry. But both these definitions fail to discriminate between poetry and eloquence. Eloquence, as well as poetry, is impassioned truth; eloquence, as well as poetry, is thoughts colored by the feelings. Yet common apprehension and philosophic criticism alike recognize a distinction between the two: there is much that everyone would call eloquence, which no one would think of classing as poetry. A question will sometimes arise, whether some particular author is a poet; and those who maintain the negative commonly allow, that, though not a poet, he is a highly

---

4. In the "Preface" to *Corn-Law Rhymes* (1828) by Ebenezer Elliott (1781–1849).

eloquent writer. The distinction between poetry and eloquence appears to us to be equally fundamental with the distinction between poetry and narrative, or between poetry and description, while it is still farther from having been satisfactorily cleared up than either of the others.

Poetry and eloquence are both alike the expression or utterance of feeling: but, if we may be excused the antithesis, we should say that eloquence is *heard*; poetry is *over*heard. Eloquence supposes an audience. The peculiarity of poetry appears to us to lie in the poet's utter unconsciousness of a listener. Poetry is feeling confessing itself to itself in moments of solitude, and embodying itself in symbols which are the nearest possible representations of the feeling in the exact shape in which it exists in the poet's mind. Eloquence is feeling pouring itself out to other minds, courting their sympathy, or endeavoring to influence their belief, or move them to passion or to action.

All poetry is of the nature of soliloquy. It may be said that poetry which is printed on hot-pressed paper, and sold at a bookseller's shop, is a soliloquy in full dress and on the stage. It is so; but there is nothing absurd in the idea of such a mode of soliloquizing. What we have said to ourselves we may tell to others afterwards; what we have said or done in solitude we may voluntarily reproduce when we know that other eyes are upon us. But no trace of consciousness that any eyes are upon us must be visible in the work itself. The actor knows that there is an audience present: but, if he act as though he knew it, he acts ill. A poet may write poetry, not only with the intention of printing it, but for the express purpose of being paid for it. That it should *be* poetry, being written under such influences, is less probable, not, however, impossible; but no otherwise possible than if he can succeed in excluding from his work every vestige of such lookings-forth into the outward and every-day world, and can express his emotions exactly as he has felt them in solitude, or as he is conscious that he should feel them, though they were to remain for ever unuttered, or (at the lowest) as he knows that others feel them in similar circumstances of solitude. But when he turns round, and addresses himself to another person; when the act of utterance is not itself the end, but a means to an end—viz., by the feelings he himself expresses, to work upon the feelings, or upon the belief or the will of another; when the expression of his emotions, or of his thoughts tinged by his emotions, is tinged also by that purpose, by that desire of making an impression upon another mind—then it ceases to be poetry, and becomes eloquence.

Poetry, accordingly, is the natural fruit of solitude and meditation; eloquence, of intercourse with the world. The persons who have most feeling of their own, if intellectual culture has given them a language in which to express it, have the highest faculty of poetry: those who best understand the feelings of others are the most eloquent. The persons and the nations who commonly excel in poetry are those whose character and tastes render them least dependent upon the applause or sympathy or concurrence of the world in general. Those to whom that applause, that sympathy, that concurrence, are most necessary, generally excel most in eloquence. And hence, perhaps, the French, who are the least poetical of all great and intellectual nations, are among the most eloquent; the French also being the most sociable, the vainest, and the least self-dependent.

If the above be, as we believe, the true theory of the distinction commonly admitted between eloquence and poetry, or even though it be not so, yet if, as we cannot doubt, the distinction above stated be a real bona fide distinction, it will be found to hold, not merely in the language of words, but in all other language, and to intersect the whole domain of art.

Take, for example, music. We shall find in that art, so peculiarly the expression of passion, two perfectly distinct styles—one of which may be called the poetry, the other the oratory, of music. This difference, being seized, would put an end to much musical sectarianism. There has been much contention whether the music of the modern Italian school, that of Rossini,[5] and his successors, be impassioned or not. Without doubt, the passion it expresses is not the musing, meditative tenderness or pathos or grief of Mozart or Beethoven; yet it is passion, but garrulous passion, the passion which pours itself into other ears, and therein the better calculated for dramatic effect, having a natural adaptation for dialogue. Mozart also is great in musical oratory; but his most touching compositions are in the opposite style, that of soliloquy. Who can imagine "Dove sono"[6] *heard*? We imagine it *over*heard.

Purely pathetic music commonly partakes of soliloquy. The soul is absorbed in its distress and, though there may be bystanders, it is not thinking of them. When the mind is looking within, and not without, its state does not often or rapidly vary; and hence the even, uninterrupted flow, approaching almost to monotony, which a good reader or a good singer will give to words or music of a pensive or melancholy cast. But grief, taking the form of a prayer or of a complaint, becomes oratorical: no longer low and even and subdued, it assumes a more emphatic rhythm, a more rapidly returning accent; instead of a few slow, equal notes, following one after another at regular intervals, it crowds note upon note, and often assumes a hurry and bustle like joy. Those who are familiar with some of the best of Rossini's serious compositions, such as the air "Tu che i miseri conforti,"[7] in the opera of "Tancredi," or the duet "Ebben per mia memoria,"[8] in "La Gazza Ladra," will at once understand and feel our meaning. Both are highly tragic and passionate: the passion of both is that of oratory, not poetry. The like may be said of that most moving invocation in Beethoven's "Fidelio,"

> "Komm, Hoffnung, lass das letzte Stern
> Der Müde nicht erbleichen"—[9]

in which Madame Schröder Devrient exhibited such consummate powers of pathetic expression. How different from Winter's beautiful "Paga fui,"[1] the very soul of melancholy exhaling itself in solitude! fuller of meaning, and therefore more profoundly poetical, than the words for which it was composed; for it seems to express, not simple melancholy, but the melancholy of remorse.

If from vocal music we now pass to instrumental, we may have a specimen

---

5. Gioacchino Rossini (1792–1868), composer of operas.
6. Where are fled [the lovely moments?] (Italian); soprano aria from Mozart's *The Marriage of Figaro*, act 3 (1786).
7. You, who give comfort to the wretched (Italian); soprano aria from Rossini's *Tancredi* (1813).
8. Indeed according to my memory (Italian); soprano aria from Rossini's *La gazza Ladra* (1817).

9. Come, Hope, let not the weary person's last star fade out (German); aria from Beethoven's *Fidelio* (1805). Mill seems to be quoting from memory. The passage should read: "Komm, Hoffnung, lass den letzten Stern / Der Müden nicht erbleichen."
1. I have been contented (Italian); aria from the once-popular opera *Il ratto di Proserpina* by Peter Winter (1754–1825), first performed in London in 1804.

of musical oratory in any fine military symphony or march; while the poetry of music seems to have attained its consummation in Beethoven's "Overture to Egmont," so wonderful in its mixed expression of grandeur and melancholy.

In the arts which speak to the eye, the same distinctions will be found to hold, not only between poetry and oratory, but between poetry, oratory, narrative, and simple imitation or description.

Pure description is exemplified in a mere portrait or a mere landscape, productions of art, it is true, but of the mechanical rather than of the fine arts; being works of simple imitation, not creation. We say, a mere portrait or a mere landscape; because it is possible for a portrait or a landscape, without ceasing to be such, to be also a picture, like Turner's[2] landscapes, and the great portraits by Titian or Vandyke.

Whatever in painting or sculpture expresses human feeling—or character, which is only a certain state of feeling grown habitual—may be called, according to circumstances, the poetry or the eloquence of the painter's or the sculptor's art: the poetry, if the feeling declares itself by such signs as escape from us when we are unconscious of being seen; the oratory, if the signs are those we use for the purpose of voluntary communication.

The narrative style answers to what is called historical painting, which it is the fashion among connoisseurs to treat as the climax of the pictorial art. That it is the most difficult branch of the art, we do not doubt, because, in its perfection, it includes the perfection of all the other branches; as, in like manner, an epic poem, though, in so far as it is epic (i.e. narrative), it is not poetry at all, is yet esteemed the greatest effort of poetic genius, because there is no kind whatever of poetry which may not appropriately find a place in it. But an historical picture as such, that is, as the representation of an incident, must necessarily, as it seems to us, be poor and ineffective. The narrative powers of painting are extremely limited. Scarcely any picture, scarcely even any series of pictures, tells its own story without the aid of an interpreter. But it is the single figures, which, to us, are the great charm even of an historical picture. It is in these that the power of the art is really seen. In the attempt to narrate, visible and permanent signs are too far behind the fugitive audible ones, which follow so fast one after another; while the faces and figures in a narrative picture, even though they be Titian's, stand still. Who would not prefer one "Virgin and Child" of Raphael to all the pictures which Rubens, with his fat, frouzy Dutch Venuses, ever painted?—though Rubens, besides excelling almost everyone in his mastery over the mechanical parts of his art, often shows real genius in *grouping* his figures, the peculiar problem of historical painting. But then, who, except a mere student of drawing and coloring, ever cared to look twice at any of the figures themselves? The power of painting lies in poetry, of which Rubens had not the slightest tincture, not in narrative, wherein he might have excelled.

The single figures, however, in an historical picture, are rather the eloquence of painting than the poetry. They mostly (unless they are quite out of place in the picture) express the feelings of one person as modified by the presence of others. Accordingly, the minds whose bent leads them

2. J. M. W. Turner (1775–1851), English landscape painter.

rather to eloquence than to poetry rush to historical painting. The French painters, for instance, seldom attempt, because they could make nothing of, single heads, like those glorious ones of the Italian masters with which they might feed themselves day after day in their own Louvre. They must all be historical; and they are, almost to a man, attitudinizers. If we wished to give any young artist the most impressive warning our imagination could devise against that kind of vice in the pictorial which corresponds to rant in the histrionic art, we would advise him to walk once up and once down the gallery of the Luxembourg.[3] Every figure in French painting or statuary seems to be showing itself off before spectators. They are not poetical, but in the worst style of corrupted eloquence.

1833, 1859

From On Liberty

From Chapter 3. Of Individuality as One of the Elements of Well-Being

*   *   *

Few persons, out of Germany, even comprehend the meaning of the doctrine which Wilhelm von Humboldt, so eminent both as a savant and as a politician, made the text of a treatise—that "the end of man, or that which is prescribed by the eternal or immutable dictates of reason, and not suggested by vague and transient desires, is the highest and most harmonious development of his powers to a complete and consistent whole"; that, therefore, the object "towards which every human being must ceaselessly direct his efforts, and on which especially those who design to influence their fellow men must ever keep their eyes, is the individuality of power and development"; that for this there are two requisites, "freedom, and variety of situations"; and that from the union of these arise "individual vigor and manifold diversity," which combine themselves in "originality."[1]

Little, however, as people are accustomed to a doctrine like that of Von Humboldt, and surprising as it may be to them to find so high a value attached to individuality, the question, one must nevertheless think, can only be one of degree. No one's idea of excellence in conduct is that people should do absolutely nothing but copy one another. No one would assert that people ought not to put into their mode of life, and into the conduct of their concerns, any impress whatever of their own judgment, or of their own individual character. On the other hand, it would be absurd to pretend that people ought to live as if nothing whatever had been known in the world before they came into it; as if experience had as yet done nothing towards showing that one mode of existence, or conduct, is preferable to another. Nobody denies that people should be so taught and trained in youth, as to know and benefit by the ascertained results of human experience. But it is the privilege and proper condition of a human being, arrived at the maturity of his faculties,

<hr>

3. A palace in Paris, where paintings of scenes from French history were exhibited.
1. From *The Sphere and Duties of Government,* by Baron Wilhelm von Humboldt (1767–1835), Prussian statesman and man of letters. Originally written in 1791, the treatise was first published in Germany in 1852 and was translated into English in 1854.

to use and interpret experience in his own way. It is for him to find out what part of recorded experience is properly applicable to his own circumstances and character. The traditions and customs of other people are, to a certain extent, evidence of what their experience has taught *them;* presumptive evidence, and as such, have a claim to his deference: but, in the first place, their experience may be too narrow; or they may not have interpreted it rightly. Secondly, their interpretation of experience may be correct, but unsuitable to him. Customs are made for customary circumstances, and customary characters; and his circumstances or his character may be uncustomary. Thirdly, though the customs be both good as customs, and suitable to him, yet to conform to custom, merely *as* custom, does not educate or develop in him any of the qualities which are the distinctive endowment of a human being. The human faculties of perception, judgment, discriminative feeling, mental activity, and even moral preference are exercised only in making a choice. He who does anything because it is the custom makes no choice. He gains no practice either in discerning or in desiring what is best. The mental and moral, like the muscular powers, are improved only by being used. The faculties are called into no exercise by doing a thing merely because others do it, no more than by believing a thing only because others believe it. If the grounds of an opinion are not conclusive to the person's own reason, his reason cannot be strengthened, but is likely to be weakened, by his adopting it: and if the inducements to an act are not such as are consentaneous[2] to his own feelings and character (where affection, or the rights of others, are not concerned) it is so much done towards rendering his feelings and character inert and torpid, instead of active and energetic.

He who lets the world, or his own portion of it, choose his plan of life for him has no need of any other faculty than the apelike one of imitation. He who chooses his plan for himself employs all his faculties. He must use observation to see, reasoning and judgment to foresee, activity to gather materials for decision, discrimination to decide, and when he has decided, firmness and self-control to hold to his deliberate decision. And these qualities he requires and exercises exactly in proportion as the part of his conduct which he determines according to his own judgment and feelings is a large one. It is possible that he might be guided in some good path, and kept out of harm's way, without any of these things. But what will be his comparative worth as a human being? It really is of importance, not only what men do, but also what manner of men they are that do it. Among the works of man, which human life is rightly employed in perfecting and beautifying, the first in importance surely is man himself. Supposing it were possible to get houses built, corn grown, battles fought, causes tried, and even churches erected and prayers said, by machinery—by automatons in human form—it would be a considerable loss to exchange for these automatons even the men and women who at present inhabit the more civilized parts of the world, and who assuredly are but starved specimens of what nature can and will produce. Human nature is not a machine to be built after a model, and set to do exactly the work prescribed for it, but a tree, which requires to grow and develop itself on all sides, according to the tendency of the inward forces which make it a living thing.

2. Agreeable.

It will probably be conceded that it is desirable people should exercise their understandings, and that an intelligent following of custom, or even occasionally an intelligent deviation from custom, is better than a blind and simply mechanical adhesion to it. To a certain extent it is admitted that our understanding should be our own: but there is not the same willingness to admit that our desires and impulses should be our own likewise; or that to possess impulses of our own, and of any strength, is anything but a peril and a snare. Yet desires and impulses are as much a part of a perfect human being, as beliefs and restraints: and strong impulses are only perilous when not properly balanced; when one set of aims and inclinations is developed into strength, while others, which ought to coexist with them, remain weak and inactive. It is not because men's desires are strong that they act ill; it is because their consciences are weak. There is no natural connection between strong impulses and a weak conscience. The natural connection is the other way. To say that one person's desires and feelings are stronger and more various than those of another is merely to say that he has more of the raw material of human nature, and is therefore capable, perhaps of more evil, but certainly of more good. Strong impulses are but another name for energy. Energy may be turned to bad uses; but more good may always be made of an energetic nature than of an indolent and impassive one. Those who have most natural feeling are always those whose cultivated feelings may be made the strongest. The same strong susceptibilities which make the personal impulses vivid and powerful are also the source from whence are generated the most passionate love of virtue, and the sternest self-control. It is through the cultivation of these that society both does its duty and protects its interests: not by rejecting the stuff of which heroes are made, because it knows not how to make them. A person whose desires and impulses are his own—are the expression of his own nature, as it has been developed and modified by his own culture—is said to have a character. One whose desires and impulses are not his own, has no character, no more than a steam engine has a character. If, in addition to being his own, his impulses are strong, and are under the government of a strong will, he has an energetic character. Whoever thinks that individuality of desires and impulses should not be encouraged to unfold itself must maintain that society has no need of strong natures—is not the better for containing many persons who have much character—and that a high general average of energy is not desirable.

In some early states of society, these forces might be, and were, too much ahead of the power which society then possessed of disciplining and controlling them. There has been a time when the element of spontaneity and individuality was in excess, and the social principle had a hard struggle with it. The difficulty then was to induce men of strong bodies or minds to pay obedience to any rules which require them to control their impulses. To overcome this difficulty, law and discipline, like the Popes struggling against the Emperors, asserted a power over the whole man, claiming to control all his life in order to control his character—which society had not found any other sufficient means of binding. But society has now fairly got the better of individuality; and the danger which threatens human nature is not the excess, but the deficiency, of personal impulses and preferences. Things are vastly changed, since the passions of those who were strong by station or by personal endowment were in a state of habitual rebellion against laws and ordinances, and required to be rigorously chained up to enable the persons within their reach to enjoy any particle of security. In our times, from the highest class of society down to the lowest, everyone lives as under the eye of a hostile and dreaded censorship. Not only in what concerns others, but in what concerns only themselves, the individual or the family do not ask themselves—what do I prefer? or, what would suit my character and disposition? or, what would allow the best and highest in me to have fair play, and enable it to grow and thrive? They ask themselves, what is suitable to my position? what is usually done by persons of my station and pecuniary circumstances? or (worse still) what is usually done by persons of a station and circumstances superior to mine? I do not mean that they choose what is customary, in preference to what suits their own inclination. It does not occur to them to have any inclination, except for what is customary. Thus the mind itself is bowed to the yoke: even in what people do for pleasure, conformity is the first thing thought of; they like in crowds; they exercise choice only among things commonly done: peculiarity of taste, eccentricity of conduct, are shunned equally with crimes: until by dint of not following their own nature, they have no nature to follow: their human capacities are withered and starved: they become incapable of any strong wishes or native pleasures, and are generally without either opinions or feelings of home growth, or properly their own. Now is this, or is it not, the desirable condition of human nature?

It is so, on the Calvinistic theory. According to that, the one great offense of man is self-will. All the good of which humanity is capable is comprised in obedience. You have no choice; thus you must do, and no otherwise: "whatever is not a duty is a sin." Human nature being radically corrupt, there is no redemption for anyone until human nature is killed within him. To one holding this theory of life, crushing out any of the human faculties, capacities, and susceptibilities is no evil: man needs no capacity but that of surrendering himself to the will of God: and if he uses any of his faculties for any other purpose but to do that supposed will more effectually, he is better without them. This is the theory of Calvinism; and it is held, in a mitigated form, by many who do not consider themselves Calvinists; the mitigation consisting in giving a less ascetic interpretation to the alleged will of God; asserting it to be his will that mankind should gratify some of their inclinations; of course not in the manner they themselves prefer, but in the way of obedience, that is, in a way prescribed to them by authority; and, therefore, by the necessary conditions of the case, the same for all.

In some such insidious form there is at present a strong tendency to this narrow theory of life, and to the pinched and hidebound type of human character which it patronizes. Many persons, no doubt, sincerely think that human beings thus cramped and dwarfed are as their Maker designed them to be; just as many have thought that trees are a much finer thing when clipped into pollards,[3] or cut out into figures of animals, than as nature made them. But if it be any part of religion to believe that man was made by a good Being, it is more consistent with that faith to believe that this Being gave all human faculties that they might be cultivated and unfolded, not rooted out and consumed, and that he takes delight in every nearer approach

---

3. Trees that acquire an artificial shape by being cut back to produce a mass of dense foliage.

made by his creatures to the ideal conception embodied in them, every increase in any of their capabilities of comprehension, of action, or of enjoyment. There is a different type of human excellence from the Calvinistic; a conception of humanity as having its nature bestowed on it for other purposes than merely to be abnegated. "Pagan self-assertion" is one of the elements of human worth, as well as "Christian self-denial."[4] There is a Greek ideal of self-development, which the Platonic and Christian ideal of self-government blends with, but does not supersede. It may be better to be a John Knox than an Alcibiades, but it is better to be a Pericles[5] than either, nor would a Pericles, if we had one in these days, be without anything good which belonged to John Knox.

It is not by wearing down into uniformity all that is individual in themselves, but by cultivating it and calling it forth, within the limits imposed by the rights and interests of others, that human beings become a noble and beautiful object of contemplation; and as the works partake the character of those who do them, by the same process human life also becomes rich, diversified, and animating, furnishing more abundant aliment to high thoughts and elevating feelings, and strengthening the tie which binds every individual to the race, by making the race infinitely better worth belonging to. In proportion to the development of his individuality, each person becomes more valuable to himself, and is therefore capable of being more valuable to others. There is a greater fullness of life about his own existence, and when there is more life in the units there is more in the mass which is composed of them. As much compression as is necessary to prevent the stronger specimens of human nature from encroaching on the rights of others cannot be dispensed with; but for this there is ample compensation even in the point of view of human development. The means of development which the individual loses by being prevented from gratifying his inclinations to the injury of others are chiefly obtained at the expense of the development of other people. And even to himself there is a full equivalent in the better development of the social part of his nature, rendered possible by the restraint put upon the selfish part. To be held to rigid rules of justice for the sake of others develops the feelings and capacities which have the good of others for their object. But to be restrained in things not affecting their good, by their mere displeasure, develops nothing valuable, except such force of character as may unfold itself in resisting the restraint. If acquiesced in, it dulls and blunts the whole nature. To give any fair play to the nature of each, it is essential that different persons should be allowed to lead different lives. In proportion as this latitude has been exercised in any age, has that age been noteworthy to posterity. Even despotism does not produce its worst effects, so long as individuality exists under it; and whatever crushes individuality is despotism, by whatever name it may be called, and whether it professes to be enforcing the will of God or the injunctions of men.

Having said that Individuality is the same thing with development, and that it is only the cultivation of individuality which produces, or can produce, well-developed human beings, I might here close the argument: for what more or better can be said of any condition of human affairs than that it

4. From the *Essays* (1848) of John Sterling, a minor writer and friend of Carlyle's.
5. A model statesman in Athens (495–429 B.C.E.).

Knox (1514–1572), a stern Scottish Calvinist reformer. Alcibiades (450–404 B.C.E.), a dissolute Athenian commander.

brings human beings themselves nearer to the best thing they can be? or what worse can be said of any obstruction to good than that it prevents this? Doubtless, however, these considerations will not suffice to convince those who most need convincing; and it is necessary further to show that these developed human beings are of some use to the undeveloped—to point out to those who do not desire liberty, and would not avail themselves of it, that they may be in some intelligible manner rewarded for allowing other people to make use of it without hindrance.

In the first place, then, I would suggest that they might possibly learn something from them. It will not be denied by anybody, that originality is a valuable element in human affairs. There is always need of persons not only to discover new truths, and point out when what were once truths are true no longer, but also to commence new practices, and set the example of more enlightened conduct, and better taste and sense in human life. This cannot well be gainsaid by anybody who does not believe that the world has already attained perfection in all its ways and practices. It is true that this benefit is not capable of being rendered by everybody alike: there are but few persons, in comparison with the whole of mankind, whose experiments, if adopted by others, would be likely to be any improvement on established practice. But these few are the salt of the earth; without them, human life would become a stagnant pool. Not only is it they who introduce good things which did not before exist; it is they who keep the life in those which already existed. If there were nothing new to be done, would human intellect cease to be necessary? Would it be a reason why those who do the old things should forget why they are done, and do them like cattle, not like human beings? There is only too great a tendency in the best beliefs and practices to degenerate into the mechanical; and unless there were a succession of persons whose ever-recurring originality prevents the grounds of those beliefs and practices from becoming merely traditional, such dead matter would not resist the smallest shock from anything really alive, and there would be no reason why civilization should not die out, as in the Byzantine Empire. Persons of genius, it is true, are, and are always likely to be, a small minority; but in order to have them, it is necessary to preserve the soil in which they grow. Genius can only breathe freely in an *atmosphere* of freedom. Persons of genius are, *ex vi termini*,[6] *more* individual than any other people—less capable, consequently, of fitting themselves, without hurtful compression, into any of the small number of molds which society provides in order to save its members the trouble of forming their own character. If from timidity they consent to be forced into one of these molds, and to let all that part of themselves which cannot expand under the pressure remain unexpanded, society will be little the better for their genius. If they are of a strong character, and break their fetters, they become a mark for the society which has not succeeded in reducing them to commonplace, to point at with solemn warning as "wild," "erratic," and the like; much as if one should complain of the Niagara River for not flowing smoothly between its banks like a Dutch canal.

I insist thus emphatically on the importance of genius, and the necessity of allowing it to unfold itself freely both in thought and in practice, being well aware that no one will deny the position in theory, but knowing also

---

6. By force of the term (Latin); i.e., by definition.

that almost everyone, in reality, is totally indifferent to it. People think genius a fine thing if it enables a man to write an exciting poem, or paint a picture. But in its true sense, that of originality in thought and action, though no one says that it is not a thing to be admired, nearly all, at heart, think that they can do very well without it. Unhappily this is too natural to be wondered at. Originality is the one thing which unoriginal minds cannot feel the use of. They cannot see what it is to do for them: how should they? If they could see what it would do for them, it would not be originality. The first service which originality has to render them is that of opening their eyes: which being once fully done, they would have a chance of being themselves original. Meanwhile, recollecting that nothing was ever yet done which someone was not the first to do, and that all good things which exist are the fruits of originality, let them be modest enough to believe that there is something still left for it to accomplish, and assure themselves that they are more in need of originality, the less they are conscious of the want.

In sober truth, whatever homage may be professed, or even paid, to real or supposed mental superiority, the general tendency of things throughout the world is to render mediocrity the ascendant power among mankind. In ancient history, in the middle ages, and in a diminishing degree through the long transition from feudality to the present time, the individual was power in himself; and if he had either great talents or a high social position, he was a considerable power. At present individuals are lost in the crowd. In politics it is almost a triviality to say that public opinion now rules the world. The only power deserving the name is that of masses, and of governments while they make themselves the organ of the tendencies and instincts of masses. This is as true in the moral and social relations of private life as in public transactions. Those whose opinions go by the name of public opinion, are not always the same sort of public: in America they are the whole white population; in England, chiefly the middle class. But they are always a mass, that is to say, collective mediocrity. And what is a still greater novelty, the mass do not now take their opinions from dignitaries in Church or State, from ostensible leaders, or from books. Their thinking is done for them by men much like themselves, addressing them or speaking in their name, on the spur of the moment, through the newspapers. I am not complaining of all this. I do not assert that anything better is compatible, as a general rule, with the present low state of the human mind. But that does not hinder the government of mediocrity from being mediocre government. No government by a democracy or a numerous aristocracy, either in its political acts or in the opinions, qualities, and tone of mind which it fosters, ever did or could rise above mediocrity, except in so far as the sovereign Many have let themselves be guided (which in their best times they always have done) by the counsels and influence of a more highly gifted and instructed One or Few. The initiation of all wise or noble things, comes and must come from individuals; generally at first from some one individual. The honor and glory of the average man is that he is capable of following that initiative; that he can respond internally to wise and noble things, and be led to them with his eyes open. I am not countenancing the sort of "hero worship" which applauds the strong man of genius for forcibly seizing on the government of the world and making it do his bidding in spite of itself. All he can claim is freedom to point out the way. The power of compelling others into it is not only inconsistent with the freedom and development of all the rest, but corrupting to the strong man himself. It does seem, however, that when the opinions of masses of merely average men are everywhere become or becoming the dominant power, the counterpoise and corrective to that tendency would be the more and more pronounced individuality of those who stand on the higher eminences of thought. It is in these circumstances most especially that exceptional individuals, instead of being deterred, should be encouraged in acting differently from the mass. In other times there was no advantage in their doing so, unless they acted not only differently, but better. In this age, the mere example of nonconformity, the mere refusal to bend the knee to custom, is itself a service. Precisely because the tyranny of opinion is such as to make eccentricity a reproach, it is desirable, in order to break through that tyranny, that people should be eccentric. Eccentricity has always abounded when and where strength of character has abounded; and the amount of eccentricity in a society has generally been proportional to the amount of genius, mental vigor, and moral courage which it contained. That so few now dare to be eccentric marks the chief danger of the time.

*   *   *

There is one characteristic of the present direction of public opinion, peculiarly calculated to make it intolerant of any marked demonstration of individuality. The general average of mankind are not only moderate in intellect, but also moderate in inclinations: they have no tastes or wishes strong enough to incline them to do anything unusual, and they consequently do not understand those who have, and class all such with the wild and intemperate whom they are accustomed to look down upon. Now, in addition to this fact which is general, we have only to suppose that a strong movement has set in towards the improvement of morals, and it is evident what we have to expect. In these days such a movement has set in; much has actually been effected in the way of increased regularity of conduct, and discouragement of excesses; and there is a philanthropic spirit abroad, for the exercise of which there is no more inviting field than the moral and prudential improvement of our fellow creatures. These tendencies of the times cause the public to be more disposed than at most former periods to prescribe general rules of conduct, and endeavor to make everyone conform to the approved standard. And that standard, express or tacit, is to desire nothing strongly. Its ideal of character is to be without any marked character; to maim by compression, like a Chinese lady's foot, every part of human nature which stands out prominently, and tends to make the person markedly dissimilar in outline to commonplace humanity.

As is usually the case with ideals which exclude one half of what is desirable, the present standard of approbation produces only an inferior imitation of the other half. Instead of great energies guided by vigorous reason, and strong feelings strongly controlled by a conscientious will, its result is weak feelings and weak energies, which therefore can be kept in outward conformity to rule without any strength either of will or reason. Already energetic characters on any large scale are becoming merely traditional. There is now scarcely any outlet for energy in this country except business. The energy expended in this may still be regarded as considerable. What little is left from that employment, is expended on some hobby; which may be a useful, even a philanthropic hobby, but is always some one thing, and generally a thing of small dimensions. The greatness of England is now all collective: individually small, we only appear capable of anything great by our habit of combining; and with this our moral and religious philanthropies are perfectly contented. But it was men of another stamp than this that made England what it has been; and men of another stamp will be needed to prevent its decline.

The despotism of custom is everywhere the standing hindrance to human advancement, being in unceasing antagonism to that disposition to aim at something better than customary, which is called, according to circumstances, the spirit of liberty, or that of progress or improvement. The spirit of improvement is not always a spirit of liberty, for it may aim at forcing improvements on an unwilling people; and the spirit of liberty, in so far as it resists such attempts, may ally itself locally and temporarily with the opponents of improvement; but the only unfailing and permanent source of improvement is liberty, since by it there are as many possible independent centers of improvement as there are individuals. The progressive principle, however, in either shape, whether as the love of liberty or of improvement, is antagonistic to the sway of Custom, involving at least emancipation from that yoke; and the contest between the two constitutes the chief interest of the history of mankind. The greater part of the world has, properly speaking, no history, because the depotism of Custom is complete. This is the case over the whole East. Custom is there, in all things, the final appeal; justice and right mean conformity to custom; the argument of custom no one, unless some tyrant intoxicated with power, thinks of resisting. And we see the result. Those nations must once have had originality; they did not start out of the ground populous, lettered, and versed in many of the arts of life; they made themselves all this, and were then the greatest and most powerful nations of the world. What are they now? The subjects or dependants of tribes whose forefathers wandered in the forests when theirs had magnificent palaces and gorgeous temples, but over whom custom exercised only a divided rule with liberty and progress. A people, it appears, may be progressive for a certain length of time, and then stop: when does it stop? When it ceases to possess individuality. If a similar change should befall the nations of Europe, it will not be in exactly the same shape: the despotism of custom with which these nations are threatened is not precisely stationariness. It proscribes singularity, but it does not preclude change, provided all change together. We have discarded the fixed costumes of our forefathers; everyone must still dress like other people, but the fashion may change once or twice a year. We thus take care that when there is change it shall be for change's sake, and not from any idea of beauty or convenience; for the same idea of beauty or convenience would not strike all the world at the same moment, and be simultaneously thrown aside by all at another moment. But we are progressive as well as changeable: we continually make new inventions in mechanical things, and keep them until they are again superseded by better; we are eager for improvement in politics, in education, even in morals, though in this last our idea of improvement chiefly consists in persuading or forcing other people to be as good as ourselves. It is not progress that we object to; on the contrary, we flatter ourselves that we are the most progressive people who ever lived. It is individuality that we war against: we should think we had done wonders if we had made ourselves all alike; forgetting that the unlikeness of one person to another is generally the first thing which draws the attention of either to the imperfection of his own type, and the superiority of another, or the possibility, by combining the advantages of both, of producing something better than either. We have a warning example in China— a nation of much talent, and, in some respects, even wisdom, owing to the rare good fortune of having been provided at an early period with a particularly good set of customs, the work, in some measure, of men to whom even the most enlightened European must accord, under certain limitations, the title of sages and philosophers. They are remarkable, too, in the excellence of their apparatus for impressing, as far as possible, the best wisdom they possess upon every mind in the community, and securing that those who have appropriated most of it shall occupy the posts of honor and power. Surely the people who did this have discovered the secret of human progressiveness, and must have kept themselves steadily at the head of the movement of the world. On the contrary, they have become stationary—have remained so for thousands of years; and if they are ever to be farther improved, it must be by foreigners. They have succeeded beyond all hope in what English philanthropists are so industriously working at—in making a people all alike, all governing their thoughts and conduct by the same maxims and rules; and these are the fruits. The modern regime of public opinion is, in an unorganized form, what the Chinese educational and political systems are in an organized; and unless individuality shall be able successfully to assert itself against this yoke, Europe, notwithstanding its noble antecedents and its professed Christianity, will tend to become another China. . . .

1859

The Subjection of Women   After its 1869 publication in England and America, Mill's *The Subjection of Women* was quickly adopted by the leaders of the suffrage movement as the definitive analysis of the position of women in society. American suffragists sold copies of the book at their conventions; at the age of seventy-nine, American reformer Sarah Grimké went door to door in her hometown to sell one hundred copies.

The book had its roots in a tradition of libertarian thought and writing dating from the late eighteenth century. Out of this context came the first major work of feminist theory, Mary Wollstonecraft's *A Vindication of the Rights of Women* (1792). (Wollstonecraft's reputation was so scandalous, Mill avoided referring to her work.) In the early decades of the century, there was much discussion of women's rights in the Unitarian and radical circles inhabited by Mill and his wife, Harriet Taylor, who wrote her own essay on women's suffrage. By the middle of the century, "the woman question," as the Victorians called it, had become a frequent subject of writing and debate; and an organized feminist movement had begun to develop. Early reform efforts focused on the conditions of women's work, particularly in mines and factories; access to better jobs and to higher education; and married women's property rights. Women's suffrage started attracting support in the 1860s. Mill himself introduced the first parliamentary motion extending the franchise to women in 1866.

From The Subjection of Women

From *Chapter 1*

The object of this Essay is to explain as clearly as I am able, the grounds of an opinion which I have held from the very earliest period when I had formed any opinions at all on social or political matters, and which, instead of being weakened or modified, has been constantly growing stronger by the progress of reflection and the experience of life: That the principle which regulates the existing social relations between the two sexes—the legal subordination of one sex to the other—is wrong in itself, and now one of the chief hindrances to human improvement; and that it ought to be replaced by a principle of perfect equality, admitting no power or privilege on the one side, nor disability on the other.

*   *   *

Some will object, that a comparison cannot fairly be made between the government of the male sex and the forms of unjust power[1] which I have adduced in illustration of it, since these are arbitrary, and the effect of mere usurpation, while it on the contrary is natural. But was there ever any domination which did not appear natural to those who possessed it? There was a time when the division of mankind into two classes, a small one of masters and a numerous one of slaves, appeared, even to the most cultivated minds, to be a natural, and the only natural, condition of the human race. No less an intellect, and one which contributed no less to the progress of human thought, than Aristotle, held this opinion without doubt or misgiving; and rested it on the same premises on which the same assertion in regard to the dominion of men over women is usually based, namely that there are different natures among mankind, free natures, and slave natures; that the Greeks were of a free nature, the barbarian races of Thracians and Asiatics of a slave nature. But why need I go back to Aristotle? Did not the slaveowners of the Southern United States maintain the same doctrine, with all the fanaticism with which men cling to the theories that justify their passions and legitimate their personal interests? Did they not call heaven and earth to witness that the dominion of the white man over the black is natural, that the black race is by nature incapable of freedom, and marked out for slavery? some even going so far as to say that the freedom of manual laborers is an unnatural order of things anywhere. Again, the theorists of absolute monarchy have always affirmed it to be the only natural form of government; issuing from the patriarchal, which was the primitive and spontaneous form of society, framed on the model of the paternal, which is anterior to society itself, and, as they contend, the most natural authority of all. Nay, for that matter, the law of force itself, to those who could not plead any other, has always seemed the most natural of all grounds for the exercise of authority. Conquering races hold it to be Nature's own dictate that the conquered should obey the conquerors, or, as they euphoniously paraphrase it, that the feebler and more unwarlike races should submit to the braver and manlier. The smallest

---

1. As examples of unjust power Mill had cited the forceful control of slaves by slave owners or of nations by military despots.

acquaintance with human life in the middle ages, shows how supremely natural the dominion of the feudal nobility over men of low condition appeared to the nobility themselves, and how unnatural the conception seemed, of a person of the inferior class claiming equality with them, or exercising authority over them. It hardly seemed less so to the class held in subjection. The emancipated serfs and burgesses, even in their most vigorous struggles, never made any pretension to a share of authority; they only demanded more or less of limitation to the power of tyrannizing over them. So true is it that unnatural generally means only uncustomary, and that everything which is usual appears natural. The subjection of women to men being a universal custom, any departure from it quite naturally appears unnatural. But how entirely, even in this case, the feeling is dependent on custom, appears by ample experience. Nothing so much astonishes the people of distant parts of the world, when they first learn anything about England, as to be told that it is under a queen: the thing seems to them so unnatural as to be almost incredible. To Englishmen this does not seem in the least degree unnatural, because they are used to it; but they do feel it unnatural that women should be soldiers or members of Parliament. In the feudal ages, on the contrary, war and politics were not thought unnatural to women, because not unusual; it seemed natural that women of the privileged classes should be of manly character, inferior in nothing but bodily strength to their husbands and fathers. The independence of women seemed rather less unnatural to the Greeks than to other ancients, on account of the fabulous Amazons (whom they believed to be historical), and the partial example afforded by the Spartan women; who, though no less subordinate by law than in other Greek states, were more free in fact, and being trained to bodily exercises in the same manner with men, gave ample proof that they were not naturally disqualified for them. There can be little doubt that Spartan experience suggested to Plato, among many other of his doctrines, that of the social and political equality of the two sexes.[2]

But, it will be said, the rule of men over women differs from all these others in not being a rule of force: it is accepted voluntarily; women make no complaint, and are consenting parties to it. In the first place, a great number of women do not accept it. Ever since there have been women able to make their sentiments known by their writings (the only mode of publicity which society permits to them), an increasing number of them have recorded protests against their present social condition: and recently many thousands of them, headed by the most eminent women known to the public, have petitioned Parliament for their admission to the Parliamentary Suffrage.[3] The claim of women to be educated as solidly, and in the same branches of knowledge, as men, is urged with growing intensity, and with a great prospect of success; while the demand for their admission into professions and occupations hitherto closed against them, becomes every year more urgent. Though there are not in this country, as there are in the United States, periodical Conventions and an organized party to agitate for the Rights of Women,[4] there is a numerous and active Society organized and managed by

---

2. Plato's *The Republic* 5.
3. As a member of the House of Commons, Mill had introduced a petition for women's suffrage in 1866.

4. Such as the Women's Rights Convention held at Worcester, Massachusetts, in October 1850, which had occasioned an essay by Mill's wife titled *Enfranchisement of Women* (1851).

women, for the more limited object of obtaining the political franchise. Nor is it only in our own country and in America that women are beginning to protest, more or less collectively, against the disabilities under which they labor. France, and Italy, and Switzerland, and Russia now afford examples of the same thing. How many more women there are who silently cherish similar aspirations, no one can possibly know; but there are abundant tokens how many *would* cherish them, were they not so strenuously taught to repress them as contrary to the proprieties of their sex. It must be remembered, also, that no enslaved class ever asked for complete liberty at once. When Simon de Montfort[5] called the deputies of the commons to sit for the first time in Parliament, did any of them dream of demanding that an assembly, elected by their constituents, should make and destroy ministries, and dictate to the king in affairs of state? No such thought entered into the imagination of the most ambitious of them. The nobility had already these pretensions; the commons pretended to nothing but to be exempt from arbitrary taxation, and from the gross individual oppression of the king's officers. It is a political law of nature that those who are under any power of ancient origin, never begin by complaining of the power itself, but only of its oppressive exercise. There is never any want of women who complain of ill usage by their husbands. There would be infinitely more, if complaint were not the greatest of all provocatives to a repetition and increase of the ill usage. It is this which frustrates all attempts to maintain the power but protect the woman against its abuses. In no other case (except that of a child) is the person who has been proved judicially to have suffered an injury, replaced under the physical power of the culprit who inflicted it. Accordingly wives, even in the most extreme and protracted cases of bodily ill usage, hardly ever dare avail themselves of the laws made for their protection: and if, in a moment of irrepressible indignation, or by the interference of neighbors, they are induced to do so, their whole effort afterward is to disclose as little as they can, and to beg off their tyrant from his merited chastisement.

All causes, social and natural, combine to make it unlikely that women should be collectively rebellious to the power of men. They are so far in a position different from all other subject classes, that their masters require something more from them than actual service. Men do not want solely the obedience of women, they want their sentiments. All men, except the most brutish, desire to have, in the woman most nearly connected with them, not a forced slave but a willing one, not a slave merely, but a favorite. They have therefore put everything in practice to enslave their minds. The masters of all other slaves rely, for maintaining obedience, on fear; either fear of themselves, or religious fears. The masters of women wanted more than simple obedience, and they turned the whole force of education to effect their purpose. All women are brought up from the very earliest years in the belief that their ideal of character is the very opposite to that of men; not self-will, and government by self-control, but submission, and yielding to the control of others. All the moralities tell them that it is the duty of women, and all the current sentimentalities that it is their nature, to live for others; to make complete abnegation of themselves, and to have no life but in their affec-

5. English nobleman and statesman (ca. 1208–1265), who assembled a parliament in 1265 that has been called the basis of the modern House of Commons.

tions. And by their affections are meant the only ones they are allowed to have—those to the men with whom they are connected, or to the children who constitute an additional and indefeasible tie between them and a man. When we put together three things—first, the natural attraction between opposite sexes; secondly, the wife's entire dependence on the husband, every privilege or pleasure she has being either his gift, or depending entirely on his will; and lastly, that the principal object of human pursuit, consideration, and all objects of social ambition, can in general be sought or obtained by her only through him, it would be a miracle if the object of being attractive to men had not become the polar star of feminine education and formation of character. And, this great means of influence over the minds of women having been acquired, an instinct of selfishness made men avail themselves of it to the utmost as a means of holding women in subjection, by representing to them meekness, submissiveness, and resignation of all individual will into the hands of a man, as an essential part of sexual attractiveness. Can it be doubted that any of the other yokes which mankind have succeeded in breaking, would have subsisted till now if the same means had existed, and had been as sedulously used, to bow down their minds to it? If it had been made the object of the life of every young plebeian to find personal favor in the eyes of some patrician, of every young serf with some seigneur; if domestication with him, and a share of his personal affections, had been held out as the prize which they all should look out for, the most gifted and aspiring being able to reckon on the most desirable prizes; and if, when this prize had been obtained, they had been shut out by a wall of brass from all interests not centering in him, all feelings and desires but those which he shared or inculcated; would not serfs and seigneurs, plebeians and patricians, have been as broadly distinguished at this day as men and women are? and would not all but a thinker here and there, have believed the distinction to be a fundamental and unalterable fact in human nature?

The preceding considerations are amply sufficient to show that custom, however universal it may be, affords in this case no presumption, and ought not to create any prejudice, in favor of the arrangements which place women in social and political subjection to men. But I may go farther, and maintain that the course of history, and the tendencies of progressive human society, afford not only no presumption in favor of this system of inequality of rights, but a strong one against it; and that, so far as the whole course of human improvement up to this time, the whole stream of modern tendencies, warrants any inference on the subject, it is, that this relic of the past is discordant with the future, and must necessarily disappear.

For, what is the peculiar character of the modern world—the difference which chiefly distinguishes modern institutions, modern social ideas, modern life itself, from those of times long past? It is, that human beings are no longer born to their place in life, and chained down by an inexorable bond to the place they are born to, but are free to employ their faculties, and such favourable chances as offer, to achieve the lot which may appear to them most desirable.

*   *   *

The social subordination of women thus stands out an isolated fact in modern social institutions; a solitary breach of what has become their fundamental law; a single relic of an old world of thought and practice exploded in everything else, but retained in the one thing of most universal interest; as if a gigantic dolmen,[6] or a vast temple of Jupiter Olympius, occupied the site of St. Paul's and received daily worship, while the surrounding Christian churches were only resorted to on fasts and festivals. This entire discrepancy between one social fact and all those which accompany it, and the radical opposition between its nature and the progressive movement which is the boast of the modern world, and which has successively swept away everything else of an analogous character, surely affords, to a conscientious observer of human tendencies, serious matter for reflection. It raises a *primâ facie* presumption on the unfavorable side, far outweighing any which custom and usage could in such circumstances create on the favorable; and should at least suffice to make this, like the choice between republicanism and royalty, a balanced question.

The least that can be demanded is, that the question should not be considered as prejudged by existing fact and existing opinion, but open to discussion on its merits, as a question of justice and expediency: the decision on this, as on any of the other social arrangements of mankind, depending on what an enlightened estimate of tendencies and consequences may show to be most advantageous to humanity in general, without distinction of sex. And the discussion must be a real discussion, descending to foundations, and not resting satisfied with vague and general assertions. It will not do, for instance, to assert in general terms, that the experience of mankind has pronounced in favor of the existing system. Experience cannot possibly have decided between two courses, so long as there has only been experience of one. If it be said that the doctrine of the equality of the sexes rests only on theory, it must be remembered that the contrary doctrine also has only theory to rest upon. All that is proved in its favor by direct experience, is that mankind have been able to exist under it, and to attain the degree of improvement and prosperity which we now see; but whether that prosperity has been attained sooner, or is now greater, than it would have been under the other system, experience does not say. On the other hand, experience does say, that every step in improvement has been so invariably accompanied by a step made in raising the social position of women, that historians and philosophers have been led to adopt their elevation or debasement as on the whole the surest test and most correct measure of the civilization of a people or an age. Through all the progressive period of human history, the condition of women has been approaching nearer to equality with men. This does not of itself prove that the assimilation must go on to complete equality; but it assuredly affords some presumption that such is the case.

Neither does it avail anything to say that the *nature* of the two sexes adapts them to their present functions and position, and renders these appropriate to them. Standing on the ground of common sense and the constitution of the human mind, I deny that any one knows, or can know, the nature of the two sexes, as long as they have only been seen in their present relation to one another. If men had ever been found in society without women, or women without men, or if there had been a society of men and women in which the women were not under the control of the men, something might

6. Prehistoric stone monument; here associated with pagan religious rites.

have been positively known about the mental and moral differences which may be inherent in the nature of each. What is now called the nature of women is an eminently artificial thing—the result of forced repression in some directions, unnatural stimulation in others. It may be asserted without scruple, that no other class of dependents have had their character so entirely distorted from its natural proportions by their relation with their masters; for, if conquered and slave races have been, in some respects, more forcibly repressed, whatever in them has not been crushed down by an iron heel has generally been let alone, and if left with any liberty of development, it has developed itself according to its own laws; but in the case of women, a hot-house and stove cultivation has always been carried on of some of the capabilities of their nature, for the benefit and pleasure of their masters. Then, because certain products of the general vital force sprout luxuriantly and reach a great development in this heated atmosphere and under this active nurture and watering, while other shoots from the same root, which are left outside in the wintry air, with ice purposely heaped all round them, have a stunted growth, and some are burnt off with fire and disappear; men, with that inability to recognize their own work which distinguishes the unanalytic mind, indolently believe that the tree grows of itself in the way they have made it grow, and that it would die if one half of it were not kept in a vapour bath and the other half in the snow.

Of all difficulties which impede the progress of thought, and the formation of well-grounded opinions on life and social arrangements, the greatest is now the unspeakable ignorance and inattention of mankind in respect to the influences which form human character. Whatever any portion of the human species now are, or seem to be, such, it is supposed, they have a natural tendency to be: even when the most elementary knowledge of the circumstances in which they have been placed, clearly points out the causes that made them what they are. Because a cottier[7] deeply in arrears to his landlord is not industrious, there are people who think that the Irish are naturally idle. Because constitutions can be overthrown when the authorities appointed to execute them turn their arms against them, there are people who think the French incapable of free government. Because the Greeks cheated the Turks, and the Turks only plundered the Greeks, there are persons who think that the Turks are naturally more sincere: and because women, as is often said, care nothing about politics except their personalities, it is supposed that the general good is naturally less interesting to women than to men. History, which is now so much better understood than formerly, teaches another lesson: if only by showing the extraordinary susceptibility of human nature to external influences, and the extreme variableness of those of its manifestations which are supposed to be most universal and uniform. But in history, as in traveling, men usually see only what they already had in their own minds; and few learn much from history, who do not bring much with them to its study.

Hence, in regard to that most difficult question, what are the natural differences between the two sexes—a subject on which it is impossible in the present state of society to obtain complete and correct knowledge—while almost everybody dogmatizes upon it, almost all neglect and make light of

7. Tenant cottager on a small Irish farm.

the only means by which any partial insight can be obtained into it. This is, an analytic study of the most important department of psychology, the laws of the influence of circumstances on character. For, however great and apparently ineradicable the moral and intellectual differences between men and women might be, the evidence of their being natural differences could only be negative. Those only could be inferred to be natural which could not possibly be artificial—the residuum, after deducting every characteristic of either sex which can admit of being explained from education or external circumstances. The profoundest knowledge of the laws of the formation of character is indispensable to entitle any one to affirm even that there is any difference, much more what the difference is, between the two sexes considered as moral and rational beings; and since no one, as yet, has that knowledge (for there is hardly any subject which, in proportion to its importance, has been so little studied), no one is thus far entitled to any positive opinion on the subject. Conjectures are all that can at present be made; conjectures more or less probable, according as more or less authorized by such knowledge as we yet have of the laws of psychology, as applied to the formation of character.

Even the preliminary knowledge, what the differences between the sexes now are, apart from all question as to how they are made what they are, is still in the crudest and most incomplete state. Medical practitioners and physiologists have ascertained, to some extent, the differences in bodily constitution; and this is an important element to the psychologist: but hardly any medical practitioner is a psychologist. Respecting the mental characteristics of women; their observations are of no more worth than those of common men. It is a subject on which nothing final can be known, so long as those who alone can really know it, women themselves, have given but little testimony, and that little, mostly suborned. It is easy to know stupid women. Stupidity is much the same all the world over. A stupid person's notions and feelings may confidently be inferred from those which prevail in the circle by which the person is surrounded. Not so with those whose opinions and feelings are an emanation from their own nature and faculties. It is only a man here and there who has any tolerable knowledge of the character even of the women of his own family. I do not mean, of their capabilities; these nobody knows, not even themselves, because most of them have never been called out. I mean their actually existing thoughts and feelings. Many a man thinks he perfectly understands women, because he has had amatory relations with several, perhaps with many of them. If he is a good observer, and his experience extends to quality as well as quantity, he may have learnt something of one narrow department of their nature—an important department, no doubt. But of all the rest of it, few persons are generally more ignorant, because there are few from whom it is so carefully hidden. The most favorable case which a man can generally have for studying the character of a woman, is that of his own wife: for the opportunities are greater, and the cases of complete sympathy not so unspeakably rare. And in fact, this is the source from which any knowledge worth having on the subject has, I believe, generally come. But most men have not had the opportunity of studying in this way more than a single case: accordingly one can, to an almost laughable degree, infer what a man's wife is like, from his opinions about women in general. To make even this one case yield any result, the woman must be worth knowing, and the man not only a competent judge, but of a character so sympathetic in itself, and so well adapted to hers, that he can either read her mind by sympathetic intuition, or has nothing in himself which makes her shy of disclosing it. Hardly anything, I believe, can be more rare than this conjunction. It often happens that there is the most complete unity of feeling and community of interests as to all external things, yet the one has as little admission into the internal life of the other as if they were common acquaintance. Even with true affection, authority on the one side and subordination on the other prevent perfect confidence. Though nothing may be intentionally withheld, much is not shown. In the analogous relation of parent and child, the corresponding phenomenon must have been in the observation of every one. As between father and son, how many are the cases in which the father, in spite of real affection on both sides, obviously to all the world does not know, nor suspect, parts of the son's character familiar to his companions and equals. The truth is, that the position of looking up to another is extremely unpropitious to complete sincerity and openness with him. The fear of losing ground in his opinion or in his feelings is so strong, that even in an upright character, there is an unconscious tendency to show only the best side, or the side which, though not the best, is that which he most likes to see: and it may be confidently said that thorough knowledge of one another hardly ever exists, but between persons who, besides being intimates, are equals. How much more true, then, must all this be, when the one is not only under the authority of the other, but has it inculcated on her as a duty to reckon everything else subordinate to his comfort and pleasure, and to let him neither see nor feel anything coming from her, except what is agreeable to him. All these difficulties stand in the way of a man's obtaining any thorough knowledge even of the one woman whom alone, in general, he has sufficient opportunity of studying. When we further consider that to understand one woman is not necessarily to understand any other woman; that even if he could study many women of one rank, or of one country, he would not thereby understand women of other ranks or countries; and even if he did, they are still only the women of a single period of history; we may safely assert that the knowledge which men can acquire of women, even as they have been and are, without reference to what they might be, is wretchedly imperfect and superficial, and always will be so, until women themselves have told all that they have to tell.

And this time has not come; nor will it come otherwise than gradually. It is but of yesterday that women have either been qualified by literary accomplishments, or permitted by society, to tell anything to the general public. As yet very few of them dare tell anything, which men, on whom their literary success depends, are unwilling to hear. Let us remember in what manner, up to a very recent time, the expression, even by a male author, of uncustomary opinions, or what are deemed eccentric feelings, usually was, and in some degree still is, received; and we may form some faint conception under what impediments a woman, who is brought up to think custom and opinion her sovereign rule, attempts to express in books anything drawn from the depths of her own nature. The greatest woman who has left writings behind her sufficient to give her an eminent rank in the literature of her country, thought it necessary to prefix as a motto to her boldest work, "Un homme peut braver l'opinion; une femme doit s'y soumettre."[8] The greater part of what women write about women is mere sycophancy to men. In the case of unmarried women, much of it seems only intended to increase their chance of a husband. Many, both married and unmarried, overstep the mark, and inculcate a servility beyond what is desired or relished by any man, except the very vulgarest. But this is not so often the case as, even at a quite late period, it still was. Literary women are becoming more freespoken, and more willing to express their real sentiments. Unfortunately, in this country especially, they are themselves such artificial products, that their sentiments are compounded of a small element of individual observation and consciousness, and a very large one of acquired associations. This will be less and less the case, but it will remain true to a great extent, as long as social institutions do not admit the same free development of originality in women which is possible to men. When that time comes, and not before, we shall see, and not merely hear, as much as it is necessary to know of the nature of women, and the adaptation of other things to it.

*   *   *

One thing we may be certain of—that what is contrary to women's nature to do, they never will be made to do by simply giving their nature free play. The anxiety of mankind to interfere in behalf of nature, for fear lest nature should not succeed in effecting its purpose, is an altogether unnecessary solicitude. What women by nature cannot do, it is quite superfluous to forbid them from doing. What they can do, but not so well as the men who are their competitors, competition suffices to exclude them from; since nobody asks for protective duties and bounties in favor of women; it is only asked that the present bounties and protective duties in favor of men should be recalled. If women have a greater natural inclination for some things than for others, there is no need of laws or social inculcation to make the majority of them do the former in preference to the latter. Whatever women's services are most wanted for, the free play of competition will hold out the strongest inducements to them to undertake. And, as the words imply, they are most wanted for the things for which they are most fit; by the apportionment of which to them, the collective faculties of the two sexes can be applied on the whole with the greatest sum of valuable result.

The general opinion of men is supposed to be, that the natural vocation of a woman is that of a wife and mother. I say, is supposed to be, because, judging from acts—from the whole of the present constitution of society— one might infer that their opinion was the direct contrary. They might be supposed to think that the alleged natural vocation of women was of all things the most repugnant to their nature; insomuch that if they are free to do anything else—if any other means of living, or occupation of their time and faculties, is open, which has any chance of appearing desirable to them—there will not be enough of them who will be willing to accept the condition said to be natural to them. If this is the real opinion of men in general, it would be well that it should be spoken out. I should like to hear somebody openly enunciating the doctrine (it is already implied in much that

8. A man can defy what is thought; a woman must submit to it (French); the epigraph to Mme. de Staël's *Delphine*.

is written on the subject)—"It is necessary to society that women should marry and produce children. They will not do so unless they are compelled. Therefore it is necessary to compel them." The merits of the case would then be clearly defined. It would be exactly that of the slaveholders of South Carolina and Louisiana. "It is necessary that cotton and sugar should be grown. White men cannot produce them. Negroes will not, for any wages which we choose to give. Ergo[9] they must be compelled." An illustration still closer to the point is that of impressment.[1] Sailors must absolutely be had to defend the country. It often happens that they will not voluntarily enlist. Therefore there must be the power of forcing them. How often has this logic been used! and, but for one flaw in it, without doubt it would have been successful up to this day. But it is open to the retort—First pay the sailors the honest value of their labor. When you have made it as well worth their while to serve you, as to work for other employers, you will have no more difficulty than others have in obtaining their services. To this there is no logical answer except "I will not:" and as people are now not only ashamed, but are not desirous, to rob the laborer of his hire, impressment is no longer advocated. Those who attempt to force women into marriage by closing all other doors against them, lay themselves open to a similar retort. If they mean what they say, their opinion must evidently be, that men do not render the married condition so desirable to women, as to induce them to accept it for its own recommendations. It is not a sign of one's thinking the boon one offers very attractive, when one allows only Hobson's choice,[2] "that or none." And here, I believe, is the clue to the feelings of those men, who have a real antipathy to the equal freedom of women. I believe they are afraid, not lest women should be unwilling to marry, for I do not think that any one in reality has that apprehension; but lest they should insist that marriage should be on equal conditions; lest all women of spirit and capacity should prefer doing almost anything else, not in their own eyes degrading, rather than marry, when marrying is giving themselves a master, and a master too of all their earthly possessions. And truly, if this consequence were necessarily incident to marriage, I think that the apprehension would be very well founded. I agree in thinking it probable that few women, capable of anything else, would, unless under an irresistible entrainement,[3] rendering them for the time insensible to anything but itself, choose such a lot, when any other means were open to them of filling a conventionally honorable place in life: and if men are determined that the law of marriage shall be a law of despotism, they are quite right, in point of mere policy, in leaving to women only Hobson's choice. But, in that case, all that has been done in the modern world to relax the chain on the minds of women, has been a mistake. They never should have been allowed to receive a literary education. Women who read, much more women who write, are, in the existing constitution of things, a contradiction and a disturbing element: and it was wrong to bring women up with any acquirements but those of an odalisque, or of a domestic servant.

1860   1869

9. Therefore (Latin).
1. The practice of seizing men and forcing them into service as sailors.
2. A choice without an alternative, so called in ref-
erence to the practice of Thomas Hobson, who rented out horses and required every customer to take the horse nearest the door.
3. Rapture.

From Autobiography

From Chapter 5. A Crisis in My Mental History.
One Stage Onward

For some years after this time[1] I wrote very little, and nothing regularly, for publication: and great were the advantages which I derived from the intermission. It was of no common importance to me, at this period, to be able to digest and mature my thoughts for my own mind only, without any immediate call for giving them out in print. Had I gone on writing, it would have much disturbed the important transformation in my opinions and character, which took place during those years. The origin of this transformation, or at least the process by which I was prepared for it, can only be explained by turning some distance back.

From the winter of 1821, when I first read Bentham, and especially from the commencement of the *Westminster Review,* I had what might truly be called an object in life; to be a reformer of the world. My conception of my own happiness was entirely identified with this object. The personal sympathies I wished for were those of fellow laborers in this enterprise. I endeavored to pick up as many followers as I could by the way; but as a serious and permanent personal satisfaction to rest upon, my whole reliance was placed on this; and I was accustomed to felicitate myself on the certainty of a happy life which I enjoyed, through placing my happiness in something durable and distant, in which some progress might be always making, while it could never be exhausted by complete attainment. This did very well for several years, during which the general improvement going on in the world and the idea of myself as engaged with others in struggling to promote it, seemed enough to fill up an interesting and animated existence. But the time came when I awakened from this as from a dream. It was in the autumn of 1826. I was in a dull state of nerves, such as everybody is occasionally liable to; unsusceptible to enjoyment or pleasurable excitement; one of those moods when what is pleasure at other times becomes insipid or indifferent; the state, I should think, in which converts to Methodism usually are, when smitten by their first "conviction of sin." In this frame of mind it occurred to me to put the question directly to myself: "Suppose that all your objects in life were realized; that all the changes in institutions and opinions which you are looking forward to could be completely effected at this very instant: would this be a great joy and happiness to you?" And an irrepressible self-consciousness distinctly answered, "No!" At this my heart sank within me: the whole foundation on which my life was constructed fell down. All my happiness was to have been found in the continual pursuit of this end. The end had ceased to charm, and how could there ever again be any interest in the means? I seemed to have nothing left to live for.

At first I hoped that the cloud would pass away of itself; but it did not. A night's sleep, the sovereign remedy for the smaller vexations of life, had no effect on it. I awoke to a renewed consciousness of the woeful fact. I carried it with me into all companies, into all occupations. Hardly anything had power to cause me even a few minutes' oblivion of it. For some months the

---

1. I.e., 1828. Mill had been contributing articles to the *Westminster Review.*

cloud seemed to grow thicker and thicker. The lines in Coleridge's *Dejection*—I was not then acquainted with them—exactly describe my case:

> A grief without a pang, void, dark and drear,
> A drowsy, stifled, unimpassioned grief,
> Which finds no natural outlet or relief
> In word, or sigh, or tear.[2]

In vain I sought relief from my favorite books; those memorials of past nobleness and greatness from which I had always hitherto drawn strength and animation. I read them now without feeling, or with the accustomed feeling minus all its charm; and I became persuaded that my love of mankind, and of excellence for its own sake, had worn itself out. I sought no comfort by speaking to others of what I felt. If I had loved anyone sufficiently to make confiding my griefs a necessity, I should not have been in the condition I was. I felt, too, that mine was not an interesting, or in any way respectable distress. There was nothing in it to attract sympathy. Advice, if I had known where to seek it, would have been most precious. The words of Macbeth to the physician[3] often occurred to my thoughts. But there was no one on whom I could build the faintest hope of such assistance. My father, to whom it would have been natural to me to have recourse in any practical difficulties, was the last person to whom, in such a case as this, I looked for help. Everything convinced me that he had no knowledge of any such mental state as I was suffering from, and that even if he could be made to understand it, he was not the physician who could heal it. My education, which was wholly his work, had been conducted without any regard to the possibility of its ending in this result; and I saw no use in giving him the pain of thinking that his plans had failed, when the failure was probably irremediable, and, at all events, beyond the power of *his* remedies. Of other friends, I had at that time none to whom I had any hope of making my condition intelligible. It was however abundantly intelligible to myself; and the more I dwelt upon it, the more hopeless it appeared.

My course of study had led me to believe that all mental and moral feelings and qualities, whether of a good or of a bad kind, were the results of association; that we love one thing, and hate another, take pleasure in one sort of action or contemplation, and pain in another sort, through the clinging of pleasurable or painful ideas to those things, from the effect of education or of experience. As a corollary from this, I had always heard it maintained by my father, and was myself convinced, that the object of education should be to form the strongest possible associations of the salutary class; associations of pleasure with all things beneficial to the great whole, and of pain with all things hurtful to it. This doctrine appeared inexpugnable; but it now seemed to me, on retrospect, that my teachers had occupied themselves but superficially with the means of forming and keeping up these salutary associations. They seemed to have trusted altogether to the old familiar instruments, praise and blame, reward and punishment. Now, I did not doubt that by these means, begun early, and applied unremittingly, intense associations of pain and pleasure, especially of pain, might be created, and might produce

---

2. *Dejection: An Ode* 21–24.
3. Shakespeare's *Macbeth* 5.3.40–44: "Canst thou not minister to a mind diseas'd?"

desires and aversions capable of lasting undiminished to the end of life. But there must always be something artificial and casual in associations thus produced. The pains and pleasures thus forcibly associated with things are not connected with them by any natural tie; and it is therefore, I thought, essential to the durability of these associations that they should have become so intense and inveterate as to be practically indissoluble, before the habitual exercise of the power of analysis had commenced. For I now saw, or thought I saw, what I had always before received with incredulity—that the habit of analysis has a tendency to wear away the feelings: as indeed it has, when no other mental habit is cultivated, and the analyzing spirit remains without its natural complements and correctives. The very excellence of analysis (I argued) is that it tends to weaken and undermine whatever is the result of prejudice; that it enables us mentally to separate ideas which have only casually clung together: and no associations whatever could ultimately resist this dissolving force, were it not that we owe to analysis our clearest knowledge of the permanent sequences in nature; the real connections between Things, not dependent on our will and feelings; natural laws, by virtue of which, in many cases, one thing is inseparable from another in fact; which laws, in proportion as they are clearly perceived and imaginatively realized, cause our ideas of things which are always joined together in Nature to cohere more and more closely in our thoughts. Analytic habits may thus even strengthen the associations between causes and effects, means and ends, but tend altogether to weaken those which are, to speak familiarly, a *mere* matter of feeling. They are therefore (I thought) favorable to prudence and clearsightedness, but a perpetual worm at the root both of the passions and of the virtues; and, above all, fearfully undermine all desires, and all pleasures, which are the effects of association, that is, according to the theory I held, all except the purely physical and organic; of the entire insufficiency of which to make life desirable, no one had a stronger conviction than I had. These were the laws of human nature, by which, as it seemed to me, I had been brought to my present state. All those to whom I looked up were of opinion that the pleasure of sympathy with human beings, and the feelings which made the good of others, and especially of mankind on a large scale, the object of existence, were the greatest and surest sources of happiness. Of the truth of this I was convinced, but to know that a feeling would make me happy if I had it, did not give me the feeling. My education, I thought, had failed to create these feelings in sufficient strength to resist the dissolving influence of analysis, while the whole course of my intellectual cultivation had made precocious and premature analysis the inveterate habit of my mind. I was thus, as I said to myself, left stranded at the commencement of my voyage, with a well-equipped ship and a rudder, but no sail; without any real desire for the ends which I had been so carefully fitted out to work for: no delight in virtue, or the general good, but also just as little in anything else. The fountains of vanity and ambition seemed to have dried up within me, as completely as those of benevolence. I had had (as I reflected) some gratification of vanity at too early an age: I had obtained some distinction, and felt myself of some importance, before the desire of distinction and of importance had grown into a passion: and little as it was which I had attained, yet having been attained too early, like all pleasures enjoyed too soon, it had made me *blasé* and indifferent to the pursuit. Thus neither selfish nor unselfish pleasures were pleasures to me. And there seemed no power in nature sufficient to begin the formation of my character anew, and create in a mind now irretrievably analytic, fresh associations of pleasure with any of the objects of human desire.

These were the thoughts which mingled with the dry heavy dejection of the melancholy winter of 1826–7. During this time I was not incapable of my usual occupations. I went on with them mechanically, by the mere force of habit. I had been so drilled in a certain sort of mental exercise that I could still carry it on when all the spirit had gone out of it. I even composed and spoke several speeches at the debating society, how, or with what degree of success, I know not. Of four years continual speaking at that society, this is the only year of which I remember next to nothing. Two lines of Coleridge, in whom alone of all writers I have found a true description of what I felt, were often in my thoughts, not at this time (for I had never read them), but in a later period of the same mental malady:

> Work without hope draws nectar in a sieve,
> And hope without an object cannot live.[4]

In all probability my case was by no means so peculiar as I fancied it, and I doubt not that many others have passed through a similar state; but the idiosyncrasies of my education had given to the general phenomenon a special character, which made it seem the natural effect of causes that it was hardly possible for time to remove. I frequently asked myself if I could, or if I was bound to go on living, when life must be passed in this manner. I generally answered to myself, that I did not think I could possibly bear it beyond a year. When, however, not more than half that duration of time had elapsed, a small ray of light broke in upon my gloom. I was reading, accidentally, Marmontel's *Mémoires*,[5] and came to the passage which relates his father's death, the distressed position of the family, and the sudden inspiration by which he, then a mere boy, felt and made them feel that he would be everything to them—would supply the place of all that they had lost. A vivid conception of that scene and its feelings came over me, and I was moved to tears. From this moment my burden grew lighter. The oppression of the thought that all feeling was dead within me was gone. I was no longer hopeless: I was not a stock or a stone. I had still, it seemed, some of the material out of which all worth of character, and all capacity for happiness, are made. Relieved from my ever present sense of irremediable wretchedness, I gradually found that the ordinary incidents of life could again give me some pleasure; that I could again find enjoyment, not intense, but sufficient for cheerfulness, in sunshine and sky, in books, in conversation, in public affairs; and that there was, once more, excitement, though of a moderate kind, in exerting myself for my opinions, and for the public good. Thus the cloud gradually drew off, and I again enjoyed life: and though I had several relapses, some of which lasted many months, I never again was as miserable as I had been.

The experiences of this period had two very marked effects on my opinions and character. In the first place, they led me to adopt a theory of life, very

---

4. The last two lines of Coleridge's short poem *Work without Hope*.

5. J. F. Marmontel (1723–1799), whose *Mémoires* were published in 1804.

unlike that on which I had before acted, and having much in common with what at that time I certainly had never heard of, the anti-self-consciousness theory of Carlyle.[6] I never, indeed, wavered in the conviction that happiness is the test of all rules of conduct, and the end of life. But I now thought that this end was only to be attained by not making it the direct end. Those only are happy (I thought) who have their minds fixed on some object other than their own happiness; on the happiness of others, on the improvement of mankind, even on some art or pursuit, followed not as a means, but as itself an ideal end. Aiming thus at something else, they find happiness by the way. The enjoyments of life (such was now my theory) are sufficient to make it a pleasant thing, when they are taken *en passant*,[7] without being made a principal object. Once make them so, and they are immediately felt to be insufficient. They will not bear a scrutinizing examination. Ask yourself whether you are happy, and you cease to be so. The only chance is to treat, not happiness, but some end external to it, as the purpose of life. Let your self-consciousness, your scrutiny, your self-interrogation exhaust themselves on that; and if otherwise fortunately circumstanced you will inhale happiness with the air you breathe, without dwelling on it or thinking about it, without either forestalling it in imagination, or putting it to flight by fatal questioning. This theory now became the basis of my philosophy of life. And I still hold to it as the best theory for all those who have but a moderate degree of sensibility and of capacity for enjoyment, that is, for the great majority of mankind.

The other important change which my opinions at this time underwent was that I, for the first time, gave its proper place, among the prime necessities of human well-being, to the internal culture of the individual. I ceased to attach almost exclusive importance to the ordering of outward circumstances, and the training of the human being for speculation and for action.

I had now learnt by experience that the passive susceptibilities needed to be cultivated as well as the active capacities, and required to be nourished and enriched as well as guided. I did not, for an instant, lose sight of, or undervalue, that part of the truth which I had seen before; I never turned recreant to intellectual culture, or ceased to consider the power and practice of analysis as an essential condition both of individual and of social improvement. But I thought that it had consequences which required to be corrected, by joining other kinds of cultivation with it. The maintenance of a due balance among the faculties now seemed to me of primary importance. The cultivation of the feelings became one of the cardinal points in my ethical and philosophical creed. And my thoughts and inclinations turned in an increasing degree toward whatever seemed capable of being instrumental to that object.

I now began to find meaning in the things which I had read or heard about the importance of poetry and art as instruments of human culture. But it was some time longer before I began to know this by personal experience. The only one of the imaginative arts in which I had from childhood taken great pleasure was music; the best effect of which (and in this it surpasses perhaps every other art) consists in exciting enthusiasm; in winding up to a

---

6. See *The Everlasting Yea* (p. 1089), of Carlyle's *Sartor Resartus*.

7. In passing (Latin).

high pitch those feelings of an elevated kind which are already in the character, but to which this excitement gives a glow and a fervor, which, though transitory at its utmost height, is precious for sustaining them at other times. This effect of music I had often experienced; but like all my pleasurable susceptibilities it was suspended during the gloomy period. I had sought relief again and again from this quarter, but found none. After the tide had turned, and I was in process of recovery, I had been helped forward by music, but in a much less elevated manner. I at this time first became acquainted with Weber's *Oberon*,[8] and the extreme pleasure which I drew from its delicious melodies did me good, by showing me a source of pleasure to which I was as susceptible as ever. The good, however, was much impaired by the thought that the pleasure of music (as is quite true of such pleasure as this was, that of mere tune) fades with familiarity, and requires either to be revived by intermittence, or fed by continual novelty. And it is very characteristic both of my then state, and of the general tone of my mind at this period of my life, that I was seriously tormented by the thought of the exhaustibility of musical combinations. The octave consists only of five tones and two semitones, which can be put together in only a limited number of ways, of which but a small proportion are beautiful: most of these, it seemed to me, must have been already discovered, and there could not be room for a long succession of Mozarts and Webers, to strike out, as these had done, entirely new and surpassingly rich veins of musical beauty. This source of anxiety may, perhaps, be thought to resemble that of the philosophers of Laputa,[9] who feared lest the sun should be burnt out. It was, however, connected with the best feature in my character, and the only good point to be found in my very unromantic and in no way honorable distress. For though my dejection, honestly looked at, could not be called other than egotistical, produced by the ruin, as I thought, of my fabric of happiness, yet the destiny of mankind in general was ever in my thoughts, and could not be separated from my own. I felt that the flaw in my life must be a flaw in life itself; that the question was whether, if the reformers of society and government could succeed in their objects, and every person in the community were free and in a state of physical comfort, the pleasures of life, being no longer kept up by struggle and privation, would cease to be pleasures. And I felt that unless I could see my way to some better hope than this for human happiness in general, my dejection must continue; but that if I could see such an outlet, I should then look on the world with pleasure; content as far as I was myself concerned, with any fair share of the general lot.

This state of my thoughts and feelings made the fact of my reading Wordsworth for the first time (in the autumn of 1828), an important event in my life. I took up the collection of his poems from curiosity, with no expectation of mental relief from it, though I had before resorted to poetry with that hope. In the worst period of my depression, I had read through the whole of Byron (then new to me), to try whether a poet, whose peculiar department was supposed to be that of the intenser feelings, could rouse any feeling in me. As might be expected, I got no good from this reading, but the reverse. The poet's state of mind was too like my own. His was the lament of a man

---

8. A romantic opera composed by Carl Maria von Weber (1786–1826).

9. In part 3 of Swift's *Gulliver's Travels*.

who had worn out all pleasures, and who seemed to think that life, to all who possess the good things of it, must necessarily be the vapid, uninteresting thing which I found it. His Harold and Manfred had the same burden on them which I had; and I was not in a frame of mind to derive any comfort from the vehement sensual passion of his Giaours, or the sullenness of his Laras.[1] But while Byron was exactly what did not suit my condition, Wordsworth was exactly what did. I had looked into *The Excursion*[2] two or three years before, and found little in it; and I should probably have found as little had I read it at this time. But the miscellaneous poems, in the two-volume edition of 1815 (to which little of value was added in the latter part of the author's life), proved to be the precise thing for my mental wants at that particular juncture.

In the first place, these poems addressed themselves powerfully to one of the strongest of my pleasurable susceptibilities, the love of rural objects and natural scenery; to which I had been indebted not only for much of the pleasure of my life, but quite recently for relief from one of my longest relapses into depression. In this power of rural beauty over me, there was a foundation laid for taking pleasure in Wordsworth's poetry; the more so, as his scenery lies mostly among mountains, which, owing to my early Pyrenean excursion,[3] were my ideal of natural beauty. But Wordsworth would never have had any great effect on me, if he had merely placed before me beautiful pictures of natural scenery. Scott does this still better than Wordsworth, and a very second-rate landscape does it more effectually than any poet. What made Wordsworth's poems a medicine for my state of mind, was that they expressed, not mere outward beauty, but states of feeling, and of thought colored by feeling, under the excitement of beauty. They seemed to be the very culture of the feelings, which I was in quest of. In them I seemed to draw from a source of inward joy, of sympathetic and imaginative pleasure, which could be shared in by all human beings; which had no connection with struggle or imperfection, but would be made richer by every improvement in the physical or social condition of mankind. From them I seemed to learn what would be the perennial sources of happiness, when all the greater evils of life shall have been removed. And I felt myself at once better and happier as I came under their influence. There have certainly been, even in our own age, greater poets than Wordsworth; but poetry of deeper and loftier feeling could not have done for me at that time what his did. I needed to be made to feel that there was real, permanent happiness in tranquil contemplation. Wordsworth taught me this, not only without turning away from, but with a greatly increased interest in the common feelings and common destiny of human beings. And the delight which these poems gave me proved that with culture of this sort, there was nothing to dread from the most confirmed habit of analysis. At the conclusion of the Poems came the famous *Ode*, falsely called Platonic, *Intimations of Immortality*: in which, along with more than his usual sweetness of melody and rhythm, and along with the two passages of grand imagery but bad philosophy so often quoted,

---

1. The heroes of some of Byron's early poems were usually gloomy and self-preoccupied. Mill refers here to *Childe Harold's Pilgrimage* (1812–18), *Manfred* (1817), *The Giaour* (1813), and *Lara* (1814).
2. A long meditative poem by Wordsworth, pub-

lished in 1814.
3. At fifteen, Mill had been deeply affected by the landscape of the Pyrenees in Spain, a mountainous region that also made a strong impression on Tennyson.

I found that he too had had similar experience to mine; that he also had felt that the first freshness of youthful enjoyment of life was not lasting; but that he had sought for compensation, and found it, in the way in which he was now teaching me to find it. The result was that I gradually, but completely, emerged from my habitual depression, and was never again subject to it. I long continued to value Wordsworth less according to his intrinsic merits than by the measure of what he had done for me. Compared with the greatest poets, he may be said to be the poet of unpoetical natures, possessed of quiet and contemplative tastes. But unpoetical natures are precisely those which require poetic cultivation. This cultivation Wordsworth is much more fitted to give than poets who are intrinsically far more poets than he.

∗   ∗   ∗

1873

ELIZABETH BARRETT BROWNING
1806–1861

During her lifetime, Elizabeth Barrett Browning was England's most famous woman poet. Passionately admired by contemporaries as diverse as Ruskin, Swinburne, and Emily Dickinson for her moral and emotional ardor and her energetic engagement with the issues of her day, she was more famous than her husband, Robert Browning, at the time of her death. Her work fell into disrepute with the modernist reaction against what was seen as the inappropriate didacticism and rhetorical excess of Victorian poetry; but recently scholars interested in her exploration of what it means to be a woman poet have restored her status as a major writer.

Barrett Browning received an unusual education for a woman of her time. Availing herself of her brother's tutor, she studied Latin and Greek. She read voraciously in history, philosophy, and literature and began to write poetry from an early age—her first volume of poetry was published when she was thirteen. But as her intellectual and literary powers matured, her personal life became increasingly circumscribed both by ill health and by a tyrannically protective father, who had forbidden any of his eleven children to marry. By the age of thirty-nine, Elizabeth Barrett was a prominent woman of letters who lived in semiseclusion as an invalid in her father's house, where she occasionally received visitors in her room. One of these visitors was Robert Browning, who, moved by his admiration of her poetry, wrote to tell her "I do as I say, love these books with all my heart—and I love you too." He thereby initiated a courtship that culminated in 1846 in their secret marriage and elopement to Italy, for which her father never forgave her. Once in Italy, she regained much health and strength, bearing and raising a son, Pen, to whom she was ardently devoted, and becoming deeply involved in Italian nationalist politics. She and her husband made their home in Florence, at the house called Casa Guidi, where she died in 1861.

Barrett Browning's poetry is characterized by a fervent moral sensibility. In her early work, she tended to use the visionary modes of Romantic narrative poetry, but she turned increasingly to contemporary topics, particularly liberal causes of her day. For example, in 1843, when government investigations had exposed the exploitation of children employed in coal mines and factories, she wrote *The Cry of the Children*, a powerful indictment of the appalling use of child labor. Like Harriet Beecher Stowe in *Uncle Tom's Cabin*, Barrett Browning uses literature as a tool of social protest and reform. In later poems she took up the cause of the *risorgimento*, the movement to unify Italy as a nation-state, in which Italy's struggle for freedom and identity found resonance with her own.

For many years Elizabeth Barrett Browning was best known for her *Sonnets from the Portuguese*, a sequence of forty-four sonnets presented under the guise of a translation from the Portuguese language, in which she recorded the stages of her love for Robert Browning. But increasingly, her verse novel *Aurora Leigh* (1857) has attracted critical attention. The poem depicts the growth of a woman poet and is thus, as Cora Kaplan observes, the first work in English by a woman writer in which the heroine herself is an author. When Barrett Browning first envisioned the poem, she wrote, "My chief *intention* just now is the writing of a sort of novel-poem . . . running into the midst of our conventions, and rushing into drawing-rooms and the like 'where angels fear to tread'; and so, meeting face to face and without mask the Humanity of the age, and speaking the truth as I conceive of it out plainly." The poem is a female *Prelude* (cf. Wordsworth's *The Prelude*), a portrait of the artist as a young woman committed to a socially inclusive realist art. It is a daring work both in its presentation of social issues concerning women and in its claims for Aurora's poetic vocation; on her twentieth birthday, to pursue her career as a poet, Aurora refuses a proposal of marriage from her cousin Romney, who wants her to be his helpmate in the liberal causes he has embraced. Later in the poem, she rescues a fallen woman and takes her to Italy, where they settle together and confront a chastened Romney.

Immensely popular in its own day, *Aurora Leigh* had extravagant admirers (like Ruskin, who asserted that it was the greatest poem written in English) and critics who found fault with both its poetry and its morality. With its crowded canvas and melodramatic plot, it seems closer to the novel than to poetry, but it is important to view the poem in the context of the debate about appropriate poetic subject that engaged other Victorian poets. Unlike Arnold, who believed that the present age had not produced actions heroic enough to be the subjects of a great poetry, and unlike Tennyson, who used Arthurian legend to represent contemporary concerns, Barrett Browning felt that the present age contained the materials for an epic poetry. Virginia Woolf writes that "Elizabeth Barrett was inspired by a flash of true genius when she rushed into the drawing-room and said that here, where we live and work, is the true place for the poet." And whatever its faults, *Aurora Leigh* succeeds in giving us what Woolf describes as "a sense of life in general, of people who are unmistakably Victorian, wrestling with the problems of their own time, all brightened, intensified, and compacted by the fire of poetry. . . . Aurora Leigh, with her passionate interest in social questions, her conflict as artist and woman, her longing for knowledge and freedom, is the true daughter of her age."

The Cry of the Children[1]

"Φεῦ, φεῦ, τί προσδέρκεσθέ μ' ὄμμασιν, τέκνα;"
—*Medea*[2]

Do ye hear the children weeping, O my brothers,
     Ere the sorrow comes with years?

1. Barrett Browning wrote *The Cry of the Children* in response to the report of a parliamentary commission written by her friend R. H. Horne on the labor of children in mines and factories. Many of the details of Barrett Browning's poem derive from the report.
2. Alas, my children, why do you look at me? (Greek), from Euripides' tragedy *Medea*. Medea speaks these lines when she kills her children in vengeance.

They are leaning their young heads against their mothers,
    And *that* cannot stop their tears.
5 The young lambs are bleating in the meadows,
    The young birds are chirping in the nest,
The young fawns are playing with the shadows,
    The young flowers are blowing toward the west—
But the young, young children, O my brothers,
10   They are weeping bitterly!
They are weeping in the playtime of the others,
    In the country of the free.

Do you question the young children in the sorrow
    Why their tears are falling so?
15 The old man may weep for his to-morrow
    Which is lost in Long Ago;
The old tree is leafless in the forest,
    The old year is ending in the frost,
The old wound, if stricken, is the sorest,
20   The old hope is hardest to be lost:
But the young, young children, O my brothers,
    Do you ask them why they stand
Weeping sore before the bosoms of their mothers,
    In our happy Fatherland?

25 They look up with their pale and sunken faces,
    And their looks are sad to see,
For the man's hoary anguish draws and presses
    Down the cheeks of infancy;
"Your old earth," they say, "is very dreary,"
30   "Our young feet," they say, "are very weak;
Few paces have we taken, yet are weary—
    Our grave-rest is very far to seek:
Ask the aged why they weep, and not the children,
    For the outside earth is cold,
35 And we young ones stand without, in our bewildering,
    And the graves are for the old."

"True," say the children, "it may happen
    That we die before our time:
Little Alice died last year, her grave is shapen
40   Like a snowball, in the rime.
We looked into the pit prepared to take her:
    Was no room for any work in the close clay!
From the sleep wherein she lieth none will wake her,
    Crying, 'Get up, little Alice! it is day.'
45 If you listen by that grave, in sun and shower,
    With your ear down, little Alice never cries;
Could we see her face, be sure we should not know her,
    For the smile has time for growing in her eyes:
And merry go her moments, lulled and stilled in
50   The shroud by the kirk° chime.   *church*

It is good when it happens," say the children,
    "That we die before our time."

Alas, alas, the children! they are seeking
    Death in life, as best to have:
55 They are binding up their hearts away from breaking,
    With a ceremen° from the grave.   *shroud*
Go out, children, from the mine and from the city,
    Sing out, children, as the little thrushes do;
Pluck your handfuls of the meadow-cowslips pretty,
60   Laugh aloud, to feel your fingers let them through!
But they answer, "Are your cowslips of the meadows
    Like our weeds anear the mine?
Leave us quiet in the dark of the coal-shadows,
    From your pleasures fair and fine!

65 "For oh," say the children, "we are weary,
    And we cannot run or leap;
If we cared for any meadows, it were merely
    To drop down in them and sleep.
Our knees tremble sorely in the stooping,
70   We fall upon our faces, trying to go;
And, underneath our heavy eyelids drooping,
    The reddest flower would look as pale as snow.
For, all day, we drag our burden tiring
    Through the coal-dark, underground;
75 Or, all day, we drive the wheels of iron
    In the factories, round and round.

"For, all day, the wheels are droning, turning;
    Their wind comes in our faces,
Till our hearts turn, our heads with pulses burning,
80   And the walls turn in their places:
Turns the sky in the high window blank and reeling,
    Turns the long light that drops adown the wall,
Turn the black flies that crawl along the ceiling,
    All are turning, all the day, and we with all.
85 And all day, the iron wheels are droning,
    And sometimes we could pray,
'O ye wheels,' (breaking out in a mad moaning)
    'Stop! be silent for to-day!' "

Ay, be silent! Let them hear each other breathing
90   For a moment, mouth to mouth!
Let them touch each other's hands, in a fresh wreathing
    Of their tender human youth!
Let them feel that this cold metallic motion
    Is not all the life God fashions or reveals:
95 Let them prove their living souls against the notion
    That they live in you, or under you, O wheels!
Still, all day, the iron wheels go onward,
    Grinding life down from its mark;

And the children's souls, which God is calling sunward,
100   Spin on blindly in the dark.

Now tell the poor young children; O my brothers,
      To look up to Him and pray;
So the blessed One who blesseth all the others,
      Will bless them another day.
105 They answer, "Who is God that He should hear us,
      While the rushing of the iron wheels is stirred?
When we sob aloud, the human creatures near us
      Pass by, hearing not, or answer not a word.
And *we* hear not (for the wheels in their resounding)
110   Strangers speaking at the door:
Is it likely God, with angels singing round Him,
      Hears our weeping any more?

Two words, indeed, of praying we remember,
      And at midnight's hour of harm,
115 'Our Father,' looking upward in the chamber,
      We say softly for a charm.
We know no other words except 'Our Father.'
      And we think that, in some pause of angels' song,
God may pluck them with the silence sweet to gather,
120   And hold both within His right hand which is strong.
'Our Father!' If He heard us, He would surely
      (For they call Him good and mild)
Answer, smiling down the steep world very purely,
      'Come and rest with me, my child.'

125 "But, no!" say the children, weeping faster,
      "He is speechless as a stone:
And they tell us, of His image is the master
      Who commands us to work on.
Go to!" say the children,— "up in Heaven,
130   Dark, wheel-like, turning clouds are all we find.
Do not mock us; grief has made us unbelieving:
      We look up for God, but tears have made us blind."
Do you hear the children weeping and disproving,
      O my brothers, what ye preach?
135 For God's possible is taught by His world's loving,
      And the children doubt of each.

And well may the children weep before you!
      They are weary ere they run;
They have never seen the sunshine, nor the glory
140   Which is brighter than the sun.
They know the grief of man, without its wisdom;
      They sink in man's despair, without its calm;
Are slaves, without the liberty in Christdom,
      Are martyrs, by the pang without the palm:
145 Are worn as if with age, yet unretrievingly
      The harvest of its memories cannot reap,—

Are orphans of the earthly love and heavenly.
    Let them weep! let them weep!

They look up with their pale and sunken faces,
150   And their look is dread to see,
For they mind you of their angels in high places,
    With eyes turned on Deity.
"How long," they say, "how long, O cruel nation,
    Will you stand, to move the world, on a child's heart,—
155 Stifle down with a mailed heel its palpitation,
    And tread onward to your throne amid the mart?
Our blood splashes upward, O gold-heaper,
    And your purple shows your path!
But the child's sob in the silence curses deeper
160   Than the strong man in his wrath."

1843

To George Sand[1]

A Desire

Thou large-brained woman and large-hearted man,
Self-called George Sand! whose soul, amid the lions
Of thy tumultuous senses, moans defiance
And answers roar for roar, as spirits can:
5   I would some mild miraculous thunder ran
Above the applauded circus,[2] in appliance
Of thine own nobler nature's strength and science,
Drawing two pinions, white as wings of swan,
From thy strong shoulders, to amaze the place
10 With holier light! that thou to woman's claim
And man's, mightst join beside the angel's grace
Of a pure genius sanctified from blame,
Till child and maiden pressed to thine embrace
To kiss upon thy lips a stainless fame.

1844

To George Sand

A Recognition

True genius, but true woman! dost deny
The woman's nature with a manly scorn,

1. French Romantic novelist (1804–1876), famous for her unconventional ideas and behavior. Barrett Browning discovered her writing when she was an invalid, "a prisoner," and asserts that Sand, together with Balzac, "kept the color in my life." Barrett Browning defended Sand's genius to her less-sympathetic friends, who were critical of Sand's morality; she writes to her friend Mary Russell Mitford, a contemporary novelist and dramatist, "She is eloquent as a fallen angel. . . . A true woman of genius!—but of a womanhood tired of itself, and scorned by *her*, while she bears it burning above her head."
2. A Roman spectacle that might include such things as combats with lions.

And break away the gauds° and armlets worn   *ornaments*
By weaker women in captivity?
5 Ah, vain denial! that revolted cry
Is sobbed in by a woman's voice forlorn,—
Thy woman's hair, my sister, all unshorn
Floats back dishevelled strength in agony,
Disproving thy man's name: and while before
10 The world thou burnest in a poet-fire,
We see thy woman-heart beat evermore
Through the large flame. Beat purer, heart, and higher,
Till God unsex thee on the heavenly shore
Where unincarnate spirits purely aspire!

1844

From Sonnets from the Portuguese

21

Say over again, and yet once over again,
That thou dost love me. Though the word repeated
Should seem "a cuckoo song,"[1] as thou dost treat it,
Remember, never to the hill or plain,
5 Valley and wood, without her cuckoo strain
Comes the fresh Spring in all her green completed.
Belovèd, I, amid the darkness greeted
By a doubtful spirit voice, in that doubt's pain
Cry, "Speak once more—thou lovest!" Who can fear
10 Too many stars, though each in heaven shall roll,
Too many flowers, though each shall crown the year?
Say thou dost love me, love me, love me—toll
The silver iterance!°—only minding, Dear,   *repetition*
To love me also in silence with thy soul.

22

When our two souls stand up erect and strong,
Face to face, silent, drawing nigh and nigher,
Until the lengthening wings break into fire
At either curvèd point—what bitter wrong
5 Can the earth do to us, that we should not long
Be here contented? Think. In mounting higher,
The angels would press on us and aspire
To drop some golden orb of perfect song
Into our deep, dear silence. Let us stay
10 Rather on earth, Belovèd,—where the unfit
Contrarious moods of men recoil away
And isolate pure spirits, and permit
A place to stand and love in for a day,
With darkness and the death-hour rounding it.

1. The cuckoo has a repeating call.

32

The first time that the sun rose on thine oath
To love me, I looked forward to the moon
To slacken all those bonds which seemed too soon
And quickly tied to make a lasting troth.
5   Quick-loving hearts, I thought, may quickly loathe;
And, looking on myself, I seemed not one
For such man's love!—more like an out-of-tune
Worn viol, a good singer would be wroth
To spoil his song with, and which, snatched in haste,
10 Is laid down at the first ill-sounding note.
I did not wrong myself so, but I placed
A wrong on *thee*. For perfect strains may float
'Neath master-hands, from instruments defaced—
And great souls, at one stroke, may do and dote.

43

How do I love thee? Let me count the ways.
I love thee to the depth and breadth and height
My soul can reach, when feeling out of sight
For the ends of Being and ideal Grace.
5   I love thee to the level of everyday's
Most quiet need, by sun and candlelight.
I love thee freely, as men strive for Right;
I love thee purely, as they turn from Praise.
I love thee with the passion put to use
10 In my old griefs, and with my childhood's faith.
I love thee with a love I seemed to lose
With my lost saints—I love thee with the breath,
Smiles, tears, of all my life!—and, if God choose,
I shall but love thee better after death.

1845–47   1850

From Aurora Leigh

From *Book 1*

[THE FEMININE EDUCATION OF AURORA LEIGH][1]

Then, land!—then, England! oh, the frosty cliffs[2]
Looked cold upon me. Could I find a home
Among those mean red houses through the fog?
And when I heard my father's language first
255 From alien lips which had no kiss for mine

---

1. Aurora Leigh, the only child of an Italian mother and an English father, was raised in Italy by her father since her mother's death when Aurora was four years old. When she was thirteen her father also died, and the orphaned girl has been sent to England to live with her father's maiden sister, who is to be responsible for the girl's education.
2. The white chalk cliffs at Dover.

I wept aloud, then laughed, then wept, then wept,
And some one near me said the child was mad
Through much sea-sickness. The train swept us on:
Was this my father's England? the great isle?
260   The ground seemed cut up from the fellowship
Of verdure, field from field,[3] as man from man;
The skies themselves looked low and positive,
As almost you could touch them with a hand,
And dared to do it they were so far off
265   From God's celestial crystals;[4] all things blurred
And dull and vague. Did Shakespeare and his mates
Absorb the light here?—not a hill or stone
With heart to strike a radiant colour up
Or active outline on the indifferent air.

270   I think I see my father's sister stand
Upon the hall-step of her country-house
To give me welcome. She stood straight and calm,
Her somewhat narrow forehead braided tight
As if for taming accidental thoughts
275   From possible pulses;[5] brown hair pricked with gray
By frigid use of life (she was not old,
Although my father's elder by a year),
A nose drawn sharply, yet in delicate lines;
A close mild mouth, a little soured about
280   The ends, through speaking unrequited loves
Or peradventure niggardly half-truths;
Eyes of no colour,—once they might have smiled,
But never, never have forgot themselves
In smiling; cheeks, in which was yet a rose
285   Of perished summers, like a rose in a book,
Kept more for ruth° than pleasure,—if past bloom,   *remorse*
Past fading also.
                 She had lived, we'll say,
A harmless life, she called a virtuous life,
A quiet life, which was not life at all
290   (But that, she had not lived enough to know),
Between the vicar and the county squires,
The lord-lieutenant[6] looking down sometimes
From the empyrean to assure their souls
Against chance vulgarisms, and, in the abyss,
295   The apothecary,[7] looked on once a year
To prove their soundness of humility.
The poor-club[8] exercised her Christian gifts
Of knitting stockings, stitching petticoats,
Because we are of one flesh, after all,
300   And need one flannel[9] (with a proper sense

3. English fields were separated from each other by hedgerows.
4. Perhaps a reference to the ancient notion that the sky was composed of several crystalline spheres orbiting around the earth.
5. I.e., pulsation in her temples from excitement.

6. Governor of the county.
7. Pharmacist, who in England at the time could prescribe as well as sell medicine.
8. Club devoted to making things for the poor.
9. I.e., flannel petticoat.

Of difference in the quality)—and still
The book-club, guarded from your modern trick
Of shaking dangerous questions from the crease,[1]
Preserved her intellectual. She had lived
305 A sort of cage-bird life, born in a cage,
Accounting that to leap from perch to perch
Was act and joy enough for any bird.
Dear heaven, how silly are the things that live
In thickets, and eat berries!
                                I, alas,
310 A wild bird scarcely fledged, was brought to her cage,
And she was there to meet me. Very kind.
Bring the clean water, give out the fresh seed.

She stood upon the steps to welcome me,
Calm, in black garb. I clung about her neck,—
315 Young babes, who catch at every shred of wool
To draw the new light closer, catch and cling
Less blindly. In my ears my father's word
Hummed ignorantly, as the sea in shells,
"Love, love, my child." She, black there with my grief,
320 Might feel my love— she was his sister once—
I clung to her. A moment she seemed moved,
Kissed me with cold lips, suffered me to cling,
And drew me feebly through the hall into
The room she sat in.
                        There, with some strange spasm
325 Of pain and passion, she wrung loose my hands
Imperiously, and held me at arm's length,
And with two grey-steel naked-bladed eyes
Searched through my face,—ay, stabbed it through and through,
Through brows and cheeks and chin, as if to find
330 A wicked murderer in my innocent face,
If not here, there perhaps. Then, drawing breath,
She struggled for her ordinary calm—
And missed it rather,—told me not to shrink,
As if she had told me not to lie or swear,—
335 "She loved my father and would love me too
As long as I deserved it." Very kind.

I understood her meaning afterward;
She thought to find my mother in my face,
And questioned it for that. For she, my aunt,
340 Had loved my father truly, as she could,
And hated, with the gall of gentle souls,
My Tuscan[2] mother who had fooled away
A wise man from wise courses, a good man
From obvious duties, and, depriving her,
345 His sister, of the household precedence,

---

1. The fold between two pages of a book, which had to be cut to open the pages. Presumably more modern books revealed more dangerous material when the crease was cut.
2. From Tuscany, a region in central Italy.

Had wronged his tenants, robbed his native land,
And made him mad, alike by life and death,
In love and sorrow. She had pored° for years   *pored over*
What sort of woman could be suitable
350   To her sort of hate, to entertain it with,
And so, her very curiosity
Became hate too, and all the idealism
She ever used in life was used for hate,
Till hate, so nourished, did exceed at last
355   The love from which it grew, in strength and heat,
And wrinkled her smooth conscience with a sense
Of disputable virtue (say not, sin)
When Christian doctrine was enforced at church.

And thus my father's sister was to me
360   My mother's hater. From that day she did
Her duty to me (I appreciate it
In her own word as spoken to herself),
Her duty, in large measure, well pressed out
But measured always. She was generous, bland,
365   More courteous than was tender, gave me still
The first place,—as if fearful that God's saints
Would look down suddenly and say "Herein
You missed a point, I think, through lack of love."
Alas, a mother never is afraid
370   Of speaking angerly to any child,
Since love, she knows, is justified of love.
And I, I was a good child on the whole,
A meek and manageable child. Why not?
I did not live, to have the faults of life:
375   There seemed more true life in my father's grave
Than in all England. Since *that* threw me off
Who fain would cleave (his latest will, they say,
Consigned me to his land), I only thought
Of lying quiet there where I was thrown
380   Like sea-weed on the rocks, and suffering her
To prick me to a pattern with her pin,[3]
Fibre from fibre, delicate leaf from leaf,
And dry out from my drowned anatomy
The last sea-salt left in me.
                    So it was.
385   I broke the copious curls upon my head
In braids, because she liked smooth-ordered hair.
I left off saying my sweet Tuscan words
Which still at any stirring of the heart
Came up to float across the English phrase
390   As lilies (*Bene* or *Che che*[4]), because
She liked my father's child to speak his tongue.
I learnt the collects[5] and the catechism,

---

3. As in embroidery.
4. No, no, indeed (Italian). *"Bene"*: it is well (Italian).

5. Seasonal opening prayers in the Anglican Church service.

The creeds,[6] from Athanasius back to Nice,
The Articles, the Tracts *against* the times[7]
395 (By no means Buonaventure's "Prick of Love"[8]),
And various popular synopses of
Inhuman doctrines never taught by John,[9]
Because she liked instructed piety.
I learnt my complement of classic French
400 (Kept pure of Balzac and neologism[1])
And German also, since she liked a range
Of liberal education,—tongues,° not books.   *languages*
I learnt a little algebra, a little
Of the mathematics,—brushed with extreme flounce
405 The circle of the sciences, because
She misliked women who are frivolous.
I learnt the royal genealogies
Of Oviedo,[2] the internal laws
Of the Burmese empire,—by how many feet
410 Mount Chimborazo outsoars Teneriffe,
What navigable river joins itself
To Lara,[3] and what census of the year five
Was taken at Klagenfurt,[4]—because she liked
A general insight into useful facts.
415 I learnt much music,—such as would have been
As quite impossible in Johnson's day[5]
As still it might be wished—fine sleights of hand
And unimagined fingering, shuffling off
The hearer's soul through hurricanes of notes
420 To a noisy Tophet;° and I drew . . . costumes   *Hell*
From French engravings, nereids° neatly draped   *sea nymphs*
(With smirks of simmering godship): I washed in[6]
Landscapes from nature (rather say, washed out).
I danced the polka and Cellarius,[7]
425 Spun glass, stuffed birds, and modeled flowers in wax,
Because she liked accomplishments in girls.
I read a score of books on womanhood
To prove, if women do not think at all,
They may teach thinking (to a maiden aunt
430 Or else the author),—books that boldly assert
Their right of comprehending husband's talk
When not too deep, and even of answering

6. Articles of Christian faith such as those proclaimed at the early church council held at Nicaea.
7. In the 1830s leaders of the conservative High Church party, such as John Henry Newman, had published *Tracts for the Times*, which expounded arguments against efforts by liberals to modernize the Anglican Church. Aurora's version of the title is hence ironic. "Articles": the thirty-nine articles are the principles of faith of the Church of England.
8. St. Bonaventure's doctrine that the power of the heart to love leads to higher illumination than the power of the mind to reason.
9. I.e., the author of the Gospel.
1. A new word or expression. Balzac (1799–1850), a French novelist whose realism made him improper reading for a young lady.
2. Spanish historian (16th century), who wrote a book on the genealogies of the grandees of Spain.
3. A town in Spain on the river Arlanza. Mount Chimborazo is one of the highest peaks of the Andes. Teneriffe is a mountain in the Canary Islands.
4. A town in Austria.
5. Allusion to the story about Samuel Johnson, who, when told how difficult a piece of music was that a young lady was playing, replied, "I would it had been impossible."
6. As in painting with watercolors.
7. A kind of waltz.

With pretty "may it please you," or "so it is,"—
Their rapid insight and fine aptitude,
435 Particular worth and general missionariness,
As long as they keep quiet by the fire
And never say "no" when the world says "ay,"
For that is fatal,—their angelic reach
Of virtue, chiefly used to sit and darn,
440 And fatten household sinners,—their, in brief,
Potential faculty in everything
Of abdicating power in it: she owned
She liked a woman to be womanly,
And English women, she thanked God and sighed
445 (Some people always sigh in thanking God),
Were models to the universe. And last
I learnt cross-stitch,[8] because she did not like
To see me wear the night with empty hands
A-doing nothing. So, my shepherdess
450 Was something after all (the pastoral saints
Be praised for't), leaning lovelorn with pink eyes
To match her shoes, when I mistook the silks;
Her head uncrushed by that round weight of hat
So strangely similar to the tortoise shell
Which slew the tragic poet.[9]
455   By the way,
The works of women are symbolical.
We sew, sew, prick our fingers, dull our sight,
Producing what? A pair of slippers, sir,
To put on when you're weary—or a stool
460 To stumble over and vex you . . . "curse that stool!"
Or else at best, a cushion, where you lean
And sleep, and dream of something we are not
But would be for your sake. Alas, alas!
This hurts most, this—that, after all, we are paid
The worth of our work, perhaps.
465   In looking down
Those years of education (to return)
I wonder if Brinvilliers suffered more
In the water-torture[1] . . . flood succeeding flood
To drench the incapable throat and split the veins . . .
470 Than I did. Certain of your feebler souls
Go out in such a process; many pine
To a sick, inodorous light; my own endured:
I had relations in the Unseen, and drew
The elemental nutriment and heat
475 From nature, as earth feels the sun at nights,
Or as a babe sucks surely in the dark.
I kept the life thrust on me, on the outside

---

8. I.e., embroidery.
9. According to tradition, the Greek playwright
Aeschylus was killed by an eagle, who, mistaking
his bald head for a stone, dropped a tortoise on it
to break the shell.

1. Marie Marguerite, Marquise de Brinvilliers, a
celebrated criminal who was beheaded in 1676,
was tortured by having water forced down her
throat.

Of the inner life with all its ample room
For heart and lungs, for will and intellect,
480 Inviolable by conventions. God,
I thank thee for that grace of thine!
                                    At first
I felt no life which was not patience,—did
The thing she bade me, without heed to a thing
Beyond it, sat in just the chair she placed,
485 With back against the window, to exclude
The sight of the great lime-tree on the lawn,[2]
Which seemed to have come on purpose from the woods
To bring the house a message,—ay, and walked
Demurely in her carpeted low rooms,
490 As if I should not, harkening my own steps,
Misdoubt I was alive. I read her books,
Was civil to her cousin, Romney Leigh,
Gave ear to her vicar, tea to her visitors,
And heard them whisper, when I changed a cup
495 (I blushed for joy at that),—"The Italian child,
For all her blue eyes and her quiet ways,
Thrives ill in England: she is paler yet
Than when we came the last time; she will die."

From *Book 2*

[AURORA'S ASPIRATIONS][3]

Times followed one another. Came a morn
I stood upon the brink of twenty years,
And looked before and after, as I stood
Woman and artist,—either incomplete,
5 Both credulous of completion. There I held
The whole creation in my little cup,
And smiled with thirsty lips before I drank
"Good health to you and me, sweet neighbour mine,
And all these peoples."
                        I was glad, that day;
10 The June was in me, with its multitudes
Of nightingales all singing in the dark,
And rosebuds reddening where the calyx[4] split.
I felt so young, so strong, so sure of God!
So glad, I could not choose be very wise!
15 And, old at twenty, was inclined to pull
My childhood backward in a childish jest
To see the face of't once more, and farewell!

---

2. Cf. Coleridge's *This Lime-Tree Bower My Prison,* in which the lime tree becomes the vehicle of a realization that Nature never deserts the wise and pure even when they seem to be cut off from her most beautiful vistas.
3. Stifled by her aunt's oppressive conventionality, Aurora has found three sources of comfort and inspiration: poetic aspirations, fostered by the dis-
covery of her father's library; the beauty of the natural world; and the intellectual companionship of her cousin Romney Leigh, an idealistic young man troubled by the misery of the poor and inspired by contemporary notions of social reform.
4. The protective outer leaves covering a flower or bud.

In which fantastic mood I bounded forth
At early morning,—would not wait so long
20   As even to snatch my bonnet by the strings,
But, brushing a green trail across the lawn
With my gown in the dew, took will and away
Among the acacias of the shrubberies,
To fly my fancies in the open air
25   And keep my birthday, till my aunt awoke
To stop good dreams. Meanwhile I murmured on
As honeyed bees keep humming to themselves,
"The worthiest poets have remained uncrowned
Till death has bleached their foreheads to the bone;
30   And so with me it must be unless I prove
Unworthy of the grand adversity,
And certainly I would not fail so much.
What, therefore, if I crown myself to-day
In sport, not pride, to learn the feel of it,
35   Before my brows be numbed as Dante's own
To all the tender pricking of such leaves?
Such leaves! what leaves?"
                                            I pulled the branches down
To choose from.
                        "Not the bay![5] I choose no bay
(The fates deny us if we are overbold),
40   Nor myrtle—which means chiefly love; and love
Is something awful which one dares not touch
So early o' mornings. This verbena strains
The point of passionate fragrance; and hard by,
This guelder-rose,° at far too slight a beck   cranberry bush
45   Of the wind; will toss about her flower-apples.
Ah—there's my choice,—that ivy on the wall,
That headlong ivy! not a leaf will grow
But thinking of a wreath. Large leaves, smooth leaves,
Serrated like my vines, and half as green.
50   I like such ivy, bold to leap a height
'Twas strong to climb; as good to grow on graves
As twist about a thyrsus;[6] pretty too
(And that's not ill) when twisted round a comb."
Thus speaking to myself, half singing it,
55   Because some thoughts are fashioned like a bell
To ring with once being touched, I drew a wreath
Drenched, blinding me with dew, across my brow,
And fastening it behind so, turning faced
. . . My public!—cousin Romney—with a mouth
Twice graver than his eyes.
60   I stood there fixed,—
My arms up, like the caryatid,[7] sole
Of some abolished temple, helplessly

5. A type of laurel tree whose leaves the ancient
Greeks used to honor athletic champions; subsequently, a symbol of poetic achievement.
6. Staff twined with ivy, carried by Dionysus in
Greek myth.
7. Classical column in the form of a draped female
figure.

Persistent in a gesture which derides
A former purpose. Yet my blush was flame,
As if from flax, not stone.

65   "Aurora Leigh,
The earliest of Auroras!"[8]

                              Hand stretched out
I clasped, as shipwrecked men will clasp a hand,
Indifferent to the sort of palm. The tide
Had caught me at my pastime, writing down

70   My foolish name too near upon the sea
Which drowned me with a blush as foolish. "You,
My cousin!"

                    The smile died out in his eyes
And dropped upon his lips, a cold dead weight,
For just a moment, "Here's a book I found!

75   No name writ on it—poems, by the form;
Some Greek upon the margin,—lady's Greek
Without the accents. Read it? Not a word.
I saw at once the thing had witchcraft in't,
Whereof the reading calls up dangerous spirits:
I rather bring it to the witch."

80   "My book.
You found it" . . .

                    "In the hollow by the stream
That beech leans down into—of which you said
The Oread in it has a Naiad's[9] heart
And pines for waters."

                    "Thank you."

                              "Thanks to *you*

85   My cousin! that I have seen you not too much
Witch, scholar, poet, dreamer, and the rest,
To be a woman also."

                    With a glance
The smile rose in his eyes again and touched
The ivy on my forehead, light as air.

90   I answered gravely "Poets needs must be
Or men or women—more's the pity."

                                        "Ah,
But men, and still less women, happily,
Scarce need be poets. Keep to the green wreath,
Since even dreaming of the stone and bronze

95   Brings headaches, pretty cousin, and defiles
The clean white morning dresses."

                                        "So you judge!
Because I love the beautiful I must
Love pleasure chiefly, and be overcharged
For ease and whiteness! well, you know the world,

100 And only miss your cousin, 'tis not much.
But learn this; I would rather take my part

---

8. Dawns; from Aurora, Roman goddess of the
dawn.

9. Water nymph's. "Oread": tree nymph.

With God's Dead, who afford to walk in white
Yet spread His glory, than keep quiet here
And gather up my feet from even a step
105 For fear to soil my gown in so much dust.
I choose to walk at all risks.—Here, if heads
That hold a rhythmic thought, must ache perforce,
For my part I choose headaches,—and to-day's
My birthday,"
        "Dear Aurora, choose instead
To cure them. You have balsams."°   *balms*
110   "I perceive.
The headache is too noble for my sex.
You think the heartache would sound decenter,
Since that's the woman's special, proper ache,
And altogether tolerable, except
115 To a woman."

[AURORA'S REJECTION OF ROMNEY][1]

                There he glowed on me
With all his face and eyes. "No other help?"
Said he—"no more than so?"
345   "What help?" I asked.
"You'd scorn my help,—as Nature's self, you say,
Has scorned to put her music in my mouth
Because a woman's. Do you now turn round
And ask for what a woman cannot give?"

350 "For what she only can, I turn and ask,"
He answered, catching up my hands in his,
And dropping on me from his high-eaved brow
The full weight of his soul,—"I ask for love,
And that, she can; for life in fellowship
355 Through bitter duties—that, I know she can;
For wifehood—will she?"
               "Now," I said, "may God
Be witness 'twixt us two!" and with the word,
Meeseemed[2] I floated into a sudden light
Above his stature,—"am I proved too weak
360 To stand alone, yet strong enough to bear
Such leaners on my shoulder? poor to think,
Yet rich enough to sympathise with thought?
Incompetent to sing, as blackbirds can,
Yet competent to love, like HIM?"
                    I paused;
365 Perhaps I darkened, as the lighthouse will

---

1. Romney and Aurora have been arguing about whether art, particularly a young woman's poetry, is useful in a world that, according to Romney, is full of human suffering. Romney claims that women have no faculty of generalizing and are, therefore, doomed to be trivial poets and ineffec-tual social reformers. Aurora is quick to agree that to be merely a poetaster would be intolerable to her, but while she admires Romney's lofty concern for humanity, she remains untempted to join forces with him.
2. It seemed to me.

That turns upon the sea. "It's always so.
Anything does for a wife."
                              "Aurora, dear,
And dearly honoured,"—he pressed in at once
With eager utterance,—"you translate me ill.
370 I do not contradict my thought of you
Which is most reverent, with another thought
Found less so. If your sex is weak for art
(And I, who said so, did but honour you
By using truth in courtship), it is strong
375 For life and duty. Place your fecund heart
In mine, and let us blossom for the world
That wants love's colour in the grey of time.
My talk, meanwhile, is arid to you, ay,
Since all my talk can only set you where
380 You look down coldly on the arena-heaps
Of headless bodies, shapeless, indistinct!
The Judgment-Angel scarce would find his way
Through such a heap of generalised distress
To the individual man with lips and eyes,
385 Much less Aurora. Ah, my sweet, come down,
And hand in hand we'll go where yours shall touch
These victims, one by one! till, one by one,
The formless, nameless trunk of every man
Shall seem to wear a head with hair you know,
390 And every woman catch your mother's face
To melt you into passion."
                              "I am a girl,"
I answered slowly; "you do well to name
My mother's face. Though far too early, alas,
God's hand did interpose 'twixt it and me,
395 I know so much of love as used to shine
In that face and another. Just so much;
No more indeed at all. I have not seen
So much love since, I pray you pardon me,
As answers even to make a marriage with
400 In this cold land of England. What you love
Is not a woman, Romney, but a cause:
You want a helpmate, not a mistress, sir,
A wife to help your ends,—in her no end.
Your cause is noble, your ends excellent,
405 But I, being most unworthy of these and that,
Do otherwise conceive of love. Farewell."

"Farewell, Aurora? you reject me thus?"
He said.
          "Sir, you were married long ago.
You have a wife already whom you love,
410 Your social theory. Bless you both, I say.
For my part, I am scarcely meek enough
To be the handmaid of a lawful spouse.

Do I look a Hagar,[3] think you?"
                              "So you jest."

"Nay, so, I speak in earnest," I replied.
415 "You treat of marriage too much like, at least,
A chief apostle: you would bear with you
A wife . . . a sister . . . shall we speak it out?
A sister of charity."
                       "Then, must it be
Indeed farewell? And was I so far wrong
420 In hope and in illusion, when I took
The woman to be nobler than the man,
Yourself the noblest woman, in the use
And comprehension of what love is,—love,
That generates the likeness of itself
425 Through all heroic duties? so far wrong,
In saying bluntly, venturing truth on love,
'Come, human creature, love and work with me,'—
Instead of 'Lady, thou art wondrous fair,
'And, where the Graces walk before, the Muse
430 'Will follow at the lightning of their eyes,
'And where the Muse walks, lovers need to creep:
'Turn round and love me, or I die of love.' "

With quiet indignation I broke in.
"You misconceive the question like a man,
435 Who sees a woman as the complement
Of his sex merely. You forget too much
That every creature, female as the male,
Stands single in responsible act and thought
As also in birth and death. Whoever says
440 To a loyal woman, 'Love and work with me,'
Will get fair answers if the work and love,
Being good themselves, are good for her—the best
She was born for. Women of a softer mood,
Surprised by men when scarcely awake to life,
445 Will sometimes only hear the first word, love,
And catch up with it any kind of work,
Indifferent, so that dear love go with it.
I do not blame such women, though, for love,
They pick much oakum;[4] earth's fanatics make
450 Too frequently heaven's saints. But *me* your work
Is not the best for,—nor your love the best,
Nor able to commend the kind of work
For love's sake merely. Ah, you force me, sir,
To be overbold in speaking of myself:
455 I too have my vocation,—work to do,
The heavens and earth have set me since I changed

---

3. In Genesis 16, Sarah's maidservant, who bore a child, Ishmael, by Sarah's husband, Abraham.

4. Fiber derived by untwisting (picking) old rope, a task frequently assigned to workhouse inmates.

My father's face for theirs, and, though your world
Were twice as wretched as you represent,
Most serious work, most necessary work
460 As any of the economists'. Reform,
Make trade a Christian possibility,
And individual right no general wrong;
Wipe out earth's furrows of the Thine and Mine,
And leave one green for men to play at bowls,[5]
465 With innings for them all! . . . What then, indeed,
If mortals are not greater by the head
Than any of their prosperities? what then,
Unless the artist keep up open roads
Betwixt the seen and unseen,—bursting through
470 The best of your conventions with his best,
The speakable, imaginable best
God bids him speak, to prove what lies beyond
Both speech and imagination? A starved man
Exceeds a fat beast: we'll not barter, sir,
475 The beautiful for barley.—And, even so,
I hold you will not compass your poor ends
Of barley-feeding and material ease,
Without a poet's individualism
To work your universal. It takes a soul,
480 To move a body: it takes a high-souled man,
To move the masses, even to a cleaner stye:
It takes the ideal, to blow a hair's-breadth off
The dust of the actual.—Ah, your Fouriers[6] failed,
Because not poets enough to understand
485 That life develops from within.——For me,
Perhaps I am not worthy, as you say,
Of work like this: perhaps a woman's soul
Aspires, and not creates: yet we aspire,
And yet I'll try out your perhapses, sir,
490 And if I fail . . . why, burn me up my straw[7]
Like other false works—I'll not ask for grace;
Your scorn is better, cousin Romney. I
Who love my art, would never wish it lower
To suit my stature. I may love my art.
495 You'll grant that even a woman may love art,
Seeing that to waste true love on anything
Is womanly, past question."

From *Book 5*

[POETS AND THE PRESENT AGE]

The critics say that epics have died out
140 With Agamemnon and the goat-nursed gods;[8]

---

5. A game of skill played on a smooth lawn with weighted wooden balls.
6. François-Marie-Charles Fourier (1772–1837), a French political theorist who advocated communal property as a basis for social harmony.
7. I.e., destroy my poetry (a deliberate archaism).
8. Zeus was nursed by a goat.

I'll not believe it. I could never deem,
As Payne Knight[9] did (the mythic mountaineer
Who travelled higher than he was born to live,
And showed sometimes the goitre[1] in his throat
145 Discoursing of an image seen through fog),
That Homer's heroes measured twelve feet high.
They were but men:—his Helen's hair turned grey
Like any plain Miss Smith's who wears a front;[2]
And Hector's infant whimpered at a plume[3]
150 As yours last Friday at a turkey-cock.
All actual heroes are essential men,
And all men possible heroes: every age,
Heroic in proportions, double-faced,
Looks backward and before, expects a morn
And claims an epos.°   *epic poem*
155   Ay, but every age
Appears to souls who live in 't (ask Carlyle)[4]
Most unheroic. Ours, for instance, ours:
The thinkers scout it, and the poets abound
Who scorn to touch it with a finger-tip:
160 A pewter age,[5]—mixed metal, silver-washed;
An age of scum, spooned off the richer past,
An age of patches for old gaberdines,°   *coats*
An age of mere transition,[6] meaning nought
Except that what succeeds must shame it quite
165 If God please. That's wrong thinking, to my mind,
And wrong thoughts make poor poems.
                                          Every age,
Through being beheld too close, is ill-discerned
By those who have not lived past it. We'll suppose
Mount Athos carved, as Alexander schemed,
170 To some colossal statue of a man.[7]
The peasants, gathering brushwood in his ear,
Had guessed as little as the browsing goats
Of form or feature of humanity
Up there,—in fact, had travelled five miles off
175 Or ere the giant image broke on them,
Full human profile, nose and chin distinct,
Mouth, muttering rhythms of silence up the sky

9. Richard Payne Knight (1750–1824), a classical philologist, who, upon England's acquisition of the Parthenon marbles, claimed that Lord Elgin had wasted his labor because they were not all Greek.
1. A disease often contracted in high mountain areas because of the low iodine content of the water.
2. A piece of false hair worn over the forehead by women.
3. In an episode in the *Iliad*, Hector tries to take his infant son in his arms; but the child clings to his nurse, frightened of his father's helmet and crest.
4. In *Heroes and Hero-Worship* (1841), Carlyle argues that the present age needs a renewed perception of the heroic.
5. Allusion to the convention, which originates in Hesiod, of describing civilization's decline through a succession of ages named for increasingly less precious materials, i.e., the Golden Age, the Silver Age, the Bronze Age.
6. In *The Spirit of the Age* (1831) John Stuart Mill calls the present age "an age of transition."
7. Dionocrates, a sculptor, is said to have suggested to Alexander that Mount Athos be carved into the statue of a conqueror with a city in his left hand and a basin in his right, where all the waters of the region could be collected and used to water the pasture lands below.

And fed at evening with the blood of suns;
Grand torso,—hand, that flung perpetually
180 The largesse of a silver river down
To all the country pastures. 'Tis even thus
With times we live in,—evermore too great
To be apprehended near.
But poets should
Exert a double vision; should have eyes
185 To see near things as comprehensively
As if afar they took their point of sight,
And distant things as intimately deep
As if they touched them. Let us strive for this.
I do distrust the poet who discerns
190 No character or glory in his times,
And trundles back his soul five hundred years,
Past moat and drawbridge, into a castle-court,
To sing—oh, not of lizard or of toad
Alive i' the ditch there,—'twere excusable,
195 But of some black chief, half knight, half sheep-lifter,
Some beauteous dame, half chattel and half queen,
As dead as must be, for the greater part,
The poems made on their chivalric bones;
And that's no wonder: death inherits death.

200 Nay, if there's room for poets in this world
A little overgrown (I think there is),
Their sole work is to represent the age,
Their age, not Charlemagne's,[8]—this live, throbbing age,
That brawls, cheats, maddens, calculates, aspires,
205 And spends more passion, more heroic heat,
Betwixt the mirrors of its drawing-rooms,
Than Roland[9] with his knights at Roncesvalles.
To flinch from modern varnish, coat or flounce,
Cry out for togas and the picturesque,
210 Is fatal,—foolish too. King Arthur's self
Was commonplace to Lady Guenever;
And Camelot to minstrels seemed as flat
As Fleet Street[1] to our poets.
Never flinch,
But still, unscrupulously epic, catch
215 Upon the burning lava of a song
The full-veined, heaving, double-breasted Age:
That, when the next shall come, the men of that
May touch the impress with reverent hand, and say
"Behold,—behold the paps° we all have sucked!   breasts
220 This bosom seems to beat still, or at least
It sets ours beating: this is living art,
Which thus presents and thus records true life."

1853–56   1857

8. Frankish conqueror (742–814), who created a
European empire.
9. Legendary medieval hero, whose adventures
are told in the epic poem *Chanson de Roland.*
1. A center for book shops and newspaper and
publishing offices in London.

Mother and Poet[1]

(Turin, After News from Gaeta, 1861)

1

DEAD! One of them shot by the sea in the east,
   And one of them shot in the west by the sea.
Dead! both my boys! When you sit at the feast
   And are wanting a great song for Italy free,
5   Let none look at *me!*

2

Yet I was a poetess only last year,
   And good at my art, for a woman, men said;
But *this* woman, *this,* who is agonised here,
   —The east sea and west sea rhyme on in her head
10   For ever instead.

3

What art can a woman be good at? Oh, vain!
   What art *is* she good at, but hurting her breast
With the milk-teeth of babes, and a smile at the pain?
   Ah boys, how you hurt! you were strong as you pressed,
15   And I proud, by that test.

4

What art's for a woman? To hold on her knees
   Both darlings! to feel all their arms round her throat,
Cling, strangle a little! to sew by degrees
   And 'broider the long-clothes and neat little coat;
20   To dream and to doat.

5

To teach them . . . It stings there! *I* made them indeed
   Speak plain the word *country. I* taught them, no doubt,
That a country's a thing men should die for at need.
   I prated of liberty, rights, and about
25   The tyrant cast out.

6

And when their eyes flashed . . . O my beautiful eyes! . . .
   I exulted; nay, let them go forth at the wheels
Of the guns, and denied not. But then the surprise
   When one sits quite alone! Then one weeps, then one kneels!
30   God, how the house feels!

1. The speaker is the Italian poet and patriot Laura Savio of Turin, both of whose sons were killed in the struggle for the unification of Italy, one in the attack on the fortress at Ancona, the other at the siege of Gaeta, the last stronghold of the Neapolitan government.

7

At first, happy news came, in gay letters moiled°　　　　*moistened*
　　With my kisses,—of camp-life and glory, and how
They both loved me; and, soon coming home to be spoiled
　　In return would fan off every fly from my brow
35　　　　With their green laurel-bough.[2]

8

Then was triumph at Turin: "Ancona was free!"
　　And some one came out of the cheers in the street,
With a face pale as stone, to say something to me.
　　My Guido was dead! I fell down at his feet,
40　　　　While they cheered in the street.

9

I bore it; friends soothed me; my grief looked sublime
　　As the ransom of Italy. One boy remained
To be leant on and walked with, recalling the time
　　When the first grew immortal, while both of us strained
45　　　　To the height he had gained.

10

And letters still came, shorter, sadder, more strong,
　　Writ now but in one hand, "I was not to faint,—
One loved me for two—would be with me ere long:
　　And *Viva l'Italia!—he* died for, our saint,
50　　　　Who forbids our complaint."

11

My Nanni would add, "he was safe, and aware
　　Of a presence that turned off the balls,°—was imprest　　*cannonballs*
It was Guido himself, who knew what I could bear,
　　And how 'twas impossible, quite dispossessed
55　　　　To live on for the rest."

12

On which, without pause, up the telegraph line
　　Swept smoothly the next news from Gaeta:—*Shot.*
Tell his mother. Ah, ah, "his," "their" mother,—not "mine,"
　　No voice says "*My* mother" again to me. What!
60　　　　You think Guido forgot?

13

Are souls straight so happy that, dizzy with Heaven,
　　They drop earth's affections, conceive not of woe?
I think not. Themselves were too lately forgiven
　　Through THAT Love and Sorrow which reconciled so
65　　　　The Above and Below.

2. A laurel crown is the conventional mark of a poet's fame.

14

O Christ of the five wounds, who look'dst through the dark
    To the face of thy mother! consider, I pray,
How we common mothers stand desolate, mark,
    Whose sons, not being Christs, die with eyes turned away
70   And no last word to say!

15

Both boys dead? but that's out of nature. We all
    Have been patriots, yet each house must always keep one.
'Twere imbecile, hewing out roads to a wall;
    And, when Italy's made, for what end is it done
75   If we have not a son?

16

Ah, ah, ah! when Gaeta's taken, what then?
    When the fair wicked queen sits no more at her sport
Of the fire-balls of death crashing souls out of men?
    When the guns of Cavalli³ with final retort
80   Have cut the game short?

17

When Venice and Rome keep their new jubilee,⁴
    When your flag takes all heaven for its white, green, and red,
When *you* have your country from mountain to sea,
    When King Victor has Italy's crown on his head,
85   (And *I* have my Dead)—

18

What then? Do not mock me. Ah, ring your bells low,
    And burn your lights faintly! *My* country is *there*,
Above the star pricked by the last peak of snow:
    My Italy's THERE, with my brave civic Pair,
90   To disfranchise despair!

19

Forgive me. Some women bear children in strength,
    And bite back the cry of their pain in self-scorn;
But the birth-pangs of nations will wring us at length
    Into wail such as this—and we sit on forlorn
95   When the man-child is born.

20

Dead! One of them shot by the sea in the east,
    And one of them shot in the west by the sea.
Both! both my boys! If in keeping the feast

3. The general commanding the siege of Gaeta.
"The fair wicked queen": Maria, wife of Francis II,
the last ruler of the Neapolitan government, who
retreated to Gaeta.
4. The celebration when they too will have been
united with the rest of Italy under King Victor
Emmanuel. In 1861, when the poem was written,
they were the two cities that were still independent
of the new state.

You want a great song for your Italy free,
100   Let none look at *me!*

1861   1862

ALFRED, LORD TENNYSON
1809–1892

Whether or not Alfred Tennyson was the greatest of the Victorian poets, as affirmed by many critics today, there is no doubt that in his own lifetime he was the most popular of poets. On the bookshelves of almost every family of readers in England and the United States, from 1850 onward, were the works of a man who had incontestably gained the title that Walt Whitman longed for: "The Poet of the People" (Whitman, in fact, called Tennyson, colorfully, "the Boss"). Popularity inevitably provided provocation for a reaction in the decades following his death. In the course of repudiating their Victorian predecessors, the Edwardians and Georgians established the fashion of making fun of Tennyson's great achievements. Samuel Butler (1835–1902), who anticipated early twentieth-century tastes, has a characteristic entry in his *Notebooks:* "Talking it over, we agreed that Blake was no good because he learnt Italian at sixty in order to study Dante, and we knew Dante was no good because he was so fond of Virgil, and Virgil was no good because Tennyson ran him, and as for Tennyson—well, Tennyson goes without saying." In the second half of the twentieth century, Butler's flippant dismissal of Tennyson expresses an attitude that is no longer fashionable. The delights to be found in this superb "lord of language"—as Tennyson himself addresses his favorite predecessor, Virgil—have been rediscovered, and Tennyson's stature as one of the major poets of any age has been reestablished.

Like his poetry, Tennyson's life and character have been reassessed in the twentieth century. To many of his contemporaries he seemed a remote wizard, secure in his laureate's robes, a man whose life had been sheltered, marred only by the loss of his best friend in youth. During much of his career Tennyson may have been isolated, but his was not a sheltered life in the real sense of the word. Although he grew up in a parsonage, it was not the kind of parsonage one encounters in the novels of Jane Austen. It was a household dominated by frictions and loyalties and broodings over ancestral inheritances, in which the children showed marked strains of instability and eccentricity.

Alfred was the fourth son in a family of twelve children. One of his brothers had to be confined to an insane asylum for life; another was long addicted to opium; another had violent quarrels with his father, the Reverend Dr. George Tennyson. This father, a man of considerable learning, had himself been born the eldest son of a wealthy landowner and had, therefore, expected to be heir to his family's estates. Instead he was disinherited in favor of his younger brother and had to make his own livelihood by joining the clergy, a profession that he disliked. After George Tennyson had settled in a small rectory in Somersby, his brooding sense of dissatisfaction led to increasingly violent bouts of drunkenness, despite which he was able to serve as tutor for his sons in classical and modern languages to prepare them for entering the university.

Before leaving this strange household for Cambridge, Alfred had already demonstrated a flair for writing verse—precocious exercises in the manner of Milton or Byron or the Elizabethan dramatists. He had even published a volume in 1827, in collaboration with his brother Charles, *Poems by Two Brothers.* This feat drew him to the attention of a group of gifted undergraduates at Cambridge, "the Apostles," who encouraged him to devote his life to poetry. Up until that time, the young man had known scarcely anyone outside the circle of his own family. Despite his massive frame and powerful physique, he was painfully shy; and the friendships he found at Cambridge as well as the intellectual and political discussions in which he participated served to give him confidence and to widen his horizons as a poet. The most important of these friendships was with Arthur Hallam, a leader of the Apostles, who later became engaged to Tennyson's sister. Hallam's sudden death, in 1833, seemed an overwhelming calamity to his friend. Not only the long elegy *In Memoriam* but many of Tennyson's other poems are tributes to this early friendship.

Alfred's career at Cambridge was interrupted and finally broken off in 1831 by family dissensions and financial need, and he returned home to study and practice the craft of poetry. His early volumes (1830 and 1832) were attacked as "obscure" or "affected" by some of the reviewers. Tennyson suffered acutely under hostile criticism, but he also profited from it. His volume of 1842 demonstrated a remarkable advance in taste and technical excellence, and in 1850 he at last attained fame and full critical recognition with *In Memoriam.* In the same year, he became poet laureate in succession to Wordsworth. The struggle during the previous twenty years had been made especially painful by the long postponement of his marriage to Emily Sellwood, whom he had loved since 1836 but could not marry, because of poverty, until 1850.

His life thereafter was a comfortable one. He was as popular as Byron had been. The earnings from his poetry (sometimes exceeding £10,000 a year) enabled him to purchase a house in the country and to enjoy the kind of seclusion he liked. His notoriety was enhanced, like that of Bernard Shaw and Walt Whitman, by his colorful appearance. Huge and shaggy, in cloak and broad-brimmed hat, gruff in manner as a farmer, he impressed everyone as what is called a "character." The pioneering photographer Julia Cameron, who took magnificent portraits of him, called him "the most beautiful old man on earth." Like Dylan Thomas in the twentieth century, he had a booming voice that electrified listeners when he read his poetry, "mouthing out his hollow o's and a's, / Deep-chested music." Moreover, for many Victorian readers, he seemed not only a great poetical phrase maker and a striking individual but also a wise man whose occasional pronouncements on politics or world affairs represented the national voice itself. In 1884 he accepted a peerage. In 1892 he died and was buried in Westminster Abbey.

It is often said that success was bad for Tennyson and that after *In Memoriam* his poetic power seriously declined. That in his last forty-two years certain of his mannerisms became accentuated is true. One of the difficulties of his dignified blank verse was, as he said himself, that it is hard to describe commonplace objects and "at the same time to retain poetical elevation." This difficulty is evident, for example, in *Enoch Arden* (1864), a long blank verse narrative of everyday life in a fishing village, in which a basketful of fish is ornately described as "Enoch's ocean spoil / In ocean-smelling osier." In others of his later poems, those dealing with national affairs, there is also an increased shrillness of tone—a mannerism accentuated by Tennyson's realizing that like Dickens he had a vast public behind him to back up his pronouncements.

It is foolish, however, to try to shelve all of Tennyson's later productions. In 1855 he published his experimental monologue *Maud,* perhaps his finest long poem, in which he displays the bitterness and despair its alienated hero feels toward society. In 1859 he published four books of his *Idylls of the King,* a large-scale epic that occupied most of his energies in the second half of his career. The *Idylls* uses the body of Arthurian legend to construct a vision of the rise and fall of civilization. In this civilization, women at once inspire men's highest efforts and sow the seeds of their destruction. The *Idylls* provides Tennyson's most extensive social vision, one whose concern with medieval ideals of social community, heroism, and courtly love and whose despairing sense of the cycles of historical change typifies much social thought of the age.

W. H. Auden stated that Tennyson had "the finest ear, perhaps, of any English poet." The interesting point is that Tennyson did not "have" such an ear: he developed it. Studies of the original versions of his poems in the 1830 and 1832 volumes demonstrate how hard he worked at his craftsmanship. Like Chaucer or Keats or Pope, Tennyson studied his predecessors assiduously to perfect his technique. Anyone wanting to learn the traditional craft of English verse can study with profit the various stages of revision that such poems as *The Lotos-Eaters* were subjected to by this painstaking and artful poet. Some lines of 1988 by the American poet Karl Shapiro effectively characterize Tennyson's accomplishments in these areas:

> Long-lived, the very image of English Poet,
> Whose songs still break out tears in the generations,
> Whose poetry for practitioners still astounds,
> Who crafted his life and letters like a watch.

Tennyson's early poetry shows other skills as well. One of these was a capacity for linking scenery to states of mind. As early as 1835, J. S. Mill identified the special kind of scene painting to be found in early poems such as *Mariana*: "not the power of producing that rather vapid species of composition usually termed descriptive poetry . . . but the power of *creating* scenery, in keeping with some state of human feeling so fitted to it as to be the embodied symbol of it, and to summon up the state of feeling itself, with a force not to be surpassed by anything but reality."

The state of feeling to which Tennyson was most intensely drawn was a melancholy isolation, often portrayed through the consciousness of an abandoned woman, as in *Mariana*. Tennyson's absorption with such emotions in his early poetry evoked considerable criticism. His friend R. C. Trench warned him, "Tennyson, we cannot live in Art," and Mill urged him to "cultivate, and with no half devotion, philosophy as well as poetry." Advice of this kind Tennyson was already predisposed to heed. The death of Hallam, the religious uncertainties that he had himself experienced, together with his own extensive study of writings by geologists, astronomers, and biologists, led him to confront many of the religious issues that bewildered his and later generations. The result was *In Memoriam* (1850), a long elegy written over a period of seventeen years, embodying the poet's reflections on our relation to God and to nature.

Was Tennyson intellectually equipped to deal with the great questions raised in *In Memoriam*? The answer may depend on a reader's religious and philosophical presuppositions. Some, such as T. H. Huxley, considered Tennyson an intellectual giant, a thinker who had mastered the scientific thought of his century and fully confronted the issues it raised. Others dismissed Tennyson, in this phase, as a lightweight. Auden went so far as to call him the "stupidest" of English poets. He went on to say, "There was little about melancholia that he didn't know; there was little else that he did." Perhaps T. S. Eliot's evaluation of *In Memoriam* is the more accurate: the poem, he wrote, is remarkable not "because of the quality of its faith but because of the quality of its doubt." Tennyson's mind was slow, ponderous, brooding; for the composition of *In Memoriam* such qualities of mind were assets, not liabilities. In these terms we can understand when Tennyson's poetry really fails to measure up: it is when he writes of events of the moment over which his thoughts and feelings have had no time to brood. Several of his poems are what he himself called "newspaper verse." They are letters to the editor, in effect, with the ephemeral heat and simplicity we expect of such productions. *The Charge of the Light Brigade,* inspired by a report in the *Times* of a cavalry charge at Balaclava during the Crimean War, is one of the best of his productions in this category.

Tennyson's poems of contemporary events were inevitably popular in his own day. So too were those poems in which, as in *Locksley Hall,* he dipped into the future.

The technological changes wrought by Victorian inventors and engineers fascinated him. Sometimes they gave him an assurance of human progress as swaggeringly exultant as that of Macaulay. At other times the horrors of industrialism's by-products in the slums, the persistence of barbarity and bloodshed, the greed of the newly rich, destroyed his hopes that humanity was evolving upward. Such a late poem as *The Dawn* embodies an attitude that he found in Virgil: "Thou majestic in thy sadness at the doubtful doom of human kind."

For despite Tennyson's fascination with technological developments, he was essentially a poet of the countryside, a man whose whole being was conditioned by the recurring rhythms of rural rather than urban life. He had the country dweller's awareness of traditional roots and sense of the past. It is appropriate that most of his best poems are about the past, not about the present or future. Even in his childhood, Tennyson said that "the words 'far, far away' had always a strange charm for me"; he was haunted by what he called "the passion of the past." The past became his great theme, whether it be his own past (as in *In the Valley of Cauteretz*), his country's past (as in *The Idylls of the King*), the past of humankind, the past of the world itself:

> There rolls the deep where grew the tree.
> O earth, what changes hast thou seen!
> There where the long street roars hath been
> The stillness of the central sea.

Tennyson is the first major writer to express this awareness of the vast extent of geological time that has haunted human consciousness since Victorian scientists exposed the history of the earth's crust. In his more usual vein, however, it is the recorded past of humankind that inspires him, the classical past in particular. Classical themes, as Douglas Bush has noted, "generally banished from his mind what was timid, parochial, sentimental . . . and evoked his special gifts and most authentic emotions, his rich and wistful sense of the past, his love of nature, and his power of style."

One returns, finally, to the question of language. At the time of his death, a critic complained that Tennyson was merely "a discoverer of words rather than of ideas." The same complaint has been made by Bernard Shaw and others—not about Tennyson but about Shakespeare.

The Kraken[1]

> Below the thunders of the upper deep,
> Far, far beneath in the abysmal sea,
> His ancient, dreamless, uninvaded sleep
> The Kraken sleepeth: faintest sunlights flee
> 5 About his shadowy sides; above him swell
> Huge sponges of millennial growth and height;
> And far away into the sickly light,
> From many a wondrous grot and secret cell
> Unnumbered and enormous polypi°   octopuses
> 10 Winnow with giant arms the slumbering green.
> There hath he lain for ages, and will lie
> Battening upon huge sea worms in his sleep,
> Until the latter fire[2] shall heat the deep;

1. A mythical sea beast of gigantic size.
2. Fire that would finally consume the world (Revelation 16.8–9).

Then once by man and angels to be seen,
15   In roaring he shall rise and on the surface die.

1830

Mariana[1]

> "Mariana in the moated grange."
> *Measure for Measure*

With blackest moss the flower-plots
  Were thickly crusted, one and all;
The rusted nails fell from the knots
  That held the pear to the gable wall.
5   The broken sheds looked sad and strange:
  Unlifted was the clinking latch;
  Weeded and worn the ancient thatch
Upon the lonely moated grange.
    She only said, "My life is dreary,
10   He cometh not," she said;
    She said, "I am aweary, aweary,
      I would that I were dead!"

Her tears fell with the dews at even;
  Her tears fell ere the dews were dried;
15   She could not look on the sweet heaven,
  Either at morn or eventide.
After the flitting of the bats,
  When thickest dark did trance° the sky,   cross
  She drew her casement curtain by,
20   And glanced athwart the glooming flats.
    She only said, "The night is dreary,
      He cometh not," she said;
    She said, "I am aweary, aweary,
      I would that I were dead!"

25   Upon the middle of the night,
  Waking she heard the nightfowl crow;
The cock sung out an hour ere light;
  From the dark fen the oxen's low
Came to her; without hope of change,
30   In sleep she seemed to walk forlorn,
  Till cold winds woke the gray-eyed morn
About the lonely moated grange.
    She only said, "The day is dreary,
      He cometh not," she said;
35   She said, "I am aweary, aweary,
      I would that I were dead!"

---

1. Mariana, in Shakespeare's *Measure for Measure* 3.1.277, waits in a grange (an outlying farmhouse) for her lover, who has deserted her.

About a stonecast from the wall
   A sluice with blackened waters slept,
And o'er it many, round and small,
40   The clustered marish-mosses[2] crept.
Hard by a poplar shook alway,
   All silver-green with gnarlèd bark:
For leagues no other tree did mark
The level waste, the rounding gray.
45   She only said, "My life is dreary,
     He cometh not," she said;
   She said, "I am aweary, aweary,
     I would that I were dead!"

And ever when the moon was low,
50   And the shrill winds were up and away,
In the white curtain, to and fro,
   She saw the gusty shadow sway.
But when the moon was very low,
   And wild winds bound within their cell,[3]
55   The shadow of the poplar fell
Upon her bed, across her brow.
     She only said, "The night is dreary,
     He cometh not," she said;
   She said, "I am aweary, aweary,
60   I would that I were dead!"

All day within the dreamy house,
   The doors upon their hinges creaked;
The blue fly sung in the pane; the mouse
   Behind the moldering wainscot shrieked,
65   Or from the crevice peered about.
     Old faces glimmered through the doors,
     Old footsteps trod the upper floors,
   Old voices called her from without.
     She only said, "My life is dreary,
70   He cometh not," she said;
   She said, "I am aweary, aweary,
     I would that I were dead!"

The sparrow's chirrup on the roof,
   The slow clock ticking, and the sound
75   Which to the wooing wind aloof
   The poplar made, did all confound
Her sense; but most she loathed the hour
   When the thick-moted sunbeam lay
   Athwart the chambers, and the day
80   Was sloping toward his western bower.
     Then, said she, "I am very dreary,
     He will not come," she said;

2. The little marsh-moss lumps that float on the surface of water [Tennyson's note].

3. According to Virgil, Aeolus, god of winds, kept the winds imprisoned in a cave (*Aeneid* 1.50–59).

> She wept, "I am aweary, aweary,
> Oh God, that I were dead!"

1830

The Lady of Shalott[1]

Part 1

On either side the river lie
Long fields of barley and of rye,
That clothe the wold° and meet the sky;   *rolling plain*
And through the field the road runs by
5   To many-towered Camelot;
And up and down the people go,
Gazing where the lilies blow°   *bloom*
Round an island there below,
The island of Shalott.

10   Willows whiten, aspens quiver,
Little breezes dusk and shiver
Through the wave that runs forever
By the island in the river
Flowing down to Camelot.
15   Four gray walls, and four gray towers,
Overlook a space of flowers,
And the silent isle imbowers
The Lady of Shalott.

By the margin, willow-veiled,
20   Slide the heavy barges trailed
By slow horses; and unhailed
The shallop° flitteth silken-sailed   *light open boat*
Skimming down to Camelot:
But who hath seen her wave her hand?
25   Or at the casement seen her stand?
Or is she known in all the land,
The Lady of Shalott?

Only reapers, reaping early
In among the bearded barley,
30   Hear a song that echoes cheerly
From the river winding clearly,
Down to towered Camelot;
And by the moon the reaper weary,
Piling sheaves in uplands airy,
35   Listening, whispers " 'Tis the fairy
Lady of Shalott."

---

1. For the author's revisions while composing this poem, see "Poems in Process," in the appendices to this volume.

Part 2

There she weaves by night and day
A magic web with colors gay.
She has heard a whisper say,
40   A curse is on her if she stay
      To look down to Camelot.
She knows not what the curse may be,
And so she weaveth steadily,
And little other care hath she,
45   The Lady of Shalott.

And moving through a mirror clear[2]
That hangs before her all the year,
Shadows of the world appear.
There she sees the highway near
50   Winding down to Camelot;
There the river eddy whirls,
And there the surly village churls,
And the red cloaks of market girls,
      Pass onward from Shalott.

55 Sometimes a troop of damsels glad,
An abbot on an ambling pad,°   *easy-paced horse*
Sometimes a curly shepherd lad,
Or long-haired page in crimson clad,
      Goes by to towered Camelot;
60 And sometimes through the mirror blue
The knights come riding two and two:
She hath no loyal knight and true,
      The Lady of Shalott.

But in her web she still delights
65 To weave the mirror's magic sights,
For often through the silent nights
A funeral, with plumes and lights
      And music, went to Camelot;
Or when the moon was overhead,
70 Came two young lovers lately wed:
"I am half sick of shadows," said
      The Lady of Shalott.

Part 3

A bowshot from her bower eaves,
He rode between the barley sheaves,
75 The sun came dazzling through the leaves,
And flamed upon the brazen greaves[3]
      Of bold Sir Lancelot.

---

2. Weavers used mirrors, placed facing their looms, to see the progress of their work.

3. Armor protecting the leg below the knee.

A red-cross knight[4] forever kneeled
To a lady in his shield,
80 That sparkled on the yellow field,
        Beside remote Shalott.

The gemmy bridle glittered free,
Like to some branch of stars we see
Hung in the golden Galaxy.
85 The bridle bells rang merrily
        As he rode down to Camelot;
And from his blazoned baldric[5] slung
A mighty silver bugle hung,
And as he rode his armor rung,
90   Beside remote Shalott.

All in the blue unclouded weather
Thick-jeweled shone the saddle leather,
The helmet and the helmet-feather
Burned like one burning flame together,
95 As he rode down to Camelot;
As often through the purple night,
Below the starry clusters bright,
Some bearded meteor, trailing light,
        Moves over still Shalott.

100 His broad clear brow in sunlight glowed;
On burnished hooves his war horse trode;
From underneath his helmet flowed
His coal-black curls as on he rode,
        As he rode down to Camelot.
105 From the bank and from the river
He flashed into the crystal mirror,
"Tirra lirra," by the river
        Sang Sir Lancelot.

She left the web, she left the loom,
110 She made three paces through the room,
She saw the water lily bloom,
She saw the helmet and the plume,
        She looked down to Camelot.
Out flew the web and floated wide;
115 The mirror cracked from side to side;
"The curse is come upon me," cried
        The Lady of Shalott.

Part 4

In the stormy east wind straining,
The pale yellow woods were waning,
120 The broad stream in his banks complaining,

---

4. Cf. *The Faerie Queene* 1 and 3.2.17–25.
5. A belt worn diagonally from one shoulder to the opposite hip; it supported a sword, bugle, etc.

Heavily the low sky raining
    Over towered Camelot;
Down she came and found a boat
Beneath a willow left afloat,
125   And round about the prow she wrote
    The Lady of Shalott.

And down the river's dim expanse
Like some bold seër in a trance,
Seeing all his own mischance—
130   With a glassy countenance
    Did she look to Camelot.
And at the closing of the day
She loosed the chain, and down she lay;
The broad steam bore her far away,
135   The Lady of Shalott.

Lying, robed in snowy white
That loosely flew to left and right—
The leaves upon her falling light—
Through the noises of the night
140   She floated down to Camelot;
And as the boat-head wound along
The willowy hills and fields among,
They heard her singing her last song,
    The Lady of Shalott.

145   Heard a carol, mournful, holy,
Chanted loudly, chanted lowly,
Till her blood was frozen slowly,
And her eyes were darkened wholly,[6]
    Turned to towered Camelot.
150   For ere she reached upon the tide
The first house by the waterside,
Singing in her song she died,
    The Lady of Shalott.

Under tower and balcony,
155   By garden wall and gallery,
A gleaming shape she floated by,
Dead-pale between the houses high,
    Silent into Camelot.
Out upon the wharfs they came,
160   Knight and burgher, lord and dame,
And round the prow they read her name,
    The Lady of Shalott.

Who is this? and what is here?
And in the lighted palace near
165   Died the sound of royal cheer;

6. In the 1832 version (reproduced in "Poems in Process") this line read: "And her smooth face sharpened slowly." George Eliot informed Tennyson that she preferred the earlier version.

And they crossed themselves for fear,
      All the knights at Camelot:
But Lancelot mused a little space;
He said, "She has a lovely face;
170   God in his mercy lend her grace,
      The Lady of Shalott."

1831–32   1832, 1842

Dante Gabriel Rossetti's 1857 engraving for publisher Edward Moxon's illustrated collection of Tennyson's poetry shows Lancelot musing "a little space" on the Lady of Shalott in her boat.

The Lotos-Eaters[1]

"Courage!" he[2] said, and pointed toward the land,
"This mounting wave will roll us shoreward soon."

1. Based on a short episode from the *Odyssey* (9.82–97) in which the weary Greek veterans of the Trojan War are tempted by a desire to abandon their long voyage homeward. As Odysseus later reported: "On the tenth day we set foot on the land of the lotos-eaters who eat a flowering food. . . . I sent forth certain of my company [who] . . . mixed with the men of the lotos-eaters who gave . . . them of the lotos to taste. Now whosoever of them did eat the honey-sweet fruit of the lotos had no more wish to bring tidings nor to come back, but there

he chose to abide . . . forgetful of his homeward way."

Tennyson expands Homer's brief account into an elaborate picture of weariness and the desire for rest and death. The descriptions in the first stanzas are similar to *Faerie Queene* 2.6 and employ the same stanza form. The final section derives, in part, from Lucretius's conception of the gods in *De rerum natura*.

2. Odysseus (or Ulysses).

In the afternoon they came unto a land[3]
In which it seemèd always afternoon.
5 All round the coast the languid air did swoon,
Breathing like one that hath a weary dream.
Full-faced above the valley stood the moon;
And, like a downward smoke, the slender stream
Along the cliff to fall and pause and fall did seem.

10 A land of streams! some, like a downward smoke,
Slow-dropping veils of thinnest lawn,° did go;   *fine, thin linen*
And some through wavering lights and shadows broke,
Rolling a slumbrous sheet of foam below.
They saw the gleaming river seaward flow
15 From the inner land; far off, three mountaintops
Three silent pinnacles of aged snow,
Stood sunset-flushed; and, dewed with showery drops,
Up-clomb the shadowy pine above the woven copse.

The charmèd sunset lingered low adown
20 In the red West; through mountain clefts the dale
Was seen far inland, and the yellow down[4]
Bordered with palm, and many a winding vale
And meadow, set with slender galingale;[5]
A land where all things always seemed the same!
25 And round about the keel with faces pale,
Dark faces pale against that rosy flame,
The mild-eyed melancholy Lotos-eaters came.

Branches they bore of that enchanted stem,
Laden with flower and fruit, whereof they gave
30 To each, but whoso did receive of them
And taste, to him the gushing of the wave
Far far away did seem to mourn and rave
On alien shores; and if his fellow spake,
His voice was thin, as voices from the grave;
35 And deep-asleep he seemed, yet all awake,
And music in his ears his beating heart did make.

They sat them down upon the yellow sand,
Between the sun and moon upon the shore;
And sweet it was to dream of Fatherland,
40 Of child, and wife, and slave; but evermore
Most weary seemed the sea, weary the oar,
Weary the wandering fields of barren foam,
Then some one said, "We will return no more";
And all at once they sang, "Our island home°   *Ithaca*
45 Is far beyond the wave; we will no longer roam."

---

3. The repetition of "land" from line 1 was deliberate; Tennyson said that this "no rhyme" was
"lazier" in its effect. Cf. "afternoon" (lines 3–4) and
the rhyming of "adown" and "down" (lines 19 and

21).
4. An open plain on high ground.
5. A plant resembling tall coarse grass.

Choric Song[6]

1

There is sweet music here that softer falls
Than petals from blown roses on the grass,
Or night-dews on still waters between walls
Of shadowy granite, in a gleaming pass;
50   Music that gentlier on the spirit lies,
Than tired[7] eyelids upon tired eyes;
Music that brings sweet sleep down from the blissful skies.
Here are cool mosses deep,
And through the moss the ivies creep,
55   And in the stream the long-leaved flowers weep,
And from the craggy ledge the poppy hangs in sleep.

2

Why are we weighed upon with heaviness,
And utterly consumed with sharp distress,
While all things else have rest from weariness?
60   All things have rest: why should we toil alone,
We only toil, who are the first of things,
And make perpetual moan,
Still from one sorrow to another thrown;
Nor ever fold our wings,
65   And cease from wanderings,
Nor steep our brows in slumber's holy balm;
Nor harken what the inner spirit sings,
"There is no joy but calm!"—
Why should we only toil, the roof and crown of things?[8]

3

70   Lo! in the middle of the wood,
The folded leaf is wooed from out the bud
With winds upon the branch, and there
Grows green and broad, and takes no care,
Sun-steeped at noon, and in the moon
75   Nightly dew-fed; and turning yellow
Falls, and floats adown the air.
Lo! sweetened with summer light,
The full-juiced apple, waxing over-mellow,
Drops in a silent autumn night.
80   All its allotted length of days
The flower ripens in its place,
Ripens and fades, and falls, and hath no toil,
Fast-rooted in the fruitful soil.

6. Sung by the mariners.
7. Tennyson wanted the word to be pronounced as *tie-yerd* rather than *tier'd* or *tire-èd*, thus "making the word neither monosyllable or disyllabic, but a dreamy child of the two."

8. Cf. *Faerie Queene* 2.6.17: "Why then dost thou, O man, that of them all / Art Lord, and eke of nature Sovereaine, / Wilfully . . . wast thy joyous houres in needlesse paine?"

4

Hateful is the dark blue sky,
85 Vaulted o'er the dark blue sea.
Death is the end of life; ah, why
Should life all labor be?
Let us alone. Time driveth onward fast,
And in a little while our lips are dumb.
90 Let us alone. What is it that will last?
All things are taken from us, and become
Portions and parcels of the dreadful past.
Let us alone. What pleasure can we have
To war with evil? Is there any peace
95 In ever climbing up the climbing wave?
All things have rest, and ripen toward the grave
In silence—ripen, fall, and cease:
Give us long rest or death, dark death, or dreamful ease.[9]

5

How sweet it were, hearing the downward stream,
100 With half-shut eyes ever to seem
Falling asleep in a half-dream!
To dream and dream, like yonder amber light,
Which will not leave the myrrh-bush on the height;
To hear each other's whispered speech;
105 Eating the Lotos day by day,
To watch the crisping° ripples on the beach,   *curling*
And tender curving lines of creamy spray;
To lend our hearts and spirits wholly
To the influence of mild-minded melancholy;
110 To muse and brood and live again in memory,
With those old faces of our infancy
Heaped over with a mound of grass,
Two handfuls of white dust, shut in an urn of brass!

6

Dear is the memory of our wedded lives,
115 And dear the last embraces of our wives
And their warm tears; but all hath suffered change;
For surely now our household hearths are cold,
Our sons inherit us, our looks are strange,
And we should come like ghosts to trouble joy.
120 Or else the island princes° overbold   *Penelope's suitors*
Have eat our substance, and the minstrel sings
Before them of the ten years' war in Troy,
And our great deeds, as half-forgotten things.
Is there confusion in the little isle?
125 Let what is broken so remain.
The Gods are hard to reconcile;

9. Cf. *Faerie Queen* 1.9.40: "Sleepe after toyle, port after stormie seas, / Ease after warre, death after life does greatly please."

'Tis hard to settle order once again.
There *is* confusion worse than death,
Trouble on trouble, pain on pain,
130 Long labor unto aged breath,
Sore tasks to hearts worn out by many wars
And eyes grown dim with gazing on the pilot-stars.

7

But, propped on beds of amaranth and moly,[1]
How sweet—while warm airs lull us, blowing lowly—
135 With half-dropped eyelid still,
Beneath a heaven dark and holy,
To watch the long bright river drawing slowly
His waters from the purple hill—
To hear the dewy echoes calling
140 From cave to cave through the thick-twined vine—
To watch the emerald-colored water falling
Through many a woven acanthus[2] wreath divine!
Only to hear and see the far-off sparkling brine,
Only to hear were sweet, stretched out beneath the pine.

8

145 The Lotos blooms below the barren peak,
The Lotos blows by every winding creek;
All day the wind breathes low with mellower tone;
Through every hollow cave and alley lone
Round and round the spicy downs the yellow Lotos dust is blown.
150 We have had enough of action, and of motion we,
Rolled to starboard, rolled to larboard, when the surge was seething free,
Where the wallowing monster spouted his foam-fountains in the sea.
Let us swear an oath, and keep it with an equal mind,
In the hollow Lotos land to live and lie reclined
155 On the hills like Gods together, careless of mankind.
For they lie beside their nectar, and the bolts° are hurled   *thunderbolts*
Far below them in the valleys, and the clouds are lightly curled
Round their golden houses, girdled with the gleaming world;
Where they smile in secret, looking over wasted lands,
160 Blight and famine, plague and earthquake, roaring deeps and fiery sands,
Clanging fights, and flaming towns, and sinking ships, and praying hands.
But they smile, they find a music centered in a doleful song
Steaming up, a lamentation and an ancient tale of wrong,
Like a tale of little meaning though the words are strong;
165 Chanted from an ill-used race of men that cleave the soil,
Sow the seed, and reap the harvest with enduring toil,
Storing yearly little dues of wheat, and wine and oil;
Till they perish and they suffer—some, 'tis whispered—down in hell
Suffer endless anguish, others in Elysian valleys dwell,
170 Resting weary limbs at last on beds of asphodel.[3]

1. A flower with magical properties mentioned by
Homer. "Amaranth": a legendary unfading flower.
2. A plant resembling a thistle. Its leaves were the
model for ornaments on Corinthian columns.
3. A yellow lilylike flower supposed to grow in the
Elysian valleys.

Surely, surely, slumber is more sweet than toil, the shore
Than labor in the deep mid-ocean, wind and wave and oar;
O, rest ye, brother mariners, we will not wander more.

1832, 1842

Ulysses[1]

It little profits that an idle king,
By this still hearth, among these barren crags,
Matched with an aged wife, I mete and dole
Unequal laws[2] unto a savage race,
5 That hoard, and sleep, and feed,[3] and know not me.
I cannot rest from travel; I will drink
Life to the lees. All times I have enjoyed
Greatly, have suffered greatly, both with those
That loved me, and alone; on shore, and when
10 Through scudding drifts the rainy Hyades[4]
Vexed the dim sea. I am become a name;
For always roaming with a hungry heart
Much have I seen and known—cities of men
And manners, climates, councils, governments,
15 Myself not least, but honored of them all—
And drunk delight of battle with my peers,
Far on the ringing plains of windy Troy,
I am a part of all that I have met;
Yet all experience is an arch wherethrough
20 Gleams that untraveled world whose margin fades
Forever and forever when I move.
How dull it is to pause, to make an end,
To rust unburnished, not to shine in use![5]
As though to breathe were life! Life piled on life
25 Were all too little, and of one to me
Little remains; but every hour is saved
From that eternal silence, something more,
A bringer of new things; and vile it were
For some three suns to store and hoard myself,
30 And this gray spirit yearning in desire

1. According to Dante, after the fall of Troy, Ulysses never returned to his island home of Ithaca. Instead he persuaded some of his followers to seek new experiences by a voyage of exploration westward out beyond the Strait of Gibraltar. In his inspiring speech to his aging crew he said: "Consider your origin: you were not made to live as brutes, but to pursue virtue and knowledge" (*Inferno* 26). Tennyson modified Dante's version by combining it with Homer's account (*Odyssey* 19–24). Thus Tennyson has Ulysses make his speech in Ithaca some time after his return home to his reunion with his wife, Penelope, and his son, Telemachus, and, presumably, his resumption of administrative responsibilities involved in governing his kingdom.

Tennyson himself stated that this poem expressed his own "need of going forward and braving the struggle of life" after the death of Hallam.
2. Measure out rewards and punishments.
3. Cf. *Hamlet* 4.4.33–35: "What is a man, / If his chief good . . . / Be but to sleep and feed? a beast, no more."
4. A group of stars whose rising was assumed to be followed by rain. "Scudding drifts": driving showers of spray and rain.
5. Cf. Ulysses' speech in *Troilus and Cressida* 3.3.150–53: "Perseverance, dear my lord, / Keeps honour bright; to have done, is to hang / Quite out of fashion, like a rusty mail / in monumental mockery."

To follow knowledge like a sinking star,
Beyond the utmost bound of human thought.

This is my son, mine own Telemachus,
To whom I leave the scepter and the isle—
35 Well-loved of me, discerning to fulfill
This labor, by slow prudence to make mild
A rugged people, and through soft degrees
Subdue them to the useful and the good.
Most blameless is he, centered in the sphere
40 Of common duties, decent not to fail
In offices of tenderness, and pay
Meet adoration to my household gods,
When I am gone. He works his work, I mine.

There lies the port; the vessel puffs her sail;
45 There gloom the dark, broad seas. My mariners,
Souls that have toiled, and wrought, and thought with me—
That ever with a frolic welcome took
The thunder and the sunshine, and opposed
Free hearts, free foreheads—you and I are old;
50 Old age hath yet his honor and his toil.
Death closes all; but something ere the end,
Some work of noble note, may yet be done,
Not unbecoming men that strove with Gods.
The lights begin to twinkle from the rocks;
55 The long day wanes; the slow moon climbs; the deep
Moans round with many voices. Come, my friends,
'Tis not too late to seek a newer world.
Push off, and sitting well in order smite
The sounding furrows; for my purpose holds
60 To sail beyond the sunset, and the baths
Of all the western stars,[6] until I die.
It may be that the gulfs will wash us down;
It may be we shall touch the Happy Isles,[7]
And see the great Achilles, whom we knew.
65 Though much is taken, much abides; and though
We are not now that strength which in old days
Moved earth and heaven, that which we are, we are—
One equal temper of heroic hearts,
Made weak by time and fate, but strong in will
70 To strive, to seek, to find, and not to yield.

1833   1842

---

6. The outer ocean or river that, in Greek cosmology, surrounded the flat circle of the earth and into which the stars descended.
7. In Greek myth the Islands of the Blessed, a paradise of perpetual summer, located in the far-western ocean. They were peopled by great heroes who, without having died, had been translated there by the gods and made immortal.

Tithonus[1]

The woods decay, the woods decay and fall,
The vapors weep their burthen to the ground,
Man comes and tills the field and lies beneath,
And after many a summer dies the swan.[2]
5   Me only cruel immortality
Consumes; I wither slowly in thine arms,[3]
Here at the quiet limit of the world,
A white-haired shadow roaming like a dream
The ever-silent spaces of the East,
10   Far-folded mists, and gleaming halls of morn.
   Alas! for this gray shadow, once a man—
So glorious in his beauty and thy choice,
Who madest him thy chosen, that he seemed
To his great heart none other than a God!
15   I asked thee, "Give me immortality."
Then didst thou grant mine asking with a smile,
Like wealthy men who care not how they give.
But thy strong Hours indignant worked their wills,
And beat me down and marred and wasted me,
20   And though they could not end me, left me maimed
To dwell in presence of immortal youth,
Immortal age beside immortal youth,
And all I was in ashes. Can thy love,
Thy beauty, make amends, though even now,
25   Close over us, the silver star,[4] thy guide,
Shines in those tremulous eyes that fill with tears
To hear me? Let me go; take back thy gift.
Why should a man desire in any way
To vary from the kindly race of men,
30   Or pass beyond the goal of ordinance[5]
Where all should pause, as is most meet for all?
   A soft air fans the cloud apart; there comes
A glimpse of that dark world where I was born.
Once more the old mysterious glimmer steals
35   From thy pure brows, and from thy shoulders pure,
And bosom beating with a heart renewed.
Thy cheek begins to redden through the gloom,
Thy sweet eyes brighten slowly close to mine,
Ere yet they blind the stars, and the wild team[6]
40   Which love thee, yearning for thy yoke, arise,
And shake the darkness from their loosened manes,
And beat the twilight into flakes of fire.
   Lo! ever thus thou growest beautiful

1. A Trojan prince loved by the goddess of the dawn, Eos or Aurora, who obtained for him the gift of living forever but neglected to obtain for him the gift of everlasting youth. For the author's revisions while composing this poem, see "Poems in Process," in the appendices to this volume.
2. Some species of swans live for at least fifty years.
3. The arms of Aurora.
4. The morning star that precedes the dawn.
5. What is decreed or ordained as human destiny.
6. The horses that draw Aurora's chariot into the sky at daybreak.

In silence, then before thine answer given
45 Departest, and thy tears are on my cheek.
        Why wilt thou ever scare me with thy tears,
And make me tremble lest a saying learnt,
In days far-off, on that dark earth, be true?
"The Gods themselves cannot recall their gifts."
50   Ay me! ay me! with what another heart
In days far-off, and with what other eyes
I used to watch—if I be he that watched—
The lucid outline forming round thee; saw
The dim curls kindle into sunny rings;
55 Changed with thy mystic change, and felt my blood
Glow with the glow that slowly crimsoned all
Thy presence and thy portals, while I lay,
Mouth, forehead, eyelids, growing dewy-warm
With kisses balmier than half-opening buds
60 Of April, and could hear the lips that kissed
Whispering I knew not what of wild and sweet,
Like that strange song I heard Apollo sing,
While Ilion like a mist rose into towers.[7]
        Yet hold me not forever in thine East;
65 How can my nature longer mix with thine?
Coldly thy rosy shadows bathe me, cold
Are all thy lights, and cold my wrinkled feet
Upon thy glimmering thresholds, when the steam
Floats up from those dim fields about the homes
70 Of happy men that have the power to die,
And grassy barrows of the happier dead.
Release me, and restore me to the ground.
Thou seest all things, thou wilt see my grave;
Thou wilt renew thy beauty morn by morn,
75 I earth in earth forget these empty courts,
And thee returning on thy silver wheels.

1833, 1859   1860

Break, Break, Break

Break, break, break,
    On thy cold gray stones, O Sea!
And I would that my tongue could utter
    The thoughts that arise in me.

5   O, well for the fisherman's boy,
    That he shouts with his sister at play!
O, well for the sailor lad,
    That he sings in his boat on the bay!

And the stately ships go on
10   To their haven under the hill;

---

7. The walls of Troy ("Ilion") were supposed to have been built to the strains of Apollo's music.

But O for the touch of a vanished hand,
And the sound of a voice that is still!

Break, break, break,
At the foot of thy crags, O Sea!
15 But the tender grace of a day that is dead
Will never come back to me.

1834   1842

The Epic [Morte d'Arthur][1]

At Francis Allen's on the Christmas eve—
The game of forfeits done—the girls all kissed
Beneath the sacred bush° and passed away—   *mistletoe*
The parson Holmes, the poet Everard Hall,
5 The host, and I sat round the wassail-bowl,
Then halfway ebbed; and there we held a talk,
How all the old honor had from Christmas gone,
Or gone or dwindled down to some odd games
In some odd nooks like this; till I, tired out
10 With cutting eights that day upon the pond,
Where, three times slipping from the outer edge,
I bumped the ice into three several stars,
Fell in a doze; and half-awake I heard
The parson taking wide and wider sweeps,
15 Now harping on the church-commissioners,[2]
Now hawking at geology and schism;
Until I woke, and found him settled down
Upon the general decay of faith
Right through the world: "at home was little left,
20 And none abroad; there was no anchor, none,
To hold by." Francis, laughing, clapped his hand
On Everard's shoulder, with "I hold by him."
"And I," quoth Everard, "by the wassail-bowl."
"Why yes," I said, "we knew your gift that way
25 At college; but another which you had—
I mean of verse (for so we held it then),
What came of that?" "You know," said Frank, "he burnt
His epic, his King Arthur, some twelve books"—
And then to me demanding why: "O, sir,
30 He thought that nothing new was said, or else

1. At age twenty-four, Tennyson proposed to write a long epic on King Arthur. Five years later he had completed one book of the twelve, the story of Arthur's death, which he published in 1842 under the title *Morte d'Arthur*. In this early version the story is given a framework titled *The Epic*, which consists of a short introductory section (fifty-one lines) and an epilogue (thirty lines), describing a party on Christmas Eve in modern times, at which the poet reads *Morte d'Arthur* to his friends. In 1869, Tennyson incorporated *Morte d'Arthur* into his long narrative poem *Idylls of the King*; it appears there as the twelfth book, under the new title, *The Passing of Arthur*. At that time *The Epic* framework was discarded and some lines added. The 1842 version can be reconstructed (only two lines are modified) by reading *The Passing of Arthur*, lines 170–440.

2. Commissioners appointed by the government in 1835 to regulate finances of the Anglican Church.

Something so said 'twas nothing—that a truth
Looks freshest in the fashion of the day;
God knows; he has a mint of reasons; ask.
It pleased *me* well enough." "Nay, nay," said Hall,
35 "Why take the style of those heroic times?
For nature brings not back the mastodon,
Nor we those times; and why should any man
Remodel models? these twelve books of mine
Were faint Homeric echoes,[3] nothing-worth,
40 Mere chaff and draff, much better burnt." "But I,"
Said Francis, "picked the eleventh from this hearth,
And have it; keep a thing, its use will come.
I hoard it as a sugarplum for Holmes."
He laughed, and I, though sleepy, like a horse
45 That hears the corn-bin open, pricked my ears;
For I remembered Everard's college fame
When we were Freshmen. Then at my request
He brought it; and the poet, little urged,
But with some prelude of disparagement,
50 Read, mouthing out his hollow o's and a's,
Deep-chested music, and to this result.[4]

         *   *   *

Here ended Hall, and our last light, that long
325 Had winked and threatened darkness, flared and fell;
At which the parson, sent to sleep with sound,
And waked with silence, grunted "Good!" but we
Sat rapt: it was the tone with which he read—
Perhaps some modern touches here and there
330 Redeemed it from the charge of nothingness—
Or else we loved the man, and prized his work;
I know not; but we sitting, as I said,
The cock crew loud, as at that time of year
The lusty bird takes every hour for dawn.[5]
335 Then Francis, muttering like a man ill-used,
"There now—that's nothing!" drew a little back,
And drove his heel into the smoldered log,
That sent a blast of sparkles up the flue.
And so to bed, where yet in sleep I seemed
340 To sail with Arthur under looming shores,
Point after point; till on to dawn, when dreams
Begin to feel the truth and stir of day,
To me, methought, who waited with the crowd,
There came a bark that, blowing forward, bore
345 King Arthur, like a modern gentleman
Of stateliest port; and all the people cried,
"Arthur is come again: he cannot die."

3. After reading *Morte d'Arthur* in manuscript, Walter Savage Landor commented: "It is more Homeric than any poem of our time, and rivals some of the noblest parts of the Odyssey."
4. Here followed the 271 lines of *Morte d'Arthur* in 1842 (see *The Passing of Arthur,* lines 170–440, pp. 1297–1303). *The Epic* then continued as follows.
5. See Shakespeare's *Hamlet* 1.1.157–60 on the legend of the cock's crowing "all night long" on Christmas Eve.

Then those that stood upon the hills behind
Repeated—"Come again, and thrice as fair";
350   And, further inland, voices echoed—"Come
With all good things, and war shall be no more."
At this a hundred bells began to peal,
That with the sound I woke, and heard indeed
The clear church bells ring in the Christmas morn.

1833–38   1842

The Eagle: A Fragment

He clasps the crag with crooked hands;
Close to the sun in lonely lands,
Ringed with the azure world, he stands.

The wrinkled sea beneath him crawls:
5   He watches from his mountain walls,
And like a thunderbolt he falls.

1851

Locksley Hall[1]

Comrades, leave me here a little, while as yet 'tis early morn;
Leave me here, and when you want me, sound upon the bugle horn.

'Tis the place, and all around it, as of old, the curlews call,
Dreary gleams[2] about the moorland flying over Locksley Hall;

5   Locksley Hall, that in the distance overlooks the sandy tracts,
And the hollow ocean-ridges roaring into cataracts.

Many a night from yonder ivied casement, ere I went to rest,
Did I look on great Orion sloping slowly to the west.

Many a night I saw the Pleiads,[3] rising through the mellow shade,
10 Glitter like a swarm of fireflies tangled in a silver braid.

Here about the beach I wandered, nourishing a youth sublime
With the fairy tales of science, and the long result of time;

1. The situation in this poem—of a young man's being jilted by a woman who chose to marry a wealthy landowner—may have been suggested to Tennyson by the experience of his brother Frederick, a hot-tempered man who had fallen in love with his cousin Julia Tennyson and who was similarly unsuccessful. It may also have been inspired by Tennyson's own frustrated courtship of Rosa Baring, who rejected the young poet in favor of a wealthy suitor. Concerning the ranting tone of the speaker (a tone accentuated by the heavily marked trochaic meter), Tennyson said: "The whole poem represents young life, its good side, its deficiencies, and its yearnings."
2. Tennyson stated that "gleams" does not refer to "curlews" flying but to streaks of light.
3. Or the Pleiades, a seven-starred constellation.

When the centuries behind me like a fruitful land reposed;
When I clung to all the present for the promise that it closed°   *enclosed*

15   When I dipped into the future far as human eye could see,
Saw the vision of the world and all the wonder that would be.—

In the spring a fuller crimson comes upon the robin's breast;
In the spring the wanton lapwing gets himself another crest;

In the spring a livelier iris changes on the burnished dove;⁴
20   In the spring a young man's fancy lightly turns to thoughts of love.

Then her cheek was pale and thinner than should be for one so young,
And her eyes on all my motions with a mute observance hung.

And I said, "My cousin Amy, speak, and speak the truth to me,
Trust me, cousin, all the current of my being sets to thee."

25   On her pallid cheek and forehead came a color and a light,
As I have seen the rosy red flushing in the northern night.

And she turned—her bosom shaken with a sudden storm of sighs—
All the spirit deeply dawning in the dark of hazel eyes—

Saying, "I have hid my feelings, fearing they should do me wrong";
30   Saying, "Dost thou love me, cousin?" weeping, "I have loved thee long."

Love took up the glass of Time, and turned it in his glowing hands;
Every moment, lightly shaken, ran itself in golden sands.

Love took up the harp of Life, and smote on all the chords with might;
Smote the chord of Self, that, trembling, passed in music out of sight.

35   Many a morning on the moorland did we hear the copses ring,
And her whisper thronged my pulses with the fullness of the spring.

Many an evening by the waters did we watch the stately ships,
And our spirits rushed together at the touching of the lips.

O my cousin, shallow-hearted! O my Amy, mine no more!
40   O the dreary, dreary moorland! O the barren, barren shore!

Falser than all fancy fathoms, falser than all songs have sung,
Puppet to a father's threat, and servile to a shrewish tongue!

Is it well to wish thee happy?—having known me—to decline
On a range of lower feelings and a narrower heart than mine!

45   Yet it shall be; thou shalt lower to his level day by day,
What is fine within thee growing coarse to sympathize with clay.

4. The rainbowlike colors of a dove's throat plumage are intensified in the mating season.

As the husband is, the wife is; thou art mated with a clown,°   *boor*
And the grossness of his nature will have weight to drag thee down.

He will hold thee, when his passion shall have spent its novel force,
50   Something better than his dog, a little dearer than his horse.

What is this? his eyes are heavy; think not they are glazed with wine.
Go to him, it is thy duty; kiss him, take his hand in thine.

It may be my lord is weary, that his brain is overwrought;
Soothe him with thy finer fancies, touch him with thy lighter thought.

55   He will answer to the purpose, easy things to understand—
Better thou wert dead before me, though I slew thee with my hand!

Better thou and I were lying, hidden from the heart's disgrace,
Rolled in one another's arms, and silent in a last embrace.

Cursed be the social wants that sin against the strength of youth!
60   Cursed be the social lies that warp us from the living truth!

Cursed be the sickly forms that err from honest Nature's rule!
Cursed be the gold that gilds the straitened° forehead of the fool!   *narrowed*

Well—'tis well that I should bluster!—Hadst thou less unworthy proved—
Would to God—for I had loved thee more than ever wife was loved.

65   Am I mad, that I should cherish that which bears but bitter fruit?
I will pluck it from my bosom, though my heart be at the root.

Never, though my mortal summers to such length of years should come
As the many-wintered crow[5] that leads the clanging rookery home.

Where is comfort? in division of the records of the mind?
70   Can I part her from herself, and love her, as I knew her, kind?

I remember one that perished; sweetly did she speak and move;
Such a one do I remember, whom to look at was to love.

Can I think of her as dead, and love her for the love she bore?
No—she never loved me truly; love is love for evermore.

75   Comfort? comfort scorned of devils! this is truth the poet[6] sings,
That a sorrow's crown of sorrow is remembering happier things.

Drug thy memories, lest thou learn it, lest thy heart be put to proof,
In the dead unhappy night, and when the rain is on the roof.

Like a dog, he hunts in dreams, and thou art staring at the wall,
80   Where the dying night-lamp flickers, and the shadows rise and fall.

5. A rook, a long-lived bird.   6. Dante's *Inferno* 5.121–23.

Then a hand shall pass before thee, pointing to his drunken sleep,
To thy widowed[7] marriage-pillows, to the tears that thou wilt weep.

Thou shalt hear the "Never, never," whispered by the phantom years.
And a song from out the distance in the ringing of thine ears;

85 And an eye shall vex thee, looking ancient kindness on thy pain.
Turn thee, turn thee on thy pillow; get thee to thy rest again.

Nay, but Nature brings thee solace; for a tender voice will cry.
'Tis a purer life than thine, a lip to drain thy trouble dry.

Baby lips will laugh me down; my latest rival brings thee rest.
90 Baby fingers, waxen touches, press me from the mother's breast.

O, the child too clothes the father with a dearness not his due.
Half is thine and half is his; it will be worthy of the two.

O, I see thee old and formal, fitted to thy petty part,
With a little hoard of maxims preaching down a daughter's heart.

95 "They were dangerous guides the feelings—she herself was not exempt—
Truly, she herself had suffered"—Perish in thy self-contempt!

Overlive it—lower yet—be happy! wherefore should I care?
I myself must mix with action, lest I wither by despair.

What is that which I should turn to, lighting upon days like these?
100 Every door is barred with gold, and opens but to golden keys.

Every gate is thronged with suitors, all the markets overflow.
I have but an angry fancy; what is that which I should do?

I had been content to perish, falling on the foeman's ground,
When the ranks are rolled in vapor, and the winds are laid with sound.[8]

105 But the jingling of the guinea helps the hurt that Honor feels,
And the nations do but murmur, snarling at each other's heels.

Can I but relive in sadness? I will turn that earlier page.
Hide me from my deep emotion, O thou wondrous Mother-Age![9]

Make me feel the wild pulsation that I felt before the strife,
110 When I heard my days before me, and the tumult of my life;

Yearning for the large excitement that the coming years would yield,
Eager-hearted as a boy when first he leaves his father's field,

7. Presumably figurative. Her marriage having become a mockery, she is widowed.
8. It was once believed that the firing of artillery stilled the winds.
9. A happier past at life's beginning, which generated a more confident anticipation of the future (see also line 185).

And at night along the dusky highway near and nearer drawn,
Sees in heaven the light of London flaring like a dreary dawn;

5　And his spirit leaps within him to be gone before him then,
Underneath the light he looks at, in among the throngs of men;

Men, my brothers, men the workers, ever reaping something new;
That which they have done but earnest° of the things that they　　　*pledge*
　　shall do.

For I dipped into the future, far as human eye could see,
20　Saw the Vision of the world, and all the wonder that would be;

Saw the heavens fill with commerce, argosies of magic sails,[1]
Pilots of the purple twilight, dropping down with costly bales;

Heard the heavens fill with shouting, and there rained a ghastly dew
From the nations' airy navies grappling in the central blue;

25　Far along the world-wide whisper of the south wind rushing warm,
With the standards of the peoples plunging through the thunderstorm;

Till the war drum throbbed no longer, and the battle flags were furled
In the Parliament of man, the Federation of the world.

There the common sense of most shall hold a fretful realm in awe,
30　And the kindly earth shall slumber, lapped in universal law.

So I triumphed ere my passion sweeping through me left me dry,
Left me with the palsied heart, and left me with the jaundiced eye;

Eye, to which all order festers, all things here are out of joint.
Science moves, but slowly, slowly, creeping on from point to point;

35　Slowly comes a hungry people, as a lion, creeping nigher,
Glares at one that nods and winks behind a slowly-dying fire.

Yet I doubt not through the ages one increasing purpose runs,
And the thoughts of men are widened with the process of the suns.

What is that to him that reaps not harvest of his youthful joys,
40　Though the deep heart of existence beat forever like a boy's?

Knowledge comes, but wisdom lingers, and I linger on the shore,
And the individual withers, and the world is more and more.

Knowledge comes, but wisdom lingers, and he bears a laden breast,
Full of sad experience, moving toward the stillness of his rest.

1. Probably airships, such as balloons.

145 Hark, my merry comrades call me, sounding on the bugle horn,
They to whom my foolish passion were a target for their scorn.

Shall it not be scorn to me to harp on such a moldered string?
I am shamed through all my nature to have loved so slight a thing.

Weakness to be wroth with weakness! woman's pleasure, woman's pain—
150 Nature made them blinder motions bounded in a shallower brain.

Woman is the lesser man, and all thy passions, matched with mine,
Are as moonlight unto sunlight, and as water unto wine—

Here at least, where nature sickens, nothing. Ah, for some retreat
Deep in yonder shining Orient, where my life began to beat.

155 Where in wild Mahratta-battle² fell my father evil-starred—
I was left a trampled orphan, and a selfish uncle's ward.

Or to burst all links of habit—there to wander far away,
On from island unto island at the gateways of the day.

Larger constellations burning, mellow moons and happy skies,
160 Breadths of tropic shade and palms in cluster, knots of Paradise.

Never comes the trader, never floats an European flag,
Slides the bird o'er lustrous woodland, swings the trailer° from   *vine*
   the crag;

Droops the heavy-blossomed bower, hangs the heavy-fruited tree—
Summer isles of Eden lying in dark purple spheres of sea.

165 There methinks would be enjoyment more than in this march of mind,
In the steamship, in the railway, in the thoughts that shake mankind.

There the passions cramped no longer shall have scope and breathing space;
I will take some savage woman, she shall rear my dusky race.

Iron-jointed, supple-sinewed, they shall dive, and they shall run,
170 Catch the wild goat by the hair, and hurl their lances in the sun;

Whistle back the parrot's call, and leap the rainbows of the brooks,
Not with blinded eyesight poring over miserable books—

Fool, again the dream, the fancy! but I *know* my words are wild,
But I count the gray barbarian lower than the Christian child.

175 I, to herd with narrow foreheads, vacant of our glorious gains,
Like a beast with lower pleasures, like a beast with lower pains!

2. Reference to wars waged by a Hindu people against the British forces in India (1803 and 1817).

Mated with a squalid savage—what to me were sun or clime?
I the heir of all the ages, in the foremost files of time—

I that rather held it better men should perish one by one,
80 Than that earth should stand at gaze like Joshua's moon in Ajalon![3]

Not in vain the distance beacons. Forward, forward let us range,
Let the great world spin forever down the ringing grooves[4] of change.

Through the shadow of the globe we sweep into the younger day;
Better fifty years of Europe than a cycle of Cathay.[5]

85 Mother-Age—for mine I knew not—help me as when life begun;
Rift the hills, and roll the waters, flash the lightnings, weigh the sun.

O, I see the crescent promise of my spirit hath not set.
Ancient founts of inspiration well through all my fancy yet.

Howsoever these things be, a long farewell to Locksley Hall!
90 Now for me the woods may wither, now for me the roof-tree fall.

Comes a vapor from the margin, blackening over heath and holt,
Cramming all the blast before it, in its breast a thunderbolt.

Let it fall on Locksley Hall, with rain or hail, or fire or snow;
For the mighty wind arises, roaring seaward, and I go.

1837–38   1842

FROM THE PRINCESS[1]

Sweet and Low

Sweet and low, sweet and low,
  Wind of the western sea,
Low, low, breathe and blow,
  Wind of the western sea!
5 Over the rolling waters go,
  Come from the dying moon, and blow,
    Blow him again to me;
  While my little one, while my pretty one, sleeps.

  Sleep and rest, sleep and rest,
10   Father will come to thee soon;

---

3. At the command of Joshua, the sun and moon stood still while the Israelites completed the slaughter of their enemies in the valley of Ajalon (Joshua 10.12–13).
4. Railroad tracks. Tennyson at one time had the impression that train wheels ran in grooved rails.
5. China, regarded in the 19th century as a static, unprogressive country.

1. *The Princess* (1847), a long narrative poem, contains interludes in which occasional songs are sung. The six songs printed here, some of which first appeared in later editions of the poem, rank among the finest of Tennyson's lyrics, and various 19th- and 20th-century composers have set them to music.

Rest, rest, on mother's breast,
   Father will come to thee soon;
Father will come to his babe in the nest,
Silver sails all out of the west
15   Under the silver moon;
Sleep, my little one, sleep, my pretty one, sleep.

1849
                                             1850

The Splendor Falls

The splendor falls on castle walls
   And snowy summits old in story;
The long light shakes across the lakes,
   And the wild cataract leaps in glory.
5 Blow, bugle, blow, set the wild echoes flying,
Blow, bugle; answer, echoes, dying, dying, dying.

O, hark, O, hear! how thin and clear,
   And thinner, clearer, farther going!
O, sweet and far from cliff and scar°   *mountainside*
10   The horns of Elfland faintly blowing!
Blow, let us hear the purple glens replying,
Blow, bugle; answer, echoes, dying, dying, dying.

O love, they die in yon rich sky,
   They faint on hill or field or river;
15 Our echoes roll from soul to soul,
   And grow forever and forever.
Blow, bugle, blow, set the wild echoes flying,
And answer, echoes, answer, dying, dying, dying.

                                             1850

Tears, Idle Tears[1]

   Tears, idle tears, I know not what they mean,
Tears from the depth of some divine despair
Rise in the heart, and gather to the eyes,
In looking on the happy autumn-fields,
5 And thinking of the days that are no more.

   Fresh as the first beam glittering on a sail,
That brings our friends up from the underworld,
Sad as the last which reddens over one
That sinks with all we love below the verge;
10 So sad, so fresh, the days that are no more.

1. Tennyson commented: "This song came to me on the yellowing autumn-tide at Tintern Abbey, full for me of its bygone memories." This locale would be for him associated both with Wordsworth's *Tintern Abbey* and with memories of Hallam, who was buried across the Bristol Channel in this area. "It is what I have always felt even from a boy, and what as a boy I called the 'passion of the past.' And it is so always with me now; it is the distance that charms me in the landscape, the picture and the past, and not the immediate today in which I move."

Ah, sad and strange as in dark summer dawns
The earliest pipe of half-awakened birds
To dying ears, when unto dying eyes
The casement slowly grows a glimmering square;
15   So sad, so strange, the days that are no more.

Dear as remembered kisses after death,
And sweet as those by hopeless fancy feigned
On lips that are for others; deep as love,
Deep as first love, and wild with all regret;
20   O Death in Life, the days that are no more!

1847

Ask Me No More

Ask me no more: the moon may draw the sea;
    The cloud may stoop from heaven and take the shape,
    With fold to fold, of mountain or of cape;
But O too fond, when have I answered thee?
5   Ask me no more.

Ask me no more: what answer should I give?
    I love not hollow cheek or faded eye:
    Yet, O my friend, I will not have thee die!
Ask me no more, lest I should bid thee live;
10   Ask me no more.

Ask me no more: thy fate and mine are sealed;
    I strove against the stream and all in vain;
    Let the great river take me to the main.
No more, dear love, for at a touch I yield;
15   Ask me no more.

1849   1850

Now Sleeps the Crimson Petal

Now sleeps the crimson petal, now the white;
Nor waves the cypress in the palace walk;
Nor winks the gold fin in the porphyry font.
The firefly wakens; waken thou with me.

5   Now droops the milk-white peacock like a ghost,
And like a ghost she glimmers on to me.

Now lies the Earth all Danaë[1] to the stars,
And all thy heart lies open unto me.

1. A Greek princess, who was confined in a metal tower by her father to prevent suitors from coming near her. Zeus, however, succeeded in visiting her in the form of a shower of gold. Their offspring was the hero Perseus.

Now slides the silent meteor on, and leaves
10   A shining furrow, as thy thoughts in me.

Now folds the lily all her sweetness up,
And slips into the bosom of the lake.
So fold thyself, my dearest, thou, and slip
Into my bosom and be lost in me.

1847

Come Down, O Maid[1]

Come down, O maid, from yonder mountain height.
What pleasure lives in height (the shepherd sang),
In height and cold, the splendor of the hills?
But cease to move so near the heavens, and cease
5   To glide a sunbeam by the blasted pine,
To sit a star upon the sparkling spire;
And come, for Love is of the valley, come,
For Love is of the valley, come thou down
And find him; by the happy threshold, he,
10   Or hand in hand with Plenty in the maize,
Or red with spirted purple of the vats,
Or foxlike in the vine; nor cares to walk
With Death and Morning on the Silver Horns,°   *mountain peaks*
Nor wilt thou snare him in the white ravine,
15   Nor find him dropped upon the firths of ice,°   *glaciers*
That huddling slant in furrow-cloven falls
To roll the torrent out of dusky doors.
But follow; let the torrent dance thee down
To find him in the valley; let the wild
20   Lean-headed eagles yelp alone, and leave
The monstrous ledges there to slope, and spill
Their thousand wreaths of dangling water-smoke,
That like a broken purpose waste in air.
So waste not thou, but come; for all the vales
25   Await thee; azure pillars of the hearth[2]
Arise to thee; the children call, and I
Thy shepherd pipe, and sweet is every sound,
Sweeter thy voice, but every sound is sweet;
Myriads of rivulets hurrying through the lawn,
30   The moan of doves in immemorial elms,
And murmuring of innumerable bees.

1847

1. Written during Tennyson's visit to the Swiss   2. Columns of smoke from the houses in the val-
Alps in 1846, after he had seen Mount Jungfrau   ley.
("The Maiden").

["The Woman's Cause Is Man's"][1]

"Blame not thyself too much," I said, "nor blame
240 Too much the sons of men and barbarous laws;
These were the rough ways of the world till now.
Henceforth thou hast a helper, me, that know
The woman's cause is man's: they rise or sink
Together, dwarfed or godlike, bond or free:
245 For she that out of Lethe scales with man
The shining steps of Nature, shares with man
His nights, his days, moves with him to one goal,
Stays all the fair young planet in her hands—
If she be small, slight-natured, miserable,
250 How shall men grow? but work no more alone!
Our place is much: as far as in us lies
We two will serve them both in aiding her—
Will clear away the parasitic forms
That seem to keep her up but drag her down—
255 Will leave her space to burgeon out of all
Within her—let her make herself her own
To give or keep, to live and learn and be
All that not harms distinctive womanhood.
For woman is not undevelopt man,
260 But diverse: could we make her as the man,
Sweet Love were slain: his dearest bond is this,
Not like to like, but like in difference.
Yet in the long years liker must they grow;
The man be more of woman, she of man;
265 He gain in sweetness and in moral height,
Nor lose the wrestling thews that throw the world;
She mental breadth, nor fail in childward care,
Nor lose the childlike in the larger mind;
Till at the last she set herself to man,
270 Like perfect music unto noble words;
And so these twain, upon the skirts of Time,
Sit side by side, full-summed in all their powers,
Dispensing harvest, sowing the To-be,
Self-reverent each and reverencing each,
275 Distinct in individualities,
But like each other even as those who love.
Then comes the statelier Eden back to men:
Then reign the world's great bridals, chaste and calm:
Then springs the crowning race of humankind.

1. *The Princess* was Tennyson's attempt to address the contemporary debate over woman's proper role. It tells the story of a prince who courts the young and beautiful Princess Ida. She has vowed she will never marry and has established a women's university from which men are excluded. The prince and his two companions dress themselves up in women's clothes to gain entrance to the university. When a battle ensues—in which King Gama, the prince's father, invades the university to rescue his son and force Ida to marry him—the university is turned into a hospital and the princess is persuaded of the error of her ways. The prince's final vision, from book 7 (reprinted here), in which he imagines a future of gradual change, by which men and women adopt the strengths of the other while maintaining their distinct natures, has been a key text in discussing Victorian patriarchy. In the operetta *Princess Ida*, Gilbert and Sullivan use Tennyson's story to satirize feminism.

May these things be!"
280   Sighing she spoke "I fear
They will not."
                Dear, but let us type them now
In our own lives, and this proud watchword rest
Of equal; seeing either sex alone
Is half itself, and in true marriage lies
285 Nor equal, nor unequal: each fulfils
Defect in each, and always thought in thought,
Purpose in purpose, will in will, they grow,
The single pure and perfect animal,
The two-celled heart beating, with one full stroke,
Life."
290   And again sighing she spoke: "A dream
That once was mine! what woman taught you this?"

1839–47   1847

In Memoriam A. H. H. When Arthur Hallam died suddenly at the age of twenty-two, Tennyson felt that his life had been shattered. Hallam was not only Tennyson's closest friend, and his sister's fiancé, but a critic and champion of his poetry. Widely regarded as the most promising young man of his generation, Hallam had written a review of Tennyson's first book of poetry that is still one of the best assessments of it. When Tennyson lost Hallam's love and support, he was overwhelmed with doubts about his own life and vocation and about the meaning of the universe and humankind's place in it, doubts reinforced by his study of geology and other sciences. To express the variety of his feelings and reflections, he began to compose a series of lyrics. Tennyson later arranged these "short swallow-flights of song," as he called them, written at intervals over a period of seventeen years, into one long elegy. Although the resulting poem has many affinities with traditional elegies like Milton's *Lycidas* and Shelley's *Adonais,* its structure is strikingly different. It is made up of individual lyric units that are seemingly self-contained but take their full meaning from their place in the whole. As T. S. Eliot has written, "It is unique: it is a long poem made by putting together lyrics, which have only the unity and continuity of a diary, the concentrated diary of a man confessing himself." Though intensely personal, it expressed the religious doubts of his age. Eliot continues, "It is not religious because of the quality of its faith but because of the quality of its doubt. . . . *In Memoriam* is a poem of despair." It is also a love poem. Like Shakespeare's sonnets, to which the poem alludes, *In Memoriam* vests its most intense emotion in male friendship.

The sections of the poem record a progressive development from despair to some sort of hope. Some of the early sections of the poem resemble traditional pastoral elegies, including those portraying the voyage during which Hallam's body was brought to England for burial (sections 9 to 15 and 19). Other early sections portraying the speaker's loneliness, in which even Christmas festivities seem joyless (sections 28 to 30), are more distinctive. With the passage of time, indicated by anniversaries and by recurring changes of the seasons, the speaker comes to accept the loss and to assert his belief in life and in an afterlife. In particular the recurring Christmases (sections 28, 78, 104) indicate the stages of his development, yet the pattern of progress in the poem is not a simple unimpeded movement upward. Dramatic conflicts recur throughout. Thus the most intense expression of doubt occurs not at the beginning of *In Memoriam* but as late as sections 54, 55, and 56.

The quatrain form in which the whole poem is written is usually called the "*In Memoriam* stanza," although it had been occasionally used by earlier poets. So rigid a form taxed Tennyson's ingenuity in achieving variety, but it is one of several means by which the diverse parts of the poem are knitted together.

The introductory section, consisting of eleven stanzas, is commonly referred to as the "Prologue," although Tennyson did not assign a title to it. It was written in 1849 after the rest of the poem was complete.

From In Memoriam A. H. H.

OBIIT MDCCCXXXIII[1]

Strong Son of God, immortal Love,
    Whom we, that have not seen thy face,
    By faith, and faith alone, embrace,
Believing where we cannot prove;[2]

5 Thine are these orbs[3] of light and shade;
    Thou madest Life in man and brute;
    Thou madest Death; and lo, thy foot
Is on the skull which thou hast made.

Thou wilt not leave us in the dust:
10   Thou madest man, he knows not why,
    He thinks he was not made to die;
And thou hast made him: thou art just.

Thou seemest human and divine,
    The highest, holiest manhood, thou.
15   Our wills are ours, we know not how;
Our wills are ours, to make them thine.

Our little systems[4] have their day;
    They have their day and cease to be;
    They are but broken lights of thee,
20 And thou, O Lord, art more than they.

We have but faith: we cannot know,
    For knowledge is of things we see;
    And yet we trust it comes from thee,
A beam in darkness: let it grow.

25 Let knowledge grow from more to more,
    But more of reverence in us dwell;
    That mind and soul, according well,
May make one music as before,[5]

1. Died 1833.
2. Cf. John 20.24–29, in which Jesus rebukes Thomas for his doubts concerning the Resurrection: "Blessed are they that have not seen, and yet have believed."

3. The sun and moon (according to Tennyson's note).
4. Of religion and philosophy.
5. As in the days of fixed religious faith.

But vaster. We are fools and slight;
30   We mock thee when we do not fear:
    But help thy foolish ones to bear;
Help thy vain worlds to bear thy light.

Forgive what seemed my sin in me,
    What seemed my worth since I began;
35   For merit lives from man to man,
And not from man, O Lord, to thee.

Forgive my grief for one removed,
    Thy creature, whom I found so fair.
    I trust he lives in thee, and there
40 I find him worthier to be loved.

Forgive these wild and wandering cries,
    Confusions of a wasted° youth;   *desolated*
    Forgive them where they fail in truth,
And in thy wisdom make me wise.

1849

1

I held it truth, with him who sings
    To one clear harp in divers tones,[6]
    That men may rise on stepping stones
Of their dead selves to higher things.

5 But who shall so forecast the years
    And find in loss a gain to match?
    Or reach a hand through time to catch
The far-off interest of tears?

Let Love clasp Grief lest both be drowned,
10   Let darkness keep her raven gloss.
    Ah, sweeter to be drunk with loss,
To dance with Death, to beat the ground,

Than that the victor Hours should scorn
    The long result of love, and boast,
15   "Behold the man that loved and lost,
But all he was is overworn."

2

Old yew, which graspest at the stones
    That name the underlying dead,

6. Identified by Tennyson as Goethe.

Thy fibers net the dreamless head,
Thy roots are wrapped about the bones.

5   The seasons bring the flower again,
    And bring the firstling to the flock;
    And in the dusk of thee the clock
Beats out the little lives of men.

O, not for thee the glow, the bloom,
10   Who changest not in any gale,
    Nor branding summer suns avail
To touch thy thousand years of gloom[7]

And gazing on thee, sullen tree,
    Sick for° thy stubborn hardihood,   *envying*
15   I seem to fail from out my blood
And grow incorporate into thee.

3

O Sorrow, cruel fellowship,
    O Priestess in the vaults of Death,
    O sweet and bitter in a breath,
What whispers from thy lying lip?

5   "The stars," she whispers, "blindly run;
    A web is woven across the sky;
    From out waste places comes a cry,
And murmurs from the dying sun;

"And all the phantom, Nature, stands—
10   With all the music in her tone,
    A hollow echo of my own—
A hollow form with empty hands."

And shall I take a thing so blind,
    Embrace her° as my natural good;   *Sorrow*
15   Or crush her, like a vice of blood,
Upon the threshold of the mind?

4

To Sleep I give my powers away;
    My will is bondsman to the dark;
    I sit within a helmless bark,
And with my heart I muse and say:

7. The ancient yew tree, growing in the grounds near the clock tower and church where Hallam was to be buried, seems neither to blossom in spring nor to change from its dark mournful color in summer. "Thousand years": cf. Book of Common Prayer Psalm 90: "For a thousand years in Thy sight are but as yesterday when it is past, and as a watch in the night."

5 O heart, how fares it with thee now,
  That thou should fail from thy desire,
  Who scarcely darest to inquire,
 "What is it makes me beat so low?"

 Something it is which thou hast lost,
10 Some pleasure from thine early years.
  Break thou deep vase of chilling tears,
 That grief hath shaken into frost![8]

 Such clouds of nameless trouble cross
  All night below the darkened eyes;
15 With morning wakes the will, and cries,
 "Thou shalt not be the fool of loss."

5

 I sometimes hold it half a sin
  To put in words the grief I feel;
  For words, like Nature, half reveal
 And half conceal the Soul within.

5 But, for the unquiet heart and brain,
  A use in measured language lies;
  The sad mechanic exercise,
 Like dull narcotics, numbing pain.

 In words, like weeds,° I'll wrap me o'er,   *garments*
10 Like coarsest clothes against the cold;
  But that large grief which these enfold
 Is given in outline and no more.

6

 One writes, that "Other friends remain,"
  That "Loss is common to the race"—
  And common is the commonplace,
 And vacant chaff well meant for grain.

5 That loss is common would not make
  My own less bitter, rather more:
  Too common! Never morning wore
 To evening, but some heart did break.

 O father, wheresoe'er thou be,
10 Who pledgest° now thy gallant son;   *toasts*
  A shot, ere half thy draft be done,
 Hath stilled the life that beat from thee.

8. Water can be brought below freezing-point and not turn into ice—if it be kept still; but if it be moved suddenly it turns into ice and may break a vase [Tennyson's note].

O mother, praying God will save
    Thy sailor—while thy head is bowed,
15   His heavy-shotted hammock-shroud
Drops in his vast and wandering grave.

Ye know no more than I who wrought
    At that last hour to please him well;[9]
    Who mused on all I had to tell,
20 And something written, something thought;

Expecting still his advent home;
    And ever met him on his way
    With wishes, thinking, "here today,"
Or "here tomorrow will he come."

25 O somewhere, meek, the unconscious dove,
    That sittest ranging° golden hair;   *arranging*
    And glad to find thyself so fair,
Poor child, that waitest for thy love!

For now her father's chimney glows
30   In expectation of a guest;
    And thinking "this will please him best,"
She takes a riband or a rose;

For he will see them on tonight;
    And with the thought her color burns;
35   And, having left the glass, she turns
Once more to set a ringlet right;

And, even when she turned, the curse
    Had fallen, and her future Lord
    Was drowned in passing through the ford,
40 Or killed in falling from his horse.

O what to her shall be the end?
    And what to me remains of good?
    To her, perpetual maidenhood,
And unto me no second friend.

7

Dark house,[1] by which once more I stand
    Here in the long unlovely street,
    Doors, where my heart was used to beat
So quickly, waiting for a hand,

9. According to Tennyson's son, his father had discovered that he had been writing a letter to Hallam during the very hour when his friend died.

1. The house on Wimpole Street, in London, where Hallam had lived.

5 A hand that can be clasped no more—
   Behold me, for I cannot sleep,
   And like a guilty thing I creep
At earliest morning to the door.

   He is not here; but far away
10   The noise of life begins again,
   And ghastly through the drizzling rain
On the bald street breaks the blank day.

8

   A happy lover who has come
   To look on her that loves him well,
   Who 'lights and rings the gateway bell,
And learns her gone and far from home;

5 He saddens, all the magic light
   Dies off at once from bower and hall,
   And all the place is dark, and all
The chambers emptied of delight:

   So find I every pleasant spot
10   In which we two were wont to meet,
   The field, the chamber, and the street,
For all is dark where thou art not.

   Yet as that other, wandering there
   In those deserted walks, may find
15   A flower beat with rain and wind,
Which once she fostered up with care;

   So seems it in my deep regret,
   O my forsaken heart, with thee
   And this poor flower of poesy
20 Which little cared for fades not yet.

   But since it pleased a vanished eye,[2]
   I go to plant it on his tomb,
   That if it can it there may bloom,
Or dying, there at least may die.

9

   Fair ship, that from the Italian shore
   Sailest the placid ocean-plains
   With my lost Arthur's loved remains,
Spread thy full wings, and waft him o'er.

2. Hallam expressed enthusiasm for Tennyson's early poetry in a review written in 1831.

5 So draw him home to those that mourn
    In vain; a favorable speed
    Ruffle thy mirrored mast, and lead
Through prosperous floods his holy urn.

    All night no ruder air perplex
10   Thy sliding keel, till Phosphor,° bright   *morning star*
    As our pure love, through early light
Shall glimmer on the dewey decks.

    Sphere all your lights around, above;
    Sleep, gentle heavens, before the prow;
15   Sleep, gentle winds, as he sleeps now,
My friend, the brother of my love;

    My Arthur, whom I shall not see
    Till all my widowed race be run;
    Dear as the mother to the son,
20   More than my brothers are to me.

10

    I hear the noise about thy keel;
    I hear the bell struck in the night;
    I see the cabin window bright;
    I see the sailor at the wheel.

5 Thou bring'st the sailor to his wife,
    And traveled men from foreign lands;
    And letters unto trembling hands;
And, thy dark freight, a vanished life.

    So bring him; we have idle dreams;
10   This look of quiet flatters thus
    Our home-bred fancies. O, to us,
The fools of habit, sweeter seems

    To rest beneath the clover sod,
    That takes the sunshine and the rains,
15   Or where the kneeling hamlet drains
The chalice of the grapes of God;[3]

    Than if with thee the roaring wells
    Should gulf him fathom-deep in brine,
    And hands so often clasped in mine,
20   Should toss with tangle° and with shells.   *seaweed*

---

3. Reference to a burial inside a church building rather than in the churchyard.

11

Calm is the morn without a sound,
   Calm as to suit a calmer grief,
   And only through the faded leaf
The chestnut pattering to the ground;

5 Calm and deep peace on this high wold,°   *open countryside*
   And on these dews that drench the furze,
   And all the silvery gossamers
That twinkle into green and gold;

Calm and still light on yon great plain
10   That sweeps with all its autumn bowers,
   And crowded farms and lessening towers,
To mingle with the bounding main;

Calm and deep peace in this wide air,
   These leaves that redden to the fall,
15   And in my heart, if calm at all,
If any calm, a calm despair;

Calm on the seas, and silver sleep,
   And waves that sway themselves in rest,
   And dead calm in that noble breast
20 Which heaves but with the heaving deep.[4]

12

Lo, as a dove when up she springs
   To bear through Heaven a tale of woe,
   Some dolorous message knit below
The wild pulsation of her wings;

5 Like her I go; I cannot stay;
   I leave this mortal ark behind,
   A weight of nerves without a mind,
And leave the cliffs, and haste away

O'er ocean-mirrors rounded large,
10   And reach the glow of southern skies,
   And see the sails at distance rise,
And linger weeping on the marge,

And saying; "Comes he thus, my friend?
   Is this the end of all my care?"
15   And circle moaning in the air:
"Is this the end? Is this the end?"

---

4. It is now the autumn of 1833, and the poet imagines that Hallam's body was already being brought back by ship to England. The date of the actual voyage seems to have been later in the year.

And forward dart again, and play
About the prow, and back return
To where the body sits, and learn
20   That I have been an hour away.

13

Tears of the widower, when he sees
A late-lost form that sleep reveals,
And moves his doubtful arms, and feels
Her place is empty, fall like these;

5   Which weep a loss forever new,
A void where heart on heart reposed;
And, where warm hands have pressed and closed,
Silence, till I be silent too;

Which weep the comrade of my choice,
10   An awful thought, a life removed,
The human-hearted man I loved,
A Spirit, not a breathing voice.

Come, Time, and teach me, many years,
I do not suffer in a dream;
15   For now so strange do these things seem,
Mine eyes have leisure for their tears,

My fancies time to rise on wing,
And glance about the approaching sails,
As though they brought but merchants' bales,
20   And not the burthen that they bring.[5]

14

If one should bring me this report,
That thou° hadst touched the land today,   *the ship*
And I went down unto the quay;[6]
And found thee lying in the port;

5   And standing, muffled round with woe,
Should see thy passengers in rank
Come stepping lightly down the plank
And beckoning unto those they know;

And if along with these should come
10   The man I held as half divine,

5. The poet asks Time to teach him to confront
the "awful" fact of what has happened (line 10) so
that he will not delude himself by fancying the ship
is bearing only merchandise and not the body of

his friend.
6. By 1850 the accepted pronunciation of "quay"
would rhyme with *key*, but Tennyson reverts to an
earlier pronunciation, *kay*.

Should strike a sudden hand in mine,
And ask a thousand things of home;

And I should tell him all my pain,
   And how my life had drooped of late,
15   And he should sorrow o'er my state
And marvel what possessed my brain;

And I perceived no touch of change,
   No hint of death in all his frame,
   But found him all in all the same,
20   I should not feel it to be strange.

15

Tonight the winds begin to rise
   And roar from yonder dropping day;
   The last red leaf is whirled away,
The rooks are blown about the skies;

5   The forest cracked, the waters curled,
   The cattle huddled on the lea;
   And wildly dashed on tower and tree
The sunbeam strikes along the world:

And but for fancies, which aver
10   That all thy motions gently pass
   Athwart a plane of molten glass,
I scarce could brook the strain and stir

That makes the barren branches loud;
   And but for fear it is not so,
15   The wild unrest that lives in woe
Would dote and pore on yonder cloud

That rises upward always higher,
   And onward drags a laboring breast,
   And topples round the dreary west,
20   A looming bastion fringed with fire.

*   *   *

19

The Danube to the Severn[7] gave
   The darkened heart that beat no more;

7. Hallam died at Vienna on the Danube. His burial place is on the banks of the Severn, a tidal river in the southwest of England.

They laid him by the pleasant shore,
And in the hearing of the wave.

5   There twice a day the Severn fills;
    The salt sea water passes by,
    And hushes half the babbling Wye,[8]
And makes a silence in the hills.

The Wye is hushed nor moved along,
10   And hushed my deepest grief of all,
    When filled with tears that cannot fall,
I brim with sorrow drowning song.

The tide flows down, the wave again
    Is vocal in its wooded walls;
15   My deeper anguish also falls,
And I can speak a little then.

           *   *   *

21

I sing to him that rests below,
    And, since the grasses round me wave,
    I take the grasses of the grave,[9]
And make them pipes whereon to blow.

5   The traveler hears me now and then,
    And sometimes harshly will he speak:
    "This fellow would make weakness weak,
And melt the waxen hearts of men."

Another answers: "Let him be,
10   He loves to make parade of pain,
    That with his piping he may gain
The praise that comes to constancy."

A third is wroth: "Is this an hour
    For private sorrow's barren song,
15   When more and more the people throng
The chairs and thrones of civil power?

"A time to sicken and to swoon,
    When Science reaches forth her arms[1]
    To feel from world to world, and charms
20 Her secret from the latest moon?"[2]

8. The water of the Wye River, a tributary of the Severn, is dammed up as the tide flows in, and its sound is silenced until, with the turn of the tide, its "wave" once more becomes "vocal" (lines 13–14); these stanzas were written at Tintern Abbey in the Wye River country.
9. The poet assumes that the burial was in the churchyard; in fact, Hallam's body was interred in a vault inside St. Andrews church at Clevedon, Somersetshire, on January 3, 1834 (see section 10, lines 11–16).
1. Astronomical instruments such as telescopes.
2. Probably alluding to the discovery in 1846 of the planet Neptune and one of its moons.

Behold, ye speak an idle thing;
    Ye never knew the sacred dust.
    I do but sing because I must,
And pipe but as the linnets sing:

25 And one is glad; her note is gay,
    For now her little ones have ranged;
    And one is sad; her note is changed,
Because her brood is stolen away.

22

The path by which we twain did go,
    Which led by tracts that pleased us well,
    Through four sweet years arose and fell,
From flower to flower, from snow to snow;

5 And we with singing cheered the way,
    And, crowned with all the season lent,
    From April on to April went,
And glad at heart from May to May.

But where the path we walked began
10   To slant the fifth autumnal slope,[3]
    As we descended following Hope,
There sat the Shadow feared of man;

Who broke our fair companionship,
    And spread his mantle dark and cold,
15   And wrapped thee formless in the fold,
And dulled the murmur on thy lip,

And bore thee where I could not see
    Nor follow, though I walk in haste,
    And think that somewhere in the waste
20 The Shadow sits and waits for me.

23

Now, sometimes in my sorrow shut,
    Or breaking into song by fits,
    Alone, alone, to where he sits,
The Shadow cloaked from head to foot,

5 Who keeps the keys of all the creeds,
    I wander, often falling lame,
    And looking back to whence I came,
Or on to where the pathway leads;

3. Hallam died just before the beginning of autumn (September 15, 1833) in the fifth year of the friendship.

And crying, How changed from where it ran
10   Through lands where not a leaf was dumb,
     But all the lavish hills would hum
     The murmur of a happy Pan;

     When each by turns was guide to each,
        And Fancy light from Fancy caught,
15   And Thought leapt out to wed with Thought
     Ere Thought could wed itself with Speech;

     And all we met was fair and good,
        And all was good that Time could bring,
        And all the secret of the Spring
20   Moved in the chambers of the blood;

     And many an old philosophy
        On Argive heights⁴ divinely sang,
        And round us all the thicket rang
     To many a flute of Arcady.⁵

24

     And was the day of my delight
        As pure and perfect as I say?
        The very source and fount of day
     Is dashed with wandering isles of night.⁶

5   If all was good and fair we met,
        This earth had been the Paradise
        It never looked to human eyes
     Since our first sun arose and set.

     And is it that the haze of grief
10   Makes former gladness loom so great?
        The lowness of the present state,
     That sets the past in this relief?

     Or that the past will always win
        A glory from its being far,
15   And orb into the perfect star
     We saw not when we moved therein?⁷

25

     I know that this was Life—the track
        Whereon with equal feet we fared;

4. Argos, a Greek city renowned for its music.
5. A sheep-raising region in Greece associated with pastoral poetry.
6. Moving spots on the sun.
7. The poet speculates whether past experiences seem so much more "pure and perfect" (line 2) than present ones because they are far distant from us in time, just as our planet earth would have the deceptive appearance of being a perfect orb if we viewed it from a great distance in space, as from another planet (cf. *Locksley Hall Sixty Years After*, lines 187–92).

And then, as now, the day prepared
The daily burden for the back.

5   But this it was that made me move
As light as carrier birds in air;
I loved the weight I had to bear,
Because it needed help of Love;

Nor could I weary, heart or limb,
10   When mighty Love would cleave in twain
The lading° of a single pain,   *burden*
And part it, giving half to him.

26

Still onward winds the dreary way;
I with it, for I long to prove
No lapse of moons can canker Love,
Whatever fickle tongues may say.

5   And if that eye which watches guilt
And goodness, and hath power to see
Within the green the mouldered tree,
And towers fallen as soon as built—

O, if indeed that eye foresee
10   Or see—in Him is no before—
In more of life true life no more
And Love the indifference to be,

Then might I find, ere yet the morn
Breaks hither over Indian seas,
15   That Shadow waiting with the keys,
To shroud me from my proper scorn.[8]

27

I envy not in any moods
The captive void of noble rage,
The linnet born within the cage,
That never knew the summer woods;

5   I envy not the beast that takes
His license in the field of time,
Unfettered by the sense of crime,
To whom a conscience never wakes;

8. The Deity, being outside time, sees (rather than foresees) whether or not the rest of life ("more of life," line 11) will be pointless. If pointless, then the way for the speaker to deal with his self-scorn ("proper scorn") might be to seek death.

Nor, what may count itself as blest,
10   The heart that never plighted troth
        But stagnates in the weeds of sloth;
Nor any want-begotten rest.[9]

I hold it true, whate'er befall;
        I feel it, when I sorrow most;
15   'Tis better to have loved and lost
Than never to have loved at all.

28

The time draws near the birth of Christ.[1]
        The moon is hid, the night is still;
        The Christmas bells from hill to hill
Answer each other in the mist.

5   Four voices of four hamlets round,
        From far and near, on mead and moor,
        Swell out and fail, as if a door
Were shut between me and the sound;

Each voice four changes[2] on the wind,
10   That now dilate, and now decrease,
        Peace and goodwill, goodwill and peace,
Peace and goodwill, to all mankind.

This year I slept and woke with pain,
        I almost wished no more to wake,
15   And that my hold on life would break
Before I heard those bells again;

But they my troubled spirit rule,
        For they controlled me when a boy;
        They bring me sorrow touched with joy,
20   The merry, merry bells of Yule.

29

With such compelling cause to grieve
        As daily vexes household peace,
        And chains regret to his decease,
How dare we keep our Christmas eve;

5   Which brings no more a welcome guest
        To enrich the threshold of the night

---

9. Complacency resulting from some deficiency ("want").
1. The first Christmas after Hallam's death (1833); the setting is Tennyson's family home in Lincolnshire.
2. Different sequences in which church bells are pealed.

With showered largess of delight
In dance and song and game and jest?

Yet go, and while the holly boughs
10   Entwine the cold baptismal font,
Make one wreath more for Use and Wont,[3]
That guard the portals of the house;

Old sisters of a day gone by,
Gray nurses, loving nothing new;
15   Why should they miss their yearly due
Before their time? They too will die.

30

With trembling fingers did we weave
The holly round the Christmas hearth;
A rainy cloud possessed the earth,
And sadly fell our Christmas eve.

5 At our old pastimes in the hall
We gamboled, making vain pretense
Of gladness, with an awful sense
Of one mute Shadow watching all.

We paused: the winds were in the beech;
10   We heard them sweep the winter land;
And in a circle hand-in-hand
Sat silent, looking each at each.

Then echo-like our voices rang;
We sung, though every eye was dim,
15   A merry song we sang with him
Last year; impetuously we sang.

We ceased; a gentler feeling crept
Upon us: surely rest is meet.[4]
"They rest," we said, "their sleep is sweet,"
20 And silence followed, and we wept.

Our voices took a higher range;
Once more we sang: "They do not die
Nor lose their mortal sympathy,
Nor change to us, although they change;

25 "Rapt[5] from the fickle and the frail
With gathered power, yet the same,
Pierces the keen seraphic flame
From orb to orb,[6] from veil to veil."

---

3. Personifying the spirits who expect customary
observances of the Christmas season to be followed.
4. Proper or appropriate.

5. Carried away from.
6. The angelic spirit ("flame") of the dead moves
from star to star.

Rise, happy morn, rise, holy morn,
30   Draw forth the cheerful day from night:
    O Father, touch the east, and light
    The light that shone when Hope was born.

*   *   *

34

My own dim life should teach me this,
    That life shall live forevermore,
    Else earth is darkness at the core,
And dust and ashes all that is;

5 This round of green, this orb of flame,
    Fantastic beauty; such as lurks
    In some wild poet, when he works
Without a conscience or an aim.

What then were God to such as I?
10   'Twere hardly worth my while to choose
    Of things all mortal, or to use
A little patience ere I die;

'Twere best at once to sink to peace,
    Like birds the charming serpent[7] draws,
15   To drop head-foremost in the jaws
    Of vacant darkness and to cease.

35

Yet if some voice that man could trust
    Should murmur from the narrow house,
    "The cheeks drop in, the body bows;
Man dies, nor is there hope in dust";

5 Might I not say? "Yet even here,
    But for one hour, O Love, I strive
    To keep so sweet a thing alive."
But I should turn mine ears and hear

The moanings of the homeless sea,
10   The sound of streams that swift or slow
    Draw down Aeonian[8] hills, and sow
The dust of continents to be;

And Love would answer with a sigh,
    "The sound of that forgetful shore

7. Some snakes are reputed to capture their prey by casting a charm.   8. Eons old, seemingly everlasting.

15   Will change my sweetness more and more,
      Half-dead to know that I shall die."

    O me, what profits it to put
      An idle case? If Death were seen
      At first as Death, Love had not been,
20 Or been in narrowest working shut,

    Mere fellowship of sluggish moods,
      Or in his coarsest Satyr-shape
      Had bruised the herb and crushed the grape,
    And basked and battened in the woods.[9]

*   *   *

39

    Old warder of these buried bones,
      And answering now my random stroke
      With fruitful cloud and living smoke,
    Dark yew, that graspest at the stones

5   And dippest toward the dreamless head,
      To thee too comes the golden hour
      When flower is feeling after flower;[1]
    But Sorrow—fixed upon the dead,

    And darkening the dark graves of men—
10   What whispered from her lying lips?
      Thy gloom is kindled at the tips,[2]
    And passes into gloom again.

*   *   *

47

    That each, who seems a separate whole,
      Should move his rounds,[3] and fusing all
      The skirts[4] of self again, should fall
    Remerging in the general Soul,

5   Is faith as vague as all unsweet.
      Eternal form shall still divide

9. Lines 18ff. may be paraphrased: if we knew death to be final and that no afterlife were possible, love could not exist except on a primitive or bestial level.

1. The ancient yew tree in the graveyard was described in section 2 as never changing. Now the poet discovers that in the flowering season, if the tree is struck ("my random stroke"), it gives off a cloud of golden pollen.

2. Only the tips of the yew branches are in flower.

3. I.e., go through the customary circuit of life.

4. Outer edges or fringes.

The eternal soul from all beside;
And I shall know him when we meet;

And we shall sit at endless feast,
10   Enjoying each the other's good.
What vaster dream can hit the mood
Of Love on earth? He seeks at least

Upon the last and sharpest height,
Before the spirits fade away,
15   Some landing place, to clasp and say,
"Farewell! We lose ourselves in light."

48

If these brief lays, of Sorrow born,
Were taken to be such as closed
Grave doubts and answers here proposed,
Then these were such as men might scorn.

5 Her care is not to part and prove;
She takes, when harsher moods remit,
What slender shade of doubt may flit,
And makes it vassal unto love;

And hence, indeed, she sports with words,
10   But better serves a wholesome law,
And holds it sin and shame to draw
The deepest measure from the chords;

Nor dare she trust a larger lay,
But rather loosens from the lip
15   Short swallow-flights of song, that dip
Their wings in tears, and skim away.

50

Be near me when my light is low,
When the blood creeps, and the nerves prick
And tingle; and the heart is sick,
And all the wheels of being slow.

5 Be near me when the sensuous frame
Is racked with pangs that conquer trust;
And Time, a maniac scattering dust,
And Life, a Fury slinging flame.

Be near me when my faith is dry,
10   And men the flies of latter spring,

That lay their eggs, and sting and sing
And weave their petty cells and die.

Be near me when I fade away,
   To point the term of human strife,
15   And on the low dark verge of life
The twilight of eternal day.

*   *   *

54

O, yet we trust that somehow good
   Will be the final goal of ill,
   To pangs of nature, sins of will,
Defects of doubt, and taints of blood;

5   That nothing walks with aimless feet;
   That not one life shall be destroyed,
   Or cast as rubbish to the void,
When God hath made the pile complete;

That not a worm is cloven in vain;
10   That not a moth with vain desire
   Is shriveled in a fruitless fire,
Or but subserves another's gain.

Behold, we know not anything;
   I can but trust that good shall fall
15   At last—far off—at last, to all,
And every winter change to spring.

So runs my dream; but what am I?
   An infant crying in the night;
   An infant crying for the light,
20   And with no language but a cry.

55

The wish, that of the living whole
   No life may fail beyond the grave,
   Derives it not from what we have
The likest God within the soul?

5   Are God and Nature then at strife,
   That Nature lends such evil dreams?
   So careful of the type she seems,
So careless of the single life,

That I, considering everywhere
10   Her secret meaning in her deeds,
    And finding that of fifty seeds
She often brings but one to bear,

I falter where I firmly trod,
    And falling with my weight of cares
15   Upon the great world's altar-stairs
That slope through darkness up to God,

I stretch lame hands of faith, and grope,
    And gather dust and chaff, and call
    To what I feel is Lord of all,
20 And faintly trust the larger hope.[5]

56

"So careful of the type?" but no.
    From scarpèd[6] cliff and quarried stone
    She° cries, "A thousand types are gone;   *i.e., Nature*
I care for nothing, all shall go.

5 "Thou makest thine appeal to me:
    I bring to life, I bring to death;
    The spirit does but mean the breath:
I know no more." And he, shall he,

Man, her last work, who seemed so fair,
10   Such splendid purpose in his eyes,
    Who rolled the psalm to wintry skies,
Who built him fanes° of fruitless prayer,   *temples*

Who trusted God was love indeed
    And love Creation's final law—
15   Though Nature, red in tooth and claw
With ravine, shrieked against his creed—

Who loved, who suffered countless ills,
    Who battled for the True, the Just,
    Be blown about the desert dust,
20 Or sealed within the iron hills?[7]

No more? A monster then, a dream,
    A discord. Dragons of the prime,
    That tare° each other in their slime,   *tore (archaic)*
Were mellow music matched with° him.   *compared to*

5. As expressed in lines 1 and 2.   7. Preserved like fossils in rock.
6. Cut away so that the strata are exposed.

25 O life as futile, then, as frail!
   O for thy voice to soothe and bless!
   What hope of answer, or redress?
Behind the veil, behind the veil.

57

Peace; come away: the song of woe
   Is after all an earthly song.
   Peace; come away: we do him wrong
To sing so wildly: let us go.

5 Come; let us go: your cheeks are pale;
   Methinks my friend is richly shrined;
   But half my life I leave behind.
But I shall pass, my work will fail.

Yet in these ears, till hearing dies,
10   One set slow bell will seem to toll
   The passing of the sweetest soul
That ever looked with human eyes.

I hear it now, and o'er and o'er,
   Eternal greetings to the dead;
15   And "Ave,° Ave, Ave," said,   Hail (Latin)
"Adieu, adieu," forevermore.

58

In those sad words I took farewell.
   Like echoes in sepulchral halls,
   As drop by drop the water falls
In vaults and catacombs, they fell;

5 And, falling, idly broke the peace
   Of hearts that beat from day to day,
   Half-conscious of their dying clay,
And those cold crypts where they shall cease.

The high Muse answered: "Wherefore grieve
10   Thy brethren with a fruitless tear?
   Abide a little longer here,
And thou shalt take a nobler leave."

59

O Sorrow, wilt thou live with me
   No casual mistress, but a wife,

My bosom friend and half of life;
As I confess it needs must be?

5   O Sorrow, wilt thou rule my blood,
        Be sometimes lovely like a bride,
        And put thy harsher moods aside,
     If thou wilt have me wise and good?

     My centered passion cannot move,
10   Nor will it lessen from today;
        But I'll have leave at times to play
     As with the creature of my love;

     And set thee forth, for thou art mine,
        With so much hope for years to come,
15   That, howsoe'er I know thee, some
     Could hardly tell what name were thine.

                    *   *   *

                    64

     Dost thou look back on what hath been,
        As some divinely gifted man,
        Whose life in low estate began
     And on a simple village green;

5   Who breaks his birth's invidious bar,
        And grasps the skirts of happy chance,
        And breasts the blows of circumstance,
     And grapples with his evil star;

     Who makes by force his merit known
10   And lives to clutch the golden keys,[8]
        To mold a mighty state's decrees,
     And shape the whisper of the throne;

     And moving up from high to higher,
        Becomes on Fortune's crowning slope
15   The pillar of a people's hope,
     The center of a world's desire;

     Yet feels, as in a pensive dream,
        When all his active powers are still,
        A distant dearness in the hill,
20   A secret sweetness in the stream,

     The limit of his narrower fate,
        While yet beside its vocal springs

8. Badges of high public office.

He played at counselors and kings,
With one that was his earliest mate;

25 Who plows with pain his native lea
And reaps the labor of his hands,
Or in the furrow musing stands:
"Does my old friend remember me?"

*   *   *

67

When on my bed the moonlight falls,
I know that in thy place of rest
By that broad water[9] of the west
There comes a glory on the walls:

5 Thy marble bright in dark appears,
As slowly steals a silver flame
Along the letters of thy name,
And o'er the number of thy years.

The mystic glory swims away,
10 From off my bed the moonlight dies;
And closing eaves of wearied eyes
I sleep till dusk is dipped in gray;

And then I know the mist is drawn
A lucid veil from coast to coast,
15 And in the dark church like a ghost
Thy tablet glimmers to the dawn.

*   *   *

70

I cannot see the features right,
When on the gloom I strive to paint
The face I know; the hues are faint
And mix with hollow masks of night;

5 Cloud-towers by ghostly masons wrought,
A gulf that ever shuts and gapes,
A hand that points, and pallèd shapes
In shadowy thoroughfares of thought;

And crowds that stream from yawning doors,
10 And shoals of puckered faces drive;

9. The Severn River.

Dark bulks that tumble half alive,
And lazy lengths on boundless shores;

Till all at once beyond the will
I hear a wizard music roll,
15   And through a lattice on the soul
Looks thy fair face and makes it still.

71

Sleep, kinsman thou to death and trance
And madness, thou has forged at last
A night-long present of the past
In which we went through summer France.[1]

5 Hadst thou such credit with the soul?
    Then bring an opiate trebly strong,
    Drug down the blindfold sense of wrong,
That so my pleasure may be whole;

While now we talk as once we talked
10   Of men and minds, the dust of change,
    The days that grow to something strange,
In walking as of old we walked

Beside the river's wooded reach,
    The fortress, and the mountain ridge,
15   The cataract flashing from the bridge,
The breaker breaking on the beach.

72

Risest thou thus, dim dawn, again,[2]
    And howlest, issuing out of night,
    With blasts that blow the poplar white,
And lash with storm the streaming pane?

5 Day, when my crowned estate[3] begun
    To pine in that reverse of doom,[4]
    Which sickened every living bloom,
And blurred the splendor of the sun;

Who usherest in the dolorous hour
10   With thy quick tears that make the rose
    Pull sideways, and the daisy close
Her crimson fringes to the shower;

1. In the summer of 1830 Hallam and Tennyson went through southern France en route to Spain.
2. September 15, 1834, the first anniversary of Hallam's death.
3. State of happiness.
4. The reversal or disaster that doom brought upon him when Hallam died.

Who mightst have heaved a windless flame
　　Up the deep East, or, whispering, played
15　　A checker-work of beam and shade
Along the hills, yet looked the same,

As wan, as chill, as wild as now;
　　Day, marked as with some hideous crime,
　　When the dark hand struck down through time,
20　And canceled nature's best: but thou,

Lift as thou mayst thy burthened brows
　　Through clouds that drench the morning star,
　　And whirl the ungarnered sheaf afar,
And sow the sky with flying boughs,

25　And up thy vault with roaring sound
　　Climb thy thick noon, disastrous day;
　　Touch thy dull goal of joyless gray,
And hide thy shame beneath the ground.

　　　　　　✻　✻　✻

75

I leave thy praises unexpressed
　　In verse that brings myself relief,
　　And by the measure of my grief
I leave thy greatness to be guessed.

5　What practice howsoe'er expert
　　In fitting aptest words to things,
　　Or voice the richest-toned that sings,
Hath power to give thee as thou wert?

I care not in these fading days
10　　To raise a cry that lasts not long,
　　And round thee with the breeze of song
To stir a little dust of praise.

Thy leaf has perished in the green,
　　And, while we breathe beneath the sun,
15　　The world which credits what is done
Is cold to all that might have been.

So here shall silence guard thy fame;
　　But somewhere, out of human view,
　　Whate'er thy hands are set to do
20　Is wrought with tumult of acclaim.

　　　　　　✻　✻　✻

78

Again at Christmas[5] did we weave
   The holly round the Christmas hearth;
   The silent snow possessed the earth,
And calmly fell our Christmas eve.

5   The yule clog° sparkled keen with frost,   *log*
   No wing of wind the region swept,
   But over all things brooding slept
The quiet sense of something lost.

As in the winters left behind,
10   Again our ancient games had place,
   The mimic picture's[6] breathing grace,
And dance and song and hoodman-blind.[7]

Who showed a token of distress?
   No single tear, no mark of pain—
15   O sorrow, then can sorrow wane?
O grief, can grief be changed to less?

O last regret, regret can die!
   No—mixed with all this mystic frame,
   Her deep relations are the same,
20   But with long use her tears are dry.

*   *   *

82

I wage not any feud with Death
   For changes wrought on form and face;
   No lower life that earth's embrace
May breed with him can fright my faith.

5   Eternal process moving on,
   From state to state the spirit walks;
   And these are but the shattered stalks,
Or ruined chrysalis of one.

Nor blame I Death, because he bare
10   The use of virtue out of earth;
   I know transplanted human worth
Will bloom to profit, otherwise.

---

5. The second Christmas (1834) after Hallam's death.
6. A game in which the participants pose in the manner of some famous statue or painting and the spectators try to guess what work of art is being portrayed.
7. The player in the game of blindman's buff who wears a blindfold or hood.

For this alone on Death I wreak
    The wrath that garners in my heart:
15   He put our lives so far apart
    We cannot hear each other speak.

83

Dip down upon the northern shore,
    O sweet new-year° delaying long;   *spring 1835*
    Thou doest expectant Nature wrong;
Delaying long, delay no more.

5   What stays thee from the clouded noons,
    Thy sweetness from its proper place?
    Can trouble live with April days,
Or sadness in the summer moons?

Bring orchis, bring the foxglove spire,
10   The little speedwell's° darling blue,   *spring flower*
    Deep tulips dashed with fiery dew,
Laburnums, dropping-wells of fire.

O thou, new-year, delaying long,
    Delayest the sorrow in my blood,
15   That longs to burst a frozen bud
And flood a fresher throat with song.

84

When I contemplate all alone
    The life that had been thine below,
    And fix my thoughts on all the glow
To which thy crescent would have grown,

5   I see thee sitting crowned with good,
    A central warmth diffusing bliss
    In glance and smile, and clasp and kiss,
On all the branches of thy blood;

Thy blood, my friend, and partly mine;
10   For now the day was drawing on,
    When thou shouldst link thy life with one
Of mine own house, and boys of thine

Had babbled "Uncle" on my knee;
    But that remorseless iron hour
15   Made cypress of her orange flower,[8]
Despair of hope, and earth of thee.

---

8. Orange blossoms are associated with brides—here the poet's sister Emily Tennyson, to whom Hallam had been engaged.

I seem to meet their least desire,
    To clap their cheeks, to call them mine.
    I see their unborn faces shine
20 Beside the never-lighted fire.

I see myself an honored guest,
    Thy partner in the flowery walk
    Of letters, genial table talk,
Or deep dispute, and graceful jest;

25 While now thy prosperous labor fills
    The lips of men with honest praise,
    And sun by sun the happy days
Descend below the golden hills

With promise of a morn as fair;
30   And all the train of bounteous hours
    Conduct, by paths of growing powers,
To reverence and the silver hair;

Till slowly worn her earthly robe,
    Her lavish mission richly wrought,
35   Leaving great legacies of thought,
Thy spirit should fail from off the globe;

What time mine own might also flee,
    As linked with thine in love and fate,
    And, hovering o'er the dolorous strait
40 To the other shore, involved in thee,

Arrive at last the blessed goal,
    And He that died in Holy Land
    Would reach us out the shining hand,
And take us as a single soul.

45 What reed was that on which I leant?
    Ah, backward fancy, wherefore wake
    The old bitterness again, and break
The low beginnings of content?

*   *   *

86

Sweet after showers, ambrosial air,
    That rollest from the gorgeous gloom
    Of evening over brake and bloom
And meadow, slowly breathing bare

5 The round of space,[9] and rapt below
    Through all the dewy-tasseled wood,

9. Air that is slowly clearing the clouds from the sky.

And shadowing down the hornèd flood[1]
In ripples, fan my brows and blow

The fever from my cheek, and sigh
10   The full new life that feeds thy breath
Throughout my frame, till Doubt and Death,
Ill brethren, let the fancy fly

From belt to belt of crimson seas
On leagues of odor streaming far,
15   To where in yonder orient star
A hundred spirits whisper "Peace."

87

I passed beside the reverend walls[2]
In which of old I wore the gown;
I roved at random through the town,
And saw the tumult of the halls;

5   And heard once more in college fanes
The storm their high-built organs make,
And thunder-music, rolling, shake
The prophet blazoned on the panes;

And caught once more the distant shout,
10   The measured pulse of racing oars
Among the willows; paced the shores
And many a bridge, and all about

The same gray flats again, and felt
The same, but not the same; and last
15   Up that long walk of limes I passed
To see the rooms in which he dwelt.

Another name was on the door.
I lingered; all within was noise
Of songs, and clapping hands, and boys
20   That crashed the glass and beat the floor;

Where once we held debate, a band
Of youthful friends,[3] on mind and art,
And labor, and the changing mart,
And all the framework of the land;

25   When one would aim an arrow fair,
But send it slackly from the string;

---

1. Between two promontories [Tennyson's note].
2. Of Trinity College, Cambridge University.

3. "The Apostles," an undergraduate club to which Tennyson and Hallam had belonged.

And one would pierce an outer ring,
And one an inner, here and there;

And last the master bowman, he,
30   Would cleave the mark. A willing ear
We lent him. Who but hung to hear
The rapt oration flowing free

From point to point, with power and grace
And music in the bounds of law,[4]
35   To those conclusions when we saw
The God within him light his face,

And seem to lift the form, and glow
In azure orbits heavenly-wise;
And over those ethereal eyes
40   The bar of Michael Angelo?[5]

88

Wild bird,[6] whose warble, liquid sweet,
Rings Eden through the budded quicks,[7]
O tell me where the senses mix,
O tell me where the passions meet,

5   Whence radiate: fierce extremes employ
Thy spirits in the darkening leaf,
And in the midmost heart of grief
Thy passion clasps a secret joy;

And I—my harp would prelude woe—
10   I cannot all command the strings;
The glory of the sum of things
Will flash along the chords and go.

89

Witch elms that counterchange the floor
Of this flat lawn with dusk and bright;[8]
And thou, with all thy breadth and height
Of foliage, towering sycamore;

5   How often, hither wandering down,
My Arthur found your shadows fair,

4. An essay presented by Hallam at Cambridge in 1831 provides an example of his skill while still an undergraduate in theological argument (cf. *The Writings of Arthur Hallam,* edited by T. H. V. Motter, 1943, pp. 198–213).
5. Hallam, like Michelangelo, had a prominent ridge of bone above his eyes.
6. Probably a nightingale.
7. Hawthorn hedges.
8. Shadows of the elm tree checker the lawn at Somersby, the Tennysons' country home.

And shook to all the liberal air
The dust and din and steam of town!

He brought an eye for all he saw;
10   He mixed in all our simple sports;
They pleased him, fresh from brawling courts
And dusty purlieus of the law.[9]

O joy to him in this retreat,
Immantled in ambrosial dark,
15   To drink the cooler air, and mark
The landscape winking through the heat!

O sound to rout the brood of cares,
The sweep of scythe in morning dew,
The gust that round the garden flew,
20 And tumbled half the mellowing pears!

O bliss, when all in circle drawn
About him, heart and ear were fed
To hear him, as he lay and read
The Tuscan poets on the lawn!

25 Or in the all-golden afternoon
A guest, or happy sister, sung,
Or here she brought the harp and flung
A ballad to the brightening moon.

Nor less it pleased in livelier moods,
30   Beyond the bounding hill to stray,
And break the livelong summer day
With banquet in the distant woods;

Whereat we glanced from theme to theme,
Discussed the books to love or hate,
35   Or touched the changes of the state,
Or threaded some Socratic dream;[1]

But if I praised the busy town,
He loved to rail against it still,
For "ground in yonder social mill
40 We rub each other's angles down,

"And merge," he said, "in form and gloss
The picturesque of man and man."
We talked: the stream beneath us ran,
The wine-flask lying couched in moss,

9. Hallam became a law student in London after leaving Cambridge.

1. I.e., worked our way through some discourse of Socrates (as recorded by Plato).

45   Or cooled within the glooming wave;
      And last, returning from afar,
      Before the crimson-circled star[2]
    Had fallen into her father's[3] grave,

    And brushing ankle-deep in flowers,
50   We heard behind the woodbine veil
      The milk that bubbled in° the pail,   *into*
    And buzzings of the honeyed hours.

      *   *   *

91

    When rosy plumelets tuft the larch,
      And rarely° pipes the mounted thrush,   *exquisitely*
      Or underneath the barren bush
    Flits by the sea-blue bird° of March;   *kingfisher*

5   Come, wear the form by which I know
      Thy spirit in time among thy peers;
      The hope of unaccomplished years
    Be large and lucid round thy brow.

    When summer's hourly-mellowing change
10   May breathe, with many roses sweet,
      Upon the thousand waves of wheat
    That ripple round the lowly grange,

    Come; not in watches of the night,
      But where the sunbeam broodeth warm,
15   Come, beauteous in thine after form,
    And like a finer light in light.

      *   *   *

93

    I shall not see thee. Dare I say
      No spirit ever brake the band
      That stays him from the native land
    Where first he walked when clasped in clay?[4]

5   No visual shade of someone lost,
      But he, the Spirit himself, may come
      Where all the nerve of sense is numb,
    Spirit to Spirit, Ghost to Ghost.

2. Venus, which will sink into the west as the sun has done.
3. According to the nebular hypothesis, planets condensed out of the sun's atmosphere; in this sense the sun is the "father" of planets.
4. I.e., when he was alive and clothed in flesh.

Oh, therefore from thy sightless° range   *invisible*
10   With gods in unconjectured bliss,
Oh, from the distance of the abyss
Of tenfold-complicated change,

Descend, and touch, and enter; hear
The wish too strong for words to name,
15   That in this blindness of the frame°   *living frame*
My Ghost may feel that thine is near.

94

How pure at heart and sound in head,
With what divine affections bold
Should be the man whose thought would hold
An hour's communion with the dead.

5 In vain shalt thou, or any, call
The spirits from their golden day,
Except, like them, thou too canst say,
My spirit is at peace with all.

They haunt the silence of the breast,
10   Imaginations calm and fair,
The memory like a cloudless air,
The conscience as a sea at rest;

But when the heart is full of din,
And doubt beside the portal waits,
15   They can but listen at the gates,
And hear the household jar within.

95

By night we lingered on the lawn,
For underfoot the herb was dry;
And genial warmth; and o'er the sky
The silvery haze of summer drawn;

5 And calm that let the tapers burn
Unwavering: not a cricket chirred;
The brook alone far off was heard,
And on the board the fluttering urn.[5]

And bats went round in fragrant skies,
10   And wheeled or lit the filmy shapes[6]
That haunt the dusk, with ermine capes
And woolly breasts and beaded eyes;

5. For boiling water for tea or coffee, heated by a fluttering flame.

6. The white-winged night moths called ermine moths.

While now we sang old songs that pealed
  From knoll to knoll, where, couched at ease,
15   The white kine° glimmered, and the trees   *cows*
Laid their dark arms[7] about the field.

But when those others, one by one,
  Withdrew themselves from me and night,
  And in the house light after light
20 Went out, and I was all alone,

A hunger seized my heart; I read
  Of that glad year which once had been,
  In those fallen leaves which kept their green,
The noble letters of the dead.

25 And strangely on the silence broke
  The silent-speaking words, and strange
  Was love's dumb cry defying change
To test his worth; and strangely spoke

The faith, the vigor, bold to dwell
30   On doubts that drive the coward back,
  And keen through wordy snares to track
Suggestion to her inmost cell.

So word by word, and line by line,
  The dead man touched me from the past,
35   And all at once it seemed at last
The[8] living soul was flashed on mine.

And mine in this was wound, and whirled
  About empyreal heights of thought,
  And came on that which is, and caught
40 The deep pulsations of the world,

Aeonian music[9] measuring out
  The steps of Time—the shocks of Chance—
  The blows of Death. At length my trance
Was canceled, stricken through with doubt.[1]

45 Vague words! but ah, how hard to frame
  In matter-molded forms of speech,

---

7. Cast the shadows of their branches.
8. It was "His" in the 1st edition, and also in the 1st edition, line 37 read, "And mine in his was wound."
9. Of the universe, which has pulsated for eons.
1. In a letter of 1874, replying to an inquiry about his experience of mystical trances, Tennyson wrote: "A kind of waking trance I have frequently had, quite up from boyhood, when I have been all alone. This has generally come upon me through repeating my own name two or three times to myself silently, till all at once, as it were out of the intensity of the consciousness of individuality, the individuality itself seemed to dissolve and fade away into boundless being, and this not a confused state, but the clearest of the clearest, the surest of the surest, the weirdest of the weirdest, utterly beyond words, where death was an almost laughable impossibility, the loss of personality (if so it were) seeming no extinction but the only true life. . . . This might . . . be the state which St. Paul describes, 'Whether in the body I cannot tell, or whether out of the body I cannot tell.' . . . I am ashamed of my feeble description. Have I not said the state is utterly beyond words? But in a moment, when I come back to my normal state of 'sanity,' I am ready to fight for *mein liebes Ich* [my dear self], and hold that it will last for aeons of aeons" (*Alfred Lord Tennyson, A Memoir*, 1897, vol. 1, 320).

Or even for intellect to reach
Through memory that which I became.

Till now the doubtful dusk revealed
50   The knolls once more where, couched at ease,
The white kine glimmered, and the trees
Laid their dark arms about the field;

And sucked from out the distant gloom
A breeze began to tremble o'er
55   The large leaves of the sycamore,
And fluctuate all the still perfume,

And gathering freshlier overhead,
Rocked the full-foliaged elms, and swung
The heavy-folded rose, and flung
60   The lilies to and fro, and said,

"The dawn, the dawn," and died away;
And East and West, without a breath,
Mixed their dim lights, like life and death,
To broaden into boundless day.

96

You say, but with no touch of scorn,
Sweet-hearted, you,[2] whose light blue eyes
Are tender over drowning flies,
You tell me, doubt is Devil-born.

5   I know not: one indeed I knew
In many a subtle question versed,
Who touched a jarring lyre at first,
But ever strove to make it true;

Perplexed in faith, but pure in deeds,
10   At last he beat his music out.
There lives more faith in honest doubt,
Believe me, than in half the creeds.

He fought his doubts and gathered strength,
He would not make his judgment blind,
15   He faced the specters of the mind
And laid them; thus he came at length

To find a stronger faith his own,
And Power was with him in the night,
Which makes the darkness and the light,
20   And dwells not in the light alone,

2. A woman of simple faith.

But in the darkness and the cloud,
  As over Sinaï's peaks of old,[3]
  While Israel made their gods of gold,
Although the trumpet blew so loud.

*   *   *

99

Risest thou thus, dim dawn, again,[4]
  So loud with voices of the birds,
  So thick with lowings of the herds,
Day, when I lost the flower of men;

5   Who tremblest through thy darkling red
  On yon swollen brook that bubbles fast[5]
  By meadows breathing of the past,
And woodlands holy to the dead;

Who murmurest in the foliage eaves
10   A song that slights the coming care,[6]
  And Autumn laying here and there
A fiery finger on the leaves;

Who wakenest with thy balmy breath
  To myriads on the genial earth,
15   Memories of bridal, or of birth,[7]
And unto myriads more, of death.

Oh, wheresoever those[8] may be,
  Betwixt the slumber of the poles,
  Today they count as kindred souls;
20   They know me not, but mourn with me.

*   *   *

103

On that last night before we went
  From out the doors where I was bred,[9]
  I dreamed a vision of the dead,
Which left my after-morn content.

3. Cf. Exodus 19.16–25. After veiling Mount
Sinai in a "cloud" of smoke, God addressed Moses
from the darkness.
4. September 15, 1835, the second anniversary of
Hallam's death.
5. I.e., reflections of the clouded red light of dawn
quiver on the surface of the fast-moving water.
6. I.e., disregards future events such as death or
the coming of autumn.

7. Cf. *Epilogue*, lines 117–28 (pp. 1279–80).
8. I.e., the many who remember death.
9. In 1837 Tennyson and his family moved away
from their home in Lincolnshire, which had been
closely associated with his friendship with Hallam.
In section 104 the move seems to occur in 1835,
the year of the third Christmas after Hallam's
death.

5   Methought I dwelt within a hall,
      And maidens with me; distant hills
      From hidden summits fed with rills
      A river sliding by the wall.

    The hall with harp and carol rang.
10   They sang of what is wise and good
      And graceful. In the center stood
      A statue veiled, to which they sang;

    And which, though veiled, was known to me,
      The shape of him I loved, and love
15   Forever. Then flew in a dove
      And brought a summons from the sea;

    And when they learnt that I must go,
      They wept and wailed, but led the way
      To where the little shallop° lay   *light open boat*
20   At anchor in the flood below;

    And on by many a level mead,
      And shadowing bluff that made the banks,
      We glided winding under ranks
      Of iris and the golden reed;

25   And still as vaster grew the shore
      And rolled the floods in grander space,
      The maidens gathered strength and grace
      And presence, lordlier than before;

    And I myself, who sat apart
30   And watched them, waxed in every limb;
      I felt the thews of Anakim,[1]
      The pulses of a Titan's[2] heart;

    As one would sing the death of war,
      And one would chant the history
35   Of that great race which is to be,[3]
      And one the shaping of a star;

    Until the forward-creeping tides
      Began to foam, and we to draw
      From deep to deep, to where we saw
40   A great ship lift her shining sides.[4]

1. Plural of *Anak*; a reference to the giant sons of
Anak (cf. Numbers 13.33).
2. Giant of Greek mythology.
3. See the account of the "crowning race" in *Epilogue*, lines 128–44.
4. Cf. *Morte d'Arthur*, lines 255–322, in which
Bedivere is left behind as Arthur's barge, the ship

of death, sails away. In the present dream vision
not only is the speaker taken aboard but also his
companions, who represent the creative arts of this
world—"all the human powers and talents that do
not pass with life but go along with it," as Tennyson
said of this passage.

The man we loved was there on deck,
But thrice as large as man he bent
To greet us. Up the side I went,
And fell in silence on his neck;

45 Whereat those maidens with one mind
Bewailed their lot; I did them wrong:
"We served thee here," they said, "so long,
And wilt thou leave us now behind?"

So rapt° I was, they could not win   *entranced*
50 An answer from my lips, but he
Replying, "Enter likewise ye
And go with us:" they entered in.

And while the wind began to sweep
A music out of sheet and shroud,
55 We steered her toward a crimson cloud
That landlike slept along the deep.

104

The time draws near the birth of Christ;[5]
The moon is hid, the night is still;
A single church below the hill
Is pealing, folded in the mist.

5 A single peal of bells below,
That wakens at this hour of rest
A single murmur in the breast,
That these are not the bells I know.

Like strangers' voices here they sound,
10 In lands where not a memory strays,
Nor landmark breathes of other days,
But all is new unhallowed ground.

105

Tonight ungathered let us leave
This laurel, let this holly stand:[6]
We live within the stranger's land,
And strangely falls our Christmas eve.

5 Our father's dust is left alone
And silent under other snows:

5. See n. 1, p. 1245.
6. Cf. section 29, in which the family in their for- / mer home still continued to gather holly. In the new home, the customary observances lapse.

There in due time the woodbine blows,
   The violet comes, but we are gone.

    No more shall wayward grief abuse
10   The genial hour with mask and mime;
     For change of place, like growth of time,
    Has broke the bond of dying use.

    Let cares that petty shadows cast,
     By which our lives are chiefly proved,
15   A little spare the night I loved,
    And hold it solemn to the past.

    But let no footstep beat the floor,
     Nor bowl of wassail mantle warm;[7]
     For who would keep an ancient form
20   Through which the spirit breathes no more?

    Be neither song, nor game, nor feast;
     Nor harp be touched, nor flute be blown;
     No dance, no motion, save alone
    What lightens in the lucid east

25   Of rising worlds[8] by yonder wood.
     Long sleeps the summer in the seed;
     Run out your measured arcs, and lead
    The closing cycle rich in good.

106

Ring out, wild bells, to the wild sky,
   The flying cloud, the frosty light:
   The year is dying in the night;
Ring out, wild bells, and let him die.

5   Ring out the old, ring in the new,
    Ring, happy bells, across the snow:
    The year is going, let him go;
   Ring out the false, ring in the true.

   Ring out the grief that saps the mind,
10   For those that here we see no more;
    Ring out the feud of rich and poor,
   Ring in redress to all mankind.

   Ring out a slowly dying cause,
    And ancient forms of party strife;

7. I.e., no bowl of hot punch warms the mantel-piece.

8. The scintillating motion of the stars that rise [Tennyson's note].

15   Ring in the nobler modes of life,
      With sweeter manners, purer laws.

      Ring out the want, the care, the sin,
        The faithless coldness of the times:
        Ring out, ring out my mournful rhymes,
20   But ring the fuller minstrel in.

      Ring out false pride in place and blood,
        The civic slander and the spite;
        Ring in the love of truth and right,
      Ring in the common love of good.

25   Ring out old shapes of foul disease;
        Ring out the narrowing lust of gold;
        Ring out the thousand wars of old,
      Ring in the thousand years of peace.

      Ring in the valiant man and free,
30   The larger heart, the kindlier hand;
        Ring out the darkness of the land,
      Ring in the Christ that is to be.[9]

107

      It is the day when he was born.°   *February 1*
        A bitter day that early sank
        Behind a purple-frosty bank
      Of vapor, leaving night forlorn.

5   The time admits not flowers or leaves
        To deck the banquet. Fiercely flies
        The blast of North and East, and ice
      Makes daggers at the sharpened eaves,

      And bristles all the brakes and thorns
10   To yon hard crescent, as she hangs
        Above the wood which grides[1] and clangs
      Its leafless ribs and iron horns

      Together, in the drifts[2] that pass
        To darken on the rolling brine
15   That breaks the coast. But fetch the wine,
      Arrange the board and brim the glass;

9. These allusions to the second coming of Christ and to the millennium are derived from Revelation 20, but Tennyson has interpreted the biblical account in his own way. He once told his son of his conviction that "the forms of Christian religion would alter; but that the spirit of Christ would still grow from more to more."
1. Clashes with a strident noise.
2. Either cloud-drifts or clouds of snow.

Bring in great logs and let them lie,
　　To make a solid core of heat;
　　Be cheerful-minded, talk and treat
20　Of all things even as he were by;

We keep the day. With festal cheer,
　　With books and music, surely we
　　Will drink to him, whate'er he be,
And sing the songs he loved to hear.

108

I will not shut me from my kind,
　　And, lest I stiffen into stone,
　　I will not eat my heart alone,
Nor feed with sighs a passing wind:

5　What profit lies in barren faith,
　　And vacant yearning, though with might
　　To scale the heaven's highest height,
Or dive below the wells of Death?

What find I in the highest place,
10　But mine own phantom chanting hymns?
　　And on the depths of death there swims
The reflex of a human face.°　　　　　　　　*his own face*

I'll rather take what fruit may be
　　Of sorrow under human skies:
15　'Tis held that sorrow makes us wise,
Whatever wisdom sleep with thee.°　　　　　　*Hallam*

109

Heart-affluence in discursive talk
　　From household fountains never dry;
　　The critic clearness of an eye
That saw through all the Muses' walk;³

5　Seraphic intellect and force
　　To seize and throw the doubts of man;
　　Impassioned logic, which outran
The hearer in its fiery course;

High nature amorous of the good,
10　But touched with no ascetic gloom;
　　And passion pure in snowy bloom
Through all the years of April blood;

3. The realm of art and literature.

A love of freedom rarely felt,
  Of freedom in her regal seat
15   Of England; not the schoolboy heat,
The blind hysterics of the Celt;[4]

And manhood fused with female grace
  In such a sort, the child would twine
  A trustful hand, unasked, in thine,
20 And find his comfort in thy face;

All these have been, and thee mine eyes
  Have looked on: if they looked in vain,
  My shame is greater who remain,
Nor let thy wisdom make me wise.

*   *   *

<h1 align="center">115</h1>

Now fades the last long streak of snow,
  Now burgeons every maze of quick°   *hawthorn hedges*
  About the flowering squares,° and thick   *fields*
By ashen roots the violets blow.

5 Now rings the woodland loud and long,
  The distance takes a lovelier hue,
  And drowned in yonder living blue
The lark becomes a sightless song.

Now dance the lights on lawn and lea,
10   The flocks are whiter down the vale,
  And milkier every milky sail
On winding stream or distant sea;

Where now the seamew pipes, or dives
  In yonder greening gleam, and fly
15   The happy birds, that change their sky
To build and brood, that live their lives

From land to land; and in my breast
  Spring wakens too, and my regret
  Becomes an April violet,
20 And buds and blossoms like the rest.

*   *   *

4. A member of one of the groups of peoples populating ancient Britain; i.e., a less-civilized people.

118

Contèmplate all this work of Time,
  The giant laboring in his youth;
  Nor dream of human love and truth,
As dying Nature's earth and lime;[5]

5   But trust that those we call the dead
  Are breathers of an ampler day
  For ever nobler ends. They[6] say,
The solid earth whereon we tread

  In tracts of fluent heat began,
10   And grew to seeming-random forms,
  The seeming prey of cyclic storms,
Till at the last arose the man;

  Who throve and branched from clime to clime,
  The herald of a higher race,
15   And of himself in higher place
If so he type[7] this work of time

  Within himself, from more to more;
  Or, crowned with attributes of woe
  Like glories, move his course, and show
20   That life is not as idle ore,

  But iron dug from central gloom,
  And heated hot with burning fears,
  And dipped in baths of hissing tears,
And battered with the shocks of doom

25   To shape and use. Arise and fly
  The reeling Faun, the sensual feast;
  Move upward, working out the beast,
And let the ape and tiger die.

119

Doors, where my heart was used to beat
  So quickly, not as one that weeps
  I come once more; the city sleeps;
I smell the meadow in the street;

5   I hear a chirp of birds; I see
  Betwixt the black fronts long-withdrawn
  A light blue lane of early dawn,
And think of early days and thee,

---

5. Alluding to the materialistic analysis of living matter into chemicals and simpler compounds [cited by Susan Shatto].

6. Geologists and astronomers.
7. Emulate, prefigure as a type.

And bless thee, for thy lips are bland,
10   And bright the friendship of thine eye;
    And in my thoughts with scarce a sigh
I take the pressure of thine hand.

120

I trust I have not wasted breath:
    I think we are not wholly brain,
    Magnetic mockeries;[8] not in vain,
Like Paul[9] with beasts, I fought with Death;

5 Not only cunning casts in clay:
    Let Science prove we are, and then
    What matters Science unto men,
At least to me? I would not stay.

Let him, the wiser man who springs
10   Hereafter, up from childhood shape
    His action like the greater ape,
But I was *born* to other things.

121

Sad Hesper° o'er the buried sun   *evening star*
    And ready, thou, to die with him,
    Thou watchest all things ever dim
And dimmer, and a glory done.

5 The team is loosened from the wain,°   *hay wagon*
    The boat is drawn upon the shore;
    Thou listenest to the closing door,
And life is darkened in the brain.

Bright Phosphor,° fresher for the night,   *morning star*
10   By thee the world's great work is heard
    Beginning, and the wakeful bird;
Behind thee comes the greater light.[1]

The market boat is on the stream,
    And voices hail it from the brink;
15   Thou hear'st the village hammer clink,
And see'st the moving of the team.

Sweet Hesper-Phosphor, double name[2]
    For what is one, the first, the last,

8. Mechanisms operated by responses to electrical forces.
9. 1 Corinthians 15.32.
1. Cf. Genesis 1.16: "The greater light to rule the day."
2. The planet Venus is both evening star and morning star.

Thou, like my present and my past,
20   Thy place is changed; thou art the same.

*   *   *

123

There rolls the deep where grew the tree.
  O earth, what changes hast thou seen!
  There where the long street roars hath been
The stillness of the central sea.[3]

5 The hills are shadows, and they flow
  From form to form, and nothing stands;
  They melt like mist, the solid lands,
Like clouds they shape themselves and go.

But in my spirit will I dwell,
10   And dream my dream, and hold it true;
  For though my lips may breathe adieu,
I cannot think the thing farewell.

124

That which we dare invoke to bless;
  Our dearest faith; our ghastliest doubt;
  He, They, One, All; within, without;
The Power in darkness whom we guess—

5 I found Him not in world or sun,
  Or eagle's wing, or insect's eye,[4]
  Nor through the questions men may try,
The petty cobwebs we have spun.

If e'er when faith had fallen asleep,
10   I heard a voice, "believe no more,"
  And heard an ever-breaking shore
That tumbled in the Godless deep,

A warmth within the breast would melt
  The freezing reason's colder part,
15   And like a man in wrath the heart
Stood up and answered, "I have felt."[5]

---

3. Cf. a passage from Sir Charles Lyell's *The Principles of Geology* (1832), a book well known to Tennyson. In discussing the "interchange of sea and land" that has occurred "on the surface of our globe" Lyell remarks: "In the Mediterranean alone, many flourishing inland towns and a still greater number of ports now stand where the sea rolled its waves since the era when civilized nations first grew in Europe."
4. He does not discover satisfactory proof of God's existence in the 18th-century argument that because objects in nature are designed there must exist a designer.
5. Cf. Carlyle's *Sartor Resartus, The Everlasting No* (p. 1077).

No, like a child in doubt and fear:
    But that blind clamor made me wise;
    Then was I as a child that cries,
20 But, crying, knows his father near;

And what I am beheld again
    What is, and no man understands;
    And out of darkness came the hands
That reach through nature, molding men.

*   *   *

126

Love is and was my lord and king,
    And in his presence I attend
    To hear the tidings of my friend,
Which every hour his couriers bring.

5 Love is and was my king and lord,
    And will be, though as yet I keep
    Within the court on earth, and sleep
Encompassed by his faithful guard,

And hear at times a sentinel
10   Who moves about from place to place,
    And whispers to the worlds of space,
In the deep night, that all is well.

127

And all is well, though faith and form[6]
    Be sundered in the night of fear;
    Well roars the storm to those that hear
A deeper voice across the storm,

5 Proclaiming social truth shall spread,
    And justice, even though thrice again
    The red fool-fury of the Seine
Should pile her barricades with dead.[7]

But ill for him that wears a crown,
10   And him, the lazar,[8] in his rags!
    They tremble, the sustaining crags;
The spires of ice are toppled down,

6. Traditional institutions through which faith was formerly expressed, such as the church.
7. Revolutionary uprisings in France, in each of which a king lost his throne (line 9): in 1789 against Louis XVI, in 1830 against Charles X, and in 1848 against Louis-Philippe. The third (line 6) would have been a prophecy if, as Tennyson recollected, section 127 were finished at a date earlier than 1848.
8. Pauper suffering from disease.

And molten up, and roar in flood;
 The fortress crashes from on high,
15 The brute earth lightens⁹ to the sky,
And the great Aeon¹ sinks in blood,

And compassed by the fires of hell,
 While thou, dear spirit, happy star,
 O'erlook'st the tumult from afar,
20 And smilest, knowing all is well.

   * * *

129

Dear friend, far off, my lost desire,
 So far, so near in woe and weal,
 O loved the most, when most I feel
There is a lower and a higher;

5 Known and unknown, human, divine;
 Sweet human hand and lips and eye;
 Dear heavenly friend that canst not die,
Mine, mine, forever, ever mine;

Strange friend, past, present, and to be;
10 Loved deeplier, darklier understood;
 Behold, I dream a dream of good,
And mingle all the world with thee.

130

Thy voice is on the rolling air
 I hear thee where the waters run;
 Thou standest in the rising sun,
And in the setting thou art fair.

5 What art thou then? I cannot guess;
 But though I seem in star and flower
 To feel thee some diffusive power,
I do not therefore love thee less.

My love involves the love before;
10 My love is vaster passion now;
 Tho' mix'd with God and Nature thou,
I seem to love thee more and more.

Far off thou art, but ever nigh;
 I have thee still, and I rejoice;

---

9. Is lit up by fire.
1. A vast tract of time, here perhaps modern Western civilization.

15   I prosper, circled with thy voice;
      I shall not lose thee tho' I die.

131

O living will[2] that shalt endure
    When all that seems shall suffer shock,
    Rise in the spiritual rock,°   *Christ*
Flow through our deeds and make them pure,

5   That we may lift from out of dust
    A voice as unto him that hears,
    A cry above the conquered years
To one that with us works, and trust,

With faith that comes of self-control,
10   The truths that never can be proved
    Until we close with all we loved,
And all we flow from, soul in soul.

From Epilogue[3]

*　*　*

And rise, O moon, from yonder down,
110   Till over down and over dale
    All night the shining vapor sail
And pass the silent-lighted town,

The white-faced halls, the glancing rills,
    And catch at every mountain head,
115   And o'er the friths° that branch and spread   *inlets of the sea*
    Their sleeping silver through the hills;

And touch with shade the bridal doors,
    With tender gloom the roof, the wall;
    And breaking let the splendor fall
120   To spangle all the happy shores

By which they rest, and ocean sounds,
    And, star and system rolling past,
    A soul shall draw from out the vast
And strike his being into bounds,

125   And, moved through life of lower phase,
    Result in man,[4] be born and think,

2. Tennyson later commented that he meant here the moral will of humankind.
3. The *Epilogue* describes the wedding day of Tennyson's sister Cecilia to Edmund Lushington. At the conclusion (printed here) the speaker reflects on the moonlit wedding night and the kind of offspring that will result from their union.
4. A child will be conceived and will develop in embryo through various stages. This development is similar to human evolution from the animal to

And act and love, a closer link
Betwixt us and the crowning race

Of those that, eye to eye, shall look
130   On knowledge; under whose command
Is Earth and Earth's, and in their hand
Is Nature like an open book;

No longer half-akin to brute,
For all we thought and loved and did,
135   And hoped, and suffered, is but seed
Of what in them is flower and fruit;

Whereof the man that with me trod
This planet was a noble type
Appearing ere the times were ripe,
140   That friend of mine who lives in God,

That God, which ever lives and loves,
One God, one law, one element,
And one far-off divine event,
To which the whole creation moves.

1833–50   1850

The Charge of the Light Brigade[1]

1

Half a league, half a league,
Half a league onward,
All in the valley of Death
    Rode the six hundred.
5   "Forward the Light Brigade!
Charge for the guns!" he said.
Into the valley of Death
    Rode the six hundred.[2]

2

"Forward, the Light Brigade!"
10   Was there a man dismayed?
Not though the soldier knew
    Someone had blundered.
Theirs not to make reply,
Theirs not to reason why,
15   Theirs but to do and die.

---

the human level and perhaps to a future higher
stage of development.
1. During the Crimean War, owing to confusion
of orders, a brigade of British cavalry charged some
entrenched batteries of Russian artillery. This
blunder cost the lives of three-quarters of the six
hundred horsemen engaged (see Cecil Woodham-

Smith, *The Reason Why*, 1954). Tennyson rapidly
composed his "ballad" (as he called the poem) after
reading an account of the battle in a newspaper.
2. In the recording Tennyson made of this poem,
"hundred" sounds like "hunderd"—a Lincolnshire
pronunciation that reinforces the rhyme with
"thundered," etc.

Into the valley of Death
    Rode the six hundred.

3

Cannon to right of them,
Cannon to left of them,
20 Cannon in front of them
    Volleyed and thundered;
Stormed at with shot and shell,
Boldly they rode and well,
Into the jaws of Death,
25 Into the mouth of hell
    Rode the six hundred.

4

Flashed all their sabers bare,
Flashed as they turned in air
Sab'ring the gunners there,
30 Charging an army, while
    All the world wondered.
Plunged in the battery smoke
Right through the line they broke;
Cossack and Russian
35 Reeled from the saber stroke
    Shattered and sundered.
Then they rode back, but not,
    Not the six hundred.

5

Cannon to right of them,
40 Cannon to left of them,
Cannon behind them
    Volleyed and thundered;
Stormed at with shot and shell,
While horse and hero fell.
45 They that had fought so well
Came through the jaws of Death,
Back from the mouth of hell,
All that was left of them,
    Left of six hundred.

6

50 When can their glory fade?
O the wild charge they made!
    All the world wondered.
Honor the charge they made!
Honor the Light Brigade,
55   Noble six hundred!

1854   1854

Idylls of the King   When John Milton was considering subjects suitable for
an epic poem, one of those he entertained was the story of the Christian British king
Arthur, a semilegendary leader of about 500 who fought off the heathen Saxon invaders who had swarmed into Britain after the withdrawal of the Roman legions. Tennyson likewise saw that the Arthurian story had epic potential and selected it for his
lifework as "the greatest of all poetical subjects." At intervals, during a period of fifty
years, he labored over the twelve books that make up his *Idylls of the King,* completing
the work in 1888.

The principal source of Tennyson's stories of Arthur and his knights was Sir Thomas
Malory's *Morte Darthur,* a version that Malory translated into English prose from
French sources in 1470. As Talbot Donaldson has suggested, one basis of the appeal of
the Arthurian stories, like the legends of Robin Hood and stories of the American West,
is that all three represent the struggle of individuals to restore order in situations of
chaos and anarchy, a task performed in the face of seemingly overwhelming odds. The
individual stories in Tennyson's *Idylls* have the same basic appeal, but the overall design
of the whole poem is more ambitious and impressive. The *Idylls of the King* represent the
rise and fall of a civilization. They imply that after two thousand years of Christianity,
Western civilization may be going through a cycle in which it must confront the possibilities of a renewal in the future or an apocalyptic extinction. The first book, *The Coming of Arthur,* introduces the basic myth of a springtime hero transforming a wasteland
and inspiring faith and hope in the highest values of civilized life among his devoted followers. Succeeding books move through summer and autumn and culminate in the
bleak wintry scene of Arthur's last battle in which his order perishes in a civil war; the
leader of the enemy forces is his own nephew, Sir Modred.

Throughout the later books of the *Idylls* the forces of opposition grow in strength,
and disaffections infect leading figures of the Round Table itself. The most glaring
example is the adulterous relationship between Guinevere, Arthur's "sumptuous"
queen (as Tennyson once described her), and the king's chief lieutenant and friend,
Sir Lancelot. Many other fallings away subsequently come to light, such as the per-
fidious betrayal by Sir Gawain in the ninth book, *Pelleas and Ettarre,* and the cynical
conduct of Sir Tristram, whose story is told in the bitter tenth book, *The Last Tour-
nament.* Even Merlin, Arthur's trusted magician and counselor, becomes corrupted
and can perform no further offices for the king (*Merlin and Vivien*). *The Passing of
Arthur* depicts the apocalyptic end of this long process of disintegration and decay.

FROM IDYLLS OF THE KING

The Coming of Arthur

Leodogran, the King of Cameliard,
Had one fair daughter, and none other child;
And she was fairest of all flesh on earth,
Guinevere, and in her his one delight.

5   For many a petty king ere Arthur came
Ruled in this isle, and ever waging war
Each upon other, wasted all the land;
And still from time to time the heathen host
Swarm'd overseas, and harried° what was left.   *ravaged*
10   And so there grew great tracts of wilderness,
Wherein the beast was ever more and more,

But man was less and less, till Arthur came.
For first Aurelius[1] lived and fought and died,
And after him King Uther fought and died,
15 But either fail'd to make the kingdom one.
And after these King Arthur for a space,
And thro' the puissance° of his Table Round,   *power*
Drew all their petty princedoms under him,
Their king and head, and made a realm, and reign'd.

20   And thus the land of Cameliard was waste,
Thick with wet woods, and many a beast therein,
And none or few to scare or chase the beast;
So that wild dog, and wolf and boar and bear
Came night and day, and rooted[2] in the fields,
25 And wallow'd in the gardens of the King.
And ever and anon the wolf would steal
The children and devour, but now and then,
Her own brood lost or dead, lent her fierce teat
To human sucklings; and the children, housed
30 In her foul den, there at their meat would growl,
And mock their foster-mother on four feet,
Till, straighten'd, they grew up to wolf-like men,
Worse than the wolves. And King Leodogran
Groan'd for the Roman legions here again,
35 And Caesar's eagle:[3] then his brother king,
Urien, assail'd him: last a heathen horde,
Reddening the sun with smoke and earth with blood,
And on the spike that split the mother's heart
Spitting° the child, brake on him, till, amazed,   *impaling*
40 He knew not whither he should turn for aid.

But—for he heard of Arthur newly crown'd,
Tho' not without an uproar made by those
Who cried, "He is not Uther's son"—the King
Sent to him, saying, "Arise, and help us thou!
45 For here between the man and beast we die."

And Arthur yet had done no deed of arms,
But heard the call, and came: and Guinevere
Stood by the castle walls to watch him pass;
But since he neither wore on helm or shield
50 The golden symbol of his kinglihood,[4]
But rode a simple knight among his knights,
And many of these in richer arms than he,
She saw him not, or mark'd not, if she saw,
One among many, tho' his face was bare,
55 But Arthur, looking downward as he past,
Felt the light of her eyes into his life
Smite on the sudden, yet rode on, and pitch'd

1. Brother of King Uther.
2. Tore up the earth.
3. Imperial protection.
4. The golden dragon [Tennyson's note].

His tents beside the forest. Then he drave°   *drove*
The heathen; after, slew the beast, and fell'd
60 The forest, letting in the sun, and made
Broad pathways for the hunter and the knight
And so return'd.

      For while he linger'd there,
A doubt that ever smoulder'd in the hearts
Of those great Lords and Barons of his realm
65 Flash'd forth and into war: for most of these,
Colleaguing with a score of petty kings,
Made head against him, crying, 'Who is he
That he should rule us? who hath proven him
King Uther's son? for lo! we look at him,
70 And find nor face nor bearing, limbs nor voice,
Are like to those of Uther whom we knew.
This is the son of Gorloïs, not the King;
This is the son of Anton, not the King.'

   And Arthur, passing thence to battle, felt
75 Travail, and throes and agonies of the life,
Desiring to be join'd with Guinevere;
And thinking as he rode, "Her father said
That there between the man and beast they die.
Shall I not lift her from this land of beasts
80 Up to my throne, and side by side with me?
What happiness to reign a lonely king,
Vext—O ye stars that shudder over me,
O earth that soundest hollow under me,
Vext with waste dreams? for saving I be join'd
85 To her that is the fairest under heaven,
I seem as nothing in the mighty world,
And cannot will my will, nor work my work
Wholly, nor make myself in mine own realm
Victor and lord. But were I join'd with her,
90 Then might we live together as one life,
And reigning with one will in everything
Have power on this dark land to lighten it,
And power on this dead world to make it live."

   Thereafter—as he speaks who tells the tale—
95 When Arthur reach'd a field-of-battle bright
With pitch'd pavilions of his foe, the world
Was all so clear about him, that he saw
The smallest rock far on the faintest hill,
And even in high day the morning star.
100 So when the King had set his banner broad,
At once from either side, with trumpet-blast,
And shouts, and clarions shrilling unto blood,
The long-lanced battle let their horses run.
And now the Barons and the kings prevail'd,
105 And now the King, as here and there that war

Went swaying; but the Powers who walk the world
Made lightnings and great thunders over him,
And dazed all eyes, till Arthur by main might,
And mightier of his hands with every blow,
110 And leading all his knighthood threw the kings
Carádos, Urien, Cradlemont of Wales,
Claudias, and Clariance of Northumberland,
The King Brandagoras of Latangor,
With Anguisant of Erin, Morganore,
115 And Lot of Orkney.[5] Then, before a voice
As dreadful as the shout of one who sees
To one who sins, and deems himself alone
And all the world asleep, they swerved and brake
Flying, and Arthur call'd to stay the brands
120 That hack'd among the flyers, "Ho! they yield!"
So like a painted battle the war stood
Silenced, the living quiet as the dead,
And in the heart of Arthur joy was lord.
He laugh'd upon his warrior° whom he loved   *Lancelot*
125 And honour'd most. "Thou dost not doubt me King,
So well thine arm hath wrought for me to-day."
"Sir and my liege," he cried, "the fire of God
Descends upon thee in the battle-field:
I know thee for my King!" Whereat the two,
130 For each had warded° either in the fight,   *guarded*
Sware on the field of death a deathless love.
And Arthur said, "Man's word is God in man:
Let chance what will, I trust thee to the death."

        Then quickly from the foughten field he sent
135 Ulfius, and Brastias, and Bedivere,
His new-made knights, to King Leodogran,
Saying, "If I in aught have served thee well,
Give me thy daughter Guinevere to wife."

        Whom when he heard, Leodogran in heart
140 Debating—"How should I that am a king,
However much he holp me at my need,
Give my one daughter saving to a king,
And a king's son?"—lifted his voice, and call'd
A hoary man, his chamberlain, to whom
145 He trusted all things, and of him required
His counsel: "Knowest thou aught of Arthur's birth?"

        Then spake the hoary chamberlain and said,
"Sir King, there be but two old men that know:
And each is twice as old as I; and one
150 Is Merlin, the wise man that ever served
King Uther thro' his magic art; and one
Is Merlin's master (so they call him) Bleys,

5. Islands north of Scotland. These kings opposed Arthur in Malory's version.

Who taught him magic; but the scholar ran
Before the master, and so far, that Bleys
155   Laid magic by, and sat him down, and wrote
All things and whatsoever Merlin did
In one great annal-book, where after-years
Will learn the secret of our Arthur's birth."

To whom the King Leodogran replied,
160   "O friend, had I been holpen half as well
By this King Arthur as by thee to-day,
Then beast and man had had their share of me:
But summon here before us yet once more
Ulfius, and Brastias, and Bedivere."

165   Then, when they came before him, the King said,
"I have seen the cuckoo chased by lesser fowl,
And reason in the chase: but wherefore now
Do these your lords stir up the heat of war,
Some calling Arthur born of Gorloïs,
170   Others of Anton? Tell me, ye yourselves,
Hold ye this Arthur for King Uther's son?"

And Ulfius and Brastias answer'd, "Ay."
Then Bedivere, the first of all his knights
Knighted by Arthur at his crowning, spake—
175   For bold in heart and act and word was he,
Whenever slander breathed against the King—

"Sir, there be many rumours on this head:
For there be those who hate him in their hearts,
Call him baseborn, and since his ways are sweet,
180   And theirs are bestial, hold him less than man:
And there be those who deem him more than man,
And dream he dropt from heaven: but my belief
In all this matter—so ye care to learn—
Sir, for ye know that in King Uther's time
185   The prince and warrior Gorloïs, he that held
Tintagil castle by the Cornish sea,
Was wedded with a winsome wife, Ygerne:
And daughters had she borne him,—one whereof,
Lot's wife, the Queen of Orkney, Bellicent,
190   Hath ever like a loyal sister cleaved
To Arthur,—but a son she had not borne.
And Uther cast upon her eyes of love:
But she, a stainless wife to Gorloïs,
So loathed the bright dishonour of his love,
195   That Gorloïs and King Uther went to war:
And overthrown was Gorloïs and slain.
Then Uther in his wrath and heat besieged
Ygerne within Tintagil, where her men,
Seeing the mighty swarm about their walls,
200   Left her and fled, and Uther enter'd in,

And there was none to call to but himself.
So, compass'd by the power of the King,
Enforced she was to wed him in her tears,
And with a shameful swiftness: afterward,
205 Not many moons, King Uther died himself,
Moaning and wailing for an heir to rule
After him, lest the realm should go to wrack.
And that same night, the night of the new year,
By reason of the bitterness and grief
210 That vext his mother, all before his time
Was Arthur born, and all as soon as born
Deliver'd at a secret postern-gate
To Merlin, to be holden far apart
Until his hour should come; because the lords
215 Of that fierce day were as the lords of this,
Wild beasts, and surely would have torn the child
Piecemeal among them, had they known; for each
But sought to rule for his own self and hand,
And many hated Uther for the sake
220 Of Gorloïs. Wherefore Merlin took the child,
And gave him to Sir Anton, an old knight
And ancient friend of Uther; and his wife
Nursed the young prince, and rear'd him with her own;
And no man knew. And ever since the lords
225 Have foughten like wild beasts among themselves,
So that the realm has gone to wrack: but now,
This year, when Merlin (for his hour had come)
Brought Arthur forth, and set him in the hall,
Proclaiming, 'Here is Uther's heir, your king,'
230 A hundred voices cried, 'Away with him!
No king of ours! a son of Gorloïs he,
Or else the child of Anton, and no king,
Or else baseborn.' Yet Merlin thro' his craft,
And while the people clamour'd for a king,
235 Had Arthur crown'd; but after, the great lords
Banded, and so brake out in open war."

    Then while the King debated with himself
If Arthur were the child of shamefulness,
Or born the son of Gorloïs, after death,
240 Or Uther's son, and born before his time,
Or whether there were truth in anything
Said by these three, there came to Cameliard,
With Gawain and young Modred, her two sons,
Lot's wife, the Queen of Orkney, Bellicent;
245 Whom as he could, not as he would, the King
Made feast for, saying, as they sat at meat,

    "A doubtful throne is ice on summer seas.
Ye come from Arthur's court. Victor his men
Report him! Yea, but ye—think ye this king—
250 So many those that hate him, and so strong,

So few his knights, however brave they be—
Hath body enow to hold his foemen down?"

"O King," she cried, "and I will tell thee: few,
Few, but all brave, all of one mind with him;
255 For I was near him when the savage yells
Of Uther's peerage died, and Arthur sat
Crown'd on the daïs, and his warriors cried,
'Be thou the king, and we will work thy will
Who love thee.' Then the King in low deep tones,
260 And simple words of great authority,
Bound them by so strait vows to his own self,
That when they rose, knighted from kneeling, some
Were pale as at the passing of a ghost,
Some flush'd, and others dazed, as one who wakes
265 Half-blinded at the coming of a light.

"But when he spake and cheer'd his Table Round
With large, divine, and comfortable words,
Beyond my tongue to tell thee—I beheld
From eye to eye thro' all their Order flash
270 A momentary likeness of the King:
And ere it left their faces, thro' the cross
And those around it and the Crucified,
Down from the casement over Arthur, smote
Flame-colour, vert° and azure, in three rays,   *green*
275 One falling upon each of three fair queens,
Who stood in silence near his throne, the friends
Of Arthur, gazing on him, tall, with bright
Sweet faces, who will help him at his need.

"And there I saw mage° Merlin, whose vast wit   *magician*
280 And hundred winters are but as the hands
Of loyal vassals toiling for their liege.

"And near him stood the Lady of the Lake,[6]
Who knows a subtler magic than his own—
Clothed in white samite,[7] mystic, wonderful.
285 She gave the King his huge cross-hilted sword,
Whereby to drive the heathen out: a mist
Of incense curl'd about her, and her face
Wellnigh was hidden in the minister gloom;
But there was heard among the holy hymns
290 A voice as of the waters,[8] for she dwells
Down in a deep; calm, whatsoever storms
May shake the world, and when the surface rolls,
Hath power to walk the waters like our Lord.

"There likewise I beheld Excalibur
295 Before him at his crowning borne, the sword

6. The Lady of the Lake in the old legends is the Church [Tennyson's note].
7. A rich silk fabric.

8. Cf. Revelation 14.2: "And I heard a voice from Heaven, as the voice of many waters."

That rose from out the bosom of the lake,
And Arthur row'd across and took it—rich
With jewels, elfin Urim,[9] on the hilt,
Bewildering heart and eye—the blade so bright
300   That men are blinded by it—on one side,
Graven in the oldest tongue of all this world,
'Take me,' but turn the blade and ye shall see,
And written in the speech ye speak yourself,
'Cast me away!' And sad was Arthur's face
305   Taking it, but old Merlin counsell'd him,
'Take thou and strike! the time to cast away
Is yet far-off.' So this great brand° the king   sword
Took, and by this will beat his foemen down."

      Thereat Leodogran rejoiced, but thought
310   To sift his doubtings to the last, and ask'd,
Fixing full eyes of question on her face,
"The swallow and the swift are near akin,
But thou art closer to this noble prince,
Being his own dear sister;" and she said,
315   "Daughter of Gorloïs and Ygerne am I;"
"And therefore Arthur's sister?" ask'd the King
She answer'd, "These be secret things," and sign'd
To those two sons to pass, and let them be.
And Gawain went, and breaking into song
320   Sprang out, and follow'd by his flying hair
Ran like a colt, and leapt at all he saw:
But Modred laid his ear beside the doors,
And there half-heard; the same that afterward
Struck for the throne, and striking found his doom.

325   And then the Queen made answer, "What know I?
For dark my mother was in eyes and hair,
And dark in hair and eyes am I; and dark
Was Gorloïs, yea and dark was Uther too,
Wellnigh to blackness; but this King is fair
330   Beyond the race of Britons and of men.
Moreover, always in my mind I hear
A cry from out the dawning of my life,
A mother weeping, and I hear her say,
'O that ye had some brother, pretty one,
335   To guard thee on the rough ways of the world.'

      "Ay," said the King, "and hear ye such a cry?
But when did Arthur chance upon thee first?"

      "O King!" she cried, "and I will tell thee true:
He found me first when yet a little maid:
340   Beaten I had been for a little fault
Whereof I was not guilty; and out I ran
And flung myself down on a bank of heath,

9. Gems used for divination.

And hated this fair world and all therein,
And wept, and wish'd that I were dead; and he—
345   I know not whether of himself he came,
Or brought by Merlin, who, they say, can walk
Unseen at pleasure—he was at my side,
And spake sweet words, and comforted my heart,
And dried my tears, being a child with me.
350   And many a time he came, and evermore
As I grew greater grew with me; and sad
At times he seem'd, and sad with him was I,
Stern too at times, and then I loved him not,
But sweet again, and then I loved him well.
355   And now of late I see him less and less,
But those first days had golden hours for me,
For then I surely thought he would be king.

"But let me tell thee now another tale:
For Bleys, our Merlin's master, as they say,
360   Died but of late, and sent his cry to me,
To hear him speak before he left his life.
Shrunk like a fairy changeling[1] lay the mage;
And when I enter'd told me that himself
And Merlin ever served about the King,
365   Uther, before he died; and on the night
When Uther in Tintagil past away
Moaning and wailing for an heir, the two
Left the still King, and passing forth to breathe,
Then from the castle gateway by the chasm
370   Descending thro' the dismal night—a night
In which the bounds of heaven and earth were lost—
Beheld, so high upon the dreary deeps
It seem'd in heaven, a ship, the shape thereof
A dragon wing'd, and all from stem to stern
375   Bright with a shining people on the decks,
And gone as soon as seen. And then the two
Dropt to the cove, and watch'd the great sea fall,
Wave after wave, each mightier than the last,
Till last, a ninth one, gathering half the deep
380   And full of voices, slowly rose and plunged
Roaring, and all the wave was in a flame:
And down the wave and in the flame was borne
A naked babe, and rode to Merlin's feet,
Who stoopt and caught the babe, and cried 'The King!
385   Here is an heir for Uther!' And the fringe
Of that great breaker, sweeping up the strand,
Lash'd at the wizard as he spake the word,
And all at once all round him rose in fire,
So that the child and he were clothed in fire.
390   And presently thereafter follow'd calm,
Free sky and stars: 'And this same child,' he said,

---

1. Child secretly substituted for another.

'Is he who reigns; nor could I part in peace
Till this were told.' And saying this the seer
Went thro' the strait and dreadful pass of death,
395 Not ever to be question'd any more
Save on the further side; but when I met
Merlin, and ask'd him if these things were truth—
The shining dragon and the naked child
Descending in the glory of the seas—
400 He laugh'd as is his wont, and answer'd me
In riddling triplets of old time, and said:

    ' "Rain, rain, and sun! a rainbow in the sky!
A young man will be wiser by and by;
An old man's wit may wander ere he die.
405 Rain, rain, and sun! a rainbow on the lea!
And truth is this to me, and that to thee;
And truth or clothed or naked let it be.
Rain, sun, and rain! and the free blossom blows:
Sun, rain, and sun! and where is he who knows?
410 From the great deep to the great deep he goes.'

    "So Merlin riddling anger'd me; but thou
Fear not to give this King thine only child,
Guinevere: so great bards of him will sing
Hereafter; and dark sayings from of old
415 Ranging and ringing thro' the minds of men,
And echo'd by old folk beside their fires
For comfort after their wage-work is done,
Speak of the King; and Merlin in our time
Hath spoken also, not in jest, and sworn
420 Tho' men may wound him that he will not die,
But pass, again to come; and then or now
Utterly smite the heathen underfoot,
Till these and all men hail him for their king."

    She spake and King Leodogran rejoiced,
425 But musing "Shall I answer yea or nay?"
Doubted, and drowsed, nodded and slept, and saw,
Dreaming, a slope of land that ever grew,
Field after field, up to a height, the peak
Haze-hidden, and thereon a phantom king,
430 Now looming, and now lost; and on the slope
The sword rose, the hind° fell, the herd was driven,   *servant*
Fire glimpsed;° and all the land from roof and rick,[2]   *glimmered*
In drifts of smoke before a rolling wind,
Stream'd to the peak, and mingled with the haze
435 And made it thicker; while the phantom king
Sent out at times a voice; and here or there
Stood one who pointed toward the voice, the rest
Slew on and burnt, crying, "No king of ours,

2. Stacks of grain.

No son of Uther, and no king of ours;"
440 Till with a wink his dream was changed, the haze
Descended, and the solid earth became
As nothing, but the King stood out in heaven,
Crown'd. And Leodogran awoke, and sent
Ulfius, and Brastias and Bedivere,
445 Back to the court of Arthur answering yea.

Then Arthur charged his warrior whom he loved
And honour'd most, Sir Lancelot, to ride forth
And bring the Queen;—and watch'd him from the gates:
And Lancelot past away among the flowers,
450 (For then was latter April) and return'd
Among the flowers, in May, with Guinevere.
To whom arrived, by Dubric the high saint,
Chief of the church in Britain, and before
The stateliest of her altar-shrines, the King
455 That morn was married, while in stainless white,
The fair beginners of a nobler time,
And glorying in their vows and him, his knights
Stood round him, and rejoicing in his joy.
Far shone the fields of May thro' open door,
460 The sacred altar blossom'd white with May,
The Sun of May descended on their King,
They gazed on all earth's beauty in their Queen,
Roll'd incense, and there past along the hymns
A voice as of the waters, while the two
465 Sware at the shrine of Christ a deathless love:
And Arthur said, "Behold, thy doom is mine.
Let chance what will, I love thee to the death!"
To whom the Queen replied with drooping eyes,
"King and my lord, I love thee to the death!"
470 And holy Dubric spread his hands and spake,
"Reign ye, and live and love, and make the world
Other, and may thy Queen be one with thee,
And all this Order of thy Table Round
Fulfil the boundless purpose of their King!"
475 So Dubric said; but when they left the shrine
Great Lords from Rome before the portal stood,
In scornful stillness gazing as they past;
Then while they paced a city all on fire
With sun and cloth of gold, the trumpets blew,
480 And Arthur's knighthood sang before the King:—

"Blow trumpet, for the world is white with May;
Blow trumpet, the long night hath roll'd away!
Blow thro' the living world—'Let the King reign.'

"Shall Rome or Heathen rule in Arthur's realm?
485 Flash brand and lance, fall battleaxe upon helm,
Fall battleaxe, and flash brand! Let the King reign.

"Strike for the King and live! his knights have heard.
That God hath told the King a secret word.
Fall battleaxe, and flash brand! Let the King reign.

490 "Blow trumpet! he will lift us from the dust.
Blow trumpet! live the strength and die the lust!
Clang battleaxe, and clash brand! Let the King reign.

"Strike for the King and die! and if thou diest,
The King is King, and ever wills the highest.
495 Clang battleaxe, and clash brand! Let the King reign.

"Blow, for our Sun is mighty in his May!
Blow, for our Sun is mightier day by day!
Clang battleaxe, and clash brand! Let the King reign.

"The King will follow Christ, and we the King
500 In whom high God hath breathed a secret thing.
Fall battleaxe, and flash brand! Let the King reign."

So sang the knighthood, moving to their hall.
There at the banquet those great Lords from Rome,
The slowly-fading mistress of the world,
505 Strode in, and claim'd their tribute as of yore.
But Arthur spake, "Behold, for these have sworn
To wage my wars, and worship me their King;
The old order changeth, yielding place to new;
And we that fight for our fair father Christ,
510 Seeing that ye be grown too weak and old
To drive the heathen from your Roman wall,
No tribute will we pay:" so those great lords
Drew back in wrath, and Arthur strove with Rome.

And Arthur and his knighthood for a space
515 Were all one will, and thro' that strength the King
Drew in the petty princedoms under him,
Fought, and in twelve great battles overcame
The heathen hordes, and made a realm and reign'd.

1869   1869

The Passing of Arthur[1]

That story which the bold Sir Bedivere,[2]
First made and latest left of all the knights,
Told, when the man was no more than a voice

1. On the composition of this final idyll and its relation to his Morte d'Arthur of 1842, see n. 1, p. 1217. The principal source was Malory's Morte Darthur 21.4–5. Preceding the action of this idyll, Arthur had been in France with his nephew Gawain fighting against the forces of Lancelot. Learning at that time of the gathering of an army against him in England, under the leadership of

his nephew, Modred, Arthur returned there to engage in his last battle. Upon landing at Dover, Gawain was slain.
2. A knight who had long been close to the king, described in The Coming of Arthur: "Bedivere, the first of all his knights / Knighted by Arthur at his crowning."

In the white winter of his age, to those
5 With whom he dwelt, new faces, other minds.

For on their march to westward, Bedivere,
Who slowly paced among the slumbering host,
Heard in his tent the moanings of the King:

"I found Him in the shining of the stars,
10 I marked Him in the flowering of His fields,
But in His ways with men I find Him not.
I waged His wars, and now I pass and die.
O me! for why is all around us here
As if some lesser god had made the world,
15 But had not force to shape it as he would,
Till the High God behold it from beyond,
And enter it, and make it beautiful?
Or else as if the world were wholly fair,
But that these eyes of men are dense and dim,
20 And have not power to see it as it is:
Perchance, because we see not to the close;—
For I, being simple, thought to work His will,
And have but stricken with the sword in vain;
And all whereon I leaned in wife and friend
25 Is traitor to my peace, and all my realm
Reels back into the beast, and is no more.
My God, thou hast forgotten me in my death:[3]
Nay—God my Christ—I pass but shall not die."

Then, ere that last weird battle in the west,
30 There came on Arthur sleeping, Gawain killed
In Lancelot's war, the ghost of Gawain blown
Along a wandering wind, and past his ear
Went shrilling. "Hollow, hollow all delight!
Hail, King! tomorrow thou shalt pass away.
35 Farewell! there is an isle of rest for thee.
And I am blown along a wandering wind,
And hollow, hollow, hollow all delight."
And fainter onward, like wild birds that change
Their season in the night and wail their way
40 From cloud to cloud, down the long wind the dream
Shrilled; but in going mingled with dim cries
Far in the moonlit haze among the hills,
As of some lonely city sacked by night,
When all is lost, and wife and child with wail
45 Pass to new lords; and Arthur woke and called,
"Who spake? A dream. O light upon the wind,
Thine, Gawain, was the voice—are these dim cries
Thine? or doth all that haunts the waste and wild
Mourn, knowing it will go along with me?"

50 This heard the bold Sir Bedivere and spake:
"O me, my King, let pass whatever will,

3. Cf. Matthew 27.46: "My God, my God, why hast thou forsaken me?"

Elves, and the harmless glamor of the field;[4]
But in their stead thy name and glory cling
To all high places like a golden cloud
55 Forever: but as yet thou shalt not pass.
Light was Gawain in life, and light in death
Is Gawain, for the ghost is as the man;
And care not thou for dreams from him, but rise—
I hear the steps of Modred in the west,
60 And with him many of thy people, and knights
Once thine, whom thou hast loved, but grosser grown
Than heathen, spitting at their vows and thee.
Right well in heart they know thee for the King.
Arise, go forth and conquer as of old."

65   Then spake King Arthur to Sir Bedivere:
"Far other is this battle in the west
Whereto we move, than when we strove in youth,
And brake the petty kings, and fought with Rome,
Or thrust the heathen from the Roman wall,
70 And shook him through the north. Ill doom is mine
To war against my people and my knights.
The king who fights his people fights himself.
And they thy knights, who loved me once, the stroke
That strikes them dead is as my death to me.
75 Yet let us hence, and find or feel a way
Through this blind haze, which ever since I saw
One lying in the dust at Almesbury,[5]
Hath folded in the passes of the world."

Then rose the King and moved his host by night,
80 And ever pushed Sir Modred, league by league,
Back to the sunset bound of Lyonnesse[6]—
A land of old upheaven from the abyss
By fire, to sink into the abyss again;
Where fragments of forgotten peoples dwelled,
85 And the long mountains ended in a coast
Of ever-shifting sand, and far away
The phantom circle of a moaning sea.
There the pursuer could pursue no more,
And he that fled no further fly the King;
90 And there, that day when the great light of heaven
Burned at his lowest in the rolling year,
On the waste sand by the waste sea they closed.
Nor ever yet had Arthur fought a fight
Like this last, dim, weird battle of the west.
95 A deathwhite mist slept over sand and sea:
Whereof the chill, to him who breathed it, drew
Down with his blood, till all his heart was cold

4. Tennyson said the reference is to "the legends which cluster round the King's name." One legend told of the elves' bestowing gifts on Arthur as a child.
5. The convent to which Guinevere had with-drawn; during the king's farewell visit to her there, she had lain in the dust at his feet.
6. Legendary land, extending west from Cornwall, which sank into the sea.

With formless fear; and even on Arthur fell
Confusion, since he saw not whom he fought.
100 For friend and foe were shadows in the mist,
And friend slew friend not knowing whom he slew;
And some had visions out of golden youth,
And some beheld the faces of old ghosts
Look in upon the battle; and in the mist
105 Was many a noble deed, many a base,
And chance and craft and strength in single fights,
And ever and anon with host to host
Shocks, and the splintering spear, the hard mail hewn,
Shield-breakings, and the clash of brands, the crash
110 Of battleaxes on shattered helms, and shrieks
After the Christ, of those who falling down
Looked up for heaven, and only saw the mist;
And shouts of heathen and the traitor knights,
Oaths, insult, filth, and monstrous blasphemies,
115 Sweat, writhings, anguish, laboring of the lungs
In that close mist, and cryings for the light,
Moans of the dying, and voices of the dead.

Last, as by some one deathbed after wail
Of suffering, silence follows, or through death
120 Or deathlike swoon, thus over all that shore,
Save for some whisper of the seething seas,
A dead hush fell; but when the dolorous day
Grew drearier toward twilight falling, came
A bitter wind, clear from the North, and blew
125 The mist aside, and with that wind the tide
Rose, and the pale King glanced across the field
Of battle: but no man was moving there;
Nor any cry of Christian heard thereon,
Nor yet of heathen; only the wan wave
130 Brake in among dead faces, to and fro
Swaying the helpless hands, and up and down
Tumbling the hollow helmets of the fallen,
And shivered brands that once had fought with Rome,
And rolling far along the gloomy shores
135 The voice of days of old and days to be.

Then spake King Arthur to Sir Bedivere,
And whiter than the mist that all day long
Had held the field of battle was the King:

"Hearest thou this great voice that shakes the world,
140 And wastes the narrow realm whereon we move,
And beats upon the faces of the dead,
My dead, as though they had not died for me?—
O Bedivere, for on my heart hath fallen
Confusion, till I know not what I am,
145 Nor whence I am, nor whether I be King.
Behold, I seem but King among the dead."

Then spake the bold Sir Bedivere: "My King,
King everywhere! and so the dead have kings,
There also will I worship thee as King.
150 Yet still thy life is whole, and still I live
Who love thee; but who hates thee, he that brought
The heathen back among us, yonder stands,
Modred, unharmed, the traitor of thine house."

Then spake the King: "My house hath been my doom.
155 But call not thou this traitor of my house
Who hath but dwelled beneath one roof with me.
My house are rather they who sware my vows,
Yea, even while they brake them, owned me King.
And well for thee, saying in my dark hour,
160 When all the purport of my throne hath failed,
That quick or dead thou holdest me for King.
King am I, whatsoever be their cry;
And one last act of kinghood shalt thou see
Yet, ere I pass." And uttering this the King
165 Made at the man: then Modred smote his liege
Hard on that helm which many a heathen sword
Had beaten thin; while Arthur at one blow,
Striking the last stroke with Excalibur,
Slew him, and all but slain himself, he fell.

170 So all day long the noise of battle rolled
Among the mountains by the winter sea;
Until King Arthur's Table, man by man,
Had fallen in Lyonnesse about their lord,
King Arthur. Then, because his wound was deep,
175 The bold Sir Bedivere uplifted him,
And bore him to a chapel nigh the field,
A broken chancel with a broken cross,
That stood on a dark strait of barren land:
On one side lay the Ocean, and on one
180 Lay a great water, and the moon was full.

Then spake King Arthur to Sir Bedivere:
"The sequel of today unsolders all
The goodliest fellowship of famous knights
Whereof this world holds record. Such a sleep
185 They sleep—the men I loved. I think that we
Shall never more, at any future time,
Delight our souls with talk of knightly deeds,
Walking about the gardens and the halls
Of Camelot, as in the days that were.
190 I perish by this people which I made,—
Though Merlin sware that I should come again
To rule once more;[7] but, let what will be, be,

---

7. Cf. Malory, *Morte Darthur* 21.7: "Some men yet say in many parts of England that King Arthur is not dead, but by the will of our Lord in another place. And men say that he will come again."

I am so deeply smitten through the helm
That without help I cannot last til morn.
195 Thou therefore take my brand Excalibur,
Which was my pride: for thou rememberest how
In those old days, one summer noon, an arm
Rose up from out the bosom of the lake,
Clothed in white samite, mystic, wonderful,
200 Holding the sword—and how I rowed across
And took it, and have worn it, like a king;
And, wheresoever I am sung or told
In aftertime, this also shall be known:
But now delay not: take Excalibur,
205 And fling him far into the middle mere:[8]
Watch what thou seëst, and lightly° bring me word."   *quickly*

To him replied the bold Sir Bedivere:
"It is not meet, Sir King, to leave thee thus,
Aidless, alone, and smitten through the helm—
210 A little thing may harm a wounded man;
Yet I thy hest° will all perform at full,   *command*
Watch what I see, and lightly bring thee word."

So saying, from the ruined shrine he stepped,
And in the moon athwart the place of tombs,
215 Where lay the mighty bones of ancient men,
Old knights, and over them the sea-wind sang
Shrill, chill, with flakes of foam. He, stepping down
By zigzag paths, and juts of pointed rock,
Came on the shining levels of the lake.

220 There drew he forth the brand Excalibur,
And o'er him, drawing it, the winter moon,
Brightening the skirts of a long cloud, ran forth
And sparkled keen with frost against the hilt:
For all the haft twinkled with diamond sparks,
225 Myriads of topaz-lights, and jacinth°-work   *red gem*
Of subtlest jewelry. He gazed so long
That both his eyes were dazzled as he stood,
This way and that dividing the swift mind,
In act to throw: but at the last it seemed
230 Better to leave Excalibur concealed
There in the many-knotted waterflags,
That whistled stiff and dry about the marge.
So strode he back slow to the wounded King.

Then spake King Arthur to Sir Bedivere:
235 "Hast thou performed my mission which I gave?
What is it thou hast seen? or what hast heard?"
And answer made the bold Sir Bedivere:
"I heard the ripple washing in the reeds,
And the wild water lapping on the crag."

8. Middle of the lake.

240   To whom replied King Arthur, faint and pale:
"Thou hast betrayed thy nature and thy name.
Not rendering true answer, as beseemed
Thy fëalty, nor like a noble knight:
For surer sign had followed, either hand,
245   Or voice, or else a motion of the mere.
This is a shameful thing for men to lie.
Yet now, I charge thee, quickly go again,
As thou art lief° and dear, and do the thing   *beloved*
I bade thee, watch, and lightly bring me word."

250   Then went Sir Bedivere the second time
Across the ridge, and paced beside the mere,
Counting the dewy pebbles, fixed in thought;
But when he saw the wonder of the hilt,
How curiously and strangely chased,[9] he smote
255   His palms together, and he cried aloud:

     "And if indeed I cast the brand away,
Surely a precious thing, one worthy note,
Should thus be lost forever from the earth,
Which might have pleased the eyes of many men.
260   What good should follow this, if this were done?
What harm, undone? Deep harm to disobey,
Seeing obedience is the bond of rule.
Were it well to obey then, if a king demand
An act unprofitable, against himself?
265   The King is sick, and knows not what he does.
What record, or what relic of my lord
Should be to aftertime, but empty breath
And rumors of a doubt? But were this kept,
Stored in some treasure-house of mighty kings,
270   Some one might show it at a joust of arms,
Saying, 'King Arthur's sword, Excalibur,
Wrought by the lonely maiden of the Lake.
Nine years she wrought it, sitting in the deeps
Upon the hidden bases of the hills.'
275   So might some old man speak in the aftertime
To all the people, winning reverence.
But now much honor and much fame were lost."

     So spake he, clouded with his own conceit,[1]
And hid Excalibur the second time,
280   And so strode back slow to the wounded king.

     Then spoke King Arthur, breathing heavily:
"What is it thou hast seen? or what hast heard?"

     And answer made the bold Sir Bedivere:
"I heard the water lapping on the crag,
285   And the long ripple washing in the reeds."

9. Adorned. "Curiously": skillfully.   1. Vain and foolish fancies.

To whom replied King Arthur, much in wrath:
"Ah, miserable and unkind, untrue,
Unknightly, traitor-hearted! Woe is me!
Authority forgets a dying king,
290   Laid widowed of the power in his eye
That bowed the will. I see thee what thou art,
For thou, the latest-left of all my knights,
In whom should meet the offices of all,
Thou wouldst betray me for the precious hilt;
295   Either from lust of gold, or like a girl
Valuing the giddy pleasure of the eyes.
Yet, for a man may fail in duty twice,
And the third time may prosper, get thee hence:
But, if thou spare to fling Excalibur,
300   I will arise and slay thee with my hands."

Then quickly rose Sir Bedivere, and ran,
And, leaping down the ridges lightly, plunged
Among the bullrush beds, and clutched the sword,
And strongly wheeled and threw it. The great brand
305   Made lightnings in the splendor of the moon,
And flashing round and round and whirled in an arch,
Shot like a streamer of the northern morn,[2]
Seen where the moving isles of winter shock[3]
By night, with noises of the Northern Sea.
310   So flashed and fell the brand Excalibur:
But ere he dipped the surface, rose an arm
Clothed in white samite, mystic, wonderful,
And caught him by the hilt, and brandished him
Three times, and drew him under in the mere.
315   And lightly went the other to the King.

Then spoke King Arthur, drawing thicker breath:
"Now see I by thine eyes that this is done.
Speak out: what is it thou hast heard, or seen?"

And answer made the bold Sir Bedivere:
320   "Sir King, I closed mine eyelids, lest the gems
Should blind my purpose, for I never saw,
Nor shall see, here or elsewhere, till I die,
Not though I live three lives of mortal men,
So great a miracle as yonder hilt.
325   Then with both hands I flung him, wheeling him;
But when I looked again, behold an arm,
Clothed in white samite, mystic, wonderful,
That caught him by the hilt, and brandished him
Three times, and drew him under in the mere."

330   And answer made King Arthur, breathing hard:
"My end draws nigh; 'tis time that I were gone.

2. The northern lights.   3. Where the icebergs collide.

Make broad thy shoulders to receive my weight,
And bear me to the margin; yet I fear
My wound hath taken cold, and I shall die."

335   So saying, from the pavement he half rose,
Slowly, with pain, reclining on his arm,
And looking wistfully with wide blue eyes
As in a picture. Him Sir Bedivere
Remorsefully regarded through his tears,
340   And would have spoken, but he found not words;
Then took with care, and kneeling on one knee,
O'er both his shoulders drew the languid hands,
And rising bore him through the place of tombs.

But, as he walked, King Arthur panted hard,
345   Like one that feels a nightmare on his bed
When all the house is mute. So sighed the King,
Muttering and murmuring at his ear, "Quick, quick!
I fear it is too late, and I shall die."
But the other swiftly strode from ridge to ridge,
350   Clothed with his breath, and looking, as he walked,
Larger than human on the frozen hills.
He heard the deep behind him, and a cry
Before. His own thought drove him like a goad.
Dry clashed his harness in the icy caves
355   And barren chasms, and all to left and right
The bare black cliff clanged round him, as he based
His feet on juts of slippery crag that rang
Sharp-smitten with the dint of armèd heels—
And on a sudden, lo! the level lake,
360   And the long glories of the winter moon.

Then saw they how there hove a dusky barge,
Dark as a funeral scarf from stem to stern,
Beneath them; and descending they were ware
That all the decks were dense with stately forms,
365   Black-stoled, black-hooded, like a dream—by these
Three Queens with crowns of gold: and from them rose
A cry that shivered to the tingling stars,
And, as it were one voice, an agony
Of lamentation, like a wind that shrills
370   All night in a waste land, where no one comes,
Or hath come, since the making of the world.

Then murmured Arthur, "Place me in the barge."
So to the barge they came. There those three Queens
Put forth their hands, and took the King, and wept.
375   But she, that rose the tallest of them all
And fairest, laid his head upon her lap,
And loosed the shattered casque,° and chafed his hands,   *helmet*
And called him by his name, complaining loud,
And dropping bitter tears against a brow

380   Striped with dark blood: for all his face was white
       And colorless, and like the withered moon
       Smote by the fresh beam of the springing east;
       And all his greaves and cuisses⁴ dashed with drops
       Of onset;⁵ and the light and lustrous curls—
385   That made his forehead like a rising sun
       High from the daïs-throne—were parched with dust;
       Or, clotted into points and hanging loose,
       Mixed with the knightly growth that fringed his lips.
       So like a shattered column lay the King;
390   Not like that Arthur who, with lance in rest,
       From spur to plume a star of tournament,
       Shot through the lists at Camelot, and charged
       Before the eyes of ladies and of kings.

       Then loudly cried the bold Sir Bedivere:
395   "Ah! my Lord Arthur, whither shall I go?
       Where shall I hide my forehead and my eyes?
       For now I see the true old times are dead,
       When every morning brought a noble chance,
       And every chance brought out a noble knight.
400   Such times have been not since the light that led
       The holy Elders⁶ with the gift of myrrh.
       But now the whole Round Table is dissolved
       Which was an image of the mighty world,
       And I, the last, go forth companionless,
405   And the days darken round me, and the years,
       Among new men, strange faces, other minds."

       And slowly answered Arthur from the barge:
       "The old order changeth, yielding place to new,
       And God fulfills himself in many ways,
410   Lest one good custom should corrupt the world.
       Comfort thyself: what comfort is in me?
       I have lived my life, and that which I have done
       May He within himself make pure! but thou,
       If thou shouldst never see my face again,
415   Pray for my soul. More things are wrought by prayer
       Than this world dreams of. Wherefore, let thy voice
       Rise like a fountain for me night and day.
       For what are men better than sheep or goats
       That nourish a blind life within the brain,
420   If, knowing God, they lift not hands of prayer
       Both for themselves and those who call them friend?
       For so the whole round earth is every way
       Bound by gold chains about the feet of God.
       But now farewell. I am going a long way
425   With these thou seëst—if indeed I go
       (For all my mind is clouded with a doubt)—

---

4. Armor to protect the front of the thighs.
"Greaves": armor to protect the leg below the knee.
5. Blood from battle.

6. I.e., the star that guided the three kings
("Elders") to the Christ child at Bethlehem.

To the island-valley of Avilion;[7]
Where falls not hail, or rain, or any snow,
Nor ever wind blows loudly: but it lies
430 Deep-meadowed, happy, fair with orchard lawns
And bowery hollows crowned with summer sea,
Where I will heal me of my grievous wound."

So said he, and the barge with oar and sail
Moved from the brink, like some full-breasted swan
435 That, fluting a wild carol ere her death,
Ruffles her pure cold plume, and takes the flood
With swarthy webs. Long stood Sir Bedivere
Revolving many memories, till the hull
Looked one black dot against the verge of dawn,
440 And on the mere the wailing died away.

But when that moan had passed for evermore,
The stillness of the dead world's winter dawn
Amazed him, and he groaned, "The King is gone."
And therewithal came on him the weird rhyme,[8]
445 "From the great deep to the great deep he goes."

Whereat he slowly turned and slowly clomb
The last hard footstep of that iron crag;
Thence marked the black hull moving yet, and cried,
"He passes to be King among the dead,
450 And after healing of his grievous wound
He comes again; but—if he come no more—
O me, be yon dark Queens in yon black boat,
Who shrieked and wailed, the three whereat we gazed
On that high day, when, clothed with living light,
455 They stood before his throne in silence, friends
Of Arthur, who should help him at his need?"

Then from the dawn it seemed there came, but faint
As from beyond the limit of the world,
Like the last echo born of a great cry,
460 Sounds, as if some fair city were one voice
Around a king returning from his wars.

Thereat once more he moved about, and clomb
Even to the highest he could climb, and saw,
Straining his eyes beneath an arch of hand,
465 Or thought he saw, the speck that bare the King,
Down that long water opening on the deep
Somewhere far off, pass on and on, and go
From less to less and vanish into light.
And the new sun rose bringing the new year.

1833–69   1869

7. Or Avalon, in Celtic mythology and medieval romance, the Vale of the Blessed where heroes enjoyed life after death.

8. A mysterious prophecy in verse had been spoken by Merlin concerning Arthur's birth; see *The Coming of Arthur,* lines 409–10, p. 1291.

Flower in the Crannied Wall

Flower in the crannied wall,
I pluck you out of the crannies,
I hold you here, root and all, in my hand,
Little flower—but if I could understand
5   What you are, root and all, and all in all,
I should know what God and man is.

                                                                        1869

Crossing the Bar[1]

Sunset and evening star,
    And one clear call for me!
And may there be no moaning of the bar,[2]
    When I put out to sea,

5   But such a tide as moving seems asleep,
    Too full for sound and foam,
When that which drew from out the boundless deep
    Turns again home.

Twilight and evening bell,
10   And after that the dark!
And may there be no sadness of farewell,
    When I embark;

For though from out our bourne° of Time and Place   boundary
    The flood may bear me far,
15   I hope to see my Pilot face to face[3]
    When I have crossed the bar.

1889   1889

1. Although not the last poem written by Tennyson, *Crossing the Bar* appears, at his request, as the
final poem in all collections of his work.
2. Mournful sound of the ocean beating on a sand
bar at the mouth of a harbor.

3. The expression "face to face" also occurs in two
lines of section 131 of *In Memoriam* not used but
left in manuscript: "And come to look on those we
loved / And That which made us, face to face."

EDWARD FITZGERALD
1809–1883

Omar Khayyám was a twelfth-century mathematician, astronomer, and teacher from
Nishapur in Persia. He was also the author of numerous rhymed quatrains, a verse
form called *rubā'i* in Persian. Omar's four-lined epigrams were subsequently brought
together in collections called *Rubáiyát* and recorded in various manuscripts.

More than seven hundred years later, in 1857, one such Omar manuscript came into the hands of Edward FitzGerald, who made from it one of the most popular poems in the English language. FitzGerald was a scholar of comfortable means who lived in the country reading the classics and cultivating his garden. He also cultivated his friendships with writers like Tennyson, Thackeray, and Carlyle, to whom he wrote charming letters. His translations from Greek and Latin were largely ignored and so too, at first, was his translation of Omar's Persian verses, which he published anonymously. In 1859, only two reviewers noticed the appearance of the *Rubáiyát of Omar Khayyám*, and the edition was soon remaindered. Two years later the volume was discovered by D. G. Rossetti, and enthusiasm for it gradually spread, until edition after edition was called for. The demand for the poem led FitzGerald to revise his translation considerably by further polishing his already finely polished stanzas (the fifth version of these revisions is printed here).

Experts have argued at great length whether FitzGerald's adaptation of Omar's poem is a faithful translation, but no one argues its beauty. One reader said of Fitz-Gerald's witty and melancholy masterpiece: "It reads like the latest and freshest expression of the perplexity and of the doubt of the generation to which we ourselves belong." This comment was made by the American Charles Eliot Norton writing in 1869. Norton's favorable opinion has been endorsed by later generations as well. The *Rubáiyát* has much in common with another late Victorian volume, *A Shropshire Lad* by A. E. Housman, and the remarkable popularity of these two collections of nostalgic lyrics is a reminder that to be popular, especially among young readers, poetry does not have to offer optimistic edification. As George Moore said, "The sadness of life is the joy of art."

The Rubáiyát of Omar Khayyám

I

Wake! For the Sun, who scattered into flight
The Stars before him from the Field of Night,
     Drives Night along with them from Heav'n and strikes
The Sultán's Turret with a Shaft of Light.

2

5   Before the phantom of False morning[1] died,
Methought a Voice within the Tavern cried,
     "When all the Temple is prepared within,
Why nods the drowsy Worshiper outside?"

3

And, as the Cock crew, those who stood before
10 The Tavern shouted—"Open, then, the Door!
     You know how little while we have to stay,
And, once departed, may return no more."

4

Now the New Year[2] reviving old Desires,
The thoughtful Soul to Solitude retires,

---

1. A transient Light on the Horizon about an hour
before the . . . True Dawn [FitzGerald's note].

2. In Persia, the beginning of spring.

15   Where the WHITE HAND OF MOSES on the Bough
       Puts out, and Jesus from the Ground suspires.[3]

                                 5
       Iram[4] indeed is gone with all his Rose,
       And Jamshyd's° Sev'n-ringed Cup where no one knows;   *legendary king*
           But still a Ruby kindles in the Vine,
20   And many a Garden by the Water blows.

                                 6
       And David's lips are locked; but in divine
       High-piping Pehleví,[5] with "Wine! Wine! Wine!
           Red Wine!"—the Nightingale cries to the Rose
       That sallow cheek of hers to incarnadine.

                                 7
25   Come, fill the Cup, and in the fire of Spring
       Your Winter-garment of Repentance fling;
           The Bird of Time has but a little way
       To flutter—and the Bird is on the Wing.

                                 8
       Whether at Naishápur or Babylon,
30   Whether the Cup with sweet or bitter run,
           The Wine of Life keeps oozing drop by drop,
       The Leaves of Life keep falling one by one.

                                 9
       Each Morn a thousand Roses brings, you say;
       Yes, but where leaves the Rose of Yesterday?
35   And this first Summer month that brings the Rose
       Shall take Jamshyd and Kaikobád[6] away.

                                 10
       Well, let it take them! What have we to do
       With Kaikobád the Great, or Kaikhosrú?°   *king*
           Let Zál and Rustum[7] bluster as they will,
40   Or Hátim[8] call to Supper—heed not you.

                                 11
       With me along the strip of Herbage strown
       That just divides the desert from the sown,
           Where name of Slave and Sultán is forgot—
       And Peace to Mahmúd[9] on his golden Throne!

---

3. Breathes. "Moses" and "Jesus": plants named in honor of prophets who came before Mohammed. The Persians believed that the healing power of Jesus was in his breath.
4. A royal Garden now sunk somewhere in the Sands of Arabia [FitzGerald's note].

5. The classical language of Persia.
6. Founder of a line of Persian kings.
7. Son and father who were warriors.
8. A generous host.
9. A sultan who conquered India.

12

45 A Book of Verses underneath the Bough,
A Jug of Wine, a Loaf of Bread—and Thou
    Beside me singing in the Wilderness—
Oh, Wilderness were Paradise enow!

13

Some for the Glories of This World; and some
50 Sigh for the Prophet's° Paradise to come;   *Mohammed's*
    Ah, take the Cash, and let the Credit go,
Nor heed the rumble of a distant Drum!

14

Look to the blowing Rose about us—"Lo,
Laughing," she says, "into the world I blow,
55   At once the silken tassel of my Purse
Tear, and its Treasure on the Garden throw."

15

And those who husbanded the Golden Grain,
And those who flung it to the winds like Rain,
    Alike to no such aureate Earth are turned
60 As, buried once, Men want dug up again.

16

The Worldly Hope men set their Hearts upon
Turns Ashes—or it prospers; and anon,
    Like Snow upon the Desert's dusty Face,
Lighting a little hour or two—is gone.

17

65 Think, in this battered Caravanserai°   *inn*
Whose Portals are alternate Night and Day,
    How Sultán after Sultán with his Pomp
Abode his destined Hour, and went his way.

18

They say the Lion and the Lizard keep
70 The Courts where Jamshyd gloried and drank deep;
    And Bahrám,[1] that great Hunter—the Wild Ass
Stamps o'er his Head, but cannot break his Sleep.

19

I sometimes think that never blows so red
The Rose as where some buried Caesar bled;
75   That every Hyacinth[2] the Garden wears
Dropped in her Lap from some once lovely Head.

1. A king who was lost while hunting a wild ass.
2. In classical myth the hyacinth had associations of sadness because the plant was supposed to have sprung from the blood of Hyacinthus, a beautiful youth who was killed in an accident. Its petals were marked AI, meaning "alas." FitzGerald, however, seems to be referring more particularly to the shape of the flower, as in *Odyssey* 6.231, where locks of hair are likened to hyacinth clusters.

20

And this reviving Herb whose tender Green
Fledges the River-Lip on which we lean—
   Ah, lean upon it lightly! for who knows
80 From what once lovely Lip it springs unseen!

21

Ah, my Belovèd, fill the Cup that clears
TODAY of past Regrets and future Fears:
   Tomorrow!—Why, Tomorrow I may be
Myself with Yesterday's Sev'n thousand Years.

22

85 For some we loved, the loveliest and the best
That from his Vintage rolling Time hath pressed,
   Have drunk their Cup a Round or two before,
And one by one crept silently to rest.

23

And we, that now make merry in the Room
90 They left, and Summer dresses in new bloom,
   Ourselves must we beneath the Couch of Earth
Descend—ourselves to make a Couch—for whom?

24

Ah, make the most of what we yet may spend,
Before we too into the Dust descend;
95   Dust into Dust, and under Dust to lie,
Sans Wine, sans Song, sans Singer, and—sans End!

25

Alike for those who for TODAY prepare,
And those that after some TOMORROW stare,
   A Muezzín[3] from the Tower of Darkness cries,
100 "Fools, your Reward is neither Here nor There."

26

Why, all the Saints and Sages who discussed
Of the Two Worlds so wisely—they are thrust
   Like foolish Prophets forth; their Words to Scorn
Are scattered, and their Mouths are stopped with Dust.

27

105 Myself when young did eagerly frequent
Doctor and Saint, and heard great argument
   About it and about; but evermore
Came out by the same door where in I went.

---

3. One who calls the hour of prayer from the tower of a mosque.

28

With them the seed of Wisdom did I sow,
110 And with mine own hand wrought to make it grow;
　　And this was all the Harvest that I reaped—
"I came like Water, and like Wind I go."

29

Into this Universe, and *Why* not knowing
Nor *Whence,* like Water willy-nilly flowing;
115 　　And out of it, as Wind along the Waste,
I know not *Whither,* willy-nilly blowing.

30

What, without asking, hither hurried *Whence?*
And, without asking, *Whither* hurried hence!
　　Oh, many a Cup of this forbidden Wine[4]
120 Must drown the memory of that insolence!

31

Up from the Earth's Center through the Seventh Gate
I rose, and on the Throne of Saturn[5] sate,
　　And many a Knot unraveled by the Road;
But not the Master-knot of Human Fate.

32

125 There was the Door to which I found no Key;
There was the Veil through which I might not see;
　　Some little talk awhile of ME and THEE
There was—and then no more of THEE and ME.

33

Earth could not answer; nor the Seas that mourn
130 In flowing Purple, of their Lord forlorn;
　　Nor rolling Heaven, with all his Signs° revealed　　　*of the zodiac*
And hidden by the sleeve of Night and Morn.

34

Then of the THEE IN ME who works behind
The Veil, I lifted up my hands to find
135 　　A lamp amid the Darkness; and I heard,
As from Without—"THE ME WITHIN THEE BLIND!"

35

Then to the Lip of this poor earthen Urn
I leaned, the Secret of my Life to learn;
　　And Lip to Lip it murmured—"While you live,
140 Drink!—for, once dead, you never shall return."

4. Alcohol is forbidden to strict Muslims.
5. The seat of knowledge. According to a note by FitzGerald, Saturn was lord of the seventh heaven.

36

I think the Vessel, that with fugitive
Articulation answered, once did live,
   And drink; and Ah! the passive Lip I kissed,
How many Kisses might it take—and give!

37

145 For I remember stopping by the way
To watch a Potter thumping his wet Clay;
   And with its all-obliterated Tongue
It murmured—"Gently, Brother, gently, pray!"

38

And has not such a Story from of Old
150 Down Man's successive generations rolled
   Of such a clod of saturated Earth
Cast by the Maker into Human mold?

39

And not a drop that from our Cups we throw
For Earth to drink of,[6] but may steal below
155   To quench the fire of Anguish in some Eye
There hidden—far beneath, and long ago.

40

As then the Tulip, for her morning sup
Of Heav'nly Vintage, from the soil looks up,
   Do you devoutly do the like, till Heav'n
160 To Earth invert you—like an empty Cup.

41

Perplexed no more with Human or Divine,
Tomorrow's tangle to the winds resign,
   And lose your fingers in the tresses of
The Cypress-slender Minister of Wine.[7]

42

165 And if the Wine you drink, the Lip you press,
End in what All begins and ends in—Yes;
   Think then you are TODAY what YESTERDAY
You were—TOMORROW you shall not be less.

43

So when that Angel of the darker Drink
170 At last shall find you by the river brink,
   And offering his Cup, invite your Soul
Forth to your Lips to quaff—you shall not shrink.

---

6. A reference to the custom of pouring some wine on the ground before drinking to refresh some dead and buried wine drinker.
7. Maiden who serves the wine.

44

Why, if the Soul can fling the Dust aside,
And naked on the Air of Heaven ride,
175   Were 't not a Shame—were 't not a Shame for him
In this clay carcass crippled to abide?

45

'Tis but a Tent where takes his one day's rest
A Sultán to the realm of Death addressed;
    The Sultán rises, and the dark Ferrásh[8]
180   Strikes, and prepares it for another Guest.

46

And fear not lest Existence closing your
Account, and mine, should know the like no more;
    The Eternal Sákí[9] from that Bowl has poured
Millions of Bubbles like us, and will pour.

47

185   When You and I behind the Veil are past,
Oh, but the long, long while the World shall last,
    Which of our Coming and Departure heeds
As the Sea's self should heed a pebble-cast.

48

A Moment's Halt—a momentary taste
190   Of BEING from the Well amid the Waste—
    And Lo!—the phantom Caravan has reached
The NOTHING it set out from—Oh, make haste!

49

Would you that spangle of Existence spend
About THE SECRET—quick about it, Friend!
195   A Hair perhaps divides the False and True—
And upon what, prithee, may life depend?

50

A Hair perhaps divides the False and True—
Yes; and a single Alif[1] were the clue—
    Could you but find it—to the Treasure-house,
200   And peradventure to THE MASTER too;

51

Whose secret Presence, through Creation's veins
Running Quicksilver-like, eludes your pains;
    Taking all shapes from Máh to Máhi;[2] and
They change and perish all—but He remains;

8. Servant who takes down ("strikes") a tent.
9. Servant who passes the wine.
1. The first letter of the Arabic alphabet, repre-sented by a single vertical line.
2. From lowest to highest.

52

205 A moment guessed—then back behind the Fold
Immersed of Darkness round the Drama rolled
    Which, for the Pastime of Eternity,
He doth Himself contrive, enact, behold.

53

But if in vain, down on the stubborn floor
210 Of Earth, and up to Heav'n's unopening Door,
    You gaze TODAY, while You are You—how then
TOMORROW, You when shall be You no more?

54

Waste not your Hour, nor in the vain pursuit
Of This and That endeavor and dispute;
215   Better be jocund with the fruitful Grape
Than sadden after none, or bitter, Fruit.

55

You know, my Friends, with what a brave Carouse
I made a Second Marriage in my house;
    Divorced old barren Reason from my Bed,
220 And took the Daughter of the Vine to Spouse.

56

For "Is" and "IS-NOT" though with Rule and Line,
And "UP-AND-DOWN" by Logic, I define,
    Of all that one should care to fathom, I
Was never deep in anything but—Wine.

57

225 Ah, but my Computations, People say,
Reduced the Year to better reckoning?[3]—Nay,
    'Twas only striking from the Calendar
Unborn Tomorrow, and dead Yesterday.

58

And lately, by the Tavern Door agape,
230 Came shining through the Dusk an Angel Shape
    Bearing a Vessel on his Shoulder; and
He bid me taste of it; and 'twas—the Grape!

59

The Grape that can with Logic absolute
The Two-and-Seventy jarring Sects[4] confute;
235   The sovereign Alchemist that in a trice
Life's leaden metal into Gold transmute;

---

3. As a mathematician, Omar had devised an improved calendar.

4. The 72 religions supposed to divide the world [FitzGerald's note].

60

The mighty Mahmúd, Allah-breathing Lord,
That all the misbelieving and black Horde[5]
    Of Fears and Sorrows that infest the Soul
240 Scatters before him with his whirlwind Sword.

61

Why, be this Juice the growth of God, who dare
Blaspheme the twisted tendril as a Snare?
    A Blessing, we should use it, should we not?
And if a Curse—why, then, Who set it there?

62

245 I must abjure the Balm of Life, I must,
Scared by some After-reckoning ta'en on trust
    Or lured with Hope of some Diviner Drink,
To fill the Cup—when crumbled into Dust!

63

Oh threats of Hell and Hopes of Paradise!
250 One thing at least is certain—*This* Life flies;
    One thing is certain and the rest is Lies—
The Flower that once has blown forever dies.

64

Strange, is it not? that of the myriads who
Before us passed the door of Darkness through,
255   Not one returns to tell us of the Road,
Which to discover we must travel too.

65

The Revelations of Devout and Learn'd
Who rose before us, and as Prophets burned,[6]
    Are all but Stories, which, awoke from Sleep,
260 They told their comrades, and to Sleep returned.

66

I sent my Soul through the Invisible,
Some letter of that After-life to spell;
    And by and by my Soul returned to me,
And answered, "I Myself am Heav'n and Hell"—

67

265 Heaven but the Vision of fulfilled Desire,
And Hell the Shadow from a Soul on fire
    Cast on the Darkness into which Ourselves,
So late emerged from, shall so soon expire.

---

5. Alluding to Sultan Mahmúd's Conquest of India and its dark people [FitzGerald's note].

6. I.e., inspired by burning zeal to spread their prophecies.

68

We are no other than a moving row
270 Of Magic Shadow-shapes that come and go
       Round with the Sun-illumined Lantern held
       In Midnight by the Master of the Show;

69

But helpless Pieces of the Game He plays
Upon this Checkerboard of Nights and Days;
275   Hither and thither moves, and checks, and slays,
       And one by one back in the Closet lays.

70

The Ball no question makes of Ayes and Noes,
But Here or There as strikes the Player° goes;   polo player
       And He that tossed you down into the Field,
280 *He* knows about it all—HE knows—HE knows!

71

The Moving Finger writes, and, having writ,
Moves on; nor all your Piety nor Wit
       Shall lure it back to cancel half a Line,
Nor all your Tears wash out a Word of it.

72

285 And that inverted Bowl they call the Sky,
Whereunder crawling cooped we live and die,
       Lift not your hands to *It* for help—for It
As impotently moves as you or I.

73

With Earth's first Clay They did the Last Man knead,
290 And there of the Last Harvest sowed the Seed;
       And the first Morning of Creation wrote
What the Last Dawn of Reckoning shall read.

74

YESTERDAY *This* Day's Madness did prepare;
TOMORROW'S Silence, Triumph, or Despair.
295   Drink! for you know not whence you came, nor why;
Drink, for you know not why you go, nor where.

75

I tell you this—When, started from the Goal,
Over the flaming shoulders of the Foal
       Of Heav'n Parwín and Mushtarí they flung,
300 In my predestined Plot of Dust and Soul[7]

7. The speaker asserts that his fate was predestined in accordance with the relationship of the
stars and planets at the moment of his birth when
he "started from the Goal." In his horoscope the
particular relationship involved the Pleiades ("Par-
wín") and the planet Jupiter ("Mushtarí") that were

76

The Vine had struck a fiber; which about
If clings my Being—let the Dervish[8] flout;
   Of my Base metal may be filed a Key,
That shall unlock the Door he howls without.

77

305 And this I know: whether the one True Light
Kindle to Love, or Wrath—consume me quite,
   One Flash of It within the Tavern caught
Better than in the Temple lost outright.

78

What! out of senseless Nothing to provoke
310 A conscious Something to resent the yoke
   Of unpermitted Pleasure, under pain
Of Everlasting Penalties, if broke!

79

What! from his helpless Creature be repaid
Pure Gold for what he lent him dross-allayed—
315   Sue for a Debt he never did contract,
And cannot answer—Oh, the sorry trade!

80

O Thou, who didst with pitfall and with gin°   *trap*
Beset the Road I was to wander in,
   Thou wilt not with Predestined Evil round
320 Enmesh, and then impute my Fall to Sin!

81

O Thou, who Man of Baser Earth didst make,
And ev'n with Paradise devise the Snake,
   For all the Sin wherewith the Face of Man
Is blackened—Man's forgiveness give—and take!

_____

82

325 As under cover of departing Day
Slunk hunger-stricken Ramazán[9] away,
   Once more within the Potter's house alone
I stood, surrounded by the Shapes of Clay—

83

Shapes of all Sorts and Sizes, great and small
330 That stood along the floor and by the wall;

"flung" by the gods into a special position in relation to the place in the sky of the constellation
Equuleus ("the Foal" or Colt).
8. Ascetic, who would despise ("flout") wine as a

means of discovering truth.
9. The month of fasting, during which no food is
eaten from sunrise to sunset.

And some loquacious Vessels were; and some
Listened perhaps, but never talked at all.

84

Said one among them—"Surely not in vain
My substance of the common Earth was ta'en
335   And to this Figure molded, to be broke,
Or trampled back to shapeless Earth again."

85

Then said a Second—"Ne'er a peevish Boy
Would break the Bowl from which he drank in joy;
And He that with his hand the Vessel made
340   Will surely not in after Wrath destroy."

86

After a momentary silence spake
Some Vessel of a more ungainly Make:
    "They sneer at me for leaning all awry;
What! did the Hand, then, of the Potter shake?"

87

345   Whereat someone of the loquacious Lot—
I think a Súfi° pipkin—waxing hot—   *mystic*
    "All this of Pot and Potter—Tell me then,
Who is the Potter, pray, and who the Pot?"

88

"Why," said another, "Some there are who tell
350   Of one who threatens he will toss to Hell
    The luckless Pots he marred in making—Pish!
He's a Good Fellow, and 'twill all be well."

89

"Well," murmured one, "Let whoso make or buy,
My Clay with long Oblivion is gone dry;
355   But fill me with the old familiar Juice,
Methinks I might recover by and by."

90

So while the Vessels one by one were speaking
The little Moon looked in that all were seeking;[1]
    And then they jogged each other, "Brother! Brother!
360   Now for the Porter's shoulder-knot[2] a-creaking!"

---

1. At the close of the Fasting Month, Ramazán . . .
the first Glimpse of the new Moon . . . is looked
for with the utmost Anxiety and hailed with all
Acclamation [FitzGerald's note].
2. The rope or strap on which were hung the wine
jars carried by the porter.

91

Ah, with the Grape my fading Life provide,
And wash the Body whence the Life has died,
 And lay me, shrouded in the living Leaf,
By some not unfrequented Garden-side—

92

365 That ev'n my buried Ashes such a snare
Of Vintage shall fling up into the Air
 As not a True-believer passing by
But shall be overtaken unaware.

93

Indeed the Idols I have loved so long
370 Have done my credit in this World much wrong,
 Have drowned my Glory in a shallow Cup,
And sold my Reputation for a Song.

94

Indeed, indeed, Repentance oft before
I swore—but was I sober when I swore?
375 And then and then came Spring, and Rose-in-hand
My threadbare Penitence apieces tore.

95

And much as Wine has played the Infidel,
And robbed me of my Robe of Honor—Well,
 I wonder often what the Vintners buy
380 One-half so precious as the stuff they sell.

96

Yet Ah, that Spring should vanish with the Rose!
That Youth's sweet-scented manuscript should close!
 The Nightingale that in the branches sang,
Ah whence, and whither flown again, who knows!

97

385 Would but the Desert of the Fountain yield
One glimpse—if dimly, yet indeed, revealed,
 To which the fainting Traveler might spring,
As springs the trampled herbage of the field.

98

Would but some wingèd Angel ere too late
390 Arrest the yet unfolded Roll of Fate,
 And make the stern Recorder otherwise
Enregister, or quite obliterate!

99

Ah, Love! could you and I with Him conspire
To grasp this sorry Scheme of Things entire,

395   Would not we shatter it to bits—and then
      Remold it nearer to the Heart's Desire!

100

    Yon rising Moon that looks for us again—
    How oft hereafter will she wax and wane;
      How oft hereafter rising look for us
400   Through this same Garden—and for *one* in vain!

101

    And when like her, O Sákí, you shall pass
    Among the Guests Star-scattered on the Grass,
      And in your joyous errand reach the spot
    Where I made One—turn down an empty Glass!

TAMÁM[3]

1857   1859, 1889

3. It is ended.

ELIZABETH GASKELL
1810–1865

It is ironic that the writer whom contemporaries and future generations knew as "Mrs. Gaskell" once instructed her sister-in-law that it was "a silly piece of bride-like affectation not to sign yourself by your proper name." Despite the wifely identity that the name Mrs. Gaskell connotes, Elizabeth Gaskell, as she always signed herself, wrote fiction on contemporary social topics that stimulated considerable controversy. Her first novel, *Mary Barton* (1848), presents a sympathetic picture of the hardships and the grievances of the working class. Another early novel, *Ruth* (1853), portrays the seduction and rehabilitation of an unwed mother.

Elizabeth Cleghorn Gaskell was born in 1810 in Chelsea, on the outskirts of London, to a Unitarian family. Her mother died when Gaskell was one, and the girl was sent to rural Knutsford, in Cheshire, to be raised by her aunt. At the age of twenty-one, she met and married William Gaskell, a Unitarian minister whose chapel was in the industrial city of Manchester. For the first ten years of her marriage, she led the life of a minister's wife, bearing five children, keeping a house, and helping her husband serve his congregation. When her fourth child and only son, William, died at the age of one year, Gaskell grew despondent. Her husband encouraged her to write as a way of allaying her grief, and so she produced *Mary Barton*, subtitled *A Tale of Manchester Life*. In the preface to the novel she wrote that she was inspired by thinking "how deep might be the romance in the lives of some of those who elbowed me daily in the busy streets of the town in which I resided. I had always felt a deep sympathy with the careworn men, who looked as if doomed to struggle through their lives in strange alternations between work and want." She observes the bitterness of their resentment against the rich and sets herself the task of creating understanding and sympathy for them.

Anonymously published, the novel was widely reviewed and discussed. Elizabeth Gaskell was soon identified as the author; she subsequently developed a wide acquaintance in literary circles. She wrote five more novels and about thirty short stories, many of which were published in Dickens's journal *Household Words*, later titled *All the Year Round*. The contrasting experiences Gaskell's life had given her of the south and the north, of rural Knutsford and industrial Manchester, defined the poles of her fiction. Her second novel, *Cranford* (1853), presents a delicate picture of the small events of country village life, a subject to which she returns with greater range and psychological depth in her last novel, *Wives and Daughters* (1866). In *North and South* (1855), Gaskell brings together the two worlds of her fiction in the story of Margaret Hale, a young woman from the south who moves to a factory town in the north.

One of the writers her literary fame led her to know was Charlotte Brontë, with whom she became friends. When Brontë died in 1855, Gaskell was approached by Patrick Brontë to write the story of his daughter's life. Gaskell's *Life of Charlotte Brontë* (1857) is a masterpiece of English biography and one of Gaskell's finest portrayals of character. Her focus in the *Life* on the relationship between Brontë's identity as a writer and her role as daughter, sister, and wife reflects the balance Gaskell herself sought between the stories she wove and the people she tended. "My dear Scheherazade," Dickens called her, words of praise and affection in which future readers have joined.

The Old Nurse's Story[1]

You know, my dears, that your mother was an orphan, and an only child; and I dare say you have heard that your grandfather was a clergyman up in Westmoreland, where I come from. I was just a girl in the village school, when, one day, your grandmother came in to ask the mistress if there was any scholar there who would do for a nurse-maid; and mighty proud I was, I can tell ye, when the mistress called me up, and spoke to my being a good girl at my needle, and a steady honest girl, and one whose parents were very respectable, though they might be poor. I thought I should like nothing better than to serve the pretty young lady, who was blushing as deep as I was, as she spoke of the coming baby, and what I should have to do with it. However, I see you don't care so much for this part of my story, as for what you think is to come, so I'll tell you at once I was engaged, and settled at the parsonage before Miss Rosamond (that was the baby, who is now your mother) was born. To be sure, I had little enough to do with her when she came, for she was never out of her mother's arms, and slept by her all night long; and proud enough was I sometimes when missis trusted her to me. There never was such baby before or since, though you've all of you been fine enough in your turns; but for sweet winning ways, you've none of you come up to your mother. She took after her mother, who was a real lady born; a Miss Furnivall, a granddaughter of Lord Furnivall's in Northumberland. I believe she had neither brother nor sister, and had been brought up in my lord's family till she had married your grandfather, who was just a curate, son to a shopkeeper in Carlisle—but a clever fine gentleman as ever was—and one who was a right-down hard worker in his parish, which was very wide, and scattered all abroad over the Westmoreland Fells. When your mother, little Miss

1. Originally published anonymously in the 1852 Christmas number of Dickens's journal *Household Words*; it was later republished in Gaskell's *Lizzie Leigh, and Other Tales* (1855).

Rosamond, was about four or five years old, both her parents died in a fort-night—one after the other. Ah! that was a sad time. My pretty young mistress and me was looking for another baby, when my master came home from one of his long rides, wet and tired, and took the fever he died of; and then she never held up her head again, but just lived to see her dead baby, and have it laid on her breast before she sighed away her life. My mistress had asked me, on her death-bed, never to leave Miss Rosamond; but if she had never spoken a word, I would have gone with the little child to the end of the world.

The next thing, and before we had well stilled our sobs, the executors and guardians came to settle the affairs. They were my poor young mistress's own cousin, Lord Furnivall, and Mr. Esthwaite, my master's brother, a shop-keeper in Manchester; not so well to do then, as he was afterwards, and with a large family rising about him. Well! I don't know if it were their settling, or because of a letter my mistress wrote on her death-bed to her cousin, my lord; but somehow it was settled that Miss Rosamond and me were to go to Furnivall Manor House, in Northumberland, and my lord spoke as if it had been her mother's wish that she should live with his family, and as if he had no objections, for that one or two more or less could make no difference in so grand a household. So, though that was not the way in which I should have wished the coming of my bright and pretty pet to have been looked at— who was like a sunbeam in any family, be it never so grand—I was well pleased that all the folks in the Dale should stare and admire, when they heard I was going to be young lady's maid at my Lord Furnivall's at Furnivall Manor.

But I made a mistake in thinking we were to go and live where my lord did. It turned out that the family had left Furnivall Manor House fifty years or more. I could not hear that my poor young mistress had ever been there, though she had been brought up in the family; and I was sorry for that, for I should have liked Miss Rosamond's youth to have passed where her mother's had been.

My lord's gentleman, from whom I asked as many questions as I durst, said that the Manor House was at the foot of the Cumberland Fells, and a very grand place; that an old Miss Furnivall, a great-aunt of my lord's, lived there, with only a few servants; but that it was a very healthy place, and my lord had thought that it would suit Miss Rosamond very well for a few years, and that her being there might perhaps amuse his old aunt.

I was bidden by my lord to have Miss Rosamond's things ready by a certain day. He was a stern, proud man, as they say all the Lord Furnivalls were; and he never spoke a word more than was necessary. Folk did say he had loved my young mistress; but that, because she knew that his father would object, she would never listen to him, and married Mr. Esthwaite; but I don't know. He never married at any rate. But he never took much notice of Miss Rosamond; which I thought he might have done if he had cared for her dead mother. He sent his gentleman with us to the Manor House, telling him to join him at Newcastle that same evening; so there was no great length of time for him to make us known to all the strangers before he, too, shook us off; and we were left, two lonely young things (I was not eighteen), in the great old Manor House. It seems like yesterday that we drove there. We had left our own dear parsonage very early, and we had both cried as if our hearts would break, though we were travelling in my lord's carriage, which I had thought so much of once. And now it was long past noon on a September day, and we stopped to change horses for the last time at a little smoky town, all full of colliers and miners. Miss Rosamond had fallen asleep, but Mr. Henry told me to waken her, that she might see the park and the Manor House as we drove up. I thought it rather a pity; but I did what he bade me, for fear he should complain of me to my lord. We had left all signs of a town or even a village, and were then inside the gates of a large wild park—not like the parks here in the south, but with rocks, and the noise of running water, and gnarled thorn-trees, and old oaks, all white and peeled with age.

The road went up about two miles, and then we saw a great and stately house, with many trees close around it, so close that in some places their branches dragged against the walls when the wind blew; and some hung broken down; for no one seemed to take much charge of the place;—to lop the wood, or to keep the moss-covered carriage-way in order. Only in front of the house all was clear. The great oval drive was without a weed; and neither tree nor creeper was allowed to grow over the long, many-windowed front; at both sides of which a wing projected, which were each the ends of other side fronts; for the house, although it was so desolate, was even grander than I expected. Behind it rose the Fells, which seemed unenclosed and bare enough; and on the left hand of the house as you stood facing it, was a little old-fashioned flower-garden, as I found out afterwards. A door opened out upon it from the west front; it had been scooped out of the thick dark wood for some old Lady Furnivall; but the branches of the great forest trees had grown and overshadowed it again, and there were very few flowers that would live there at that time.

When we drove up to the great front entrance, and went into the hall I thought we should be lost—it was so large, and vast, and grand. There was a chandelier all of bronze, hung down from the middle of the ceiling; and I had never seen one before, and looked at it all in amaze. Then, at one end of the hall, was a great fire-place, as large as the sides of the houses in my country, with massy andirons and dogs to hold the wood; and by it were heavy old-fashioned sofas. At the opposite end of the hall, to the left as you went in—on the western side—was an organ built into the wall, and so large that it filled up the best part of that end. Beyond it, on the same side, was a door; and opposite, on each side of the fire-place, were also doors leading to the east front; but those I never went through as long as I stayed in the house, so I can't tell you what lay beyond.

The afternoon was closing in, and the hall, which had no fire lighted in it, looked dark and gloomy; but we did not stay there a moment. The old servant who had opened the door for us bowed to Mr. Henry, and took us in through the door at the further side of the great organ, and led us through several smaller halls and passages into the west drawing-room, where he said that Miss Furnivall was sitting. Poor little Miss Rosamond held very tight to me, as if she were scared and lost in that great place, and, as for myself, I was not much better. The west drawing-room was very cheerful-looking, with a warm fire in it, and plenty of good comfortable furniture about. Miss Furnivall was an old lady not far from eighty, I should think, but I do not know. She was thin and tall, and had a face as full of fine wrinkles as if they had been drawn all over it with a needle's point. Her eyes were very watchful, to make up, I suppose, for her being so deaf as to be obliged to use a trumpet.[2]

2. A horn-shaped device used by the hard of hearing to amplify sound.

Sitting with her, working at the same great piece of tapestry, was Mrs. Stark, her maid and companion, and almost as old as she was. She had lived with Miss Furnivall ever since they both were young, and now she seemed more like a friend than a servant; she looked so cold and grey, and stony, as if she had never loved or cared for any one; and I don't suppose she did care for any one, except her mistress; and, owing to the great deafness of the latter, Mrs. Stark treated her very much as if she were a child. Mr. Henry gave some message from my lord, and then he bowed good-bye to us all,—taking no notice of my sweet little Miss Rosamond's out-stretched hand—and left us standing there, being looked at by the two old ladies through their spectacles.

I was right glad when they rung for the old footman who had shown us in at first, and told him to take us to our rooms. So we went out of that great drawing-room, and into another sitting-room, and out of that, and then up a great flight of stairs, and along a broad gallery—which was something like a library, having books all down one side, and windows and writing-tables all down the other—till we came to our rooms, which I was not sorry to hear were just over the kitchens; for I began to think I should be lost in that wilderness of a house. There was an old nursery, that had been used for all the little lords and ladies long ago, with a pleasant fire burning in the grate, and the kettle boiling on the hob, and tea things spread out on the table; and out of that room was the night-nursery, with a little crib for Miss Rosamond close to my bed. And old James called up Dorothy, his wife, to bid us welcome; and both he and she were so hospitable and kind, that by-and-by Miss Rosamond and me felt quite at home; and by the time tea was over, she was sitting on Dorothy's knee, and chattering away as fast as her little tongue could go. I soon found out that Dorothy was from Westmoreland, and that bound her and me together, as it were; and I would never wish to meet with kinder people than were old James and his wife. James had lived pretty nearly all his life in my lord's family, and thought there was no one so grand as they. He even looked down a little on his wife; because, till he had married her, she had never lived in any but a farmer's household. But he was very fond of her, as well he might be. They had one servant under them, to do all the rough work. Agnes they called her; and she and me, and James and Dorothy, with Miss Furnivall and Mrs. Stark, made up the family; always remembering my sweet little Miss Rosamond! I used to wonder what they had done before she came, they thought so much of her now. Kitchen and drawing-room, it was all the same. The hard, sad Miss Furnivall, and the cold Mrs. Stark, looked pleased when she came fluttering in like a bird, playing and pranking hither and thither, with a continual murmur, and pretty prattle of gladness. I am sure, they were sorry many a time when she flitted away into the kitchen, though they were too proud to ask her to stay with them, and were a little surprised at her taste; though, to be sure, as Mrs. Stark said, it was not to be wondered at, remembering what stock her father had come of. The great, old rambling house, was a famous place for little Miss Rosamond. She made expeditions all over it, with me at her heels; all, except the east wing, which was never opened, and whither we never thought of going. But in the western and northern part was many a pleasant room; full of things that were curiosities to us, though they might not have been to people who had seen more. The windows were darkened by the sweeping boughs of the trees, and the ivy which had overgrown them: but, in the green gloom, we could manage to see old China jars and carved ivory boxes, and great heavy books, and, above all, the old pictures!

Once, I remember, my darling would have Dorothy go with us to tell us who they all were; for they were all portraits of some of my lord's family, though Dorothy could not tell us the names of every one. We had gone through most of the rooms, when we came to the old state drawing-room over the hall, and there was a picture of Miss Furnivall; or, as she was called in those days, Miss Grace, for she was the younger sister. Such a beauty she must have been! but with such a set, proud look, and such scorn looking out of her handsome eyes, with her eyebrows just a little raised, as if she wondered how any one could have the impertinence to look at her; and her lip curled at us, as we stood there gazing. She had a dress on, the like of which I had never seen before, but it was all the fashion when she was young; a hat of some soft white stuff like beaver, pulled a little over her brows, and a beautiful plume of feathers sweeping round it on one side; and her gown of blue satin was open in front to a quilted white stomacher.[3]

"Well, to be sure!" said I, when I had gazed my fill. "Flesh is grass, they do say; but who would have thought that Miss Furnivall had been such an out-and-out beauty, to see her now?"

"Yes," said Dorothy. "Folks change sadly. But if what my master's father used to say was true, Miss Furnivall, the elder sister, was handsomer than Miss Grace. Her picture is here somewhere; but, if I show it you, you must never let on, even to James, that you have seen it. Can the little lady hold her tongue, think you?" asked she.

I was not so sure, for she was such a little sweet, bold, open-spoken child, so I set her to hide herself; and then I helped Dorothy to turn a great picture, that leaned with its face towards the wall, and was not hung up as the others were. To be sure, it beat Miss Grace for beauty; and, I think, for scornful pride, too, though in that matter it might be hard to choose. I could have looked at it an hour, but Dorothy seemed half frightened of having shown it to me, and hurried it back again, and bade me run and find Miss Rosamond, for that there were some ugly places about the house, where she should like ill for the child to go. I was a brave, high-spirited girl, and thought little of what the old woman said, for I liked hide-and-seek as well as any child in the parish; so off I ran to find my little one.

As winter drew on, and the days grew shorter, I was sometimes almost certain that I heard a noise as if some one was playing on the great organ in the hall. I did not hear it every evening; but, certainly, I did very often; usually when I was sitting with Miss Rosamond, after I had put her to bed, and keeping quite still and silent in the bedroom. Then I used to hear it booming and swelling away in the distance. The first night, when I went down to my supper, I asked Dorothy who had been playing music, and James said very shortly that I was a gowk to take the wind soughing[4] among the trees for music; but I saw Dorothy look at him very fearfully, and Bessy, the kitchen-maid, said something beneath her breath, and went quite white. I saw they did not like my question, so I held my peace till I was with Dorothy alone,

3. Ornamental covering for the front of the body.   4. Moaning.
"Beaver": felted wool.

when I knew I could get a good deal out of her. So, the next day, I watched my time, and I coaxed and asked her who it was that played the organ; for I knew that it was the organ and not the wind well enough, for all I had kept silence before James. But Dorothy had had her lesson, I'll warrant, and never a word could I get from her. So then I tried Bessy, though I had always held my head rather above her, as I was evened to James and Dorothy, and she was little better than their servant. So she said I must never, never tell; and, if I ever told, I was never to say *she* had told me; but it was a very strange noise, and she had heard it many a time, but most of all on winter nights, and before storms; and folks did say, it was the old lord playing on the great organ in the hall, just as he used to do when he was alive; but who the old lord was, or why he played, and why he played on stormy winter evenings in particular, she either could not or would not tell me. Well! I told you I had a brave heart; and I thought it was rather pleasant to have that grand music rolling about the house, let who would be the player; for now it rose above the great gusts of wind, and wailed and triumphed just like a living creature, and then it fell to a softness most complete; only it was always music and tunes, so it was nonsense to call it the wind. I thought, at first, it might be Miss Furnivall who played, unknown to Bessy; but, one day when I was in the hall by myself, I opened the organ and peeped all about it, and around it, as I had done to the organ in Crosthwaite Church once before, and I saw it was all broken and destroyed inside, though it looked so brave and fine; and then, though it was noon-day, my flesh began to creep a little, and I shut it up, and ran away pretty quickly to my own bright nursery; and I did not like hearing the music for some time after that, any more than James and Dorothy did. All this time Miss Rosamond was making herself more and more beloved. The old ladies liked her to dine with them at their early dinner; James stood behind Miss Furnivall's chair, and I behind Miss Rosamond's, all in state; and, after dinner, she would play about in a corner of the great drawing-room, as still as any mouse, while Miss Furnivall slept, and I had my dinner in the kitchen. But she was glad enough to come to me in the nursery afterwards; for, as she said, Miss Furnivall was so sad, and Mrs. Stark so dull; but she and I were merry enough; and, by-and-by, I got not to care for that weird rolling music, which did one no harm, if we did not know where it came from.

That winter was very cold. In the middle of October the frosts began, and lasted many, many weeks. I remember, one day at dinner, Miss Furnivall lifted up her sad, heavy eyes, and said to Mrs. Stark, "I am afraid we shall have a terrible winter," in a strange kind of meaning way. But Mrs. Stark pretended not to hear, and talked very loud of something else. My little lady and I did not care for the frost;—not we! As long as it was dry we climbed up the steep brows, behind the house, and went up on the Fells, which were bleak and bare enough, and there we ran races in the fresh, sharp air; and once we came down by a new path that took us past the two old gnarled holly-trees, which grew about half-way down by the east side of the house. But the days grew shorter and shorter; and the old lord, if it was he, played away more and more stormily and sadly on the great organ. One Sunday afternoon,—it must have been towards the end of November—I asked Dorothy to take charge of little Missey when she came out of the drawing-room, after Miss Furnivall had had her nap; for it was too cold to take her with me to church, and yet I wanted to go. And Dorothy was glad enough to promise, and was so fond of the child that all seemed well; and Bessy and I set off very briskly, though the sky hung heavy and black over the white earth, as if the night had never fully gone away; and the air, though still, was very biting and keen.

"We shall have a fall of snow," said Bessy to me. And sure enough, even while we were in church, it came down thick, in great large flakes, so thick it almost darkened the windows. It had stopped snowing before we came out, but it lay soft, thick and deep beneath our feet, as we tramped home. Before we got to the hall the moon rose, and I think it was lighter then,—what with the moon, and what with the white dazzling snow—than it had been when we went to church, between two and three o'clock. I have not told you that Miss Furnivall and Mrs. Stark never went to church: they used to read the prayers together, in their quiet gloomy way; they seemed to feel the Sunday very long without their tapestry-work to be busy at. So when I went to Doro-thy in the kitchen, to fetch Miss Rosamond and take her up-stairs with me, I did not much wonder when the old woman told me that the ladies had kept the child with them, and that she had never come to the kitchen, as I had bidden her, when she was tired of behaving pretty in the drawing-room. So I took off my things and went to find her, and bring her to her supper in the nursery. But when I went into the best drawing-room, there sat the two old ladies, very still and quiet, dropping out a word now and then, but looking as if nothing so bright and merry as Miss Rosamond had ever been near them. Still I thought she might be hiding from me; it was one of her pretty ways; and that she had persuaded them to look as if they knew nothing about her; so I went softly peeping under this sofa, and behind that chair, making believe I was sadly frightened at not finding her.

"What's the matter, Hester?" said Mrs. Stark sharply. I don't know if Miss Furnivall had seen me, for, as I told you, she was very deaf, and she sat quite still, idly staring into the fire, with her hopeless face. "I'm only looking for my little Rosy-Posy," replied I, still thinking that the child was there, and near me, though I could not see her.

"Miss Rosamond is not here," said Mrs. Stark. "She went away more than an hour ago to find Dorothy." And she too turned and went on looking into the fire.

My heart sank at this, and I began to wish I had never left my darling. I went back to Dorothy and told her. James was gone out for the day, but she and me and Bessy took lights, and went up into the nursery first and then we roamed over the great large house, calling and entreating Miss Rosamond to come out of her hiding place, and not frighten us to death in that way. But there was no answer; no sound.

"Oh!" said I at last, "Can she have got into the east wing and hidden there?" But Dorothy said it was not possible, for that she herself had never been in there; that the doors were always locked, and my lord's steward had the keys, she believed; at any rate, neither she nor James had ever seen them: so, I said I would go back and see it, after all, she was not hidden in the drawing-room, unknown to the old ladies; and if I found her there, I said, I would whip her well for the fright she had given me; but I never meant to do it. Well, I went back to the west drawing-room, and I told Mrs. Stark we could not find her anywhere, and asked for leave to look all about the furniture there, for I thought now, that she might have fallen asleep in some warm hidden corner; but no! we looked, Miss Furnivall got up and looked, trembling all over, and she was no where there; then we set off again, every one in the house, and looked in all the places we had searched before, but we could not find her. Miss Furnivall shivered and shook so much, that Mrs. Stark took her back into the warm drawing-room; but not before they had made me promise to bring her to them when she was found. Well-a-day! I began to think she never would be found, when I bethought me to look out into the great front court, all covered with snow. I was up-stairs when I looked out; but, it was such clear moonlight, I could see quite plain two little footprints, which might be traced from the hall door, and round the corner of the east wing. I don't know how I got down, but I tugged open the great, stiff hall door; and, throwing the skirt of my gown over my head for a cloak, I ran out. I turned the east corner, and there a black shadow fell on the snow; but when I came again into the moonlight, there were the little footmarks going up—up to the Fells. It was bitter cold; so cold that the air almost took the skin off my face as I ran, but I ran on, crying to think how my poor little darling must be perished and frightened. I was within sight of the holly-trees, when I saw a shepherd coming down the hill, bearing something in his arms wrapped in his maud.[5] He shouted to me, and asked me if I had lost a bairn;[6] and, when I could not speak for crying, he bore towards me, and I saw my wee bairnie lying still, and white, and stiff, in his arms, as if she had been dead. He told me he had been up the Fells to gather in his sheep, before the deep cold of night came on, and that under the holly-trees (black marks on the hill-side, where no other bush was for miles around) he had found my little lady—my lamb—my queen—my darling—stiff and cold, in the terrible sleep which is frost-begotten. Oh! the joy, and the tears of having her in my arms once again! for I would not let him carry her; but took her, maud and all, into my own arms, and held her near my own warm neck and heart, and felt the life stealing slowly back again into her little gentle limbs. But she was still insensible when we reached the hall, and I had no breath for speech. We went in by the kitchen door.

"Bring the warming-pan," said I; and I carried her up-stairs and began undressing her by the nursery fire, which Bessy had kept up. I called my little lammie all the sweet and playful names I could think of,—even while my eyes were blinded by my tears; and at last, oh! at length she opened her large blue eyes. Then I put her into her warm bed, and sent Dorothy down to tell Miss Furnivall that all was well; and I made up my mind to sit by my darling's bedside the live-long night. She fell away into a soft sleep as soon as her pretty head had touched the pillow, and I watched by her till morning light; when she wakened up bright and clear—or so I thought at first—and, my dears, so I think now.

She said, that she had fancied that she should like to go to Dorothy, for that both the old ladies were asleep, and it was very dull in the drawing-room; and that, as she was going through the west lobby, she saw the snow through the high window falling—falling—soft and steady; but she wanted to see it lying pretty and white on the ground; so she made her way into the

5. Shawl of gray plaid used by shepherds in the region.   6. Child.

great hall; and then, going to the window, she saw it bright and soft upon the drive; but while she stood there, she saw a little girl, not so old as she was, "but so pretty," said my darling, "and this little girl beckoned to me to come out; and oh, she was so pretty and so sweet, I could not choose but go." And then this other little girl had taken her by the hand, and side by side the two had gone round the east corner.

"Now you are a naughty little girl, and telling stories," said I. "What would your good mamma, that is in heaven, and never told a story in her life, say to her little Rosamond, if she heard her—and I dare say she does—telling stories!"

"Indeed, Hester," sobbed out my child; "I'm telling you true. Indeed I am."

"Don't tell me!" said I, very stern. "I tracked you by your foot-marks through the snow; there were only yours to be seen: and if you had had a little girl to go hand-in-hand with you up the hill, don't you think the foot-prints would have gone along with yours?"

"I can't help it, dear, dear Hester," said she, crying, "if they did not; I never looked at her feet, but she held my hand fast and tight in her little one, and it was very, very cold. She took me up the Fell-path, up to the holly trees; and there I saw a lady weeping and crying; but when she saw me, she hushed her weeping, and smiled very proud and grand, and took me on her knees, and began to lull me to sleep; and that's all, Hester—but that is true; and my dear mamma knows it is," said she, crying. So I thought the child was in a fever, and pretended to believe her, as she went over her story—over and over again, and always the same. At last Dorothy knocked at the door with Miss Rosamond's breakfast; and she told me the old ladies were down in the eating-parlour, and that they wanted to speak to me. They had both been into the night-nursery the evening before, but it was after Miss Rosamond was asleep; so they had only looked at her—not asked me any questions.

"I shall catch it," thought I to myself, as I went along the north gallery. "And yet," I thought, taking courage, "it was in their charge I left her; and it's they that's to blame for letting her steal away unknown and unwatched." So I went in boldly, and told my story. I told it all to Miss Furnivall, shouting it close to her ear; but when I came to the mention of the other little girl out in the snow, coaxing and tempting her out, and willing her up to the grand and beautiful lady by the Holly-tree, she threw her arms up—her old and withered arms—and cried aloud, "Oh! Heaven, forgive! Have mercy!"

Mrs. Stark took hold of her; roughly enough, I thought; but she was past Mrs. Stark's management, and spoke to me, in a kind of wild warning and authority.

"Hester! keep her from that child! It will lure her to her death! That evil child! Tell her it is a wicked, naughty child." Then, Mrs. Stark hurried me out of the room; where, indeed, I was glad enough to go; but Miss Furnivall kept shrieking out, "Oh! have mercy! Wilt Thou never forgive! It is many a long year ago——"

I was very uneasy in my mind after that. I durst never leave Miss Rosamond, night or day, for fear lest she might slip off again, after some fancy or other; and all the more, because I thought I could make out that Miss Furnivall was crazy, from their odd ways about her; and I was afraid lest something of the same kind (which might be in the family, you know) hung over my darling. And the great frost never ceased all this time; and, whenever it was a more stormy night than usual, between the gusts, and through the wind, we heard the old lord playing on the great organ. But, old lord, or not, wherever Miss Rosamond went, there I followed; for my love for her, pretty helpless orphan, was stronger than my fear for the grand and terrible sound. Besides, it rested with me to keep her cheerful and merry, as beseemed her age. So we played together, and wandered together, here and there, and everywhere; for I never dared to lose sight of her again in that large and rambling house. And so it happened, that one afternoon, not long before Christmas day, we were playing together on the billiard-table in the great hall (not that we knew the right way of playing, but she liked to roll the smooth ivory balls with her pretty hands, and I liked to do whatever she did); and, by-and-bye, without our noticing it, it grew dusk indoors, though it was still light in the open air, and I was thinking of taking her back into the nursery, when, all of a sudden, she cried out:

"Look, Hester! look! there is my poor little girl out in the snow!"

I turned towards the long narrow windows, and there, sure enough, I saw a little girl, less than my Miss Rosamond—dressed all unfit to be out-of-doors such a bitter night—crying, and beating against the window-panes, as if, she wanted to be let in. She seemed to sob and wail, till Miss Rosamond could bear it no longer, and was flying to the door to open it, when, all of a sudden, and close upon us, the great organ pealed out so loud and thundering, it fairly made me tremble; and all the more, when I remembered me that, even in the stillness of that dead-cold weather, I had heard no sound of little battering hands upon the window-glass, although the Phantom Child had seemed to put forth all its force; and, although I had seen it wail and cry, no faintest touch of sound had fallen upon my ears. Whether I remembered all this at the very moment, I do not know; the great organ sound had so stunned me into terror; but this I know, I caught up Miss Rosamond before she got the hall-door opened, and clutched her, and carried her away, kicking and screaming, into the large bright kitchen, where Dorothy and Agnes were busy with their mince-pies.

"What is the matter with my sweet one?" cried Dorothy, as I bore in Miss Rosamond, who was sobbing as if her heart would break.

"She won't let me open the door for my little girl to come in; and she'll die if she is out on the Fells all night. Cruel, naughty Hester," she said, slapping me; but she might have struck harder, for I had seen a look of ghastly terror on Dorothy's face, which made my very blood run cold.

"Shut the back kitchen door fast, and bolt it well," said she to Agnes. She said no more; she gave me raisins and almonds to quiet Miss Rosamond: but she sobbed about the little girl in the snow, and would not touch any of the good things. I was thankful when she cried herself to sleep in bed. Then I stole down to the kitchen, and told Dorothy I had made up my mind. I would carry my darling back to my father's house in Applethwaite; where, if we lived humbly, we lived at peace. I said I had been frightened enough with the old lord's organ-playing; but now, that I had seen for myself this little moaning child, all decked out as no child in the neighborhood could be, beating and battering to get in, yet always without any sound or noise—with the dark wound on its right shoulder; and that Miss Rosamond had known it again for the phantom that had nearly lured her to her death (which Dorothy knew was true); I would stand it no longer.

I saw Dorothy change color once or twice. When I had done, she told me she did not think I could take Miss Rosamond with me, for that she was my lord's ward, and I had no right over her; and she asked me, would I leave the child that I was so fond of, just for sounds and sights that could do me no harm; and that they had all had to get used to in their turns? I was all in a hot, trembling passion; and I said it was very well for her to talk, that knew what these sights and noises betokened, and that had, perhaps, had something to do with the Spectre-child while it was alive. And I taunted her so, that she told me all she knew, at last; and then I wished I had never been told, for it only made me more afraid than ever.

She said she had heard the tale from old neighbors, that were alive when she was first married; when folks used to come to the hall sometimes, before it had got such a bad name on the country side: it might not be true, or it might, what she had been told.

The old lord was Miss Furnivall's father—Miss Grace, as Dorothy called her, for Miss Maude was the elder, and Miss Furnivall by rights. The old lord was eaten up with pride. Such a proud man was never seen or heard of; and his daughters were like him. No one was good enough to wed them, although they had choice enough; for they were the great beauties of their day, as I had seen by their portraits, where they hung in the state drawing-room. But, as the old saying is, "Pride will have a fall;" and these two haughty beauties fell in love with the same man, and he no better than a foreign musician, whom their father had down from London to play music with him at the Manor House. For, above all things, next to his pride, the old lord loved music. He could play on nearly every instrument that ever was heard of; and it was a strange thing it did not soften him; but he was a fierce dour old man, and had broken his poor wife's heart with his cruelty, they said. He was mad after music, and would pay any money for it. So he got this foreigner to come; who made such beautiful music, that they said the very birds on the trees stopped their singing to listen. And, by degrees, this foreign gentleman got such a hold over the old lord, that nothing would serve him but that he must come every year; and it was he that had the great organ brought from Holland and built up in the hall, where it stood now. He taught the old lord to play on it; but many and many a time, when Lord Furnivall was thinking of nothing but his fine organ, and his finer music, the dark foreigner was walking abroad in the woods with one of the young ladies; now Miss Maude, and then Miss Grace.

Miss Maude won the day and carried off the prize, such as it was; and he and she were married, all unknown to any one; and before he made his next yearly visit, she had been confined of a little girl at a farm-house on the Moors, while her father and Miss Grace thought she was away at Doncaster Races. But though she was a wife and a mother, she was not a bit softened, but as haughty and as passionate as ever; and perhaps more so, for she was jealous of Miss Grace, to whom her foreign husband paid a deal of court— by way of blinding her—as he told his wife. But Miss Grace triumphed over Miss Maude, and Miss Maude grew fiercer and fiercer, both with her husband and with her sister; and the former—who could easily shake off what was disagreeable, and hide himself in foreign countries—went away a month before his usual time that summer, and half threatened that he would never come back again. Meanwhile, the little girl was left at the farm-house, and her mother used to have her horse saddled and gallop wildly over the hills to see her once every week, at the very least—for where she loved, she loved; and where she hated, she hated. And the old lord went on playing—playing on his organ; and the servants thought the sweet music he made had soothed down his awful temper, of which (Dorothy said) some terrible tales could be told. He grew infirm too, and had to walk with a crutch; and his son—that was the present Lord Furnivall's father—was with the army in America, and the other son at sea; so Miss Maude had it pretty much her own way, and she and Miss Grace grew colder and bitterer to each other every day; till at last they hardly ever spoke, except when the old lord was by. The foreign musician came again the next summer, but it was for the last time; for they led him such a life with their jealously and their passions, that he grew weary, and went away, and never was heard of again. And Miss Maude, who had always meant to have her marriage acknowledged when her father should be dead, was left now a deserted wife—whom nobody knew to have been married—with a child that she dared not own, although she loved it to distraction; living with a father whom she feared, and a sister whom she hated. When the next summer passed over and the dark foreigner never came, both Miss Maude and Miss Grace grew gloomy and sad; they had a haggard look about them, though they looked handsome as ever. But by and by Miss Maude brightened; for her father grew more and more infirm, and more than ever carried away by his music; and she and Miss Grace lived almost entirely apart, having separate rooms, the one on the west side—Miss Maude on the east—those very rooms which were now shut up. So she thought she might have her little girl with her, and no one need ever know except those who dared not speak about it, and were bound to believe that it was, as she said, a cottager's child she had taken a fancy to. All this, Dorothy said, was pretty well known; but what came afterwards no one knew, except Miss Grace, and Mrs. Stark, who was even then her maid, and much more of a friend to her than ever her sister had been. But the servants supposed, from words that were dropped, that Miss Maude had triumphed over Miss Grace, and told her that all the time the dark foreigner had been mocking her with pretended love—he was her own husband; the color left Miss Grace's cheek and lips that very day for ever, and she was heard to say many a time that sooner or later she would have her revenge; and Mrs. Stark was for ever spying about the east rooms.

One fearful night, just after the New Year had come in, when the snow was lying thick and deep, and the flakes were still falling—fast enough to blind any one who might be out and abroad—there was a great and violent noise heard, and the old lord's voice above all, cursing and swearing awfully,—and the cries of a little child,—and the proud defiance of a fierce woman,—and the sound of a blow,—and a dead stillness,—and moans and wailings dying away on the hill-side! Then the old lord summoned all his servants, and told them, with terrible oaths, and words more terrible, that his daughter had disgraced herself, and that he had turned her out of doors,—her, and her child,—and that if ever they gave her help,—or food— or shelter,—he prayed that they might never enter Heaven. And, all the while, Miss Grace stood by him, white and still as any stone; and when he had ended she heaved a great sigh, as much as to say her work was done, and her end was accomplished. But the old lord never touched his organ again, and died within the year; and no wonder! for, on the morrow of that wild and fearful night, the shepherds, coming down the Fell side, found Miss Maude sitting, all crazy and smiling, under the holly-trees, nursing a dead child,—with a terrible mark on its right shoulder. "But that was not what killed it," said Dorothy; "it was the frost and the cold—every wild creature was in its hole, and every beast in its fold,—while the child and its mother were turned out to wander on the Fells! And now you know all! and I wonder if you are less frightened now?"

I was more frightened than ever; but I said I was not. I wished Miss Rosamond and myself well out of that dreadful house for ever; but I would not leave her, and I dared not take her away. But oh! how I watched her, and guarded her! We bolted the doors, and shut the window-shutters fast, an hour or more before dark, rather than leave them open five minutes too late. But my little lady still heard the weird child crying and mourning; and not all we could do or say, could keep her from wanting to go to her, and let her in from the cruel wind and the snow. All this time, I kept away from Miss Furnivall and Mrs. Stark, as much as ever I could; for I feared them—I knew no good could be about them, with their grey hard faces, and their dreamy eyes, looking back into the ghastly years that were gone. But, even in my fear, I had a kind of pity—for Miss Furnivall, at least. Those gone down to the pit can hardly have a more hopeless look than that which was ever on her face. At last I even got so sorry for her—who never said a word but what was quite forced from her—that I prayed for her; and I taught Miss Rosamond to pray for one who had done a deadly sin; but often when she came to those words, she would listen, and start up from her knees, and say, "I hear my little girl plaining and crying very sad—Oh! let her in, or she will die!"

One night—just after New Year's Day had come at last, and the long winter had taken a turn as I hoped—I heard the west drawing-room bell ring three times, which was the signal for me. I would not leave Miss Rosamond alone, for all she was asleep—for the old lord had been playing wilder than ever—and I feared lest my darling should waken to hear the spectre child; see her I knew she could not, I had fastened the windows too well for that. So, I took her out of her bed and wrapped her up in such outer clothes as were most handy, and carried her down to the drawing-room, where the old ladies sat at their tapestry work as usual. They looked up when I came in, and Mrs. Stark asked, quite astounded, "Why did I bring Miss Rosamond there, out of her warm bed?" I had begun to whisper, "Because I was afraid of her being tempted out while I was away, by the wild child in the snow," when she stopped me short (with a glance at Miss Furnivall) and said Miss Furnivall wanted me to undo some work she had done wrong, and which neither of them could see to unpick. So, I laid my pretty dear on the sofa, and sat down on a stool by them, and hardened my heart against them as I heard the wind rising and howling.

Miss Rosamond slept on sound, for all the wind blew so; and Miss Furnivall said never a word, nor looked round when the gusts shook the windows. All at once she started up to her full height, and put up one hand as if to bid us listen.

"I hear voices!" said she. "I hear terrible screams—I hear my father's voice!"

Just at that moment, my darling wakened with a sudden start: "My little girl is crying, oh, how she is crying!" and she tried to get up and go to her, but she got her feet entangled in the blanket, and I caught her up; for my flesh had begun to creep at these noises, which they heard while we could catch no sound. In a minute or two the noises came, and gathered fast, and filled our ears; we, too, heard voices and screams, and no longer heard the winter's wind that raged abroad. Mrs. Stark looked at me, and I at her, but we dared not speak. Suddenly Miss Furnivall went towards the door, out into the ante-room, through the west lobby, and opened the door into the great hall. Mrs. Stark followed, and I durst not be left, though my heart almost stopped beating for fear. I wrapped my darling tight in my arms, and went out with them. In the hall the screams were louder than ever; they sounded to come from the east wing—nearer and nearer—close on the other side of the locked-up doors—close behind them. Then I noticed that the great bronze chandelier seemed all alight, though the hall was dim, and that a fire was blazing in the vast hearth-place, though it gave no heat; and I shuddered up with terror, and folded my darling closer to me. But as I did so, the east door shook, and she, suddenly struggling to get free from me, cried, "Hester! I must go! My little girl is there; I hear her; she is coming! Hester, I must go!"

I held her tight with all my strength; with a set will, I held her. If I had died, my hands would have grasped her still; I was so resolved in my mind. Miss Furnivall stood listening, and paid no regard to my darling, who had got down to the ground, and whom I, upon my knees now, was holding with both my arms clasped round her neck; she still striving and crying to get free.

All at once, the east door gave way with a thundering crash, as if torn open in a violent passion, and there came into that broad and mysterious light, the figure of a tall old man, with grey hair and gleaming eyes. He drove before him, with many a relentless gesture of abhorrence, a stern and beautiful woman, with a little child clinging to her dress.

"Oh Hester! Hester!" cried Miss Rosamond. "It's the lady! the lady below the holly-trees; and my little girl is with her. Hester! Hester! let me go to her; they are drawing me to them. I feel them—I feel them. I must go!"

Again she was almost convulsed by her efforts to get away; but I held her tighter and tighter; till I feared I should do her a hurt; but rather that than let her go towards those terrible phantoms. They passed along towards the great hall-door, where the winds howled and ravened for their prey; but before they reached that, the lady turned; and I could see that she defied the old man with a fierce and proud defiance; but then she quailed—and then she threw up her arms wildly and piteously to save her child—her little child—from a blow from his uplifted crutch.

And Miss Rosamond was torn as by a power stronger than mine, and writhed in my arms, and sobbed (for by this time the poor darling was growing faint).

"They want me to go with them on to the Fells—they are drawing me to them. Oh, my little girl! I would come, but cruel, wicked Hester holds me very tight." But when she saw the uplifted crutch she swooned away, and I thanked God for it. Just at this moment—when the tall old man, his hair streaming as in the blast of a furnace, was going to strike the little shrinking child—Miss Furnivall, the old woman by my side, cried out, "Oh, father! father! spare the little innocent child!" But just then I saw—we all saw— another phantom shape itself, and grow clear out of the blue and misty light that filled the hall; we had not seen her till now, for it was another lady who stood by the old man, with a look of relentless hate and triumphant scorn. That figure was very beautiful to look upon, with a soft white hat drawn down over the proud brows, and a red and curling lip. It was dressed in an open robe of blue satin. I had seen that figure before. It was the likeness of Miss Furnivall in her youth; and the terrible phantoms moved on, regardless of old Miss Furnivall's wild entreaty,—and the uplifted crutch fell on the right shoulder of the little child, and the younger sister looked on, stony and deadly serene. But at that moment, the dim lights, and the fire that gave no heat, went out of themselves, and Miss Furnivall lay at our feet stricken down by the palsy—death-stricken.

Yes! she was carried to her bed that night never to rise again. She lay with her face to the wall, muttering low but muttering alway: "Alas! alas! what is done in youth can never be undone in age! What is done in youth can never be undone in age!"

1852

CHARLES DICKENS
1812–1870

Charles Dickens was Victorian England's most beloved and distinctive novelist. In the words of the eulogy that the classicist Benjamin Jowett spoke at his funeral serv- ice, Dickens "occupied a greater space than any other writer during the last thirty- five years. We read him, talked about him, acted him; we laughed with him, we were roused by him to a consciousness of the misery of others, and to a pathetic interest in human life."

Charles Dickens was born the second of eight children in the coastal town of Portsmouth in southern England. His father, a clerk in the Naval Pay Office, found it difficult to keep his family out of debt. Plagued by financial insecurity, the family moved from place to place, to increasingly poorer lodgings, finally ending up in Lon- don. In an effort to help the family out, a friend of his father's offered Charles a job in a shoe-blacking factory. Two days before his twelfth birthday, he began work, labeling bottles for six shillings a week. Two weeks later his father was arrested and sent to the Marshalsea Prison for debt. His family went to live in prison with him, as was the custom; but they decided that Charles should remain outside, boarding with a woman who took in young lodgers and continuing to work.

The months in which Charles lived alone and worked in the blacking warehouse were traumatic, and the intense feeling Dickens had of injury and abandonment shaped his fiction in profound ways. The sense he had of himself as "a child of singular abilities: quick, eager, delicate, and soon hurt, bodily or mentally," who had been cast away to suffer unjustly, formed the basis for characters such as Oliver Twist, the young David Copperfield, and Pip in *Great Expectations*, whose mistreatment repre- sents Dickens's harshest indictment of society.

Dickens's father was able to leave debtors prison after three months, upon receipt of a legacy from his mother. He removed Charles from the factory and sent him to school. At fifteen Dickens began work as a junior clerk at a law office; eighteen months later he became a freelance newspaper reporter, first reporting court proceedings and later debates in the House of Commons. Reporting led him to fiction. He began publishing literary sketches, at first anonymously and then under the pseudonym Boz. In 1836, on his twenty-fourth birthday, he published the collection *Sketches by Boz*. The success of the volume led to a commission from the publishers Chapman & Hall to publish a book in serial installments with companion illustrations. The result, *Pickwick Papers* (1836–37), brought Dickens fame and prosperity. This picaresque novel, relating the adventures of Mr. Pickwick and his friends as they travel around England, set the pattern of illustrated serial publication that was to define Dickens's writing career and to shape the reading habits of his generation. Families would wait in suspense for the next installment of a novel to be issued, which they would read aloud as an evening's entertainment. Successes followed quickly: *Oliver Twist* (1838), *Nicholas Nickleby* (1838–39), and *The Old Curiosity Shop* (1840–41).

By the time of *Pickwick's* completion, Dickens had married Catherine Hogarth, the daughter of a fellow journalist, and had begun a family; they eventually had ten children, and household chaos would come increasingly to frustrate him. Dickens's portrayal of women, both as unreachable ideals and as inadequate keepers of domestic order, was influenced by two other women. Maria Beadnell, the daughter of a banker, was his first love; but his courtship was discouraged by her family, who felt he was beneath her. He was left with a painful sense that he had lost his ideal love. Dickens experienced another traumatic loss when Mary, his seventeen-year-old sister-in-law to whom he had become devoted, died in his arms.

Through the 1840s and 1850s Dickens continued to write novels at an intense pace, producing *Barnaby Rudge* (1841), *Martin Chuzzlewit* (1843–44), *Dombey and Son* (1846–48), *David Copperfield* (1849–50), *Bleak House* (1852–53), *Hard Times* (1854), *Little Dorrit* (1855–57), and *A Tale of Two Cities* (1859). He also became deeply involved in a number of other activities, including traveling, working for charities, and acting. During this time he founded and edited the weekly magazine *Household Words* (incorporated in 1859 into *All the Year Round*), which published fiction by Elizabeth Gaskell, Wilkie Collins, Dickens himself, and other novelists as well as opinion pieces about political and social issues. And he began a series of Christmas books, the first of which was *A Christmas Carol* (1843).

In 1858 when Dickens separated from his wife, his life and work changed. He became involved with the actress Ellen Ternan, and he took up residence at Gad's Hill, a gentleman's house in Kent. Abandoning amateur theatricals, he embarked on a series of lucrative professional readings, which were so emotionally and physically exhausting his doctor finally instructed him to stop. He slowed the pace of his writing, publishing only two novels in the 1860s: *Great Expectations* (1860–61) and *Our Mutual Friend* (1864–65). He died suddenly in 1870, leaving his last novel, *The Mystery of Edwin Drood* (1870), unfinished.

Dickens's early fiction is remarkable for its extravagance, which Franz Kafka calls "Dickens' opulence and great, careless prodigality." It marks many elements of his novels—their baggy plots, filled with incident; the constant metaphorical invention of their language; and the multitude of their characters. Anthony Trollope observed that no other writer except Shakespeare has left so many "characters which are known by their names familiarly as household words, and which bring to our minds vividly and at once, a certain well-understood set of ideas, habits, phrases and costumes, making together a man, or woman, or child, whom we know at a glance and recognize at a sound, as we do our own intimate friends."

Dickens builds character from a repeated set of gestures, phrases, and metaphors. For example, whenever Mrs. Micawber enters the story of *David Copperfield*, she repeats, "I will never desert Mr. Micawber." Dickens identifies Wemmick in *Great Expectations* with his post office mouth and Mr. Gradgrind in *Hard Times* with the squareness of each of his physical attributes. This way of creating character led the novelist E. M. Forster to use Dickens to illustrate what he means by a flat, as opposed to a round, character. Such a reductive technique of characterization might seem to have little to offer by way of depth of insight, yet such is not the case. In particular, as Dickens's fiction becomes more complex in the course of his career, the repeated tics that identify his characters come to represent emotional fixations and social distortions. Dickens's early fiction exults in a comedy of humors. In his later fiction, that comedy becomes grotesque, as the distortions of caricature reflect failures of humanity in his increasingly dark social vision.

Bernard Shaw wrote that "Dickens never regarded himself as a revolutionist, though he certainly was one." Dickens's early novels often concern social abuses—the workhouses in which pauper children were confined in *Oliver Twist*, abusive and fraudulent schools in *Nicholas Nickleby*. As his career progressed, Dickens felt an increasing urgency about the social criticism his novels made. He gave *Hard Times* the subtitle *For These Times* and dedicated the book to Thomas Carlyle, indicating his ambition to write a work in the tradition of Carlyle's social indictment, *Signs of the Times*. In his middle novels, Dickens's criticism of society becomes increasingly systemic, and he begins to use organizing metaphors to express his social vision. *Bleak House*, for example, concerns the failings of the legal system, but the obfuscation and self-interest of the law is symptomatic of a larger social ill, symbolized in the smothering fog whose description begins the novel.

Despite the bleakness of Dickens's view of society and the fierceness of his criticism of it, his novels always end with a sentimental assertion of the virtues of home and heart. A number of critics have thought this sentimentality blunts his social analysis. Whatever the claims Dickens makes for fellow feeling, however, his sentimental endings are never completely consistent with his social analysis. Although Dickens tries to use fiction to stir the human heart and evoke humanitarian feelings, the domestic refuges of his novels never change the world outside. The modern novelist Graham Greene has written that Dickens's inability to believe in his own good characters creates the real tension of his fiction. Without sharing Greene's incredulity, one can see the novels as polyphonic, as giving expression to many voices that together create a structural sense not only of Victorian society but also of the values that give shape to its perceptions, including its sentimentality.

The distinctive character of Dickens's fiction is so pronounced that critics often talk of his world as if the individual worlds of all of his novels were continuous. In part, Dickens's tendency to return repeatedly to the subjects that possessed his imagination supports this impression. One of those subjects is prisons. *A Visit to Newgate* is his earliest piece about prisons; but he returns to the subject many times, as in *Great Expectations, Oliver Twist, Pickwick Papers,* and *Little Dorrit.* Prison for Dickens is a particular social abuse, the most harrowing setting in which to contemplate criminality and guilt, a metaphor for the psychological captivity his characters create for themselves, and the system through which society enforces its discipline. In the many layers of significance that the main elements of Victorian society take on in his fiction, Dickens's creative vision, as the critic J. Hillis Miller observes, in part determines the Victorian spirit itself.

A Visit to Newgate[1]

"The force of habit" is a trite phrase in everybody's mouth; and it is not a little remarkable that those who use it most as applied to others, uncon-

1. First published in *Sketches by Boz* (1836). Newgate was London's main criminal prison.

sciously afford in their own persons singular examples of the power which habit and custom exercise over the minds of men, and of the little reflection they are apt to bestow on subjects with which every day's experience has rendered them familiar. If Bedlam could be suddenly removed like another Aladdin's palace,[2] and set down on the space now occupied by Newgate, scarcely one man out of a hundred, whose road to business every morning lies through Newgate-street, or the Old Bailey,[3] would pass the building without bestowing a hasty glance on its small, grated windows, and a transient thought upon the condition of the unhappy beings immured in its dismal cells; and yet these same men, day by day, and hour by hour, pass and repass this gloomy depository of the guilt and misery of London, in one perpetual stream of life and bustle, utterly unmindful of the throng of wretched creatures pent up within it—nay, not even knowing, or if they do, not heeding, the fact, that as they pass one particular angle of the massive wall with a light laugh or a merry whistle, they stand within one yard of a fellow-creature, bound and helpless, whose hours are numbered, from whom the last feeble ray of hope has fled for ever, and whose miserable career will shortly terminate in a violent and shameful death. Contact with death even in its least terrible shape, is solemn and appalling. How much more awful is it to reflect on this near vicinity to the dying—to men in full health and vigour, in the flower of youth or the prime of life, with all their faculties and perceptions as acute and perfect as your own; but dying, nevertheless—dying as surely—with the hand of death imprinted upon them as indelibly—as if mortal disease had wasted their frames to shadows, and corruption had already begun!

It was with some such thoughts as these that we determined, not many weeks since, to visit the interior of Newgate—in an amateur capacity, of course; and, having carried our intention into effect, we proceed to lay its results before our readers, in the hope—founded more upon the nature of the subject, than on any presumptuous confidence in our own descriptive powers—that this paper may not be found wholly devoid of interest. We have only to premise, that we do not intend to fatigue the reader with any statistical accounts of the prison; they will be found at length in numerous reports of numerous committees, and a variety of authorities of equal weight. We took no notes, made no memoranda, measured none of the yards, ascertained the exact number of inches in no particular room, are unable even to report of how many apartments the gaol is composed.

We saw the prison, and saw the prisoners; and what we did see, and what we thought, we will tell at once in our own way.

Having delivered our credentials to the servant who answered our knock at the door of the governor's[4] house, we were ushered into the "office;" a little room, on the right-hand side as you enter, with two windows looking into the Old Bailey: fitted up like an ordinary attorney's office, or merchant's counting-house, with the usual fixtures—a wainscoted partition, a shelf or two, a desk, a couple of stools, a pair of clerks, an almanack, a clock, and a few maps. After a little delay, occasioned by sending into the interior of the

2. In *Tales of the Arabian Nights*, an evil magician temporarily gets control of Aladdin's magic lamp and transports his palace to Africa. "Bedlam": a London hospital for the insane.

3. London's criminal court, which is located on the street of the same name.
4. The head of the prison.

prison for the officer whose duty it was to conduct us, that functionary arrived; a respectable-looking man of about two or three and fifty, in a broad-brimmed hat, and full suit of black, who, but for his keys, would have looked quite as much like a clergyman as a turnkey. We were disappointed; he had not even top-boots on. Following our conductor by a door opposite to that at which we had entered, we arrived at a small room, without any other furniture than a little desk, with a book for visitors' autographs, and a shelf, on which were a few boxes for papers, and casts of the heads and faces of the two notorious murderers, Bishop and Williams;[5] the former, in particular, exhibiting a style of head and set of features, which might have afforded sufficient moral grounds for his instant execution at any time, even had there been no other evidence against him. Leaving this room also, by an opposite door, we found ourself in the lodge which opens on the Old Bailey; one side of which is plentifully garnished with a choice collection of heavy sets of irons, including those worn by the redoubtable Jack Sheppard—genuine; and those *said* to have been graced by the sturdy limbs of the no less celebrated Dick Turpin[6]—doubtful. From this lodge, a heavy oaken gate, bound with iron, studded with nails of the same material, and guarded by another turn-key, opens on a few steps, if we remember right, which terminate in a narrow and dismal stone passage, running parallel with the Old Bailey, and leading to the different yards, through a number of tortuous and intricate windings, guarded in their turn by huge gates and gratings, whose appearance is sufficient to dispel at once the slightest hope of escape that any new comer may have entertained; and the very recollection of which, on eventually traversing the place again, involves one in a maze of confusion.

It is necessary to explain here, that the buildings in the prison, or in other words the different wards—form a square, of which the four sides abut respectively on the Old Bailey, the old College of Physicians (now forming a part of Newgate-market), the Sessions-house, and Newgate-street. The intermediate space is divided into several paved yards, in which the prisoners take such air and exercise as can be had in such a place. These yards, with the exception of that in which prisoners under sentence of death are confined (of which we shall presently give a more detailed description), run parallel with Newgate-street, and consequently from the Old Bailey, as it were, to Newgate-market. The women's side is in the right wing of the prison nearest the Sessions-house. As we were introduced into this part of the building first, we will adopt the same order, and introduce our readers to it also.

Turning to the right, then, down the passage to which we just now adverted, omitting any mention of intervening gates—for if we noticed every gate that was unlocked for us to pass through, and locked again as soon as we had passed, we should require a gate at every comma—we came to a door composed of thick bars of wood, through which were discernible, passing to and fro in a narrow yard, some twenty women: the majority of whom, however, as soon as they were aware of the presence of strangers, retreated to their wards. One side of this yard is railed off at a considerable distance, and formed into a kind of iron cage, about five feet ten inches in height, roofed at the top, and defended in front by iron bars, from which the friends of the

---

5. John Bishop and Thomas Head (aka "Williams"), notorious body snatchers who were hanged for murdering a young boy in 1831.

6. Notorious 18th-century thieves and highwaymen. "Irons": shackles.

female prisoners communicate with them. In one corner of this singular-looking den, was a yellow, haggard, decrepit old woman, in a tattered gown that had once been black, and the remains of an old straw bonnet, with faded ribbon of the same hue, in earnest conversation with a young girl—a prisoner, of course—of about two-and-twenty. It is impossible to imagine a more poverty-stricken object, or a creature so borne down in soul and body, by excess of misery and destitution as the old woman. The girl was a good-looking robust female, with a profusion of hair streaming about in the wind—for she had no bonnet on—and a man's silk pocket-handkerchief loosely thrown over a most ample pair of shoulders. The old woman was talking in that low, stifled tone of voice which tells so forcibly of mental anguish; and every now and then burst into an irrepressible sharp, abrupt cry of grief, the most distressing sound that ears can hear. The girl was perfectly unmoved. Hardened beyond all hope of redemption, she listened doggedly to her mother's entreaties, whatever they were: and, beyond inquiring after "Jem," and eagerly catching at the few halfpence her miserable parent had brought her, took no more apparent interest in the conversation than the most unconcerned spectators. Heaven knows there were enough of them, in the persons of the other prisoners in the yard, who were no more concerned by what was passing before their eyes, and within their hearing, than if they were blind and deaf. Why should they be? Inside the prison, and out, such scenes were too familiar to them, to excite even a passing thought, unless of ridicule or contempt for feelings which they had long since forgotten.

A little farther on, a squalid-looking woman in a slovenly, thick-bordered cap, with her arms muffled in a large red shawl, the fringed ends of which straggled nearly to the bottom of a dirty white apron, was communicating some instructions to *her* visitor—her daughter evidently. The girl was thinly clad, and shaking with the cold. Some ordinary word of recognition passed between her and her mother when she appeared at the grating, but neither hope, condolence, regret, nor affection was expressed on either side. The mother whispered her instructions, and the girl received them with her pinched-up half-starved features twisted into an expression of careful cunning. It was some scheme for the woman's defence that she was disclosing, perhaps; and a sullen smile came over the girl's face for an instant, as if she were pleased: not so much at the probability of her mother's liberation, as at the chance of her "getting off" in spite of her prosecutors. The dialogue was soon concluded; and with the same careless indifference with which they had approached each other, the mother turned towards the inner end of the yard, and the girl to the gate at which she had entered.

The girl belonged to a class—unhappily but too extensive—the very existence of which, should make men's hearts bleed. Barely past her childhood, it required but a glance to discover that she was one of those children, born and bred in neglect and vice, who have never known what childhood is: who have never been taught to love and court a parent's smile, or to dread a parent's frown. The thousand nameless endearments of childhood, its gaiety and its innocence, are alike unknown to them. They have entered at once upon the stern realities and miseries of life, and to their better nature it is almost hopeless to appeal in aftertimes, by any of the references which will awaken, if it be only for a moment, some good feeling in ordinary bosoms, however corrupt they may have become. Talk to *them* of parental solicitude, the happy days of childhood, and the merry games of infancy! Tell them of hunger and the streets, beggary and stripes, the gin-shop, the station-house, and the pawnbroker's, and they will understand you.

Two or three women were standing at different parts of the grating, conversing with their friends, but a very large proportion of the prisoners appeared to have no friends at all, beyond such of their old companions as might happen to be within the walls. So, passing hastily down the yard, and pausing only for an instant to notice the little incidents we have just recorded, we were conducted up a clean and well-lighted flight of stone stairs to one of the wards. There are several in this part of the building, but a description of one is a description of the whole.

It was a spacious, bare, whitewashed apartment, lighted of course, by windows looking into the interior of the prison, but far more light and airy than one could reasonably expect to find in such a situation. There was a large fire with a deal table before it, round which ten or a dozen women were seated on wooden forms at dinner. Along both sides of the room ran a shelf; below it, at regular intervals, a row of large hooks were fixed in the wall, on each of which was hung the sleeping mat of a prisoner: her rug and blanket being folded up, and placed on the shelf above. At night, these mats are placed on the floor, each beneath the hook on which it hangs during the day; and the ward is thus made to answer the purposes both of a day-room and sleeping apartment. Over the fireplace, was a large sheet of pasteboard, on which were displayed a variety of texts from Scripture, which were also scattered about the room in scraps about the size and shape of the copy-slips which are used in schools. On the table was a sufficient provision of a kind of stewed beef and brown bread, in pewter dishes, which are kept perfectly bright, and displayed on shelves in great order and regularity when they are not in use.

The women rose hastily, on our entrance, and retired in a hurried manner to either side of the fireplace. They were all cleanly—many of them decently—attired, and there was nothing peculiar, either in their appearance or demeanour. One or two resumed the needlework which they had probably laid aside at the commencement of their meal; others gazed at the visitors with listless curiosity; and a few retired behind their companions to the very end of the room, as if desirous to avoid even the casual observation of the strangers. Some old Irish women, both in this and other wards, to whom the thing was no novelty, appeared perfectly indifferent to our presence, and remained standing close to the seats from which they had just risen; but the general feeling among the females seemed to be one of uneasiness during the period of our stay among them: which was very brief. Not a word was uttered during the time of our remaining, unless, indeed, by the wardswoman in reply to some question which we put to the turnkey who accompanied us. In every ward on the female side, a wardswoman is appointed to preserve order, and a similar regulation is adopted among the males. The wardsmen and wardswomen are all prisoners, selected for good conduct. They alone are allowed the privilege of sleeping on bedsteads; a small stump bedstead[7] being placed in every ward for that purpose. On both sides of the gaol, is a small receiving-room, to which prisoners are conducted on their first recep-

7. Bedframe that ends at the level of the mattress.

tion, and whence they cannot be removed until they have been examined by the surgeon of the prison.[8]

Retracing our steps to the dismal passage in which we found ourselves at first (and which, by-the-bye, contains three or four dark cells for the accommodation of refractory prisoners), we were led through a narrow yard to the "school"—a portion of the prison set apart for boys under fourteen years of age. In a tolerable-sized room, in which were writing-materials and some copy-books, was the school-master, with a couple of his pupils; the remainder having been fetched from an adjoining apartment, the whole were drawn up in line for our inspection. There were fourteen of them in all, some with shoes, some without; some in pinafores[9] without jackets, others in jackets without pinafores, and one in scarce anything at all. The whole number, without an exception we believe, had been committed for trial on charges of pocket-picking; and fourteen such terrible little faces we never beheld.— There was not one redeeming feature among them—not a glance of honesty—not a wink expressive of anything but the gallows and the hulks,[1] in the whole collection. As to anything like shame or contrition, that was entirely out of the question. They were evidently quite gratified at being thought worth the trouble of looking at; their idea appeared to be, that we had come to see Newgate as a grand affair, and that they were an indispensable part of the show; and every boy as he "fell in" to the line, actually seemed as pleased and important as if he had done something excessively meritorious in getting there at all. We never looked upon a more disagreeable sight, because we never saw fourteen such hopeless creatures of neglect, before.

On either side of the school-yard is a yard for men, in one of which—that towards Newgate-street—prisoners of the more respectable class are confined. Of the other, we have little description to offer, as the different wards necessarily partake of the same character. They are provided, like the wards on the women's side, with mats and rugs, which are disposed of in the same manner during the day; the only very striking difference between their appearance and that of the wards inhabited by the females, is the utter absence of any employment. Huddled together on two opposite forms, by the fireside, sit twenty men perhaps; here, a boy in livery; there, a man in a rough great-coat and top-boots; farther on, a desperate-looking fellow in his shirt sleeves, with an old Scotch cap[2] upon his shaggy head; near him again, a tall ruffian, in a smock-frock; next to him, a miserable being of distressed appearance, with his head resting on his hand;—all alike in one respect, all idle and listless. When they do leave the fire, sauntering moodily about, lounging in the window, or leaning against the wall, vacantly swinging their bodies to and fro. With the exception of a man reading an old newspaper, in two or three instances, this was the case in every ward we entered.

The only communication these men have with their friends, is through two close iron gratings, with an intermediate space of about a yard in width between the two, so that nothing can be handed across, nor can the prisoner

<hr>

8. The regulations of the prison relative to the confinement of prisoners during the day, their sleeping at night, their taking their meals, and other matters of gaol economy, have been all altered—greatly for the better—since this sketch was published. Even the construction of the prison itself has been changed [Dickens's note].
9. Aprons.
1. Prison ships.
2. Brimless woolen hat with two tails.

have any communication by touch with the person who visits him. The married men have a separate grating, at which to see their wives, but its construction is the same.

The prison chapel is situated at the back of the governor's house: the latter having no windows looking into the interior of the prison. Whether the associations connected with the place—the knowledge that here a portion of the burial service is, on some dreadful occasions, performed over the quick[3] and not upon the dead—cast over it a still more gloomy and sombre air than art has imparted to it, we know not, but its appearance is very striking. There is something in a silent and deserted place of worship, solemn and impressive at any time; and the very dissimilarity of this one from any we have been accustomed to, only enhances the impression. The meanness of its appointments—the bare and scanty pulpit, with the paltry painted pillars on either side—the women's gallery with its great heavy curtain—the men's with its unpainted benches and dingy front—the tottering little table at the altar, with the commandments on the wall above it, scarcely legible through lack of paint, and dust and damp—so unlike the velvet and gilding, the marble and wood, of a modern church—are strange and striking. There is one object, too, which rivets the attention and fascinates the gaze, and from which we may turn horror-stricken in vain, for the recollection of it will haunt us, waking and sleeping, for a long time afterwards. Immediately below the reading-desk, on the floor of the chapel, and forming the most conspicuous object in its little area, is *the condemned pew*; a huge black pen, in which the wretched people, who are singled out for death, are placed on the Sunday preceding their execution, in sight of all their fellow-prisoners, from many of whom they may have been separated but a week before, to hear prayers for their own souls, to join in the responses of their own burial service, and to listen to an address, warning their recent companions to take example by their fate, and urging themselves, while there is yet time—nearly four-and-twenty hours—to "turn, and flee from the wrath to come!"[4] Imagine what have been the feelings of the men whom that fearful pew has enclosed, and of whom, between the gallows and the knife, no mortal remnant may now remain! Think of the hopeless clinging to life to the last, and the wild despair, far exceeding in anguish the felon's death itself, by which they have heard the certainty of their speedy transmission to another world, with all their crimes upon their heads, rung into their ears by the officiating clergyman!

At one time—and at no distant period either—the coffins of the men about to be executed, were placed in that pew, upon the seat by their side, during the whole service. It may seem incredible, but it is true. Let us hope that the increased spirit of civilization and humanity which abolished this frightful and degrading custom, may extend itself to other usages equally barbarous; usages which have not even the plea of utility in their defense, as every year's experience has shown them to be more and more inefficacious.

Leaving the chapel, descending to the passage so frequently alluded to, and crossing the yard before noticed as being allotted to prisoners of a more respectable description than the generality of men confined here, the visitor arrives at a thick iron gate of great size and strength. Having been admitted

3. Living.
4. Cf. Matthew 3.7 and Luke 3.7: "O generation of vipers, who hath warned you to flee from the wrath to come?"

through it by the turnkey on duty, he turns sharp round to the left, and pauses before another gate; and, having passed this last barrier, he stands in the most terrible part of this gloomy building—the condemned ward.

The press-yard,[5] well known by name to newspaper readers, from its frequent mention in accounts of executions, is at the corner of the building, and next to the ordinary's[6] house, in Newgate-street: running from Newgate-street, towards the centre of the prison, parallel with Newgate-market. It is a long, narrow court, of which a portion of the wall in Newgate-street forms one end, and the gate the other. At the upper end, on the left-hand—that is, adjoining the wall in Newgate-street—is a cistern of water, and at the bottom a double grating (of which the gate itself forms a part) similar to that before described. Through these grates the prisoners are allowed to see their friends; a turnkey always remaining in the vacant space between, during the whole interview. Immediately on the right as you enter, is a building containing the press-room, day-room, and cells; the yard is on every side surrounded by lofty walls guarded by *chevaux de frise*;[7] and the whole is under the constant inspection of vigilant and experienced turnkeys.

In the first apartment into which we were conducted—which was at the top of a staircase, and immediately over the press-room—were five-and-twenty or thirty prisoners, all under sentence of death, awaiting the result of the recorder's report—men of all ages and appearances, from a hardened old offender with swarthy face and grizzly beard of three days' growth, to a handsome boy, not fourteen years old, and of singularly youthful appearance even for that age, who had been condemned for burglary. There was nothing remarkable in the appearance of these prisoners. One or two decently-dressed men were brooding with a dejected air over the fire; several little groups of two or three had been engaged in conversation at the upper end of the room, or in the windows; and the remainder were crowded round a young man seated at a table, who appeared to be engaged in teaching the younger ones to write. The room was large, airy, and clean. There was very little anxiety or mental suffering depicted in the countenance of any of the men;—they had all been sentenced to death, it is true, and the recorder's report had not yet been made; but, we question whether there was a man among them, notwithstanding, who did not *know* that although he had undergone the ceremony, it never was intended that his life should be sacrificed. On the table lay a Testament, but there were no tokens of its having been in recent use.

In the press-room below, were three men, the nature of whose offence rendered it necessary to separate them, even from their companions in guilt. It is a long, sombre room, with two windows sunk into the stone wall, and here the wretched men are pinioned on the morning of their execution, before moving towards the scaffold. The fate of one of these prisoners was uncertain; some mitigatory circumstances having come to light since his trial, which had been humanely represented in the proper quarter. The other two had nothing to expect from the mercy of the crown; their doom was sealed; no plea could be urged in extenuation of their crime, and they well knew that for them there was no hope in this world. "The two short ones," the turnkey whispered, "were dead men."

---

5. Area from which criminals condemned to death started for the place of execution.
6. Clergyman appointed to prepare criminals for execution.
7. Line of spikes (French).

The man to whom we have alluded as entertaining some hopes of escape, was lounging, at the greatest distance he could place between himself and his companions, in the window nearest to the door. He was probably aware of our approach, and had assumed an air of courageous indifference; his face was purposely averted towards the window, and he stirred not an inch while we were present. The other two men were at the upper end of the room. One of them, who was imperfectly seen in the dim light, had his back towards us, and was stooping over the fire, with his right arm on the mantel-piece, and his head sunk upon it. The other, was leaning on the sill of the farthest window. The light fell full upon him, and communicated to his pale, haggard face, and disordered hair, an appearance which, at that distance, was ghastly. His cheek rested upon his hand; and, with his face a little raised, and his eyes wildly staring before him, he seemed to be unconsciously intent on counting the chinks in the opposite wall. We passed this room again afterwards. The first man was pacing up and down the court with a firm military step—he had been a soldier in the foot-guards—and a cloth cap jauntily thrown on one side of his head. He bowed respectfully to our conductor, and the salute was returned. The other two still remained in the positions we have described, and were as motionless as statues.[8]

A few paces up the yard, and forming a continuation of the building, in which are the two rooms we have just quitted, lie the condemned cells. The entrance is by a narrow and obscure staircase leading to a dark passage, in which a charcoal stove casts a lurid tint over the objects in its immediate vicinity, and diffuses something like warmth around. From the left-hand side of this passage, the massive door of every cell on the story opens; and from it alone can they be approached. There are three of these passages, and three of these ranges of cells, one above the other; but in size, furniture and appearance, they are all precisely alike. Prior to the recorder's report being made, all the prisoners under sentence of death are removed from the day-room at five o'clock in the afternoon, and locked up in these cells, where they are allowed a candle until ten o'clock; and here they remain until seven next morning. When the warrant for a prisoner's execution arrives, he is removed to the cells and confined in one of them until he leaves it for the scaffold. He is at liberty to walk in the yard; but, both in his walks and in his cell, he is constantly attended by a turnkey who never leaves him on any pretence.

We entered the first cell. It was a stone dungeon, eight feet long by six wide, with a bench at the upper end, under which were a common rug, a bible, and prayer-book. An iron candlestick was fixed into the wall at the side; and a small high window in the back admitted as much air and light as could struggle in between a double row of heavy, crossed iron bars. It contained no other furniture of any description.

Conceive the situation of a man, spending his last night on earth in this cell. Buoyed up with some vague and undefined hope of reprieve, he knew not why—indulging in some wild and visionary idea of escaping, he knew not how—hour after hour of the three preceding days allowed him for preparation, has fled with a speed which no man living would deem possible, for none but this dying man can know. He has wearied his friends with entreaties, exhausted the attendants with importunities, neglected in his feverish

8. These two men were executed shortly afterwards. The other was respited during his Majesty's pleasure [Dickens's note].

restlessness the timely warnings of his spiritual consoler; and, now that the illusion is at last dispelled, now that eternity is before him and guilt behind, now that his fears of death amount almost to madness, and an overwhelming sense of his helpless, hopeless state rushes upon him, he is lost and stupified, and has neither thoughts to turn to, nor power to call upon, the Almighty Being, from whom alone he can seek mercy and forgiveness, and before whom his repentance can alone avail.

Hours have glided by, and still he sits upon the same stone bench with folded arms, heedless alike of the fast decreasing time before him, and the urgent entreaties of the good man at his side. The feeble light is wasting gradually, and the deathlike stillness of the street without, broken only by the rumbling of some passing vehicle which echoes mournfully through the empty yards, warns him that the night is waning fast away. The deep bell of St. Paul's strikes—one! He heard it; it has roused him. Seven hours left! He paces the narrow limits of his cell with rapid strides, cold drops of terror starting on his forehead, and every muscle of his frame quivering with agony. Seven hours! He suffers himself to be led to his seat, mechanically takes the bible which is placed in his hand, and tries to read and listen. No: his thoughts will wander. The book is torn and soiled by use—and like the book he read his lessons in, at school, just forty years ago! He has never bestowed a thought upon it, perhaps, since he left it as a child: and yet the place, the time, the room—nay, the very boys he played with, crowd as vividly before him as if they were scenes of yesterday; and some forgotten phrase, some childish word, rings in his ears like the echo of one uttered but a minute since. The voice of the clergyman recalls him to himself. He is reading from the sacred book its solemn promises of pardon for repentance, and its awful denunciation of obdurate men. He falls upon his knees and clasps his hands to pray. Hush! what sound was that? He starts upon his feet. It cannot be two yet. Hark! Two quarters have struck;—the third—the fourth. It is! Six hours left. Tell him not of repentance! Six hours' repentance for eight times six years of guilt and sin! He buries his face in his hands, and throws himself on the bench.

Worn with watching and excitement, he sleeps, and the same unsettled state of mind pursues him in his dreams. An insupportable load is taken from his breast; he is walking with his wife in a pleasant field, with the bright sky above them, and a fresh and boundless prospect on every side—how different from the stone walls of Newgate! She is looking—not as she did when he saw her for the last time in that dreadful place, but as she used when he loved her—long, long ago, before misery and ill-treatment had altered her looks, and vice had changed his nature, and she is leaning upon his arm, and looking up into his face with tenderness and affection—and he does *not* strike her now, nor rudely shake her from him. And oh! how glad he is to tell her all he had forgotten in that last hurried interview, and to fall on his knees before her and fervently beseech her pardon for all the unkindness and cruelty that wasted her form and broke her heart! The scene suddenly changes. He is on his trial again: there are the judge and jury, and prosecutors, and witnesses, just as they were before. How full the court is—what a sea of heads—with a gallows, too, and a scaffold—and how all those people stare at *him*! Verdict, "Guilty." No matter; he will escape.

The night is dark and cold, the gates have been left open, and in an instant he is in the street, flying from the scene of his imprisonment like the wind. The streets are cleared, the open fields are gained and the broad wide country lies before him. Onward he dashes in the midst of darkness, over hedge and ditch, through mud and pool, bounding from spot to spot with a speed and lightness, astonishing even to himself. At length he pauses; he must be safe from pursuit now; he will stretch himself on that bank and sleep till sunrise.

A period of unconsciousness succeeds. He wakes, cold and wretched. The dull gray light of morning is stealing into the cell, and falls upon the form of the attendant turnkey. Confused by his dreams, he starts from his uneasy bed in momentary uncertainty. It is but momentary. Every object in the narrow cell is too frightfully real to admit of doubt or mistake. He is the condemned felon again, guilty and despairing; and in two hours more will be dead.

1835   1836

ROBERT BROWNING
1812–1889

During the years of his marriage Robert Browning was sometimes referred to as "Mrs. Browning's husband." Elizabeth Barrett was at that time a famous poet, whereas her husband was a relatively unknown experimenter whose poems were greeted with misunderstanding or indifference. Not until the 1860s did he at last gain a public and become recognized as the rival or equal of Tennyson. In the twentieth century his reputation has persisted but in an unusual way: his poetry is admired by two groups of readers widely different in tastes. To one group, among whom are the Browning societies that have flourished in England and America, Browning is a wise philosopher and religious teacher who resolved the doubts that had troubled Arnold and Tennyson.

The second group of readers enjoy Browning less for his attempt to solve problems of religious doubt than for his attempt to solve the problems of how poetry should be written. Such poets as Ezra Pound and Robert Lowell have recognized that more than any other nineteenth-century poet, it was Browning who energetically hacked through a trail that has subsequently become the main road of twentieth-century poetry. In *Poetry and the Age* (1953) Randall Jarrell remarked how "the dramatic monologue, which once had depended for its effect upon being a departure from the norm of poetry, now became in one form or another the norm."

The dramatic monologue, as Browning uses it, separates the speaker from the poet in such a way that the reader must work through the words of the speaker to discover the meaning of the poet. For example, in the well-known early monologue *My Last Duchess*, we listen to the duke as he speaks of his dead wife. From his one-sided conversation we piece together the situation, both past and present, and we infer what sort of woman the duchess really was and what sort of man the duke is. Ultimately, we may also infer what the poet himself thinks of the speaker he has created. In this poem, it is fairly easy to reach such a judgment, although the pleasure of the poem results from our reconstruction of a story quite different from the one the duke thinks he is telling. Many of Browning's poems are far less stable, and it is difficult to discern the relationship of the poet to his speaker. In reading *A Gram-*

marian's Funeral, for example, can we be sure that the central character is a hero? Or is he merely a fool? In *"Childe Roland to the Dark Tower Came"* is the speaker describing a phantasmagoric landscape of his own paranoid imagining or is the poem a fable of courage and defiance in a modern wasteland?

In addition to his experiments with the dramatic monologue, Browning also experimented with language and syntax. The grotesque rhymes and jaw-breaking diction that he often employs have been repugnant to some critics; George Santayana, for instance, dismissed him as a clumsy barbarian. But to those who appreciate Browning, the incongruities of language are a humorous and appropriate counterpart to an imperfect world. Ezra Pound's tribute to "Old Hippety-Hop o' the accents," as he addresses Browning, is both affectionate and memorable:

> Heart that was big as the bowels of Vesuvius
> Words that were winged as her sparks in eruption,
> Eagled and thundered as Jupiter Pluvius
> Sound in your wind past all signs o' corruption.

Robert Browning was born in Camberwell, a London suburb. His father, a bank clerk, was a learned man with an extensive library. His mother was a kindly, religious-minded woman, interested in music, whose love for her brilliant son was warmly reciprocated. Until the time of his marriage, at the age of thirty-four, Browning was rarely absent from his parents' home. He attended a boarding school near Camberwell, traveled a little (to Russia and Italy), and was a student at the University of London for a short period, but he preferred to pursue his education at home, where he was tutored in foreign languages, music, boxing, and horsemanship and where he read omnivorously. From this unusual education he acquired a store of knowledge on which to draw for the background of his poems.

The "obscurity" of which his contemporaries complained in his earlier poetry may be partly accounted for by the circumstances of Browning's education, but it also reflects his anxious desire to avoid exposing himself too explicitly before his readers. His first poem, *Pauline,* published when he was twenty-one, had been modeled on the example of Shelley, the most personal of poets. When an otherwise admiring review by John Stuart Mill noted that the young author was afflicted with an "intense and morbid self-consciousness," Browning was overwhelmed with embarrassment. He resolved to avoid confessional writings thereafter.

One way of reducing the personal element in his poetry was to write plays instead of soul-searching narratives or lyrics. In 1836, encouraged by the actor W. C. Macready, Browning began work on his first play, *Strafford,* a historical tragedy that lasted only four nights when it was produced in London in 1837. For ten years, the young writer struggled to write for the theater, but all his stage productions remained failures. Nevertheless, writing dialogue for actors led him to explore another form more congenial to his genius, the dramatic monologue, a form that enabled him through imaginary speakers to avoid explicit autobiography. His first collection of such monologues, *Dramatic Lyrics,* appeared in 1842; but it received no more critical enthusiasm than did his plays.

Browning's resolution to avoid the subjective manner of Shelley did not preclude his being influenced by the earlier poet in other ways. At fourteen, when he first discovered Shelley's works, he became an atheist and liberal. Although he grew away from the atheism, after a struggle, and also the extreme phases of his liberalism, he retained from Shelley's influence something permanent and more difficult to define: an ardent dedication to ideals (often undefined ideals) and an energetic striving toward goals (often undefined goals).

Browning's ardent romanticism also found expression in his love affair with Elizabeth Barrett, which had the dramatic ingredients of Browning's own favorite story of St. George rescuing the maiden from the dragon. Almost everything seemed unpropitious when Browning met Elizabeth Barrett in 1845. She was six years older than he was, a semi-invalid, jealously guarded by her possessively tyrannical father. But love, as the poet was to say later, is best; and love swept aside all obstacles. After their elopement to Italy, the former semi-invalid was soon enjoying good health and a full life. The husband likewise seemed to thrive during the years of this remarkable marriage. His most memorable volume of poems, *Men and Women* (1855), reflects his enjoyment of Italy: its picturesque landscapes and lively street scenes as well as its monuments from the past— its Renaissance past in particular.

The happy fifteen-year sojourn in Italy ended in 1861 with Elizabeth's death. The widower returned to London with his son. During the twenty-eight years remaining to him, the quantity of verse he produced did not diminish. Nor, during the first decade, did it decrease in quality. *Dramatis Personae* (1864) is a volume containing some of his finest monologues, such as *Caliban upon Setebos*. And in 1868 he published his greatest single poem, *The Ring and the Book*, which was inspired by his discovery of an old book of legal records concerning a murder trial in seventeenth-century Rome. His poem tells the story of a brutally sadistic husband, Count Guido Franceschini. The middle-aged Guido grows dissatisfied with his young wife, Pompilia, and accuses her of having adulterous relations with a handsome priest who, like St. George, had tried to rescue her from the dragon's den in which her husband confined her. Eventually Guido stabs his wife to death and is himself executed. In a series of twelve books, Browning retells this tale of violence, presenting it from the contrasting points of view of participants and spectators. Because of its vast scale, *The Ring and the Book* is like a Victorian novel, but in its experiments with multiple points of view it anticipates later novels such as Conrad's *Lord Jim* (1900).

After *The Ring and the Book* several more volumes appeared. In general, Browning's writings during the last two decades of his life suffer from a certain mechanical repetition of mannerism and an excess of argumentation—faults into which he may have been led by the unqualified enthusiasm of his admirers, for it was during this period that he gained his great following. When he died, in 1889, he was buried in Westminster Abbey.

During the London years, Browning became abundantly fond of social life. He dined at the homes of friends and at clubs, where he enjoyed port wine and conversation. He would talk loudly and emphatically about many topics—except his own poetry, about which he was usually reticent.

Despite his bursts of outspokenness, Browning's character seemed, in Hardy's words, "*the* literary puzzle of the nineteenth century." Like Yeats, he was a poet preoccupied with masks. On the occasion of his burial, his friend Henry James reflected that many oddities and many great writers have been buried in Westminster Abbey, "but none of the odd ones have been so great and none of the great ones been so odd."

Just as Browning's character is hard to identify so also are his poems difficult to relate to the age in which they were written. Bishops and painters of the Renaissance, physicians of the Roman Empire, musicians of eighteenth-century Germany—as we explore this gallery of talking portraits we seem to be in a world of time long past, remote from the world of steam engines and disputes about human beings' descent from the ape.

Yet our first impression is misleading. Many of these portraits explore problems that confronted Browning's contemporaries, especially problems of faith and doubt, good and evil, and problems of the function of the artist in modern life. *Caliban upon Setebos*, for example, is a highly topical critique of Darwinism and of natural (as opposed to supernatural) religions. Browning's own attitude toward these topics is partially concealed because of his use of speakers and of settings from earlier ages, yet we do encounter certain recurrent religious assumptions that we can safely assign to the poet himself. The most recurrent is that God has created an imperfect world as a kind of testing ground, a "vale of soul-making," as Keats had said. It followed, for Browning's purposes, that the human soul must be immortal and that heaven itself be perfect. As Abt Vogler affirms: "On the earth the broken arcs; in the heaven, a perfect round." Armed with such a faith, Browning sometimes gives the impression that he was himself untroubled by the doubts that gnawed at the hearts of Arnold and Clough and Tennyson. Yet Browning's apparent optimism is consistently being tested by his bringing to light the evils of human nature. His gallery of villains— murderers, sadistic husbands, mean and petty manipulators—is an extraordinary one. Few writers, in fact, seem to have been more aware of the existence of evil.

A second aspect of Browning's poetry that separates it from the Victorian age is its style. The most representative Victorian poets such as Tennyson and Dante Gabriel Rossetti write in the manner of Keats, Milton, Spenser, and of classical poets such as Virgil. Theirs is the central stylistic tradition in English poetry, one that favors smoothly polished texture, elevated diction and subjects, and pleasing liquidity of sound. Browning draws from a different tradition, more colloquial and discordant, a tradition that includes the poetry of John Donne, the soliloquies of Shakespeare, and certain features of the narrative style of Chaucer. Of most significance are Browning's affinities with Donne. Both poets sacrifice, on occasion, the pleasures of harmony and of a consistent elevation of tone by using a harshly discordant style and unexpected juxtapositions that startle us into an awareness of a world of everyday realities and trivialities. Readers who dislike this kind of poetry in Browning or in Donne argue that it suffers from prosiness. Oscar Wilde once described the novelist George Meredith as "a prose Browning." And so, he added, was Browning. Wilde's joke may help us to relate Browning to his contemporaries. For if Browning seems out of step with other Victorian poets, he is by no means out of step with his contemporaries in prose. The grotesque, which plays such a prominent role in the style and subject matter of Carlyle and Dickens and in the aesthetic theories of John Ruskin, is equally prominent in Browning's verse:

> Fee, faw, fum! bubble and squeak!
> Blessedest Thursday's the fat of the week.
> Rumble and tumble, sleek and rough,
> Stinking and savory, smug and gruff.

Like Carlyle's *Sartor Resartus* these lines from *Holy-Cross Day* present a situation of grave seriousness with noisy jocularity. It was fitting that Browning and Carlyle remained good friends, even though the elder writer kept urging Browning to give up verse in favor of prose.

The link between Browning and the Victorian prose writers is not limited to style. With the later generation of Victorian novelists, George Eliot, George Meredith, and Henry James, Browning shares a central preoccupation. Like Eliot in particular, he was interested in exposing the devious ways in which our minds work and the complexity of our motives. "My stress lay on incidents in the development of a human soul," he wrote; "little else is worth study." His psychological insights can be illustrated in such poems as *The Bishop Orders His Tomb* and *Andrea del Sarto*. Although these are spoken monologues, not inner monologues in the manner of James Joyce, the insight into the workings of the mind is similarly acute. As in reading Joyce, we must be on our guard to follow the rapid shifts of the speakers' mental processes as jumps are made from one cluster of associations to another. A further challenge for the reader of Browning is to identify what has been left out. As was remarked in a letter by the 1890s poet Ernest Dowson, Browning's "masterpieces in verse" demonstrate both "subtlety" and "the tact of omission." *My Last Duchess*, he added, "is pure Henry James."

But Browning's role as a forerunner of twentieth-century literature should not blind us to his essential Victorianism. Energy is the most characteristic aspect of his writing and of the man (Turgenev compared Browning's handshake to an electric shock). Gerard Manley Hopkins described Browning as "a man bouncing up from table with his mouth full of bread and cheese and saying that he meant to stand no blasted nonsense." This buoyancy imparts a creative vitality to all of Browning's writings.

Porphyria's Lover[1]

The rain set early in tonight,
        The sullen wind was soon awake,
It tore the elm-tops down for spite,
        And did its worst to vex the lake:
5   I listened with heart fit to break.
When glided in Porphyria; straight
        She shut the cold out and the storm,
And kneeled and made the cheerless grate
        Blaze up, and all the cottage warm;
10   Which done, she rose, and from her form
Withdrew the dripping cloak and shawl,
        And laid her soiled gloves by, untied
Her hat and let the damp hair fall,
        And, last, she sat down by my side
15   And called me. When no voice replied,
She put my arm about her waist,
        And made her smooth white shoulder bare,
And all her yellow hair displaced,
        And, stooping, made my cheek lie there,
20   And spread, o'er all, her yellow hair,
Murmuring how she loved me—she
        Too weak, for all her heart's endeavor,
To set its struggling passion free
        From pride, and vainer ties dissever,
25   And give herself to me forever.
But passion sometimes would prevail,
        Nor could tonight's gay feast restrain
A sudden thought of one so pale
        For love of her, and all in vain:
30   So, she was come through wind and rain.
Be sure I looked up at her eyes
        Happy and proud; at last I knew
Porphyria worshiped me: surprise
        Made my heart swell, and still it grew
35   While I debated what to do.
That moment she was mine, mine, fair,
        Perfectly pure and good: I found
A thing to do, and all her hair
        In one long yellow string I wound
40   Three times her little throat around,
And strangled her. No pain felt she;
        I am quite sure she felt no pain.

1. One of a pair of monologues originally published under the title *Madhouse Cells,* a title that emphasized the abnormal state of mind of the speaker.

As a shut bud that holds a bee,
    I warily oped her lids: again
45   Laughed the blue eyes without a stain.
And I untightened next the tress
    About her neck; her cheek once more
Blushed bright beneath my burning kiss:
    I propped her head up as before,
50   Only, this time my shoulder bore
Her head, which droops upon it still:
    The smiling rosy little head,
So glad it has its utmost will,
    That all it scorned at once is fled,
55   And I, its love, am gained instead!
Porphyria's love: she guessed not how
    Her darling one wish would be heard.
And thus we sit together now,
    And all night long we have not stirred,
60   And yet God has not said a word!

1834   1836, 1842

Soliloquy of the Spanish Cloister

1

Gr-r-r—there go, my heart's abhorrence!
    Water your damned flowerpots, do!
If hate killed men, Brother Lawrence,
    God's blood, would not mine kill you!
5 What? your myrtle bush wants trimming?
    Oh, that rose has prior claims—
Needs its leaden vase filled brimming?
    Hell dry you up with its flames!

2

At the meal we sit together:
10   *Salve tibi!*[1] I must hear
Wise talk of the kind of weather,
    Sort of season, time of year:
Not a plenteous cork crop: scarcely
    Dare we hope oak-galls,[2] *I doubt:*
15 *What's the Latin name for "parsley"?*
    What's the Greek name for Swine's Snout?[3]

3

Whew! We'll have our platter burnished,
    Laid with care on our own shelf!
With a fire-new spoon we're furnished,

1. Hail to thee! (Latin). This and other speeches in italics in this stanza are the words of Brother Lawrence.

2. Abnormal outgrowths on oak trees, used for tanning.
3. Dandelion (19th-century use).

20   And a goblet for ourself,
     Rinsed like something sacrificial
          Ere 'tis fit to touch our chaps°   *jaws*
     Marked with L. for our initial!
     (He-he! There his lily snaps!)

                    4
25   *Saint*, forsooth! While brown Dolores
          Squats outside the Convent bank
     With Sanchicha, telling stories,
          Steeping tresses in the tank,
     Blue-black, lustrous, thick like horsehairs,
30   —Can't I see his dead eye glow,
     Bright as 'twere a Barbary corsair's?⁴
          (That is, if he'd let it show!)

                    5
     When he finishes refection,°   *dinner*
          Knife and fork he never lays
35   Cross-wise, to my recollection,
          As do I, in Jesu's praise.
     I the Trinity illustrate,
          Drinking watered orange pulp—
     In three sips the Arian⁵ frustrate;
40   While he drains his at one gulp.

                    6
     Oh, those melons? If he's able
          We're to have a feast! so nice!
     One goes to the Abbot's table,
          All of us get each a slice.
45   How go on your flowers? None double?
          Not one fruit-sort can you spy?
     Strange!—And I, too, at such trouble,
          Keep them close-nipped on the sly!

                    7
     There's a great text in Galatians,⁶
50   Once you trip on it, entails
     Twenty-nine distinct damnations,
          One sure, if another fails:
     If I trip him just a-dying,
          Sure of heaven as sure can be,
55   Spin him round and send him flying
          Off to hell, a Manichee?⁷

4. Pirate of the Barbary Coast of northern Africa, renowned for fierceness and lechery.
5. Heretical follower of Arius (256–336), who denied the doctrine of the Trinity.
6. The speaker hopes to obtain Lawrence's damnation by luring him into a heresy, this to be accomplished by exposing him to the difficult task

of interpreting "Galatians" in an unswervingly orthodox way. In Galatians 5.15–23, St. Paul specifies an assortment of "works of the flesh" that lead to damnation, which could make up a total of "twenty-nine" (line 51).
7. A heretic, a follower of Mani (3rd century), Persian prophet.

8

Or, my scrofulous French novel
    On gray paper with blunt type!
Simply glance at it, you grovel
60   Hand and foot in Belial's gripe:
If I double down its pages
    At the woeful sixteenth print,
When he gathers his greengages,
    Ope a sieve and slip it in't?

9

65 Or, there's Satan!—one might venture
    Pledge one's soul to him, yet leave
Such a flaw in the indenture
    As he'd miss till, past retrieve,
Blasted lay that rose-acacia[8]
70   We're so proud of! *Hy, Zy, Hine*[9]
'St, there's Vespers! *Plena gratiâ*
    Ave, Virgo![1] Gr-r-r—you swine!

ca. 1839   1842

My Last Duchess[1]

Ferrara

That's my last Duchess painted on the wall,
Looking as if she were alive. I call
That piece a wonder, now: Frà Pandolf's[2] hands
Worked busily a day, and there she stands.
5 Will 't please you sit and look at her? I said
"Frà Pandolf" by design, for never read
Strangers like you that pictured countenance,
The depth and passion of its earnest glance,
But to myself they turned (since none puts by
10 The curtain I have drawn for you, but I)
And seemed as they would ask me, if they durst,
How such a glance came there; so, not the first
Are you to turn and ask thus. Sir, 'twas not
Her husband's presence only, called that spot
15 Of joy into the Duchess' cheek: perhaps
Frà Pandolf chanced to say "Her mantle laps
Over my lady's wrist too much," or "Paint
Must never hope to reproduce the faint

8. The speaker would pledge his own soul to Satan in return for blasting Lawrence and his "rose-acacia," but the pledge would be so cleverly worded that the speaker himself would not have to pay his debt to Satan. There would be an escape clause ("flaw in the indenture") for himself.
9. Perhaps the opening of a mysterious curse against Lawrence.
1. Full of grace, Hail, Virgin! (Latin). The speaker's twisted state of mind may be reflected in his mixed-up version of the prayer to Mary: "Ave, Maria, gratia plena."
1. The poem is based on incidents in the life of Alfonso II, duke of Ferrara in Italy, whose first wife, Lucrezia, a young woman, died in 1561 after three years of marriage. Following her death, the duke negotiated through an agent to marry a niece of the count of Tyrol. Browning represents the duke as addressing this agent.
2. Brother Pandolf, an imaginary painter.

Half-flush that dies along her throat": such stuff
20 Was courtesy, she thought, and cause enough
For calling up that spot of joy. She had
A heart—how shall I say?—too soon made glad,
Too easily impressed; she liked whate'er
She looked on, and her looks went everywhere.
25 Sir, 'twas all one! My favor at her breast,
The dropping of the daylight in the West,
The bough of cherries some officious fool
Broke in the orchard for her, the white mule
She rode with round the terrace—all and each
30 Would draw from her alike the approving speech,
Or blush, at least. She thanked men—good! but thanked
Somehow—I know not how—as if she ranked
My gift of a nine-hundred-years-old name
With anybody's gift. Who'd stoop to blame
35 This sort of trifling? Even had you skill
In speech—(which I have not)—to make your will
Quite clear to such an one, and say, "Just this
Or that in you disgusts me; here you miss,
Or there exceed the mark"—and if she let
40 Herself be lessoned so, nor plainly set
Her wits to yours, forsooth, and made excuse
—E'en then would be some stooping; and I choose
Never to stoop. Oh sir, she smiled, no doubt,
Whene'er I passed her; but who passed without
45 Much the same smile? This grew; I gave commands;
Then all smiles stopped together. There she stands
As if alive. Will 't please you rise? We'll meet
The company below, then. I repeat,
The Count your master's known munificence
50 Is ample warrant that no just pretense
Of mine for dowry will be disallowed;
Though his fair daughter's self, as I avowed
At starting, is my object. Nay, we'll go
Together down, sir. Notice Neptune, though,
55 Taming a sea horse, thought a rarity,
Which Claus of Innsbruck[3] cast in bronze for me!

1842   1842

The Laboratory

Ancien Régime[1]

I

Now that I, tying thy glass mask tightly,
May gaze thro' these faint smokes curling whitely,

3. An unidentified or imaginary sculptor. The count of Tyrol had his capital at Innsbruck.

1. The regime in France before the Revolution of 1789.

As thou pliest thy trade in this devil's-smithy—
Which is the poison to poison her, prithee?

2

5   He is with her, and they know that I know
Where they are, what they do: they believe my tears flow
While they laugh, laugh at me, at me fled to the drear
Empty church, to pray God in, for them!—I am here.

3

Grind away, moisten and mash up thy paste,
10 Pound at thy powder—I am not in haste!
Better sit thus, and observe thy strange things,
Than go where men wait me and dance at the King's.

4

That in the mortar—you call it a gum?
Ah, the brave tree whence such gold oozings come!
15 And yonder soft phial, the exquisite blue,
Sure to taste sweetly, is that poison too?

5

Had I but all of them, thee and thy treasures,
What a wild crowd of invisible pleasures!
To carry pure death in an earring, a casket,
20 A signet, a fan-mount, a filigree basket!

6

Soon, at the King's,[2] a mere lozenge to give,
And Pauline should have just thirty minutes to live!
But to light a pastile, and Elise, with her head
And her breast and her arms and her hands, should drop dead!

7

25 Quick—is it finished? The color's too grim!
Why not soft like the phial's, enticing and dim?
Let it brighten her drink, let her turn it and stir,
And try it and taste, ere she fix and prefer!

8

What a drop! She's not little, no minion[3] like me!
30 That's why she ensnared him: this never will free
The soul from those masculine eyes—say, "no!"
To that pulse's magnificent come-and-go.

2. Probably King Louis XIV of France (1643–
1715). In the 1670s, a police investigation disclosed that an extraordinary number of women and
men attached to the king's court had been disposing of rivals and enemies by poisonings. Some
thirty-six of the accused courtiers and the dealers
from whom they had purchased poisons were punished by torture and burned to death.
3. A dainty and delicate person.

9

For only last night, as they whispered, I brought
My own eyes to bear on her so, that I thought
35 Could I keep them one half minute fixed, she would fall
Shriveled; she fell not; yet this does it all!

10

Not that I bid you spare her the pain;
Let death be felt and the proof remain:
Brand, burn up, bite into its grace—
40 He is sure to remember her dying face!

11

Is it done? Take my mask off! Nay, be not morose;
It kills her, and this prevents seeing it close:
The delicate droplet, my whole fortune's fee!
If it hurts her, beside, can it ever hurt me?

12

45 Now, take all my jewels, gorge gold to your fill,
You may kiss me, old man, on my mouth if you will!
But brush this dust off me, lest horror it brings
Ere I know it—next moment I dance at the King's!

ca. 1844   1844

The Lost Leader[1]

1

Just for a handful of silver he left us,
    Just for a riband[2] to stick in his coat—
Found the one gift of which fortune bereft us,
    Lost all the others she lets us devote;
5 They, with the gold to give, doled him out silver,
    So much was theirs who so little allowed:
How all our copper had gone for his service!
    Rags—were they purple, his heart had been proud!
We that had loved him so, followed him, honored him,
10   Lived in his mild and magnificent eye,
Learned his great language, caught his clear accents,
    Made him our pattern to live and to die!
Shakespeare was of us, Milton was for us,
    Burns, Shelley, were with us—they watch from their graves!
15 He alone breaks from the van[3] and the freemen
    —He alone sinks to the rear and the slaves!

1. William Wordsworth, who had been an ardent liberal in his youth, had become a political conservative in later years. In old age, when he accepted a grant of money from the government and the office of poet laureate, he alienated some of his young admirers such as Browning, whose liberalism was then as ardent as Wordsworth's had once been.
2. Symbol of the office of poet laureate.
3. Vanguard of the army of liberalism.

2

We shall march prospering—not through his presence;
 Songs may inspirit us—not from his lyre;
Deeds will be done—while he boasts his quiescence,
20 Still bidding crouch whom the rest bade aspire:
Blot out his name, then, record one lost soul more,
 One task more declined, one more footpath untrod,
One more devils'-triumph and sorrow for angels,
 One wrong more to man, one more insult to God!
25 Life's night begins: let him never come back to us!
 There would be doubt, hesitation and pain,
Forced praise on our part—the glimmer of twilight,
 Never glad confident morning again!
Best fight on well, for we taught him—strike gallantly,
30 Menace our heart ere we master his own;
Then let him receive the new knowledge and wait us,
 Pardoned in heaven, the first by the throne!

1843
                    1845

How They Brought the Good News from Ghent to Aix[1]

(16—)

I

I sprang to the stirrup, and Joris, and he;
I galloped, Dirck galloped, we galloped all three;
"Good speed!" cried the watch, as the gate-bolts undrew;
"Speed!" echoed the wall to us galloping through;
5 Behind shut the postern, the lights sank to rest,
And into the midnight we galloped abreast.

2

Not a word to each other; we kept the great pace
Neck by neck, stride by stride, never changing our place;
I turned in my saddle and made its girths tight,
10 Then shortened each stirrup, and set the pique° right, *spur or pommel*
Rebuckled the cheek-strap, chained slacker the bit,
Nor galloped less steadily Roland a whit.

3

'Twas moonset at starting; but while we drew near
Lokeren, the cocks crew and twilight dawned clear;
15 At Boom, a great yellow star came out to see;
At Düffeld, 'twas morning as plain as could be;
And from Mecheln church-steeple we heard the half-chime,
So, Joris broke silence with, "Yet there is time!"

1. The distance between Ghent, in Flanders, and Aix-la-Chapelle is about one hundred miles. Browning said that the incident, occurring during the wars between Flanders and Spain, was an imaginary one. In 1889, Thomas Edison prepared a cylinder recording of Browning's reciting of the opening lines of this poem.

4

At Aershot, up leaped of a sudden the sun,
20   And against him the cattle stood black every one,
To stare through the mist at us galloping past,
And I saw my stout galloper Roland at last,
With resolute shoulders, each butting away
The haze, as some bluff river headland its spray:

5

25   And his low head and crest, just one sharp ear bent back
For my voice, and the other pricked out on his track;
And one eye's black intelligence—ever that glance
O'er its white edge at me, his own master, askance!
And the thick heavy spume-flakes which ay and anon
30   His fierce lips shook upwards in galloping on.

6

By Hasselt, Dirck groaned; and cried Joris, "Stay spur!
Your Roos galloped bravely, the fault's not in her,
We'll remember at Aix"—for one heard the quick wheeze
Of her chest, saw the stretched neck and staggering knees,
35   And sunk tail, and horrible heave of the flank
As down on her haunches she shuddered and sank.

7

So, we were left galloping, Joris and I,
Past Looz and past Tongres, no cloud in the sky;
The broad sun above laughed a pitiless laugh,
40   'Neath our feet broke the brittle bright stubble like chaff;
Till over by Dalhem a dome-spire sprang white,
And "Gallop," gasped Joris, "for Aix is in sight!"

8

"How they'll greet us!"—and all in a moment his roan
Rolled neck and croup over, lay dead as a stone;
45   And there was my Roland to bear the whole weight
Of the news which alone could save Aix from her fate,
With his nostrils like pits full of blood to the brim,
And with circles of red for his eye-sockets' rim.

9

Then I cast loose my buffcoat, each holster let fall,
50   Shook off both my jack boots, let go belt and all,
Stood up in the stirrup, leaned, patted his ear,
Called my Roland his pet name, my horse without peer;
Clapped my hands, laughed and sang, any noise, bad or good,
Till at length into Aix Roland galloped and stood.

10

55   And all I remember is—friends flocking round
As I sat with his head 'twixt my knees on the ground;

And no voice but was praising this Roland of mine,
As I poured down his throat our last measure of wine,
Which (the burgesses voted by common consent)
60 Was no more than his due who brought good news from Ghent.

ca. 1844   1845

Home-Thoughts, from Abroad

1

Oh, to be in England
Now that April's there,
And whoever wakes in England
Sees, some morning, unaware,
5 That the lowest boughs and the brushwood sheaf
Round the elm-tree bole are in tiny leaf,
While the chaffinch sings on the orchard bough
In England—now!

2

And after April, when May follows,
10 And the whitethroat builds, and all the swallows!
Hark, where my blossomed peartree in the hedge
Leans to the field and scatters on the clover
Blossoms and dewdrops—at the bent spray's edge—
That's the wise thrush; he sings each song twice over,
15 Lest you should think he never could recapture
The first fine careless rapture!
And though the fields look rough with hoary dew,
All will be gay when noontide wakes anew
The buttercups, the little children's dower
20 —Far brighter than this gaudy melon-flower!

ca. 1845   1845

Home-Thoughts, from the Sea

Nobly, nobly Cape Saint Vincent[1] to the northwest died away;
Sunset ran, one glorious blood-red, reeking into Cadiz Bay;
Bluish 'mid the burning water, full in face Trafalgar[2] lay;
In the dimmest northeast distance dawned Gibraltar grand and gray;
5 "Here and here did England help me: how can I help England?"—say,
Whoso turns as I, this evening, turn to God to praise and pray,
While Jove's planet° rises yonder, silent over Africa.   Jupiter

1844   1845

1. Off the coast of Portugal, scene of British naval   2. A cape in Spain, where Nelson won his great
victory under Commodore Nelson (1797).   victory over Napoleon's fleets (1805).

The Bishop Orders His Tomb at Saint Praxed's Church[1]

Rome, 15—

Vanity, saith the preacher, vanity![2]
Draw round my bed: is Anselm keeping back?
Nephews—sons mine . . . ah God, I know not! Well—
She, men would have to be your mother once,
5 Old Gandolf envied me, so fair she was!
What's done is done, and she is dead beside,
Dead long ago, and I am Bishop since,
And as she died so must we die ourselves,
And thence ye may perceive the world's a dream.
10 Life, how and what is it? As here I lie
In this state chamber, dying by degrees,
Hours and long hours in the dead night, I ask
"Do I live, am I dead?" Peace, peace seems all.
Saint Praxed's ever was the church for peace;
15 And so, about this tomb of mine. I fought
With tooth and nail to save my niche, ye know:
—Old Gandolf cozened° me, despite my care;   *cheated*
Shrewd was that snatch from out the corner south
He graced his carrion with, God curse the same!
20 Yet still my niche is not so cramped but thence
One sees the pulpit o' the epistle side,[3]
And somewhat of the choir, those silent seats,
And up into the aery dome where live
The angels, and a sunbeam's sure to lurk:
25 And I shall fill my slab of basalt[4] there,
And 'neath my tabernacle[5] take my rest,
With those nine columns round me, two and two,
The odd one at my feet where Anselm stands:
Peach-blossom marble all, the rare, the ripe
30 As fresh-poured red wine of a mighty pulse.[6]
—Old Gandolf with his paltry onion-stone,[7]

1. In *Fra Lippo Lippi*, Browning represents the dawn of the Renaissance in Italy, with its fresh zest for human experiences in this world. In this monologue, he portrays a later stage of the Renaissance when such worldliness, full-blown, had infected some of the leading clergy of Italy. Browning's portrait of the dying bishop is, however, not primarily a satire against corruption in the church. It is a brilliant exposition of the workings of a mind, a mind that has been conditioned by special historical circumstances. The Victorian historian of art John Ruskin said of this poem:

I know of no other piece of modern English, prose or poetry, in which there is so much told, as in these lines, of the Renaissance spirit—its worldliness, inconsistency, pride, hypocrisy, ignorance of itself, love of art, of luxury, and of good Latin. It is nearly all that I have said of the central Renaissance in thirty pages of the *Stones of Venice*, put into as many lines, Browning's

also being the antecedent work.

St. Praxed's Church was named in honor of St. Praxedes, a Roman virgin of the 2nd century who gave her riches to poor Christians. Both the bishop and his predecessor, Gandolf, are imaginary persons.
2. Cf. Ecclesiastes 1.2.
3. The Epistles of the New Testament are read from the right-hand side of the altar (as one faces it).
4. Dark-colored igneous rock.
5. Stone canopy or tentlike roof, presumably supported by the "nine columns" under which the sculptured effigy of the bishop would lie on the "slab of basalt."
6. Browning uses "pulse" in the special sense of a pulpy mash of fermented grapes from which a strong wine might be poured off.
7. An inferior marble that peels in layers.

Put me where I may look at him! True peach,
Rosy and flawless: how I earned the prize!
Draw close: that conflagration of my church
35 —What then? So much was saved if aught were missed!
My sons, ye would not be my death? Go dig
The white-grape vineyard where the oil-press stood,
Drop water gently till the surface sink,
And if ye find . . . Ah God, I know not, I! . . .
40 Bedded in store of rotten fig leaves soft,
And corded up in a tight olive-frail,[8]
Some lump, ah God, of *lapis lazuli*,[9]
Big as a jew's head cut off at the nape,[1]
Blue as a vein o'er the Madonna's breast . . .
45 Sons, all have I bequeathed you, villas, all,
That brave Frascati[2] villa with its bath,
So, let the blue lump poise between my knees,
Like God the Father's globe on both his hands
Ye worship in the Jesu Church[3] so gay,
50 For Gandolf shall not choose but see and burst!
Swift as a weaver's shuttle fleet our years:[4]
Man goeth to the grave, and where is he?
Did I say basalt for my slab, sons? Black[5]—
'Twas ever antique-black I meant! How else
55 Shall ye contrast my frieze[6] to come beneath?
The bas-relief[7] in bronze ye promised me,
Those Pans and Nymphs ye wot of, and perchance
Some tripod, thyrsus, with a vase or so,
The Saviour at his sermon on the mount,
60 Saint Praxed in a glory, and one Pan
Ready to twitch the Nymph's last garment off,
And Moses with the tables[8] . . . but I know
Ye mark me not! What do they whisper thee,
Child of my bowels, Anselm? Ah, ye hope
65 To revel down my villas while I gasp
Bricked o'er with beggar's moldy travertine°   *Italian limestone*
Which Gandolf from his tomb-top chuckles at!
Nay, boys, ye love me—all of jasper, then!
'Tis jasper ye stand pledged to, lest I grieve
70 My bath must needs be left behind, alas!
One block, pure green as a pistachio nut,
There's plenty jasper somewhere in the world—
And have I not Saint Praxed's ear to pray

---

8. Basket for holding olives.
9. Valuable bright blue stone.
1. Perhaps a reference to the head of John the Baptist, cut off at the request of Salomé.
2. Suburb of Rome, used as a resort by wealthy Italians.
3. Il Gesù, a Jesuit church in Rome. In a chapel in this church the figure of an angel (rather than God) holds a huge lump of lapis lazuli in his hands.
4. Cf. Job 7.6.
5. I.e., black marble.
6. Continuous band of sculpture.
7. Sculpture in which the figures do not project far from the background surface.
8. Sculpture in which the figures do not project far from the background surface. The sculpture would consist of a mixture of pagan and Christian iconography. "Tripod": seat on which the Oracle of Delphi made prophecies. "Thyrsus": a long staff carried in processions in honor of Bacchus, the god of wine. "Glory": halo. "Tables": the stone tablets on which the Ten Commandments were written. Such intermingling of pagan and Christian traditions, characteristic of the Renaissance, had been attacked in 1841 in *Contrasts*, a book on architecture by A. W. Pugin, a Roman Catholic.

Horses for ye, and brown Greek manuscripts,
75 And mistresses with great smooth marbly limbs?
—That's if ye carve my epitaph aright,
Choice Latin, picked phrase, Tully's[9] every word,
No gaudy ware like Gandolf's second line—
Tully, my masters? Ulpian[1] serves his need!
80 And then how I shall lie through centuries,
And hear the blessed mutter of the mass,
And see God made and eaten all day long,[2]
And feel the steady candle flame, and taste
Good strong thick stupefying incense-smoke!
85 For as I lie here, hours of the dead night,
Dying in state and by such slow degrees,
I fold my arms as if they clasped a crook,°   *bishop's staff*
And stretch my feet forth straight as stone can point,
And let the bedclothes, for a mortcloth,[3] drop
90 Into great laps and folds of sculptor's-work:
And as yon tapers dwindle, and strange thoughts
Grow, with a certain humming in my ears,
About the life before I lived this life,
And this life too, popes, cardinals, and priests,
95 Saint Praxed at his sermon on the mount,[4]
Your tall pale mother with her talking eyes,
And new-found agate urns as fresh as day,
And marble's language, Latin pure, discreet
—Aha, ELUCESCEBAT[5] quoth our friend?
100 No Tully, said I, Ulpian at the best!
Evil and brief hath been my pilgrimage.[6]
All *lapis*, all, sons! Else I give the Pope
My villas! Will ye ever eat my heart?
Ever your eyes were as a lizard's quick,
105 They glitter like your mother's for my soul,
Or ye would heighten my impoverished frieze,
Piece out its starved design, and fill my vase
With grapes, and add a vizor and a Term,[7]
And to the tripod ye would tie a lynx
110 That in his struggle throws the thyrsus down,
To comfort me on my entablature[8]
Whereon I am to lie till I must ask
"Do I live, am I dead?" There, leave me, there!
For ye have stabbed me with ingratitude
115 To death—ye wish it—God, ye wish it! Stone—
Gritstone,[9] a-crumble! Clammy squares which sweat

9. I.e., Marcus Tullius Cicero, whose writing was the model, during the Renaissance, of classical Latin prose.
1. Late Latin prose writer, not a model of good style.
2. Reference to the doctrine of transubstantiation.
3. Rich cloth spread over a dead body or coffin.
4. The bishop is confusing St. Praxed (a woman) with Christ—an indication that his mind is wandering.
5. He was illustrious (Latin); word from Gandolf's

epitaph. The bishop considers the form of the verb to be in "gaudy" bad taste (line 78). If the epitaph had been copied from Cicero instead of from Ulpian, the word would have been *elucebat*.
6. Cf. Genesis 47.9.
7. Statue of Terminus, the Roman god of boundaries, usually represented without arms. "Vizor": part of a helmet, often represented in sculpture.
8. Horizontal platform supporting a statue or effigy.
9. Coarse sandstone.

As if the corpse they keep were oozing through—
And no more *lapis* to delight the world!
Well go! I bless ye. Fewer tapers there,
120 But in a row: and, going, turn your backs
—Aye, like departing altar-ministrants,
And leave me in my church, the church for peace,
That I may watch at leisure if he leers—
Old Gandolf, at me, from his onion-stone,
125 As still he envied me, so fair she was!

1844   1845

Meeting at Night[1]

1

The gray sea and the long black land;
And the yellow half-moon large and low;
And the startled little waves that leap
In fiery ringlets from their sleep,
5 As I gain the cove with pushing prow,
And quench its speed i' the slushy sand.

2

Then a mile of warm sea-scented beach;
Three fields to cross till a farm appears;
A tap at the pane, the quick sharp scratch
10 And blue spurt of a lighted match,
And a voice less loud, through its joys and fears,
Than the two hearts beating each to each!

1845

Parting at Morning

Round the cape of a sudden came the sea,
And the sun looked over the mountain's rim:
And straight was a path of gold for him,°   *the sun*
And the need of a world of men for me.

1845

---

1. This poem and the one that follows it appeared originally under the single title *Night and Morning*. The speaker in both is a man.

A Toccata of Galuppi's[1]

I

Oh, Galuppi, Baldassaro, this is very sad to find!
I can hardly misconceive you; it would prove me deaf and blind;
But although I take your meaning, 'tis with such a heavy mind!

2

Here you come with your old music, and here's all the good it brings.
5   What, they lived once thus at Venice where the merchants were the kings,
Where Saint Mark's is, where the Doges used to wed the sea with rings?[2]

3

Aye, because the sea's the street there; and 'tis arched by . . . what you call
. . . Shylock's bridge[3] with houses on it, where they kept the carnival:
I was never out of England—it's as if I saw it all.

4

10 Did young people take their pleasure when the sea was warm in May?
Balls and masks° begun at midnight, burning ever to midday,   *masquerades*
When they made up fresh adventures for the morrow, do you say?

5

Was a lady such a lady, cheeks so round and lips so red—
On her neck the small face buoyant, like a bellflower on its bed,
15 O'er the breast's superb abundance where a man might base his head?

6

Well, and it was graceful of them—they'd break talk off and afford
—She, to bite her mask's black velvet—he, to finger on his sword,
While you sat and played toccatas, stately at the clavichord?[4]

7

What? Those lesser thirds so plaintive, sixths diminished, sigh on sigh,
20 Told them something? Those suspensions, those solutions—"Must we die?"
Those commiserating sevenths—"Life might last! we can but try!"

1. There are three speakers in this short poem. The first is a 19th-century scientist in England who is listening to a musical composition by Baldassaro Galuppi (1706–1785), a Venetian. The music evokes for this scientist the voice of the dead composer (the third speaker) who comments on the pointless and butterfly-like frivolity of his 18th-century contemporaries. The second group of voices is made up of comments by members of Galuppi's audience as they respond to the different moods of his clavichord playing during a party that the scientist imagines to have taken place in Venice. "Toccata": according to *Grove's Dictionary of Music*, a "touch-piece, or a composition intended to exhibit the touch and execution of the performer." The same authority states that "no particular composition was taken as the basis of the poem."
2. An annual ceremony in which the doge, the Venetian chief magistrate, threw a ring into the water to symbolize the bond between his city, with its maritime empire, and the sea.
3. The Rialto, a bridge over the Grand Canal.
4. A keyboard instrument in which the strings are struck by metal hammers. As a mechanism, it resembles a piano, but the sound is more like that of a harpsichord.

8

"Were you happy?"—"Yes."—"And are you still as happy?"—"Yes. And you?"
—"Then, more kisses!"—"Did *I* stop them, when a million seemed so few?"
Hark, the dominant's persistence till it must be answered to!

9

25 So, an octave struck the answer.[5] Oh, they praised you, I dare say!
"Brave Galuppi! that was music; good alike at grave and gay!
I can always leave off talking when I hear a master play!"

10

Then they left you for their pleasure: till in due time, one by one,
Some with lives that came to nothing, some with deeds as well undone,
30 Death stepped tacitly and took them where they never see the sun.

11

But when I sit down to reason, think to take my stand nor swerve,
While I triumph o'er a secret wrung from nature's close reserve,
In you come with your cold music till I creep through every nerve.

12

Yes, you, like a ghostly cricket, creaking where a house was burned:
35 "Dust and ashes, dead and done with, Venice spent what Venice earned.
The soul, doubtless, is immortal—where a soul can be discerned.

13

"Yours for instance: you know physics, something of geology,
Mathematics are your pastime; souls shall rise in their degree;
Butterflies may dread extinction—you'll not die, it cannot be!

14

40 "As for Venice and her people, merely born to bloom and drop,
Here on earth they bore their fruitage, mirth and folly were the crop:
What of soul was left, I wonder, when the kissing had to stop?

15

"Dust and ashes!" So you creak it, and I want° the heart to scold.   lack
Dear dead women, with such hair, too—what's become of all the gold
45 Used to hang and brush their bosoms? I feel chilly and grown old.

ca. 1847   1855

---

5. The terms in these lines refer to the technical devices used by Galuppi to produce alternating moods in his music, conflict in each instance being resolved into harmony. Thus the "dominant" (the fifth note of the scale), after being persistently sounded, is answered by a resolving chord (lines 24–25).

Memorabilia[1]

1

Ah, did you once see Shelley plain,
    And did he stop and speak to you
And did you speak to him again?
    How strange it seems and new!

2

5 But you were living before that,
    And also you are living after;
And the memory I started at—
    My starting moves your laughter.

3

I crossed a moor, with a name of its own
10   And a certain use in the world no doubt,
Yet a hand's-breadth of it shines alone
    'Mid the blank miles round about:

4

For there I picked up on the heather
    And there I put inside my breast
15 A molted feather, an eagle feather!
    Well, I forget the rest.

ca. 1851   1855

Love among the Ruins[1]

1

Where the quiet-colored end of evening smiles,
    Miles and miles
On the solitary pastures where our sheep
    Half-asleep
5 Tinkle homeward through the twilight, stray or stop
    As they crop—
Was the site once of a city great and gay
    (So they say),
Of our country's very capital, its prince
10   Ages since
Held his court in, gathered councils, wielding far
    Peace or war.

1. Things worth remembering. Browning reports that he once met a stranger in a bookstore who mentioned having talked with Shelley. "Suddenly the stranger paused, and burst into laughter as he observed me staring at him with blanched face. . . . I still vividly remember how strangely the presence of a man who had seen and spoken with Shelley affected me."

1. The ruins may be those of such cities as Babylon and Nineveh or the site of the Circus Maximus in Rome. The unusual stanza used in this poem was invented by Browning. The contrast between past and present, which is the core of the poem, is reinforced by devoting one half of each stanza to the past and the other half to the present.

2

Now—the country does not even boast a tree,
    As you see,
15 To distinguish slopes of verdure, certain rills
    From the hills
Intersect and give a name to (else they run
    Into one),
Where the domed and daring palace shot its spires
20   Up like fires
O'er the hundred-gated circuit of a wall
    Bounding all,
Made of marble, men might march on nor be pressed,
    Twelve abreast.

3

25 And such plenty and perfection, see, of grass
    Never was!
Such a carpet as, this summertime, o'erspreads
    And embeds
Every vestige of the city, guessed alone,
30   Stock or stone—
Where a multitude of men breathed joy and woe
    Long ago;
Lust of glory pricked their hearts up, dread of shame
    Struck them tame;
35 And that glory and that shame alike, the gold
    Bought and sold.

4

Now—the single little turret that remains
    On the plains,
By the caper overrooted, by the gourd
40   Overscored,
While the patching houseleek's[2] head of blossom winks
    Through the chinks—
Marks the basement whence a tower in ancient time
    Sprang sublime,
45 And a burning ring, all round, the chariots traced
    As they raced,
And the monarch and his minions and his dames
    Viewed the games.

5

And I know, while thus the quiet-colored eve
50   Smiles to leave
To their folding, all our many-tinkling fleece
    In such peace,
And the slopes and rills in undistinguished gray
    Melt away—
55 That a girl with eager eyes and yellow hair
    Waits me there

---

2. Common European plant, with petals clustered in the shape of rosettes.

In the turret whence the charioteers caught soul
    For the goal,
When the king looked, where she looks now, breathless, dumb
60   Till I come.

6

But he looked upon the city, every side,
    Far and wide,
All the mountains topped with temples, all the glades'
    Colonnades,
65 All the causeys,[3] bridges, aqueducts—and then,
    All the men!
When I do come, she will speak not, she will stand,
    Either hand
On my shoulder, give her eyes the first embrace
70   Of my face,
Ere we rush, ere we extinguish sight and speech
    Each on each.

7

In one year they sent a million fighters forth
    South and north,
75 And they built their gods a brazen pillar high
    As the sky,
Yet reserved a thousand chariots in full force—
    Gold, of course.
Oh heart! oh blood that freezes, blood that burns!
80   Earth's returns
For whole centuries of folly, noise, and sin!
    Shut them in,
With their triumphs and their glories and the rest!
    Love is best.

1853   1855

"Childe Roland to the Dark Tower Came"[1]

(See Edgar's Song in "Lear")

I

My first thought was, he lied in every word,
   That hoary cripple, with malicious eye

---

3. Causeways or roads raised above low ground.
1. Browning stated that this poem "came upon me as a kind of dream," and that it was written in one day. Although the poem was among those of his own writings that pleased him most, he was reluctant to explain what the dream (or nightmare) signified. He once agreed with a friend's suggestion that the meaning might be expressed in the statement: "He that endureth to the end shall be saved." Most readers have responded to the poem in this way, finding in the story of Roland's quest an inspiring expression of defiance and courage. Other readers find the poem to be more expressive of despair than of enduring hope, and it is at least true that the landscape is as grim and nightmare-

like as in such 20th-century writings as T. S. Eliot's *Hollow Men* or Franz Kafka's *Penal Colony*. It has been said of *"Childe Roland"* that every reader can be his own allegorist.

The lines from Shakespeare's *King Lear* 3.4 (lines 163–65), from which the title is taken, are spoken when Lear is about to enter a hovel on the heath, and Edgar, feigning madness, chants the fragment of a song reminiscent of quests and challenges in fairy tales: "Child Rowland to the dark tower came, / His word was still,—Fie, foh, and fum, / I smell the blood of a British man." "Childe": a youth of gentle birth, usually a candidate for knighthood.

Askance° to watch the working of his lie   *squinting sidewise*
On mine, and mouth scarce able to afford
5   Suppression of the glee, that pursed and scored
        Its edge, at one more victim gained thereby.

2

What else should he be set for, with his staff?
        What, save to waylay with his lies, ensnare
        All travelers who might find him posted there,
10   And ask the road? I guessed what skull-like laugh
Would break, what crutch 'gin write my epitaph
        For pastime in the dusty thoroughfare,

3

If at his counsel I should turn aside
        Into that ominous tract which, all agree,
15   Hides the Dark Tower. Yet acquiescingly
I did turn as he pointed: neither pride
Nor hope rekindling at the end descried,
        So much as gladness that some end might be.

4

For, what with my whole world-wide wandering,
20   What with my search drawn out through years, my hope
        Dwindled into a ghost not fit to cope
With that obstreperous joy success would bring,
I hardly tried now to rebuke the spring
        My heart made, finding failure in its scope.

5

25   As when a sick man very near to death
        Seems dead indeed, and feels begin and end
        The tears and takes the farewell of each friend,
And hears one bid the other go, draw breath
Freelier outside ("since all is o'er," he saith,
30   "And the blow fallen no grieving can amend"),

6

While some discuss if near the other graves
        Be room enough for this, and when a day
        Suits best for carrying the corpse away,
With care about the banners, scarves and staves:
35   And still the man hears all, and only craves
        He may not shame such tender love and stay.

7

Thus, I had so long suffered in this quest,
        Heard failure prophesied so oft, been writ
        So many times among "The Band"—to wit,
40   The knights who to the Dark Tower's search addressed

Their steps—that just to fail as they, seemed best,
And all the doubt was now—should I be fit?

8

So, quiet as despair, I turned from him,
    That hateful cripple, out of his highway
45   Into the path he pointed. All the day
Had been a dreary one at best, and dim
Was settling to its close, yet shot one grim
    Red leer to see the plain catch its estray.[2]

9

For mark! no sooner was I fairly found
50   Pledged to the plain, after a pace or two,
    Than, pausing to throw backward a last view
O'er the safe road, 'twas gone; gray plain all round:
Nothing but plain to the horizon's bound.
    I might go on; naught else remained to do.

10

55 So, on I went. I think I never saw
    Such starved ignoble nature; nothing throve:
    For flowers—as well expect a cedar grove!
But, cockle, spurge,[3] according to their law
Might propagate their kind, with none to awe,
60   You'd think; a burr had been a treasure trove.

11

No! penury, inertness and grimace,
    In some strange sort, were the land's portion. "See
    Or shut your eyes," said Nature peevishly,
"It nothing skills: I cannot help my case;
65   'Tis the Last Judgment's fire must cure this place,
    Calcine[4] its clods and set my prisoners free."

12

If there pushed any ragged thistle stalk
    Above its mates, the head was chopped; the bents[5]
    Were jealous else. What made those holes and rents
70 In the dock's° harsh swarth leaves, bruised as to balk   *coarse plant*
All hope of greenness? 'tis a brute must walk
    Pashing their life out, with a brute's intents.

13

As for the grass, it grew as scant as hair
    In leprosy; thin dry blades pricked the mud

2. Literally, a domestic animal that has strayed
away from its home.
3. A bitter-juiced weed. "Cockle": a weed that
bears burrs.
4. Turn to powder by heat.
5. Coarse, stiff grasses.

75　　　Which underneath looked kneaded up with blood.
　　One stiff blind horse, his every bone a-stare,
　　Stood stupefied, however he came there:
　　　　Thrust out past service from the devil's stud!

14

　　Alive? he might be dead for aught I know,
80　　　With that red gaunt and colloped° neck a-strain,　　　　　*ridged*
　　　And shut eyes underneath the rusty mane;
　　Seldom went such grotesqueness with such woe;
　　I never saw a brute I hated so;
　　　　He must be wicked to deserve such pain.

15

85　I shut my eyes and turned them on my heart.
　　　As a man calls for wine before he fights,
　　　I asked one draught of earlier, happier sights,
　　Ere fitly I could hope to play my part.
　　Think first, fight afterwards—the soldier's art:
90　　　One taste of the old time sets all to rights.

16

　　Not it! I fancied Cuthbert's reddening face
　　　Beneath its garniture of curly gold,
　　　Dear fellow, till I almost felt him fold
　　An arm in mine to fix me to the place,
95　That way he used. Alas, one night's disgrace!
　　　Out went my heart's new fire and left it cold.

17

　　Giles then, the soul of honor—there he stands
　　　Frank as ten years ago when knighted first.
　　　What honest man should dare (he said) he durst.
100　Good—but the scene shifts—faugh! what hangman hands
　　Pin to his breast a parchment? His own bands
　　　Read it. Poor traitor, spit upon and cursed!

18

　　Better this present than a past like that;
　　　Back therefore to my darkening path again!
105　　　No sound, no sight as far as eye could strain.
　　Will the night send a howlet° or a bat?　　　　　*owl*
　　I asked: when something on the dismal flat
　　　Came to arrest my thoughts and change their train.

19

　　A sudden little river crossed my path
110　　　As unexpected as a serpent comes.
　　　No sluggish tide congenial to the glooms;
　　This, as it frothed by, might have been a bath

For the fiend's glowing hoof—to see the wrath
Of its black eddy bespate° with flakes and spumes.   *bespattered*

20

115 So petty yet so spiteful! All along,
  Low scrubby alders kneeled down over it;
  Drenched willows flung them headlong in a fit
Of mute despair, a suicidal throng:
The river which had done them all the wrong,
120   Whate'er that was, rolled by, deterred no whit.

21

Which, while I forded—good saints, how I feared
  To set my foot upon a dead man's cheek,
  Each step, or feel the spear I thrust to seek
For hollows, tangled in his hair or beard!
125 —It may have been a water rat I speared,
  But, ugh! it sounded like a baby's shriek.

22

Glad was I when I reached the other bank.
  Now for a better country. Vain presage!
  Who were the strugglers, what war did they wage,
130 Whose savage trample thus could pad the dank
Soil to a plash? Toads in a poisoned tank,
  Or wild cats in a red-hot iron cage—

23

The fight must so have seemed in that fell cirque.°   *dreadful arena*
  What penned them there, with all the plain to choose?
135   No footprint leading to that horrid mews,[6]
None out of it. Mad brewage set to work
Their brains, no doubt, like galley slaves the Turk
  Pits for his pastime, Christians against Jews.

24

And more than that—a furlong on—why, there!
140   What bad use was that engine for, that wheel,
  Or brake,[7] not wheel—that harrow fit to reel
Men's bodies out like silk? with all the air
Of Tophet's° tool, on earth left unaware,   *Hell's*
  Or brought to sharpen its rusty teeth of steel.

25

145 Then came a bit of stubbed ground, once a wood,
  Next a marsh, it would seem, and now mere earth
  Desperate and done with; (so a fool finds mirth,

6. Enclosed stable yard.
7. A toothed machine used for separating the
fibers of flax or hemp; here an instrument of torture.

Makes a thing and then mars it, till his mood
Changes and off he goes!) within a rood[8]
150   Bog, clay and rubble, sand and stark black dearth.

26

Now blotches rankling, colored gay and grim,
      Now patches where some leanness of the soil's
      Broke into moss or substances like boils;
Then came some palsied oak, a cleft in him
155 Like a distorted mouth that splits its rim
      Gaping at death, and dies while it recoils.

27

And just as far as ever from the end!
      Naught in the distance but the evening, naught
      To point my footstep further! At the thought,
160 A great black bird, Apollyon's[9] bosom friend,
      Sailed past, nor beat his wide wing dragon-penned[1]
      That brushed my cap—perchance the guide I sought.

28

For, looking up, aware I somehow grew,
      'Spite of the dusk, the plain had given place
165   All round to mountains—with such name to grace
Mere ugly heights and heaps now stolen in view.
      How thus they had surprised me—solve it, you!
      How to get from them was no clearer case.

29

Yet half I seemed to recognize some trick
170   Of mischief happened to me, God knows when—
      In a bad dream perhaps. Here ended, then,
Progress this way. When, in the very nick
Of giving up, one time more, came a click
      As when a trap shuts—you're inside the den!

30

175 Burningly it came on me all at once,
      This was the place! those two hills on the right,
      Crouched like two bulls locked horn in horn in fight;
While to the left, a tall scalped mountain . . . Dunce,
Dotard, a-dozing at the very nonce,°   moment
180   After a life spent training for the sight!

31

What in the midst lay but the Tower itself?
      The round squat turret, blind as the fool's heart,[2]

---

8. Quarter acre of land.
9. In Revelation 9.11 Apollyon is "the angel of the bottomless pit." In Bunyan's *Pilgrim's Progress*, he is a hideous "monster"; "he had wings like a

dragon."
1. With wings or pinions like those of a dragon.
2. Cf. Psalm 14.1: "The fool hath said in his heart, There is no God."

Built of brown stone, without a counterpart
In the whole world. The tempest's mocking elf
185   Points to the shipman thus the unseen shelf
He strikes on, only when the timbers start.

32

Not see? because of night perhaps?—why, day
Came back again for that! before it left,
The dying sunset kindled through a cleft:
190   The hills, like giants at a hunting, lay,
Chin upon hand, to see the game at bay—
"Now stab and end the creature—to the heft!"[3]

33

Not hear? when noise was everywhere! it tolled
Increasing like a bell. Names in my ears
195   Of all the lost adventurers my peers—
How such a one was strong, and such was bold,
And such was fortunate, yet each of old
Lost, lost! one moment knelled the woe of years.

34

There they stood, ranged along the hillsides, met
200   To view the last of me, a living frame
For one more picture! in a sheet of flame
I saw them and I knew them all. And yet
Dauntless the slug-horn[4] to my lips I set,
And blew. *"Childe Roland to the Dark Tower came."*

1852   1855

Fra Lippo Lippi[1]

I am poor brother Lippo, by your leave!
You need not clap your torches to my face.
Zooks,[2] what's to blame? you think you see a monk!
What, 'tis past midnight, and you go the rounds,
5   And here you catch me at an alley's end
Where sportive ladies leave their doors ajar?
The Carmine's[3] my cloister: hunt it up,
Do—harry out, if you must show your zeal,

---

3. Handle of dagger or sword.
4. The war cry or slogan of a clan about to engage in battle (Scottish). In 1770, however, the poet Chatterton was misled into using it to mean a kind of trumpet or horn. Browning followed Chatterton's example, although the original meaning would also be relevant here.
1. This monologue portrays the dawn of the Renaissance in Italy at a point when the medieval attitude toward life and art was about to be displaced by a fresh appreciation of earthly pleasures. It was from Giorgio Vasari's *Lives of the Painters*

that Browning derived most of his information about the life of the Florentine painter and friar Lippo Lippi (1406–1469), but the theory of art propounded by Lippi in the poem was developed by the poet himself.
2. A shortened version of *Gadzooks,* a mild oath now obscure in meaning but perhaps resembling a phrase still in use: "God's truth."
3. Santa Maria del Carmine, a church and cloister of the Carmelite order of friars to which Lippi belonged.

Whatever rat, there, haps on his wrong hole,
10 And nip each softling of a wee white mouse,
Weke, weke, that's crept to keep him company!
Aha, you know your betters! Then, you'll take
Your hand away that's fiddling on my throat,
And please to know me likewise. Who am I?
15 Why, one, sir, who is lodging with a friend
Three streets off—he's a certain . . . how d'ye call?
Master—a . . . Cosimo of the Medici,⁴
I' the house that caps the corner. Boh! you were best!
Remember and tell me, the day you're hanged,
20 How you affected such a gullet's gripe!⁵
But you,⁶ sir, it concerns you that your knaves
Pick up a manner nor discredit you:
Zooks, are we pilchards,° that they sweep the streets   *small fish*
And count fair prize what comes into this net?
25 He's Judas to a tittle, that man is!⁷
Just such a face! Why, sir, you make amends.
Lord, I'm not angry! Bid your hangdogs go
Drink out this quarter-florin to the health
Of the munificent House that harbors me
30 (And many more beside, lads! more beside!)
And all's come square again. I'd like his face—
His, elbowing on his comrade in the door
With the pike and lantern—for the slave that holds
John Baptist's head a-dangle by the hair
35 With one hand ("Look you, now," as who should say)
And his weapon in the other, yet unwiped!
It's not your chance to have a bit of chalk,
A wood-coal or the like? or you should see!
Yes, I'm the painter, since you style me so.
40 What, brother Lippo's doings, up and down,
You know them and they take you? like enough!
I saw the proper twinkle in your eye—
'Tell you, I liked your looks at very first.
Let's sit and set things straight now, hip to haunch.
45 Here's spring come, and the nights one makes up bands
To roam the town and sing out carnival,⁸
And I've been three weeks shut within my mew,°   *private den*
A-painting for the great man, saints and saints
And saints again. I could not paint all night—
50 Ouf! I leaned out of window for fresh air.
There came a hurry of feet and little feet,
A sweep of lute-strings, laughs, and whiffs of song—
Flower o' the broom,
Take away love, and our earth is a tomb!
55 *Flower o' the quince,*
*I let Lisa go, and what good in life since?*⁹

4. Lippi's patron, banker and virtual ruler of Florence.
5. I.e., how you had the arrogance to choke the gullet of someone with my connections.
6. The officer in charge of the patrol of policemen or watchmen.
7. I.e., one of the watchmen has a face that would serve as a model for a painting of Judas.
8. Season of revelry before the commencement of Lent.
9. This and other interspersed flower songs are called *stornelli* in Italy.

Flower o' the thyme—and so on. Round they went.
Scarce had they turned the corner when a titter
Like the skipping of rabbits by moonlight—three slim shapes,
60 And a face that looked up . . . zooks, sir, flesh and blood,
That's all I'm made of! Into shreds it went,
Curtain and counterpane and coverlet,
All the bed-furniture—a dozen knots,
There was a ladder! Down I let myself,
65 Hands and feet, scrambling somehow, and so dropped,
And after them. I came up with the fun
Hard by Saint Laurence,[1] hail fellow, well met—
Flower o' the rose,
If I've been merry, what matter who knows!
70 And so as I was stealing back again
To get to bed and have a bit of sleep
Ere I rise up tomorrow and go work
On Jerome knocking at his poor old breast
With his great round stone to subdue the flesh,[2]
75 You snap me of the sudden. Ah, I see!
Though your eye twinkles still, you shake your head—
Mine's shaved—a monk, you say—the sting's in that!
If Master Cosimo announced himself,
Mum's the word naturally; but a monk!
80 Come, what am I a beast for? tell us, now!
I was a baby when my mother died
And father died and left me in the street.
I starved there, God knows how, a year or two
On fig skins, melon parings, rinds and shucks,
85 Refuse and rubbish. One fine frosty day,
My stomach being empty as your hat,
The wind doubled me up and down I went.
Old Aunt Lapaccia trussed me with one hand
(Its fellow was a stinger as I knew),
90 And so along the wall, over the bridge,
By the straight cut to the convent. Six words there,
While I stood munching my first bread that month:
"So, boy, you're minded," quoth the good fat father
Wiping his own mouth, 'twas refection time°—   *mealtime*
95 "To quit this very miserable world?
Will you renounce" . . . "the mouthful of bread?" thought I;
By no means! Brief, they made a monk of me;
I did renounce the world, its pride and greed,
Palace, farm, villa, shop, and banking house,
100 Trash, such as these poor devils of Medici
Have given their hearts to—all at eight years old.
Well, sir, I found in time, you may be sure,
'Twas not for nothing—the good bellyful,
The warm serge and the rope that goes all round,
105 And day-long blessed idleness beside!
"Let's see what the urchin's fit for"—that came next.

1. San Lorenzo, a church in Florence.
2. A picture of Saint Jerome (ca. 340–420), whose ascetic observances were hardly a congenial subject for such a painter as Lippi.

Not overmuch their way, I must confess.
Such a to-do! They tried me with their books:
Lord, they'd have taught me Latin in pure waste!
110 *Flower o' the clove,*
All the Latin I construe is "amo," I love!
But, mind you, when a boy starves in the streets
Eight years together, as my fortune was,
Watching folk's faces to know who will fling
115 The bit of half-stripped grape bunch he desires,
And who will curse or kick him for his pains—
Which gentleman processional and fine,
Holding a candle to the Sacrament,
Will wink and let him lift a plate and catch
120 The droppings of the wax to sell again,
Or holla for the Eight° and have him whipped—   *Florentine magistrates*
How say I?—nay, which dog bites, which lets drop
His bone from the heap of offal in the street—
Why, soul and sense of him grow sharp alike,
125 He learns the look of things, and none the less
For admonition from the hunger-pinch.
I had a store of such remarks, be sure,
Which, after I found leisure, turned to use.
I drew men's faces on my copybooks,
130 Scrawled them within the antiphonary's marge,[3]
Joined legs and arms to the long music-notes,
Found eyes and nose and chin for A's and B's,
And made a string of pictures of the world
Betwixt the ins and outs of verb and noun,
135 On the wall, the bench, the door. The monks looked black.
"Nay," quoth the Prior,[4] "turn him out, d' ye say?
In no wise. Lose a crow and catch a lark.
What if at last we get our man of parts,
We Carmelites, like those Camaldolese
140 And Preaching Friars,[5] to do our church up fine
And put the front on it that ought to be!"
And hereupon he bade me daub away.
Thank you! my head being crammed, the walls a blank,
Never was such prompt disemburdening.
145 First, every sort of monk, the black and white,
I drew them, fat and lean: then, folk at church,
From good old gossips waiting to confess
Their cribs of barrel droppings, candle ends—
To the breathless fellow at the altar-foot,
150 Fresh from his murder, safe and sitting there
With the little children round him in a row
Of admiration, half for his beard and half
For that white anger of his victim's son
Shaking a fist at him with one fierce arm,
155 Signing himself with the other because of Christ

---

3. Margin of music book used for choral singing.
4. Head of a Carmelite convent.
5. Benedictine and Dominican religious orders, respectively.

(Whose sad face on the cross sees only this
After the passion° of a thousand years)   *sufferings*
Till some poor girl, her apron o'er her head
(Which the intense eyes looked through), came at eve
160 On tiptoe, said a word, dropped in a loaf,
Her pair of earrings and a bunch of flowers
(The brute took growling), prayed, and so was gone.
I painted all, then cried " 'Tis ask and have;
Choose, for more's ready!"—laid the ladder flat,
165 And showed my covered bit of cloister wall.
The monks closed in a circle and praised loud
Till checked, taught what to see and not to see,
Being simple bodies—"That's the very man!
Look at the boy who stoops to pat the dog!
170 That woman's like the Prior's niece who comes
To care about his asthma: it's the life!"
But there my triumph's straw-fire flared and funked;[6]
Their betters took their turn to see and say:
The Prior and the learned pulled a face
175 And stopped all that in no time. "How? what's here?
Quite from the mark of painting, bless us all!
Faces, arms, legs and bodies like the true
As much as pea and pea! it's devil's game!
Your business is not to catch men with show,
180 With homage to the perishable clay,
But lift them over it, ignore it all,
Make them forget there's such a thing as flesh.
Your business is to paint the souls of men—
Man's soul, and it's a fire, smoke . . . no, it's not . . .
185 It's vapor done up like a newborn babe—
(In that shape when you die it leaves your mouth)
It's . . . well, what matters talking, it's the soul!
Give us no more of body than shows soul!
Here's Giotto,[7] with his Saint a-praising God,
190 That sets us praising—why not stop with him?
Why put all thoughts of praise out of our head
With wonder at lines, colors, and what not?
Paint the soul, never mind the legs and arms!
Rub all out, try at it a second time.
195 Oh, that white smallish female with the breasts,
She's just my niece . . . Herodias,[8] I would say—
Who went and danced and got men's heads cut off!
Have it all out!" Now, is this sense, I ask?
A fine way to paint soul, by painting body
200 So ill, the eye can't stop there, must go further
And can't fare worse! Thus, yellow does for white
When what you put for yellow's simply black,

6. Went up in smoke.
7. Great Florentine painter (1276–1337), whose stylized pictures of religious subjects were admired as models of pre-Renaissance art.
8. Also called Salomé, had the same name as her

mother (Herodias), sister-in-law of King Herod. The daughter's dance coincided with the beheading of John the Baptist, who had aroused her mother's displeasure (Matthew 14.6–11).

And any sort of meaning looks intense
When all beside itself means and looks naught.
205 Why can't a painter lift each foot in turn,
Left foot and right foot, go a double step,
Make his flesh liker and his soul more like,
Both in their order? Take the prettiest face,
The Prior's niece . . . patron-saint—is it so pretty
210 You can't discover if it means hope, fear,
Sorrow or joy? won't beauty go with these?
Suppose I've made her eyes all right and blue,
Can't I take breath and try to add life's flash,
And then add soul and heighten them threefold?
215 Or say there's beauty with no soul at all—
(I never saw it—put the case the same—)
If you get simple beauty and naught else,
You get about the best thing God invents:
That's somewhat: and you'll find the soul you have missed,
220 Within yourself, when you return him thanks.
"Rub all out!" Well, well, there's my life, in short,
And so the thing has gone on ever since.
I'm grown a man no doubt, I've broken bounds:
You should not take a fellow eight years old
225 And make him swear to never kiss the girls.
I'm my own master, paint now as I please—
Having a friend, you see, in the Corner-house![9]
Lord, it's fast holding by the rings in front—
Those great rings serve more purposes than just
230 To plant a flag in, or tie up a horse!
And yet the old schooling sticks, the old grave eyes
Are peeping o'er my shoulder as I work,
The heads shake still—"It's art's decline, my son!
You're not of the true painters, great and old;
235 Brother Angelico's the man, you'll find;
Brother Lorenzo[1] stands his single peer:
Fag on at flesh, you'll never make the third!"
Flower o' the pine,
You keep your mistr . . . manners, and I'll stick to mine!
240 I'm not the third, then: bless us, they must know!
Don't you think they're the likeliest to know,
They with their Latin? So, I swallow my rage,
Clench my teeth, suck my lips in tight, and paint
To please them—sometimes do and sometimes don't;
245 For, doing most, there's pretty sure to come
A turn, some warm eve finds me at my saints—
A laugh, a cry, the business of the world—
(Flower o' the peach,
Death for us all, and his own life for each!)
250 And my whole soul revolves, the cup runs over,

9. The Medici palace.
1. Fra Angelico (1387–1455) and Lorenzo Mon-
aco (1370–1425), whose paintings were in the
approved traditional manner.

The world and life's too big to pass for a dream,
And I do these wild things in sheer despite,
And play the fooleries you catch me at,
In pure rage! The old mill-horse, out at grass
255 After hard years, throws up his stiff heels so,
Although the miller does not preach to him
The only good of grass is to make chaff.°   straw
What would men have? Do they like grass or no—
May they or mayn't they? all I want's the thing
260 Settled forever one way. As it is,
You tell too many lies and hurt yourself:
You don't like what you only like too much,
You do like what, if given you at your word,
You find abundantly detestable.
265 For me, I think I speak as I was taught;
I always see the garden and God there
A-making man's wife: and, my lesson learned,
The value and significance of flesh,
I can't unlearn ten minutes afterwards.

270   You understand me: I'm a beast, I know.
But see, now—why, I see as certainly
As that the morning star's about to shine,
What will hap some day. We've a youngster here
Comes to our convent, studies what I do,
275 Slouches and stares and lets no atom drop:
His name is Guidi²—he'll not mind the monks—
They call him Hulking Tom, he lets them talk—
He picks my practice up—he'll paint apace,
I hope so—though I never live so long,
280 I know what's sure to follow. You be judge!
You speak no Latin more than I, belike;
However, you're my man, you've seen the world
—The beauty and the wonder and the power,
The shapes of things, their colors, lights and shades,
285 Changes, surprises—and God made it all!
—For what? Do you feel thankful, aye or no,
For this fair town's face, yonder river's line,
The mountain round it and the sky above,
Much more the figures of man, woman, child,
290 These are the frame to? What's it all about?
To be passed over, despised? or dwelt upon,
Wondered at? oh, this last of course!—you say.
But why not do as well as say—paint these
Just as they are, careless what comes of it?
295 God's works—paint any one, and count it crime
To let a truth slip. Don't object, "His works

2. Guidi or Masaccio (1401–1428), a painter who may have been Lippi's master rather than his pupil, although Browning, in a letter to the press in 1870, argued that Lippi had been born earlier. Like Lippi, Masaccio was in revolt against the medieval theory of art. His frescoes in the chapel of Santa Maria del Carmine are considered his masterpiece.

Are here already; nature is complete:
Suppose you reproduce her—(which you can't)
There's no advantage! You must beat her, then."
300 For, don't you mark? we're made so that we love
First when we see them painted, things we have passed
Perhaps a hundred times nor cared to see;
And so they are better, painted—better to us,
Which is the same thing. Art was given for that;
305 God uses us to help each other so,
Lending our minds out. Have you noticed, now,
Your cullion's° hanging face? A bit of chalk,   *rascal's*
And trust me but you should, though! How much more,
If I drew higher things with the same truth!
310 That were to take the Prior's pulpit-place,
Interpret God to all of you! Oh, oh,
It makes me mad to see what men shall do
And we in our graves! This world's no blot for us,
Nor blank; it means intensely, and means good:
315 To find its meaning is my meat and drink.
"Aye, but you don't so instigate to prayer!"
Strikes in the Prior: "when your meaning's plain
It does not say to folk—remember matins,
Or, mind you fast next Friday!" Why, for this
320 What need of art at all? A skull and bones,
Two bits of stick nailed crosswise, or, what's best,
A bell to chime the hour with, does as well.
I painted a Saint Laurence[3] six months since
At Prato, splashed the fresco[4] in fine style:
325 "How looks my painting, now the scaffold's down?"
I ask a brother: "Hugely," he returns—
"Already not one phiz of your three slaves
Who turn the Deacon off his toasted side,
But it's scratched and prodded to our heart's content,
330 The pious people have so eased their own
With coming to say prayers there in a rage:
We get on fast to see the bricks beneath.
Expect another job this time next year,
For pity and religion grow i' the crowd—
335 Your painting serves its purpose!" Hang the fools!

—That is—you'll not mistake an idle word
Spoke in a huff by a poor monk, God wot,
Tasting the air this spicy night which turns
The unaccustomed head like Chianti wine!
340 Oh, the church knows! don't misreport me, now!
It's natural a poor monk out of bounds
Should have his apt word to excuse himself:
And hearken how I plot to make amends.

3. A scene representing the fiery martyrdom of Saint Laurence.
4. Painted on a freshly plastered surface. It must be painted quickly before the plaster dries. Prato is a town near Florence

I have bethought me: I shall paint a piece
345 . . . There's for you! Give me six months, then go, see
Something in Sant' Ambrogio's![5] Bless the nuns!
They want a cast o' my office.[6] I shall paint
God in the midst, Madonna and her babe,
Ringed by a bowery flowery angel brood,
350 Lilies and vestments and white faces, sweet
As puff on puff of grated orris-root[7]
When ladies crowd to Church at midsummer.
And then i' the front, of course a saint or two—
Saint John, because he saves the Florentines,
355 Saint Ambrose, who puts down in black and white
The convent's friends and gives them a long day,
And Job, I must have him there past mistake,
The man of Uz (and Us without the z,
Painters who need his patience). Well, all these
360 Secured at their devotion, up shall come
Out of a corner when you least expect,
As one by a dark stair into a great light,
Music and talking, who but Lippo! I!—
Mazed, motionless and moonstruck—I'm the man!
365 Back I shrink—what is this I see and hear?
I, caught up with my monk's things by mistake,
My old serge gown and rope that goes all round,
I, in this presence, this pure company!
Where's a hole, where's a corner for escape?
370 Then steps a sweet angelic slip of a thing
Forward, puts out a soft palm—"Not so fast!"
—Addresses the celestial presence, "nay—
He made you and devised you, after all,
Though he's none of you! Could Saint John there draw—
375 His camel-hair[8] make up a painting-brush?
We come to brother Lippo for all that,
Iste perfecit opus!"[9] So, all smile—
I shuffle sideways with my blushing face
Under the cover of a hundred wings
380 Thrown like a spread of kirtles° when you're gay   skirts°
And play hot cockles,[1] all the doors being shut,
Till, wholly unexpected, in there pops
The hothead husband! Thus I scuttle off
To some safe bench behind, not letting go
385 The palm of her, the little lily thing
That spoke the good word for me in the nick,
Like the Prior's niece . . . Saint Lucy, I would say.
And so all's saved for me, and for the church

5. A convent church in Florence.
6. Sample of my work. The completed painting,
which Browning saw in Florence, is Lippi's *Coronation of the Virgin*.
7. Powder (like talcum) made from sweet-smelling
roots of a flower.
8. Cf. Mark 1.6: "And John was clothed with

camel's hair."
9. This man made the work! (Latin). In this painting, as later completed, these words appear beside
a figure that Browning took to be Lippi's self-portrait.
1. A game in which a player wears a blindfold.

A pretty picture gained. Go, six months hence!
390   Your hand, sir, and good-by: no lights, no lights!
The street's hushed, and I know my own way back,
Don't fear me! There's the gray beginning. Zooks!

ca. 1853   1855

The Last Ride Together

I

I said—Then, dearest, since 'tis so,
Since now at length my fate I know,
Since nothing all my love avails,
Since all, my life seemed meant for, fails,
5   Since this was written and needs must be—
My whole heart rises up to bless
Your name in pride and thankfulness!
Take back the hope you gave—I claim
Only a memory of the same,
10   —And this beside, if you will not blame,
        Your leave for one more last ride with me.

2

My mistress bent that brow of hers;
Those deep dark eyes where pride demurs
When pity would be softening through,
15   Fixed me a breathing-while or two
        With life or death in the balance: right!
The blood replenished me again;
My last thought was at least not vain:
I and my mistress, side by side
20   Shall be together, breathe and ride,
So, one day more am I deified.
        Who knows but the world may end tonight?

3

Hush! if you saw some western cloud
All billowy-bosomed, over-bowed
25   By many benedictions—sun's
And moon's and evening star's at once—
        And so, you, looking and loving best,
Conscious grew, your passion drew
Cloud, sunset, moonrise, star-shine too,
30   Down on you, near and yet more near,
Till flesh must fade for heaven was here!—
Thus leant she and lingered[1]—joy and fear!
        Thus lay she a moment on my breast.

_____

1. Before she mounted her horse.

4

Then we began to ride. My soul
35 Smoothed itself out, a long-cramped scroll
Freshening and fluttering in the wind.
Past hopes already lay behind.
     What need to strive with a life awry?
Had I said that, had I done this,
40 So might I gain, so might I miss.
Might she have loved me? just as well
She might have hated, who can tell!
Where had I been now if the worst befell?
     And here we are riding, she and I.

5

45 Fail I alone, in words and deeds?
Why, all men strive and who succeeds?
We rode; it seemed my spirit flew,
Saw other regions, cities new,
     As the world rushed by on either side.
50 I thought—All labor, yet no less
Bear up beneath their unsuccess.
Look at the end of work, contrast
The petty done, the undone vast,
     This present of theirs with the hopeful past!
55   I hoped she would love me; here we ride.

6

What hand and brain went ever paired?
What heart alike conceived and dared?
What act proved all its thought had been?
What will but felt the fleshly screen?
60   We ride and I see her bosom heave.
There's many a crown for who can reach.
Ten lines, a statesman's life in each![2]
The flag stuck on a heap of bones,
A soldier's doing! what atones?
65 They scratch his name on the Abbey stones.[3]
     My riding is better, by their leave.

7

What does it all mean, poet? Well,
Your brains beat into rhythm, you tell
What we felt only; you expressed
70 You hold things beautiful the best,
     And pace them in rhyme so, side by side.
'Tis something, nay 'tis much: but then,

---

2. If a man tries hard enough, he may be crowned
with what seems to be success. He might become,
for example, an eminent "statesman." Yet his only
memorial would be a short sketch of his career
("ten lines") in some history or biographical
dictionary.
3. I.e., he is honored by burial in Westminster
Abbey.

Have you yourself what's best for men?
Are you—poor, sick, old ere your time—
75 Nearer one whit your own sublime
Than we who never have turned a rhyme?
Sing, riding's a joy! For me, I ride.

8

And you, great sculptor—so, you gave
A score of years to Art, her slave,
80 And that's your Venus, whence we turn
To yonder girl that fords the burn!⁴
You acquiesce, and shall I repine?
What, man of music, you grown gray
With notes and nothing else to say,
85 Is this your sole praise from a friend,
"Greatly his opera's strains intend,
But in music we know how fashions end!"
I gave my youth; but we ride, in fine.°   *in short*

9

Who knows what's fit for us? Had fate
90 Proposed bliss here should sublimate
My being—had I signed the bond—
Still one must lead some life beyond,
Have a bliss to die with, dim-descried.
This foot once planted on the goal,
95 This glory-garland round my soul,
Could I descry such? Try and test!
I sink back shuddering from the quest.
Earth being so good, would Heaven seem best?⁵
Now, Heaven and she are beyond this ride.

10

100 And yet—she has not spoke so long!
What if heaven be that, fair and strong
At life's best, with our eyes upturned
Whither life's flower is first discerned,
We, fixed so, ever should so abide?
105 What if we still ride on, we two
With life forever old yet new,
Changed not in kind but in degree,
The instant made eternity—
And heaven just prove that I and she
110 Ride, ride together, forever ride?

1855

4. Crosses the brook.
5. If fate had decreed that he could possess his mistress fully, life on earth would have been so blissful that heaven could offer nothing for him to look forward to after death. Hence (he argues) to preserve "a bliss to die with" (line 93), it is better that she never really became his on earth.

Andrea del Sarto[1]

(called "The Faultless Painter")

But do not let us quarrel any more,
No, my Lucrezia; bear with me for once:
Sit down and all shall happen as you wish.
You turn your face, but does it bring your heart?
5 I'll work then for your friend's friend, never fear,
Treat his own subject after his own way,
Fix his own time, accept too his own price,
And shut the money into this small hand
When next it takes mine. Will it? tenderly?
10 Oh, I'll content him—but tomorrow, Love!
I often am much wearier than you think,
This evening more than usual, and it seems
As if—forgive now—should you let me sit
Here by the window with your hand in mine
15 And look a half-hour forth on Fiesole,[2]
Both of one mind, as married people use,
Quietly, quietly the evening through,
I might get up tomorrow to my work
Cheerful and fresh as ever. Let us try.
20 Tomorrow, how you shall be glad for this!
Your soft hand is a woman of itself,
And mine the man's bared breast she curls inside.
Don't count the time lost, neither; you must serve
For each of the five pictures we require:
25 It saves a model. So! keep looking so—
My serpentining beauty, rounds on rounds![3]
—How could you ever prick those perfect ears,
Even to put the pearl there! oh, so sweet—
My face, my moon, my everybody's moon,
30 Which everybody looks on and calls his,
And, I suppose, is looked on by in turn,
While she looks—no one's: very dear, no less.[4]
You smile? why, there's my picture ready made,
There's what we painters call our harmony!

1. This portrait of Andrea del Sarto (1486–1531) was derived from a biography written by his pupil Giorgio Vasari, author of *The Lives of the Painters.* Vasari's account seeks to explain why his Florentine master, one of the most skillful painters of the Renaissance, never altogether fulfilled the promise he had shown early in his career and why he had never arrived (in Vasari's opinion) at the level of such artists as Raphael. Vasari noted that Andrea suffered from "a certain timidity of mind . . . which rendered it impossible that those evidences of ardor and animation, which are proper to the more exalted character, should ever appear in him."

Browning also follows Vasari's account of Andrea's marriage to a beautiful widow, Lucrezia, "an artful woman who made him do as she pleased in all things." Vasari reports that Andrea's "immoderate love for her soon caused him to neglect the

studies demanded by his art" and that this infatuation had "more influence over him than the glory and honor towards which he had begun to make such hopeful advances."

Browning's poem has often been praised for its exposition of a paradoxical theory of success and failure, but it has other qualities as well. Its slow-paced, enervated blank verse, its setting of a quiet evening in autumn, its comparative lack of the movement and noise that we expect in Browning's energetic verse create a unity of impression that is unobtrusive yet effective.
2. A suburb on the hills overlooking Florence.
3. Coils of hair like the coils of a serpent.
4. Her affections are centered on no one person, not even on her husband, yet she is nevertheless dear to him.

35   A common grayness silvers everything[5]—
      All in a twilight, you and I alike
      —You, at the point of your first pride in me
      (That's gone you know)—but I, at every point;
      My youth, my hope, my art, being all toned down
40   To yonder sober pleasant Fiesole.
      There's the bell clinking from the chapel top;
      That length of convent wall across the way
      Holds the trees safer, huddled more inside;
      The last monk leaves the garden; days decrease,
45   And autumn grows, autumn in everything.
      Eh? the whole seems to fall into a shape
      As if I saw alike my work and self
      And all that I was born to be and do,
      A twilight-piece. Love, we are in God's hand.
50   How strange now, looks the life he makes us lead;
      So free we seem, so fettered fast we are!
      I feel he laid the fetter: let it lie!
      This chamber for example—turn your head—
      All that's behind us! You don't understand
55   Nor care to understand about my art,
      But you can hear at least when people speak:
      And that cartoon,° the second from the door   *drawing*
      —It is the thing, Love! so such things should be—
      Behold Madonna!—I am bold to say.
60   I can do with my pencil what I know,
      What I see, what at bottom of my heart
      I wish for, if I ever wish so deep—
      Do easily, too—when I say, perfectly,
      I do not boast, perhaps: yourself are judge,
65   Who listened to the Legate's[6] talk last week,
      And just as much they used to say in France.
      At any rate 'tis easy, all of it!
      No sketches first, no studies, that's long past:
      I do what many dream of, all their lives,
70   —Dream? strive to do, and agonize to do,
      And fail in doing. I could count twenty such
      On twice your fingers, and not leave this town,
      Who strive—you don't know how the others strive
      To paint a little thing like that you smeared
75   Carelessly passing with your robes afloat—
      Yet do much less, so much less, Someone[7] says
      (I know his name, no matter)—so much less!
      Well, less is more, Lucrezia: I am judged.
      There burns a truer light of God in them,
80   In their vexed beating stuffed and stopped-up brain,
      Heart, or whate'er else, than goes on to prompt
      This low-pulsed forthright craftsman's hand of mine.
      Their works drop groundward, but themselves, I know,

---

5. The predominant color in many of Andrea's paintings is silver gray.

6. A deputy of the pope.

7. Probably Michelangelo (1475–1564).

Reach many a time a heaven that's shut to me,
85   Enter and take their place there sure enough,
Though they come back and cannot tell the world.
My works are nearer heaven, but I sit here.
The sudden blood of these men! at a word—
Praise them, it boils, or blame them, it boils too.
90   I, painting from myself and to myself,
Know what I do, am unmoved by men's blame
Or their praise either. Somebody remarks
Morello's[8] outline there is wrongly traced,
His hue mistaken; what of that? or else,
95   Rightly traced and well ordered; what of that?
Speak as they please, what does the mountain care?
Ah, but a man's reach should exceed his grasp,
Or what's a heaven for? All is silver-gray
Placid and perfect with my art: the worse!
100   I know both what I want and what might gain,
And yet how profitless to know, to sigh
"Had I been two, another and myself,
Our head would have o'erlooked the world!" No doubt.
Yonder's a work now, of that famous youth
105   The Urbinate[9] who died five years ago.
('Tis copied,[1] George Vasari sent it me.)
Well, I can fancy how he did it all,
Pouring his soul, with kings and popes to see,
Reaching, that heaven might so replenish him,
110   Above and through his art—for it gives way;
That arm is wrongly put —and there again—
A fault to pardon in the drawing's lines,
Its body, so to speak: its soul is right,
He means right—that, a child may understand.
115   Still, what an arm! and I could alter it:
But all the play, the insight and the stretch—
Out of me, out of me! And wherefore out?
Had you enjoined them on me, given me soul,
We might have risen to Rafael, I and you!
120   Nay, Love, you did give all I asked, I think—
More than I merit, yes, by many times.
But had you—oh, with the same perfect brow,
And perfect eyes, and more than perfect mouth,
And the low voice my soul hears, as a bird
125   The fowler's pipe,[2] and follows to the snare—
Had you, with these same, but brought a mind!
Some women do so. Had the mouth there urged
"God and the glory! never care for gain.
The present by the future, what is that?
130   Live for fame, side by side with Agnolo!°   *Michelangelo*
Rafael is waiting: up to God, all three!"

---

8. A mountain peak outside Florence.
9. Raphael (1483–1520), born at Urbino.
1. In saying that the painting is a copy, Andrea may perhaps be concerned to prevent Lucrezia

from selling it.
2. Whistle or call used by hunters to lure wild fowl into range.

I might have done it for you. So it seems:
Perhaps not. All is as God overrules.
Beside, incentives come from the soul's self;
135   The rest avail not. Why do I need you?
What wife had Rafael, or has Agnolo?
In this world, who can do a thing, will not;
And who would do it, cannot, I perceive:
Yet the will's somewhat—somewhat, too, the power—
140   And thus we half-men struggle. At the end,
God, I conclude, compensates, punishes.
'Tis safer for me, if the award be strict,
That I am something underrated here.
Poor this long while, despised, to speak the truth.
145   I dared not, do you know, leave home all day,
For fear of chancing on the Paris lords.
The best is when they pass and look aside;
But they speak sometimes; I must bear it all.
Well may they speak! That Francis,[3] that first time,
150   And that long festal year at Fontainebleau!
I surely then could sometimes leave the ground,
Put on the glory, Rafael's daily wear,
In that humane great monarch's golden look—
One finger in his beard or twisted curl
155   Over his mouth's good mark that made the smile,
One arm about my shoulder, round my neck,
The jingle of his gold chain in my ear,
I painting proudly with his breath on me,
All his court round him, seeing with his eyes,
160   Such frank French eyes, and such a fire of souls
Profuse, my hand kept plying by those hearts—
And, best of all, this, this, this face beyond,
This in the background, waiting on my work,
To crown the issue with a last reward!
165   A good time, was it not, my kingly days?
And had you not grown restless . . . but I know—
'Tis done and past; 'twas right, my instinct said;
Too live the life grew, golden and not gray,
And I'm the weak-eyed bat no sun should tempt
170   Out of the grange whose four walls make his world.
How could it end in any other way?
You called me, and I came home to your heart.
The triumph was—to reach and stay there; since
I reached it ere the triumph, what is lost?
175   Let my hands frame your face in your hair's gold,
You beautiful Lucrezia that are mine!
"Rafael did this, Andrea painted that;
The Roman's is the better when you pray,
But still the other's Virgin was his wife—"
180   Men will excuse me. I am glad to judge

---

3. King Francis I of France had invited Andrea to his court at Fontainebleau and warmly encouraged him in his painting. On returning to Florence, however, Andrea is reputed to have stolen some funds entrusted to him by Francis; and to please Lucrezia he built a house with the money. Now he is afraid of being insulted by "Paris lords" on the streets.

Both pictures in your presence; clearer grows
My better fortune, I resolve to think.
For, do you know, Lucrezia, as God lives,
Said one day Agnolo, his very self,
185   To Rafael . . . I have known it all these years . . .
(When the young man was flaming out his thoughts
Upon a palace wall for Rome to see,
Too lifted up in heart because of it)
"Friend, there's a certain sorry little scrub
190   Goes up and down our Florence, none cares how,
Who, were he set to plan and execute
As you are, pricked on by your popes and kings,
Would bring the sweat into that brow of yours!"
To Rafael's—And indeed the arm is wrong.
195   I hardly dare . . . yet, only you to see,
Give the chalk here—quick, thus the line should go!
Aye, but the soul! he's Rafael! rub it out!
Still, all I care for, if he spoke the truth,
(What he? why, who but Michel Agnolo?
200   Do you forget already words like those?)
If really there was such a chance, so lost—
Is, whether you're—not grateful—but more pleased.
Well, let me think so. And you smile indeed!
This hour has been an hour! Another smile?
205   If you would sit thus by me every night
I should work better, do you comprehend?
I mean that I should earn more, give you more.
See, it is settled dusk now; there's a star;
Morello's gone, the watch-lights show the wall,
210   The cue-owls[4] speak the name we call them by.
Come from the window, love—come in, at last,
Inside the melancholy little house
We built to be so gay with. God is just.
King Francis may forgive me: oft at nights
215   When I look up from painting, eyes tired out,
The walls become illumined, brick from brick
Distinct, instead of mortar, fierce bright gold,
That gold of his I did cement them with!
Let us but love each other. Must you go?
220   That Cousin here again? he waits outside?
Must see you—you, and not with me? Those loans?
More gaming debts to pay?[5] you smiled for that?
Well, let smiles buy me! have you more to spend?
While hand and eye and something of a heart
225   Are left me, work's my ware, and what's it worth?
I'll pay my fancy. Only let me sit
The gray remainder of the evening out,
Idle, you call it, and muse perfectly
How I could paint, were I but back in France,

---

4. A kind of owl named for its cry, which sounds like *cue*.
5. Lucrezia's "Cousin" (or lover or friend) owes gambling debts to a creditor. Andrea has already contracted (lines 5–10) to pay off these debts by painting some pictures according to the creditor's specifications. Now he agrees to pay off further debts.

230   One picture, just one more—the Virgin's face,
    Not yours this time! I want you at my side
    To hear them—that is, Michel Agnolo—
    Judge all I do and tell you of its worth.
    Will you? Tomorrow, satisfy your friend.
235   I take the subjects for his corridor,
    Finish the portrait out of hand—there, there,
    And throw him in another thing or two
    If he demurs; the whole should prove enough
    To pay for this same Cousin's freak. Beside,
240   What's better and what's all I care about,
    Get you the thirteen scudi° for the ruff!   *Italian coins*
    Love, does that please you? Ah, but what does he,
    The Cousin! What does he to please you more?

    I am grown peaceful as old age tonight.
245   I regret little, I would change still less.
    Since there my past life lies, why alter it?
    The very wrong to Francis!—it is true
    I took his coin, was tempted and complied,
    And built this house and sinned, and all is said.
250   My father and my mother died of want.[6]
    Well, had I riches of my own? you see
    How one gets rich! Let each one bear his lot.
    They were born poor, lived poor, and poor they died:
    And I have labored somewhat in my time
255   And not been paid profusely. Some good son
    Paint my two hundred pictures—let him try!
    No doubt, there's something strikes a balance. Yes,
    You loved me quite enough, it seems tonight.
    This must suffice me here. What would one have?
260   In heaven, perhaps, new chances, one more chance—
    Four great walls in the New Jerusalem,[7]
    Meted on each side by the angel's reed,°   *measuring rod*
    For Leonard,[8] Rafael, Agnolo and me
    To cover—the three first without a wife,
265   While I have mine! So—still they overcome
    Because there's still Lucrezia—as I choose.

    Again the Cousin's whistle! Go, my Love.

ca. 1853   1855

Two in the Campagna[1]

I

I wonder do you feel today
    As I have felt since, hand in hand,

---

6. According to Vasari, Andrea's infatuation for Lucrezia prompted him to stop supporting his poverty-stricken parents.
7. Cf. Revelation 21.10–21.

8. Leonardo da Vinci (1452–1519).
1. The level plains and pasture lands near Rome where the ruins of ancient cities are overrun with wildflowers.

We sat down on the grass, to stray
　　In spirit better through the land,
5　This morn of Rome and May?

2

For me, I touched a thought, I know,
　　Has tantalized me many times,
(Like turns of thread the spiders throw
　　Mocking across our path) for rhymes
10　To catch at and let go.

3

Help me to hold it! First it left
　　The yellowing fennel,[2] run to seed
There, branching from the brickwork's cleft,
　　Some old tomb's ruin: yonder weed
15　Took up the floating weft,[3]

4

Where one small orange cup amassed
　　Five beetles—blind and green they grope
Among the honey-meal: and last,
　　Everywhere on the grassy slope
20　I traced it. Hold it fast!

5

The champaign° with its endless fleece　　　*the Campagna*
　　Of feathery grasses everywhere!
Silence and passion, joy and peace,
　　An everlasting wash of air—
25　Rome's ghost since her decease.

6

Such life here, through such lengths of hours,
　　Such miracles performed in play,
Such primal naked forms of flowers,
　　Such letting nature have her way
30　While heaven looks from its towers!

7

How say you? Let us, O my dove,
　　Let us be unashamed of soul,
As earth lies bare to heaven above!
　　How is it under our control
35　To love or not to love?

8

I would that you were all to me,
　　You that are just so much, no more.

2. A yellow-flowered plant from which a pungent　　　3. Threads crossing from side to side of a web.
spice is derived.

Nor yours nor mine, nor slave nor free!
　　Where does the fault lie? What the core
40　O' the wound, since wound must be?

9

I would I could adopt your will,
　　See with your eyes, and set my heart
Beating by yours, and drink my fill
　　At your soul's springs—your part my part
45　In life, for good and ill.

10

No. I yearn upward, touch you close,
　　Then stand away. I kiss your cheek,
Catch your soul's warmth—I pluck the rose
　　And love it more than tongue can speak—
50　Then the good minute goes.

11

Already how am I so far
　　Out of that minute? Must I go
Still like the thistle-ball, no bar,
　　Onward, whenever light winds blow,
55　Fixed by no friendly star?[4]

12

Just when I seemed about to learn!
　　Where is the thread now? Off again!
The old trick! Only I discern—
　　Infinite passion, and the pain
60　Of finite hearts that yearn.

1854　　　　　　　　　　　　　　　　　　　　　　　　1855

A Grammarian's Funeral[1]

Shortly after the Revival of Learning in Europe

Let us begin and carry up this corpse,
　　Singing together.
Leave we the common crofts,[2] the vulgar thorpes°　　　　*villages*
　　Each in its tether[3]
5　Sleeping safe on the bosom of the plain,
　　Cared for till cock-crow:

---

4. Cf. Shakespeare's Sonnet 116.
1. The speaker is one of the students who are bearing the body of their scholarly master to the mountaintop for burial. The student's defense of the dead grammarian's idealistic dedication to knowledge and faith in a future life is expressed in some of the harshest-sounding and most laborious verse ever written by Browning. It is this grotesque combination of opposites (soaring idealism in conjunction with harsh or petty realities) that gives *A*

Grammarian's Funeral its distinctive tone.
　No model for the grammarian has been specifically identified. Browning seems to have had in mind the kind of early Renaissance scholar whose devotion to the Greek language made it possible for others to enjoy the more recognizably significant aspects of the revival of learning.
2. Small tracts of land farmed by peasants.
3. Restricted to a narrow sphere like an animal tied to a stake.

Look out if yonder be not day again
    Rimming the rock-row!
That's the appropriate country; there, man's thought,
10   Rarer, intenser,
Self-gathered for an outbreak, as it ought,
    Chafes in the censer.
Leave we the unlettered plain[4] its herd and crop;
    Seek we sepulture°   *burial place*
15 On a tall mountain, citied to the top,
    Crowded with culture!
All the peaks soar, but one the rest excels;
    Clouds overcome it;
No! yonder sparkle is the citadel's
20   Circling its summit.
Thither our path lies; wind we up the heights:
    Wait ye the warning?
Our low life was the level's and the night's;
    He's for the morning.
25 Step to a tune, square chests, erect each head,
    'Ware° the beholders!   *beware*
This is our master, famous, calm, and dead,
    Borne on our shoulders.

Sleep, crop and herd! sleep, darkling thorpe and croft,
30   Safe from the weather!
He, whom we convoy to his grave aloft,
    Singing together,
He was a man born with thy face and throat,
    Lyric Apollo![5]
35 Long he lived nameless: how should spring take note
    Winter would follow?
Till lo, the little touch, and youth was gone!
    Cramped and diminished,
Moaned he, "New measures, other feet anon!
40   My dance is finished?"
No, that's the world's way: (keep the mountain-side,
    Make for the city!)
He knew the signal, and stepped on with pride
    Over men's pity;
45 Left play for work, and grappled with the world
    Bent on escaping:
"What's in the scroll," quoth he, "thou keepest furled?
    Show me their shaping,
Theirs who most studied man, the bard and sage—
50   Give!"—So, he gowned him,[6]
Straight got by heart that book to its last page:
    Learned, we found him.
Yea, but we found him bald too, eyes like lead,
    Accents uncertain:
55 "Time to taste life," another would have said,
    "Up with the curtain!"

---

4. Flatlands at the base of the mountain that are populated by illiterate shepherds and peasants.

5. God of music and embodiment of male beauty.
6. Dressed in academic gown; became a scholar.

This man said rather, "Actual life comes next?
        Patience a moment!
Grant I have mastered learning's crabbed text,
60   Still there's the comment.[7]
Let me know all! Prate not of most or least,
        Painful or easy!
Even to the crumbs I'd fain eat up the feast,
        Aye, nor feel queasy."
65 Oh, such a life as he resolved to live,
        When he had learned it,
When he had gathered all books had to give!
        Sooner, he spurned it.
Image the whole, then execute the parts—
70   Fancy the fabric
Quite, ere you build, ere steel strike fire from quartz,
        Ere mortar dab brick!

(Here's the town gate reached: there's the market place
        Gaping before us.)
75 Yea, this in him was the peculiar grace
        (Hearten our chorus!)
That before living he'd learn how to live—
        No end to learning:
Earn the means first—God surely will contrive
80   Use for our earning.
Others mistrust and say, "But time escapes:
        Live now or never!"
He said, "What's time? Leave Now for dogs and apes!
        Man has Forever."
85 Back to his book then: deeper drooped his head:
        Calculus[8] racked him:
Leaden before, his eyes grew dross of lead:
        Tussis° attacked him.   *a cough*
"Now, master, take a little rest!"—not he!
90   (Caution redoubled,
Step two abreast, the way winds narrowly!)
        Not a whit troubled
Back to his studies, fresher than at first,
        Fierce as a dragon
95 He (soul-hydroptic[9] with a sacred thirst)
        Sucked at the flagon.
Oh, if we draw a circle premature,
        Heedless of far gain,
Greedy for quick returns of profit, sure
100   Bad is our bargain!
Was it not great? did not he throw on God
        (He loves the burthen)—
God's task to make the heavenly period
        Perfect the earthen?

7. Commentaries or annotations on a text.   9. Insatiably soul thirsty.
8. A stone such as a gallstone.

105 Did not he magnify the mind, show clear
      Just what it all meant?
  He would not discount life, as fools do here,
      Paid by installment.
  He ventured neck or nothing—heaven's success
110   Found, or earth's failure:
  "Wilt thou trust death or not?" He answered "Yes:
      Hence with life's pale lure!"
  That low man seeks a little thing to do,
      Sees it and does it:
115 This high man, with a great thing to pursue,
      Dies ere he knows it.
  That low man goes on adding one to one,
      His hundred's soon hit:
  This high man, aiming at a million,
120   Misses an unit.[1]
  That, has the world here—should he need the next,
      Let the world mind him!
  This, throws himself on God, and unperplexed
      Seeking shall find him.
125 So, with the throttling hands of death at strife,
      Ground he at grammar;
  Still, through the rattle, parts of speech were rife:
      While he could stammer
  He settled *Hoti's* business—let it be!—
130   Properly based *Oun*—
  Gave us the doctrine of the enclitic *De*,[2]
      Dead from the waist down.
  Well, here's the platform, here's the proper place:
      Hail to your purlieus,
135 All ye highfliers of the feathered race,
      Swallows and curlews!
  Here's the top peak; the multitude below
      Live, for they can, there:
  This man decided not to Live but Know—
140   Bury this man there?
  Here—here's his place, where meteors shoot, clouds form,
      Lightnings are loosened,
  Stars come and go! Let joy break with the storm,
      Peace let the dew send!
145 Lofty designs must close in like effects:
      Loftily lying,
  Leave him—still loftier than the world suspects,
      Living and dying.

ca. 1854   1855

---

1. A small item such as some trifling worldly pleasure.
2. "*Hoti,*" "*Oun,*" and "*De*": Greek particles meaning "that," "then," and "toward." An unaccented word such as *de* is "enclitic" when it affects the accentuation of a word adjacent to it. In a letter of 1863, Browning commented to Tennyson that he wanted his grammarian to have been working on "the biggest of the littlenesses."

An Epistle Containing the Strange Medical Experience of Karshish, the Arab Physician[1]

Karshish, the picker-up of learning's crumbs,
The not-incurious in God's handiwork
(This man's-flesh he hath admirably made,
Blown like a bubble, kneaded like a paste,
5   To coop up and keep down on earth a space
That puff of vapor from his mouth, man's soul)[2]
—To Abib, all-sagacious in our art,
Breeder in me of what poor skill I boast,
Like me inquisitive how pricks and cracks
10   Befall the flesh through too much stress and strain,
Whereby the wily vapor fain would slip
Back and rejoin its source before the term,—
And aptest in contrivance (under God)
To baffle it by deftly stopping such:—
15   The vagrant° Scholar to his Sage at home   *wandering*
Sends greeting (health and knowledge, fame with peace)
Three samples of true snakestone[3]—rarer still,
One of the other sort, the melon-shaped,
(But fitter, pounded fine, for charms than drugs)
20   And writeth now the twenty-second time.

    My journeyings were brought to Jericho:
Thus I resume. Who studious in our art
Shall count a little labor unrepaid?
I have shed sweat enough, left flesh and bone
25   On many a flinty furlong of this land.
Also, the country-side is all on fire
With rumors of a marching hitherward:
Some say Vespasian[4] cometh, some, his son.
A black lynx snarled and pricked a tufted ear;
30   Lust of my blood inflamed his yellow balls:°   *eyeballs*
I cried and threw my staff and he was gone.
Twice have the robbers stripped and beaten me,
And once a town declared me for a spy;
But at the end, I reach Jerusalem,
35   Since this poor covert where I pass the night,
This Bethany,[5] lies scarce the distance thence
A man with plague-sores at the third degree

1. The letter is written in 66 C.E., when the Romans, under Vespasian, were to invade Palestine. During a journey across the country, Karshish, whose name in Arabic means "one who gathers" (or roughly, "the picker-up of learning's crumbs"), has been collecting information on medical and scientific developments he has encountered. The "case" that has intrigued him most recently is that of Lazarus, a Jew who is reputed to have died and been miraculously brought back to life by a "Nazarene physician" many years earlier (cf. John 11.1–46). Karshish's letter is addressed from Bethlehem to Abib, formerly his science teacher and now his colleague and friend. Both scientists are imaginary characters.
2. Karshish is referring to the old belief that the soul leaves the body with the last breath in the form of a vapor.
3. A stone used to treat snake bites.
4. The Roman commander (and later emperor) who invaded Palestine in 66 C.E. His son Titus destroyed Jerusalem four years later.
5. The small village where Lazarus lives, located two miles south of Jerusalem.

Runs till he drops down dead. Thou laughest here!
'Sooth,[6] it elates me, thus reposed and safe,
40　To void the stuffing of my travel-scrip°　　　　　　*small bag*
And share with thee whatever Jewry yields.
A viscid choler is observable
In tertians,[7] I was nearly bold to say;
And falling-sickness° hath a happier cure　　　　　　*epilepsy*
45　Than our school wots° of: there's a spider here　　*knows*
Weaves no web, watches on the ledge of tombs,
Sprinkled with mottles on an ash-gray back;
Take five and drop them . . . but who knows his mind,
The Syrian runagate° I trust this to?　　　　　　　*renegade*
50　His service payeth me a sublimate[8]
Blown up his nose to help the ailing eye.
Best wait: I reach Jerusalem at morn,
There set in order my experiences,
Gather what most deserves, and give thee all—
55　Or I might add, Judea's gum-tragacanth[9]
Scales off in purer flakes, shines clearer-grained,
Cracks 'twixt the pestle and the porphyry,[1]
In fine exceeds our produce. Scalp-disease
Confounds me, crossing so with leprosy—
60　Thou hadst admired one sort I gained at Zoar[2]
But zeal outruns discretion. Here I end.

　　Yet stay: my Syrian blinketh gratefully,
Protesteth his devotion is my price—
Suppose I write what harms not, though he steal?
65　I half resolve to tell thee, yet I blush,
What set me off a-writing first of all.
An itch I had, a sting to write, a tang!
For, be it this town's barrenness—or else
The Man° had something in the look of him—　　　*Lazarus*
70　His case has struck me far more than 'tis worth.
So, pardon if—(lest presently I lose
In the great press of novelty at hand
The care and pains this somehow stole from me)
I bid thee take the thing while fresh in mind,
75　Almost in sight—for, wilt thou have the truth?
The very man is gone from me but now,
Whose ailment is the subject of discourse.
Thus then, and let thy better wit help all!

　　'Tis but a case of mania—subinduced[3]
80　By epilepsy, at the turning-point
Of trance prolonged° unduly some three days:

6. Forsooth; in truth.
7. A sticky bile is observable in fevers occurring every other day.
8. I.e., pays me for a medicine.
9. A salve derived from a plant.

1. A hard rock against which the substance is pounded with a pestle.
2. Town north of the Dead Sea.
3. Brought about as a result of something else.

When, by the exhibition° of some drug   *administration*
Or spell, exorcization, stroke of art
Unknown to me and which 'twere well to know,
85 The evil thing out-breaking all at once
Left the man whole and sound of body indeed,—
But, flinging (so to speak) life's gates too wide,
Making a clear house of it too suddenly,
The first conceit° that entered might inscribe   *idea*
90 Whatever it was minded on the wall
So plainly at that vantage, as it were,
(First come, first served) that nothing subsequent
Attaineth to erase those fancy-scrawls
The just-returned and new-established soul
95 Hath gotten now so thoroughly by heart
That henceforth she will read or these or none.
And first—the man's own firm conviction rests
That he was dead (in fact they buried him)
—That he was dead and then restored to life
100 By a Nazarene physician of his tribe:
—'Sayeth, the same bade "Rise," and he did rise.
"Such cases are diurnal,"[4] thou wilt cry.
Not so this figment!—not, that such a fume,[5]
Instead of giving way to time and health,
105 Should eat itself into the life of life,
As saffron[6] tingeth flesh, blood, bones and all!
For see, how he takes up the after-life.
The man—it is one Lazarus a Jew,
Sanguine,° proportioned, fifty years of age,   *robust*
110 The body's habit wholly laudable,°   *healthy*
As much, indeed, beyond the common health
As he were made and put aside to show.
Think, could we penetrate by any drug
And bathe the wearied soul and worried flesh,
115 And bring it clear and fair, by three days' sleep!
Whence has the man the balm that brightens all?
This grown man eyes the world now like a child.
Some elders of his tribe, I should premise,[7]
Led in their friend, obedient as a sheep,
120 To bear my inquisition. While they spoke,
Now sharply, now with sorrow,—told the case,—
He listened not except I spoke to him,
But folded his two hands and let them talk,
Watching the flies that buzzed: and yet no fool.
125 And that's a sample how his years must go.
Look, if a beggar, in fixed middle-life,
Should find a treasure,—can he use the same
With straitened habits and with tastes starved small,
And take at once to his impoverished brain
130 The sudden element that changes things,

4. Occur every day.
5. A vapor standing for a hallucinated belief.
6. Yellow-colored dye made from the plant of the

same name, also used as a spice.
7. Set forth beforehand.

That sets the undreamed-of rapture at his hand
And puts the cheap old joy in the scorned dust?
Is he not such an one as moves to mirth—
Warily parsimonious, when no need,
135 Wasteful as drunkenness at undue times?
All prudent counsel as to what befits
The golden mean, is lost on such an one:
The man's fantastic will is the man's law.
So here—we call the treasure knowledge, say,
140 Increased beyond the fleshly faculty—
Heaven opened to a soul while yet on earth,
Earth forced on a soul's use while seeing heaven:
The man is witless of the size, the sum,
The value in proportion of all things,
145 Or whether it be little or be much.
Discourse to him of prodigious armaments
Assembled to besiege his city now,
And of the passing of a mule with gourds—
'Tis one! Then take it on the other side,
150 Speak of some trifling fact,—he will gaze rapt
With stupor at its very littleness
(Far as I see), as if in that indeed
He caught prodigious import, whole results;
And so will turn to us the bystanders
155 In ever the same stupor (note this point)
That we too see not with his opened eyes.
Wonder and doubt come wrongly into play,
Preposterously, at cross-purposes.
Should his child sicken unto death,—why, look
160 For scarce abatement of his cheerfulness,
Or pretermission° of the daily craft!   *interruption*
While a word, gesture, glance from that same child
At play or in the school or laid asleep,
Will startle him to an agony of fear,
165 Exasperation, just as like. Demand
The reason why—" 'tis but a word," object—
"A gesture"—he regards thee as our lord[8]
Who lived there in the pyramid alone,
Looked at us (dost thou mind?) when, being young,
170 We both would unadvisedly recite
Some charm's beginning, from that book of his,
Able to bid the sun throb wide and burst
All into stars, as suns grown old are wont.
Thou and the child have each a veil alike
175 Thrown o'er your heads, from under which ye both
Stretch your blind hands and trifle with a match
Over a mine of Greek fire,[9] did ye know!
He holds on firmly to some thread of life—
(It is the life to lead perforcedly)

8. A magician or wise man under whom Karshish   9. Weapon made of sulfur, naphtha, and saltpeter.
and Abib had studied.

180 Which runs across some vast distracting orb
Of glory on either side that meager thread,
Which, conscious of, he must not enter yet—
The spiritual life around the earthly life:
The law of that is known to him as this,[1]
185 His heart and brain move there, his feet stay here.
So is the man perplexed with impulses
Sudden to start off crosswise, not straight on,
Proclaiming what is right and wrong across,
And not along, this black thread through the blaze—
190 "It should be" balked by "here it cannot be."
And oft the man's soul springs into his face
As if he saw again and heard again
His sage that bade him "Rise" and he did rise.
Something, a word, a tick o' the blood° within   *pulse beat*
195 Admonishes: then back he sinks at once
To ashes, who was very fire before,
In sedulous recurrence to his trade
Whereby he earneth him the daily bread;
And studiously the humbler for that pride,
200 Professedly the faultier that he knows
God's secret, while he holds the thread of life.
Indeed the especial marking of the man
Is prone submission to the heavenly will—
Seeing it, what it is, and why it is.
205 'Sayeth,° he will wait patient to the last   *he says*
For that same death which must restore his being
To equilibrium, body loosening soul
Divorced even now by premature full growth:
He will live, nay, it pleaseth him to live
210 So long as God please, and just how God please.
He even seeketh not to please God more
(Which meaneth, otherwise) than as God please.
Hence, I perceive not he affects° to preach   *aspires*
The doctrine of his sect whate'er it be,
215 Make proselytes as madmen thirst to do:
How can he give his neighbor the real ground,
His own conviction? Ardent as he is—
Call his great truth a lie, why, still the old
"Be it as God please" reassureth him.
220 I probed the sore[2] as thy disciple should:
"How, beast," said I, "this stolid carelessness
Sufficeth thee, when Rome is on her march
To stamp out like a little spark thy town,
Thy tribe, thy crazy tale and thee at once?"
225 He merely looked with his large eyes on me.
The man is apathetic, you deduce?
Contrariwise, he loves both old and young,
Able and weak, affects[3] the very brutes

1. I.e., he knows the law of the spiritual life as well
as that of the earthly life.
2. Investigated the case.
3. Has affection for.

And birds—how say I? flowers of the field—
230   As a wise workman recognizes tools
In a master's workshop, loving what they make.
Thus is the man, as harmless as a lamb:
Only impatient, let him do his best,
At ignorance and carelessness and sin—
235   An indignation which is promptly curbed:
As when in certain travels I have feigned
To be an ignoramus in our art
According to some preconceived design,
And happed to hear the land's practitioners
240   Steeped in conceit sublimed[4] by ignorance,
Prattle fantastically on disease,
Its cause and cure—and I must hold my peace!

    Thou wilt object—Why have I not ere this
Sought out the sage himself, the Nazarene
245   Who wrought this cure, inquiring at the source,
Conferring with the frankness that befits?
Alas! it grieveth me, the learnèd leech°   *doctor*
Perished in a tumult many years ago,
Accused,—our learning's fate,—of wizardry,
250   Rebellion, to the setting up a rule
And creed prodigious as described to me.
His death, which happened when the earthquake fell[5]
(Prefiguring, as soon appeared, the loss
To occult learning in our lord the sage
255   Who lived there in the pyramid alone)
Was wrought by the mad people—that's their wont!
On vain recourse, as I conjecture it,
To his tried virtue, for miraculous help—
How could he stop the earthquake? That's their way!
260   The other imputations must be lies:
But take one, though I loathe to give it thee,
In mere respect for any good man's fame.
(And after all, our patient Lazarus
Is stark mad; should we count on what he says?
265   Perhaps not: though in writing to a leech
'Tis well to keep back nothing of a case.)
This man so cured regards the curer, then,
As—God forgive me! who but God himself,
Creator and sustainer of the world,
270   That came and dwelt in flesh on it awhile!
—'Sayeth that such an one was born and lived,
Taught, healed the sick, broke bread at his own house,
Then died, with Lazarus by, for aught I know,
And yet was . . . what I said nor choose repeat,
275   And must have so avouched himself, in fact,
In hearing of this very Lazarus

---

4. Exalted. "Conceit": foolish fancy.
5. The earthquake at the time of Christ's crucifixion reported in Matthew 27.51.

Who saith—but why all this of what he saith?
Why write of trivial matters, things of price
Calling at every moment for remark?
280   I noticed on the margin of a pool
Blue-flowering borage, the Aleppo[6] sort,
Aboundeth, very nitrous. It is strange!

    Thy pardon for this long and tedious case,
Which, now that I review it, needs must seem
285   Unduly dwelt on, prolixly set forth!
Nor I myself discern in what is writ
Good cause for the peculiar interest
And awe indeed this man has touched me with.
Perhaps the journey's end, the weariness
290   Had wrought upon me first. I met him thus:
I crossed a ridge of short sharp broken hills
Like an old lion's cheek teeth. Out there came
A moon made like a face with certain spots
Multiform, manifold and menacing:
295   Then a wind rose behind me. So we met
In this old sleepy town at unaware,
The man and I. I send thee what is writ.
Regard it as a chance, a matter risked
To this ambiguous Syrian—he may lose,
300   Or steal, or give it thee with equal good,
Jerusalem's repose shall make amends
For time this letter wastes, thy time and mine;
Till when, once more thy pardon and farewell!

    The very God! think, Abib; dost thou think?
305   So, the All-Great, were the All-Loving too—
So, through the thunder comes a human voice
Saying, "O heart I made, a heart beats here!
Face, my hands fashioned, see it in myself!
Thou hast no power nor mayst conceive of mine,
310   But love I gave thee, with myself to love,
And thou must love me who have died for thee!"
The madman saith He said so: it is strange.

1855

Caliban upon Setebos   Two closely related controversies of the Victorian period led Browning to write this poem (the title of which means "Caliban's thoughts about Setebos"). The first, stimulated by Darwin, was concerned with humanity's origins and our relation to other animals (the poem teems with animal life; in 295 lines, as Park Honan has shown, there are sixty-three references to animals). Caliban, the half-man and half-monster of Shakespeare's *Tempest,* provided the poet with a model of how the mind of a primitive creature may operate. The second controversy

6. Town in northern Syria. "Borage": herb used medicinally that contains niter.

concerned the nature of God and God's responsibility for the existence of suffering in the world. Like many humans, Caliban thinks of God's nature as similar to his own. His anthropomorphic conception of the deity, whom he calls Setebos, is confined to what he has observed of life on his island and to what he has observed of himself. From the former derives his "natural theology," that is, his identifying the character of God from evidences provided by nature rather than from the evidence of supernatural revelation. From the latter, his observation of his own character, derives Caliban's conception of God's willful power. Caliban himself admires power and thinks of God in Calvinistic terms as a being who selects at random some creatures who are to be saved and others who are to be condemned to suffer.

An obstacle for the reader is Caliban's use of the third-person pronoun to refer to himself. Thus " 'Will sprawl" means "Caliban will sprawl" (an apostrophe before the verb usually indicates that Caliban himself is the implied subject). The deity is also referred to in the third person but with an initial capital letter ("He").

Caliban upon Setebos

Or Natural Theology in the Island

"Thou thoughtest that I was altogether such a one as thyself."[1]

['Will sprawl, now that the heat of day is best,
Flat on his belly in the pit's much mire,
With elbows wide, fists clenched to prop his chin.
And, while he kicks both feet in the cool slush,
5   And feels about his spine small eft-things° course,   *water lizards*
Run in and out each arm, and make him laugh:
And while above his head a pompion° plant,   *pumpkin*
Coating the cave-top as a brow its eye,
Creeps down to touch and tickle hair and beard,
10   And now a flower drops with a bee inside,
And now a fruit to snap at, catch and crunch—
He looks out o'er yon sea which sunbeams cross
And recross till they weave a spider web
(Meshes of fire, some great fish breaks at times)
15   And talks to his own self, howe'er he please,
Touching that other, whom his dam[2] called God.
Because to talk about Him, vexes—ha,
Could He but know! and time to vex is now,
When talk is safer than in wintertime.
20   Moreover Prosper and Miranda[3] sleep
In confidence he drudges at their task,
And it is good to cheat the pair, and gibe,
Letting the rank tongue blossom into speech.]

Setebos, Setebos, and Setebos!
25   'Thinketh, He dwelleth i' the cold o' the moon.

'Thinketh He made it, with the sun to match,
But not the stars; the stars came otherwise;

1. Psalm 50.21. The speaker is God.
2. Caliban's mother, Sycorax.

3. The daughter of Prospero, the magician, who is Caliban's master in *The Tempest*.

Only made clouds, winds, meteors, such as that:
Also this isle, what lives and grows thereon,
30   And snaky sea which rounds and ends the same.

'Thinketh, it came of being ill at ease:
He hated that He cannot change His cold,
Nor cure its ache. 'Hath spied an icy fish
That longed to 'scape the rock-stream where she lived,
35   And thaw herself within the lukewarm brine
O' the lazy sea her stream thrusts far amid,
A crystal spike 'twixt two warm walls of wave;[4]
Only, she ever sickened, found repulse
At the other kind of water, not her life,
40   (Green-dense and dim-delicious, bred o' the sun)
Flounced back from bliss she was not born to breathe,
And in her old bounds buried her despair,
Hating and loving warmth alike: so He.

'Thinketh, He made thereat the sun, this isle,
45   Trees and the fowls here, beast and creeping thing.
Yon otter, sleek-wet, black, lithe as a leech;
Yon auk,° one fire-eye in a ball of foam,   sea bird
That floats and feeds; a certain badger brown
He hath watched hunt with that slant white-wedge eye
50   By moonlight; and the pie° with the long tongue   magpie
That pricks deep into oakwarts for a worm,
And says a plain word when she finds her prize,
But will not eat the ants; the ants themselves
That build a wall of seeds and settled stalks
55   About their hole—He made all these and more,
Made all we see, and us, in spite: how else?
He could not, Himself, make a second self
To be His mate; as well have made Himself:
He would not make what he mislikes or slights,
60   An eyesore to Him, or not worth His pains:
But did, in envy, listlessness, or sport,
Make what Himself would fain, in a manner, be—
Weaker in most points, stronger in a few,
Worthy, and yet mere playthings all the while,
65   Things He admires and mocks too—that is it.
Because, so brave, so better though they be,
It nothing skills if He begin to plague.[5]
Look now, I melt a gourd-fruit into mash,
Add honeycomb and pods, I have perceived,
70   Which bite like finches when they bill and kiss—
Then, when froth rises bladdery,° drink up all,   bubbly
Quick, quick, till maggots scamper through my brain;
Last, throw me on my back i' the seeded thyme,
And wanton, wishing I were born a bird.

4. I.e., the thin stream of cold water that is driven into the warm ocean like a spike between walls.

5. I.e., our superior virtues are of no help to us if God elects to inflict plagues on us.

75 Put case, unable to be what I wish,
    I yet could make a live bird out of clay:
    Would not I take clay, pinch my Caliban
    Able to fly?—for, there, see, he hath wings,
    And great comb like the hoopoe's[6] to admire,
80 And there, a sting to do his foes offense,
    There, and I will that he begin to live,
    Fly to yon rock-top, nip me off the horns
    Of griggs° high up that make the merry din,   *grasshoppers*
    Saucy through their veined wings, and mind me not.
85 In which feat, if his leg snapped, brittle clay,
    And he lay stupid-like—why, I should laugh;
    And if he, spying me, should fall to weep,
    Beseech me to be good, repair his wrong,
    Bid his poor leg smart less or grow again—
90 Well, as the chance were, this might take or else
    Not take my fancy: I might hear his cry,
    And give the mankin three sound legs for one,
    Or pluck the other off, leave him like an egg,
    And lessoned he was mine and merely clay.
95 Were this no pleasure, lying in the thyme,
    Drinking the mash, with brain become alive,
    Making and marring clay at will? So He.
    'Thinketh, such shows nor right nor wrong in Him,
    Nor kind, nor cruel: He is strong and Lord.
100 'Am strong myself compared to yonder crabs
    That march now from the mountain to the sea;
    'Let twenty pass, and stone the twenty-first,
    Loving not, hating not, just choosing so.
    'Say, the first straggler that boasts purple spots
105 Shall join the file, one pincer twisted off;
    'Say, this bruised fellow shall receive a worm,
    And two worms he whose nippers end in red;
    As it likes me each time, I do: so He.

    Well then, 'supposeth He is good i' the main,
110 Placable if His mind and ways were guessed,
    But rougher than His handiwork, be sure!
    Oh, He hath made things worthier than Himself,
    And envieth that, so helped, such things do more
    Than He who made them! What consoles but this?
115 That they, unless through Him, do naught at all,
    And must submit: what other use in things?
    'Hath cut a pipe of pithless elder-joint
    That, blown through, gives exact the scream o' the jay
    When from her wing you twitch the feathers blue:
120 Sound this, and little birds that hate the jay
    Flock within stone's throw, glad their foe is hurt:
    Put case such pipe could prattle and boast forsooth,
    "I catch the birds, I am the crafty thing,

6. Bird with bright plumage.

I make the cry my maker cannot make
125 With his great round mouth; he must blow through mine!"
Would not I smash it with my foot? So He.

But wherefore rough, why cold and ill at ease?
Aha, that is a question! Ask, for that,
What knows—the something over Setebos
130 That made Him, or He, may be, found and fought,
Worsted, drove off and did to nothing,° perchance.   completely overcame
There may be something quiet o'er His head,
Out of His reach, that feels nor joy nor grief,
Since both derive from weakness in some way.
135 I joy because the quails come; would not joy
Could I bring quails here when I have a mind:
This Quiet, all it hath a mind to, doth.
'Esteemeth stars the outposts of its couch,
But never spends much thought nor care that way.
140 It may look up, work up—the worse for those
It works on! 'Careth but for Setebos[7]
The many-handed as a cuttlefish,
Who, making Himself feared through what He does,
Looks up, first, and perceives he cannot soar
145 To what is quiet and hath happy life;
Next looks down here, and out of very spite
Makes this a bauble-world to ape yon real,
These good things to match those as hips[8] do grapes.
'Tis solace making baubles, aye, and sport.
150 Himself peeped late, eyed Prosper at his books
Careless and lofty, lord now of the isle:
Vexed, 'stitched a book of broad leaves, arrow-shaped,
Wrote thereon, he knows what, prodigious words;
Has peeled a wand and called it by a name;
155 Weareth at whiles for an enchanter's robe
The eyed skin of a supple oncelot;[9]
And hath an ounce[1] sleeker than youngling mole,
A four-legged serpent he makes cower and couch,
Now snarl, now hold its breath and mind his eye,
160 And saith she is Miranda and my wife:
'Keeps for his Ariel[2] a tall pouch-bill crane
He bids go wade for fish and straight disgorge;
Also a sea beast, lumpish, which he snared,
Blinded the eyes of, and brought somewhat tame,
165 And split its toe-webs, and now pens the drudge
In a hole o' the rock and calls him Caliban;
A bitter heart that bides its time and bites.
'Plays thus at being Prosper in a way,
Taketh his mirth with make-believes: so He.

7. Caliban's concern is to appease only Setebos, not the other deity—the Quiet.
8. Hard fruits produced by wild roses.
9. Browning may have invented this term from the Spanish *oncela* or from the French *ocelot*. Both words signify a leopard or spotted wildcat.
1. A large, ferocious leopard, six or seven feet in length.
2. In *The Tempest*, a spirit who serves Prospero.

170   His dam held that the Quiet made all things
     Which Setebos vexed only: 'holds not so.
     Who made them weak, meant weakness He might vex.
     Had He meant other, while His hand was in,
     Why not make horny eyes no thorn could prick,
175   Or plate my scalp with bone against the snow,
     Or overscale my flesh 'neath joint and joint,
     Like an orc's° armor? Aye—so spoil His sport!   *sea monster's*
     He is the One now: only He doth all.

     'Saith, He may like, perchance, what profits Him.
180   Aye, himself loves what does him good; but why?
     'Gets good no otherwise. This blinded beast
     Loves whoso places flesh-meat on his nose,
     But, had he eyes, would want no help, but hate
     Or love, just as it liked him: He hath eyes.
185   Also it pleaseth Setebos to work,
     Use all His hands, and exercise much craft,
     By no means for the love of what is worked.
     'Tasteth, himself, no finer good i' the world
     When all goes right, in this safe summertime,
190   And he wants little, hungers, aches not much,
     Than trying what to do with wit and strength.
     'Falls to make something: 'piled yon pile of turfs,
     And squared and stuck there squares of soft white chalk,
     And, with a fish-tooth, scratched a moon on each,
195   And set up endwise certain spikes of tree,
     And crowned the whole with a sloth's skull a-top,
     Found dead i' the woods, too hard for one to kill.
     No use at all i' the work, for work's sole sake;
     'Shall some day knock it down again: so He.

200   'Saith He is terrible: watch His feats in proof!
     One hurricane will spoil six good months' hope.
     He hath a spite against me, that I know,
     Just as He favors Prosper, who knows why?
     So it is, all the same, as well I find.
205   'Wove wattles half the winter, fenced them firm
     With stone and stake to stop she-tortoises
     Crawling to lay their eggs here: well, one wave,
     Feeling the foot of Him upon its neck,
     Gaped as a snake does, lolled out its large tongue,
210   And licked the whole labor flat; so much for spite.
     'Saw a ball° flame down late (yonder it lies)   *meteorite*
     Where, half an hour before, I slept i' the shade:
     Often they scatter sparkles: there is force!
     'Dug up a newt He may have envied once
215   And turned to stone, shut up inside a stone.
     Please Him and hinder this?—What Prosper does?[3]

---

3. I.e., shall I please Setebos, as Prospero does, and thus prevent my being punished as the newt was punished?

Aha, if He would tell me how! Not He!
There is the sport: discover how or die!
All need not die, for of the things o' the isle
220   Some flee afar, some dive, some run up trees;
Those at His mercy—why, they please Him most
When . . . when . . . well, never try the same way twice!
Repeat what act has pleased, He may grow wroth.
You must not know His ways, and play Him off,
225   Sure of the issue. 'Doth the like himself:
'Spareth a squirrel that it nothing fears
But steals the nut from underneath my thumb,
And when I threat, bites stoutly in defense:
'Spareth an urchin° that contrariwise   hedgehog
230   Curls up into a ball, pretending death
For fright at my approach: the two ways please.
But what would move my choler more than this,
That either creature counted on its life
Tomorrow and next day and all days to come,
235   Saying, forsooth, in the inmost of its heart,
"Because he did so yesterday with me,
And otherwise with such another brute,
So must he do henceforth and always."—Aye?
Would teach the reasoning couple what "must" means!
240   'Doth as he likes, or wherefore Lord? So He.

'Conceiveth all things will continue thus,
And we shall have to live in fear of Him
So long as He lives, keeps His strength: no change,
If He have done His best, make no new world
245   To please Him more, so leave off watching this—
If He surprise not even the Quiet's self
Some strange day—or, suppose, grow into it
As grubs grow butterflies: else, here are we,
And there is He, and nowhere help at all.
250   'Believeth with the life, the pain shall stop.
His dam held different, that after death
He both plagued enemies and feasted friends:
Idly!⁴ He doth His worst in this our life,
Giving just respite lest we die through pain,
255   Saving last pain for worst—with which, an end.
Meanwhile, the best way to escape His ire
Is, not to seem too happy. 'Sees, himself,
Yonder two flies, with purple films and pink,
Bask on the pompion-bell above: kills both.
260   'Sees two black painful beetles roll their ball
On head and tail as if to save their lives:
Moves them the stick away they strive to clear.

Even so, 'would have Him misconceive, suppose
This Caliban strives hard and ails no less,

---

4. I.e., Caliban thinks his mother's opinion was wrong or idle. God's sport with humankind is confined to this world: there is no afterlife.

265 And always, above all else, envies Him;
Wherefore he mainly dances on dark nights,
Moans in the sun, gets under holes to laugh,
And never speaks his mind save housed as now:
Outside, 'groans, curses. If He caught me here,
270 O'erheard this speech, and asked "What chucklest at?"
'Would, to appease Him, cut a finger off,
Or of my three kid yearlings burn the best,
Or let the toothsome apples rot on tree,
Or push my tame beast for the orc to taste:
275 While myself lit a fire, and made a song
And sung it, *"What I hate, be consecrate*
To celebrate Thee and Thy state, no mate
For Thee; what see for envy in poor me?"
Hoping the while, since evils sometimes mend,
280 Warts rub away and sores are cured with slime,
That some strange day, will either the Quiet catch
And conquer Setebos, or likelier He
Decrepit may doze, doze, as good as die.

———

[What, what? A curtain o'er the world at once!
285 Crickets stop hissing; not a bird—or, yes,
There scuds His raven that has told Him all!
It was fool's play this prattling! Ha! The wind
Shoulders the pillared dust, death's house o' the move,[5]
And fast invading fires begin! White blaze—
290 A tree's head snaps—and there, there, there, there, there,
His thunder follows! Fool to gibe at Him!
Lo! 'Lieth flat and loveth Setebos!
'Maketh his teeth meet through his upper lip,
Will let those quails fly, will not eat this month
295 One little mess of whelks,° so he may 'scape!]   *shellfish*

ca. 1860   1864

Prospice[1]

Fear death?—to feel the fog in my throat,
    The mist in my face,
When the snows begin, and the blasts denote
    I am nearing the place,
5 The power of the night, the press of the storm,
    The post of the foe;
Where he stands, the Arch Fear in a visible form,
    Yet the strong man must go:
For the journey is done and the summit attained,
10   And the barriers fall,
Though a battle's to fight ere the guerdon be gained,
    The reward of it all.

---

5. The whirlwind stirs up a column of dust that Caliban associates with a house of death.

1. The title means "Look forward."

I was ever a fighter, so—one fight more,
    The best and the last!
15 I would hate that death bandaged my eyes, and forbore,
    And bade me creep past.
No! let me taste the whole of it, fare like my peers
    The heroes of old,
Bear the brunt, in a minute pay glad life's arrears
20   Of pain, darkness, and cold.
For sudden the worst turns the best to the brave,
    The black minute's at end,
And the elements' rage, the fiend-voices that rave,
    Shall dwindle, shall blend,
25 Shall change, shall become first a peace out of pain,
    Then a light, then thy breast,
O thou soul of my soul![2] I shall clasp thee again,
    And with God be the rest!

ca. 1861   1864

Abt Vogler[1]

(After He has Been Extemporizing Upon the Musical Instrument of His Invention[2])

1

Would that the structure brave, the manifold music I build,
    Bidding my organ obey, calling its keys to their work,
Claiming each slave of the sound, at a touch, as when Solomon willed
    Armies of angels that soar, legions of demons that lurk,
5 Man, brute, reptile, fly—alien of end and of aim,
    Adverse, each from the other heaven-high, hell-deep removed—
Should rush into sight at once as he named the ineffable Name,[3]
    And pile him a palace straight, to pleasure the princess[4] he loved!

2

Would it might tarry like his, the beautiful building of mine,
10   This which my keys in a crowd pressed and importuned to raise!
Ah, one and all, how they helped, would dispart now and now combine,
    Zealous to hasten the work, heighten their master his praise!
And one would bury his brow with a blind plunge down to hell,

2. Browning's wife.
1. Georg Joseph Vogler (1749–1814), a German priest and musician, held the honorary title of *Abbé* or *Abt*. As a composer, teacher, and designer of musical instruments he was well known in his own day, but he was most famous as an extemporizer at the organ. Browning's soliloquy represents Vogler at the organ joyfully improvising a piece of music and then reflecting on the ephemeral existence of such a unique work of art and of its possible relation to God's purposes in heaven and on earth.
A characteristic feature of *Abt Vogler* is the use

of exceptionally long sentences, densely packed with details, which may evoke for us the effects of rolling organ music. The resulting movement is markedly different from the brisk staccato rhythms of *A Toccata of Galuppi's*.
2. A compact organ called the orchestrion.
3. According to Jewish legend King Solomon (because he possessed a seal inscribed with the "ineffable Name" of God) had the power of compelling the demons of earth and air to perform his bidding.
4. Pharaoh's daughter (1 Kings 7.8).

Burrow awhile and build, broad on the roots of things,
Then up again swim into sight, having based me my palace well,
Founded it, fearless of flame, flat on the nether springs.

3

And another would mount and march, like the excellent minion he was,
Aye, another and yet another, one crowd but with many a crest,
Raising my rampired walls of gold as transparent as glass,
Eager to do and die, yield each his place to the rest:
For higher still and higher (as a runner tips with fire,
When a great illumination surprises a festal night—
Outlining round and round Rome's dome from space to spire)[5]
Up, the pinnacled glory reached, and the pride of my soul was in sight.

4

In sight? Not half! for it seemed, it was certain, to match man's birth,
Nature in turn conceived, obeying an impulse as I;
And the emulous heaven yearned down, made effort to reach the earth,
As the earth had done her best, in my passion, to scale the sky:
Novel splendors burst forth, grew familiar and dwelt with mine,
Not a point nor peak but found and fixed its wandering star;
Meteor-moons, balls of blaze: and they did not pale nor pine,
For earth had attained to heaven, there was no more near nor far.

5

Nay more; for there wanted not who walked in the glare and glow,
Presences plain in the place; or, fresh from the Protoplast,[6]
Furnished for ages to come, when a kindlier wind should blow,
Lured now to begin and live, in a house to their liking at last;
Or else the wonderful Dead who have passed through the body and gone,
But were back once more to breathe in an old world worth their new:
What never had been, was now; what was, as it shall be anon;
And what is—shall I say, matched both? for I was made perfect too.

6

All through my keys that gave their sounds to a wish of my soul,
All through my soul that praised as its wish flowed visibly forth,
All through music and me! For think, had I painted the whole,
Why, there it had stood, to see, nor the process so wonderworth:
Had I written the same, made verse—still, effect proceeds from cause,
Ye know why the forms are fair, ye hear how the tale is told;
It is all triumphant art, but art in obedience to laws,
Painter and poet are proud in the artist-list enrolled—

7

But here is the finger of God, a flash of the will that can,
Existent behind all laws, that made them and, lo, they are!

---

5. On festival nights the dome of Saint Peter's in Rome is illuminated by a series of lights ignited by a torch-bearer.

6. The original or archetypal form of a species. "Presences": beings of the future, not yet existing, who are "lured" into life by the music (line 36).

And I know not if, save in this, such gift be allowed to man,
    That out of three sounds he frame, not a fourth sound, but a star.[7]
Consider it well: each tone of our scale in itself is naught;
    It is everywhere in the world—loud, soft, and all is said:
55 Give it to me to use! I mix it with two in my thought:
    And, there! Ye have heard and seen: consider and bow the head!

8

Well, it is gone at last, the palace of music I reared;
    Gone! and the good tears start, the praises that come too slow;
For one is assured at first, one scarce can say that he feared,
60   That he even gave it a thought, the gone thing was to go.
Never to be again! But many more of the kind
    As good, nay, better perchance: is this your comfort to me?
To me, who must be saved because I cling with my mind
    To the same, same self, same love, same God: aye, what was, shall be.

9

65 Therefore to whom turn I but to thee, the ineffable Name?
    Builder and maker, thou, of houses not made with hands![8]
What, have fear of change from thee who art ever the same?
    Doubt that thy power can fill the heart that thy power expands?
There shall never be one lost good! What was, shall live as before;
70   The evil is null, is naught, is silence implying sound;
What was good shall be good, with, for evil, so much good more;
    On the earth the broken arcs; in the heaven, a perfect round.

10

All we have willed or hoped or dreamed of good shall exist;
    Not its semblance, but itself; no beauty, nor good, nor power
75 Whose voice has gone forth, but each survives for the melodist
    When eternity affirms the conception of an hour.
The high that proved too high, the heroic for earth too hard,
    The passion that left the ground to lose itself in the sky,
Are music sent up to God by the lover and the bard;
80   Enough that he heard it once: we shall hear it by-and-by.

11

And what is our failure here but a triumph's evidence
    For the fullness of the days? Have we withered or agonized?
Why else was the pause prolonged but that singing might issue thence?
    Why rushed the discords in but that harmony should be prized?
85 Sorrow is hard to bear, and doubt is slow to clear,
    Each sufferer says his say, his scheme of the weal and woe:
But God has a few of us whom he whispers in the ear;
    The rest may reason and welcome: 'tis we musicians know.

---

7. I.e., the musician's combining of three notes into a new harmonic unit is a creative act as miraculous as the creation of a star.

8. Cf. 2 Corinthians 5.1, in which Saint Paul speaks of "a building of God, an house not made with hands, eternal in the heavens."

12

Well, it is earth with me; silence resumes her reign:
90   I will be patient and proud, and soberly acquiesce.
Give me the keys. I feel for the common chord again,
        Sliding by semitones, till I sink to the minor—yes,
And I blunt it into a ninth,[9] and I stand on alien ground,
        Surveying awhile the heights I rolled from into the deep;
95 Which, hark, I have dared and done, for my resting place is found,
        The C Major[1] of this life: so, now I will try to sleep.

1864

Rabbi Ben Ezra[1]

1

        Grow old along with me!
        The best is yet to be,
The last of life, for which the first was made:
        Our times are in His hand
5   Who saith, "A whole I planned,
Youth shows but half; trust God: see all nor be afraid!"

2

        Not that, amassing flowers,
        Youth sighed, "Which rose make ours,
Which lily leave and then as best recall?"
10   Not that, admiring stars,
        It yearned, "Nor Jove, nor Mars;
Mine be some figured flame which blends, transcends them all!"

3

        Not for such hopes and fears
        Annulling youth's brief years,
15 Do I remonstrate: folly wide the mark!
        Rather I prize the doubt
        Low kinds exist without,
Finished and finite clods, untroubled by a spark.

4

        Poor vaunt of life indeed,
20   Were man but formed to feed
On joy, to solely seek and find and feast:
        Such feasting ended, then

---

9. A discord that requires resolution.
1. A key without sharps or flats, representing the plane of ordinary life.
1. The speaker, Abraham Ibn Ezra (ca. 1092–1167), was an eminent biblical scholar of Spain, but Browning makes little attempt to present him as a distinct individual or to relate him to the age in which he lived. Unlike the more characteristic monologues, *Rabbi Ben Ezra* is not dramatic but declamatory.

As sure an end to men;
Irks care the crop-full bird? Frets doubt the maw-crammed beast?[2]

5

25   Rejoice we are allied
   To That which doth provide
And not partake, effect and not receive!
   A spark disturbs our clod;
   Nearer we hold of God
30 Who gives, than of His tribes that take, I must believe.

6

   Then, welcome each rebuff
   That turns earth's smoothness rough,
Each sting that bids nor sit nor stand but go!
   Be our joys three parts pain!
35   Strive, and hold cheap the strain;
Learn, nor account the pang; dare, never grudge the throe!°   *anguish*

7

   For thence—a paradox
   Which comforts while it mocks—
Shall life succeed in that it seems to fail:
40   What I aspired to be,
   And was not, comforts me:
A brute I might have been, but would not sink i' the scale.

8

   What is he but a brute
   Whose flesh has soul to suit,
45 Whose spirit works lest arms and legs want play?
   To man, propose this test—
   Thy body at its best,
How far can that project thy soul on its lone way?

9

   Yet gifts should prove their use:
50   I own the Past profuse
Of power each side, perfection every turn:
   Eyes, ears took in their dole,
   Brain treasured up the whole;
Should not the heart beat once, "How good to live and learn"?

10

55   Not once beat, "Praise be Thine!
   I see the whole design,
I, who saw power, see now love perfect too:
   Perfect I call Thy plan:

---

2. I.e., does care disturb a bird whose gullet ("crop") is full of food? Does doubt trouble an animal whose stomach ("maw") is full?

Thanks that I was a man!
60 Maker, remake, complete—I trust what Thou shalt do!"

11

For pleasant is this flesh;
Our soul, in its rose-mesh[3]
Pulled ever to the earth, still yearns for rest;
Would we some prize might hold
65 To match those manifold
Possessions of the brute—gain most, as we did best!

12

Let us not always say,
"Spite of this flesh today
I strove, made head, gained ground upon the whole!"
70 As the bird wings and sings,
Let us cry, "All good things
Are ours, nor soul helps flesh more, now, than flesh helps soul!"

13

Therefore I summon age
To grant youth's heritage,
75 Life's struggle having so far reached its term:
Thence shall I pass, approved
A man, for aye removed
From the developed brute; a god though in the germ.

14

And I shall thereupon
80 Take rest, ere I be gone
Once more on my adventure brave and new;[4]
Fearless and unperplexed,
When I wage battle next,
What weapons to select, what armor to indue.°   *put on*

15

Youth ended, I shall try
85 My gain or loss thereby;
Leave the fire ashes,[5] what survives is gold:
And I shall weigh the same,
Give life its praise or blame:
90 Young, all lay in dispute; I shall know, being old.

16

For note, when evening shuts,
A certain moment cuts
The deed off, calls the glory from the gray:
A whisper from the west

3. The body, which holds the soul in its net.   5. If the fire leaves ashes.
4. In the next life.

95   Shoots—"Add this to the rest,
Take it and try its worth: here dies another day."

17

So, still within this life,
Though lifted o'er its strife,
Let me discern, compare, pronounce at last,
100   "This rage was right i' the main,
That acquiescence vain:
The Future I may face now I have proved the Past."

18

For more is not reserved
To man, with soul just nerved
105 To act tomorrow what he learns today:
Here, work enough to watch
The Master work, and catch
Hints of the proper craft, tricks of the tool's true play.

19

As it was better, youth
110   Should strive, through acts uncouth,
Toward making, than repose on aught found made:
So, better, age, exempt
From strife, should know, than tempt°   *attempt*
Further. Thou waitedst age: wait death nor be afraid!

20

115   Enough now, if the Right
And Good and Infinite
Be named here, as thou callest thy hand thine own,
With knowledge absolute,
Subject to no dispute
120 From fools that crowded youth, nor let thee feel alone.

21

Be there, for once and all,
Severed great minds from small,
Announced to each his station in the Past!
Was I, the world arraigned,[6]
125   Were they, my soul disdained,
Right? Let age speak the truth and give us peace at last![7]

22

Now, who shall arbitrate?
Ten men love what I hate,
Shun what I follow, slight what I receive;
130   Ten, who in ears and eyes

---

6. I.e., was I, whom the world arraigned.
7. Stanzas 20 and 21 affirm that in age we can more readily think independently than in youth.

Maturity enables us to ignore the pressure of having to conform to the thinking of the crowd of small-minded people.

Match me: we all surmise,
They this thing, and I that: whom shall my soul believe?

23

Not on the vulgar mass
Called "work," must sentence pass,
135   Things done, that took the eye and had the price;
O'er which, from level stand,
The low world laid its hand,
Found straightway to its mind, could value in a trice:

24

But all, the world's coarse thumb
140   And finger failed to plumb,
So passed in making up the main account;
All instincts immature,
All purposes unsure,
That weighed not as his work, yet swelled the man's amount:

25

145   Thoughts hardly to be packed
Into a narrow act,
Fancies that broke through language and escaped;
All I could never be,
All, men ignored in me,
150   This, I was worth to God, whose wheel the pitcher shaped.[8]

26

Aye, note that Potter's wheel,
That metaphor! and feel
Why time spins fast, why passive lies our clay—
Thou, to whom fools propound,[9]
155   When the wine makes its round,
"Since life fleets, all is change; the Past gone, seize today!"

27

Fool! All that is, at all,
Lasts ever, past recall;
Earth changes, but thy soul and God stand sure:
160   What entered into thee,
That was, is, and shall be:
Time's wheel runs back or stops: Potter and clay endure.

28

He fixed thee 'mid this dance
Of plastic circumstance,
165   This Present, thou, forsooth, wouldst fain arrest:[1]

8. The speaker's highest qualities of soul were
shaped on a potting wheel into an enduring
"pitcher" by God. Cf. Isaiah 64.8.
9. Perhaps addressed to Omar Khayyám, whose
poem, *The Rubáiyát*, urged men to eat, drink, and

be merry. Edward FitzGerald's translation of
Omar's poem had appeared in 1859.
1. I.e., you would be glad to stop ("arrest") time at
this present point of your life.

Machinery just meant
To give thy soul its bent,
Try thee and turn thee forth, sufficiently impressed.

29

What though the earlier grooves
170   Which ran the laughing loves
Around thy base,[2] no longer pause and press?
What though, about thy rim,
Skull-things in order grim
Grow out, in graver mood, obey the sterner stress?

30

175   Look not thou down but up!
To uses of a cup,
The festal board, lamp's flash, and trumpet's peal,
The new wine's foaming flow,
The Master's lips a-glow!
180 Thou, heaven's consummate cup, what need'st thou with earth's wheel?

31

But I need, now as then,
Thee, God, who moldest men;
And since, not even while the whirl was worst,
Did I—to the wheel of life
185   With shapes and colors rife,
Bound dizzily—mistake my end, to slake Thy thirst:

32

So, take and use Thy work:
Amend what flaws may lurk,
What strain o' the stuff, what warpings past the aim!
190   My times be in Thy hand!
Perfect the cup as planned!
Let age approve of youth, and death complete the same!

ca. 1862   1864

2. Of the clay pitcher.

EMILY BRONTË
1818–1848

Emily Brontë spent most of her life in a stone parsonage in the small village of Haworth on the wild and bleak Yorkshire moors. She was the fifth of Patrick and Maria Brontë's six children. Her father was a clergyman; her mother died when she was two. At the age of six, she was sent away to a school for the daughters of poor clergy with her three elder sisters; within a year, the two oldest girls had died, in part the result of the school's harsh and unhealthful conditions, which Charlotte Brontë was later to portray in *Jane Eyre*. Mr. Brontë brought his two remaining daughters home, where, together with their brother and younger sister, he educated them himself. Emily was the most reclusive and private of the children; she shunned the company of those outside her family and suffered acutely from homesickness in her few short stays away from the parsonage.

Despite the isolation of Haworth, the Brontë family shared a rich literary life. Mr. Brontë discussed poetry, history, and politics with his children, and the children themselves created an extraordinary fantasy world together. When Mr. Brontë gave his son a box of wooden soldiers, each child excitedly seized one and named it. The soldiers became for them the centers of an increasingly elaborate set of stories that they first acted out in plays and later recorded in a series of book-length manuscripts, composed for the most part by Charlotte and her brother, Branwell. The two younger children, Emily and Anne, later started a separate series, a chronicle about an imaginary island called Gondal.

In Charlotte Brontë's preface to the second edition of *Wuthering Heights,* she tells the story of how she and her sister came to write for publication. One day when she accidentally came upon a manuscript volume of verse in Emily's handwriting, she was struck by the conviction "that these were not common effusions, nor at all like the poetry women generally write." With some difficulty, Charlotte persuaded her intensely private sister to publish some of her poems in a selection of poetry by all three Brontë sisters. Averse to personal publicity and afraid that "authoresses are liable to be looked on with prejudice," Charlotte, Emily, and Anne adopted the pseudonyms of Currer, Ellis, and Acton Bell. Although the book sold only two copies, its publication inspired each of the Brontë sisters to begin work on a novel; Emily's, of course, was *Wuthering Heights.* She began work on a second novel, but a year after the publication of *Wuthering Heights,* she died of consumption.

Many of Emily's poems—*Remembrance* and *The Prisoner,* for example—were written for the Gondal saga and express its preoccupation with political intrigue, passionate love, rebellion, war, imprisonment, and exile. Brontë also wrote personal lyrics unconnected with the Gondal stories; but both groups of poems share a drive to break through the constrictions of ordinary life, whether by the transfigurative power of the imagination, by union with another, or by death itself. Like Catherine and Heathcliff in *Wuthering Heights,* the speakers of Brontë's poems yearn for a fuller, freer world of spirit, transcending the forms and limits of mortal life. Her concern with a visionary world links her to the Romantic poets, particularly to Byron and Shelley; but her hymnlike stanzas have a haunting quality that distinguishes her individual voice.

The texts printed here are from the edition of *Poems* published by the Brontë sisters for the poems it includes and C. W. Hatfield's edition of Brontë's manuscripts for the poems she did not publish during her life.

I'm Happiest When Most Away

I'm happiest when most away
I can bear my soul from its home of clay
On a windy night when the moon is bright
And the eye can wander through worlds of light—

5 When I am not and none beside—
Nor earth nor sea nor cloudless sky—
But only spirit wandering wide
Through infinite immensity.

1838   1910

The Night-Wind

In summer's mellow midnight,
A cloudless moon shone through
Our open parlour window
And rosetrees wet with dew.

5   I sat in silent musing,
The soft wind waved my hair:
It told me Heaven was glorious.
And sleeping Earth was fair.

I needed not its breathing
10   To bring such thoughts to me,
But still it whispered lowly,
"How dark the woods will be!

"The thick leaves in my murmur
Are rustling like a dream,
15   And all their myriad voices
Instinct with spirit seem."

I said, "Go, gentle singer,
Thy wooing voice is kind,
But do not think its music
20   Has power to reach my mind.

"Play with the scented flower,
The young tree's supple bough,
And leave my human feelings
In their own course to flow."

25   The wanderer would not leave me;
Its kiss grew warmer still—
"O come," it sighed so sweetly,
"I'll win thee 'gainst thy will.

"Have we not been from childhood friends?
30   Have I not loved thee long?
As long as thou hast loved the night
Whose silence wakes my song.

"And when thy heart is laid at rest
Beneath the church-yard stone
35   I shall have time enough to mourn
And thou to be alone."

1840   1850

Remembrance[1]

Cold in the earth, and the deep snow piled above thee!
Far, far removed, cold in the dreary grave!
Have I forgot, my Only Love, to love thee,
Severed at last by Time's all-wearing wave?

5 Now, when alone, do my thoughts no longer hover
Over the mountains, on that northern shore;
Resting their wings where heath and fern-leaves cover
Thy noble heart for ever, ever more?

Cold in the earth, and fifteen wild Decembers
10 From those brown hills have melted into spring—
Faithful indeed is the spirit that remembers
After such years of change and suffering!

Sweet Love of youth, forgive if I forget thee
While the World's tide is bearing me along:
15 Other desires and other hopes beset me,
Hopes which obscure but cannot do thee wrong.

No later light has lightened up my heaven,
No second morn has ever shone for me:
All my life's bliss from thy dear life was given—
20 All my life's bliss is in the grave with thee.

But when the days of golden dreams had perished
And even Despair was powerless to destroy,
Then did I learn how existence could be cherished,
Strengthened and fed without the aid of joy;

25 Then did I check the tears of useless passion,
Weaned my young soul from yearning after thine;
Sternly denied its burning wish to hasten
Down to that tomb already more than mine!

And even yet, I dare not let it languish,
30 Dare not indulge in Memory's rapturous pain;
Once drinking deep of that divinest anguish,
How could I seek the empty world again?

1845   1846

Stars

Ah! why, because the dazzling sun
Restored our earth to joy

1. Titled in manuscript *R. Alcona to J. Breznaida,* this poem was originally composed as a lament by the heroine of the Gondal saga for the hero's death.

Have you departed, every one,
And left a desert sky?

5   All through the night, your glorious eyes
Were gazing down in mine,
And with a full heart's thankful sighs
I blessed that watch divine!

    I was at peace, and drank your beams
10 As they were life to me
And revelled in my changeful dreams
Like petrel° on the sea.   *small dark seabirds*

    Thought followed thought—star followed star
Through boundless regions on,
15 While one sweet influence, near and far,
Thrilled through and proved us one.

    Why did the morning dawn to break
So great, so pure a spell,
And scorch with fire the tranquil cheek
20 Where your cool radiance fell?

    Blood-red he rose, and arrow-straight
His fierce beams struck my brow:
The soul of Nature sprang elate,
But mine sank sad and low!

25 My lids closed down—yet through their veil
I saw him blazing still;
And steep in gold the misty dale
And flash upon the hill.

    I turned me to the pillow then
30 To call back Night, and see
Your worlds of solemn light, again
Throb with my heart and me!

    It would not do—the pillow glowed
And glowed both roof and floor,
35 And birds sang loudly in the wood,
And fresh winds shook the door.

    The curtains waved, the wakened flies
Were murmuring round my room,
Imprisoned there, till I should rise
40 And give them leave to roam.

    O Stars and Dreams and Gentle Night;
O Night and Stars return!
And hide me from the hostile light
That does not warm, but burn—

45   That drains the blood of suffering men;
      Drinks tears, instead of dew:
      Let me sleep through his blinding reign,
      And only wake with you!

1845   1846

The Prisoner. A Fragment[1]

In the dungeon crypts idly did I stray,
Reckless of the lives wasting there away;
"Draw the ponderous bars; open, Warder stern!"
He dare not say me nay—the hinges harshly turn.

5   "Our guests are darkly lodged," I whispered, gazing through
    The vault whose grated eye showed heaven more grey than blue.
    (This was when glad spring laughed in awaking pride.)
    "Aye, darkly lodged enough!" returned my sullen guide.

    Then, God forgive my youth, forgive my careless tongue!
10 I scoffed, as the chill chains on the damp flagstones rung;
    "Confined in triple walls, art thou so much to fear,
    That we must bind thee down and clench thy fetters here?"

    The captive raised her face; it was as soft and mild
    As sculptured marble saint or slumbering, unweaned child;
15 It was so soft and mild, it was so sweet and fair,
    Pain could not trace a line nor grief a shadow there!

    The captive raised her hand and pressed it to her brow:
    "I have been struck," she said, "and I am suffering now;
    Yet these are little worth, your bolts and irons strong;
20 And were they forged in steel they could not hold me long."

    Hoarse laughed the jailor grim: "Shall I be won to hear;
    Dost think, fond° dreaming wretch, that *I* shall grant thy prayer?   *foolish*
    Or, better still, wilt melt my master's heart with groans?
    Ah, sooner might the sun thaw down these granite stones!

25 "My master's voice is low, his aspect bland and kind,
    But hard as hardest flint the soul that lurks behind;
    And I am rough and rude, yet not more rough to see
    Than is the hidden ghost which has its home in me!

    About her lips there played a smile of almost scorn:
30 "My friend," she gently said, "you have not heard me mourn;
    When you my kindred's lives—*my* lost life, can restore
    Then may I weep and sue—but *never,* Friend, before!"

1. An excerpt from a poem in the Gondal manuscript, *Julian M. and A. G. Rochelle,* describing an event unplaced in the story, this poem was printed as *The Prisoner: A Fragment* in *Poems* by the Brontë sisters. The speaker, a man, is visiting a dungeon in his father's castle.

"Still, let my tyrants know, I am not doomed to wear
Year after year in gloom and desolate despair;
35 A messenger of Hope comes every night to me,
And offers, for short life, eternal liberty.

He comes with western winds, with evening's wandering airs,
With that clear dusk of heaven that brings the thickest stars;
Winds take a pensive tone, and stars a tender fire,
40 And visions rise and change that kill me with desire—

"Desire for nothing known in my maturer years
When joy grew mad with awe at counting future tears;
When, if my spirit's sky was full of flashes warm,
I knew not whence they came, from sun or thunderstorm;

45 "But first a hush of peace, a soundless calm descends;
The struggle of distress and fierce impatience ends;
Mute music soothes my breast—unuttered harmony
That I could never dream till earth was lost to me.

"Then dawns the Invisible, the Unseen its truth reveals;
50 My outward sense is gone, my inward essence feels—
Its wings are almost free, its home, its harbour found;
Measuring the gulf it stoops and dares the final bound!

"Oh, dreadful is the check—intense the agony
When the ear begins to hear and the eye begins to see;
55 When the pulse begins to throb, the brain to think again,
The soul to feel the flesh and the flesh to feel the chain!

"Yet I would lose no sting, would wish no torture less;
The more that anguish racks the earlier it will bless;
And robed in fires of Hell, or bright with heavenly shine,
60 If it but herald Death, the vision is divine."[2]

She ceased to speak, and we, unanswering turned to go—
We had no further power to work the captive woe;
Her cheek, her gleaming eye, declared that man had given
A sentence unapproved, and overruled by Heaven.

1845   1846

No Coward Soul Is Mine[1]

No coward soul is mine
No trembler in the world's storm-troubled sphere

---

2. Cf. the words of the dying Catherine in *Wuthering Heights*: "The thing that irks me most is this shattered prison [my body]. . . . I'm tired, tired of being enclosed here. I'm wearying to escape into that glorious world, and to be always there. . . . I shall be incomparably beyond and above you all."
1. According to Charlotte Brontë, these are the last lines written by her sister.

I see Heaven's glories shine
And Faith shines equal arming me from Fear

5   O God within my breast
Almighty ever-present Deity
Life, that in me hast rest
As I Undying Life, have power in Thee

Vain are the thousand creeds
10   That move men's hearts, unutterably vain,
Worthless as withered weeds
Or idlest froth amid the boundless main

To waken doubt in one
Holding so fast by thy infinity
15   So surely anchored on
The steadfast rock of Immortality

With wide-embracing love
Thy spirit animates eternal years
Pervades and broods above,
20   Changes, sustains, dissolves, creates and rears

Though Earth and moon were gone
And suns and universes ceased to be
And thou wert left alone
Every Existence would exist in thee

25   There is not room for Death
Nor atom that his might could render void
Since thou art Being and Breath
And what thou art may never be destroyed.

1846   1850

JOHN RUSKIN
1819–1900

John Ruskin was both the leading Victorian critic of art and an important critic of society. These two roles can be traced back to two important influences of his childhood. His father, a wealthy wine merchant, was fond of travel, and on tours of the Continent he introduced his son to landscape, architecture, and art. From this exposure Ruskin acquired a zest for beauty that animates even the most theoretical of his discussions of aesthetics. In his autobiography he describes his first view of the Swiss Alps at sunset: "the seen walls of lost Eden could not have been more beautiful" (he was fourteen at the time):

It is not possible to imagine, in any time of the world, a more blessed entrance into life, for a child of such a temperament as mine. True, the temperament belonged to the age: a very few years,—within the hundred,—before that, no child could have been born to care for mountains, or for the men that lived among them, in that way. Till Rousseau's time, there had been no "sentimental" love of nature; and till Scott's, no such apprehensive love of "all sorts and conditions of men," not in the soul merely, but in the flesh . . . I went down that evening from the garden-terrace of Schaffhausen with my destiny fixed in all of it that was to be sacred and useful.

Such a rapturous response to the beauties of nature was later to be duplicated by his response to the beauties of architecture and art. During a tour of "this Holy Land of Italy" (as he called it), he visited Venice and recorded in his diary (May 6, 1841) his response to Saint Mark's cathedral square in that city: "Thank God I am here! It is the Paradise of cities and there is moon enough to make herself the sanities of earth lunatic, striking its pure flashes of light against the grey water before the window; and I am happier than I have been these five years. . . . I feel fresh and young when my foot is on these pavements."

Ruskin's choice of phrase in these accounts of how beauty affected him reflects the second influence in his life, often at variance with the first: his daily Bible readings under the direction of his mother. From this biblical indoctrination, Ruskin derived some elements of his lush and highly rhythmical prose style but more especially his sense of prophecy and mission as a critic of modern society.

Ruskin's life was spent in traveling, lecturing, and writing. His prodigious literary output can be roughly divided into three phases. At first he was preoccupied with problems of art. *Modern Painters,* which he began writing at the age of twenty-three after his graduation from Oxford, was a defense of the English landscape painter J. M. W. Turner (1775–1851). This defense (which was to extend to five volumes) involved Ruskin in problems of truth in art (as in his chapter "Pathetic Fallacy") and in the ultimate importance of imagination (as in his discussion of Turner's painting *The Slave Ship*).

During the 1850s Ruskin's principal interest shifted from art to architecture, especially to the problem of determining what kind of society is capable of producing great buildings. His enthusiasm for Gothic architecture was infectious, and he has sometimes been blamed for the prevalence of Gothic buildings on college campuses in America. A study of *The Stones of Venice* (1851–53), however (especially the chapter printed here), will show that merely to revive the Gothic style was not his concern. What he wanted to revive was the kind of society that had produced such architecture, a society in which the individual workers could express themselves and enjoy what Ruskin's disciple William Morris called "work-pleasure." A mechanized production-line society, such as Ruskin's or our own, could not produce Gothic architecture but only imitations of its mannerisms. Ruskin's concern was to change industrial society not to decorate concrete towers with gargoyles.

This interest in the stultifying effects of industrialism led Ruskin gradually into economics. After 1860 the critic of art became (like his master, Carlyle) an outspoken critic of laissez-faire economics. His conception of the responsibilities of employers toward their workers, as expounded in *Unto This Last* (1860), was dismissed by his contemporaries as an absurdity. What he was laboring to show was that self-seeking business relationships might be made over on the principle of dedicated service, taking as a model the learned professions and also the military. The soldier, however crude, is more highly regarded by society than the capitalist, Ruskin said, "for the soldier's trade . . . is not slaying, but being slain." Although his position was essentially conservative in the proper sense of the word (he styled himself "a violent Tory of the old school;—Walter Scott's school"), he was regarded as a radical eccentric. It was many years before his social criticism gained a following among writers as diverse as William Morris, Bernard Shaw, and D. H. Lawrence; and in particular among the founders of the British Labour Party, his influence was to be profound and lasting.

Ruskin's realization, after 1860, that despite his fame he was becoming isolated and that the world was continuing to move in directions opposite from those to which he pointed may have contributed to the recurrent mental breakdowns from which he suffered between 1870 and 1900. As he reports in *Fors Clavigera* (1880): "The doctors said I went mad, this time two years ago, from overwork," but he had not then been working harder than usual. "I went mad because nothing came of my work . . . because after I got [my manuscripts] published, nobody believed a word of them."Also contributing to his breakdowns may have been his unhappiness in his relations with women. His marriage to Effie Gray in 1848 was a disaster. After six years of living together an annulment was arranged on the grounds that the marriage had not been consummated. Ruskin testified that he had not found his wife's person physically attractive, although by others she was considered a great beauty. One of these admirers was the Pre-Raphaelite painter John Millais, who fell in love with her at a time when he was painting her husband's portrait; shortly after the annulment he married her. In later years Ruskin fell pathetically in love with a young Irish girl, Rose La Touche, whom he first met when he was nearly forty and she was a child of nine. They were divided not only by the gap of age but by religious differences. She was an intensely pious believer; and for several years after Ruskin proposed marriage to her, when she was eighteen, she tried unsuccessfully to persuade him to return to the Evangelical faith that he had abandoned. In 1875, after herself suffering attacks of mental illness, La Touche died at the age of twenty-five. In his autobiography Ruskin commented: "I wonder mightily what sort of creature I should have turned out, if instead of the distracting and useless pain, I had had the joy of approved love, and the untellable, incalculable motive of its sympathy and praise. It seems to me such things are not allowed in the world. The men capable of the highest imaginative passion are always tossed on fiery waves by it." Despite both the despair that he suffered following La Touche's death and the recurring attacks of mental illness that blighted the last thirty-five years of his life, Ruskin remained active and productive up until his final silent decade of the 1890s. His publications during his active period included six volumes of his lectures on art that he had delivered as Slade Professor of Fine Arts at Oxford and his letters to laborers, *Fors Clavigera* (1871–84). One topic that becomes especially prominent in these later writings is pollution of air and water—an ideal subject for Ruskin's eloquence. In discussing it he combines his lifelong love for beautiful landscape and landscape painting with his later acquired conviction that modern industrial leadership was woefully irresponsible. A letter of A. E. Housman, who was an undergraduate at Oxford in 1877, provides a vivid record of how effective Ruskin could be:

> This afternoon Ruskin gave us a great outburst against modern times. He had got a picture of Turner's, framed and glassed, representing Leicester and the Abbey in the distance at sunset, over a river. He read the account of Wolsey's death out of *Henry VIII*. Then he pointed to the picture as representing Leicester when Turner had drawn it. Then he said, "You, if you like, may go to Leicester to see what it is like now. I never shall. But I can make a pretty good guess." Then he caught up a paintbrush. "These stepping-stones of course have been done away with, and are replaced by a be-au-ti-ful iron bridge." Then he dashed in the iron bridge on the glass of the picture. "The color of the stream is supplied on one side by the indigo factory." Forthwith one side of the stream became indigo. "On the other side by the soap factory." Soap dashed in. "They mix in the middle—like curds," he said, working them together with a sort of malicious deliberation. "This field, over which you see the sun setting behind the abbey, is

now occupied in a *proper* manner." Then there went a flame of scarlet across the picture, which developed itself into windows and roofs and red brick, and rushed up into a chimney. "The atmosphere is supplied—thus!" A puff and cloud of smoke all over Turner's sky: and then the brush thrown down, and Ruskin confronting modern civilization amidst a tempest of applause, which he always elicits now, as he has this term become immensely popular, his lectures being crowded, whereas of old he used to prophesy to empty benches.

Among Ruskin's publications that illustrate this crusade against pollution is his tirade of 1884, *The Storm-Cloud of the Nineteenth Century*. And finally, following this awesome vision of the future, Ruskin concluded his long writing career with a dramatic shift of focus from time future to time past—in his delightful autobiography, *Praeterita* (meaning "the past"), written from 1885 to 1889.

From Modern Painters

[A DEFINITION OF GREATNESS IN ART][1]

Painting, or art generally, as such, with all its technicalities, difficulties, and particular ends, is nothing but a noble and expressive language, invaluable as the vehicle of thought, but by itself nothing. He who has learned what is commonly considered the whole art of painting, that is, the art of representing any natural object faithfully, has as yet only learned the language by which his thoughts are to be expressed. He has done just as much towards being that which we ought to respect as a great painter, as a man who has learnt how to express himself grammatically and melodiously has towards being a great poet. The language is, indeed, more difficult of acquirement in the one case than in the other, and possesses more power of delighting the sense, while it speaks to the intellect; but it is, nevertheless, nothing more than language, and all those excellences which are peculiar to the painter as such, are merely what rhythm, melody, precision, and force are in the words of the orator and the poet, necessary to their greatness, but not the tests of their greatness. It is not by the mode of representing and saying, but by what is represented and said, that the respective greatness either of the painter or the writer is to be finally determined.

* * *

* * * So that, if I say that the greatest picture is that which conveys to the mind of the spectator the greatest number of the greatest ideas, I have a definition which will include as subjects of comparison every pleasure which art is capable of conveying. If I were to say, on the contrary, that the best picture was that which most closely imitated nature, I should assume that art could only please by imitating nature; and I should cast out of the pale of criticism those parts of works of art which are not imitative, that is to say, intrinsic beauties of color and form, and those works of art wholly, which, like the Arabesques of Raffaelle in the Loggias,[2] are not imitative at all. Now, I want a definition of art wide enough to include all its varieties of aim. I do not say, therefore, that the art is greatest which gives most pleasure, because

1. From vol. 1, part 1, section 1, chap. 2.
2. The arabesques in the Loggia of the Vatican, designed by Raphael, were decorative wall paint-ings that feature a complex pattern of leaves, animals, and human figures.

perhaps there is some art whose end is to teach, and not to please. I do not say that the art is greatest which teaches us most, because perhaps there is some art whose end is to please, and not to teach. I do not say that the art is greatest which imitates best, because perhaps there is some art whose end is to create and not to imitate. But I say that the art is greatest which conveys to the mind of the spectator, by any means whatsoever, the greatest number of the greatest ideas; and I call an idea great in proportion as it is received by a higher faculty of the mind, and as it more fully occupies, and in occupying, exercises and exalts, the faculty by which it is received.

If this, then, be the definition of great art, that of a great artist naturally follows. He is the greatest artist who has embodied, in the sum of his works, the greatest number of the greatest ideas.

["THE SLAVE SHIP"]³

But I think the noblest sea that Turner has ever painted, and, if so, the noblest certainly ever painted by man, is that of "The Slave Ship," the chief Academy⁴ picture of the exhibition of 1840. It is a sunset on the Atlantic after prolonged storm; but the storm is partially lulled, and the torn and streaming rain clouds are moving in scarlet lines to lose themselves in the hollow of the night. The whole surface of sea included in the picture is divided into two ridges of enormous swell, not high, nor local, but a low, broad heaving of the whole ocean, like the lifting of its bosom by deep-drawn breath after the torture of the storm. Between these two ridges the fire of the sunset falls along the trough of the sea, dyeing it with an awful but glorious light, the intense and lurid splendor which burns like gold and bathes like blood. Along this fiery path and valley the tossing waves by which the swell of the sea is restlessly divided lift themselves in dark, indefinite, fantastic forms, each casting a faint and ghastly shadow behind it along the illumined foam. They do not rise everywhere, but three or four together in wild groups, fitfully and furiously, as the under-strength of the swell compels or permits them; leaving between them treacherous spaces of level and whirling water, now lighted with green and lamplike fire, now flashing back the gold of the declining sun, now fearfully shed from above with the indistinguishable images of the burning clouds, which fall upon them in flakes of crimson and scarlet and give to the reckless waves the added motion of their own fiery being. Purple and blue, the lurid shadows of the hollow breakers are cast upon the mist of night, which gathers cold and low, advancing like the shadow of death upon the guilty ship as it labors amidst the lightning of the sea, its thin masts written upon the sky in lines of blood, girded with condemnation in that fearful hue which signs the sky with horror, and mixes its flaming flood with the sunlight, and, cast far along the desolate heave of the sepulchral waves, incarnadines the multitudinous sea.⁵

I believe, if I were reduced to rest Turner's immortality upon any single

3. From vol. 1, part 2, section 5, chap. 3. The painting is of a ship in which slaves are being transported. Victims who have died during the passage are being thrown overboard at sunset; as Ruskin noted, "the near sea is encumbered with corpses."
4. The Royal Academy of Arts, founded in London in 1768. The painting was given to Ruskin by his father as a New Year's present in 1844 and hung in the Ruskin household for a number of years until Ruskin decided to sell it because he found its subject "too painful to live with." The painting now hangs in the Museum of Fine Arts in Boston.
5. Shakespeare's *Macbeth* 2.2.60.

work, I should choose this. Its daring conception—ideal in the highest sense of the word—is based on the purest truth, and wrought out with the concentrated knowledge of a life; its color is absolutely perfect, not one false or morbid hue in any part or line, and so modulated that every square inch of canvas is a perfect composition; its drawing as accurate as fearless; the ship buoyant, bending, and full of motion; its tones as true as they are wonderful; and the whole picture dedicated to the most sublime of subjects and impressions—completing thus the perfect system of all truth which we have shown to be formed by Turner's works—the power, majesty, and deathfulness of the open, deep, illimitable Sea.

1843

From *Of the Pathetic Fallacy*[6]

*   *   *

Now therefore, putting these tiresome and absurd words[7] quite out of our way, we may go on at our ease to examine the point in question—namely, the difference between the ordinary, proper, and true appearances of things to us; and the extraordinary, or false appearances, when we are under the influence of emotion, or contemplative fancy; false appearances, I say, as being entirely unconnected with any real power of character in the object, and only imputed to it by us.

For instance—

> The spendthrift crocus, bursting through the mold
> Naked and shivering, with his cup of gold.[8]

This is very beautiful, and yet very untrue. The crocus is not a spendthrift, but a hardy plant; its yellow is not gold, but saffron. How is it that we enjoy so much the having it put into our heads that it is anything else than a plain crocus?

It is an important question. For, throughout our past reasonings about art, we have always found that nothing could be good or useful, or ultimately pleasurable, which was untrue. But here is something pleasurable in written poetry, which is nevertheless *un*true. And what is more, if we think over our favorite poetry, we shall find it full of this kind of fallacy, and that we like it all the more for being so.

It will appear also, on consideration of the matter, that this fallacy is of two principal kinds. Either, as in this case of the crocus, it is the fallacy of willful fancy, which involves no real expectation that it will be believed; or else it is a fallacy caused by an excited state of the feelings, making us, for the time, more or less irrational. Of the cheating of the fancy we shall have to speak presently; but, in this chapter, I want to examine the nature of the

6. From vol. 3, part 4, chap. 12. In this celebrated chapter, Ruskin shifts from discussing problems of truth and realism in art to the same problems in literature. The term *pathetic* refers not to something feebly ineffective but to the emotion (pathos) with which a writer invests descriptions of objects and of the distortion (fallacy) that may result. Poets such as Tennyson protested that Ruskin was being unfairly rigorous in pointing up the fallacy, and it may be noted that Ruskin himself falls into it often. See, e.g., his reference to the "guilty ship" in his discussion of Turner's *The Slave Ship*, p. 1429.

7. The metaphysical terms *objective* and *subjective* as applied to kinds of truth.

8. From a poem by Oliver Wendell Holmes.

other error, that which the mind admits when affected strongly by emotion. Thus, for instance, in *Alton Locke*—

> They rowed her in across the rolling foam—
> The cruel, crawling foam.[9]

The foam is not cruel, neither does it crawl. The state of mind which attributes to it these characters of a living creature is one in which the reason is unhinged by grief. All violent feelings have the same effect. They produce in us a falseness in all our impressions of external things, which I would generally characterize as the "pathetic fallacy."

Now we are in the habit of considering this fallacy as eminently a character of poetical description, and the temper of mind in which we allow it, as one eminently poetical, because passionate. But, I believe, if we look well into the matter, that we shall find the greatest poets do not often admit this kind of falseness—that it is only the second order of poets who much delight in it.

Thus, when Dante describes the spirits falling from the bank of Acheron "as dead leaves flutter from a bough,"[1] he gives the most perfect image possible of their utter lightness, feebleness, passiveness, and scattering agony of despair, without, however, for an instant losing his own clear perception that *these* are souls, and *those* are leaves: he makes no confusion of one with the other. But when Coleridge speaks of

> The one red leaf, the last of its clan,
> That dances as often as dance it can,[2]

he has a morbid, that is to say, a so far false, idea about the leaf: he fancies a life in it, and will, which there are not; confuses its powerlessness with choice, its fading death with merriment, and the wind that shakes it with music. Here, however, there is some beauty, even in the morbid passage; but take an instance in Homer and Pope. Without the knowledge of Ulysses, Elpenor, his youngest follower, has fallen from an upper chamber in the Circean palace, and has been left dead, unmissed by his leader or companions, in the haste of their departure. They cross the sea to the Cimmerian land; and Ulysses summons the shades from Tartarus. The first which appears is that of the lost Elpenor. Ulysses, amazed, and in exactly the spirit of bitter and terrified lightness which is seen in Hamlet, addresses the spirit with the simple, startled words: "Elpenor! How camest thou under the shadowy darkness? Hast thou come faster on foot than I in my black ship?"[3] Which Pope renders thus:

> O, say, what angry power Elpenor led
> To glide in shades, and wander with the dead?
> How could thy soul, by realms and seas disjoined,
> Outfly the nimble sail, and leave the lagging wind?

I sincerely hope the reader finds no pleasure here, either in the nimbleness of the sail, or the laziness of the wind! And yet how is it that these conceits are so painful now, when they have been pleasant to us in the other instances?

For a very simple reason. They are not a *pathetic* fallacy at all, for they are

---

9. From chap. 26 of Charles Kingsley's novel *Alton Locke* (1850).
1. *Inferno* 3.112.
2. *Christabel* 49–50.
3. *Odyssey* 11.51.

put into the mouth of the wrong passion—a passion which never could possibly have spoken them—agonized curiosity. Ulysses wants to know the facts of the matter; and the very last thing his mind could do at the moment would be to pause, or suggest in anywise what was *not* a fact. The delay in the first three lines, and conceit in the last, jar upon us instantly, like the most frightful discord in music. No poet of true imaginative power would possibly have written the passage.

Therefore, we see that the spirit of truth must guide us in some sort, even in our enjoyment of fallacy. Coleridge's fallacy has no discord in it, but Pope's has set our teeth on edge. * * *

1856

From The Stones of Venice

[THE SAVAGENESS OF GOTHIC ARCHITECTURE][1]

I am not sure when the word "Gothic" was first generically applied to the architecture of the North; but I presume that, whatever the date of its original usage, it was intended to imply reproach, and express the barbaric character of the nations among whom that architecture arose. It never implied that they were literally of Gothic lineage, far less that their architecture had been originally invented by the Goths themselves; but it did imply that they and their buildings together exhibited a degree of sternness and rudeness, which, in contradistinction to the character of Southern and Eastern nations, appeared like a perpetual reflection of the contrast between the Goth and the Roman in their first encounter. And when that fallen Roman, in the utmost impotence of his luxury, and insolence of his guilt, became the model for the imitation of civilized Europe,[2] at the close of the so-called Dark Ages, the word Gothic became a term of unmitigated contempt, not unmixed with aversion. From that contempt, by the exertion of the antiquaries and architects of this century, Gothic architecture has been sufficiently vindicated; and perhaps some among us, in our admiration of the magnificent science of its structure, and sacredness of its expression, might desire that the term of ancient reproach should be withdrawn, and some other, of more apparent honorableness, adopted in its place. There is no chance, as there is no need, of such a substitution. As far as the epithet was used scornfully, it was used falsely; but there is no reproach in the word, rightly understood; on the contrary, there is a profound truth, which the instinct of mankind almost unconsciously recognizes. It is true, greatly and deeply true, that the architecture of the North is rude and wild; but it is not true that, for this reason, we are to condemn it, or despise. Far otherwise: I believe it is in this very character that it deserves our profoundest reverence.

The charts of the world which have been drawn up by modern science have thrown into a narrow space the expression of a vast amount of knowledge, but I have never yet seen any one pictorial enough to enable the spec-

1. From vol. 2, chap. 6.
2. Renaissance architecture, based on imitating classical buildings, was distasteful to Ruskin. He later stated that his aim in *The Stones of Venice* had been "to show that the Gothic architecture of

Venice had risen out of . . . a state of pure national faith and domestic virtue; and that its Renaissance architecture had arisen out of . . . a state of concealed national infidelity and domestic corruption."

tator to imagine the kind of contrast in physical character which exists between Northern and Southern countries. We know the differences in detail, but we have not that broad glance and grasp which would enable us to feel them in their fullness. We know that gentians grow on the Alps, and olives on the Apennines; but we do not enough conceive for ourselves that variegated mosaic of the world's surface which a bird sees in its migration, that difference between the district of the gentian and of the olive which the stork and the swallow see far off, as they lean upon the sirocco wind.[3] Let us, for a moment, try to raise ourselves even above the level of their flight, and imagine the Mediterranean lying beneath us like an irregular lake, and all its ancient promontories sleeping in the sun: here and there an angry spot of thunder, a gray stain of storm, moving upon the burning field; and here and there a fixed wreath of white volcano smoke, surrounded by its circle of ashes; but for the most part a great peacefulness of light, Syria and Greece, Italy and Spain, laid like pieces of a golden pavement into the sea-blue, chased, as we stoop nearer to them, with bossy beaten work of mountain chains, and glowing softly with terraced gardens, and flowers heavy with frankincense, mixed among masses of laurel, and orange, and plumy palm, that abate with their gray-green shadows the burning of the marble rocks, and of the ledges of porphyry sloping under lucent sand. Then let us pass farther towards the north, until we see the orient colors change gradually into a vast belt of rainy green, where the pastures of Switzerland, and poplar valleys of France, and dark forests of the Danube and Carpathians stretch from the mouths of the Loire to those of the Volga, seen through clefts in gray swirls of rain cloud and flaky veils of the mist of the brooks, spreading low along the pasture lands: and then, farther north still, to see the earth heave into mighty masses of leaden rock and heathy moor, bordering with a broad waste of gloomy purple that belt of field and wood, and splintering into irregular and grisly islands amidst the northern seas, beaten by storm, and chilled by ice drift, and tormented by furious pulses of contending tide, until the roots of the last forests fail from among the hill ravines, and the hunger of the north wind bites their peaks into barrenness; and, at last, the wall of ice, durable like iron, sets, deathlike, its white teeth against us out of the polar twilight. And, having once traversed in thought this gradation of the zoned iris of the earth in all its material vastness, let us go down nearer to it, and watch the parallel change in the belt of animal life: the multitudes of swift and brilliant creatures that glance in the air and sea, or tread the sands of the southern zone; striped zebras and spotted leopards, glistening serpents, and birds arrayed in purple and scarlet. Let us contrast their delicacy and brilliancy of color, and swiftness of motion, with the frost-cramped strength, and shaggy covering, and dusky plumage of the northern tribes; contrast the Arabian horse with the Shetland, the tiger and leopard with the wolf and bear, the antelope with the elk, the bird of paradise with the osprey: and then, submissively acknowledging the great laws by which the earth and all that it bears are ruled throughout their being, let us not condemn, but rejoice in the expression by man of his own rest in the statutes of the lands that gave him birth. Let us watch him with reverence as he sets side by side the burning gems, and smooths with soft sculpture the jasper pillars, that

3. Hot wind from the southern Mediterranean.

are to reflect a ceaseless sunshine, and rise into a cloudless sky: but not with less reverence let us stand by him, when, with rough strength and hurried stroke, he smites an uncouth animation out of the rocks which he has torn from among the moss of the moorland, and heaves into the darkened air the pile of iron buttress and rugged wall, instinct with work of an imagination as wild and wayward as the northern sea; creations of ungainly shape and rigid limb, but full of wolfish life; fierce as the winds that beat, and changeful as the clouds that shade them.

There is, I repeat, no degradation, no reproach in this, but all dignity and honorableness: and we should err grievously in refusing either to recognize as an essential character of the existing architecture of the North, or to admit as a desirable character in that which it yet may be, this wildness of thought, and roughness of work; this look of mountain brotherhood between the cathedral and the Alp; this magnificence of sturdy power, put forth only the more energetically because the fine finger-touch was chilled away by the frosty wind, and the eye dimmed by the moor mist, or blinded by the hail; this outspeaking of the strong spirit of men who may not gather redundant fruitage from the earth, nor bask in dreamy benignity of sunshine, but must break the rock for bread, and cleave the forest for fire, and show, even in what they did for their delight, some of the hard habits of the arm and heart that grew on them as they swung the ax or pressed the plow.

If, however, the savageness of Gothic architecture, merely as an expression of its origin among Northern nations, may be considered, in some sort, a noble character, it possesses a higher nobility still, when considered as an index, not of climate, but of religious principle.

In the 13th and 14th paragraphs of Chapter XXI of the first volume of this work, it was noticed that the systems of architectural ornament, properly so called, might be divided into three: (1) Servile ornament, in which the execution or power of the inferior workman is entirely subjected to the intellect of the higher; (2) Constitutional ornament, in which the executive inferior power is, to a certain point, emancipated and independent, having a will of its own, yet confessing its inferiority and rendering obedience to higher powers; and (3) Revolutionary ornament, in which no executive inferiority is admitted at all. I must here explain the nature of these divisions at somewhat greater length.

Of Servile ornament, the principal schools are the Greek, Ninevite, and Egyptian; but their servility is of different kinds. The Greek master-workman was far advanced in knowledge and power above the Assyrian or Egyptian. Neither he nor those for whom he worked could endure the appearance of imperfection in anything; and, therefore, what ornament he appointed to be done by those beneath him was composed of mere geometrical forms—balls, ridges, and perfectly symmetrical foliage—which could be executed with absolute precision by line and rule, and were as perfect in their way, when completed, as his own figure sculpture. The Assyrian and Egyptian, on the contrary, less cognizant of accurate form in anything, were content to allow their figure sculpture to be executed by inferior workmen, but lowered the method of its treatment to a standard which every workman could reach, and then trained him by discipline so rigid that there was no chance of his falling beneath the standard appointed. The Greek gave to the lower workman no subject which he could not perfectly execute. The Assyrian gave him subjects which he could only execute imperfectly, but fixed a legal standard for his imperfection. The workman was, in both systems, a slave.

But in the medieval, or especially Christian, system of ornament, this slavery is done away with altogether; Christianity having recognized, in small things as well as great, the individual value of every soul. But it not only recognizes its value; it confesses its imperfection, in only bestowing dignity upon the acknowledgment of unworthiness. That admission of lost power and fallen nature, which the Greek or Ninevite felt to be intensely painful, and, as far as might be, altogether refused, the Christian makes daily and hourly, contemplating the fact of it without fear, as tending, in the end, to God's greater glory. Therefore, to every spirit which Christianity summons to her service, her exhortation is: Do what you can, and confess frankly what you are unable to do; neither let your effort be shortened for fear of failure, nor your confession silenced for fear of shame. And it is, perhaps, the principal admirableness of the Gothic schools of architecture, that they thus receive the results of the labor of inferior minds; and out of fragments full of imperfection, and betraying that imperfection in every touch, indulgently raise up a stately and unaccusable whole.

But the modern English mind has this much in common with that of the Greek, that it intensely desires, in all things, the utmost completion or perfection compatible with their nature. This is a noble character in the abstract, but becomes ignoble when it causes us to forget the relative dignities of that nature itself, and to prefer the perfectness of the lower nature to the imperfection of the higher; not considering that as, judged by such a rule, all the brute animals would be preferable to man, because more perfect in their functions and kind, and yet are always held inferior to him, so also in the works of man, those which are more perfect in their kind are always inferior to those which are, in their nature, liable to more faults and shortcomings. For the finer the nature, the more flaws it will show through the clearness of it; and it is a law of this universe that the best things shall be seldomest seen in their best form. The wild grass grows well and strongly, one year with another; but the wheat is, according to the greater nobleness of its nature, liable to the bitterer blight. And therefore, while in all things that we see, or do, we are to desire perfection, and strive for it, we are nevertheless not to set the meaner thing, in its narrow accomplishment, above the nobler thing, in its mighty progress; not to esteem smooth minuteness above shattered majesty; not to prefer mean victory to honorable defeat; not to lower the level of our aim, that we may the more surely enjoy the complacency of success. But above all, in our dealings with the souls of other men, we are to take care how we check, by severe requirement or narrow caution, efforts which might otherwise lead to a noble issue; and, still more, how we withhold our admiration from great excellencies, because they are mingled with rough faults. Now, in the make and nature of every man, however rude or simple, whom we employ in manual labor, there are some powers for better things: some tardy imagination, torpid capacity of emotion, tottering steps of thought, there are, even at the worst; and in most cases it is all our own fault that they *are* tardy or torpid. But they cannot be strengthened, unless we are content to take them in their feebleness, and unless we prize and honor them in their imperfection above the best and most perfect manual skill. And this is what we have to do with all our laborers; to look for the *thoughtful* part of them, and get that out of them, whatever we lose for it, whatever faults and errors we are obliged to take with it. For the best that is in them cannot manifest itself, but in company with much error. Understand this clearly: You can teach a man to draw a straight line, and to cut one; to strike a curved line, and to carve it; and to copy and carve any number of given lines or forms, with admirable speed and perfect precision; and you find his work perfect of its kind: but if you ask him to think about any of those forms, to consider if he cannot find any better in his own head, he stops; his execution becomes hesitating; he thinks, and ten to one he thinks wrong; ten to one he makes a mistake in the first touch he gives to his work as a thinking being. But you have made a man of him for all that. He was only a machine before, an animated tool.

And observe, you are put to stern choice in this matter. You must either make a tool of the creature, or a man of him. You cannot make both. Men were not intended to work with the accuracy of tools, to be precise and perfect in all their actions. If you will have that precision out of them, and make their fingers measure degrees like cogwheels, and their arms strike curves like compasses, you must unhumanize them. All the energy of their spirits must be given to make cogs and compasses of themselves. All their attention and strength must go to the accomplishment of the mean act. The eye of the soul must be bent upon the finger point, and the soul's force must fill all the invisible nerves that guide it, ten hours a day, that it may not err from its steely precision, and so soul and sight be worn away, and the whole human being be lost at last—a heap of sawdust, so far as its intellectual work in this world is concerned; saved only by its Heart, which cannot go into the form of cogs and compasses, but expands, after the ten hours are over, into fireside humanity. On the other hand, if you will make a man of the working creature, you cannot make a tool. Let him but begin to imagine, to think, to try to do anything worth doing; and the engine-turned precision is lost at once. Out come all his roughness, all his dullness, all his incapability; shame upon shame, failure upon failure, pause after pause: but out comes the whole majesty of him also; and we know the height of it only, when we see the clouds settling upon him. And, whether the clouds be bright or dark, there will be transfiguration behind and within them.

And now, reader, look around this English room of yours, about which you have been proud so often, because the work of it was so good and strong, and the ornaments of it so finished. Examine again all those accurate moldings, and perfect polishings, and unerring adjustments of the seasoned wood and tempered steel. Many a time you have exulted over them, and thought how great England was, because her slightest work was done so thoroughly. Alas! if read rightly, these perfectnesses are signs of a slavery in our England a thousand times more bitter and more degrading than that of the scourged African, or helot[4] Greek. Men may be beaten, chained, tormented, yoked like cattle, slaughtered like summer flies, and yet remain in one sense, and the best sense, free. But to smother their souls within them, to blight and hew into rotting pollards[5] the suckling branches of their human intelligence, to make the flesh and skin which, after the worm's work on it, is to see God, into leathern thongs to yoke machinery with—this it is to be slave-masters

---

4. A class of serfs in Sparta.   5. Trees with top branches cut back to the trunk.

indeed; and there might be more freedom in England, though her feudal lords' lightest words were worth men's lives, and though the blood of the vexed husbandman dropped in the furrows of her fields, than there is while the animation of her multitudes is sent like fuel to feed the factory smoke, and the strength of them is given daily to be wasted into the fineness of a web, or racked into the exactness of a line.

And, on the other hand, go forth again to gaze upon the old cathedral front, where you have smiled so often at the fantastic ignorance of the old sculptors: examine once more those ugly goblins, and formless monsters, and stern statues, anatomiless[6] and rigid; but do not mock at them, for they are signs of the life and liberty of every workman who struck the stone; a freedom of thought, and rank in scale of being, such as no laws, no charters, no charities can secure; but which it must be the first aim of all Europe at this day to regain for her children.

Let me not be thought to speak wildly or extravagantly. It is verily this degradation of the operative into a machine, which, more than any other evil of the times, is leading the mass of the nations everywhere into vain, incoherent, destructive struggling for a freedom of which they cannot explain the nature to themselves. Their universal outcry against wealth, and against nobility, is not forced from them either by the pressure of famine, or the sting of mortified pride. These do much, and have done much in all ages; but the foundations of society were never yet shaken as they are at this day. It is not that men are ill fed, but that they have no pleasure in the work by which they make their bread, and therefore look to wealth as the only means of pleasure. It is not that men are pained by the scorn of the upper classes, but they cannot endure their own; for they feel that the kind of labor to which they are condemned is verily a degrading one, and makes them less than men. Never had the upper classes so much sympathy with the lower, or charity for them, as they have at this day, and yet never were they so much hated by them: for, of old, the separation between the noble and the poor was merely a wall built by law; now it is a veritable difference in level of standing, a precipice between upper and lower grounds in the field of humanity, and there is pestilential air at the bottom of it. I know not if a day is ever to come when the nature of right freedom will be understood, and when men will see that to obey another man, to labor for him, yield reverence to him or to his place, is not slavery. It is often the best kind of liberty—liberty from care. The man who says to one, Go, and he goeth, and to another, Come, and he cometh,[7] has, in most cases, more sense of restraint and difficulty than the man who obeys him. The movements of the one are hindered by the burden on his shoulder; of the other, by the bridle on his lips: there is no way by which the burden may be lightened; but we need not suffer from the bridle if we do not champ at it. To yield reverence to another, to hold ourselves and our lives at his disposal, is not slavery; often, it is the noblest state in which a man can live in this world. There is, indeed, a reverence which is servile, that is to say irrational or selfish: but there is also noble reverence, that is to say, reasonable and loving; and a man is never so noble as when he is reverent in this kind; nay, even if the feeling pass the bounds

6. A coinage by Ruskin meaning devoid of anatomy.   7. Matthew 8.9.

of mere reason, so that it be loving, a man is raised by it. Which had, in reality, most of the serf nature in him—the Irish peasant who was lying in wait yesterday for his landlord, with his musket muzzle thrust through the ragged hedge; or that old mountain servant, who, 200 years ago, at Inverkeithing, gave up his own life and the lives of his seven sons for his chief?[8]— as each fell, calling forth his brother to the death, "Another for Hector!" And therefore, in all ages and all countries, reverence has been paid and sacrifice made by men to each other, not only without complaint, but rejoicingly; and famine, and peril, and sword, and all evil, and all shame, have been borne willingly in the causes of masters and kings; for all these gifts of the heart ennobled the men who gave not less than the men who received them, and nature prompted, and God rewarded the sacrifice. But to feel their souls withering within them, unthanked, to find their whole being sunk into an unrecognized abyss, to be counted off into a heap of mechanism, numbered with its wheels, and weighed with its hammer strokes—this nature bade not—this God blesses not—this humanity for no long time is able to endure.

We have much studied and much perfected, of late, the great civilized invention of the division of labor; only we give it a false name. It is not, truly speaking, the labor that is divided; but the men: Divided into mere segments of men—broken into small fragments and crumbs of life; so that all the little piece of intelligence that is left in a man is not enough to make a pin, or a nail, but exhausts itself in making the point of a pin, or the head of a nail. Now it is a good and desirable thing, truly, to make many pins in a day; but if we could only see with what crystal sand their points were polished—sand of human soul, much to be magnified before it can be discerned for what it is—we should think there might be some loss in it also. And the great cry that rises from all our manufacturing cities, louder than their furnace blast, is all in very deed for this—that we manufacture everything there except men; we blanch cotton, and strengthen steel, and refine sugar, and shape pottery; but to brighten, to strengthen, to refine, or to form a single living spirit, never enters into our estimate of advantages. And all the evil to which that cry is urging our myriads can be met only in one way: not by teaching nor preaching, for to teach them is but to show them their misery, and to preach to them, if we do nothing more than preach, is to mock at it. It can be met only by a right understanding, on the part of all classes, of what kinds of labor are good for men, raising them, and making them happy; by a determined sacrifice of such convenience, or beauty, or cheapness as is to be got only by the degradation of the workman; and by equally determined demand for the products and results of healthy and ennobling labor.

And how, it will be asked, are these products to be recognized, and this demand to be regulated? Easily: by the observance of three broad and simple rules:

1. Never encourage the manufacture of any article not absolutely necessary, in the production of which *Invention* has no share.

2. Never demand an exact finish for its own sake, but only for some practical or noble end.

---

8. An incident described in the preface to Walter Scott's novel *The Fair Maid of Perth*.

3. Never encourage imitation or copying of any kind, except for the sake of preserving record of great works.

The second of these principles is the only one which directly rises out of the consideration of our immediate subject; but I shall briefly explain the meaning and extent of the first also, reserving the enforcement of the third for another place.

1. Never encourage the manufacture of anything not necessary, in the production of which invention has no share.

For instance. Glass beads are utterly unnecessary, and there is no design or thought employed in their manufacture. They are formed by first drawing out the glass into rods; these rods are chopped up into fragments of the size of beads by the human hand, and the fragments are then rounded in the furnace. The men who chop up the rods sit at their work all day, their hands vibrating with a perpetual and exquisitely timed palsy, and the beads dropping beneath their vibration like hail. Neither they, nor the men who draw out the rods or fuse the fragments, have the smallest occasion for the use of any single humanfaculty; and every young lady, therefore, who buys glass beads is engaged in the slave trade, and in a much more cruel one than that which we have so long been endeavoring to put down.

But glass cups and vessels may become the subjects of exquisite invention; and if in buying these we pay for the invention, that is to say for the beautiful form, or color, or engraving, and not for mere finish of execution, we are doing good to humanity.

So, again, the cutting of precious stones, in all ordinary cases, requires little exertion of any mental faculty; some tact and judgment in avoiding flaws, and so on, but nothing to bring out the whole mind. Every person who wears cut jewels merely for the sake of their value is, therefore, a slave driver.

But the working of the goldsmith, and the various designing of grouped jewelry and enamel-work, may become the subject of the most noble human intelligence. Therefore, money spent in the purchase of well-designed plate, of precious engraved vases, cameos, or enamels, does good to humanity; and, in work of this kind, jewels may be employed to heighten its splendor; and their cutting is then a price paid for the attainment of a noble end, and thus perfectly allowable.

I shall perhaps press this law farther elsewhere, but our immediate concern is chiefly with the second, namely, never to demand an exact finish, when it does not lead to a noble end. For observe, I have only dwelt upon the rudeness of Gothic, or any other kind of imperfectness, as admirable, where it was impossible to get design or thought without it. If you are to have the thought of a rough and untaught man, you must have it in a rough and untaught way; but from an educated man, who can without effort express his thoughts in an educated way, take the graceful expression, and be thankful. Only *get* the thought, and do not silence the peasant because he cannot speak good grammar, or until you have taught him his grammar. Grammar and refinement are good things, both, only be sure of the better thing first. And thus in art, delicate finish is desirable from the greatest masters, and is always given by them. In some places Michael Angelo, Leonardo, Phidias, Perugino, Turner all finished with the most exquisite care; and the finish they give always leads to the fuller accomplishment of their noble purposes.

But lower men than these cannot finish, for it requires consummate knowledge to finish consummately, and then we must take their thoughts as they are able to give them. So the rule is simple: Always look for invention first, and after that, for such execution as will help the invention, and as the inventor is capable of without painful effort, and *no more*. Above all, demand no refinement of execution where there is no thought, for that is slaves' work, unredeemed. Rather choose rough work than smooth work, so only that the practical purpose be answered, and never imagine there is reason to be proud of anything that may be accomplished by patience and sandpaper.

I shall only give one example, which however will show the reader what I mean, from the manufacture already alluded to, that of glass. Our modern glass is exquisitely clear in its substance, true in its form, accurate in its cutting. We are proud of this. We ought to be ashamed of it. The old Venice glass was muddy, inaccurate in all its forms, and clumsily cut, if at all. And the old Venetian was justly proud of it. For there is this difference between the English and Venetian workman, that the former thinks only of accurately matching his patterns, and getting his curves perfectly true and his edges perfectly sharp, and becomes a mere machine for rounding curves and sharpening edges, while the old Venetian cared not a whit whether his edges were sharp or not, but he invented a new design for every glass that he made, and never molded a handle or a lip without a new fancy in it. And therefore, though some Venetian glass is ugly and clumsy enough, when made by clumsy and uninventive workmen, other Venetian glass is so lovely in its forms that no price is too great for it; and we never see the same form in it twice. Now you cannot have the finish and the varied form too. If the workman is thinking about his edges, he cannot be thinking of his design; if of his design, he cannot think of his edges. Choose whether you will pay for the lovely form or the perfect finish, and choose at the same moment whether you will make the worker a man or a grindstone.

Nay, but the reader interrupts me—"If the workman can design beautifully, I would not have him kept at the furnace. Let him be taken away and made a gentleman, and have a studio, and design his glass there, and I will have it blown and cut for him by common workmen, and so I will have my design and my finish too."

All ideas of this kind are founded upon two mistaken suppositions: the first, that one man's thoughts can be, or ought to be, executed by another man's hands; the second, that manual labor is a degradation, when it is governed by intellect.

On a large scale, and in work determinable by line and rule, it is indeed both possible and necessary that the thoughts of one man should be carried out by the labor of others; in this sense I have already defined the best architecture to be the expression of the mind of manhood by the hands of childhood. But on a smaller scale, and in a design which cannot be mathematically defined, one man's thoughts can never be expressed by another: and the difference between the spirit of touch of the man who is inventing, and of the man who is obeying directions, is often all the difference between a great and a common work of art. How wide the separation is between original and secondhand execution, I shall endeavor to show elsewhere; it is not so much to our purpose here as to mark the other and more fatal error

of despising manual labor when governed by intellect; for it is no less fatal
an error to despise it when thus regulated by intellect, than to value it for
its own sake. We are always in these days endeavoring to separate the two;
we want one man to be always thinking, and another to be always working,
and we call one a gentleman, and the other an operative; whereas the workman ought often to be thinking, and the thinker often to be working, and
both should be gentlemen, in the best sense. As it is, we make both ungentle,
the one envying, the other despising, his brother; and the mass of society is
made up of morbid thinkers, and miserable workers. Now it is only by labor
that thought can be made healthy, and only by thought that labor can be
made happy, and the two cannot be separated with impunity. It would be
well if all of us were good handicraftsmen in some kind, and the dishonor of
manual labor done away with altogether; so that though there should still be
a trenchant distinction of race between nobles and commoners, there should
not, among the latter, be a trenchant distinction of employment, as between
idle and working men, or between men of liberal and illiberal professions.
All professions should be liberal, and there should be less pride felt in peculiarity of employment, and more in excellence of achievement. And yet more,
in each several profession, no master should be too proud to do its hardest
work. The painter should grind his own colors; the architect work in the
mason's yard with his men; the master manufacturer be himself a more skillful operative than any man in his mills; and the distinction between one man
and another be only in experience and skill, and the authority and wealth
which these must naturally and justly obtain.

I should be led far from the matter in hand, if I were to pursue this interesting subject. Enough, I trust, has been said to show the reader that the
rudeness or imperfection which at first rendered the term "Gothic" one of
reproach is indeed, when rightly understood, one of the most noble characters of Christian architecture, and not only a noble but an *essential* one.
It seems a fantastic paradox, but it is nevertheless a most important truth,
that no architecture can be truly noble which is *not* imperfect. And this is
easily demonstrable. For since the architect, whom we will suppose capable
of doing all in perfection, cannot execute the whole with his own hands, he
must either make slaves of his workmen in the old Greek, and present
English fashion, and level his work to a slave's capacities, which is to degrade
it; or else he must take his workmen as he finds them, and let them show
their weaknesses together with their strength, which will involve the Gothic
imperfection, but render the whole work as noble as the the intellect of the
age can make it.

But the principle may be stated more broadly still. I have confined the
illustration of it to architecture, but I must not leave it as if true of architecture only. Hitherto I have used the words imperfect and perfect merely to
distinguish between work grossly unskillful, and work executed with average
precision and science; and I have been pleading that any degree of unskill-
fulness should be admitted, so only that the laborer's mind had room for
expression. But, accurately speaking, no good work whatever can be perfect,
and *the demand for perfection is always a sign of a misunderstanding of the
ends of art.*

This for two reasons, both based on everlasting laws. The first, that no great man ever stops working till he has reached his point of failure; that is to say, his mind is always far in advance of his powers of execution, and the latter will now and then give way in trying to follow it; besides that he will always give to the inferior portions of his work only such inferior attention as they require; and according to his greatness he becomes so accustomed to the feeling of dissatisfaction with the best he can do, that in moments of lassitude or anger with himself he will not care though the beholder be dissatisfied also. I believe there has only been one man who would not acknowledge this necessity, and strove always to reach perfection, Leonardo; the end of his vain effort being merely that he would take ten years to a picture, and leave it unfinished. And therefore, if we are to have great men working at all, or less men doing their best, the work will be imperfect, however beautiful. Of human work none but what is bad can be perfect, in its own bad way.[9]

The second reason is that imperfection is in some sort essential to all that we know of life. It is the sign of life in a mortal body, that is to say, of a state of progress and change. Nothing that lives is, or can be, rigidly perfect; part of it is decaying, part nascent. The foxglove blossom—a third part bud, a third part past, a third part in full bloom—is a type of the life of this world. And in all things that live there are certain irregularities and deficiencies which are not only signs of life, but sources of beauty. No human face is exactly the same in its lines on each side, no leaf perfect in its lobes, no branch in its symmetry. All admit irregularity as they imply change; and to banish imperfection is to destroy expression, to check exertion, to paralyze vitality. All things are literally better, lovelier, and more beloved for the imperfections which have been divinely appointed, that the law of human life may be Effort, and the law of human judgment, Mercy.

Accept this then for a universal law, that neither architecture nor any other noble work of man can be good unless it be imperfect; and let us be prepared for the otherwise strange fact, which we shall discern clearly as we approach the period of the Renaissance, that the first cause of the fall of the arts of Europe was a relentless requirement of perfection, incapable alike either of being silenced by veneration for greatness, or softened into forgiveness of simplicity.

Thus far then of the Rudeness or Savageness, which is the first mental element of Gothic architecture. It is an element in many other healthy architectures also, as in Byzantine and Romanesque; but true Gothic cannot exist without it.

1851–53

---

9. "The Elgin marbles are supposed by many persons to be 'perfect.' In the most important portions they indeed approach perfection, but only there. The draperies are unfinished, the hair and wool of the animals are unfinished, and the entire bas-reliefs of the frieze are roughly cut" [Ruskin's note]. Ruskin is referring to the collection of statues brought from Athens to England by Lord Elgin, statues that were considered models of perfect realism. Cf. Keats, *On Seeing the Elgin Marbles*, p. 828.

The Storm-Cloud of the Nineteenth Century

Lecture 1[1]

Let me first assure my audience that I have no *arrière pensée*[2] in the title chosen for this lecture. I might, indeed, have meant, and it would have been only too like me to mean, any number of things by such a title;—but, tonight, I mean simply what I have said, and propose to bring to your notice a series of cloud phenomena, which, so far as I can weigh existing evidence, are peculiar to our own times; yet which have not hitherto received any special notice or description from meteorologists.

So far as the existing evidence, I say, of former literature can be interpreted, the storm-cloud—or more accurately plague-cloud, for it is not alway stormy—which I am about to describe to you, never was seen but by now living, or *lately* living eyes. It is not yet twenty years that this—I may well call it, wonderful—cloud has been, in its essence, recognizable. There is no description of it, so far as I have read, or by any ancient observer. Neither Homer nor Virgil, neither Aristophanes nor Horace, acknowledge any such clouds among those compelled by Jove. Chaucer has no word of them, nor Dante; Milton none, nor Thomson. In modern times, Scott, Wordsworth, and Byron are alike unconscious of them; and the most observant and descriptive of scientific men, De Saussure,[3] is utterly silent concerning them. Taking up the traditions of air from the year before Scott's death, I am able, by my own constant and close observation, to certify you that in the forty following years (1831 to 1871 approximately—for the phenomena in question came on gradually)—no such clouds as these are, and are now often for months without intermission, were ever seen in the skies of England, France or Italy.

In those old days, when weather was fine, it was luxuriously fine; when it was bad—it was often abominably bad, but it had its fit of temper and was done with it—it didn't sulk for three months without letting you see the sun,—nor send you one cyclone inside out, every Saturday afternoon, and another outside in, every Monday morning.

In fine weather the sky was either blue or clear in its light; the clouds, either white or golden, adding to, not abating, the luster of the sky. In wet weather, there were two different species of clouds,—those of beneficent rain, which for distinction's sake I will call the non-electric rain-cloud, and

---

1. Delivered February 4, 1884, at the London Institution. Some newspapers complained that the lecture seemed merely to blame air pollution on the devil; however, what Ruskin was blaming was the devil of industrialism, the source of the "Manchester devil's darkness" and of the "dense manufacturing mist." As E. T. Cook noted:

> industrial statistics fully bear out the date which Ruskin fixes for the growth of the phenomena in question: the storm-cloud thickened just when the consumption of coal went up by leaps and bounds, both in this country [England] and in the industrialized parts of central Europe.

Much of the evidence cited in the lecture derives from diaries and sketchbooks in which, over a period of fifty years, Ruskin had recorded observations of sunsets and storms, a record that enabled him to point out the changes. As he stated in his second lecture:

> Had the weather when I was young been such as it is now, no book such as *Modern Painters* ever would or *could* have been written; for every argument, and every sentiment in that book, was founded on the personal experience of the beauty and blessing of nature, all spring and summer long; and on the then demonstrable fact that over a great portion of the world's surface the air and the earth were fitted to the education of the spirit of man as closely as a schoolboy's primer is to his labor, and as gloriously as a lover's mistress is to his eyes.
>
> That harmony is now broken and broken the world round.

2. Afterthought or hidden meaning (French).
3. Horace Bénédict de Saussure (1740–1799), Swiss geologist and alpinist.

those of storm, usually charged highly with electricity. The beneficent rain-cloud was indeed often extremely dull and gray for days together, but gracious nevertheless, felt to be doing good, and often to be delightful after drought; capable also of the most exquisite coloring, under certain conditions; and continually traversed in clearing by the rainbow:—and, secondly, the storm-cloud, always majestic, often dazzlingly beautiful, and felt also to be beneficent in its own way, affecting the mass of the air with vital agitation, and purging it from the impurity of all morbific elements.

In the entire system of the Firmament, thus seen and understood, there appeared to be, to all the thinkers of those ages, the incontrovertible and unmistakable evidence of a Divine Power in creation, which had fitted, as the air for human breath, so the clouds for human sight and nourishment;—the Father who was in heaven feeding day by day the souls of His children with marvels, and satisfying them with bread, and so filling their hearts with food and gladness.[4]

* * *

Thus far then of clouds that were once familiar; now at last, entering on my immediate subject, I shall best introduce it to you by reading an entry in my diary which gives progressive description of the most gentle aspect of the modern plague-cloud.

Bolton Abbey, 4th July, 1875.

Half-past eight, morning; the first bright morning for the last fortnight.

At half-past five it was entirely clear, and entirely calm; the moorlands glowing, and the Wharfe[5] glittering in sacred light, and even the thin-stemmed field-flowers quiet as stars, in the peace in which—

All trees and simples, great and small,
    That balmy leaf do bear,
Than they were painted on a wall,
    No more do move, no steir.[6]

But, an hour ago, the leaves at my window first shook slightly. They are now trembling *continuously,* as those of all the trees, under a gradually rising wind, of which the tremulous action scarcely permits the direction to be defined,—but which falls and returns in fits of varying force, like those which precede a thunderstorm—never wholly ceasing: the direction of its upper current is shown by a few ragged white clouds, moving fast from the north, which rose, at the time of the first leaf-shaking, behind the edge of the moors in the east.

This wind is the plague-wind of the eighth decade of years in the nineteenth century; a period which will assuredly be recognized in future meteorological history as one of phenomena hitherto unrecorded in the courses of nature, and characterized preeminently by the almost ceaseless action of this calamitous wind. While I have been writing these sentences, the white clouds above specified have increased to twice the size they had when I began to write; and in about two hours from this time—say by eleven o'clock, if the wind continue,—the whole sky will be dark with

4. Cf. Acts 14.17.
5. River near Bolton Abbey in Yorkshire.
6. Stir. From a hymn by Alexander Herne (1560–1609), Scottish clergyman.

them, as it was yesterday, and has been through prolonged periods during the last five years. I first noticed the definite character of this wind, and of the clouds it brings with it, in the year 1871, describing it then in the July number of *Fors Clavigera;* but little, at the time, apprehending either its universality, or any probability of its annual continuance. I am able now to state positively that its range of power extends from the North of England to Sicily; and that it blows more or less during the whole of the year, except the early autumn. This autumnal abdication is, I hope, beginning: it blew but feebly yesterday, though without intermission, from the north, making every shady place cold, while the sun was burning; its effect on the sky being only to dim the blue of it between masses of ragged cumulus. Today it has entirely fallen; and there seems hope of bright weather, the first for me since the end of May, when I had two fine days at Aylesbury; the third, May 28th, being black again from morning to evening. There seems to be some reference to the blackness caused by the prevalence of this wind in the old French name of Bise, *"grey* wind"; and, indeed, one of the darkest and bitterest days of it I ever saw was at Vevay in 1872.

The first time I recognized the clouds brought by the plague-wind as distinct in character was in walking back from Oxford, after a hard day's work, to Abingdon, in the early spring of 1871: it would take too long to give you any account this evening of the particulars which drew my attention to them; but during the following months I had too frequent opportunities of verifying my first thoughts of them, and on the first of July in that year wrote the description of them which begins the *Fors Clavigera* of August, thus:—

It is the first of July, and I sit down to write by the dismalest light that ever yet I wrote by; namely, the light of this midsummer morning, in mid-England (Matlock, Derbyshire), in the year 1871.

For the sky is covered with gray cloud;—not rain-cloud, but a dry black veil which no ray of sunshine can pierce; partly diffused in mist, feeble mist, enough to make distant objects unintelligible, yet without any substance, or wreathing, or color of its own. And everywhere the leaves of the trees are shaking fitfully, as they do before a thunderstorm; only not violently, but enough to show the passing to and fro of a strange, bitter, blighting wind. Dismal enough, had it been the first morning of its kind that summer had sent. But during all this spring, in London, and at Oxford, through meager March, through changelessly sullen April, through despondent May, and darkened June, morning after morning has come gray-shrouded thus.

And it is a new thing to me, and a very dreadful one. I am fifty years old, and more; and since I was five, have gleaned the best hours of my life in the sun of spring and summer mornings; and I never saw such as these, till now.

And the scientific men are busy as ants, examining the sun and the moon, and the seven stars, and can tell me all about *them,* I believe, by this time; and how they move, and what they are made of.

And I do not care, for my part, two copper spangles how they move, nor what they are made of. I can't move them any other way than they go, nor make them of anything else, better than they are made. But I would care much and give much, if I could be told where this bitter wind comes from, and what *it* is made of.

For, perhaps, with forethought, and fine laboratory science, one might make it of something else.

It looks partly as if it were made of poisonous smoke; very possibly it may be: there are at least two hundred furnace chimneys in a square of two miles on every side of me. But mere smoke would not blow to and fro in that wild way. It looks more to me as if it were made of dead men's souls—such of them as are not gone yet where they have to go, and may be flitting hither and thither, doubting, themselves, of the fittest place for them.

You know, if there *are* such things as souls, and if ever any of them haunt places where they have been hurt, there must be many above us, just now, displeased enough!

The last sentence refers of course to the battles of the Franco-German campaign, which was especially horrible to me, in its digging, as the Germans should have known, a moat flooded with waters of death between the two nations for a century to come.

Since that Midsummer day, my attention, however otherwise occupied, has never relaxed in its record of the phenomena characteristic of the plague-wind; and I now define for you, as briefly as possible, the essential signs of it.

(1.) It is a wind of darkness,—all the former conditions of tormenting winds, whether from the north or east, were more or less capable of co-existing with sunlight, and often with steady and bright sunlight; but when-ever, and wherever the plague-wind blows, be it but for ten minutes, the sky is darkened instantly.

(2.) It is a malignant *quality* of wind, unconnected with any one quarter of the compass; it blows indifferently from all, attaching its own bitterness and malice to the worst characters of the proper winds of each quarter. It will blow either with drenching rain, or dry rage, from the south,—with ruinous blasts from the west,—with bitterest chills from the north,—and with venomous blight from the east.

Its own favorite quarter, however, is the southwest, so that it is distinguished in its malignity equally from the Bise of Provence, which is a north wind always, and from our own old friend, the east.

(3.) It always blows *tremulously*, making the leaves of the trees shudder as if they were all aspens, but with a peculiar fitfulness which gives them—and I watch them this moment as I write—an expression of anger as well as of fear and distress. You may see the kind of quivering, and hear the ominous whimpering, in the gusts that precede a great thunderstorm; but plague-wind is more panic-struck, and feverish; and its sound is a hiss instead of a wail.

When I was last at Avallon, in South France, I went to see *Faust*[7] played at the little country theater: it was done with scarcely any means of pictorial effect, except a few old curtains, and a blue light or two. But the night on the Brocken was nevertheless extremely appalling to me,—a strange ghast-liness being obtained in some of the witch scenes merely by fine management of gesture and drapery; and in the phantom scenes, by the half-palsied, half-furious, faltering or fluttering past of phantoms stumbling as into graves; as if of not only soulless, but senseless, Dead, moving with the very action, the rage, the decrepitude, and the trembling of the plague-wind.

---

7. Goethe's drama, which Ruskin saw in 1882.

(4.) Not only tremulous at every moment, it is also *intermittent* with a rapidity quite unexampled in former weather. There are, indeed, days—and weeks, on which it blows without cessation, and is as inevitable as the Gulf Stream; but also there are days when it is contending with healthy weather, and on such days it will remit for half an hour, and the sun will begin to show itself, and then the wind will come back and cover the whole sky with clouds in ten minutes; and so on, every half-hour, through the whole day; so that it is often impossible to go on with any kind of drawing in color, the light being never for two seconds the same from morning till evening.

(5.) It degrades, while it intensifies, ordinary storm; but before I read you any description of its efforts in this kind, I must correct an impression which has got abroad through the papers, that I speak as if the plague-wind blew now always, and there were no more any natural weather. On the contrary, the winter of 1878–9 was one of the most healthy and lovely I ever saw ice in;—Coniston lake[8] shone under the calm clear frost in one marble field, as strong as the floor of Milan Cathedral, half a mile across and four miles down; and the first entries in my diary which I read you shall be from the 22nd to 26th June, 1876, of perfectly lovely and natural weather:—

Sunday, 25th June, 1876.

Yesterday, an entirely glorious sunset, unmatched in beauty since that at Abbeville,[9]—deep scarlet, and purest rose, on purple gray, in bars; and stationary, plumy, sweeping filaments above in upper sky, like *"using up the brush,"* said Joanie; remaining in glory, every moment best, changing from one good into another, (but only in color or light—*form steady,*) for half an hour full, and the clouds afterwards fading into the gray against amber twilight, *stationary in the same form for about two hours,* at least. The darkening rose tint remained till half-past ten, the grand time being at nine.

The day had been fine,—exquisite green light on afternoon hills.

Monday, 26th June, 1876.

Yesterday an entirely perfect summer light on the Old Man;[1] Lancaster Bay all clear; Ingleborough and the great Pennine fault as on a map. Divine beauty of western color on thyme and rose,—then twilight of clearest *warm* amber far into night, of *pale* amber all night long; hills dark-clear against it.

And so it continued, only growing more intense in blue and sunlight, all day. After breakfast, I came in from the well under strawberry bed, to say I had never seen anything like it, so pure or intense, in Italy; and so it went glowing on, cloudless, with soft north wind, all day.

16th July.

The sunset almost too bright *through the blinds* for me to read Humboldt at tea by,—finally, new moon like a lime-light, reflected on breeze-struck water; traces, across dark calm, of reflected hills.

8. In the Lake District of north Lancashire, where Ruskin's house, Brantwood, was located.
9. Ruskin had made a sketch of this sunset, in October 1868, and described it as "a beautiful example of what . . . a sunset could then be, in the districts of Kent and Picardy unaffected by smoke."
1. Mountain near Ruskin's home.

These extracts are, I hope, enough to guard you against the absurdity of supposing that it all only means that I am myself soured, or doting, in my old age, and always in an ill humor. Depend upon it, when old men are worth anything, they are better-humored than young ones; and have learned to see what good there is, and pleasantness, in the world they are likely so soon to have orders to quit.

Now then—take the following sequences of accurate description of thunderstorm, *with* plague-wind.

22nd June, 1876.

Thunderstorm; pitch dark, with no *blackness,*—but deep, high, *filthiness* of lurid, yet not sublimely lurid, smoke-cloud; dense manufacturing mist; fearful squalls of shivery wind, making Mr. Severn's sails[2] quiver like a man in a fever fit—all about four, afternoon—but only two or three claps of thunder, and feeble, though near, flashes. I never saw such a dirty, weak, foul storm. It cleared suddenly after raining all afternoon, at half-past eight to nine, into pure, natural weather,—low rain-clouds on quite clear, green, wet hills.

Brantwood, 13th August, 1879.

The most terrific and horrible thunderstorm, this morning, I ever remember. It waked me at six, or a little before—then rolling incessantly, like railway luggage trains, quite ghastly in its mockery of them—the air one loathsome mass of sultry and foul fog, like smoke; scarcely raining at all, but increasing to heavier rollings, with flashes quivering vaguely through all the air, and at last terrific double streams of reddish-violet fire, not forked or zigzag, but rippled rivulets—two at the same instant some twenty to thirty degrees apart, and lasting on the eye at least half a second, with grand artillery-peals following; not rattling crashes, or irregular cracklings, but delivered volleys. It lasted an hour, then passed off, clearing a little, without rain to speak of,—not a glimpse of blue,— and now, half-past seven, seems settling down again into Manchester devil's darkness.

Quarter to eight, morning.—Thunder returned, all the air collapsed into one black fog, the hills invisible, and scarcely visible the opposite shore; heavy rain in short fits, and frequent, though less formidable, flashes, and shorter thunder. While I have written this sentence the cloud has again dissolved itself, like a nasty solution in a bottle, with miraculous and unnatural rapidity, and the hills are in sight again; a double-forked flash—rippled, I mean, like the others—starts into its frightful ladder of light between me and Wetherlam, as I raise my eyes. All black above, a rugged spray cloud on the Eaglet. The "Eaglet" is my own name for the bold and elevated crag to the west of the little lake above Coniston mines. It had no name among the country people, and is one of the most conspicuous features of the mountain chain, as seen from Brantwood.

Half-past eight.—Three times light and three times dark since last I wrote, and the darkness seeming each time as it settles more loathsome,

---

2. A neighbor's sailboat on Coniston Lake.

at last stopping my reading in mere blindness. One lurid gleam of white cumulus in upper lead-blue sky, seen for half a minute through the sulphurous chimney-pot vomit of blackguardly cloud beneath, where its rags were thinnest.

Thursday, 22nd Feb. 1883.

Yesterday a fearfully dark mist all afternoon, with steady, south plague-wind of the bitterest, nastiest, poisonous blight, and fretful flutter. I could scarcely stay in the wood for the horror of it. Today, really rather bright blue, and bright semi-cumuli, with the frantic Old Man blowing sheaves of lancets and chisels across the lake—not in strength enough, or whirl enough, to raise it in spray, but tracing every squall's outline in black on the silver grey waves, and whistling meanly, and as if on a flute made of a file.

Sunday, 17th August, 1879.

Raining in foul drizzle, slow and steady; sky pitch-dark, and I just get a little light by sitting in the bow-window; diabolic clouds over everything: and looking over my kitchen garden yesterday, I found it one miserable mass of weeds gone to seed, the roses in the higher garden putrefied into brown sponges, feeling like dead snails; and the half-ripe strawberries all rotten at the stalks.

And now I come to the most important sign of the plague-wind and the plague-cloud: that in bringing on their peculiar darkness, they *blanch* the sun instead of reddening it. And here I must note briefly to you the uselessness of observation by instruments, or machines, instead of eyes. In the first year when I had begun to notice the specialty of the plague-wind, I went of course to the Oxford observatory to consult its registrars. They have their anemometer always on the twirl, and can tell you the force, or at least the pace, of a gale, by day or night. But the anemometer can only record for you how often it has been driven round, not at all whether it went round *steadily*, or went round *trembling*. And on that point depends the entire question whether it is a plague breeze or a healthy one: and what's the use of telling you whether the wind's strong or not, when it can't tell you whether it's a strong medicine, or a strong poison?

But again—you have your *sun*-measure, and can tell exactly at any moment how strong, or how weak, or how wanting, the sun is. But the sun-measurer can't tell you whether the rays are stopped by a dense *shallow* cloud, or a thin *deep* one. In healthy weather, the sun is hidden behind a cloud, as it is behind a tree; and, when the cloud is past, it comes out again, as bright as before. But in plague-wind, the sun is choked out of the whole heaven, all day long, by a cloud which may be a thousand miles square and five miles deep.

And yet observe: that thin, scraggy, filthy, mangy, miserable cloud, for all the depth of it, can't turn the sun red, as a good, business-like fog does with a hundred feet or so of itself. By the plague-wind every breath of air you draw is polluted, half round the world; in a London fog the air itself is pure, though you choose to mix up dirt with it, and choke yourself with your own nastiness.

Now I'm going to show you a diagram of a sunset in entirely pure weather, above London smoke.[3] I saw it and sketched it from my old post of observation—the top garret of my father's house at Herne Hill. There, when the wind is south, we are outside of the smoke and above it; and this diagram, admirably enlarged from my own drawing by my, now in all things best aide-de-camp, Mr. Collingwood, shows you an old-fashioned sunset—the sort of thing Turner and I used to have to look at,—(nobody else ever would) constantly. Every sunset and every dawn, in fine weather, had something of the sort to show us. This is one of the last pure sunsets I ever saw, about the year 1876,—and the point I want you to note in it is, that the air being pure, the smoke on the horizon, though at last it hides the sun, yet hides it through gold and vermilion. Now, don't go away fancying there's any exaggeration in that study. The *prismatic* colors, I told you, were simply impossible to paint; these, which are transmitted colors, can indeed be suggested, but no more. The brightest pigment we have would look dim beside the truth.

I should have liked to have blotted down for you a bit of plague-cloud to put beside this; but Heaven knows, you can see enough of it nowadays without any trouble of mine; and if you want, in a hurry, to see what the sun looks like through it, you've only to throw a bad half-crown into a basin of soap and water.

Blanched Sun,—blighted grass,—blinded man.—If, in conclusion, you ask me for any conceivable cause or meaning of these things—I can tell you none, according to your modern beliefs; but I can tell you what meaning it would have borne to the men of old time. Remember, for the last twenty years, England, and all foreign nations, either tempting her, or following her, have blasphemed[4] the name of God deliberately and openly; and have done iniquity by proclamation, every man doing as much injustice to his brother as it is in his power to do. Of states in such moral gloom every seer of old predicted the physical gloom, saying, "The light shall be darkened in the heavens thereof, and the stars shall withdraw their shining."[5] All Greek, all Christian, all Jewish prophecy insists on the same truth through a thousand myths; but of all the chief, to former thought, was the fable of the Jewish warrior and prophet, for whom the sun hasted not to go down,[6] with which I leave you to compare at leisure the physical result of your own wars and prophecies, as declared by your own elect journal not fourteen days ago,— that the Empire of England, on which formerly the sun never set, has become one on which he never rises.[7]

What is best to be done, do you ask me? The answer is plain. Whether you can affect the signs of the sky or not, you *can* the signs of the times. Whether you can bring the *sun* back or not, you can assuredly bring back your own cheerfulness, and your own honesty. You may not be able to say to the winds, "Peace; be still,"[8] but you can cease from the insolence of your

---

3. The illustration shown at the lecture was titled *An Old-Fashioned Sunset, 1876.*
4. Ruskin defined blasphemy as

"harmful speaking"—not against God only, but against man, and against all the good works and purposes of Nature. The word is accurately opposed to "Euphemy," the right or well-speaking of God and His world . . . And the universal instinct of blasphemy in the modern scientific mind is above all manifested in its love

of what is ugly, and natural enthrallment by the abominable.
5. Cf. Joel 2.10.
6. On Joshua's commanding the sun to stand still, see Joshua 10.13.
7. In January 1884, after weeks of sunless weather, the *Pall Mall Gazette* had made joking references to the popular boast about the sun never setting on the British dominions, for the good reason that it never rises.
8. Mark 4.39.

own lips, and the troubling of your own passions. And all *that* it would be extremely well to do, even though the day *were* coming when the sun should be as darkness, and the moon as blood.[9] But, the paths of rectitude and piety once regained, who shall say that the promise of old time would not be found to hold for us also?—"Bring ye all the tithes into my storehouse, and prove me now herewith, saith the Lord God, if I will not open you the windows of heaven, and pour you out a blessing, that there shall not be room enough to receive it."[1]

1884

9. Cf. the prophecy in Revelation 6.12: "the sun became black as sackcloth of hair, and the moon became as blood."
1. Malachi 3.10.

ARTHUR HUGH CLOUGH
1819–1861

The writings of Arthur Hugh Clough (whose name is pronounced so as to rhyme with *rough*) are usually treated as a kind of footnote to those of his friend Matthew Arnold. Read in this way they can indeed add to our understanding of Arnold's early poems written during the phase of religious stress shared by both young men. Some of Clough's admirers argue, however, that such a reading is to be deplored because Clough, despite his frequent clumsiness in versification, is a poet of considerable stature in his own right. What is beyond dispute is that he provides exceptional insights into the intellectual history of his century.

Like many Victorians (including John Ruskin, his exact contemporary), Clough was permanently influenced by his mother's pious religious convictions, her influence being reinforced by his years at Rugby School, where he was the prize pupil of Dr. Thomas Arnold. Later, at Oxford, his earnest preoccupation with religious duty was undermined by a number of different intellectual developments. He was forced to think through questions of High Church authoritarianism and traditionalism—provoked by John Henry Newman's presence at Oxford—and to confront the evidence of scientific critics who challenged the authority and authenticity of the Scriptures. Clough emerged as a skeptic in the real sense of the word. In a letter to his sister in 1847, speaking of the Atonement as an article of Christian faith, he remarks: "I think others are more right who say boldly, we don't understand it, and therefore we won't fall down and worship it. Though there is no occasion for adding—'there *is* nothing in it'—I should say, until I know, I will wait, and if I am not born with the power to discover, I will do what I can . . . and neither pretend to know, nor, without knowing, pretend to embrace: nor yet oppose those who, by whatever means, are increasing or trying to increase knowledge." A year later, reflections of this kind led Clough to resign his fellowship at Oxford where he was expected to subscribe to the doctrines of the Church of England. For the rest of his life he held various educational posts. On one occasion, his application for a chair of classics in Australia was unsuccessful. His failure may be attributed to the refusal of his principal referee at Oxford to write a recommendation for him on the grounds that "no one ought to be appointed to such a situation who is at all in a state of doubt or difficulty as to his religious beliefs." Such obstacles did not prevent Clough's obtaining other employments in London and, in 1852–53 (under the auspices of Emerson), in America, where he had spent his early childhood. Clough was fond of travel, especially in Italy, which served as the setting for several of his poems, including *Amours de Voyage,* the most modern of his poems, an epistolary narrative about a young intellectual whose ironic self-conscoiusness causes him the loss of his love.

Much of Clough's poetry was published posthumously. His first volume, *The Bothie of Tober-na-Vuolich* (1848), is a delightful novel in verse, an undergraduate love story exhibiting aspects of his character omitted in Arnold's picture of him in *Thyrsis*. For despite his painful exposure to religious uncertainties, Clough had a strain of high spirits and fun that gives flavor to his best poems. In his later poems, including *Dipsychus* (1850), a series of debates between idealism and worldliness, the strains of earnestness, uncertainty, and humor are blended into an ironic point of view different from Matthew Arnold's and, in fact, different from the characteristic tone of most of his contemporaries. Perhaps one of the reasons that Clough's poetry has been inadequately appreciated is that this distinctive tone of his is most evident in his full-length poems rather than in the short hymnlike verses by which he is usually represented in anthologies.

Epi-strauss-ium[1]

Matthew and Mark and Luke and holy John
Evanished all and gone!
Yea, he[2] that erst, his dusky curtains quitting,
Through Eastern pictured panes his level beams transmitting,
5   With gorgeous portraits blent,
On them his glories intercepted spent,
Southwestering now, through windows plainly glassed,
On the inside face his radiance keen hath cast,
And in the luster lost, invisible, and gone,
10 Are, say you, Matthew, Mark, and Luke and holy John?
Lost, is it? lost, to be recovered never?
However,
The place of worship the meantime with light
Is, if less richly, more sincerely bright,
15 And in blue skies the Orb is manifest to sight.

1847   1869

The Latest Decalogue

Thou shalt have one God only; who
Would be at the expense of two?
No graven images may be
Worshiped, except the currency.
5 Swear not at all; for, for thy curse
Thine enemy is none the worse.
At church on Sunday to attend

---

1. The title is a play on *epi-thalamium,* which means "concerning the bridal chamber." The word usually refers to a song in honor of a bride and bridegroom (as in Spenser's poem). Clough's title means "concerning Strauss-ism," a reference to D. F. Strauss, a German biblical scholar whose *Life of Jesus* was translated into English by George Eliot in 1846. The "light" of Strauss's analysis reputedly showed up the historical inaccuracy of parts of the Gospels in the Bible.
2. The sun. Cf. lines 13–16 of *Say Not the Struggle Nought Availeth* (p. 1453).

Will serve to keep the world thy friend.
Honor thy parents; that is, all
10 From whom advancement may befall.
Thou shalt not kill; but need'st not strive
Officiously to keep alive.
Do not adultery commit;
Advantage rarely comes of it.
15 Thou shalt not steal; an empty feat,
When it's so lucrative to cheat.
Bear not false witness; let the lie
Have time on its own wings to fly.
Thou shalt not covet, but tradition
20 Approves all forms of competition.

The sum of all is, thou shalt love,
If anybody, God above:
At any rate shall never labor
More than thyself to love thy neighbor.[1]

1862

Say Not the Struggle Nought Availeth

Say not the struggle nought availeth,
    The labor and the wounds are vain,
The enemy faints not, nor faileth,
    And as things have been they remain.

5 If hopes were dupes, fears may be liars;
    It may be, in yon smoke concealed,
Your comrades chase e'en now the fliers,
    And, but for you, possess the field.

For while the tired waves, vainly breaking,
10   Seem here no painful inch to gain,
Far back, through creeks and inlets making,
    Comes silent, flooding in, the main.

And not by eastern windows only,
    When daylight comes, comes in the light,
15 In front, the sun climbs slow, how slowly,
    But westward, look, the land is bright.

1849   1862

---

1. Lines 21–24 were discovered in one of Clough's manuscripts and were not originally included in published versions of the poem.

GEORGE ELIOT
1819–1880

Like many English novelists (Dickens being an exception) George Eliot came to novel writing relatively late in life. She was forty when her first novel, *Adam Bede,* an outstandingly popular work, was published. The lives of her characters are, therefore, viewed from the vantage point of maturity and extensive experience; and this perspective is accentuated by her practice of setting her stories back in time to the period of her own childhood, or even earlier. In most of her novels, she evokes a preindustrial rural scene or the small-town life of the English Midlands, which she views with a combination of nostalgia and candid awareness of their limitations.

The place Eliot looks back on is usually the Warwickshire countryside, where, under her real name, Marian Evans, she spent her childhood at Arbury Farm, of which her father, Robert Evans, was supervisor and land agent. The time was the 1820s and 1830s (1819, the year of her birth, was an *annus mirabilis* for the nineteenth century, for in the same year were born John Ruskin, Herman Melville, Walt Whitman, Arthur Hugh Clough, and Queen Victoria). During these decades, Evans read widely in and out of school and was also strongly affected by Evangelicism; she even advocated, at one point in her girlhood, giving up novelists such as Scott (who was later to influence her own novel writing) on the grounds that fiction was frivolous and time wasting. Her mother's death led to her leaving school at sixteen, and in the next four or five years she seems to have experienced bouts of depression and self-doubt. In a letter of 1871, looking back to the period, she likened her state of mind to that of Mary Wollstonecraft at the time of her attempted suicide: "Hopelessness has been to me, all through my life, but especially in the painful years of my youth, the chief source of wasted energy with all the consequent bitterness of regret. Remember, it has happened to many to be glad they did not commit suicide, though they once ran for the final leap, or as Mary Wollstonecraft did, wetted their garments well in the rain hoping to sink the better when they plunged."

At the age of twenty-one Evans moved with her father to the town of Coventry, and in this new setting, her intellectual horizons were extensively widened. As the result of her association with a group of freethinking intellectuals, and her own studies of theology, she reluctantly decided that she could no longer believe in the Christian religion. Her decision created a painful break with her father, finally resolved when she agreed to observe the formality of attending church with him and he agreed, tacitly at least, that while there she could think what she liked.

These preoccupations with theological issues led to her first book, a translation of *The Life of Jesus* by D. F. Strauss, one of the leading figures of the Higher Criticism in Germany. This criticism was the work of a group of scholars dedicated to testing the historical authenticity of biblical narratives in the light of modern methods of research. For the rest of her life, Evans continued to read extensively in English and Continental philosophy; and when she moved to London in 1851, after her father's death, her impressive intellectual credentials led to her appointment as an assistant editor of the *Westminster Review,* a learned journal formerly edited by John Stuart Mill. In the years in which she served as editor, she wrote a number of essays, including *Margaret Fuller and Mary Wollstonecraft* and *Silly Novels by Lady Novelists,* which she contributed to various periodicals, in addition to the *Westminster Review.*

Her work at the *Review* brought her into contact with many important writers and thinkers. Among them was George Henry Lewes, a brilliant critic of literature and philosophy, with whom she fell in love. Lewes, a married man and father of three children, could not obtain a divorce. Evans, therefore, elected to live with him as a common-law wife, and what they called their "marriage" lasted happily until his death in 1878. In the last year of her life, she married an admirer and friend, J. W. Cross, who became her biographer.

Her earlier decision to live with Lewes was painfully made: "Light and easily broken ties are what I neither desire theoretically nor could live for practically. Women who are satisfied with such ties do *not* act as I have done—they obtain what they desire and are still invited to dinner." Mrs. Lewes, as she called herself, was not invited to dinner; instead, those who wanted to visit with her had themselves to seek her company at the house that she shared with Lewes, where she received visitors on Sunday afternoons. These Sunday afternoons became legendary occasions, over which she presided almost like a sibyl. However, her decision to live with Lewes cost her a number of social and family ties, including her relationship with her brother, Isaac, to whom she had been deeply attached since childhood. Isaac never spoke to her again after her elopement. It is reasonable to conjecture that this experience affects the stress, in all of her novels, on incidents involving choice. All of her characters are tested by situations in which they must choose, and the choices, as in *The Mill on the Floss,* are often agonizingly painful.

Although she had occasionally tried her hand at fiction earlier in life, it was only after her relationship with Lewes became established that she turned her full attention to this form. *Scenes from Clerical Life* appeared in magazine installments in 1857 under the pen name that misled most of her readers (Dickens excepted) into believing the author to be a man—a "university man," it was commonly said, to Eliot's amusement and satisfaction. This work was followed by seven full-length novels in the 1860s and 1870s, most of which repeated the success of *Adam Bede* with the Victorian reading public and which, after a period of being out of favor earlier in our century, are now once more deeply admired by readers and critics. Virginia Woolf praised *Middlemarch* as "one of the few English novels written for grown-up people," and later readers have found a similar maturity combined with a powerful creative energy in other novels by Eliot such as *The Mill on the Floss* and *Daniel Deronda* (1876).

When Eliot began writing fiction, she and Lewes were reading to each other the novels of Jane Austen. Eliot's fiction owes much to Austen's with its concern with provincial society, its satire of human motives, its focus on courtship. But Eliot brings to these subjects a philosophical and psychological depth very different in character from that of the novel of manners. Eliot's fiction typically combines expansive philosophic meditation with an acute dissection of her characters' motives and feelings.

In a famous passage from *Middlemarch,* Eliot compares herself with the great eighteenth-century novelist Henry Fielding:

> A great historian, as he insisted on calling himself, who had the happiness to be dead a hundred and twenty years ago, and so to take his place among the colossi whose huge legs our living pettiness is observed to walk under, glories in his copious remarks and digressions as the least imitable part of his work. . . . But Fielding lived when the days were longer. . . . We belated historians must not linger after his example; I at least have so much to do in unravelling certain human lots, and seeing how they were woven and interwoven, that all the light I can command must be concentrated on this particular web, and not dispersed over that tempting range of relevancies called the universe.

Despite her ironic disclaimer Eliot too prides herself on her remarks and digressions— as this passage, itself a digression, suggests. As a "belated historian," however, she focuses on the intersection of a few human lives at a particular time and place in her country's history. She frequently likened herself not only to a historian but to a scientist, who, with a microscope, observes and analyzes the tangled web of character and circumstance that determines human history. As both comparisons imply, Eliot strives to present her fiction as a mirror that reflects without distortion our experience of life. But her insistence on art's transparency is often troubled both by her consciousness of its fictions and by her sense of the way in which the egoism we all share distorts our perceptions. Hence she portrays this egoism with a combination of acuity and compassion. It is this distinctive compounding of realism and sympathy that makes her, according to the French critic Brunetiere, a better realist than her famous French contemporary Flaubert, author of *Madame Bovary.* Often compared with Tolstoy, she is, perhaps, the greatest English realist.

Eliot's definition of herself as a historian leads us to expect her novels to offer considerable insight into contemporary issues. The Woman Question, as her essay *Margaret Fuller and Mary Wollstonecraft* suggests, held particular interest for her. She typically chooses for her heroine a young woman, like Maggie Tulliver of *The Mill on the Floss* or Dorothea Brooke of *Middlemarch*, of powerful imagination and of yearning to be more than her society allows her to be. The prelude to *Middlemarch* speaks of the modern-day Saint Teresa, with the ardor and vision to found a religious order, caught at a historical moment that gives no outlet for her ambition. In her portrayal of the frustrations and yearnings of such a heroine, Eliot seems sympathetic to a feminist point of view. Yet her stress on the values of loyalty to one's past; of adherence to duty, despite personal desire; and of what Wordsworth calls "little, nameless, unremembered acts of kindness and of love" suggests that her attitude toward the Woman Question is complex.

George Eliot wrote, "My function is that of the *aesthetic* not the doctrinal teacher." The largeness of vision through which Eliot enters into the consciousness of all her characters makes the perspective of her novels on many issues a complex one, for it is finally issues as they are refracted through the lens of human character that interest her.

Margaret Fuller and Mary Wollstonecraft[1]

The dearth of new books just now gives us time to recur to less recent ones which we have hitherto noticed but slightly; and among these we choose the late edition of Margaret Fuller's *Woman in the Nineteenth Century*, because we think it has been unduly thrust into the background by less comprehensive and candid productions on the same subject. Notwithstanding certain defects of taste and a sort of vague spiritualism and grandiloquence which belong to all but the very best American writers, the book is a valuable one; it has the enthusiasm of a noble and sympathetic nature, with the moderation and breadth and large allowance of a vigorous and cultivated understanding. There is no exaggeration of woman's moral excellence or intellectual capabilities; no injudicious insistence on her fitness for this or that function hitherto engrossed by men; but a calm plea for the removal of unjust laws and artificial restrictions, so that the possibilities of her nature may have room for full development, a wisely stated demand to disencumber her of the

> Parasitic forms
> That seem to keep her up, but drag her down—
> And leave her field to burgeon and to bloom

1. Published in *The Leader* in 1855, this essay is a retrospective book review of two important feminist publications—*A Vindication of the Rights of Woman* (1792) by Mary Wollstonecraft and *Woman in the Nineteenth Century* (1855; published originally as *The Great Lawsuit*, 1843), by Margaret Fuller (1810–1850), an American essayist and editor whom Eliot warmly admired.

As Barbara Hardy notes, despite "her generous sympathy with Victorian feminism," George Eliot "played no active part in the movement." Eliot seems to have shared the view of women's relation to men expressed by the Prince in Tennyson's *Princess*, whose speeches she cites in this essay. As she herself wrote in 1854, in another essay, *Women in France:*

Women became superior in France by being admitted to a common fund of ideas, to common objects of interest with men; and this must ever be the essential condition at once of true womanly culture and of true social well-being. . . . Let the whole field of reality be laid open to woman as well as to man, and then that which is peculiar in the mental modification, instead of being, as it is now, a source of discord and repulsion between the sexes, will be found to be a necessary complement to the truth and beauty of life.

From all within her, make herself her own
To give or keep, to live and learn and be
All that not harms distinctive womanhood.[2]

It is interesting to compare this essay of Margaret Fuller's published in its earliest form in 1843,[3] with a work on the position of woman, written between sixty and seventy years ago—we mean Mary Wollstonecraft's *Rights of Woman*. The latter work was not continued beyond the first volume; but so far as this carries the subject, the comparison, at least in relation to strong sense and loftiness of moral tone, is not at all disadvantageous to the woman of the last century. There is in some quarters a vague prejudice against the *Rights of Woman* as in some way or other a reprehensible book, but readers who go to it with this impression will be surprised to find it eminently serious, severely moral, and withal rather heavy—the true reason, perhaps, that no edition has been published since 1796, and that it is now rather scarce. There are several points of resemblance, as well as of striking difference, between the two books. A strong understanding is present in both; but Margaret Fuller's mind was like some regions of her own American continent, where you are constantly stepping from the sunny "clearings" into the mysterious twilight of the tangled forest—she often passes in one breath from forcible reasoning to dreamy vagueness; moreover, her unusually varied culture gives her great command of illustration. Mary Wollstonecraft, on the other hand, is nothing if not rational; she has no erudition, and her grave pages are lit up by no ray of fancy. In both writers we discern, under the brave bearing of a strong and truthful nature, the beating of a loving woman's heart, which teaches them not to undervalue the smallest offices of domestic care or kindliness. But Margaret Fuller, with all her passionate sensibility, is more of the literary woman, who would not have been satisfied without intellectual production; Mary Wollstonecraft, we imagine, wrote not at all for writing's sake, but from the pressure of other motives. So far as the difference of date allows, there is a striking coincidence in their trains of thought; indeed, every important idea in the *Rights of Woman,* except the combination of home education with a common day-school for boys and girls, reappears in Margaret Fuller's essay.

One point on which they both write forcibly is the fact that, while men have a horror of such faculty or culture in the other sex as tends to place it on a level with their own, they are really in a state of subjection to ignorant and feeble-minded women. Margaret Fuller says:

> Wherever man is sufficiently raised above extreme poverty or brutal stupidity, to care for the comforts of the fireside, or the bloom and ornament of life, woman has always power enough, if she chooses to exert it, and is usually disposed to do so, in proportion to her ignorance and childish vanity. Unacquainted with the importance of life and its purposes, trained to a selfish coquetry and love of petty power, she does not look beyond the pleasure of making herself felt at the moment, and governments are shaken and commerce broken up to gratify the pique

---

2. Tennyson's *The Princess* 7.253–258. As noted by Thomas Pinney, the quotation, slightly inaccurate, is from the unrevised 1847 text of the poem. See the passage containing these lines ["The

Woman's Cause Is Man's"], p. 1229.
3. I.e., the original version published in *The Dial;* revised and expanded in 1855.

of a female favorite. The English shopkeeper's wife does not vote, but it
is for her interest that the politician canvasses by the coarsest flattery.

Again:

> All wives, bad or good, loved or unloved, inevitably influence their
> husbands from the power their position not merely gives, but necessi-
> tates of coloring evidence and infusing feelings in hours when the—
> patient, shall I call him?—is off his guard.

Hear now what Mary Wollstonecraft says on the same subject:

> Women have been allowed to remain in ignorance and slavish depend-
> ence many, very many years, and still we hear of nothing but their fond-
> ness of pleasure and sway, their preference of rakes and soldiers, their
> childish attachment to toys, and the vanity that makes them value
> accomplishments more than virtues. History brings forward a fearful
> catalogue of the crimes which their cunning has produced, when the
> weak slaves have had sufficient address to overreach their masters. . . .
> When, therefore, I call women slaves, I mean in a political and civil
> sense; for indirectly they obtain too much power, and are debased by
> their exertions to obtain illicit sway. . . . The libertinism, and even the
> virtues of superior men, will always give women of some description
> great power over them; and these weak women, under the influence of
> childish passions and selfish vanity, *will throw a false light over the objects
> which the very men view with their eyes who ought to enlighten their
> judgment.* Men of fancy, and those sanguine characters who mostly hold
> the helm of human affairs in general, relax in the society of women; and
> surely I need not cite to the most superficial reader of history the numer-
> ous examples of vice and oppression which the private intrigues of
> female favorites have produced; not to dwell on the mischief that nat-
> urally arises from the blundering interposition of well-meaning folly. *For
> in the transactions of business it is much better to have to deal with a
> knave than a fool, because a knave adheres to some plan, and any plan of
> reason may be seen through sooner than a sudden flight of folly.* The power
> which vile and foolish women have had over wise men who possessed
> sensibility is notorious.

There is a notion commonly entertained among men that an instructed
woman, capable of having opinions, is likely to prove an unpracticable yoke-
fellow, always pulling one way when her husband wants to go the other,
oracular in tone, and prone to give curtain lectures[4] on metaphysics. But
surely, so far as obstinacy is concerned, your unreasoning animal is the most
unmanageable of creatures, where you are not allowed to settle the question
by a cudgel, a whip and bridle, or even a string to the leg. For our own parts,
we see no consistent or commodious medium between the old plan of cor-
poral discipline and that thorough education of women which will make
them rational beings in the highest sense of the word. Wherever weakness
is not harshly controlled it must *govern,* as you may see when a strong man
holds a little child by the hand, how he is pulled hither and thither, and

---

4. See Douglas Jerrold's comic sketches of a wife who delivers nightly lectures to her husband from behind
their bed curtains, *Mrs. Caudle's Curtain Lectures* (1846).

wearied in his walk by his submission to the whims and feeble movements of his companion. A really cultured woman, like a really cultured man, will be ready to yield in trifles. So far as we see, there is no indissoluble connection between infirmity of logic and infirmity of will, and a woman quite innocent of an opinion in philosophy, is as likely as not to have an indomitable opinion about the kitchen. As to airs of superiority, no woman ever had them in consequence of true culture, but only because her culture was shallow or unreal, only as a result of what Mrs. Malaprop well calls "the ineffectual qualities in a woman"[5]—mere acquisitions carried about, and not knowledge thoroughly assimilated so as to enter into the growth of the character.

To return to Margaret Fuller, some of the best things she says are on the folly of absolute definitions of woman's nature and absolute demarcations of woman's mission. "Nature," she says, "seems to delight in varying the arrangements, as if to show that she will be fettered by no rule; and we must admit the same varieties that she admits." Again: "If nature is never bound down, nor the voice of inspiration stifled, that is enough. We are pleased that women should write and speak, if they feel need of it, from having something to tell; but silence for ages would be no misfortune, if that silence be from divine command, and not from man's tradition." And here is a passage, the beginning of which has been often quoted:

> If you ask me what offices they [women] may fill, I reply—any. I do not care what case you put; let them be sea-captains if you will. I do not doubt there are women well fitted for such an office, and, if so, I should be as glad as to welcome the Maid of Saragossa, or the Maid of Missolonghi, or the Suliote heroine, or Emily Plater.[6] I think women need, especially at this juncture, a much greater range of occupation than they have, to rouse their latent powers. . . . In families that I know, some little girls like to saw wood, others to use carpenter's tools. Where these tastes are indulged, cheerfulness and good-humor are promoted. Where they are forbidden, because "such things are not proper for girls," they grow sullen and mischievous. Fourier had observed these wants of women, as no one can fail to do who watches the desires of little girls, or knows the *ennui* that haunts grown women, except where they make to themselves a serene little world by art of some kind. He, therefore, in proposing a great variety of employments, in manufactures or the care of plants and animals, allows for one-third of women as likely to have a taste for masculine pursuits, one-third of men for feminine.[7] . . . I have no doubt, however, that a large proportion of women would give themselves to the same employments as now, because there are circumstances that must lead them. Mothers will delight to make the nest soft and warm. Nature

5. In response to compliments about her "intellectual accomplishments," Mrs. Malaprop exclaims: "Ah! few gentlemen, nowadays, know how to value the ineffectual qualities in a woman!" Richard Brinsley Sheridan, *The Rivals* 3.2 (1775).
6. A Polish patriot, who became a captain in command of a company in the insurgent army fighting the Russians in 1831. "Maid of Saragossa": Maria Agustin, who fought against the French at the siege of Saragossa, in Spain, in 1808 (see Byron, *Childe Harold's Pilgrimage* 1.54–56). "Maid of

Missolonghi": an unidentified Greek, who must have made some heroic exploit during the Turkish sieges of that town in 1822 or 1826. "The Suliote heroine": probably Moscha, who led a band of three hundred women to rout the Turks during the siege of Souli, in Albania, in 1803.
7. Charles Fourier (1772–1837), in his utopian treatise *The New Industrial World* (1829–30), develops these theories in his discussion of "the Little Hordes."

would take care of that; no need to clip the wings of any bird that wants to soar and sing, or finds in itself the strength of pinion for a migratory flight unusual to its kind. The difference would be that *all* need not be constrained to employments for which *some* are unfit.

Apropos of the same subject, we find Mary Wollstonecraft offering a suggestion which the women of the United States have already begun to carry out. She says:

> Women, in particular, all want to be ladies, which is simply to have nothing to do, but listlessly to go they scarcely care where, for they cannot tell what. But what have women to do in society? I may be asked, but to loiter with easy grace; surely you would not condemn them all to suckle fools and chronicle small beer.[8] No. *Women might certainly study the art of healing, and be physicians as well as nurses. . . .* Business of various kinds they might likewise pursue, if they were educated in a more orderly manner. . . . Women would not then marry for a support, as men accept of places under government, and neglect the implied duties.

Men pay a heavy price for their reluctance to encourage self-help and independent resources in women. The precious meridian years of many a man of genius have to be spent in the toil of routine, that an "establishment" may be kept up for a woman who can understand none of his secret yearnings,[9] who is fit for nothing but to sit in her drawing-room like a doll-Madonna in her shrine. No matter. Anything is more endurable than to change our established formulae about women, or to run the risk of looking up to our wives instead of looking down on them. *Sit divus, dummodo non sit vivus* (let him be a god, provided he be not living), said the Roman magnates of Romulus;[1] and so men say of women, let them be idols, useless absorbents of previous things, provided we are not obliged to admit them to be strictly fellow-beings, to be treated, one and all, with justice and sober reverence.

On one side we hear that woman's position can never be improved until women themselves are better; and, on the other, that women can never become better until their position is improved—until the laws are made more just, and a wider field opened to feminine activity. But we constantly hear the same difficulty stated about the human race in general. There is a perpetual action and reaction between individuals and institutions; we must try and mend both by little and little—the only way in which human things can be mended. Unfortunately, many over-zealous champions of women assert their actual equality with men—nay, even their moral superiority to men—as a ground for their release from oppressive laws and restrictions. They lose strength immensely by this false position. If it were true, then there would be a case in which slavery and ignorance nourished virtue, and so far we should have an argument for the continuance of bondage. But we want freedom and culture for woman, because subjection and ignorance have debased her, and with her, Man; for—

---

8. Iago on the role of women, Shakespeare's *Othello* 2.1.160.
9. Cf. Eliot's fictional representation of such a situation in her account of Dr. Lydgate's married life in *Middlemarch*.
1. Cf. *Historia Augusta, Geta* 2, in which the same cynical comment is made on a proposal to have a man deified.

> If she be small, slight-natured, miserable,
> How shall men grow?[2]

Both Margaret Fuller and Mary Wollstonecraft have too much sagacity to fall into this sentimental exaggeration. Their ardent hopes of what women may become do not prevent them from seeing and painting women as they are. On the relative moral excellence of men and women Mary Wollstonecraft speaks with the most decision:

> Women are supposed to possess more sensibility, and even humanity, than men, and their strong attachments and instantaneous emotions of compassion are given as proofs; but the clinging affection of ignorance has seldom anything noble in it, and may mostly be resolved into selfishness, as well as the affection of children and brutes. I have known many weak women whose sensibility was entirely engrossed by their husbands; and as for their humanity, it was very faint indeed, or rather it was only a transient emotion of compassion. Humanity does not consist "in a squeamish ear," says an eminent orator.[3] "It belongs to the mind as well as to the nerves." But this kind of exclusive affection, though it degrades the individual, should not be brought forward as a proof of the inferiority of the sex, because it is the natural consequence of confined views; for even women of superior sense, having their attention turned to little employments and private plans, rarely rise to heroism, unless when spurred on by love! and love, as an heroic passion, like genius, appears but once in an age. I therefore agree with the moralist who asserts "that women have seldom so much generosity as men"; and that their narrow affections, to which justice and humanity are often sacrificed, render the sex apparently inferior, especially as they are commonly inspired by men; but I contend that the heart would expand as the understanding gained strength, if women were not depressed from their cradles.

We had marked several other passages of Margaret Fuller's for extract, but as we do not aim at an exhaustive treatment of our subject, and are only touching a few of its points, we have, perhaps, already claimed as much of the reader's attention as he will be willing to give to such desultory material.

1855

Silly Novels by Lady Novelists[1]

Silly Novels by Lady Novelists are a genus with many species, determined by the particular quality of silliness that predominates in them—the frothy, the prosy, the pious, or the pedantic. But it is a mixture of all these—a composite order of feminine fatuity, that produces the largest class of such novels, which we shall distinguish as the *mind-and-millinery* species. The

---

2. Tennyson's *The Princess* 7.249–50.
3. Perhaps Edmund Burke (1729–1797).
1. Published anonymously in the *Westminster Review*, this review essay, satirizing a number of

contemporary novels, provides a good indication of Eliot's ideas about fiction at the time she was beginning her first story, *The Sad Fortunes of the Rev. Amos Barton*.

heroine is usually an heiress, probably a peeress in her own right, with perhaps a vicious baronet, an amiable duke, and an irresistible younger son of a marquis as lovers in the foreground, a clergyman and a poet sighing for her in the middle distance, and a crowd of undefined adorers dimly indicated beyond. Her eyes and her wit are both dazzling; her nose and her morals are alike free from any tendency to irregularity; she has a superb *contralto* and a superb intellect; she is perfectly well-dressed and perfectly religious; she dances like a sylph, and reads the Bible in the original tongues. Or it may be that the heroine is not an heiress—that rank and wealth are the only things in which she is deficient; but she infallibly gets into high society, she has the triumph of refusing many matches and securing the best, and she wears some family jewels or other as a sort of crown of righteousness at the end. Rakish men either bite their lips in impotent confusion at her repartees, or are touched to penitence by her reproofs, which, on appropriate occasions, rise to a lofty strain of rhetoric; indeed, there is a general propensity in her to make speeches, and to rhapsodize at some length when she retires to her bedroom. In her recorded conversations she is amazingly eloquent, and in her unrecorded conversations, amazingly witty. She is understood to have a depth of insight that looks through and through the shallow theories of philosophers, and her superior instincts are a sort of dial by which men have only to set their clocks and watches, and all will go well. The men play a very subordinate part by her side. You are consoled now and then by a hint that they have affairs, which keeps you in mind that the working-day business of the world is somehow being carried on, but ostensibly the final cause of their existence is that they may accompany the heroine on her "starring" expedition through life. They see her at a ball, and are dazzled; at a flower-show, and they are fascinated; on a riding excursion, and they are witched[2] by her noble horsemanship; at church, and they are awed by the sweet solemnity of her demeanour. She is the ideal woman in feelings, faculties, and flounces. For all this, she as often as not marries the wrong person to begin with, and she suffers terribly from the plots and intrigues of the vicious baronet; but even death has a soft place in his heart for such a paragon, and remedies all mistakes for her just at the right moment. The vicious baronet is sure to be killed in a duel, and the tedious husband dies in his bed requesting his wife, as a particular favour to him, to marry the man she loves best, and having already dispatched a note to the lover informing him of the comfortable arrangement. Before matters arrive at this desirable issue our feelings are tried by seeing the noble, lovely, and gifted heroine pass through many *mauvais*[3] *moments*, but we have the satisfaction of knowing that her sorrows are wept into embroidered pocket-handkerchiefs, that her fainting form reclines on the very best upholstery, and that whatever vicissitudes she may undergo, from being dashed out of her carriage to having her head shaved in a fever, she comes out of them all with a complexion more blooming and locks more redundant than ever.

We may remark, by the way, that we have been relieved from a serious scruple by discovering that silly novels by lady novelists rarely introduce us into any other than very lofty and fashionable society. We had imagined that destitute women turned novelists, as they turned governesses, because they

---

2. Bewitched.   3. Bad (French).

had no other "lady-like" means of getting their bread. On this supposition, vacillating syntax and improbable incident had a certain pathos for us, like the extremely supererogatory pincushions and ill-devised nightcaps that are offered for sale by a blind man. We felt the commodity to be a nuisance, but we were glad to think that the money went to relieve the necessitous, and we pictured to ourselves lonely women struggling for a maintenance, or wives and daughters devoting themselves to the production of "copy" out of pure heroism,—perhaps to pay their husband's debts, or to purchase luxuries for a sick father. Under these impressions we shrank from criticising a lady's novel: her English might be faulty, but, we said to ourselves, her motives are irreproachable; her imagination may be uninventive, but her patience is untiring. Empty writing was excused by an empty stomach, and twaddle was consecrated by tears. But no! This theory of ours, like many other pretty theories, has had to give way before observation. Women's silly novels, we are now convinced, are written under totally different circumstances. The fair writers have evidently never talked to a tradesman except from a carriage window; they have no notion of the working-classes except as "dependents; " they think five hundred a-year a miserable pittance; Belgravia[4] and "baronial halls" are their primary truths; and they have no idea of feeling interest in any man who is not at least a great landed proprietor, if not a prime minister. It is clear that they write in elegant boudoirs, with violet-colored ink and a ruby pen; that they must be entirely indifferent to publishers' accounts, and inexperienced in every form of poverty except poverty of brains. It is true that we are constantly struck with the want of verisimilitude in their representations of the high society in which they seem to live; but then they betray no closer acquaintance with any other form of life. If their peers and peeresses are improbable, their literary men, tradespeople, and cottagers are impossible; and their intellect seems to have the peculiar impartiality of reproducing both what they *have* seen and heard, and what they have *not* seen and heard, with equal unfaithfulness.

✳   ✳   ✳

Writers of the mind-and-millinery school are remarkably unanimous in their choice of diction. In their novels, there is usually a lady or gentleman who is more or less of a upas tree:[5] the lover has a manly breast; minds are redolent of various things; hearts are hollow; events are utilized; friends are consigned to the tomb; infancy is an engaging period; the sun is a luminary that goes to his western couch, or gathers the rain-drops into his refulgent bosom; life is a melancholy boon; Albion and Scotia[6] are conversational epithets. There is a striking resemblance, too, in the character of their moral comments, such, for instance, as that "It is a fact, no less true than melancholy, that all people, more or less, richer or poorer, are swayed by bad example;" that "Books, however trivial, contain some subjects from which useful information may be drawn;" that "Vice can too often borrow the language of virtue;" that "Merit and nobility of nature must exist, to be accepted, for clamour and pretension cannot impose upon those too well read in human nature to be easily deceived;" and that, "In order to forgive, we must

---

4. A wealthy district of London.
5. A Javanese tree from which an arrow poison is derived; here, a figurative cliché meaning "a poi-

sonous influence."
6. Poetic clichés for England and Scotland, respectively.

have been injured." There is, doubtless, a class of readers to whom these remarks appear peculiarly pointed and pungent; for we often find them doubly and trebly scored with the pencil, and delicate hands giving in their determined adhesion to these hardy novelties by a distinct *très vrai*,[7] emphasized by many notes of exclamation. The colloquial style of these novels is often marked by much ingenious inversion, and a careful avoidance of such cheap phraseology as can be heard every day. Angry young gentlemen exclaim—" 'Tis ever thus, methinks;" and in the half-hour before dinner a young lady informs her next neighbour that the first day she read Shakspeare she "stole away into the park, and beneath the shadow of the greenwood tree, devoured with rapture the inspired page of the great magician." But the most remarkable efforts of the mind-and-millinery writers lie in their philosophic reflections. The authoress of "Laura Gay,"[8] for example, having married her hero and heroine, improves the event by observing that "if those sceptics, whose eyes have so long gazed on matter that they can no longer see aught else in man, could once enter with heart and soul into such bliss as this, they would come to say that the soul of man and the polypus are not of common origin, or of the same texture." Lady novelists, it appears, can see something else besides matter; they are not limited to phenomena, but can relieve their eyesight by occasional glimpses of the *noumenon*,[9] and are, therefore, naturally better able than any one else to confound sceptics, even of that remarkable, but to us unknown school, which maintains that the soul of man is of the same texture as the polypus.[1]

The most pitiable of all silly novels by lady novelists are what we may call the *oracular* species—novels intended to expound the writer's religious, philosophical, or moral theories. There seems to be a notion abroad among women, rather akin to the superstition that the speech and actions of idiots are inspired, and that the human being most entirely exhausted of common sense is the fittest vehicle of revelation. To judge from their writings, there are certain ladies who think that an amazing ignorance, both of science and of life, is the best possible qualification for forming an opinion on the knottiest moral and speculative questions. Apparently, their recipe for solving all such difficulties is something like this:—Take a woman's head, stuff it with a smattering of philosophy and literature chopped small, and with false notions of society baked hard, let it hang over a desk a few hours every day, and serve up hot in feeble English, when not required. You will rarely meet with a lady novelist of the oracular class who is diffident of her ability to decide on theological questions,—who has any suspicion that she is not capable of discriminating with the nicest accuracy between the good and evil in all church parties,—who does not see precisely how it is that men have gone wrong hitherto,—and pity philosophers in general that they have not had the opportunity of consulting her. Great writers, who have modestly contented themselves with putting their experience into fiction, and have thought it quite a sufficient task to exhibit men and things as they are, she sighs over as deplorably deficient in the application of their powers. "They have solved no great questions"—and she is ready to remedy their omission by setting before you a complete theory of life and manual of divinity, in a

---

7. Very true (French).
8. The novel Eliot has just satirized in the preceding section.

9. An object of purely rational, as opposed to sensual, perception.
1. Polyp.

love story, where ladies and gentlemen of good family go through genteel vicissitudes, to the utter confusion of Deists, Puseyites,[2] and ultra-Protestants, and to the perfect establishment of that particular view of Christianity which either condenses itself into a sentence of small caps, or explodes into a cluster of stars on the three hundred and thirtieth page. It is true, the ladies and gentlemen will probably seem to you remarkably little like any you have had the fortune or misfortune to meet with, for, as a general rule, the ability of a lady novelist to describe actual life and her fellow-men, is in inverse proportion to her confident eloquence about God and the other world, and the means by which she usually chooses to conduct you to true ideas of the invisible is a totally false picture of the visible.

* * *

The epithet "silly" may seem impertinent, applied to a novel which indicates so much reading and intellectual activity as "The Enigma;"[3] but we use this epithet advisedly. If, as the world has long agreed, a very great amount of instruction will not make a wise man, still less will a very mediocre amount of instruction make a wise woman. And the most mischievous form of feminine silliness is the literary form, because it tends to confirm the popular prejudice against the more solid education of women. When men see girls wasting their time in consultations about bonnets and ball dresses, and in giggling or sentimental love-confidences, or middle-aged women mismanaging their children, and solacing themselves with acrid gossip, they can hardly help saying, "For Heaven's sake, let girls be better educated; let them have some better objects of thought—some more solid occupations." But after a few hours' conversation with an oracular literary woman, or a few hours' reading of her books, they are likely enough to say, "After all, when a woman gets some knowledge, see what use she makes of it! Her knowledge remains acquisition, instead of passing into culture; instead of being subdued into modesty and simplicity by a larger acquaintance with thought and fact, she has a feverish consciousness of her attainments; she keeps a sort of mental pocket-mirror, and is continually looking in it at her own 'intellectuality;' she spoils the taste of one's muffin by questions of metaphysics; 'puts down' men at a dinner table with her superior information; and seizes the opportunity of a *soirée* to catechise us on the vital question of the relation between mind and matter. And then, look at her writings! She mistakes vagueness for depth, bombast for eloquence, and affectation for originality; she struts on one page, rolls her eyes on another, grimaces in a third, and is hysterical in a fourth. She may have read many writings of great men, and a few writings of great women; but she is as unable to discern the difference between her own style and theirs as a Yorkshireman is to discern the difference between his own English and a Londoner's: rhodomontade[4] is the native accent of her intellect. No—the average nature of women is too shallow and feeble a soil to bear much tillage; it is only fit for the very lightest crops."

It is true that the men who come to such a decision on such very superficial

2. Protestants who believed in the importance of liturgical sacraments. "Deists": Protestants who believed in a personal God who created the universe but who was completely beyond human experience.
3. The novel Eliot has just satirized in the preced-

ing section.
4. Inflated diction. It is assumed a Yorkshireman cannot discern the difference between his provincial northern dialect and the sophisticated speech of a Londoner.

and imperfect observation may not be among the wisest in the world; but we have not now to contest their opinion—we are only pointing out how it is unconsciously encouraged by many women who have volunteered themselves as representatives of the feminine intellect. We do not believe that a man was ever strengthened in such an opinion by associating with a woman of true culture, whose mind had absorbed her knowledge instead of being absorbed by it. A really cultured woman, like a really cultured man, is all the simpler and the less obtrusive for her knowledge; it has made her see herself and her opinions in something like just proportions; she does not make it a pedestal from which she flatters herself that she commands a complete view of men and things, but makes it a point of observation from which to form a right estimate of herself. She neither spouts poetry nor quotes Cicero[5] on slight provocation; not because she thinks that a sacrifice must be made to the prejudices of men, but because that mode of exhibiting her memory and Latinity does not present itself to her as edifying or graceful. She does not write books to confound philosophers, perhaps because she is able to write books that delight them. In conversation she is the least formidable of women, because she understands you, without wanting to make you aware that you *can't* understand her. She does not give you information, which is the raw material of culture,—she gives you sympathy, which is its subtlest essence.

A more numerous class of silly novels than the oracular, (which are generally inspired by some form of High Church, or transcendental Christianity,) is what we may call the *white neck-cloth* species, which represent the tone of thought and feeling in the Evangelical party. This species is a kind of genteel tract on a large scale, intended as a sort of medicinal sweetmeat for Low Church young ladies; an Evangelical substitute for the fashionable novel, as the May Meetings[6] are a substitute for the Opera. Even Quaker children, one would think, can hardly have been denied the indulgence of a doll; but it must be a doll dressed in a drab gown and a coal-scuttle bonnet— not a worldly doll, in gauze and spangles. And there are no young ladies, we imagine,—unless they belong to the Church of the United Brethren, in which people are married without any love-making—who can dispense with love stories. Thus, for Evangelical young ladies there are Evangelical love stories, in which the vicissitudes of the tender passion are sanctified by saving views of Regeneration and the Atonement. These novels differ from the oracular ones, as a Low Churchwoman often differs from a High Churchwoman: they are a little less supercilious, and a great deal more ignorant, a little less correct in their syntax, and a great deal more vulgar.

The Orlando[7] of Evangelical literature is the young curate, looked at from the point of view of the middle class, where cambric bands are understood to have as thrilling an effect on the hearts of young ladies as epaulettes have in the classes above and below it. In the ordinary type of these novels, the hero is almost sure to be a young curate, frowned upon, perhaps, by worldly mammas, but carrying captive the hearts of their daughters, who can "never forget *that* sermon;" tender glances are seized from the pulpit stairs instead of the opera-box; *tête-à-têtes* are seasoned with quotations from Scripture, instead of quotations from the poets; and questions as to the state of the

---

5. Roman statesman and orator (106–43 B.C.E.).
6. The Church of England's Missionary Society's annual spring meetings.

7. The romantic hero (in allusion to the hero of Shakespeare's *As You Like It*).

heroine's affections are mingled with anxieties as to the state of her soul. The young curate always has a background of well-dressed and wealthy, if not fashionable society;—for Evangelical silliness is as snobbish as any other kind of silliness; and the Evangelical lady novelist, while she explains to you the type of the scapegoat on one page, is ambitious on another to represent the manners and conversation of aristocratic people. Her pictures of fashionable society are often curious studies considered as efforts of the Evangelical imagination; but in one particular the novels of the White Neck-cloth School are meritoriously realistic,—their favourite hero, the Evangelical young curate is always rather an insipid personage.

*   *   *

But, perhaps, the least readable of silly women's novels, are the *modern-antique* species, which unfold to us the domestic life of Jannes and Jambres, the private love affairs of Sennacherib, or the mental struggles and ultimate conversion of Demetrius the silversmith.[8] From most silly novels we can at least extract a laugh; but those of the modern antique school have a ponderous, a leaden kind of fatuity, under which we groan. What can be more demonstrative of the inability of literary women to measure their own powers, than their frequent assumption of a task which can only be justified by the rarest concurrence of acquirement with genius? The finest effort to reanimate the past is of course only approximative—is always more or less an infusion of the modern spirit into the ancient form,—

> Was ihr den Geist der Zeiten heisst,
> Das ist im Grund der Herren eigner Geist,
> In dem die Zeiten sich bespiegeln.[9]

Admitting that genius which has familiarized itself with all the relics of an ancient period can sometimes, by the force of its sympathetic divination, restore the missing notes in the "music of humanity," and reconstruct the fragments into a whole which will really bring the remote past nearer to us, and interpret it to our duller apprehension,—this form of imaginative power must always be among the very rarest, because it demands as much accurate and minute knowledge as creative vigour. Yet we find ladies constantly choosing to make their mental mediocrity more conspicuous, by clothing it in a masquerade of ancient names; by putting their feeble sentimentality into the mouths of Roman vestals or Egyptian princesses, and attributing their rhetorical arguments to Jewish high-priests and Greek philosophers. * * *

"Be not a baker if your head be made of butter," says a homely proverb, which, being interpreted, may mean, let no woman rush into print who is not prepared for the consequences. We are aware that our remarks are in a very different tone from that of the reviewers who, with a perennial recurrence of precisely similar emotions, only paralleled, we imagine, in the experience of monthly nurses,[1] tell one lady novelist after another that they "hail"

---

8. In Acts 19.24–27 he makes statues of the Roman goddess Diana and denounces Paul for taking business away from him and his fellow craftsmen by converting people to Christianity. Jannes and Jambres were Egyptian magicians who opposed Moses at Pharaoh's court (2 Timothy 3.8). Sennacherib was an Assyrian king who ruled from 705 to 681 B.C.E.

9. What they call the spirit of the age / is at the base the gentlemen's own spirit, / in which the ages are reflected (German; Goethe's *Faust I, Nacht*, lines 577–79).

1. Women hired to nurse infants.

her productions "with delight." We are aware that the ladies at whom our criticism is pointed are accustomed to be told, in the choicest phraseology of puffery, that their pictures of life are brilliant, their characters well drawn, their style fascinating, and their sentiments lofty. But if they are inclined to resent our plainness of speech, we ask them to reflect for a moment on the chary praise, and often captious blame, which their panegyrists give to writers whose works are on the way to become classics. No sooner does a woman show that she has genius or effective talent, than she receives the tribute of being moderately praised and severely criticised. By a peculiar thermometric adjustment, when a woman's talent is at zero, journalistic approbation is at the boiling pitch; when she attains mediocrity, it is already at no more than summer heat; and if ever she reaches excellence, critical enthusiasm drops to the freezing point. Harriet Martineau, Currer Bell,[2] and Mrs. Gaskell have been treated as cavalierly as if they had been men. And every critic who forms a high estimate of the share women may ultimately take in literature, will, on principle, abstain from any exceptional indulgence towards the productions of literary women. For it must be plain to every one who looks impartially and extensively into feminine literature, that its greatest deficiencies are due hardly more to the want of intellectual power than to the want of those moral qualities that contribute to literary excellence—patient diligence, a sense of the responsibility involved in publication, and an appreciation of the sacredness of the writer's art. In the majority of women's books you see that kind of facility which springs from the absence of any high standard; that fertility in imbecile combination or feeble imitation which a little self-criticism would check and reduce to barrenness; just as with a total want of musical ear people will sing out of tune, while a degree more melodic sensibility would suffice to render them silent. The foolish vanity of wishing to appear in print, instead of being counterbalanced by any consciousness of the intellectual or moral derogation implied in futile authorship, seems to be encouraged by the extremely false impression that to write *at all* is a proof of superiority in a woman. On this ground, we believe that the average intellect of women is unfairly represented by the mass of feminine literature, and that while the few women who write well are very far above the ordinary intellectual level of their sex, the many women who write ill are very far below it. So that, after all, the severer critics are fulfilling a chivalrous duty in depriving the mere fact of feminine authorship of any false prestige which may give it a delusive attraction, and in recommending women of mediocre faculties—as at least a negative service they can render their sex—to abstain from writing.

The standing apology for women who become writers without any special qualification is, that society shuts them out from other spheres of occupation. Society is a very culpable entity, and has to answer for the manufacture of many unwholesome commodities, from bad pickles to bad poetry. But society, like "matter," and Her Majesty's Government, and other lofty abstractions, has its share of excessive blame as well as excessive praise. Where there is one woman who writes from necessity, we believe there are three women who write from vanity; and, besides, there is something so antiseptic in the mere healthy fact of working for one's bread, that the most

2. Pseudonym of Charlotte Brontë.

trashy and rotten kind of feminine literature is not likely to have been produced under such circumstances. "In all labour there is profit;" but ladies' silly novels, we imagine, are less the result of labour than of busy idleness.

Happily, we are not dependent on argument to prove that Fiction is a department of literature in which women can, after their kind, fully equal men. A cluster of great names, both living and dead, rush to our memories in evidence that women can produce novels not only fine, but among the very finest;—novels, too, that have a precious speciality, lying quite apart from masculine aptitudes and experience. No educational restrictions can shut women out from the materials of fiction, and there is no species of art which is so free from rigid requirements. Like crystalline masses, it may take any form, and yet be beautiful; we have only to pour in the right elements— genuine observation, humour, and passion. But it is precisely this absence of rigid requirement which constitutes the fatal seduction of novel-writing to incompetent women. Ladies are not wont to be very grossly deceived as to their power of playing on the piano; here certain positive difficulties of execution have to be conquered, and incompetence inevitably breaks down. Every art which has its absolute *technique* is, to a certain extent, guarded from the intrusions of mere left-handed imbecility. But in novel-writing there are no barriers for incapacity to stumble against, no external criteria to prevent a writer from mistaking foolish facility for mastery. And so we have again and again the old story of La Fontaine's ass, who puts his nose to the flute, and, finding that he elicits some sound, exclaims, "Moi, aussi, je joue de la flute;"[3]—a fable which we commend, at parting, to the consideration of any feminine reader who is in danger of adding to the number of "silly novels by lady novelists."

1856   1856

From The Mill on the Floss[1]

From *Book First. Boy and Girl*

CHAPTER 1. OUTSIDE DORLCOTE MILL

A wide plain, where the broadening Floss hurries on between its green banks to the sea, and the loving tide, rushing to meet it, checks its passage with an impetuous embrace. On this mighty tide the black ships—laden with the fresh-scented fir-planks, with rounded sacks of oil-bearing seed, or with the dark glitter of coal—are borne along to the town of St. Ogg's, which shows its aged, fluted red roofs and the broad gables of its wharves between the low wooded hill and the river brink, tinging the water with a soft purple hue under the transient glance of this February sun. Far away on each hand stretch the rich pastures, and the patches of dark earth, made ready for the

3. I also play the flute (French). Jean de La Fontaine (1621–1695), French author of beast fables.
1. Published in 1860, *The Mill on the Floss* draws on George Eliot's Warwickshire childhood. Beginning in 1829, when its heroine, Maggie, is ten years old (as Eliot was in that year), the novel represents in idealized form Eliot's relationship with her brother, Isaac, in Maggie and Tom Tulliver. Like many of Eliot's novels, *The Mill on the Floss*

portrays a passionate, rapidly developing consciousness in conflict with a conservative social order. It is also, however, a panoramic depiction, at once nostalgic and critical, of a rural middle class whose values were undergoing transformation. Printed here is the first chapter of *The Mill on the Floss*, Eliot's retrospective meditation on the scene of the novel that Marcel Proust claimed reduced him to tears.

seed of broad-leaved green crops, or touched already with the tint of the tender-bladed autumn-sown corn.[2] There is a remnant still of the last year's golden clusters of beehive ricks rising at intervals beyond the hedgerows; and everywhere the hedgerows are studded with trees: the distant ships seem to be lifting their masts and stretching their red-brown sails close among the branches of the spreading ash. Just by the red-roofed town the tributary Ripple flows with a lively current into the Floss. How lovely the little river is, with its dark, changing wavelets! It seems to me like a living companion while I wander along the bank and listen to its low placid voice, as to the voice of one who is deaf and loving. I remember those large dipping willows. I remember the stone bridge.

And this is Dorlcote Mill. I must stand a minute or two here on the bridge and look at it, though the clouds are threatening, and it is far on in the afternoon. Even in this leafless time of departing February it is pleasant to look at—perhaps the chill damp season adds a charm to the trimly-kept, comfortable dwelling-house, as old as the elms and chestnuts that shelter it from the northern blast. The stream is brimful now, and lies high in this little withy plantation, and half drowns the grassy fringe of the croft[3] in front of the house. As I look at the full stream, the vivid grass, the delicate bright-green powder softening the outline of the great trunks and branches that gleam from under the bare purple boughs, I am in love with moistness, and envy the white ducks that are dipping their heads far into the water here among the withes, unmindful of the awkward appearance they make in the drier world above.

The rush of the water, and the booming of the mill, bring a dreamy deaf-ness, which seems to heighten the peacefulness of the scene. They are like a great curtain of sound, shutting one out from the world beyond. And now there is the thunder of the huge covered waggon coming home with sacks of grain. That honest waggoner is thinking of his dinner, getting sadly dry in the oven at this late hour; but he will not touch it till he has fed his horses,—the strong, submissive, meek-eyed beasts, who, I fancy, are looking mild reproach at him from between their blinkers, that he should crack his whip at them in that awful manner as if they needed that hint! See how they stretch their shoulders up the slope towards the bridge, with all the more energy because they are so near home. Look at their grand shaggy feet that seem to grasp the firm earth, at the patient strength of their necks, bowed under the heavy collar, at the mighty muscles of their struggling haunches! I should like well to hear them neigh over their hardly-earned feed of corn, and see them, with their moist necks freed from the harness, dipping their eager nostrils into the muddy pond. Now they are on the bridge, and down they go again at a swifter pace, and the arch of the covered waggon disappears at the turning behind the trees.

Now I can turn my eyes towards the mill again, and watch the unresting wheel sending out its diamond jets of water. That little girl[4] is watching it too: she has been standing on just the same spot at the edge of the water ever since I paused on the bridge. And that queer white cur with the brown ear seems to be leaping and barking in ineffectual remonstrance with the

2. Wheat.
3. A patch of farmland adjacent to a house or cottage. "Withy": willow.
4. Maggie Tulliver, the heroine.

wheel; perhaps he is jealous, because his playfellow in the beaver bonnet is so rapt in its movement. It is time the little playfellow went in, I think; and there is a very bright fire to tempt her: the red light shines out under the deepening grey of the sky. It is time, too, for me to leave off resting my arms on the cold stone of this bridge. . . .

Ah, my arms are really benumbed. I have been pressing my elbows on the arms of my chair, and dreaming that I was standing on the bridge in front of Dorlcote Mill, as it looked one February afternoon many years ago. Before I dozed off, I was going to tell you what Mr. and Mrs. Tulliver were talking about, as they sat by the bright fire in the left-hand parlour, on that very afternoon I have been dreaming of.

1860

MATTHEW ARNOLD
1822–1888

How is a full and enjoyable life to be lived in a modern industrial society? This was the recurrent topic in the poetry and prose of Matthew Arnold. In his poetry the question itself is raised; in his prose some answers are attempted. "The misapprehensiveness of his age is exactly what a poet is sent to remedy," wrote Browning. Oddly enough it is to Arnold's work rather than to Browning's that the statement seems more appropriate. And its applicability to Arnold has persisted from Victorian times to ours, in part because the "misapprehensiveness" has also persisted.

Matthew Arnold was born in Laleham, a village in the valley of the Thames. That his childhood was spent in the vicinity of a river seems appropriate, for clear-flowing streams were later to appear in his poems as symbols of serenity. At six, Arnold was moved to Rugby School, where his father, Dr. Thomas Arnold, had become headmaster. As a clergyman Dr. Arnold was a leader of the liberal or Broad Church and hence one of the principal opponents of John Henry Newman. As a headmaster he became famous as an educational reformer, a teacher who instilled into his pupils an earnest preoccupation with moral and social issues and also an awareness of the connection between liberal studies and modern life. At Rugby his eldest son, Matthew, was directly exposed to the powerful force of the father's mind and character. The son's attitude toward this force was a mixture of attraction and repulsion. That he was permanently influenced by his father is evident in his poems and in his writings on religion and politics, but like many sons of clergymen, he made a determined effort in his youth to be different. At Oxford he behaved like a character from one of Evelyn Waugh's early novels. Elegantly and colorfully dressed, alternately languid or merry in manner, he attracted attention as a dandy whose irreverent jokes irritated his more solemn undergraduate friends and acquaintances. "His manner displeases, from its seeming foppery," wrote Charlotte Brontë after talking with the young man. "The shade of Dr. Arnold," she added, "seemed to me to frown on his young representative." Thus with Rugby School's standards of earnestness the son of Dr. Arnold appeared to have no connection. Even his studies did not seem to occupy him seriously. By a session of cramming, he managed to earn second-class honors in his final examinations, a near disaster that was redeemed by his election to a fellowship at Oriel College.

Arnold's biographers usually dismiss his youthful frivolity of spirit as a temporary pose or mask, but it was more. It remained to color his prose style, brightening his most serious criticism with geniality and wit. For most readers the jauntiness of his prose is a virtue, although for others it is offensive. Anyone suspicious of urbanity and irony would applaud Whitman's sour comment that Arnold is "one of the dudes of literature." A more appropriate estimate of his manner is provided by Arnold's own description of Sainte-Beuve as a critic: "a critic of measure, not exuberant; of the center, not provincial . . . with gay and amiable temper, his manner as good as his matter—the *'critique souriant'* [smiling critic]."

Unlike Tennyson or Carlyle, Arnold had to confine his writing and reading to his spare time. In 1847 he took the post of private secretary to Lord Lansdowne, and in 1851, the year of his marriage, he became an inspector of schools, a position that he held for thirty-five years. Although his work as an inspector may have reduced his output as a writer, it had several advantages. His extensive traveling in England took him to the homes of the more ardently Protestant middle classes, and when he criticized the dullness of middle-class life (as he often did), Arnold knew his subject intimately. His position also led to travel on the Continent to study the schools of Europe. As a critic of English education, he was thus able to make helpful comparisons and to draw on a stock of fresh ideas in the same way as in his literary criticism he used his knowledge of French, German, Italian, and classical literatures to measure the achievements of English writers. Despite the monotony of much of his work as an inspector, Arnold became convinced of its importance. It was work that contributed to what he regarded as the most important need of his century: the development of a satisfactory system of education for the middle classes.

In 1849, Arnold published *The Strayed Reveler,* the first of his volumes of poetry. Eight years later, as a tribute to his poetic achievement, he was elected to the professorship of poetry at Oxford, a part-time position that he held for ten years. Later, like Dickens and Thackeray before him, Arnold toured America to make money by lecturing. The reception accorded his lectures was varied. Sometimes his audiences were indifferent, but it is of interest to learn from the *Washington Post* of his stunning success in that city, where, following a two-hour address, the great African American leader Frederick Douglass "moved that a tremendous vote of thanks be tendered to the speaker." For his two visits (1883 and 1886), there was the further inducement of seeing his daughter Lucy, who had married an American. Two years after his second visit to the United States, Arnold died of a sudden heart attack.

Arnold's career as a writer can be divided roughly into four periods. In the 1850s most of his poems appeared; in the 1860s, his literary criticism and social criticism; in the 1870s, his religious and educational writings; and in the 1880s, his second set of essays in literary criticism.

About his career as a poet, two questions are repeatedly asked. The first is whether his poetry is as effective as or better than his prose; the second is why he virtually stopped writing poetry after 1860. The first has, of course, been variously answered. Many would endorse Tennyson's request in a letter: "Tell Mat not to write any more of those prose things like *Literature and Dogma,* but to give us something like his *Thyrsis, Scholar Gypsy,* or *Forsaken Merman."* At the opposite extreme is a recent critic, J. D. Jump, who has a high regard for Arnold's prose but considers only one of the poems (*Dover Beach*) to have merit. Such readers complain, and with good cause, of Arnold's bad habits as a poet: for example, his excessive reliance on italics instead of on meter as a method of emphasizing the meaning of a line. Or they cite the prosy flatness of some of his lines. Contrariwise, when Arnold leaves the flat plane of versified reflections and attempts to scale the heights of what he called "the grand style," there is a different kind of uncertainty that becomes evident, as in *Sohrab and Rustum,* in the overelaborated similes. Yet the success of such lovely poems as *Thyrsis* is more than enough to overcome the indictments of the critics. Often, as in *Thyrsis,* he is at his best as a poet of nature. Settings of seashore or river or mountaintop provide something more than picturesque backdrops for these poems; they function to draw the meaning together. A concern for rendering outdoor nature may seem a curious accomplishment for so sophisticated a writer, but as his contemporaries noted, Arnold is in this respect, as in several others, similar to Thomas Gray.

Arnold's own verdict on the qualities of his poetry is a reasonable one. In a letter to his mother, in 1869, he writes:

> My poems represent, on the whole, the main movement of mind of the last quarter of a century, and thus they will probably have their day as people become conscious to themselves of what that movement of mind is, and interested in the literary productions which reflect it. It might be fairly urged that I have less poetical sentiment than Tennyson, and less intellectual vigor and abundance than Browning; yet, because I have perhaps more of a fusion of the two than either of them, and have more regularly applied that fusion to the main line of modern development, I am likely enough to have my turn, as they have had theirs.

The emphasis in the letter on "movement of mind" suggests that Arnold's poetry and prose should be studied together. Such an approach can be fruitful provided that it does not obscure the important difference between Arnold the poet and Arnold the critic. T. S. Eliot once said of his own writings that "in one's prose reflections one may be legitimately occupied with ideals, whereas in the writing of verse, one can deal only with actuality." Arnold's writings provide a nice verification of Eliot's seeming paradox. As a poet he usually records his own experiences, his own feelings of loneliness and isolation as a lover, his longing for a serenity that he cannot find, his melancholy sense of the passing of youth (more than for many men, Arnold's thirtieth birthday was an awesome landmark after which he felt, he said, "three parts iced over"). Above all he records his despair in a universe in which humanity's role seemed as incongruous as it was later to seem to Thomas Hardy. In a memorable passage of his *Stanzas from the Grande Chartreuse,* he describes himself as "wandering between two worlds, one dead, / The other powerless to be born." And addressing the representatives of a faith that seems to him dead, he cries: "Take me, cowled forms, and fence me round, / Till I possess my soul again."

As a poet, then, like T. S. Eliot and W. H. Auden, Arnold provides a record of a sick individual in a sick society. This was "actuality" as he experienced it—an actuality, like Eliot's and Auden's, representative of his era. As a prose writer, a formulator of "ideals," he seeks a different role. It is the role of what Auden calls the "healer" of a sick society, or as he himself called Goethe, the "Physician of the iron age." And in this difference we have a clue to the question previously raised: why did Arnold virtually abandon the writing of poetry and shift into criticism? Among other reasons, he abandoned it because he was dissatisfied with the kind of poetry he himself was writing.

In one of his excellent letters to his friend Arthur Hugh Clough in the 1850s (letters that provide the best insight we have into Arnold's mind and tastes) this note of dissatisfaction is struck: "I am glad you like the *Gypsy Scholar*—but what does it *do* for you? Homer *animates*—Shakespeare *animates*—in its poor way I think *Sohrab and Rustum animates*—the *Gypsy Scholar* at best awakens a pleasing melancholy. But this is not what we want." It is evident that early in his career Arnold had evolved a theory of what poetry should do for its readers, a theory based, in part, on his impression of what classical poetry had achieved. To help make life bearable, poetry, in Arnold's view, must bring joy. As he says in the preface to his *Poems* in 1853, it must "inspirit and rejoice the reader"; it must "convey a charm, and infuse delight." Such a demand does not exclude tragic poetry but does exclude works "in which suffering finds no vent in action; in which a continual state of mental distress is prolonged." Of Charlotte Brontë's novel *Villette* he says witheringly: "The writer's mind contains nothing but hunger, rebellion, and rage. . . . No fine writing can hide this thoroughly, and it will be fatal to her in the long run." Judged by such a standard, most nineteenth-century poems, including *Empedocles on Etna* and others by Arnold, were unsatisfactory. And when Arnold tried himself to write poems that would meet his own requirements—*Sohrab and Rustum* or *Balder Dead*—he was not at his best. By the late 1850s he thus found himself at a dead end. By turning aside to literary criticism he was able partially to escape the dilemma. In his prose his melancholy and "morbid" personality was subordinated to the resolutely cheerful and purposeful character he had created for himself by an effort of will.

Arnold's two volumes of *Essays in Criticism* (1865 and 1888) repeatedly show how authors as different as Marcus Aurelius, Tolstoy, Homer, and Wordsworth provide the virtues he sought in his reading. Among these virtues was plainness of style. Although he could on occasion recommend the richness of language of such poets as Keats or Tennyson—their "natural magic" as he himself called it—Arnold's usual preference was for literature that was unadorned. And beyond stylistic excellences the principal virtue he admired as a critic was what he called the quality of "high seriousness." Given a world in which formal religion appeared to be of subordinate importance, it became increasingly important to Arnold that the poet must be a serious thinker who could offer guidance for his readers. Arnold's attitude toward religion helps to account for his finally asking perhaps too much from literature. Excessive expectations underlie his most glaring blunder as a critic: his solemnly inadequate discussion of Chaucer's lack of high seriousness in *The Study of Poetry*.

In *The Function of Criticism,* it is apparent that Arnold regarded good literary criticism, as he regarded literature itself, as a potent force in producing what he conceived as a civilized society. From a close study of this basic essay one could forecast the third stage of his career: his excursion into the criticism of society that was to culminate in *Culture and Anarchy* (1869) and *Friendship's Garland* (1871).

Arnold's starting point as a critic of society is different from that of Carlyle and John Ruskin. The older prophets attacked the Victorian middle classes on the grounds of their materialism, their selfish indifference to the sufferings of the poor—their immorality, in effect. Arnold argued instead that the "Philistines," as he called them, were not so much wicked as ignorant, narrow-minded, and suffering from the dullness of their private lives. This novel analysis was reinforced by Arnold's conviction that the world of the future, both in England and America, would be a middle-class world, a world dominated therefore by a class inadequately equipped for leadership and inadequately equipped to enjoy civilized living.

To establish this point, Arnold employed cajolery, satire, and even quotations from the newspapers with considerable effect. He also employed memorable catchwords (such as "sweetness and light") that sometimes pose an obstacle to understanding the complexities of his position. His view of civilization, for example, was pared down to a four-point formula of the four "powers": conduct, intellect and knowledge, beauty, social life and manners. The formula was simple and workable. Applying it to French or American civilizations, he had a scale by which to show up the virtues of different countries as well as their inadequacies. Applying the formula to his own country, Arnold usually awarded the Victorian middle classes an A in the first category (of conduct) but a failing grade in the other three categories.

Arnold's relentless exposure of middle-class narrow-mindedness eventually led him into the arena of religious controversy. As a critic of religious institutions he was arguing, in effect, that just as the middle classes did not know how to lead full lives, so also did they not know how to read the Bible intelligently or attend church intelligently. Of the Christian religion, he remarked that there are two things "that surely must be clear to anybody with eyes in his head. One is, that men cannot do without it; the other that they cannot do with it as it is." His three full-length studies of the Bible, including *Literature and Dogma* (1873), are best considered in this way as a postscript to his social criticism. The Bible, to Arnold, was a great work of literature like the *Odyssey,* and the Church of England was a great national institution like Parliament. Both Bible and church must be preserved not because historical Christianity was credible but because both, when properly understood, were agents of what he called "culture"—they contributed to making humanity more civilized.

The term *culture* is perhaps Arnold's most familiar catchword, although what he meant by it has sometimes been misunderstood. For him the term connotes the qualities of an open-minded intelligence (as described in *The Function of Criticism*)—a refusal to take things on authority. In this respect, Arnold appears close to T. H. Huxley and J. S. Mill. But the word also connotes a full awareness of humanity's past and a capacity to enjoy the best works of art, literature, history, and philosophy that have come down to us from that past. As a way of viewing life in all its aspects, including the social, political, and religious, culture represents for Arnold the most effective way of curing the ills of a sick society. It is his principal prescription.

To attempt to define culture brings one to a final aspect of Arnold's career as a critic: his writings on education, in which he sought to make cultural values, as he said, "prevail." Most obviously these writings comprise his reply to Huxley in his admirably reasoned essay *Literature and Science,* and his volumes of official reports written as an inspector of schools. Less obviously, they comprise all his prose. At the core of these writings is his belief that good education is *the* crucial need. Arnold was essentially a great teacher. He has the faults of a teacher: a tendency to repeat himself, to lean too hard on formulated phrases, and he displays something of the lectern manner at times. He also has the great teacher's virtues, in particular the virtue of skillfully conveying to us the conviction on which all his arguments are based. This conviction is that the humanist tradition of which he is the expositor can enable the individual man or woman to live life more fully and to change the course of society. He believes that a democratic society can thrive only if its citizens become educated in what he saw as the great Western tradition, "the best that is known and thought." These values, which some readers find elitist, make Arnold both timely and controversial. It is for these values Arnold fought. He boxed with the gloves on—kid gloves, his opponents used to say—and he provided a lively exhibition of footwork that is a pleasure in itself for us to witness. Yet the gracefulness of the display should not obscure the fact that he is landing hard blows squarely on his opponents.

Although his lifelong attacks against the inadequacies of puritanism make Arnold one of the most anti-Victorian figures of the Victorian age, there is an assumption behind his attacks that is itself characteristically Victorian. This assumption is that the puritan middle classes *can* be changed, that they are, as we would more clumsily say, educable. In 1852, writing to Clough on the subject of equality (a political objective in which he believed by conviction if not by instinct), he observed: "I am more and more convinced that the world tends to become more comfortable for the mass, and more uncomfortable for those of any natural gift or distinction—and it is as well perhaps that it should be so—for hitherto the gifted have astonished and delighted the world, but not trained or inspired or in any real way changed it." Arnold's gifts as a poet and critic enabled him to do both: to delight the world and also to change it.

The Forsaken Merman

Come, dear children, let us away;
Down and away below!
Now my brothers call from the bay,
Now the great winds shoreward blow,
5   Now the salt tides seaward flow;
Now the wild white horses play,
Champ and chafe and toss in the spray.
Children dear, let us away!
This way, this way!

10   Call her once before you go—
Call once yet!

In a voice that she will know:
"Margaret! Margaret!"
Children's voices should be dear
15 (Call once more) to a mother's ear;
Children's voices, wild with pain—
Surely she will come again!
Call her once and come away;
This way, this way!
20 "Mother dear, we cannot stay!
The wild white horses foam and fret."
Margaret! Margaret!

Come, dear children, come away down;
Call no more!
25 One last look at the white-walled town,
And the little gray church on the windy shore,
Then come down!
She will not come though you call all day;
Come away, come away!

30 Children dear, was it yesterday
We heard the sweet bells over the bay?
In the caverns where we lay,
Through the surf and through the swell,
The far-off sound of a silver bell?
35 Sand-strewn caverns, cool and deep,
Where the winds are all asleep;
Where the spent lights quiver and gleam,
Where the salt weed sways in the stream,
Where the sea beasts, ranged all round,
40 Feed in the ooze of their pasture ground;
Where the sea snakes coil and twine,
Dry their mail and bask in the brine;
Where great whales come sailing by,
Sail and sail, with unshut eye,
45 Round the world for ever and aye?
When did music come this way?
Children dear, was it yesterday?

Children dear, was it yesterday
(Call yet once) that she went away?
50 Once she sate with you and me,
On a red gold throne in the heart of the sea,
And the youngest sate on her knee.
She combed its bright hair, and she tended it well,
When down swung the sound of a far-off bell.
55 She sighed, she looked up through the clear green sea;
She said: "I must go, for my kinsfolk pray
In the little gray church on the shore today.
'Twill be Easter time in the world—ah me!
And I lose my poor soul, Merman! here with thee."
60 I said: "Go up, dear heart, through the waves;

Say thy prayer, and come back to the kind sea-caves!"
She smiled, she went up through the surf in the bay.
Children dear, was it yesterday?

Children dear, were we long alone?
65 "The sea grows stormy, the little ones moan;
Long prayers," I said, "in the world they say;
Come!" I said; and we rose through the surf in the bay.
We went up the beach, by the sandy down
Where the sea-stocks bloom, to the white-walled town;
70 Through the narrow paved streets, where all was still,
To the little gray church on the windy hill.
From the church came a murmur of folk at their prayers,
But we stood without in the cold blowing airs.
We climbed on the graves, on the stones worn with rains,
75 And we gazed up the aisle through the small leaded panes.
She sate by the pillar; we saw her clear:
"Margaret, hist! come quick, we are here!
Dear heart," I said, "we are long alone;
The sea grows stormy, the little ones moan."
80 But, ah, she gave me never a look,
For her eyes were sealed to the holy book!
Loud prays the priest; shut stands the door.
Come away, children, call no more!
Come away, come down, call no more!

85 Down, down, down!
Down to the depths of the sea!
She sits at her wheel in the humming town,
Singing most joyfully.
Hark what she sings: "O joy, O joy,
90 For the humming street, and the child with its toy!
For the priest, and the bell, and the holy well;
For the wheel where I spun,
And the blessed light of the sun!"
And so she sings her fill,
95 Singing most joyfully,
Till the spindle drops from her hand,
And the whizzing wheel stands still.
She steals to the window, and looks at the sand,
And over the sand at the sea;
100 And her eyes are set in a stare;
And anon there breaks a sigh,
And anon there drops a tear,
From a sorrow-clouded eye,
And a heart sorrow-laden,
105 A long, long sigh;
For the cold strange eyes of a little Mermaiden
And the gleam of her golden hair.

Come away, away children;
Come children, come down!

110 The hoarse wind blows coldly;
Lights shine in the town.
She will start from her slumber
When gusts shake the door;
She will hear the winds howling,
115 Will hear the waves roar.
We shall see, while above us
The waves roar and whirl,
A ceiling of amber,
A pavement of pearl.
120 Singing: "Here came a mortal,
But faithless was she!
And alone dwell forever
The kings of the sea."

But, children, at midnight,
125 When soft the winds blow,
When clear falls the moonlight,
When spring tides are low;
When sweet airs come seaward
From heaths starred with broom,
130 And high rocks throw mildly
On the blanched sands a gloom;
Up the still, glistening beaches,
Up the creek we will hie,
Over banks of bright seaweed
135 The ebb-tide leaves dry.
We will gaze, from the sand-hills,
At the white, sleeping town;
At the church on the hillside—
And then come back down.
140 Singing: "There dwells a loved one,
But cruel is she!
She left lonely forever
The kings of the sea."

1849

Isolation. To Marguerite[1]

We were apart; yet, day by day,
I bade my heart more constant be.
I bade it keep the world away,
And grow a home for only thee;
5 Nor feared but thy love likewise grew,
Like mine, each day, more tried, more true.

The fault was grave! I might have known,
What far too soon, alas! I learned—

1. Addressed to a woman Arnold is reputed to have met in Switzerland in the 1840s. It has been commonly assumed that she was French or Swiss; but some recent biographies speculate she might have been Mary Claude, a woman Arnold knew in England at this same period, who, although English, had connections with Germany and had translated German prose and verse.

The heart can bind itself alone,
10 And faith may oft be unreturned.
Self-swayed our feelings ebb and swell—
Thou lov'st no more—Farewell! Farewell!

Farewell!—and thou, thou lonely heart,[2]
Which never yet without remorse
15 Even for a moment didst depart
From thy remote and spherèd course
To haunt the place where passions reign—
Back to thy solitude again!

Back with the conscious thrill of shame
20 Which Luna felt, that summer night,
Flash through her pure immortal frame,
When she forsook the starry height
To hang over Endymion's sleep
Upon the pine-grown Latmian steep.[3]
25 Yet she, chaste queen, had never proved
How vain a thing is mortal love,
Wandering in Heaven, far removed.
But thou hast long had place to prove
This truth—to prove, and make thine own:
30 "Thou hast been, shalt be, art, alone."

Or, if not quite alone, yet they
Which touch thee are unmating things—
Ocean and clouds and night and day;
Lorn autumns and triumphant springs;
35 And life, and others' joy and pain,
And love, if love, of happier men.

Of happier men—for they, at least,
Have *dreamed* two human hearts might blend
In one, and were through faith released
40 From isolation without end
Prolonged; nor knew, although not less
Alone than thou, their loneliness.

1849   1857

To Marguerite—Continued

Yes! in the sea of life enisled,
With echoing straits between us thrown,
Dotting the shoreless watery wild,
We mortal millions live *alone*.
5 The islands feel the enclasping flow,
And then their endless bounds they know.
But when the moon their hollows lights,

2. Presumably the speaker's heart, not Marguerite's.
3. Luna (or Diana), goddess of chastity and the
moon, fell in love with Endymion, a handsome
shepherd, whom she discovered asleep on Mount
Latmos.

And they are swept by balms of spring,
And in their glens, on starry nights,
10   The nightingales divinely sing;
And lovely notes, from shore to shore,
Across the sounds and channels pour—

Oh! then a longing like despair
Is to their farthest caverns sent;
15   For surely once, they feel, we were
Parts of a single continent!
Now round us spreads the watery plain—
Oh might our marges meet again!

Who ordered that their longing's fire
20   Should be, as soon as kindled, cooled?
Who renders vain their deep desire?—
A God, a God their severance ruled!
And bade betwixt their shores to be
The unplumbed, salt, estranging sea.

1849   1852

The Buried Life

Light flows our war of mocking words, and yet,
Behold, with tears mine eyes are wet!
I feel a nameless sadness o'er me roll.
Yes, yes, we know that we can jest,
5   We know, we know that we can smile!
But there's a something in this breast,
To which thy light words bring no rest,
And thy gay smiles no anodyne.
Give me thy hand, and hush awhile,
10   And turn those limpid eyes on mine,
And let me read there, love! thy inmost soul.

Alas! is even love too weak
To unlock the heart, and let it speak?
Are even lovers powerless to reveal
15   To one another what indeed they feel?
I knew the mass of men concealed
Their thoughts, for fear that if revealed
They would by other men be met
With blank indifference, or with blame reproved;
20   I knew they lived and moved
Tricked in disguises, alien to the rest
Of men, and alien to themselves—and yet
The same heart beats in every human breast!

But we, my love!—doth a like spell benumb
25   Our hearts, our voices?—must we too be dumb?

Ah! well for us, if even we,
Even for a moment, can get free
Our heart, and have our lips unchained;
For that which seals them hath been deep-ordained!

30 Fate, which foresaw
How frivolous a baby man would be—
By what distractions he would be possessed,
How he would pour himself in every strife,
And well-nigh change his own identity—
35 That it might keep from his capricious play
His genuine self, and force him to obey
Even in his own despite his being's law,
Bade through the deep recesses of our breast
The unregarded river of our life
40 Pursue with indiscernible flow its way;
And that we should not see
The buried stream, and seem to be
Eddying at large in blind uncertainty,
Though driving on with it eternally.

45 But often, in the world's most crowded streets,[1]
But often, in the din of strife,
There rises an unspeakable desire
After the knowledge of our buried life;
A thirst to spend our fire and restless force
50 In tracking out our true, original course;
A longing to inquire
Into the mystery of this heart which beats
So wild, so deep in us—to know
Whence our lives come and where they go.
55 And many a man in his own breast then delves,
But deep enough, alas! none ever mines.
And we have been on many thousand lines,
And we have shown, on each, spirit and power;
But hardly have we, for one little hour,
60 Been on our own line, have we been ourselves—
Hardly had skill to utter one of all
The nameless feelings that course through our breast,
But they course on forever unexpressed.
And long we try in vain to speak and act
65 Our hidden self, and what we say and do
Is eloquent, is well—but 'tis not true!
And then we will no more be racked
With inward striving, and demand
Of all the thousand nothings of the hour
70 Their stupefying power;
Ah yes, and they benumb us at our call!
Yet still, from time to time, vague and forlorn,

1. This passage, like many others in Arnold's poetry, illustrates Wordsworth's effect on his writings. In this instance cf. Wordsworth's *Tintern* *Abbey* 25–27: "But oft, in lonely rooms, and 'mid the din / Of towns and cities, I have owed to them, / In hours of weariness, sensations sweet."

From the soul's subterranean depth upborne
As from an infinitely distant land,
75 Come airs, and floating echoes, and convey
A melancholy into all our day.[2]

Only—but this is rare—
When a beloved hand is laid in ours,
When, jaded with the rush and glare
80 Of the interminable hours,
Our eyes can in another's eyes read clear,
When our world-deafened ear
Is by the tones of a loved voice caressed—
A bolt is shot back somewhere in our breast,
85 And a lost pulse of feeling stirs again.
The eye sinks inward, and the heart lies plain,
And what we mean, we say, and what we would, we know.
A man becomes aware of his life's flow,
And hears its winding murmur; and he sees
90 The meadows where it glides, the sun, the breeze.

And there arrives a lull in the hot race
Wherein he doth forever chase
That flying and elusive shadow, rest.
An air of coolness plays upon his face,
95 And an unwonted calm pervades his breast.
And then he thinks he knows
The hills where his life rose,
And the sea where it goes.

1852

Memorial Verses[1]

April 1850

Goethe in Weimar sleeps, and Greece,
Long since, saw Byron's struggle cease.
But one such death remained to come;
The last poetic voice is dumb—
5 We stand today by Wordsworth's tomb.

When Byron's eyes were shut in death,
We bowed our head and held our breath.
He taught us little; but our soul
Had *felt* him like the thunder's roll.
10 With shivering heart the strife we saw

---

2. Cf. Wordworth's *Ode: Intimations of Immortality*, lines 149–51: "Those shadowy recollections, / Which, be they what they may, / Are yet the fountain light of all our day."
1. This elegy was written shortly after Wordsworth had died in April 1850, at the age of eighty. Arnold had known the poet as a man and deeply admired his writings—as is evident not only in this poem but in his late essay *Wordsworth*. Byron, who died

in Greece in 1824, had affected Arnold profoundly in his youth, but later that strenuous "Titanic" (line 14) poetry seemed to him less satisfactory, its value limited by its lack of serenity. His final verdict on Byron can be encountered in his essay in *Essays in Criticism: Second Series*. Goethe, who died in 1832, was regarded by Arnold as a great philosophical poet and the most significant man of letters of the early 19th century.

Of passion with eternal law;
And yet with reverential awe
We watched the fount of fiery life
Which served for that Titanic strife.
15 When Goethe's death was told, we said:
Sunk, then, is Europe's sagest head.
Physician of the iron age,
Goethe has done his pilgrimage.
He took the suffering human race,
20 He read each wound, each weakness clear;
And struck his finger on the place,
And said: *Thou ailest here, and here!*
He looked on Europe's dying hour
Of fitful dream and feverish power;
25 His eye plunged down the weltering strife,
The turmoil of expiring life—
He said: *The end is everywhere,*
Art still has truth, take refuge there!
And he was happy, if to know
30 Causes of things, and far below
His feet to see the lurid flow
Of terror, and insane distress,
And headlong fate, be happiness.

And Wordsworth!—Ah, pale ghosts, rejoice!
35 For never has such soothing voice
Been to your shadowy world conveyed,
Since erst, at morn, some wandering shade
Heard the clear song of Orpheus[2] come
Through Hades, and the mournful gloom.
40 Wordsworth has gone from us—and ye,
Ah, may ye feel his voice as we!
He too upon a wintry clime
Had fallen—on this iron time
Of doubts, disputes, distractions, fears.
45 He found us when the age had bound
Our souls in its benumbing round;
He spoke, and loosed our heart in tears.
He laid us as we lay at birth
On the cool flowery lap of earth,
50 Smiles broke from us and we had ease;
The hills were round us, and the breeze
Went o'er the sunlit fields again;
Our foreheads felt the wind and rain.
Our youth returned; for there was shed
55 On spirits that had long been dead,
Spirits dried up and closely furled,
The freshness of the early world.

Ah! since dark days still bring to light
Man's prudence and man's fiery might,

---

2. By means of his beautiful music, Orpheus won his way through Hades in his search for the "shade" of his dead wife, Eurydice.

60   Time may restore us in his course
     Goethe's sage mind and Byron's force;
     But where will Europe's latter hour
     Again find Wordsworth's healing power?
     Others will teach us how to dare,
65   And against fear our breast to steel;
     Others will strengthen us to bear—
     But who, ah! who, will make us feel?
     The cloud of mortal destiny,
     Others will front it fearlessly—
70   But who, like him, will put it by?

     Keep fresh the grass upon his grave
     O Rotha,[3] with thy living wave!
     Sing him thy best! for few or none
     Hears thy voice right, now he is gone.

1850
                                              1850

Lines Written in Kensington Gardens[1]

    In this lone, open glade I lie,
    Screened by deep boughs on either hand;
    And at its end, to stay the eye,
    Those black-crowned, red-boled pine trees stand!

5   Birds here make song, each bird has his,
    Across the girdling city's hum.
    How green under the boughs it is!
    How thick the tremulous sheep-cries come![2]

    Sometimes a child will cross the glade
10 To take his nurse his broken toy;
    Sometimes a thrush flit overhead
    Deep in her unknown day's employ.

    Here at my feet what wonders pass,
    What endless, active life is here!
15 What blowing daisies, fragrant grass!
    An air-stirred forest, fresh and clear.

    Scarce fresher is the mountain sod
    Where the tired angler lies, stretched out,
    And, eased of basket and of rod,
20 Counts his day's spoil, the spotted trout.

    In the huge world, which roars hard by,
    Be others happy if they can!

3. A river near Wordsworth's burial place.   2. Sheep sometimes grazed in London parks.
1. A park in the heart of London.

But in my helpless cradle I
Was breathed on by the rural Pan.

25 I, on men's impious uproar hurled,
Think often, as I hear them rave,
That peace has left the upper world
And now keeps only in the grave.

Yet here is peace forever new!
30 When I who watch them am away,
Still all things in this glade go through
The changes of their quiet day.

Then to their happy rest they pass!
The flowers upclose, the birds are fed,
35 The night comes down upon the grass,
The child sleeps warmly in his bed.

Calm soul of all things! make it mine
To feel, amid the city's jar,
That there abides a peace of thine,
40 Man did not make, and cannot mar.

The will to neither strive nor cry,
The power to feel with others give!
Calm, calm me more! nor let me die
Before I have begun to live.

1852

The Scholar Gypsy   The story of a seventeenth-century student who left
Oxford and joined a band of gypsies had made a strong impression on Arnold. In the
poem he wistfully imagines that the spirit of this scholar is still to be encountered in
the Cumner countryside near Oxford, having achieved immortality by a serene pursuit
of the secret of human existence. Like Keats's nightingale, the scholar has escaped
"the weariness, the fever, and the fret" of modern life.
    At the outset, the poet addresses a shepherd who has been helping him in his search
for traces of the scholar. The shepherd is addressed as *you*. After line 61, with the
shift to *thou* and *thy*, the person addressed is the scholar himself, and the poet
thereafter sometimes uses the pronoun *we* to indicate he is speaking for all humanity
of later generations.
    About the setting Arnold wrote to his brother Tom on May 15, 1857: "You alone
of my brothers are associated with that life at Oxford, the *freest* and most delightful
part, perhaps, of my life, when with you and Clough and Walrond I shook off all the
bonds and formalities of the place, and enjoyed the spring of life and that unforgotten
Oxfordshire and Berkshire country. Do you remember a poem of mine called 'The
Scholar Gipsy'? It was meant to fix the remembrance of those delightful wanderings
of ours in the Cumner Hills."
    The passage from Joseph Glanvill's *Vanity of Dogmatizing* (1661) that inspired the
poem was included by Arnold as a note:

There was very lately a lad in the University of Oxford, who was by his poverty
forced to leave his studies there; and at last to join himself to a company of
vagabond gypsies. Among these extravagant people, by the insinuating subtilty
of his carriage, he quickly got so much of their love and esteem as that they
discovered to him their mystery. After he had been a pretty while exercised in
the trade, there chanced to ride by a couple of scholars, who had formerly been
of his acquaintance. They quickly spied out their old friend among the gypsies;
and he gave them an account of the necessity which drove him to that kind of
life, and told them that the people he went with were not such imposters as they
were taken for, but that they had a traditional kind of learning among them, and
could do wonders by the power of imagination, their fancy binding that of others:
that himself had learned much of their art, and when he had compassed the
whole secret, he intended, he said, to leave their company, and give the world
an account of what he had learned.

The Scholar Gypsy

Go, for they call you, shepherd, from the hill;
  Go, shepherd, and untie the wattled cotes![1]
    No longer leave thy wistful flock unfed,
    Nor let thy bawling fellows rack their throats,
5   Nor the cropped herbage shoot another head.
      But when the fields are still,
    And the tired men and dogs all gone to rest,
    And only the white sheep are sometimes seen
    Cross and recross the strips of moon-blanched green,
10 Come, shepherd, and again begin the quest!

Here, where the reaper was at work of late—
  In this high field's dark corner, where he leaves
    His coat, his basket, and his earthen cruse,[2]
    And in the sun all morning binds the sheaves,
15   Then here, at noon, comes back his stores to use—
      Here will I sit and wait,
    While to my ear from uplands far away
    The bleating of the folded° flocks is borne,   *penned up*
    With distant cries of reapers in the corn[3]—
20 All the live murmur of a summer's day.

Screened is this nook o'er the high, half-reaped field,
  And here till sundown, shepherd! will I be.
    Through the thick corn the scarlet poppies peep,
    And round green roots and yellowing stalks I see
25   Pale pink convolvulus in tendrils creep;
      And air-swept lindens yield
    Their scent, and rustle down their perfumed showers
    Of bloom on the bent grass[4] where I am laid,
    And bower me from the August sun with shade;
30 And the eye travels down to Oxford's towers.

1. Sheepfolds woven from sticks.
2. Pot or jug for carrying his drink.

3. Grain or wheat.
4. A stiff kind of grass.

And near me on the grass lies Glanvill's book—
  Come, let me read the oft-read tale again!
    The story of the Oxford scholar poor,
    Of pregnant parts[5] and quick inventive brain,
35   Who, tired of knocking at preferment's door,
        One summer morn forsook
  His friends, and went to learn the gypsy lore,
    And roamed the world with that wild brotherhood,
    And came, as most men deemed, to little good,
40 But came to Oxford and his friends no more.

But once, years after, in the country lanes,
  Two scholars, whom at college erst he knew,
    Met him, and of his way of life inquired;
    Whereat he answered, that the gypsy crew,
45   His mates, had arts to rule as they desired
        The workings of men's brains,
  And they can bind them to what thoughts they will.
    "And I," he said, "the secret of their art,
    When fully learned, will to the world impart;
50 But it needs heaven-sent moments for this skill."

This said, he left them, and returned no more.—
  But rumors hung about the countryside,
    That the lost Scholar long was seen to stray,
    Seen by rare glimpses, pensive and tongue-tied,
55   In hat of antique shape, and cloak of grey,
        The same the gypsies wore.
  Shepherds had met him on the Hurst[6] in spring;
    At some lone alehouse in the Berkshire moors,
    On the warm ingle-bench, the smock-frocked boors[7]
60 Had found him seated at their entering,

But, 'mid their drink and clatter, he would fly.
  And I myself seem half to know thy looks,
    And put the shepherds, wanderer! on thy trace;
    And boys who in lone wheatfields scare the rooks[8]
65   I ask if thou hast passed their quiet place;
        Or in my boat I lie
  Moored to the cool bank in the summer heats,
    'Mid wide grass meadows which the sunshine fills,
    And watch the warm, green-muffled Cumner hills,
70 And wonder if thou haunt'st their shy retreats.

For most, I know, thou lov'st retired ground!
  Thee at the ferry Oxford riders blithe,
    Returning home on summer nights, have met
    Crossing the stripling Thames[9] at Bab-lock-hithe,

5. Teeming with ideas.
6. A hill near Oxford. All the place names in the poem (except those in the final two stanzas) refer to the countryside near Oxford.
7. Rustics. "Ingle-bench": fireside bench.

8. Boys hired to frighten crows away from eating wheat grains.
9. The narrow upper reaches of the river before it broadens out to its full width.

75　　　　Trailing in the cool stream thy fingers wet,
　　　　　　As the punt's rope chops round;[1]
　　　　And leaning backward in a pensive dream,
　　　　And fostering in thy lap a heap of flowers
　　　　　Plucked in shy fields and distant Wychwood bowers,
80　　　And thine eyes resting on the moonlit stream.

　　　　And then they land, and thou art seen no more!—
　　　　Maidens, who from the distant hamlets come
　　　　　To dance around the Fyfield elm in May,
　　　　Oft through the darkening fields have seen thee roam,
85　　　　Or cross a stile into the public way.
　　　　　　Oft thou hast given them store
　　　　Of flowers—the frail-leafed, white anemone,
　　　　Dark bluebells drenched with dews of summer eves,
　　　　And purple orchises with spotted leaves—
90　　　But none hath words she can report of thee.

　　　　And, above Godstow Bridge, when hay time's here
　　　　In June, and many a scythe in sunshine flames,
　　　　　Men who through those wide fields of breezy grass
　　　　Where black-winged swallows haunt the glittering Thames,
95　　　　To bathe in the abandoned lasher pass,[2]
　　　　　　Have often passed thee near
　　　　Sitting upon the river bank o'ergrown;
　　　　Marked thine outlandish garb, thy figure spare,
　　　　Thy dark vague eyes, and soft abstracted air—
100　　But, when they came from bathing, thou wast gone!

　　　　At some lone homestead in the Cumner hills,
　　　　Where at her open door the housewife darns,
　　　　　Thou hast been seen, or hanging on a gate
　　　　To watch the threshers in the mossy barns.
105　　　Children, who early range these slopes and late
　　　　　　For cresses from the rills,
　　　　Have known thee eying, all an April day,
　　　　The springing pastures and the feeding kine;
　　　　And marked thee, when the stars come out and shine,
110　　Through the long dewy grass move slow away.

　　　　In autumn, on the skirts of Bagley Wood—
　　　　Where most the gypsies by the turf-edged way
　　　　　Pitch their smoked tents, and every bush you see
　　　　With scarlet patches tagged and shreds of grey,
115　　　Above the forest ground called Thessaly—
　　　　　　The blackbird, picking food,
　　　　Sees thee, nor stops his meal, nor fears at all;
　　　　So often has he known thee past him stray,
　　　　Rapt, twirling in thy hand a withered spray,
120　　And waiting for the spark from heaven to fall.

1. The scholar's flat-bottomed boat ("punt") is tied up by a rope at the riverbank near the ferry crossing like the speaker's boat (in the previous stanza), which was "moored to the cool bank." The motion of the boat as it is stirred by the current of the river causes the chopping sound of the rope in the water.
2. Water that spills over a dam or weir.

And once, in winter, on the causeway chill
  Where home through flooded fields foot-travelers go,
    Have I not passed thee on the wooden bridge,
    Wrapped in thy cloak and battling with the snow,
125   Thy face tow'rd Hinksey and its wintry ridge?
      And thou hast climbed the hill,
    And gained the white brow of the Cumner range;
      Turned once to watch, while thick the snowflakes fall,
      The line of festal light in Christ Church hall[3]—
130   Then sought thy straw in some sequestered grange.

But what—I dream! Two hundred years are flown
  Since first thy story ran through Oxford halls,
    And the grave Glanvill did the tale inscribe
    That thou wert wandered from the studious walls
135   To learn strange arts, and join a gypsy tribe;
      And thou from earth art gone
    Long since, and in some quiet churchyard laid—
      Some country nook, where o'er thy unknown grave
      Tall grasses and white flowering nettles wave,
140   Under a dark, red-fruited yew tree's shade.

—No, no, thou hast not felt the lapse of hours!
  For what wears out the life of mortal men?
    'Tis that from change to change their being rolls;
    'Tis that repeated shocks, again, again,
145   Exhaust the energy of strongest souls
      And numb the elastic powers.
    Till having used our nerves with bliss and teen,°   *vexation*
      And tired upon a thousand schemes our wit,
      To the just-pausing Genius[4] we remit
150   Our worn-out life, and are—what we have been.

Thou hast not lived, why should'st thou perish, so?
  Thou hadst *one* aim, *one* business, *one* desire;
    Else wert thou long since numbered with the dead!
    Else hadst thou spent, like other men, thy fire!
155   The generations of thy peers are fled,
      And we ourselves shall go;
    But thou possessest an immortal lot,
      And we imagine thee exempt from age
      And living as thou liv'st on Glanvill's page,
160   Because thou hadst—what we, alas! have not.

For early didst thou leave the world, with powers
  Fresh, undiverted to the world without,
    Firm to their mark, not spent on other things;
    Free from the sick fatigue, the languid doubt,
165   Which much to have tried, in much been baffled, brings.
      O life unlike to ours!

---

3. The dining hall of an Oxford college.
4. Perhaps the spirit of the universe, which pauses briefly to receive back the life given to us.

Who fluctuate idly without term or scope,
　　Of whom each strives, nor knows for what he strives,
　　　And each half⁵ lives a hundred different lives;
170　Who wait like thee, but not, like thee, in hope.

Thou waitest for the spark from heaven! and we,
　　Light half-believers of our casual creeds,
　　　Who never deeply felt, nor clearly willed,
　　Whose insight never has borne fruit in deeds,
175　　　Whose vague resolves never have been fulfilled;
　　　　For whom each year we see
　　Breeds new beginnings, disappointments new;
　　　Who hesitate and falter life away,
　　　And lose tomorrow the ground won today—
180　Ah! do not we, wanderer! await it too?

Yes, we await it!—but it still delays,
　　And then we suffer! and amongst us one,⁶
　　　Who most has suffered, takes dejectedly
　　His seat upon the intellectual throne;
185　　　And all his store of sad experience he
　　　　Lays bare of wretched days;
　　Tells us his misery's birth and growth and signs,
　　　And how the dying spark of hope was fed,
　　　And how the breast was soothed, and how the head,
190　And all his hourly varied anodynes.

This for our wisest! and we others pine,
　　And wish the long unhappy dream would end,
　　　And waive all claim to bliss, and try to bear;
　　With close-lipped patience for our only friend,
195　　　Sad patience, too near neighbor to despair—
　　　　But none has hope like thine!
　　Thou through the fields and through the woods dost stray,
　　　Roaming the countryside, a truant boy,
　　　Nursing thy project in unclouded joy,
200　And every doubt long blown by time away.

O born in days when wits were fresh and clear,
　　And life ran gaily as the sparkling Thames;
　　　Before this strange disease of modern life,
　　With its sick hurry, its divided aims,
205　　　Its heads o'ertaxed, its palsied hearts, was rife—
　　　　Fly hence, our contact fear!
　　Still fly, plunge deeper in the bowering wood!
　　　Averse, as Dido did with gesture stern
　　　From her false friend's approach in Hades turn,⁷
210　Wave us away, and keep thy solitude!

---

5. An adverb modifying "lives."
6. Probably Goethe, although possibly referring to Tennyson, whose In Memoriam had appeared in 1850.

7. Dido committed suicide after her lover, Aeneas, deserted her. When he later encountered her in Hades, she turned sternly away from him.

Still nursing the unconquerable hope,
  Still clutching the inviolable shade,
    With a free, onward impulse brushing through,
  By night, the silvered branches of the glade—
215   Far on the forest skirts, where none pursue.
      On some mild pastoral slope
  Emerge, and resting on the moonlit pales
  Freshen thy flowers as in former years
  With dew, or listen with enchanted ears,
220 From the dark dingles,° to the nightingales!   *small deep valleys*

But fly our paths, our feverish contact fly!
  For strong the infection of our mental strife,
    Which, though it gives no bliss, yet spoils for rest;
  And we should win thee from thy own fair life,
225   Like us distracted, and like us unblest.
      Soon, soon thy cheer would die,
  Thy hopes grow timorous, and unfixed thy powers,
  And thy clear aims be cross and shifting made;
  And then thy glad perennial youth would fade,
230 Fade, and grow old at last, and die like ours.

Then fly our greetings, fly our speech and smiles!
  —As some grave Tyrian trader, from the sea,
    Descried at sunrise an emerging prow
  Lifting the cool-haired creepers stealthily,
235   The fringes of a southward-facing brow
      Among the Aegean isles;
  And saw the merry Grecian coaster come,
  Freighted with amber grapes, and Chian wine,
  Green, bursting figs, and tunnies° steeped in brine—   *tuna fish*
240 And knew the intruders on his ancient home,

The young lighthearted masters of the waves—
  And snatched his rudder, and shook out more sail;
    And day and night held on indignantly
  O'er the blue Midland waters with the gale,
245   Betwixt the Syrtes[8] and soft Sicily,
      To where the Atlantic raves
  Outside the western straits; and unbent sails
  There, where down cloudy cliffs, through sheets of foam,
  Shy traffickers, the dark Iberians[9] come;
250 And on the beach undid his corded bales.[1]

1853

8. Shoals off the coast of North Africa.
9. Dark inhabitants of Spain and Portugal—perhaps associated with gypsies.
1. The elaborate simile of the final two stanzas has been variously interpreted. The trader from Tyre is disconcerted when, peering out through the foliage ("fringes," line 235) that screens his hiding place, he sees noisy intruders entering his harbor. Like the Scholar Gypsy, when similarly intruded on by hearty extroverts, he resolves to flee and seek a new home.

The reference (line 249) to the Iberians as "shy traffickers" (traders) is explained by Kenneth Allott as having been derived from Herodotus's *History* (4.196). Herodotus describes a distinctive method of selling goods established by Carthaginian merchants who used to sail through the Strait of Gibraltar to trade with the inhabitants of the coast of West Africa. The Carthaginians would leave bales of their merchandise on display along the beaches and, without having seen their prospective customers, would return to their ships. The shy natives

Dover Beach

The sea is calm tonight.
The tide is full, the moon lies fair
Upon the straits—on the French coast the light
Gleams and is gone; the cliffs of England stand,
5   Glimmering and vast, out in the tranquil bay.
Come to the window, sweet is the night air!
Only, from the long line of spray
Where the sea meets the moon-blanched land,
Listen! you hear the grating roar[1]
10   Of pebbles which the waves draw back, and fling,
At their return, up the high strand,
Begin, and cease, and then again begin,
With tremulous cadence slow, and bring
The eternal note of sadness in.

15   Sophocles long ago
Heard it on the Aegean, and it brought
Into his mind the turbid ebb and flow
Of human misery;[2] we
Find also in the sound a thought,
20   Hearing it by this distant northern sea.

The Sea of Faith
Was once, too, at the full, and round earth's shore
Lay like the folds of a bright girdle furled.[3]
But now I only hear
25   Its melancholy, long, withdrawing roar,
Retreating, to the breath
Of the night wind, down the vast edges drear
And naked shingles[4] of the world.

Ah, love, let us be true
30   To one another! for the world, which seems
To lie before us like a land of dreams,
So various, so beautiful, so new,
Hath really neither joy, nor love, nor light,
Nor certitude, nor peace, nor help for pain;

would then come down from their inland hiding places and set gold beside the bales they wished to buy. When the natives withdrew in their turn, the Carthaginians would return to the beach and decide whether payments were adequate, a process repeated until agreement was reached. On the Atlantic coasts this method of bargaining persisted into the 19th century. As William Beloe, a translator of Herodotus, noted in 1844: "In this manner they transact their exchange without seeing one another, or without the least instance of dishonesty . . . on either side." For the solitary Tyrian trader such a procedure, with its avoidance of "contact" (line 221), would have been especially appropriate.

1. Cf. Wordsworth's It Is a Beauteous Evening, lines 6–8: "Listen! the mighty Being is awake, /And doth with his eternal motion make/A sound like thunder—everlastingly."

2. A reference to a chorus in Antigone, which compares human sorrow to the sound of the waves moving the sand beneath them (lines 585–91).

3. This difficult line means, in general, that at high tide the sea envelops the land closely. Its forces are "gathered" up (to use Wordsworth's term for it) like the "folds" of bright clothing ("girdle") that have been compressed ("furled"). At ebb tide, as the sea retreats, it is unfurled and spread out. It still surrounds the shoreline but not as an "enclasping flow" (as in To Marguerite—Continued).

4. Beaches covered with pebbles.

35 And we are here as on a darkling plain
Swept with confused alarms of struggle and flight,
Where ignorant armies[5] clash by night.

ca. 1851   1867

Stanzas from the Grande Chartreuse[1]

Through Alpine meadows soft-suffused
With rain, where thick the crocus blows,
Past the dark forges long disused,
The mule track from Saint Laurent goes.
5   The bridge is crossed, and slow we ride,
Through forest, up the mountainside.

The autumnal evening darkens round,
The wind is up, and drives the rain;
While, hark! far down, with strangled sound
10 Doth the Dead Guier's[2] stream complain,
Where that wet smoke, among the woods,
Over his boiling cauldron broods.

Swift rush the spectral vapors white
Past limestone scars° with ragged pines,   *precipices*
15 Showing—then blotting from our sight!—
Halt—through the cloud-drift something shines!
High in the valley, wet and drear,
The huts of Courrerie appear.

Strike leftward! cries our guide; and higher
20 Mounts up the stony forest way.
At last the encircling trees retire;
Look! through the showery twilight grey
What pointed roofs are these advance?—
A palace of the Kings of France?

25 Approach, for what we seek is here!
Alight, and sparely sup, and wait
For rest in this outbuilding near;
Then cross the sward and reach that gate.

5. Perhaps alluding to conflicts in Arnold's own time such as occurred during the revolutions of 1848 in Europe, or at the Siege of Rome by the French in 1849 (the date of composition of the poem is unknown, although generally assumed to be 1851.) But the passage also refers back to another battle, one that occurred more than two thousand years earlier when an Athenian army was attempting an invasion of Sicily at nighttime. As this "night battle" was described by Thucydides in his *History of the Peloponnesian War* (7, chap.44), the invaders became confused by darkness and slaughtered many of their own men. Hence "ignorant armies."

1. A monastery situated high in the French Alps. It was established in 1084 by Saint Bruno, founder of the Carthusians (line 30), whose austere regimen of solitary contemplation, fasting, and religious exercises (lines 37–44) had remained virtually unchanged for centuries. Arnold visited the site on September 7, 1851, accompanied by his bride. His account may be compared with that by Wordsworth (*Prelude* 6.416–88), who had made a similar visit in 1790.
2. The Guiers Mort River flows down from the monastery and joins the Guiers Vif in the valley below. Wordsworth speaks of the two rivers as "the sister streams of Life and Death."

Knock; pass the wicket! Thou art come
30   To the Carthusians' world-famed home.

The silent courts, where night and day
Into their stone-carved basins cold
The splashing icy fountains play—
The humid corridors behold!
35   Where, ghostlike in the deepening night,
Cowled forms brush by in gleaming white.

The chapel, where no organ's peal
Invests the stern and naked prayer—
With penitential cries they kneel
40   And wrestle; rising then, with bare
And white uplifted faces stand,
Passing the Host from hand to hand;[3]

Each takes, and then his visage wan
Is buried in his cowl once more.
45   The cells!—the suffering Son of Man
Upon the wall—the knee-worn floor—
And where they sleep, that wooden bed,
Which shall their coffin be, when dead![4]

The library, where tract and tome
50   Not to feed priestly pride are there,
To hymn the conquering march of Rome,
Nor yet to amuse, as ours are!
They paint of souls the inner strife,
Their drops of blood, their death in life.

55   The garden, overgrown—yet mild,
See, fragrant herbs[5] are flowering there!
Strong children of the Alpine wild
Whose culture is the brethren's care;
Of human tasks their only one,
60   And cheerful works beneath the sun.

Those halls, too, destined to contain
Each its own pilgrim-host of old,
From England, Germany, or Spain—
All are before me! I behold
65   The House, the Brotherhood austere!
—And what am I, that I am here?

For rigorous teachers seized my youth,
And purged its faith, and trimmed its fire,

---

3. Arnold, during his short visit, may not actually have witnessed the service of the Mass in the monastery. The consecrated wafer ("the Host") is not passed from the hand of the officiating priest to the hands of the communicant (as is the practice in Arnold's own Anglican Church) but placed, instead, on the tongue of the communicant (who kneels rather than stands).
4. A Carthusian is buried on a wooden plank but does not sleep in a coffin.
5. From which the liqueur Chartreuse is manufactured. Sales of this liqueur provide the principal revenues for upkeep of the monastery.

Showed me the high, white star of Truth,
70 There bade me gaze, and there aspire.
Even now their whispers pierce the gloom:
What dost thou in this living tomb?

Forgive me, masters of the mind![6]
At whose behest I long ago
75 So much unlearnt, so much resigned—
I come not here to be your foe!
I seek these anchorites, not in ruth,[7]
To curse and to deny your truth;

Not as their friend, or child, I speak!
80 But as, on some far northern strand,
Thinking of his own Gods, a Greek
In pity and mournful awe might stand
Before some fallen Runic stone[8]—
For both were faiths, and both are gone.

85 Wandering between two worlds, one dead,
The other powerless to be born,
With nowhere yet to rest my head,
Like these, on earth I wait forlorn.
Their faith, my tears, the world deride—
90 I come to shed them at their side.

Oh, hide me in your gloom profound,
Ye solemn seats of holy pain!
Take me, cowled forms, and fence me round,
Till I possess my soul again;
95 Till free my thoughts before me roll,
Not chafed by hourly false control!

For the world cries your faith is now
But a dead time's exploded dream;
My melancholy, sciolists[9] say,
100 Is a passed mode, an outworn theme—
As if the world had ever had
A faith, or sciolists been sad!

Ah, if it *be* passed, take away,
At least, the restlessness, the pain;
105 Be man henceforth no more a prey
To these out-dated stings again!

6. Writers whose insistence on testing religious beliefs in the light of fact and reason persuaded Arnold that faith in Christianity (especially in the Roman Catholic or Anglo Catholic forms) was no longer tenable in the modern world.
7. Remorse for having adopted the rationalist view of Christianity.
8. A monument inscribed in Teutonic letters (runes), emblematic of a Nordic religion that has become extinct. The relic reminds the Greek that his own religion is likewise dying and will soon be extinct (see *Preface to Poems* [1853], p. 1504, para. 2).
9. Superficial-minded persons who pretend to know the answers to all questions.

The nobleness of grief is gone—
Ah, leave us not the fret alone!

But—if you[1] cannot give us ease—
110 Last of the race of them who grieve
Here leave us to die out with these
Last of the people who believe!
Silent, while years engrave the brow;
Silent—the best are silent now.

115 Achilles[2] ponders in his tent,
The kings of modern thought[3] are dumb;
Silent they are, though not content,
And wait to see the future come.
They have the grief men had of yore,
120 But they contend and cry no more.

Our fathers[4] watered with their tears
This sea of time whereon we sail,
Their voices were in all men's ears
Who passed within their puissant hail.
125 Still the same ocean round us raves,
But we stand mute, and watch the waves.

For what availed it, all the noise
And outcry of the former men?—
Say, have their sons achieved more joys,
130 Say, is life lighter now than then?
The sufferers died, they left their pain—
The pangs which tortured them remain.

What helps it now, that Byron bore,
With haughty scorn which mocked the smart,
135 Through Europe to the Aetolian shore[5]
The pageant of his bleeding heart?
That thousands counted every groan,
And Europe made his woe her own?

What boots it, Shelley! that the breeze
140 Carried thy lovely wail away,
Musical through Italian trees
Which fringe thy soft blue Spezzian bay?[6]
Inheritors of thy distress
Have restless hearts one throb the less?

---

1. It is not clear whether the speaker has resumed addressing his "rigorous teachers" (line 67) or (as would seem more likely) a combination of the sciolists, who scorn the speaker's melancholy, and the worldly, who scorn the faith of the monks. See his address to the "sons of the world" (lines 161–68).
2. Until the death of Patroclus, he refused to participate in the Trojan war, hence similar to modern intellectual leaders who refuse to speak out about their frustrated sense of alienation.

3. Variously but never satisfactorily identified as Newman or Carlyle (the latter was said to have preached the gospel of silence in forty volumes). Another advocate of stoical silence was the French poet Alfred de Vigny (1797–1863).
4. Predecessors among the Romantic writers such as Byron.
5. Region in Greece where Byron died.
6. The Gulf of Spezia in Italy, where Shelley was drowned.

145 Or are we easier, to have read,
O Obermann![7] the sad, stern page,
Which tells us how thou hidd'st thy head
From the fierce tempest of thine age
In the lone brakes of Fontainebleau,
150 Or chalets near the Alpine snow?

Ye slumber in your silent grave!
The world, which for an idle day
Grace to your mood of sadness gave,
Long since hath flung her weeds° away. *mourning clothes*
155 The eternal trifler[8] breaks your spell;
But we—we learnt your lore too well!

Years hence, perhaps, may dawn an age,
More fortunate, alas! than we,
Which without hardness will be sage,
160 And gay without frivolity.
Sons of the world, oh, speed those years;
But, while we wait, allow our tears!

Allow them! We admire with awe
The exulting thunder of your race;
165 You give the universe your law,
You triumph over time and space!
Your pride of life, your tireless powers,
We laud them, but they are not ours.

We are like children reared in shade
170 Beneath some old-world abbey wall,
Forgotten in a forest glade,
And secret from the eyes of all.
Deep, deep the greenwood round them waves,
Their abbey, and its close° of graves! *enclosure*

175 But, where the road runs near the stream,
Oft through the trees they catch a glance
Of passing troops in the sun's beam—
Pennon, and plume, and flashing lance!
Forth to the world those soldiers fare,
180 To life, to cities, and to war!

And through the wood, another way,
Faint bugle notes from far are borne,
Where hunters gather, staghounds bay,[9]
Round some fair forest-lodge at morn.
185 Gay dames are there, in sylvan green;
Laughter and cries—those notes between!

7. Melancholy hero of *Obermann* (1804), a novel
by the French writer Senancour.
8. The sciolist, as in line 99.

9. Cf. the contrast between recluses and hunters
in *The Scholar Gypsy,* lines 71–81 (pp. 1487–
88).

The banners flashing through the trees
Make their blood dance and chain their eyes;
That bugle music on the breeze
190   Arrests them with a charmed surprise.
Banner by turns and bugle woo:
Ye shy recluses, follow too!

O children, what do ye reply?—
"Action and pleasure, will ye roam
195   Through these secluded dells to cry
And call us?—but too late ye come!
Too late for us your call ye blow,
Whose bent was taken long ago.

"Long since we pace this shadowed nave;
200   We watch those yellow tapers shine,
Emblems of hope over the grave,
In the high altar's depth divine;
The organ carries to our ear
Its accents of another sphere.[1]

205   "Fenced early in this cloistral round
Of reverie, of shade, of prayer,
How should we grow in other ground?
How can we flower in foreign air?
—Pass, banners, pass, and bugles, cease;
210   And leave our desert to its peace!"

1852(?)   1855

Thyrsis[1]

*A Monody, to Commemorate the Author's Friend, Arthur Hugh Clough,
Who Died at Florence, 1861*

How changed is here each spot man makes or fills!
In the two Hinkseys[2] nothing keeps the same;
The village street its haunted mansion lacks,
And from the sign is gone Sibylla's[3] name,
5   And from the roofs the twisted chimney stacks—

1. The organ music is from the abbey in the greenwood (line 174), as contrasted with the monastery on the mountaintop in which there is no organ (line 37).

1. In the 1840s, at Oxford, Clough had been one of Arnold's closest friends. After the death of this fellow poet twenty years later, Arnold revisited the Thames valley countryside that they had explored together. The familiar scenes prompted him to review the changes wrought by time on the ideals shared in his Oxford days with Clough, ideals symbolized, in part, by a distant elm and by the story of the Scholar Gypsy. The survival of these ideals in the face of the difficulties of modern life is the subject of this elegy. Unlike Tennyson in such elegies as *In Memoriam*, Arnold rarely touches here on other kinds of immortality.

As a framework for his elegy, Arnold draws on the same Greek and Latin pastoral tradition from which Milton's *Lycidas* and Shelley's *Adonais* were derived. Hence Clough is referred to by one of the traditional names for a shepherd poet, Thyrsis, and Arnold himself as Corydon. The sense of distancing that results from this traditional elegiac mode is reduced considerably by the realism of the setting with its bleak wintry landscape at twilight, a landscape that is brightened, in turn, by evocations of the return of hopeful springtime.
2. The villages of North Hinksey and South Hinksey.
3. Sibylla Kerr had been the proprietress of a tavern in South Hinksey.

Are ye too changed, ye hills?
See, 'tis no foot of unfamiliar men
  Tonight from Oxford up your pathway strays!
Here came I often, often, in old days—
10 Thyrsis and I; we still had Thyrsis then.

Runs it not here, the track by Childsworth Farm,
  Past the high wood, to where the elm tree crowns
  The hill behind whose ridge the sunset flames?
The signal-elm, that looks on Ilsley Downs,
15 The Vale, the three lone weirs, the youthful Thames?—
    This winter eve is warm,
  Humid the air! leafless, yet soft as spring,
  The tender purple spray on copse and briers!
And that sweet city with her dreaming spires,
20 She needs not June for beauty's heightening,

Lovely all times she lies, lovely tonight!—
  Only, methinks, some loss of habit's power
  Befalls me wandering through this upland dim.
Once passed I blindfold here, at any hour;
25 Now seldom come I, since I came with him.
    That single elm tree bright
  Against the west—I miss it! is it gone?
  We prized it dearly; while it stood, we said,
  Our friend, the Gypsy Scholar, was not dead;
30 While the tree lived, he in these fields lived on.

Too rare, too rare, grow now my visits here,
  But once I knew each field, each flower, each stick;
  And with the countryfolk acquaintance made
By barn in threshing time, by new-built rick.
35 Here, too, our shepherd pipes we first assayed.
    Ah me! this many a year
  My pipe is lost, my shepherd's holiday!
  Needs must I lose them, needs with heavy heart
  Into the world and wave of men depart;
40 But Thyrsis of his own will went away.[4]

It irked him to be here, he could not rest.
  He loved each simple joy the country yields,
  He loved his mates; but yet he could not keep,°   *stay*
For that a shadow loured on the fields,
45 Here with the shepherds and the silly° sheep.   *innocent*
    Some life of men unblest
  He knew, which made him droop, and filled his head.
  He went; his piping took a troubled sound
  Of storms[5] that rage outside our happy ground;
50 He could not wait their passing, he is dead.

So, some tempestuous morn in early June,
    When the year's primal burst of bloom is o'er,
        Before the roses and the longest day—
    When garden walks and all the grassy floor
55   With blossoms red and white of fallen May
            And chestnut flowers are strewn—
    So have I heard the cuckoo's parting cry,
        From the wet field, through the vexed garden trees,
        Come with the volleying rain and tossing breeze:
60   *The bloom is gone, and with the bloom go I!*

Too quick despairer, wherefore wilt thou go?
    Soon will the high Midsummer pomps come on,
        Soon will the musk carnations break and swell,
    Soon shall we have gold-dusted snapdragon,
65   Sweet-William with his homely cottage-smell,
            And stocks in fragrant blow;
    Roses that down the alleys shine afar,
        And open, jasmine-muffled lattices,
        And groups under the dreaming garden trees,
70   And the full moon, and the white evening star.

He hearkens not! light comer, he is flown!
    What matters it? next year he will return,
        And we shall have him in the sweet spring days,
    With whitening hedges, and uncrumpling fern,
75   And bluebells trembling by the forest ways,
            And scent of hay new-mown.
    But Thyrsis never more we swains shall see,
        See him come back, and cut a smoother reed,
        And blow a strain the world at last shall heed—
80   For Time, not Corydon, hath conquered thee!

Alack, for Corydon no rival now!—
    But when Sicilian shepherds lost a mate,
        Some good survivor with his flute would go,
    Piping a ditty sad for Bion's fate;[6]
85   And cross the unpermitted ferry's flow,[7]
            And relax Pluto's brow,
    And make leap up with joy the beauteous head
        Of Proserpine, among whose crownèd hair
        Are flowers first opened on Sicilian air,[8]
90   And flute his friend, like Orpheus,[9] from the dead.

O easy access to the hearer's grace
    When Dorian shepherds[1] sang to Proserpine!

6. Moschus, a Greek poet, composed a pastoral elegy upon the death of the poet Bion in Sicily.
7. The river Styx across which the dead were ferried to the underworld.
8. Pluto ruled the underworld with his queen, Proserpine. In spring, Proserpine's returning above ground in Sicily would cause the flowers to blossom.
9. His music enabled him to enter the "unpermitted" realms of the dead and to bring his wife, Eurydice, back with him to the land of the living.
1. Greeks who colonized Sicily, the home of pastoral poetry.

For she herself had trod Sicilian fields,
She knew the Dorian water's gush divine,
95   She knew each lily white which Enna[2] yields,
Each rose with blushing face;
She loved the Dorian pipe, the Dorian strain.
But ah, of our poor Thames she never heard!
Her foot the Cumner cowslips never stirred;
100 And we should tease her with our plaint in vain!

Well! wind-dispersed and vain the words will be,
Yet, Thyrsis, let me give my grief its hour
In the old haunt, and find our tree-topped hill!
Who, if not I, for questing here hath power?
105   I know the wood which hides the daffodil,
I know the Fyfield tree,
I know what white, what purple fritillaries[3]
The grassy harvest of the river fields,
Above by Ensham, down by Sandford, yields,
110 And what sedged brooks are Thames's tributaries;

I know these slopes; who knows them if not I?—
But many a dingle[4] on the loved hillside,
With thorns once studded, old, white-blossomed trees,
Where thick the cowslips grew, and far descried
115   High towered the spikes of purple orchises,
Hath since our day put by
The coronals of that forgotten time;
Down each green bank hath gone the plowboy's team,
And only in the hidden brookside gleam
120 Primroses, orphans of the flowery prime.

Where is the girl, who by the boatman's door,
Above the locks, above the boating throng,
Unmoored our skiff when through the Wytham flats,
Red loosestrife[5] and blond meadowsweet among
125   And darting swallows and light water-gnats,
We tracked the shy Thames shore?
Where are the mowers, who, as the tiny swell
Of our boat passing heaved the river grass,
Stood with suspended scythe to see us pass?—
130 They all are gone, and thou art gone as well!

Yes, thou art gone! and round me too the night
In ever-nearing circle weaves her shade.
I see her veil draw soft across the day,
I feel her slowly chilling breath invade
135   The cheek grown thin, the brown hair sprent° with grey;   *sprinkled*
I feel her finger light
Laid pausefully upon life's headlong train;

2. From a meadow near the Sicilian town of Enna, Proserpine had been carried off to the underworld by Pluto (or Dis).
3. Flowers commonly found in moist meadows.
4. Small deep valley.
5. Flowers that grow on banks of streams.

The foot less prompt to meet the morning dew,
The heart less bounding at emotion new,
140   And hope, once crushed, less quick to spring again.

And long the way appears, which seemed so short
    To the less practiced eye of sanguine youth;
    And high the mountaintops, in cloudy air,
    The mountaintops where is the throne of Truth,
145   Tops in life's morning sun so bright and bare!
        Unbreachable the fort
Of the long-battered world uplifts its wall;
    And strange and vain the earthly turmoil grows,
    And near and real the charm of thy repose,
150   And night as welcome as a friend would fall.

But hush! the upland hath a sudden loss
    Of quiet!—Look, adown the dusk hillside,
    A troop of Oxford hunters going home,
    As in old days, jovial and talking, ride!
155   From hunting with the Berkshire hounds they come.
        Quick! let me fly, and cross
Into yon farther field!—'Tis done; and see,
    Backed by the sunset, which doth glorify
    The orange and pale violet evening sky,
160   Bare on its lonely ridge, the Tree! the Tree!

I take the omen! Eve lets down her veil,
    The white fog creeps from bush to bush about,
    The west unflushes, the high stars grow bright,
    And in the scattered farms the lights come out.
165   I cannot reach the signal-tree tonight,
        Yet, happy omen, hail!
Hear it from thy broad lucent Arno vale[6]
    (For there thine earth-forgetting eyelids keep
    The morningless and unawakening sleep
170   Under the flowery oleanders pale),

Hear it, O Thyrsis, still our tree is there!—
    Ah, vain! These English fields, this upland dim,
    These brambles pale with mist engarlanded,
    That lone, sky-pointing tree, are not for him;
175   To a boon southern country he is fled,
        And now in happier air,
Wandering with the great Mother's train divine[7]
    (And purer or more subtle soul than thee,
    I trow, the mighty Mother doth not see)
180   Within a folding of the Apennine,[8]

Thou hearest the immortal chants[9] of old!—
    Putting his sickle to the perilous grain

---

6. Clough was buried in Florence, which is situated in the valley of the Arno River.
7. Followers of Demeter (whose name may mean Earth Mother), who was worshiped as the goddess of agriculture.
8. Mountains near Florence.
9. Sung in Demeter's honor.

In the hot cornfield of the Phrygian king,[1]
For thee the Lityerses song again
185   Young Daphnis with his silver voice doth sing;
Sings his Sicilian fold,
His sheep, his hapless love, his blinded eyes—
And how a call celestial round him rang,
And heavenward from the fountain brink he sprang,
190   And all the marvel of the golden skies.

There thou art gone, and me thou leavest here
Sole in these fields! yet will I not despair.
Despair I will not, while I yet descry
'Neath the mild canopy of English air
195   That lonely tree against the western sky.
Still, still these slopes, 'tis clear,
Our Gypsy Scholar haunts, outliving thee!
Fields where soft sheep from cages pull the hay,
Woods with anemones in flower till May,
200   Know him a wanderer still; then why not me?

A fugitive and gracious light he seeks,
Shy to illumine; and I seek it too.
This does not come with houses or with gold,
With place, with honor, and a flattering crew;
205   'Tis not in the world's market bought and sold—
But the smooth-slipping weeks
Drop by, and leave its seeker still untired;
Out of the heed of mortals he is gone,
He wends unfollowed, he must house alone;
210   Yet on he fares, by his own heart inspired.

Thou too, O Thyrsis, on like quest wast bound;
Thou wanderedst with me for a little hour!
Men gave thee nothing; but this happy quest,
If men esteemed thee feeble, gave thee power,
215   If men procured thee trouble, gave thee rest.
And this rude Cumner ground,
Its fir-topped Hurst, its farms, its quiet fields,
Here cam'st thou in thy jocund youthful time,
Here was thine height of strength, thy golden prime!
220   And still the haunt beloved a virtue yields.

What though the music of thy rustic flute
Kept not for long its happy, country tone;
Lost it too soon, and learnt a stormy note[2]

1. Daphnis, the ideal Sicilian shepherd of Greek pastoral poetry, was said to have followed into Phrygia his mistress Piplea, who had been carried off by robbers, and to have found her in the power of the king of Phrygia, Lityerses. Lityerses used to make strangers try a contest with him in reaping corn, and to put them to death if he overcame them. Hercules arrived in time to save Daphnis, took upon himself the reaping contest with Lityerses, overcame him, and slew him. The Lityerses song connected with this tradition was, like the Linus song, one of the early plaintive strains of Greek popular poetry, and used to be sung by corn reapers. Other traditions represented Daphnis as beloved by a nymph who exacted from him an oath to love no one else. He fell in love with a princess, and was struck blind by the jealous nymph. Mercury, who was his father, raised him to heaven, and made a fountain spring up in the place from which he ascended. At this fountain the Sicilians offered yearly sacrifices [from Servius's commentary on Virgil's *Ecologues*; Arnold's note].
2. Clough's poetry often dealt with contemporary religious problems.

Of men contention-tossed, of men who groan,
225   Which tasked thy pipe too sore, and tired thy throat—
It failed, and thou wast mute!
Yet hadst thou always visions of our light,
And long with men of care thou couldst not stay,
And soon thy foot resumed its wandering way,
230   Left human haunt, and on alone till night.

Too rare, too rare, grow now my visits here!
'Mid city noise, not, as with thee of yore,
Thyrsis! in reach of sheep-bells is my home.
—Then through the great town's harsh, heart-wearying roar,
235   Let in thy voice a whisper often come,
To chase fatigue and fear:
Why faintest thou? I wandered till I died.
Roam on! The light we sought is shining still.
Dost thou ask proof? Our tree yet crowns the hill,
240   *Our Scholar travels yet the loved hillside.*

1866

Preface to *Poems* (1853)

In two small volumes of poems, published anonymously, one in 1849, the other in 1852, many of the poems which compose the present volume have already appeared. The rest are now published for the first time.

I have, in the present collection, omitted the poem from which the volume published in 1852 took its title.[1] I have done so, not because the subject of it was a Sicilian Greek born between two and three thousand years ago, although many persons would think this a sufficient reason. Neither have I done so because I had, in my own opinion, failed in the delineation which I intended to effect. I intended to delineate the feelings of one of the last of the Greek religious philosophers, one of the family of Orpheus and Musaeus,[2] having survived his fellows, living on into a time when the habits of Greek thought and feeling had begun fast to change, character to dwindle, the influence of the Sophists[3] to prevail. Into the feelings of a man so situated there entered much that we are accustomed to consider as exclusively modern; how much, the fragments of Empedocles[4] himself which remain to us

---

1. *Empedocles on Etna,* the long poem that supplied the title for Arnold's second collection of poems, portrays the disillusioned reflections of the Greek philosopher and scientist Empedocles and culminates in the speaker's suicide on Mount Etna in Sicily, in the 5th century B.C.E. Because of his dissatisfaction with what he calls the "morbid" tone of *Empedocles on Etna,* Arnold continued to exclude it from his volumes of poetry until 1867 when he reprinted it at the request, he said, "of a man of genius, whom it had the honor and good fortune to interest—Mr. Robert Browning." It should be noted that in the arguments developed in the Preface against his own poem (and against 19th-century poetry in general), Arnold is exclusively concerned with narrative and dramatic

poetry. The Preface, as he himself remarked in 1854, "leaves . . . untouched the question, how far, and in what manner, the opinions there expressed respecting the choice of subjects apply to lyric poetry; that region of the poetical field which is chiefly cultivated at present."
2. Pupil of the poet and musician Orpheus. The latter was the legendary founder of the Orphic religion that flourished in 6th-century Greece and later declined.
3. Greek rhetoricians, often criticized because of their reputed concern for niceties of expression over substance of knowledge.
4. Empedocles' writings (medical and scientific treatises in verse) have survived only in fragments.

are sufficient at least to indicate. What those who are familiar only with the great monuments of early Greek genius suppose to be its exclusive characteristics, have disappeared; the calm, the cheerfulness, the disinterested objectivity have disappeared; the dialogue of the mind with itself has commenced; modern problems have presented themselves, we hear already the doubts, we witness the discouragement, of Hamlet and of Faust.

The representation of such a man's feelings must be interesting, if consistently drawn. We all naturally take pleasure, says Aristotle, in any imitation or representation whatever;[5] this is the basis of our love of poetry; and we take pleasure in them, he adds, because all knowledge is naturally agreeable to us; not to the philosopher only, but to mankind at large. Every representation therefore which is consistently drawn may be supposed to be interesting, inasmuch as it gratifies this natural interest in knowledge of all kinds. What is *not* interesting is that which does not add to our knowledge of any kind; that which is vaguely conceived and loosely drawn; a representation which is general, indeterminate, and faint, instead of being particular, precise, and firm.

Any accurate representation may therefore be expected to be interesting; but, if the representation be a poetical one, more than this is demanded. It is demanded, not only that it shall interest, but also that it shall inspirit and rejoice the reader; that it shall convey a charm, and infuse delight. For the muses, as Hesiod says, were born that they might be "a forgetfulness of evils, and a truce from cares":[6] and it is not enough that the poet should add to the knowledge of men, it is required of him also that he should add to their happiness. "All art," says Schiller, "is dedicated to Joy, and there is no higher and no more serious problem, than how to make men happy. The right art is that alone, which creates the highest enjoyment."[7]

A poetical work, therefore, is not yet justified when it has been shown to be an accurate, and therefore interesting representation; it has to be shown also that it is a representation from which men can derive enjoyment. In presence of the most tragic circumstances, represented in a work of Art, the feeling of enjoyment, as is well known, may still subsist; the representation of the most utter calamity, of the liveliest anguish, is not sufficient to destroy it; the more tragic the situation, the deeper becomes the enjoyment; and the situation is more tragic in proportion as it becomes more terrible.

What then are the situations, from the representation of which, though accurate, no poetical enjoyment can be derived? They are those in which the suffering finds no vent in action; in which a continuous state of mental distress is prolonged, unrelieved by incident, hope, or resistance; in which there is everything to be endured, nothing to be done. In such situations there is inevitably something morbid, in the description of them something monotonous. When they occur in actual life, they are painful, not tragic; the representation of them in poetry is painful also.

To this class of situations, poetically faulty as it appears to me, that of Empedocles, as I have endeavored to represent him, belongs; and I have therefore excluded the poem from the present collection.

---

5. See Aristotle's *Poetics,* especially 1, 2, 4, 7, 14.
6. From *Theogony* 52–56, by Hesiod, early Greek poet.
7. J. C. F. von Schiller's *On the Use of the Chorus*

in *Tragedy,* prefatory essay to *The Bride of Messina* (1803). See *Friedrich Schiller's Works* (1903) 8.224.

And why, it may be asked, have I entered into this explanation respecting a matter so unimportant as the admission or exclusion of the poem in question? I have done so, because I was anxious to avow that the sole reason for its exclusion was that which has been stated above; and that it has not been excluded in deference to the opinion which many critics of the present day appear to entertain against subjects chosen from distant times and countries: against the choice, in short, of any subjects but modern ones.

"The poet," it is said, and by an intelligent critic, "the poet who would really fix the public attention must leave the exhausted past, and draw his subjects from matters of present import, and *therefore* both of interest and novelty."[8]

Now this view I believe to be completely false. It is worth examining, inasmuch as it is a fair sample of a class of critical dicta everywhere current at the present day, having a philosophical form and air, but no real basis in fact; and which are calculated to vitiate the judgment of readers of poetry, while they exert, so far as they are adopted, a misleading influence on the practice of those who write it.

What are the eternal objects of poetry, among all nations and at all times? They are actions; human actions; possessing an inherent interest in themselves, and which are to be communicated in an interesting manner by the art of the poet.[9] Vainly will the latter imagine that he has everything in his own power; that he can make an intrinsically inferior action equally delightful with a more excellent one by his treatment of it; he may indeed compel us to admire his skill, but his work will possess, within itself, an incurable defect.

The poet, then, has in the first place to select an excellent action; and what actions are the most excellent? Those, certainly, which most powerfully appeal to the great primary human affections: to those elementary feelings which subsist permanently in the race, and which are independent of time. These feelings are permanent and the same; that which interests them is permanent and the same also. The modernness or antiquity of an action, therefore, has nothing to do with its fitness for poetical representation; this depends upon its inherent qualities. To the elementary part of our nature, to our passions, that which is great and passionate is eternally interesting; and interesting solely in proportion to its greatness and to its passion. A great human action of a thousand years ago is more interesting to it than a smaller human action of today, even though upon the representation of this last the most consummate skill may have been expended, and though it has the advantage of appealing by its modern language, familiar manners, and contemporary allusions, to all our transient feelings and interests. These, however, have no right to demand of a poetical work that it shall satisfy them; their claims are to be directed elsewhere. Poetical works belong to the domain of our permanent passions; let them interest these, and the voice of all subordinate claims upon them is at once silenced.

Achilles, Prometheus, Clytemnestra, Dido—what modern poem presents personages as interesting, even to us moderns, as these personages of an

---

8. In the *Spectator* of April 2nd, 1853. The words quoted were not used with reference to poems of mine [Arnold's note]. According to Arnold the

"intelligent critic" was R. S. Rintoul, editor of the *Spectator*.
9. Cf. Aristotle's *Poetics* 6.

"exhausted past"? We have the domestic epic dealing with the details of modern life which pass daily under our eyes;[1] we have poems representing modern personages in contact with the problems of modern life, moral, intellectual, and social; these works have been produced by poets the most distinguished of their nation and time; yet I fearlessly assert that *Hermann and Dorothea, Childe Harold, Jocelyn, The Excursion,*[2] leave the reader cold in comparison with the effect produced upon him by the latter books of the *Iliad,* by the *Oresteia,* or by the episode of Dido.[3] And why is this? Simply because in the three last-named cases the action is greater, the personages nobler, the situations more intense: and this is the true basis of the interest in a poetical work, and this alone.

It may be urged, however, that past actions may be interesting in themselves, but that they are not to be adopted by the modern poet, because it is impossible for him to have them clearly present to his own mind, and he cannot therefore feel them deeply, nor represent them forcibly. But this is not necessarily the case. The externals of a past action, indeed, he cannot know with the precision of a contemporary; but his business is with its essentials. The outward man of Oedipus or of Macbeth, the houses in which they lived, the ceremonies of their courts, he cannot accurately figure to himself; but neither do they essentially concern him. His business is with their inward man; with their feelings and behavior in certain tragic situations, which engage their passions as men; these have in them nothing local and casual; they are as accessible to the modern poet as to a contemporary.

The date of an action, then, signifies nothing: the action itself, its selection and construction, this is what is all-important. This the Greeks understood far more clearly than we do. The radical difference between their poetical theory and ours consists, as it appears to me, in this: that, with them, the poetical character of the action in itself, and the conduct of it, was the first consideration; with us, attention is fixed mainly on the value of the separate thoughts and images which occur in the treatment of an action. They regarded the whole; we regard the parts. With them, the action predominated over the expression of it; with us, the expression predominates over the action. Not that they failed in expression, or were inattentive to it; on the contrary, they are the highest models of expression, the unapproached masters of the *grand style:* but their expression is so excellent because it is so admirably kept in its right degree of prominence; because it is so simple and so well subordinated; because it draws its force directly from the pregnancy of the matter which it conveys. For what reason was the Greek tragic poet confined to so limited a range of subjects? Because there are so few actions which unite in themselves, in the highest degree, the conditions of excellence: and it was not thought that on any but an excellent subject could an excellent poem be constructed. A few actions, therefore, eminently adapted for tragedy, maintained almost exclusive possession of the Greek tragic stage; their significance appeared inexhaustible; they were as permanent problems,

---

1. Perhaps alluding to such poems as Tennyson's *The Princess* (1847) or to Alexander Smith's *Life Drama* (1853) or to the modern novel.
2. Long poems by Goethe (1797), Byron (1818), Lamartine (1836), and Wordsworth (1814),

respectively.
3. See Virgil's *Aeneid* 4. *"Oresteia"*: a trilogy of plays by Aeschylus concerned with the stories of Agamemnon, Clytemnestra, and their son, Orestes.

perpetually offered to the genius of every fresh poet. This too is the reason of what appears to us moderns a certain baldness of expression in Greek tragedy; of the triviality with which we often reproach the remarks of the chorus, where it takes part in the dialogue: that the action itself, the situation of Orestes, or Merope, or Alcmaeon,[4] was to stand the central point of interest, unforgotten, absorbing, principal; that no accessories were for a moment to distract the spectator's attention from this; that the tone of the parts was to be perpetually kept down, in order not to impair the grandiose effect of the whole. The terrible old mythic story on which the drama was founded stood, before he entered the theater, traced in its bare outlines upon the spectator's mind; it stood in his memory, as a group of statuary, faintly seen, at the end of a long and dark vista: then came the poet, embodying outlines, developing situations, not a word wasted, not a sentiment capriciously thrown in: stroke upon stroke, the drama proceeded: the light deepened upon the group; more and more it revealed itself to the riveted gaze of the spectator: until at last, when the final words were spoken, it stood before him in broad sunlight, a model of immortal beauty.

This was what a Greek critic demanded; this was what a Greek poet endeavored to effect. It signified nothing to what time an action belonged; we do not find that the *Persae* occupied a particularly high rank among the dramas of Aeschylus, because it represented a matter of contemporary interest:[5] this was not what a cultivated Athenian required, he required that the permanent elements of his nature should be moved; and dramas of which the action, though taken from a long-distant mythic time, yet was calculated to accomplish this in a higher degree than that of the *Persae,* stood higher in his estimation accordingly. The Greeks felt, no doubt, with their exquisite sagacity of taste, that an action of present times was too near them, too much mixed up with what was accidental and passing, to form a sufficiently grand, detached, and self-subsistent object for a tragic poem: such objects belonged to the domain of the comic poet, and of the lighter kinds of poetry. For the more serious kinds, for *pragmatic* poetry, to use an excellent expression of Polybius,[6] they were more difficult and severe in the range of subjects which they permitted. Their theory and practice alike, the admirable treatise of Aristotle, and the unrivaled works of their poets, exclaim with a thousand tongues—"All depends upon the subject; choose a fitting action, penetrate yourself with the feeling of its situations; this done, everything else will follow."

But for all kinds of poetry alike there was one point on which they were rigidly exacting; the adaptability of the subject to the kind of poetry selected, and the careful construction of the poem.

How different a way of thinking from this is ours! We can hardly at the present day understand what Menander[7] meant when he told a man who inquired as to the progress of his comedy that he had finished it, not having yet written a single line, because he had constructed the action of it in his mind. A modern critic would have assured him that the merit of his piece

---

4. The son of a legendary Greek hero, who, like Orestes, avenged his father's death by killing his mother. He was the subject of several Greek plays now lost. Merope, queen of Messene in Greece, appears in plays by Euripides and in Arnold's own play *Merope* (1858).

5. Aeschylus's *Persians* (472 B.C.E.) portrays the Greek victory over the Persian invaders, which had occurred only a few years before the play was produced.

6. Greek historian (202–120 B.C.E.).

7. Greek writer of comedies (342–292 B.C.E.).

depended on the brilliant things which arose under his pen as he went along. We have poems which seem to exist merely for the sake of single lines and passages; not for the sake of producing any total impression. We have critics who seem to direct their attention merely to detached expressions, to the language about the action, not to the action itself, I verily think that the majority of them do not in their hearts believe that there is such a thing as a total impression to be derived from a poem at all, or to be demanded from a poet; they think the term a commonplace of metaphysical criticism. They will permit the poet to select any action he pleases, and to suffer that action to go as it will, provided he gratifies them with occasional bursts of fine writing, and with a shower of isolated thoughts and images. That is, they permit him to leave their poetical sense ungratified, provided that he gratifies their rhetorical sense and their curiosity. Of his neglecting to gratify these, there is little danger. He needs rather to be warned against the danger of attempting to gratify these alone; he needs rather to be perpetually reminded to prefer his action to everything else; so to treat this, as to permit its inherent excellences to develop themselves, without interruption from the intrusion of his personal peculiarities; most fortunate, when he most entirely succeeds in effacing himself, and in enabling a noble action to subsist as it did in nature.

But the modern critic not only permits a false practice; he absolutely prescribes false aims.—"A true allegory of the state of one's own mind in a representative history," the poet is told, "is perhaps the highest thing that one can attempt in the way of poetry."[8] And accordingly he attempts it. An allegory of the state of one's own mind, the highest problem of an art which imitates actions! No assuredly, it is not, it never can be so: no great poetical work has ever been produced with such an aim. *Faust* itself, in which something of the kind is attempted, wonderful passages as it contains, and in spite of the unsurpassed beauty of the scenes which relate to Margaret, *Faust* itself, judged as a whole, and judged strictly as a poetical work, is defective: its illustrious author, the greatest poet of modern times, the greatest critic of all times, would have been the first to acknowledge it; he only defended his work, indeed, by asserting it to be "something incommensurable."[9]

The confusion of the present times is great, the multitude of voices counseling different things bewildering, the number of existing works capable of attracting a young writer's attention and of becoming his models, immense. What he wants is a hand to guide him through the confusion, a voice to prescribe to him the aim which he should keep in view, and to explain to him that the value of the literary works which offer themselves to his attention is relative to their power of helping him forward on his road towards this aim. Such a guide the English writer at the present day will nowhere find. Failing this, all that can be looked for, all indeed that can be desired is, that his attention should be fixed on excellent models; that he may reproduce, at any rate, something of their excellence, by penetrating himself with their works and by catching their spirit, if he cannot be taught to produce what is excellent independently.

8. *North British Review* 19 (Aug. 1853): 180 (U.S. edition). Arnold seems not to have noticed that Goethe (a critic he revered) had been cited earlier in the article as the authority for this critical generalization.

9. J. Eckermann's *Conversations with Goethe*, Jan. 3, 1830.

Foremost among these models for the English writer stands Shakespeare: a name the greatest perhaps of all poetical names; a name never to be mentioned without reverence. I will venture, however, to express a doubt, whether the influence of his works, excellent and fruitful for the readers of poetry, for the great majority, has been of unmixed advantage to the writers of it. Shakespeare indeed chose excellent subjects; the world could afford no better than Macbeth, or Romeo and Juliet, or Othello: he had no theory respecting the necessity of choosing subjects of present import, or the paramount interest attaching to allegories of the state of one's own mind; like all great poets, he knew well what constituted a poetical action; like them, wherever he found such an action, he took it; like them, too, he found his best in past times. But to these general characteristics of all great poets he added a special one of his own; a gift, namely, of happy, abundant, and ingenious expression, eminent and unrivaled: so eminent as irresistibly to strike the attention first in him, and even to throw into comparative shade his other excellences as a poet. Here has been the mischief. These other excellences were his fundamental excellences *as a poet*; what distinguishes the artist from the mere amateur, says Goethe, is *Architectonicè* in the highest sense;[1] that power of execution, which creates, forms, and constitutes: not the profoundness of single thoughts, not the richness of imagery, not the abundance of illustration. But these attractive accessories of a poetical work being more easily seized than the spirit of the whole, and these accessories being possessed by Shakespeare in an unequaled degree, a young writer having recourse to Shakespeare as his model runs great risk of being vanquished and absorbed by them, and, in consequence, of reproducing, according to the measure of his power, these, and these alone.[2] Of this preponderating quality of Shakespeare's genius, accordingly almost the whole of modern English poetry has, it appears to me, felt the influence. To the exclusive attention on the part of his imitators to this it is in a great degree owing, that of the majority of modern poetical works the details alone are valuable, the composition worthless. In reading them one is perpetually reminded of that terrible sentence on a modern French poet: *Il dit tout ce qu'il veut, mais malheureusement il n'a rien à dire.*[3]

Let me give an instance of what I mean. I will take it from the works of the very chief among those who seem to have been formed in the school of Shakespeare: of one whose exquisite genius and pathetic death render him forever interesting. I will take the poem of *Isabella, or the Pot of Basil*, by Keats. I choose this rather than the *Endymion*, because the latter work (which a modern critic has classed with the *Fairy Queen*!)[4] although undoubtedly there blows through it the breath of genius, is yet as a whole so utterly incoherent, as not strictly to merit the name of a poem at all. The poem of *Isabella*, then, is a perfect treasure house of graceful and felicitous

1. In the essay *Concerning the So-called Dilettantism* (1799) in his *Werke* (1851) 25.322.
2. Cf. Arnold's letter to Clough (Oct. 28, 1852):

> More and more I feel that the difference between a mature and a youthful age of the world compels the poetry of the former to use great plainness of speech . . . and that Keats and Shelley were on a false track when they set themselves to reproduce the exuberance of expression, the charm, the richness of images,

and the felicity, of the Elizabethan poets.
3. He says everything he wishes to, but unfortunately he has nothing to say (French). A comment on Théophile Gautier (1811–1872), whose emphasis on style was severely criticized by Arnold in his late essay *Wordsworth*.
4. In the *North British Review* 19 (Aug. 1853): 172–74, Keats's *Endymion* is twice linked with Spenser's *Faerie Queene* as "leisurely compositions of the sweet sensuous order."

words and images: almost in every stanza there occurs one of those vivid and picturesque turns of expression, by which the object is made to flash upon the eye of the mind, and which thrill the reader with a sudden delight. This one short poem contains, perhaps, a greater number of happy single expressions which one could quote than all the extant tragedies of Sophocles. But the action, the story? The action in itself is an excellent one; but so feebly is it conceived by the poet, so loosely constructed, that the effect produced by it, in and for itself, is absolutely null. Let the reader, after he has finished the poem of Keats, turn to the same story in the *Decameron:*[5] he will then feel how pregnant and interesting the same action has become in the hands of a great artist, who above all things delineates his object; who subordinates expression to that which it is designed to express.

I have said that the imitators of Shakespeare, fixing their attention on his wonderful gift of expression, have directed their imitation to this, neglecting his other excellences. These excellences, the fundamental excellences of poetical art, Shakespeare no doubt possessed them—possessed many of them in a splendid degree; but it may perhaps be doubted whether even he himself did not sometimes give scope to his faculty of expression to the prejudice of a higher poetical duty. For we must never forget that Shakespeare is the great poet he is from his skill in discerning and firmly conceiving an excellent action, from his power of intensely feeling a situation, of intimately associating himself with a character; not from his gift of expression, which rather even leads him astray, degenerating sometimes into a fondness for curiosity of expression, into an irritability of fancy, which seems to make it impossible for him to say a thing plainly, even when the press of the action demands the very direct language, or its level character the very simplest. Mr. Hallam, than whom it is impossible to find a saner and more judicious critic, has had the courage (for at the present day it needs courage) to remark, how extremely and faultily difficult Shakespeare's language often is.[6] It is so: you may find main scenes in some of his greatest tragedies, *King Lear* for instance, where the language is so artificial, so curiously tortured, and so difficult, that every speech has to be read two or three times before its meaning can be comprehended. This overcuriousness of expression is indeed but the excessive employment of a wonderful gift—of the power of saying a thing in a happier way than any other man; nevertheless, it is carried so far that one understands what M. Guizot meant, when he said that Shakespeare appears in his language to have tried all styles except that of simplicity.[7] He has not the severe and scrupulous self-restraint of the ancients, partly no doubt, because he had a far less cultivated and exacting audience. He has indeed a far wider range than they had, a far richer fertility of thought; in this respect he rises above them. In his strong conception of his subject, in the genuine way in which he is penetrated with it, he resembles them, and is unlike the moderns. But in the accurate limitation of it, the conscientious rejection of superfluities, the simple and rigorous development of it from the first line of his work to the last, he falls below them, and comes nearer to the moderns. In his chief works, besides what he has of his own, he has the

---

5. By Boccaccio: fourth day, fifth story.
6. *Introduction to the Literature of Europe* (1838–39), chap. 23, by Henry Hallam (1779–1859), historian.

7. F. P. G. Guizot (1787–1874), French historian discussing Shakespeare's sonnets in his *Shakespeare et son temps* (1852), 114.

elementary soundness of the ancients; he has their important action and their large and broad manner; but he has not their purity of method. He is therefore a less safe model; for what he has of his own is personal, and inseparable from his own rich nature; it may be imitated and exaggerated, it cannot be learned or applied as an art. He is above all suggestive; more valuable, therefore, to young writers as men than as artists. But clearness of arrangement, rigor of development, simplicity of style—these may to a certain extent be learned; and these may, I am convinced, be learned best from the ancients, who although infinitely less suggestive than Shakespeare, are thus, to the artist, more instructive.

What, then, it will be asked, are the ancients to be our sole models? the ancients with their comparatively narrow range of experience, and their widely different circumstances? Not, certainly, that which is narrow in the ancients, nor that in which we can no longer sympathize. An action like the action of the *Antigone* of Sophocles, which turns upon the conflict between the heroine's duty to her brother's corpse and that to the laws of her country, is no longer one in which it is possible that we should feel a deep interest. I am speaking too, it will be remembered, not of the best sources of intellectual stimulus for the general reader, but of the best models of instruction for the individual writer. This last may certainly learn of the ancients, better than anywhere else, three things which it is vitally important for him to know: the all-importance of the choice of a subject; the necessity of accurate construction; and the subordinate character of expression. He will learn from them how unspeakably superior is the effect of the one moral impression left by a great action treated as a whole, to the effect produced by the most striking single thought or by the happiest image. As he penetrates into the spirit of the great classical works, as he becomes gradually aware of their intense significance, their noble simplicity, and their calm pathos, he will be convinced that it is this effect, unity and profoundness of moral impression, at which the ancient poets aimed; that it is this which constitutes the grandeur of their works, and which makes them immortal. He will desire to direct his own efforts towards producing the same effect. Above all, he will deliver himself from the jargon of modern criticism, and escape the danger of producing poetical works conceived in the spirit of the passing time, and which partake of its transitoriness.

The present age makes great claims upon us; we owe it service, it will not be satisfied without our admiration. I know not how it is, but their commerce with the ancients appears to me to produce, in those who constantly practice it, a steadying and composing effect upon their judgment, not of literary works only, but of men and events in general. They are like persons who have had a very weighty and impressive experience; they are more truly than others under the empire of facts, and more independent of the language current among those with whom they live. They wish neither to applaud nor to revile their age; they wish to know what it is, what it can give them, and whether this is what they want. What they want, they know very well; they want to educe and cultivate what is best and noblest in themselves; they know, too, that this is no easy task—χαλεπὸν, as Pittacus said, χαλεπὸν ἐσθλὸν ἔμμεναι[8]—and they ask themselves sincerely whether their age and its literature can assist them in the attempt. If they are endeavoring to prac-

---

8. It is hard to be good (Greek); an aphorism of Pittacus (7th century B.C.E.).

tice any art, they remember the plain and simple proceedings of the old artists, who attained their grand results by penetrating themselves with some noble and significant action, not by inflating themselves with a belief in the pre-eminent importance and greatness of their own times. They do not talk of their mission, nor of interpreting their age, nor of the coming poet; all this, they know, is the mere delirium of vanity; their business is not to praise their age, but to afford to the men who live in it the highest pleasure which they are capable of feeling. If asked to afford this by means of subjects drawn from the age itself, they ask what special fitness the present age has for supplying them. They are told that it is an era of progress, an age commissioned to carry out the great ideas of industrial development and social amelioration. They reply that with all this they can do nothing; that the elements they need for the exercise of their art are great actions, calculated powerfully and delightfully to affect what is permanent in the human soul; that so far as the present age can supply such actions, they will gladly make use of them; but that an age wanting in moral grandeur can with difficulty supply such, and an age of spiritual discomfort with difficulty be powerfully and delightfully affected by them.

A host of voices will indignantly rejoin that the present age is inferior to the past neither in moral grandeur nor in spiritual health. He who possesses the discipline I speak of will content himself with remembering the judgments passed upon the present age, in this respect, by the two men, the one of strongest head, the other of widest culture, whom it has produced; by Goethe and by Niebuhr.[9] It will be sufficient for him that he knows the opinions held by these two great men respecting the present age and its literature; and that he feels assured in his own mind that their aims and demands upon life were such as he would wish, at any rate, his own to be; and their judgment as to what is impeding and disabling such as he may safely follow. He will not, however, maintain a hostile attitude towards the false pretensions of his age: he will content himself with not being overwhelmed by them. He will esteem himself fortunate if he can succeed in banishing from his mind all feelings of contradiction, and irritation, and impatience; in order to delight himself with the contemplation of some noble action of a heroic time, and to enable others, through his representation of it, to delight in it also.

I am far indeed from making any claim, for myself, that I possess this discipline; or for the following poems, that they breathe its spirit. But I say, that in the sincere endeavor to learn and practice, amid the bewildering confusion of our times, what is sound and true in poetical art, I seemed to myself to find the only sure guidance, the only solid footing, among the ancients. They, at any rate, knew what they wanted in art, and we do not. It is this uncertainty which is disheartening, and not hostile criticism. How often have I felt this when reading words of disparagement or of cavil: that it is the uncertainty as to what is really to be aimed at which makes our difficulty, not the dissatisfaction of the critic, who himself suffers from the same uncertainty. *Non me tua fervida terrent Dicta; . . . Dii me terrent, et Jupiter hostis.*[1]

9. B. G. Niebuhr (1776–1831), German historian.
1. Your fiery speeches do not frighten me; . . . it is the gods and the enmity of Jupiter that frighten me (Latin); from Virgil's *Aeneid* 12.894–95. Turnus, a warrior abandoned by the gods, is replying to Aeneas, who has taunted him with being afraid.

Two kinds of *dilettanti,* says Goethe, there are in poetry: he who neglects the indispensable mechanical part, and thinks he has done enough if he shows spirituality and feeling; and he who seeks to arrive at poetry merely by mechanism, in which he can acquire an artisan's readiness, and is without soul and matter. And he adds, that the first does most harm to art, and the last to himself. If we must be *dilettanti;* if it is impossible for us, under the circumstances amidst which we live, to think clearly, to feel nobly, and to delineate firmly; if we cannot attain to the mastery of the great artists; let us, at least, have so much respect for our art as to prefer it to ourselves. Let us not bewilder our successors; let us transmit to them the practice of poetry, with its boundaries and wholesome regulative laws, under which excellent works may again, perhaps, at some future time, be produced, not yet fallen into oblivion through our neglect, not yet condemned and canceled by the influence of their eternal enemy, caprice.

From The Function of Criticism at the Present Time[1]

Many objections have been made to a proposition which, in some remarks of mine on translating Homer,[2] I ventured to put forth; a proposition about criticism, and its importance at the present day. I said: "Of the literature of France and Germany, as of the intellect of Europe in general, the main effort, for now many years, has been a critical effort; the endeavor, in all branches of knowledge, theology, philosophy, history, art, science, to see the object as in itself it really is." I added, that owing to the operation in English literature of certain causes, "almost the last thing for which one would come to English literature is just that very thing which now Europe most desires—criticism"; and that the power and value of English literature was thereby impaired. More than one rejoinder declared that the importance I here assigned to criticism was excessive, and asserted the inherent superiority of the creative effort of the human spirit over its critical effort. And the other day, having been led by a Mr. Shairp's excellent notice of Wordsworth[3] to turn again to his biography, I found, in the words of this great man, whom I, for one, must always listen to with the profoundest respect, a sentence passed on the critic's business, which seems to justify every possible disparagement of it. Wordsworth says in one of his letters:

---

1. This essay served as an introduction to *Essays in Criticism* (1865). As a declaration of intentions it can serve as a standard for measuring his total accomplishment in criticism. The essay makes us aware that criticism, for Arnold, meant a great deal more than casual book reviewing or mere censoriousness. He was not a Utilitarian, yet his object in this essay is to show that good criticism is useful. Creative writers, he argues, can profit in a special way from good criticism, but all of us can also derive from it benefits of the greatest value. In particular, we may develop a civilized attitude of mind in which to examine the social, political, aesthetic, and religious problems that confront us.
2. *On Translating Homer* (1861).
3. J. C. Shairp's essay *Wordsworth: The Man and the Poet* was published in 1864. Arnold comments in a footnote:

> I cannot help thinking that a practice, common in England during the last century, and still followed in France, of printing a notice of this kind—a notice by a competent critic—to serve as an introduction to an eminent author's works, might be revived among us with advantage. To introduce all succeeding editions of Wordsworth, Mr. Shairp's notice might, it seems to me, excellently serve; it is written from the point of view of an admirer, nay, of a disciple, and that is right; but then the disciple must be also, as in this case he is, a critic, a man of letters, not, as too often happens, some relation or friend with no qualification for his task except affection for his author.

The writers in these publications (the Reviews), while they prosecute their inglorious employment, cannot be supposed to be in a state of mind very favorable for being affected by the finer influences of a thing so pure as genuine poetry.

And a trustworthy reporter of his conversation quotes a more elaborate judgment to the same effect:

> Wordsworth holds the critical power very low, infinitely lower than the inventive; and he said today that if the quantity of time consumed in writing critiques on the works of others were given to original composition, of whatever kind it might be, it would be much better employed; it would make a man find out sooner his own level, and it would do infinitely less mischief. A false or malicious criticism may do much injury to the minds of others; a stupid invention, either in prose or verse, is quite harmless.

It is almost too much to expect of poor human nature, that a man capable of producing some effect in one line of literature, should, for the greater good of society, voluntarily doom himself to impotence and obscurity in another. Still less is this to be expected from men addicted to the composition of the "false or malicious criticism" of which Wordsworth speaks. However, everybody would admit that a false or malicious criticism had better never have been written. Everybody, too, would be willing to admit, as a general proposition, that the critical faculty is lower than the inventive. But is it true that criticism is really, in itself, a baneful and injurious employment; is it true that all time given to writing critiques on the works of others would be much better employed if it were given to original composition, of whatever kind this may be? Is it true that Johnson had better have gone on producing more Irenes[4] instead of writing his Lives of the Poets; nay, is it certain that Wordsworth himself was better employed in making his Ecclesiastical Sonnets than when he made his celebrated Preface[5] so full of criticism, and criticism of the works of others? Wordsworth was himself a great critic, and it is to be sincerely regretted that he has not left us more criticism; Goethe was one of the greatest of critics, and we may sincerely congratulate ourselves that he has left us so much criticism. Without wasting time over the exaggeration which Wordsworth's judgment on criticism clearly contains, or over an attempt to trace the causes—not difficult, I think, to be traced—which may have led Wordsworth to this exaggeration, a critic may with advantage seize an occasion for trying his own conscience, and for asking himself of what real service, at any given moment, the practice of criticism either is or may be made to his own mind and spirit, and to the minds and spirits of others.

The critical power is of lower rank than the creative. True; but in assenting to this proposition, one or two things are to be kept in mind. It is undeniable that the exercise of a creative power, that a free creative activity, is the highest function of man; it is proved to be so by man's finding in it his true happiness. But it is undeniable, also, that men may have the sense of exer-

---

4. *Irene* is the name of a clumsy play by Samuel Johnson.
5. To *Lyrical Ballads* (1800). "Ecclesiastical Sonnets": a sonnet sequence by Wordsworth, usually regarded as minor verse.

cising this free creative activity in other ways than in producing great works of literature or art; if it were not so, all but a very few men would be shut out from the true happiness of all men. They may have it in well-doing, they may have it in learning, they may have it even in criticizing. This is one thing to be kept in mind. Another is, that the exercise of the creative power in the production of great works of literature or art, however high this exercise of it may rank, is not at all epochs and under all conditions possible; and that therefore labor may be vainly spent in attempting it, which might with more fruit be used in preparing for it, in rendering it possible. This creative power works with elements, with materials; what if it has not those materials, those elements, ready for its use? In that case it must surely wait till they are ready. Now, in literature—I will limit myself to literature, for it is about literature that the question arises—the elements with which the creative power works are ideas; the best ideas on every matter which literature touches, current at the time. At any rate we may lay it down as certain that in modern literature no manifestation of the creative power not working with these can be very important or fruitful. And I say *current* at the time, not merely accessible at the time; for creative literary genius does not principally show itself in discovering new ideas, that is rather the business of the philosopher. The grand work of literary genius is a work of synthesis and exposition, not of analysis and discovery; its gift lies in the faculty of being happily inspired by a certain intellectual and spiritual atmosphere, by a certain order of ideas, when it finds itself in them; of dealing divinely with these ideas, presenting them in the most effective and attractive combinations—making beautiful works with them, in short. But it must have the atmosphere, it must find itself amidst the order of ideas, in order to work freely; and these it is not so easy to command. This is why great creative epochs in literature are so rare, this is why there is so much that is unsatisfactory in the productions of many men of real genius; because, for the creation of a masterwork of literature two powers must concur, the power of the man and the power of the moment, and the man is not enough without the moment; the creative power has, for its happy exercise, appointed elements, and those elements are not in its own control.

Nay, they are more within the control of the critical power. It is the business of the critical power, as I said in the words already quoted, "in all branches of knowledge, theology, philosophy, history, art, science, to see the object as in itself it really is." Thus it tends, at last, to make an intellectual situation of which the creative power can profitably avail itself. It tends to establish an order of ideas, if not absolutely true, yet true by comparison with that which it displaces; to make the best ideas prevail. Presently these new ideas reach society, the touch of truth is the touch of life, and there is a stir and growth everywhere; out of this stir and growth come the creative epochs of literature.

Or, to narrow our range, and quit these considerations of the general march of genius and of society—considerations which are apt to become too abstract and impalpable—everyone can see that a poet, for instance, ought to know life and the world before dealing with them in poetry; and life and the world being in modern times very complex things, the creation of a modern poet, to be worth much, implies a great critical effort behind it; else it must be a comparatively poor, barren, and short-lived affair. This is why Byron's poetry had so little endurance in it, and Goethe's so much; both

Byron and Goethe had a great productive power, but Goethe's was nourished by a great critical effort providing the true materials for it, and Byron's was not; Goethe knew life and the world, the poet's necessary subjects, much more comprehensively and thoroughly than Byron. He knew a great deal more of them, and he knew them much more as they really are.

It has long seemed to me that the burst of creative activity in our literature, through the first quarter of this century, had about it in fact something premature; and that from this cause its productions are doomed, most of them, in spite of the sanguine hopes which accompanied and do still accompany them, to prove hardly more lasting than the productions of far less splendid epochs. And this prematureness comes from its having proceeded without having its proper data, without sufficient materials to work with. In other words, the English poetry of the first quarter of this century, with plenty of energy, plenty of creative force, did not know enough. This makes Byron so empty of matter, Shelley so incoherent, Wordsworth even, profound as he is, yet so wanting in completeness and variety. Wordsworth cared little for books, and disparaged Goethe. I admire Wordsworth, as he is, so much that I cannot wish him different; and it is vain, no doubt, to imagine such a man different from what he is, to suppose that he *could* have been different. But surely the one thing wanting to make Wordsworth an even greater poet than he is—his thought richer, and his influence of wider application—was that he should have read more books, among them, no doubt, those of that Goethe whom he disparaged without reading him.

But to speak of books and reading may easily lead to a misunderstanding here. It was not really books and reading that lacked to our poetry at this epoch: Shelley had plenty of reading, Coleridge had immense reading. Pindar and Sophocles—as we all say so glibly, and often with so little discernment of the real import of what we are saying—had not many books; Shakespeare was no deep reader. True; but in the Greece of Pindar and Sophocles, in the England of Shakespeare, the poet lived in a current of ideas in the highest degree animating and nourishing to the creative power; society was, in the fullest measure, permeated by fresh thought, intelligent and alive. And this state of things is the true basis for the creative power's exercise, in this it finds its data, its materials, truly ready for its hand; all the books and reading in the world are only valuable as they are helps to this. Even when this does not actually exist, books and reading may enable a man to construct a kind of semblance of it in his own mind, a world of knowledge and intelligence in which he may live and work. This is by no means an equivalent to the artist for the nationally diffused life and thought of the epochs of Sophocles or Shakespeare; but, besides that it may be a means of preparation for such epochs, it does really constitute, if many share in it, a quickening and sustaining atmosphere of great value. Such an atmosphere the many-sided learning and the long and widely combined critical effort of Germany formed for Goethe, when he lived and worked. There was no national glow of life and thought there as in the Athens of Pericles[6] or the England of Elizabeth. That was the poet's weakness. But there was a sort of equivalent for it in the complete culture and unfettered thinking of a large body of Germans. That

---

6. The leading statesman of Athens (d. 429 B.C.E.) during a period of the city's most outstanding achievements in art, literature, and politics.

was his strength. In the England of the first quarter of this century there was neither a national glow of life and thought, such as we had in the age of Elizabeth, nor yet a culture and a force of learning and criticism such as were to be found in Germany. Therefore the creative power of poetry wanted, for success in the highest sense, materials and a basis; a thorough interpretation of the world was necessarily denied to it.

At first sight it seems strange that out of the immense stir of the French Revolution and its age should not have come a crop of works of genius equal to that which came out of the stir of the great productive time of Greece, or out of that of the Renascence, with its powerful episode the Reformation. But the truth is that the stir of the French Revolution took a character which essentially distinguished it from such movements as these. These were, in the main, disinterestedly intellectual and spiritual movements; movements in which the human spirit looked for its satisfaction in itself and in the increased play of its own activity. The French Revolution took a political, practical character. The movement, which went on in France under the old *régime*, from 1700 to 1789, was far more really akin than that of the Revolution itself to the movement of the Renascence; the France of Voltaire and Rousseau told far more powerfully upon the mind of Europe than the France of the Revolution. Goethe reproached this last expressly with having "thrown quiet culture back." Nay, and the true key to how much in our Byron, even in our Wordsworth, is this!—that they had their source in a great movement of feeling, not in a great movement of mind. The French Revolution, however— that object of so much blind love and so much blind hatred—found undoubtedly its motive power in the intelligence of men, and not in their practical sense; this is what distinguishes it from the English Revolution of Charles the First's time. This is what makes it a more spiritual event than our Revolution, an event of much more powerful and worldwide interest, though practically less successful; it appeals to an order of ideas which are universal, certain, permanent. 1789 asked of a thing, Is it rational? 1642 asked of a thing, Is it legal? or, when it went furthest, Is it according to conscience? This is the English fashion, a fashion to be treated, within its own sphere, with the highest respect; for its success, within its own sphere, has been prodigious. But what is law in one place is not law in another; what is law here today is not law even here tomorrow; and as for conscience, what is binding on one man's conscience is not binding on another's. The old woman who threw her stool at the head of the surpliced minister in St. Giles's Church at Edinburgh[7] obeyed an impulse to which millions of the human race may be permitted to remain strangers. But the prescriptions of reason are absolute, unchanging, of universal validity; *to count by tens is the easiest way of counting*—that is a proposition of which everyone, from here to the Antipodes, feels the force; at least I should say so if we did not live in a country where it is not impossible that any morning we may find a letter in the *Times* declaring that a decimal coinage is an absurdity.[8] That a whole nation should have been penetrated with an enthusiasm for pure reason, and with an ardent zeal for making its prescriptions triumph, is a very remarkable thing, when we consider how lit-

7. In 1637 rioting broke out in Scotland against a new kind of church service prescribed by Charles I. The riot was started by an old woman hurling a stool at a clergyman.
8. In 1863 a proposal in Parliament to introduce

the French decimal system for weights and measures had provoked articles in the *Times* defending the English system (of ounces and pounds or inches and feet) as more practical.

tle of mind, or anything so worthy and quickening as mind, comes into the motives which alone, in general, impel great masses of men. In spite of the extravagant direction given to this enthusiasm, in spite of the crimes and follies in which it lost itself, the French Revolution derives from the force, truth, and universality of the ideas which it took for its law, and from the passion with which it could inspire a multitude for these ideas, a unique and still living power; it is—it will probably long remain—the greatest, the most animating event in history. And as no sincere passion for the things of the mind, even though it turn out in many respects an unfortunate passion, is ever quite thrown away and quite barren of good, France has reaped from hers one fruit—the natural and legitimate fruit though not precisely the grand fruit she expected: she is the country in Europe where *the people* is most alive.

But the mania for giving an immediate political and practical application to all these fine ideas of the reason was fatal. Here an Englishman is in his element: on this theme we can all go on for hours. And all we are in the habit of saying on it has undoubtedly a great deal of truth. Ideas cannot be too much prized in and for themselves, cannot be too much lived with; but to transport them abruptly into the world of politics and practice, violently to revolutionize this world to their bidding—that is quite another thing. There is the world of ideas and there is the world of practice; the French are often for suppressing the one and the English the other; but neither is to be suppressed. A member of the House of Commons said to me the other day: "That a thing is an anomaly, I consider to be no objection to it whatever." I venture to think he was wrong; that a thing is an anomaly *is* an objection to it, but absolutely and in the sphere of ideas: it is not necessarily, under such and such circumstances, or at such and such a moment, an objection to it in the sphere of politics and practice. Joubert[9] has said beautifully: "*C'est la force et le droit qui règlent toutes choses dans le monde; la force en attendant le droit.*"—"Force and right are the governors of this world; force till right is ready." *Force till right is ready*; and till right is ready, force, the existing order of things, is justified, is the legitimate ruler. But right is something moral, and implies inward recognition, free assent of the will; we are not ready for right—*right*, so far as we are concerned, is *not ready*—until we have attained this sense of seeing it and willing it. The way in which for us it may change and transform force, the existing order of things, and become, in its turn, the legitimate ruler of the world, should depend on the way in which, when our time comes, we see it and will it. Therefore for other people enamored of their own newly discerned right, to attempt to impose it upon us as ours, and violently to substitute their right for our force, is an act of tyranny, and to be resisted. It sets at nought the second great half of our maxim, *force till right is ready*. This was the grand error of the French Revolution; and its movement of ideas, by quitting the intellectual sphere and rushing furiously into the political sphere, ran, indeed a prodigious and memorable course, but produced no such intellectual fruit as the movement of ideas of the Renascence, and created, in opposition to itself, what I may call an *epoch of concentration*. The great force of that epoch of concentration was England; and the great voice of that epoch of concentration was Burke.[1] It is the

9. Joseph Joubert (1754–1824), French moralist about whom Arnold wrote one of his *Essays in Criticism*.
1. Edmund Burke (1729–1797), prominent statesman and author of *Reflections on the French Revolution* (1790), which expressed the conservative opposition to revolutionary theories.

fashion to treat Burke's writings on the French Revolution as superannuated and conquered by the event; as the eloquent but unphilosophical tirades of bigotry and prejudice. I will not deny that they are often disfigured by the violence and passion of the moment, and that in some directions Burke's view was bounded, and his observation therefore at fault. But on the whole, and for those who can make the needful corrections, what distinguishes these writings is their profound, permanent, fruitful, philosophical truth, They contain the true philosophy of an epoch of concentration, dissipate the heavy atmosphere which its own nature is apt to engender round it, and make its resistance rational instead of mechanical.

But Burke is so great because, almost alone in England, he brings thought to bear upon politics, he saturates politics with thought. It is his accident that his ideas were at the service of an epoch of concentration, not of an epoch of expansion; it is his characteristic that he so lived by ideas, and had such a source of them welling up within him, that he could float even an epoch of concentration and English Tory politics with them. It does not hurt him that Dr. Price[2] and the Liberals were enraged with him; it does not even hurt him that George the Third and the Tories were enchanted with him. His greatness is that he lived in a world which neither English Liberalism nor English Toryism is apt to enter—the world of ideas, not the world of catchwords and party habits. So far is it from being really true of him that he "to party gave up what was meant for mankind,"[3] that at the very end of his fierce struggle with the French Revolution, after all his invectives against its false pretensions, hollowness, and madness, with his sincere convictions of its mischievousness, he can close a memorandum on the best means of combating it, some of the last pages he ever wrote[4]—the *Thoughts on French Affairs*, in December 1791—with these striking words:

> The evil is stated, in my opinion, as it exists. The remedy must be where power, wisdom, and information, I hope, are more united with good intentions than they can be with me. I have done with this subject, I believe, forever. It has given me many anxious moments for the last two years. *If a great change is to be made in human affairs, the minds of men will be fitted to it; the general opinions and feelings will draw that way. Every fear, every hope will forward it; and then they who persist in opposing this mighty current in human affairs, will appear rather to resist the decrees of Providence itself, than the mere designs of men. They will not be resolute and firm, but perverse and obstinate.*

That return of Burke upon himself has always seemed to me one of the finest things in English literature, or indeed in any literature. That is what I call living by ideas: when one side of a question has long had your earnest support, when all your feelings are engaged, when you hear all round you no language but one, when your party talks this language like a steam engine and can imagine no other—still to be able to think, still to be irresistibly carried, if so it be, by the current of thought to the opposite side of the

---

2. Richard Price (1723–1791), a prorevolutionary clergyman who was an opponent of Burke's.
3. From Oliver Goldsmith's poem *Retaliation* (1774).
4. Arnold was mistaken; Burke continued to write for another six years after 1791. According to Arnold's editor, R. H. Super, the mistake was caused by misunderstanding a passage in one of Burke's letters.

question, and, like Balaam, to be unable to speak anything *but what the Lord has put in your mouth.*[5] I know nothing more striking, and I must add that I know nothing more un-English.

For the Englishman in general is like my friend the Member of Parliament, and believes, point-blank, that for a thing to be an anomaly is absolutely no objection to it whatever. He is like the Lord Auckland of Burke's day, who, in a memorandum on the French Revolution, talks of certain "miscreants, assuming the name of philosophers, who have presumed themselves capable of establishing a new system of society." The Englishman has been called a political animal, and he values what is political and practical so much that ideas easily become objects of dislike in his eyes, and thinkers, "miscreants," because ideas and thinkers have rashly meddled with politics and practice. This would be all very well if the dislike and neglect confined themselves to ideas transported out of their own sphere, and meddling rashly with practice; but they are inevitably extended to ideas as such, and to the whole life of intelligence; practice is everything, a free play of the mind is nothing. The notion of the free play of the mind upon all subjects being a pleasure in itself, being an object of desire, being an essential provider of elements without which a nation's spirit, whatever compensations it may have for them, must, in the long run, die of inanition, hardly enters into an Englishman's thoughts. It is noticeable that the word *curiosity,* which in other languages is used in a good sense, to mean, as a high and fine quality of man's nature, just this disinterested love of a free play of the mind on all subjects, for its own sake— it is noticeable, I say, that this word has in our language no sense of the kind, no sense but a rather bad and disparaging one. But criticism, real criticism, is essentially the exercise of this very quality. It obeys an instinct prompting it to try to know the best that is known and thought in the world, irrespectively of practice, politics, and everything of the kind; and to value knowledge and thought as they approach this best, without the intrusion of any other considerations whatever. This is an instinct for which there is, I think, little original sympathy in the practical English nature, and what there was of it has undergone a long benumbing period of blight and suppression in the epoch of concentration which followed the French Revolution.

But epochs of concentration cannot well endure forever; epochs of expansion, in the due course of things, follow them. Such an epoch of expansion seems to be opening in this country. In the first place all danger of a hostile forcible pressure of foreign ideas upon our practice has long disappeared; like the traveler in the fable, therefore, we begin to wear our cloak a little more loosely.[6] Then, with a long peace, the ideas of Europe steal gradually and amicably in, and mingle, though in infinitesimally small quantities at a time, with our own notions. Then, too, in spite of all that is said about the absorbing and brutalizing influence of our passionate material progress, it seems to me indisputable that this progress is likely, though not certain, to lead in the end to an apparition of intellectual life; and that man, after he has made himself perfectly comfortable and has now to determine what to do with himself next, may begin to remember that he has a mind, and that the mind may be made the source of great pleasure. I grant it is mainly the

5. Cf. Numbers 22.38.
6. See Aesop's fable of the wind and the sun, in which the wind and the sun compete to see who is more powerful. The sun wins because he causes the traveler to take off his coat, whereas the wind makes him hold it closely.

privilege of faith, at present, to discern this end to our railways, our business, and our fortune-making; but we shall see if, here as elsewhere, faith is not in the end the true prophet. Our ease, our traveling, and our unbounded liberty to hold just as hard and securely as we please to the practice to which our notions have given birth, all tend to beget an inclination to deal a little more freely with these notions themselves, to canvass them a little, to penetrate a little into their real nature. Flutterings of curiosity, in the foreign sense of the word, appear amongst us, and it is in these that criticism must look to find its account. Criticism first; a time of true creative activity, perhaps—which, as I have said, must inevitably be preceded amongst us by a time of criticism—hereafter, when criticism has done its work.

It is of the last importance that English criticism should clearly discern what rule for its course, in order to avail itself of the field now opening to it, and to produce fruit for the future, it ought to take. The rule may be summed up in one word—*disinterestedness*.[7] And how is criticism to show disinterestedness? By keeping aloof from what is called "the practical view of things"; by resolutely following the law of its own nature, which is to be a free play of the mind on all subjects which it touches. By steadily refusing to lend itself to any of those ulterior, political, practical considerations about ideas, which plenty of people will be sure to attach to them, which perhaps ought often to be attached to them, which in this country at any rate are certain to be attached to them quite sufficiently, but which criticism has really nothing to do with. Its business is, as I have said, simply to know the best that is known and thought in the world, and by in its turn making this known, to create a current of true and fresh ideas. Its business is to do this with inflexible honesty, with due ability; but its business is to do no more, and to leave alone all questions of practical consequences and applications, questions which will never fail to have due prominence given to them. Else criticism, besides being really false to its own nature, merely continues in the old rut which it has hitherto followed in this country, and will certainly miss the chance now given to it. For what is at present the bane of criticism in this country? It is that practical considerations cling to it and stifle it. It subserves interests not its own. Our organs of criticism are organs of men and parties having practical ends to serve, and with them those practical ends are the first thing and the play of mind the second; so much play of mind as is compatible with the prosecution of those practical ends is all that is wanted. An organ like the *Revue des Deux Mondes*,[8] having for its main function to understand and utter the best that is known and thought in the world, existing, it may be said, as just an organ for a free play of the mind, we have not. But we have the *Edinburgh Review*, existing as an organ of the old Whigs, and for as much play of mind as may suit its being that; we have the *Quarterly Review*, existing as an organ of the Tories, and for as much play of mind as may suit its being that; we have the *British Quarterly Review*, existing as an organ of the political Dissenters, and for as much play of mind as may suit its being that; we have the *Times*, existing as an organ of the common, satisfied, well-to-do Englishman, and for as much play of mind as may suit its being that. And so on through all the various fractions, political and religious, of our society; every fraction has, as such, its organ of criticism, but the

7. This key word in Arnold's argument connotes independence and objectivity of mind. It means not having an interest, in the sense of an ax to grind. It does not mean lack of interest.
8. An international magazine of exceptionally high quality, founded in Paris in 1829.

notion of combining all fractions in the common pleasure of a free disinterested play of mind meets with no favor. Directly this play of mind wants to have more scope, and to forget the pressure of practical considerations a little, it is checked, it is made to feel the chain. We saw this the other day in the extinction, so much to be regretted, of the *Home and Foreign Review*.[9] Perhaps in no organ of criticism in this country was there so much knowledge, so much play of mind; but these could not save it. The *Dublin Review* subordinates play of mind to the practical business of English and Irish Catholicism, and lives. It must needs be that men should act in sects and parties, that each of these sects and parties should have its organ, and should make this organ subserve the interests of its action; but it would be well, too, that there should be a criticism, not the minister of these interests, not their enemy, but absolutely and entirely independent of them. No other criticism will ever attain any real authority or make any real way towards its end—the creating a current of true and fresh ideas.

It is because criticism has so little kept in the pure intellectual sphere, has so little detached itself from practice, has been so directly polemical and controversial, that it has so ill accomplished, in this country, its best spiritual work, which is to keep man from a self-satisfaction which is retarding and vulgarizing, to lead him towards perfection, by making his mind dwell upon what is excellent in itself, and the absolute beauty and fitness of things. A polemical practical criticism makes men blind even to the ideal imperfection of their practice, makes them willingly assert its ideal perfection, in order the better to secure it against attack; and clearly this is narrowing and baneful for them. If they were reassured on the practical side, speculative considerations of ideal perfection they might be brought to entertain, and their spiritual horizon would thus gradually widen. Sir Charles Adderley[1] says to the Warwickshire farmers:

> Talk of the improvement of breed! Why, the race we ourselves represent, the men and women, the old Anglo-Saxon race, are the best breed in the whole world. . . . The absence of a too enervating climate, too unclouded skies, and a too luxurious nature, has produced so vigorous a race of people, and has rendered us so superior to all the world.

Mr. Roebuck[2] says to the Sheffield cutlers:

> I look around me and ask what is the state of England? Is not property safe? Is not every man able to say what he likes? Can you not walk from one end of England to the other in perfect security? I ask you whether, the world over or in past history, there is anything like it? Nothing. I pray that our unrivaled happiness may last.

Now obviously there is a peril for poor human nature in words and thoughts of such exuberant self-satisfaction, until we find ourselves safe in the streets of the Celestial City.

> *Das wenige verschwindet leicht dem Blicke*
> *Der vorwärts sieht, wie viel noch übrig bleibt—*[3]

9. A liberal Catholic periodical, founded in 1862, which ceased publication in 1864.
1. Conservative politician and wealthy landowner (1814–1905).

2. John Arthur Roebuck (1801–1879), radical politician and representative in Parliament for the industrial city of Sheffield.
3. Goethe's *Iphigenie auf Tauris* 1.2.91–92.

says Goethe; "the little that is done seems nothing when we look forward and see how much we have yet to do." Clearly this is a better line of reflection for weak humanity, so long as it remains on this earthly field of labor and trial.

But neither Sir Charles Adderley nor Mr. Roebuck is by nature inaccessible to considerations of this sort. They only lose sight of them owing to the controversial life we all lead, and the practical form which all speculation takes with us. They have in view opponents whose aim is not ideal, but practical; and in their zeal to uphold their own practice against these innovators, they go so far as even to attribute to this practice an ideal perfection. Somebody has been wanting to introduce a six-pound franchise, or to abolish church-rates,[4] or to collect agricultural statistics by force, or to diminish local self-government. How natural, in reply to such proposals, very likely improper or ill-timed, to go a little beyond the mark and to say stoutly, "Such a race of people as we stand, so superior to all the world! The old Anglo-Saxon race, the best breed in the whole world! I pray that our unrivaled happiness may last! I ask you whether, the world over or in past history, there is anything like it?" And so long as criticism answers this dithyramb by insisting that the old Anglo-Saxon race would be still more superior to all others if it had no church-rates, or that our unrivaled happiness would last yet longer with a six-pound franchise, so long will the strain, "The best breed in the whole world!" swell louder and louder, everything ideal and refining will be lost out of sight, and both the assailed and their critics will remain in a sphere, to say the truth, perfectly unvital, a sphere in which spiritual progression is impossible. But let criticism leave church-rates and the franchise alone, and in the most candid spirit, without a single lurking thought of practical innovation, confront with our dithyramb this paragraph on which I stumbled in a newspaper immediately after reading Mr. Roebuck:

> A shocking child murder has just been committed at Nottingham. A girl named Wragg left the workhouse there on Saturday morning with her young illegitimate child. The child was soon afterwards found dead on Mapperly Hills, having been strangled. Wragg is in custody.

Nothing but that; but, in juxtaposition with the absolute eulogies of Sir Charles Adderley and Mr. Roebuck, how eloquent, how suggestive are those few lines! "Our old Anglo-Saxon breed, the best in the whole world!"—how much that is harsh and ill-favored there is in this best! *Wragg!* If we are to talk of ideal perfection, of "the best in the whole world," has anyone reflected what a touch of grossness in our race, what an original shortcoming in the more delicate spiritual perceptions, is shown by the natural growth amongst us of such hideous names—Higginbottom, Stiggins, Bugg! In Ionia and Attica they were luckier in this respect than "the best race in the world"; by the Ilissus[5] there was no Wragg, poor thing! And "our unrivaled happiness"—what an element of grimness, bareness, and hideousness mixes with it and blurs it; the workhouse, the dismal Mapperly Hills[6]—how dismal those who have seen them will remember—the gloom, the smoke, the cold, the stran-

---

4. Taxes supporting the Church of England. "Six-pound franchise": a radical proposal to extend the right to vote to anyone owning land worth £6 annual rent.

5. A stream in Attica, Greece.
6. Adjacent to the coal-mining and industrial area of Nottingham (later associated with the writings of D. H. Lawrence).

gled illegitimate child! "I ask you whether, the world over or in past history, there is anything like it?" Perhaps not, one is inclined to answer; but at any rate, in that case, the world is very much to be pitied. And the final touch— short, bleak and inhuman: *Wragg is in custody.* The sex lost in the confusion of our unrivaled happiness; or (shall I say?) the superfluous Christian name lopped off by the straightforward vigor of our old Anglo-Saxon breed! There is profit for the spirit in such contrasts as this; criticism serves the cause of perfection by establishing them. By eluding sterile conflict, by refusing to remain in the sphere where alone narrow and relative conceptions have any worth and validity, criticism may diminish its momentary importance, but only in this way has it a chance of gaining admittance for those wider and more perfect conceptions to which all its duty is really owed. Mr. Roebuck will have a poor opinion of an adversary who replies to his defiant songs of triumph only by murmuring under his breath, *Wragg is in custody;* but in no other way will these songs of triumph be induced gradually to moderate themselves, to get rid of what in them is excessive and offensive, and to fall into a softer and truer key.

It will be said that it is a very subtle and indirect action which I am thus prescribing for criticism, and that, by embracing in this manner the Indian virtue of detachment and abandoning the sphere of practical life, it condemns itself to a slow and obscure work. Slow and obscure it may be, but it is the only proper work of criticism. The mass of mankind will never have any ardent zeal for seeing things as they are; very inadequate ideas will always satisfy them. On these inadequate ideas reposes, and must repose, the general practice of the world. That is as much as saying that whoever sets himself to see things as they are will find himself one of a very small circle; but it is only by this small circle resolutely doing its own work that adequate ideas will ever get current at all. The rush and roar of practical life will always have a dizzying and attracting effect upon the most collected spectator, and tend to draw him into its vortex; most of all will this be the case where that life is so powerful as it is in England. But it is only by remaining collected, and refusing to lend himself to the point of view of the practical man, that the critic can do the practical man any service, and it is only by the greatest sincerity in pursuing his own course, and by at last convincing even the practical man of his sincerity, that he can escape misunderstandings which perpetually threaten him.

For the practical man is not apt for fine distinctions, and yet in these distinctions truth and the highest culture greatly find their account. But it is not easy to lead a practical man—unless you reassure him as to your practical intentions, you have no chance of leading him—to see that a thing which he has always been used to look at from one side only, which he greatly values, and which, looked at from that side, quite deserves, perhaps, all the prizing and admiring which he bestows upon it—that this thing, looked at from another side, may appear much less beneficent and beautiful, and yet retain all its claims to our practical allegiance. Where shall we find language innocent enough, how shall we make the spotless purity of our intentions evident enough, to enable us to say to the political Englishman that the British Constitution itself, which, seen from the practical side, looks such a magnificent organ of progress and virtue, seen from the speculative side— with its compromises, its love of facts, its horror of theory, its studied avoidance of clear thoughts—that, seen from this side, our august Constitution sometimes looks—forgive me, shade of Lord Somers!—a colossal machine for the manufacture of Philistines?[7] How is Cobbett[8] to say this and not be misunderstood, blackened as he is with the smoke of a lifelong conflict in the field of political practice? how is Mr. Carlyle to say it and not be misunderstood, after his furious raid into this field with his *Latter-day Pamphlets?* how is Mr. Ruskin, after his pugnacious political economy?[9] I say, the critic must keep out of the region of immediate practice in the political, social, humanitarian sphere if he wants to make a beginning for that more free speculative treatment of things, which may perhaps one day make its benefits felt even in this sphere, but in a natural and thence irresistible manner.

*　*　*

If I have insisted so much on the course which criticism must take where politics and religion are concerned, it is because, where these burning matters are in question, it is most likely to go astray. I have wished, above all, to insist on the attitude which criticism should adopt towards things in general; on its right tone and temper of mind. But then comes another question as to the subject matter which literary criticism should most seek. Here, in general, its course is determined for it by the idea which is the law of its being; the idea of a disinterested endeavor to learn and propagate the best that is known and thought in the world, and thus to establish a current of fresh and true ideas. By the very nature of things, as England is not all the world, much of the best that is known and thought in the world cannot be of English growth, must be foreign; by the nature of things, again, it is just this that we are least likely to know, while English thought is streaming in upon us from all sides, and takes excellent care that we shall not be ignorant of its existence. The English critic of literature, therefore, must dwell much on foreign thought, and with particular heed on any part of it, which, while significant and fruitful in itself, is for any reason specially likely to escape him. Again, judging is often spoken of as the critic's one business, and so in some sense it is; but the judgment which almost insensibly forms itself in a fair and clear mind, along with fresh knowledge, is the valuable one; and thus knowledge, and ever fresh knowledge, must be the critic's great concern for himself. And it is by communicating fresh knowledge, and letting his own judgment pass along with it—but insensibly, and in the second place, not the first, as a sort of companion and clue, not as an abstract lawgiver—that the critic will generally do most good to his readers. Sometimes, no doubt, for the sake of establishing an author's place in literature, and his relation to a central standard (and if this is not done, how are we to get at our *best in the world?*) criticism may have to deal with a subject matter so familiar that fresh knowledge is out of the question, and then it must be all judgment; an enunciation and detailed application of principles. Here the great safe-

---

7. The unenlightened middle classes, whose opposition to the defenders of culture is parallel to the biblical tribe that fought against the people of Israel, "the children of light." Arnold's repeated use of this parallel has established the term in our language. John Somers (1651–1716), statesman responsible for formulating the Declaration of Rights.

8. William Cobbett (1762–1835), vehement reformer whose political position anticipated that of Dickens.

9. Reference to *Unto This Last* (1862), in which Ruskin shifted from art criticism to an attack on traditional theories of economics.

guard is never to let oneself become abstract, always to retain an intimate and lively consciousness of the truth of what one is saying, and, the moment this fails us, to be sure that something is wrong. Still under all circumstances, this mere judgment and application of principles is, in itself, not the most satisfactory work to the critic; like mathematics, it is tautological, and cannot well give us, like fresh learning, the sense of creative activity.

But stop, some one will say; all this talk is of no practical use to us whatever; this criticism of yours is not what we have in our minds when we speak of criticism; when we speak of critics and criticism, we mean critics and criticism of the current English literature of the day; when you offer to tell criticism its function, it is to this criticism that we expect you to address yourself. I am sorry for it, for I am afraid I must disappoint these expectations. I am bound by my own definition of criticism: *a disinterested endeavor to learn and propagate the best that is known and thought in the world.* How much of current English literature comes into this "best that is known and thought in the world"? Not very much I fear; certainly less, at this moment, than of the current literature of France or Germany. Well, then, am I to alter my definition of criticism, in order to meet the requirements of a number of practicing English critics, who, after all, are free in their choice of a business? That would be making criticism lend itself just to one of those alien practical considerations, which, I have said, are so fatal to it. One may say, indeed, to those who have to deal with the mass—so much better disregarded—of current English literature, that they may at all events endeavor, in dealing with this, to try it, so far as they can, by the standard of the best that is known and thought in the world; one may say, that to get anywhere near this standard, every critic should try and possess one great literature, at least, besides his own; and the more unlike his own, the better. But, after all, the criticism I am really concerned with—the criticism which alone can much help us for the future, the criticism which, throughout Europe, is at the present day meant, when so much stress is laid on the importance of criticism and the critical spirit—is a criticism which regards Europe as being, for intellectual and spiritual purposes, one great confederation, bound to a joint action and working to a common result, and whose members have, for their proper outfit, a knowledge of Greek, Roman, and Eastern antiquity, and of one another. Special, local, and temporary advantages being put out of account, that modern nation will in the intellectual and spiritual sphere make most progress, which most thoroughly carries out this program. And what is that but saying that we too, all of us, as individuals, the more thoroughly we carry it out, shall make the more progress?

There is so much inviting us!—what are we to take? what will nourish us in growth towards perfection? That is the question which, with the immense field of life and of literature lying before him, the critic has to answer; for himself first, and afterwards for others. In this idea of the critic's business the essays brought together in the following pages have had their origin; in this idea, widely different as are their subjects, they have, perhaps, their unity.

I conclude with what I said at the beginning: to have the sense of creative activity is the great happiness and the great proof of being alive, and it is not denied to criticism to have it; but then criticism must be sincere, simple, flexible, ardent, ever widening its knowledge. Then it may have, in no contemptible measure, a joyful sense of creative activity; a sense which a man of insight and conscience will prefer to what he might derive from a poor, starved, fragmentary, inadequate creation. And at some epochs no other creation is possible.

Still, in full measure, the sense of creative activity belongs only to genuine creation; in literature we must never forget that. But what true man of letters ever can forget it? It is no such common matter for a gifted nature to come into possession of a current of true and living ideas, and to produce amidst the inspiration of them, that we are likely to underrate it. The epochs of Aeschylus and Shakespeare make us feel their pre-eminence. In an epoch like those is, no doubt, the true life of literature; there is the promised land, towards which criticism can only beckon. That promised land it will not be ours to enter, and we shall die in the wilderness: but to have desired to enter it, to have saluted it from afar, is already, perhaps, the best distinction among contemporaries; it will certainly be the best title to esteem with posterity.

1864, 1865

From Culture and Anarchy[1]

From Chapter 1. Sweetness and Light

The impulse of the English race towards moral development and self-conquest has nowhere so powerfully manifested itself as in Puritanism. Nowhere has Puritanism found so adequate an expression as in the religious organization of the Independents.[2] The modern Independents have a newspaper, the *Nonconformist*, written with great sincerity and ability. The motto, the standard, the profession of faith which this organ of theirs carries aloft, is: "The Dissidence of Dissent and the Protestantism of the Protestant religion." There is sweetness and light, and an ideal of complete harmonious human perfection! One need not go to culture and poetry to find language to judge it. Religion, with its instinct for perfection, supplies language to judge it, language, too, which is in our mouths every day. "Finally, be of one mind, united in feeling," says St. Peter.[3] There is an ideal which judges the Puritan ideal: "The Dissidence of Dissent and the Protestantism of the Protestant religion!" And religious organizations like this are what people believe

---

1. Arnold began *Culture and Anarchy* in the context of the turbulent political debate that preceded the passage of the second Reform Bill in 1867. The political climate seemed to some to threaten anarchy, to which Arnold opposed culture. A characteristic quality of the cultured state of mind is summed up, for his purposes, in his formula "sweetness and light," a phrase suggesting reasonableness of temper and intellectual insight. Arnold derived the phrase from a fable contrasting the spider with the bee in Swift's *Battle of the Books*. The spider (representing a narrow, self-centered, and uncultured mind) spins out of itself "nothing at all but flybane and cobweb." The bee (representing a cultured mind that has drawn nourishment from the humanist tradition) ranges far and wide and brings to its hive honey and also wax out of which candles may be made. Therefore, the bee, Swift says, furnishes humankind "with the two noblest

of things, which are sweetness and light."
The selections printed here illustrate aspects of Arnold's indictment of the middle classes for their lack of sweetness and light. The first and third expose the narrowness and dullness of middle-class Puritan religious institutions in both the 17th and 19th centuries. The second, *Doing As One Likes*, shows the limitations of the middle-class political bias and the irresponsibility of laissez-faire. Here Arnold is most close to Carlyle and Ruskin. These three extracts indicate why it has been said that Matthew Arnold discovered the foibles of Main Street fifty years before Sinclair Lewis exposed them in his novels of American life.
2. A 17th-century Puritan group (of which Cromwell was an adherent), allied with the Congregationalists.
3. Cf. 1 Peter 3.8.

in, rest in, would give their lives for! Such, I say, is the wonderful virtue of even the beginnings of perfection, of having conquered even the plain faults of our animality, that the religious organization which has helped us to do it can seem to us something precious, salutary, and to be propagated, even when it wears such a brand of imperfection on its forehead as this. And men have got such a habit of giving to the language of religion a special application, of making it a mere jargon, that for the condemnation which religion itself passes on the shortcomings of their religious organizations they have no ear; they are sure to cheat themselves and to explain this condemnation away. They can only be reached by the criticism which culture, like poetry, speaking of language not to be sophisticated, and resolutely testing these organizations by the ideal of a human perfection complete on all sides, applies to them.

But men of culture and poetry, it will be said, are again and again failing, and failing conspicuously, in the necessary first stage to a harmonious perfection, in the subduing of the great obvious faults of our animality, which it is the glory of these religious organizations to have helped us to subdue. True, they do often so fail. They have often been without the virtues as well as the faults of the Puritan; it has been one of their dangers that they so felt the Puritan's faults that they too much neglected the practice of his virtues. I will not, however, exculpate them at the Puritan's expense. They have often failed in morality, and morality is indispensable. And they have been punished for their failure, as the Puritan has been rewarded for his performance. They have been punished wherein they erred; but their ideal of beauty, of sweetness and light, and a human nature complete on all its sides, remains the true ideal of perfection still; just as the Puritan's ideal of perfection remains narrow and inadequate, although for what he did well he has been richly rewarded. Notwithstanding the mighty results of the Pilgrim Fathers' voyage, they and their standard of perfection are rightly judged when we figure to ourselves Shakespeare or Virgil—souls in whom sweetness and light, and all that in human nature is most humane, were eminent—accompanying them on their voyage, and think what intolerable company Shakespeare and Virgil would have found them! In the same way let us judge the religious organizations which we see all around us. Do not let us deny the good and the happiness which they have accomplished; but do not let us fail to see clearly that their idea of human perfection is narrow and inadequate, and that the Dissidence of Dissent and the Protestantism of the Protestant religion will never bring humanity to its true goal. As I said with regard to wealth: Let us look at the life of those who live in and for it—so I say with regard to the religious organizations. Look at the life imaged in such a newspaper as the *Nonconformist*—a life of jealousy of the Establishment,[4] disputes, tea-meetings, openings of chapels, sermons; and then think of it as an ideal of a human life completing itself on all sides, and aspiring with all its organs after sweetness, light, and perfection!

4. The Church of England or the Established Church.

From *Chapter 2. Doing As One Likes*

* * *

When I began to speak of culture, I insisted on our bondage to machinery, on our proneness to value machinery as an end in itself, without looking beyond it to the end for which alone, in truth, it is valuable. Freedom, I said, was one of those things which we thus worshiped in itself, without enough regarding the ends for which freedom is to be desired. In our common notions and talk about freedom, we eminently show our idolatry of machinery. Our prevalent notion is—and I quoted a number of instances to prove it—that it is a most happy and important thing for a man merely to be able to do as he likes. On what he is to do when he is thus free to do as he likes, we do not lay so much stress. Our familiar praise of the British Constitution under which we live, is that it is a system of checks—a system which stops and paralyzes any power in interfering with the free action of individuals. To this effect Mr. Bright,[5] who loves to walk in the old ways of the Constitution, said forcibly in one of his great speeches, what many other people are every day saying less forcibly, that the central idea of English life and politics is *the assertion of personal liberty.* Evidently this is so; but evidently, also, as feudalism, which with its ideas, and habits of subordination was for many centuries silently behind the British Constitution, dies out, and we are left with nothing but our system of checks, and our notion of its being the great right and happiness of an Englishman to do as far as possible what he likes, we are in danger of drifting towards anarchy. We have not the notion, so familiar on the Continent and to antiquity, of *the State*—the nation in its collective and corporate character, entrusted with stringent powers for the general advantage, and controlling individual wills in the name of an interest wider than that of individuals. We say, what is very true, that this notion is often made instrumental to tyranny; we say that a State is in reality made up of the individuals who compose it, and that every individual is the best judge of his own interests. Our leading class is an aristocracy, and no aristocracy likes the notion of a State-authority greater than itself, with a stringent administrative machinery superseding the decorative inutilities of lord-lieutenancy, deputy-lieutenancy, and the *posse comitatus,*[6] which are all in its own hands. Our middle class, the great representative of trade and Dissent, with its maxims of every man for himself in business, every man for himself in religion, dreads a powerful administration which might somehow interfere with it; and besides, it has its own decorative inutilities of vestry-manship and guardianship, which are to this class what lord-lieutenancy and the county magistracy are to the aristocratic class, and a stringent administration might either take these functions out of its hands, or prevent its exercising them in its own comfortable, independent manner, as at present.

Then as to our working class. This class, pressed constantly by the hard daily compulsion of material wants, is naturally the very center and stronghold of our national idea, that it is man's ideal right and felicity to do as he likes. I think I have somewhere related how M. Michelet[7] said to me of the

5. John Bright (19th century), orator and reformer.
6. Power of the county (Latin); a feudal method of enforcing law by local authorities instead of by agencies of the central government.
7. Jules Michelet (1798–1874), French historian.

people of France, that it was "a nation of barbarians civilized by the conscription." He meant that through their military service the idea of public
duty and of discipline was brought to the mind of these masses, in other
respects so raw and uncultivated. Our masses are quite as raw and uncultivated as the French; and so far from their having the idea of public duty and
of discipline, superior to the individual's self-will, brought to their mind by
a universal obligation of military service, such as that of the conscription—
so far from their having this, the very idea of a conscription is so at variance
with our English notion of the prime right and blessedness of doing as one
likes, that I remember the manager of the Clay Cross works in Derbyshire
told me during the Crimean war, when our want of soldiers was much felt
and some people were talking of a conscription, that sooner than submit to
a conscription the population of that district would flee to the mines, and
lead a sort of Robin Hood life underground.

For a long time, as I have said, the strong feudal habits of subordination
and deference continued to tell upon the working class. The modern spirit
has now almost entirely dissolved those habits, and the anarchical tendency
of our worship of freedom in and for itself, of our superstitious faith, as I
say, in machinery, is becoming very manifest. More and more, because of
this our blind faith in machinery, because of our want of light to enable us
to look beyond machinery to the end for which machinery is valuable, this
and that man, and this and that body of men, all over the country, are beginning to assert and put in practice an Englishman's right to do what he likes;
his right to march where he likes, meet where he likes, enter where he likes,
hoot as he likes, threaten as he likes, smash as he likes.[8] All this, I say, tends
to anarchy; and though a number of excellent people, and particularly my
friends of the Liberal or progressive party, as they call themselves, are kind
enough to reassure us by saying that these are trifles, that a few transient
outbreaks of rowdyism signify nothing, that our system of liberty is one which
itself cures all the evils which it works, that the educated and intelligent
classes stand in overwhelming strength and majestic repose, ready, like our
military force in riots, to act at a moment's notice—yet one finds that one's
Liberal friends generally say this because they have such faith in themselves
and their nostrums, when they shall return, as the public welfare requires,
to place and power. But this faith of theirs one cannot exactly share, when
one has so long had them and their nostrums at work, and see that they have
not prevented our coming to our present embarrassed condition. And one
finds, also, that the outbreaks of rowdyism tend to become less and less of
trifles, to become more frequent rather than less frequent; and that meanwhile our educated and intelligent classes remain in their majestic repose,
and somehow or other, whatever happens, their overwhelming strength, like
our military force in riots, never does act.

How indeed, *should* their overwhelming strength act, when the man who
gives an inflammatory lecture, or breaks down the park railings, or invades
a Secretary of State's office, is only following an Englishman's impulse to do
as he likes; and our own conscience tells us that we ourselves have always
regarded this impulse as something primary and sacred? Mr. Murphy[9] lec-

---

8. A reference to the riots of 1866 in which a London mob demolished the iron railings enclosing
Hyde Park.

9. An orator whose inflammatory anti-Catholic
public speech *The Errors of the Roman Church* led
to rioting in Birmingham and other cities in 1867.

tures at Birmingham, and showers on the Catholic population of that town "words," says the Home Secretary, "only fit to be addressed to thieves or murderers." What then? Mr. Murphy has his own reasons of several kinds. He suspects the Roman Catholic Church of designs upon Mrs. Murphy; and he says if mayors and magistrates do not care for their wives and daughters, he does. But, above all, he is doing as he likes; or, in worthier language, asserting his personal liberty. "I will carry out my lectures if they walk over my body as a dead corpse, and I say to the Mayor of Birmingham that he is my servant while I am in Birmingham, and as my servant he must do his duty and protect me." Touching and beautiful words, which find a sympathetic chord in every British bosom! The moment it is plainly put before us that a man is asserting his personal liberty, we are half disarmed; because we are believers in freedom, and not in some dream of a right reason to which the assertion of our freedom is to be subordinated. Accordingly, the Secretary of State had to say that although the lecturer's language was "only fit to be addressed to thieves or murderers," yet, "I do not think he is to be deprived, I do not think that anything I have said could justify the inference that he is to be deprived, of the right of protection in a place built by him for the purpose of these lectures; because the language was not language which afforded grounds for a criminal prosecution." No, nor to be silenced by Mayor, or Home Secretary, or any administrative authority on earth, simply on their notion of what is discreet and reasonable! This is in perfect consonance with our public opinion, and with our national love for the assertion of personal liberty.

* * *

From *Chapter* 5. Porro Unum Est Necessarium[1]

* * *

* * * Sweetness and light evidently have to do with the bent or side in humanity which we call Hellenic. Greek intelligence has obviously for its essence the instinct for what Plato calls the true, firm, intelligible law of things; the law of light, of seeing things as they are. Even in the natural sciences, where the Greeks had not time and means adequately to apply this instinct, and where we have gone a great deal further than they did, it is this instinct which is the root of the whole matter and the ground of all our success; and this instinct the world has mainly learnt of the Greeks, inasmuch as they are humanity's most signal manifestation of it. Greek art, again, Greek beauty, have their root in the same impulse to see things as they really are, inasmuch as Greek art and beauty rest on fidelity to nature—the *best* nature—and on a delicate discrimination of what this best nature is. To say we work for sweetness and light, then, is only another way of saying that we work for Hellenism. But, oh! cry many people, sweetness and light are not enough; you must put strength or energy along with them, and make a kind of trinity of strength, sweetness and light, and then, perhaps, you may do some good. That is to say, we are to join Hebraism, strictness of the moral

1. But one thing is needful (Latin; Luke 10.42). This chapter develops a contrast established in chap. 4 between *Hebraism* (Puritan morality and energetic devotion to work) and *Hellenism* (culti- vation of the aesthetic and intellectual understanding of life). The Puritan middle classes, according to Arnold, think that the "one thing needful" is the Hebraic form of virtue.

conscience, and manful walking by the best light we have, together with Hellenism, inculcate both, and rehearse the praises of both.

Or, rather, we may praise both in conjunction, but we must be careful to praise Hebraism most. "Culture," says an acute, though somewhat rigid critic, Mr. Sidgwick,[2] "diffuses sweetness and light. I do not undervalue these blessings, but religion gives fire and strength, and the world wants fire and strength even more than sweetness and light." By religion, let me explain, Mr. Sidgwick here means particularly that Puritanism on the insufficiency of which I have been commenting and to which he says I am unfair. Now, no doubt, it is possible to be a fanatical partisan of light and the instincts which push us to it, a fanatical enemy of strictness of moral conscience and the instincts which push us to it. A fanaticism of this sort deforms and vulgarizes the well-known work, in some respects so remarkable, of the late Mr. Buckle.[3] Such a fanaticism carries its own mark with it, in lacking sweetness; and its own penalty, in that, lacking sweetness, it comes in the end to lack light too. And the Greeks—the great exponents of humanity's bent for sweetness and light united, of its perception that the truth of things must be at the same time beauty—singularly escaped the fanaticism which we moderns, whether we Hellenize or whether we Hebraize, are so apt to show. They arrived—though failing, as has been said, to give adequate practical satisfaction to the claims of man's moral side—at the idea of a comprehensive adjustment of the claims of both the sides in man, the moral as well as the intellectual, of a full estimate of both, and of a reconciliation of both; an idea which is philosophically of the greatest value, and the best of lessons for us moderns. So we ought to have no difficulty in conceding to Mr. Sidgwick that manful walking by the best light one has—fire and strength as he calls it—has its high value as well as culture, the endeavor to see things in their truth and beauty, the pursuit of sweetness and light. But whether at this or that time, and to this or that set of persons, one ought to insist most on the praises of fire and strength, or on the praises of sweetness and light, must depend, one would think, on the circumstances and needs of that particular time and those particular persons. And all that we have been saying, and indeed any glance at the world around us, shows that with us, with the most respectable and strongest part of us, the ruling force is now, and long has been, a Puritan force—the care for fire and strength, strictness of conscience, Hebraism, rather than the care for sweetness and light, spontaneity of consciousness, Hellenism.

Well, then, what is the good of our now rehearsing the praises of fire and strength to ourselves, who dwell too exclusively on them already? When Mr. Sidgwick says so broadly, that the world wants fire and strength even more than sweetness and light, is he not carried away by a turn for broad generalization? does he not forget that the world is not all of one piece, and every piece with the same needs at the same time? It may be true that the Roman world at the beginning of our era, or Leo the Tenth's Court at the time of the Reformation, or French society in the eighteenth century,[4] needed fire

2. Henry Sidgwick (1838–1900), philosopher, whose article on Arnold appeared in *Macmillan's Magazine* (Aug. 1867).
3. Henry Thomas Buckle (1821–1862), author of *A History of Civilization*.

4. Societies representing an excess of sophisticated worldliness as at the courts of such a Roman emperor as Nero (54–68 C.E.) or Pope Leo X (1513–1521) or Louis XV (1715–1774), respectively.

and strength even more than sweetness and light. But can it be said that the Barbarians who overran the empire needed fire and strength even more than sweetness and light; or that the Puritans needed them more; or that Mr. Murphy, the Birmingham lecturer, and the Rev. W. Cattle[5] and his friends, need them more?

The Puritan's great danger is that he imagines himself in possession of a rule telling him the *unum necessarium,* or one thing needful, and that he then remains satisfied with a very crude conception of what this rule really is and what it tells him, thinks he has now knowledge and henceforth needs only to act, and, in this dangerous state of assurance and self-satisfaction, proceeds to give full swing to a number of the instincts of his ordinary self. Some of the instincts of his ordinary self he has, by the help of his rule of life, conquered; but others which he has not conquered by this help he is so far from perceiving to need subjugation, and to be instincts of an inferior self, that he even fancies it to be his right and duty, in virtue of having conquered a limited part of himself, to give unchecked swing to the remainder. He is, I say, a victim of Hebraism, of the tendency to cultivate strictness of conscience rather than spontaneity of consciousness. And what he wants is a larger conception of human nature, showing him the number of other points at which his nature must come to its best, besides the points which he himself knows and thinks of. There is no *unum necessarium,* or one thing needful, which can free human nature from the obligation of trying to come to its best at all these points. The real *unum necessarium* for us is to come to our best at all points. Instead of our "one thing needful," justifying in us vulgarity, hideousness, ignorance, violence—our vulgarity, hideousness, ignorance, violence, are really so many touchstones which try our one thing needful, and which prove that in the state, at any rate, in which we ourselves have it, it is not all we want. And as the force which encourages us to stand staunch and fast by the rule and ground we have is Hebraism, so the force which encourages us to go back upon this rule, and to try the very ground on which we appear to stand, is Hellenism—a turn for giving our consciousness free play and enlarging its range. And what I say is, not that Hellenism is always for everybody more wanted than Hebraism, but that for the Rev. W. Cattle at this particular moment, and for the great majority of us his fellow countrymen, it is more wanted.

*   *   *

1868, 1869

From The Study of Poetry[1]

"The future of poetry is immense, because in poetry, where it is worthy of its high destinies, our race, as time goes on, will find an ever surer

---

5. A Nonconformist clergyman who was chairman of the anti-Catholic meeting addressed by Murphy in 1867 (see *Chapter 2. Doing As One Likes,* p. 1530).
1. Aside from its vindication of the importance of literature, this essay is an interesting example of the variety of Arnold's own reading. To know literature in only one language seemed to him not to know literature. His personal *Notebooks* show that throughout his active life he continued to read books in French, German, Italian, Latin, and Greek. His favorite authors in these languages are used by him as a means of testing English poetry.

The testing is sometimes a severe one. Readers may also protest that despite Arnold's own wit, his essay is limited by an incomplete recognition of the values of comic literature, a shortcoming abundantly evident in the discussion of Chaucer. Nevertheless, whether we agree or disagree with some of Arnold's verdicts, we can be attracted by the combination of traditionalism and impressionism on which these verdicts are based, and we can enjoy the memorable phrasemaking in which the verdicts are expressed. *The Study of Poetry* has been extraordinarily potent in shaping literary tastes in England and in America.

and surer stay. There is not a creed which is not shaken, not an accredited dogma which is not shown to be questionable, not a received tradition which does not threaten to dissolve. Our religion has materialized itself in the fact, in the supposed fact; it has attached its emotion to the fact, and now the fact is failing it. But for poetry the idea is everything; the rest is a world of illusion, of divine illusion. Poetry attaches its emotion to the idea; the idea *is* the fact. The strongest part of our religion today is its unconscious poetry."

Let me be permitted to quote these words of my own, as uttering the thought which should, in my opinion, go with us and govern us in all our study of poetry. In the present work[2] it is the course of one great contributory stream to the world-river of poetry that we are invited to follow. We are here invited to trace the stream of English poetry. But whether we set ourselves, as here, to follow only one of the several streams that make the mighty river of poetry, or whether we seek to know them all, our governing thought should be the same. We should conceive of poetry worthily, and more highly than it has been the custom to conceive of it. We should conceive of it as capable of higher uses, and called to higher destinies, than those which in general men have assigned to it hitherto. More and more mankind will discover that we have to turn to poetry to interpret life for us, to console us, to sustain us. Without poetry, our science will appear incomplete; and most of what now passes with us for religion and philosophy will be replaced by poetry. Science, I say, will appear incomplete without it. For finely and truly does Wordsworth call poetry "the impassioned expression which is in the countenance of all science";[3] and what is a countenance without its expression? Again, Wordsworth finely and truly calls poetry "the breath and finer spirit of all knowledge": our religion, parading evidences such as those on which the popular mind relies now; our philosophy, pluming itself on its reasonings about causation and finite and infinite being; what are they but the shadows and dreams and false shows of knowledge? The day will come when we shall wonder at ourselves for having trusted to them, for having taken them seriously; and the more we perceive their hollowness, the more we shall prize "the breath and finer spirit of knowledge" offered to us by poetry.

But if we conceive thus highly of the destinies of poetry, we must also set our standared for poetry high, since poetry, to be capable of fulfilling such high destinies, must be poetry of a high order of excellence. We must accustom ourselves to a high standard and to a strict judgment. * * *

The best poetry is what we want; the best poetry will be found to have a power of forming, sustaining, and delighting us, as nothing else can. A clearer, deeper sense of the best in poetry, and of the strength and joy to be drawn from it, is the most precious benefit which we can gather from a poetical collection such as the present. And yet in the very nature and conduct of such a collection there is inevitably something which tends to obscure in us the consciousness of what our benefit should be, and to distract us from the pursuit of it. We should therefore steadily set it before our minds at the outset, and should compel ourselves to revert constantly to the thought of it as we proceed.

Yes; constantly in reading poetry, a sense for the best, the really excellent,

2. An anthology of English poetry for which this essay served as the introduction.

3. Preface to *Lyrical Ballads.*

and of the strength and joy to be drawn from it, should be present in our minds and should govern our estimate of what we read. But this real estimate, the only true one, is liable to be superseded, if we are not watchful, by two other kinds of estimate, the historic estimate and the personal estimate, both of which are fallacious. A poet or a poem may count to us historically, they may count to us on grounds personal to ourselves, and they may count to us really. They may count to us historically. The course of development of a nation's language, thought, and poetry, is profoundly interesting; and by regarding a poet's work as a stage in this course of development we may easily bring ourselves to make it of more importance as poetry than in itself it really is, we may come to use a language of quite exaggerated praise in criticizing it; in short, to overrate it. So arises in our poetic judgments the fallacy caused by the estimate which we may call historic. Then, again, a poet or a poem may count to us on grounds personal to ourselves. Our personal affinities, likings, and circumstances, have great power to sway our estimate of this or that poet's work, and to make us attach more importance to it as poetry than in itself it really possesses, because to us it is, or has been, of high importance. Here also we overrate the object of our interest, and apply to it a language of praise which is quite exaggerated. And thus we get the source of a second fallacy in our poetic judgments—the fallacy caused by an estimate which we may call personal.

* * *

* * * The historic estimate is likely in especial to affect our judgment and our language when we are dealing with ancient poets; the personal estimate when we are dealing with poets our contemporaries, or at any rate modern. The exaggerations due to the historic estimate are not in themselves, perhaps, of very much gravity. Their report hardly enters the general ear; probably they do not always impose even on the literary men who adopt them. But they lead to a dangerous abuse of language. So we hear Caedmon,[4] amongst our own poets, compared to Milton. I have already noticed the enthusiasm of one accomplished French critic for "historic origins."[5] Another eminent French critic, M. Vitet, comments upon that famous document of the early poetry of his nation, the *Chanson de Roland*.[6] It is indeed a most interesting document. The *joculator* or *jongleur*[7] Taillefer, who was with William the Conqueror's army at Hastings, marched before the Norman troops, so said the tradition, singing "of Charlemagne and of Roland and of Oliver, and of the vassals who died at Roncevaux"; and it is suggested that in the *Chanson de Roland* by one Turoldus or *Theroulde*, a poem preserved in a manuscript of the twelfth century in the Bodleian Library at Oxford, we have certainly the matter, perhaps even some of the words, of the chant which Taillefer sang. The poem has vigor and freshness; it is not without pathos. But M. Vitet is not satisfied with seeing in it a document of some poetic value, and of very high historic and linguistic value; he sees in it a grand and beautiful work, a monument of epic genius. In its general design he finds the grandiose conception, in its details he finds the constant union

4. A 7th-century Old English poet.
5. Charles d'Héricault, a critic cited earlier in a passage omitted here. Arnold had mildly reprimanded him for his "historical" bias in praising a 15th-century poet, Clement Marot, at the expense of such classical 17th-century poets as Racine.

6. An 11th-century epic poem in Old French that tells of the wars of Charlemagne against the Moors in Spain and of the bravery of the French leaders Roland and Oliver.
7. Minstrel.

of simplicity with greatness, which are the marks, he truly says, of the genuine epic, and distinguish it from the artificial epic of literary ages. One thinks of Homer; this is the sort of praise which is given to Homer, and justly given. Higher praise there cannot well be, and it is the praise due to epic poetry of the highest order only, and to no other. Let us try, then, the *Chanson de Roland* at its best. Roland, mortally wounded, lays himself down under a pine tree, with his face turned towards Spain and the enemy—

> *De plusurs choses à remembrer li prist,*
> *De tantes teres cume li bers cunquist,*
> *De dulce France, des humes de sun lign,*
> *De Carlemagne sun seignor ki l'nurrit.*[8]

That is primitive work, I repeat, with an undeniable poetic quality of its own. It deserves such praise, and such praise is sufficient for it. But now turn to Homer—

> Ὡς φάτο τοὺς δ' ἤδη κάτεχεν φυσίζοος αἶα
> ἐν Λακεδαίμονι αὖθι, φίλῃ ἐν πατρίδι γαίῃ.[9]

We are here in another world, another order of poetry altogether; here is rightly due such supreme praise as that which M. Vitet gives to the *Chanson de Roland*. If our words are to have any meaning, if our judgments are to have any solidity, we must not heap that supreme praise upon poetry of an order immeasurably inferior.

Indeed there can be no more useful help for discovering what poetry belongs to the class of the truly excellent, and can therefore do us most good, than to have always in one's mind lines and expressions of the great masters, and to apply them as a touchstone to other poetry. Of course we are not to require this other poetry to resemble them; it may be very dissimilar. But if we have any tact we shall find them, when we have lodged them well in our minds, an infallible touchstone for detecting the presence or absence of high poetic quality, and also the degree of this quality, in all other poetry which we may place beside them. Short passages, even single lines, will serve our turn quite sufficiently. Take the two lines which I have just quoted from Homer, the poet's comment on Helen's mention of her brothers—or take his

> Ἃ δειλώ, τί σφῶϊ δόμεν Πηλῆϊ ἄνακτι
> θνητῷ; ὑμεῖς δ' ἐστὸν ἀγήρω τ' ἀθανάτω τε.
> ἦ ἵνα δυστήνοισι μετ' ἀνδράσιν ἄλγε' ἔχητον;[1]

the address of Zeus to the horses of Peleus—or take finally his

> Καὶ σέ, γέρον, τὸ πρὶν μὲν ἀκούομεν ὄλβιον εἶναι·[2]

the words of Achilles to Priam, a suppliant before him. Take that incomparable line and a half of Dante, Ugolino's tremendous words—

> *Io no piangeva; sì dentro impietrai.*
> *Piangevan elli . . .*[3]

8. "Then began he to call many things to remembrance—all the lands which his valor conquered and pleasant France, and the men of his lineage, and Charlemagne his liege lord who nourished him." *Chanson de Roland* 3.939–42 [Arnold's note].
9. "So said she; they long since in Earth's soft arms were reposing, / There, in their own dear land, their fatherland, Lacedaemon." *Iliad* 3.243–44 (translated by Dr. Hawtrey) [Arnold's note].

1. "Ah, unhappy pair, why gave we you to King Peleus, to a mortal? but ye are without old age, and immortal. Was it that with men born to misery ye might have sorrow?" *Iliad* 17.443–45 [Arnold's note].
2. "Nay, and thou too, old man, in former days wast, as we hear, happy." *Iliad* 14.543 [Arnold's note].
3. "I wailed not, so of stone I grew within; *they* wailed." *Inferno* 33.49–50 [Arnold's note].

take the lovely words of Beatrice to Virgil—

> Io son fatta da Dio, sua mercè, tale,
> Che la vostra miseria non mi tange,
> Nè fiamma d'esto incendio non m'assale . . . [4]

take the simple, but perfect, single line—

> In la sua volontade è nostra pace. [5]

Take of Shakespeare a line or two of Henry the Fourth's expostulation with sleep—

> Wilt thou upon the high and giddy mast
> Seal up the shipboy's eyes, and rock his brains
> In cradle of the rude imperious surge . . . [6]

and take, as well, Hamlet's dying request to Horatio—

> If thou didst ever hold me in thy heart,
> Absent thee from felicity awhile,
> And in this harsh world draw thy breath in pain,
> To tell my story . . . [7]

Take of Milton that Miltonic passage—

> Darkened so, yet shone
> Above them all the archangel; but his face
> Deep scars of thunder had intrenched, and care
> Sat on his faded cheek . . . [8]

add two such lines as—

> And courage never to submit or yield
> And what is else not to be overcome . . . [9]

and finish with the exquisite close to the loss of Proserpine, the loss

> . . . which cost Ceres all that pain
> To seek her through the world. [1]

These few lines, if we have tact and can use them, are enough even of themselves to keep clear and sound our judgments about poetry, to save us from fallacious estimates of it, to conduct us to a real estimate.

The specimens I have quoted differ widely from one another, but they have in common this: the possession of the very highest poetical quality. If we are thoroughly penetrated by their power, we shall find that we have acquired a sense enabling us, whatever poetry may be laid before us, to feel the degree in which a high poetical quality is present or wanting there. Critics give themselves great labor to draw out what in the abstract constitutes the characters of a high quality of poetry. It is much better simply to have recourse to concrete examples—to take specimens of poetry of the high, the

---

4. "Of such sort hath God, thanked be His mercy, made me, that your misery toucheth me not, neither doth the flame of this fire strike me." *Inferno* 2.91–93 [Arnold's note].
5. "In His will is our peace." *Paradiso* 3.85 [Arnold's note].

6. *2 Henry IV* 3.1.18–20.
7. *Hamlet* 5.2.357–60.
8. *Paradise Lost* 1.599–602.
9. *Paradise Lost* 1.108–9.
1. *Paradise Lost* 4.271–72.

very highest quality, and to say: The characters of a high quality of poetry are what is expressed *there*. They are far better recognized by being felt in the verse of the master, than by being perused in the prose of the critic. Nevertheless if we are urgently pressed to give some critical account of them, we may safely, perhaps, venture on laying down, not indeed how and why the characters arise, but where and in what they arise. They are in the matter and substance of the poetry, and they are in its manner and style. Both of these, the substance and matter on the one hand, the style and manner on the other, have a mark, an accent, of high beauty, worth, and power. But if we are asked to define this mark and accent in the abstract, our answer must be: No, for we should thereby be darkening the question, not clearing it. The mark and accent are as given by the substance and matter of that poetry, by the style and manner of that poetry, and of all other poetry which is akin to it in quality.

Only one thing we may add as to the substance and matter of poetry, guiding ourselves by Aristotle's profound observation that the superiority of poetry over history consists in its possessing a higher truth and a higher seriousness ($\phi\iota\lambda o\sigma o\phi\acute{\omega}\tau\epsilon\rho o\nu$ $\kappa a\grave{\iota}$ $\sigma\pi o\nu\delta a\iota\acute{o}\tau\epsilon\rho o\nu$).[2] Let us add, therefore, to what we have said, this: that the substance and matter of the best poetry acquire their special character from possessing, in an eminent degree, truth and seriousness. We may add yet further, what is in itself evident, that to the style and manner of the best poetry their special character, their accent, is given by their diction, and, even yet more, by their movement. And though we distinguish between the two characters, the two accents, of superiority, yet they are nevertheless vitally connected one with the other. The superior character of truth and seriousness, in the matter and substance of the best poetry, is inseparable from the superiority of diction and movement marking its style and manner. The two superiorities are closely related, and are in steadfast proportion one to the other. So far as high poetic truth and seriousness are wanting to a poet's matter and substance, so far also, we may be sure, will a high poetic stamp of diction and movement be wanting to his style and manner. In proportion as this high stamp of diction and movement, again, is absent from a poet's style and manner, we shall find, also, that high poetic truth and seriousness are absent from his substance and matter.

So stated, these are but dry generalities; their whole force lies in their application. And I could wish every student of poetry to make the application of them for himself. Made by himself, the application would impress itself upon his mind far more deeply than made by me. Neither will my limits allow me to make any full application of the generalities above propounded; but in the hope of bringing out, at any rate, some significance in them, and of establishing an important principle more firmly by their means, I will, in the space which remains to me, follow rapidly from the commencement the course of our English poetry with them in my view.

* * *

Chaucer's * * * poetical importance does not need the assistance of the historic estimate; it is real. He is a genuine source of joy and strength, which is flowing still for us and will flow always. He will be read, as time goes on,

2. Aristotle's *Poetics* 9.

far more generally than he is read now. His language is a cause of difficulty for us; but so also, and I think in quite as great a degree, is the language of Burns. In Chaucer's case, as in that of Burns, it is a difficulty to be unhesitatingly accepted and overcome.

If we ask ourselves wherein consists the immense superiority of Chaucer's poetry over the romance poetry—why it is that in passing from this to Chaucer we suddenly feel ourselves to be in another world, we shall find that his superiority is both in the substance of his poetry and in the style of his poetry. His superiority in substance is given by his large, free, simple, clear yet kindly view of human life—so unlike the total want, in the romance poets, of all intelligent command of it. Chaucer has not their helplessness; he has gained the power to survey the world from a central, a truly human point of view. We have only to call to mind the Prologue to *The Canterbury Tales*. The right comment upon it is Dryden's: "It is sufficient to say, according to the proverb, that *here is God's plenty*." And again: "He is a perpetual fountain of good sense."[3] It is by a large, free, sound representation of things, that poetry, this high criticism of life, has truth of substance; and Chaucer's poetry has truth of substance.

Of his style and manner, if we think first of the romance poetry and then of Chaucer's divine liquidness of diction, his divine fluidity of movement, it is difficult to speak temperately. They are irresistible, and justify all the rapture with which his successors speak of his "gold dewdrops of speech."[4] Johnson misses the point entirely when he finds fault with Dryden for ascribing to Chaucer the first refinement of our numbers, and says that Gower[5] also can show smooth numbers and easy rhymes. The refinement of our numbers means something far more than this. A nation may have versifiers with smooth numbers and easy rhymes, and yet may have no real poetry at all. Chaucer is the father of our splendid English poetry; he is our "well of English undefiled,"[6] because by the lovely charm of his diction, the lovely charm of his movement, he makes an epoch and founds a tradition. In Spenser, Shakespeare, Milton, Keats, we can follow the tradition of the liquid diction, the fluid movement, of Chaucer; at one time it is his liquid diction of which in these poets we feel the virtue, and at another time it is his fluid movement. And the virtue is irresistible.

Bounded as is my space, I must yet find room for an example of Chaucer's virtue, as I have given examples to show the virtue of the great classics. I feel disposed to say that a single line is enough to show the charm of Chaucer's verse; that merely one line like this—

O martyr souded[7] in virginitee!

has a virtue of manner and movement such as we shall not find in all the verse of romance poetry—but this is saying nothing. The virtue is such as we shall not find, perhaps, in all English poetry, outside the poets whom I have named as the special inheritors of Chaucer's tradition. A single line,

3. Both quotations are from Dryden's preface to his *Fables Ancient and Modern* (1700).
4. *The Life of Our Lady*, a poem by John Lydgate (ca. 1370–ca.1451).
5. John Gower (ca. 1325–1408), friend of Chaucer and author of the *Confessio Amantis*, a long poem in octosyllabic couplets.

6. Said of Chaucer by Spenser in *Faerie Queene* 4.2.32.
7. The French *soudé*: soldered, fixed fast [Arnold's note]. From *The Canterbury Tales*, *The Prioress's Tale* (line 127); Chaucer wrote "souded to" rather than "souded in."

however, is too little if we have not the strain of Chaucer's verse well in our memory; let us take a stanza. It is from *The Prioress's Tale,* the story of the Christian child murdered in a Jewry—

> My throte is cut unto my nekke-bone
> Saidè this child, and as by way of kinde
> I should have deyd, yea, longè time agone;
> But Jesu Christ, as ye in bookès finde,
> Will that his glory last and be in minde,
> And for the worship of his mother dere
> Yet may I sing O *Alma* loud and clere.

Wordsworth has modernized this Tale, and to feel how delicate and evanescent is the charm of verse, we have only to read Wordsworth's first three lines of this stanza after Chaucer's—

> My throat is cut unto the bone, I trow,
> Said this young child, and by the law of kind
> I should have died, yea, many hours ago.

The charm is departed. It is often said that the power of liquidness and fluidity in Chaucer's verse was dependent upon a free, a licentious dealing with language, such as is now impossible; upon a liberty, such as Burns too enjoyed, of making words like *neck, bird,* into a dissyllable by adding to them, and words like *cause, rhyme,* into a dissyllable by sounding the *e* mute. It is true that Chaucer's fluidity is conjoined with this liberty, and is admirably served by it; but we ought not to say that it was dependent upon it. It was dependent upon his talent. Other poets with a like liberty do not attain to the fluidity of Chaucer; Burns himself does not attain to it. Poets, again, who have a talent akin to Chaucer's, such as Shakespeare or Keats, have known how to attain to his fluidity without the like liberty.

And yet Chaucer is not one of the great classics. His poetry transcends and effaces, easily and without effort, all the romance poetry of Catholic Christendom; it transcends and effaces all the English poetry contemporary with it, it transcends and effaces all the English poetry subsequent to it down to the age of Elizabeth. Of such avail is poetic truth of substance, in its natural and necessary union with poetic truth of style. And yet, I say, Chaucer is not one of the great classics. He has not their accent. What is wanting to him is suggested by the mere mention of the name of the first great classic of Christendom, the immortal poet who died eighty years before Chaucer— Dante. The accent of such verse as

> *In la sua volontade è nostra pace . . .*

is altogether beyond Chaucer's reach; we praise him, but we feel that this accent is out of the question for him. It may be said that it was necessarily out of the reach of any poet in the England of that stage of growth. Possibly; but we are to adopt a real, not a historic, estimate of poetry. However we may account for its absence, something is wanting, then, to the poetry of Chaucer, which poetry must have before it can be placed in the glorious class of the best. And there is no doubt what that something is. It is the spoudaiotes, the high and excellent seriousness, which Aristotle assigns as one of the grand virtues of poetry. The substance of Chaucer's poetry, his view of things and his criticism of life, has largeness, freedom, shrewdness, benignity; but it has not this high seriousness. Homer's criticism of life has it, Dante's has it, Shakespeare's has it. It is this chiefly which gives to our spirits what they can rest upon; and with the increasing demands of our modern ages upon poetry, this virtue of giving us what we can rest upon will be more and more highly esteemed. A voice from the slums of Paris, fifty or sixty years after Chaucer, the voice of poor Villon[8] out of his life of riot and crime, has at its happy moments (as, for instance, in the last stanza of *La Belle Heaulmière*)[9] more of this important poetic virtue of seriousness than all the productions of Chaucer. But its apparition in Villon, and in men like Villon, is fitful; the greatness of the great poets, the power of their criticism of life, is that their virtue is sustained.

To our praise, therefore, of Chaucer as a poet there must be this limitation: he lacks the high seriousness of the great classics, and therewith an important part of their virtue. Still, the main fact for us to bear in mind about Chaucer is his sterling value according to that real estimate which we firmly adopt for all poets. He has poetic truth of substance, though he has not high poetic seriousness, and corresponding to his truth of substance he has an exquisite virtue of style and manner. With him is born our real poetry.

For my present purpose I need not dwell on our Elizabethan poetry, or on the continuation and close of this poetry in Milton. We all of us profess to be agreed in the estimate of this poetry; we all of us recognize it as great poetry, our greatest, and Shakespeare and Milton as our poetical classics. The real estimate, here, has universal currency. With the next age of our poetry divergency and difficulty begin. An historic estimate of that poetry has established itself; and the question is, whether it will be found to coincide with the real estimate.

The age of Dryden, together with our whole eighteenth century which followed it, sincerely believed itself to have produced poetical classics of its own, and even to have made advance, in poetry, beyond all its predecessors. Dryden regards as not seriously disputable the opinion "that the sweetness of English verse was never understood or practiced by our fathers."[1] Cowley[2] could see nothing at all in Chaucer's poetry. Dryden heartily admired it, and, as we have seen, praised its matter admirably; but of its exquisite manner and movement all he can find to say is that "there is the rude sweetness of a Scotch tune in it, which is natural and pleasing, though not perfect."[3] Addison, wishing to praise Chaucer's numbers, compares them with Dryden's own. And all through the eighteenth century, and down even into our own times, the stereotyped phrase of approbation for good verse found in our early poetry has been, that it even approached the verse of Dryden, Addison, Pope, and Johnson.

---

8. François Villon (1431–1484), French poet and vagabond.
9. The name *Heaulmière* is said to be derived from a headdress (helm) worn as a mask by courtesans. In Villon's ballad, a poor old creature of this class laments her days of youth and beauty. The last stanza of the ballad runs thus—"*Ainsi le bon temps regretons / Entrenous, pauvres vieilles sottes, / Assises bas, à croppetons, / Tout en ung tas comme pelottes; / A petit feu de chenevottes / Tost allumeés, tost estaincles, / Et jadis fusmes si mignottes! / Ainsi*

en prend à maintz et maintes." [It may be translated:] "Thus amongst ourselves we regret the good time, poor silly old things, low-seated on our heels, all in a heap like so many balls; by a little fire of hemp stalks, soon lighted, soon spent. And once we were such darlings! So fares it with many and many a one" [Arnold's note].
1. *Essay on Dramatic Poesy*.
2. Abraham Cowley (1618–1667), English poet.
3. Preface to his *Fables*.

Are Dryden and Pope poetical classics? Is the historic estimate, which represents them as such, and which has been so long established that it cannot easily give way, the real estimate? Wordsworth and Coleridge, as is well known, denied it; but the authority of Wordsworth and Coleridge does not weigh much with the young generation, and there are many signs to show that the eighteenth century and its judgments are coming into favor again. Are the favorite poets of the eighteenth century classics?

It is impossible within my present limits to discuss the question fully. And what man of letters would not shrink from seeming to dispose dictatorially of the claims of two men who are, at any rate, such masters in letters as Dryden and Pope; two men of such admirable talent, both of them, and one of them, Dryden, a man, on all sides, of such energetic and genial power? And yet, if we are to gain the full benefit from poetry, we must have the real estimate of it. I cast about for some mode of arriving, in the present case, at such an estimate without offense. And perhaps the best way is to begin, as it is easy to begin, with cordial praise.

When we find Chapman, the Elizabethan translator of Homer, expressing himself in his preface thus: "Though truth in her very nakedness sits in so deep a pit, that from Gades to Aurora and Ganges few eyes can sound her, I hope yet those few here will so discover and confirm that, the date being out of her darkness in this morning of our poet, he shall now gird his temples with the sun," we pronounce that such a prose is intolerable. When we find Milton writing: "And long it was not after, when I was confirmed in this opinion, that he, who would not be frustrate of his hope to write well hereafter in laudable things, ought himself to be a true poem"[4]—we pronounce that such a prose has its own grandeur, but that it is obsolete and inconvenient. But when we find Dryden telling us: "What Virgil wrote in the vigor of his age, in plenty and at ease, I have undertaken to translate in my declining years; struggling with wants, oppressed with sickness, curbed in my genius, liable to be misconstrued in all I write"[5]—then we exclaim that here at last we have the true English prose, a prose such as we would all gladly use if we only knew how. Yet Dryden was Milton's contemporary.

But after the Restoration the time had come when our nation felt the imperious need of a fit prose. So, too, the time had likewise come when our nation felt the imperious need of freeing itself from the absorbing preoccupation which religion in the Puritan age had exercised. It was impossible that this freedom should be brought about without some negative excess, without some neglect and impairment of the religious life of the soul; and the spiritual history of the eighteenth century shows us that the freedom was not achieved without them. Still, the freedom was achieved; the preoccupation, an undoubtedly baneful and retarding one if it had continued, was got rid of. And as with religion amongst us at that period, so it was also with letters. A fit prose was a necessity; but it was impossible that a fit prose should establish itself amongst us without some touch of frost to the imaginative life of the soul. The needful qualities for a fit prose are regularity, uniformity, precision, balance. The men of letters, whose destiny it may be to bring their nation to the attainment of a fit prose, must of necessity, whether they work

4. *Apology for Smectymnuus.*
5. *Postscript to the Reader* in his translation of Virgil.

in prose or in verse, give a predominating, an almost exclusive attention to the qualities of regularity, uniformity, precision, balance. But an almost exclusive attention to these qualities involves some repression and silencing of poetry.

We are to regard Dryden as the puissant and glorious founder, Pope as the splendid high priest, of our age of prose and reason, of our excellent and indispensable eighteenth century. For the purposes of their mission and destiny their poetry, like their prose, is admirable. Do you ask me whether Dryden's verse, take it almost where you will, is not good?

> A milk-white Hind, immortal and unchanged,
> Fed on the lawns and in the forest ranged.[6]

I answer: Admirable for the purposes of the inaugurator of an age of prose and reason. Do you ask me whether Pope's verse, take it almost where you will, is not good?

> To Hounslow Heath I point, and Banstead Down;
> Thence comes your mutton, and these chicks my own.[7]

I answer: Admirable for the purposes of the high priest of an age of prose and reason. But do you ask me whether such verse proceeds from men with an adequate poetic criticism of life, from men whose criticism of life has a high seriousness, or even, without that high seriousness, has poetic largeness, freedom, insight, benignity? Do you ask me whether the application of ideas to life in the verse of these men, often a powerful application, no doubt, is a powerful *poetic* application? Do you ask me whether the poetry of these men has either the matter or the inseparable manner of such an adequate poetic criticism; whether it has the accent of

> Absent thee from felicity awhile . . .

or of

> And what is else not to be overcome . . .

or of

> O martyr souded in virginitee!

I answer: It has not and cannot have them; it is the poetry of the builders of an age of prose and reason. Though they may write in verse, though they may in a certain sense be masters of the art of versification, Dryden and Pope are not classics of our poetry, they are classics of our prose.

Gray is our poetical classic of that literature and age; the position of Gray is singular, and demands a word of notice here. He has not the volume or the power of poets who, coming in times more favorable, have attained to an independent criticism of life. But he lived with the great poets, he lived, above all, with the Greeks, through perpetually studying and enjoying them; and he caught their poetic point of view for regarding life, caught their poetic manner. The point of view and the manner are not self-sprung in him, he caught them of others; and he had not the free and abundant use of them. But whereas Addison and Pope never had the use of them, Gray had the use

---

6. *The Hind and the Panther* 1.1–2.   7. *Imitations of Horace*, Satire 2.2.143–144.

of them at times. He is the scantiest and frailest of classics in our poetry, but he is a classic.[8]

* * *

At any rate the end to which the method and the estimate are designed to lead, and from leading to which, if they do lead to it, they get their whole value—the benefit of being able clearly to feel and deeply to enjoy the best, the truly classic, in poetry—is an end, let me say it once more at parting, of supreme importance. We are often told that an era is opening in which we are to see multitudes of a common sort of readers, and masses of a common sort of literature; that such readers do not want and could not relish anything better than such literature, and that to provide it is becoming a vast and profitable industry. Even if good literature entirely lost currency with the world, it would still be abundantly worth while to continue to enjoy it by oneself. But it never will lose currency with the world, in spite of momentary appearances; it never will lose supremacy. Currency and supremacy are insured to it, not indeed by the world's deliberate and conscious choice, but by something far deeper—by the instinct of self-preservation in humanity.

1880

Literature and Science[1]

Practical people talk with a smile of Plato and of his absolute ideas: and it is impossible to deny that Plato's ideas do often seem unpractical and unpracticable, and especially when one views them in connection with the life of a great work-a-day world like the United States. The necessary staple of the life of such a world Plato regards with disdain; handicraft and trade and the working professions he regards with disdain; but what becomes of the life of an industrial modern community if you take handicraft and trade and the working professions out of it? The base mechanic arts and handicrafts, says Plato, bring about a natural weakness in the principle of excellence in a man, so that he cannot govern the ignoble growths in him, but nurses them, and cannot understand fostering any other. Those who exercise such arts and trades, as they have their bodies, he says, marred by their vulgar businesses, so they have their souls, too, bowed and broken by them. And if one of these uncomely people has a mind to seek self-culture and philosophy, Plato compares him to a bald little tinker, who has scraped together money, and has got his release from service, and has had a bath, and bought a new coat, and is rigged out like a bridegroom about to marry the daughter of his master who has fallen into poor and helpless estate.

Nor do the working professions fare any better than trade at the hands of Plato. He draws for us an inimitable picture of the working lawyer, and of

8. After Gray, the only other poet discussed by Arnold is Burns (not printed here). Arnold concludes that "Burns, like Chaucer, comes short of the high seriousness of the great classics."
1. Delivered as a lecture during Arnold's tour of the United States in 1883 and published in *Discourses in America* (1885), this essay has become a classic contribution to a subject endlessly debated. Its main argument was summed up by Stuart P. Sherman: "If Arnold had said outright that the study of letters helps us to *bear* the grand results of science, he would not have been guilty of a superficial epigram; he would have spoken from the depths of his experience."

his life of bondage; he shows how this bondage from his youth up has stunted and warped him, and made him small and crooked of soul, encompassing him with difficulties which he is not man enough to rely on justice and truth as means to encounter, but has recourse, for help out of them, to falsehood and wrong. And so, says Plato, this poor creature is bent and broken, and grows up from boy to man without a particle of soundness in him, although exceedingly smart and clever in his own esteem.

One cannot refuse to admire the artist who draws these pictures. But we say to ourselves that his ideas show the influence of a primitive and obsolete order of things, when the warrior caste and the priestly caste were alone in honor, and the humble work of the world was done by slaves. We have now changed all that; the modern majesty consists in work, as Emerson declares; and in work, we may add, principally of such plain and dusty kind as the work of cultivators of the ground, handicraftsmen, men of trade and business, men of the working professions. Above all is this true in a great industrious community such as that of the United States.

Now education, many people go on to say, is still mainly governed by the ideas of men like Plato, who lived when the warrior caste and the priestly or philosophical class were alone in honor, and the really useful part of the community were slaves. It is an education fitted for persons of leisure in such a community. This education passed from Greece and Rome to the feudal communities of Europe, where also the warrior caste and the priestly caste were alone held in honor, and where the really useful and working part of the community, though not nominally slaves as in the pagan world, were practically not much better off than slaves, and not more seriously regarded. And how absurd it is, people end by saying, to inflict this education upon an industrious modern community, where very few indeed are persons of leisure, and the mass to be considered has not leisure, but is bound, for its own great good, and for the great good of the world at large, to plain labor and to industrial pursuits, and the education in question tends necessarily to make men dissatisfied with these pursuits and unfitted for them!

That is what is said. So far I must defend Plato, as to plead that his view of education and studies is in the general, as it seems to me, sound enough, and fitted for all sorts and conditions of men, whatever their pursuits may be. "An intelligent man," says Plato, "will prize those studies which result in his soul getting soberness, righteousness, and wisdom, and will less value the others."[2] I cannot consider *that* a bad description of the aim of education, and of the motives which should govern us in the choice of studies, whether we are preparing ourselves for a hereditary seat in the English House of Lords or for the pork trade in Chicago.

Still I admit that Plato's world was not ours, that his scorn of trade and handicraft is fantastic, that he had no conception of a great industrial community such as that of the United States, and that such a community must and will shape its education to suit its own needs. If the usual education handed down to it from the past does not suit it, it will certainly before long drop this and try another. The usual education in the past has been mainly literary. The question is whether the studies which were long supposed to be the best for all of us are practically the best now; whether others are not

2. *Republic* 9.591.

better. The tyranny of the past, many think, weighs on us injuriously in the predominance given to letters in education. The question is raised whether, to meet the needs of our modern life, the predominance ought not now to pass from letters to science; and naturally the question is nowhere raised with more energy than here in the United States. The design of abasing what is called "mere literary instruction and education," and of exalting what is called "sound, extensive, and practical scientific knowledge," is, in this intensely modern world of the United States, even more perhaps than in Europe, a very popular design, and makes great and rapid progress.

I am going to ask whether the present movement for ousting letters from their old predominance in education, and for transferring the predominance in education to the natural sciences, whether this brisk and flourishing movement ought to prevail, and whether it is likely that in the end it really will prevail. An objection may be raised which I will anticipate. My own studies have been almost wholly in letters, and my visits to the field of the natural sciences have been very slight and inadequate, although those sciences have always strongly moved my curiosity. A man of letters, it will perhaps be said, is not competent to discuss the comparative merits of letters and natural science as means of education. To this objection I reply, first of all, that his incompetence, if he attempts the discussion but is really incompetent for it, will be abundantly visible; nobody will be taken in; he will have plenty of sharp observers and critics to save mankind from that danger. But the line I am going to follow is, as you will soon discover, so extremely simple, that perhaps it may be followed without failure even by one who for a more ambitious line of discussion would be quite incompetent.

Some of you may possibly remember a phrase of mine which has been the object of a good deal of comment; an observation to the effect that in our culture, the aim being *to know ourselves and the world*, we have, as the means to this end, *to know the best which has been thought and said in the world.*[3] A man of science, who is also an excellent writer and the very prince of debaters, Professor Huxley, in a discourse at the opening of Sir Josiah Mason's college at Birmingham,[4] laying hold of this phrase, expanded it by quoting some more words of mine, which are these: "The civilized world is to be regarded as now being, for intellectual and spiritual purposes, one great confederation, bound to a joint action and working to a common result; and whose members have for their proper outfit a knowledge of Greek, Roman, and Eastern antiquity, and of one another. Special local and temporary advantages being put out of account, that modern nation will in the intellectual and spiritual sphere make most progress, which most thoroughly carries out this program."

Now on my phrase, thus enlarged, Professor Huxley remarks that when I speak of the above-mentioned knowledge as enabling us to know ourselves and the world, I assert *literature* to contain the materials which suffice for thus making us know ourselves and the world. But it is not by any means clear, says he, that after having learnt all which ancient and modern literatures have to tell us, we have laid a sufficiently broad and deep foundation for that criticism of life, that knowledge of ourselves and the world, which

3. See *The Function of Criticism at the Present Time* (p. 1514). 4. See *Science and Culture* (p. 1559).

constitutes culture. On the contrary, Professor Huxley declares that he finds himself "wholly unable to admit that either nations or individuals will really advance, if their outfit draws nothing from the stores of physical science. An army without weapons of precision, and with no particular base of operations, might more hopefully enter upon a campaign on the Rhine, than a man, devoid of a knowledge of what physical science has done in the last century, upon a criticism of life."

This shows how needful it is for those who are to discuss any matter together, to have a common understanding as to the sense of the terms they employ—how needful, and how difficult. What Professor Huxley says, implies just the reproach which is so often brought against the study of belles-lettres, as they are called: that the study is an elegant one, but slight and ineffectual; a smattering of Greek and Latin and other ornamental things, of little use for anyone whose object is to get at truth, and to be a practical man. So, too, M. Renan[5] talks of the "superficial humanism" of a school course which treats us as if we were all going to be poets, writers, preachers, orators, and he opposes this humanism to positive science, or the critical search after truth. And there is always a tendency in those who are remonstrating against the predominance of letters in education, to understand by letters belles-lettres, and by belles-lettres a superficial humanism, the opposite of science or true knowledge.

But when we talk of knowing Greek and Roman antiquity, for instance, which is the knowledge people have called the humanities, I for my part mean a knowledge which is something more than a superficial humanism, mainly decorative. "I call all teaching *scientific*," says Wolf,[6] the critic of Homer, "which is systematically laid out and followed up to its original sources. For example: a knowledge of classical antiquity is scientific when the remains of classical antiquity are correctly studied in the original languages." There can be no doubt that Wolf is perfectly right; that all learning is scientific which is systematically laid out and followed up to its original sources, and that a genuine humanism is scientific.

When I speak of knowing Greek and Roman antiquity, therefore, as a help to knowing ourselves and the world, I mean more than a knowledge of so much vocabulary, so much grammar, so many portions of authors in the Greek and Latin languages, I mean knowing the Greeks and Romans, and their life and genius, and what they were and did in the world; what we get from them, and what is its value. That, at least, is the ideal; and when we talk of endeavoring to know Greek and Roman antiquity, as a help to knowing ourselves and the world, we mean endeavoring so to know them as to satisfy this ideal, however much we may still fall short of it.

The same also as to knowing our own and other modern nations, with the like aim of getting to understand ourselves and the world. To know the best that has been thought and said by the modern nations, is to know, says Professor Huxley, "only what modern *literatures* have to tell us; it is the criticism of life contained in modern literature." And yet "the distinctive character of our times," he urges, "lies in the vast and constantly increasing part which is played by natural knowledge." And how, therefore, can a man,

---

5. Ernest Renan (1823–1892), French religious philosopher and author of *The Life of Jesus*.

6. Friedrich August Wolf (1759–1824), German scholar.

devoid of knowledge of what physical science has done in the last century, enter hopefully upon a criticism of modern life?

Let us, I say, be agreed about the meaning of the terms we are using. I talk of knowing the best which has been thought and uttered in the world; Professor Huxley says this means knowing *literature*. Literature is a large word; it may mean everything written with letters or printed in a book. Euclid's *Elements* and Newton's *Principia* are thus literature. All knowledge that reaches us through books is literature. But by literature Professor Huxley means belles-lettres. He means to make me say, that knowing the best which has been thought and said by the modern nations is knowing their belles-lettres and no more. And this is no sufficient equipment, he argues, for a criticism of modern life. But as I do not mean, by knowing ancient Rome, knowing merely more or less of Latin belles-lettres, and taking no account of Rome's military, and political, and legal, and administrative work in the world; and as, by knowing ancient Greece, I understand knowing her as the giver of Greek art, and the guide to a free and right use of reason and to scientific method, and the founder of our mathematics and physics and astronomy and biology—I understand knowing her as all this, and not merely knowing certain Greek poems, and histories, and treatises, and speeches— so as to the knowledge of modern nations also. By knowing modern nations, I mean not merely knowing their belles-lettres, but knowing also what has been done by such men as Copernicus, Galileo, Newton, Darwin. "Our ancestors learned," says Professor Huxley, "that the earth is the center of the visible universe, and that man is the cynosure of things terrestrial; and more especially was it inculcated that the course of nature had no fixed order, but that it could be, and constantly was, altered." "But for us now," continues Professor Huxley, "the notions of the beginning and the end of the world entertained by our forefathers are no longer credible. It is very certain that the earth is not the chief body in the material universe, and that the world is not subordinated to man's use. It is even more certain that nature is the expression of a definite order, with which nothing interferes." "And yet," he cries, "the purely classical education advocated by the representatives of the humanists in our day gives no inkling of all this."

In due place and time I will just touch upon that vexed question of classical education; but at present the question is as to what is meant by knowing the best which modern nations have thought and said. It is not knowing their belles-lettres merely which is meant. To know Italian belles-lettres is not to know Italy, and to know English belles-lettres is not to know England. Into knowing Italy and England there comes a great deal more, Galileo and New- ton amongst it. The reproach of being a superficial humanism, a tincture of belles-lettres, may attach rightly enough to some other disciplines; but to the particular discipline recommended when I proposed knowing the best that has been thought and said in the world, it does not apply. In that best I certainly include what in modern times has been thought and said by the great observers and knowers of nature.

There is, therefore, really no question between Professor Huxley and me as to whether knowing the great results of the modern scientific study of nature is not required as a part of our culture, as well as knowing the prod- ucts of literature and art. But to follow the processes by which those results are reached, ought, say the friends of physical science, to be made the staple of education for the bulk of mankind. And here there does arise a question between those whom Professor Huxley calls with playful sarcasm "the Levites of culture," and those whom the poor humanist is sometimes apt to regard as its Nebuchadnezzars.[7]

The great results of the scientific investigation of nature we are agreed upon knowing, but how much of our study are we bound to give to the processes by which those results are reached? The results have their visible bearing on human life. But all the processes, too, all the items of fact, by which those results are reached and established, are interesting. All knowledge is interesting to a wise man, and the knowledge of nature is interesting to all men. It is very interesting to know, that, from the albuminous white of the egg, the chick in the egg gets the materials for its flesh, bones, blood, and feathers; while, from the fatty yolk of the egg, it gets the heat and energy which enable it at length to break its shell and begin the world. It is less interesting, perhaps, but still it is interesting, to know that when a taper burns, the wax is converted into carbonic acid and water. Moreover, it is quite true that the habit of dealing with facts, which is given by the study of nature, is, as the friends of physical science praise it for being, an excellent discipline. The appeal, in the study of nature, is constantly to observation and experiment; not only is it said that the thing is so, but we can be made to see that it is so. Not only does a man tell us that when a taper burns the wax is converted into carbonic acid and water, as a man may tell us, if he likes, that Charon[8] is punting his ferry boat on the river Styx, or that Victor Hugo is a sublime poet, or Mr. Gladstone the most admirable of statesmen; but we are made to see that the conversion into carbonic acid and water does actually happen. This reality of natural knowledge it is, which makes the friends of physical science contrast it, as a knowledge of things, with the humanist's knowledge, which is, say they, a knowledge of words. And hence Professor Huxley is moved to lay it down that, "for the purpose of attaining real culture, an exclusively scientific education is at least as effectual as an exclusively literary education." And a certain President of the Section for Mechanical Science in the British Association is, in Scripture phrase, "very bold," and declares that if a man, in his mental training, "has substituted literature and history for natural science, he has chosen the less useful alternative." But whether we go these lengths or not, we must all admit that in natural science the habit gained of dealing with facts is a most valuable discipline, and that everyone should have some experience of it.

More than this, however, is demanded by the reformers. It is proposed to make the training in natural science the main part of education, for the great majority of mankind at any rate. And here, I confess, I part company with the friends of physical science, with whom up to this point I have been agreeing. In differing from them, however, I wish to proceed with the utmost caution and diffidence. The smallness of my own acquaintance with the disciplines of natural science is ever before my mind, and I am fearful of doing these disciplines an injustice. The ability and pugnacity of the partisans of natural science make them formidable persons to contradict. The tone of tentative inquiry, which befits a being of dim faculties and bounded knowl-

---

7. Huxley implied that the humanists are hidebound conservatives like the Levites, priests who were preoccupied with traditional ritual observances. Arnold implies that the scientists may be like Nebuchadnezzar, a Babylonian king who destroyed the temple of Jerusalem.
8. In Greek mythology, the boatman who conducted the souls of the dead across the river Styx.

edge, is the tone I would wish to take and not to depart from. At present it seems to me, that those who are for giving to natural knowledge, as they call it, the chief place in the education of the majority of mankind, leave one important thing out of their account: the constitution of human nature. But I put this forward on the strength of some facts not at all recondite, very far from it; facts capable of being stated in the simplest possible fashion, and to which, if I so state them, the man of science will, I am sure, be willing to allow their due weight.

Deny the facts altogether, I think, he hardly can. He can hardly deny, that when we set ourselves to enumerate the powers which go to the building up of human life, and say that they are the power of conduct, the power of intellect and knowledge, the power of beauty, and the power of social life and manners—he can hardly deny that this scheme, though drawn in rough and plain lines enough, and not pretending to scientific exactness, does yet give a fairly true representation of the matter. Human nature is built up by these powers; we have the need for them all. When we have rightly met and adjusted the claims of them all, we shall then be in a fair way for getting soberness and righteousness, with wisdom. This is evident enough, and the friends of physical science would admit it.

But perhaps they may not have sufficiently observed another thing: namely, that the several powers just mentioned are not isolated, but there is, in the generality of mankind, a perpetual tendency to relate them one to another in divers ways. With one such way of relating them I am particularly concerned now. Following our instinct for intellect and knowledge, we acquire pieces of knowledge; and presently, in the generality of men, there arises the desire to relate these pieces of knowledge to our sense for conduct, to our sense for beauty—and there is weariness and dissatisfaction if the desire is balked. Now in this desire lies, I think, the strength of that hold which letters have upon us.

All knowledge is, as I said just now, interesting; and even items of knowledge which from the nature of the case cannot well be related, but must stand isolated in our thoughts, have their interest. Even lists of exceptions have their interest. If we are studying Greek accents, it is interesting to know that *pais* and *pas,* and some other monosyllables of the same form of declension, do not take the circumflex upon the last syllable of the genitive plural, but vary, in this respect, from the common rule. If we are studying physiology, it is interesting to know that the pulmonary artery carries dark blood and the pulmonary vein carries bright blood, departing in this respect from the common rule for the division of labor between the veins and the arteries. But everyone knows how we seek naturally to combine the pieces of our knowledge together, to bring them under general rules, to relate them to principles; and how unsatisfactory and tiresome it would be to go on forever learning lists of exceptions, or accumulating items of fact which must stand isolated.

Well, that same need of relating our knowledge, which operates here within the sphere of our knowledge itself, we shall find operating, also, outside that sphere. We experience, as we go on learning and knowing—the vast majority of us experience—the need of relating what we have learnt and known to the sense which we have in us for conduct, to the sense which we have in us for beauty.

A certain Greek prophetess of Mantineia in Arcadia, Diotima by name, once explained to the philosopher Socrates that love, and impulse, and bent of all kinds, is, in fact, nothing else but the desire in men that good should forever be present to them. This desire for good, Diotima assured Socrates, is our fundamental desire, of which fundamental desire every impulse in us is only some one particular form.[9] And therefore this fundamental desire it is, I suppose—this desire in men that good should be forever present to them—which acts in us when we feel the impulse for relating our knowledge to our sense for conduct and to our sense for beauty. At any rate, with men in general the instinct exists. Such is human nature. And the instinct, it will be admitted, is innocent, and human nature is preserved by our following the lead of its innocent instincts. Therefore, in seeking to gratify this instinct in question, we are following the instinct of self-preservation in humanity.

But, no doubt, some kinds of knowledge cannot be made to directly serve the instinct in question, cannot be directly related to the sense for beauty, to the sense for conduct. These are instrument knowledges; they lead on to other knowledges, which can. A man who passes his life in instrument knowledges is a specialist. They may be invaluable as instruments to something beyond, for those who have the gift thus to employ them; and they may be disciplines in themselves wherein it is useful for everyone to have some schooling. But it is inconceivable that the generality of men should pass all their mental life with Greek accents or with formal logic. My friend Professor Sylvester,[1] who is one of the first mathematicians in the world, holds transcendental doctrines as to the virtue of mathematics, but those doctrines are not for common men. In the very Senate House and heart of our English Cambridge[2] I once ventured, though not without an apology for my profaneness, to hazard the opinion that for the majority of mankind a little of mathematics, even, goes a long way. Of course this is quite consistent with their being of immense importance as an instrument to something else; but it is the few who have the aptitude for thus using them, not the bulk of mankind.

The natural sciences do not, however, stand on the same footing with these instrument knowledges. Experience shows us that the generality of men will find more interest in learning that, when a taper burns, the wax is converted into carbonic acid and water, or in learning the explanation of the phenomenon of dew, or in learning how the circulation of the blood is carried on, than they find in learning that the genitive plural of *pais* and *pas* does not take the circumflex on the termination. And one piece of natural knowledge is added to another, and others are added to that, and at last we come to propositions so interesting as Mr. Darwin's famous proposition that "our ancestor was a hairy quadruped furnished with a tail and pointed ears, probably arboreal in his habits." Or we come to propositions of such reach and magnitude as those which Professor Huxley delivers, when he says that the notions of our forefathers about the beginning and the end of the world were all wrong, and that nature is the expression of a definite order with which nothing interferes.

Interesting, indeed, these results of science are, important they are, and

9. Plato's *Symposium* 201–07.
1. James T. Sylvester, professor of mathematics at Johns Hopkins University.
2. At Cambridge University mathematics has been

traditionally emphasized. In its original form *Literature and Science* had been delivered as a lecture at Cambridge.

we should all of us be acquainted with them. But what I now wish you to mark is, that we are still, when they are propounded to us and we receive them, we are still in the sphere of intellect and knowledge. And for the generality of men there will be found, I say, to arise, when they have duly taken in the proposition that their ancestor was "a hairy quadruped furnished with a tail and pointed ears, probably arboreal in his habits," there will be found to arise an invincible desire to relate this proposition to the sense in us for conduct, and to the sense in us for beauty. But this the men of science will not do for us, and will hardly even profess to do. They will give us other pieces of knowledge, other facts, about other animals and their ancestors, or about plants, or about stones, or about stars; and they may finally bring us to those great "general conceptions of the universe, which are forced upon us all," says Professor Huxley, "by the progress of physical science." But still it will be *knowledge* only which they give us; knowledge not put for us into relation with our sense for conduct, our sense for beauty, and touched with emotion by being so put; not thus put for us, and therefore, to the majority of mankind, after a certain while, unsatisfying, wearying.

Not to the born naturalist, I admit. But what do we mean by a born naturalist? We mean a man in whom the zeal for observing nature is so uncommonly strong and eminent, that it marks him off from the bulk of mankind. Such a man will pass his life happily in collecting natural knowledge and reasoning upon it, and will ask for nothing, or hardly anything, more. I have heard it said that the sagacious and admirable naturalist whom we lost not very long ago, Mr. Darwin, once owned to a friend that for his part he did not experience the necessity for two things which most men find so necessary to them—religion and poetry; science and the domestic affections, he thought, were enough. To a born naturalist, I can well understand that this should seem so. So absorbing is his occupation with nature, so strong his love for his occupation, that he goes on acquiring natural knowledge and reasoning upon it, and has little time or inclination for thinking about getting it related to the desire in man for conduct, the desire in man for beauty. He relates it to them for himself as he goes along, so far as he feels the need; and he draws from the domestic affections all the additional solace necessary. But then Darwins are extremely rare. Another great and admirable master of natural knowledge, Faraday,[3] was a Sandemanian. That is to say, he related his knowledge to his instinct for conduct and to his instinct for beauty, by the aid of that respectable Scottish sectary, Robert Sandeman.[4] And so strong, in general, is the demand of religion and poetry to have their share in a man, to associate themselves with his knowing, and to relieve and rejoice it, that, probably, for one man amongst us with the disposition to do as Darwin did in this respect, there are at least fifty with the disposition to do as Faraday.

Education lays hold upon us, in fact, by satisfying this demand. Professor Huxley holds up to scorn medieval education, with its neglect of the knowledge of nature, its poverty even of literary studies, its formal logic devoted to "showing how and why that which the Church said was true must be true." But the great medieval Universities were not brought into being, we

---

3. Michael Faraday (1791–1867), chemist.
4. Founder of a Scottish sect bearing his name (1718–1771). "Sectary": zealous member of a sect.

may be sure, by the zeal for giving a jejune and contemptible education. Kings have been their nursing fathers, and queens have been their nursing mothers, but not for this. The medieval Universities came into being, because the supposed knowledge, delivered by Scripture and the Church, so deeply engaged men's hearts, by so simply, easily, and powerfully relating itself to their desire for conduct, their desire for beauty. All other knowledge was dominated by this supposed knowledge and was subordinated to it, because of the surpassing strength of the hold which it gained upon the affections of men, by allying itself profoundly with their sense for conduct, their sense for beauty.

But now, says Professor Huxley, conceptions of the universe fatal to the notions held by our forefathers have been forced upon us by physical science. Grant to him that they are thus fatal, that the new conceptions must and will soon become current everywhere, and that everyone will finally perceive them to be fatal to the beliefs of our forefathers. The need of humane letters, as they are truly called, because they serve the paramount desire in men that good should be forever present to them—the need of humane letters, to establish a relation between the new conceptions, and our instinct for beauty, our instinct for conduct, is only the more visible. The Middle Age could do without humane letters, as it could do without the study of nature, because its supposed knowledge was made to engage its emotions so powerfully. Grant that the supposed knowledge disappears, its power of being made to engage the emotions will of course disappear along with it—but the emotions themselves, and their claim to be engaged and satisfied, will remain. Now if we find by experience that humane letters have an undeniable power of engaging the emotions, the importance of humane letters in a man's training becomes not less, but greater, in proportion to the success of modern science in extirpating what it calls "medieval thinking."

Have humane letters, then, have poetry and eloquence, the power here attributed to them of engaging the emotions, and do they exercise it? And if they have it and exercise it, *how* do they exercise it, so as to exert an influence upon man's sense for conduct, his sense for beauty? Finally, even if they both can and do exert an influence upon the senses in question, how are they to relate to them the results—the modern results—of natural science? All these questions may be asked. First, have poetry and eloquence the power of calling out the emotions? The appeal is to experience. Experience shows that for the vast majority of men, for mankind in general, they have the power. Next, do they exercise it? They do. But then, *how* do they exercise it so as to affect man's sense for conduct, his sense for beauty? And this is perhaps a case for applying the Preacher's words: "Though a man labor to seek it out, yet he shall not find it; yea, father, though a wise man think to know it, yet shall he not be able to find it."[5] Why should it be one thing, in its effect upon the emotions, to say, "Patience is a virtue," and quite another thing, in its effect upon the emotions, to say with Homer,

τλητὸν γὰρ Μοῖραι θυμὸν θέσαν ἀνθρώποισιν[6]—

"for an enduring heart have the destinies appointed to the children of men"? Why should it be one thing, in its effect upon the emotions, to say with the

---

5. Ecclesiastes 8.17 [Arnold's note].   6. *Iliad* 24.49 [Arnold's note].

philosopher Spinoza, *Felicitas in eo consistit quod homo suum esse conservare potest*—"Man's happiness consists in his being able to preserve his own essence,"[7] and quite another thing, in its effect upon the emotions, to say with the Gospel, "What is a man advantaged, if he gain the whole world, and lose himself, forfeit himself?"[8] How does this difference of effect arise? I cannot tell, and I am not much concerned to know; the important thing is that it does arise, and that we can profit by it. But how, finally, are poetry and eloquence to exercise the power of relating the modern results of natural science to man's instinct for conduct, his instinct for beauty? And here again I answer that I do not know *how* they will exercise it, but that they can and will exercise it I am sure. I do not mean that modern philosophical poets and modern philosophical moralists are to come and relate for us, in express terms, the results of modern scientific research to our instinct for conduct, our instinct for beauty. But I mean that we shall find, as a matter of experience, if we know the best that has been thought and uttered in the world, we shall find that the art and poetry and eloquence of men who lived, perhaps, long ago, who had the most limited natural knowledge, who had the most erroneous conceptions about many important matters, we shall find that this art, and poetry, and eloquence, have in fact not only the power of refreshing and delighting us, they have also the power—such is the strength and worth, in essentials, of their authors' criticism of life—they have a fortifying, and elevating, and quickening, and suggestive power, capable of wonderfully helping us to relate the results of modern science to our need for conduct, our need for beauty. Homer's conceptions of the physical universe were, I imagine, grotesque; but really, under the shock of hearing from modern science that "the world is not subordinated to man's use, and that man is not the cynosure of things terrestrial," I could, for my own part, desire no better comfort than Homer's line which I quoted just now,

τλητὸν γὰρ Μοῖραι θυμὸν θέσαν ἀνθρώποισιν—

"for an enduring heart have the destinies appointed to the children of men"!

And the more that men's minds are cleared, the more that the results of science are frankly accepted, the more that poetry and eloquence come to be received and studied as what in truth they really are—the criticism of life by gifted men, alive and active with extraordinary power at an unusual number of points—so much the more will the value of humane letters, and of art also, which is an utterance having a like kind of power with theirs, be felt and acknowledged, and their place in education be secured.

Let us therefore, all of us, avoid indeed as much as possible any invidious comparison between the merits of humane letters, as means of education, and the merits of the natural sciences. But when some President of a Section for Mechanical Science insists on making the comparison, and tells us that "he who in his training has substituted literature and history for natural science has chosen the less useful alternative," let us make answer to him that the student of humane letters only, will, at least, know also the great general conceptions brought in by modern physical science; for science, as Professor Huxley says, forces them upon us all. But the student of the natural sciences only, will, by our very hypothesis, know nothing of humane letters;

---

7. *Ethics* 4.18.   8. Cf. Luke 9.25.

not to mention that in setting himself to be perpetually accumulating natural knowledge, he sets himself to do what only specialists have in general the gift for doing genially. And so he will probably be unsatisfied, or at any rate incomplete, and even more incomplete than the student of humane letters only.

I once mentioned in a school report, how a young man in one of our English training colleges having to paraphrase the passage in *Macbeth* beginning,

> Can'st thou not minister to a mind diseased?[9]

turned this line into, "Can you not wait upon the lunatic?" And I remarked what a curious state of things it would be, if every pupil of our national schools knew, let us say, that the moon is two thousand one hundred and sixty miles in diameter, and thought at the same time that a good paraphrase for

> Can'st thou not minister to a mind diseased?

was, "Can you not wait upon the lunatic?" If one is driven to choose, I think I would rather have a young person ignorant about the moon's diameter, but aware that "Can you not wait upon the lunatic?" is bad, than a young person whose education had been such as to manage things the other way.

Or to go higher than the pupils of our national schools. I have in my mind's eye a member of our British Parliament who comes to travel here in America, who afterwards relates his travels, and who shows a really masterly knowledge of the geology of this great country and of its mining capabilities, but who ends by gravely suggesting that the United States should borrow a prince from our Royal Family, and should make him their king, and should create a House of Lords of great landed proprietors after the pattern of ours; and then America, he thinks, would have her future happily and perfectly secured. Surely, in this case, the President of the Section for Mechanical Science would himself hardly say that our member of Parliament, by concentrating himself upon geology and mineralogy, and so on, and not attending to literature and history, had "chosen the more useful alternative."

If then there is to be separation and option between humane letters on the one hand, and the natural sciences on the other, the great majority of mankind, all who have not exceptional and overpowering aptitudes for the study of nature, would do well, I cannot but think, to chose to be educated in humane letters rather than in the natural sciences. Letters will call out their being at more points, will make them live more.

I said that before I ended I would just touch on the question of classical education, and I will keep my word. Even if literature is to retain a large place in our education, yet Latin and Greek, say the friends of progress, will certainly have to go. Greek is the grand offender in the eyes of these gentlemen. The attackers of the established course of study think that against Greek, at any rate, they have irresistible arguments. Literature may perhaps be needed in education, they say; but why on earth should it be Greek literature? Why not French or German? Nay, "has not an Englishman models in his own literature of every kind of excellence?"[1] As before, it is not on any weak pleadings of my own that I rely for convincing the gainsayers; it is on

9. *Macbeth* 5.3.40.   1. *Science and Culture.*

the constitution of human nature itself, and on the instinct of self-preservation in humanity. The instinct for beauty is set in human nature, as surely as the instinct for knowledge is set there, or the instinct for conduct. If the instinct for beauty is served by Greek literature and art as it is served by no other literature and art, we may trust to the instinct of self-preservation in humanity for keeping Greek as part of our culture. We may trust to it for even making the study of Greek more prevalent than it is now. Greek will come, I hope, some day to be studied more rationally than at present; but it will be increasingly studied as men increasingly feel the need in them for beauty, and how powerfully Greek art and Greek literature can serve this need. Women will again study Greek, as Lady Jane Grey[2] did; I believe that in that chain of forts, with which the fair host of the Amazons are now engirdling our English universities,[3] I find that here in America, in colleges like Smith College in Massachusetts, and Vassar College in the State of New York, and in the happy families of the mixed universities out West, they are studying it already.

Defuit una mihi symmetria prisca—"The antique symmetry was the one thing wanting to me," said Leonardo da Vinci; and he was an Italian. I will not presume to speak for the Americans, but I am sure that, in the Englishman, the want of this admirable symmetry of the Greeks is a thousand times more great and crying than in any Italian. The results of the want show themselves most glaringly, perhaps, in our architecture, but they show themselves, also, in all our art. *Fit details strictly combined, in view of a large general result nobly conceived;* that is just the beautiful *symmetria prisca* of the Greeks, and it is just where we English fail, where all our art fails. Striking ideas we have, and well-executed details we have; but that high symmetry which, with satisfying and delightful effect, combines them, we seldom or never have. The glorious beauty of the Acropolis at Athens did not come from single fine things stuck about on that hill, a statue here, a gateway there—no, it arose from all things being perfectly combined for a supreme total effect. What must not an Englishman feel about our deficiencies in this respect, as the sense for beauty, whereof this symmetry is an essential element, awakens and strengthens within him! what will not one day be his respect and desire for Greece and its *symmetria prisca,* when the scales drop from his eyes as he walks the London streets, and he sees such a lesson in meanness as the Strand, for instance, in its true deformity! But here we are coming to our friend Mr. Ruskin's province,[4] and I will not intrude upon it, for he is its very sufficient guardian.

And so we at last find, it seems, we find flowing in favor of the humanities the natural and necessary stream of things, which seemed against them when we started. The "hairy quadruped furnished with a tail and pointed ears, probably arboreal in his habits," this good fellow carried hidden in his nature, apparently, something destined to develop into a necessity for humane letters. Nay, more; we seem finally to be even led to the further conclusion that our hairy ancestor carried in his nature, also, a necessity for Greek.

And therefore, to say the truth, I cannot really think that humane letters

---

2. Reputed to be a learned scholar in Greek. Grey (1537–1554) was proclaimed queen of England in 1553 but was forced to abdicate the throne nine days later. She was executed by order of Queen Mary.

3. Colleges for women at Oxford and Cambridge.
4. In such books as *The Stones of Venice,* Ruskin had criticized the "meanness" of Victorian architecture.

are in much actual danger of being thrust out from their leading place in education, in spite of the array of authorities against them at this moment. So long as human nature is what it is, their attractions will remain irresistible. As with Greek, so with letters generally: they will some day come, we may hope, to be studied more rationally, but they will not lose their place. What will happen will rather be that there will be crowded into education other matters besides, far too many; there will be, perhaps, a period of unsettlement and confusion and false tendency; but letters will not in the end lose their leading place. If they lose it for a time, they will get it back again. We shall be brought back to them by our wants and aspirations. And a poor humanist may possess his soul in patience, neither strive nor cry, admit the energy and brilliancy of the partisans of physical science, and their present favor with the public, to be far greater than his own, and still have a happy faith that the nature of things works silently on behalf of the studies which he loves, and that, while we shall all have to acquaint ourselves with the great results reached by modern science, and to give ourselves as much training in its disciplines as we can conveniently carry, yet the majority of men will always require humane letters; and so much the more, as they have the more and the greater results of science to relate to the need in man for conduct, and to the need in him for beauty.

1882, 1885

THOMAS HENRY HUXLEY
1825–1895

In Victorian controversies over religion and education, one of the most distinctive participants was Thomas Henry Huxley, a scientist who wrote clear, readable, and very persuasive English prose. Huxley's literary skill was responsible for his being lured out of his laboratory onto the platforms of public debate where his role was to champion, as he said, "the application of scientific methods of investigation to all the problems of life."

Huxley, a schoolmaster's son, was born in a London suburb. Until beginning the study of medicine, at seventeen, he had had little formal education, having taught himself classical and modern languages and the rudiments of scientific theory. In 1846, after receiving his degree in medicine, he embarked on a long voyage to the South Seas during which he studied the marine life of the tropical oceans and established a considerable reputation as a zoologist. Later he made investigations in geology and physiology, completing a total of 250 research papers during his lifetime. He also held teaching positions and served on public committees, but it was as a popularizer of science that he made his real mark. His popularizing was of two kinds. The first was to make the results of scientific investigations intelligible to a large audience. Such lectures as On a Piece of Chalk (not included here) are models of clear, vivid exposition that can be studied with profit by anyone interested in the art of teaching. His second kind of popularizing consisted of expounding the values of scientific education or of the application of scientific thinking to problems in religion. Here Huxley excels not so much as a teacher as a debater. In 1860 he demonstrated his argumentative skill when, as Darwin's defender or "bulldog," he demolished Bishop Wilberforce in a battle over *The Origin of Species*. In the 1870s, in such lectures as *Science and Culture*, he engaged in more genial fencing with Matthew Arnold concerning the relative importance of the study of science or the humanities in education. And in the 1880s he debated with William Gladstone on the topic of interpreting the Bible. His essay *Agnosticism and Christianity* indicates his premises in this controversy.

Summing up his own career in his *Autobiography*, Huxley noted that he had subordinated his ambition for scientific fame to other ends: "to the popularization of science; to the development and organization of scientific education; to the endless series of battles and skirmishes over evolution; and to untiring opposition to that ecclesiastical spirit, that clericalism, which . . . to whatever denomination it may belong, is the deadly enemy of science." In fighting these "battles" Huxley operated from different bases. Most of the time he wrote as a biologist engaged in assessing all assumptions by the tests of laboratory science. In this role he argued that humans are merely animals and that traditional religion is a tissue of superstitions and lies. At other times, however, Huxley wrote as a humanist and even as a follower of Carlyle. As he stated in a letter: "*Sartor Resartus* led me to know that a deep sense of religion was compatible with the entire absence of theology." In this second role he argued that humans are a very special kind of animal whose great distinction is that they are endowed with a moral sense and with freedom of the will; creatures who are admirable not for following nature but for departing from nature. The humanistic streak muddies the seemingly clear current of Huxley's thinking yet makes him a more interesting figure than he might otherwise have been. It is noteworthy that in the writings of his grandsons, Julian Huxley, the biologist, and Aldous Huxley, the novelist, a similar division of mind can once more be detected.

Even in his dying, T. H. Huxley continued his role as controversialist. The words he asked to be engraved on his tomb are typical of his view of life and typical, also, in the effect they had on his contemporaries, some of whom found the epitaph to be shocking:

> Be not afraid, ye waiting hearts that weep
> For still he giveth His beloved sleep,
> And if an endless sleep He wills, so best.

From Science and Culture[1]

[THE VALUES OF EDUCATION IN THE SCIENCES]

From the time that the first suggestion to introduce physical science into ordinary education was timidly whispered, until now, the advocates of scientific education have met with opposition of two kinds. On the one hand, they have been pooh-poohed by the men of business who pride themselves on being the representatives of practicality; while, on the other hand, they have been excommunicated by the classical scholars, in their capacity of Levites in charge of the ark of culture[2] and monopolists of liberal education.

The practical men believed that the idol whom they worship—rule of thumb—has been the source of the past prosperity, and will suffice for the future welfare of the arts and manufactures. They are of opinion that science is speculative rubbish; that theory and practice have nothing to do with one

1. This essay was first delivered as an address in 1880. The occasion had been the opening of a new Scientific College at Birmingham, which had been endowed by Sir Josiah Mason (1795–1881), a self-made businessman. For Matthew Arnold's reply to Huxley's argument see his essay *Literature and Science* (p. 1545).
2. In the Old Testament, the Levites were the priests preoccupied with traditional ritual observances (cf. Joshua 6).

another; and that the scientific habit of mind is an impediment, rather than an aid, in the conduct of ordinary affairs.

I have used the past tense in speaking of the practical men—for although they were very formidable thirty years ago, I am not sure that the pure species has not been extirpated. In fact, so far as mere argument goes, they have been subjected to such a *feu d'enfer*[3] that it is a miracle if any have escaped. But I have remarked that your typical practical man has an unexpected resemblance to one of Milton's angels. His spiritual wounds, such as are inflicted by logical weapons, may be as deep as a well and as wide as a church door,[4] but beyond shedding a few drops of ichor,[5] celestial or otherwise, he is no whit the worse. So, if any of these opponents be left, I will not waste time in vain repetition of the demonstrative evidence of the practical value of science; but knowing that a parable will sometimes penetrate where syllogisms fail to effect an entrance, I will offer a story for their consideration.

Once upon a time, a boy, with nothing to depend upon but his own vigorous nature, was thrown into the thick of the struggle for existence in the midst of a great manufacturing population. He seems to have had a hard fight, inasmuch as, by the time he was thirty years of age, his total disposable funds amounted to twenty pounds. Nevertheless, middle life found him giving proof of his comprehension of the practical problems he had been roughly called upon to solve, by a career of remarkable prosperity.

Finally, having reached old age with its well-earned surroundings of "honor, troops of friends,"[6] the hero of my story bethought himself of those who were making a like start in life, and how he could stretch out a helping hand to them.

After long and anxious reflection this successful practical man of business could devise nothing better than to provide them with the means of obtaining "sound, extensive, and practical scientific knowledge." And he devoted a large part of his wealth and five years of incessant work to this end.

I need not point the moral of a tale which, as the solid and spacious fabric of the Scientific College assures us, is no fable, nor can anything which I could say intensify the force of this practical answer to practical objections.

We may take it for granted then, that, in the opinion of those best qualified to judge, the diffusion of thorough scientific education is an absolutely essential condition of industrial progress; and that the College which has been opened today will confer an inestimable boon upon those whose livelihood is to be gained by the practice of the arts and manufactures of the district.

The only question worth discussion is whether the conditions under which the work of the College is to be carried out are such as to give it the best possible chance of achieving permanent success.

Sir Josiah Mason, without doubt most wisely, has left very large freedom of action to the trustees, to whom he proposes ultimately to commit the administration of the College, so that they may be able to adjust its arrangements in accordance with the changing conditions of the future. But, with respect to three points, he has laid most explicit injunctions upon both administrators and teachers.

---

3. Hellfire (French).
4. Shakespeare's *Romeo and Juliet* 3.1.99–100.
5. Ethereal fluid that supposedly flows through

the veins of the gods.
6. Cf. Shakespeare's *Macbeth* 5.3.25.

Party politics are forbidden to enter into the minds of either, so far as the work of the College is concerned; theology is as sternly banished from its precincts; and finally, it is especially declared that the College shall make no provision for "mere literary instruction and education."

It does not concern me at present to dwell upon the first two injunctions any longer than may be needful to express my full conviction of their wisdom. But the third prohibition brings us face to face with those other opponents of scientific education, who are by no means in the moribund condition of the practical man, but alive, alert, and formidable.

It is not impossible that we shall hear this express exclusion of "literary instruction and education" from a College which, nevertheless, professes to give a high and efficient education, sharply criticized. Certainly the time was that the Levites of culture would have sounded their trumpets against its walls as against an educational Jericho.[7]

How often have we not been told that the study of physical science is incompetent to confer culture; that it touches none of the higher problems of life; and, what is worse, that the continual devotion to scientific studies tends to generate a narrow and bigoted belief in the applicability of scientific methods to the search after truth of all kinds? How frequently one has reason to observe that no reply to a troublesome argument tells so well as calling its author a "mere scientific specialist." And, as I am afraid it is not permissible to speak of this form of opposition to scientific education in the past tense; may we not expect to be told that this, not only omission, but prohibition, of "mere literary instruction and education" is a patent example of scientific narrow-mindedness?

I am not acquainted with Sir Josiah Mason's reasons for the action which he has taken; but if, as I apprehend is the case, he refers to the ordinary classical course of our schools and universities by the name of "mere literary instruction and education," I venture to offer sundry reasons of my own in support of that action.

For I hold very strongly by two convictions: The first is that neither the discipline nor the subject matter of classical education is of such direct value to the student of physical science as to justify the expenditure of valuable time upon either; and the second is that for the purpose of attaining real culture, an exclusively scientific education is at least as effectual as an exclusively literary education.

I need hardly point out to you that these opinions, especially the latter, are diametrically opposed to those of the great majority of educated Englishmen, influenced as they are by school and university traditions. In their belief, culture is obtainable only by a liberal education; and a liberal education is synonymous, not merely with education and instruction in literature, but in one particular form of literature, namely, that of Greek and Roman antiquity. They hold that the man who has learned Latin and Greek, however little, is educated; while he who is versed in other branches of knowledge, however deeply, is a more or less respectable specialist, not admissible into the cultured caste. The stamp of the educated man, the University degree, is not for him.

I am too well acquainted with the generous catholicity of spirit, the true

---

7. The Levites blew their trumpets before the city walls of Jericho to bring them down (Joshua 6).

sympathy with scientific thought, which pervades the writings of our chief apostle of culture[8] to identify him with these opinions; and yet one may cull from one and another of those epistles to the Philistines, which so much delight all who do not answer to that name, sentences which lend them some support.

Mr. Arnold tells us that the meaning of culture is "to know the best that has been thought and said in the world." It is the criticism of life contained in literature. That criticism regards "Europe as being, for intellectual and spiritual purposes, one great confederation, bound to a joint action and working to a common result; and whose members have, for their common outfit, a knowledge of Greek, Roman, and Eastern antiquity, and of one another. Special, local, and temporary advantages being put out of account, that modern nation will in the intellectual and spiritual sphere make most progress, which most thoroughly carries out this program. And what is that but saying that we too, all of us, as individuals, the more thoroughly we carry it out, shall make the more progress?"[9]

We have here to deal with two distinct propositions. The first, that a criticism of life is the essence of culture; the second, that literature contains the materials which suffice for the construction of such criticism.

I think that we must all assent to the first proposition. For culture certainly means something quite different from learning or technical skill. It implies the possession of an ideal, and the habit of critically estimating the value of things by comparison with a theoretic standard. Perfect culture should supply a complete theory of life, based upon a clear knowledge alike of its possibilities and of its limitations.

But we may agree to all this, and yet strongly dissent from the assumption that literature alone is competent to supply this knowledge. After having learnt all that Greek, Roman, and Eastern antiquity have thought and said, and all that modern literature have to tell us, it is not self-evident that we have laid a sufficiently broad and deep foundation for that criticism of life which constitutes culture.

Indeed, to anyone acquainted with the scope of physical science, it is not at all evident. Considering progress only in the "intellectual and spiritual sphere," I find myself wholly unable to admit that either nations or individuals will really advance, if their common outfit draws nothing from the stores of physical science. I should say that an army, without weapons of precision and with no particular base of operations, might more hopefully enter upon a campaign on the Rhine than a man, devoid of a knowledge of what physical science has done in the last century, upon a criticism of life.

When a biologist meets with an anomaly, he instinctively turns to the study of development to clear it up. The rationale of contradictory opinions may with equal confidence be sought in history.

It is, happily, no new thing that Englishmen should employ their wealth in building and endowing institutions for educational purposes. But, five or six hundred years ago, deeds of foundation expressed or implied conditions as nearly as possible contrary to those which have been thought expedient

---

8. I.e., Matthew Arnold. For his discussion of the Philistines, see *Culture and Anarchy* (p. 1528).

9. Arnold, *The Function of Criticism at the Present Time,* para. 4 from the end.

by Sir Josiah Mason. That is to say, physical science was practically ignored, while a certain literary training was enjoined as a means to the acquirement of knowledge which was essentially theological.

The reason of this singular contradiction between the actions of men alike animated by a strong and disinterested desire to promote the welfare of their fellows, is easily discovered.

At that time, in fact, if anyone desired knowledge beyond such as could be obtained by his own observation, or by common conversation, his first necessity was to learn the Latin language, inasmuch as all the higher knowledge of the western world was contained in words written in that language. Hence, Latin grammar, with logic and rhetoric, studied through Latin, were the fundamentals of education. With respect to the substance of the knowledge imparted through this channel, the Jewish and Christian Scriptures, as interpreted and supplemented by the Romish Church, were held to contain a complete and infallibly true body of information.

Theological dicta were, to the thinkers of those days, that which the axioms and definitions of Euclid are to the geometers of these. The business of the philosophers of the Middle Ages was to deduce from the data furnished by the theologians, conclusions in accordance with ecclesiastical decrees. They were allowed the high privilege of showing, by logical process, how and why that which the Church said was true, must be true. And if their demonstrations fell short of or exceeded this limit, the Church was maternally ready to check their aberrations; if need were, by the help of the secular arm.

Between the two, our ancestors were furnished with a compact and complete criticism of life. They were told how the world began and how it would end; they learned that all material existence was but a base and insignificant blot upon the fair face of the spiritual world, and that nature was, to all intents and purposes, the playground of the devil; they learned that the earth is the center of the visible universe, and that man is the cynosure of things terrestrial, and more especially was it inculcated that the course of nature had no fixed order, but that it could be, and constantly was, altered by the agency of innumerable spiritual beings, good and bad, according as they were moved by the deeds and prayers of men. The sum and substance of the whole doctrine was to produce the conviction that the only thing really worth knowing in this world was how to secure that place in a better which, under certain conditions, the Church promised.

Our ancestors had a living belief in this theory of life, and acted upon it in their dealings with education, as in all other matters. Culture meant saintliness—after the fashion of the saints of those days; the education that led to it was, of necessity, theological; and the way to theology lay through Latin.

That the study of nature—further than was requisite for the satisfaction of everyday wants—should have any bearing on human life was far from the thoughts of men thus trained. Indeed, as nature had been cursed for man's sake, it was an obvious conclusion that those who meddled with nature were likely to come into pretty close contact with Satan. And, if any born scientific investigator followed his instincts, he might safely reckon upon earning the reputation, and probably upon suffering the fate, of a sorcerer.

Had the western world been left to itself in Chinese isolation, there is no saying how long this state of things might have endured. But, happily, it was not left to itself. Even earlier than the thirteenth century, the development of Moorish civilization in Spain and the great movement of the Crusades had introduced the leaven which, from that day to this, has never ceased to work. At first, through the intermediation of Arabic translations, afterwards by the study of the originals, the western nations of Europe became acquainted with the writings of the ancient philosophers and poets, and, in time, with the whole of the vast literature of antiquity.

Whatever there was of high intellectual aspiration or dominant capacity in Italy, France, Germany, and England, spent itself for centuries in taking possession of the rich inheritance left by the dead civilizations of Greece and Rome. Marvelously aided by the invention of printing,[1] classical learning spread and flourished. Those who possessed it prided themselves on having attained the highest culture then within the reach of mankind.

And justly. For, saving Dante on his solitary pinnacle, there was no figure in modern literature at the time of the Renaissance to compare with the men of antiquity; there was no art to compete with their sculpture; there was no physical science but that which Greece had created. Above all, there was no other example of perfect intellectual freedom—of the unhesitating acceptance of reason as the sole guide to truth and the supreme arbiter of conduct.

The new learning necessarily soon exerted a profound influence upon education. The language of the monks and schoolmen[2] seemed little better than gibberish to scholars fresh from Virgil and Cicero, and the study of Latin was placed upon a new foundation. Moreover, Latin itself ceased to afford the sole key to knowledge. The student who sought the highest thought of antiquity found only a secondhand reflection of it in Roman literature, and turned his face to the full light of the Greeks. And after a battle, not altogether dissimilar to that which is at present being fought over the teaching of physical science, the study of Greek was recognized as an essential element of all higher education.

Then the Humanists, as they were called, won the day; and the great reform which they effected was of incalculable service to mankind. But the nemesis of all reformers is finality; and the reformers of education, like those of religion, fell into the profound, however common, error of mistaking the beginning for the end of the work of reformation.

The representatives of the Humanists, in the nineteenth century, take their stand upon classical education as the sole avenue to culture as firmly as if we were still in the age of Renaissance. Yet, surely, the present intellectual relations of the modern and the ancient worlds are profoundly different from those which obtained three centuries ago. Leaving aside the existence of a great and characteristically modern literature, of modern painting, and, especially, of modern music, there is one feature of the present state of the civilized world which separates it more widely from the Renaissance than the Renaissance was separated from the Middle Ages.

This distinctive character of our own times lies in the vast and constantly increasing part which is played by natural knowledge. Not only is our daily life shaped by it; not only does the prosperity of millions of men depend upon it, but our whole theory of life has long been influenced, consciously or unconsciously, by the general conceptions of the universe which have been forced upon us by physical science.

---

1. In the mid-15th century.
2. Exponents of the theology, philosophy, and logic of the medieval period in Europe.

In fact, the most elementary acquaintance with the results of scientific investigation shows us that they offer a broad and striking contradiction to the opinion so implicitly credited and taught in the Middle Ages.

The notions of the beginning and the end of the world entertained by our forefathers are no longer credible. It is very certain that the earth is not the chief body in the material universe, and that the world is not subordinated to man's use. It is even more certain that nature is the expression of a definite order with which nothing interferes, and that the chief business of mankind is to learn that order and govern themselves accordingly. Moreover this scientific "criticism of life" presents itself to us with different credentials from any other. It appeals not to authority, nor to what anybody may have thought or said, but to nature. It admits that all our interpretations of natural fact are more or less imperfect and symbolic, and bids the learner seek for truth not among words but among things. It warns us that the assertion which outstrips evidence is not only a blunder but a crime.

The purely classical education advocated by the representatives of the Humanists in our day gives no inkling of all this. A man may be a better scholar than Erasmus,[3] and know no more of the chief causes of the present intellectual fermentation than Erasmus did. Scholarly and pious persons, worthy of all respect, favor us with allocutions upon the sadness of the antagonism of science to their medieval way of thinking, which betray an ignorance of the first principles of scientific investigation, an incapacity for understanding what a man of science means by veracity, and an unconsciousness of the weight of established scientific truths, which is almost comical.

* * *

Thus I venture to think that the pretensions of our modern Humanists to the possession of the monopoly of culture and to the exclusive inheritance of the spirit of antiquity must be abated, if not abandoned. But I should be very sorry that anything I have said should be taken to imply a desire on my part to depreciate the value of classical education, as it might be and as it sometimes is. The native capacities of mankind vary no less than their opportunities; and while culture is one, the road by which one man may best reach it is widely different from that which is most advantageous to another. Again, while scientific education is yet inchoate and tentative, classical education is thoroughly well organized upon the practical experience of generations of teachers. So that, given ample time for learning and estimation for ordinary life, or for a literary career, I do not think that a young Englishman in search of culture can do better than follow the course usually marked out for him, supplementing its deficiencies by his own efforts.

But for those who mean to make science their serious occupation; or who intend to follow the profession of medicine; or who have to enter early upon the business of life; for all these, in my opinion, classical education is a mistake; and it is for this reason that I am glad to see "mere literary education and instruction" shut out from the curriculum of Sir Josiah Mason's College, seeing that its inclusion would probably lead to the introduction of the ordinary smattering of Latin and Greek.

Nevertheless, I am the last person to question the importance of genuine

3. Eminent Dutch humanist and scholar (1466–1536).

literary education, or to suppose that intellectual culture can be complete without it. An exclusively scientific training will bring about a mental twist as surely as an exclusively literary training. The value of the cargo does not compensate for a ship's being out of trim; and I should be very sorry to think that the Scientific College would turn out none but lopsided men.

There is no need, however, that such a catastrophe should happen. Instruction in English, French, and German is provided, and thus the three greatest literatures of the modern world are made accessible to the student.

French and German, and especially the latter language, are absolutely indispensable to those who desire full knowledge in any department of science. But even supposing that the knowledge of these languages acquired is not more than sufficient for purely scientific purposes, every Englishman has, in his native tongue, an almost perfect instrument of literary expression; and, in his own literature, models of every kind of literary excellence. If an Englishman cannot get literary culture out of his Bible, his Shakespeare, his Milton, neither, in my belief, will the profoundest study of Homer and Sophocles, Virgil and Horace, give it to him.

Thus, since the constitution of the College makes sufficient provision for literary as well as for scientific education, and since artistic instruction is also contemplated, it seems to me that a fairly complete culture is offered to all who are willing to take advantage of it.

1880, 1881

From Agnosticism and Christianity[1]

[AGNOSTICISM DEFINED]

Nemo ergo ex me scire quaerat, quod me nescire scio, nisi forte ut nescire discat.
—AUGUSTINUS, *De Civ. Dei*, XII.7.[2]

The present discussion has arisen out of the use, which has become general in the last few years, of the terms "Agnostic"[3] and "Agnosticism."

The people who call themselves "Agnostics" have been charged with doing so because they have not the courage to declare themselves "Infidels." It has been insinuated that they have adopted a new name in order to escape the unpleasantness which attaches to their proper denomination. To this wholly erroneous imputation I have replied by showing that the term "Agnostic" did, as a matter of fact, arise in a manner which negatives it; and my statement has not been, and cannot be, refuted. Moreover, speaking for myself, and without impugning the right of any other person to use the term in another sense, I further say that Agnosticism is not properly described as a "negative" creed, nor indeed as a creed of any kind, except in so far as it expresses absolute faith in the validity of a principle, which is as much ethical as intellectual. This principle may be stated in various ways, but they all amount

---

1. This essay appeared in a magazine in 1889 as a reply to critics who had argued that agnostics were simply infidels under a new name. It was later included in Huxley's volume *Essays on Some Controverted Questions* (1892).

2. No one, therefore, should seek to learn knowledge from me, for I know that I do not know—unless indeed he wishes to learn that he does not know (Latin; Saint Augustine, *City of God* 12.7).
3. The term *agnostic* was coined by Huxley.

to this: that it is wrong for a man to say that he is certain of the objective truth of any proposition unless he can produce evidence which logically justifies that certainty. This is what Agnosticism asserts; and, in my opinion, it is all that is essential to Agnosticism. That which Agnostics deny and repudiate, as immoral, is the contrary doctrine, that there are propositions which men ought to believe, without logically satisfactory evidence; and that reprobation ought to attach to the profession of disbelief in such inadequately supported propositions. The justification of the Agnostic principles lies in the success which follows upon its application, whether in the field of natural, or in that of civil, history; and in the fact that, so far as these topics are concerned, no sane man thinks of denying its validity.

Still speaking for myself, I add that though Agnosticism is not, and cannot be, a creed, except in so far as its general principle is concerned; yet that the application of that principle results in the denial of, or the suspension of judgment concerning, a number of propositions respecting which our contemporary ecclesiastical "gnostics" profess entire certainty. And, in so far as these ecclesiastical persons can be justified in their old-established custom (which many nowadays think more honored in the breach than the observance) of using opprobrious names to those who differ from them, I fully admit their right to call me and those who think with me "Infidels"; all I have ventured to urge is that they must not expect us to speak of ourselves by that title.

The extent of the region of the uncertain, the number of the problems the investigation of which ends in a verdict of not proven, will vary according to the knowledge and the intellectual habits of the individual Agnostic. I do not very much care to speak of anything as "unknowable." What I am sure about is that there are many topics about which I know nothing; and which, so far as I can see, are out of reach of my faculties. But whether these things are knowable by anyone else is exactly one of those matters which is beyond my knowledge, though I may have a tolerably strong opinion as to the probabilities of the case. Relatively to myself, I am quite sure that the region of uncertainty—the nebulous country in which words play the part of realities—is far more extensive than I could wish. Materialism and Idealism; Theism and Atheism; the doctrine of the soul and its mortality or immortality—appear in the history of philosophy like the shades of Scandinavian heroes, eternally slaying one another and eternally coming to life again in a metaphysical "Nifelheim."[4] It is getting on for twenty-five centuries, at least, since mankind began seriously to give their minds to these topics. Generation after generation, philosophy has been doomed to roll the stone uphill; and, just as all the world swore it was at the top, down it has rolled to the bottom again.[5] All this is written in innumerable books; and he who will toil through them will discover that the stone is just where it was when the work began. Hume saw this; Kant saw it; since their time, more and more eyes have been cleansed of the films which prevented them from seeing it; until now the weight and number of those who refuse to be the prey of verbal mystifications has begun to tell in practical life.

It was inevitable that a conflict should arise between Agnosticism and

4. In Norse mythology, realms of cold and darkness.
5. Cf. the Greek story of Sisyphus in Hades, who was condemned to keep rolling a stone uphill, which always rolled downhill again before it reached the summit.

Theology; or rather, I ought to say, between Agnosticism and Ecclesiasticism. For Theology, the science, is one thing; and Ecclesiasticism, the championship of a foregone conclusion[6] as to the truth of a particular form of Theology, is another. With scientific Theology, Agnosticism has no quarrel. On the contrary, the Agnostic, knowing too well the influence of prejudice and idiosyncrasy, even on those who desire most earnestly to be impartial, can wish for nothing more urgently than that the scientific theologian should not only be at perfect liberty to thresh out the matter in his own fashion; but that he should, if he can, find flaws in the Agnostic position; and, even if demonstration is not to be had, that he should put, in their full force, the grounds of the conclusions he thinks probable. The scientific theologian admits the Agnostic principle, however widely his results may differ from those reached by the majority of Agnostics.

But, as between Agnosticism and Ecclesiasticism, or, as our neighbors across the Channel call it, Clericalism, there can be neither peace nor truce. The Cleric asserts that it is morally wrong not to believe certain propositions, whatever the results of a strict scientific investigation of the evidence of these propositions. He tells us "that religious error is, in itself, of an immoral nature."[7] He declares that he has prejudged certain conclusions, and looks upon those who show cause for arrest of judgment as emissaries of Satan. It necessarily follows that, for him, the attainment of faith, not the ascertainment of truth, is the highest aim of mental life. And, on careful analysis of the nature of this faith, it will too often be found to be, not the mystic process of unity with the Divine, understood by the religious enthusiast; but that which the candid simplicity of a Sunday scholar once defined it to be. "Faith," said this unconscious plagiarist of Tertullian,[8] "is the power of saying you believe things which are incredible."

Now I, and many other Agnostics, believe that faith, in this sense, is an abomination; and though we do not indulge in the luxury of self-righteousness so far as to call those who are not of our way of thinking hard names, we do feel that the disagreement between ourselves and those who hold this doctrine is even more moral than intellectual. It is desirable there should be an end of any mistakes on this topic. If our clerical opponents were clearly aware of the real state of the case, there would be an end of the curious delusion, which often appears between the lines of their writings, that those whom they are so fond of calling "Infidels" are people who not only ought to be, but in their hearts are, ashamed of themselves. It would be discourteous to do more than hint the antipodal opposition of this pleasant dream of theirs to facts.

The clerics and their lay allies commonly tell us that if we refuse to admit that there is good ground for expressing definite convictions about certain topics, the bonds of human society will dissolve and mankind lapse into savagery. There are several answers to this assertion. One is that the bonds of human society were formed without the aid of their theology; and, in the opinion of not a few competent judges, have been weakened rather than strengthened by a good deal of it. Greek science, Greek art, the ethics of old

---

6. Let us maintain, before we have proved. This seeming paradox is the secret of happiness. (Dr. Newman, Tract 85) [Huxley's note].
7. Dr. Newman, Essay on Development [Huxley's note].
8. Roman author and church father (ca. 155–ca. 222).

Israel, the social organization of old Rome, contrived to come into being, without the help of anyone who believed in a single distinctive article of the simplest of the Christian creeds. The science, the art, the jurisprudence, the chief political and social theories, of the modern world have grown out of those of Greece and Rome—not by favor of, but in the teeth of, the fundamental teachings of early Christianity, to which science, art, and any serious occupation with the things of this world, were alike despicable.

Again, all that is best in the ethics of the modern world, in so far as it has not grown out of Greek thought, or Barbarian manhood, is the direct development of the ethics of old Israel. There is no code of legislation, ancient or modern, at once so just and so merciful, so tender to the weak and poor, as the Jewish law; and, if the Gospels are to be trusted, Jesus of Nazareth himself declared that he taught nothing but that which lay implicitly, or explicitly, in the religious and ethical system of his people.

> And the scribe said unto him, Of a truth, Teacher, thou hast well said that he is one; and there is none other but he and to love him with all the heart, and with all the understanding, and with all the strength, and to love his neighbour as himself, is much more than all whole burnt offerings and sacrifices. (Mark xii.32–33)

Here is the briefest of summaries of the teaching of the prophets of Israel of the eighth century; does the Teacher, whose doctrine is thus set forth in his presence, repudiate the exposition? Nay; we are told, on the contrary, that Jesus saw that he "answered discreetly," and replied, "Thou are not far from the kingdom of God."

So that I think that even if the creeds,[9] from the so-called "Apostles' " to the so-called "Athanasian," were swept into oblivion; and even if the human race should arrive at the conclusion that, whether a bishop washes a cup or leaves it unwashed, is not a matter of the least consequence, it will get on very well. The causes which have led to the development of morality in mankind, which have guided or impelled us all the way from the savage to the civilized state, will not cease to operate because a number of ecclesiastical hypotheses turn out to be baseless. And, even if the absurd notion that morality is more the child of speculation than of practical necessity and inherited instinct, had any foundation; if all the world is going to thieve, murder, and otherwise misconduct itself as soon as it discovers that certain portions of ancient history are mythical; what is the relevance of such arguments to any one who holds by the Agnostic principle?

Surely, the attempt to cast out Beelzebub by the aid of Beelzebub is a hopeful procedure as compared to that of preserving morality by the aid of immorality. For I suppose it is admitted that an Agnostic may be perfectly sincere, may be competent, and may have studied the question at issue with as much care as his clerical opponents. But, if the Agnostic really believes what he says, the "dreadful consequence" argufier (consistently, I admit, with his own principles) virtually asks him to abstain from telling the truth, or to say what he believes to be untrue, because of the supposed injurious consequences to morality. "Beloved brethren, that we may be spotlessly moral, before all things let us lie," is the sum total of many an exhortation addressed

9. Summaries of Christian doctrine.

to the "Infidel." Now, as I have already pointed out, we cannot oblige our exhorters. We leave the practical application of the convenient doctrines of "Reserve" and "Non-natural interpretation" to those who invented them.

I trust that I have now made amends for any ambiguity, or want of fullness, in my previous exposition of that which I hold to be the essence of the Agnostic doctrine. Henceforward, I might hope to hear no more of the assertion that we are necessarily Materialists, Idealists, Atheists, Theists, or any other ists, if experience had led me to think that the proved falsity of a statement was any guarantee against its repetition. And those who appreciate the nature of our position will see, at once, that when Ecclesiasticism declares that we ought to believe this, that, and the other, and are very wicked if we don't, it is impossible for us to give any answer but this: We have not the slightest objection to believe anything you like, if you will give us good grounds for belief; but, if you cannot, we must respectfully refuse, even if that refusal should wreck morality and insure our own damnation several times over. We are quite content to leave that to the decision of the future. The course of the past has impressed us with the firm conviction that no good ever comes of falsehood, and we feel warranted in refusing even to experiment in that direction. * * *

1889, 1892

GEORGE MEREDITH
1828–1909

Like Thomas Hardy, George Meredith preferred writing poetry to writing novels, but it was as the author of *The Ordeal of Richard Feverel* (1859), *The Egoist* (1879), and other novels that he made his mark. His poems nevertheless deserve more attention than they have yet received, especially *Modern Love* (1862), a brilliant narrative poem that was greeted by the *Saturday Review* as "a grave moral mistake." This sequence of fifty 16-line sonnets is a kind of novel in verse that analyzes the sufferings of a husband and wife whose marriage is breaking up. The story is told, for the most part, by the husband speaking in the first person, but the opening and closing sections are in third person. *Modern Love* was probably derived, in part, from Meredith's own experiences. At twenty-one, at the outset of his career as a writer in London, he married a daughter of the satirist Thomas Love Peacock. Nine years later, after a series of quarrels, his wife eloped to Europe with another artist. The Merediths were never reconciled, and in 1861 she died.

From Modern Love

1

By this he knew she wept with waking eyes:
That, at his hand's light quiver by her head,
The strange low sobs that shook their common bed
Were called into her with a sharp surprise,
5   And strangled mute, like little gaping snakes,

Dreadfully venomous to him. She lay
Stone-still, and the long darkness flowed away
With muffled pulses. Then, as midnight makes
Her giant heart of Memory and Tears
10 Drink the pale drug of silence, and so beat
Sleep's heavy measure, they from head to feet
Were moveless, looking through their dead black years
By vain regret scrawled over the blank wall.
Like sculptured effigies they might be seen
15 Upon their marriage tomb, the sword between;[1]
Each wishing for the sword that severs all.

2

It ended, and the morrow brought the task.
Her eyes were guilty gates, that let him in
By shutting all too zealous for their sin:
Each sucked a secret, and each wore a mask.
5 But, oh, the bitter taste her beauty had!
He sickened as at breath of poison-flowers:
A languid humor stole among the hours,
And if their smiles encountered, he went mad,
And raged deep inward, till the light was brown
10 Before his vision, and the world, forgot,
Looked wicked as some old dull murder spot.
A star with lurid beams, she seemed to crown
The pit of infamy: and then again
He fainted on his vengefulness, and strove
15 To ape the magnanimity of love,
And smote himself, a shuddering heap of pain.

17

At dinner, she is hostess, I am host.
Went the feast ever cheerfuller? She keeps
The Topic over intellectual deeps
In buoyancy afloat. They see no ghost.
5 With sparkling surface-eyes we ply the ball:
It is in truth a most contagious game:
HIDING THE SKELETON, shall be its name.
Such play as this the devils might appall!
But here's the greater wonder: in that we,
10 Enamored of an acting naught can tire.
Each other, like true hypocrites, admire;
Warm-lighted looks, Love's ephemeridae,[2]
Shoot gayly o'er the dishes and the wine.
We waken envy of our happy lot.
15 Fast, sweet, and golden, shows the marriage knot.
Dear guests, you now have seen Love's corpse-light[3] shine.

---

1. The now silent couple are as motionless as recumbent stone statues on top of a tomb. In medieval legend, a naked sword between lovers ensured chastity.

2. Insects that live for one day only.
3. Phosphorescent light such as seen in marshes. When appearing in a cemetery it was believed to portend a funeral.

49

He found her by the ocean's moaning verge,
Nor any wicked change in her discerned;
And she believed his old love had returned,
Which was her exultation, and her scourge.
5   She took his hand, and walked with him, and seemed
The wife he sought, though shadowlike and dry.
She had one terror, lest her heart should sigh,
And tell her loudly she no longer dreamed.
She dared not say, "This is my breast: look in."
10   But there's a strength to help the desperate weak.
That night he learned how silence best can speak
The awful things when Pity pleads for Sin.
About the middle of the night her call
Was heard, and he came wondering to the bed.
15   "Now kiss me, dear! it may be, now!" she said.
Lethe[4] had passed those lips, and he knew all.

50

Thus piteously Love closed what he begat:
The union of this ever diverse pair!
These two were rapid falcons in a snare,
Condemned to do the flitting of the bat.
5   Lovers beneath the singing sky of May,
They wandered once; clear as the dew on flowers:
But they fed not on the advancing hours:
Their hearts held cravings for the buried day.
Then each applied to each that fatal knife,
10   Deep questioning, which probes to endless dole.
Ah, what a dusty answer gets the soul
When hot for certainties in this our life!—
In tragic hints here see what evermore
Moves dark as yonder midnight ocean's force,
15   Thundering like ramping hosts of warrior horse,
To throw that faint thin line upon the shore!

1862

Lucifer in Starlight

On a starred night Prince Lucifer uprose.
Tired of his dark dominion, swung the fiend
Above the rolling ball, in cloud part screened,
Where sinners hugged their specter of repose.
5   Poor prey to his hot fit of pride were those.
And now upon his western wing he leaned,
Now his huge bulk o'er Afric's sands careened,
Now the black planet shadowed Arctic snows.

---

4. River of forgetfulness in Hades, the Greek underworld.

Soaring through wider zones that pricked his scars[1]
10   With memory of the old revolt from Awe,
He reached a middle height, and at the stars,
Which are the brain of heaven, he looked, and sank.
Around the ancient track marched, rank on rank,
The army of unalterable law.

1883

1. The vast expanse of sky reminds Satan of the wounds he suffered when his revolt against God was crushed and he was hurled from heaven to hell.

DANTE GABRIEL ROSSETTI
1828–1882

Dante Gabriel Rossetti was the son of an Italian patriot whose political activities had led to his being exiled to England. The Rossetti household in London was one in which liberal politics and artistic topics were hotly debated; all three children—Dante Gabriel, William Michael, and Christina—wrote and drew from an early age. Displaying extraordinary early promise both as a painter and as a poet, Rossetti valued the beauty of colors and textures, above all the beauty of a woman's face and figure. His view of life and art, derived in part from his close study of Keats's poems and letters, anticipated by many years the aesthetic movement later to be represented by such men as Walter Pater, Oscar Wilde, and the painter James McNeill Whistler, who were to insist that art must be exclusively concerned with the beautiful, not with the useful or didactic.

The beauty that Rossetti admired in the faces of women was of a distinctive kind. In at least two of his models he found what he sought. The first was his wife, Elizabeth Siddal, whose suicide in 1862 haunted him with a sense of guilt for the rest of his life. The other was Jane Morris, the wife of his friend William Morris. In Rossetti's paintings both of these models are shown with dreamy stares, as if they were breathless from visions of heaven, but counteracting this impression is an emphasis on parted lips and voluptuous curves suggesting a more earthly kind of ecstasy. A similar combination is to be found in Rossetti's poems. *The Blessed Damozel*, first written when he was eighteen, portrays a heaven that is warm with physical bodies. And *The House of Life* (1870), his sonnet sequence, undertakes to explore the relationship of spirit to body in love. Some Victorian readers saw no Dante-like spirituality in *The House of Life*. Robert Buchanan saw in the poem nothing but lewd sensuality, and in 1871 he published a pamphlet, *The Fleshly School of Poetry*, that treated Rossetti's poetry to the most severe abuse. Buchanan's attack hurt the poet profoundly and contributed to the recurring seizures of nervous depression from which he suffered in the remaining years of his life.

Rossetti and his artist friends used to call such women as Jane Morris "stunners." The epithet can also be applied to Rossetti's own poetry, especially his later writings. In his maturity he used stunning polysyllabic diction to give an effect of opulence and density to his lines. His earlier poems such as *My Sister's Sleep* are usually much less elaborate in manner and can be related to the Pre-Raphaelite movement of which, in 1848, he became a founder and energetic leader.

This Pre-Raphaelite Brotherhood, as it was called, was a group of young artists and writers. The most prominent members were painters such as John Everett Millais,

William Holman Hunt, and Rossetti himself. Their principal object was to reform English painting by repudiating the established academic style in favor of a revival of the simplicity and pure colors of pre-Renaissance art. Because each artist preferred to develop his own individual manner, the Brotherhood did not cohere for more than a few years. Rossetti himself grew away from the Pre-Raphaelite manner and cultivated a more richly ornate style of painting. In both the early and late phases of his writing and painting, however, it can be said that he remained a poet in his painting and a painter in his poetry. "Color and meter," he once said, "these are the true patents of nobility in painting and poetry, taking precedence of all intellectual claims."

The Blessed Damozel[1]

The blessed damozel leaned out
　　From the gold bar of heaven;
Her eyes were deeper than the depth
　　Of waters stilled at even;
5　She had three lilies in her hand,
　　And the stars in her hair were seven.

Her robe, ungirt from clasp to hem,
　　No wrought flowers did adorn,
But a white rose of Mary's gift,
10　　For service meetly worn;
Her hair that lay along her back
　　Was yellow like ripe corn.°　　　　　　　　　　　*grain*

Herseemed[2] she scarce had been a day
　　One of God's choristers;
15　The wonder was not yet quite gone
　　From that still look of hers;
Albeit, to them she left, her day
　　Had counted as ten years.

(To one it is ten years of years.
20　　. . . Yet now, and in this place,
Surely she leaned o'er me—her hair
　　Fell all about my face. . . .
Nothing: the autumn-fall of leaves.
　　The whole year sets apace.)

25　It was the rampart of God's house
　　That she was standing on;
By God built over the sheer depth
　　The which is Space begun;
So high, that looking downward thence
30　　She scarce could see the sun.

1. A poetic version of "damsel," signifying a young unmarried lady. Rossetti once explained that *The Blessed Damozel* is related to Poe's *Raven*, a poem that he admired. "I saw that Poe had done the utmost it was possible to do with the grief of the lover on earth, and so I determined to reverse the conditions, and give utterance to the yearning of the loved one in heaven."
2. It seemed to her.

The Blessed Damozel (1875–78). In the second phase of his painting career, Rossetti turned from the flat, intricately patterned illustrations of literary subjects that had characterized his early work (a good example is his drawing for *The Lady of Shalott*, p. 1208) to huge, sensual portraits of women, often designed as companion pieces to his poems.

It lies in heaven, across the flood
  Of ether, as a bridge.
Beneath the tides of day and night
  With flame and darkness ridge
35 The void, as low as where this earth
  Spins like a fretful midge.

Around her, lovers, newly met
  'Mid deathless love's acclaims,
Spoke evermore among themselves
40 Their heart-remembered names;
And the souls mounting up to God
  Went by her like thin flames.

And still she bowed herself and stooped
  Out of the circling charm;
45 Until her bosom must have made
  The bar she leaned on warm,
And the lilies lay as if asleep
  Along her bended arm.

From the fixed place of heaven she saw
50 Time like a pulse shake fierce
Through all the worlds. Her gaze still strove
  Within the gulf to pierce
Its path; and now she spoke as when
  The stars sang in their spheres.

55　　The sun was gone now; the curled moon
　　　　Was like a little feather
　　　Fluttering far down the gulf; and now
　　　　She spoke through the still weather.
　　　Her voice was like the voice the stars
60　　　Had when they sang together.

　　　(Ah, sweet! Even now, in that bird's song,
　　　　Strove not her accents there,
　　　Fain to be harkened? When those bells
　　　　Possessed the midday air,
65　　Strove not her steps to reach my side
　　　　Down all the echoing stair?)

　　　"I wish that he were come to me,
　　　　For he will come," she said.
　　　"Have I not prayed in heaven?—on earth,
70　　Lord, Lord, has he not prayed?
　　　Are not two prayers a perfect strength?
　　　　And shall I feel afraid?

　　　"When round his head the aureole clings,
　　　　And he is clothed in white,
75　　I'll take his hand and go with him
　　　　To the deep wells of light;
　　　As unto a stream we will step down,
　　　　And bathe there in God's sight.

　　　"We two will stand beside that shrine,
80　　　Occult, withheld, untrod,
　　　Whose lamps are stirred continually
　　　　With prayer sent up to God;
　　　And see our old prayers, granted, melt
　　　　Each like a little cloud.

85　　"We two will lie i' the shadow of
　　　　That living mystic tree[3]
　　　Within whose secret growth the Dove
　　　　Is sometimes felt to be,
　　　While every leaf that His plumes touch
90　　　Saith His Name audibly.

　　　"And I myself will teach to him,
　　　　I myself, lying so,
　　　The songs I sing here; which his voice
　　　　Shall pause in, hushed and slow,
95　　And find some knowledge at each pause,
　　　　Or some new thing to know."

　　　(Alas! We two, we two, thou say'st!
　　　　Yea, one wast thou with me

3. Cf. Revelation 22.2.

That once of old. But shall God lift
100   To endless unity
The soul whose likeness with thy soul
    Was but its love for thee?)

"We two," she said, "will seek the groves
    Where the lady Mary is,
105 With her five handmaidens, whose names
    Are five sweet symphonies,
Cecily, Gertrude, Magdalen,
    Margaret, and Rosalys.

"Circlewise sit they, with bound locks
110   And foreheads garlanded;
Into the fine cloth white like flame
    Weaving the golden thread,
To fashion the birth-robes for them
    Who are just born, being dead.

115 "He shall fear, haply, and be dumb;
    Then will I lay my cheek
To his, and tell about our love,
    Not once abashed or weak;
And the dear Mother will approve
120   My pride, and let me speak.

"Herself shall bring us, hand in hand,
    To Him round whom all souls
Kneel, the clear-ranged unnumbered heads
    Bowed with their aureoles;
125 And angels meeting us shall sing
    To their citherns and citoles.[4]

"There will I ask of Christ the Lord
    Thus much for him and me—
Only to live as once on earth
130   With Love—only to be,
As then awhile, forever now,
    Together, I and he."

She gazed and listened and then said,
    Less sad of speech than mild—
135 "All this is when he comes." She ceased.
    The light thrilled toward her, filled
With angels in strong, level flight.
    Her eyes prayed, and she smiled.

(I saw her smile.) But soon their path
140   Was vague in distant spheres;
And then she cast her arms along

4. Guitarlike instruments.

The golden barriers,
And laid her face between her hands,
And wept. (I heard her tears.)

1846

1850

My Sister's Sleep[1]

She fell asleep on Christmas Eve.
  At length the long-ungranted shade
  Of weary eyelids overweighed
The pain nought else might yet relieve.

5 Our mother, who had leaned all day
  Over the bed from chime to chime,
  Then raised herself for the first time,
And as she sat her down, did pray.

Her little worktable was spread
10 With work to finish. For the glare
  Made by her candle, she had care
To work some distance from the bed.

Without, there was a cold moon up,
  Of winter radiance sheer and thin;
15 The hollow halo it was in
Was like an icy crystal cup.

Through the small room, with subtle sound
  Of flame, by vents the fireshine drove
  And reddened. In its dim alcove
20 The mirror shed a clearness round.

I had been sitting up some nights,
  And my tired mind felt weak and blank;
  Like a sharp strengthening wine it drank
The stillness and the broken lights.

25 Twelve struck. That sound, by dwindling years
  Heard in each hour, crept off; and then
  The ruffled silence spread again,
Like water that a pebble stirs.

Our mother rose from where she sat;
30 Her needles, as she laid them down,
  Met lightly, and her silken gown
Settled—no other noise than that.

---

1. The incident in this poem is imaginary, not autobiographical.

"Glory unto the Newly Born!"
   So, as said angels, she did say,
35   Because we were in Christmas Day,
Though it would still be long till morn.

Just then in the room over us
   There was a pushing back of chairs,
   As some who had sat unawares
40   So late, now heard the hour, and rose.

With anxious softly-stepping haste
   Our mother went where Margaret lay,
   Fearing the sounds o'erhead—should they
Have broken her long watched-for rest!

45 She stooped an instant, calm, and turned,
   But suddenly turned back again;
   And all her features seemed in pain
With woe, and her eyes gazed and yearned.

For my part, I but hid my face,
50   And held my breath, and spoke no word.
   There was none spoken; but I heard
The silence for a little space.

Our mother bowed herself and wept;
   And both my arms fell, and I said,
55   "God knows I knew that she was dead."
And there, all white, my sister slept.

Then kneeling, upon Christmas morn
   A little after twelve o'clock,
   We said, ere the first quarter struck,
60   "Christ's blessing on the newly born!"

1847   1850

The Woodspurge

The wind flapped loose, the wind was still,
Shaken out dead from tree and hill;
I had walked on at the wind's will—
I sat now, for the wind was still.

5 Between my knees my forehead was—
My lips, drawn in, said not Alas!
My hair was over in the grass,
My naked ears heard the day pass.

My eyes, wide open, had the run
10 Of some ten weeds to fix upon;

Among those few, out of the sun,
The woodspurge flowered, three cups in one.

From perfect grief there need not be
Wisdom or even memory;
15 One thing then learned remains to me—
The woodspurge has a cup of three.

1856   1870

From The House of Life

The Sonnet

A Sonnet is a moment's monument—
Memorial from the Soul's eternity
To one dead deathless hour. Look that it be,
Whether for lustral° rite or dire portent,   *purification*
5 Of its own arduous fullness reverent;
Carve it in ivory or in ebony,
As Day or Night may rule; and let Time see
Its flowering crest impearled and orient.

A Sonnet is a coin; its face reveals
10 The soul—its converse, to what Power 'tis due—
Whether for tribute to the august appeals
Of Life, or dower in Love's high retinue,
It serve; or, 'mid the dark wharf's cavernous breath,
In Charon's¹ palm it pay the toll to Death.

Nuptial Sleep²

At length their long kiss severed, with sweet smart:
And as the last slow sudden drops are shed
From sparkling eaves when all the storm has fled,
So singly flagged the pulses of each heart.
5 Their bosoms sundered, with the opening start
Of married flowers to either side outspread
From the knit stem; yet still their mouths, burnt red,
Fawned on each other where they lay apart.

Sleep sank them lower than the tide of dreams,
10 And their dreams watched them sink, and slid away.
Slowly their souls swam up again, through gleams
Of watered light and dull drowned waifs of day;
Till from some wonder of new woods and streams
He woke, and wondered more: for there she lay.

1. The ferryman who, for a fee, rowed the souls of the dead across the river Styx.
2. In *The Fleshly School of Poetry*, Robert Buchanan made this poem the focus of his attack on what he felt was Rossetti's lewd sensuality in the 1870 volume *Poems*. In 1881, when Rossetti published his next collection of poems, he omitted this sonnet from *The House of Life*.

19. Silent Noon

Your hands lie open in the long fresh grass—
    The finger-points look through like rosy blooms;
    Your eyes smile peace. The pasture gleams and glooms
'Neath billowing skies that scatter and amass.
5 All round our nest, far as the eye can pass,
    Are golden kingcup-fields with silver edge
    Where the cow-parsley skirts the hawthorn hedge.
'Tis visible silence, still as the hourglass.

    Deep in the sun-searched growths the dragonfly
10 Hangs like a blue thread loosened from the sky—
    So this winged hour is dropped to us from above.
Oh! clasp we to our hearts, for deathless dower,
This close-companioned inarticulate hour
    When twofold silence was the song of love.

77. Soul's Beauty[3]

Under the arch of Life, where love and death,
    Terror and mystery, guard her shrine, I saw
    Beauty enthroned; and though her gaze struck awe,
I drew it in as simply as my breath.
5 Hers are the eyes which, over and beneath,
    The sky and sea bend on thee,—which can draw,
    By sea or sky or woman, to one law,
The allotted bondman of her palm and wreath.

    This is that Lady Beauty, in whose praise
10 Thy voice and hand shake still,—long known to thee
    By flying hair and fluttering hem,—the beat
    Following her daily of thy heart and feet,
How passionately and irretrievably,
    In what fond flight, how many ways and days!

78. Body's Beauty

Of Adams's first wife, Lilith, it is told
    (The witch he loved before the gift of Eve,)
    That, ere the snake's, her sweet tongue could deceive,
And her enchanted hair was the first gold.
5 And still she sits, young while the earth is old,
    And subtly of herself contemplative,
    Draws men to watch the bright web she can weave,
Till heart and body and life are in its hold.

3. This sonnet and the next were not originally part of *The House of Life*, but were composed to accompany paintings with the same names as the sonnets' original titles. The original title of *Soul's Beauty* was "Sibylla Palmifera," or "palm-bearing sibyl." Sibyls are prophetesses; one of them, the Sibyl of Cumae, wrote her prophecies on palm leaves. The original title of *Body's Beauty* was "Lilith," in Talmudic legend, the first wife of Adam, who ran away from him to become a witch.

The rose and poppy are her flowers; for where
10   Is he not found, O Lilith, whom shed scent
And soft-shed kisses and soft sleep shall snare?
        Lo! as that youth's eyes burned at thine, so went
        Thy spell through him, and left his straight neck bent
And round his heart one strangling golden hair

97. A Superscription

Look in my face; my name is Might-have-been;
        I am also called No-more, Too-late, Farewell;
        Unto thine ear I hold the dead-sea shell
Cast up thy Life's foam-fretted feet between;
5   Unto thine eyes the glass° where that is seen   *mirror*
        Which had Life's form and Love's, but by my spell
        Is now a shaken shadow intolerable,
Of ultimate things unuttered the frail screen.

Mark me, how still I am! But should there dart
10   One moment through thy soul the soft surprise
        Of that winged Peace which lulls the breath of sighs—
Then shalt thou see me smile, and turn apart
Thy visage to mine ambush at thy heart
        Sleepless with cold commemorative eyes.

101. The One Hope

When vain desire at last and vain regret
        Go hand in hand to death, and all is vain,
        What shall assuage the unforgotten pain
And teach the unforgetful to forget?
5   Shall Peace be still a sunk stream long unmet—
        Or may the soul at once in a green plain
        Stoop through the spray of some sweet life-fountain
And cull the dew-drenched flowering amulet?[4]

Ah! when the wan soul in that golden air
10   Between the scriptured petals softly blown
        Peers breathless for the gift of grace unknown,
Ah! let none other alien spell soe'er
But only the one Hope's one name be there—
        Not less nor more, but even that word alone.

1848–80   1870, 1881

---

4. A charm to protect the wearer from harm.

CHRISTINA ROSSETTI
1830–1894

Referring to the title of George Gissing's novel about women who choose not to marry, the critic Jerome McGann calls Christina Rossetti "one of nineteenth-century England's greatest 'Odd Women.' " Her life had little apparent incident. She was the youngest child in the Rossetti family. Her father was an exiled Italian patriot who wrote poetry and commentaries on Dante that tried to show evidence in his poems of mysterious ancient conspiracies; her mother was an Anglo-Italian who had worked as a governess. Their household was a lively gathering place for Italian exiles, full of conversation of politics and culture, which encouraged Christina, like her brothers Dante Gabriel and William Michael, to develop an early love for art and literature and to draw and write poetry from a very early age. When she was an adolescent, her life changed dramatically: her father became a permanent invalid, the family's economic situation worsened, and her own health deteriorated. At this point, she, her mother, and her sister became intensely involved with the Anglo-Catholic movement within the Church of England. For the rest of her life, Christina Rossetti governed herself by strict religious principles, giving up theater, opera, and chess; on two occasions, she canceled plans for marriage because of religious scruples, breaking her first engagement when her fiancé reverted to Roman Catholicism and ultimately refusing to marry a second suitor because he seemed insufficiently concerned with religion. She lived a quiet life, occupying herself with charitable work—including ten years of volunteer service at a penitentiary for fallen women—with caring for her family, and with writing poetry.

Christina Rossetti's first volume of poetry, *Goblin Market and Other Poems* (1862), contains all the different poetic modes that mark her achievement—pure lyric, narrative fable, ballad, and the devotional verse to which she increasingly turned in her later years. The most remarkable poem in the book is the title piece, which early established its popularity as a seemingly simple moral fable for children. Later readers have likened it to Coleridge's *Rime of the Ancient Mariner* and have detected in it a complex representation of the religious themes of temptation and sin, and of redemption by vicarious suffering; the fruit that tempts Laura, however, is clearly not from the Tree of Knowledge but from an orchard of sensual delights. In its deceptively simple style, *Goblin Market,* like many of her poems, demonstrates her affinity with the early aims of the Pre-Raphaelite group, but her work as a whole resists this classification. A consciousness of gender often leads her to criticize the conventional representation of women in Pre-Raphaelite art, as in her sonnet *In An Artist's Studio,* and a stern religious vision controls the sensuous impulses typical of Pre-Raphaelite poetry and painting. Virginia Woolf has described the distinctive combination of sensuousness and religious severity in Rossetti's work.

> Your poems are full of gold dust and "sweet geraniums' varied brightness"; your eye noted incessantly how rushes are "velvet headed," and lizards have a "strange metallic mail"—your eye, indeed, observed with a sensual pre-Raphaelite intensity that must have surprised Christina the Anglo-Catholic. But to her you owed perhaps the fixity and sadness of your muse. . . . No sooner have you feasted on beauty with your eyes than your mind tells you that beauty is vain and beauty passes. Death, oblivion, and rest lap round your songs with their dark wave.

William Michael Rossetti wrote of his sister, "She was replete with the spirit of self-postponement." Christina Rossetti was a poet who created, in Sandra M. Gilbert and Susan Gubar's term, "an aesthetics of renunciation." She writes a poetry of deferral, of deflection, of negation, whose very denials and constraints give her a powerful way to articulate a poetic self in critical relationship to the little that the world offers.

Like Emily Dickinson, she often, as in *Winter: My Secret,* uses a coy playfulness and sardonic wit to reduce the self but at the same time to preserve for it a secret inner space. And like Dickinson, she wrote many poems of an extraordinarily pure lyric beauty that made Virginia Woolf remark, "Your instinct was so sure, so direct, so intense that it produced poems that sing like music in one's ears—like a melody by Mozart or an air by Gluck."

Song

She sat and sang alway
  By the green margin of a stream,
Watching the fishes leap and play
  Beneath the glad sunbeam.

5 I sat and wept alway
  Beneath the moon's most shadowy beam,
Watching the blossoms of the May
  Weep leaves into the stream.

I wept for memory;
10 She sang for hope that is so fair:
My tears were swallowed by the sea;
  Her songs died on the air.

1848   1862

Song

When I am dead, my dearest,
  Sing no sad songs for me;
Plant thou no roses at my head,
  Nor shady cypress tree:
5 Be the green grass above me
  With showers and dewdrops wet;
And if thou wilt, remember,
  And if thou wilt, forget.

I shall not see the shadows,
10 I shall not feel the rain;
I shall not hear the nightingale
  Sing on, as if in pain:
And dreaming through the twilight
  That doth not rise nor set,
15 Haply I may remember,
  And haply may forget.

1848   1862

After Death

The curtains were half drawn, the floor was swept
   And strewn with rushes, rosemary and may[1]
   Lay thick upon the bed on which I lay,
Where thro' the lattice ivy-shadows crept.
5   He leaned above me, thinking that I slept
   And could not hear him; but I heard him say:
   "Poor child, poor child": and as he turned away
Came a deep silence, and I knew he wept.
He did not touch the shroud, or raise the fold
10   That hid my face, or take my hand in his,
   Or ruffle the smooth pillows for my head:
   He did not love me living; but once dead
He pitied me; and very sweet it is
To know he still is warm tho' I am cold.

1849
                                                       1862

Dead before Death

Ah! changed and cold, how changed and very cold!
   With stiffened smiling lips and cold calm eyes:
   Changed, yet the same; much knowing, little wise;
This was the promise of the days of old!
5   Grown hard and stubborn in the ancient mould,
   Grown rigid in the sham of lifelong lies:
   We hoped for better things as years would rise,
But it is over as a tale once told.
All fallen the blossom that no fruitage bore,
10   All lost the present and the future time,
All lost, all lost, the lapse that went before:
So lost till death shut-to the opened door,
   So lost from chime to everlasting chime,
So cold and lost for ever evermore.

1854
                                                       1862

Cobwebs

It is a land with neither night nor day,
   Nor heat nor cold, nor any wind, nor rain,
   Nor hills nor valleys; but one even plain
Stretches thro' long unbroken miles away:
5   While thro' the sluggish air a twilight grey
   Broodeth; no moons or seasons wax and wane,
   No ebb and flow are there along the main,

---

1. Flowers associated with death.

No bud-time no leaf-falling, there for aye:—
No ripple on the sea, no shifting sand,
10   No beat of wings to stir the stagnant space,
No pulse of life thro' all the loveless land:
And loveless sea; no trace of days before,
    No guarded home, no toil-won resting place,
No future hope no fear for evermore.

1855

1896

A Triad

Three sang of love together: one with lips
    Crimson, with cheeks and bosom in a glow,
Flushed to the yellow hair and finger tips;
    And one there sang who soft and smooth as snow
5   Bloomed like a tinted hyacinth at a show;
And one was blue with famine after love,
    Who like a harpstring snapped rang harsh and low
The burden of what those were singing of.
One shamed herself in love; one temperately
10   Grew gross in soulless love, a sluggish wife;
One famished died for love. Thus two of three
    Took death for love and won him after strife;
One droned in sweetness like a fattened bee:
    All on the threshold, yet all short of life.

1856

1862

In an Artist's Studio[1]

One face looks out from all his canvases,
    One selfsame figure sits or walks or leans;
    We found her hidden just behind those screens,
That mirror gave back all her loveliness.
5   A queen in opal or in ruby dress,
    A nameless girl in freshest summer-greens,
    A saint, an angel;—every canvass means
The same one meaning, neither more nor less.
He feeds upon her face by day and night,
10   And she with true kind eyes looks back on him
Fair as the moon and joyful as the light:
    Not wan with waiting, not with sorrow dim;
Not as she is, but was when hope shone bright;
    Not as she is, but as she fills his dream.

1856

1896

---

1. William Michael Rossetti, the younger of Christina's older brothers, noted, "The reference is apparently to our brother's studio, and to his con-stantly repeated heads of the lady whom he afterwards married, Miss Siddal."

A Birthday

My heart is like a singing bird
    Whose nest is in a watered shoot;
My heart is like an apple tree
    Whose boughs are bent with thickset fruit;
5 My heart is like a rainbow shell
    That paddles in a halcyon° sea;   *tranquil*
My heart is gladder than all these
    Because my love is come to me.

Raise me a dais of silk and down;
10   Hang it with vair° and purple dyes;   *squirrel fur*
Carve it in doves and pomegranates,
    And peacocks with a hundred eyes;
Work it in gold and silver grapes,
    In leaves and silver fleurs-de-lys;
15 Because the birthday of my life
    Is come, my love is come to me.

1857   1862

An Apple-Gathering

I plucked pink blossoms from mine apple tree
    And wore them all that evening in my hair:
Then in due season when I went to see
    I found no apples there.

5 With dangling basket all along the grass
    As I had come I went the selfsame track:
My neighbours mocked me while they saw me pass
    So empty-handed back.

Lilian and Lilias smiled in trudging by,
10   Their heaped-up basket teazed me like a jeer;
Sweet-voiced they sang beneath the sunset sky,
    Their mother's home was near.

Plump Gertrude passed me with her basket full,
    A stronger hand than hers helped it along;
15 A voice talked with her thro' the shadows cool
    More sweet to me than song.

Ah Willie, Willie, was my love less worth
    Than apples with their green leaves piled above?
I counted rosiest apples on the earth
20   Of far less worth than love.

So once it was with me you stooped to talk
    Laughing and listening in this very lane:

To think that by this way we used to walk
We shall not walk again!

25 I let my neighbours pass me, ones and twos
And groups; the latest said the night grew chill,
And hastened: but I loitered, while the dews
Fell fast I loitered still.

1857   1862

Winter: My Secret

I tell my secret? No indeed, not I:
Perhaps some day, who knows?
But not today; it froze, and blows, and snows,
And you're too curious: fie!
5 You want to hear it? well:
Only, my secret's mine, and I won't tell.

Or, after all, perhaps there's none:
Suppose there is no secret after all,
But only just my fun.
10 Today's a nipping day, a biting day;
In which one wants a shawl,
A veil, a cloak, and other wraps:
I cannot ope to every one who taps,
And let the draughts come whistling thro' my hall;
15 Come bounding and surrounding me,
Come buffeting, astounding me,
Nipping and clipping thro' my wraps and all.
I wear my mask for warmth: who ever shows
His nose to Russian snows
20 To be pecked at by every wind that blows?
You would not peck? I thank you for good will,
Believe, but leave that truth untested still.

Spring's an expansive time: yet I don't trust
March with its peck of dust,
25 Nor April with its rainbow-crowned brief showers,
Nor even May, whose flowers
One frost may wither thro' the sunless hours.

Perhaps some languid summer day,
When drowsy birds sing less and less,
30 And golden fruit is ripening to excess,
If there's not too much sun nor too much cloud,
And the warm wind is neither still nor loud,
Perhaps my secret I may say,
Or you may guess.

1857   1862

Up-Hill

Does the road wind up-hill all the way?
   Yes, to the very end.
Will the day's journey take the whole long day?
   From morn to night, my friend.

5 But is there for the night a resting-place?
   A roof for when the slow dark hours begin.
May not the darkness hide it from my face?
   You cannot miss that inn.

Shall I meet other wayfarers at night?
10   Those who have gone before.
Then must I knock, or call when just in sight?
   They will not keep you standing at that door.

Shall I find comfort, travel-sore and weak?
   Of labour you shall find the sum.
15 Will there be beds for me and all who seek?
   Yea, beds for all who come.

1858   1862

Goblin Market

Morning and evening
Maids heard the goblins cry:
"Come buy our orchard fruits,
Come buy, come buy:
5 Apples and quinces,
Lemons and oranges,
Plump unpecked cherries,
Melons and raspberries,
Bloom-down-cheeked peaches,
10 Swart-headed mulberries,
Wild free-born cranberries,
Crab-apples, dewberries,
Pine-apples, blackberries,
Apricots, strawberries;—
15 All ripe together
In summer weather,—
Morns that pass by,
Fair eves that fly;
Come buy, come buy:
20 Our grapes fresh from the vine,
Pomegranates full and fine,
Dates and sharp bullaces,
Rare pears and greengages,
Damsons[1] and bilberries,

---

1. "Bullaces," "greengages," and "damsons" are varieties of plums.

25　Taste them and try:
　　Currants and gooseberries,
　　Bright-fire-like barberries,
　　Figs to fill your mouth,
　　Citrons from the South,
30　Sweet to tongue and sound to eye;
　　Come buy, come buy."

　　Evening by evening
　　Among the brookside rushes,
　　Laura bowed her head to hear,
35　Lizzie veiled her blushes:
　　Crouching close together
　　In the cooling weather,
　　With clasping arms and cautioning lips,
　　With tingling cheeks and finger tips.
40　"Lie close," Laura said,
　　Pricking up her golden head:
　　"We must not look at goblin men,
　　We must not buy their fruits:
　　Who knows upon what soil they fed
45　Their hungry thirsty roots?"
　　"Come buy," call the goblins
　　Hobbling down the glen.
　　"Oh," cried Lizzie, "Laura, Laura,
　　You should not peep at goblin men."
50　Lizzie covered up her eyes,
　　Covered close lest they should look;
　　Laura reared her glossy head,
　　And whispered like the restless brook:
　　"Look, Lizzie, look, Lizzie,
55　Down the glen tramp little men.
　　One hauls a basket,
　　One bears a plate,
　　One lugs a golden dish
　　Of many pounds weight.
60　How fair the vine must grow
　　Whose grapes are so luscious;
　　How warm the wind must blow
　　Thro' those fruit bushes."
　　"No," said Lizzie: "No, no, no;
65　Their offers should not charm us,
　　Their evil gifts would harm us."
　　She thrust a dimpled finger
　　In each ear, shut eyes and ran:
　　Curious Laura chose to linger
70　Wondering at each merchant man.
　　One had a cat's face,
　　One whisked a tail,
　　One tramped at a rat's pace,
　　One crawled like a snail,
75　One like a wombat prowled obtuse and furry,

One like a ratel[2] tumbled hurry skurry.
She heard a voice like voice of doves
Cooing all together:
They sounded kind and full of loves
80 In the pleasant weather.

Laura stretched her gleaming neck
Like a rush-imbedded swan,
Like a lily from the beck,°   small brook
Like a moonlit poplar branch,
85 Like a vessel at the launch
When its last restraint is gone.

Backwards up the mossy glen
Turned and trooped the goblin men,
With their shrill repeated cry,
90 "Come buy, come buy."
When they reached where Laura was
They stood stock still upon the moss,
Leering at each other,
Brother with queer brother;
95 Signalling each other,
Brother with sly brother.
One set his basket down,
One reared his plate;
One began to weave a crown
100 Of tendrils, leaves and rough nuts brown
(Men sell not such in any town);
One heaved the golden weight
Of dish and fruit to offer her:
"Come buy, come buy," was still their cry.
105 Laura stared but did not stir,
Longed but had no money:
The whisk-tailed merchant bade her taste
In tones as smooth as honey,
The cat-faced purr'd,
110 The rat-paced spoke a word
Of welcome, and the snail-paced even was heard;
One parrot-voiced and jolly
Cried "Pretty Goblin" still for "Pretty Polly;"—
One whistled like a bird.

115 But sweet-tooth Laura spoke in haste:
"Good folk, I have no coin;
To take were to purloin:
I have no copper in my purse,
I have no silver either,
120 And all my gold is on the furze
That shakes in windy weather
Above the rusty heather."

2. South African mammal resembling a badger (pronounced *ray-tell*).

"You have much gold upon your head,"
They answered all together:
125   "Buy from us with a golden curl."
She clipped a precious golden lock,
She dropped a tear more rare than pearl,
Then sucked their fruit globes fair or red:
Sweeter than honey from the rock.
130   Stronger than man-rejoicing wine,
Clearer than water flowed that juice;
She never tasted such before,
How should it cloy with length of use?
She sucked and sucked and sucked the more
135   Fruits which that unknown orchard bore;
She sucked until her lips were sore;
Then flung the emptied rinds away
But gathered up one kernel-stone,
And knew not was it night or day
140   As she turned home alone.

Lizzie met her at the gate
Full of wise upbraidings:
"Dear, you should not stay so late,
Twilight is not good for maidens;
145   Should not loiter in the glen
In the haunts of goblin men.
Do you not remember Jeanie,
How she met them in the moonlight,
Took their gifts both choice and many,
150   Ate their fruits and wore their flowers
Plucked from bowers
Where summer ripens at all hours?
But ever in the noonlight
She pined and pined away;
155   Sought them by night and day,
Found them no more but dwindled and grew grey;
Then fell with the first snow,
While to this day no grass will grow
Where she lies low:
160   I planted daisies there a year ago
That never blow.
You should not loiter so."
"Nay, hush," said Laura:
"Nay, hush, my sister:
165   I ate and ate my fill,
Yet my mouth waters still;
Tomorrow night I will
Buy more:" and kissed her:
"Have done with sorrow;
170   I'll bring you plums tomorrow
Fresh on their mother twigs,
Cherries worth getting;

You cannot think what figs
My teeth have met in,
175 What melons icy-cold
Piled on a dish of gold
Too huge for me to hold,
What peaches with a velvet nap,
Pellucid grapes without one seed:
180 Odorous indeed must be the mead
Whereon they grow, and pure the wave they drink
With lilies at the brink,
And sugar-sweet their sap."

Golden head by golden head,
185 Like two pigeons in one nest
Folded in each other's wings,
They lay down in their curtained bed:
Like two blossoms on one stem,
Like two flakes of new-fall'n snow,
190 Like two wands of ivory
Tipped with gold for awful° kings.   *awe-inspiring*
Moon and stars gazed in at them,

This frontispiece is one of the two illustrations that Dante Gabriel Rossetti provided for his sister's first volume of poetry in 1862.

Wind sang to them lullaby,
Lumbering owls forbore to fly,
195 Not a bat flapped to and fro
Round their rest:
Cheek to cheek and breast to breast
Locked together in one nest.

Early in the morning
200 When the first cock crowed his warning,
Neat like bees, as sweet and busy,
Laura rose with Lizzie:
Fetched in honey, milked the cows,
Aired and set to rights the house,
205 Kneaded cakes of whitest wheat,
Cakes for dainty mouths to eat,
Next churned butter, whipped up cream,
Fed their poultry, sat and sewed;
Talked as modest maidens should:
210 Lizzie with an open heart,
Laura in an absent dream,
One content, one sick in part;
One warbling for the mere bright day's delight,
One longing for the night.

215 At length slow evening came:
They went with pitchers to the reedy brook;
Lizzie most placid in her look,
Laura most like a leaping flame.
They drew the gurgling water from its deep;
220 Lizzie plucked purple and rich golden flags,
Then turning homewards said: "The sunset flushes
Those furthest loftiest crags;
Come, Laura, not another maiden lags,
No wilful squirrel wags,
225 The beasts and birds are fast asleep."
But Laura loitered still among the rushes
And said the bank was steep.

And said the hour was early still,
The dew not fall'n, the wind not chill:
230 Listening ever, but not catching
The customary cry,
"Come buy, come buy,"
With its iterated jingle
Of sugar-baited words:
235 Not for all her watching
Once discerning even one goblin
Racing, whisking, tumbling, hobbling;
Let alone the herds
That used to tramp along the glen,
240 In groups or single,
Of brisk fruit-merchant men.

Till Lizzie urged, "O Laura, come;
I hear the fruit-call but I dare not look:
You should not loiter longer at this brook:
245 Come with me home.
The stars rise, the moon bends her arc,
Each glowworm winks her spark,
Let us get home before the night grows dark:
For clouds may gather
250 Tho' this is summer weather,
Put out the lights and drench us thro';
Then if we lost our way what should we do?"

Laura turned cold as stone
To find her sister heard that cry alone,
255 That goblin cry,
"Come buy our fruits, come buy."
Must she then buy no more such dainty fruit?
Must she no more such succous° pasture find,   *juicy, succulent*
Gone deaf and blind?
260 Her tree of life drooped from the root:
She said not one word in her heart's sore ache;
But peering thro' the dimness, nought discerning,
Trudged home, her pitcher dripping all the way;
So crept to bed, and lay
265 Silent till Lizzie slept;
Then sat up in a passionate yearning,
And gnashed her teeth for baulked desire, and wept
As if her heart would break.

Day after day, night after night,
270 Laura kept watch in vain
In sullen silence of exceeding pain.
She never caught again the goblin cry:
"Come buy, come buy;"—
She never spied the goblin men
275 Hawking their fruits along the glen:
But when the noon waxed bright
Her hair grew thin and gray;
She dwindled, as the fair full moon doth turn
To swift decay and burn
280 Her fire away.

One day remembering her kernel-stone
She set it by a wall that faced the south;
Dewed it with tears, hoped for a root,
Watched for a waxing shoot,
285 But there came none;
It never saw the sun,
It never felt the trickling moisture run:
While with sunk eyes and faded mouth
She dreamed of melons, as a traveller sees
290 False waves in desert drouth

With shade of leaf-crowned trees,
And burns the thirstier in the sandful breeze.

She no more swept the house,
Tended the fowls or cows,
295 Fetched honey, kneaded cakes of wheat,
Brought water from the brook:
But sat down listless in the chimney-nook
And would not eat.

Tender Lizzie could not bear
300 To watch her sister's cankerous care
Yet not to share.
She night and morning
Caught the goblins' cry:
"Come buy our orchard fruits,
305 Come buy, come buy:"—
Beside the brook, along the glen,
She heard the tramp of goblin men,
The voice and stir
Poor Laura could not hear;
310 Longed to buy fruit to comfort her,
But feared to pay too dear.
She thought of Jeanie in her grave,
Who should have been a bride;
But who for joys brides hope to have
315 Fell sick and died
In her gay prime,
In earliest Winter time,
With the first glazing rime,
With the first snow-fall of crisp Winter time.

320 Till Laura dwindling
Seemed knocking at Death's door:
Then Lizzie weighed no more
Better and worse;
But put a silver penny in her purse,
325 Kissed Laura, crossed the heath with clumps of furze
At twilight, halted by the brook:
And for the first time in her life
Began to listen and look.

Laughed every goblin
330 When they spied her peeping:
Came towards her hobbling,
Flying, running, leaping,
Puffing and blowing,
Chuckling, clapping, crowing,
335 Clucking and gobbling,
Mopping and mowing,
Full of airs and graces,
Pulling wry faces,

Demure grimaces,
340   Cat-like and rat-like,
Ratel- and wombat-like,
Snail-paced in a hurry,
Parrot-voiced and whistler,
Helter skelter, hurry skurry,
345   Chattering like magpies,
Fluttering like pigeons,
Gliding like fishes,—
Hugged her and kissed her,
Squeezed and caressed her:
350   Stretched up their dishes,
Panniers, and plates:
"Look at our apples
Russet and dun,
Bob at our cherries,
355   Bite at our peaches,
Citrons and dates,
Grapes for the asking,
Pears red with basking
Out in the sun,
360   Plums on their twigs;
Pluck them and suck them,
Pomegranates, figs."—

"Good folk," said Lizzie,
Mindful of Jeanie:
365   "Give me much and many:"—
Held out her apron,
Tossed them her penny.
"Nay, take a seat with us,
Honour and eat with us,"
370   They answered grinning:
"Our feast is but beginning.
Night yet is early,
Warm and dew-pearly,
Wakeful and starry:
375   Such fruits as these
No man can carry;
Half their bloom would fly,
Half their dew would dry,
Half their flavour would pass by.
380   Sit down and feast with us,
Be welcome guest with us,
Cheer you and rest with us."—
"Thank you," said Lizzie: "But one waits
At home alone for me:
385   So without further parleying,
If you will not sell me any
Of your fruits tho' much and many,
Give me back my silver penny
I tossed you for a fee."—

390 They began to scratch their pates,
No longer wagging, purring,
But visibly demurring,
Grunting and snarling.
One called her proud,
395 Cross-grained, uncivil;
Their tones waxed loud,
Their looks were evil.
Lashing their tails
They trod and hustled her,
400 Elbowed and jostled her,
Clawed with their nails,
Barking, mewing, hissing, mocking,
Tore her gown and soiled her stocking,
Twitched her hair out by the roots,
405 Stamped upon her tender feet,
Held her hands and squeezed their fruits
Against her mouth to make her eat.

White and golden Lizzie stood,
Like a lily in a flood,—
410 Like a rock of blue-veined stone
Lashed by tides obstreperously,—
Like a beacon left alone
In a hoary roaring sea,
Sending up a golden fire,—
415 Like a fruit-crowned orange-tree
White with blossoms honey-sweet
Sore beset by wasp and bee,—
Like a royal virgin town
Topped with gilded dome and spire
420 Close beleaguerred by a fleet
Mad to tug her standard down.

One may lead a horse to water,
Twenty cannot make him drink.
Tho' the goblins cuffed and caught her,
425 Coaxed and fought her,
Bullied and besought her,
Scratched her, pinched her black as ink,
Kicked and knocked her,
Mauled and mocked her,
430 Lizzie uttered not a word;
Would not open lip from lip
Lest they should cram a mouthful in:
But laughed in heart to feel the drip
Of juice that syruped all her face,
435 And lodged in dimples of her chin,
And streaked her neck which quaked like curd.
At last the evil people
Worn out by her resistance
Flung back her penny, kicked their fruit

440 Along whichever road they took,
     Not leaving root or stone or shoot;
     Some writhed into the ground,
     Some dived into the brook
     With ring and ripple,
445 Some scudded on the gale without a sound,
     Some vanished in the distance.

     In a smart, ache, tingle,
     Lizzie went her way;
     Knew not was it night or day;
450 Sprang up the bank, tore thro' the furze,
     Threaded copse and dingle,
     And heard her penny jingle
     Bouncing in her purse,
     Its bounce was music to her ear.
455 She ran and ran
     As if she feared some goblin man
     Dogged her with gibe or curse
     Or something worse:
     But not one goblin skurried after,
460 Nor was she pricked by fear;
     The kind heart made her windy-paced
     That urged her home quite out of breath with haste
     And inward laughter.

     She cried "Laura," up the garden,
465 "Did you miss me?
     Come and kiss me.
     Never mind my bruises,
     Hug me, kiss me, suck my juices
     Squeezed from goblin fruits for you,
470 Goblin pulp and goblin dew.
     Eat me, drink me, love me;
     Laura, make much of me:
     For your sake I have braved the glen
     And had to do with goblin merchant men."

475 Laura started from her chair,
     Flung her arms up in the air,
     Clutched her hair:
     "Lizzie, Lizzie, have you tasted
     For my sake the fruit forbidden?
480 Must your light like mine be hidden,
     Your young life like mine be wasted,
     Undone in mine undoing
     And ruined in my ruin,
     Thirsty, cankered, goblin-ridden?"—
485 She clung about her sister,
     Kissed and kissed and kissed her:
     Tears once again
     Refreshed her shrunken eyes,

Dropping like rain
490 After long sultry drouth;
Shaking with aguish fear, and pain,
She kissed and kissed her with a hungry mouth.

Her lips began to scorch,
That juice was wormwood to her tongue,
495 She loathed the feast:
Writhing as one possessed she leaped and sung,
Rent all her robe, and wrung
Her hands in lamentable haste,
And beat her breast.
500 Her locks streamed like the torch
Borne by a racer at full speed,
Or like the mane of horses in their flight,
Or like an eagle when she stems[3] the light
Straight toward the sun,
505 Or like a caged thing freed,
Or like a flying flag when armies run.

Swift fire spread thro' her veins, knocked at her heart,
Met the fire smouldering there
And overbore its lesser flame;
510 She gorged on bitterness without a name:
Ah! fool, to choose such part
Of soul-consuming care!
Sense failed in the mortal strife:
Like the watch-tower of a town
515 Which an earthquake shatters down,
Like a lightning-stricken mast,
Like a wind-uprooted tree
Spun about,
Like a foam-topped waterspout
520 Cast down headlong in the sea,
She fell at last;
Pleasure past and anguish past,
Is it death or is it life?

Life out of death.
525 That night long Lizzie watched by her,
Counted her pulse's flagging stir,
Felt for her breath,
Held water to her lips, and cooled her face
With tears and fanning leaves:
530 But when the first birds chirped about their eaves,
And early reapers plodded to the place
Of golden sheaves,
And dew-wet grass
Bowed in the morning winds so brisk to pass,
535 And new buds with new day
Opened of cup-like lilies on the stream,

---

3. Makes headway against.

Laura awoke as from a dream,
Laughed in the innocent old way,
Hugged Lizzie but not twice or thrice;
540 Her gleaming locks showed not one thread of grey,
Her breath was sweet as May
And light danced in her eyes.

Days, weeks, months, years
Afterwards, when both were wives
545 With children of their own;
Their mother-hearts beset with fears,
Their lives bound up in tender lives;
Laura would call the little ones
And tell them of her early prime,
550 Those pleasant days long gone
Of not-returning time:
Would talk about the haunted glen,
The wicked, quaint fruit-merchant men,
Their fruits like honey to the throat
555 But poison in the blood;
(Men sell not such in any town:)
Would tell them how her sister stood
In deadly peril to do her good,
And win the fiery antidote:
560 Then joining hands to little hands
Would bid them cling together,
"For there is no friend like a sister
In calm or stormy weather;
To cheer one on the tedious way,
565 To fetch one if one goes astray,
To lift one if one totters down,
To strengthen whilst one stands."

1859   1862

"No, Thank You, John"

I never said I loved you, John:
    Why will you teaze me day by day,
And wax a weariness to think upon
    With always "do" and "pray"?

5   You know I never loved you, John;
    No fault of mine made me your toast:
Why will you haunt me with a face as wan
    As shows an hour-old ghost?

I dare say Meg or Moll would take
10   Pity upon you, if you'd ask:
And pray don't remain single for my sake
    Who can't perform that task.

I have no heart?—Perhaps I have not;
    But then you're mad to take offence

15　That I don't give you what I have not got:
　　　Use your own common sense.

Let bygones be bygones:
　　Don't call me false, who owed not to be true:
I'd rather answer "No" to fifty Johns
20　　Than answer "Yes" to you.

Let's mar our pleasant days no more,
　　Song-birds of passage, days of youth:
Catch at today, forget the days before:
　　I'll wink at your untruth.

25　Let us strike hands as hearty friends;
　　No more, no less; and friendship's good:
Only don't keep in view ulterior ends,
　　And points not understood

In open treaty. Rise above
30　　Quibbles and shuffling off and on:
Here's friendship for you if you like; but love,—
　　No, thank you, John.

1860   1862

Promises Like Pie-Crust

Promise me no promises,
　　So will I not promise you:
Keep we both our liberties,
　　Never false and never true:
5　Let us hold the die uncast,
　　Free to come as free to go:
For I cannot know your past,
　　And of mine what can you know?

You, so warm, may once have been
10　　Warmer towards another one:
I, so cold, may once have seen
　　Sunlight, once have felt the sun:
Who shall show us if it was
　　Thus indeed in time of old?
15　Fades the image from the glass,
　　And the fortune is not told.

If you promised, you might grieve
　　For lost liberty again:
If I promised, I believe
20　　I should fret to break the chain.
Let us be the friends we were,
　　Nothing more but nothing less:

Many thrive on frugal fare
Who would perish of excess.

1861   1896

In Progress

Ten years ago it seemed impossible
   That she should ever grow so calm as this,
   With self-remembrance in her warmest kiss
And dim dried eyes like an exhausted well.
5   Slow-speaking when she has some fact to tell,
   Silent with long-unbroken silences,
   Centred in self yet not unpleased to please,
Gravely monotonous like a passing bell.
Mindful of drudging daily common things,
10   Patient at pastime, patient at her work,
   Wearied perhaps but strenuous certainly.
   Sometimes I fancy we may one day see
Her head shoot forth seven stars from where they lurk
And her eyes lightnings and her shoulders wings.

1862   1896

A Life's Parallels

Never on this side of the grave again,
   On this side of the river,
On this side of the garner of the grain,
   Never,—

5   Ever while time flows on and on and on,
   That narrow noiseless river,
Ever while corn bows heavy-headed, wan,
   Ever,—

Never despairing, often fainting, rueing,
10   But looking back, ah never!
Faint yet pursuing, faint yet still pursuing
   Ever.

1881

From Later Life

17

Something this foggy day, a something which
   Is neither of this fog nor of today,
   Has set me dreaming of the winds that play
Past certain cliffs, along one certain beach,

5   And turn the topmost edge of waves to spray:
      Ah pleasant pebbly strand so far away,
So out of reach while quite within my reach,
      As out of reach as India or Cathay!
I am sick of where I am and where I am not,
10   I am sick of foresight and of memory,
      I am sick of all I have and all I see,
         I am sick of self, and there is nothing new;
Oh weary impatient patience of my lot!—
      Thus with myself: how fares it, Friends, with you?

1881

Cardinal Newman[1]

In the grave, whither thou goest[2]

O weary Champion of the Cross, lie still:
      Sleep thou at length the all-embracing sleep:
      Long was thy sowing-day, rest now and reap:
Thy fast was long, feast now thy spirit's fill.
5   Yea, take thy fill of love, because thy will
      Chose love not in the shallows but the deep:
      Thy tides were springtides, set against the neap[3]
Of calmer souls: thy flood rebuked their rill.
Now night has come to thee—please God, of rest:
10   So some time must it come to every man;
      To first and last, where many last are first.
Now fixed and finished thine eternal plan,
      Thy best has done its best, thy worst its worst:
Thy best its best, Please God, thy best its best.

1890

Sleeping at Last

Sleeping at last, the trouble & tumult over,
      Sleeping at last, the struggle & horror past,
Cold & white out of sight of friend & of lover
      Sleeping at last.

5   No more a tired heart downcast or overcast,
   No more pangs that wring or shifting fears that hover,
      Sleeping at last in a dreamless sleep locked fast.

Fast asleep.   Singing birds in their leafy cover
      Cannot wake her, nor shake her the gusty blast.

---

1. Written on the occasion of the death of John
Henry Newman.
2. Ecclesiastes 9.10.

3. Tides that do not rise to the high-water mark of
the spring tides.

10   Under the purple thyme and the purple clover
        Sleeping at last.

1896

WILLIAM MORRIS
1834–1896

In his autobiography William Butler Yeats observes that if some angel offered him the choice, he would rather live William Morris's life than his own or any other man's. Morris's career was more multifaceted than that of any other Victorian writer. He was a poet, a writer of prose romances, a painter, a designer of furniture, a business-man, a printer, and a leader of the British socialist movement.

Born of wealthy parents and brought up in the Essex countryside, he went to Oxford with the intention of becoming a clergyman. However, art for him soon displaced religion. At Oxford he discovered the work of John Ruskin, which was, in his words, "a revelation." Later in life he wrote, "It was through him that I learned to give form to my discontent. . . . Apart from the desire to produce beautiful things, the leading passion of my life has been and is hatred of modern civilization." Morris's career in many ways realizes Ruskin's views. In 1861 Morris and several friends founded a company to design and produce furniture, wallpaper, textiles, stained glass, tapestries, and carpets, objects still prized today as masterpieces of decorative art. Morris's aim was not only to make beautiful things but, much as Ruskin had urged in *The Nature of Gothic*, to restore creativity to modern manufacture. The minor arts, he believed, were in a state of complete degradation; through his firm he wanted to restore beauty of design and individual craftsmanship.

In his design work, Morris developed close ties with the Pre-Raphaelites. In 1858, he published a remarkable book of poetry, *The Defense of Guenevere*, which some critics regard as the finest book of Pre-Raphaelite verse. Using medieval materials, the poems plunge the reader into the middle of dramatic situations with little sense of larger narrative context or even right and wrong, where little is clear but the viv-idness of the characters' perceptions. After *The Defense of Guenevere*, Morris turned from lyric to narrative, publishing *The Life and Death of Jason* (1867) and *The Earthly Paradise* (1868–70), a series of twenty-four classical and medieval tales. He then discovered the Icelandic sagas. He co-translated the *Volsunga Saga* and wrote a poem based on it, *The Story of Sigurd the Volsung* (1876). In 1877, he founded the Society for the Protection of Ancient Buildings.

In the late 1870s, after Morris came to the conclusion that art could not have real life and growth under the commercialism of modern society, he turned to socialism. In 1883 he joined the Socialist Democratic Federation; the next year he led the secession of a large faction to found the Socialist League. He was at the center of socialist activity in England through the rest of the decade. At the famous debates held on Sunday evenings at Morris's house, political and literary figures regularly gathered, including Yeats and Bernard Shaw. Morris lectured and wrote tirelessly for the cause, producing essays, columns, and a series of socialist literary works including *A Dream of John Ball* (1887) and *News from Nowhere* (1890), a utopian vision of life under communism in twenty-first-century England.

In 1890, Morris's health failed and factionalism brought his leadership of the Socialist League to an end. In 1891, he co-founded the Kelmscott Press, the first fine art press in England, whose masterpiece was the Kelmscott Chaucer, an edition of *The Canterbury Tales* with illustrations by the Pre-Raphaelite painter Edward Burne Jones and designs by Morris himself.

In the obituary he published after Morris's death, Shaw wrote, "He was ultramodern—not merely up-to-date, but far ahead of it: his wall papers, his hangings, his tapestries, and his printed books have the twentieth century in every touch of them." Not only did Morris develop design principles that remained important in the twentieth century but he had a radical vision of the relationship of aesthetics to politics. He was, as Shaw said, "a complete artist."

The Defense of Guenevere   Several episodes in Thomas Malory's *Morte Darthur* (1470), one of Morris's favorite books, provided the materials on which he based this poem, although how he presents them is strikingly original. In Malory's narrative, Arthur's kingdom is eventually destroyed by dissensions among his followers; one chief focus of dissension concerned rumors of an adulterous relation between Queen Guenevere and Arthur's chief knight, Launcelot. On two occasions Guenevere had been discovered in apparently compromising circumstances, both of which led to public accusations of adultery. On the first occasion (lines 167–220), her accuser, Sir Mellyagraunce, was challenged by Launcelot to a trial by battle, in which Mellyagraunce was slain. The queen's honor was thereby restored, although, in the poem, the Mellyagraunce scandal is revived by Sir Gauwaine in his accusations against her. The second occasion, which occurred just before the poem opens, was more seriously incriminating. A band of thirteen knights had plotted to trap Launcelot when he was enjoying a visit at night in the queen's chamber, at her invitation (lines 242–77). In making his escape, Launcelot killed all but one of the knights—an event that would later lead to civil war. In Malory's version there is no formal trial of the queen after this event; she is simply told of her sentence, which is to be burned to death at the stake, and is thereafter rescued by Launcelot who takes her away to safety in his castle. Morris's trial scene is hence his own invention, although he probably drew from another episode, in chapter 18 of Malory, which shows Guenevere being accused of treason by Sir Gauwaine in the presence of twenty-four of his knights.

According to Morris's daughter, this poem originally opened with a long introductory passage of description and background, which Morris wisely decided to omit. As a result we are plunged at once into a dramatic scene reminiscent of the openings of some of the dramatic monologues of Robert Browning (the Victorian poet whom Morris most admired). Also like Browning is the way Guenevere's speech keeps shifting back and forth from present to past events such as her recalling the spring day, early in her marriage to Arthur, when Launcelot first kissed her.

During the same year in which Morris's poem appeared, one of Tennyson's *Idylls of the King,* also focused on Guenevere, was published. It is interesting to compare the two portraits of the queen, especially in terms of their pictorial qualities, although Morris's seductively eloquent Guenevere is very different from Tennyson's subdued representation of a guilt-ridden wife.

The Defense of Guenevere

But, knowing now that they would have her speak,
She threw her wet hair backward from her brow,
Her hand close to her mouth touching her cheek,

As though she had had there a shameful blow,
5   And feeling it shameful to feel aught but shame
All through her heart, yet felt her cheek burned so,

She must a little touch it; like one lame
She walked away from Gauwaine, with her head
Still lifted up; and on her cheek of flame

10 The tears dried quick; she stopped at last and said:
"O knights and lords, it seems but little skill°   *use*
To talk of well-known things past now and dead.

"God wot° I ought to say, I have done ill,   *knows*
And pray you all forgiveness heartily!
15 Because you must be right such great lords—still

"Listen, suppose your time were come to die,
And you were quite alone and very weak;
Yea, laid a dying while very mightily

"The wind was ruffling up the narrow streak
20 Of river through your broad lands running well:
Suppose a hush should come, then someone speak:

" 'One of these cloths is heaven, and one is hell,
Now choose one cloth forever, which they be,
I will not tell you, you must somehow tell

25 " 'Of your own strength and mightiness; here, see!'
Yea, yea, my lord, and you to ope your eyes,
At foot of your familiar bed to see

"A great God's angel standing, with such dyes,
Not known on earth, on his great wings, and hands,
30 Held out two ways, light from the inner skies

"Showing him well, and making his commands
Seem to be God's commands, moreover, too,
Holding within his hands the cloths on wands;

"And one of these strange choosing cloths was blue,
35 Wavy and long, and one cut short and red;
No man could tell the better of the two.

"After a shivering half hour you said,
'God help! heaven's color, the blue'; and he said, 'hell.'
Perhaps you then would roll upon your bed,

40 "And cry to all good men that loved you well,
'Ah Christ! if only I had known, known, known';
Launcelot went away, then I could tell,

"Like wisest man how all things would be, moan,
And roll and hurt myself, and long to die,
45 And yet fear much to die for what was sown.

"Nevertheless you, O Sir Gauwaine, lie,
Whatever may have happened through these years,
God knows I speak truth, saying that you lie."

Her voice was low at first, being full of tears,
50 But as it cleared, it grew full loud and shrill,
Growing a windy shriek in all men's ears,

A ringing in their startled brains, until
She said that Gauwaine lied, then her voice sunk,
And her great eyes began again to fill,

55 Though still she stood right up, and never shrunk,
But spoke on bravely, glorious lady fair!
Whatever tears her full lips may have drunk,

She stood, and seemed to think, and wrung her hair,
Spoke out at last with no more trace of shame,
60 With passionate twisting of her body there:

"It chanced upon a day that Launcelot came
To dwell at Arthur's court: at Christmas time
This happened; when the heralds sung his name,

" 'Son of King Ban[1] of Benwick,' seemed to chime
65 Along with all the bells that rang that day,
O'er the white roofs, with little change of rhyme.

"Christmas and whitened winter passed away,
And over me the April sunshine came,
Made very awful with black hail-clouds, yea.

70 "And in Summer I grew white with flame,
And bowed my head down—Autumn, and the sick
Sure knowledge things would never be the same,

"However often Spring might be most thick
Of blossoms and buds, smote on me, and I grew
75 Careless of most things, let the clock tick, tick,

"To my unhappy pulse, that beat right through
My eager body; while I laughed out loud,
And let my lips curl up at false or true,

---

1. Launcelot's father, a king of Brittany.

"Seemed cold and shallow without any cloud.
80 Behold my judges, then the cloths were brought:
While I was dizzied thus, old thoughts would crowd,

"Belonging to the time ere I was bought
By Arthur's great name and his little love,
Must I give up forever then, I thought,

85 "That which I deemed would ever round me move
Glorifying all things; for a little word,[2]
Scarce ever meant at all, must I now prove

"Stone-cold for ever? Pray you, does the Lord
Will that all folks should be quite happy and good?
90 I love God now a little, if this cord[3]

"Were broken, once for all what striving could
Make me love anything in earth or heaven.
So day by day it grew, as if one should

"Slip slowly down some path worn smooth and even,
95 Down to a cool sea on a summer day;
Yet still in slipping there was some small leaven

"Of stretched hands catching small stones by the way,
Until one surely reached the sea at last,
And felt strange new joy as the worn head lay

100 "Back, with the hair like seaweed; yea all past
Sweat of the forehead, dryness of the lips,
Washed utterly out by the dear waves o'ercast,

"In the lone sea, far off from any ships!
Do I not know now of a day in Spring?
105 No minute of that wild day ever slips

"From out my memory; I hear thrushes sing,
And wheresoever I may be, straightway
Thoughts of it all come up with most fresh sting:

"I was half mad with beauty on that day,
110 And went without my ladies all alone,
In a quiet garden walled round every way;

"I was right joyful of that wall of stone,
That shut the flowers and trees up with the sky,
And trebled all the beauty: to the bone,

2. Her marriage vow. 3. Her ties with Launcelot.

115 "Yea right through to my heart, grown very shy
With weary thoughts, it pierced, and made me glad;
Exceedingly glad, and I knew verily,

"A little thing just then had made me mad;
I dared not think, as I was wont to do,
120 Sometimes, upon my beauty; If I had

"Held out my long hand up against the blue,
And, looking on the tenderly darkened fingers,
Thought that by rights one ought to see quite through,

"There, see you, where the soft still light yet lingers,
125 Round by the edges; what should I have done,
If this had joined with yellow spotted singers,

"And startling green drawn upward by the sun?
But shouting, loosed out, see now! all my hair,
And trancedly stood watching the west wind run

130 "With faintest half-heard breathing sound—why there
I lose my head e'en now in doing this;
But shortly listen—In that garden fair

"Came Launcelot walking; this is true, the kiss
Wherewith we kissed in meeting that spring day,
135 I scarce dare talk of the remembered bliss,

"When both our mouths went wandering in one way,
And aching sorely, met among the leaves;
Our hands being left behind strained far away.

"Never within a yard of my bright sleeves
140 Had Launcelot come before—and now, so nigh!
After that day why is it Guenevere grieves?

"Nevertheless you, O Sir Gauwaine, lie,
Whatever happened on through all those years,
God knows I speak truth, saying that you lie.

145 "Being such a lady could I weep these tears
If this were true? A great queen such as I
Having sinned this way, straight her conscience sears;

"And afterwards she liveth hatefully,
Slaying and poisoning, certes° never weeps—   certainly
150 Gauwaine be friends now, speak me lovingly.

"Do I not see how God's dear pity creeps
All through your frame, and trembles in your mouth?
Remember in what grave your mother sleeps,

"Buried in some place far down in the south,
155   Men are forgetting as I speak to you;
By her head severed in that awful drouth

"Of pity that drew Agravaine's fell blow,[4]
I pray your pity! let me not scream out
Forever after, when the shrill winds blow

160   "Through half your castle-locks! let me not shout
Forever after in the winter night
When you ride out alone! in battle rout

"Let not my rusting tears make your sword light!°   *weak*
Ah! God of mercy how he turns away!
165   So, ever must I dress me to the fight,

"So—let God's justice work! Gauwaine, I say,
See me hew down your proofs: yea all men know
Even as you said how Mellyagraunce one day,

"One bitter day in *la Fausse Garde*,[5] for so
170   All good knights held it after, saw—
Yea, sirs, by cursed unknightly outrage; though

"You, Gauwaine, held his word without a flaw,
This Mellyagraunce saw blood upon my bed[6]—
Whose blood then pray you? is there any law

175   "To make a queen say why some spots of red
Lie on her coverlet? or will you say,
'Your hands are white, lady, as when you wed,

" 'Where did you bleed?' and must I stammer out—'Nay,
I blush indeed, fair lord, only to rend
180   My sleeve up to my shoulder, where there lay

" 'A knife-point last night': so must I defend
The honor of the lady Guenevere?
Not so, fair lords, even if the world should end

"This very day, and you were judges here
185   Instead of God. Did you see Mellyagraunce
When Launcelot stood by him? what white fear

"Curdled his blood, and how his teeth did dance,
His side sink in? as my knight cried and said,
'Slayer of unarmed men, here is a chance!

4. Gauwaine's brother, Agravaine, had beheaded their mother after she had been accused of adultery.
5. The False Castle (French); a term expressing her contempt.
6. Guenevere and some of her young knights who had been wounded in a skirmish were confined for a night in a room in Mellyagraunce's castle. Discovering bloodstains on her bedclothes the following morning, Mellyagraunce accused her of adulterous relations with one of the wounded knights. Actually her visiting bedfellow had been Launcelot, who had cut his hand on the window bars as he climbed into her room.

190   " 'Setter of traps,[7] I pray you guard your head,
By God I am so glad to fight with you,
Stripper of ladies, that my hand feels lead

" 'For driving weight; hurrah now! draw and do,
For all my wounds are moving in my breast,
195   And I am getting mad with waiting so.'

"He struck his hands together o'er the beast,
Who fell down flat, and groveled at his feet,
And groaned at being slain so young—'at least.'

"My knight said, 'Rise you, sir, who are so fleet
200   At catching ladies, half-armed will I fight,
My left side all uncovered!' then I weet,°   *know*

"Up sprang Sir Mellyagraunce with great delight
Upon his knave's face; not until just then
Did I quite hate him, as I saw my knight

205   "Along the lists look to my stake and pen
With such a joyous smile, it made me sigh
From agony beneath my waist-chain,[8] when

"The fight began, and to me they drew nigh;
Ever Sir Launcelot kept him on the right,
210   And traversed warily, and ever high

"And fast leaped caitiff's sword, until my knight
Sudden threw up his sword to his left hand,
Caught it, and swung it; that was all the fight.

"Except a spout of blood on the hot land;
215   For it was hottest summer; and I know
I wondered how the fire, while I should stand,

"And burn, against the heat, would quiver so,
Yards above my head; thus these matters went:
Which things were only warnings of the woe

220   "That fell on me. Yet Mellyagraunce was shent,°   *destroyed*
For Mellyagraunce had fought against the Lord;
Therefore, my lords, take heed lest you be blent°   *blinded*

"With all this wickedness; say no rash word
Against me, being so beautiful; my eyes,
225   Wept all away to gray, may bring some sword

---

7. Mellyagraunce had tried to prevent Launcelot from coming to defend the queen's honor by making him fall through a trapdoor into a dungeon.

8. She is chained to a stake, at which she will be burned if Launcelot fails to overcome her accuser.

"To drown you in your blood; see my breast rise,
Like waves of purple sea, as here I stand;
And how my arms are moved in wonderful wise,

"Yea also at my full heart's strong command,
230 See through my long throat how the words go up
In ripples to my mouth; how in my hand

"The shadow lies like wine within a cup
Of marvelously colored gold; yea now
This little wind is rising, look you up,

235 "And wonder how the light is falling so
Within my moving tresses: will you dare,
When you have looked a little on my brow,

"To say this thing is vile? or will you care
For any plausible lies of cunning woof,
240 When you can see my face with no lie there

"Forever? am I not a gracious proof—
'But in your chamber Launcelot was found'—
Is there a good knight then would stand aloof,

"When a queen says with gentle queenly sound:
245 'O true as steel come now and talk with me,
I love to see your step upon the ground

" 'Unwavering, also well I love to see
That gracious smile light up your face, and hear
Your wonderful words, that all mean verily

250 " 'The thing they seem to mean: good friend, so dear
To me in everything, come here tonight,
Or else the hours will pass most dull and drear;

" 'If you come not, I fear this time I might
Get thinking over much of times gone by,
255 When I was young, and green hope was in sight:

" 'For no man cares now to know why I sigh;
And no man comes to sing me pleasant songs,
Nor any brings me the sweet flowers that lie

" 'So thick in the gardens; therefore one so longs
260 To see you, Launcelot; that we may be
Like children once again, free from all wrongs

" 'Just for one night.' Did he not come to me?
What thing could keep true Launcelot away
If I said 'Come?' there was one less than three

265   "In my quiet room that night, and we were gay;
      Till sudden I rose up, weak, pale, and sick,
      Because a bawling broke our dream up, yea

      "I looked at Launcelot's face and could not speak,
      For he looked helpless too, for a little while;
270   Then I remember how I tried to shriek,

      "And could not, but fell down; from tile to tile
      The stones they threw up rattled o'er my head
      And made me dizzier; till within a while

      "My maids were all about me, and my head
275   On Launcelot's breast was being soothed away
      From its white chattering, until Launcelot said—

      "By God! I will not tell you more today,
      Judge any way you will—what matters it?
      You know quite well the story of that fray,

280   "How Launcelot stilled their bawling, the mad fit
      That caught up Gauwaine—all, all, verily,
      But just that which would save me; these things flit.

      "Nevertheless you, O Sir Gauwaine, lie,
      Whatever may have happened these long years,
285   God knows I speak truth, saying that you lie!

      "All I have said is truth, by Christ's dear tears."
      She would not speak another word, but stood.
      Turned sideways; listening, like a man who hears

      His brother's trumpet sounding through the wood
290   Of his foes' lances. She leaned eagerly,
      And gave a slight spring sometimes, as she could

      At last hear something really; joyfully
      Her cheek grew crimson, as the headlong speed
      Of the roan charger drew all men to see,
295   The knight who came was Launcelot at good need.

                      1859

The Haystack in the Floods[1]

      Had she come all the way for this,
      To part at last without a kiss?
      Yea, had she borne the dirt and rain

---

1. After the defeat of the French at Poitiers in 1356, an English knight, Sir Robert de Marny, is riding with Jehane, his mistress, to reach the frontier of Gascony, which was in English hands.

That her own eyes might see him slain
5   Beside the haystack in the floods?

Along the dripping leafless woods,
The stirrup touching either shoe,
She rode astride as troopers do;
With kirtle° kilted to her knee,   *long skirt*
10   To which the mud splashed wretchedly;
And the wet dripped from every tree
Upon her head and heavy hair,
And on her eyelids broad and fair;
The tears and rain ran down her face.
15   By fits and starts they rode apace,
And very often was his place
Far off from her; he had to ride
Ahead, to see what might betide
When the roads crossed; and sometimes, when
20   There rose a murmuring from his men,
Had to turn back with promises.
Ah me! she had but little ease;
And often for pure doubt and dread
She sobbed, made giddy in the head
25   By the swift riding; while, for cold,
Her slender fingers scarce could hold
The wet reins; yea, and scarcely, too,
She felt the foot within her shoe
Against the stirrup: all for this,
30   To part at last without a kiss
Beside the haystack in the floods.

For when they neared that old soaked hay,
They saw across the only way
That Judas, Godmar, and the three
35   Red running lions dismally
Grinned from his pennon, under which
In one straight line along the ditch,
They counted thirty heads.

              So then
While Robert turned round to his men,
40   She saw at once the wretched end,
And, stooping down, tried hard to rend
Her coif the wrong way from her head,
And hid her eyes; while Robert said:
"Nay, love, 'tis scarcely two to one;
45   At Poitiers where we made them run
So fast—why, sweet my love, good cheer,
The Gascon frontier is so near,
Nought after this."

             But: "O!" she said,
"My God! my God! I have to tread

50　The long way back without you; then
　　The court at Paris; those six men,°　　　　　　*the judges*
　　The gratings of the Chatelet°　　　　　　　　*Paris prison*
　　The swift Seine on some rainy day
　　Like this, and people standing by,
55　And laughing, while my weak hands try
　　To recollect how strong men swim.[2]
　　All this, or else a life with him,
　　For which I should be damned at last,
　　Would God that this next hour were past!"

60　He answered not, but cried his cry,
　　"St. George for Marny!" cheerily;
　　And laid his hand upon her rein.
　　Alas! no man of all this train
　　Gave back that cheery cry again;
65　And, while for rage his thumb beat fast
　　Upon his sword hilt, someone cast
　　About his neck a kerchief long,
　　And bound him.

　　　　　　　Then they went along
　　To Godmar; who said: "Now, Jehane,
70　Your lover's life is on the wane
　　So fast, that, if this very hour
　　You yield not as my paramour,
　　He will not see the rain leave off:
　　Nay, keep your tongue from gibe and scoff,
75　Sir Robert, or I slay you now."

　　She laid her hand upon her brow,
　　Then gazed upon the palm, as though
　　She thought her forehead bled, and: "No!"
　　She said, and turned her head away,
80　As there was nothing else to say,
　　And everything were settled: red
　　Grew Godmar's face from chin to head:
　　"Jehane, on yonder hill there stands
　　My castle, guarding well my lands;
85　What hinders me from taking you,
　　And doing that I list to do
　　To your fair willful body, while
　　Your knight lies dead?"

　　　　　　　A wicked smile
　　Wrinkled her face, her lips grew thin,
90　A long way out she thrust her chin:

2. In trial by water a woman accused of witchcraft or other crimes was thrown into the river to determine her guilt or innocence. For this ordeal the accused would customarily have her hands tied. If she sank she was deemed innocent and thereafter spared by being hauled from the water. If she floated she was guilty and thereafter burned. In Morris's version Jehane would have no chance of escaping death; if she swam she would be burned, and if she sank she would be drowned (line 108).

"You know that I should strangle you
While you were sleeping; or bite through
Your throat, by God's help: ah!" she said,
"Lord Jesus, pity your poor maid!
95   For in such wise they hem me in,
I cannot choose but sin and sin,
Whatever happens: yet I think
They could not make me eat or drink,
And so should I just reach my rest."
100   "Nay, if you do not my behest,
O Jehane! though I love you well,"
Said Godmar, "would I fail to tell
All that I know?" "Foul lies," she said.
"Eh? lies, my Jehane? by God's head,
105   At Paris folks would deem them true!
Do you know, Jehane, they cry for you:
'Jehane the brown! Jehane the brown!
Give us Jehane to burn or drown!'
Eh!—gag me Robert!—sweet my friend,
110   This were indeed a piteous end
For those long fingers, and long feet,
And long neck, and smooth shoulders sweet;
An end that few men would forget
That saw it. So, an hour yet:
115   Consider, Jehane, which to take
Of life or death!"

                 So, scarce awake,
Dismounting, did she leave that place,
And totter some yards: with her face
Turned upward to the sky she lay,
120   Her head on a wet heap of hay,
And fell asleep: and while she slept,
And did not dream, the minutes crept
Round to the twelve again; but she,
Being waked at last, sighed quietly,
125   And strangely childlike came, and said:
"I will not." Straightway Godmar's head,
As though it hung on strong wires, turned
Most sharply round, and his face burned.

For Robert, both his eyes were dry,
130   He could not weep, but gloomily
He seemed to watch the rain; yea, too,
His lips were firm; he tried once more
To touch her lips; she reached out, sore
And vain desire so tortured them,
135   The poor gray lips, and now the hem
Of his sleeve brushed them.

                  With a start
Up Godmar rose, thrust them apart;

From Robert's throat he loosed the bands
Of silk and mail; with empty hands
140 Held out, she stood and gazed, and saw,
The long bright blade without a flaw
Glide out from Godmar's sheath, his hand
In Robert's hair; she saw him bend
Back Robert's head; she saw him send
145 The thin steel down; the blow told well,
Right backward the knight Robert fell,
And moaned as dogs do, being half dead,
Unwitting, as I deem: so then
Godmar turned grinning to his men,
150 Who ran, some five or six, and beat
His head to pieces at their feet.

Then Godmar turned again and said:
"So, Jehane, the first fitte³ is read!
Take note, my lady, that your way
155 Lies backward to the Chatelet!"
She shook her head and gazed awhile
At her cold hands with a rueful smile,
As though this thing had made her mad.

This was the parting that they had
160 Beside the haystack in the floods.

1858

How I Became a Socialist[1]

I am asked by the Editor to give some sort of a history of the above conversion, and I feel that it may be of some use to do so, if my readers will look
upon me as a type of a certain group of people, but not so easy to do clearly,
briefly and truly. Let me, however, try. But first, I will say what I mean by
being a Socialist, since I am told that the word no longer expresses definitely
and with certainty what it did ten years ago. Well, what I mean by Socialism
is a condition of society in which there should be neither rich nor poor,
neither master nor master's man, neither idle nor overworked, neither brain-
sick brain workers, nor heart-sick hand workers, in a word, in which all men
would be living in equality of condition, and would manage their affairs
unwastefully, and with the full consciousness that harm to one would mean
harm to all—the realization at last of the meaning of the word COMMON-
WEALTH.

Now this view of Socialism which I hold to-day, and hope to die holding,
is what I began with; I had no transitional period, unless you may call such
a brief period of political radicalism during which I saw my ideal clear

---

3. Canto of a poem.
1. Written for the socialist magazine *Justice* in 1894.

enough, but had no hope of any realization of it. That came to an end some months before I joined the (then) Democratic Federation,[2] and the meaning of my joining that body was that I had conceived a hope of the realization of my ideal. If you ask me how much of a hope, or what I thought we Socialists then living and working would accomplish towards it, or when there would be effected any change in the face of society, I must say, I do not know. I can only say that I did not measure my hope, nor the joy that it brought me at the time. For the rest, when I took that step I was blankly ignorant of economics; I had never so much as opened Adam Smith, or heard of Ricardo, or of Karl Marx.[3] Oddly enough, I *had* read some of Mill,[4] to wit, those posthumous papers of his (published, was it in the *Westminster Review* or the *Fortnightly?*) in which he attacks Socialism in its Fourierist[5] guise. In those papers he put the arguments, as far as they go, clearly and honestly, and the result, so far as I was concerned, was to convince me that Socialism was a necessary change, and that it was possible to bring it about in our own days. Those papers put the finishing touch to my conversion to Socialism. Well, having joined a Socialist body (for the Federation soon became definitely Socialist), I put some conscience into trying to learn the economical side of Socialism, and even tackled Marx, though I must confess that, whereas I thoroughly enjoyed the historical part of "Capital," I suffered agonies of confusion of the brain over reading the pure economics of that great work. Anyhow, I read what I could, and will hope that some information stuck to me from my reading; but more, I must think, from continuous conversation with such friends as Bax and Hyndman and Scheu,[6] and the brisk course of propaganda meetings which were going on at the time, and in which I took my share. Such finish to what of education in practical Socialism as I am capable of I received afterwards from some of my Anarchist friends, from whom I learned, quite against their intention, that Anarchism was impossible, much as I learned from Mill against *his* intention that Socialism was necessary.

But in this telling how I fell into *practical* Socialism I have begun, as I perceive, in the middle, for in my position of a well-to-do man, not suffering from the disabilities which oppress a working-man at every step, I feel that I might never have been drawn into the practical side of the question if an ideal had not forced me to seek towards it. For politics as politics, *i.e.*, not regarded as a necessary if cumbersome and disgustful means to an end, would never have attracted me, nor when I had become conscious of the wrongs of society as it now is, and the oppression of poor people, could I have ever believed in the possibility of a *partial* setting right of those wrongs. In other words, I could never have been such a fool as to believe in the happy and "respectable" poor.

If, therefore, my ideal forced me to look for practical Socialism, what was

2. The first socialist organization in London, founded in 1881.
3. Political philosopher (1818–1883), who developed the concept of communism. Smith (1723–1790), Scottish economist whose argument that natural laws of production and exchange govern economies and produce wealth was an important justification of capitalism. David Ricardo (1772–1823), English economist.

4. James Mill (1773–1836), father of John Stuart Mill, philosopher and political economist.
5. Political philosophy, developed by Charles Fourier (1772–1837), that advocated a social reorganization that equalized wealth.
6. Ernest Belfort Bax, H. M. Hyndman, and Andreas Sheu, leaders in the early English socialist movement.

it that forced me to conceive of an ideal? Now, here comes in what I said (in this paper) of my being a type of a certain group of mind.

Before the uprising of *modern* Socialism almost all intelligent people either were, or professed themselves to be, quite contented with the civilization of this century. Again, almost all of these really were thus contented, and saw nothing to do but to perfect the said civilization by getting rid of a few ridiculous survivals of the barbarous ages. To be short, this was the *Whig*[7] frame of mind, natural to the modern prosperous middle-class men, who, in fact, as far as mechanical progress is concerned, have nothing to ask for, if only Socialism would leave them alone to enjoy their plentiful style.

But besides these contented ones there were others who were not really contented, but had a vague sentiment of repulsion to the triumph of civilization, but were coerced into silence by the measureless power of Whiggery. Lastly, there were a few who were in open rebellion against the said Whiggery—a few, say two, Carlyle and Ruskin. The latter, before my days of practical Socialism, was my master towards the ideal aforesaid, and, looking backward, I cannot help saying, by the way, how deadly dull the world would have been twenty years ago but for Ruskin! It was through him that I learned to give form to my discontent, which I must say was not by any means vague. Apart from the desire to produce beautiful things, the leading passion of my life has been and is hatred of modern civilization. What shall I say of it now, when the words are put into my mouth, my hope of its destruction—what shall I say of its supplanting by Socialism?

What shall I say concerning its mastery of and its waste of mechanical power, its commonwealth so poor, its enemies of the commonwealth so rich, its stupendous organization—for the misery of life! Its contempt of simple pleasures which everyone could enjoy but for its folly? Its eyeless vulgarity which has destroyed art, the one certain solace of labour? All this I felt then as now, but I did not know why it was so. The hope of the past times was gone, the struggles of mankind for many ages had produced nothing but this sordid, aimless, ugly confusion; the immediate future seemed to me likely to intensify all the present evils by sweeping away the last survivals of the days before the dull squalor of civilization had settled down on the world. This was a bad look-out indeed, and, if I may mention myself as a personality and not as a mere type, especially so to a man of my disposition, careless of metaphysics and religion, as well as of scientific analysis, but with a deep love of the earth and the life on it, and a passion for the history of the past of mankind. Think of it! Was it all to end in a counting-house on the top of a cinder-heap, with Podsnap's[8] drawing-room in the offing, and a Whig committee dealing out champagne to the rich and margarine to the poor in such convenient proportions as would make all men contented together, though the pleasure of the eyes was gone from the world, and the place of Homer was to be taken by Huxley?[9] Yet, believe me, in my heart, when I really forced myself to look towards the future, that is what I saw in it, and, as far as I could tell, scarce anyone seemed to think it worth while to struggle against such a consummation of civilization. So there I was in for a fine pessimistic

7. Political party largely identified with industry and with parliamentary and social reform; became part of the Liberal party in the early 1840s.
8. Character in Dickens's *Our Mutual Friend*, the epitome of pretentious middle-class respectability.
9. T. H. Huxley (1825–1895), writer on science and philosophy.

end of life, if it had not somehow dawned on me that amidst all this filth of civilization the seeds of a great chance, what we others call Social-Revolution, were beginning to germinate. The whole face of things was changed to me by that discovery, and all I had to do then in order to become a Socialist was to hook myself on to the practical movement, which, as before said, I have tried to do as well as I could.

To sum up, then, the study of history and the love and practice of art forced me into a hatred of the civilization which, if things were to stop as they are, would turn history into inconsequent nonsense, and make art a collection of the curiosities of the past which would have no serious relation to the life of the present.

But the consciousness of revolution stirring amidst our hateful modern society prevented me, luckier than many others of artistic perceptions, from crystallizing into a mere railer against "progress" on the one hand, and on the other from wasting time and energy in any of the numerous schemes by which the quasi-artistic of the middle classes hope to make art grow when it has no longer any root, and thus I became a practical Socialist.

A last word or two. Perhaps some of our friends will say, what have we to do with these matters of history and art? We want by means of Social-Democracy to win a decent livelihood, we want in some sort to live, and that at once. Surely any one who professes to think that the question of art and cultivation must go before that of the knife and fork (and there are some who do propose that) does not understand what art means, or how that its roots must have a soil of a thriving and unanxious life. Yet it must be remembered that civilization has reduced the workman to such a skinny and pitiful existence, that he scarcely knows how to frame a desire for any life much better than that which he now endures perforce. It is the province of art to set the true ideal of a full and reasonable life before him, a life to which the perception and creation of beauty, the enjoyment of real pleasure that is, shall be felt to be as necessary to man as his daily bread, and that no man, and no set of men, can be deprived of this except by mere opposition, which should be resisted to the utmost.

1894   1894

ALGERNON CHARLES SWINBURNE
1837–1909

In a review of Baudelaire's *Fleurs du Mal* Algernon Charles Swinburne remarked that "the mass of readers seem actually to think that a poem is the better for containing a moral lesson." He goes on to praise the courage and sense of a man who acts on the conviction "that the art of poetry has nothing to do with didactic matter at all." Certainly Swinburne's poems are not didactic in the sense of containing traditional moral values. As John Morley commented in a review of Swinburne's first volume of poems, "He is so firmly and avowedly fixed in an attitude of revolt against the current notions of decency and dignity and social duty that to beg of him to be a little more decent, to fly a little less persistently and gleefully to the animal side of human nature, is simply to beg him to be something different from Mr. Swinburne." Like the fat boy in *Pickwick Papers* who terrified the old lady by announcing, "I wants to make your flesh creep," Swinburne set about shocking his elders by a variety of rebellious gestures. In religion he appeared to be a pagan; in politics, a liberal republican dedicated to the overthrow of established governments. And on the subject of love he was often preoccupied with the pleasures of the lover who inflicts pain or accepts pain, pleasures of which he had read in the writings of the Marquis de Sade. As Arnold Bennett said of *Anactoria,* a dramatic monologue in which the poet Sappho addresses a woman with whom she is madly in love, Swinburne played "a rare trick" on England by "enshrining in the topmost heights of its literature a lovely poem that cannot be discussed."

To a more limited extent, Swinburne also expressed his rebellion against established codes by his personal behavior. He came from a distinguished family and attended Eton and Oxford, but sought the company of the bohemians of Paris and of London, where he became temporarily associated with Dante Gabriel Rossetti and other Pre-Raphaelites. By 1879 his alcoholism had profoundly affected his frail physique, and he was obliged to put himself into the protective custody of a friend, Theodore Watts-Dunton, who removed him to the countryside and kept him alive although sobered and tamed.

Swinburne continued to write voluminously and sometimes memorably, but most of his best poetry is in his early publications. His early play *Atalanta in Calydon* (1865) was described by Swinburne himself as "pure Greek," and his command of classical allusions here, as well as in other poems, is indeed impressive. Yet the kind of spirit that he found in Greek literature was not the traditional quality of classic serenity admired by Matthew Arnold. Like Shelley (the poet he most closely resembles), Swinburne loved Greece as a land of liberty in which men had expressed themselves with the most complete unrestraint. To call such an ardently romantic poet "classical" requires a series of qualifying clauses that makes the term meaningless.

In his play and in the volume that followed it, *Poems and Ballads* (1866), Swinburne demonstrated a metrical virtuosity that dazzled his early readers and is still dazzling. Those who demand that poetry should make sense, first and foremost, may find that much of his poetry is not to their taste. What he offers, instead, are heady rhythmical patterns in which words are relished as much for their sound as for their sense.

> There lived a singer in France of old
> By the tideless dolorous midland sea.
> In a land of sand and ruin and gold
> There shone one woman, and none but she.

These lines from *The Triumph of Time* have often been cited to illustrate Swinburne's qualities. Like some of the poems of the later French symbolists, such passages defy traditional kinds of critical analysis and oblige us to reconsider the variety of ways in which poetry may achieve its effects.

Another noteworthy aspect of these poems is their recurring preoccupation with death, as in the memorable re-creations of the underworld garden of Proserpine, frozen in timelessness. And as the critic Jerome McGann notes: "No English poet has composed more elegies than Swinburne." The death of any prominent figure, such as Browning, almost always prompted Swinburne to compose a poem for the occasion. Some of these are merely competent editorials in verse; others, especially his moving *Ave Atque Vale* in honor of Charles Baudelaire, are of a different dimension. Swinburne modestly hoped that *Ave Atque Vale* might find its niche as a fourth in line among the major elegies in English, following Milton's *Lycidas,* Shelley's *Adonais,* and Arnold's *Thyrsis.* McGann argues that the "elusive beauty and enigmatic greatness" of Swinburne's elegy make his poem clearly superior to *Thyrsis* and assure *Ave Atque Vale* the third place (at least) in this distinguished quartet.

Choruses from Atalanta in Calydon

When the Hounds of Spring[1]

When the hounds of spring are on winter's traces,
    The mother of months in meadow or plain
Fills the shadows and windy places
    With lisp of leaves and ripple of rain;
5 And the brown bright nightingale[2] amorous
Is half assuaged for Itylus,
For the Thracian ships and the foreign faces,
    The tongueless vigil and all the pain.

    Come with bows bent and with emptying of quivers,
10   Maiden most perfect, lady of light,
With a noise of winds and many rivers,
    With a clamor of waters, and with might;
Bind on thy sandals, O thou most fleet,
    Over the splendor and speed of thy feet;
15 For the faint east quickens, the wan west shivers,
    Round the feet of the day and the feet of the night.

    Where shall we find her, how shall we sing to her,
    Fold our hands round her knees, and cling?
O that man's heart were as fire and could spring to her,
20   Fire, or the strength of the streams that spring!
For the stars and the winds are unto her
    As raiment, as songs of the harp player;
For the risen stars and the fallen cling to her,
    And the southwest wind and the west wind sing.

25 For winter's rains and ruins are over,
    And all the season of snows and sins;
The days dividing lover and lover,
    The light that loses, the night that wins;
And time remembered is grief forgotten,
30   And frosts are slain and flowers begotten,
    And in green underwood and cover
    Blossom by blossom the spring begins.

    The full streams feed on flower of rushes,
    Ripe grasses trammel a traveling foot,

1. This choral hymn, with which Swinburne's tragedy opens, is addressed to Artemis (or Diana), virgin goddess and huntress. Artemis was also goddess of the moon and hence, as affecting the seasons, the "mother of months" (line 2).
2. Philomela, after being raped by her brother-in-law and having her tongue cut out, was changed into a nightingale. To obtain revenge, her sister, Procne, killed her own son, Itylus, and fed the child's body to her husband, Tereus, a Thracian king.

35   The faint fresh flame of the young year flushes
        From leaf to flower and flower to fruit;
     And fruit and leaf are as gold and fire,
     And the oat[3] is heard above the lyre,
     And the hoofèd heel of a satyr crushes
40   The chestnut husk at the chestnut root.

     And Pan by noon and Bacchus by night,
        Fleeter of foot than the fleet-foot kid,
     Follows with dancing and fills with delight
        The Maenad and the Bassarid;[4]
45   And soft as lips that laugh and hide,
     The laughing leaves of the trees divide,
     And screen from seeing and leave in sight
        The god pursuing, the maiden hid.

     The ivy falls with the Bacchanal's hair
50   Over her eyebrows hiding her eyes;
     The wild vine slipping down leaves bare
        Her bright breast shortening into sighs;
     The wild vine slips with the weight of its leaves,
     But the berried ivy catches and cleaves
55   To the limbs that glitter, the feet that scare
        The wolf that follows, the fawn that flies.

Before the Beginning of Years

     Before the beginning of years
        There came to the making of man
     Time, with a gift of tears;
        Grief, with a glass that ran;
5   Pleasure, with pain for leaven;
        Summer, with flowers that fell;
     Remembrance fallen from heaven,
        And madness risen from hell;
     Strength without hands to smite;
10   Love that endures for a breath;
     Night, the shadow of light,
        And life, the shadow of death.

     And the high gods took in hand
        Fire, and the falling of tears,
15   And a measure of sliding sand
        From under the feet of the years;
     And froth and drift of the sea;
        And dust of the laboring earth;
     And bodies of things to be
20   In the houses of death and of birth;
     And wrought with weeping and laughter,

---

3. Musical pipe made from an oaten straw.
4. Participants in the spring festival honoring Dionysus (or Bacchus). Such festivals sometimes
developed into frenzied sexual orgies.

And fashioned with loathing and love,
   With life before and after
   And death beneath and above,
25 For a day and a night and a morrow,
   That his strength might endure for a span
With travail and heavy sorrow,
   The holy spirit of man.

From the winds of the north and the south
30   They gathered as unto strife;
They breathed upon his mouth,
   They filled his body with life;
Eyesight and speech they wrought
   For the veils of the soul therein,
35 A time for labor and thought,
   A time to serve and to sin;
They gave him light in his ways,
   And love, and a space for delight,
And beauty and length of days,
40   And night, and sleep in the night.
His speech is a burning fire;
   With his lips he travaileth;
In his heart is a blind desire,
   In his eyes foreknowledge of death;
45 He weaves, and is clothed with derision;
   Sows, and he shall not reap;
His life is a watch or a vision
   Between a sleep and a sleep.

1865

Hymn to Proserpine

(After the Proclamation in Rome of the Christian Faith)

Vicisti, Galilaee[1]

I have lived long enough, having seen one thing, that love hath an end;
Goddess and maiden and queen, be near me now and befriend.
Thou art more than the day or the morrow, the seasons that laugh or
   that weep;
For these give joy and sorrow; but thou, Proserpina, sleep.
5 Sweet is the treading of wine, and sweet the feet of the dove;

---

1. Thou hast conquered, O Galilean (Latin); words supposedly addressed to Christ by the Roman emperor Julian the Apostate, on his deathbed in 363. Julian had tried to revive paganism and to discourage Christianity, which, after a proclamation in 313, had been tolerated in Rome. His efforts, however, were unsuccessful. The speaker of the poem, a Roman patrician and also a poet (line 9), is like Emperor Julian: he prefers the old order of pagan gods. His hymn is addressed to the goddess Proserpine, who was carried off by Hades (or Pluto) to be queen of the lower world. In this role, she is addressed in the poem as goddess of death and of sleep. The speaker also associates her with the earth itself (line 93) because she was the daughter of Demeter (or Ceres), goddess of agriculture, whose name means "Earth Mother." Swinburne may have derived some details here from the 4th-century Latin poet Claudian, whose long narrative *The Rape of Proserpine* provides helpful background for this hymn.

But a goodlier gift is thine than foam of the grapes or love.
Yea, is not even Apollo, with hair and harpstring of gold,
A bitter god to follow, a beautiful god to behold?
I am sick of singing; the bays[2] burn deep and chafe. I am fain
10   To rest a little from praise and grievous pleasure and pain.
For the gods we know not of, who give us our daily breath,
We know they are cruel as love or life, and lovely as death.

O gods dethroned and deceased, cast forth, wiped out in a day!
From your wrath is the world released, redeemed from your chains, men
    say.
15   New gods are crowned in the city; their flowers have broken your rods;
They are merciful, clothed with pity, the young compassionate gods.
But for me their new device is barren, the days are bare;
Things long past over suffice, and men forgotten that were.
Time and the gods are at strife; ye dwell in the midst thereof,
20   Draining a little life from the barren breasts of love.
I say to you, cease, take rest; yea, I say to you all, be at peace,
Till the bitter milk of her breast and the barren bosom shall cease.
Wilt thou yet take all, Galilean? But these thou shalt not take—
The laurel, the palms, and the paean, the breasts of the nymphs in the
    brake,
25   Breasts more soft than a dove's, that tremble with tenderer breath;
And all the wings of the Loves, and all the joy before death;
All the feet of the hours that sound as a single lyre,
Dropped and deep in the flowers, with strings that flicker like fire.
More than these wilt thou give, things fairer than all these things?
30   Nay, for a little we live, and life hath mutable wings.
A little while and we die; shall life not thrive as it may?
For no man under the sky lives twice, outliving his day.
And grief is a grievous thing, and a man hath enough of his tears;
Why should he labor, and bring fresh grief to blacken his years?

35   Thou hast conquered, O pale Galilean; the world has grown gray from
    thy breath;
We have drunken of things Lethean,[3] and fed on the fullness of death.
Laurel is green for a season, and love is sweet for a day;
But love grows bitter with treason, and laurel outlives not May.
Sleep, shall we sleep after all? for the world is not sweet in the end;
40   For the old faiths loosen and fall, the new years ruin and rend.
Fate is a sea without shore, and the soul is a rock that abides;
But her ears are vexed with the roar and her face with the foam of the
    tides.
O lips that the live blood faints in, the leavings of racks and rods!
O ghastly glories of saints, dead limbs of gibbeted gods!
45   Though all men abase them before you in spirit, and all knees bend,
I kneel not, neither adore you, but standing look to the end.

All delicate days and pleasant, all spirits and sorrows are cast
Far out with the foam of the present that sweeps to the surf of the past;

2. Laurel leaves of a poet's crown.
3. I.e., of Lethe, a river in the lower world. By drinking its waters the dead forgot the past.

Where beyond the extreme sea wall, and between the remote sea gates,
50 Waste water washes, and tall ships founder, and deep death waits;
Where, mighty with deepening sides, clad about with the seas as with
    wings,
And impelled of invisible tides, and fulfilled of unspeakable things,
White-eyed and poisonous-finned, shark-toothed and serpentinecurled,
Rolls, under the whitening wind of the future, the wave of the world.
55 The depths stand naked in sunder behind it, the storms flee away;
In the hollow before it the thunder is taken and snared as a prey;
In its sides is the north wind bound; and its salt is of all men's tears,
With light of ruin, and sound of changes, and pulse of years;
With travail of day after day, and with trouble of hour upon hour.
60 And bitter as blood is the spray; and the crests are as fangs that devour;
And its vapor and storm of its steam as the sighing of spirits to be;
And its noise as the noise in a dream; and its depths as the roots of the
    sea;
And the height of its heads as the height of the utmost stars of the air;
And the ends of the earth at the might thereof tremble, and time is
    made bare.
65 Will ye bridle the deep sea with reins, will ye chasten the high sea with
    rods?
Will ye take her to chain her with chains, who is older than all ye gods?
All ye as a wind shall go by, as a fire shall ye pass and be past;
Ye are gods, and behold, ye shall die, and the waves be upon you at last.
In the darkness of time, in the deeps of the years, in the changes of
    things,
70 Ye shall sleep as a slain man sleeps, and the world shall forget you or
    kings.
Though the feet of thine high priests tread where thy lords and our
    forefathers trod,
Though these that were gods are dead, and thou being dead art a god,
Though before thee the throned Cytherean[4] be fallen, and hidden her
    head,
Yet thy kingdom shall pass, Galilean, thy dead shall go down to thee
    dead.

75 Of the maiden thy mother men sing as a goddess with grace clad around;
Thou art throned where another was king; where another was queen
    she is crowned.
Yea, once we had sight of another; but now she is queen, say these.
Not as thine, not as thine was our mother, a blossom of flowering seas,
Clothed round with the world's desire as with raiment, and fair as the
    foam.
80 And fleeter than kindled fire, and a goddess, and mother of Rome.[5]
For thine came pale and a maiden, and sister to sorrow; but ours,
Her deep hair heavily laden with odor and color of flowers,
White rose of the rose-white water, a silver splendor, a flame,
Bent down unto us that besought her, and earth grew sweet with her
    name.

---

4. Aphrodite (or Venus), who was born from the waves near the island of Cythera.

5. Aeneas, the founder of Rome, was said to have been the son of Aphrodite.

85 For thine came weeping, a slave among slaves, and rejected; but she
  Came flushed from the full-flushed wave, and imperial, her foot on the
    sea.
  And the wonderful waters knew her, the winds and the viewless ways,
  And the roses grew rosier, and bluer the sea-blue stream of the bays.

  Ye are fallen, our lords, by what token? we wist that ye should not fall.
90 Ye were all so fair that are broken; and one more fair than ye all.
  But I turn to her° still, having seen she shall surely abide in   *Proserpine*
    the end.
  Goddess and maiden and queen, be near me now and befriend.
  O daughter of earth, of my mother, her crown and blossom of birth,
  I am also, I also, thy brother; I go as I came unto earth.
95 In the night where thine eyes are as moons are in heaven, the night
    where thou art,
  Where the silence is more than all tunes, where sleep overflows from
    the heart,
  Where the poppies are sweet as the rose in our world, and the red rose
    is white,
  And the wind falls faint as it blows with the fume of the flowers of the
    night,
  And the murmur of spirits that sleep in the shadow of gods from afar
100 Grows dim in thine ears and deep as the deep dim soul of a star,
  In the sweet low light of thy face, under heavens untrod by the sun,
  Let my soul with their souls find place, and forget what is done and
    undone.
  Thou art more than the gods who number the days of our temporal
    breath;
  For these give labor and slumber; but thou, Proserpina, death.
105 Therefore now at thy feet I abide for a season in silence. I know
  I shall die as my fathers died, and sleep as they sleep; even so.
  For the glass of the years is brittle wherein we gaze for a span.
  A little soul for a little bears up this corpse which is man.
  So long I endure, no longer; and laugh not again, neither weep.
110 For there is no god found stronger than death; and death is a sleep.

1866

The Garden of Proserpine[1]

Here, where the world is quiet;
  Here, where all trouble seems
Dead winds' and spent waves' riot
  In doubtful dreams of dreams;
5   I watch the green field growing

1. Or Proserpina, the goddess who was carried off by Hades (or Pluto) to be queen of the lower world. According to some accounts, she had there a garden of ever-blooming flowers. The Greek and Roman festivals honoring her and her mother, Ceres, emphasized Proserpine's return to the upper world in spring. In Swinburne's poems, however, the emphasis is on her role as goddess of death and eternal sleep. Swinburne also associates her with the sea, which he usually represents as eternally unchanging despite its surface changefulness.

For reaping folk and sowing,
For harvest time and mowing,
  A sleepy world of streams.

    I am tired of tears and laughter,
10   And men that laugh and weep;
Of what may come hereafter
  For men that sow to reap;
I am weary of days and hours,
Blown buds of barren flowers,
15 Desires and dreams and powers
  And everything but sleep.

    Here life has death for neighbor,
  And far from eye or ear
Wan waves and wet winds labor,
20   Weak ships and spirits steer;
They drive adrift, and whither
They wot not who make thither;
But no such winds blow hither,
  And no such things grow here.

25 No growth of moor or coppice,
  No heather flower or vine,
But bloomless buds of poppies,
  Green grapes of Proserpine,
Pale beds of blowing rushes,
30 Where no leaf blooms or blushes
Save this whereout she crushes
  For dead men deadly wine.

    Pale, without name or number,
  In fruitless fields of corn,°   *wheat*
35 They bow themselves and slumber
  All night till light is born;
And like a soul belated,
In hell and heaven unmated,
By cloud and mist abated
40   Comes out of darkness morn.

    Though one were strong as seven,
  He too with death shall dwell,
Nor wake with wings in heaven,
  Nor weep for pains in hell;
45 Though one were fair as roses,
His beauty clouds and closes;
And well though love reposes,
  In the end it is not well.

    Pale, beyond porch and portal,
50   Crowned with calm leaves, she stands
Who gathers all things mortal

With cold immortal hands;
Her languid lips are sweeter
Than love's who fears to greet her
55   To men that mix and meet her
From many times and lands.

She waits for each and other,
She waits for all men born;
Forgets the earth her mother,
60   The life of fruits and corn;
And spring and seed and swallow
Take wing for her and follow
Where summer song rings hollow
And flowers are put to scorn.

65   There go the loves that wither,
The old loves with wearier wings;
And all dead years draw thither,
And all disastrous things;
Dead dreams of days forsaken,
70   Blind buds that snows have shaken,
Wild leaves that winds have taken,
Red strays of ruined springs.

We are not sure of sorrow,
And joy was never sure;
75   Today will die tomorrow;
Time stoops to no man's lure;
And love, grown faint and fretful,
With lips but half regretful
Sighs, and with eyes forgetful
80   Weeps that no loves endure.

From too much love of living,
From hope and fear set free,
We thank with brief thanksgiving
Whatever gods may be
85   That no life lives forever;
That dead men rise up never;
That even the weariest river
Winds somewhere safe to sea.

Then star nor sun shall waken,
90   Nor any change of light:
Nor sound of waters shaken,
Nor any sound or sight:
Nor wintry leaves nor vernal,
Nor days nor things diurnal;
95   Only the sleep eternal
In an eternal night.

1866

Ave Atque Vale[1]

In Memory of Charles Baudelaire

Nous devrions pourtant lui porter quelques fleurs;
Les morts, les pauvres morts, ont de grandes douleurs,
Et quand Octobre souffle, émondeur des vieux arbres,
Son vent mélancolique à l'entour de leurs marbres,
Certe, ils doivent trouver les vivants bien ingrats.
—*"Les Fleurs du Mal."*[2]

I

Shall I strew on thee rose or rue or laurel,[3]
Brother, on this that was the veil[4] of thee?
Or quiet sea-flower molded by the sea,
Or simplest growth of meadow-sweet or sorrel,
5   Such as the summer-sleepy Dryads° weave,   wood nymphs
Waked up by snow-soft sudden rains at eve?
Or wilt thou rather, as on earth before,
Half-faded fiery blossoms, pale with heat
And full of bitter summer, but more sweet
10   To thee than gleanings of a northern shore
Trod by no tropic feet?[5]

2

For always thee the fervid languid glories
Allured of heavier suns in mightier skies;
Thine ears knew all the wandering watery sighs
15   Where the sea sobs round Lesbian promontories,
The barren kiss of piteous wave to wave
That knows not where is that Leucadian grave[6]
Which hides too deep the supreme head of song.
Ah, salt and sterile as her kisses were,
20   The wild sea winds her and the green gulfs bear
Hither and thither, and vex and work her wrong,
Blind gods that cannot spare.

1. Hail and farewell (Latin); a line from an elegy by Catullus occasioned by a farewell visit to the grave of his brother, to whom he brought gifts, a situation closely echoed in Swinburne's final stanza. Swinburne's elegy likewise begins with a visit to the grave of a man whom the poet regards as a brother but had never met. Charles Baudelaire (1821–1867) had impressed Swinburne as one of the "most perfect poets of the century." In 1861, in an essay on the 2nd edition of Baudelaire's collection *Les Fleurs du Mal* (Flowers of evil, 1857), Swinburne had commented on the French poet's preoccupation with "sad and strange things"—"the sharp and cruel enjoyments of pain, the acrid relish of suffering felt or inflicted"; "it has the languid, lurid beauty of close and threatening weather—a heavy, heated temperature, with dangerous hothouse scents in it." These qualities are also celebrated in Swinburne's elegy, into which are woven many allusions to Baudelaire's poems, especially his *Litanies de Satan,* which Swinburne regarded as the keynote poem of *Les Fleurs du Mal.*
2. From *La servante au grand coeur* (The great-hearted servant): We must nevertheless bring some flowers to her [or him]. / The dead, the poor dead, have great sadnesses, / And when October, the pruner of old trees, blows, / Its melancholy wind in the vicinity of their marble tombs, / Then indeed they must find the living highly ungrateful (French).
3. Respectively, symbols of love, mourning, and poetic fame.
4. I.e., the body as a veil for the soul.
5. A voyage to the tropics in Baudelaire's youth made a lasting impact on his poetry.
6. According to legend, the poetess Sappho, who was born on the island of Lesbos, destroyed herself by leaping from the rock of Leucas into the Ionian Sea. In this section Swinburne makes allusions to Baudelaire's *Lesbos.*

3

Thou sawest, in thine old singing season, brother,
    Secrets and sorrows unbeheld of us:
25   Fierce loves, and lovely leaf-buds poisonous,
Bare to thy subtler eye, but for none other
      Blowing by night in some unbreathed-in clime;
    The hidden harvest of luxurious time,
Sin without shape, and pleasure without speech;
30   And where strange dreams in a tumultuous sleep
    Make the shut eyes of stricken spirits weep;
And with each face thou sawest the shadow on each,
    Seeing as men sow men reap.[7]

4

O sleepless heart and somber soul unsleeping,
35   That were athirst for sleep and no more life
    And no more love, for peace and no more strife!
Now the dim gods of death have in their keeping
      Spirit and body and all the springs of song,
    Is it well now where love can do no wrong,
40   Where stingless pleasure has no foam or fang
      Behind the unopening closure of her lips?
    Is it not well where soul from body slips
And flesh from bone divides without a pang
    As dew from flower-bell drips?

5

45 It is enough; the end and the beginning
      Are one thing to thee, who art past the end.
    O hand unclasped of unbeholden friend,
For thee no fruits to pluck, no palms for winning,
      No triumph and no labor and no lust,
50   Only dead yew-leaves and a little dust.
O quiet eyes wherein the light saith naught,
      Whereto the day is dumb, nor any night
    With obscure finger silences your sight,
Nor in your speech the sudden soul speaks thought,
55   Sleep, and have sleep for light.

6

Now all strange hours and all strange loves are over,
    Dreams and desires and somber songs and sweet,
    Hast thou found place at the great knees and feet
Of some pale Titan-woman like a lover,
60   Such as thy vision here solicited,[8]
    Under the shadow of her fair vast head,
The deep division of prodigious breasts,
    The solemn slope of mighty limbs asleep,

---

7. Cf. Galatians 6.7: "Whatsoever a man soweth, that shall he also reap."

8. An allusion to Baudelaire's La Géante (The giantess).

The weight of awful tresses that still keep
65 The savor and shade of old-world pine forests
      Where the wet hill-winds weep?

7

Hast thou found any likeness for thy vision?
      O gardener of strange flowers, what bud, what bloom,
      Hast thou found sown, what gathered in the gloom?
70 What of despair, of rapture, of derision,
      What of life is there, what of ill or good?
      Are the fruits gray like dust or bright like blood?
Does the dim ground grow any seed of ours,
      The faint fields quicken any terrene root,
75   In low lands where the sun and moon are mute
And all the stars keep silence? Are there flowers
      At all, or any fruit?

8

Alas, but though my flying song flies after,
      O sweet strange elder singer, thy more fleet
80   Singing, and footprints of thy fleeter feet,
Some dim derision of mysterious laughter
      From the blind tongueless warders of the dead,
      Some gainless glimpse of Proserpine's[9] veiled head,
Some little sound of unregarded tears
85   Wept by effaced unprofitable eyes,
      And from pale mouths some cadence of dead sighs—
These only, these the hearkening spirit hears,
      Sees only such things rise.

9

Thou art far too far for wings of words to follow,
90   Far too far off for thought or any prayer.
      What ails us with thee, who are wind and air?
What ails us gazing where all seen is hollow?
      Yet with some fancy, yet with some desire,
      Dreams pursue death as winds a flying fire,
95 Our dreams pursue our dead and do not find.
      Still, and more swift than they, the thin flame flies,
      The low light fails us in elusive skies,
Still the foiled earnest ear is deaf, and blind
      Are still the eluded eyes.

10

100 Not thee, O never thee, in all time's changes,
      Not thee, but this the sound of thy sad soul,
      The shadow of thy swift spirit, this shut scroll
I lay my hand on, and not death estranges

9. Queen of the underworld.

My spirit from communion of thy song—
105   These memories and these melodies that throng
Veiled porches of a Muse funereal[1]—
    These I salute, these touch, these clasp and fold
    As though a hand were in my hand to hold,
Or through mine ears a mourning musical
110   Of many mourners rolled.

11

I among these, I also, in such station
    As when the pyre was charred, and piled the sods,
    And offering to the dead made, and their gods,
The old mourners had, standing to make libation,
115   I stand, and to the gods and to the dead
    Do reverence without prayer or praise, and shed
Offering to these unknown, the gods of gloom,
    And what of honey and spice my seedlands bear,
    And what I may of fruits in this chilled air,
120 And lay, Orestes-like, across the tomb
    A curl of severed hair.

12

But by no hand nor any treason stricken,
    Not like the low-lying head of Him, the King,
    The flame that made of Troy a ruinous thing,
125 Thou liest, and on this dust no tears could quicken
    There fall no tears like theirs[2] that all men hear
    Fall tear by sweet imperishable tear
Down the opening leaves of holy poets' pages.
    Thee not Orestes, not Electra mourns;[3]
130   But bending us-ward with memorial urns
The most high Muses that fulfill all ages
    Weep, and our God's heart yearns.

13

For, sparing of his sacred strength, not often
    Among us darkling here the lord of light[4]
135   Makes manifest his music and his might
In hearts that open and in lips that soften
    With the soft flame and heat of songs that shine.
    Thy lips indeed he touched with bitter wine,
And nourished them indeed with bitter bread;
140   Yet surely from his hand thy soul's food came;
    The fire that scarred thy spirit at his flame

1. According to Jerome McGann, Swinburne associates Baudelaire's distinctive kind of poetry with a tenth muse, one who inspires songs of lamentation ("funereal"). What is meant by this muse's "veiled porches" seems tantalizingly obscure.
2. Referring to the muses and holy poets, not to Orestes and Electra [noted by Jerome McGann].
3. For lines 120–29, see Aeschylus's Choëphoroe

4–8. King Agamemnon, after returning from Troy, had been treacherously slain, an event that made "a ruinous thing" of the Greek victory. His son, Orestes, visits Agamemnon's grave and dedicates on it a lock of his own hair, which is later discovered by his sister, Electra, who mournfully visits her father's grave to offer libations.
4. Apollo, god of light and poetry.

Was lighted, and thine hungering heart he fed
Who feeds our hearts with fame.

14

Therefore he too now at thy soul's sunsetting,
145   God of all suns and songs he too bends down
To mix his laurel with thy cypress[5] crown.
And save thy dust from blame and from forgetting,
Therefore he too, seeing all thou wert and art,
Compassionate, with sad and sacred heart,
150   Mourns thee of many his children the last dead,
And hallows with strange tears and alien sighs
Thine unmelodious mouth and sunless eyes,
And over thine irrevocable head
Sheds light from the under skies.[6]

15

155   And one weeps with him in the ways Lethean,[7]
And stains with tears her changing bosom chill;
That obscure Venus of the hollow hill,
That thing transformed which was the Cytherean,
With lips that lost their Grecian laugh divine
160   Long since, and face no more called Erycine;[8]
A ghost, a bitter and luxurious god.
Thee also with fair flesh and singing spell
Did she, a sad and second prey,[9] compel
Into the footless places once more trod,
165   And shadows hot from hell.

16

And now no sacred staff shall break in blossom,[1]
No choral salutation lure to light
A spirit sick with perfume and sweet night
And love's tired eyes and hands and barren bosom.
170   There is no help for these things; none to mend
And none to mar; not all our songs, O friend,
Will make death clear or make life durable.
Howbeit with rose and ivy and wild vine
And with wild notes about this dust of thine
175   At least I fill the place where white dreams dwell[2]
And wreathe an unseen shrine.

5. Associated with mourning. "Laurel": the crown of Apollo, a wreath honoring poets.
6. I.e., flickering flaming light of the underworld.
7. Lethe was the river of oblivion in Hades.
8. The Venus of medieval legends held her court inside a mountain in Germany (the Hörselberg). This later Venus is a transformed version of the joyous foam-born goddess associated with the island of Cythera and also worshiped in Sicily at a shrine on Mount Eryx (hence "Erycine"). Horace described her as "blithe goddess of Eryx, about whom hover mirth and desire" (*Odes* 1.2.33–34).

9. The first "prey" of Venus had been Tannhäuser, whom she had lured into the "footless places" of her cave. Baudelaire is her "second prey." Swinburne, after reading Baudelaire's pamphlet on Wagner's *Tannhäuser*, described this Venus as "the queen of evil, the lady of lust."
1. After Tannhäuser's pilgrimage to Rome to seek absolution for having lived in sin with Venus, a miraculous event occurred: the pope having denied such absolution until his staff should bloom, it burst into blossom.
2. Presumably the abode of the ghosts of the dead.

17

Sleep; and if life was bitter to thee, pardon,
   If sweet, give thanks; thou hast no more to live;
   And to give thanks is good, and to forgive.
180   Out of the mystic and the mournful garden
      Where all day through thine hands in barren braid
      Wove the sick flowers of secrecy and shade,
   Green buds of sorrow and sin, and remnants grey,
      Sweet-smelling, pale with poison, sanguine-hearted,
185   Passions that sprang from sleep and thoughts that started,
   Shall death not bring us all as thee one day
      Among the days departed?

18

For thee, O now a silent soul, my brother,
   Take at my hands this garland, and farewell.
190   Thin is the leaf, and chill the wintry smell,
And chill the solemn earth, a fatal mother,
   With sadder than the Niobean womb,[3]
   And in the hollow of her breasts a tomb.
Content thee, howsoe'er, whose days are done;
195   There lies not any troublous thing before,
   Nor sight nor sound to war against thee more,
For whom all winds are quiet as the sun,
   All waters as the shore.

1866–67   1868

3. Niobe's fourteen children were slain by Apollo and Artemis.

WALTER PATER
1839–1894

Studies in the History of the Renaissance, a collection of essays published in 1873, was the first of several volumes that established Walter Pater as the most important critical writer of the late Victorian period. His flair for critical writing may have first been sparked when he was an undergraduate at Oxford (1858–62), where he heard and enjoyed the lectures of Matthew Arnold, who was then professor of poetry. After graduation, Pater remained at Oxford, a shy bachelor who spent his life as a tutor of classics (for the story of his earlier years see *The Child in the House,* an autobiographical sketch that provides a helpful introduction to all of his writings). In view of his retiring disposition Pater was surprised and even alarmed by the impact made by his books on young readers of the 1870s and 1880s. Some of his younger followers such as Oscar Wilde and George Moore may have misread him. As T. S. Eliot wrote somewhat primly, "[Pater's] view of art, as expressed in *The Renaissance,* impressed itself upon a number of writers in the nineties, and propagated some confusion between life and art which is not wholly irresponsible for some untidy lives." It can be demonstrated that Pater's writings (especially his historical novel *Marius the Epicurean,* 1885) have much in common with his earnest-minded mid-Victorian predecessors, but his disciples overlooked these similarities. To them, his work seemed strikingly different and, in its quiet way, more subversive than the head-on attacks against traditional Victorianism made by Swinburne or Samuel Butler. Instead of recommending a continuation of the painful quest for Truth that had dominated Oxford in the days of Newman, Pater assured his readers that the quest was pointless. Truth, he said, is relative. And instead of echoing Carlyle's call to duty and social responsibilities, Pater reminded his readers that life passes quickly and that our only responsibility is to enjoy fully "this short day of frost and sun," to relish its sensations, especially those sensations provoked by works of art.

This epicurean gospel was conveyed in a highly wrought prose style that baffles anyone who likes to read quickly. Pater believed that prose was as difficult an art as poetry, and he expected his own elaborate sentences to be savored. Like Gustave Flaubert (1821–1880), the French novelist whom he admired, Pater painstakingly revised his sentences with special attention to their rhythms, seeking always the right word, *le mot juste,* as Flaubert had called it. For many years, Pater's day would begin with his making a careful study of a dictionary. What Pater said of Dante is an apt description of his own polished style: "He is one of those artists whose general effect largely depends on vocabulary, on the minute particles of which his work is wrought, on the color and outline of single words and phrases." An additional characteristic of his highly wrought style is its relative absence of humor. Pater was valued among his friends for his flashes of wit in conversation and for his lively and irreverent sallies. In his writings such traits are suppressed. As Michael Levey observed in *The Case of Walter Pater,* "Even for irony the mood of his writing is almost too intense."

In addition to being a key figure in the transition from mid-Victorianism to the "decadence" of the 1890s, Pater commands our attention as the writer of exemplary impressionistic criticism. In each of his essays he seeks to communicate what he called the "special unique impression of pleasure" made on him by the works of some artist or writer. His range of subjects included the dialogues of Plato, the paintings of Leonardo da Vinci, the plays of Shakespeare, and the writings of the French Romantic school of the nineteenth century. Of particular value to students of English literature are his discriminating studies of Wordsworth, Coleridge, Lamb, and Sir Thomas Browne in his volume of *Appreciations* (1889) and his essay on the poetry of William Morris titled *Aesthetic Poetry* (1868). These and other essays by Pater were praised by Oscar Wilde in a review in 1890 as "absolutely modern, in the true meaning of the term modernity. For he to whom the present is the only thing that is present, knows nothing of the age in which he lives. . . . The true critic is he who bears within himself the dreams and ideas and feelings of myriad generations, and to whom no form of thought is alien, no emotional impulse obscure."

The final sentences of his *Appreciations* volume are a revealing indication of Pater's critical position. After having attempted to show the differences between the classical and romantic schools of art, he concludes that most great artists combine the qualities of both. "To discriminate schools, of art, of literature," he writes, "is, of course, part of the obvious business of literary criticism: but, in the work of literary production, it is easy to be overmuch occupied concerning them. For, in truth, the legitimate contention is, not of one age or school of literary art against another, but of all successive schools alike, against the stupidity which is dead to the substance, and the vulgarity which is dead to form."

From The Renaissance

Preface

Many attempts have been made by writers on art and poetry to define beauty in the abstract, to express it in the most general terms, to find some universal formula for it. The value of these attempts has most often been in the suggestive and penetrating things said by the way. Such discussions help us very little to enjoy what has been well done in art or poetry, to discriminate between what is more and what is less excellent in them, or to use words like beauty, excellence, art, poetry, with a more precise meaning than they would otherwise have. Beauty, like all other qualities presented to human experience, is relative; and the definition of it becomes unmeaning and useless in proportion to its abstractness. To define beauty, not in the most abstract but in the most concrete terms possible, to find not its universal formula, but the formula which expresses most adequately this or that special manifestation of it, is the aim of the true student of aesthetics.

"To see the object as in itself it really is,"[1] has been justly said to be the aim of all true criticism whatever; and in aesthetic criticism the first step towards seeing one's object as it really is, is to know one's own impression as it really is, to discriminate it, to realize it distinctly. The objects with which aesthetic criticism deals—music, poetry, artistic and accomplished forms of human life—are indeed receptacles of so many powers or forces: they possess, like the products of nature, so many virtues or qualities. What is this song or picture, this engaging personality presented in life or in a book, to *me*? What effect does it really produce on me? Does it give me pleasure? and if so, what sort or degree of pleasure? How is my nature modified by its presence, and under its influence? The answers to these questions are the original facts with which the aesthetic critic has to do; and, as in the study of light, of morals, of number, one must realize such primary data for one's self, or not at all. And he who experiences these impressions strongly, and drives directly at the discrimination and analysis of them, has no need to trouble himself with the abstract question what beauty is in itself, or what its exact relation to truth or experience—metaphysical questions, as unprofitable as metaphysical questions elsewhere. He may pass them all by as being, answerable or not, of no interest to him.

The aesthetic critic, then, regards all the objects with which he has to do, all works of art, and the fairer forms of nature and human life, as powers or forces producing pleasurable sensations, each of a more or less peculiar or unique kind. This influence he feels, and wishes to explain, by analyzing and reducing it to its elements. To him, the picture, the landscape, the engaging personality in life or in a book, "La Gioconda," the hills of Carrara, Pico of Mirandola,[2] are valuable for their virtues, as we say, in speaking of a herb, a wine, a gem; for the property each has of affecting one with a special, a unique, impression of pleasure. Our education becomes complete in proportion as our susceptibility to these impressions increases in depth and

---

1. Cf. Matthew Arnold, *The Function of Criticism at the Present Time*, para. 1.
2. Pico della Mirandola (1463–1494), Italian philosopher and classical scholar, subject of an essay by Pater that was included in *The Renaissance*. "La Gioconda": Leonardo da Vinci's famous painting, the *Mona Lisa*. "The hills of Carrara": marble quarries in Italy.

variety. And the function of the aesthetic critic is to distinguish, to analyze, and separate from its adjuncts, the virtue by which a picture, a landscape, a fair personality in life or in a book, produces this special impression of beauty or pleasure, to indicate what the source of that impression is, and under what conditions it is experienced. His end is reached when he has disengaged that virtue, and noted it, as a chemist notes some natural element, for himself and others; and the rule for those who would reach this end is stated with great exactness in the words of a recent critic of Sainte-Beuve: *De se borner à connaître de près les belles choses, et à s'en nourrir en exquis amateurs, en humanistes accomplis.*[3]

What is important, then, is not that the critic should possess a correct abstract definition of beauty for the intellect, but a certain kind of temperament, the power of being deeply moved by the presence of beautiful objects. He will remember always that beauty exists in many forms. To him all periods, types, schools of taste, are in themselves equal. In all ages there have been some excellent workmen, and some excellent work done. The question he asks is always: In whom did the stir, the genius, the sentiment of the period find itself? where was the receptacle of its refinement, its elevation, its taste? "The ages are all equal," says William Blake, "but genius is always above its age."[4]

Often it will require great nicety to disengage this virtue from the commoner elements with which it may be found in combination. Few artists, not Goethe or Byron even, work quite cleanly, casting off all debris, and leaving us only what the heat of their imagination has wholly fused and transformed. Take, for instance, the writings of Wordsworth. The heat of his genius, entering into the substance of his work, has crystallized a part, but only a part, of it; and in that great mass of verse there is much which might well be forgotten. But scattered up and down it, sometimes fusing and transforming entire compositions, like the stanzas on *Resolution and Independence,* or the *Ode on the Recollections of Childhood,*[5] sometimes, as if at random, depositing a fine crystal here or there, in a matter it does not wholly search through and transmute, we trace the action of his unique, incommunicable faculty, that strange, mystical sense of a life in natural things, and of man's life as a part of nature, drawing strength and color and character from local influences, from the hills and streams, and from natural sights and sounds. Well! that is the *virtue,* the active principle in Wordsworth's poetry; and then the function of the critic of Wordsworth is to follow up that active principle, to disengage it, to mark the degree in which it penetrates his verse.

The subjects of the following studies are taken from the history of the *Renaissance,* and touch what I think the chief points in that complex, many-sided movement. I have explained in the first of them what I understand by the word, giving it a much wider scope than was intended by those who originally used it to denote that revival of classical antiquity in the fifteenth century which was only one of many results of a general excitement and

3. To confine themselves to knowing beautiful things intimately, and to sustain themselves by these, as sensitive amateurs and accomplished humanists do (French). In 1980 editor Donald J. Hill discovered that this quotation is *by* Sainte-Beuve rather than about him; therefore, Hill conjectures that "a recent critic" ought to be "a recent critique."
4. From Blake's annotations to *The Works of Sir Joshua Reynolds.* The "genius" was the German painter Albrecht Dürer (1471–1528).
5. Wordsworth's ode was titled *Intimations of Immortality from Recollections of Early Childhood.*

enlightening of the human mind, but of which the great aim and achievements of what, as Christian art, is often falsely opposed to the Renaissance, were another result. This outbreak of the human spirit may be traced far into the Middle Age itself, with its motives already clearly pronounced, the care for physical beauty, the worship of the body, the breaking down of those limits which the religious system of the Middle Age imposed on the heart and the imagination. I have taken as an example of this movement, this earlier Renaissance within the Middle Age itself, and as an expression of its qualities, two little compositions in early French; not because they constitute the best possible expression of them, but because they help the unity of my series, inasmuch as the Renaissance ends also in France, in French poetry, in a phase of which the writings of Joachim du Bellay[6] are in many ways the most perfect illustration. The Renaissance, in truth, put forth in France an aftermath, a wonderful later growth, the products of which have to the full that subtle and delicate sweetness which belongs to a refined and comely decadence, just as its earliest phases have the freshness which belongs to all periods of growth in art, the charm of *ascêsis*,[7] of the austere and serious girding of the loins in youth.

But it is in Italy, in the fifteenth century, that the interest of the Renaissance mainly lies—in that solemn fifteenth century which can hardly be studied too much, not merely for its positive results in the things of the intellect and the imagination, its concrete works of art, its special and prominent personalities, with their profound aesthetic charm, but for its general spirit and character, for the ethical qualities of which it is a consummate type.

The various forms of intellectual activity which together make up the culture of an age, move for the most part from different starting points, and by unconnected roads. As products of the same generation they partake indeed of a common character, and unconsciously illustrate each other; but of the producers themselves, each group is solitary, gaining what advantage or disadvantage there may be in intellectual isolation. Art and poetry, philosophy and the religious life, and that other life of refined pleasure and action in the conspicuous places of the world, are each of them confined to its own circle of ideas, and those who prosecute either of them are generally little curious of the thoughts of others. There come, however, from time to time, eras of more favorable conditions, in which the thoughts of men draw nearer together than is their wont, and the many interests of the intellectual world combine in one complete type of general culture. The fifteenth century in Italy is one of these happier eras, and what is sometimes said of the age of Pericles is true of that of Lorenzo: it is an age productive in personalities, many-sided, centralized, complete. Here, artists and philosophers and those whom the action of the world has elevated and made keen, do not live in isolation, but breathe a common air, and catch light and heat from each other's thoughts. There is a spirit of general elevation and enlightenment in which all alike communicate. The unity of this spirit gives unity to all the various products of the Renaissance; and it is to this intimate alliance with mind, this participation in the best thoughts which that age produced, that

6. French poet and critic (ca.1522–1560); subject of another essay in *The Renaissance*.

7. Asceticism.

the art of Italy in the fifteenth century owes much of its grave dignity and influence.

I have added an essay on Winckelmann,[8] as not incongruous with the studies which precede it, because Winckelmann, coming in the eighteenth century, really belongs in spirit to an earlier age. By his enthusiasm for the things of the intellect and the imagination for their own sake, by his Hellenism, his lifelong struggle to attain to the Greek spirit, he is in sympathy with the humanists of a previous century. He is the last fruit of the Renaissance, and explains in a striking way its motive and tendencies.

["LA GIOCONDA"][9]

"La Gioconda" is, in the truest sense, Leonardo's masterpiece, the revealing instance of his mode of thought and work. In suggestiveness, only the "Melancholia" of Dürer is comparable to it; and no crude symbolism disturbs the effect of its subdued and graceful mystery. We all know the face and hands of the figure, set in its marble chair, in that circle of fantastic rocks, as in some faint light under sea. Perhaps of all ancient pictures time has chilled it least. As often happens with works in which invention seems to reach its limit, there is an element in it given to, not invented by, the master. In that inestimable folio of drawings, once in the possession of Vasari, were certain designs by Verrocchio,[1] faces of such impressive beauty that Leonardo in his boyhood copied them many times. It is hard not to connect with these designs of the elder, by-past master, as with its germinal principle, the unfathomable smile, always with a touch of something sinister in it, which plays over all Leonardo's work. Besides, the picture is a portrait. From childhood we see this image defining itself on the fabric of his dreams, and but for express historical testimony, we might fancy that this was but his ideal lady, embodied and beheld at last. What was the relationship of a living Florentine to this creature of his thought? By what strange affinities had the dream and the person grown up thus apart, and yet so closely together? Present from the first incorporeally in Leonardo's brain, dimly traced in the designs of Verrocchio, she is found present at last in Il Giocondo's house. That there is much of mere portraiture in the picture is attested by the legend that by artificial means, the presence of mimes[2] and flute-players, that subtle expression was protracted on the face. Again, was it in four years and by renewed labor never really completed, or in four months and as by stroke of magic, that the image was projected?

The presence that rose thus so strangely beside the waters, is expressive of what in the ways of a thousand years men had come to desire. Hers is the head upon which all "the ends of the world are come,"[3] and the eyelids are a little weary. It is a beauty wrought out from within upon the flesh, the deposit, little cell by cell, of strange thoughts and fantastic reveries and

8. Johann Joachim Winckelmann (1717–1768), German classicist.
9. Or *Mona Lisa*, the famous painting by Leonardo da Vinci that now hangs in the Louvre in Paris. The sitter for the portrait may have been Lisa, the third wife of the Florentine Francesco del Giocondo (to whom Pater refers as "Il Giocondo")—hence her title, La Gioconda. *Mona* (more cor-

rectly *Monna*) *Lisa* means "Madonna Lisa" or "My Lady Lisa." This selection is drawn from the essay on Leonardo da Vinci.
1. Andrea del Verrocchio (1435–1488), Florentine painter and sculptor. Giorgio Vasari, author of *Lives of the Most Excellent Italian Painters* (1550).
2. Mimics or clowns.
3. 1 Corinthians 10.11.

exquisite passions. Set it for a moment beside one of those white Greek goddesses or beautiful women of antiquity, and how would they be troubled by this beauty, into which the soul with all its maladies has passed! All the thoughts and experience of the world have etched and molded there, in that which they have of power to refine and make expressive the outward form, the animalism of Greece, the lust of Rome, the mysticism of the Middle Age with its spiritual ambition and imaginative loves, the return of the Pagan world, the sins of the Borgias.[4] She is older than the rocks among which she sits; like the vampire, she has been dead many times, and learned the secrets of the grave; and has been a diver in deep seas, and keeps their fallen day about her; and trafficked for strange webs with Eastern merchants, and, as Leda, was the mother of Helen of Troy,[5] and, as Saint Anne, the mother of Mary; and all this has been to her but as the sound of lyres and flutes, and lives only in the delicacy with which it has molded the changing lineaments, and tinged the eyelids and the hands. The fancy of a perpetual life, sweeping together ten thousand experiences, is an old one; and modern philosophy has conceived the idea of humanity as wrought upon by, and summing up in itself, all modes of thought and life. Certainly Lady Lisa might stand as the embodiment of the old fancy, the symbol of the modern idea.

Conclusion[6]

Λέγει που Ἡράκλειτος ὅτι πάντα χωρεῖ καὶ οὐδὲν μένει[7]

To regard all things and principles of things as inconstant modes or fashions has more and more become the tendency of modern thought. Let us begin with that which is without—our physical life. Fix upon it in one of its more exquisite intervals, the moment, for instance, of delicious recoil from the flood of water in summer heat. What is the whole physical life in that moment but a combination of natural elements to which science gives their names? But those elements, phosphorus and lime and delicate fibers, are present not in the human body alone: we detect them in places most remote from it. Our physical life is a perpetual motion of them—the passage of the blood, the waste and repairing of the lenses of the eye, the modification of the tissues of the brain under every ray of light and sound—processes which science reduces to simpler and more elementary forces. Like the elements of which we are composed, the action of these forces extends beyond us: it rusts iron and ripens corn. Far out on every side of us those elements are broadcast, driven in many currents; and birth and gesture and death and the springing of violets from the grave are but a few out of ten thousand resultant combinations. That clear, perpetual outline of face and limb is but an image of ours, under which we group them—a design in a web, the actual threads of which pass out beyond it. This at least of flamelike our life has, that it is

4. An Italian family during the Renaissance whose reputation for scandalous conduct was notorious.
5. Her father was Zeus (who approached Leda in the form of a swan).
6. This brief "Conclusion" was omitted in the second edition of this book, as I conceived it might possibly mislead some of those young men into whose hands it might fall. On the whole, I have

thought it best to reprint it here, with some slight changes which bring it closer to my original meaning. I have dealt more fully in *Marius the Epicurean* with the thoughts suggested by it [Pater's note to the 3rd edition, 1888].
7. Heraclitus says, "All things give way; nothing remaineth" [Pater's translation].

but the concurrence, renewed from moment to moment, of forces parting sooner or later on their ways.

Or, if we begin with the inward world of thought and feeling, the whirlpool is still more rapid, the flame more eager and devouring. There it is no longer the gradual darkening of the eye, the gradual fading of color from the wall—movements of the shore-side, where the water flows down indeed, though in apparent rest—but the race of the midstream, a drift of momentary acts of sight and passion and thought. At first sight experience seems to bury us under a flood of external objects, pressing upon us with a sharp and importunate reality, calling us out of ourselves in a thousand forms of action. But when reflection begins to play upon those objects they are dissipated under its influence; the cohesive force seems suspended like some trick of magic; each object is loosed into a group of impressions—color, odor, texture—in the mind of the observer. And if we continue to dwell in thought on this world, not of objects in the solidity with which language invests them, but of impressions, unstable, flickering, inconsistent, which burn and are extinguished with our consciousness of them, it contracts still further: the whole scope of observation is dwarfed into the narrow chamber of the individual mind. Experience, already reduced to a group of impressions, is ringed round for each one of us by that thick wall of personality through which no real voice has ever pierced on its way to us, or from us to that which we can only conjecture to be without. Every one of those impressions is the impression of the individual in his isolation, each mind keeping as a solitary prisoner its own dream of a world. Analysis goes a step farther still, and assures us that those impressions of the individual mind to which, for each one of us, experience dwindles down, are in perpetual flight; that each of them is limited by time, and that as time is infinitely divisible, each of them is infinitely divisible also; all that is actual in it being a single moment, gone while we try to apprehend it, of which it may ever be more truly said that it has ceased to be than that it is. To such a tremulous wisp constantly reforming itself on the stream, to a single sharp impression, with a sense in it, a relic more or less fleeting, of such moments gone by, what is real in our life fines itself down. It is with this movement, with the passage and dissolution of impressions, images, sensations, that analysis leaves off—that continual vanishing away, that strange, perpetual weaving and unweaving of ourselves.

Philosophiren, says Novalis, *ist dephlegmatisiren, vivificiren*.[8] The service of philosophy, of speculative culture, towards the human spirit is to rouse, to startle it to a life of constant and eager observation. Every moment some form grows perfect in hand or face; some tone on the hills or the sea is choicer than the rest; some mood of passion or insight or intellectual excitement is irresistibly real and attractive to us—for that moment only. Not the fruit of experience, but experience itself, is the end. A counted number of pulses only is given to us of a variegated, dramatic life. How may we see in them all that is to be seen in them by the finest senses? How shall we pass most swiftly from point to point, and be present always at the focus where the greatest number of vital forces unite in their purest energy?

To burn always with this hard, gemlike flame, to maintain this ecstasy, is

---

8. To philosophize is to cast off inertia, to make oneself alive (German). "Novalis" was the pseudonym of Friedrich von Hardenberg (1772–1801), German Romantic writer.

success in life. In a sense it might even be said that our failure is to form habits: for, after all, habit is relative to a stereotyped world, and meantime it is only the roughness of the eye that makes any two persons, things, situations, seem alike. While all melts under our feet, we may well grasp at any exquisite passion, or any contribution to knowledge that seems by a lifted horizon to set the spirit free for a moment, or any stirring of the senses, strange dyes, strange colors, and curious odors, or work of the artist's hands, or the face of one's friend. Not to discriminate every moment some passionate attitude in those about us, and in the very brilliancy of their gifts some tragic dividing of forces on their ways, is, on this short day of frost and sun, to sleep before evening. With this sense of the splendor of our experience and of its awful brevity, gathering all we are into one desperate effort to see and touch, we shall hardly have time to make theories about the things we see and touch. What we have to do is to be forever curiously testing new opinions and courting new impressions, never acquiescing in a facile orthodoxy of Comte, or of Hegel,[9] or of our own. Philosophical theories or ideas, as points of view, instruments of criticism, may help us to gather up what might otherwise pass unregarded by us. "Philosophy is the microscope of thought." The theory or idea or system which requires of us the sacrifice of any part of this experience, in consideration of some interest into which we cannot enter, or some abstract theory we have not identified with ourselves, or of what is only conventional, has no real claim upon us.

One of the most beautiful passages of Rousseau is that in the sixth book of the *Confessions,* where he describes the awakening in him of the literary sense. An undefinable taint of death had clung always about him, and now in early manhood he believed himself smitten by mortal disease. He asked himself how he might make as much as possible of the interval that remained; and he was not biased by anything in his previous life when he decided that it must be by intellectual excitement, which he found just then in the clear, fresh writings of Voltaire. Well! we are all *condamnés* as Victor Hugo says: we are all under sentence of death but with a sort of indefinite reprieve—*les hommes sont tous condamnés à mort avec des sursis indéfinis:* we have an interval, and then our place knows us no more. Some spend this interval in listlessness, some in high passions, the wisest, at least among "the children of this world,"[1] in art and song. For our one chance lies in expanding that interval, in getting as many pulsations as possible into the given time. Great passions may give us this quickened sense of life, ecstasy and sorrow of love, the various forms of enthusiastic activity, disinterested or otherwise, which come naturally to many of us. Only be sure it is passion—that it does yield you this fruit of a quickened, multiplied consciousness. Of such wisdom, the poetic passion, the desire of beauty, the love of art for its own sake, has most. For art comes to you proposing frankly to give nothing but the highest quality to your moments as they pass, and simply for those moments' sake.

1868

1873

---

9. Georg W. F. Hegel (1770–1831), German idealistic philosopher. Auguste Comte (1798–1857), French founder of positivism.
1. Luke 16.8.

From Appreciations

From *Style*

Since all progress of mind consists for the most part in differentiation, in the resolution of an obscure and complex object into its component aspects, it is surely the stupidest of losses to confuse things which right reason has put asunder, to lose the sense of achieved distinctions, the distinction between poetry and prose, for instance, or, to speak more exactly, between the laws and characteristic excellences of verse and prose composition. On the other hand, those who have dwelt most emphatically on the distinction between prose and verse, prose and poetry, may sometimes have been tempted to limit the proper functions of prose too narrowly; and this again is at least false economy, as being, in effect, the renunciation of a certain means or faculty, in a world where after all we must needs make the most of things. Critical efforts to limit art *a priori*,[1] by anticipations regarding the natural incapacity of the material with which this or that artist works, as the sculptor with solid form, or the prose-writer with the ordinary language of men, are always liable to be discredited by the facts of artistic production; and while prose is actually found to be a colored thing with Bacon, picturesque with Livy and Carlyle, musical with Cicero and Newman, mystical and intimate with Plato and Michelet and Sir Thomas Browne, exalted or florid, it may be, with Milton and Taylor,[2] it will be useless to protest that it can be nothing at all, except something very tamely and narrowly confined to mainly practical ends—a kind of "good round hand"; as useless as the protest that poetry might not touch prosaic subjects as with Wordsworth, or an abstruse matter as with Browning, or treat contemporary life nobly as with Tennyson. In subordination to one essential beauty in all good literary style, in all literature as a fine art, as there are many beauties of poetry so the beauties of prose are many, and it is the business of criticism to estimate them as such; as it is good in the criticism of verse to look for those hard, logical, and quasi-prosaic excellences which that too has, or needs. To find in the poem, amid the flowers, the allusions, the mixed perspectives, of *Lycidas* for instance, the thought, the logical structure: how wholesome! how delightful! as to identify in prose what we call the poetry, the imaginative power, not treating it as out of place and a kind of vagrant intruder, but by way of an estimate of its rights, that is, of its achieved powers, there.

Dryden, with the characteristic instinct of his age, loved to emphasize the distinction between poetry and prose, the protest against their confusion with each other, coming with somewhat diminished effect from one whose poetry was so prosaic. In truth, his sense of prosaic excellence affected his verse rather than his prose, which is not only fervid, richly figured, poetic, as we say, but vitiated, all unconsciously, by many a scanning line. Setting up correctness, that humble merit of prose, as the central literary excellence, he is really a less correct writer than he may seem, still with an imperfect mastery of the relative pronoun. It might have been foreseen that, in the

1. Prior to experience (Latin).
2. Jeremy Taylor (1613–1667), famous for the

elaborate style of his sermons. Jules Michelet (1798–1874), French historian.

rotations of mind, the province of poetry in prose would find its assertor; and, a century after Dryden, amid very different intellectual needs, and with the need therefore of great modifications in literary form, the range of the poetic force in literature was effectively enlarged by Wordsworth. The true distinction between prose and poetry he regarded as the almost technical or accidental one of the absence or presence of metrical beauty, or, say! metrical restraint; and for him the opposition came to be between verse and prose of course; but, as the essential dichotomy in this matter, between imaginative and unimaginative writing, parallel to De Quincey's distinction between "the literature of power and the literature of knowledge,"[3] in the former of which the composer gives us not fact, but his peculiar sense of fact, whether past or present.

Dismissing then, under sanction of Wordsworth, that harsher opposition of poetry to prose, as savoring in fact of the arbitrary psychology of the last century, and with it the prejudice that there can be but one only beauty of prose style, I propose here to point out certain qualities of all literature as a fine art, which, if they apply to the literature of fact, apply still more to the literature of the imaginative sense of fact, while they apply indifferently to verse and prose, so far as either is really imaginative—certain conditions of true art in both alike, which conditions may also contain in them the secret of the proper discrimination and guardianship of the peculiar excellences of either.

The line between fact and something quite different from external fact is, indeed, hard to draw. In Pascal,[4] for instance, in the persuasive writers generally, how difficult to define the point where, from time to time, argument which, if it is to be worth anything at all, must consist of facts or groups of facts, becomes a pleading—a theorem no longer, but essentially an appeal to the reader to catch the writer's spirit, to think with him, if one can or will—an expression no longer of fact but of his sense of it, his peculiar intuition of a world, prospective, or discerned below the faulty conditions of the present, in either case changed somewhat from the actual world. In science, on the other hand, in history so far as it conforms to scientific rule, we have a literary domain where the imagination may be thought to be always an intruder. And as, in all science, the functions of literature reduce themselves eventually to the transcribing of fact, so all the excellences of literary form in regard to science are reducible to various kinds of painstaking; this good quality being involved in all "skilled work" whatever, in the drafting of an act of parliament, as in sewing. Yet here again, the writer's sense of fact, in history especially, and in all those complex subjects which do but lie on the borders of science, will still take the place of fact, in various degrees. Your historian, for instance, with absolutely truthful intention, amid the multitude of facts presented to him must needs select, and in selecting assert something of his own humor, something that comes not of the world without but of a vision within. So Gibbon molds his unwieldy material to a preconceived view. Livy, Tacitus, Michelet, moving full of poignant sensibility amid the records of the past, each, after his own sense, modifies—who can tell where and to what degree?—and becomes something else than a transcriber; each, as he thus modifies, passing into the domain of art proper. For just in proportion as the

---

3. De Quincey's essay on this topic appeared in 1848.

4. Blaise Pascal (1623–1662), French scientist, philosopher, and theologian.

writer's aim, consciously or unconsciously, comes to be the transcribing, not of the world, not of mere fact, but of his sense of it, he becomes an artist, his work *fine* art; and good art (as I hope ultimately to show) in proportion to the truth of his presentment of that sense; as in those humbler or plainer functions of literature also, truth—truth to bare fact, there—is the essence of such artistic quality as they may have. Truth! there can be no merit, no craft at all, without that. And further, all beauty is in the long run only *fineness* of truth, or what we call expression, the finer accommodation of speech to that vision within.

—The transcript of his sense of fact rather than the fact, as being preferable, pleasanter, more beautiful to the writer himself. In literature, as in every other product of human skill, in the molding of a bell or a platter for instance, wherever this sense asserts itself, wherever the producer so modifies his work as, over and above its primary use or intention, to make it pleasing (to himself, of course, in the first instance) there, "fine" as opposed to merely serviceable art, exists. Literary art, that is, like all art which is in any way imitative or reproductive of fact—form, or color, or incident—is the representation of such fact as connected with soul, of a specific personality, in its preferences, its volition and power.

Such is the matter of imaginative or artistic literature—this transcript, not of mere fact, but of fact in its infinite variety, as modified by human preference in all its infinitely varied forms. It will be good literary art not because it is brilliant or sober, or rich, or impulsive, or severe, but just in proportion as its representation of that sense, that soul-fact, is true, verse being only one department of such literature, and imaginative prose, it may be thought, being the special art of the modern world. That imaginative prose should be the special and opportune art of the modern world results from two important facts about the latter: first, the chaotic variety and complexity of its interests, making the intellectual issue, the really master currents of the present time incalculable—a condition of mind little susceptible of the restraint proper to verse form, so that the most characteristic verse of the nineteenth century has been lawless verse; and secondly, an all-pervading naturalism, a curiosity about everything whatever as it really is, involving a certain humility of attitude, cognate to what must, after all, be the less ambitious form of literature. And prose thus asserting itself as the special and privileged artistic faculty of the present day, will be, however critics may try to narrow its scope, as varied in its excellence as humanity itself reflecting on the facts of its latest experience—an instrument of many stops, meditative, observant, descriptive, eloquent, analytic, plaintive, fervid. Its beauties will not be exclusively "pedestrian": it will exert, in due measure, all the varied charms of poetry, down to the rhythm which, as in Cicero, or Michelet, or Newman, at their best, gives its musical value to every syllable.

*　　*　　*

If the style be the man, in all the color and intensity of a veritable apprehension, it will be in a real sense "impersonal."

I said, thinking of books like Victor Hugo's *Les Misérables,* that prose literature was the characteristic art of the nineteenth century, as others, thinking of its triumphs since the youth of Bach, have assigned that place to music. Music and prose literature are, in one sense, the opposite terms of art; the art of literature presenting to the imagination, through the intelligence, a range of interests, as free and various as those which music presents to it through sense. And certainly the tendency of what has been here said is to bring literature too under those conditions, by conformity to which music takes rank as the typically perfect art. If music be the ideal of all art whatever, precisely because in music it is impossible to distinguish the form from the substance or matter, the subject from the expression, then, literature, by finding its specific excellence in the absolute correspondence of the term to its import, will be but fulfilling the condition of all artistic quality in things everywhere, of all good art.

Good art, but not necessarily great art; the distinction between great art and good art depending immediately, as regards literature at all events, not on its form, but on the matter. Thackeray's *Esmond,* surely, is greater art than *Vanity Fair,* by the greater dignity of its interests. It is on the quality of the matter it informs or controls, its compass, its variety, its alliance to great ends, or the depth of the note of revolt, or the largeness of hope in it, that the greatness of literary art depends, as *The Divine Comedy, Paradise Lost, Les Misérables,* the English Bible, are great art. Given the conditions I have tried to explain as constituting good art—then, if it be devoted further to the increase of men's happiness, to the redemption of the oppressed, or the enlargement of our sympathies with each other, or to such presentment of new or old truth about ourselves and our relation to the world as may ennoble and fortify us in our sojourn here, or immediately, as with Dante, to the glory of God, it will be also great art; if, over and above those qualities I summed up as mind and soul—that color and mystic perfume, and that reasonable structure, it has something of the soul of humanity in it, and finds its logical, architectural place, in the great structure of human life.

1889

GERARD MANLEY HOPKINS
1844–1889

It has been said that the most important date in Gerard Manley Hopkins's career was 1918, twenty-nine years after his death, for it was then that the first publication of his poems made them accessible to the world of readers. During his lifetime, these remarkable poems, most of them celebrating the wonders of God's creation, had been known only to a small circle of friends, including his literary executor, the poet Robert Bridges, who waited until 1918 before releasing them to a publisher. Partly because his work was first made public in a twentieth-century volume, but especially because of his striking experiments in meter and diction, Hopkins was widely hailed as a pioneering figure of "modern" literature, miraculously unconnected with his fellow Victorian poets (who during the 1920s and 1930s were largely out of fashion among critical readers). And this way of classifying and evaluating his writings has long persisted. In 1936 a substantial selection of his poems led off *The Faber Book of Modern Verse,* one of the most influential anthologies of the century, featuring poets such as W. H. Auden, Dylan Thomas, and T. S. Eliot (the only one whose selections occupy more pages than those allotted to Hopkins). And the first four editions of *The Norton Anthology of English Literature* (1962–79) grouped Hopkins with these same twentieth-century poets. To reclassify him is not to repudiate his earlier reputation as a "modern" but rather to suggest that his work can be better understood and appreciated if it is restored to the Victorian world out of which it developed.

Hopkins was born near London into a large and cultivated family in comfortable circumstances. After a brilliant career at Highgate School, he entered Oxford in 1863, where he was exposed to a variety of Victorian ways of thinking, both secular and religious. Among influential leaders at Oxford was Matthew Arnold, professor of poetry, but more important for Hopkins was his tutor, Walter Pater, an aesthetician whose emphasis on the intense apprehension of sensuous beauty struck a responsive chord in Hopkins. At Oxford he was also exposed to the Broad Church theology of one of the tutors at his college (Balliol), Benjamin Jowett. But Hopkins became increasingly attracted first to the High Church movement represented at Oxford by Edward Pusey, and then to Roman Catholicism. Profoundly influenced by John Henry Newman's conversion to Rome and by subsequent conversations with Newman himself, Hopkins entered the Roman Catholic Church in 1866. The estrangement from his family that resulted from his conversion was very painful for him; his parents' letters to him were so "terrible" (he reported to Newman) that he could not bear to "read them twice." And this alienation was heightened by his decision not only to become a Roman Catholic but to become a priest and, in particular, a Jesuit priest, for in the eyes of many Victorian Protestants, the Jesuit order was regarded with a special distrust. For the rest of his life, Hopkins served as a priest and teacher in various places, among them Oxford, Liverpool, and Lancashire. In 1884 he was appointed professor of classics at University College in Dublin, where Newman had served as rector in the 1850s and where James Joyce would be enrolled as a student at the turn of the century.

At school and at Oxford in the early 1860s, Hopkins had written poems in the vein of Keats. He burned most of these early writings after his conversion (although drafts survive), for he believed that his vocation must require renouncing such personal satisfactions as the writing of poems. Only after his superiors in the church encouraged him to do so did he resume writing poetry, but during the seven years of silence, as his letters show, he had been thinking about experimenting with what he called a "new rhythm." The result, in 1876, was his rhapsodic lyric-narrative, *The Wreck of the Deutschland,* a long ode about the wreck of a ship in which five Franciscan nuns were drowned. The style of the poem was so distinctive that the editor of the Jesuit magazine to which he had submitted it "dared not print it," as Hopkins himself reported. During the remaining fourteen years of his life, Hopkins continued to write poems but seldom submitted them for publication, partly because he was convinced that poetic fame was incompatible with his religious vocation but also because of a fear that readers would be discouraged by the eccentricity of his work.

Hopkins's sense of his own singularity gives us an indication of the organizing structure of his poetry. Drawing on the theology of Duns Scotus, a medieval philosopher, he felt that everything in the universe was characterized by what he called *inscape,* the distinctive design that constitutes individual identity. This identity is not static but dynamic. Each being in the universe "selves," that is, enacts its identity. And the human being, the most highly selved, the most individually distinctive being in the universe, recognizes the inscape of other beings in an act that Hopkins calls *instress,* the apprehension of an object in an intense thrust of energy toward it that enables one to realize its specific distinctiveness. Ultimately, the instress of inscape leads one to Christ, for the individual identity of any object is the stamp of divine creation on it. In the act of instress, therefore, the human being becomes a celebrant of the divine, at once recognizing God's creation and enacting his or her own God-given identity within it.

Poetry for Hopkins enacts this celebration. It is instress, and it realizes the inscape of its subject in its own distinctive design. Hopkins wrote, "But as air, melody, is what strikes me most of all in music and design in painting, so design, pattern or what I am in the habit of calling 'inscape' is what I above all aim at in poetry." To create inscape, Hopkins seeks to give each poem a unique design that captures the initial inspiration when he is "caught" by his subject. Many of the characteristics of Hopkins's style—his disruption of conventional syntax, his coining and compounding of words, his use of ellipsis and repetition—can be understood as ways of representing the stress and action of the brain in moments of inspiration. He creates compounds to represent the unique interlocking of the characteristics of an object—"piece-bright," "dapple-dawn-drawn," "blue-bleak." He omits syntactical connections to fuse qualities more intensely—"the dearest freshness deep down things." He creates puns to suggest how God's creation rhymes and chimes in a divine patterning. He violates conventional syntactic order to represent the shape of mental experience. In the act of imaginative apprehension, a language particular to the moment generates itself.

Hopkins also uses a new rhythm to give each poem its distinctive design. In the new metric system he created, which he called *sprung rhythm*, lines have a given number of stresses, but the number and placement of unstressed syllables is highly variable. Hopkins rarely marks all the intended stresses, only those that readers might not anticipate. To indicate stressed syllables, Hopkins often uses both the stress (´) and the "great stress" (˝). A curved line marks an "outride"—one or more syllables added to a foot but not counted in the scansion of the line; they indicate a stronger stress on the preceding syllable and a short pause after the outride. Here, for example, is the scansion for the first three lines of *The Windhover*:

> I caúght this mórning mórning's mínion, kíng-
>   dom of dáylight's daúphin, dapple-dawn-drawn Fálcon, in his ríding
>   Of the rólling level underneáth him steady aír, and stríding

Hopkins argued that sprung rhythm was the natural rhythm of common speech and written prose, as well as of music. He found a model for it in Old English poetry and in nursery rhymes, but he claimed that it had not been used in English poetry since the Elizabethan Age.

The density and difficulty that result from Hopkins's unconventional rhythm and syntax make his poetry seem modern, but his concern with the imagination's shaping of the natural world puts him very much in the Romantic tradition, and his creation of a rough and difficult style, designed to capture the mind's own motion, resembles the style of Browning. "A horrible thing has happened to me," Hopkins wrote in 1864, "I have begun to *doubt* Tennyson." He goes on to criticize Tennyson for using the grand style as a smooth and habitual poetic speech. Like Swinburne, Pater, and Henry James as well as Browning, Hopkins displays a new mannerism, characteristic of the latter part of the nineteenth century, which paradoxically combines an elaborate aestheticism with a more complex representation of consciousness.

In Hopkins's early poetry, his singular apprehension of the beauty of individual objects always brings him to an ecstatic illumination of the presence of God. But in his late poems, the so-called terrible sonnets, his distinctive individuality comes to isolate him from the God who made him thus. Hopkins wrote, "To me there is no resemblance: searching nature, I taste *self* but at one tankard, that of my own being." In the terrible sonnets, Hopkins confronts the solipsism to which his own stress on individuality seems to lead him. Like the mad speakers of so many Victorian dramatic monologues, he cannot escape a world solely of his own imagining. Yet even these poems of despair, which seem so distinctively modern, reflect a traditional religious vision, the dark night of the soul as described by the Spanish mystic Saint John of the Cross.

In his introduction to *The Oxford Book of Modern Verse*, Yeats calls Hopkins's poetry "a last development of poetical diction." Yeats's remark indicates the anomaly that Hopkins's work poses. Perhaps it is only appropriate for a writer who stressed the uniqueness of inscape to strike us with the individuality of his achievement.

God's Grandeur

The world is charged with the grandeur of God.
It will flame out, like shining from shook foil;[1]
It gathers to a greatness, like the ooze of oil
Crushed.[2] Why do men then now not reck his rod?
5   Generations have trod, have trod, have trod;
And all is seared with trade; bleared, smeared with toil;
And wears man's smudge and shares man's smell: the soil
Is bare now, nor can foot feel, being shod.

And for° all this, nature is never spent;   *despite*
10   There lives the dearest freshness deep down things;
And though the last lights off the black West went
Oh, morning, at the brown brink eastward, springs—
Because the Holy Ghost over the bent
World broods with warm breast and with ah! bright wings.

1877   1918

The Starlight Night

Look at the stars! look, look up at the skies!
O look at all the fire-folk sitting in the air!
The bright boroughs, the circle-citadels there!
Down in dim woods the diamond delves!° the elves'-eyes!   *quarries*
5   The grey lawns cold where gold, where quickgold;[1] lies!
Wind-beat whitebeam! airy abeles° set on a flare!   *white poplars*
Flake-doves sent floating forth at a farmyard scare!—
Ah well! it is all a purchase, all is a prize.

Buy then! bid then!—What?—Prayer, patience, alms, vows.
10   Look, look: a May-mess,[2] like on orchard boughs!
Look! March-bloom, like on mealed-with-yellow sallows![3]
These are indeed the barn; withindoors house
The shocks. This piece-bright paling[4] shuts the spouse
Christ home, Christ and his mother and all his hallows.°   *saints*

1877   1918

---

1. Hopkins explained this image in a letter: "I mean foil in its sense of leaf or tinsel. . . . Shaken goldfoil gives off broad glares like sheet lightning and also, and this is true of nothing else, owing to its zigzag dints and creasings and network of small many cornered facets, a sort of fork lightning too."
2. I.e., from the crushing of olives.

1. Coined by analogy with quicksilver. The starlight night resembles the lawns below it where the dew, reflecting the starlight, looks like gold.
2. A profusion of growing things such as May blossoms.
3. Willows, here with yellow spots like meal.
4. Picket fence. "Shocks": sheaves of grain.

As Kingfishers Catch Fire

As kingfishers catch fire, dragonflies draw flame;
  As tumbled over rim in roundy wells
  Stones ring; like each tucked° string tells, each hung bell's   *plucked*
Bow swung finds tongue to fling out broad its name;
5 Each mortal thing does one thing and the same:
  Deals out that being indoors° each one dwells;   *within*
  Selves[1]—goes itself; *myself* it speaks and spells,
Crying *What I do is me: for that I came.*

  I say more: the just man justices;[2]
10   Keeps gráce: thát keeps all his goings graces;
Acts in God's eye what in God's eye he is—
  Chríst. For Christ plays in ten thousand places,
Lovely in limbs, and lovely in eyes not his
  To the Father through the features of men's faces.

1877   1918

Spring

Nothing is so beautiful as Spring—
  When weeds, in wheels, shoot long and lovely and lush;
  Thrush's eggs look little low heavens, and thrush
Through the echoing timber does so rinse and wring
5 The ear, it strikes like lightnings to hear him sing;
  The glassy peartree leaves and blooms, they brush
  The descending blue; that blue is all in a rush
With richness; the racing lambs too have fair their fling.

  What is all this juice and all this joy?
10   A strain of the earth's sweet being in the beginning
In Eden garden.—Have, get, before it cloy,
  Before it cloud, Christ, lord, and sour with sinning,
Innocent mind and Mayday in girl and boy,
  Most, O maid's child,[1] thy choice and worthy the winning.

1877   1918

The Windhover[1]

To Christ our Lord

I caught this morning morning's minion,° king-   *darling*
  dom of daylight's dauphin,[2] dapple-dawn-drawn Falcon, in his riding

---

1. Fulfills its individuality.
2. Acts in a just manner.
1. Jesus, son of the Virgin Mary.

1. Kestrel, a small falcon noted for hovering in the air.
2. A prince who is heir to the French throne.

Of the rolling level underneath him steady air, and striding
High there, how he rung upon the rein of a wimpling[3] wing
5 In his ecstasy! then off, off forth on swing,
　As a skate's heel sweeps smooth on a bow-bend: the hurl and gliding
　Rebuffed the big wind. My heart in hiding
Stirred for a bird,—the achieve of, the mastery of the thing!

Brute beauty and valour and act, oh, air, pride, plume, here
10 　Buckle![4] AND the fire that breaks from thee then, a billion
Times told lovelier, more dangerous, O my chevalier!°　　　　　*knight*

No wonder of it: shéer plód makes plough down sillion[5]
Shine, and blue-bleak embers, ah my dear,
　Fall, gall[6] themselves, and gash gold-vermilion.

1877　　　　　　　　　　　　　　　　　　　　　　　　1918

Pied[1] Beauty

Glory be to God for dappled things—
　For skies of couple-colour as a brinded[2] cow;
　　For rose-moles all in stipple upon trout that swim;
Fresh-firecoal chestnut-falls,[3] finches' wings;
5 　Landscape plotted and pieced—fold, fallow, and plough;[4]
　　And áll trádes, their gear and tackle and trim.°　　　*equipment*

All things counter, original, spare,[5] strange;
　Whatever is fickle, freckled (who knows how?)
　　With swift, slow; sweet, sour; adazzle, dim;
10 He fathers-forth whose beauty is past change:
　　　　　Praise him.

1877　　　　　　　　　　　　　　　　　　　　　　　　1918

Hurrahing in Harvest

Summer ends now; now, barbarous in beauty, the stooks[1] rise
Around; up above, what wind-walks! what lovely behavior
Of silk-sack clouds! has wilder, wilful-wavier
Meal-drift moulded ever and melted across skies?

5 　I walk, I lift up, I lift up heart, eyes,
　Down all that glory in the heavens to glean our Saviour;

3. Rippling. "Rung upon the rein": circled at the end of a rein.
4. The verb can be read as imperative or indicative. All three meanings are relevant: to prepare for action, to fasten together, to collapse.
5. The ridge between two furrows of a plowed field.
6. Break the surface of.

1. Of two or more colors in blotches, variegated.
2. Brownish orange in color with streaks of gray.
3. I.e., freshly fallen chestnuts, bright as coals.
4. Divided into fields used as pastures ("fold"), lying fallow, or plowed for cultivation. The landscape thus appears like patches of different colors.
5. Rare. "Counter": contrary.
1. Sheaves of grain.

And, éyes, heárt, what looks, what lips yet gave you a
Rapturous love's greeting of realer, of rounder replies?

And the azurous hung hills are his world-wielding shoulder
10   Majestic—as a stallion stalwart, very-violet-sweet!—
These things, these things were here and but the beholder
Wanting; which two when they once meet,
The heart rears wings bold and bolder
And hurls for him, O half hurls earth for him off under his feet.

1877   1918

Binsey Poplars

felled 1879

My aspens dear, whose airy cages quelled,
Quelled or quenched in leaves the leaping sun,
All felled, felled, are all felled;
   Of a fresh and following folded rank
5   Not spared, not one
         That dandled a sandalled
     Shadow that swam or sank
On meadow and river and wind-wandering
   weed-winding bank.

10   O if we but knew what we do
        When we delve° or hew—   *dig*
   Hack and rack° the growing green!   *torture*
      Since country is so tender
     To touch, her being só slender,
15   That, like this sleek and seeing ball°   *the eye*
    But a prick will make no eye at all,

    Where we, even where we mean
      To mend her we end her,
      When we hew or delve:
20 After-comers cannot guess the beauty been.
   Ten or twelve, only ten or twelve
     Strokes of havoc únselve[1]
      The sweet especial scene,
    Rural scene, a rural scene,
25   Sweet especial rural scene.

1879   1918

Duns Scotus's Oxford[1]

Towery city and branchy between towers;
Cuckoo-echoing, bell-swarmèd, lark-charmèd, rook-racked, river-rounded;

1. Rob it of self.
1. Duns Scotus, the medieval theologian, lectured at Oxford about 1301. His idea that individuality is the final perfection of any creature influenced Hopkins's conception of inscape. When Hopkins came on two of Scotus's commentaries in 1872, he wrote that he was immediately "flush with a new stroke of enthusiasm . . . when I took in any inscape of the sky or sea I thought of Scotus."

The dapple-eared lily below thee; that country and town did
Once encounter in, here coped[2] and poisèd powers;

5 Thou hast a base and brickish skirt[3] there, sours
That neighbour-nature thy grey beauty is grounded
Best in; graceless growth, thou hast confounded
Rural rural keeping[4]—folk, flocks, and flowers.

Yet ah! this air I gather and I release
10 He lived on; these weeds and waters, these walls are what
He haunted who of all men most sways my spirits to peace;

Of realty° the rarest-veinèd unraveller; a not   *reality*
Rivalled insight, be rival Italy or Greece;
Who fired France for Mary without spot.[5]

1879   1918

Felix Randal

Felix Randal the farrier,° O is he dead then? my duty   *blacksmith*
    all ended,
Who have watched his mould of man, big-boned and hardy-handsome
Pining, pining, till time when reason rambled in it and some
Fatal four disorders, fleshed there, all contended?

5 Sickness broke him. Impatient, he cursed at first, but mended
Being anointed[1] and all; though a heavenlier heart began some
Months earlier, since I had our sweet reprieve and ransom[2]
Tendered to him. Ah well, God rest him all road ever[3] he offended!

This seeing the sick endears them to us, us too it endears.
10 My tongue had taught thee comfort, touch had quenched thy tears,
Thy tears that touched my heart, child, Felix, poor Felix Randal;
How far from then forethought of, all thy more boisterous years,
When thou at the random[4] grim forge, powerful amidst peers,
Didst fettle° for the great grey drayhorse his bright and battering   *prepare*
    sandal!

1880   1918

Spring and Fall:

to a young child

Márgarét, áre you gríeving
Over Goldengrove unleaving?

2. Set off against one another.
3. Redbrick housing developments and industrial complexes, built in the 19th century on the north edge of Oxford, are in marked contrast with the "gray" stone buildings of the medieval city.
4. The "brickish skirt" has destroyed the way in which the rural landscape and the old city have tended and preserved each other.
5. In Paris, Scotus was the first to defend the doc-

trine of the Immaculate Conception, that Mary was born without original sin.
1. In Extreme Unction, the sacrament for the dying.
2. Holy Communion preceded by confession and absolution.
3. In whatever way.
4. Built with stones of irregular size and shape.

Leáves, líke the things of man, you
With your fresh thoughts care for, can you?
5 Áh! ás the heart grows older
It will come to such sights colder
By and by, nor spare a sigh
Though worlds of wanwood leafmeal[1] lie;
And yet you *will* weep and know why.
10 Now no matter, child, the name:
Sórrow's spríngs áre the same.
Nor mouth had, no nor mind, expressed
What heart heard of, ghost° guessed: *spirit*
It ís the blight man was born for,
15 It is Margaret you mourn for.

1880   1918

[Carrion Comfort][1]

Not, I'll not, carrion comfort, Despair, not feast on thee,[2]
Not untwist—slack they may be—these last strands of man
In me ór, most weary, cry *I can no more.* I can;
Can something, hope, wish day come, not choose not to be.

5 But ah, but O thou terrible, why wouldst thou rude on me
Thy wring-world right foot rock?[3] lay a lionlimb against me?
        scan
With darksome devouring eyes my bruisèd bones? and fan,
O in turns of tempest, me heaped there; me frantic to avoid
        thee and flee?

Why? That my chaff might fly; my grain lie, sheer and clear.
10 Nay in all that toil, that coil,° since (seems) I kissed the rod,   *tumult*
Hand rather,[4] my heart lo! lapped strength, stole joy, would
        laugh, chéer.
Cheer whom though? The Hero whose heaven-handling
        flung me, fóot tród
Me? or me that fought him? O which one? is it each one?
        That night, that year
Of now done darkness I wretch lay wrestling with (my God!)
        my God.

1885   1918

---

1. Coined by analogy with piecemeal. "Wanwood": pale or dim; the forest may be pale because
of light-colored autumn leaves or dim because light
is filtered through the leaves.
1. The title of this poem was supplied by Bridges.
It is one of the "terrible sonnets," as are the three
following poems.

2. The satisfaction of giving in to despair as a kind
of "comfort" is implicitly likened to a vulture's satisfaction in feasting on dead flesh.
3. I.e., why wouldst thou roughly against me rock
thy right foot that wrings the world?
4. I.e., the hand that wields the rod.

No Worst, There Is None

No worst, there is none. Pitched past pitch of grief,
More pangs will, schooled at forepangs, wilder wring.
Comforter, where, where is your comforting?
Mary, mother of us, where is your relief?
5 My cries heave, herds-long;[1] huddle in a main, a chief-
woe, world-sorrow; on an age-old anvil wince and sing—
Then lull, then leave off. Fury had shrieked "No ling-
ering! Let me be fell: force[2] I must be brief."
O the mind, mind has mountains; cliffs of fall
10 Frightful, sheer, no-man-fathomed. Hold them cheap
May who ne'er hung there. Nor does long our small
Durance° deal with that steep or deep. Here! creep,   *endurance*
Wretch, under a comfort serves in a whirlwind: all
Life death does end and each day dies with sleep.

1885   1918

I Wake and Feel the Fell of Dark, Not Day

I wake and feel the fell° of dark, not day.   *bitterness*
What hours, O what black hoürs we have spent
This night! what sights you, heart, saw; ways you went!
And more must, in yet longer light's delay.

5 With witness I speak this. But where I say
Hours I mean years, mean life. And my lament
Is cries countless, cries like dead letters[1] sent
To dearest him that lives alas! away.

I am gall, I am heartburn. God's most deep decree
10 Bitter would have me taste: my taste was me;
Bones built in me, flesh filled, blood brimmed the curse.

Selfyeast of spirit a dull dough sours. I see
The lost are like this, and their scourge to be
As I am mine, their sweating selves; but worse.

1885   1918

---

1. Like the succession of cries made by cattle that
have been following one another in a long line.
2. Perforce. "Fell": fierce.

1. Letters undelivered or returned to the sender
by the post office.

That Nature Is a Heraclitean Fire[1] and of the Comfort of the Resurrection

Cloud-puffball, torn tufts, tossed pillows | flaunt forth, then chevy°   *race*
   on an air-
built thoroughfare: heaven-roysterers,° in gay-gangs | they   *swaggerers*
   throng; they glitter in marches.
Down roughcast, down dazzling whitewash, | wherever an elm arches.
Shivelights and shadowtackle[2] in long | lashes lace, lance, and pair.
5 Delightfully the bright wind boisterous | ropes, wrestles, beats earth bare
Of yestertempest's creases; in pool and rut peel parches[3]
Squandering ooze to squeezed | dough, crust, dust; stanches, starches
Squadroned masks and manmarks[4] | treadmire toil there
Footfretted in it. Million-fuelèd, | nature's bonfire burns on.
10 But quench her bonniest, dearest | to her, her clearest-selvèd°   *most individual*
   spark
Man, how fast his firedint | his mark on mind, is gone!
Both are in an unfathomable, all is in an enormous dark
Drowned. O pity and indig | nation! Manshape, that shone
Sheer off, disseveral,° a star, | death blots black out; nor mark   *separate*
15   Is any of him at all so stark
But vastness blurs and time | beats level. Enough! the Resurrection,
A heart's-clarion! Away grief's gasping, | joyless days, dejection.
       Across my foundering deck shone
A beacon, an eternal beam. | Flesh fade, and mortal trash
20 Fall to the residuary worm; | world's wildfire, leave but ash:
       In a flash, at a trumpet crash,
I am all at once what Christ is, | since he was what I am, and
This Jack, joke, poor potsherd, | patch, matchwood,[5] immortal diamond,
       Is immortal diamond.

1888   1918

Thou Art Indeed Just, Lord

*Justus quidem tu es, Domine, si disputem tecum; verumtamen
justa loquar ad te: Quare via impiorum prosperatur? &c.*[1]

Thou art indeed just, Lord, if I contend
With thee; but, sir, so what I plead is just.
Why do sinners' ways prosper? and why must
Disappointment all I endeavour end?

5 Wert thou my enemy, O thou my friend,
   How wouldst thou worse, I wonder, than thou dost

---

1. Heraclitus (ca. 535–ca. 475 B.C.E.) taught that all things are in flux and that they ultimately return to the basic principle of fire.
2. Branches imagined as the shadows of a ship's rigging. "Shivelights": strips of light.
3. Ruts described as peeled places. "Parches" is a verb whose subject is *wind*.

4. The marks that people have made on the earth by walking ("Footfretted") on it.
5. Kindling. "Jack": ordinary man.
1. "Righteous art thou, O Lord, when I plead with thee: yet let me talk with thee of thy judgments: Wherefore doth the way of the wicked prosper?" (Jeremiah 12.1). The Latin was Hopkins's title.

Defeat, thwart me? Oh, the sots and thralls of lust
Do in spare hours more thrive than I that spend,

Sir, life upon thy cause. See, banks and brakes°   *thickets*
10 Now, leavèd how thick! lacèd they are again
With fretty chervil,² look, and fresh wind shakes

Them; birds build—but not I build; no, but strain,
Time's eunuch, and not breed one work that wakes.
Mine, O thou lord of life, send my roots rain.

1889   1918

From Journal¹

May 3 [1866]. Cold. Morning raw and wet, afternoon fine. Walked then with Addis, crossing Bablock Hythe, round by Skinner's Weir² through many fields into the Witney road. Sky sleepy blue without liquidity. From Cumnor Hill saw St. Philip's and the other spires through blue haze rising pale in a pink light. On further side of the Witney road hills, just fleeced with grain or other green growth, by their dips and waves foreshortened here and there and so differenced in brightness and opacity the green on them, with delicate effect. On left, brow of the near hill glistening with very bright newly turned sods and a scarf of vivid green slanting away beyond the skyline, against which the clouds shewed the slightest tinge of rose or purple. Copses in grey-red or grey-yellow—the tinges immediately forerunning the opening of full leaf. Meadows skirting Seven-bridge road voluptuous green. Some oaks are out in small leaf. Ashes not out, only tufted with their fringy blooms. Hedges springing richly. Elms in small leaf, with more or less opacity. White poplars most beautiful in small grey crisp spray-like leaf. Cowslips capriciously colouring meadows in creamy drifts. Bluebells, purple orchis. Over the green water of the river passing the slums of the town and under its bridges swallows shooting, blue and purple above and shewing their amber-tinged breasts reflected in the water, their flight unsteady with wagging wings and leaning first to one side then the other. Peewits flying. Towards sunset the sky partly swept, as often, with moist white cloud, tailing off across which are morsels of grey-black woolly clouds. Sun seemed to make a bright liquid hole in this, its texture had an upward northerly sweep or drift from the W, marked softly in grey. Dog violets. Eastward after sunset range of clouds rising in bulky heads moulded softly in tufts or bunches of snow—so it looks—and membered somewhat elaborately, rose-coloured. Notice often imperfect fairy rings. Apple and other fruit trees blossomed beautifully.

*   *   *

2. A kind of herb, related to parsley.
1. With the exception of one year, Hopkins kept a journal from May 1866 to Feb. 1875. Its most interesting entries are minutely observed descriptions of natural phenomena, which reveal the character of his imagination. The brackets and abbreviations are Hopkins's own.
2. Dam. William E. Addis (1844–1917), friend of Hopkins at Oxford; like him he became a Catholic convert and priest. The places mentioned are around Oxford. "Hythe": landing place on a river.

Feb.—1870. One day in the Long Retreat (which ended on Xmas Day) they were reading in the refectory Sister Emmerich's[3] account of the Agony in the Garden and I suddenly began to cry and sob and could not stop. I put it down for this reason, that if I had been asked a minute beforehand I should have said that nothing of the sort was going to happen and even when it did I stood in a manner wondering at myself not seeing in my reason the traces of an adequate cause for such strong emotion—the traces of it I say because of course the cause in itself is adequate for the sorrow of a lifetime. I remember much the same thing on Maundy Thursday when the presanctified Host[4] was carried to the sacristy. But neither the weight nor the stress of sorrow, that is to say of the thing which should cause sorrow, by themselves move us or bring the tears as a sharp knife does not cut for being pressed as long as it is pressed without any shaking of the hand but there is always one touch, something striking sideways and unlooked for, which in both cases undoes resistance and pierces, and this may be so delicate that the pathos seems to have gone directly to the body and cleared the understanding in its passage. On the other hand the pathetic touch by itself, as in dramatic pathos, will only draw slight tears if its matter is not important or not of import to us, the strong emotion coming from a force which was gathered before it was discharged: in this way a knife may pierce the flesh which it had happened only to graze and only grazing will go no deeper.

* * *

May 18 [1870]. —Great brilliancy and projection: the eye seemed to fall perpendicular from level to level along our trees, the nearer and further Park; all things hitting the sense with double but direct instress. * * *

This was later. One day when the bluebells were in bloom I wrote the following. I do not think I have ever seen anything more beautiful than the bluebell I have been looking at. I know the beauty of our Lord by it. It[s inscape] is [mixed of] strength and grace, like an ash [tree]. The head is strongly drawn over [backwards] and arched down like a cutwater [drawing itself back from the line of the keel.] The lines of the bells strike and overlie this, rayed but not symmetrically, some lie parallel. They look steely against [the] paper, the shades lying between the bells and behind the cockled petal-ends and nursing up the precision of their distinctness, the petal-ends themselves being delicately lit. Then there is the straightness of the trumpets in the bells softened by the slight entasis and [by] the square splay of the mouth. One bell, the lowest, some way detached and carried on a longer footstalk, touched out with the tips of the petals on oval / not like the rest in a plane perpendicular of the axis of the bell but a little atilt, and so with [the] square-in-rounding turns of the petals

* * *

Aug. 10 [1872]. —I was looking at high waves. The breakers always are parallel to the coast and shape themselves to it except where the curve is sharp however the wind blows. They are rolled out by the shallowing shore just as a piece of putty between the palms whatever its shape runs into a

---

3. *The Dolorous Passion of Our Lord Jesus Christ; from the Meditations of Anne Catherine Emmerich,* an Augustinian nun (1774–1824).

4. The bread wafer sanctified for Holy Communion. "Maundy Thursday": the Thursday before Easter, day of the Last Supper.

long roll. The slant ruck[5] or crease one sees in them shows the way of the wind. The regularity of the barrels surprised and charmed the eye; the edge behind the comb or crest was as smooth and bright as glass. It may be noticed to be green behind and silver white in front: the silver marks where the air begins, the pure white is foam, the green / solid water. Then looked at to the right or left they are scrolled over like mouldboards[6] or feathers or jibsails seen by the edge. It is pretty to see the hollow of the barrel disappearing as the white combs on each side run along the wave gaining ground till the two meet at a pitch and crush and overlap each other.

About all the turns of the scaping from the break and flooding of wave to its run out again I have not yet satisfied myself. The shores are swimming and the eyes have before them a region of milky surf but it is hard for them to unpack the huddling and gnarls of the water and law out the shapes and the sequence of the running: I catch however the looped or forked wisp made by every big pebble the backwater runs over—if it were clear and smooth there would be a network from their overlapping, such as can in fact be seen on smooth sand after the tide is out—; then I saw it run browner, the foam dwindling and twitched into long chains of suds, while the strength of the back-draught shrugged the stones together and clocked them one against another

1959

---

5. Fold or crease.　　　　　6. Curved iron plates attached to plowshares.

Light Verse

Despite its later reputation as an age of solemnity, the Victorian age produced a remarkable outburst of humorous prose and verse from the time of Dickens's *Pickwick Papers* at the beginning of the period to the operas of Gilbert and Sullivan near the end. The following selections provide examples of two varieties of Victorian light verse. One, represented by W. S. Gilbert, makes playful mockery of institutions such as the Court of Chancery and marriage. Gilbert's burlesque mode is also to be found, though managed by less inspired writers, in many pages of *Punch*, a humorous and satirical magazine that began publication in 1841. Although exaggeration and absurdities are important ingredients in these writings, the world of Gilbert is still recognizably related to the ordinary world.

The other variety is a more distinctive Victorian specialty—nonsense writing—represented here by the verse of Edward Lear and Lewis Carroll. Nonsense writing was occasionally used by Shakespeare and, in the twentieth century, by James Joyce and James Thurber, but the period in which this genre had its finest flowering was, without question, the Victorian age. Freudian explanations can be devised to account for its appearance during this particular period; and indeed, if nonsense writing does originate in a writer's repressions, we may have a clue to the undertone of melancholy that some readers detect in the verses of Lear and Carroll. The best nonsense writing, however, raises its own less solemn problems. Lear and Carroll created a zany upside-down world full of puzzles; the attempt to solve such puzzles, even when they cannot be solved, is in itself a perennial satisfaction.

EDWARD LEAR
1812–1888

Edward Lear was a landscape painter who spent much of his life in Mediterranean countries. In 1846 he published his first *Book of Nonsense*, a collection of limericks for children. The form of the limerick was not invented by Lear, but his use of it served to establish its popularity. In later volumes of the *Book of Nonsense*, he used other forms of verse, some of them modeled on rhythms that had been developed by his close friend Tennyson. All of his own poems were characteristically classified by Lear as "nonsense pure and absolute," yet it is as the author of *The Owl and the Pussy-Cat, The Jumblies,* and other poems that Lear is remembered. Evidently pure and absolute nonsense is a rare art.

Limerick

There was an Old Man who supposed
That the street door was partially closed;
But some very large rats ate his coats and his hats,
While that futile old gentleman dozed.

1846

How Pleasant to Know Mr. Lear

"How pleasant to know Mr. Lear!"
    Who has written such volumes of stuff!
Some think him ill-tempered and queer,
    But a few think him pleasant enough.

5   His mind is concrete and fastidious,
        His nose is remarkably big;
His visage is more or less hideous,
        His beard it resembles a wig.

He has ears, and two eyes, and ten fingers,
10   Leastways if you reckon two thumbs;
Long ago he was one of the singers,
        But now he is one of the dumbs.

He sits in a beautiful parlor,
        With hundreds of books on the wall;
15 He drinks a great deal of Marsala,
        But never gets tipsy at all.

He has many friends, lay men and clerical,
        Old Foss is the name of his cat;
His body is perfectly spherical,
20   He weareth a runcible¹ hat.

When he walks in waterproof white,
        The children run after him so!
Calling out, "He's come out in his night-
        Gown, that crazy old Englishman, oh!"

25 He weeps by the side of the ocean,
        He weeps on the top of the hill;
He purchases pancakes and lotion,
        And chocolate shrimps from the mill.

He reads, but he cannot speak, Spanish,
30   He cannot abide ginger beer:

---

1. A runcible spoon is a spoon-shaped fork with a cutting edge.

Ere the days of his pilgrimage vanish,
How pleasant to know Mr. Lear!

1871

The Jumblies

They went to sea in a sieve, they did;
  In a sieve they went to sea;
In spite of all their friends could say,
On a winter's morn, on a stormy day,
5   In a sieve they went to sea.
And when the sieve turned round and round,
And everyone cried, "You'll be drowned!"
They called aloud, "Our sieve ain't big,
But we don't care a button; we don't care a fig—
10   In a sieve we'll go to sea!"
    Far and few, far and few,
      Are the lands where the Jumblies live.
    Their heads are green, and their hands are blue;
      And they went to sea in a sieve.

15   They sailed away in a sieve, they did,
    In a sieve they sailed so fast,
With only a beautiful pea-green veil
Tied with a ribbon, by way of a sail,
    To a small tobacco-pipe mast.
20   And everyone said who saw them go,
"Oh! won't they be soon upset, you know,
For the sky is dark, and the voyage is long;
And, happen what may, it's extremely wrong
    In a sieve to sail so fast."

25   The water it soon came in, it did;
    The water it soon came in.
So, to keep them dry, they wrapped their feet
In a pinky paper all folded neat;
    And they fastened it down with a pin.
30   And they passed the night in a crockery-jar;
And each of them said, "How wise we are!
Though the sky be dark, and the voyage be long,
Yet we never can think we were rash or wrong,
    While round in our sieve we spin."

35   And all night long they sailed away;
    And, when the sun went down,
They whistled and warbled a moony song
To the echoing sound of a coppery gong,
    In the shade of the mountains brown,
40   "O Timballoo! how happy we are
When we live in a sieve and a crockery-jar!

And all night long, in the moonlight pale,
We sail away with a pea-green sail
    In the shade of the mountains brown."

45   They sailed to the Western Sea, they did—
        To a land all covered with trees;
    And they bought an owl, and a useful cart,
    And a pound of rice, and a cranberry tart,
        And a hive of silvery bees;
50   And they bought a pig, and some green jackdaws,
    And a lovely monkey with lollipop paws,
    And seventeen bags of edelweiss tea,
    And forty bottles of ring-bo-ree,
        And no end of Stilton cheese.

55   And in twenty years they all came back—
        In twenty years or more;
    And everyone said, "How tall they've grown!
    For they've been to the Lakes, and the Torrible Zone,
        And the hills of the Chankly Bore."
60   And they drank their health, and gave them a feast
    Of dumplings made of beautiful yeast;
    And everyone said, "If we only live,
    We, too, will go to sea in a sieve,
        To the hills of the Chankly Bore."
65   Far and few, far and few,
            Are the lands where the Jumblies live.
        Their heads are green, and their hands are blue;
            And they went to sea in a sieve.

                                                        1871

Cold Are the Crabs

    Cold are the crabs that crawl on yonder hills,
    Colder the cucumbers that grow beneath,
    And colder still the brazen chops that wreathe
        The tedious gloom of philosophic pills!
5   For when the tardy film of nectar fills
    The ample bowls of demons and of men,
    There lurks the feeble mouse, the homely hen,
        And there the porcupine with all her quills.
    Yet much remains—to weave a solemn strain
10   That lingering sadly—slowly dies away,
    Daily departing with departing day.
    A pea-green gamut on a distant plain
    When wily walruses in congress meet—
        Such such is life—

                                                        1953

LEWIS CARROLL
1832–1898

Charles Lutwidge Dodgson was a deacon in the Anglican Church and a lecturer in mathematics at Oxford as well as a pioneer in the art of portrait photography. Most of his publications were mathematical treatises, but his fame rests on the strange pair of books he wrote for children: *Alice in Wonderland* (1865) and *Through the Looking-Glass* (1871), both published under the pseudonym Lewis Carroll. Like *Gulliver's Travels,* these narratives have long been enjoyed, at different levels, by both children and adults. The various songs scattered through the stories are sometimes parodies, as, for example, *The White Knight's Song,* but more often they are classic examples of nonsense verse. Poems such as *Jabberwocky* exhibit a mathematician's fondness for puzzles combined with a literary person's fondness for word games. At this level, *Jabberwocky* can be enjoyed as a small-scale *Finnegans Wake.*

Carroll's art has obviously many affinities with that of another eccentric Victorian, Edward Lear, although the two men never met and (so far as we know) never referred to each other. Despite these affinities, Carroll's nonsense, often on the brink of satire, is more pointed than Lear's.

Jabberwocky[1]

'Twas brillig, and the slithy toves
    Did gyre and gimble in the wabe;
All mimsy were the borogoves,
    And the mome raths outgrabe.

5   "Beware the Jabberwock, my son!
    The jaws that bite, the claws that catch!
Beware the Jubjub bird, and shun
    The frumious Bandersnatch!"

He took his vorpal sword in hand;
10   Long time the manxome foe he sought—
So rested he by the Tumtum tree,
    And stood awhile in thought.

And, as in uffish thought he stood,
    The Jabberwock, with eyes of flame,
15 Came whiffling through the tulgey wood,
    And burbled as it came!

One, two! One, two! And through and through
    The vorpal blade went snicker-snack!
He left it dead, and with its head
20   He went galumphing back.

"And hast thou slain the Jabberwock?
    Come to my arms, my beamish boy!

---

1. From *Through the Looking-Glass,* chap. 1.

O frabjous day! Callooh! Callay!"
    He chortled in his joy.

25   'Twas brillig, and the slithy toves
      Did gyre and gimble in the wabe;
    All mimsy were the borogoves,
      And the mome raths outgrabe.

1855   1871

[Humpty Dumpty's Explication of *Jabberwocky*][1]

"You seem very clever at explaining words, Sir," said Alice. "Would you kindly tell me the meaning of the poem *Jabberwocky*?"

"Let's hear it," said Humpty Dumpty. "I can explain all the poems that ever were invented—and a good many that haven't been invented just yet."

This sounded very hopeful, so Alice repeated the first verse:

" 'Twas brillig, and the slithy toves
    Did gyre and gimble in the wabe;
All mimsy were the borogoves,
    And the mome raths outgrabe."

"That's enough to begin with," Humpty Dumpty interrupted: "there are plenty of hard words there. 'Brillig' means four o'clock in the afternoon— the time when you begin *broiling* things for dinner."

"That'll do very well," said Alice: "and 'slithy'?"[2]

"Well, 'slithy' means 'lithe and slimy.' 'Lithe' is the same as 'active.' You see it's like a portmanteau[3]—there are two meanings packed up into one word."

"I see it now," Alice remarked thoughtfully: "and what are 'toves'?"

"Well, 'toves' are something like badgers—they're something like lizards— and they're something like corkscrews."

"They must be very curious creatures."

"They are that," said Humpty Dumpty: "also they make their nests under sundials—also they live on cheese."

"And what's to 'gyre' and to 'gimble'?"

"To 'gyre' is to go round and round like a gyroscope. To 'gimble' is to make holes like a gimlet."

"And the 'wabe' is the grass plot round a sundial, I suppose?" said Alice, surprised at her own ingenuity.

"Of course it is. It's called 'wabe,' you know, because it goes a long way before it, and a long way behind it——"

"And a long way beyond it on each side," Alice added.

"Exactly so. Well then, 'mimsy' is 'flimsy and miserable' (there's another

---

1. From *Through the Looking-Glass*, chap. 6.
2. Concerning the pronunciation of these words, Carroll later said: "The 'i' in 'slithy' is long, as in 'writhe'; and 'toves' is pronounced so as to rhyme with 'groves.' Again, the first 'o' in 'borogroves' is pronounced like the 'o' in 'borrow.' I have heard people try to give it the sound of the 'o' in 'worry.' Such is Human Perversity."
3. Large suitcase.

portmanteau for you). And a 'borogove' is a thin shabby-looking bird with its feathers sticking out all round—something like a live mop."

"And then 'mome raths'?" said Alice. "If I'm not giving you too much trouble."

"Well, a 'rath' is a sort of green pig: but 'mome' I'm not certain about. I think it's short for 'from home'—meaning that they'd lost their way, you know."

"And what does 'outgrabe' mean?"

"Well, 'outgribing' is something between bellowing and whistling, with a kind of sneeze in the middle: however, you'll hear it done, maybe—down in the wood yonder—and when you've once heard it you'll be *quite* content. Who's been repeating all that hard stuff to you?"

"I read it in a book," said Alice.

1871

The White Knight's Song[1]

I'll tell thee everything I can;
　　There's little to relate.
I saw an aged, aged man,
　　A-sitting on a gate.
5　"Who are you, aged man?" I said.
　　"And how is it you live?"
And his answer trickled through my head
　　Like water through a sieve.

He said "I look for butterflies
10　　That sleep among the wheat;
I make them into mutton-pies,
　　And sell them in the street.
I sell them unto men," he said,
　　"Who sail on stormy seas;
15　And that's the way I get my bread—
　　A trifle, if you please."

But I was thinking of a plan
　　To dye one's whiskers green,
And always use so large a fan
20　　That they could not be seen.
So, having no reply to give
　　To what the old man said,
I cried, "Come, tell me how you live!"
　　And thumped him on the head.

25　His accents mild took up the tale;
　　He said, "I go my ways,
And when I find a mountain-rill,

---

1. From *Through the Looking-Glass*, chap. 8. Cf. Wordsworth's poem concerning the aged leech gatherer: *Resolution and Independence*.

I set it in a blaze;
And thence they make a stuff they call
30   Rowland's Macassar Oil—
Yet twopence-halfpenny is all
    They give me for my toil."

But I was thinking of a way
    To feed oneself on batter,
35 And so go on from day to day
    Getting a little fatter.
I shook him well from side to side,
    Until his face was blue;
"Come, tell me how you live," I cried
40   "And what it is you do!"

He said, "I hunt for haddocks' eyes
    Among the heather bright,
And work them into waistcoat-buttons
    In the silent night.
45 And these I do not sell for gold
    Or coin of silvery shine,
But for a copper halfpenny,
    And that will purchase nine.

"I sometimes dig for buttered rolls,
50   Or set limed twigs for crabs;
I sometimes search the grassy knolls
    For wheels of hansom-cabs.
And that's the way" (he gave a wink)
    "By which I get my wealth—
55 And very gladly will I drink
    Your Honor's noble health."

I heard him then, for I had just
    Completed my design
To keep the Menai bridge[2] from rust
60   By boiling it in wine.
I thanked him much for telling me
    The way he got his wealth,
But chiefly for his wish that he
    Might drink my noble health.

65 And now, if e'er by chance I put
    My fingers into glue,
Or madly squeeze a right-hand foot
    Into a left-hand shoe,
Or if I drop upon my toe
70   A very heavy weight,
I weep, for it reminds me so
    Of that old man I used to know—

_____

2. Railway bridge in Wales (completed in 1850).

Whose look was mild, whose speech was slow,
Whose hair was whiter than the snow,
75 Whose face was very like a crow,
With eyes, like cinders, all aglow,
Who seemed distracted with his woe.
Who rocked his body to and fro,
And muttered mumblingly and low,
80 As if his mouth were full of dough,
Who snorted like a buffalo—
That summer evening long ago
    A-sitting on a gate.

1856   1871

The Walrus and the Carpenter[1]

The sun was shining on the sea,
  Shining with all his might;
He did his very best to make
  The billows smooth and bright—
5 And this was odd, because it was
  The middle of the night.

The moon was shining sulkily,
  Because she thought the sun
Had got no business to be there
10   After the day was done—
"It's very rude of him," she said,
  "To come and spoil the fun!"

The sea was wet as wet could be,
  The sands were dry as dry.
15 You could not see a cloud, because
  No cloud was in the sky;
No birds were flying overhead—
  There were no birds to fly.

The Walrus and the Carpenter
20   Were walking close at hand;
They wept like anything to see
  Such quantities of sand.
"If this were only cleared away,"
  They said, "it *would* be grand!"

25 "If seven maids with seven mops
  Swept it for half a year,
Do you suppose," the Walrus said,
  "That they could get it clear?"

---

1. Recited by Tweedledee in chap. 4 of *Through the Looking-Glass.*

"I doubt it," said the Carpenter,
30   And shed a bitter tear.

"O Oysters, come and walk with us!"
    The Walrus did beseech.
"A pleasant walk, a pleasant talk,
    Along the briny beach;
35 We cannot do with more than four,
    To give a hand to each."

The eldest Oyster looked at him,
    But never a word he said;
The eldest Oyster winked his eye,
40   And shook his heavy head—
Meaning to say he did not choose
    To leave the oyster-bed.

But four young Oysters hurried up,
    All eager for the treat;
45 Their coats were brushed, their faces washed,
    Their shoes were clean and neat—
And this was odd, because, you know,
    They hadn't any feet.

Four other Oysters followed them,
50   And yet another four;
And thick and fast they came at last,
    And more, and more, and more—
All hopping through the frothy waves,
    And scrambling to the shore.

55 The Walrus and the Carpenter
    Walked on a mile or so,
And then they rested on a rock
    Conveniently low;
And all the little Oysters stood
60   And waited in a row.

"The time has come," the Walrus said,
    "To talk of many things:
Of shoes—and ships—and sealing-wax—
    Of cabbages—and kings—
65 And why the sea is boiling hot—
    And whether pigs have wings."

"But wait a bit," the Oysters cried,
    "Before we have our chat;
For some of us are out of breath,
70   And all of us are fat!"
"No hurry!" said the Carpenter.
    They thanked him much for that.

"A loaf of bread," the Walrus said,
  "Is what we chiefly need;
75 Pepper and vinegar besides
  Are very good indeed—
Now, if you're ready, Oysters dear,
  We can begin to feed."

"But not on us!" the Oysters cried,
80   Turning a little blue.
"After such kindness, that would be
  A dismal thing to do!"
"The night is fine," the Walrus said,
  "Do you admire the view?

85 "It was so kind of you to come!
  And you are very nice!"
The Carpenter said nothing but
  "Cut us another slice.
I wish you were not quite so deaf—
90   I've had to ask you twice!"

"It seems a shame," the Walrus said,
  "To play them such a trick,
After we've brought them out so far,
  And made them trot so quick!"
95 The Carpenter said nothing but
  "The butter's spread too thick!"

"I weep for you," the Walrus said;
  "I deeply sympathize."
With sobs and tears he sorted out
100   Those of the largest size,
Holding his pocket-handkerchief
  Before his streaming eyes.

"O Oysters," said the Carpenter,
  "You've had a pleasant run!
105 Shall we be trotting home again?"
  But answer came there none—
And this was scarcely odd, because
  They'd eaten every one.

1871

From The Hunting of the Snark

The Baker's Tale

They roused him[1] with muffins—they roused him with ice—
  They roused him with mustard and cress—

---

1. I.e., the Baker, a member of the Snark-hunting expedition. He had fainted when the leader of the crew, the Bellman, had mentioned that one species of Snark is called Boojum. The nameless Baker's fear of Boojums turns out later to have been well founded: at the end of the poem he encounters a Boojum and is never seen again.

They roused him with jam and judicious advice—
   They set him conundrums to guess.

5 When at length he sat up and was able to speak,
     His sad story he offered to tell;
   And the Bellman cried, "Silence! Not even a shriek!"
     And excitedly tingled his bell.[2]

   There was silence supreme! Not a shriek, not a scream,
10   Scarcely even a howl or a groan,
   As the man they called "Ho!" told his story of woe
     In an antediluvian tone.

   "My father and mother were honest though poor—"
     "Skip all that!" cried the Bellman in haste.
15 "If it once becomes dark, there's no chance of a Snark—
     We have hardly a minute to waste!"

   "I skip forty years," said the Baker, in tears,
     "And proceed without further remark
   To the day when you took me aboard of your ship
20   To help you in hunting the Snark.

   "A dear uncle of mine (after whom I was named)
     Remarked, when I bade him farewell—"
   "Oh, skip your dear uncle!" the Bellman exclaimed,
     As he angrily tingled his bell.

25 "He remarked to me then," said that mildest of men,
     " 'If your Snark be a Snark, that is right;
   Fetch it home by all means—you may serve it with greens,
     And it's handy for striking a light.

   " 'You may seek it with thimbles—and seek it with care;
30   You may hunt it with forks and hope;
   You may threaten its life with a railway-share;
     You may charm it with smiles and soap—' "

   ("That's exactly the method," the Bellman bold
     In a hasty parenthesis cried,
35 "That's exactly the way I have always been told
     That the capture of Snarks should be tried!")

   " 'But oh, beamish[3] nephew, beware of the day,
     If your Snark be a Boojum! For then
   You will softly and suddenly vanish away,
40   And never be met with again!'

   "It is this, it is this that oppresses my soul,
     When I think of my uncle's last words;

---

2. A Bellman sold muffins (carried on a tray) on city streets. He would announce his wares by "tin- gling" a bell.
3. See *Jabberwocky,* line 22 (p. 1666).

And my heart is like nothing so much as a bowl
　　Brimming over with quivering curds!

45 "It is this, it is this—" "We have had that before!"
　　The Bellman indignantly said.
And the Baker replied, "Let me say it once more.
　　It is this, it is this that I dread!

"I engage with the Snark—every night after dark—
50 　　In a dreamy, delirious fight;
I serve it with greens in those shadowy scenes,
　　And I use it for striking a light;

"But if ever I meet with a Boojum, that day,
　　In a moment (of this I am sure),
55 I shall softly and suddenly vanish away—
　　And the notion I cannot endure!"

1874–76　　　　　　　　　　　　　　　　　　　　1876

W. S. GILBERT
1836–1911

Before becoming a full-time writer William Schwenck Gilbert had worked in the civil service and as a lawyer. In 1869, he published *Bab Ballads*, a collection of narrative verses he had contributed to a magazine called *Fun*. These ballads are indeed funny but also curiously macabre in their imperturbable accounts of disasters, cannibalism, and murders. Gilbert's skills as a writer of light verse, together with his experience in devising plays for the London theater, were responsible for his triumphant success as a librettist in a series of light operas that he composed in collaboration with the eminent musician Sir Arthur Sullivan. For twenty-five years (1871–96) Gilbert and Sullivan captivated audiences in London and New York with such delightfully entertaining productions as *H.M.S. Pinafore* and *The Mikado*. Most of these operas exhibit Gilbert's satirical flair; good-hearted fun is made of the pretentious ineffectuality of the House of Lords and of corner-cutting lawyers and politicians as well as of bumbling admirals and generals. The good-hearted quality is especially evident in the happy endings of the operas: the satire is usually blunted in the finales by a jovial-spirited acceptance of characters who in earlier scenes were exposed as foolish or inept.

Gilbert was knighted in 1907 (some twenty-five years after Sullivan had received the same honor in token of Queen Victoria's interest in his "serious" music). He died on May 29, 1911, while attempting to save a young woman from drowning.

When I, Good Friends, Was Called to the Bar[1]

When I, good friends, was called to the bar,
    I'd an appetite fresh and hearty,
But I was, as many young barristers are,
    An impecunious party.
5 I'd a swallow-tail coat of a beautiful blue—
    A brief which I bought of a booby[2]—
A couple of shirts and a collar or two,
    And a ring that looked like a ruby!

CHORUS.   A couple of shirts, etc.

In Westminster Hall[3] I danced a dance,
10   Like a semidespondent fury;
For I thought I should never hit on a chance
    Of addressing a British jury—
But I soon got tired of third-class journeys,
    And dinners of bread and water;
15 So I fell in love with a rich attorney's
    Elderly, ugly daughter.

CHORUS.   So he fell in love, etc.

The rich attorney, he jumped with joy,
    And replied to my fond professions:
"You shall reap the reward of your pluck, my boy
20   At the Bailey and Middlesex Sessions.[4]
You'll soon get used to her looks," said he,
    "And a very nice girl you'll find her!
She may very well pass for forty-three
    In the dusk, with a light behind her!"

CHORUS.   She may very well, etc.

25 The rich attorney was good as his word;
    The briefs came trooping gaily,
And every day my voice was heard
    At the Sessions or Ancient Bailey.
All thieves who could my fees afford
30   Relied on my orations,
And many a burglar I've restored
    To his friends and his relations.

CHORUS.   And many a burglar, etc.

---

1. Before a breach of promise suit begins in *Trial by Jury*, the judge in this song tells the court "how I came to be a Judge."
2. A fool or dunce. "Brief": a summary of the facts of a case that is prepared (usually by a solicitor) to assist a barrister in presenting the case in court.

3. Courtrooms of the Court of Chancery in London.
4. Meetings of the county court of Middlesex (which includes London). "Bailey": the Old Bailey was a court where criminals were tried.

At length I became as rich as the Gurneys[5]—
An incubus[6] then I thought her,
35 So I threw over that rich attorney's
Elderly, ugly daughter.
The rich attorney my character high
Tried vainly to disparage—
And now, if you please, I'm ready to try
40 This Breach of Promise of Marriage!

1875

If You're Anxious for to Shine in the High Aesthetic Line[1]

Am I alone,
And unobserved? I am!
Then let me own
I'm an aesthetic sham!

5 This air severe
Is but a mere
Veneer!

This cynic smile
Is but a wile
10 Of guile!

This costume chaste
Is but good taste
Misplaced!

Let me confess!
15 A languid love for lilies does *not* blight me!
Lank limbs and haggard cheeks do *not* delight me!
I do *not* care for dirty greens
By any means.
I do *not* long for all one sees
20 That's Japanese.[2]
I am *not* fond of uttering platitudes
In stained-glass attitudes.
In short, my medievalism's affectation,
Born of a morbid love of admiration!

5. A wealthy banking family.
6. Oppressive demon as encountered in a nightmare.
1. Sung in *Patience* (act 1) by Reginald Bunthorne, a caricature of such poets of the "aesthetic school" as Oscar Wilde.
2. To admire Japanese vases and paintings had become a cult among aesthetes like the painter James McNeill Whistler (1834–1903). Bunthorne's other references are probably to Pre-Raphaelite paintings such as Rossetti's portraits of languidly gazing women (sometimes in green dresses) in which the subject might be posed in a cramped posture like a figure in a stained-glass window.

25 If you're anxious for to shine in the high aesthetic line as a man of
    culture rare,
You must get up all the germs of the transcendental terms, and plant
    them everywhere.
You must lie upon the daisies and discourse in novel phrases of your
    complicated state of mind,
The meaning doesn't matter if it's only idle chatter of a transcendental
    kind.
                And everyone will say,
30   As you walk your mystic way,
"If this young man expresses himself in terms too deep for *me*,
Why, what a very singularly deep young man this deep young man
    must be!"

Be eloquent in praise of the very dull old days which have long since
    passed away,
And convince 'em, if you can, that the reign of good Queen Anne was
    Culture's palmiest day.
35 Of course you will pooh-pooh whatever's fresh and new, and declare
    it's crude and mean,
For Art stopped short in the cultivated court of the Empress Jose-
    phine.[3]
                And everyone will say,
                As you walk your mystic way,
"If that's not good enough for him which is good enough for *me*,
40 Why, what a very cultivated kind of youth this kind of youth must
    be!"

Then a sentimental passion of a vegetable fashion must excite your
    languid spleen,
An attachment *à la* Plato[4] for a bashful young potato, or a not-too-
    French French bean!
Though the Philistines[5] may jostle, you will rank as an apostle in the
    high aesthetic band,
If you walk down Piccadilly with a poppy or a lily in your medieval
    hand.
45   And everyone will say,
                As you walk your flowery way,
"If he's content with a vegetable love which would certainly not suit
    me,
Why, what a most particularly pure young man this pure young man
    must be!"

1881

---

3. Napoleon's wife and empress of France from
1804 to 1811.
4. Platonic love denotes a spiritual relationship,
devoid of sexual desire.

5. A term used by Matthew Arnold to describe the
respectable middle classes, who predictably dis-
approved of the aesthetes' flamboyant behavior.

When Britain Really Ruled the Waves[1]

When Britain really ruled the waves
   (In good Queen Bess's time)—
The House of Peers made no pretense
To intellectual eminence,
5   Or scholarship sublime;
Yet Britain won her proudest bays°   *honors*
In good Queen Bess's glorious days!

CHORUS.   Yes, Britain won, etc.

When Wellington thrashed Bonaparte,
   As every child can tell,
10 The House of Peers, throughout the war,
Did nothing in particular,
   And did it very well:
Yet Britain set the world ablaze
In good King George's glorious days![2]

CHORUS.   Yes, Britain set, etc.

15 And while the House of Peers withholds
   Its legislative hand,
And noble statesmen do not itch
To interfere with matters which
   They do not understand,
20 As bright will shine Great Britain's rays
As in King George's glorious days!

CHORUS.   As bright will shine, etc.

1882

---

1. From *Iolanthe* (act 2), sung by Lord Mount-ararat, following a discussion about whether or not members of the House of Lords should obtain their titles by competitive examination instead of by inheritance. His Lordship prefaces his song by affirming "that if there is any institution in Great Britain which is not susceptible of any improvement at all, it is the House of Peers!"
2. At the time of the Battle of Waterloo (1815), Britain's king was George III (1760–1820).

Victorian Issues

EVOLUTION

One of the most dramatic controversies in the Victorian age concerned theories of evolution. This controversy exploded into prominence in 1859 when Charles Darwin's *Origin of Species* was published, but it had been rumbling for many years previously. Sir Charles Lyell's *Principles of Geology* (1830) and Robert Chambers's popular book *Vestiges of Creation* (1843–46) had already raised issues that Tennyson aired in his *In Memoriam* (1850). It was Darwin, however, with his monumental marshaling of evidence to establish his theory of natural selection, who finally brought the topic fully into the open, and the public, as well as the experts, took sides.

The opposition aroused by Darwin's treatise came from two different quarters. The first consisted of some of his fellow scientists, who affirmed that his theory was unsound. The second consisted of religious leaders who attacked his theory because it seemed to contradict a literal interpretation of the Bible. Sometimes the two kinds of opposition combined forces, as in 1860 when his scientific opponents selected Bishop Wilberforce to be their spokesman in spearheading their attack on *The Origin of Species*. In replying to such attacks, Darwin had the good fortune to be supported by two of the ablest popularizers of science in his day, T. H. Huxley and John Tyndall. Moreover, although shy by temperament, Darwin was himself (as Tyndall affirms and the selections printed here will illustrate) an exceptionally effective expositor of his own theories.

CHARLES DARWIN

Charles Darwin (1809–1882) developed an interest in geology and biology at Cambridge, where he was studying to become a clergyman. Aided by a private income, he resolved to devote the rest of his life to scientific research. The observations he made during a long voyage to the South Seas on the HMS *Beagle* (on which he served as a naturalist) led Darwin to construct hypotheses about evolution. In 1858, more than twenty years after his return to England from his voyage, he ventured to submit a paper developing his theory of the origin of species. A year later, when his theory appeared in book form, as *The Origin of Species*, Darwin emerged as a famous and controversial figure.

From The Origin of Species

Struggle for Existence

We will now discuss in a little more detail the struggle for existence. . . . Nothing is easier than to admit in words the truth of the universal struggle for life, or more difficult—at least I have found it so—than constantly to bear this conclusion in mind. Yet unless it be thoroughly engrained in the mind, the whole economy of nature, with every fact on distribution, rarity, abundance, extinction, and variation, will be dimly seen or quite misunderstood. We behold the face of nature bright with gladness, we often see superabundance of food; we do not see or we forget, that the birds which are idly singing round us mostly live on insects or seeds, and are thus constantly destroying life; or we forget how largely these songsters, or their eggs, or their nestlings, are destroyed by birds and beasts of prey; we do not always bear in mind, that, though food may be now superabundant, it is not so at all seasons of each recurring year.

THE TERM, STRUGGLE FOR EXISTENCE, USED IN A LARGE SENSE

I should premise that I use this term in a large and metaphorical sense including dependence of one being on another, and including (which is more important) not only the life of the individual, but success in leaving progeny. Two canine animals, in a time of dearth, may be truly said to struggle with each other which shall get food and live. But a plant on the edge of a desert is said to struggle for life against the drought, though more properly it should be said to be dependent on the moisture. A plant which annually produces a thousand seeds, of which only one of an average comes to maturity, may be more truly said to struggle with the plants of the same and other kinds which already clothe the ground. The mistletoe is dependent on the apple and a few other trees, but can only in a farfetched sense be said to struggle with these trees, for, if too many of these parasites grow on the same tree, it languishes and dies. But several seedling mistletoes, growing close together on the same branch, may more truly be said to struggle with each other. As the mistletoe is disseminated by birds, its existence depends on them; and it may methodically be said to struggle with other fruit-bearing plants, in tempting the birds to devour and thus disseminate its seeds. In these several senses, which pass into each other, I use for convenience' sake the general term of Struggle for Existence.

GEOMETRICAL RATIO OF INCREASE

A struggle for existence inevitably follows from the high rate at which all organic beings tend to increase. Every being, which during its natural lifetime produces several eggs or seeds, must suffer destruction during some period of its life, and during some season or occasional year, otherwise, on the principle of geometrical increase, its numbers would quickly become so inordinately great that no country could support the product. Hence, as more individuals are produced than can possibly survive, there must in every case be a struggle for existence, either one individual with another of the same species, or with the individuals of distinct species, or with the physical conditions of life. It is the doctrine of Malthus[1] applied with manifold force to the whole animal and vegetable kingdoms; for in this case there can be no artificial increase of food, and no prudential restraint from marriage.

1. Thomas Robert Malthus (1766–1834), British social theorist who argued that because the population, increasing geometrically, would grow beyond the means of subsistence, which increased arithmetically, poverty, disease, and starvation were necessary natural checks.

Although some species may be now increasing, more or less rapidly, in numbers, all cannot do so, for the world would not hold them.

There is no exception to the rule that every organic being naturally increases at so high a rate, that, if not destroyed, the earth would soon be covered by the progeny of a single pair. Even slow-breeding man has doubled in twenty-five years, and at this rate, in less than a thousand years, there would literally not be standing-room for his progeny. Linnæus[2] has calculated that if an annual plant produced only two seeds—and there is no plant so unproductive as this—and their seedlings next year produced two, and so on, then in twenty years there should be a million plants. The elephant is reckoned the slowest breeder of all known animals, and I have taken some pains to estimate its probable minimum rate of natural increase; it will be safest to assume that it begins breeding when thirty years old, and goes on breeding till ninety years old, bringing forth six young in the interval, and surviving till one hundred years old; if this be so, after a period of from 740 to 750 years there would be nearly nineteen million elephants alive, descended from the first pair.

* * *

COMPLEX RELATIONS OF ALL ANIMALS AND PLANTS TO EACH OTHER IN THE STRUGGLE FOR EXISTENCE

Many cases are on record showing how complex and unexpected are the checks and relations between organic beings, which have to struggle together in the same country.

* * *

Nearly all our orchidaceous plants absolutely require the visits of insects to remove their pollen-masses and thus to fertilise them. I find from experiments that humble-bees are almost indispensable to the fertilisation of the heartsease (Viola tricolor), for other bees do not visit this flower. I have also found that the visits of bees are necessary for the fertilisation of some kinds of clover; for instance, 20 heads of Dutch clover (Trifolium repens) yielded 2,290 seeds, but 20 other heads protected from bees produced not one. Again, 100 heads of red clover (T. pratense) produced 2,700 seeds, but the same number of protected heads produced not a single seed. Humble-bees alone visit red clover, as other bees cannot reach the nectar. It has been suggested that moths may fertilise the clovers; but I doubt whether they could do so in the case of the red clover, from their weight not being sufficient to depress the wing petals. Hence we may infer as highly probable that, if the whole genus of humble-bees became extinct or very rare in England, the heartsease and red clover would become very rare, or wholly disappear. The number of humble-bees in any district depends in a great measure upon the number of field-mice, which destroy their combs and nests; and Col. Newman, who has long attended to the habits of humble-bees, believes that "more than two-thirds of them are thus destroyed all over England." Now the number of mice is largely dependent, as every one knows, on the number of cats; and Col. Newman says, "Near villages and small towns I have found

2. Carl Linnaeus (1707–1778), Swedish naturalist who developed the binomial system for naming plants and animals.

the nests of humble-bees more numerous than elsewhere, which I attribute to the number of cats that destroy the mice." Hence it is quite credible that the presence of a feline animal in large numbers in a district might determine, through the intervention first of mice and then of bees, the frequency of certain flowers in that district!

In the case of every species, many different checks, acting at different periods of life, and during different seasons or years, probably come into play; some one check or some few being generally the most potent; but all will concur in determining the average number or even the existence of the species. In some cases it can be shown that widely-different checks act on the same species in different districts. When we look at the plants and bushes clothing an entangled bank, we are tempted to attribute their proportional numbers and kinds to what we call chance. But how false a view is this! Every one has heard that when an American forest is cut down a very different vegetation springs up; but it has been observed that ancient Indian ruins in the Southern United States, which must formerly have been cleared of trees, now display the same beautiful diversity and proportion of kinds as in the surrounding virgin forest. What a struggle must have gone on during long centuries between the several kinds of trees each annually scattering its seeds by the thousand; what war between insect and insect—between insects, snails, and other animals with birds and beasts of prey—all striving to increase, all feeding on each other, or on the trees, their seeds and seedlings, or on the other plants which first clothed the ground and thus checked the growth of the trees! Throw up a handful of feathers, and all fall to the ground according to definite laws; but how simple is the problem where each shall fall compared to that of the action and reaction of the innumerable plants and animals which have determined, in the course of centuries, the proportional numbers and kinds of trees now growing on the old Indian ruins!

Recapitulation and Conclusion[3]

I see no good reason why the views given in this volume should shock the religious feelings of any one. It is satisfactory, as showing how transient such impressions are, to remember that the greatest discovery ever made by man, namely, the law of the attraction of gravity, was also attacked by Leibnitz,[4] "as subversive of natural, and inferentially of revealed, religion." A celebrated author and divine has written to me that "he has gradually learnt to see that it is just as noble a conception of the Deity to believe that He created a few original forms capable of self-development into other and needful forms, as to believe that He required a fresh act of creation to supply the voids caused by the action of His laws."

Why, it may be asked, until recently did nearly all the most eminent living naturalists and geologists disbelieve in the mutability of species? It cannot be asserted that organic beings in a state of nature are subject to no variation; it cannot be proved that the amount of variation in the course of long ages is a limited quality; no clear distinction has been, or can be, drawn between species and well-marked varieties. It cannot be maintained that species when

---

3. From chap. 15.
4. Gottfried Wilhelm Leibniz (1646–1716),

German philosopher and mathematician, contemporary of Isaac Newton.

intercrossed are invariably sterile, and varieties invariably fertile; or that sterility is a special endowment and sign of creation. The belief that species were immutable productions was almost unavoidable as long as the history of the world was thought to be of short duration; and now that we have acquired some idea of the lapse of time, we are too apt to assume, without proof, that the geological record is so perfect that it would have afforded us plain evidence of the mutation of species, if they had undergone mutation.

But the chief cause of our natural unwillingness to admit that one species has given birth to clear and distinct species, is that we are always slow in admitting great changes of which we do not see the steps. The difficulty is the same as that felt by so many geologists, when Lyell[5] first insisted that long lines of inland cliffs had been formed, and great valleys excavated, by the agencies which we see still at work. The mind cannot possibly grasp the full meaning of the term of even a million years; it cannot add up and perceive the full effects of many slight variations, accumulated during an almost infinite number of generations.

Although I am fully convinced of the truth of the views given in this volume under the form of an abstract, I by no means expect to convince experienced naturalists whose minds are stocked with a multitude of facts all viewed, during a long course of years, from a point of view directly opposite to mine. It is so easy to hide our ignorance under such expressions as the "plan of creation," "unity of design," &c., and to think that we give an explanation when we only re-state a fact. Any one whose disposition leads him to attach more weight to unexplained difficulties than to the explanation of a certain number of facts will certainly reject the theory. A few naturalists, endowed with much flexibility of mind, and who have already begun to doubt the immutability of species, may be influenced by this volume; but I look with confidence to the future,—to young and rising naturalists, who will be able to view both sides of the question with impartiality. Whoever is led to believe that species are mutable will do good service by conscientiously expressing his conviction; for thus only can the load of prejudice by which this subject is overwhelmed be removed.

* * *

It may be asked how far I extend the doctrine of the modification of species. The question is difficult to answer, because the more distinct the forms are which we consider, by so much the arguments in favour of community of descent become fewer in number and less in force. But some arguments of the greatest weight extend very far. All the members of whole classes are connected together by a chain of affinities, and all can be classed on the same principle, in groups subordinate to groups. Fossil remains sometimes tend to fill up very wide intervals between existing orders.

Organs in a rudimentary condition plainly show that an early progenitor had the organ in a fully developed condition; and this in some cases implies an enormous amount of modification in the descendants. Throughout whole classes various structures are formed on the same pattern, and at a very early

5. Charles Lyell (1797–1875), geologist whose book *Principles of Geology* (1830–33) was important in dissociating geological theory from the Bible and in establishing nature as the record of the earth's history, which he saw as a record of lengthy and gradual change rather than swift catastrophic events.

age the embryos closely resemble each other. Therefore I cannot doubt that the theory of descent with modification embraces all the members of the same great class or kingdom. I believe that animals are descended from at most only four or five progenitors, and plants from an equal or lesser number.

Analogy would lead me one step farther, namely, to the belief that all animals and plants are descended from some one prototype. But analogy may be a deceitful guide. Nevertheless all living things have much in common, in their chemical composition, their cellular structure, their laws of growth, and their liability to injurious influences. We see this even in so trifling a fact as that the same poison often similarly affects plants and animals; or that the poison secreted by the gall-fly produces monstrous growths on the wild rose or oak-tree. With all organic beings excepting perhaps some of the very lowest, sexual production seems to be essentially similar. With all, as far as is at present known the germinal vesicle is the same; so that all organisms start from a common origin. If we look even to the two main divisions—namely, to the animal and vegetable kingdoms—certain low forms are so far intermediate in character that naturalists have disputed to which kingdom they should be referred. As Professor Asa Gray[6] has remarked, "the spores and other reproductive bodies of many of the lower algae may claim to have first a characteristically animal, and then an unequivocally vegetable existence." Therefore, on the principle of natural selection with divergence of character, it does not seem incredible that, from such low and intermediate form, both animals and plants may have been developed; and, if we admit this, we must likewise admit that all the organic beings which have ever lived on this earth may be descended from some one primordial form.

* * *

When we feel assured that all the individuals of the same species, and all the closely allied species of most genera, have within a not very remote period descended from one parent, and have migrated from some one birth-place; and when we better know the many means of migration, then, by the light which geology now throws, and will continue to throw, on former changes of climate and of the level of the land, we shall surely be enabled to trace in an admirable manner the former migrations of the inhabitants of the whole world. Even at present, by comparing the differences between the inhabitants of the sea on the opposite sides of a continent, and the nature of the various inhabitants on that continent, in relation to their apparent means of immigration, some light can be thrown on ancient geography.

The noble science of Geology loses glory from the extreme imperfection of the record. The crust of the earth with its imbedded remains must not be looked at as a well-filled museum, but as a poor collection made at hazard and at rare intervals. The accumulation of each great fossiliferous formation will be recognised as having depended on an unusual concurrence of favourable circumstances, and the blank intervals between the successive stages as having been of vast duration. But we shall be able to gauge with some security the duration of these intervals by a comparison of the preceding and succeeding organic forms. We must be cautious in attempting to correlate

6. American botanist (1810–1888).

as strictly contemporaneous two formations, which do not include many identical species, by the general succession of the forms of life. As species are produced and exterminated by slowly acting and still existing causes, and not by miraculous acts of creation; and as the most important of all causes of organic change is one which is almost independent of altered and perhaps suddenly altered physical conditions, namely, the mutual relation of organism to organism,—the improvement of one organism entailing the improvement or the extermination of others; it follows, that the amount of organic change in the fossils of consecutive formations probably serves as a fair measure of the relative though not actual lapse of time. A number of species, however, keeping in a body might remain for a long period unchanged, whilst within the same period several of these species by migrating into new countries and coming into competition with foreign associates, might become modified; so that we must not overrate the accuracy of organic change as a measure of time.

In the future I see open fields for far more important researches. Psychology will be securely based on the foundation already well laid by Mr. Herbert Spencer,[7] that of the necessary acquirement of each mental power and capacity by gradation. Much light will be thrown on the origin of man and his history.

Authors of the highest eminence seem to be fully satisfied with the view that each species has been independently created. To my mind it accords better with what we know of the laws impressed on matter by the Creator, that the production and extinction of the past and present inhabitants of the world should have been due to secondary causes, like those determining the birth and death of the individual. When I view all beings not as special creations, but as the lineal descendants of some few beings which lived long before the first bed of the Cambrian system was deposited, they seem to me to become ennobled. Judging from the past, we may safely infer that not one living species will transmit its unaltered likeness to a distant futurity. And of the species now living very few will transmit progeny of any kind to a far distant futurity; for the manner in which all organic beings are grouped, shows that the greater number of species in each genus, and all the species in many genera, have left no descendants, but have become utterly extinct. We can so far take a prophetic glance into futurity as to foretell that it will be the common and widely-spread species, belonging to the larger and dominant groups within each class, which will ultimately prevail and procreate new and dominant species. As all the living forms of life are the lineal descendants of those which lived long before the Cambrian epoch, we may feel certain that the ordinary succession by generation has never once been broken, and that no cataclysm has desolated the whole world. Hence we may look with some confidence to a secure future of great length. And as natural selection works solely by and for the good of each being, all corporeal and mental endowments will tend to progress towards perfection.

It is interesting to contemplate a tangled bank, clothed with many plants of many kinds, with birds singing on the bushes, with various insects flitting about, and with worms crawling through the damp earth, and to reflect that these elaborately constructed forms, so different from each other, and

7. Social theorist (1820–1903), who developed the concept of social Darwinism.

dependent upon each other in so complex a manner, have all been produced by laws acting around us. These laws, taken in the largest sense, being Growth with Reproduction; Inheritance which is almost implied by reproduction; Variability from the indirect and direct action of the conditions of life, and from use and disuse: a Ratio of Increase so high as to lead to a Struggle for Life, and as a consequence to Natural Selection, entailing Divergence of Character and the Extinction of less-improved forms. Thus, from the war of nature, from famine and death, the most exalted object which we are capable of conceiving, namely, the production of the higher animals, directly follows. There is grandeur in this view of life, with its several powers, having been originally breathed by the Creator into a few forms or into one; and that, whilst this planet has gone cycling on according to the fixed law of gravity, from so simple a beginning endless forms most beautiful and most wonderful have been, and are being evolved.

1859

CHARLES DARWIN

After he published *The Origin of Species*, Darwin wrote several treatises, some of which develop and clarify the theory of *The Origin of Species*. One of these works, *The Descent of Man* (1871), was especially provocative in its stress on the similarities between humans and animals and in its naturalistic explanations of the beautiful colorings of birds, insects, and flowers.

From The Descent of Man

[NATURAL SELECTION AND SEXUAL SELECTION][1]

A brief summary will here be sufficient to recall to the reader's mind the more salient points in this work. Many of the views which have been advanced are highly speculative, and some no doubt will prove erroneous; but I have in every case given the reasons which have led me to one view rather than to another. It seemed worth while to try how far the principle of evolution would throw light on some of the more complex problems in the natural history of man. False facts are highly injurious to the progress of science, for they often long endure; but false views, if supported by some evidence, do little harm, as everyone takes a salutary pleasure in proving their falseness; and when this is done, one path towards error is closed and the road to truth is often at the same time opened.

The main conclusion arrived at in this work, and now held by many naturalists who are well competent to form a sound judgment, is that man is descended from some less highly organized form. The grounds upon which

1. From chap. 21.

this conclusion rests will never be shaken, for the close similarity between man and the lower animals in embryonic development, as well as in innumerable points of structure and constitution, both of high and of the most trifling importance—the rudiments which he retains, and the abnormal reversions to which he is occasionally liable—are facts which cannot be disputed. They have long been known, but until recently they told us nothing with respect to the origin of man. Now when viewed by the light of our knowledge of the whole organic world, their meaning is unmistakable. The great principle of evolution stands up clear and firm, when these groups of facts are considered in connection with others, such as the mutual affinities of the members of the same group, their geographical distribution in past and present times, and their geological succession. It is incredible that all these facts should speak falsely. He who is not content to look, like a savage, at the phenomena of nature as disconnected cannot any longer believe that man is the work of a separate act of creation. He will be forced to admit that the close resemblance of the embryo of man to that, for instance, of a dog—the construction of his skull, limbs, and whole frame, independently of the uses to which the parts may be put, on the same plan with that of other mammals—the occasional reappearance of various structures, for instance of several distinct muscles, which man does not normally possess, but which are common to the Quadrumana[2]—and a crowd of analogous facts—all point in the plainest manner to the conclusion that man is the codescendant with other mammals of a common progenitor.

*   *   *

By considering the embryological structure of man—the homologies which he presents with the lower animals, the rudiments which he retains, and the reversions to which he is liable—we can partly recall in imagination the former condition of our early progenitors; and can approximately place them in their proper position in the zoological series. We thus learn that man is descended from a hairy quadruped, furnished with a tail and pointed ears, probably arboreal in its habits, and an inhabitant of the Old World. This creature, if its whole structure had been examined by a naturalist, would have been classed amongst the Quadrumana, as surely as would the common and still more ancient progenitor of the Old and New World monkeys. The Quadrumana and all the higher mammals are probably derived from an ancient marsupial animal, and this through a long line of diversified forms, either from some reptile-like or some amphibianlike creature, and this again from some fishlike animal. In the dim obscurity of the past we can see that the early progenitor of all the Vertebrata must have been an aquatic animal, provided with branchae, with the two sexes united in the same individual, and with the most important organs of the body (such as the brain and heart) imperfectly developed. This animal seems to have been more like the larvae of our existing marine ascidians[3] than any other known form.

*   *   *

2. Animals, such as monkeys, whose hind feet and forefeet can be used as hands—hence "four-handed."

3. Part of a group of marine animals called tunicata, or popularly "sea squirts," sometimes assumed to be ancestors of the vertebrate animals.

Sexual selection has been treated at great length in these volumes; for, as I have attempted to show, it has played an important part in the history of the organic world.

           *   *   *

The belief in the power of sexual selection rests chiefly on the following considerations. The characters which we have the best reason for supposing to have been thus acquired are confined to one sex; and this alone renders it probable that they are in some way connected with the act of reproduction. These characters in innumerable instances are fully developed only at maturity; and often during only a part of the year, which is always the breeding season. The males (passing over a few exceptional cases) are the most active in courtship; they are the best armed, and are rendered the most attractive in various ways. It is to be especially observed that the males display their attractions with elaborate care in the presence of the females; and that they rarely or never display them excepting during the season of love. It is incredible that all this display should be purposeless. Lastly we have distinct evidence with some quadrupeds and birds that the individuals of the one sex are capable of feeling a strong antipathy or preference for certain individuals of the opposite sex.

Bearing these facts in mind, and not forgetting the marked results of man's unconscious selection, it seems to me almost certain that if the individuals of one sex were during a long series of generations to prefer pairing with certain individuals of the other sex, characterized in some peculiar manner, the offspring would slowly but surely become modified in this same manner. I have not attempted to conceal that, excepting when the males are more numerous than the females, or when polygamy prevails, it is doubtful how the more attractive males succeed in leaving a larger number of offspring to inherit their superiority in ornaments or other charms than the less attractive males; but I have shown that this would probably follow from the females—especially the more vigorous females which would be the first to breed, preferring not only the more attractive but at the same time the more vigorous and victorious males.

Although we have some positive evidence that birds appreciate bright and beautiful objects, as with the bowerbirds of Australia, and although they certainly appreciate the power of song, yet I fully admit that it is an astonishing fact that the females of many birds and some mammals should be endowed with sufficient taste for what has apparently been effected through sexual selection; and this is even more astonishing in the case of reptiles, fish, and insects. But we really know very little about the minds of the lower animals. It cannot be supposed that male birds of paradise or peacocks, for instance, should take so much pains in erecting, spreading, and vibrating their beautiful plumes before the females for no purpose. We should remember the fact given on excellent authority in a former chapter, namely that several peahens, when debarred from an admired male, remained widows during a whole season rather than pair with another bird.

Nevertheless I know of no fact in natural history more wonderful than that the female argus pheasant should be able to appreciate the exquisite shading of the ball-and-socket ornaments and the elegant patterns on the wing feathers of the male. He who thinks that the male was created as he now exists must admit that the great plumes, which prevent the wings from being used for flight, and which, as well as the primary feathers, are displayed in a manner quite peculiar to this one species during the act of courtship, and at no other time, were given to him as an ornament. If so, he must likewise admit that the female was created and endowed with the capacity of appreciating such ornaments. I differ only in the conviction that the male argus pheasant acquired his beauty gradually, through the females having preferred during many generations the more highly ornamented males; the aesthetic capacity of the females having been advanced through exercise or habit in the same manner as our own taste is gradually improved. In the male, through the fortunate chance of a few feathers not having been modified, we can distinctly see how simple spots with a little fulvous[4] shading on one side might have been developed by small and graduated steps into the wonderful ball-and-socket ornaments; and it is probable that they were actually thus developed.

* * *

He who admits the principle of sexual selection will be led to the remarkable conclusion that the cerebral system not only regulates most of the existing functions of the body, but has indirectly influenced the progressive development of various bodily structures and of certain mental qualities. Courage, pugnacity, perseverance, strength and size of body, weapons of all kinds, musical organs, both vocal and instrumental, bright colors, stripes and marks, and ornamental appendages have all been indirectly gained by the one sex or the other, through the influence of love and jealousy, through the appreciation of the beautiful in sound, color or form, and through the exertion of a choice; and these powers of the mind manifestly depend on the development of the cerebral system.

* * *

The main conclusion arrived at in this work, namely that man is descended from some lowly-organized form, will, I regret to think, be highly distasteful to many persons. But there can hardly be a doubt that we are descended from barbarians. The astonishment which I felt on first seeing a party of Fuegians[5] on a wild and broken shore will never be forgotten by me, for the reflection at once rushed into my mind—such were our ancestors. These men were absolutely naked and bedaubed with paint, their long hair was tangled, their mouths frothed with excitement, and their expression was wild, startled, and distrustful. They possessed hardly any arts, and like wild animals lived on what they could catch; they had no government, and were merciless to everyone not of their own small tribe. He who has seen a savage in his native land will not feel much shame, if forced to acknowledge that the blood of some more humble creature flows in his veins. For my own part I would as soon be descended from that heroic little monkey, who braved his dreaded enemy in order to save the life of his keeper; or from that old baboon, who, descending from the mountains, carried away in triumph his

4. Dull yellow.
5. Natives inhabiting the islands off the southern tip of South America, Tierra del Fuego, which Darwin had visited in 1832. See his *Voyage of the Beagle*, chap. 10.

young comrade from a crowd of astonished dogs[6]—as from a savage who delights to torture his enemies, offers up bloody sacrifices, practices infanticide without remorse, treats his wives like slaves, knows no decency, and is haunted by the grossest superstitions.

Man may be excused for feeling some pride at having risen, though not through his own exertions, to the very summit of the organic scale; and the fact of his having thus risen, instead of having been aboriginally placed there, may give him hopes for a still higher destiny in the distant future. But we are not here concerned with hopes or fears, only with the truth as far as our reason allows us to discover it. I have given the evidence to the best of my ability; and we must acknowledge, as it seems to me, that man with all his noble qualities, with sympathy which feels for the most debased, with benevolence which extends not only to other men but to the humblest living creature, with his godlike intellect which has penetrated into the movements and constitution of the solar system—with all these exalted powers—Man still bears in his bodily frame the indelible stamp of his lowly origin.

1871

6. Incidents described in chap. 4 to demonstrate that animals may be endowed with a moral sense.

LEONARD HUXLEY

At meetings of the British Association for the Advancement of Science, the reading of a paper is followed by a discussion. In 1860, at Oxford, this discussion developed into a debate between Thomas Henry Huxley (1825–1895), a defender of Darwin's theories, and Bishop Samuel Wilberforce (1805–1873). Although he had majored in mathematics as an undergraduate, Wilberforce could hardly lay claim to be a scientist. He was willing, nevertheless, to serve as a spokesperson for those scientists who disagreed with *The Origin of Species,* and he reportedly came to the meeting ready to "smash Darwin." The bishop's principal qualifications for this role were his great powers as a smoothly persuasive orator (he was commonly known by his detractors as "Soapy Sam"), but he met more than his match in Huxley.

Because no complete transcript of this celebrated debate was made at the time, Huxley's son Leonard (1860–1933), in writing his father's biography, had to reconstruct the scene by combining quotations from reports made by magazine writers and other witnesses. The account given here is from chapter 14.

From The Life and Letters
of Thomas Henry Huxley

[THE HUXLEY-WILBERFORCE DEBATE AT OXFORD]

The famous Oxford Meeting of 1860 was of no small importance in Huxley's career. It was not merely that he helped to save a great cause from being stifled under misrepresentation and ridicule—that he helped to extort for it a fair hearing; it was now that he first made himself known in popular estimation as a dangerous adversary in debate—a personal force in the world of science which could not be neglected. From this moment he entered the front fighting line in the most exposed quarter of the field. * * *

It was the merest chance, as I have already said, that Huxley attended the meeting of the section that morning. Dr. Draper of New York was to read a paper on the *Intellectual Development of Europe considered with reference to the views of Mr. Darwin.* "I can still hear," writes one who was present, "the American accents of Dr. Draper's opening address when he asked 'Air we a fortuitous concourse of atoms?' " However, it was not to hear him, but the eloquence of the Bishop, that the members of the Association crowded in such numbers into the Lecture Room of the Museum, that this, the appointed meeting place of the section, had to be abandoned for the long west room, since cut in two by a partition for the purposes of the library. It was not term time, nor were the general public admitted; nevertheless the room was crowded to suffocation long before the protagonists appeared on the scene, 700 persons or more managing to find places. The very windows by which the room was lighted down the length of its west side were packed with ladies, whose white handkerchiefs, waving and fluttering in the air at the end of the Bishop's speech, were an unforgettable factor in the acclamation of the crowd.

On the east side between the two doors was the platform. Professor Henslow, the President of the section, took his seat in the center; upon his right was the Bishop, and beyond him again Dr. Draper; on his extreme left was Mr. Dingle, a clergyman from Lanchester, near Durham, with Sir J. Hooker and Sir J. Lubbock in front of him, and nearer the center, Professor Beale of King's College, London, and Huxley.

The clergy, who shouted lustily for the Bishop, were massed in the middle of the room; behind them in the northwest corner a knot of undergraduates (one of these was T. H. Green, who listened but took no part in the cheering) had gathered together beside Professor Brodie, ready to lift their voices, poor minority though they were, for the opposite party. Close to them stood one of the few men among the audience already in Holy orders, who joined in— and indeed led—the cheers for the Darwinians.

So "Dr. Draper droned out his paper, turning first to the right hand and then to the left, of course bringing in a reference to the *Origin of Species* which set the ball rolling."

An hour or more that paper lasted, and then discussion began. The President "wisely announced *in limine*[1] that none who had not valid arguments to bring forward on one side or the other would be allowed to address the meeting; a caution that proved necessary, for no fewer than four combatants had their utterances burked by him, because of their indulgence in vague declamation."

> First spoke (writes Professor Farrar) a layman from Brompton, who gave his name as being one of the Committee of the (newly formed) Economic section of the Association. He, in a stentorian voice, let off his theological venom. Then jumped up Richard Greswell with a thin voice, saying much the same, but speaking as a scholar; but we did not merely want any theological discussion, so we shouted them down. Then

1. As a starting point (Latin).

a Mr. Dingle got up and tried to show that Darwin would have done much better if he had taken him into consultation. He used the blackboard and began a mathematical demonstration on the question—"Let this point A be man, and let that point B be the mawnkey." He got no further; he was shouted down with cries of "mawnkey." None of these had spoken more than three minutes. It was when these were shouted down that Henslow said he must demand that the discussion should rest on *scientific* grounds only.

Then there were calls for the Bishop, but he rose and said he understood his friend Professor Beale had something to say first. Beale, who was an excellent histologist,[2] spoke to the effect that the new theory ought to meet with fair discussion, but added, with great modesty, that he himself had not sufficient knowledge to discuss the subject adequately. Then the Bishop spoke the speech that you know, and the question about his mother being an ape, or his grandmother.

From the scientific point of view, the speech was of small value. It was evident from his mode of handling the subject that he had been "crammed up to the throat," and knew nothing at first hand; he used no argument beyond those to be found in his *Quarterly* article, which appeared a few days later, and is now admitted to have been inspired by Owen.[3] "He ridiculed Darwin badly and Huxley savagely; but," confesses one of his strongest opponents, "all in such dulcet tones, so persuasive a manner, and in such well turned periods, that I who had been inclined to blame the President for allowing a discussion that could serve no scientific purpose, now forgave him from the bottom of my heart."

The Bishop spoke thus "for full half an hour with inimitable spirit, emptiness and unfairness." "In a light, scoffing tone, florid and fluent, he assured us there was nothing in the idea of evolution; rock pigeons were what rock pigeons had always been. Then, turning to his antagonist with a smiling insolence, he begged to know, was it through his grandfather or his grandmother that he claimed his descent from a monkey?"

This was the fatal mistake of his speech. Huxley instantly grasped the tactical advantage which the descent to personalities gave him. He turned to Sir Benjamin Brodie, who was sitting beside him, and emphatically striking his hand upon his knee, exclaimed, "The Lord hath delivered him into mine hands." The bearing of the exclamation did not dawn upon Sir Benjamin until after Huxley had completed his "forcible and eloquent" answer to the scientific part of the Bishop's argument, and proceeded to make his famous retort.

On this (continues the writer in *Macmillan's Magazine*) Mr. Huxley slowly and deliberately arose. A slight tall figure, stern and pale, very quiet and very grave, he stood before us and spoke those tremendous words—words which no one seems sure of now, nor, I think, could remember just after they were spoken, for their meaning took away our breath, though it left us in no doubt as to what it was. He was not

---

2. A biologist specializing in the study of the minute structure of the tissues of plants and animals.
3. Sir Richard Owen (1804–1892), a leading zoologist and paleontologist who was opposed to Darwin's theories.

ashamed to have a monkey for his ancestor; but he would be ashamed to be connected with a man who used great gifts to obscure the truth. No one doubted his meaning, and the effect was tremendous. One lady fainted and had to be carried out; I, for one, jumped out of my seat.

The fullest and probably most accurate account of these concluding words is the following, from a letter of the late John Richard Green, then an undergraduate, to his friend, afterwards Professor Boyd Dawkins:

> I asserted—and I repeat—that a man has no reason to be ashamed of having an ape for his grandfather. If there were an ancestor whom I should feel shame in recalling it would rather be a man—a man of restless and versatile intellect—who, not content with an equivocal success in his own sphere of activity, plunges into scientific questions with which he has no real acquaintance, only to obscure them by an aimless rhetoric, and distract the attention of his hearers from the real point at issue by eloquent digressions and skilled appeals to religious prejudice.

The result of this encounter, though a check to the other side, cannot, of course, be represented as an immediate and complete triumph for evolutionary doctrine. This was precluded by the character and temper of the audience, most of whom were less capable of being convinced by the arguments than shocked by the boldness of the retort, although, being gentlefolk, as Professor Farrar remarks, they were disposed to admit on reflection that the Bishop had erred on the score of taste and good manners. Nevertheless, it was a noticeable feature of the occasion, Sir M. Foster tells me, that when Huxley rose he was received coldly, just a cheer of encouragement from his friends, the audience as a whole not joining in it. But as he made his points the applause grew and widened, until, when he sat down, the cheering was not very much less than that given to the Bishop. To that extent he carried an unwilling audience with him by the force of his speech. The debate on the ape question, however, was continued elsewhere during the next two years, and the evidence was completed by the unanswerable demonstrations of Sir W. H. Flower at the Cambridge meeting of the Association in 1862.

The importance of the Oxford meeting lay in the open resistance that was made to authority, at a moment when even a drawn battle was hardly less effectual than acknowledged victory. Instead of being crushed under ridicule, the new theories secured a hearing, all the wider, indeed, for the startling nature of their defense.

1901

SIR EDMUND GOSSE

Philip Henry Gosse (1810–1888) was a zoologist of some repute and also an ardent adherent of a strict Protestant sect, the Plymouth Brethren. To reconcile his scientific knowledge with his fundamentalist position in religion, Gosse published a book called *Omphalos*, which pleased no one. His dilemma is described by his son, the literary critic Sir Edmund Gosse (1849–1928), in an autobiography published in 1907. This selection is from chapter 5.

From Father and Son

[THE DILEMMA OF THE FUNDAMENTALIST AND SCIENTIST]

So, through my Father's brain, in that year of scientific crisis, 1857, there rushed two kinds of thought, each absorbing, each convincing, yet totally irreconcilable. There is a peculiar agony in the paradox that truth has two forms, each of them indisputable, yet each antagonistic to the other. It was this discovery, that there were two theories of physical life, each of which was true, but the truth of each incompatible with the truth of the other, which shook the spirit of my Father with perturbation. It was not, really, a paradox, it was a fallacy, if he could only have known it, but he allowed the turbid volume of superstition to drown the delicate stream of reason. He took one step in the service of truth, and then he drew back in an agony, and accepted the servitude of error.

This was the great moment in the history of thought when the theory of the mutability of species was preparing to throw a flood of light upon all departments of human speculation and action. It was becoming necessary to stand emphatically in one army or the other. Lyell was surrounding himself with disciples, who were making strides in the direction of discovery. Darwin had long been collecting facts with regard to the variation of animals and plants. Hooker and Wallace, Asa Gray and even Agassiz, each in his own sphere, were coming closer and closer to a perception of that secret which was first to reveal itself clearly to the patient and humble genius of Darwin. In the year before, in 1856, Darwin, under pressure from Lyell, had begun that modest statement of the new revelation, that "abstract of an essay," which developed so mightily into *The Origin of Species*. Wollaston's *Variation of Species* had just appeared, and had been a nine days' wonder in the wilderness.

On the other side, the reactionaries, although never dreaming of the fate which hung over them, had not been idle. In 1857 the astounding question had for the first time been propounded with contumely, "What, then, did we come from orangoutang?" The famous *Vestiges of Creation* had been supplying a sugar-and-water panacea for those who could not escape from the trend of evidence, and who yet clung to revelation. Owen was encouraging reaction by resisting, with all the strength of his prestige, the theory of the mutability of species.

In this period of intellectual ferment, as when a great political revolution is being planned, many possible adherents were confidentially tested with hints and encouraged to reveal their bias in a whisper. It was the notion of Lyell, himself a great mover of men, that, before the doctrine of natural selection was given to a world which would be sure to lift up at it a howl of execration, a certain bodyguard of sound and experienced naturalists, expert in the description of species, should be privately made aware of its tenor. Among those who were thus initiated, or approached with a view towards possible illumination, was my Father. He was spoken to by Hooker, and later on by Darwin, after meetings of the Royal Society in the summer of 1857.

My Father's attitude towards the theory of natural selection was critical in his career, and oddly enough, it exercised an immense influence on my own experience as a child. Let it be admitted at once, mournful as the admission is, that every instinct in his intelligence went out at first to greet the new light. It had hardly done so, when a recollection of the opening chapter of Genesis checked it at the outset. He consulted with Carpenter, a great investigator, but one who was fully as incapable as himself of remodeling his ideas with regard to the old, accepted hypotheses. They both determined, on various grounds, to have nothing to do with the terrible theory, but to hold steadily to the law of the fixity of species. * * *

My Father had never admired Sir Charles Lyell. I think that the famous Lord Chancellor manner of the geologist intimidated him, and we undervalue the intelligence of those whose conversation puts us at a disadvantage. For Darwin and Hooker, on the other hand, he had a profound esteem, and I know not whether this had anything to do with the fact that he chose, for his impetuous experiment in reaction, the field of geology, rather than that of zoology or botany. Lyell had been threatening to publish a book on the geological history of Man, which was to be a bombshell flung into the camp of the catastrophists. My Father, after long reflection, prepared a theory of his own, which, as he fondly hoped, would take the wind out of Lyell's sails, and justify geology to godly readers of Genesis. It was, very briefly, that there had been no gradual modification of the surface of the earth, or slow development of organic forms, but that when the catastrophic act of creation took place, the world presented, instantly, the structural appearance of a planet on which life had long existed.

The theory, coarsely enough, and to my Father's great indignation, was defined by a hasty press as being this—that God hid the fossils in the rocks in order to tempt geologists into infidelity. In truth, it was the logical and inevitable conclusion of accepting, literally, the doctrine of a sudden act of creation; it emphasized the fact that any breach in the circular course of nature could be conceived only on the supposition that the object created bore false witness to past processes, which had never taken place.

Never was a book cast upon the waters with greater anticipations of success than was this curious, this obstinate, this fanatical volume. My Father lived in a fever of suspense, waiting for the tremendous issue. This *Omphalos* of his, he thought, was to bring all the turmoil of scientific speculation to a close, fling geology into the arms of Scripture, and make the lion eat grass with the lamb. It was not surprising, he admitted, that there had been experienced an ever-increasing discord between the facts which geology brings to light and the direct statements of the early chapters of Genesis. Nobody was to blame for that. My Father, and my Father alone, possessed the secret of the enigma; he alone held the key which could smoothly open the lock of geological mystery. He offered it, with a glowing gesture, to atheists and Christians alike. This was to be the universal panacea; this the system of intellectual therapeutics which could not but heal all the maladies of the age. But, alas! atheists and Christians alike looked at it, and laughed, and threw it away.

In the course of that dismal winter, as the post began to bring in private letters, few and chilly, and public reviews, many and scornful, my Father looked in vain for the approval of the churches, and in vain for the acquiescence of the scientific societies, and in vain for the gratitude of those "thousands of thinking persons," which he had rashly assured himself of receiving. As his reconciliation of Scripture statements and geological deductions was welcomed nowhere; as Darwin continued silent, and the youthful Huxley was scornful, and even Charles Kingsley,[1] from whom my Father had expected the most instant appreciation, wrote that he could not "give up the painful and slow conclusion of five and twenty years' study of geology, and believe that God has written on the rocks one enormous and superfluous lie"—as all this happened or failed to happen, a gloom, cold and dismal, descended upon our morning teacups. * * *

1907

1. Clergyman and novelist (1819–1875).

INDUSTRIALISM: PROGRESS OR DECLINE?

In 1835, the French statesman and author Alexis de Tocqueville wrote of Manchester: "From this foul drain, the greatest stream of human industry flows out to fertilize the whole world. From this filthy sewer pure gold flows. Here humanity attains its most complete development and its most brutish, here civilization works its miracles and civilized man is turned almost into a savage." De Tocqueville's graphic sense of the wealth and the wretchedness that the Industrial Revolution created epitomized contemporary responses to the way in which manufacturing had transformed nineteenth-century England. Victorians debated whether the machine age was a blessing or a curse, whether the middle-class economic system was making humanity happier or more miserable. Did the Industrial Revolution represent progress, and how, in fact, was progress to be defined?

The Industrial Revolution began with a set of inventions for spinning and weaving developed in England in the eighteenth century. At first this new machinery was operated by workers in their homes, but in the 1780s the introduction of the steam engine to drive these new machines led manufacturers to install them in large buildings called at first mills and later factories. Mill towns, producing cotton cloth for the world's markets, quickly grew in central and northern England; the population of the city of Manchester, for example, increased by ten times in the years between 1760 and 1830. The development of the railways in the 1830s initiated a new phase in industrial development, marked by an enormous expansion in the production of iron and coal. By the beginning of the Victorian period, the Industrial Revolution had created profound economic and social changes. Hundreds of thousands of workers had migrated to industrial towns, where they lived in horribly crowded, unsanitary housing and worked very long hours—fourteen a day or even more—at very low wages. Employers often preferred to hire women and children, who worked for even less than men.

Moved by the terrible suffering of the workers, which was intensified by a severe depression in the early 1840s, writers and legislators drew increasingly urgent attention to the condition of the working class. A number of parliamentary committees and commissions in the 1830s and 1840s introduced testimony about working conditions in mines and factories that led to the beginning of government regulation and inspection, particularly of the working conditions of women and children. Other eye-witness accounts created a growing consciousness of the plight of the workers. In *The Condition of the Working Class* (1845), Friedrich Engels described the conclusions he drew in the twenty months he spent observing industrial conditions in Manchester. In a series of interviews written for the *Morning Chronicle* (1849–52), later published as *London Labour and the London Poor* (1861–62), the journalist Henry Mayhew created a portrait of working London by collecting scores of interviews in the voices of the workers. Novels began to appear, such as Elizabeth Gaskell's *Mary Barton* (1848) and *North and South* (1855) and Charles Dickens's *Hard Times* (1854), portraying the painful consequences of industrialism.

The terrible living and working conditions of industrial laborers led a number of writers to see the Industrial Revolution as an appalling retrogression. Carlyle and Ruskin both lamented the changed conditions of labor, the loss of craftsmanship and individual creativity, and the disappearance of what Karl Marx called the "feudal, patriarchal, idyllic relations" between employer and employee that they believed had existed in earlier economies. They criticized industrial manufacture not only for the misery of the conditions it created but also for its regimentation of minds and hearts as well as bodies and resources. In works like *Past and Present* and *Unto This Last*, Carlyle and Ruskin advocated a nostalgic and conservative ideal, in which employers and workers returned to a medieval relationship to craft and to authority and responsibility. Other writers drew more radical conclusions. William Morris's perception of the workers' plight led him to socialism, though a socialism with a medieval ideal, and Marx, in collaboration with Engels, based *The Communist Manifesto* of 1848 in part on Engels's observation of Manchester in *The Condition of the Working Class*. All of these writers seem very distant from the satisfaction the historian Thomas Babington Macaulay voiced in the progress industrialism had enabled.

It is instructive to compare the selections in this section with Carlyle's chapter *Captains of Industry* from *Past and Present*; Elizabeth Barrett Browning's poem about child labor, *The Cry of the Children*; John Ruskin's arguments about manufacture in *The Stones of Venice*; his apocalyptic vision of industrial pollution in *The Storm Cloud of the Nineteenth Century*; and William Morris's explanation in *How I Became a Socialist*.

THOMAS BABINGTON MACAULAY

In a book titled *Colloquies on the Progress and Prospects of Society* (1829), the poet Robert Southey (1774–1843) had sought to expose the evils of industrialism and to assert the superiority of the traditional feudal and agricultural way of life of England's past. His romantic Toryism provoked Macaulay (1800–1859) to review the book in a long and characteristic essay, published in the *Edinburgh Review* (1830). As in his popular *History of England* (1849–61), Macaulay seeks here to demolish his opponent with a bombardment of facts and figures, demonstrating that industrialism and middle-class government have resulted in progress and increased comforts for humankind.

From A Review of Southey's *Colloquies*

[EVIDENCE OF PROGRESS]

* * * Perhaps we could not select a better instance of the spirit which pervades the whole book than the passages in which Mr. Southey gives his

opinion of the manufacturing system. There is nothing which he hates so bitterly. It is, according to him, a system more tyrannical than that of the feudal ages, a system of actual servitude, a system which destroys the bodies and degrades the minds of those who are engaged in it. He expresses a hope that the competition of other nations may drive us out of the field; that our foreign trade may decline; and that we may thus enjoy a restoration of national sanity and strength. But he seems to think that the extermination of the whole manufacturing population would be a blessing, if the evil could be removed in no other way.

Mr. Southey does not bring forward a single fact in support of these views; and, as it seems to us, there are facts which lead to a very different conclusion. In the first place, the poor rate[1] is very decidedly lower in the manufacturing than in the agricultural districts. If Mr. Southey will look over the Parliamentary returns on this subject, he will find that the amount of parochial relief required by the laborers in the different counties of England is almost exactly in inverse proportion to the degree in which the manufacturing system has been introduced into those counties. The returns for the years ending in March, 1825, and in March, 1828, are now before us. In the former year we find the poor rate highest in Sussex,[2] about twenty shillings to every inhabitant. Then come Buckinghamshire, Essex, Suffolk, Bedfordshire, Huntingdonshire, Kent, and Norfolk. In all these the rate is above fifteen shillings a head. We will not go through the whole. Even in Westmoreland and the North Riding of Yorkshire, the rate is at more than eight shillings. In Cumberland and Monmouthshire, the most fortunate of all the agricultural districts, it is at six shillings. But in the West Riding of Yorkshire,[3] it is as low as five shillings: and when we come to Lancashire, we find it at four shillings, one-fifth of what it is in Sussex. The returns of the year ending in March, 1828, are a little, and but a little, more unfavorable to the manufacturing districts. Lancashire, even in that season of distress, required a smaller poor rate than any other district, and little more than one-fourth of the poor rate raised in Sussex. Cumberland alone, of the agricultural districts, was as well off as the West Riding of Yorkshire. These facts seem to indicate that the manufacturer is both in a more comfortable and in a less dependent situation than the agricultural laborer.

As to the effect of the manufacturing system on the bodily health, we must beg leave to estimate it by a standard far too low and vulgar for a mind so imaginative as that of Mr. Southey, the proportion of births and deaths. We know that, during the growth of this atrocious system, this new misery, to use the phrases of Mr. Southey, this new enormity, this birth of a portentous age, this pest which no man can approve whose heart is not seared or whose understanding has not been darkened, there has been a great diminution of mortality, and that this diminution has been greater in the manufacturing towns than anywhere else. The mortality still is, as it always was, greater in towns than in the country. But the difference has diminished in an extraordinary degree. There is the best reason to believe that the annual mortality of Manchester, about the middle of the last century, was one in twenty-eight.

1. Taxes on property, to provide food and lodging for the unemployed or unemployable. The amount or rate of such taxes varied from district to district in England, depending on local conditions of unemployment.
2. A predominantly agricultural district.
3. A manufacturing district.

It is now reckoned at one in forty-five. In Glasgow and Leeds a similar improvement has taken place. Nay, the rate of mortality in those three great capitals of the manufacturing districts is now considerably less than it was, fifty years ago, over England and Wales, taken together, open country and all. We might with some plausibility maintain that the people live longer because they are better fed, better lodged, better clothed, and better attended in sickness, and that these improvements are owing to that increase of national wealth which the manufacturing system has produced.

Much more might be said on this subject. But to what end? It is not from bills of mortality and statistical tables that Mr. Southey has learned his political creed. He cannot stoop to study the history of the system which he abuses, to strike the balance between the good and evil which it has produced, to compare district with district, or generation with generation. We will give his own reason for his opinion, the only reason which he gives for it, in his own words:

> We remained a while in silence looking upon the assemblage of dwellings below. Here, and in the adjoining hamlet of Millbeck, the effects of manufacturer and of agriculture may be seen and compared. The old cottages are such as the poet and the painter equally delight in beholding. Substantially built of the native stone without mortar, dirtied with no white lime, and their long low roofs covered with slate, if they had been raised by the magic of some indigenous Amphion's[4] music, the materials could not have adjusted themselves more beautifully in accord with the surrounding scene; and time has still further harmonized them with weather stains, lichens, and moss, short grasses, and short fern, and stoneplants of various kinds. The ornamented chimneys, round or square, less adorned than those which, like little turrets, crest the houses of the Portuguese peasantry, and yet not less happily suited to their place; the hedge of clipped box beneath the windows, the rose bushes beside the door, the little patch of flower ground, with its tall hollyhocks in front; the garden beside, the beehives, and the orchard with its bank of daffodils and snowdrops, the earliest and the profusest in these parts, indicate in the owners some portion of ease and leisure, some regard to neatness and comfort, some sense of natural, and innocent, and healthful enjoyment. The new cottages of the manufacturers are upon the manufacturing pattern—naked, and in a row.
>
> "How is it," said I, "that everything which is connected with manufactures presents such features of unqualified deformity? From the largest of Mammon's temples down to the poorest hovel in which his helotry are stalled, these edifices have all one character. Time will not mellow them; nature will neither clothe nor conceal them; and they will remain always as offensive to the eye as to the mind."

Here is wisdom. Here are the principles on which nations are to be governed. Rosebushes and poor rates, rather than steam engines and independence. Mortality and cottages with weather stains, rather than health and long life with edifices which time cannot mellow. We are told that our age

---

4. According to Greek mythology, Amphion's magical skill as a harp player caused the walls of Thebes to be erected without human aid.

has invented atrocities beyond the imagination of our fathers; that society has been brought into a state compared with which extermination would be a blessing; and all because the dwellings of cotton-spinners are naked and rectangular. Mr. Southey has found out a way, he tells us, in which the effects of manufactures and agriculture may be compared. And what is this way? To stand on a hill, to look at a cottage and a factory, and to see which is the prettier. Does Mr. Southey think that the body of the English peasantry live, or ever lived, in substantial or ornamented cottages, with boxhedges, flower gardens, beehives, and orchards? If not, what is his parallel worth? We despise those mock philosophers,[5] who think that they serve the cause of science by depreciating literature and the fine arts. But if anything could excuse their narrowness of mind, it would be such a book as this. It is not strange that, when one enthusiast makes the picturesque the test of political good, another should feel inclined to proscribe altogether the pleasures of taste and imagination.

* * *

It is not strange that, differing so widely from Mr. Southey as to the past progress of society, we should differ from him also as to its probable destiny. He thinks, that to all outward appearance, the country is hastening to destruction; but he relies firmly on the goodness of God. We do not see either the piety or the rationality of thus confidently expecting that the Supreme Being will interfere to disturb the common succession of causes and effects. We, too, rely on his goodness, on his goodness as manifested, not in extraordinary interpositions, but in those general laws which it has pleased him to establish in the physical and in the moral world. We rely on the natural tendency of the human intellect to truth, and on the natural tendency of society to improvement. We know no well-authenticated instance of a people which has decidedly retrograded in civilization and prosperity, except from the influence of violent and terrible calamities, such as those which laid the Roman Empire in ruins, or those which, about the beginning of the sixteenth century, desolated Italy. We know of no country which, at the end of fifty years of peace and tolerably good government, has been less prosperous than at the beginning of that period. The political importance of a state may decline, as the balance of power is disturbed by the introduction of new forces. Thus the influence of Holland and of Spain is much diminished. But are Holland and Spain poorer than formerly? We doubt it. Other countries have outrun them. But we suspect that they have been positively, though not relatively, advancing. We suspect that Holland is richer than when she sent her navies up the Thames,[6] that Spain is richer than when a French king was brought captive to the footstool of Charles the Fifth.[7]

History is full of the signs of this natural progress of society. We see in almost every part of the annals of mankind how the industry of individuals, struggling up against wars, taxes, famines, conflagrations, mischievous pro-

5. Presumably such Utilitarian philosophers as Jeremy Bentham, who had equated poetry with pushpin, a trifling game. It should be noted, however, that although Macaulay often attacked the Utilitarians for their narrow preoccupation with theory, his own position had much in common with theirs.

6. In 1667 a Dutch fleet displayed its power by sailing up the river Thames without being challenged by the English navy.

7. The Spanish king Charles V captured the king of France, Francis I, in the battle of Pavia (1525).

hibitions, and more mischievous protections, creates faster than governments can squander, and repairs whatever invaders can destroy. We see the wealth of nations increasing, and all the arts of life approaching nearer and nearer to perfection, in spite of the grossest corruption and the wildest profusion on the part of rulers.

The present moment is one of great distress. But how small will that distress appear when we think over the history of the last forty years; a war,[8] compared with which all other wars sink into insignificance; taxation, such as the most heavily taxed people of former times could not have conceived; a debt larger than all the public debts that ever existed in the world added together; the food of the people studiously rendered dear; the currency imprudently debased, and imprudently restored. Yet is the country poorer than in 1790? We firmly believe that, in spite of all the misgovernment of her rulers, she has been almost constantly becoming richer and richer. Now and then there has been a stoppage, now and then a short retrogression; but as to the general tendency there can be no doubt. A single breaker may recede; but the tide is evidently coming in.

If we were to prophesy that in the year 1930 a population of fifty millions, better fed, clad, and lodged than the English of our time, will cover these islands, that Sussex and Huntingdonshire will be wealthier than the wealthiest parts of the West Riding of Yorkshire now are, that cultivation, rich as that of a flower garden, will be carried up to the very tops of Ben Nevis and Helvellyn,[9] that machines constructed on principles yet undiscovered will be in every house, that there will be no highways but railroads, no traveling but by steam, that our debt, vast as it seems to us, will appear to our great-grandchildren a trifling encumbrance, which might easily be paid off in a year or two, many people would think us insane. We prophesy nothing; but this we say: If any person had told the Parliament which met in perplexity and terror after the crash in 1720 that in 1830 the wealth of England would surpass all their wildest dreams, that the annual revenue would equal the principal of that debt which they considered as an intolerable burden, that for one man of ten thousand pounds then living there would be five men of fifty thousand pounds, that London would be twice as large and twice as populous, and that nevertheless the rate of mortality would have diminished to one-half of what it then was, that the post office would bring more into the exchequer than the excise and customs had brought in together under Charles the Second, that stage coaches would run from London to York in twenty-four hours, that men would be in the habit of sailing without wind, and would be beginning to ride without horses, our ancestors would have given as much credit to the prediction as they gave to *Gulliver's Travels*. Yet the prediction would have been true; and they would have perceived that it was not altogether absurd, if they had considered that the country was then raising every year a sum which would have purchased the fee-simple of the revenue of the Plantagenets,[1] ten times what supported the Government of Elizabeth, three times what, in the time of Cromwell, had been thought intolerably oppressive. To almost all men the state of things under which

---

8. The wars against France and Napoleon, extending, with some interruptions, from 1792 to 1815.
9. Mountains, in Scotland and in the English Lake District, respectively.

1. The Plantagenet family provided the monarchs of England from 1145 to 1485. "Fee-simple": absolute ownership of their estates.

they have been used to live seems to be the necessary state of things. We have heard it said that five per cent is the natural interest of money, that twelve is the natural number of a jury, that forty shillings is the natural qualification of a county voter. Hence it is that, though in every age everybody knows that up to his own time progressive improvement has been taking place, nobody seems to reckon on any improvement during the next generation. We cannot absolutely prove that those are in error who tell us that society has reached a turning point, that we have seen our best days. But so said all who came before us, and with just as much apparent reason. "A million a year will beggar us," said the patriots of 1640. "Two millions a year will grind the country to powder," was the cry in 1660. "Six millions a year, and a debt of fifty millions!" exclaimed Swift, "the high allies have been the ruin of us." "A hundred and forty millions of debt!" said Junius;[2] "well may we say that we owe Lord Chatham more than we shall ever pay, if we owe him such a load as this." "Two hundred and forty millions of debt!" cried all the statesmen of 1783 in chorus; "what abilities, or what economy on the part of a minister, can save a country so burdened?" We know that if, since 1783, no fresh debt had been incurred, the increased resources of the country would have enabled us to defray that debt at which Pitt, Fox, and Burke stood aghast, nay, to defray it over and over again, and that with much lighter taxation than what we have actually borne. On what principle is it that, when we see nothing but improvement behind us, we are to expect nothing but deterioration before us?

It is not by the intermeddling of Mr. Southey's idol, the omniscient and omnipotent State, but by the prudence and energy of the people, that England has hitherto been carried forward in civilization; and it is to the same prudence and the same energy that we now look with comfort and good hope. Our rulers will best promote the improvement of the nation by strictly confining themselves to their own legitimate duties, by leaving capital to find its most lucrative course, commodities their fair price, industry and intelligence their natural reward, idleness and folly their natural punishment, by maintaining peace, by defending property, by diminishing the price of law, and by observing strict economy in every department of the State. Let the Government do this: the People will assuredly do the rest.

1830

2. Pseudonym of a political commentator whose letters (1769–72) usually praised William Pitt, earl of Chatham. Pitt, as leader of the war against France, which gained Canada for England, could have been blamed for running his country into debt.

FRIEDRICH ENGELS

These eyewitness accounts from *The Condition of the Working Class* (1845) describe conditions of 1844, when Engels (1820–1895) had been living in England, chiefly in Manchester. The book was first translated from the German into English in 1892; this translation is by W. O. Henderson and W. H. Chaloner (1958). The first two paragraphs are the conclusion of chapter 2, *The Industrial Proletariat*; the balance is from chapter 3.

From The Great Towns

Industry and commerce attain their highest stage of development in the big towns, so that it is here that the effects of industrialization on the wage earners can be most clearly seen. It is in these big towns that the concentration of property has reached its highest point. Here the manners and customs of the good old days have been most effectively destroyed. Here the very name of "Merry England" has long since been forgotten, because the inhabitants of the great manufacturing centers have never even heard from their grandparents what life was like in those days. In these towns there are only rich and poor, because the lower middle classes are fast disappearing. At one time this section of the middle classes was the most stable social group, but now it has become the least stable. It is represented in the big factory towns today partly by a few survivors from a bygone age and partly by a group of people who are anxious to get rich as quickly as possible. Of these shady speculators and dubious traders one becomes rich while ninety-nine go bankrupt. Indeed, for more than half of those who have failed, bankruptcy has become a habit.

The vast majority of the inhabitants of these towns are the workers. We propose to discuss their condition and to discover how they have been influenced by life and work in the great factory towns.

*   *   *

London is unique, because it is a city in which one can roam for hours without leaving the built-up area and without seeing the slightest sign of the approach of open country. This enormous agglomeration of population on a single spot has multiplied a hundred-fold the economic strength of the two and a half million inhabitants concentrated there. This great population has made London the commercial capital of the world and has created the gigantic docks in which are assembled the thousands of ships which always cover the River Thames. I know nothing more imposing than the view one obtains of the river when sailing from the sea up to London Bridge. Especially above Woolwich the houses and docks are packed tightly together on both banks of the river. The further one goes up the river the thicker becomes the concentration of ships lying at anchor, so that eventually only a narrow shipping lane is left free in midstream. Here hundreds of steamships dart rapidly to and fro. All this is so magnificent and impressive that one is lost in admiration. The traveler has good reason to marvel at England's greatness even before he steps on English soil.

It is only later that the traveler appreciates the human suffering which has made all this possible. He can only realize the price that has been paid for all this magnificence after he has tramped the pavements of the main streets of London for some days and has tired himself out by jostling his way through the crowds and dodging the endless stream of coaches and carts which fills the streets. It is only when he has visited the slums of this great city that it dawns upon him that the inhabitants of modern London have had to sacrifice so much that is best in human nature in order to create those wonders of civilization with which their city teems. The vast majority of Londoners have had to let so many of their potential creative faculties lie dormant, stunted and unused in order that a small, closely-knit group of their fellow citizens could develop to the full the qualities with which nature has endowed them. The restless and noisy activity of the crowded streets is highly distasteful, and it is surely abhorrent to human nature itself. Hundreds of thousands of men and women drawn from all classes and ranks of society pack the streets of London. Are they not all human beings with the same innate characteristics and potentialities? Are they not all equally interested in the pursuit of happiness? And do they not all aim at happiness by following similar methods? Yet they rush past each other as if they had nothing in common. They are tacitly agreed on one thing only—that everyone should keep to the right of the pavement so as not to collide with the stream of people moving in the opposite direction. No one even thinks of sparing a glance for his neighbor in the streets. The more that Londoners are packed into a tiny space, the more repulsive and disgraceful becomes the brutal indifference with which they ignore their neighbors and selfishly concentrate upon their private affairs. We know well enough that this isolation of the individual—this narrow-minded egotism—is everywhere the fundamental principle of modern society. But nowhere is this selfish egotism so blatantly evident as in the frantic bustle of the great city. The disintegration of society into individuals, each guided by his private principles and each pursuing his own aims has been pushed to its furthest limits in London. Here indeed human society has been split into its component atoms.

From this it follows that the social conflict—the war of all against all—is fought in the open. * * * Here men regard their fellows not as human beings, but as pawns in the struggle for existence. Everyone exploits his neighbor with the result that the stronger tramples the weaker under foot. The strongest of all, a tiny group of capitalists, monopolize everything, while the weakest, who are in the vast majority, succumb to the most abject poverty.

What is true of London is true also of all the great towns, such as Manchester, Birmingham, and Leeds. Everywhere one finds on the one hand the most barbarous indifference and selfish egotism and on the other the most distressing scenes of misery and poverty. Signs of social conflict are to be found everywhere. Everyone turns his house into a fortress to defend himself—under the protection of the law—from the depredations of his neighbors. Class warfare is so open and shameless that it has to be seen to be believed. The observer of such an appalling state of affairs must shudder at the consequences of such feverish activity and can only marvel that so crazy a social and economic structure should survive at all.

* * *

Every great town has one or more slum areas into which the working classes are packed. Sometimes, of course, poverty is to be found hidden away in alleys close to the stately homes of the wealthy. Generally, however, the workers are segregated in separate districts where they struggle through life as best they can out of sight of the more fortunate classes of society. The slums of the English towns have much in common—the worst houses in a town being found in the worst districts. They are generally unplanned wildernesses of one- or two-storied terrace houses built of brick. Wherever possible these have cellars which are also used as dwellings. These little houses of three or four rooms and a kitchen are called cottages, and throughout England, except for some parts of London, are where the working classes normally live. These streets themselves are usually unpaved and full of holes. They are filthy and strewn with animal and vegetable refuse. Since they have neither gutters nor drains the refuse accumulates in stagnant, stinking puddles. Ventilation in the slums is inadequate owing to the hopelessly unplanned nature of these areas. A great many people live huddled together in a very small area, and so it is easy to imagine the nature of the air in these workers' quarters. However, in fine weather the streets are used for the drying of washing, and clothes lines are stretched across the streets from house to house and wet garments are hung out on them.

We propose to describe some of these slums in detail.

* * *

If we cross Blackstone Edge on foot or take the train we reach Manchester, the regional capital of South Lancashire, and enter the classic home of English industry. This is the masterpiece of the Industrial Revolution and at the same time the mainspring of all the workers' movements. Once more we are in a beautiful hilly countryside. The land slopes gently down toward the Irish Sea, intersected by the charming green valleys of the Ribble, the Irwell, the Mersey, and their tributaries. A hundred years ago this region was to a great extent thinly populated marshland. Now it is covered with towns and villages and is the most densely populated part of England. In Lancashire—particularly in Manchester—is to be found not only the origin but the heart of the industry of the United Kingdom. Manchester Exchange is the thermometer which records all the fluctuations of industrial and commercial activity. The evolution of the modern system of manufacture has reached its climax in Manchester. It was in the South Lancashire cotton industry that water and steam power first replaced hand machines. It was here that such machines as the power-loom and the self-acting mule replaced the old hand-loom and spinning wheel. It is here that the division of labor has been pushed to its furthest limits. These three factors are the essence of modern industry. In all three of them the cotton industry was the pioneer and remains ahead in all branches of industry. In the circumstances it is to be expected that it is in this region that the inevitable consequences of industrialization in so far as they affect the working classes are most strikingly evident. Nowhere else can the life and conditions of the industrial proletariat be studied in all their aspects as in South Lancashire. Here can be seen most clearly the degradation into which the worker sinks owing to the introduction of steam power, machinery, and the division of labor. Here, too, can be seen most the strenuous efforts of the proletariat to raise themselves from their degraded situation. I propose to examine conditions in Manchester in greater detail for two reasons. In the first place, Manchester is the classic type of modern industrial town. Secondly, I know Manchester as well as I know my native town and I know more about it than most of its inhabitants.

* * *

* * * Owing to the curious lay-out of the town it is quite possible for someone to live for years in Manchester and to travel daily to and from his work without ever seeing a working-class quarter or coming into contact with an artisan. He who visits Manchester simply on business or for pleasure need never see the slums, mainly because the working-class districts and the middle-class districts are quite distinct. This division is due partly to deliberate policy and partly to instinctive and tacit agreement between the two social groups. In those areas where the two social groups happen to come into contact with each other the middle classes sanctimoniously ignore the existence of their less fortunate neighbors. In the center of Manchester there is a fairly large commercial district, which is about half a mile long and half a mile broad. This district is almost entirely given over to offices and warehouses. Nearly the whole of this district has no permanent residents and is deserted at night, when only policemen patrol its dark, narrow thoroughfares with their bull's-eye lanterns. This district is intersected by certain main streets which carry an enormous volume of traffic. The lower floors of the buildings are occupied by shops of dazzling splendor. A few of the upper stories on these premises are used as dwellings and the streets present a relatively busy appearance until late in the evening. Around this commercial quarter there is a belt of built-up areas on the average one and a half miles in width, which is occupied entirely by working-class dwellings. This area of workers' houses includes all Manchester proper, except the center, all Salford and Hulme, an important part of Pendleton and Chorlton, two-thirds of Ardwick, and certain small areas of Cheetham Hill and Broughton. Beyond this belt of working-class houses or dwellings lie the districts inhabited by the middle classes and the upper classes. The former are to be found in regularly laid out streets near the working-class districts—in Chorlton and in the remoter parts of Cheetham Hill. The villas of the upper classes are surrounded by gardens and lie in the higher and remoter parts of Chorlton and Ardwick or on the breezy heights of Cheetham Hill, Broughton, and Pendleton. The upper class enjoy healthy country air and live in luxurious and comfortable dwellings which are linked to the center of Manchester by omnibuses which run every fifteen or thirty minutes. To such an extent has the convenience of the rich been considered in the planning of Manchester that these plutocrats can travel from their houses to their places of business in the center of the town by the shortest routes, which run entirely through working-class districts, without even realizing how close they are to the misery and filth which lie on both sides of the road.

* * *

* * * I will now give a description of the working-class districts of Manchester. The first of them is the Old Town, which lies between the northern limit of the commercial quarter and the River Irk. Here even the better streets, such Todd Street, Long Millgate, Withy Grove, and Shudehill are narrow and tortuous. The houses are dirty, old, and tumble-down. The side-streets have been built in a disgraceful fashion. If one enters the district near the "Old Church" and goes down Long Millgate, one sees immediately on the right hand side a row of antiquated houses where not a single front wall is standing upright. This is a remnant of the old Manchester of the days before the town became industrialized. The original inhabitants and their children have left for better houses in other districts, while the houses in Long Millgate, which no longer satisfied them, were left to a tribe of workers containing a strong Irish element. Here one is really and truly in a district which is quite obviously given over entirely to the working classes, because even the shopkeepers and the publicans of Long Millgate make no effort to give their establishments a semblance of cleanliness. The condition of this street may be deplorable, but it is by no means as bad as the alleys and courts which lie behind it, and which can be approached only by covered passages so narrow that two people cannot pass. Anyone who has never visited these courts and alleys can have no idea of the fantastic way in which the houses have been packed together in disorderly confusion in impudent defiance of all reasonable principles of town planning. And the fault lies not merely in the survival of old property from earlier periods in Manchester's history. Only in quite modern times has the policy of cramming as many houses as possible on to such space as was not utilized in earlier periods reached its climax. The result is that today not an inch of space remains between the houses and any further building is now physically impossible. To prove my point I reproduce a small section of a plan of Manchester.[1] It is by no means the worst slum in Manchester and it does not cover one-tenth of the area of Manchester.

This sketch will be sufficient to illustrate the crazy layout of the whole district lying near the River Irk. There is a very sharp drop of some 15 to 30 feet down to the south bank of the Irk at this point. As many as three rows of houses have generally been squeezed onto this precipitous slope. The lowest row of houses stands directly on the bank of the river while the front walls of the highest row stand on the crest of the ridge in Long Millgate. Moreover, factory buildings are also to be found on the banks of the river. In short the layout of the upper part of Long Millgate at the top of the rise is just as disorderly and congested as the lower part of the street. To the right and left a number of covered passages from Long Millgate give access to several courts. On reaching them one meets with a degree of dirt and revolting filth the like of which is not to be found elsewhere. The worst courts are those leading down to the Irk, which contain unquestionably the most dreadful dwellings I have ever seen. In one of these courts, just at the entrance where the covered passage ends, there is a privy without a door. This privy is so dirty that the inhabitants of the court can only enter or leave the court if they are prepared to wade through puddles of stale urine and excrement. Anyone who wishes to confirm this description should go to the first court on the bank of the Irk above Ducie Bridge. Several tanneries are situated on the bank of the river and they fill the neighborhood with the stench of animal putrefaction. The only way of getting to the courts below Ducie Bridge is by going down flights of narrow dirty steps and one can only reach the houses by treading over heaps of dirt and filth. The first court below Ducie Bridge is called Allen's Court. At the time of the cholera [1832] this court was in such a disgraceful state that the sanitary inspectors [of the local Board of Health] evacuated the inhabitants. The court was then swept and fumigated with chlorine. In his pamphlet Dr. Kay gives a horrifying description of conditions in this court at that time. Since Kay wrote this pamphlet, this court appears to have been at any rate partly demolished and rebuilt. If one looks down the river from Ducie Bridge one does at least see several ruined walls

---

1. Not reprinted here.

and high piles of rubble, side by side with some recently built houses. The view from this bridge, which is mercifully concealed by a high parapet from all but the tallest mortals, is quite characteristic of the whole district. At the bottom the Irk flows, or rather, stagnates. It is a narrow, coal-black, stinking river full of filth and rubbish which it deposits on the more low-lying right bank. In dry weather this bank presents the spectacle of a series of the most revolting blackish-green puddles of slime from the depths of which bubbles of miasmatic gases constantly rise and create a stench which is unbearable even to those standing on the bridge forty or fifty feet above the level of the water. Moreover, the flow of the river is continually interrupted by numerous high weirs, behind which large quantities of slime and refuse collect and putrefy. Above Ducie Bridge there are some tall tannery buildings, and further up there are dye-works, bone mills, and gasworks. All the filth, both liquid and solid, discharged by these works finds its way into the River Irk, which also receives the contents of the adjacent sewers and privies. The nature of the filth deposited by this river may well be imagined. If one looks at the heaps of garbage below Ducie Bridge one can gauge the extent to which accumulated dirt, filth, and decay permeate the courts on the steep left bank of the river. The houses are packed very closely together and since the bank of the river is very steep it is possible to see a part of every house. All of them have been blackened by soot, all of them are crumbling with age and all have broken window panes and window frames. In the background there are old factory buildings which look like barracks. On the opposite, low-lying bank of the river, one sees a long row of houses and factories. The second house is a roofless ruin, filled with refuse, and the third is built in such a low situation that the ground floor is uninhabitable and has neither doors nor windows. In the background one sees the paupers' cemetery, and the stations of the railways to Liverpool and Leeds. Behind these buildings is situated the workhouse, Manchester's "Poor Law Bastille."[2] The workhouse is built on a hill and from behind its high walls and battlements seems to threaten the whole adjacent working-class quarter like a fortress.

Above Ducie Bridge the left bank of the Irk becomes flatter and the right bank of the Irk becomes steeper and so the condition of the houses on both sides of the river becomes worse rather than better. Turning left from the main street which is still Long Millgate, the visitor can easily lose his way. He wanders aimlessly from one court to another. He turns one corner after another through innumerable narrow dirty alleyways and passages, and in only a few minutes he has lost all sense of direction and does not know which way to turn. The area is full of ruined or half-ruined buildings. Some of them are actually uninhabited and that means a great deal in this quarter of the town. In the houses one seldom sees a wooden or a stone floor, while the doors and windows are nearly always broken and badly fitting. And as for the dirt! Everywhere one sees heaps of refuse, garbage, and filth. There are stagnant pools instead of gutters and the stench alone is so overpowering that no human being, even partially civilized, would find it bearable to live in such

---

2. The workhouses established by the Poor Laws of the 1830s, because of the strict regimens enforced on inmates, were commonly likened to prisons such as the Bastille in Paris.

a district.[3] The recently constructed extension of the Leeds railway which crosses the Irk at this point has swept away some of these courts and alleys, but it has thrown open to public gaze some of the others. So it comes about that there is to be found immediately under the railway bridge a court which is even filthier and more revolting than all the others. This is simply because it was formerly so hidden and secluded that it could only be reached with considerable difficulty, [but is now exposed to the human eye]. I thought I knew this district well, but even I would never have found it had not the railway viaduct made a breach in the slums at this point. One walks along a very rough path on the river bank, in between clothes-posts and washing lines to reach a chaotic group of little, one-storied, one-roomed cabins. Most of them have earth floors, and working, living, and sleeping all take place in the one room. In such a hole, barely six feet long and five feet wide, I saw two beds—and what beds and bedding!—which filled the room, except for the fireplace and the doorstep. Several of these huts, as far as I could see, were completely empty, although the door was open and the inhabitants were leaning against the door posts. In front of the doors filth and garbage abounded. I could not see the pavement, but from time to time, I felt it was there because my feet scraped it. This whole collection of cattle sheds for human beings was surrounded on two sides by houses and a factory and on a third side by the river. [It was possible to get to this slum by only two routes]. One was the narrow path along the river bank, while the other was a narrow gateway which led to another human rabbit warren which was nearly as badly built and was nearly in such a bad condition as the one I have just described.

Enough of this! All along the Irk slums of this type abound. There is an unplanned and chaotic conglomeration of houses, most of which are more or less uninhabitable. The dirtiness of the interiors of these premises is fully in keeping with the filth that surrounds them. How can people dwelling in such places keep clean! There are not even adequate facilities for satisfying the most natural daily needs. There are so few privies that they are either filled up everyday or are too far away for those who need to use them. How can these people wash when all that is available is the dirty water of the Irk? Pumps and piped water are to be found only in the better-class districts of the town. Indeed no one can blame these helots of modern civilization if their homes are no cleaner than the occasional pigsties which are a feature of these slums. There are actually some property owners who are not ashamed to let dwellings such as those which are to be found below Scotland Bridge. Here on the quayside a mere six feet from the water's edge is to be found a row of six or seven cellars, the bottoms of which are at least two feet

3. Cf. another account of Manchester slums of the same decade in Elizabeth Gaskell's novel *Mary Barton* (1848), chap. 6:

Women from their doors tossed household slops of *every* description into the gutter; they ran into the next pool, which overflowed and stagnated. Heaps of ashes were stepping-stones, on which the passer-by, who cared in the least for cleanliness, took care not to put his foot. Our friends [two factory workers] were not dainty, but even they picked their way, till they got to some steps leading down . . . into the cellar in which a fam-

ily of human beings lived. . . . After the account I have given of the state of the street, no one can be surprised that on going into the cellar inhabited by Davenport, the smell was so foetid as almost to knock the two men down. Quickly recovering themselves, as those inured to such things do, they began to penetrate the thick darkness of the place, and to see three or four children rolling on the damp, nay wet brick floor, through which the stagnant, filthy moisture of the street oozed up; the fireplace was empty and black; the wife sat on her husband's lair [couch], and cried in the dank loneliness.

beneath the low-water level of the Irk. [What can one say of the owner of] the corner house—situated on the opposite bank of the river above Scotland Bridge—who actually lets the upper floor although the premises downstairs are quite uninhabitable and no attempt has been made to board up the gaps left by the disappearance of doors and windows? This sort of thing is by no means uncommon in this part of Manchester, where, owing to the lack of conveniences, such deserted ground floors are often used by the whole neighborhood as privies.

* * *

1845

CHARLES KINGSLEY

The following selection is from chapter 8 of *Alton Locke*, a novel by Charles Kingsley (1819–1875). Under the influence of Carlyle's writings and also as a result of his own observations, Kingsley, a clergyman, became deeply concerned with the sufferings of the working classes. The speaker here is a young tailor who is accompanied by an elderly Scottish bookseller, Sandy Mackaye.

From Alton Locke

[A LONDON SLUM]

It was a foul, chilly, foggy Saturday night. From the butchers' and greengrocers' shops the gaslights flared and flickered, wild and ghastly, over haggard groups of slipshod dirty women, bargaining for scraps of stale meat and frostbitten vegetables, wrangling about short weight and bad quality. Fish stalls and fruit stalls lined the edge of the greasy pavement, sending up odors as foul as the language of sellers and buyers. Blood and sewer water crawled from under doors and out of spouts, and reeked down the gutters among offal, animal and vegetable, in every stage of putrefaction. Foul vapors rose from cow sheds and slaughterhouses, and the doorways of undrained alleys, where the inhabitants carried the filth out on their shoes from the backyard into the court, and from the court up into the main street; while above, hanging like cliffs over the streets—those narrow, brawling torrents of filth, and poverty, and sin—the houses with their teeming load of life were piled up into the dingy, choking night. A ghastly, deafening, sickening sight it was. Go, scented Belgravian![1] and see what London is! and then go to the library which God has given thee—one often fears in vain—and see what science says this London might be!

* * *

We went on through a back street or two, and then into a huge, miserable house, which, a hundred years ago, perhaps, had witnessed the luxury, and

---

1. Inhabitant of Belgravia, a wealthy residential district of London.

rung to the laughter of some one great fashionable family, alone there in their glory. Now every room of it held its family, or its group of families—a phalanstery[2] of all the fiends—its grand staircase, with the carved balustrades rotting and crumbling away piecemeal, converted into a common sewer for all its inmates. Up stair after stair we went, while wails of children, and curses of men, steamed out upon the hot stifling rush of air from every doorway, till, at the topmost story, we knocked at a garret door. We entered. Bare it was of furniture, comfortless, and freezing cold; but, with the exception of the plaster dropping from the roof, and the broken windows, patched with rags and paper, there was a scrupulous neatness about the whole, which contrasted strangely with the filth and slovenliness outside. There was no bed in the room—no table. On a broken chair by the chimney sat a miserable old woman, fancying that she was warming her hands over embers which had long been cold, shaking her head, and muttering to herself, with palsied lips, about the guardians and the workhouse; while upon a few rags on the floor lay a girl, ugly, small-pox-marked, hollow-eyed, emaciated, her only bedclothes the skirt of a large handsome new riding habit, at which two other girls, wan and tawdry, were stitching busily, as they sat right and left of her on the floor. The old woman took no notice of us as we entered; but one of the girls looked up, and, with a pleased gesture of recognition, put her finger up to her lips, and whispered, "Ellen's asleep."

"I'm not asleep, dears," answered a faint unearthly voice; "I was only praying. Is that Mr. Mackaye?"

"Aye, my lassies; but ha' ye gotten na fire the nicht?"

"No," said one of them, bitterly, "we've earned no fire tonight, by fair trade or foul either."

1850

2. A kind of model housing development proposed by the French socialist Charles Fourier (1772–1837).

CHARLES DICKENS

The following selection is from chapter 5 of *Hard Times*, a novel by Charles Dickens (1812–1870). The picture of Coketown was based on Dickens's impressions of the raw industrial towns of central and northern England such as Manchester and, in particular, Preston, a cotton-manufacturing center in Lancashire.

From Hard Times

[COKETOWN]

It was a town of red brick, or of brick that would have been red if the smoke and ashes had allowed it; but as matters stood it was a town of unnatural red and black like the painted face of a savage. It was a town of machinery and tall chimneys, out of which interminable serpents of smoke trailed themselves forever and ever, and never got uncoiled. It had a black canal in it, and a river that ran purple with ill-smelling dye, and vast piles of buildings full of windows where there was a rattling and a trembling all day long, and where the piston of the steam engine worked monotonously up and down like the head of an elephant in a state of melancholy madness. It contained several large streets all very like one another, and many small streets still more like one another, inhabited by people equally like one another, who all went in and out at the same hours, with the same sound upon the same pavements, to do the same work, and to whom every day was the same as yesterday and tomorrow, and every year the counterpart of the last and the next.

These attributes of Coketown were in the main inseparable from the work by which it was sustained; against them were to be set off, comforts of life which found their way all over the world, and elegancies of life which made, we will not ask how much of the fine lady, who could scarcely bear to hear the place mentioned. The rest of its features were voluntary, and they were these.

You saw nothing in Coketown but what was severely workful. If the members of a religious persuasion built a chapel there—as the members of eighteen religious persuasions had done—they made it a pious warehouse of red brick, with sometimes (but this is only in highly ornamented examples) a bell in a birdcage on the top of it. The solitary exception was the New Church; a stuccoed edifice with a square steeple over the door terminating in four short pinnacles like florid wooden legs. All the public inscriptions in the town were painted alike, in severe characters of black and white. The jail might have been the infirmary, the infirmary might have been the jail, the town hall might have been either, or both, or anything else, for anything that appeared to the contrary in the graces of their construction. Fact, fact, fact, everywhere in the material aspect of the town; fact, fact, fact, everywhere in the immaterial. The M'Choakumchild school was all fact, and the school of design was all fact, and the relations between master and man were all fact, and everything was fact between the lying-in hospital and the cemetery, and what you couldn't state in figures, or show to be purchasable in the cheapest market and salable in the dearest, was not, and never should be, world without end, Amen.

1854

ANONYMOUS

A. L. Lloyd, a collector of British folk songs, heard *Poverty Knock* from a weaver in 1965, who had learned it sixty years earlier. The song certainly dates from before that.

Poverty Knock[1]

REFRAIN[2]

Poverty, poverty knock!
Me loom is a-sayin' all day.
Poverty, poverty knock!
Gaffer's too skinny[3] to pay.
Poverty, poverty knock!
Keepin' one eye on the clock.
Ah know ah can guttle°   *eat*
When ah hear me shuttle
Go: Poverty, poverty knock!

Up every mornin' at five.
Ah wonder that we keep alive.
Tired an' yawnin' on the cold mornin',
It's back to the dreary old drive.

5   Oh dear, we're goin' to be late.
Gaffer is stood at the gate.
We're out o' pocket, our wages they're docket°   *docked*
We'll 'a' to buy grub on the slate.[4]

An' when our wages they'll bring,
10 We're often short of a string.[5]
While we are fratchin' wi' gaffer for snatchin',[6]
We know to his brass° he will cling.   *money*

We've got to wet our own yarn
By dippin' it into the tarn.°   *pool*
15 It's wet an' soggy an' makes us feel groggy,
An' there's mice in that dirty old barn.

Oh dear, me poor 'ead it sings.
Ah should have woven three strings,
But threads are breakin' and my back is achin'.
20 Oh dear, ah wish ah had wings.

Sometimes a shuttle flies out,
Gives some poor woman a clout.
Ther she lies bleedin', but nobody's 'eedin'.
Who's goin' t'carry her out?

25 Tuner[7] should tackle me loom.
'E'd rather sit on his bum.
'E's far too busy a-courtin' our Lizzie,
An' ah cannat get 'im to come.

---

1. The sound of a 19th-century loom.
2. Repeated after each stanza.
3. Stingy. "Gaffer's": the foreman's.
4. On credit, as recorded on a piece of slate.
5. Short payment for a piece of cloth.
6. Cheating. "Fratchin' ": quarreling.
7. Man who maintains the loom.

Lizzie is so easy led.
30   Ah think that 'e teks her to bed.
She allus was skinny, now look at her pinny.°   *pinafore*
It's just about time they was wed.

1967

HENRY MAYHEW

In 1849, Henry Mayhew (1812–1887) was asked by the *Morning Chronicle* to be the metropolitan correspondent for its series "Labour and the Poor." His interviews of workers and of street folk, later published as a book, convey a vivid sense of the lives of London's poor.

From London Labour and the London Poor

[BOY INMATE OF THE CASUAL WARDS[1]]

I am now seventeen, My father was a cotton-spinner in Manchester, but has been dead ten years; and soon after that my mother went into the workhouse, leaving me with an aunt; and I had to work in a cotton factory. As young as I was, I earned 2s. 2d.[2] a-week at first. I can read well, and write a little. I worked at the factory two years, and was then earning 7s. a-week. I then ran away, for I had always a roving mind; but I should have stayed if my master hadn't knocked me about so. I thought I should make my fortune in London—I'd heard it was such a grand place. I had read in novels and romances,—halfpenny and penny books,—about such things, but I've met with nothing of the kind. I started without money, and begged my way from Manchester to London, saying I was going up to look for work. I wanted to see the place more than anything else. I suffered very much on the road, having to be out all night often; and the nights were cold, though it was summer. When I got to London all my hopes were blighted. I could get no further. I never tried for work in London, for I believe there are no cotton factories in it; besides, I wanted to see life. I begged, and slept in the unions.[3] I got acquainted with plenty of boys like myself. We met at the casual wards, both in London and the country. I have now been five years at this life. We were merry enough in the wards, we boys, singing and telling stories.

*   *   *

I live a roving life, at first, being my own master. I was fond of going to plays, and such-like, when I got money; but now I'm getting tired of it, and wish for something else. I have tried for work at cotton factories in Lancashire and Yorkshire, but never could get any. I'm sure I could settle now. I couldn't have done that two years ago, the roving spirit was so strong upon me and the company I kept got a strong hold on me. Two winters back, there

1. Short-term poor shelters.
2. Two shillings, two pence.

3. Shelters for the poor maintained by two or more parishes

was a regular gang of us boys in London. After sleeping at a union, we would fix where to meet at night to get into another union to sleep. There were thirty of us that way, all boys; besides forty young men, and thirty young women. Sometimes we walked the streets all night. We didn't rob, at least I never saw any robbing. We had pleasure in chaffing[4] the policemen, and some of us got taken up. I always escaped. We got broken up in time,— some's dead, some's gone to sea, some into the country, some home, and some lagged.[5] Among them were many young lads very expert in reading, writing, and arithmetic. One young man—he was only twenty-five—could speak several languages: he had been to sea. He was then begging, though a strong young man. I suppose he liked that life: some soon got tired of it.

I often have suffered from cold and hunger. I never made more than 3*d*. a-day in money, take the year round, by begging; some make more than 6*d* . . . but then, I've had meat and bread given besides. I say nothing when I beg, but that I am a poor boy out of work and starving. I never stole anything in my life. I've often been asked to do so by my mates. I never would. The young women steal the most. I know, least, I did know, two that kept young men, their partners, going about the country with them, chiefly by their stealing. Some do so by their prostitution. Those go as partners are all prostitutes. There is a great deal of sickness among the young men and women, but I never was ill these last seven years. Fevers, colds, and venereal diseases, are very common.

1851

4. Making fun of.

5. Fell behind.

ANNIE BESANT

In 1873 Annie Besant (1847–1933) left the church and her marriage to an Anglican clergyman to become active in feminist and socialist causes. When she heard about the high dividends and low wages at the match factory of Bryant and May, she wrote a series of articles, including this one published in the magazine *Link*, that led to a public boycott and a strike of fourteen hundred match workers.

The "White Slavery" of London Match Workers

Bryant and May, now a limited liability company, paid last year a dividend of 23 per cent to its shareholders; two years ago it paid a dividend of 25 per cent, and the original £5 shares were then quoted for sale at £18 7s. 6d.[1] The highest dividend paid has been 38 per cent.

Let us see how the money is made with which these monstrous dividends are paid. . . .

1. Eighteen pounds, seven shillings, six pence.

The hour for commencing work is 6.30 in summer and 8 in winter; work concludes at 6 P.M. Half-an-hour is allowed for breakfast and an hour for dinner. This long day of work is performed by young girls, who have to stand the whole of the time. A typical case is that of a girl of 16, a piece-worker; she earns 4s. a week, and lives with a sister, employed by the same firm, who "earns good money, as much as 8s. or 9s. per week." Out of the earnings 2s. is paid for the rent of one room; the child lives on only bread-and-butter and tea, alike for breakfast and dinner, but related with dancing eyes that once a month she went to a meal where "you get coffee, and bread and butter, and jam, and marmalade, and lots of it." . . . The splendid salary of 4s. is subject to deductions in the shape of fines; if the feet are dirty, or the ground under the bench is left untidy, a fine of 3d. is inflicted; for putting "burnts"— matches that have caught fire during the work—on the bench 1s. has been forfeited, and one unhappy girl was once fined 2s. 6d. for some unknown crime. If a girl leaves four or five matches on her bench when she goes for a fresh "frame" she is fined 3d., and in some departments a fine of 3d. is inflicted for talking. If a girl is late she is shut out for "half the day," that is for the morning six hours, and 5d. is deducted out of her day's 8d. One girl was fined 1s. for letting the web twist around a machine in the endeavor to save her fingers from being cut, and was sharply told to take care of the machine, "never mind your fingers." Another, who carried out the instructions and lost a finger thereby, was left unsupported while she was helpless. The wage covers the duty of submitting to an occasional blow from a foreman; one, who appears to be a gentleman of variable temper, "clouts" them "when he is mad."

One department of the work consists in taking matches out of a frame and putting them into boxes; about three frames can be done in an hour, and ½d. is paid for each frame emptied; only one frame is given out at a time, and the girls have to run downstairs and upstairs each time to fetch the frame, thus much increasing their fatigue. One of the delights of the frame work is the accidental firing of the matches: when this happens the worker loses the work, and if the frame is injured she is fined or "sacked." 5s. a week had been earned at this by one girl I talked to.

The "fillers" get ¾d. a gross for filling boxes; at "boxing," i.e. wrapping papers round the boxes, they can earn from 4s 6d. to 5s. a week. A very rapid "filler" has been known to earn once "as much as 9s." in a week, and 6s. a week "sometimes." The making of boxes is not done in the factory; for these 2 ¼d. a gross is paid to people who work in their own homes, and "find your own paste." Daywork is a little better paid than piecework, and is done chiefly by married women, who earn as much sometimes as 10s. a week, the piecework falling to the girls. Four women day workers, spoken of with reverent awe, earn—13s. a week.

A very bitter memory survives in the factory. Mr. Theodore Bryant, to show his admiration of Mr. Gladstone[2] and the greatness of his own public spirit, bethought him to erect a statue to that eminent statesman. In order that his workgirls might have the privilege of contributing, he stopped 1s. each out of their wages, and further deprived them of half-a-day's work by closing the

---

2. William Ewart Gladstone (1809–1898), leader of the Liberal Party from 1868 to 1875 and 1880 to 1894 and prime minister on four occasions.

factory, "giving them a holiday." ("We don't want no holidays," said one of the girls pathetically, for—needless to say—the poorer employees of such a firm lose their wages when a holiday is "given.") So furious were the girls at this cruel plundering, that many went to the unveiling of the statue with stones and bricks in their pockets, and I was conscious of a wish that some of those bricks had made an impression on Mr. Bryant's conscience. Later on they surrounded the statue—"we paid for it" they cried savagely—shouting and yelling, and a gruesome story is told that some cut their arms and let their blood trickle on the marble paid for, in very truth, by their blood. . . .

Such is a bald account of one form of white slavery as it exists in London. With chattel slaves Mr. Bryant could not have made his huge fortune, for he could not have fed, clothed, and housed them for 4s. a week each, and they would have had a definite money value which would have served as a protection. But who cares for the fate of these white wage slaves? Born in slums, driven to work while still children, undersized because underfed, oppressed because helpless, flung aside as soon as worked out, who cares if they die or go on the streets, provided only that the Bryant and May shareholders get their 23 per cent, and Mr. Theodore Bryant can erect statues and buy parks? Oh if we had but a people's Dante, to make a special circle in the Inferno for those who live on this misery, and suck wealth out of the starvation of helpless girls.

Failing a poet to hold up their conduct to the execration of posterity, enshrined in deathless verse, let us strive to touch their consciences, *i.e.* their pockets, and let us at least avoid being "partakers of their sins," by abstaining from using their commodities.

1888

ADA NIELD CHEW

Born on a farm in North Staffordshire, Ada Nield Chew (1870–1945) left school at the age of eleven to help her mother with taking care of house and family. In her early twenties, she worked as a tailor in a factory in Crewe. She wrote a series of letters to the *Crewe Chronicle* about working conditions in the factory. When her identity was discovered, an uproar ensued, and she was fired. She became active in politics and continued to write for political causes.

A Living Wage for Factory Girls at Crewe, 5 May 1894

Sir,

—Will you grant me space in your sensible and widely read paper to complain of a great grievance of the class—that of tailoresses in some of the Crewe factories—to which I belong? I have hoped against hope that some influential man (or woman) would take up our cause and put us in the right way to remedy—for of course there is a remedy—for the evils we are suffering from. But although one cannot open a newspaper without seeing what all sorts and conditions of men are constantly agitating for and slowly but surely obtaining—as in the miners' eight hour bill[1]— only very vague mention is ever made of the under-paid, over-worked "Factory Girl." And I have come to the conclusion, sir, that as long as we are silent ourselves and apparently content with our lot, so long shall we be left in the enjoyment [?] of that lot.

The rates paid for the work done by us are so fearfully low as to be totally inadequate to—I had almost said keep body and soul together. Well, sir, it is a fact which I could prove, if necessary, that we are compelled, not by our employers, but by stern necessity, in order to keep ourselves in independence, which self-respecting girls even in our class of life like to do, to work so many hours—I would rather not say how many—that life loses its savour, and our toil, which in moderation and at a fair rate of remuneration would be pleasurable, becomes drudgery of the most wearisome kind.

To take what may be considered a good week's wage the work has to be so close and unremitting that we cannot be said to "live"—we merely exist. We eat, we sleep, we work, endlessly, ceaselessly work, from Monday morning till Saturday night, without remission. Cultivation of the mind? How is it possible? Reading? Those of us who are determined to live like human beings and require food for mind as well as body are obliged to take time which is necessary for sleep to gratify this desire. As for recreation and enjoying the beauties of nature, the seasons come and go, and we have barely time to notice whether it is spring or summer.

Certainly we have Sundays: but Sunday is to many of us, after our week of slavery, a day of exhaustion. It has frequently been so in my case, and I am not delicate. This, you will understand, sir, is when work is plentiful. Of course we have slack times, of which the present is one (otherwise I should not have time to write to you). It may be said that we should utilise these slack times for recruiting our bodies and cultivating our minds. Many of us do so, as far as is possible in the anxious state we necessarily in, knowing that we are not earning our "keep," for it is not possible, absolutely not possible, for the average ordinary "hand" to earn enough in busy seasons, even with the overtime I have mentioned, to make up for slack ones.

"A living wage!" Ours is a lingering, dying wage. Who reaps the benefit of our toil? I read sometimes of a different state of things in other factories, and if in others, why not those in Crewe? I have just read the report of the Royal Commission on Labour. Very good, but while Royal Commissions are enquiring and reporting and making suggestions, some of the workers are being hurried to their graves.

I am afraid I am trespassing a great deal on your space, sir, but my subject has such serious interest for me—I sometimes wax very warm as I sit stitching and thinking over our wrongs—that they, and the knowledge that your columns are always open to the needy, however humble, must be my excuse.

I am, sir, yours sincerely,
A CREWE FACTORY GIRL
Crewe, 1 May 1894

---

1. Bill limiting miners' workshifts to eight hours.

Editor's note: Our correspondent writes a most intelligent letter; and if she is a specimen of the factory girl, then Crewe factory proprietors should be proud of their "hands." We shall be glad to hear further from our correspondent as to the wages paid, the numbers of hours worked, and the conditions of their employment. *Crewe Chronicle*, 5 May 1894

1894

THE "WOMAN QUESTION":
THE VICTORIAN DEBATE ABOUT GENDER

"The greatest social difficulty in England today is the relationship between men and women. The principal difference between ourselves and our ancestors is that they took society as they found it while we are self-conscious and perplexed. The institution of marriage might almost seem just now to be upon trial." This assertion by Justin M'Carthy (1830–1912), appearing in an essay on novels in the *Westminster Review* (July 1864), could be further extended, for on trial throughout the Victorian period was not only the institution of marriage but the family itself, and, most particularly, the traditional roles of women as wives, mothers, and daughters. The "Woman Question," as it was called, engaged many Victorians, both male and female.

As indicated in a section of the introduction to the Victorian age, "The Role of Women" (p. 1055), the Woman Question was not one but many. The mixed opinions of Queen Victoria herself make an interesting illustration of some of its different aspects. Believing in education for her sex, she gave support and encouragement to the founding of a college for women in 1847. On the other hand, she opposed the movement to give women the right to vote, which she described in a letter as "this mad folly." But most interesting, for our purposes, is another letter in which she comments on women and marriage. In 1858, writing to her recently married daughter, Victoria remarks: "There is great happiness . . . in devoting oneself to another who is worthy of one's affection; still, men are very selfish and the woman's devotion is always one of submission which makes our poor sex so very unenviable. This you will feel hereafter—I know; though it cannot be otherwise as God has willed it so."

Many of the queen's female subjects shared her assumptions that woman's role was to be accepted as divinely willed—as illustrated in the selections from Sarah Ellis's popular guidebook, *The Women of England* (1839). The required "submission" of which the queen wrote was justified in many quarters on the grounds of the supposed intellectual inferiority of women. As popularly accepted lore expressed it: "Average Weight of Man's Brain 3½ lbs; Woman's 2 lbs, 11 ozs." Such inferiority justified woman's dependent role. Another early Victorian guidebook, *The Female Instructor*, in reminding wives of their dependent roles, recommended always wearing one's wedding ring so that whenever a wife felt "ruffled," she might "cast [her] eyes upon it, and call to mind who gave it to [her]." In such quarters it would follow that a woman who tried to cultivate her intellect beyond drawing-room accomplishments was violating the order of Nature and of religious tradition. Woman was to be valued, instead, for other qualities considered to be especially characteristic of her sex: tenderness of understanding, unworldliness and innocence, domestic affection, and, in various degrees, submissiveness. By virtue of these qualities, woman became an object to be worshiped—an "angel in the house," as Coventry Patmore describes her in the title of his popular poem. Although a number of feminists as well as more traditional thinkers held this ideal view of woman's character, the exalted pedestal on which women were placed, as George Eliot argued in her essay on Mary Wollstonecraft, was one of the principal obstacles to their achieving any change of status.

It is commonly said that, as a result, Victorian women, married or unmarried, suffered painfully from boredom, as the experiences of Caroline Helstone in Charlotte Brontë's *Shirley* (1849) illustrate. Living in the home of her uncle, a clergyman, she finds no outlet for her energies, and her boredom becomes so intense that she longs for death. A reviewer of *Shirley* commented:

> The author is very bitter against *men* . . . she speaks as one outraged and aggrieved by their contemptuous treatment of her sex. We discern symptoms of a bitterness . . . almost a fierceness—for which there is probably some good cause. But there are few women of strong powers of mind, such as the author of this book unquestionably is, who do not feel that the social position of women is not at all what it should be, and hence she speaks in her angry and indignant tone.

Yet generalizations about bored Victorian females need to be severely qualified; by the year in which *Shirley* appeared, one-quarter of England's female population had jobs, most of them onerous and low paying. Although the millions of women employed as domestics, seamstresses, factory workers, or farm laborers had many problems, excessive leisure was not one of them. To be bored was the privilege of wives and daughters in upper- and middle-class families in which feminine idleness was treasured as a status symbol. It was only among this small and important segment of the population, as the novelist Dinah Maria Mulock emphasizes, that there was "nothing to do" for these comfortably well-off wives and daughters, because in such households the servants ran everything, even taking over the principal role in the rearing of children. Another group in which frustration was common consisted of women from the same classes whose families had lost their fortunes, thereby obliging their daughters to seek employment as governesses. Charlotte Brontë's governess-heroine Jane Eyre, reflecting that among both men and women, "millions are in silent revolt against their lot," adds:

> Women are supposed to be very calm generally: but women feel just as men feel; they need exercise for their faculties and a field for their efforts as much as their brothers do; they suffer from too rigid a restraint, too absolute a stagnation, precisely as men would suffer; and it is narrow-minded in their more privileged fellow-creatures to say that they ought to confine themselves to making puddings and knitting stockings, to playing on the piano and embroidering bags. It is thoughtless to condemn them, or laugh at them, if they seek to do more or learn more than custom has pronounced necessary for their sex.

George Meredith, in his *Essay on Comedy* (1873), develops the same argument; the test of a civilization, he writes, is whether men "consent to talk on equal terms with their women, and to listen to them." Yet at least two reviewers of *Jane Eyre*, both women, regarded such proposals as virtually seditious. Margaret Oliphant called the novel "A wild declaration of the 'Rights of Women' in a new aspect." And Elizabeth Rigby attacked its "pervading tone of ungodly discontent."

In some households such discontent, whether godly or ungodly, led to a daughter's open rebellion. A remarkable instance was Florence Nightingale, who found family life in the 1850s intolerably pointless and, despite parental opposition, cut loose from home to carve out a career for herself in nursing and hospital administration.

According to Sir Walter Besant, similar drives for independence produced an extraordinary change in the status of women during the late Victorian period, opening up for them a wide variety of professional opportunities. Many women became successful novelists, but embarking on such a career was no easy choice. The selections from Harriet Martineau's autobiography included here suggest some of the obstacles, internal and external, against which the aspiring woman writer struggled. Inevitably, some women writers were hacks, of whom Eliot made fun in her essay *Silly Novels by Lady Novelists* (1855). Nonetheless, women emerge as major literary artists during the period, as illustrated in the careers of the Brontë sisters and of George Eliot, one of the great novelists of the language.

It is instructive to compare the selections in this section with Eliot's judicious essay on the Woman Question, inspired by her rereading of Mary Wollstonecraft (p. 1456). It should be noted, however, that it was not only as an essayist but as a novelist that the Woman Question engaged her attention, as in her highly complex portrait of the frustrations of Maggie Tulliver, the bookish early-Victorian heroine of *The Mill on the Floss*. And her portraits of women were not restricted to the frustrated and discontented. As a realist, Eliot recognized that many upper- and middle-class women apparently found their leisurely lives fully enjoyable. In *Middlemarch,* for example, she portrays one of these in Celia Brooke Chetham, who rejoices in her comfortable life as wife and mother on a country estate. Her sister Dorothea, however (whom Celia regards with affectionate indulgence as an eccentric misfit), finds the traditional womanly dispensation as painfully frustrating as Florence Nightingale had found it. And it was on behalf of such women as Dorothea that Mill developed his argument in *The Subjection of Women* (1869; p. 1155), a classic essay that should be read in conjunction with the selections in this section. It is also interesting to compare these discussions of the Woman Question with Elizabeth Barrett Browning's *Aurora Leigh* (p. 1180), a novel in verse that represents the life of a woman poet; the *Anthology* includes a selection portraying the way the typical girl's education constricts her mind and one portraying Aurora's defense of her vocation as a poet.

SARAH STICKNEY ELLIS

Sarah Stickney (d. 1872), an essayist, married in 1837 William Ellis, a missionary, and worked with him for the temperance movement and other evangelical causes. Ellis's book on women's education and domestic roles (1839) became a best-seller and went through sixteen editions in two years. In the 1840s, she founded a school for girls that sought to inculcate her theories that feminine education should cultivate what she called "the heart" rather than the intellectual faculties of her pupils.

From The Women of England: Their Social Duties and Domestic Habits

[DISINTERESTED KINDNESS]

To men belongs the potent—(I had almost said the *omnipotent*) consideration of worldly aggrandizement; and it is constantly misleading their steps, closing their ears against the voice of conscience, and beguiling them with the promise of peace, where peace was never found.

* * *

How often has man returned to his home with a mind confused by the many voices, which in the mart, the exchange, or the public assembly, have addressed themselves to his inborn selfishness, or his worldly pride; and while his integrity was shaken, and his resolution gave way beneath the pressure of apparent necessity, or the insidious pretenses of expediency, he has stood corrected before the clear eye of woman, as it looked directly to the naked truth, and detected the lurking evil of the specious act he was about to commit. Nay, so potent may have become this secret influence, that he may have borne it about with him like a kind of second conscience, for mental reference, and spiritual counsel, in moments of trial; and when the snares of the world were around him, and temptations from within and without have bribed over the witness in his own bosom, he has thought of the humble monitress who sat alone, guarding the fireside comforts of his distant home; and the remembrance of her character, clothed in moral beauty, has scattered the clouds before his mental vision, and sent him back to that beloved home, a wiser and a better man.

The women of England, possessing the grand privilege of being better instructed than those of any other country, in the minutiae of domestic comfort, have obtained a degree of importance in society far beyond what their unobtrusive virtues would appear to claim. The long-established customs of their country have placed in their hands the high and holy duty of cherishing and protecting the minor morals of life, from whence springs all that is elevated in purpose, and glorious in action. The sphere of their direct personal influence is central, and consequently small; but its extreme operations are as widely extended as the range of human feeling. They may be less striking in society than some of the women of other countries, and may feel themselves, on brilliant and stirring occasions, as simple, rude, and unsophisticated in the popular science of excitement; but as far as the noble daring of Britain has sent forth her adventurous sons, and that is to every point of danger on the habitable globe, they have borne along with them a generosity, a disinterestedness, and a moral courage, derived in no small measure from the female influence of their native country.

It is a fact well worthy of our serious attention, and one which bears immediately upon the subject under consideration, that the present state of our national affairs is such as to indicate that the influence of woman in counteracting the growing evils of society is about to be more needed than ever.

*   *   *

In order to ascertain what kind of education is most effective in making woman what she ought to be, the best method is to inquire into the character, station, and peculiar duties of woman throughout the largest portion of her earthly career; and then ask, for what she is most valued, admired, and beloved?

In answer to this, I have little hesitation in saying—for her disinterested kindness. Look at all the heroines, whether of romance or reality—at all the female characters that are held up to universal admiration—at all who have gone down to honored graves, amongst the tears and lamentations of their survivors. Have these been the learned, the accomplished women; the women who could solve problems, and elucidate systems of philosophy? No: or if they have, they have also been women who were dignified with the majesty of moral greatness.

*   *   *

Let us single out from any particular seminary a child who has been there from the years of ten to fifteen, and reckon, if it can be reckoned, the pains that have been spent in making that child proficient in Latin. Have the same pains been spent in making her disinterestedly kind? And yet what man is there in existence who would not rather his wife should be free from selfishness, than be able to read Virgil without the use of a dictionary?

* * *

I still cling fondly to the hope that some system of female instruction will be discovered, by which the young women of England may be sent from school to the homes of their parents, habituated to be on the watch for every opportunity of doing good to others; making it the first and the last inquiry of every day, "What can I do to make my parents, my brothers, or my sisters, more happy? I am but a feeble instrument in the hands of Providence, but as He will give me strength, I hope to pursue the plan to which I have been accustomed, of seeking my own happiness only in the happiness of others."

1839

COVENTRY PATMORE

First published in 1854–62, this long poem about courtship and marriage became a best-seller first in the United States and later in Britain. Dedicated to Patmore's first wife, Emily Augusta Andrews, the poem celebrated their fifteen years of married life. (She died in 1862, and Patmore, who lived from 1823 to 1896, twice remarried.) The popularity of the poem among Patmore's contemporaries (including Hopkins and Ruskin) plummeted in later years. Feminist critics, such as Virginia Woolf, criticized *The Angel in the House* both for the sentimentality of its ideal of woman and for the oppressive effect of this ideal on women's lives. Since Woolf, the phrase "the angel in the house" has often been used to characterize a patronizing Victorian sentimentality toward women, with the implication that, if the woman is the angel in the house, her husband is its lord.

From The Angel in the House

The Paragon

When I behold the skies aloft
    Passing the pageantry of dreams,
The cloud whose bosom, cygnet-soft,
    A couch for nuptial Juno seems,
5   The ocean broad, the mountains bright,
    The shadowy vales with feeding herds,
I from my lyre the music smite,
    Nor want for justly matching words.
All forces of the sea and air,
10   All interests of hill and plain,
I so can sing, in seasons fair,
    That who hath felt may feel again.
Elated oft by such free songs,

I think with utterance free to raise
15 That hymn for which the whole world longs,
A worthy hymn in woman's praise;
A hymn bright-noted like a bird's,
Arousing these song-sleepy times
With rhapsodies of perfect words,
20 Ruled by returning kiss of rhymes.
But when I look on her and hope
To tell with joy what I admire,
My thoughts lie cramp'd in narrow scope,
Or in the feeble birth expire;
25 No mystery of well-woven speech,
No simplest phrase of tenderest fall,
No liken'd excellence can reach
Her, the most excellent of all,
The best half of creation's best,
30 Its heart to feel, its eye to see,
The crown and complex of the rest,
Its aim and its epitome.
Nay, might I utter my conceit,
'Twere after all a vulgar song,
35 For she's so simply, subtly sweet,
My deepest rapture does her wrong.
Yet is it now my chosen task
To sing her worth as Maid and Wife;
Nor happier post than this I ask,
40 To live her laureate all my life.
On wings of love uplifted free,
And by her gentleness made great,
I'll teach how noble man should be
To match with such a lovely mate;
45 And then in her may move the more
The woman's wish to be desired,
(By praise increased,) till both shall soar,
With blissful emulations fired.
And, as geranium, pink, or rose
50 Is thrice itself through power of art,
So may my happy skill disclose
New fairness even in her fair heart;
Until that churl shall nowhere be
Who bends not, awed, before the throne
55 Of her affecting majesty,
So meek, so far unlike our own;
Until (for who may hope too much
From her who wields the powers of love?)
Our lifted lives at last shall touch
60 That happy goal to which they move;
Until we find, as darkness rolls
Away, and evil mists dissolve,
The nuptial contrasts are the poles
On which the heavenly spheres revolve.

1854–62

HARRIET MARTINEAU

Harriet Martineau (1802–1876), who grew up in the town of Norwich, suffered a painfully unhappy childhood and adolescence both because of recurring illnesses and because of the strict and narrow lifestyle of her middle-class Unitarian family. She was a prolific author, who produced many kinds of books—history, political and economic theory, travel narratives, fiction, translation. She was best known for her collection of instructive stories, *Illustrations of Political Economy* (1832 and later); but she also dealt with a wide variety of other issues, such as slavery in the United States (she was an early supporter of the Abolitionists). Her *Autobiography*, written in 1855, was published in 1877. In the first selection, she is eighteen years old.

From Autobiography

When I was young, it was not thought proper for young ladies to study very conspicuously; and especially with pen in hand. Young ladies (at least in provincial towns) were expected to sit down in the parlour to sew,—during which reading aloud was permitted,—or to practice their music; but so as to be fit to receive callers, without any signs of bluestockingism which could be reported abroad. Jane Austen herself, the Queen of novelists, the immortal creator of Anne Elliott, Mr. Knightley, and a score or two more of unrivalled intimate friends of the whole public, was compelled by the feelings of her family to cover up her manuscripts with a large piece of muslin work, kept on the table for the purpose, whenever any genteel people came in. So it was with other young ladies, for some time after Jane Austen was in her grave; and thus my first studies in philosophy were carried on with great care and reserve. I was at the work table regularly after breakfast,—making my own clothes, or the shirts of the household, or about some fancy work: I went out walking with the rest,—before dinner in winter, and after tea in summer: and if ever I shut myself into my own room for an hour of solitude, I knew it was at the risk of being sent for to join the sewing-circle, or to read aloud,— I being the reader, on account of my growing deafness. But I won time for what my heart was set upon, nevertheless,—either in the early morning, or late at night. I had a strange passion for translating, in those days; and a good preparation it proved for the subsequent work of my life. Now, it was meeting James at seven in the morning to read Lowth's Prelections[1] in the Latin, after having been busy since five about something else, in my own room. Now it was translating Tacitus,[2] in order to try what was the utmost compression of style that I could attain.—About this I may mention an incident while it occurs. We had all grown up with a great reverence for Mrs. Barbauld[3] (which she fully deserved from much wiser people than ourselves) and, reflectively, for Dr. Aikin,[4] her brother,—also able in his way, and far more industrious, but without her genius. Among a multitude of other

---

1. *Praelectiones de Sacra Poesi Herbraeorum* (*Lectures on Hebrew Poetry*, 1753–70), by Robert Lowth (1710–1787), an English bishop and scholar. "James": James Martineau (1805–1900), her younger brother, who later became a renowned Unitarian preacher and moral philosopher.

2. Roman historian (ca. 55–ca. 118).
3. Anna Laetitia Barbauld (1743–1825), poet and writer of prose for children.
4. John Aikin (1747–1822), English physician, author, and biographer.

labours, Dr. Aikin had translated the Agricola[5] of Tacitus. I went into such an enthusiasm over the original, and especially over the celebrated concluding passage, that I thought I would translate it, and correct it by Dr. Aikin's, which I could procure from our public library. I did it, and found my own translation unquestionably the best of the two. I had spent an infinity of pains over it,—word by word; and I am confident I was not wrong in my judgment. I stood pained and mortified before my desk, I remember, thinking how strange and small a matter was human achievement, if Dr. Aikin's fame was to be taken as a testimony of literary desert. I had beaten him whom I had taken for my master. I need not point out that, in the first place, Dr. Aikin's fame did not hang on this particular work; nor that, in the second place, I had exaggerated his fame by our sectarian estimate of him. I give the incident as a curious little piece of personal experience, and one which helped to make me like literary labour more for its own sake, and less for its rewards, than I might otherwise have done.—Well: to return to my translating propensities. Our cousin J. M. L., then studying for his profession in Norwich, used to read Italian with Rachel[6] and me,—also before breakfast. We made some considerable progress, through the usual course of prose authors and poets; and out of this grew a fit which Rachel and I at one time took, in concert with our companions and neighbours, the C.'s, to translate Petrarch.[7] Nothing could be better as an exercise in composition than translating Petrarch's sonnets into English of the same limits. It was putting ourselves under compulsion to do with the Italian what I had set myself voluntarily to do with the Latin author. I believe we really succeeded pretty well; and I am sure that all these exercises were a singularly apt preparation for my after work. At the same time, I went on studying Blair's Rhetoric[8] (for want of a better guide) and inclining mightily to every kind of book or process which could improve my literary skill,—really as if I had foreseen how I was to spend my life.

* * *

At this time,—(I think it must have been in 1821,) was my first appearance in print. * * * My brother James, then my idolized companion, discovered how wretched I was when he left me for his college, after the vacation; and he told me that I must not permit myself to be so miserable. He advised me to take refuge, on each occasion, in a new pursuit; and on that particular occasion, in an attempt at authorship. I said, as usual, that I would if he would: to which he answered that it would never do for him, a young student, to rush into print before the eyes of his tutors; but he desired me to write something that was in my head, and try my chance with it in the "Monthly Repository,"—the poor little Unitarian periodical in which I have mentioned that Talfourd[9] tried his young powers. What James desired, I always did, as of course; and after he had left me to my widowhood soon after six o'clock, one bright September morning, I was at my desk before seven, beginning a letter to the Editor of the "Monthly Repository,"—that editor being the formidable prime minister of his sect,—Rev. Robert Aspland.[1] I suppose I must

5. A biography of Julius Agricola (40–93), Tacitus's father-in-law and a Roman senator and general.
6. Martineau's sister.
7. Italian poet (1304–1374).
8. *Lectures on Rhetoric and Belles Lettres* (1784)

by Hugh Blair (1718–1800), a Scottish divine and professor of rhetoric, which expressed 18th-century ideals of prose style.
9. Sir Thomas Noon Talfourd (1795–1854), English lawyer and author.
1. A Unitarian divine (1782–1845).

tell what that first paper was, though I had much rather not; for I am so heartily ashamed of the whole business as never to have looked at the article since the first flutter of it went off. It was on Female Writers on Practical Divinity. I wrote away, in my abominable scrawl of those days, on foolscap paper,[2] feeling mightily like a fool all the time. I told no one, and carried my expensive packet to the post-office myself, to pay the postage. I took the letter V for my signature,—I cannot at all remember why. The time was very near the end of the month: I had no definite expectation that I should ever hear any thing of my paper; and certainly did not suppose it could be in the forthcoming number. That number was sent in before service-time on a Sunday morning. My heart may have been beating when I laid hands on it; but it thumped prodigiously when I saw my article there, and, in the Notices to Correspondents, a request to hear more from V. of Norwich. There is certainly something entirely peculiar in the sensation of seeing oneself in print for the first time:—the lines burn themselves in upon the brain in a way of which black ink is incapable, in any other mode. So I felt that day, when I went about with my secret.—I have said what my eldest brother was to us,—in what reverence we held him. He was just married, and he and his bride asked me to return from chapel with them to tea. After tea he said, "Come now, we have had plenty of talk; I will read you something;" and he held out his hand for the new "Repository." After glancing at it, he exclaimed, "They have got a new hand here. Listen." After a paragraph, he repeated, "Ah! this is a new hand; they have had nothing so good as this for a long while." (It would be impossible to convey to any who do not know the "Monthly Repository" of that day, how very small a compliment this was.) I was silent, of course. At the end of the first column, he exclaimed about the style, looking at me in some wonder at my being as still as a mouse. Next (and well I remember his tone, and thrill to it still) his words were—"What a fine sentence that is! Why, do you not think so?" I mumbled out, sillily enough, that it did not seem any thing particular. "Then," said he, "you were not listening. I will read it again. There now!" As he still got nothing out of me, he turned round upon me, as we sat side by side on the sofa, with "Harriet, what is the matter with you? I never knew you so slow to praise any thing before." I replied, in utter confusion,—"I never could baffle any body. The truth is, that paper is mine." He made no reply; read on in silence, and spoke no more till I was on my feet to come away. He then laid his hand on my shoulder, and said gravely (calling me 'dear' for the first time) "Now, dear, leave it to other women to make shirts and darn stockings; and do you devote yourself to this." I went home in a sort of dream, so that the squares of the pavement seemed to float before my eyes. That evening made me an authoress.

*   *   *

While I was at Newcastle [1829], a change, which turned out a very happy one, was made in our domestic arrangements. * * * I call it a misfortune, because in common parlance it would be so treated; but I believe that my mother and all her other daughters would have joined heartily, if asked, in my conviction that it was one of the best things that ever happened to us. My mother and her daughters lost, at a stroke, nearly all they had in the world by the failure of the house,—the old manufactory,—in which their

---

2. A thirteen-by-sixteen-inch sheet of paper.

money was placed. We never recovered more than the merest pittance; and at the time, I, for one, was left destitute;—that is to say, with precisely one shilling in my purse. The effect upon me of this new "calamity," as people called it, was like that of a blister upon a dull, weary pain, or series of pains. I rather enjoyed it, even at the time; for there was scope for action; whereas, in the long, dreary series of preceding trials, there was nothing possible but endurance. In a very short time, my two sisters at home and I began to feel the blessing of a wholly new freedom. I, who had been obliged to write before breakfast, or in some private way, had henceforth liberty to do my own work in my own way; for we had lost our gentility. Many and many a time since have we said that, but for that loss of money, we might have lived on in the ordinary provincial method of ladies with small means, sewing, and economizing, and growing narrower every year; whereas, by being thrown, while it was yet time, on our own resources, we have worked hard and usefully, won friends, reputation and independence, seen the world abundantly, abroad and at home, and, in short, have truly lived instead of vegetated.

1855   1877

ANONYMOUS

In early January 1858 a prostitute, signing herself "One More Unfortunate," wrote a letter to *The Times*, describing her respectable upbringing and her experience as a governess, lamenting her disgrace, and calling on men to be compassionate in their reform efforts. "The Great Social Evil," another letter from a prostitute, published on February 24, 1858, responds in part to the first.

The Great Social Evil

To the Editor of the Times

Sir,—another "Unfortunate," but of a class entirely different from the one who has already instructed the public in your columns, presumes to address you.

I am a stranger to all the fine sentiments which still linger in the bosom of your correspondent. I have none of those youthful recollections which, contrasting her early days with her present life, aggravate the misery of the latter. My parents did not give me any education; they did not instil into my mind virtuous precepts nor set me a good example. All my experiences in early life were gleaned among associates who knew nothing of the laws of God but by dim tradition and faint report, and whose chiefest triumphs of wisdom consisted in picking their way through the paths of destitution in which they were cast by cunning evasion or in open defiance of the laws of man.

*   *   *

Let me tell you something of my parents. My father's most profitable occupation was brickmaking. When not employed at this he did anything he could get to do. My mother worked with him in the brickfield, and so did I and a progeny of brothers and sisters; for, somehow or other, although my parents occupied a very unimportant space in the world, it pleased God to make them fruitful. We all slept in the same room. There were few privacies, few family secrets in our house.

✻   ✻   ✻

I was a very pretty child, and had a sweet voice; of course I used to sing. Most London boys and girls of the lower classes sing. "My face is my fortune, kind Sir, she said" was the ditty on which I bestowed most pains, and my father and mother would wink knowingly as I sang it. The latter would also tell me how pretty she was when young, and how she sang, and what a fool she had been, and how well she might have done had she been wise.

Frequently we had quite a stir in our colony. Some young lady who had quitted the paternal restraints, or perhaps, been started off, none knew whither or how, to seek her fortune, would reappear among us with a profusion of ribands, fine clothes, and lots of cash. Visiting the neighbors, treating indiscriminately, was the order of the day on such occasions, without any more definite information of the means by which the dazzling transformation had been effected than could be conveyed by knowing winks and the words "luck" and "friends." Then she would disappear and leave us in our dirt, penury, and obscurity. You cannot conceive, Sir, how our young ambition was stirred by these visitations.

Now commences an important era in my life. I was a fine, robust, healthy girl, 13 years of age. I had larked with the boys of my own age. I had huddled with them, boys and girls together, all night long in our common haunts. I had seen much and heard abundantly of the mysteries of the sexes. To me such things had been matters of common sight and common talk. For some time I had trembled and coquetted on the verge of a strong curiosity, and a natural desire, and without a particle of affection, scarce a partiality, I lost what? not my virtue, for I never had any. That which is commonly, but untruly called virtue, I gave away.

You reverend Mr. Philanthropist—what call you virtue? Is it not the principle, the essence, which keeps watch and ward over the conduct, over the substance, the materiality? No such principle ever kept watch and ward over me, and I repeat that I never lost that which I never had—my virtue.

According to my own ideas at the time I only extended my rightful enjoyments. Opportunity was not long wanting to put my newly-acquired knowledge to profitable use. In the commencement of my fifteenth year one of our be-ribanded visitors took me off, and introduced me to the great world, and thus commenced my career as what you better classes call a prostitute. I cannot say that I felt any other shame than the bashfulness of a noviciate introduced to strange society. Remarkable for good looks, and no less so for good temper, I gained money, dressed gaily, and soon agreeably astonished my parents and old neighbors by making a descent upon them.

Passing over the vicissitudes of my course, alternating between reckless gaiety and extreme destitution, I improved myself greatly; and at the age of 18 was living partly under the protection of one who thought he discovered that I had talent, and some good qualities as well as beauty, who treated me more kindly and considerately than I had ever before been treated, and thus drew from me something like a feeling of regard, but not sufficiently strong to lift me to that sense of my position which the so-called virtuous and respectable members of society seem to entertain. Under the protection of this gentleman, and encouraged by him, I commenced the work of my education; that portion of education which is comprised in some knowledge of my own language and the ordinary accomplishments of my sex;—moral science, as I believe it is called, has always been an enigma to me, and is so to this day

* * *

Now, what if I am a prostitute, what business has society to abuse me? Have I received any favours at the hands of society? If I am a hideous cancer in society, are not the causes of the disease to be sought in the rottenness of the carcass? Am I not its legitimate child; no bastard, Sir? Why does my unnatural parent repudiate me, and what has society ever done for me, that I should do anything for it, and what have I ever done against society that it should drive me into a corner and crush me to the earth? I have neither stolen (at least not since I was a child), nor murdered, nor defrauded. I earn my money and pay my way, and try to do good with it, according to my ideas of good. I do not get drunk, nor fight, nor create uproar in the streets or out of them. I do not use bad language. I do not offend the public eye by open indecencies. I go to the Opera, I go to Almack's,[1] I go to the theatres, I go to quiet, well-conducted casinos, I go to all places of public amusement, behaving myself with as much propriety as society can exact. I pay business visits to my tradespeople, the most fashionable of the West-end.[2] My milliners, my silk-mercers,[3] my bootmaker know, all of them, who I am and how I live, and they solicit my patronage as earnestly and cringingly as if I were Madam, the lady of the right rev. patron of the Society for the Suppression of Vice. They find my money as good and my pay better (for we are robbed on every hand) than that of Madam, my Lady; and, if all the circumstances and conditions of our lives had been reversed, would Madam, my Lady, have done better or been better than I?

I speak for others as well as for myself, for the very great majority, nearly all of the real undisguised prostitutes in London, spring from my class, and are made by and under pretty much such conditions of life as I have narrated, and particularly by untutored and unrestrained intercourse of the sexes in early life. We come from the dregs of society, as our so-called betters term it. What business has society to have dregs—such dregs as we? You railers of the Society for the Suppression of Vice, you the pious, the moral, the respectable, as you call yourselves, who stand on your smooth and pleasant side of the great gulf you have dug and keep between yourselves and the dregs, why don't you bridge it over, or fill it up, and by some humane and generous process absorb us into your leavened mass, until we become interpenetrated with goodness like yourselves? Why stand on your eminence

---

1. Assembly rooms, the scene of social functions.   3. Dealers in textiles.
2. A fashionable shopping district in London.

shouting that we should be ashamed of ourselves? What have we to be ashamed of, we who do not know what shame is—the shame you mean? I conduct myself prudently, and defy you and your policemen too. Why stand you there mouthing with sleek face about morality? What is morality? Will you make us responsible for what we never knew? Teach us what is right and tutor us in good before you punish us for doing wrong. We who are the real prostitutes of the true natural growth of society, and no impostors, will not be judged by "One more Unfortunate," nor measured by any standard of her setting up. She is a mere chance intruder in our ranks, and has no business there.

* * *

Hurling big figures at us, it is said that there are 80,000 of us in London alone—which is a monstrous falsehood—and of this 80,000, poor hard-working sewing girls, sewing women, are numbered in by thousands and called indiscriminately prostitutes; writing, preaching, speechifying, that they have lost their virtue too.

It is a cruel calumny to call them in mass prostitutes; and, as for their virtue, they lose it as one loses his watch who is robbed by the highway thief. Their virtue is the watch, and society is the thief. These poor women toiling on starvation wages, while penury, misery, and famine clutch them by the throat and say, "Render up your body or die."

* * *

Admire this magnificent shop in this fashionable street; its front, fittings, and decorations cost not less than a thousand pounds. The respectable master of the establishment keeps his carriage, and lives in his countryhouse. He has daughters too; his patronesses are fine ladies, the choicest imperson-ations of society. Do they think, as they admire the taste and elegance of that tradesman's show, of the poor creatures who wrought it, and of what they were paid for it? Do they reflect on the weary toiling fingers, on the eyes dim with watching, on the bowels yearning with hunger, on the bended frames, on the broken constitutions, on poor human nature driven to its coldest corner and reduced to its narrowest means in the production of these luxuries and adornments? This is an old story! Would it not be truer and more charitable to call these poor souls "victims?"—some gentler, some more humane name than prostitute—to soften by some Christian expression, if you cannot better the un-Christian system, the oppobrium of a fate to which society has itself driven them by the direst straits? What business has society to point its finger in scorn, and to raise its voice in reprobation of them? Are they not its children, born of its cold indifference, of its callous selfishness, of its cruel pride?

Sir, I have trespassed on your patience beyond limit, and yet much remains to be said, which I leave for further communication if you think proper to insert this. The difficulty of dealing with the evil is not so great as society considers it. Setting aside "the sin," we are not so bad as we are thought to be. The difficulty is for society to set itself, with the necessary earnestness, self-humiliation, and self-denial to the work. But of this hereafter. To deprive us of proper and harmless amusements, to subject us in mass to the pressure of force—of force wielded, for the most part, by ignorant, and often by brutal men—is only to add the cruelty of active persecution to the cruelty of the passive indifference which made us as we are.

I remain your humble servant,
ANOTHER UNFORTUNATE

1858

DINAH MARIA MULOCK

In 1857, a year earlier than her book on women, Dinah Mulock (1826–1887) had published her best-known novel, a Victorian best-seller, *John Halifax, Gentleman*. In 1864, she married George Craik.

From A Woman's Thoughts about Women

[SOMETHING TO DO]

Man and woman were made for, and not like one another. Only one "right" we have to assert in common with mankind—and that is as much in our hands as theirs—the right of having something to do.

* * *

But how few parents ever consider this! Tom, Dick, and Harry, aforesaid, leave school and plunge into life; "the girls" likewise finish their education, come home, and stay at home. That is enough. Nobody thinks it needful to waste a care upon them. Bless them, pretty dears, how sweet they are! papa's nosegay of beauty to adorn his drawing-room. He delights to give them all they can desire—clothes, amusements, society; he and mamma together take every domestic care off their hands; they have abundance of time and nothing to occupy it; plenty of money, and little use for it; pleasure without end, but not one definite object of interest or employment; flattery and flummery enough, but no solid food whatever to satisfy mind or heart—if they happen to possess either—at the very emptiest and most craving season of both. They have literally nothing whatever to do. * * *

* * *

And so their whole energies are devoted to the massacre of old Time. They prick him to death with crochet and embroidery needles; strum him deaf with piano and harp playing—*not* music; cut him up with morning visitors, or leave his carcass in ten-minute parcels at every "friend's" house they can think of. Finally, they dance him defunct at all sort of unnatural hours; and then, rejoicing in the excellent excuse, smother him in sleep for a third of the following day. Thus he dies, a slow, inoffensive, perfectly natural death; and they will never recognize his murder till, on the confines of this world, or from the unknown shores of the next, the question meets them: "What have you done with Time?"—Time, the only mortal gift bestowed equally on every living soul, and excepting the soul, the only mortal loss which is totally irretrievable.

* * *

But "what am I to do with my life?" as once asked me one girl out of the numbers who begin to feel aware that, whether marrying or not, each possesses an individual life, to spend, to use, or to lose. And herein lies the momentous question.

* * *

A definite answer to this question is simply impossible. Generally—and this is the best and safest guide—she will find her work lying very near at hand: some desultory tastes to condense into regular studies, some faulty household quietly to remodel, some child to teach, or parent to watch over. All these being needless or unattainable, she may extend her service out of the home into the world, which perhaps never at any time so much needed the help of us women. And hardly one of its charities and duties can be done so thoroughly as by a wise and tender woman's hand.

* * *

These are they who are little spoken of in the world at large. * * * They have made for themselves a place in the world: the harsh, practical, yet no ill-meaning world, where all find their level soon or late, and where a frivolous young maid sunk into a helpless old one, can no more expect to keep her pristine position than a last year's leaf to flutter upon a spring bough. But an old maid who deserves well of this same world, by her ceaseless work therein, having won her position, keeps it to the end.

Not an ill position either, or unkindly; often higher and more honorable than that of many a mother of ten sons. In households, where "Auntie" is the universal referee, nurse, playmate, comforter, and counselor: in society, where "that nice Miss So-and-so," though neither clever, handsome, nor young, is yet such a person as can neither be omitted nor overlooked: in charitable works, where she is "such a practical body—always knows exactly what to do, and how to do it": or perhaps, in her own house, solitary indeed, as every single woman's home must be, yet neither dull nor unhappy in itself, and the nucleus of cheerfulness and happiness to many another home besides.

* * *

Published or unpublished, this woman's life is a goodly chronicle, the title page of which you may read in her quiet countenance; her manner, settled, cheerful, and at ease; her unfailing interest in all things and all people. You will rarely find she thinks much about herself; she has never had time for it. And this her life-chronicle, which, out of its very fullness, has taught her that the more one does, the more one finds to do—she will never flourish in your face, or the face of Heaven, as something uncommonly virtuous and extraordinary. She knows that, after all, she has simply done what it was her duty to do.

But—and when her place is vacant on earth, this will be said of her assuredly, both here and Otherwhere—"*She hath done what she could.*"

1858

FLORENCE NIGHTINGALE

Florence Nightingale (1820–1910) was in 1854 to become world famous for organizing a contingent of nurses to take care of sick and wounded soldiers in the Crimean War, an event that provided an outlet for her passionate desire to change the world of hospital treatments. At the time she was writing *Cassandra*, however, she had not yet been able to realize her aims; at thirty-two she was still living at home, unmarried (having declined several proposals), with her well-to-do family. Some members of her family, in particular her mother, strongly opposed her nursing ambitions and kept pressure on her to remain at home. In 1852, so bored with family and social life that she had thoughts of suicide, she began writing *Cassandra*, which she called her "family manuscript"; it is a record of her frustrations before she escaped into a professional world where there was "something to do." In 1859 she revised the manuscript, and a few copies were privately printed that year, but it was not published until 1928. The title refers to the Trojan princess whose true prophecies went unheeded by those around her.

From Cassandra

[NOTHING TO DO]

Why have women passion, intellect, moral activity—these three—and a place in society where no one of the three can be exercised? Men say that God punishes for complaining. No, but men are angry with misery. They are irritated with women for not being happy. They take it as a personal offense. To God alone may women complain without insulting Him!

* * *

Is discontent a privilege?

Yes, it is a privilege for you to suffer for your race—a privilege not reserved to the Redeemer, and the martyrs alone, but one enjoyed by numbers in every age.

The commonplace life of thousands; and in that is its only interest—its only merit as a history; viz., that it *is* the type of common sufferings—the story of one who has not the courage to resist nor to submit to the civilization of her time—is this.

Poetry and imagination begin life. A child will fall on its knees on the gravel walk at the sight of a pink hawthorn in full flower, when it is by itself, to praise God for it.

Then comes intellect. It wishes to satisfy the wants which intellect creates for it. But there is a physical, not moral, impossibility of supplying the wants of the intellect in the state of civilization at which we have arrived. The stimulus, the training, the time, are all three wanting to us; or, in other words, the means and inducements are not there.

Look at the poor lives we lead. It is a wonder that we are so good as we are, not that we are so bad. In looking round we are struck with the power of the organizations we see, not with their want of power. Now and then, it is true, we are conscious that *there* is an inferior organization, but, in general, just the contrary. Mrs A. has the imagination, the poetry of a Murillo,[1] and has sufficient power of execution to show that she might have had a great deal more. Why is she not a Murillo? From a material difficulty, not a mental one. If she has a knife and fork in her hands for three hours of the day, she cannot have a pencil or brush. Dinner is the great sacred ceremony of this day, the great sacrament. To be absent from dinner is equivalent to being ill. Nothing else will excuse us from it. Bodily incapacity is the only apology valid. If she has a pen and ink in her hands during other three hours, writing answers for the penny post, again, she cannot have her pencil, and so *ad infinitum* through life. People have no type before them in their lives, neither fathers nor mothers, nor the children themselves. They look at things in detail. They say, "It is very desirable that A., my daughter, should go to such a party, should know such a lady, should sit by such a person." It is true. But what standard have they before them of the nature and destination of man? The very words are rejected as pedantic. But might they not, at least, have a type in their minds that such an one might be a discoverer through her intellect, such another through her art, a third through her moral power?

Women often try one branch of intellect after another in their youth, e.g., mathematics. But that, least of all, is compatible with the life of "society." It is impossible to follow up anything systematically. Women often long to enter some man's profession where they would find direction, competition (or rather opportunity of measuring the intellect with others) and, above all, time.

In those wise institutions, mixed as they are with many follies, which will last as long as the human race lasts, because they are adapted to the wants of the human race; those institutions which we call monasteries, and which, embracing much that is contrary to the laws of nature, are yet better adapted to the union of the life of action and that of thought than any other mode of life with which we are acquainted; in many such, four and a half hours, at least, are daily set aside for thought, rules are given for thought, training and opportunity afforded. Among us there is *no* time appointed for this purpose, and the difficulty is that, in our social life, we must be always doubtful whether we ought not to be with somebody else or be doing something else.

Are men better off than women in this?

If one calls upon a friend in London and sees her son in the drawing room, it strikes one as odd to find a young man sitting idle in his mother's drawing room in the morning. For men, who are seen much in those haunts, there is no end of the epithets we have: "knights of the carpet," "drawing-room heroes," "ladies' men." But suppose we were to see a number of men in the morning sitting round a table in the drawing-room, looking at prints, doing worsted work, and reading little books, how we should laugh! A member of the House of Commons was once known to do worsted work. Of another

1. Bartolomé Murillo (1617–1682), Spanish painter.

man was said, "His only fault is that he is too good; he drives out with his mother every day in the carriage, and if he is asked anywhere he answers that he must dine with his mother, but, if she can spare him, he will come in to tea, and he does not come."

Now, why is it more ridiculous for a man than for a woman to do worsted work and drive out every day in the carriage? Why should we laugh if we were to see a parcel of men sitting round a drawing room table in the morning, and think it all right if they were women?

Is man's time more valuable than woman's? or is the difference between man and woman this, that woman has confessedly nothing to do?

Women are never supposed to have any occupation of sufficient importance *not* to be interrupted, except "suckling their fools";[2] and women themselves have accepted this, have written books to support it, and have trained themselves so as to consider whatever they do as *not* of such value to the world or to others, but that they can throw it up at the first "claim of social life." They have accustomed themselves to consider intellectual occupation as a merely selfish amusement, which it is their "duty" to give up for every trifler more selfish than themselves.

*　*　*

Women have no means given them, whereby they *can* resist the "claims of social life." They are taught from their infancy upwards that it is a wrong, ill-tempered, and a misunderstanding of "woman's mission" (with a great M) if they do not allow themselves *willingly* to be interrupted at all hours. If a woman has once put in a claim to be treated as a man by some work of science or art or literature, which she can *show* as the "fruit of her leisure," then she will be considered justified in *having* leisure (hardly, perhaps, even then). But if not, not. If she has nothing to show, she must resign herself to her fate.

"I like riding about this beautiful place, why don't you? I like walking about the garden, why don't you?" is the common expostulation—as if we were children, whose spirits rise during a fortnight's holiday, who think that they will last forever—and look neither backwards nor forwards.

Society triumphs over many. They wish to regenerate the world with their institutions, with their moral philosophy, with their love. Then they sink to living from breakfast till dinner, from dinner till tea, with a little worsted work, and to looking forward to nothing but bed.

When shall we see a life full of steady enthusiasm, walking straight to its aim, flying home, as that bird is now, against the wind—with the calmness and the confidence of one who knows the laws of God and can apply them?

*　*　*

When shall we see a woman making a *study* of what she does? Married women cannot; for a man would think, if his wife undertook any great work with the intention of carrying it out—of making anything but a sham of it— that she would "suckle his fools and chronicle his small beer" less well for

---

2. See Iago's cynical comments on the role of women, *Othello* 2.1.160: "To suckle fools, and chronicle small beer."

it—that he would not have so good a dinner—that she would destroy, as it is called, his domestic life.

The intercourse of man and woman—how frivolous, how unworthy it is! Can we call *that* the true vocation of woman—her high career? Look round at the marriages which you know. The true marriage—that noble union, by which a man and woman become together the one perfect being—probably does not exist at present upon earth.

It is not surprising that husbands and wives seem so little part of one another. It is surprising that there is so much love as there is. For there is no food for it. What does it live upon—what nourishes it? Husbands and wives never seem to have anything to say to one another. What do they talk about? Not about any great religious, social, political questions or feelings. They talk about who shall come to dinner, who is to live in this lodge and who in that, about the improvement of the place, or when they shall go to London. If there are children, they form a common subject of some nourishment. But, even then, the case is oftenest thus—the husband is to think of how they are to get on in life; the wife of bringing them up at home.

But any real communion between husband and wife—any descending into the depths of their being, and drawing out thence what they find and comparing it—do we ever dream of such a thing? Yes, we may dream of it during the season of "passion," but we shall not find it afterwards. We even expect it to go off, and lay our account that it will. If the husband has, by chance, gone into the depths of *his* being, and found there anything unorthodox, he, oftenest, conceals it carefully from his wife—he is afraid of "unsettling her opinions."

＊   ＊   ＊

＊ ＊ ＊ For a woman is "by birth a Tory"—has often been said—by education a "Tory," we mean.

Women dream till they have no longer the strength to dream; those dreams against which they so struggle, so honestly, vigorously, and conscientiously, and so in vain, yet which are their life, without which they could not have lived; those dreams go at last. All their plans and visions seem vanished, and they know not where; gone, and they cannot recall them. They do not even remember them. And they are left without the food of reality or of hope.

Later in life, they neither desire nor dream, neither of activity, nor of love, nor of intellect. The last often survives the longest. They wish, if their experiences would benefit anybody, to give them to someone. But they never find an hour free in which to collect their thoughts, and so discouragement becomes ever deeper and deeper, and they less and less capable of undertaking anything.

It seems as if the female spirit of the world were mourning everlastingly over blessings, not *lost*, but which she has never had, and which, in her discouragement she feels that she never will have, they are so far off.

The more complete a woman's organization, the more she will feel it, till at last there shall arise a woman, who will resume, in her own soul, all the sufferings of her race, and that woman will be the Saviour of her race.

1852–59   1928

WALTER BESANT

Walter Besant (1836–1901) was a literary critic, historian, and novelist. His history *The Queen's Reign* (1897) celebrated the improvements that he thought had occurred during his lifetime.

From The Queen's Reign

[THE TRANSFORMATION OF WOMEN'S STATUS BETWEEN 1837 AND 1897]

Let me present to you, first, an early Victorian girl, born about the Waterloo year; next, her granddaughter, born about 1875. * * *

The young lady of 1837 * * * cannot reason on any subject whatever because of her ignorance—as she herself would say, because she is a woman. In her presence, and indeed in the presence of ladies generally, men talk trivialities. * * * It has often been charged against Thackeray[1] that his good women were insipid. Thackeray, like most artists, could only draw the women of his own time, and at that time they were undoubtedly insipid. Men, I suppose, liked them so. To be childishly ignorant; to carry shrinking modesty so far as to find the point of a shoe projecting beyond the folds of a frock indelicate; to confess that serious subjects were beyond a woman's grasp; never even to pretend to form an independent judgment; to know nothing of Art, History, Science, Literature, Politics, Sociology, Manners—men liked these things; women yielded to please the men; her very ignorance formed a subject of laudable pride with the Englishwoman of the Forties. * * * There was something Oriental in the seclusion of women in the home, and their exclusion from active and practical life.

* * *

Let us turn to the Englishwoman—the young Englishwoman—of 1897. She is educated. Whatever things are taught to the young man are taught to the young woman. If she wants to explore the wickedness of the world she can do so, for it is all in the books. The secrets of Nature are not closed to her; she can learn the structure of the body if she wishes. At school, at college, she studies just as the young man studies, but harder and with greater concentration. * * * She has invaded the professions. She cannot become a priest, because the Oriental prejudice against women still prevails, so that women in High Church places are not allowed to sing in the choir, or to play the organ, not to speak of preaching. * * * In the same way she cannot enter the Law. Some day she will get over this restriction, but not yet. For a long time she was kept out of medicine. That restriction is now removed; she can, and she does, practice as a physician or a surgeon, generally the former. I believe that she has shown in this profession, as in her university studies, she can stand, *inter pares,*[2] among her equals and her peers, not her superiors. There is no branch of literature in which women have not distinguished themselves. * * * In music they compose, but not

1. William Makepeace Thackeray (1811–1863), novelist. The character of Amelia Sedley, in his novel *Vanity Fair* (1848), is cited by Besant as typ- ical of the "insipid" women of the 1840s.
2. Between equals (Latin).

greatly; they play and sing divinely. The acting of the best among them is equal to that of any living man. They have become journalists, in some cases of remarkable ability; in fact, there are thousands of women who now make their livelihood by writing in all its branches. As for the less common professions—the accountants, architects, actuaries, agents—they are rapidly being taken over by women.

It is no longer a question of necessity; women do not ask themselves whether they must earn their own bread, or live a life of dependence. Necessity or no necessity they demand work, with independence and personal liberty. Whether they will take upon them the duties and responsibilities of marriage, they postpone for further consideration. I believe that, although in the first eager running there are many who profess to despise marriage, the voice of nature and the instinctive yearning for love will prevail.

Personal independence: that is the keynote of the situation. Mothers no longer attempt the old control over their daughters: they would find it impossible. The girls go off by themselves on their bicycles; they go about as they please; they neither compromise themselves nor get talked about. For the first time in man's history it is regarded as a right and proper thing to trust a girl as a boy insists upon being trusted. Out of this personal freedom will come, I daresay, a change in the old feelings of young man to maiden. He will not see in her a frail, tender plant which must be protected from cold winds; she can protect herself perfectly well. He will not see in her any longer a creature of sweet emotions and pure aspirations, coupled with a complete ignorance of the world, because she already knows all that she wants to know. Nor will he see in her a companion whose mind is a blank, and whose conversation is insipid, because she already knows as much as he knows himself. Nor, again, will he see in her a housewife whose whole time will be occupied in superintending servants or in making, brewing, confecting things with her own hand.

1897

The Nineties

The state of mind prevailing during the final decade of the nineteenth century was characterized previously (in the introduction to the Victorian age) as typical neither of the earlier Victorians nor of the twentieth century. As a result of their between-centuries role, writers of the 1890s are sometimes styled "Late Victorians"—a perfectly legitimate label in chronological terms—and sometimes (more ambiguously) "the first of the 'Moderns.' " In the *Anthology*, we retain as "Late Victorians" those writers who made their chief contribution before 1900. And we reserve for the twentieth century a number of writers—already on the scene in the 1890s—whose work achieved particular prominence in the twentieth century: these are William Butler Yeats, Joseph Conrad, A. E. Housman, and Thomas Hardy. Hardy's writings offer an example of the principle. He was born fifteen to twenty years before most of the writers of the nineties, and his last two great novels, *Tess of the D'Urbervilles* and *Jude the Obscure,* were published during that decade. But since it was only after 1900 that Hardy made his name as a poet, we include him in the twentieth century, even though many of the attitudes toward life and literature in his poetry are recognizably Victorian and his writings can be considered as having contributed, in part, to the overall accomplishments of Victorian literature. (The same generalizations may be made about Gerard Manley Hopkins, whom we include in the Victorian section because he wrote during the Victorian period but whose work was not published until 1918, when it had a great effect on modernist poets and critics.) The problem of placing Hardy or Hopkins in one age or another is a striking reminder that literary history, as is sometimes said of all history, is a seamless web, resistant to the divisive time categories that we set up for ease of reference.

The writers most closely identified with the decade of the nineties, epitomized by the career of Oscar Wilde, were proponents of "art for art's sake": they believed that art should be unconcerned with controversial issues, such as politics, and that it should be restricted to celebrating beauty in a highly polished style. The "aesthetes," as these writers and artists were called, included in their group painters such as James McNeill Whistler, critics such as Arthur Symons, and the young Yeats. In 1936, when Yeats in old age was compiling an anthology of "modern verse," he looked back, as he often did, to the group of poets of the 1890s to which he himself had once been attached, a group styling itself The Rhymers' Club, whose members used to meet at a restaurant to read their poems aloud to each other. Among this coterie, an admiration for the writings of Walter Pater was, according to Yeats, a badge of membership. Indeed the first "poem" in Yeats's anthology is a passage of Pater's prose that Yeats prints as verse—the passage about the Mona Lisa in *The Renaissance* that begins: "She is older than the rocks among which she sits."

The Rhymers' Club poets liked to think of themselves as anti-Victorians, and they had some cause to do so in view of their revolt against the moral earnestness of such early Victorian prophets as Thomas Carlyle and against a whole set of middle-class opinions that they enjoyed mocking. Even Matthew Arnold, although appreciated for his ridicule of middle-class Philistines, was suspect in the eyes of the aesthetes because he had attacked, in his essay on Wordsworth, the French poet Théophile Gautier, who was regarded as a chief progenitor of the aesthetic movement. What Tennyson called in 1873 "poisonous honey stolen from France" was, in the 1890s, favored fare. Nevertheless it can be shown that the aesthetes' credo of art for art's sake was also rooted in the writings of some of their nineteenth-century predecessors in England. The poets of the aesthetic movement were in a sense the last heirs of the Romantics; the appeal to sensation in their imagery goes back through Rossetti and Tennyson to Keats. They developed this sensationalism, however, much more histrionically than their predecessors, seeking compensation for the drabness of ordinary life in melancholy suggestiveness, antibourgeois sensationalism, heady ritualism, world weariness, or mere emotional debauchery, qualities that led some critics to denounce the nineties as a time of decadence and degeneration. What makes the nineties important as a period of English literary history is not, however, its writers' sensationalism and desire to shock. It is their strongly held belief in the independence of art, their view that a work of art has its own unique kind of value—that, in T. S. Eliot's phrase, poetry must be judged "as poetry and not another thing"—which has most strongly influenced later generations. Not only did the aesthetic movement nurse the young Yeats and provide him with his lifelong belief in poetry as poetry rather than as a means to some moral or other end; it is also provided some of the principal schools of modern criticism with their basic assumptions. "Art for art's sake" was in the nineties a provocative slogan; in the modern period, many leading critics have been largely concerned with demonstrating the uniqueness of the literary use of language and with training us to see works of literary art as possessing their special kind of form, their special kind of meaning, and hence their special kind of value. In this these critics are the heir of the nineties, however much they may have modified or enriched the legacy. It was the poets of the 1890s, too, who first absorbed the influence of the French *symboliste* poets, an influence that has proved pervasive in the twentieth century and is especially strong (although in different ways) in the poetry of Yeats and Eliot.

Despite the characterization of the nineties as the Decadence, the poetry of the period was more various than this label suggests. Much as Wilde and Beardsley expanded the range of male literary identity through their dandyism and effeminacy, women writers of the aesthetic movement such as the pseudonymous Michael Field (Katherine Harris Bradley and her niece Edith Emma Cooper) and Mary Elizabeth Coleridge made equally untraditional claims for women's experience, Field translating and elaborating on Sappho's poems and Coleridge taking on the voice of the witch. There were also poets, such as William Earnest Henley and Rudyard Kipling, whose tone, in contrast to the aesthetes, was strenuously masculine. They embraced the values not of languid contemplation but of a life of action, and they shared a belief in the civilizing mission of British imperial power and the responsibilities called for in exercising that power—what Kipling called "The White Man's Burden." They also shared a commitment to realism that links them to naturalist novelists of the decade like George Gissing and George Moore. Henley's realism appears in his grim sketches of hospital experiences, and Kipling's in his distinctive recreation of the lives of common soldiers in the British army in India and Africa.

Ironically, perhaps, it was Kipling who in 1897 wrote, in his hymn *Recessional,* not a jingoistic celebration of sixty years of Victoria's reign but, instead, a haunting elegy that evokes the achievement of his country and his century but also, from the vaster perspectives of human history, the fragility of that achievement.

MICHAEL FIELD
Katherine Bradley (1846–1914)
Edith Cooper (1862–1913)

Michael Field was the pseudonym adopted by Katherine Bradley and her niece Edith Cooper, who together published twenty-seven verse plays and eight volumes of poems. When Robert Browning wrote to Michael Field to praise a volume of plays, Edith Cooper responded, "My Aunt and I work together after the fashion of Beaumont and Fletcher. She is my senior, by but fifteen years. She has lived with me, taught me, encouraged me and joined me to her poetic life." When Browning let slip the secret of their authorship, Katherine Bradley begged him to maintain the disguise. The revelation of their secret, she pleaded, "would indeed be utter ruin to us," adding, "We have many things to say that the world will not tolerate from a woman's lips."

Katherine Bradley, lost her father, a tobacco manufacturer, when she was two and her mother when she was twenty-two. After her mother's death, she attended Newnham College, Cambridge, and the Collège de France in Paris. When she returned home, she joined John Ruskin's Guild of Saint George, a small utopian society. When Katherine wrote to Ruskin telling him that she had lost God and found a Skye terrier, he angrily ended their friendship. Shortly thereafter she began attending classes at Bristol University with her niece, Edith Cooper, whom she had adopted and raised after Edith's mother became ill. The two became lovers and began a life of writing and traveling together. Their first joint volume of poetry, *Long Ago* (1889), was inspired by Henry Wharton's edition of Sappho (1885), which was the first English translation to represent the object of Sappho's love poems as a woman. The preface to *Long Ago* explains their attempt to create poems elaborating on Sappho's fragments: "Devoutly as the fiery-bosomed Greek turned in her anguish to Aphrodite to accomplish her heart's desires, I have turned to the one woman who has dared to speak unfalteringly of the fearful mastery of love."

Bradley and Cooper knew most of the literary figures of the nineties, including Pater, Wilde, and Yeats, although their relationship to the decadent movement was complex. The eroticism of their early poetry, with its frank expression of love between women, seems consistent with the spirit of the decade; but Bradley and Cooper sharply criticized the work of Beardsley for its depravity and withdrew one of their poems from publication in *The Yellow Book* in protest against its style. In 1906, they converted to Roman Catholicism when their beloved chow dog died, thus reversing the substitution of dog for God Katherine had flippantly described to Ruskin three decades earlier. In 1911, Edith was diagnosed with cancer. Suffering too from cancer, which she kept a secret from Edith to spare her pain, Katherine survived her by only eight months.

[Maids, not to you my mind doth change]

Ταῖς κάλαις ἴμμιν [τὸ] νόημα τῶμον οὐ διάμειπτον.[1]

Maids, not to you my mind doth change;
Men I defy, allure, estrange,
Prostrate, make bond or free:
Soft as the stream beneath the plane

---

1. A fragment from the works of the Greek poet Sappho (mid-7th century B.C.E.), which is translated in the first line of the poem.

5   To you I sing my love's refrain;
     Between us is no thought of pain,
         Peril, satiety.

     Soon doth a lover's patience tire,
     But ye to manifold desire
10   Can yield response, ye know
     When for long, museful days I pine,
     The presage at my heart divine;
     To you I never breathe a sign
     Of inward want or woe.

15   When injuries my spirit bruise,
     Allaying virtue ye infuse
     With unobtrusive skill:
     And if care frets ye come to me
     As fresh as nymph from stream or tree,
20   And with your soft vitality
         My weary bosom fill.

                                 1889

[A girl]

     A girl,
     Her soul a deep-wave pearl
   Dim, lucent of all lovely mysteries;
     A face flowered for heart's ease,
5   A brow's grace soft as seas
     Seen through faint forest-trees:
     A mouth, the lips apart,
   Like aspen-leaflets trembling in the breeze
   From her tempestuous heart.
10   Such: and our souls so knit,
     I leave a page half-writ—
        The work begun
   Will be to heaven's conception done,
        If she come to it.

                                 1893

Unbosoming

   The love that breeds
   In my heart for thee!
   As the iris is full, brimful of seeds,
   And all that it flowered for among the reeds
5   Is packed in a thousand vermilion-beads
   That push, and riot, and squeeze, and clip,
   Till they burst the sides of the silver scrip,

And at last we see
What the bloom, with its tremulous, bowery fold
10   Of zephyr-petal at heart did hold:
So my breast is rent
With the burthen and strain of its great content;
For the summer of fragrance and sighs is dead,
The harvest-secret is burning red,
15   And I would give thee, after my kind,
The final issues of heart and mind.

1893

[It was deep April, and the morn]

It was deep April, and the morn
    Shakspere was born;
The world was on us, pressing sore;
My Love and I took hands and swore,
5   Against the world, to be
Poets and lovers evermore,
To laugh and dream on Lethe's[1] shore,
To sing to Charon[2] in his boat,
Heartening the timid souls afloat;
10   Of judgment never to take heed,
But to those fast-locked souls to speed,
Who never from Apollo fled,
Who spent no hour among the dead;
      Continually
15   With them to dwell,
Indifferent to heaven and hell.

1893

To Christina Rossetti

Lady, we would behold thee moving bright
As Beatrice or Matilda[1] mid the trees,
Alas! thy moan was as a moan for ease
And passage through cool shadows to the night:
5   Fleeing from love, hadst thou not poet's right
To slip into the universe? The seas
Are fathomless to rivers drowned in these,
And sorrow is secure in leafy light.
Ah, had this secret touched thee, in a tomb
10   Thou hadst not buried thy enchanting self,
As happy Syrinx[2] murmuring with the wind,
Or Daphne,[3] thrilled through all her mystic bloom,

1. The river of forgetfulness in the underworld.
2. The ferryman who rows the dead across the river Styx to the underworld.
1. An idealized virgin in Dante's *Purgatorio* (28. 30), who explains to the poet that he's in the Garden of Eden. Beatrice, Dante's idealized beloved, appears to the poet in the Earthly Paradise at the top of the mountain of Purgatory.
2. A nymph who, when pursued by Pan, fled into the river Ladon, where she was transformed into a reed, from which Pan made his flute.
3. A nymph who, to escape Apollo's pursuit, was transformed into a laurel tree.

From safe recess as genius or as elf,
Thou hadst breathed joy in earth and in thy kind.

1896

Nests in Elms

The rooks are cawing up and down the trees!
Among their nests they caw. O sound I treasure,
Ripe as old music is, the summer's measure,
Sleep at her gossip, sylvan mysteries,
5   With prate and clamour to give zest of these—
In rune I trace the ancient law of pleasure,
Of love, of all the busy-ness of leisure,
With dream on dream of never-thwarted ease.
O homely birds, whose cry is harbinger
10 Of nothing sad, who know not anything
Of sea-birds' loneliness, of Procne's[1] strife,
Rock round me when I die! So sweet it were
To die by open doors, with you on wing
Humming the deep security of life.

1908

Eros

O Eros of the mountains, of the earth,
One thing I know of thee that thou art old,
Far, sovereign, lonesome tyrant of the dearth
Of chaos, ruler of the primal cold!
5   None gave thee nurture: chaos' icy rings
Pressed on thy plenitude. O fostering power,
Thine the first voice, first warmth, first golden wings,
First blowing zephyr, earliest opened flower,
Thine the first smile of Time: thou hast no mate,
10 Thou art alone forever, giving all:
After thine image, Love, thou did'st create
Man to be poor, man to be prodigal;
And thus, O awful god, he is endued
With the raw hungers of thy solitude.

1908

1. In Greek myth her husband, King Tereus, raped her sister, Philomela. Tereus then ripped out Philomela's tongue to keep her from revealing the crime, but she wove the story into a tapestry. Procne in revenge killed her son and served him to Tereus in a stew. When the sisters fled Tereus, Procne was changed into a swallow and Philomela, into a nightingale.

WILLIAM ERNEST HENLEY
1849–1903

During the 1880s and 1890s William Ernest Henley edited the *National Observer* and other periodicals in London, where he became a powerful figure in literary circles. The affectionate regard in which he was held by his contemporaries was enhanced by his courageous confrontation of long years of crippling physical pain caused by tuberculosis of the bone. Yeats said of him: "I disagreed with him about everything, but I admired him beyond words."

Most of Henley's poems, such as his vivid accounts of his hospital experiences, are realistic sketches of city life, often in free verse. Also characteristic, but in a different vein, are his hearty affirmations of faith in the indomitable human spirit, as in *Invictus,* and his patriotic verses expressing his pride in England's imperial role and her shouldering the responsibility for a world order. In *England, My England* he writes

> They call you proud and hard,
>   England, my England:
> You with worlds to watch and ward,
>   England, my own!
> You whose mailed hand keeps the keys
>   Of such teeming destinies
> You could know nor dread nor ease
>   Were the Song on your bugles blown,
>   England
> Round the Pit on your bugles blown!

The spirit in poems such as these links Henley's writings to the poetry of his friend Rudyard Kipling.

In Hospital

Waiting

A square, squat room (a cellar on promotion),
Drab to the soul, drab to the very daylight;
Plasters astray in unnatural-looking tinware;
Scissors and lint and apothecary's jars.

5 Here, on a bench a skeleton would writhe from,
Angry and sore, I wait to be admitted;
Wait till my heart is lead upon my stomach,
While at their ease two dressers do their chores.

One has a probe—it feels to me a crowbar.
10 A small boy sniffs and shudders after bluestone.[1]
A poor old tramp explains his poor old ulcers.
Life is (I think) a blunder and a shame.

1875

---

1. Or hydrated copper sulfate, commonly used in emergency wards as an emetic for patients who have taken poison.

Invictus[1]

Out of the night that covers me,
  Black as the Pit from pole to pole,
I thank whatever gods may be
  For my unconquerable soul.

5 In the fell clutch of circumstance
  I have not winced nor cried aloud.
Under the bludgeonings of chance
  My head is bloody, but unbowed.

Beyond this place of wrath and tears
10   Looms but the Horror of the shade,
And yet the menace of the years
  Finds, and shall find, me unafraid.

It matters not how strait the gate,
  How charged with punishments the scroll,
15 I am the master of my fate;
  I am the captain of my soul.

1875
                                                            1888

1. Unconquered (Latin).

OSCAR WILDE
1854–1900

In Oscar Wilde's comedy *The Importance of Being Earnest* (1895) there is an account of a rakish character, Ernest Worthing, whose death in a Paris hotel is reported by the manager. Five years later, Wilde himself died in Paris (where he was living in exile) attended by a hotel manager. The coincidence seems a curious paradigm of Wilde's whole career, for with him the connections between his life and his art were unusually close. Indeed, in his last years, he told André Gide that he seemed to have put his genius into his life and only his talent into his writings.

His father, Sir William, was a distinguished surgeon in Dublin, where Wilde was born and grew up. After majoring in classical studies at Trinity College, Dublin, he won a scholarship to Oxford and there established a brilliant academic record. At Oxford he came under the influence of the aesthetic theories of John Ruskin (who was at the time professor of fine arts) and, more important, of Walter Pater. With characteristic hyperbole, Wilde affirmed of Pater's *Renaissance:* "It is my golden book; I never travel anywhere without it. But it is the very flower of decadence; the last trumpet should have sounded the moment it was written."

After graduating in 1878, Wilde settled in London, where his fellow Irishmen, Bernard Shaw and William Butler Yeats, were also to settle. Here Wilde quickly established himself both as a writer and as a spokesperson for the school of "art for art's sake." In Wilde's view this school included not only French poets and critics but also a line of English poets going back through Rossetti and the Pre-Raphaelites to Keats. In 1882 he visited America for a lengthy (and successful) lecture tour during which he startled audiences by airing the gospel of the "aesthetic movement." In one of these lectures, he asserted that "to disagree with three fourths of all England on all points of view is one of the first elements of sanity."

For his role as a spokesperson for aestheticism, Wilde had many gifts. From all accounts he was a dazzling conversationalist. Yeats reported, after first listening to him: "I never before heard a man talking with perfect sentences, as if he had written them all overnight with labor and yet all spontaneous." Wilde delighted his listeners not only by his polished wordplay but also by uttering opinions that were both outrageous and incongruous, as for example, his solemn affirmation that Queen Victoria was one of the three women he most admired and whom he would have married "with pleasure" (the other two were Sarah Bernhardt, the actress, and Lillie Langtry, reputedly a mistress of Victoria's son Edward, prince of Wales).

In addition to his mastery of witty conversation, Wilde had the gifts of an actor who delights in gaining attention. Pater had been a most shy and reticent man, but there was nothing reticent about his disciple who had discovered, early, that a flamboyant style of dress was one of the most effective means of gaining attention. Like the dandies of the earlier decades of the nineteenth century (including Benjamin Disraeli and Charles Dickens), Wilde favored colorful costumes in marked contrast to the sober black suits of the late-Victorian middle classes. A green carnation in his buttonhole and velvet knee breeches became for Wilde badges of his youthful iconoclasm, and even when he approached middle age, he continued to emphasize the gap between generations. In a letter written when he was forty-two years old, he remarks: "The opinions of the old on matters of Art are, of course, of no value whatever."

Wilde's campaign early prompted an amused response from middle-class quarters. In 1881, Gilbert and Sullivan staged their comic opera *Patience,* which mocked the affectations of the aesthetes in the character of Bunthorne, especially in his song, "If You're Anxious for to Shine in the High Aesthetic Line."

Wilde's successes for seventeen years in England and America were, of course, not limited to his self-advertising stunts as a dandy. In his writings, he excelled in a variety of genres: as a critic of literature and of society (*The Decay of Lying,* 1889, and *The Soul of Man under Socialism,* 1891) and also as a novelist, poet, and dramatist. Much of his prose, including *The Critic as Artist,* develops Pater's aestheticism, particularly its sense of the superiority of art to life and its lack of obligation to any standards of mimesis. His novel *The Picture of Dorian Gray,* which created a sensation when it was published in 1891, takes a somewhat different perspective. The novel is a strikingly ingenious story of a handsome young man and his selfish pursuit of sensual pleasures. Until the end of the book he himself remains fresh and healthy in appearance while his portrait mysteriously changes into a horrible image of his corrupted soul. Although the preface to the novel (reprinted here) emphasizes that art and morality are totally separate, in the novel itself, at least in its later chapters, Wilde seems to be portraying the evils of self-regarding hedonism.

As a poet Wilde felt overshadowed by the Victorian predecessors whom he admired—Robert Browning, D. G. Rossetti, and Swinburne—and had trouble finding his own voice. Many of the poems in his first volume (1881) are highly derivative, but such pieces as *The Harlot's House* and *Impression du Matin* offer a distinctive perspective on city streets that seems to anticipate early poems by T. S. Eliot. His most outstanding success, however, was as a writer of comedies, which were staged in London and New York from 1892 through 1895, including *Lady Windermere's Fan, A Woman of No Importance, An Ideal Husband,* and *The Importance of Being Earnest.*

By the spring of 1895 this triumphant success suddenly crumbled when Wilde was arrested and sentenced to jail, with hard labor, for two years. Although Wilde was married and the father of two children, he did not hide his homosexual relationships. When he began a romance (in 1891) with the handsome young poet Lord Alfred Douglas, he set in motion the events that brought about his ruin. In 1895, Lord Alfred's father, the marquis of Queensberry, accused Wilde of homosexuality; Wilde recklessly sued for libel, lost the case, and was thereupon arrested and convicted for what was then on the statute books a serious criminal offense. The revulsion of feeling against him in England and in America was violent, and the aesthetic movement itself suffered a severe setback not only with the public but among writers as well.

His two years in jail led Wilde to write two sober and emotionally high-pitched works, his poem *The Ballad of Reading Gaol* (1898) and his prose confession *De Profundis* (1905). After leaving jail, Wilde, a ruined man, emigrated to France, where he lived out the last three years of his life under an assumed name. Before his departure from England he had been divorced and declared a bankrupt, and in France he had to rely on friends for financial support. Wilde is buried in Paris in the Père Lachaise cemetery.

Impression du Matin[1]

    The Thames nocturne of blue and gold[2]
        Changed to a harmony in gray;
        A barge with ocher-colored hay
    Dropped from the wharf:[3] and chill and cold

5   The yellow fog came creeping down
        The bridges, till the houses' walls
        Seemed changed to shadows, and St. Paul's
    Loomed like a bubble o'er the town.

    Then suddenly arose the clang
10   Of waking life; the streets were stirred
        With country wagons; and a bird
    Flew to the glistening roofs and sang.

    But one pale woman all alone,
        The daylight kissing her wan hair,
15   Loitered beneath the gas lamps' flare,
    With lips of flame and heart of stone.

                        1881

Hélas[1]

    To drift with every passion till my soul
    Is a stringed lute on which all winds can play,
    Is it for this that I have given away

1. Impression of the morning (French).
2. Cf. the "Nocturnes" (paintings of nighttime scenes) by James McNeill Whistler in the 1870s. *Nocturne in Blue and Gold: Old Battersea Bridge* was one of this series; it was painted by 1875 but given its present title in 1892. An earlier painting by Whistler, *Harmony in Gray,* may be referred to in the next line.
3. I.e., left the wharf and went down river with the ebb tide.
1. "Alas!"

Mine ancient wisdom, and austere control?
5   Methinks my life is a twice-written scroll
Scrawled over on some boyish holiday
With idle songs for pipe and virelay,[2]
Which do but mar the secret of the whole.
Surely there was a time I might have trod
10   The sunlit heights, and from life's dissonance
Struck one clear chord to reach the ears of God.
Is that time dead? lo! with a little rod
I did but touch the honey of romance—
And must I lose a soul's inheritance?[3]

1881

E Tenebris[1]

Come down, O Christ, and help me! reach thy hand,
   For I am drowning in a stormier sea
   Than Simon on thy lake of Galilee:[2]
The wine of life is spilt upon the sand,
5   My heart is as some famine-murdered land
   Whence all good things have perished utterly,
   And well I know my soul in Hell must lie
If I this night before God's throne should stand.
"He sleeps perchance, or rideth to the chase,
10   Like Baal, when his prophets howled that name
From morn to noon on Carmel's smitten height."[3]
Nay, peace, I shall behold, before the night,
   The feet of brass,[4] the robe more white than flame,
The wounded hands, the weary human face.

1881

The Harlot's House

We caught the tread of dancing feet,
We loitered down the moonlit street,
And stopped beneath the Harlot's house.

Inside, above the din and fray,
5   We heard the loud musicians play
The "Treues Liebes Herz" of Strauss.[1]

2. A song or short lyric in stanzas.
3. Perhaps referring to Numbers 20.10–13. After Moses had obtained water for his people by striking a rock with his rod, he was denied the privilege of entering the Promised Land.
1. Out of darkness (Latin).
2. Simon Peter, one of the twelve apostles, came close to drowning in a storm until rescued by Christ (Matthew 14.28–31).
3. The poet imagines an ironic voice discouraging

him; it uses the language of Elijah when he mocked the priests of Baal for their god's impotence by suggesting that perhaps Baal was on a journey or asleep (1 Kings 18.19–40).
4. Cf. Revelation 1.13–16, where the "Son of man" is seen in a vision, "his feet like unto fine brass, as if they burned in a furnace."
1. *Heart of True Love*, a waltz by the Austrian composer and "Waltz King" Johann Strauss (1825–1899).

Like strange mechanical grotesques,
Making fantastic arabesques,
The shadows raced across the blind.

10 We watched the ghostly dancers spin
To sound of horn and violin,
Like black leaves wheeling in the wind.

Like wire-pulled automatons,
Slim silhouetted skeletons
15 Went sidling through the slow quadrille,[2]

Then took each other by the hand,
And danced a stately saraband;[3]
Their laughter echoed thin and shrill.

Sometimes a clockwork puppet pressed
20 A phantom lover to her breast,
Sometimes they seemed to try to sing,

Sometimes a horrible marionette
Came out, and smoked its cigarette
Upon the steps like a live thing.[4]

25 Then turning to my love I said,
"The dead are dancing with the dead,
The dust is whirling with the dust."

But she, she heard the violin,
And left my side, and entered in;
30 Love passed into the house of Lust.

Then suddenly the tune went false,
The dancers wearied of the waltz,
The shadows ceased to wheel and whirl,

And down the long and silent street,
35 The dawn, with silver-sandaled feet,
Crept like a frightened girl.

1885, 1908

2. Intricate dance involving four couples facing
each other in a square.
3. A slow and stately dance, originating in Spain.

4. In an illustration for the poem by Althea Gyles
(approved by Wilde), the marionette is pictured as
a man in evening dress.

From The Critic as Artist[1]

ERNEST   Gilbert, you sound too harsh a note. Let us go back to the more gracious fields of literature. What was it you said? That it was more difficult to talk about a thing than to do it?

GILBERT   [*after a pause*] Yes: I believe I ventured upon that simple truth. Surely you see now that I am right? When man acts he is a puppet. When he describes he is a poet. The whole secret lies in that. It was easy enough on the sandy plains by windy Ilion[2] to send the notched arrow from the painted bow, or to hurl against the shield of hide and flamelike brass the long ash-handled spear. It was easy for the adulterous queen[3] to spread the Tyrian carpets for her lord, and then, as he lay couched in the marble bath, to throw over his head the purple net, and call to her smooth-faced lover to stab through the meshes at the heart that should have broken at Aulis.[4] For Antigone[5] even, with Death waiting for her as her bridegroom, it was easy to pass through the tainted air at noon, and climb the hill, and strew with kindly earth the wretched naked corse that had no tomb. But what of those who wrote about these things? What of those who gave them reality, and made them live forever? Are they not greater than the men and women they sing of? "Hector that sweet knight is dead."[6] And Lucian[7] tells us how in the dim underworld Menippus saw the bleaching skull of Helen, and marveled that it was for so grim a favor that all those horned ships were launched, those beautiful mailed men laid low, those towered cities brought to dust. Yet, every day the swanlike daughter of Leda comes out on the battlements, and looks down at the tide of war. The graybeards wonder at her loveliness, and she stands by the side of the king.[8] In his chamber of stained ivory lies her leman.[9] He is polishing his dainty armor, and combing the scarlet plume. With squire and page, her husband passes from tent to tent. She can see his bright hair, and hears, or fancies that she hears, that clear cold voice. In the courtyard below, the son of Priam is buckling on his brazen cuirass. The white arms of Andromache[1] are around his neck. He sets his helmet on the ground, lest their babe should be frightened. Behind the embroidered curtains of his pavilion sits Achilles,[2] in perfumed raiment, while in har-

---

1. In "the library of a house in Piccadilly," Gilbert and Ernest, two sophisticated young men, are talking about the use and function of criticism. Earlier in the dialogue, Ernest had complained that criticism is officious and useless: "Why should the artist be troubled by the shrill clamor of criticism? Why should those who cannot create take upon themselves to estimate the value of creative work?" Gilbert, in his reply, argues that criticism is creative in its own right. He digresses to compare the life of action unfavorably with the life of art: actions are dangerous and their results unpredictable; "if we lived long enough to see the results of our actions it may be that those who call themselves good would be sickened by a dull remorse, and those whom the world calls evil stirred by a noble joy." The excerpt printed here begins immediately following this digression.
2. Troy. Gilbert is referring to Homer's *Iliad*.
3. Clytemnestra, whose murder of her husband, Agamemnon, provides the plot for Aeschylus's

tragedy of that name.
4. Where Agamemnon sacrificed his daughter Iphigenia, thus incurring Clytemnestra's wrath.
5. Antigone defied Creon, king of Thebes, by burying the body of her brother, an act that Creon had forbidden, and was punished by death; see Sophocles' play *Antigone*.
6. Cf. Shakespeare's *Love's Labour's Lost* 5.2.663: "The sweet war-man [Hector] is dead and rotten."
7. Late Greek satirical writer, influenced by the earlier Greek seriocomic writer Menippus.
8. Priam. Homer in the *Iliad* describes the old men of Troy admiring the beauty of Helen, "swanlike daughter of Leda" and of Zeus (Zeus came to Leda in the form of a swan).
9. Lover (i.e., Paris).
1. Wife of Hector, one of the sons of Priam.
2. Son of Peleus and of the sea nymph Thetis; Achilles was the Greek hero, opposite of Hector, the Trojan hero, in the Trojan war. The scene set here is a tissue of recollections from the *Iliad*.

ness of gilt and silver the friend of his soul[3] arrays himself to go forth to fight. From a curiously carven chest that his mother Thetis had brought to his shipside, the Lord of the Myrmidons takes out that mystic chalice that the lip of man had never touched, and cleanses it with brimstone, and with fresh water cools it, and, having washed his hands, fills with black wine its burnished hollow, and spills the thick grape-blood upon the ground in honor of Him whom at Dodona[4] barefooted prophets worshiped, and prays to Him, and knows not that he prays in vain, and that by the hands of two knights from Troy, Panthous' son, Euphorbus, whose love-locks were looped with gold, and the Priamid,[5] the lion-hearted, Patroclus, the comrade of comrades, must meet his doom. Phantoms, are they? Heroes of mist and mountain? Shadows in a song? No: they are real. Action! What is action? It dies at the moment of its energy. It is a base concession to fact. The world is made by the singer for the dreamer.

ERNEST While you talk it seems to me to be so.

GILBERT It is so in truth. On the moldering citadel of Troy lies the lizard like a thing of green bronze. The owl has built her nest in the palace of Priam. Over the empty plain wander shepherd and goatherd with their flocks,[6] and where, on the wine-surfaced, oily sea, οἶνοψ πόντος,[6] as Homer calls it, copper-prowed and streaked with vermilion, the great galleys of the Danaoi[7] came in their gleaming crescent, the lonely tunny-fisher sits in his little boat and watches the bobbing corks of his net. Yet, every morning the doors of the city are thrown open, and on foot, or in horse-drawn chariot, the warriors go forth to battle, and mock their enemies from behind their iron masks. All day long the fight rages, and when night comes the torches gleam by the tents, and the cresset[8] burns in the hall. Those who live in marble or on painted panel know of life but a single exquisite instant, eternal indeed in its beauty, but limited to one note of passion or one mood of calm. Those whom the poet makes live have their myriad emotions of joy and terror, of courage and despair, of pleasure and of suffering. The seasons come and go in glad or saddening pageant, and with winged or leaden feet the years pass by before them. They have their youth and their manhood, they are children, and they grow old. It is always dawn for St. Helena, as Veronese saw her at the window.[9] Through the still morning air the angels bring her the symbol of God's pain. The cool breezes of the morning lift the gilt threads from her brow. On that little hill by the city of Florence, where the lovers of Giorgione[1] are lying, it is always the solstice of noon, made so languorous by summer suns that hardly can the slim naked girl dip into the marble tank the round bubble of clear glass, and the long fingers of the lute player rest idly upon the chords. It is twilight always for the dancing nymphs whom Corot[2] set free among the silver poplars of France. In eternal twilight they move, those frail diaphanous figures, whose trem-

3. I.e., Patroclus.
4. Seat of a very ancient oracle of Zeus.
5. "Son of Priam," i.e., Hector. With the help of Euphorbus, one of the bravest of the Trojans, he slew Patroclus and was in turn slain by Achilles.
6. Wine-dark sea (Greek).
7. Greeks.
8. Metal basket holding fuel burned for illumina-

tion, often hung from the ceiling.
9. One of the best-known paintings of the 16th-century Italian painter Paolo Veronese is *Helena's Vision.*
1. Italian painter (ca. 1477–1511), the most brilliant colorist of his time.
2. Jean-Baptiste-Camille Corot, 19th-century French painter, best-known for his shimmering trees.

ulous white feet seem not to touch the dew-drenched grass they tread on. But those who walk in epos,[3] drama, or romance, see through the laboring months the young moons wax and wane, and watch the night from evening unto morning star, and from sunrise unto sunsetting can note the shifting day with all its gold and shadow. For them, as for us, the flowers bloom and wither, and the Earth, that Green-tressed Goddess as Coleridge calls her, alters her raiment for their pleasure. The statue is concentrated to one moment of perfection. The image stained upon the canvas possesses no spiritual element of growth or change. If they know nothing of death, it is because they know little of life, for the secrets of life and death belong to those, and those only, whom the sequence of time affects, and who possess not merely the present but the future, and can rise or fall from a past of glory or of shame. Movement, that problem of the visible arts, can be truly realized by Literature alone. It is Literature that shows us the body in its swiftness and the soul in its unrest.

ERNEST Yes; I see now what you mean. But, surely, the higher you place the creative artist, the lower must the critic rank.

GILBERT Why so?

ERNEST Because the best that he can give us will be but an echo of rich music, a dim shadow of clear-outlined form. It may, indeed, be that life is chaos, as you tell me that it is; that its martyrdoms are mean and its heroisms ignoble; and that it is the function of Literature to create, from the rough material of actual existence, a new world that will be more marvelous, more enduring, and more true than the world that common eyes look upon, and through which common natures seek to realize their perfection. But surely, if this new world has been made by the spirit and touch of a great artist, it will be a thing so complete and perfect that there will be nothing left for the critic to do. I quite understand now, and indeed admit most readily, that it is far more difficult to talk about a thing than to do it. But it seems to me that this sound and sensible maxim, which is really extremely soothing to one's feelings, and should be adopted as its motto by every Academy of Literature all over the world, applies only to the relations that exist between Art and Life, and not to any relations that there may be between Art and Criticism.

GILBERT But, surely, Criticism is itself an art. And just as artistic creation implies the working of the critical faculty, and, indeed, without it cannot be said to exist at all, so Criticism is really creative in the highest sense of the word. Criticism is, in fact, both creative and independent.

ERNEST Independent?

GILBERT Yes; independent. Criticism is no more to be judged by any low standard of imitation or resemblance than is the work of poet or sculptor. The critic occupies the same relation to the work of art that he criticizes as the artist does to the visible world of form and color, or the unseen world of passion and of thought. He does not even require for the perfection of his art the finest materials. Anything will serve his purpose. And just as out of the sordid and sentimental amours of the silly wife of a small country doctor in the squalid village of Yonville-l'Abbaye, near

3. Epic poetry.

Rouen, Gustave Flaubert[4] was able to create a classic, and make a masterpiece of style, so, from subjects of little or of no importance, such as the pictures in this year's Royal Academy, or in any year's Royal Academy for that matter, Mr. Lewis Morris's poems, M. Ohnet's novels, or the plays of Mr. Henry Arthur Jones,[5] the true critic can, if it be his pleasure so to direct or waste his faculty of contemplation, produce work that will be flawless in beauty and instinct with intellectual subtlety. Why not? Dullness is always an irresistible temptation for brilliancy, and stupidity is the permanent *Bestia Trionfans*[6] that calls wisdom from its cave. To an artist so creative as the critic, what does subject matter signify? No more and no less than it does to the novelist and the painter. Like them, he can find his motives everywhere. Treatment is the test. There is nothing that has not in it suggestion or challenge.

ERNEST   But is Criticism really a creative art?

GILBERT   Why should it not be? It works with materials, and puts them into a form that is at once new and delightful. What more can one say of poetry? Indeed, I would call criticism a creation within a creation. For just as the great artists, from Homer and Aeschylus, down to Shakespeare and Keats, did not go directly to life for their subject matter, but sought for it in myth, and legend, and ancient tale, so the critic deals with materials that others have, as it were, purified for him, and to which imaginative form and color have been already added. Nay, more, I would say that the highest Criticism, being the purest form of personal impression, is in its way more creative than creation, as it has least reference to any standard external to itself, and is, in fact, its own reason for existing, and, as the Greeks would put it, in itself, and to itself, an end. Certainly, it is never trammeled by any shackles of verisimilitude. No ignoble considerations of probability, that cowardly concession to the tedious repetitions of domestic or public life, affect it ever. One may appeal from fiction unto fact. But from the soul there is no appeal.

ERNEST   From the soul?

GILBERT   Yes, from the soul. That is what the highest criticism really is, the record of one's own soul. It is more fascinating than history, as it is concerned simply with oneself. It is more delightful than philosophy, as its subject is concrete and not abstract, real and not vague. It is the only civilized form of autobiography, as it deals not with the events, but with the thoughts of one's life, not with life's physical accidents of deed or circumstance, but with the spiritual moods and imaginative passions of the mind. I am always amused by the silly vanity of those writers and artists of our day who seem to imagine that the primary function of the critic is to chatter about their second-rate work. The best that one can say of most modern creative art is that it is just a little less vulgar than reality, and so the critic, with his fine sense of distinction and sure instinct of delicate refinement, will prefer to look into the silver mirror or through the woven veil, and will turn his eyes away from the chaos

4. French novelist (1821–1880); the reference is to his novel *Madame Bovary* (1857).
5. Wilde is mischievously suggesting his low opinion of the contemporary writers just named. Morris was a Welsh poet and essayist often ridiculed by the critics. Georges Ohnet was a French novelist

and dramatist. Jones was one of the leading English playwrights of his time.
6. Triumphant beast (Latin). A reference to *Spaccio della Bestia Trionfante* (Expulsion of the triumphant beast, 1584), a philosophical allegory by the Italian philosopher Giordano Bruno.

and clamor of actual existence, though the mirror be tarnished and the veil be torn. His sole aim is to chronicle his own impressions. It is for him that pictures are painted, books written, and marble hewn into form.

ERNEST   I seem to have heard another theory of Criticism.

GILBERT   Yes: it has been said by one whose gracious memory we all revere,[7] and the music of whose pipe once lured Proserpina from her Sicilian fields, and made those white feet stir, and not in vain, the Cumnor cowslips, that the proper aim of Criticism is to see the object as in itself it really is. But this is a very serious error, and takes no cognizance of Criticism's most perfect form, which is in its essence purely subjective, and seeks to reveal its own secret and not the secret of another. For the highest Criticism deals with art not as expressive but as impressive purely.

ERNEST   But is that really so?

GILBERT   Of course it is. Who cares whether Mr. Ruskin's views on Turner[8] are sound or not? What does it matter? That mighty and majestic prose of his, so fervid and so fiery-colored in its noble eloquence, so rich in its elaborate symphonic music, so sure and certain, at its best, in subtle choice of word and epithet, is at least as great a work of art as any of those wonderful sunsets that bleach or rot on their corrupted canvases in England's Gallery; greater indeed, one is apt to think at times, not merely because its equal beauty is more enduring, but on account of the fuller variety of its appeal, soul speaking to soul in those long-cadenced lines, not through form and color alone, though through these, indeed, completely and without loss, but with intellectual and emotional utterance, with lofty passion and with loftier thought, with imaginative insight, and with poetic aim; greater, I always think, even as Literature is the greater art. Who, again, cares whether Mr. Pater has put into the portrait of Mona Lisa[9] something that Leonardo never dreamed of? The painter may have been merely the slave of an archaic smile, as some have fancied, but whenever I pass into the cool galleries of the Palace of the Louvre, and stand before that strange figure "set in its marble chair in that cirque of fantastic rocks, as in some faint light under sea," I murmur to myself, "She is older than the rocks among which she sits; like the vampire, she has been dead many times, and learned the secrets of the grave; and has been a diver in deep seas, and keeps their fallen day about her: and trafficked for strange webs with Eastern merchants; and, as Leda, was the mother of Helen of Troy, and, as St. Anne, the mother of Mary; and all this has been to her but as the sound of lyres and flutes, and lives only in the delicacy with which it has molded the changing lineaments, and tinged the eyelids and the hands." And I say to my friend, "The presence that thus so strangely rose beside the waters is expressive of what in the ways of a thousand years man had come to desire"; and

---

7. I.e., Matthew Arnold, whose poem *Thyrsis* (lines 91–100) evokes the legend of Proserpina, a goddess associated with the pastoral landscapes of Sicily. Arnold believed that it would be "in vain" to summon Proserpina to visit the Cumnor hills landscape (near Oxford), but Wilde's speaker here flatters Arnold that the summons was so beautiful that it was "not in vain." For the prose passage about the "aim of Criticism," see Arnold's *The Function of Criticism at the Present Time* (para. 1, p. 1514).
8. For Ruskin's defense of the paintings of Turner, see *Modern Painters*, especially his praise of Turner's *The Slave Ship* (p. 1429).
9. All remaining references in this paragraph are to Pater's essay *La Gioconda* (p. 1641).

he answers me, "Hers is the head upon which all 'the ends of the world are come,' and the eyelids are a little weary."

And so the picture becomes more wonderful to us than it really is, and reveals to us a secret of which, in truth, it knows nothing, and the music of the mystical prose is as sweet in our ears as was that flute-player's music that lent to the lips of La Gioconda[1] those subtle and poisonous curves. Do you ask me what Leonardo would have said had any one told him of this picture that "all the thoughts and experience of the world had etched and molded therein that which they had of power to refine and make expressive the outward form, the animalism of Greece, the lust of Rome, the reverie of the Middle Age with its spiritual ambition and imaginative loves, the return of the Pagan world, the sins of the Borgias?" He would probably have answered that he had contemplated none of these things, but had concerned himself simply with certain arrangements of lines and masses, and with new and curious color-harmonies of blue and green. And it is for this very reason that the criticism which I have quoted is criticism of the highest kind. It treats the work of art simply as a starting point for a new creation. It does not confine itself— let us at least suppose so for the moment—to discovering the real intention of the artist and accepting that as final. And in this it is right, for the meaning of any beautiful created thing is, at least, as much in the soul of him who looks at it, as it was in his soul who wrought it. Nay, it is rather the beholder who lends to the beautiful thing its myriad meanings, and makes it marvelous for us, and sets it in some new relation to the age, so that it becomes a vital portion of our lives, and symbol of what we pray for, or perhaps of what, having prayed for, we fear that we may receive. The longer I study, Ernest, the more clearly I see that the beauty of the visible arts is, as the beauty of music, impressive[2] primarily, and that it may be marred, and indeed often is so, by any excess of intellectual intention on the part of the artist. For when the work is finished it has, as it were, an independent life of its own, and may deliver a message far other than that which was put into its lips to say. Sometimes, when I listen to the overture to *Tannhäuser*,[3] I seem indeed to see that comely knight treading delicately on the flower-strewn grass, and to hear the voice of Venus calling to him from the caverned hill. But at other times it speaks to me of a thousand different things, of myself, it may be, and my own life, or of the lives of others whom one has loved and grown weary of loving, or of the passions that man has known, or of the passions that man has not known, and so has sought for. Tonight it may fill one with that ΕΡΩΣ ΤΩΝ ΑΔΥΝΑΤΩΝ, that *amour de l'impossible*,[4] which falls like a madness on many who think they live securely and out of reach of harm, so that they sicken suddenly with the poison of unlimited desire, and, in the infinite pursuit of what they may not obtain, grow faint and swoon or stumble. Tomorrow, like the music of which Aristotle and Plato tell us, the noble Dorian music of the Greek, it may perform

1. I.e., the *Mona Lisa* (she was the wife of Francesco del Gioconda—hence "La Gioconda").
2. I.e., designed to create an impression of the senses.
3. An opera by Richard Wagner (1845) based on the legend of a 14th-century German poet who fell

under the spell of Venus and lived with her in the Venusberg.
4. Love of the impossible, in Greek (in capital letters, perhaps to give the effect of an inscription) and in French.

the office of a physician, and give us an anodyne against pain, and heal the spirit that is wounded, and "bring the soul into harmony with all right things." And what is true about music is true about all the arts. Beauty has as many meanings as man has moods. Beauty is the symbol of symbols. Beauty reveals everything, because it expresses nothing. When it shows us itself, it shows us the whole fiery-colored world.

ERNEST But is such work as you have talked about really criticism?

GILBERT It is the highest Criticism, for it criticizes not merely the individual work of art, but Beauty itself, and fills with wonder a form which the artist may have left void, or not understood, or understood incompletely.

ERNEST The highest Criticism, then, is more creative than creation, and the primary aim of the critic is to see the object as in itself it really is not; that is your theory, I believe?

GILBERT Yes, that is my theory. To the critic the work of art is simply a suggestion for a new work of his own, that need not necessarily bear any obvious resemblance to the thing it criticizes. The one characteristic of a beautiful form is that one can put into it whatever one wishes, and see in it whatever one chooses to see; and the Beauty, that gives to creation its universal and aesthetic element, makes the critic a creator in his turn, and whispers of a thousand different things which were not present in the mind of him who carved the statue or painted the panel or graved the gem.

It is sometimes said by those who understand neither the nature of the highest Criticism nor the charm of the highest Art, that the pictures that the critic loves most to write about are those that belong to the anecdotage of painting, and that deal with scenes taken out of literature or history. But this is not so. Indeed, pictures of this kind are far too intelligible. As a class, they rank with illustrations, and even considered from this point of view are failures, as they do not stir the imagination, but set definite bounds to it. For the domain of the painter is, as I suggested before, widely different from that of the poet. To the latter belongs life in its full and absolute entirety; not merely the beauty that men look at, but the beauty that men listen to also; not merely the momentary grace of form or the transient gladness of color, but the whole sphere of feeling, the perfect cycle of thought. The painter is so far limited that it is only through the mask of the body that he can show us the mystery of the soul; only through conventional images that he can handle ideas; only through its physical equivalents that he can deal with psychology. And how inadequately does he do it then, asking us to accept the torn turban of the Moor for the noble rage of Othello, or a dotard in a storm for the wild madness of Lear! Yet it seems as if nothing could stop him. Most of our elderly English painters spend their wicked and wasted lives in poaching upon the domain of the poets, marring their motives by clumsy treatment, and striving to render, by visible form or color, the marvel of what is invisible, the splendor of what is not seen. Their picures are, as a natural consequence, insufferably tedious. They have degraded the invisible arts into the obvious arts, and the one thing not worth looking at is the obvious. I do not say that poet and painter may not treat of the same subject. They have always done so, and will always do so. But while the poet can be pictorial or not, as he chooses, the painter must be pictorial always. For a painter is limited, not to what he sees in nature, but to what upon canvas may be seen.

And so, my dear Ernest, pictures of this kind will not really fascinate the critic. He will turn from them to such works as make him brood and dream and fancy, to works that possess the subtle quality of suggestion, and seem to tell one that even from them there is an escape into a wider world. It is sometimes said that the tragedy of an artist's life is that he cannot realize his ideal. But the true tragedy that dogs the steps of most artists is that they realize their ideal too absolutely. For, when the ideal is realized, it is robbed of its wonder and its mystery, and becomes simply a new starting point for an ideal that is other than itself. This is the reason why music is the perfect type of art. Music can never reveal its ultimate secret. This, also, is the explanation of the value of limitations in art. The sculptor gladly surrenders imitative color, and the painter the actual dimensions of form, because by such renunciations they are able to avoid too definite a presentation of the Real, which would be mere imitation, and too definite a realization of the Ideal, which would be too purely intellectual. It is through its very incompleteness that Art becomes complete in beauty, and so addresses itself, not to the faculty of recognition nor to the faculty of reason, but to the aesthetic sense alone, which, while accepting both reason and recognition as stages of apprehension, subordinates them both to a pure synthetic impression of the work of art as a whole, and, taking whatever alien emotional elements the work may possess, uses their very complexity as a means by which a richer unity may be added to the ultimate impression itself. You see, then, how it is that the aesthetic critic rejects these obvious modes of art that have but one message to deliver, and having delivered it become dumb and sterile, and seeks rather for such modes as suggest reverie and mood, and by their imaginative beauty make all interpretations true, and no interpretation final. Some resemblance, no doubt, the creative work of the critic will have to the work that has stirred him to creation, but it will be such resemblance as exists, not between Nature and the mirror that the painter of landscape or figure may be supposed to hold up to her, but between Nature and the work of the decorative artist. Just as on the flowerless carpets of Persia, tulip and rose blossom indeed and are lovely to look on, though they are not reproduced in visible shape or line; just as the pearl and purple of the sea shell is echoed in the church of St. Mark at Venice; just as the vaulted ceiling of the wondrous chapel at Ravenna is made gorgeous by the gold and green and sapphire of the peacock's tail, though the birds of Juno fly not across it; so the critic reproduces the work that he criticizes in a mode that is never imitative, and part of whose charm may really consist in the rejection of resemblance, and shows us in this way not merely the meaning but also the mystery of Beauty, and, by transforming each art into literature, solves once for all the problem of Art's unity.

But I see it is time for supper. After we have discussed some Chambertin and a few ortolans,[5] we will pass on to the question of the critic considered in the light of the interpreter.

ERNEST   Ah! you admit, then, that the critic may occasionally be allowed to see the object as in itself it really is.

GILBERT   I am not quite sure. Perhaps I may admit it after supper. There is a subtle influence in supper.

1890, 1891

Preface to *The Picture of Dorian Gray*

The artist is the creator of beautiful things.

To reveal art and conceal the artist is art's aim.

The critic is he who can translate into another manner or a new material his impression of beautiful things.

The highest, as the lowest, form of criticism is a mode of autobiography.

Those who find ugly meanings in beautiful things are corrupt without being charming. This is a fault.

Those who find beautiful meanings in beautiful things are the cultivated. For these there is hope.

They are the elect to whom beautiful things mean only Beauty.

There is no such thing as a moral or an immoral book.

Books are well written, or badly written. That is all.

The nineteenth-century dislike of Realism is the rage of Caliban[1] seeing his own face in a glass.

The nineteenth-century dislike of Romanticism is the rage of Caliban not seeing his own face in a glass.

The moral life of man forms part of the subject matter of the artist, but the morality of art consists in the perfect use of an imperfect medium. No artist desires to prove anything. Even things that are true can be proved.

No artist has ethical sympathies. An ethical sympathy in an artist is an unpardonable mannerism of style.

No artist is ever morbid. The artist can express everything.

Thought and language are to the artist instruments of an art.

Vice and Virtue are to the artist materials for an art.

From the point of view of form, the type of all the arts is the art of the musician. From the point of view of feeling, the actor's craft is the type.

All art is at once surface and symbol.

Those who go beneath the surface do so at their peril.

Those who read the symbol do so at their peril.

It is the spectator, and not life, that art really mirrors.

Diversity of opinion about a work of art shows that the work is new, complex, and vital.

When critics disagree the artist is in accord with himself. We can forgive a man for making a useful thing as long as he does not admire

---

5. Birds esteemed by epicures for their delicate flavor. "Chambertin": one of the finest wines of Burgundy.

1. The character in Shakespeare's *Tempest* is half-human, half-monster.

it. The only excuse for making a useless thing is that one admires it
intensely.

> All art is quite useless.

1891

The Importance of Being Earnest   Of the four stage comedies by Wilde,

his last, *The Importance of Being Earnest*, is generally regarded as his masterpiece. It
was first staged in February 1895 and was an immediate hit. Only one critic failed to
find it delightful; curiously, this was Wilde's fellow playwright from Ireland, Bernard
Shaw, who, though amused, found Wilde's wit "hateful" and "sinister," and thought
the play exhibited "real degeneracy." Despite Shaw's complaints, the first London
production ran for eighty-six performances, but when Wilde was sentenced to prison,
production ceased for several years. Shortly before his death it was revived in London
and New York, and has subsequently become a classic of the theater.

In its original version, the play was in four acts. At the request of the stage producer,
Wilde reduced it to three acts—the version almost always used in performances and
therefore the version reprinted here. A few of the notes in the text cite passages from
the four-act version.

The play was first published in 1899. Earlier, in an interview, Wilde had described
his overall aim in writing it: "It has as its philosophy . . . that we should treat all the
trivial things of life seriously, and all the serious things of life with sincere and studied
triviality." Just before his death he remarked that although he was pleased with the
"bright and happy" tone and temper of his play, he wished it might have had a "higher
seriousness of intent." Later critics have found this seriousness of intent in the play's
deconstruction of Victorian moral and social values. Like another Victorian masterpiece of the absurd, *Alice's Adventures in Wonderland*, *The Importance of Being Earnest* empties manners and morals of their underlying sense to create a nominalist
world where earnest is not a quality of character but a name, where words, to paraphrase Humpty Dumpty in *Through the Looking-Glass*, mean what you choose them
to mean, neither more nor less.

The literary ancestry of Wilde's play has been variously identified. In its witty wordplay and worldly attitudes it has been likened to comedies of the Restoration period
such as Congreve's *Love for Love*. In its genial and lighthearted tone, it has some
affinities with the festive comedies of Shakespeare, such as *Twelfth Night*, and with
Goldsmith's *She Stoops to Conquer*. A more immediate predecessor was *Engaged*
(1877), a comic play by W. S. Gilbert that anticipated some of the burlesque effects
exploited by Wilde, such as the interrupting of sentimental scenes by the consumption
of food, and the inviolable imperturbability of the speakers. Gilbert's advice to the
actors who were putting on his *Engaged* is worth citing as a clue to how *The Importance of Being Earnest* may be most effectively imagined as a stage representation:

> It is absolutely essential to the success of this piece that it should be played with
> the most perfect earnestness and gravity throughout. . . . Directly the actors
> show that they are conscious of the absurdity of their utterances the piece begins
> to drag.

The Importance of Being Earnest

First Act

SCENE—*Morning room in* ALGERNON's *flat in Half-Moon Street.*[1]

The room is luxuriously and artistically furnished. The sound of a piano is heard in the adjoining room.

[LANE *is arranging afternoon tea on the table, and after the music has ceased,* ALGERNON *enters.*]

ALGERNON   Did you hear what I was playing, Lane?

LANE   I didn't think it polite to listen, sir.

ALGERNON   I'm sorry for that, for your sake. I don't play accurately—anyone can play accurately—but I play with wonderful expression. As far as the piano is concerned, sentiment is my forte. I keep science for Life.

LANE   Yes, sir.

ALGERNON   And, speaking of the science of Life, have you got the cucumber sandwiches cut for Lady Bracknell?[2]

LANE   Yes, sir. [*Hands them on a salver.*]

ALGERNON   [*Inspects them, takes two, and sits down on the sofa.*]   Oh! . . . by the way, Lane, I see from your book[3] that on Thursday night, when Lord Shoreham and Mr. Worthing were dining with me, eight bottles of champagne are entered as having been consumed.

LANE   Yes, sir; eight bottles and a pint.

ALGERNON   Why is it that at a bachelor's establishment the servants invariably drink the champagne? I ask merely for information.

LANE   I attribute it to the superior quality of the wine, sir. I have often observed that in married households the champagne is rarely of a first-rate brand.

ALGERNON   Good Heavens! Is marriage so demoralizing as that?

LANE   I believe it *is* a very pleasant state, sir. I have had very little experience of it myself up to the present. I have only been married once. That was in consequence of a misunderstanding between myself and a young person.

ALGERNON   [*Languidly.*]   I don't know that I am much interested in your family life, Lane.

LANE   No, sir; it is not a very interesting subject. I never think of it myself.

ALGERNON   Very natural, I am sure. That will do, Lane, thank you.

LANE   Thank you, sir.   [LANE *goes out.*]

ALGERNON   Lane's views on marriage seem somewhat lax. Really, if the lower orders don't set us a good example, what on earth is the use of them? They seem, as a class, to have absolutely no sense of moral responsibility.

[*Enter* LANE.]

LANE   Mr. Ernest Worthing.

---

1. A highly fashionable location (at the time of the play) in the West End of London.
2. The name of a place in Berkshire where the mother of Lord Alfred Douglas had her summer home, which Wilde had visited.
3. Cellar book, in which records were kept of wines.

[*Enter* JACK.]   [LANE *goes out.*]

ALGERNON   How are you, my dear Ernest? What brings you up to town?

JACK   Oh, pleasure, pleasure! What else should bring one anywhere? Eating as usual, I see, Algy!

ALGERNON [*Stiffly.*]   I believe it is customary in good society to take some slight refreshment at five o'clock. Where have you been since last Thursday?

JACK [*Sitting down on the sofa.*]   In the country.

ALGERNON   What on earth do you do there?

JACK [*Pulling off his gloves.*]   When one is in town one amuses oneself. When one is in the country one amuses other people. It is excessively boring.

ALGERNON   And who are the people you amuse?

JACK [*Airily.*]   Oh, neighbors, neighbors.

ALGERNON   Got nice neighbors in your part of Shropshire?

JACK   Perfectly horrid! Never speak to one of them.

ALGERNON   How immensely you must amuse them! [*Goes over and takes sandwich.*] By the way, Shropshire is your county, is it not?

JACK   Eh? Shropshire?⁴ Yes, of course. Hallo! Why all these cups? Why cucumber sandwiches? Why such reckless extravagance in one so young? Who is coming to tea?

ALGERNON   Oh! merely Aunt Augusta and Gwendolen.

JACK   How perfectly delightful!

ALGERNON   Yes, that is all very well; but I am afraid Aunt Augusta won't quite approve of your being here.

JACK   May I ask why?

ALGERNON   My dear fellow, the way you flirt with Gwendolen is perfectly disgraceful. It is almost as bad as the way Gwendolen flirts with you.

JACK   I am in love with Gwendolen. I have come up to town expressly to propose to her.

ALGERNON   I thought you had come up for pleasure? . . . I call that business.

JACK   How utterly unromantic you are!

ALGERNON   I really don't see anything romantic in proposing. It is very romantic to be in love. But there is nothing romantic about a definite proposal. Why, one may be accepted. One usually is, I believe. Then the excitement is all over. The very essence of romance is uncertainty. If ever I get married, I'll certainly try to forget the fact.

JACK   I have no doubt about that, dear Algy. The Divorce Court was specially invented for people whose memories are so curiously constituted.

ALGERNON   Oh! there is no use speculating on that subject. Divorces are made in Heaven—[JACK *puts out his hand to take a sandwich.* ALGERNON *at once interferes.*] Please don't touch the cucumber sandwiches. They are ordered specially for Aunt Augusta. [*Takes one and eats it.*]

JACK   Well, you have been eating them all the time.

4. As we learn later, the estate is in Hertfordshire, a very long distance from Shropshire. In the four-act version of the play, when this discrepancy is pointed out by Algernon, Jack replies: "My dear fellow! Surely you don't expect me to be accurate about geography? No gentleman is accurate about geography. Why, I got a prize for geography when I was at school. I can't be expected to know anything about it now."

ALGERNON   That is quite a different matter. She is my aunt. [*Takes plate from below.*] Have some bread and butter. The bread and butter is for Gwendolen. Gwendolen is devoted to bread and butter.

JACK [*Advancing to table and helping himself.*]   And very good bread and butter it is too.

ALGERNON   Well, my dear fellow, you need not eat as if you were going to eat it all. You behave as if you were married to her already. You are not married to her already, and I don't think you ever will be.

JACK   Why on earth do you say that?

ALGERNON   Well, in the first place, girls never marry the men they flirt with. Girls don't think it right.

JACK   Oh, that is nonsense!

ALGERNON   It isn't. It is a great truth. It accounts for the extraordinary number of bachelors that one sees all over the place. In the second place, I don't give my consent.

JACK   Your consent!

ALGERNON   My dear fellow, Gwendolen is my first cousin. And before I allow you to marry her, you will have to clear up the whole question of Cecily. [*Rings bell.*]

JACK   Cecily! What on earth do you mean? What do you mean, Algy, by Cecily? I don't know anyone of the name of Cecily.
   [*Enter* LANE.]

ALGERNON   Bring me that cigarette case Mr. Worthing left in the smoking-room the last time he dined here.

LANE   Yes, sir.   [LANE *goes out.*]

JACK   Do you mean to say you have had my cigarette case all this time? I wish to goodness you had let me know. I have been writing frantic letters to Scotland Yard[5] about it. I was very nearly offering a large reward.

ALGERNON   Well, I wish you would offer one. I happen to be more than usually hard up.

JACK   There is no good offering a large reward now that the thing is found.
   [*Enter* LANE *with the cigarette case on a salver.* ALGERNON *takes it at once.* LANE *goes out.*]

ALGERNON   I think that is rather mean of you, Ernest, I must say. [*Opens case and examines it.*] However, it makes no matter, for, now that I look at the inscription inside, I find that the thing isn't yours after all.

JACK   Of course it's mine. [*Moving to him.*] You have seen me with it a hundred times, and you have no right whatsoever to read what is written inside. It is a very ungentlemanly thing to read a private cigarette case.

ALGERNON   Oh! it is absurd to have a hard-and-fast rule about what one should read and what one shouldn't. More than half of modern culture depends on what one shouldn't read.

JACK   I am quite aware of the fact, and I don't propose to discuss modern culture. It isn't the sort of thing one should talk of in private. I simply want my cigarette case back.

ALGERNON   Yes; but this isn't your cigarette case. This cigarette case is a present from someone of the name of Cecily, and you said you didn't know anyone of that name.

5. Police headquarters in London.

JACK Well, if you want to know, Cecily happens to be my aunt.

ALGERNON Your aunt!

JACK Yes. Charming old lady she is, too. Lives at Tunbridge Wells.[6] Just give it back to me, Algy.

ALGERNON [*retreating to back of sofa.*] But why does she call herself little Cecily if she is your aunt and lives at Tunbridge Wells? [*Reading.*] "From little Cecily with her fondest love."

JACK [*Moving to sofa and kneeling upon it.*] My dear fellow, what on earth is there in that? Some aunts are tall, some aunts are not tall. That is a matter that surely an aunt may be allowed to decide for herself. You seem to think that every aunt should be exactly like your aunt! That is absurd! For Heaven's sake give me back my cigarette case. [*Follows Algy round the room.*]

ALGERNON Yes. But why does your aunt call you her uncle? "From little Cecily, with her fondest love to her dear Uncle Jack." There is no objection, I admit, to an aunt being a small aunt, but why an aunt, no matter what her size may be, should call her own nephew her uncle, I can't quite make out. Besides, your name isn't Jack at all; it is Ernest.

JACK It isn't Ernest; it's Jack.

ALGERNON You have always told me it was Ernest. I have introduced you to everyone as Ernest. You answer to the name of Ernest. You look as if your name was Ernest. You are the most earnest looking person I ever saw in my life. It is perfectly absurd your saying that your name isn't Ernest. It's on your cards. Here is one of them. [*Taking it from case.*] "Mr. Ernest Worthing, B. 4, The Albany."[7] I'll keep this as a proof that your name is Ernest if ever you attempt to deny it to me, or to Gwendolen, or to anyone else. [*Puts the card in his pocket.*]

JACK Well, my name is Ernest in town and Jack in the country, and the cigarette case was given to me in the country.

ALGERNON Yes, but that does not account for the fact that your small Aunt Cecily, who lives at Tunbridge Wells, calls you her dear uncle. Come, old boy, you had much better have the thing out at once.

JACK My dear Algy, you talk exactly as if you were a dentist. It is very vulgar to talk like a dentist when one isn't a dentist. It produces a false impression.

ALGERNON Well, that is exactly what dentists always do. Now, go on! Tell me the whole thing. I may mention that I have always suspected you of being a confirmed and secret Bunburyist; and I am quite sure of it now.

JACK Bunburyist? What on earth do you mean by a Bunburyist?

ALGERNON I'll reveal to you the meaning of that incomparable expression as soon as you are kind enough to inform me why you are Ernest in town and Jack in the country.

JACK Well, produce my cigarette case first.

ALGERNON Here it is. [*Hands cigarette case.*] Now produce your explanation, and pray make it improbable. [*Sits on sofa.*]

JACK My dear fellow, there is nothing improbable about my explanation at all. In fact it's perfectly ordinary. Old Mr. Thomas Cardew, who

6. A fashionable resort town south of London.
7. A former residence of the duke of Albany (brother of George IV) near Piccadilly that had been converted into elegant apartments often rented by country gentry for visits to London.

adopted me when I was a little boy, made me in his will guardian to his granddaughter, Miss Cecily Cardew. Cecily, who addresses me as her uncle from motives of respect that you could not possibly appreciate, lives at my place in the country under the charge of her admirable governess, Miss Prism.

ALGERNON   Where is that place in the country, by the way?

JACK   That is nothing to you, dear boy. You are not going to be invited. . . . I may tell you candidly that the place is not in Shropshire.

ALGERNON   I suspected that, my dear fellow! I have Bunburyed all over Shropshire on two separate occasions. Now, go on. Why are you Ernest in town and Jack in the country?

JACK   My dear Algy, I don't know whether you will be able to understand my real motives. You are hardly serious enough. When one is placed in the position of guardian, one has to adopt a very high moral tone on all subjects. It's one's duty to do so. And as a high moral tone can hardly be said to conduce very much to either one's health or one's happiness, in order to get up to town I have always pretended to have a younger brother of the name of Ernest, who lives in the Albany, and gets into the most dreadful scrapes. That, my dear Algy, is the whole truth pure and simple.

ALGERNON   The truth is rarely pure and never simple. Modern life would be very tedious if it were either, and modern literature a complete impossibility!

JACK   That wouldn't be at all a bad thing.

ALGERNON   Literary criticism is not your forte, my dear fellow. Don't try it. You should leave that to people who haven't been at a University. They do it so well in the daily papers. What you really are is a Bunburyist. I was quite right in saying you were a Bunburyist. You are one of the most advanced Bunburyists I know.

JACK   What on earth do you mean?

ALGERNON   You have invented a very useful young brother called Ernest, in order that you may be able to come up to town as often as you like. I have invented an invaluable permanent invalid called Bunbury, in order that I may be able to go down into the country whenever I choose. Bunbury is perfectly invaluable. If it wasn't for Bunbury's extraordinary bad health, for instance, I wouldn't be able to dine with you at Willis's tonight, for I have been really engaged[8] to Aunt Augusta for more than a week.

JACK   I haven't asked you to dine with me anywhere tonight.

ALGERNON   I know. You are absurdly careless about sending out invitations. It is very foolish of you. Nothing annoys people so much as not receiving invitations.

JACK   You had much better dine with your Aunt Augusta.

ALGERNON   I haven't the smallest intention of doing anything of the kind. To begin with, I dined there on Monday, and once a week is quite enough to dine with one's own relations. In the second place, whenever I do dine there I am always treated as a member of the family, and sent down with[9] either no woman at all, or two. In the third place, I know perfectly well whom she will place me next to, tonight. She will place me next Mary

8. I.e., committed to attend her dinner party. "Willis's": a first-class restaurant in the vicinity of   St. James's Street.
9. I.e., required to escort, as a dinner partner.

Farquhar, who always flirts with her own husband across the dinner table. That is not very pleasant. Indeed, it is not even decent . . . and that sort of thing is enormously on the increase. The amount of women in London who flirt with their own husbands is perfectly scandalous. It looks so bad. It is simply washing one's clean linen in public. Besides, now that I know you to be a confirmed Bunburyist, I naturally want to talk to you about Bunburying. I want to tell you the rules.

JACK   I'm not a Bunburyist at all. If Gwendolen accepts me, I am going to kill my brother, indeed I think I'll kill him in any case. Cecily is a little too much interested in him. It is rather a bore. So I am going to get rid of Ernest. And I strongly advise you to do the same with Mr. . . . with your invalid friend who has the absurd name.

ALGERNON   Nothing will induce me to part with Bunbury, and if you ever get married, which seems to me extremely problematic, you will be very glad to know Bunbury. A man who marries without knowing Bunbury has a very tedious time of it.

JACK   That is nonsense. If I marry a charming girl like Gwendolen, and she is the only girl I ever saw in my life that I would marry, I certainly won't want to know Bunbury.

ALGERNON   Then your wife will. You don't seem to realize, that in married life three is company and two is none.

JACK [*Sententiously.*]   That, my dear young friend, is the theory that the corrupt French Drama has been propounding for the last fifty years.[1]

ALGERNON   Yes; and that the happy English home has proved in half the time.

JACK   For heaven's sake, don't try to be cynical. It's perfectly easy to be cynical.

ALGERNON   My dear fellow, it isn't easy to be anything nowadays. There's such a lot of beastly competition about. [*The sound of an electric bell is heard.*] Ah! that must be Aunt Augusta. Only relatives, or creditors, ever ring in that Wagnerian manner.[2] Now, if I get her out of the way for ten minutes, so that you can have an opportunity for proposing to Gwendolen, may I dine with you tonight at Willis's?

JACK   I suppose so, if you want to.

ALGERNON   Yes, but you must be serious about it. I hate people who are not serious about meals. It is so shallow of them.
   [*Enter* LANE.]

LANE   Lady Bracknell and Miss Fairfax.
   [ALGERNON *goes forward to meet them. Enter* LADY BRACKNELL *and* GWENDOLEN.]

LADY BRACKNELL   Good afternoon, dear Algernon, I hope you are behaving very well.

ALGERNON   I'm feeling very well, Aunt Augusta.

LADY BRACKNELL   That's not quite the same thing. In fact the two things rarely go together. [*Sees* JACK *and bows to him with icy coldness.*]

ALGERNON [*To* GWENDOLEN.]   Dear me, you are smart![3]

---

1. Almost all the plays by the leading French playwrights of the second half of the 19th century (Alexandre Dumas *fils,* Émile Augier, and Victorien Sardou) focus on the topic of marital infidelity. As Brander Matthews, an American critic, noted in 1882, "the trio—husband, wife, and lover" had become "almost universal" in the French theater.
2. Insistently loud, like some of the music in Richard Wagner's large-scale operas.
3. Elegantly fashionable.

GWENDOLEN   I am always smart! Aren't I, Mr. Worthing?

JACK   You're quite perfect, Miss Fairfax.

GWENDOLEN   Oh! I hope I am not that. It would leave no room for developments, and I intend to develop in many directions. [GWENDOLEN *and* JACK *sit down together in the corner.*]

LADY BRACKNELL   I'm sorry if we are a little late, Algernon, but I was obliged to call on dear Lady Harbury. I hadn't been there since her poor husband's death. I never saw a woman so altered; she looks quite twenty years younger. And now I'll have a cup of tea, and one of those nice cucumber sandwiches you promised me.

ALGERNON   Certainly, Aunt Augusta. [*Goes over to teatable.*]

LADY BRACKNELL   Won't you come and sit here, Gwendolen?

GWENDOLEN   Thanks, mamma,[4] I'm quite comfortable where I am.

ALGERNON [*Picking up empty plate in horror.*]   Good heavens! Lane! Why are there no cucumber sandwiches? I ordered them specially.

LANE [*Gravely.*]   There were no cucumbers in the market this morning, sir. I went down twice.

ALGERNON   No cucumbers!

LANE   No, sir. Not even for ready money.

ALGERNON   That will do, Lane, thank you.

LANE   Thank you, sir.

ALGERNON   I am greatly distressed, Aunt Augusta, about there being no cucumbers, not even for ready money.

LADY BRACKNELL   It really makes no matter, Algernon. I had some crumpets[5] with Lady Harbury, who seems to me to be living entirely for pleasure now.

ALGERNON   I hear her hair has turned quite gold from grief.

LADY BRACKNELL   It certainly has changed its color. From what cause I, of course, cannot say. [ALGERNON *crosses and hands tea.*] Thank you. I've quite a treat for you tonight, Algernon. I am going to send you down with Mary Farquhar. She is such a nice woman, and so attentive to her husband. It's delightful to watch them.

ALGERNON   I am afraid, Aunt Augusta, I shall have to give up the pleasure of dining with you tonight after all.

LADY BRACKNELL [*Frowning.*]   I hope not, Algernon. It would put my table completely out. Your uncle would have to dine upstairs. Fortunately he is accustomed to that.

ALGERNON   It is a great bore, and, I need hardly say, a terrible disappointment to me, but the fact is I have just had a telegram to say that my poor friend Bunbury is very ill again. [*Exchanges glances with* JACK.] They seem to think I should be with him.

LADY BRACKNELL   It is very strange. This Mr. Bunbury seems to suffer from curiously bad health.

ALGERNON   Yes; poor Bunbury is a dreadful invalid.

LADY BRACKNELL   Well, I must say, Algernon, that I think it is high time that Mr. Bunbury made up his mind whether he was going to live or to die. This shilly-shallying with the question is absurd. Nor do I in any way

---

4. Pronounced with the accent on the second syllable.

5. A kind of toasted muffin.

approve of the modern sympathy with invalids. I consider it morbid. Illness of any kind is hardly a thing to be encouraged in others. Health is the primary duty of life. I am always telling that to your poor uncle, but he never seems to take much notice . . . as far as any improvement in his ailments goes. I should be obliged if you would ask Mr. Bunbury, from me, to be kind enough not to have a relapse on Saturday, for I rely on you to arrange my music for me. It is my last reception, and one wants something that will encourage conversation, particularly at the end of the season[6] when everyone has practically said whatever they had to say, which, in most cases, was probably not much.

ALGERNON   I'll speak to Bunbury, Aunt Augusta, if he is still conscious, and I think I can promise you he'll be all right by Saturday. Of course the music is a great difficulty. You see, if one plays good music, people don't listen, and if one plays bad music, people don't talk. But I'll run over the program I've drawn out, if you will kindly come into the next room for a moment.

LADY BRACKNELL   Thank you, Algernon. It is very thoughtful of you. [*Rising, and following* ALGERNON.] I'm sure the program will be delightful, after a few expurgations. French songs I cannot possibly allow. People always seem to think that they are improper, and either look shocked, which is vulgar, or laugh, which is worse. But German sounds a thoroughly respectable language, and indeed, I believe is so. Gwendolen, you will accompany me.

GWENDOLEN   Certainly, mamma.

[LADY BRACKNELL *and* ALGERNON *go into the music room,* GWENDOLEN *remains behind.*]

JACK   Charming day it has been, Miss Fairfax.

GWENDOLEN   Pray don't talk to me about the weather, Mr. Worthing. Whenever people talk to me about the weather, I always feel quite certain that they mean something else. And that makes me so nervous.

JACK   I do mean something else.

GWENDOLEN   I thought so. In fact, I am never wrong.

JACK   And I would like to be allowed to take advantage of Lady Bracknell's temporary absence . . .

GWENDOLEN   I would certainly advise you to do so. Mamma has a way of coming back suddenly into a room that I have often had to speak to her about.

JACK [*Nervously.*]   Miss Fairfax, ever since I met you I have admired you more than any girl . . . I have ever met since . . . I met you.

GWENDOLEN   Yes, I am quite aware of the fact. And I often wish that in public, at any rate, you had been more demonstrative. For me you have always had an irresistible fascination. Even before I met you I was far from indifferent to you. [JACK *looks at her in amazement.*] We live, as I hope you know, Mr. Worthing, in an age of ideals. The fact is constantly mentioned in the more expensive monthly magazines, and has reached the provincial pulpits, I am told: and my ideal has always been to love someone of the name of Ernest. There is something in that name that

---

6. The social season, extending from May through July, when people of fashion came into London from their country estates for entertainments and parties.

inspires absolute confidence. The moment Algernon first mentioned to me that he had a friend called Ernest, I knew I was destined to love you.

JACK   You really love me, Gwendolen?

GWENDOLEN   Passionately!

JACK   Darling! You don't know how happy you've made me.

GWENDOLEN   My own Ernest!

JACK   But you don't really mean to say that you couldn't love me if my name wasn't Ernest?

GWENDOLEN   But your name is Ernest.

JACK   Yes, I know it is. But supposing it was something else? Do you mean to say you couldn't love me then?

GWENDOLEN   [Glibly.]   Ah! that is clearly a metaphysical speculation, and like most metaphysical speculations has very little reference at all to the actual facts of real life, as we know them.

JACK   Personally, darling, to speak quite candidly, I don't much care about the name of Ernest . . . I don't think the name suits me at all.

GWENDOLEN   It suits you perfectly. It is a divine name. It has a music of its own. It produces vibrations.

JACK   Well, really, Gwendolen, I must say that I think there are lots of other much nicer names. I think Jack, for instance, a charming name.

GWENDOLEN   Jack? . . . No, there is very little music in the name Jack, if any at all, indeed. It does not thrill. It produces absolutely no vibrations. . . . I have known several Jacks, and they all, without exception, were more than usually plain. Besides, Jack is a notorious domesticity for John! And I pity any woman who is married to a man called John. She would probably never be allowed to know the entrancing pleasure of a single moment's solitude. The only really safe name is Ernest.

JACK   Gwendolen, I must get christened at once—I mean we must get married at once. There is no time to be lost.

GWENDOLEN   Married, Mr. Worthing?

JACK [Astounded.]   Well . . . surely. You know that I love you, and you led me to believe, Miss Fairfax, that you were not absolutely indifferent to me.

GWENDOLEN   I adore you. But you haven't proposed to me yet. Nothing has been said at all about marriage. The subject has not even been touched on.

JACK   Well . . . may I propose to you now?

GWENDOLEN   I think it would be an admirable opportunity. And to spare you any possible disappointment, Mr. Worthing, I think it only fair to tell you quite frankly beforehand that I am fully determined to accept you.

JACK   Gwendolen!

GWENDOLEN   Yes, Mr. Worthing, what have you got to say to me?

JACK   You know what I have got to say to you.

GWENDOLEN   Yes, but you don't say it.

JACK   Gwendolen, will you marry me? [Goes on his knees.]

GWENDOLEN   Of course I will, darling. How long you have been about it! I am afraid you have had very little experience in how to propose.

JACK   My own one, I have never loved anyone in the world but you.

GWENDOLEN   Yes, but men often propose for practice. I know my brother Gerald does. All my girlfriends tell me so. What wonderfully blue eyes you have, Ernest! They are quite, quite blue. I hope you will always look at me just like that, especially when there are other people present.

[*Enter* LADY BRACKNELL.]

LADY BRACKNELL Mr. Worthing! Rise, sir, from this semi-recumbent posture. It is most indecorous.

GWENDOLEN Mamma! [*He tries to rise; she restrains him.*] I must beg you to retire. This is no place for you. Besides, Mr. Worthing has not quite finished yet.

LADY BRACKNELL Finished what, may I ask?

GWENDOLEN I am engaged to Mr. Worthing, mamma.

[*They rise together.*]

LADY BRACKNELL Pardon me, you are not engaged to anyone. When you do become engaged to someone, I, or your father, should his health permit him, will inform you of the fact. An engagement should come on a young girl as a surprise, pleasant or unpleasant, as the case may be. It is hardly a matter that she could be allowed to arrange for herself. . . . And now I have a few questions to put to you, Mr. Worthing. While I am making these inquiries, you, Gwendolen, will wait for me below in the carriage.

GWENDOLEN [*Reproachfully.*] Mamma!

LADY BRACKNELL In the carriage, Gwendolen! [GWENDOLEN *goes to the door. She and* JACK *blow kisses to each other behind* LADY BRACKNELL's *back.* LADY BRACKNELL *looks vaguely about as if she could not understand what the noise was. Finally turns round.*] Gwendolen, the carriage!

GWENDOLEN Yes, mamma. [*Goes out, looking back at* JACK.]

LADY BRACKNELL [*Sitting down.*] You can take a seat, Mr. Worthing.

[*Looks in her pocket for notebook and pencil.*]

JACK Thank you, Lady Bracknell, I prefer standing.

LADY BRACKNELL [*Pencil and notebook in hand.*] I feel bound to tell you that you are not down on my list of eligible young men, although I have the same list as the dear Duchess of Bolton has. We work together, in fact. However, I am quite ready to enter your name, should your answers be what a really affectionate mother requires. Do you smoke?

JACK Well, yes, I must admit I smoke.

LADY BRACKNELL I am glad to hear it. A man should always have an occupation of some kind. There are far too many idle men in London as it is. How old are you?

JACK Twenty-nine.

LADY BRACKNELL A very good age to be married at. I have always been of opinion that a man who desires to get married should know either everything or nothing. Which do you know?

JACK [*After some hesitation.*] I know nothing, Lady Bracknell.

LADY BRACKNELL I am pleased to hear it. I do not approve of anything that tampers with natural ignorance. Ignorance is like a delicate exotic fruit; touch it and the bloom is gone. The whole theory of modern education is radically unsound. Fortunately in England, at any rate, education produces no effect whatsoever. If it did, it would prove a serious danger to the upper classes, and probably lead to acts of violence in Grosvenor Square.[7] What is your income?

---

7. A fashionable residential area in the West End of London.

JACK   Between seven and eight thousand a year.

LADY BRACKNELL [*Makes a note in her book.*]   In land, or in investments?

JACK   In investments, chiefly.

LADY BRACKNELL   That is satisfactory. What between the duties expected of one during one's lifetime, and the duties exacted from one after one's death,[8] land has ceased to be either a profit or a pleasure. It gives one position, and prevents one from keeping it up. That's all that can be said about land.

JACK   I have a country house with some land, of course, attached to it, about fifteen hundred acres, I believe; but I don't depend on that for my real income. In fact, as far as I can make out, the poachers are the only people who make anything out of it.

LADY BRACKNELL   A country house! How many bedrooms? Well, that point can be cleared up afterwards. You have a town house, I hope? A girl with a simple, unspoiled nature, like Gwendolen, could hardly be expected to reside in the country.

JACK   Well, I own a house in Belgrave Square,[9] but it is let by the year to Lady Bloxham. Of course, I can get it back whenever I like, at six months' notice.

LADY BRACKNELL   Lady Bloxham? I don't know her.

JACK   Oh, she goes about very little. She is a lady considerably advanced in years.

LADY BRACKNELL   Ah, nowadays that is no guarantee of respectability of character. What number in Belgrave Square?

JACK   149.

LADY BRACKNELL [*Shaking her head.*]   The unfashionable side. I thought there was something. However, that could easily be altered.

JACK   Do you mean the fashion, or the side?

LADY BRACKNELL [*Sternly.*]   Both, if necessary, I presume. What are your politics?

JACK   Well, I am afraid I really have none. I am a Liberal Unionist.[1]

LADY BRACKNELL   Oh, they count as Tories. They dine with us. Or come in the evening, at any rate. Now to minor matters. Are your parents living?

JACK   I have lost both my parents.

LADY BRACKNELL   Both? To lose one parent may be regarded as a misfortune—to lose *both* seems like carelessness. Who was your father? He was evidently a man of some wealth. Was he born in what the Radical papers call the purple of commerce, or did he rise from the ranks of aristocracy?

JACK   I am afraid I really don't know. The fact is, Lady Bracknell, I said I had lost my parents. It would be nearer the truth to say that my parents seem to have lost me. . . . I don't actually know who I am by birth. I was . . . well, I was found.

LADY BRACKNELL   Found!

JACK   The late Mr. Thomas Cardew, an old gentleman of a very charitable

---

8. The wordplay is on "death duties"—i.e., inheritance taxes.
9. Another fashionable residential area in the West End known as Belgravia.

1. A splinter group of members of the Liberal Party who, in 1886, led by Joseph Chamberlain, joined forces with the Conservative Party (the "Tories") in opposing Home Rule for Ireland.

and kindly disposition, found me, and gave me the name of Worthing, because he happened to have a first-class ticket for Worthing in his pocket at the time. Worthing is a place in Sussex. It is a seaside resort.

LADY BRACKNELL   Where did the charitable gentleman who had a first-class ticket for this seaside resort find you?

JACK [Gravely.]   In a handbag.

LADY BRACKNELL   A handbag?

JACK. [Very seriously.] Yes, Lady Bracknell. I was in a handbag—a somewhat large, black leather handbag, with handles to it—an ordinary handbag, in fact.

LADY BRACKNELL   In what locality did this Mr. James, or Thomas, Cardew come across this ordinary handbag?

JACK   In the cloak room at Victoria Station. It was given to him in mistake for his own.[2]

LADY BRACKNELL   The cloak room at Victoria Station?

JACK   Yes. The Brighton line.

LADY BRACKNELL   The line is immaterial. Mr. Worthing, I confess I feel somewhat bewildered by what you have just told me. To be born, or at any rate, bred in a handbag, whether it had handles or not, seems to me to display a contempt for the ordinary decencies of family life that reminds one of the worst excesses of the French Revolution. And I presume you know what that unfortunate movement led to? As for the particular locality in which the handbag was found, a cloak room at a railway station might serve to conceal a social indiscretion—has probably, indeed, been used for that purpose before now—but it could hardly be regarded as an assured basis for a recognized position in good society.

JACK   May I ask you then what you would advise me to do? I need hardly say I would do anything in the world to ensure Gwendolen's happiness.

LADY BRACKNELL   I would strongly advise you, Mr. Worthing, to try and acquire some relations as soon as possible, and to make a definite effort to produce at any rate one parent, of either sex, before the season is quite over.[3]

JACK   Well, I don't see how I could possibly manage to do that. I can produce the handbag at any moment, it is in my dressing room at home. I really think that should satisfy you, Lady Bracknell.

LADY BRACKNELL   Me, sir! What has it to do with me? You can hardly imagine that I and Lord Bracknell would dream of allowing our only daughter—a girl brought up with the utmost care—to marry into a cloak room, and form an alliance with a parcel? Good morning, Mr. Worthing!

[LADY BRACKNELL sweeps out in majestic indignation.]

JACK   Good morning! [ALGERNON, from the other room, strikes up the Wedding March. JACK looks perfectly furious, and goes to the door.] For goodness' sake don't play that ghastly tune, Algy! How idiotic you are!

[The music stops, and ALGERNON enters cheerily.]

---

2. In the four-act version of the play, Jack explains further what happened to Mr. Cardew: "He did not discover the error till he arrived at his own house. All subsequent efforts to ascertain who I was were unavailing."
3. In the four-act version of the play, Jack later comments to Algernon about Lady Bracknell's demands about locating parents: "After all what does it matter whether a man has ever had a father and mother or not? Mothers, of course, are all right. They pay a chap's bills and don't bother him. But fathers bother a chap and never pay his bills. I don't know a single chap at the club who speaks to his father." And Algernon remarks: "Yes. Fathers are certainly not popular just at present. . . . They are like these chaps, the minor poets. They are never quoted."

ALGERNON   Didn't it go off all right, old boy? You don't mean to say Gwendolen refused you? I know it is a way she has. She is always refusing people. I think it is most ill-natured of her.

JACK   Oh, Gwendolen is as right as a trivet.[4] As far as she is concerned, we are engaged. Her mother is perfectly unbearable. Never met such a Gorgon[5] . . . I don't really know what a Gorgon is like, but I am quite sure that Lady Bracknell is one. In any case, she is a monster, without being a myth, which is rather unfair . . . I beg your pardon, Algy, I suppose I shouldn't talk about your own aunt in that way before you.

ALGERNON   My dear boy, I love hearing my relations abused. It is the only thing that makes me put up with them at all. Relations are simply a tedious pack of people who haven't got the remotest knowledge of how to live, nor the smallest instinct about when to die.

JACK   Oh, that is nonsense!

ALGERNON   It isn't!

JACK   Well, I won't argue about the matter. You always want to argue about things.

ALGERNON   That is exactly what things were originally made for.

JACK   Upon my word, if I thought that, I'd shoot myself . . . [A pause.] You don't think there is any chance of Gwendolen becoming like her mother in about a hundred and fifty years, do you, Algy?

ALGERNON   All women become like their mothers. That is their tragedy. No man does. That's his.

JACK   Is that clever?

ALGERNON   It is perfectly phrased! and quite as true as any observation in civilized life should be.

JACK   I am sick to death of cleverness. Everybody is clever nowadays. You can't go anywhere without meeting clever people. The thing has become an absolute public nuisance. I wish to goodness we had a few fools left.

ALGERNON   We have.

JACK   I should extremely like to meet them. What do they talk about?

ALGERNON   The fools? Oh! about the clever people, of course.

JACK   What fools!

ALGERNON   By the way, did you tell Gwendolen the truth about your being Ernest in town, and Jack in the country?

JACK [In a very patronizing manner.]   My dear fellow, the truth isn't quite the sort of thing one tells to a nice sweet refined girl. What extraordinary ideas you have about the way to behave to a woman!

ALGERNON   The only way to behave to a woman is to make love to her, if she is pretty, and to someone else if she is plain.

JACK   Oh, that is nonsense.

ALGERNON   What about your brother? What about the profligate Ernest?

JACK   Oh, before the end of the week I shall have got rid of him. I'll say he died in Paris of apoplexy. Lots of people die of apoplexy, quite suddenly, don't they?

ALGERNON   Yes, but it's hereditary, my dear fellow. It's a sort of thing that runs in families. You had much better say a severe chill.

---

4. Proverbial expression meaning reliably steady, like a tripod ("trivet") used to support pots over a fire.

5. A mythical female creature, like Medusa, whose look turned into stone anyone beholding her.

JACK   You are sure a severe chill isn't hereditary, or anything of that kind?

ALGERNON   Of course it isn't!

JACK   Very well, then. My poor brother Ernest is carried off suddenly in Paris, by a severe chill. That gets rid of him.[6]

ALGERNON   But I thought you said that . . . Miss Cardew was a little too much interested in your poor brother Ernest? Won't she feel his loss a good deal?

JACK   Oh, that is all right. Cecily is not a silly romantic girl, I am glad to say. She has got a capital appetite, goes on long walks, and pays no attention at all to her lessons.

ALGERNON   I would rather like to see Cecily.

JACK   I will take very good care you never do. She is excessively pretty, and she is only just eighteen.

ALGERNON   Have you told Gwendolen yet that you have an excessively pretty ward who is only just eighteen?

JACK   Oh! one doesn't blurt these things out to people. Cecily and Gwendolen are perfectly certain to be extremely great friends. I'll bet you anything you like that half an hour after they have met, they will be calling each other sister.

ALGERNON   Women only do that when they have called each other a lot of other things first. Now, my dear boy, if we want to get a good table at Willis's, we really must go and dress. Do you know it is nearly seven?

JACK   [Irritably.] Oh! it always is nearly seven.

ALGERNON   Well, I'm hungry.

JACK   I never knew you when you weren't. . . .

ALGERNON   What shall we do after dinner? Go to the theater?

JACK   Oh no! I loathe listening.

ALGERNON   Well, let us go to the club?

JACK   Oh, no! I hate talking.

ALGERNON   Well, we might trot around to the Empire[7] at ten?

JACK   Oh no! I can't bear looking at things. It is so silly.

ALGERNON   Well, what shall we do?

JACK   Nothing!

ALGERNON   It is awfully hard work doing nothing. However, I don't mind hard work where there is no definite object of any kind.

[Enter LANE.]

LANE   Miss Fairfax.

[Enter GWENDOLEN. LANE goes out.]

ALGERNON   Gwendolen, upon my word!

GWENDOLEN   Algy, kindly turn your back. I have something very particular to say to Mr. Worthing.

ALGERNON   Really, Gwendolen, I don't think I can allow this at all.

GWENDOLEN   Algy, you always adopt a strictly immoral attitude towards life. You are not quite old enough to do that. [ALGERNON retires to the fireplace.]

JACK   My own darling!

---

6. In the four-act version of the play Jack explains further: "I'll wear mourning for him, of course; that would be only decent. I don't at all mind wearing mourning. I think that all black, with a good pearl pin, rather smart. Then I'll go down home and break the news to my household."

7. A music hall in Leicester Square that featured light entertainment.

GWENDOLEN   Ernest, we may never be married. From the expression on mamma's face I fear we never shall. Few parents nowadays pay any regard to what their children say to them. The old-fashioned respect for the young is fast dying out. Whatever influence I ever had over mamma, I lost at the age of three. But although she may prevent us from becoming man and wife, and I may marry someone else, and marry often, nothing that she can possibly do can alter my eternal devotion to you.

JACK   Dear Gwendolen!

GWENDOLEN   The story of your romantic origin, as related to me by mamma, with unpleasing comments, has naturally stirred the deeper fibers of my nature. Your Christian name has an irresistible fascination. The simplicity of your character makes you exquisitely incomprehensible to me. Your town address at the Albany I have. What is your address in the country?

JACK   The Manor House, Woolton, Hertfordshire.

[ALGERNON, *who has been carefully listening, smiles to himself, and writes the address on his shirt-cuff.*[8] *Then picks up the Railway Guide.*]

GWENDOLEN   There is a good postal service, I suppose? It may be necessary to do something desperate. That of course will require serious consideration. I will communicate with you daily.

JACK   My own one!

GWENDOLEN   How long do you remain in town?

JACK   Till Monday.

GWENDOLEN   Good! Algy, you may turn round now.

ALGERNON   Thanks, I've turned round already.

GWENDOLEN   You may also ring the bell.

JACK   You will let me see you to your carriage, my own darling?

GWENDOLEN   Certainly.

JACK [*To* LANE, *who now enters.*]   I will see Miss Fairfax out.

LANE   Yes, sir. [JACK *and* GWENDOLEN *go off.*]

[LANE *presents several letters on a salver to* ALGERNON. *It is to be surmised that they are bills, as* ALGERNON *after looking at the envelopes, tears them up.*]

ALGERNON   A glass of sherry, Lane.

LANE   Yes, sir.

ALGERNON   Tomorrow, Lane, I'm going Bunburying.

LANE   Yes, sir.

ALGERNON   I shall probably not be back till Monday. You can put up my dress clothes, my smoking jacket,[9] and all the Bunbury suits . . .

LANE   Yes, sir. [*Handing sherry.*]

ALGERNON   I hope tomorrow will be a fine day, Lane.

LANE   It never is, sir.

ALGERNON   Lane, you're a perfect pessimist.

LANE   I do my best to give satisfaction, sir.

[*Enter* JACK. LANE *goes off.*]

JACK   There's a sensible, intellectual girl! the only girl I ever cared for in

---

8. Because shirt cuffs were heavily starched they provided a good surface on which to make notes.
9. Coat worn when gentlemen assembled in a room designated for smoking. The object was to avoid contaminating their regular clothing with the smell of cigars or pipes, which was considered offensive to ladies.

my life. [ALGERNON *is laughing immoderately.*] What on earth are you so amused at?

ALGERNON   Oh, I'm a little anxious about poor Bunbury, that is all.

JACK   If you don't take care, your friend Bunbury will get you into a serious scrape some day.

ALGERNON   I love scrapes. They are the only things that are never serious.

JACK   Oh, that's nonsense, Algy. You never talk anything but nonsense.

ALGERNON   Nobody ever does.

> [JACK *looks indignantly at him, and leaves the room.* ALGERNON *lights a cigarette, reads his shirt-cuff, and smiles.*]
> ACT-DROP[1]

Second Act

SCENE—*Garden at the Manor House. A flight of gray stone steps leads up to the house. The garden, an old-fashioned one, full of roses. Time of year, July. Basket chairs, and a table covered with books, are set under a large yew tree.*

> [MISS PRISM[2] *discovered seated at the table.* CECILY *is at the back watering flowers.*]

MISS PRISM [*Calling.*]   Cecily, Cecily! Surely such a utilitarian occupation as the watering of flowers is rather Moulton's duty than yours? Especially at a moment when intellectual pleasures await you. Your German grammar is on the table. Pray open it at page fifteen. We will repeat yesterday's lesson.

CECILY [*Coming over very slowly.*]   But I don't like German. It isn't at all a becoming language. I know perfectly well that I look quite plain after my German lesson.

MISS PRISM   Child, you know how anxious your guardian is that you should improve yourself in every way. He laid particular stress on your German, as he was leaving for town yesterday. Indeed, he always lays stress on your German when he is leaving for town.

CECILY   Dear Uncle Jack is so very serious! Sometime he is so serious that I think he cannot be quite well.

MISS PRISM [*Drawing herself up.*]   Your guardian enjoys the best of health, and his gravity of demeanor is especially to be commended in one so comparatively young as he is. I know no one who has a higher sense of duty and responsibility.

CECILY   I suppose that is why he often looks a little bored when we three are together.

MISS PRISM   Cecily! I am surprised at you. Mr. Worthing has many troubles in his life. Idle merriment and triviality would be out of place in his conversation. You must remember his constant anxiety about that unfortunate young man his brother.

CECILY   I wish Uncle Jack would allow that unfortunate young man, his

---

1. A special curtain lowered during theatrical performances to denote intervals between acts or scenes.

2. The name has connotations with the expression "prunes and prism" from Dickens's *Little Dorrit*, in which Mrs. General, a prim and proper teacher of manners for young ladies, trains them to repeat "prunes and prism" aloud because this exercise "gives a pretty form to the lips."

brother, to come down here sometimes. We might have a good influence over him, Miss Prism. I am sure you certainly would. You know German, and geology, and things of that kind influence a man very much. [CECILY *begins to write in her diary.*]

MISS PRISM [*Shaking her head.*]   I do not think that even I could produce any effect on a character that according to his own brother's admission is irretrievably weak and vacillating. Indeed I am not sure that I would desire to reclaim him. I am not in favor of this modern mania for turning bad people into good people at a moment's notice. As a man sows so let him reap.[3] You must put away your diary, Cecily. I really don't see why you should keep a diary at all.

CECILY   I keep a diary in order to enter the wonderful secrets of my life. If I didn't write them down I should probably forget all about them.

MISS PRISM   Memory, my dear Cecily, is the diary that we all carry about with us.

CECILY   Yes, but it usually chronicles the things that have never happened, and couldn't possibly have happened. I believe that Memory is responsible for nearly all the three-volume novels that Mudie[4] sends us.

MISS PRISM   Do not speak slightingly of the three-volume novel, Cecily. I wrote one myself in earlier days.

CECILY   Did you really, Miss Prism? How wonderfully clever you are! I hope it did not end happily? I don't like novels that end happily. They depress me so much.

MISS PRISM   The good ended happily, and the bad unhappily. That is what Fiction means.

CECILY   I suppose so. But it seems very unfair. And was your novel ever published?

MISS PRISM   Alas! no. The manuscript unfortunately was abandoned. I use the word in the sense of lost or mislaid. To your work, child, these speculations are profitless.

CECILY [*Smiling.*]   But I see dear Dr. Chasuble coming up through the garden.

MISS PRISM [*Rising and advancing.*]   Dr. Chasuble! This is indeed a pleasure.

[*Enter* CANON CHASUBLE.]

CHASUBLE   And how are we this morning? Miss Prism, you are, I trust, well?

CECILY   Miss Prism has just been complaining of a slight headache. I think it would do her so much good to have a short stroll with you in the Park, Dr. Chasuble.

MISS PRISM   Cecily, I have not mentioned anything about a headache.

CECILY   No, dear Miss Prism, I know that, but I felt instinctively that you had a headache. Indeed I was thinking about that, and not about my German lesson, when the Rector came in.

CHASUBLE   I hope, Cecily, you are not inattentive.

CECILY   Oh, I am afraid I am.

---

3. Cf. Galatians 6.7.
4. Mudie's Circulating Library lent copies of new three-volume novels (usually sentimental tales) to subscribers for a moderate fee. Mudie's power in controlling the book market, especially for novels, was on the wane by 1895.

CHASUBLE   That is strange. Were I fortunate enough to be Miss Prism's pupil, I would hang upon her lips. [MISS PRISM *glares.*] I spoke metaphorically.—My metaphor was drawn from bees. Ahem! Mr. Worthing, I suppose, has not returned from town yet?

MISS PRISM   We do not expect him till Monday afternoon.

CHASUBLE   Ah yes, he usually likes to spend his Sunday in London. He is not one of those whose sole aim is enjoyment, as, by all accounts, that unfortunate young man his brother seems to be. But I must not disturb Egeria[5] and her pupil any longer.

MISS PRISM   Egeria? My name is Laetitia, Doctor.

CHASUBLE [*Bowing.*]   A classical allusion merely, drawn from the Pagan authors. I shall see you both no doubt at Evensong?[6]

MISS PRISM   I think, dear Doctor, I will have a stroll with you. I find I have a headache after all, and a walk might do it good.

CHASUBLE   With pleasure, Miss Prism, with pleasure. We might go as far as the schools and back.

MISS PRISM   That would be delightful. Cecily, you will read your Political Economy[7] in my absence. The chapter on the Fall of the Rupee[8] you may omit. It is somewhat too sensational. Even these metallic problems have their melodramatic side. [*Goes down the garden with* DR. CHASUBLE.]

CECILY [*Picks up books and throws them back on table.*]   Horrid Political Economy! Horrid Geography! Horrid, horrid German!

[*Enter* MERRIMAN *with a card on a salver.*]

MERRIMAN   Mr. Ernest Worthing has just driven over from the station. He has brought his luggage with him.

CECILY [*Takes the card and reads it.*]   "Mr. Ernest Worthing, B. 4, The Albany, W." Uncle Jack's brother! Did you tell him Mr. Worthing was in town?

MERRIMAN   Yes, Miss. He seemed very much disappointed. I mentioned that you and Miss Prism were in the garden. He said he was anxious to speak to you privately for a moment.

CECILY.   Ask Mr. Ernest Worthing to come here. I suppose you had better talk to the housekeeper about a room for him.

MERRIMAN   Yes, Miss.   [MERRIMAN *goes off.*]

CECILY   I have never met any really wicked person before. I feel rather frightened. I am so afraid he will look just like everyone else. [*Enter* ALGERNON, *very gay and debonair.*] He does!

ALGERNON [*Raising his hat.*]   You are my little cousin Cecily, I'm sure.

CECILY   You are under some strange mistake. I am not little. In fact, I believe I am more than usually tall for my age. [ALGERNON *is rather taken aback.*] But I am your cousin Cecily. You, I see from your card, are Uncle Jack's brother, my cousin Ernest, my wicked cousin Ernest.

ALGERNON   Oh! I am not really wicked at all, cousin Cecily. You mustn't think that I am wicked.

CECILY   If you are not, then you have certainly been deceiving us all in a

---

5. Roman goddess of fountains. Her name was also used as an epithet for a woman who provides guidance for other women.
6. Evening church services.

7. I.e., book about economics.
8. The basic unit of currency in India. British civil servants who worked in India were paid in rupees and would suffer from its fall in value.

very inexcusable manner. I hope you have not been leading a double life, pretending to be wicked and being really good all the time. That would be hypocrisy.

ALGERNON [*Looks at her in amazement.*] Oh! Of course I have been rather reckless.

CECILY I am glad to hear it.

ALGERNON In fact, now you mention the subject, I have been very bad in my own small way.

CECILY I don't think you should be so proud of that, though I am sure it must have been very pleasant.

ALGERNON It is much pleasanter being here with you.

CECILY I can't understand how you are here at all. Uncle Jack won't be back till Monday afternoon.

ALGERNON That is a great disappointment. I am obliged to go up by the first train on Monday morning. I have a business appointment that I am anxious . . . to miss.

CECILY Couldn't you miss it anywhere but in London?

ALGERNON No: the appointment is in London.

CECILY Well, I know, of course, how important it is not to keep a business engagement, if one wants to retain any sense of the beauty of life, but still I think you had better wait till Uncle Jack arrives. I know he wants to speak to you about your emigrating.

ALGERNON About my what?

CECILY Your emigrating. He has gone up to buy your outfit.

ALGERNON I certainly wouldn't let Jack buy my outfit. He has no taste in neckties at all.

CECILY I don't think you will require neckties. Uncle Jack is sending you to Australia.[9]

ALGERNON Australia? I'd sooner die.

CECILY Well, he said at dinner on Wednesday night, that you would have to choose between this world, the next world, and Australia.

ALGERNON Oh, well! The accounts I have received of Australia and the next world are not particularly encouraging. This world is good enough for me, cousin Cecily.

CECILY Yes, but are you good enough for it?

ALGERNON I'm afraid I'm not that. That is why I want you to reform me. You might make that your mission, if you don't mind, cousin Cecily.

CECILY I'm afraid I've no time, this afternoon.

ALGERNON Well, would you mind my reforming myself this afternoon?

CECILY It is rather Quixotic of you. But I think you should try.

ALGERNON I will. I feel better already.

CECILY You are looking a little worse.

ALGERNON That is because I am hungry.

CECILY How thoughtless of me. I should have remembered that when one is going to lead an entirely new life, one requires regular and wholesome meals. Won't you come in?

---

9. Although Australia had originally been a place to which criminals were banished, it was, by this time, like Canada, a place to which families might send harmless but useless members, who would be paid an allowance to remain abroad.

ALGERNON   Thank you. Might I have a buttonhole[1] first? I never have any appetite unless I have a buttonhole first.

CECILY   A Maréchal Niel?[2] [*Picks up scissors.*]

ALGERNON   No, I'd sooner have a pink rose.

CECILY   Why? [*Cuts a flower.*]

ALGERNON   Because you are like a pink rose, cousin Cecily.

CECILY   I don't think it can be right for you to talk to me like that. Miss Prism never says such things to me.

ALGERNON   Then Miss Prism is a shortsighted old lady. [CECILY *puts the rose in his buttonhole.*] You are the prettiest girl I ever saw.

CECILY   Miss Prism says that all good looks are a snare.

ALGERNON   They are a snare that every sensible man would like to be caught in.

CECILY   Oh! I don't think I would care to catch a sensible man. I shouldn't know what to talk to him about.

[*They pass into the house.* MISS PRISM *and* DR. CHASUBLE *return.*]

MISS PRISM   You are too much alone, dear Dr. Chasuble. You should get married. A misanthrope I can understand—a womanthrope, never!

CHASUBLE   [*With a scholar's shudder.*][3]   Believe me, I do not deserve so neologistic a phrase. The precept as well as the practice of the Primitive Church was distinctly against matrimony.

MISS PRISM   [*Sententiously.*]   That is obviously the reason why the Primitive Church has not lasted up to the present day. And you do not seem to realize, dear Doctor, that by persistently remaining single, a man converts himself into a permanent public temptation. Men should be more careful; this very celibacy leads weaker vessels astray.

CHASUBLE   But is a man not equally attractive when married?

MISS PRISM   No married man is ever attractive except to his wife.

CHASUBLE   And often, I've been told, not even to her.

MISS PRISM   That depends on the intellectual sympathies of the woman. Maturity can always be depended on. Ripeness can be trusted. Young women are green. [DR. CHASUBLE *starts.*] I spoke horticulturally. My metaphor was drawn from fruits. But where is Cecily?

CHASUBLE   Perhaps she followed us to the schools.

[*Enter* JACK *slowly from the back of the garden. He is dressed in the deepest mourning, with crape hat-band and black gloves.*]

MISS PRISM   Mr. Worthing!

CHASUBLE   Mr. Worthing?

MISS PRISM   This is indeed a surprise. We did not look for you till Monday afternoon.

JACK   [*Shakes* MISS PRISM's *hand in a tragic manner.*]   I have returned sooner than I expected. Dr. Chasuble, I hope you are well?

CHASUBLE   Dear Mr. Worthing, I trust this garb of woe does not betoken some terrible calamity?

JACK   My brother.

MISS PRISM   More shameful debts and extravagance?

---

1. I.e., a flower worn in the buttonhole of a man's coat lapel.
2. A chrome yellow variety of rose named after one of the generals of Napoleon III.

3. He shudders because instead of using the correct word for woman hater, *misogynist*, she has coined her own expression.

CHASUBLE   Still leading his life of pleasure?

JACK [*Shaking his head.*]   Dead!

CHASUBLE   Your brother Ernest dead?

JACK   Quite dead.

MISS PRISM   What a lesson for him! I trust he will profit by it.

CHASUBLE   Mr. Worthing, I offer you my sincere condolence. You have at least the consolation of knowing that you were always the most generous and forgiving of brothers.

JACK   Poor Ernest! He had many faults, but it is a sad, sad blow.

CHASUBLE   Very sad indeed. Were you with him at the end?

JACK   No. He died abroad; in Paris, in fact. I had a telegram last night from the manager of the Grand Hotel.

CHASUBLE   Was the cause of death mentioned?

JACK   A severe chill, it seems.

MISS PRISM   As a man sows, so shall he reap.

CHASUBLE [*Raising his hand.*]   Charity, dear Miss Prism, charity! None of us are perfect. I myself am peculiarly susceptible to drafts. Will the interment take place here?

JACK   No. He seemed to have expressed a desire to be buried in Paris.

CHASUBLE   In Paris! [*Shakes his head.*] I fear that hardly points to any very serious state of mind at the last. You would no doubt wish me to make some slight allusion to this tragic domestic affliction next Sunday. [JACK *presses his hand convulsively.*] My sermon on the meaning of the manna in the wilderness can be adapted to almost any occasion, joyful, or, as in the present case, distressing. [*All sigh.*] I have preached it at harvest celebrations, christenings, confirmations, on days of humiliation and festal days. The last time I delivered it was in the Cathedral, as a charity sermon on behalf of the Society for the Prevention of Discontent among the Upper Orders. The Bishop, who was present, was much struck by some of the analogies I drew.

JACK   Ah! That reminds me, you mentioned christenings, I think, Dr. Chasuble? I suppose you know how to christen all right? [DR. CHASUBLE *looks astounded.*] I mean, of course, you are continually christening, aren't you?

MISS PRISM   It is, I regret to say, one of the Rector's most constant duties in this parish. I have often spoken to the poorer classes on the subject. But they don't seem to know what thrift is.

CHASUBLE   But is there any particular infant in whom you are interested, Mr. Worthing? Your brother was, I believe, unmarried, was he not?

JACK   Oh yes.

MISS PRISM [*Bitterly.*]   People who live entirely for pleasure usually are.

JACK   But it is not for any child, dear Doctor. I am very fond of children. No! the fact is, I would like to be christened myself, this afternoon, if you have nothing better to do.

CHASUBLE   But surely, Mr. Worthing, you have been christened already?

JACK   I don't remember anything about it.

CHASUBLE   But have you any grave doubts on the subject?

JACK   I certainly intend to have. Of course I don't know if the thing would bother you in any way, or if you think I am a little too old now.

CHASUBLE Not at all. The sprinkling, and, indeed, the immersion of adults is a perfectly canonical practice.

JACK Immersion!

CHASUBLE You need have no apprehensions. Sprinkling is all that is necessary, or indeed I think advisable. Our weather is so changeable. At what hour would you wish the ceremony performed?

JACK Oh, I might trot round about five if that would suit you.

CHASUBLE Perfectly, perfectly! In fact I have two similar ceremonies to perform at that time. A case of twins that occurred recently in one of the outlying cottages on your own estate. Poor Jenkins the carter, a most hard-working man.

JACK Oh! I don't see much fun in being christened along with other babies. It would be childish. Would half-past five do?

CHASUBLE Admirably! Admirably! [*Takes out watch.*] And now, dear Mr. Worthing, I will not intrude any longer into a house of sorrow. I would merely beg you not to be too much bowed down by grief. What seem to us bitter trials are often blessings in disguise.

MISS PRISM This seems to me a blessing of an extremely obvious kind.
    [*Enter* CECILY *from the house.*]

CECILY Uncle Jack! Oh, I am pleased to see you back. But what horrid clothes you have got on! Do go and change them.

MISS PRISM Cecily!

CHASUBLE My child! my child! [CECILY *goes towards* JACK; *he kisses her brow in a melancholy manner.*]

CECILY What is the matter, Uncle Jack? Do look happy! You look as if you had toothache, and I have got such a surprise for you. Who do you think is in the dining room? Your brother!

JACK Who?

CECILY Your brother Ernest. He arrived about half an hour ago.

JACK What nonsense! I haven't got a brother!

CECILY Oh, don't say that. However badly he may have behaved to you in the past he is still your brother. You couldn't be so heartless as to disown him. I'll tell him to come out. And you will shake hands with him, won't you, Uncle Jack? [*Runs back into the house.*]

CHASUBLE These are very joyful tidings.

MISS PRISM After we had all been resigned to his loss, his sudden return seems to me peculiarly distressing.

JACK My brother is in the dining room? I don't know what it all means. I think it is perfectly absurd.
    [*Enter* ALGERNON *and* CECILY *hand in hand. They come slowly up to* JACK.]

JACK Good heavens! [*Motions* ALGERNON *away.*]

ALGERNON Brother John, I have come down from town to tell you that I am very sorry for all the trouble I have given you, and that I intend to lead a better life in the future. [JACK *glares at him and does not take his hand.*]

CECILY Uncle Jack, you are not going to refuse your own brother's hand?

JACK Nothing will induce me to take his hand. I think his coming down here disgraceful. He knows perfectly well why.

CECILY Uncle Jack, do be nice. There is some good in everyone. Ernest has just been telling me about his poor invalid friend Mr. Bunbury whom he goes to visit so often. And surely there must be much good in one who is kind to an invalid, and leaves the pleasures of London to sit by a bed of pain.

JACK   Oh! he has been talking about Bunbury, has he?

CECILY   Yes, he has told me all about poor Mr. Bunbury, and his terrible state of health.

JACK   Bunbury! Well, I won't have him talk to you about Bunbury or about anything else. It is enough to drive one perfectly frantic.

ALGERNON   Of course I admit that the faults were all on my side. But I must say that I think that Brother John's coldness to me is peculiarly painful. I expected a more enthusiastic welcome, especially considering it is the first time I have come here.

CECILY   Uncle Jack, if you don't shake hands with Ernest, I will never forgive you.

JACK   Never forgive me?

CECILY   Never, never, never!

JACK   Well, this is the last time I shall ever do it. [*Shakes hands with* ALGERNON *and glares.*]

CHASUBLE   It's pleasant, is it not, to see so perfect a reconciliation? I think we might leave the two brothers together.

MISS PRISM   Cecily, you will come with us.

CECILY   Certainly, Miss Prism. My little task of reconciliation is over.

CHASUBLE   You have done a beautiful action today, dear child.

MISS PRISM   We must not be premature in our judgments.

CECILY   I feel very happy. [*They all go off.*]

JACK   You young scoundrel, Algy, you must get out of this place as soon as possible. I don't allow any Bunburying here.

[*Enter* MERRIMAN.]

MERRIMAN   I have put Mr. Ernest's things in the room next to yours, sir. I suppose that is all right?

JACK   What?

MERRIMAN   Mr. Ernest's luggage, sir. I have unpacked it and put it in the room next to your own.

JACK   His luggage?

MERRIMAN   Yes, sir. Three portmanteaus, a dressing case, two hat-boxes, and a large luncheon basket.[4]

ALGERNON   I am afraid I can't stay more than a week this time.

JACK   Merriman, order the dogcart[5] at once. Mr. Ernest has been suddenly called back to town.

MERRIMAN   Yes, sir.   [*Goes back into the house.*]

ALGERNON   What a fearful liar you are, Jack. I have not been called back to town at all.

JACK   Yes, you have.

---

4. According to *Cassell's Domestic Dictionary*, "a convenient little receptacle in which gentlemen who are going out shooting for the day, or artists who wish to sketch, can carry their luncheon with them." "Portmanteaus": large leather suitcases. A "dressing case" (also according to *Cassell's*) was "ordinarily made of rosewood, mahogany or cormandel wood." It was supposed to include "scent bottles, jars for pomade and tooth-powders, hair brushes and combs, shaving, nail and tooth brushes, razors and strop, nail scissors, buttonhook, tweezer, nail file and penknife" [noted by Russell Jackson].

5. A horse-drawn cart with seats, originally designed to carry hunters and their hunting dogs.

ALGERNON   I haven't heard anyone call me.

JACK   Your duty as a gentleman calls you back.

ALGERNON   My duty as a gentleman has never interfered with my pleasures in the smallest degree.

JACK   I can quite understand that.

ALGERNON   Well, Cecily is a darling.

JACK   You are not to talk of Miss Cardew like that. I don't like it.

ALGERNON   Well, I don't like your clothes. You look perfectly ridiculous in them. Why on earth don't you go up and change? It is perfectly childish to be in deep mourning for a man who is actually staying for a whole week with you in your house as a guest. I call it grotesque.

JACK   You are certainly not staying with me for a whole week as a guest or anything else. You have got to leave . . . by the four-five train.

ALGERNON   I certainly won't leave you so long as you are in mourning. It would be most unfriendly. If I were in mourning you would stay with me, I suppose. I should think it very unkind if you didn't.

JACK   Well, will you go if I change my clothes?

ALGERNON   Yes, if you are not too long. I never saw anybody take so long to dress, and with such little result.

JACK   Well, at any rate, that is better than being always overdressed as you are.

ALGERNON   If I am occasionally a little overdressed, I make up for it by being always immensely overeducated.

JACK   Your vanity is ridiculous, your conduct an outrage, and your presence in my garden utterly absurd. However, you have got to catch the four-five, and I hope you will have a pleasant journey back to town. This Bunburying, as you call it, has not been a great success for you. [*Goes into the house.*]

ALGERNON   I think it has been a great success. I'm in love with Cecily, and that is everything.

[*Enter* CECILY *at the back of the garden. She picks up the can and begins to water the flowers.*]

But I must see her before I go, and make arrangements for another Bunbury. Ah, there she is.

CECILY   Oh, I merely came back to water the roses. I thought you were with Uncle Jack.

ALGERNON   He's gone to order the dogcart for me.

CECILY   Oh, is he going to take you for a nice drive?

ALGERNON   He's going to send me away.

CECILY   Then have we got to part?

ALGERNON   I am afraid so. It's very painful parting.

CECILY   It is always painful to part from people whom one has known for a very brief space of time. The absence of old friends one can endure with equanimity. But even a momentary separation from anyone to whom one has just been introduced is almost unbearable.

ALGERNON   Thank you.

[*Enter* MERRIMAN.]

MERRIMAN   The dogcart is at the door, sir. [ALGERNON *looks appealingly at* CECILY.]

CECILY   It can wait, Merriman . . . for . . . five minutes.

MERRIMAN   Yes, Miss.   [*Exit* MERRIMAN.]

ALGERNON I hope, Cecily, I shall not offend you if I state quite frankly and openly that you seem to me to be in every way the visible personification of absolute perfection.

CECILY I think your frankness does you great credit, Ernest. If you will allow me I will copy your remarks into my diary. [*Goes over to table and begins writing in diary.*]

ALGERNON Do you really keep a diary? I'd give anything to look at it. May I?

CECILY Oh no. [*Puts her hand over it.*] You see, it is simply a very young girl's record of her own thoughts and impressions, and consequently meant for publication. When it appears in volume form I hope you will order a copy. But pray, Ernest, don't stop. I delight in taking down from dictation. I have reached "absolute perfection." You can go on. I am quite ready for more.

ALGERNON [*Somewhat taken aback.*] Ahem! Ahem!

CECILY Oh, don't cough, Ernest. When one is dictating one should speak fluently and not cough. Besides, I don't know how to spell a cough. [*Writes as* ALGERNON *speaks.*]

ALGERNON [*Speaking very rapidly.*] Cecily, ever since I first looked upon your wonderful and incomparable beauty, I have dared to love you wildly, passionately, devotedly, hopelessly.

CECILY I don't think that you should tell me that you love me wildly, passionately, devotedly, hopelessly. Hopelessly doesn't seem to make much sense, does it?

ALGERNON Cecily!
        [*Enter* MERRIMAN.]

MERRIMAN The dogcart is waiting, sir.

ALGERNON Tell it to come round next week, at the same hour.

MERRIMAN [*Looks at* CECILY, *who makes no sign.*] Yes, sir.
                                        [MERRIMAN *retires.*]

CECILY Uncle Jack would be very much annoyed if he knew you were staying on till next week, at the same hour.

ALGERNON Oh, I don't care about Jack. I don't care for anybody in the whole world but you. I love you, Cecily. You will marry me, won't you?

CECILY You silly boy! Of course. Why, we have been engaged for the last three months.

ALGERNON For the last three months?

CECILY Yes, it will be exactly three months on Thursday.

ALGERNON But how did we become engaged?

CECILY Well, ever since dear Uncle Jack first confessed to us that he had a younger brother who was very wicked and bad, you of course have formed the chief topic of conversation between myself and Miss Prism. And of course a man who is much talked about is always very attractive. One feels there must be something in him after all. I daresay it was foolish of me, but I fell in love with you, Ernest.

ALGERNON Darling! And when was the engagement actually settled?

CECILY On the 14th of February last. Worn out by your entire ignorance of my existence, I determined to end the matter one way or the other, and after a long struggle with myself I accepted you under this dear old tree here. The next day I bought this little ring in your name, and this is the little bangle with the true lovers' knot I promised you always to wear.

ALGERNON   Did I give you this? It's very pretty, isn't it?

CECILY   Yes, you've wonderfully good taste, Ernest. It's the excuse I've always given for your leading such a bad life. And this is the box in which I keep all your dear letters. [*Kneels at table, opens box, and produces letters tied up with blue ribbon.*]

ALGERNON   My letters! But my own sweet Cecily, I have never written you any letters.

CECILY   You need hardly remind me of that, Ernest. I remember only too well that I was forced to write your letters for you. I always wrote three times a week, and sometimes oftener.

ALGERNON   Oh, do let me read them, Cecily?

CECILY   Oh, I couldn't possibly. They would make you far too conceited. [*Replaces box.*] The three you wrote me after I had broken off the engagement are so beautiful, and so badly spelled, that even now I can hardly read them without crying a little.

ALGERNON   But was our engagement ever broken off?

CECILY   Of course it was. On the 22nd of last March. You can see the entry if you like. [*Shows diary.*] "Today I broke off my engagement with Ernest. I feel it is better to do so. The weather still continues charming."

ALGERNON   But why on earth did you break if off? What had I done? I had done nothing at all. Cecily, I am very much hurt indeed to hear you broke it off. Particularly when the weather was so charming.

CECILY   It would hardly have been a really serious engagement if it hadn't been broken off at least once. But I forgave you before the week was out.

ALGERNON   [*Crossing to her, and kneeling.*]   What a perfect angel you are, Cecily.

CECILY   You dear romantic boy. [*He kisses her, she puts her fingers through his hair.*] I hope your hair curls naturally, does it?

ALGERNON   Yes, darling, with a little help from others.

CECILY   I am so glad.

ALGERNON   You'll never break off our engagement again, Cecily?

CECILY   I don't think I could break it off now that I have actually met you. Besides, of course, there is the question of your name.

ALGERNON   Yes, of course. [*Nervously.*]

CECILY   You must not laugh at me, darling, but it had always been a girlish dream of mine to love someone whose name was Ernest. [ALGERNON *rises,* CECILY *also.*] There is something in that name that seems to inspire absolute confidence. I pity any poor married woman whose husband is not called Ernest.

ALGERNON   But, my dear child, do you mean to say you could not love me if I had some other name?

CECILY   But what name?

ALGERNON   Oh, any name you like—Algernon—for instance . . .

CECILY   But I don't like the name of Algernon.

ALGERNON   Well, my own dear, sweet, loving little darling, I really can't see why you should object to the name of Algernon. It is not at all a bad name. In fact, it is rather an aristocratic name. Half of the chaps who get into the Bankruptcy Court are called Algernon. But seriously, Cecily . . . [*Moving to her.*] . . . if my name was Algy, couldn't you love me?

CECILY   [*Rising.*]   I might respect you, Ernest, I might admire your character, but I fear that I should not be able to give you my undivided attention.

ALGERNON Ahem! Cecily! [*Picking up hat.*] Your Rector here is, I suppose, thoroughly experienced in the practice of all the rites and ceremonials of the Church?

CECILY Oh, yes. Dr. Chasuble is a most learned man. He has never written a single book, so you can imagine how much he knows.

ALGERNON I must see him at once on a most important christening—I mean on most important business.

CECILY Oh!

ALGERNON I shan't be away more than half an hour.

CECILY Considering that we have been engaged since February the 14th, and that I only met you today for the first time, I think it is rather hard that you should leave me for so long a period as half an hour. Couldn't you make it twenty minutes?

ALGERNON I'll be back in no time. [*Kisses her and rushes down the garden.*]

CECILY What an impetuous boy he is! I like his hair so much. I must enter his proposal in my diary.

[*Enter* MERRIMAN.]

MERRIMAN A Miss Fairfax has just called to see Mr. Worthing. On very important business, Miss Fairfax states.

CECILY Isn't Mr. Worthing in his library?

MERRIMAN Mr. Worthing went over in the direction of the Rectory some time ago.

CECILY Pray ask the lady to come out here; Mr. Worthing is sure to be back soon. And you can bring tea.

MERRIMAN Yes, Miss. [*Goes out.*]

CECILY Miss Fairfax! I suppose one of the many good elderly women who are associated with Uncle Jack in some of his philanthropic work in London. I don't quite like women who are interested in philanthropic work. I think it is so forward of them.

[*Enter* MERRIMAN.]

MERRIMAN Miss Fairfax.

[*Enter* GWENDOLEN.] [*Exit* MERRIMAN.]

CECILY [*Advancing to meet her.*] Pray let me introduce myself to you. My name is Cecily Cardew.

GWENDOLEN Cecily Cardew? [*Moving to her and shaking hands.*] What a very sweet name! Something tells me that we are going to be great friends. I like you already more than I can say. My first impressions of people are never wrong.

CECILY How nice of you to like me so much after we have known each other such a comparatively short time. Pray sit down.

GWENDOLEN [*Still standing up.*] I may call you Cecily, may I not?

CECILY With pleasure!

GWENDOLEN And you will always call me Gwendolen, won't you?

CECILY If you wish.

GWENDOLEN Then that is all quite settled, is it not?

CECILY I hope so. [*A pause. They both sit down together.*]

GWENDOLEN Perhaps this might be a favorable opportunity for my mentioning who I am. My father is Lord Bracknell. You have never heard of papa, I suppose?

CECILY   I don't think so.

GWENDOLEN   Outside the family circle, papa, I am glad to say, is entirely unknown. I think that is quite as it should be. The home seems to me to be the proper sphere for the man. And certainly once a man begins to neglect his domestic duties he becomes painfully effeminate, does he not? And I don't like that. It makes men so very attractive. Cecily, mamma, whose views on education are remarkably strict, has brought me up to be extremely shortsighted; it is part of her system; so do you mind my looking at you through my glasses?

CECILY   Oh! not at all, Gwendolen. I am very fond of being looked at.

GWENDOLEN   [*After examining* CECILY *carefully through a lorgnette.*]   You are here on a short visit, I suppose.

CECILY   Oh no! I live here.

GWENDOLEN   [*Severely.*]   Really? Your mother, no doubt, or some female relative of advanced years, resides here also?

CECILY   Oh no! I have no mother, nor, in fact, any relations.

GWENDOLEN   Indeed?

CECILY   My dear guardian, with the assistance of Miss Prism, has the arduous task of looking after me.

GWENDOLEN   Your guardian?

CECILY   Yes, I am Mr. Worthing's ward.

GWENDOLEN   Oh! It is strange he never mentioned to me that he had a ward. How secretive of him! He grows more interesting hourly. I am not sure, however, that the news inspires me with feelings of unmixed delight. [*Rising and going to her.*] I am very fond of you, Cecily; I have liked you ever since I met you! But I am bound to state that now that I know that you are Mr. Worthing's ward, I cannot help expressing a wish you were—well just a little older than you seem to be—and not quite so very alluring in appearance. In fact, if I may speak candidly——

CECILY   Pray do! I think that whenever one has anything unpleasant to say, one should always be quite candid.

GWENDOLEN   Well, to speak with perfect candor, Cecily, I wish that you were fully forty-two, and more than usually plain for your age. Ernest has a strong upright nature. He is the very soul of truth and honor. Disloyalty would be as impossible to him as deception. But even men of the noblest possible moral character are extremely susceptible to the influence of the physical charms of others. Modern, no less than Ancient History, supplies us with many most painful examples of what I refer to. If it were not so, indeed, History would be quite unreadable.

CECILY   I beg your pardon, Gwendolen, did you say Ernest?

GWENDOLEN   Yes.

CECILY   Oh, but it is not Mr. Ernest Worthing who is my guardian. It is his brother—his elder brother.

GWENDOLEN   [*Sitting down again.*]   Ernest never mentioned to me that he had a brother.

CECILY   I am sorry to say they have not been on good terms for a long time.

GWENDOLEN   Ah! that accounts for it. And now that I think of it I have never heard any man mention his brother. The subject seems distasteful to most men. Cecily, you have lifted a load from my mind. I was growing almost anxious. It would have been terrible if any cloud had come across a friendship like ours, would it not? Of course you are quite, quite sure that it is not Mr. Ernest Worthing who is your guardian?

CECILY   Quite sure. [*A pause.*] In fact, I am going to be his.

GWENDOLEN [*Inquiringly.*]   I beg your pardon?

CECILY [*Rather shy and confidingly.*]   Dearest Gwendolen, there is no reason why I should make a secret of it to you. Our little county newspaper is sure to chronicle the fact next week. Mr. Ernest Worthing and I are engaged to be married.

GWENDOLEN [*Quite politely, rising.*]   My darling Cecily, I think there must be some slight error. Mr. Ernest Worthing is engaged to me. The announcement will appear in the *Morning Post*[6] on Saturday at the latest.

CECILY [*Very politely, rising.*]   I am afraid you must be under some misconception. Ernest proposed to me exactly ten minutes ago. [*Shows diary.*]

GWENDOLEN [*Examines diary through her lorgnette carefully.*]   It is certainly very curious, for he asked me to be his wife yesterday afternoon at 5:30. If you would care to verify the incident, pray do so. [*Produces diary of her own.*] I never travel without my diary. One should always have something sensational to read in the train. I am so sorry, dear Cecily, if it is any disappointment to you, but I am afraid *I* have the prior claim.

CECILY   It would distress me more than I can tell you, dear Gwendolen, if it caused you any mental or physical anguish, but I feel bound to point out that since Ernest proposed to you he clearly has changed his mind.

GWENDOLEN [*Meditatively.*]   If the poor fellow has been entrapped into any foolish promise I shall consider it my duty to rescue him at once, and with a firm hand.

CECILY [*Thoughtfully and sadly.*]   Whatever unfortunate entanglement my dear boy may have got into, I will never reproach him with it after we are married.

GWENDOLEN   Do you allude to me, Miss Cardew, as an entanglement? You are presumptuous. On an occasion of this kind it becomes more than a moral duty to speak one's mind. It becomes a pleasure.

CECILY   Do you suggest, Miss Fairfax, that I entrapped Ernest into an engagement? How dare you? This is no time for wearing the shallow mask of manners. When I see a spade I call it a spade.

GWENDOLEN [*Satirically.*]   I am glad to say that I have never seen a spade. It is obvious that our social spheres have been widely different.

[*Enter* MERRIMAN, *followed by the footman. He carries a salver, tablecloth, and plate stand.* CECILY *is about to retort. The presence of the servants exercises a restraining influence, under which both girls chafe.*]

MERRIMAN   Shall I lay tea here as usual, Miss?

CECILY [*Sternly, in a calm voice.*]   Yes, as usual.

[MERRIMAN *begins to clear table and lay cloth. A long pause.* CECILY *and* GWENDOLEN *glare at each other.*]

GWENDOLEN   Are there many interesting walks in the vicinity, Miss Cardew?

CECILY   Oh! yes! a great many. From the top of one of the hills quite close one can see five counties.

---

6. A popular journal featuring society gossip and also announcements of engagements and marriages.

GWENDOLEN   Five counties! I don't think I should like that. I hate crowds.

CECILY [Sweetly.]   I suppose that is why you live in town?

[GWENDOLEN *bites her lip, and beats her foot nervously with her parasol.*]

GWENDOLEN [Looking round.]   Quite a well-kept garden this is, Miss Cardew.

CECILY   So glad you like it, Miss Fairfax.

GWENDOLEN   I had no idea there were any flowers in the country.

CECILY   Oh, flowers are as common here, Miss Fairfax, as people are in London.

GWENDOLEN   Personally I cannot understand how anybody manages to exist in the country, if anybody who is anybody does. The country always bores me to death.

CECILY   Ah! This is what the newspapers call agricultural depression, is it not? I believe the aristocracy are suffering very much from it just at present.[7] It is almost an epidemic amongst them, I have been told. May I offer you some tea, Miss Fairfax?

GWENDOLEN [With elaborate politeness.]   Thank you. [Aside.] Detestable girl! But I require tea!

CECILY [Sweetly.]   Sugar?

GWENDOLEN [Superciliously.]   No, thank you. Sugar is not fashionable any more. [CECILY *looks angrily at her, takes up the tongs and puts four lumps of sugar into the cup.*]

CECILY [Severely.]   Cake or bread and butter?

GWENDOLEN [In a bored manner.]   Bread and butter, please. Cake is rarely seen at the best houses nowadays.

CECILY [Cuts a very large slice of cake, and puts it on the tray.]   Hand that to Miss Fairfax.

[MERRIMAN *does so, and goes out with footman.* GWENDOLEN *drinks the tea and makes a grimace. Puts down cup at once, reaches out her hand to the bread and butter, looks at it, and finds it is cake. Rises in indignation.*]

GWENDOLEN   You have filled my tea with lumps of sugar, and though I asked most distinctly for bread and butter, you have given me cake. I am known for the gentleness of my disposition, and the extraordinary sweetness of my nature, but I warn you, Miss Cardew, you may go too far.

CECILY [Rising.]   To save my poor, innocent, trusting boy from the machinations of any other girl there are no lengths to which I would not go.

GWENDOLEN   From the moment I saw you I distrusted you. I felt that you were false and deceitful. I am never deceived in such matters. My first impressions of people are invariably right.

CECILY   It seems to me, Miss Fairfax, that I am trespassing on your valuable time. No doubt you have many other calls of a similar character to make in the neighborhood.

[Enter JACK.]

GWENDOLEN [Catching sight of him.]   Ernest! My own Ernest!

JACK   Gwendolen! Darling! [Offers to kiss her.]

---

7. From the 1870s on, landowners (including aristocrats) had been suffering severe losses because of adverse economic conditions.

GWENDOLEN [*Drawing back.*] A moment! May I ask if you are engaged to be married to this young lady? [*Points to* CECILY.]

JACK [*Laughing.*] To dear little Cecily! Of course not! What could have put such an idea into your pretty little head?

GWENDOLEN Thank you. You may! [*Offers her cheek.*]

CECILY [*Very sweetly.*] I knew there must be some misunderstanding, Miss Fairfax. The gentleman whose arm is at present round your waist is my dear guardian, Mr. John Worthing.

GWENDOLEN I beg your pardon?

CECILY This is Uncle Jack.

GWENDOLEN [*Receding.*] Jack! Oh!

[*Enter* ALGERNON.]

CECILY Here is Ernest.

ALGERNON [*Goes straight over to* CECILY *without noticing anyone else.*] My own love! [*Offers to kiss her.*]

CECILY [*Drawing back.*] A moment, Ernest! May I ask you—are you engaged to be married to this young lady?

ALGERNON [*Looking round.*] To what young lady? Good heavens! Gwendolen!

CECILY Yes! to good heavens, Gwendolen, I mean to Gwendolen.

ALGERNON [*Laughing.*] Of course not! What could have put such an idea into your pretty little head?

CECILY Thank you. [*Presenting her cheek to be kissed.*] You may. [ALGERNON *kisses her.*]

GWENDOLEN I felt there was some slight error, Miss Cardew. The gentleman who is now embracing you is my cousin, Mr. Algernon Moncrieff.

CECILY. [*Breaking away from* ALGERNON.] Algernon Moncrieff! Oh! [*The two girls move towards each other and put their arms round each other's waists as if for protection.*]

CECILY Are you called Algernon?

ALGERNON I cannot deny it.

CECILY Oh!

GWENDOLEN Is your name really John?

JACK [*Standing rather proudly.*] I could deny it if I liked, I could deny anything if I liked. But my name certainly is John. It has been John for years.

CECILY [*To* GWENDOLEN.] A gross deception has been practiced on both of us.

GWENDOLEN My poor wounded Cecily!

CECILY My sweet wronged Gwendolen!

GWENDOLEN [*Slowly and seriously.*] You will call me sister, will you not? [*They embrace.* JACK *and* ALGERNON *groan and walk up and down.*]

CECILY [*Rather brightly.*] There is just one question I would like to be allowed to ask my guardian.

GWENDOLEN An admirable idea! Mr. Worthing, there is just one question I would like to be permitted to put to you. Where is your brother Ernest? We are both engaged to be married to your brother Ernest, so it is a matter of some importance to us to know where your brother Ernest is at present.

JACK [*Slowly and hesitatingly.*] Gwendolen—Cecily—it is very painful for me to be forced to speak the truth. It is the first time in my life that I have ever been reduced to such a painful position, and I am really quite inexperienced in doing anything of the kind. However I will tell you quite frankly that I have no brother Ernest. I have no brother at all. I never had a brother in my life, and I certainly have not the smallest intention of ever having one in the future.

CECILY [*Surprised.*] No brother at all?

JACK [*Cheerily.*] None!

GWENDOLEN [*Severely.*] Had you never a brother of any kind?

JACK [*Pleasantly.*] Never. Not even of any kind.

GWENDOLEN I am afraid it is quite clear, Cecily, that neither of us is engaged to be married to anyone.

CECILY It is not a very pleasant position for a young girl suddenly to find herself in. Is it?

GWENDOLEN Let us go into the house. They will hardly venture to come after us there.

CECILY No, men are so cowardly, aren't they?

[*They retire into the house with scornful looks.*]

JACK This ghastly state of things is what you call Bunburying, I suppose?

ALGERNON Yes, and a perfectly wonderful Bunbury it is. The most wonderful Bunbury I have ever had in my life.

JACK Well, you've no right whatsoever to Bunbury here.

ALGERNON That is absurd. One has a right to Bunbury anywhere one chooses. Every serious Bunburyist knows that.

JACK Serious Bunburyist! Good heavens!

ALGERNON Well, one must be serious about something, if one wants to have any amusement in life. I happen to be serious about Bunburying. What on earth you are serious about I haven't got the remotest idea. About everything, I should fancy. You have such an absolutely trivial nature.

JACK Well, the only small satisfaction I have in the whole of this wretched business is that your friend Bunbury is quite exploded. You won't be able to run down to the country quite so often as you used to do, dear Algy. And a very good thing too.

ALGERNON Your brother is a little off-color, isn't he, dear Jack? You won't be able to disappear to London quite so frequently as your wicked custom was. And not a bad thing either.

JACK As for your conduct towards Miss Cardew, I must say that your taking in a sweet, simple, innocent girl like that is quite inexcusable. To say nothing of the fact that she is my ward.

ALGERNON I can see no possible defense at all for your deceiving a brilliant, clever, thoroughly experienced young lady like Miss Fairfax. To say nothing of the fact that she is my cousin.

JACK I wanted to be engaged to Gwendolen, that is all. I love her.

ALGERNON Well, I simply wanted to be engaged to Cecily. I adore her.

JACK There is certainly no chance of your marrying Miss Cardew.

ALGERNON I don't think there is much likelihood, Jack, of you and Miss Fairfax being united.

JACK   Well, that is no business of yours.

ALGERNON   If it was my business, I wouldn't talk about it. [*Begins to eat muffins.*] It is very vulgar to talk about one's business. Only people like stockbrokers do that, and then merely at dinner parties.

JACK   How can you sit there, calmly eating muffins when we are in this horrible trouble, I can't make out. You seem to me to be perfectly heartless.

ALGERNON   Well, I can't eat muffins in an agitated manner. The butter would probably get on my cuffs. One should always eat muffins quite calmly. It is the only way to eat them.

JACK   I say it's perfectly heartless your eating muffins at all, under the circumstances.

ALGERNON   When I am in trouble, eating is the only thing that consoles me. Indeed, when I am in really great trouble, as anyone who knows me intimately will tell you, I refuse everything except food and drink. At the present moment I am eating muffins because I am unhappy. Besides, I am particularly fond of muffins. [*Rising.*]

JACK [*Rising.*]   Well, that is no reason why you should eat them all in that greedy way. [*Takes muffins from* ALGERNON.]

ALGERNON [*Offering tea cake.*]   I wish you would have tea cake instead. I don't like tea cake.

JACK   Good heavens! I suppose a man may eat his own muffins in his own garden.

ALGERNON   But you have just said it was perfectly heartless to eat muffins.

JACK   I said it was perfectly heartless of you, under the circumstances. That is a very different thing.

ALGERNON   That may be. But the muffins are the same. [*He seizes the muffin dish from* JACK.]

JACK   Algy, I wish to goodness you would go.

ALGERNON   You can't possibly ask me to go without having some dinner. It's absurd. I never go without my dinner. No one ever does, except vegetarians and people like that. Besides I have just made arrangements with Dr. Chasuble to be christened at a quarter to six under the name of Ernest.

JACK   My dear fellow, the sooner you give up that nonsense the better. I made arrangements this morning with Dr. Chasuble to be christened myself at 5:30, and I naturally will take the name of Ernest. Gwendolen would wish it. We can't both be christened Ernest. It's absurd. Besides, I have a perfect right to be christened if I like. There is no evidence at all that I ever have been christened by anybody. I should think it extremely probable I never was, and so does Dr. Chasuble. It is entirely different in your case. You have been christened already.

ALGERNON   Yes, but I have not been christened for years.

JACK   Yes, but you have been christened. That is the important thing.

ALGERNON   Quite so. So I know my constitution can stand it. If you are not quite sure about your ever having been christened, I must say I think it rather dangerous your venturing on it now. It might make you very unwell. You can hardly have forgotten that someone very closely connected with you was very nearly carried off this week in Paris by a severe chill.

JACK   Yes, but you said yourself that a severe chill was not hereditary.

ALGERNON   It usen't to be, I know—but I daresay it is now. Science is always making wonderful improvements in things.

JACK [*Picking up the muffin dish.*]   Oh, that is nonsense; you are always talking nonsense.

ALGERNON   Jack, you are at the muffins again! I wish you wouldn't. There are only two left. [*Takes them.*] I told you I was particularly fond of muffins.

JACK   But I hate tea cake.

ALGERNON   Why on earth then do you allow tea cake to be served up for your guests? What ideas you have of hospitality!

JACK   Algernon! I have already told you to go. I don't want you here. Why don't you go!

ALGERNON   I haven't quite finished my tea yet! and there is still one muffin left. [*Jack groans, and sinks into a chair.* ALGERNON *still continues eating.*]

ACT-DROP

Third Act

SCENE—*Morning room*[8] *at the Manor House.*

[GWENDOLEN *and* CECILY *are at the window, looking out into the garden.*]

GWENDOLEN   The fact that they did not follow us at once into the house, as anyone else would have done, seems to me to show that they have some sense of shame left.

CECILY   They have been eating muffins. That looks like repentance.

GWENDOLEN [*After a pause.*]   They don't seem to notice us at all. Couldn't you cough?

CECILY   But I haven't got a cough.

GWENDOLEN   They're looking at us. What effrontery!

CECILY   They're approaching. That's very forward of them.

GWENDOLEN   Let us preserve a dignified silence.

CECILY   Certainly. It's the only thing to do now.

[*Enter* JACK *followed by* ALGERNON. *They whistle some dreadful popular air from a British Opera.*[9]]

GWENDOLEN   This dignified silence seems to produce an unpleasant effect.

CECILY   A most distasteful one.

GWENDOLEN   But we will not be the first to speak.

CECILY   Certainly not.

GWENDOLEN   Mr. Worthing, I have something very particular to ask you. Much depends on your reply.

CECILY   Gwendolen, your common sense is invaluable. Mr. Moncrieff, kindly answer me the following question. Why did you pretend to be my guardian's brother?

8. A relatively informally furnished room for receiving visitors making morning calls (usually close friends of the host or hostess). Afternoon visitors, on the other hand, would be received in the drawing room, a much more formal and elegant setting.
9. Probably a reference to one of the operas of Gilbert and Sullivan.

ALGERNON   In order that I might have an opportunity of meeting you.

CECILY [*To* GWENDOLEN.]   That certainly seems a satisfactory explanation, does it not?

GWENDOLEN   Yes, dear, if you can believe him.

CECILY   I don't. But that does not affect the wonderful beauty of his answer.

GWENDOLEN   True. In matters of grave importance, style, not sincerity is the vital thing. Mr. Worthing, what explanation can you offer to me for pretending to have a brother? Was it in order that you might have an opportunity of coming up to town to see me as often as possible?

JACK   Can you doubt it, Miss Fairfax?

GWENDOLEN   I have the gravest doubts upon the subject. But I intend to crush them. This is not the moment for German skepticism.[1] [*Moving to* CECILY.] Their explanations appear to be quite satisfactory, especially Mr. Worthing's. That seems to me to have the stamp of truth upon it.

CECILY   I am more than content with what Mr. Moncrieff said. His voice alone inspires one with absolute credulity.

GWENDOLEN   Then you think we should forgive them?

CECILY   Yes. I mean no.

GWENDOLEN   True! I had forgotten. There are principles at stake that one cannot surrender. Which of us should tell them? The task is not a pleasant one.

CECILY   Could we not both speak at the same time?

GWENDOLEN   An excellent idea! I nearly always speak at the same time as other people. Will you take the time from me?

CECILY   Certainly. [GWENDOLEN *beats time with uplifted finger.*]

GWENDOLEN AND CECILY [*Speaking together.*]   Your Christian names are still an insuperable barrier. That is all!

JACK AND ALGERNON [*Speaking together.*]   Our Christian names! Is that all? But we are going to be christened this afternoon.

GWENDOLEN [*To* JACK.]   For my sake you are prepared to do this terrible thing?

JACK   I am.

CECILY [*To* ALGERNON.]   To please me you are ready to face this fearful ordeal?

ALGERNON   I am!

GWENDOLEN   How absurd to talk of the equality of the sexes! Where questions of self-sacrifice are concerned, men are infinitely beyond us.

JACK   We are. [*Clasps hands with* ALGERNON.]

CECILY   They have moments of physical courage of which we women know absolutely nothing.

GWENDOLEN [*To* JACK.]   Darling!

ALGERNON [*To* CECILY.]   Darling. [*They fall into each other's arms.*]

[*Enter* MERRIMAN. *When he enters he coughs loudly, seeing the situation.*]

MERRIMAN   Ahem! Ahem! Lady Bracknell!

JACK   Good heavens!

---

1. Many 19th-century German scholars (e.g., D. F. Strauss) seemed, in England, to be notoriously skeptical in their analyses of religious texts.

[*Enter* LADY BRACKNELL. *The couples separate in alarm. Exit* MERRI-MAN.]

LADY BRACKNELL   Gwendolen! What does this mean?

GWENDOLEN   Merely that I am engaged to be married to Mr. Worthing, mamma.

LADY BRACKNELL   Come here. Sit down. Sit down immediately. Hesitation of any kind is a sign of mental decay in the young, of physical weakness in the old. [*Turns to* JACK.] Apprised, sir, of my daughter's sudden flight by her trusty maid, whose confidence I purchased by means of a small coin, I followed her at once by a luggage train. Her unhappy father is, I am glad to say, under the impression that she is attending a more than usually lengthy lecture by the University Extension Scheme on the Influence of a Permanent Income on Thought. I do not propose to undeceive him. Indeed I have never undeceived him on any question. I would consider it wrong. But of course, you will clearly understand that all communication between yourself and my daughter must cease immediately from this moment. On this point, as indeed on all points, I am firm.

JACK   I am engaged to be married to Gwendolen, Lady Bracknell!

LADY BRACKNELL   You are nothing of the kind, sir. And now, as regards Algernon! . . . Algernon!

ALGERNON   Yes, Aunt Augusta.

LADY BRACKNELL   May I ask if it is in this house that your invalid friend Mr. Bunbury resides?

ALGERNON [*Stammering.*]   Oh! No! Bunbury doesn't live here. Bunbury is somewhere else at present. In fact, Bunbury is dead.

LADY BRACKNELL   Dead! When did Mr. Bunbury die? His death must have been extremely sudden.

ALGERNON [*Airily.*]   Oh! I killed Bunbury this afternoon. I mean poor Bunbury died this afternoon.

LADY BRACKNELL   What did he die of?

ALGERNON   Bunbury? Oh, he was quite exploded.

LADY BRACKNELL   Exploded! Was he the victim of a revolutionary outrage? I was not aware that Mr. Bunbury was interested in social legislation. If so, he is well punished for his morbidity.

ALGERNON   My dear Aunt Augusta, I mean he was found out! The doctors found out that Bunbury could not live, that is what I mean—so Bunbury died.

LADY BRACKNELL   He seems to have had great confidence in the opinion of his physicians. I am glad, however, that he made up his mind at the last to some definite course of action, and acted under proper medical advice. And now that we have finally got rid of this Mr. Bunbury, may I ask, Mr. Worthing, who is that young person whose hand my nephew Algernon is now holding in what seems to me a peculiarly unnecessary manner?

JACK   That lady is Miss Cecily Cardew, my ward.

[LADY BRACKNELL *bows coldly to* CECILY.]

ALGERNON   I am engaged to be married to Cecily, Aunt Augusta.

LADY BRACKNELL   I beg your pardon?

CECILY   Mr. Moncrieff and I are engaged to be married, Lady Bracknell.

LADY BRACKNELL [*With a shiver, crossing to the sofa and sitting down.*] I do not know whether there is anything peculiarly exciting in the air of this particular part of Hertfordshire, but the number of engagements that go on seems to me considerably above the proper average that statistics have laid down for our guidance. I think some preliminary inquiry on my part would not be out of place. Mr. Worthing, is Miss Cardew at all connected with any of the larger railway stations in London? I merely desire information. Until yesterday I had no idea that there were any families or persons whose origin was a Terminus.[2] [JACK *looks perfectly furious, but restrains himself.*]

JACK [*In a clear, cold voice.*] Miss Cardew is the granddaughter of the late Mr. Thomas Cardew of 149, Belgrave Square, S.W.; Gervase Park, Dorking, Surrey; and the Sporran, Fifeshire, N.B.[3]

LADY BRACKNELL That sounds not unsatisfactory. Three addresses always inspire confidence, even in tradesmen. But what proof have I of their authenticity?

JACK I have carefully preserved the Court Guides of the period. They are open to your inspection, Lady Bracknell.

LADY BRACKNELL [*Grimly.*] I have known strange errors in that publication.

JACK Miss Cardew's family solicitors are Messrs. Markby, Markby, and Markby.

LADY BRACKNELL Markby, Markby, and Markby? A firm of the very highest position in their profession. Indeed I am told that one of the Mr. Markbys is occasionally to be seen at dinner parties. So far I am satisfied.

JACK [*Very irritably.*] How extremely kind of you, Lady Bracknell! I have also in my possession, you will be pleased to hear, certificates of Miss Cardew's birth, baptism, whooping cough, registration, vaccination, confirmation, and the measles; both the German and the English variety.

LADY BRACKNELL Ah! A life crowded with incident, I see; though perhaps somewhat too exciting for a young girl. I am not myself in favor of premature experiences. [*Rises, looks at her watch.*] Gwendolen! the time approaches for our departure. We have not a moment to lose. As a matter of form, Mr. Worthing, I had better ask you if Miss Cardew has any little fortune?

JACK Oh! about a hundred and thirty thousand pounds in the Funds.[4] That is all. Good-bye, Lady Bracknell. So pleased to have seen you.

LADY BRACKNELL [*Sitting down again.*] A moment, Mr. Worthing. A hundred and thirty thousand pounds! And in the Funds! Miss Cardew seems to me a most attractive young lady, now that I look at her. Few girls of the present day have any really solid qualities, any of the qualities that last, and improve with time. We live, I regret to say, in an age of surfaces. [*To* CECILY.] Come over here, dear. [CECILY *goes across.*] Pretty child! your dress is sadly simple, and your hair seems almost as Nature might have left it. But we can soon alter all that. A thoroughly experienced French maid produces a really marvelous result in a very brief space of

---

2. Station at the end of a railway line.
3. Presumably North Britain, i.e., Scotland.

4. Interest-bearing government bonds.

time. I remember recommending one to young Lady Lancing, and after three months her own husband did not know her.

JACK [*Aside.*]   And after six months nobody knew her.

LADY BRACKNELL [*Glares at* JACK *for a few moments. Then bends, with a practiced smile, to* CECILY.]   Kindly turn round, sweet child. [CECILY *turns completely round.*] No, the side view is what I want. [CECILY *presents her profile.*] Yes, quite as I expected. There are distinct social possibilities in your profile. The two weak points in our age are its want of principle and its want of profile. The chin a little higher, dear. Style largely depends on the way the chin is worn. They are worn very high, just at present. Algernon!

ALGERNON   Yes, Aunt Augusta!

LADY BRACKNELL   There are distinct social possibilities in Miss Cardew's profile.

ALGERNON   Cecily is the sweetest, dearest, prettiest girl in the whole world. And I don't care twopence about social possibilities.

LADY BRACKNELL   Never speak disrespectfully of Society, Algernon. Only people who can't get into it do that. [*To* CECILY.] Dear child, of course you know that Algernon has nothing but his debts to depend upon. But I do not approve of mercenary marriages. When I married Lord Bracknell I had no fortune of any kind. But I never dreamed for a moment of allowing that to stand in my way. Well, I suppose I must give my consent.

ALGERNON   Thank you, Aunt Augusta.

LADY BRACKNELL   Cecily, you may kiss me!

CECILY [*Kisses her.*]   Thank you, Lady Bracknell.

LADY BRACKNELL. You may also address me as Aunt Augusta for the future.

CECILY   Thank you, Aunt Augusta.

LADY BRACKNELL   The marriage, I think, had better take place quite soon.

ALGERNON   Thank you, Aunt Augusta.

CECILY   Thank you, Aunt Augusta.

LADY BRACKNELL   To speak frankly, I am not in favor of long engagements. They give people the opportunity of finding out each other's character before marriage, which I think is never advisable.

JACK   I beg your pardon for interrupting you, Lady Bracknell, but this engagement is quite out of the question. I am Miss Cardew's guardian, and she cannot marry without my consent until she comes of age. That consent I absolutely decline to give.

LADY BRACKNELL   Upon what grounds may I ask? Algernon is an extremely, I may almost say an ostentatiously, eligible young man. He has nothing, but he looks everything. What more can one desire?

JACK   It pains me very much to have to speak frankly to you, Lady Bracknell, about your nephew, but the fact is that I do not approve at all of his moral character. I suspect him of being untruthful. [ALGERNON *and* CECILY *look at him in indignant amazement.*]

LADY BRACKNELL   Untruthful! My nephew Algernon? Impossible! He is an Oxonian.[5]

JACK   I fear there can be no possible doubt about the matter. This afternoon, during my temporary absence in London on an important question

5. I.e., he had been a student at Oxford (originally spelled *Oxenford*).

of romance, he obtained admission to my house by means of the false pretense of being my brother. Under an assumed name he drank, I've just been informed by my butler, an entire pint bottle of my Perrier-Jouet, Brut, '89;[6] a wine I was specially reserving for myself. Continuing his disgraceful deception, he succeeded in the course of the afternoon in alienating the affections of my only ward. He subsequently stayed to tea, and devoured every single muffin. And what makes his conduct all the more heartless is, that he was perfectly well aware from the first that I have no brother, that I never had a brother, and that I don't intend to have a brother, not even of any kind. I distinctly told him so myself yesterday afternoon.

LADY BRACKNELL Ahem! Mr. Worthing, after careful consideration I have decided entirely to overlook my nephew's conduct to you.

JACK That is very generous of you, Lady Bracknell. My own decision, however, is unalterable. I decline to give my consent.

LADY BRACKNELL [*To* CECILY.] Come here, sweet child. [CECILY *goes over.*] How old are you, dear?

CECILY Well, I am really only eighteen, but I always admit to twenty when I go to evening parties.

LADY BRACKNELL You are perfectly right in making some slight alteration. Indeed, no woman should ever be quite accurate about her age. It looks so calculating. . . . [*In a meditative manner.*] Eighteen, but admitting to twenty at evening parties. Well, it will not be very long before you are of age and free from the restraints of tutelage. So I don't think your guardian's consent is, after all, a matter of any importance.

JACK Pray excuse me, Lady Bracknell, for interrupting you again, but it is only fair to tell you that according to the terms of her grandfather's will Miss Cardew does not come legally of age till she is thirty-five.

LADY BRACKNELL That does not seem to me to be a grave objection. Thirty-five is a very attractive age. London society is full of women of the very highest birth who have, of their own free choice, remained thirty-five for years. Lady Dumbleton is an instance in point. To my own knowledge she has been thirty-five ever since she arrived at the age of forty, which was many years ago now. I see no reason why our dear Cecily should not be even still more attractive at the age you mention than she is at present. There will be a large accumulation of property.

CECILY Algy, could you wait for me till I was thirty-five?

ALGERNON Of course I could, Cecily. You know I could.

CECILY Yes, I felt it instinctively, but I couldn't wait all that time. I hate waiting even five minutes for anybody. It always makes me rather cross. I am not punctual myself, I know, but I do like punctuality in others, and waiting, even to be married, is quite out of the question.

ALGERNON Then what is to be done, Cecily?

CECILY I don't know, Mr. Moncrieff.

LADY BRACKNELL My dear Mr. Worthing, as Miss Cardew states positively that she cannot wait till she is thirty-five—a remark which I am bound to say seems to me to show a somewhat impatient nature—I would beg of you to reconsider your decision.

6. An outstanding brand and year of dry champagne.

JACK But my dear Lady Bracknell, the matter is entirely in your own hands. The moment you consent to my marriage with Gwendolen, I will most gladly allow your nephew to form an alliance with my ward.

LADY BRACKNELL [*Rising and drawing herself up.*] You must be quite aware that what you propose is out of the question.

JACK Then a passionate celibacy is all that any of us can look forward to.

LADY BRACKNELL This is not the destiny I propose for Gwendolen. Algernon, of course, can choose for himself. [*Pulls out her watch.*] Come, dear; [GWENDOLEN *rises.*] we have already missed five, if not six, trains. To miss any more might expose us to comment on the platform.

[*Enter* DR. CHASUBLE.]

CHASUBLE Everything is quite ready for the christenings.

LADY BRACKNELL The christenings, sir! Is not that somewhat premature!

CHASUBLE [*Looking rather puzzled, and pointing to* JACK *and* ALGERNON.] Both these gentlemen have expressed a desire for immediate baptism.

LADY BRACKNELL At their age? The idea is grotesque and irreligious! Algernon, I forbid you to be baptized. I will not hear of such excesses. Lord Bracknell would be highly displeased if he learned that that was the way in which you wasted your time and money.

CHASUBLE Am I to understand then that there are to be no christenings at all this afternoon?

JACK I don't think that, as things are now, it would be of much practical value to either of us, Dr. Chasuble.

CHASUBLE I am grieved to hear such sentiments from you, Mr. Worthing. They savor of the heretical views of the Anabaptists,[7] views that I have completely refuted in four of my unpublished sermons. However, as your present mood seems to be one peculiarly secular, I will return to the church at once. Indeed, I have just been informed by the pew-opener[8] that for the last hour and a half Miss Prism has been waiting for me in the vestry.

LADY BRACKNELL [*Starting.*] Miss Prism! Did I hear you mention a Miss Prism?

CHASUBLE Yes, Lady Bracknell. I am on my way to join her.

LADY BRACKNELL Pray allow me to detain you for a moment. This matter may prove to be one of vital importance to Lord Bracknell and myself. Is this Miss Prism a female of repellent aspect, remotely connected with education?

CHASUBLE [*Somewhat indignantly.*] She is the most cultivated of ladies, and the very picture of respectability.

LADY BRACKNELL It is obviously the same person. May I ask what position she holds in your household?

CHASUBLE [*Severely.*] I am a celibate, madam.

JACK [*Interposing.*] Miss Prism, Lady Bracknell, has been for the last three years Miss Cardew's esteemed governess and valued companion.

LADY BRACKNELL In spite of what I hear of her, I must see her at once. Let her be sent for.

---

7. A radical Protestant sect of the 17th century, whose views about baptism were regarded as heretical by Anglicans.

8. A person employed at church services to usher worshipers to their pews and open the doors for them.

CHASUBLE [*Looking off.*]   She approaches; she is nigh.
[*Enter* MISS PRISM *hurriedly.*]

MISS PRISM   I was told you expected me in the vestry, dear Canon. I have been waiting for you there for an hour and three quarters. [*Catches sight of* LADY BRACKNELL *who has fixed her with a stony glare.* MISS PRISM *grows pale and quails. She looks anxiously round as if desirous to escape.*]

LADY BRACKNELL [*In a severe, judicial voice.*]   Prism! [MISS PRISM *bows her head in shame.*] Come here, Prism! [MISS PRISM *approaches in a humble manner.*] Prism! Where is that baby? [*General consternation.* THE CANON *starts back in horror.* ALGERNON *and* JACK *pretend to be anxious to shield* CECILY *and* GWENDOLEN *from hearing the details of a terrible public scandal.*] Twenty-eight years ago, Prism, you left Lord Bracknell's house, Number 104, Upper Grosvenor Street, in charge of a perambulator that contained a baby, of the male sex. You never returned. A few weeks later, through the elaborate investigations of the Metropolitan police, the perambulator was discovered at midnight, standing by itself in a remote corner of Bayswater.[9] It contained the manuscript of a three-volume novel of more than usually revolting sentimentality. [MISS PRISM *starts in involuntary indignation.*] But the baby was not there! [*Everyone looks at* MISS PRISM.] Prism! Where is that baby? [*A pause.*]

MISS PRISM   Lady Bracknell, I admit with shame that I do not know. I only wish I did. The plain facts of the case are these. On the morning of the day you mention, a day that is forever branded on my memory, I prepared as usual to take the baby out in its perambulator. I had also with me a somewhat old, but capacious handbag, in which I had intended to place the manuscript of a work of fiction that I had written during my few unoccupied hours. In a moment of mental abstraction, for which I never can forgive myself, I deposited the manuscript in the bassinette, and placed the baby in the handbag.

JACK   [*Who has been listening attentively.*] But where did you deposit the handbag?

MISS PRISM. Do not ask me, Mr. Worthing.

JACK   Miss Prism, this is a matter of no small importance to me. I insist on knowing where you deposited the handbag that contained that infant.

MISS PRISM   I left it in the cloak room of one of the larger railway stations in London.

JACK   What railway station?

MISS PRISM [*Quite crushed.*]   Victoria. The Brighton line. [*Sinks into a chair.*]

JACK   I must retire to my room for a moment. Gwendolen, wait here for me.

GWENDOLEN   If you are not too long, I will wait here for you all my life.
[*Exit* JACK *in great excitement.*]

CHASUBLE   What do you think this means, Lady Bracknell?

LADY BRACKNELL   I dare not even suspect, Dr. Chasuble. I need hardly tell you that in families of high position strange coincidences are not supposed to occur. They are hardly considered the thing.

---

9. A once fashionable locality in the West End near Kensington Gardens.

[*Noises heard overhead as if someone was throwing trunks about. Everyone looks up.*]

CECILY   Uncle Jack seems strangely agitated.

CHASUBLE   Your guardian has a very emotional nature.

LADY BRACKNELL   This noise is extremely unpleasant. It sounds as if he was having an argument. I dislike arguments of any kind. They are always vulgar, and often convincing.

CHASUBLE [*Looking up.*]   It has stopped now. [*The noise is redoubled.*]

LADY BRACKNELL   I wish he would arrive at some conclusion.

GWENDOLEN   This suspense is terrible. I hope it will last.

[*Enter* JACK *with a handbag of black leather in his hand.*]

JACK [*Rushing over to* MISS PRISM.]   Is this the handbag, Miss Prism? Examine it carefully before you speak. The happiness of more than one life depends on your answer.

MISS PRISM [*Calmly.*]   It seems to be mine. Yes, here is the injury it received through the upsetting of a Gower Street omnibus in younger and happier days. Here is the stain on the lining caused by the explosion of a temperance beverage, an incident that occurred at Leamington. And here, on the lock, are my initials. I had forgotten that in an extravagant mood I had had them placed there. The bag is undoubtedly mine. I am delighted to have it so unexpectedly restored to me. It has been a great inconvenience being without it all these years.

JACK [*In a pathetic voice.*]   Miss Prism, more is restored to you than this handbag. I was the baby you placed in it.

MISS PRISM [*Amazed.*]   You!

JACK [*Embracing her.*]   Yes . . . mother!

MISS PRISM [*Recoiling in indignant astonishment.*]   Mr. Worthing! I am unmarried!

JACK   Unmarried! I do not deny that is a serious blow. But after all, who has the right to cast a stone against one who has suffered? Cannot repentance wipe out an act of folly? Why should there be one law for men, and another for women? Mother, I forgive you. [*Tries to embrace her again.*]

MISS PRISM [*Still more indignant.*]   Mr. Worthing, there is some error. [*Pointing to* LADY BRACKNELL.] There is the lady who can tell you who you really are.

JACK [*After a pause.*]   Lady Bracknell, I hate to seem inquisitive, but would you kindly inform me who I am?

LADY BRACKNELL   I am afraid that the news I have to give you will not altogether please you. You are the son of my poor sister, Mrs. Moncrieff, and consequently Algernon's elder brother.

JACK   Algy's elder brother! Then I have a brother after all. I knew I had a brother! I always said I had a brother! Cecily—how could you have ever doubted that I had a brother? [*Seizes hold of* ALGERNON.] Dr. Chasuble, my unfortunate brother. Miss Prism, my unfortunate brother. Gwendolen, my unfortunate brother. Algy, you young scoundrel, you will have to treat me with more respect in the future. You have never behaved to me like a brother in all your life.

ALGERNON   Well, not till today, old boy, I admit. I did my best, however, though I was out of practice. [*Shakes hands.*]

GWENDOLEN [*To* JACK.]   My own! But what own are you? What is your Christian name, now that you have become someone else?

JACK   Good heavens! . . . I had quite forgotten that point. Your decision on the subject of my name is irrevocable, I suppose?

GWENDOLEN   I never change, except in my affections.

CECILY   What a noble nature you have, Gwendolen!

JACK   Then the question had better be cleared up at once. Aunt Augusta, a moment. At the time when Miss Prism left me in the handbag, had I been christened already?

LADY BRACKNELL   Every luxury that money could buy, including christening, had been lavished on you by your fond and doting parents.

JACK   Then I was christened! That is settled. Now, what name was I given? Let me know the worst.

LADY BRACKNELL   Being the eldest son you were naturally christened after your father.

JACK [*Irritably.*]   Yes, but what was my father's Christian name?

LADY BRACKNELL [*Meditatively.*]   I cannot at the present moment recall what the General's Christian name was. But I have no doubt he had one. He was eccentric, I admit. But only in later years. And that was the result of the Indian climate, and marriage, and indigestion, and other things of that kind.

JACK   Algy! Can't you recollect what our father's Christian name was?

ALGERNON   My dear boy, we were never even on speaking terms. He died before I was a year old.

JACK   His name would appear in the Army Lists of the period, I suppose, Aunt Augusta?

LADY BRACKNELL   The General was essentially a man of peace, except in his domestic life. But I have no doubt his name would appear in any military directory.

JACK   The Army Lists of the last forty years are here. These delightful records should have been my constant study. [*Rushes to bookcase and tears the books out.*] M. Generals . . . Mallam, Maxbohm,[1] Magley, what ghastly names they have—Markby, Migsby, Mobbs, Moncrieff! Lieutenant 1840, Captain, Lieutenant Colonel, Colonel, General 1869, Christian names, Ernest John. [*Puts book very quietly down and speaks quite calmly.*] I always told you, Gwendolen, my name was Ernest, didn't I? Well it is Ernest after all. I mean it naturally is Ernest.

LADY BRACKNELL   Yes, I remember now that the General was called Ernest. I knew I had some particular reason for disliking the name.

GWENDOLEN   Ernest! My own Ernest! I felt from the first that you could have no other name!

JACK   Gwendolen, it is a terrible thing for a man to find out suddenly that all his life he has been speaking nothing but the truth. Can you forgive me?

GWENDOLEN   I can. For I feel that you are sure to change.

JACK   My own one!

CHASUBLE [*To* MISS PRISM.]   Laetitia! [*Embraces her.*]

MISS PRISM [*Enthusiastically.*]   Frederick! At last!

---

1. A play on the name of Max Beerbohm (1872–1956), English essayist, caricaturist, and parodist.

ALGERNON   Cecily! [*Embraces her.*] At last!
JACK   Gwendolen! [*Embraces her.*] At last!
LADY BRACKNELL   My nephew, you seem to be displaying signs of triviality.
JACK   On the contrary, Aunt Augusta, I've now realized for the first time in my life the vital Importance of Being Earnest.
                              CURTAIN

performed 1895   1899

From De Profundis[1]

*   *   *

And the end of it all is that I have got to forgive you. I must do so. I don't write this letter to put bitterness into your heart, but to pluck it out of mine. For my own sake I must forgive you. One cannot always keep an adder in one's breast to feed on one, nor rise up every night to sow thorns in the garden of one's soul. It will not be difficult at all for me to do so, if you help me a little. Whatever you did to me in old days I always readily forgave. It did you no good then. Only one whose life is without stain of any kind can forgive sins. But now when I sit in humiliation and disgrace it is different. My forgiveness should mean a great deal to you now. Some day you will realise it. Whether you do so early or late, soon or not at all, my way is clear before me. I cannot allow you to go through life bearing in your heart the burden of having ruined a man like me. The thought might make you callously indifferent, or morbidly sad. I must take the burden from you and put it on my own shoulders.

I must say to myself that neither you nor your father, multiplied a thousand times over, could possibly have ruined a man like me: that I ruined myself: and that nobody, great or small, can be ruined except by his own hand. I am quite ready to do so. I am trying to do so, though you may not think it at the present moment. If I have brought this pitiless indictment against you, think what an indictment I bring without pity against myself. Terrible as what you did to me was, what I did to myself was far more terrible still.

I was a man who stood in symbolic relations to the art and culture of my age. I had realized this for myself at the very dawn of my manhood, and had forced my age to realize it afterwards. Few men hold such a position in their own lifetime and have it so acknowledged. It is usually discerned, if discerned at all, by the historian, or the critic, long after both the man and his age have passed away. With me it was different. I felt it myself, and made others feel it. Byron[2] was a symbolic figure, but his relations were to the passion of his

1. Out of the depths (Latin); Psalm 130.1: "Out of the depths have I cried unto thee, O Lord." While in prison in Reading Gaol, Wilde was allowed a pen and paper only to write letters. Given one sheet of paper at a time, which was taken away after it was filled, Wilde wrote this work as a letter to Lord Alfred Douglas, or Bosie. Wilde titled it *Epistola: In Carcere et Vinculis* (Letter: in prison and in chains). He was given the manuscript on his release and turned it over to a friend, Robert Ross, who gave it its current title and published it in an abridged version in 1905, after Wilde's death. After Douglas's death in 1945 a fuller text was published by Wilde's son, Vyvyan Holland; but only in 1962, when scholars could consult the original manuscript, did a complete version appear.
2. George Gordon, Lord Byron (1788–1824), the Romantic poet.

age and its weariness of passion. Mine were to something more noble, more permanent, of more vital issue, of larger scope.

The gods had given me almost everything. I had genius, a distinguished name, high social position, brilliancy, intellectual daring: I made art a philosophy, and philosophy an art: I altered the minds of men and the colors of things: there was nothing I said or did that did not make people wonder: I took the drama, the most objective form known to art, and made it as personal a mode of expression as the lyric or the sonnet, at the same time that I widened its range and enriched its characterization: drama, novel, poem in rhyme, poem in prose, subtle or fantastic dialogue, whatever I touched I made beautiful in a new mode of beauty: to truth itself I gave what is false no less than what is true as its rightful province, and showed that the false and the true are merely forms of intellectual existence. I treated Art as the supreme reality, and life as a mere mode of fiction: I awoke the imagination of my century so that it created myth and legend around me: I summed up all systems in a phrase, and all existence in an epigram.

Along with these things, I had things that were different. I let myself be lured into long spells of senseless and sensual ease. I amused myself with being a *flâneur*,[3] a dandy, a man of fashion. I surrounded myself with the smaller natures and the meaner minds. I became the spendthrift of my own genius, and to waste an eternal youth gave me a curious joy. Tired of being on the heights I deliberately went to the depths in the search for new sensations. What the paradox was to me in the sphere of thought, perversity became to me in the sphere of passion. Desire, at the end, was a malady, or a madness, or both. I grew careless of the lives of others. I took pleasure where it pleased me and passed on. I forgot that every little action of the common day makes or unmakes character, and that therefore what one has done in the secret chamber one has some day to cry aloud on the housetops. I ceased to be Lord over myself. I was no longer the Captain of my Soul, and did not know it. I allowed you to dominate me, and your father to frighten me. I ended in horrible disgrace. There is only one thing for me now, absolute Humility: just as there is only one thing for you, absolute Humility also. You had better come down into the dust and learn it beside me.

I have lain in prison for nearly two years. Out of my nature has come wild despair; an abandonment to grief that was piteous even to look at: terrible and impotent rage: bitterness and scorn: anguish that wept aloud: misery that could find no voice: sorrow that was dumb. I have passed through every possible mood of suffering. Better than Wordsworth himself I know what Wordsworth meant when he said:

> Suffering is permanent, obscure, and dark
> And has the nature of Infinity.[4]

But while there were times when I rejoiced in the idea that my sufferings were to be endless, I could not bear them to be without meaning. Now I find hidden away in my nature something that tells me that nothing in the whole world is meaningless, and suffering least of all. That something hidden away in my nature, like a treasure in a field, is Humility.

It is the last thing left in me, and the best: the ultimate discovery at which

---

3. Idle stroller (French).

4. From *The Borderers*, lines 1543–44.

I have arrived: the starting-point for a fresh development. It has come to me right out of myself, so I know that it has come at the proper time. It could not have come before, nor later. Had anyone told me of it, I would have rejected it. Had it been brought to me, I would have refused it. As I found it, I want to keep it. I must do so. It is the one thing that has in it the elements of life, of a new life, a *Vita Nuova*[5] for me.

✻   ✻   ✻

Morality does not help me. I am a born antinomian.[6] I am one of those who are made for exceptions, not for laws. But while I see that there is nothing wrong in what one does, I see that there is something wrong in what one becomes. It is well to have learned that.

Religion does not help me. The faith that others give to what is unseen, I give to what one can touch, and look at. My Gods dwell in temples made with hands, and within the circle of actual experience is my creed made perfect and complete: too complete it may be, for like many or all of those who have placed their Heaven in this earth, I have found in it not merely the beauty of Heaven, but the horror of Hell also. When I think about Religion at all, I feel as if I would like to found an order for those who cannot believe: the Confraternity of the Fatherless one might call it, where on an altar, on which no taper burned, a priest, in whose heart peace had no dwelling, might celebrate with unblessed bread and a chalice empty of wine. Everything to be true must become a religion. And agnosticism should have its ritual no less than faith. It has sown its martyrs, it should reap its saints, and praise God daily for having hidden Himself from man. But whether it be faith or agnosticism, it must be nothing external to me. Its symbols must be of my own creating. Only that is spiritual which makes its own form. If I may not find its secret within myself, I shall never find it. If I have not got it already, it will never come to me.

Reason does not help me. It tells me that the laws under which I am convicted are wrong and unjust laws, and the system under which I have suffered a wrong and unjust system. But, somehow, I have got to make both of these things just and right to me. And exactly as in Art one is only concerned with what a particular thing is at a particular moment to oneself, so it is also in the ethical evolution of one's character. I have got to make everything that has happened to me good for me. The plank-bed, the loathsome food, the hard ropes shredded into oakum[7] till one's fingertips grow dull with pain, the menial offices with which each day begins and finishes, the harsh orders that routine seems to necessitate, the dreadful dress that makes sorrow grotesque to look at, the silence, the solitude, the shame—each and all of these things I have to transform into a spiritual experience. There is not a single degradation of the body which I must not try and make into a spiritualizing of the soul.

I want to get to the point when I shall be able to say, quite simply and without affection, that the two great turning-points of my life were when my father sent me to Oxford, and when society sent me to prison. I will not say that it is the best thing that could have happened to me, for that phrase

---

5. New life (Italian); here Dante's earliest work (1292–94) about his love for Beatrice.
6. One who believes that faith alone, and not obe-
dience of the moral law, is necessary for salvation.
7. Loose fiber from old hemp ropes, which prisoners were often made to shred.

would savour of too great bitterness towards myself. I would sooner say, or hear it said of me, that I was so typical a child of my age that in my perversity, and for that perversity's sake, I turned the good things of my life to evil, and the evil things of my life to good. What is said, however, by myself or by others matters little. The important thing, the thing that lies before me, the thing that I have to do, or be for the brief remainder of my days one maimed, marred, and incomplete, is to absorb into my nature all that has been done to me, to make it part of me, to accept it without complaint, fear, or reluctance. The supreme vice is shallowness. Whatever is realized is right.

1897

1962

BERNARD SHAW
1856–1950

Winston Churchill described Bernard Shaw as a "bright, nimble, fierce, and comprehending being, Jack Frost dancing bespangled in the sunshine." Churchill's words not only name essential qualities of the man but also suggest how long his life and historical reach were. Born and raised in the Victorian period, Shaw continued an important public figure until his death in 1950. His experience encompassed the momentous historical changes of the last half of the nineteenth century and the first half of the twentieth. Shaw made it his business to pronounce on them all in the witty epigrammatic style that characterizes his plays. He was an engaged public intellectual, who created himself as a remarkable public character.

Like Oscar Wilde, the other playwright whose work changed the course of British drama, Shaw was an Irishman. He was born in Dublin, in Shaw's own words, "the fruit of an unsuitable marriage between two quite amiable people who finally separated in the friendliest fashion." His mother, an aspiring singer, went to London to pursue her musical career; Shaw followed five years later, in 1876, quitting the job he had held since the age of fifteen at a land agent's office. His intention was to become a novelist. He spent much of his time in the Reading Room of the British Museum, where a young journalist named William Archer introduced himself because he was so intrigued by the combination of things Shaw was studying—Marx's *Das Kapital* and the score of Wagner's opera, *Tristan and Isolde*.

These two works indicate the main involvements of Shaw's life in London. *Das Kapital* convinced him that socialism was the answer to society's problems. With the socialist economist Sidney Webb and his wife, also a socialist economist, Beatrice Webb, Shaw joined the Fabian Society, a socialist organization that had committed itself to gradual reform rather than revolution. Shaw quickly became a leader in the group and its principal spokesman. His pronouncements and tracts had a wit absent from most political writing. *In Fabian Tract No. 2*, for example, he argued that nineteenth-century capitalism had divided society "into hostile classes, with large appetites and no dinners at one extreme and large dinners and no appetites at the other." Though painfully shy, he disciplined himself to become an accomplished public speaker. Accepting fees from no one, he spoke everywhere, stipulating only that he could speak on whatever subject he liked.

Meanwhile, his acquaintance with William Archer led him to journalism. He worked first as an art critic, then as a music critic, championing the operas of Richard Wagner and introducing a new standard of wit and judgment to music reviewing, writing of a hapless soprano who "fell fearlessly on Mozart and was defeated with heavy loss to the hearers," a corps de ballet, that "wandered about in the prompt corner as if some vivisector had removed from their heads that portion of the brain which enables us to find our way out the door," or Schubert's "Death and the Maiden" quartet, which makes one "reconciled to Death and indifferent to the Maiden." Shaw then turned to drama criticism, where he later described his work as "a siege laid to the theater of the XIXth Century by an author who had to cut his own way into it at the point of the pen, and throw some of its defenders into the moat." Just as he championed the music of Wagner, he now championed the plays of the Norwegian dramatist, Henrik Ibsen. In 1891 he published *The Quintessence of Ibsenism*, in which, in setting out the reasons for his admiration of Ibsen, he defined the kind of drama he wanted to write.

In the first ten years of his life in London, Shaw had written five unsuccessful novels. When he turned to drama in the 1890s, he found his medium. Shaw's first play, *Widowers' Houses* (1892), dealt with the problem of slum landlords. Though it ran only two performances, Shaw's career as a dramatist was launched. In the course of his career he wrote more than fifty plays. Among the most famous are *Mrs. Warren's Profession* (1893), *Arms and the Man* (1894), *Candida* (1894), *The Devil's Disciple* (1896), *Caesar and Cleopatra* (1898), *Man and Superman* (1903), *Major Barbara* (1905), *Androcles and the Lion* (1912), *Pygmalion* (1912; later the basis of the musical *My Fair Lady*), *Heartbreak House* (1919), *Back to Methuselah* (1920), and *Saint Joan* (1923). (Because the production and publication history of Shaw's plays is so complex, this list gives the date of composition.) Shaw at first had difficulty getting his plays performed. Therefore, in 1898 he decided to publish them in book form as *Plays Pleasant and Unpleasant*, for which he wrote a didactic preface, the first of many that he provided his plays. Then in 1904, the producer and Shakespearean Harley Granville-Barker put on *Candida* at the Royal Court Theater, which he was managing. The play was a success, and Shaw went on to work with Barker in making the Royal Court the center for avant-garde drama in London.

In *The Quintessence of Ibsenism*, Shaw defines the elements of the kind of theater he aspired to create:

> first, the introduction of the discussion and its development until it so overspreads and interpenetrates the action that it finally assimilates it, making play and discussion practically identical; and second, as a consequence of making the spectators themselves the persons of the drama, and the incidents of their own lives its incidents, the disuse of the old stage tricks by which audiences had to be induced to take an interest in unreal people and improbable circumstances, and the substitution of a forensic technique of recrimination, disillusion, and penetration through ideals to the truth, with a free use of all the rhetorical and lyrical arts of the orator, the preacher, the pleader, and the rhapsodist.

Shaw created a drama of ideas, in which his characters strenuously argue points of view that justify their social positions—the prostitute in *Mrs. Warren's Profession*, the munitions manufacturer in *Major Barbara*. His object is to attack the complacencies and conventional moralism of his audience. By the rhetorical brilliance of his dialogue and by surprising reversals of plot conventions, Shaw manipulates his audience into a position of uncomfortable sympathy with points of view and characters that violate traditional assumptions.

By the end of the first decade of the twentieth century, as a result of the success of his plays at the Royal Court Theater, Shaw had become a literary celebrity. Like Oscar Wilde, he had worked to develop a public persona, but with a substantial difference in aim. Whereas Wilde used his public image to define an aesthetic point of view, Shaw used his public personality—iconoclastic, clownish, argumentative—to advocate social ideas. He was radical in many respects. He was a vegetarian, a nonsmoker, and a nondrinker. He was courageous enough to be a pacifist in World War I. He championed the reform of English spelling and punctuation. He believed in women's rights and the abolition of private property. He also believed in the Life Force and progressive evolution, driven by the power of the human will, a point of view that led to sympathy with Mussolini and other dictators before World War II. Shaw's insistent rationality made some of his contemporaries view him as bloodless. After seeing *Arms and the Man*, Yeats described a nightmare in which he was haunted by a sewing machine, "that clicked and shone, but the incredible thing was that the machine smiled, smiled perpetually." However, Yeats goes on to say, "Yet I delighted in Shaw the formidable man. He could hit my enemies and the enemies of all I loved, as I could never hit, as no living author that was dear to me could ever hit."

Shaw wrote *Mrs. Warren's Profession* in 1893, but though it was published in *Plays Pleasant and Unpleasant* in 1898, public performance was long prohibited by British censors. In 1902, the Stage Society, technically a private club and so not under the jurisdiction of the censors, gave performances for its own members. The play was produced in New York in 1905; but it was closed down by the police, and the producer and his company were arrested. They were eventually acquitted, and the play was allowed to continue. Legal public performance in England did not take place until 1926, the year after Shaw won the Nobel Prize.

Shaw's preface to the play attacks the confusions and contradictions involved in the censorship of plays and contains an eloquent plea for the recognition of the seriousness and morality of *Mrs. Warren's Profession*. The play was written, he tells us, "to draw attention to the truth that prostitution is caused, not by female depravity and male licentiousness, but simply by underpaying, undervaluing, and overworking women so shamefully that the poorest of them are forced to resort to prostitution to keep body and soul together. He argues that Mrs. Warren's defense of herself in the play is "valid and unanswerable." (It is interesting to compare Mrs. Warren's defense with that of the prostitute who wrote *The Great Social Evil* [p. 1728] as a letter to the *Times*.) Shaw's discussion of Mrs. Warren's self-justification continues:

> But it is no defense at all of the vice which she organizes. It is no defense of an immoral life to say that the alternative offered by society collectively to poor women is a miserable life, starved, overworked, fetid, ailing, ugly. Though it is quite natural and *right* for Mrs. Warren to choose what is, according to her lights, the least immoral alternative, it is none the less infamous of society to offer such alternatives. For the alternatives offered are not morality and immorality but two sorts of immorality. The man who cannot see that starvation, overwork, dirt, and disease are as anti-social as prostitution—that they are the vices and crimes of a nation, and not merely its misfortunes—is (to put it as politely as possible) a hopelessly Private Person.

This is Shaw's way of saying that such a man is a hopeless idiot; the word *idiot* comes from the Greek *idiotes*, "a private person," as distinct from one interested in public affairs.

Shaw's belief in spelling reform led him to introduce simplifications in his own texts that he insisted on his publishers retaining. These simplifications (omission of the apostrophe in a number of contractions, and the use of widely spaced letters rather than italics to indicate emphasis, for example) are retained in the selection reprinted here.

Mrs. Warren's Profession

Act 1

Summer afternoon in a cottage garden on the eastern slope of a hill a little south of Haslemere in Surrey. Looking up the hill, the cottage is seen in the left hand corner of the garden, with its thatched roof and porch, and a large latticed window to the left of the porch. A paling completely shuts in the gar-

*den, except for a gate on the right. The common rises uphill beyond the paling
to the sky line. Some folded canvas garden chairs are leaning against the side
bench in the porch. A lady's bicycle is propped against the wall, under the
window. A little to the right of the porch a hammock is slung from two posts.
A big canvas umbrella, stuck in the ground, keeps the sun off the hammock,
in which a young lady lies reading and making notes, her head towards the
cottage and her feet towards the gate. In front of the hammock, and within
reach of her hand, is a common kitchen chair, with a pile of serious-looking
books and a supply of writing paper on it.*

*A gentleman walking on the common comes into sight from behind the
cottage. He is hardly past middle age, with something of the artist about him,
unconventionally but carefully dressed, and clean-shaven except for a moustache, with an eager susceptible face and very amiable and considerate manners. He has silky black hair, with waves of grey and white in it. His eyebrows
are white, his moustache black. He seems not certain of his way. He looks over
the paling; takes stock of the place; and sees the young lady.*

THE GENTLEMAN [*Taking off his hat.*]   I beg your pardon. Can you direct
me to Hindhead View—Mrs Alison's?

THE YOUNG LADY [*Glancing up from her book.*]   This is Mrs Alison's. [*She
resumes her work.*]

THE GENTLEMAN   Indeed! Perhaps—may I ask are you Miss Vivie Warren?

THE YOUNG LADY [*Sharply, as she turns on her elbow to get a good look at
him.*]   Yes.

THE GENTLEMAN [*Daunted and conciliatory.*]   I'm afraid I appear intrusive.
My name is Praed. [VIVIE *at once throws her books upon the chair, and
gets out of the hammock.*]   Oh, pray dont let me disturb you.

VIVIE [*Striding to the gate and opening it for him.*]   Come in, Mr Praed.
[*He comes in.*] Glad to see you. [*She proffers her hand and takes his with
a resolute and hearty grip. She is an attractive specimen of the sensible,
able, highly-educated young middle-class Englishwoman. Age 22. Prompt,
strong, confident, self-possessed. Plain business-like dress, but not dowdy.
She wears a chatelaine*[1] *at her belt, with a fountain pen and a paper knife
among its pendants.*]

PRAED   Very kind of you indeed, Miss Warren. [*She shuts the gate with a
vigorous slam. He passes in to the middle of the garden, exercising his
fingers, which are slightly numbed by her greeting.*] Has your mother
arrived?

VIVIE [*Quickly, evidently scenting aggression.*]   Is she coming?

PRAED [*Surprised.*]   Didnt you expect us?

VIVIE   No.

PRAED   Now, goodness me, I hope Ive not mistaken the day. That would
be just like me, you know. Your mother arranged that she was to come
down from London and that I was to come over from Horsham to be
introduced to you.

VIVIE [*Not at all pleased.*]   Did she? Hm! My mother has rather a trick of
taking me by surprise—to see how I behave myself when she's away, I
suppose. I fancy I shall take my mother very much by surprise one of

1. Clasp or hook.

these days, if she makes arrangements that concern me without consulting me beforehand. She hasnt come.

PRAED [*Embarrassed.*] I'm really very sorry.

VIVIE [*Throwing off her displeasure.*] It's not your fault, Mr Praed, is it? And I'm very glad youve come. You are the only one of my mother's friends I have ever asked her to bring to see me.

PRAED [*Relieved and delighted.*] Oh, now this is really very good of you, Miss Warren!

VIVIE Will you come indoors; or would you rather sit out here and talk?

PRAED It will be nicer out here, dont you think?

VIVIE Then I'll go and get you a chair. [*She goes to the porch for a garden chair.*]

PRAED [*Following her.*] Oh, pray, pray! Allow me. [*He lays hands on the chair.*]

VIVIE [*Letting him take it.*] Take care of your fingers: theyre rather dodgy things, those chairs. [*She goes across to the chair with the books on it; pitches them into the hammock; and brings the chair forward with one swing.*]

PRAED [*Who has just unfolded his chair.*] Oh, now d o let me take that hard chair. I like hard chairs.

VIVIE So do I. Sit down, Mr Praed. [*This invitation she gives with genial peremptoriness, his anxiety to please her clearly striking her as a sign of weakness of character on his part. But he does not immediately obey.*]

PRAED By the way, though, hadnt we better go to the station to meet your mother?

VIVIE [*Coolly.*] Why? She knows the way.

PRAED [*Disconcerted.*] Er—I suppose she does. [*He sits down.*]

VIVIE Do you know, you are just like what I expected. I hope you are disposed to be friends with me.

PRAED [*Again beaming.*] Thank you, my d e a r Miss Warren: thank you. Dear me! I'm glad your mother hasnt spoilt you!

VIVIE How?

PRAED Well, in making you too conventional. You know, my dear Miss Warren, I am a born anarchist. I hate authority. It spoils the relations between parent and child: even between mother and daughter. Now I was always afraid that your mother would strain her authority to make you very conventional. It's such a relief to find that she hasnt.

VIVIE Oh! have I been behaving unconventionally?

PRAED Oh no; oh dear no. At least not conventionally unconventionally, you understand. [*She nods and sits down. He goes on, with a cordial outburst.*] But it was so charming of you to say that you were disposed to be friends with me! You modern young ladies are splendid: perfectly splendid!

VIVIE [*Dubiously.*] Eh? [*Watching him with dawning disappointment as to the quality of his brains and character.*]

PRAED When I was your age, young men and women were afraid of each other: there was no good fellowship. Nothing real. Only gallantry copied out of novels, and as vulgar and affected as it could be. Maidenly reserve! gentlemanly chivalry! always saying no when you meant yes! simple purgatory for shy and sincere souls.

VIVIE   Yes, I imagine there must have been a frightful waste of time. Especially women's time.

PRAED   Oh, waste of life, waste of everything. But things are improving. Do you know, I have been in a positive state of excitement about meeting you ever since your magnificent achievements at Cambridge: a thing unheard of in my day. It was perfectly splendid, you tieing with the third wrangler.[2] Just the right place, you know. The first wrangler is always a dreamy, morbid fellow, in whom the thing is pushed to the length of a disease.

VIVIE   It doesnt pay. I wouldnt do it again for the same money.

PRAED   [Aghast.]   The same money!

VIVIE   I did it for £50.

PRAED   Fifty pounds!

VIVIE   Yes. Fifty pounds. Perhaps you dont know how it was. Mrs. Latham, my tutor at Newnham,[3] told my mother that I could distinguish myself in the mathematical tripos if I went in for it in earnest. The papers were full just then of Phillipa Summers beating the senior wrangler. You remember about it, of course.

PRAED   [Shakes his head energetically.]!!!

VIVIE   Well anyhow she did; and nothing would please my mother but that I should do the same thing. I said flatly it was not worth my while to face the grind since I was not going in for teaching; but I offered to try for fourth wrangler, or thereabouts, for £50. She closed with me at that, after a little grumbling; and I was better than my bargain. But I wouldn't do it again for that. Two hundred pounds would have been nearer the mark.

PRAED   [Much damped.]   Lord bless me! Thats a very practical way of looking at it.

VIVIE   Did you expect to find me an unpractical person?

PRAED   But surely it's practical to consider not only the work these honors cost, but also the culture they bring.

VIVIE   Culture! My dear Mr Praed: do you know what the mathematical tripos means? It means grind, grind, grind for six to eight hours a day at mathematics, and nothing but mathematics. I'm supposed to know something about science; but I know nothing except the mathematics it involves. I can make calculations for engineers, electricians, insurance companies, and so on; but I know next to nothing about engineering or electricity or insurance. I dont even know arithmetic well. Outside mathematics, lawn-tennis, eating, sleeping, cycling, and walking, I'm a more ignorant barbarian than any woman could possibly be who hadnt gone in for the tripos.

PRAED   [Revolted.]   What a monstrous, wicked, rascally system! I knew it! I felt at once that it meant destroying all that makes womanhood beautiful.

VIVIE   I dont object to it on that score in the least. I shall turn it to very good account, I assure you.

PRAED   Pooh! In what way?

---

2. A unique Cambridge term denoting distinction in the final honors examination (known as the tripos) leading to an A.B. in mathematics. The person who achieved the top mark was the senior wrangler; then came the junior wrangler, and then the third wrangler.

3. Women's college at Cambridge University.

VIVIE   I shall set up in chambers in the City, and work at actuarial calculations and conveyancing. Under cover of that I shall do some law,
with one eye on the Stock Exchange all the time. Ive come down here
by myself to read law: not for a holiday, as my mother imagines. I hate
holidays.

PRAED   You make my blood run cold. Are you to have no romance, no
beauty in your life?

VIVIE   I don't care for either, I assure you.

PRAED   You cant mean that.

VIVIE   Oh yes I do. I like working and getting paid for it. When I'm tired
of working, I like a comfortable chair, a cigar, a little whisky, and a novel
with a good detective story in it.

PRAED [Rising in a frenzy of repudiation.]   I dont believe it. I am an artist;
and I cant believe it: I refuse to believe it. It's only that you havnt discovered yet what a wonderful world art can open up to you.

VIVIE   Yes I have. Last May I spent six weeks in London with Honoria
Fraser. Mamma thought we were doing a round of sightseeing together;
but I was really at Honoria's chambers in Chancery Lane[4] every day,
working away at actuarial calculations for her, and helping her as well
as a greenhorn could. In the evenings we smoked and talked, and never
dreamt of going out except for exercise. And I never enjoyed myself more
in my life. I cleared all my expenses, and got initiated into the business
without a fee into the bargain.

PRAED   But bless my heart and soul, Miss Warren, do you call that discovering art?

VIVIE   Wait a bit. That wasnt the beginning. I went up to town on an
invitation from some artistic people in Fitzjohn's Avenue: one of the girls
was a Newnham chum. They took me to the National Gallery—

PRAED [Approving.]   Ah!! [He sits down, much relieved.]

VIVIE [Continuing.]—to the Opera—

PRAED [Still more pleased.]   Good!

VIVIE—and to a concert where the band played all the evening: Beethoven
and Wagner and so on. I wouldnt go through that experience again for
anything you could offer me. I held out for civility's sake until the third
day; and then I said, plump out, that I couldnt stand any more of it, and
went off to Chancery Lane. N o w you know the sort of perfectly splendid
modern young lady I am. How do you think I shall get on with my
mother?

PRAED [Startled.]   Well, I hope—er—

VIVIE   It's not so much what you hope as what you believe, that I want to
know.

PRAED   Well, frankly, I am afraid your mother will be a little disappointed.
Not from any shortcoming on your part, you know: I dont mean that.
But you are so different from her ideal.

VIVIE   Her what?!

PRAED   Her ideal.

VIVIE   Do you mean her ideal of ME?

PRAED   Yes.

4. I.e., office in the legal quarter of London.

VIVIE   What on earth is it like?

PRAED   Well, you must have observed, Miss Warren, that people who are dissatisfied with their own bringing-up generally think that the world would be all right if everybody were to be brought up quite differently. Now your mother's life has been—er—I suppose you know—

VIVIE   Dont suppose anything, Mr Praed. I hardly know my mother. Since I was a child I have lived in England, at school or college, or with people paid to take charge of me. I have been boarded out all my life. My mother has lived in Brussels or Vienna and never let me go to her. I only see her when she visits England for a few days. I dont complain: it's been very pleasant; for people have been very good to me; and there has always been plenty of money to make things smooth. But dont imagine I know anything about my mother. I know far less than you do.

PRAED   [*Very ill at ease.*]   In that case—[*He stops, quite at a loss. Then, with a forced attempt at gaiety*] But what nonsense we are talking! Of course you and your mother will get on capitally. [*He rises, and looks abroad at the view.*] What a charming little place you have here!

VIVIE   [*Unmoved.*]   Rather a violent change of subject, Mr Praed. Why wont my mother's life bear being talked about?

PRAED   Oh, you really mustnt say that. Isnt it natural that I should have a certain delicacy in talking to my old friend's daughter about her behind her back? You and she will have plenty of opportunity of talking about it when she comes.

VIVIE   No: s h e wont talk about it either. [*Rising.*] However, I daresay you have good reasons for telling me nothing. Only, mind this, Mr Praed. I expect there will be a battle royal when my mother hears of my Chancery Lane project.

PRAED   [*Ruefully.*]   I'm afraid there will.

VIVIE   Well, I shall win, because I want nothing but my fare to London to start there to-morrow earning my own living by devilling[5] for Honoria. Besides, I have no mysteries to keep up; and it seems she has. I shall use that advantage over her if necessary.

PRAED   [*Greatly shocked.*]   Oh no! No, pray. Youd not do such a thing.

VIVIE   Then tell me why not.

PRAED   I really cannot. I appeal to your good feeling. [*She smiles at his sentimentality.*] Besides you may be too bold. Your mother is not to be trifled with when she's angry.

VIVIE   You cant frighten me, Mr Praed. In that month at Chancery Lane I had opportunities of taking the measure of one or two women v e r y like my mother. You may back me to win. But if I hit harder in my ignorance than I need, remember that it is you who refuse to enlighten me. Now, let us drop the subject. [*She takes her chair and replaces it near the hammock with the same vigorous swing as before.*]

PRAED   [*Taking a desperate resolution.*]   One word, Miss Warren. I had better tell you. It's very difficult; but—

[MRS WARREN *and* SIR GEORGE CROFTS *arrive at the gate.* MRS WARREN *is between 40 and 50, formerly pretty, showily dressed in a brilliant hat and a gay blouse fitting tightly over her bust and flanked by fashionable*

---

5. Acting as assistant to a barrister (trial lawyer) as a way of gaining legal experience.

sleeves, Rather spoilt and domineering, and decidedly vulgar, but, on the whole, a genial and fairly presentable old blackguard of a woman.

CROFTS is a tall powerfully-built man of about 50, fashionably dressed in the style of a young man. Nasal voice, reedier than might be expected from his strong frame. Clean-shaven bulldog jaws, large flat ears, and thick neck: gentlemanly combination of the most brutal types of city man, sporting man, and man about town.]

VIVIE   Here they are. [*Coming to them as they enter the garden.*] How do, mater? Mr Praed's been here this half hour waiting for you.

MRS WARREN   Well, if youve been waiting, Praddy, it's your own fault: I thought youd have the gumption to know I was coming by the 3.10 train. Vivie: put your hat on, dear: youll get sunburnt. Oh, I forgot to introduce you. Sir George Crofts: my little Vivie.

[*CROFTS advances to VIVIE with his most courtly manner. She nods, but makes no motion to shake hands.*]

CROFTS   May I shake hands with a young lady whom I have known by reputation very long as the daughter of one of my oldest friends?

VIVIE [*Who has been looking him up and down sharply.*]   If you like. [*She takes his tenderly proffered hand and gives it a squeeze that makes him open his eyes; then turns away, and says to her mother*] Will you come in, or shall I get a couple more chairs? [*She goes into the porch for the chairs.*] ·

MRS WARREN   Well George, what do you think of her?

CROFTS [*Ruefully.*]   She has a powerful fist. Did you shake hands with her, Praed?

PRAED   Yes: it will pass off presently.

CROFTS   I hope so. [VIVIE *reappears with two more chairs. He hurries to her assistance.*] Allow me.

MRS WARREN [*Patronizingly.*]   Let Sir George help you with the chairs, dear.

VIVIE [*Pitching them into his arms.*]   Here you are. [*She dusts her hands and turns to* MRS WARREN.] Youd like some tea, wouldnt you?

MRS WARREN [*Sitting in* PRAED's *chair and fanning herself.*]   I'm dying for a drop to drink.

VIVIE   I'll see about it. [*She goes into the cottage.*]

[SIR GEORGE *has by this time managed to unfold a chair and plant it beside* MRS WARREN, *on her left. He throws the other on the grass and sits down, looking dejected and rather foolish, with the handle of his stick in his mouth.* PRAED, *still very uneasy, fidgets about the garden on their right.*]

MRS WARREN [*To* PRAED, *looking at* CROFTS.]   Just look at him, Praddy: he looks cheerful, dont he? He's been worrying my life out these three years to have that little girl of mine shewn to him; and now that Ive done it, he's quite out of countenance. [*Briskly.*] Come! sit up, George; and take your stick out of your mouth. [CROFTS *sulkily obeys.*]

PRAED   I think, you know—if you dont mind my saying so—that we had better get out of the habit of thinking of her as a little girl. You see she has really distinguished herself; and I'm not sure, from what I have seen of her, that she is not older than any of us.

MRS WARREN [*Greatly amused.*]   Only listen to him, George! Older than any of us! Well, she has been stuffing you nicely with her importance.

PRAED   But young people are particularly sensitive about being treated in that way.

MRS WARREN   Yes; and young people have to get all that nonsense taken out of them, and a good deal more besides. Dont you interfere, Praddy: I know how to treat my own child as well as you do. [PRAED, *with a grave shake of his head, walks up the garden with his hands behind his back.* MRS WARREN *pretends to laugh, but looks after him with perceptible concern. Then she whispers to* CROFTS] Whats the matter with him? What does he take it like that for?

CROFTS [*Morosely.*]   Youre afraid of Praed.

MRS WARREN   What! Me! Afraid of dear old Praddy! Why, a fly wouldnt be afraid of him.

CROFTS   Y o u r e afraid of him.

MRS WARREN [*Angry.*]   I'll trouble you to mind your own business, and not try any of your sulks on me. I'm not afraid of y o u, anyhow. If you cant make yourself agreeable, youd better go home. [*She gets up, and turning her back on him, finds herself face to face with* PRAED.] Come, Praddy, I know it was only your tender-heartedness. Youre afraid I'll bully her.

PRAED   My dear Kitty: you think I'm offended. Dont imagine that: pray dont. But you know I often notice things that escape you; and though you never take my advice, you sometimes admit afterwards that you ought to have taken it.

MRS WARREN   Well, what do you notice now?

PRAED   Only that Vivie is a grown woman. Pray, Kitty, treat her with every respect.

MRS WARREN [*With genuine amazement.*]   Respect! Treat my own daughter with respect! What next, pray!

VIVIE [*Appearing at the cottage door and calling to* MRS WARREN.]   Mother: will you come to my room before tea?

MRS WARREN   Yes, dearie. [*She laughs indulgently at* PRAED's *gravity, and pats him on the cheek as she passes him on her way to the porch.*] Dont be cross, Praddy. [*She follows* VIVIE *into the cottage.*]

CROFTS [*Furtively.*]   I say, Praed.

PRAED   Yes.

CROFTS   I want to ask you a rather particular question.

PRAED   Certainly. [*He takes* MRS WARREN's *chair and sits close to* CROFTS.]

CROFTS   Thats right: they might hear us from the window. Look here: did Kitty ever tell you who that girl's father is?

PRAED   Never.

CROFTS   Have you any suspicion of who it might be?

PRAED   None.

CROFTS [*Not believing him.*]   I know, of course, that you perhaps might feel bound not to tell if she had said anything to you. But it's very awkward to be uncertain about it now that we shall be meeting the girl every day. We dont exactly know how we ought to feel towards her.

PRAED   What difference can that make? We take her on her own merits. What does it matter who her father was?

CROFTS [*Suspiciously.*]   Then you know who he was?

PRAED [*With a touch of temper.*]   I said no just now. Did you not hear me?

CROFTS   Look here, Praed. I ask you as a particular favor. If you do know

[*Movement of protest from* PRAED.]—I only say, if you know you might at least set my mind at rest about her. The fact is, I feel attracted.

PRAED [*Sternly.*] What do you mean?

CROFTS Oh, dont be alarmed: it's quite an innocent feeling. Thats what puzzles me about it. Why, for all I know, I might be her father.

PRAED You! Impossible!

CROFTS [*Catching him up cunningly.*] You know for certain that I'm not?

PRAED I know nothing about it, I tell you, any more than you. But really, Crofts—oh no, it's out of the question. Theres not the least resemblance.

CROFTS As to that, theres no resemblance between her and her mother that I can see. I suppose she's not y o u r daughter, is she?

PRAED [*Rising indignantly.*] Really, Crofts—!

CROFTS No offence, Praed. Quite allowable as between two men of the world.

PRAED [*Recovering himself with an effort and speaking gently and gravely.*] Now listen to me, my dear Crofts. [*He sits down again.*] I have nothing to do with that side of Mrs Warren's life, and never had. She has never spoken to me about it; and of course I have never spoken to her about it. Your delicacy will tell you that a handsome woman needs s o m e friends who are not—well, not on that footing with her. The effect of her own beauty would become a torment to her if she could not escape from it occasionally. You are probably on much more confidential terms with Kitty than I am. Surely you can ask her the question yourself.

CROFTS I have asked her, often enough. But she's so determined to keep the child all to herself that she would deny that it ever had a father if she could. [*Rising.*] I'm thoroughly uncomfortable about it, Praed.

PRAED [*Rising also.*] Well, as you are, at all events, old enough to be her father, I dont mind agreeing that we both regard Miss Vivie in a parental way, as a young girl whom we are bound to protect and help. What do you say?

CROFTS [*Aggressively.*] I'm no older than you, if you come to that.

PRAED Yes you are, my dear fellow: you were born old. I was born a boy: Ive never been able to feel the assurance of a grown-up man in my life. [*He folds his chair and carries it to the porch.*]

MRS WARREN [*Calling from within the cottage.*] Prad-dee! George! Tea-ea-ea-ea!

CROFTS [*Hastily.*] She's calling us. [*He hurries in.*]

   [PRAED *shakes his head bodingly, and is following* CROFTS *when he is hailed by a young gentleman who has just appeared on the common, and is making for the gate. He is pleasant, pretty, smartly dressed, cleverly good-for-nothing, not long turned 20, with a charming voice and agreeably disrespectful manners. He carries a light sporting magazine rifle.*]

THE YOUNG GENTLEMAN Hallo! Praed!

PRAED Why, Frank Gardner! [FRANK *comes in and shakes hands cordially.*] What on earth are you doing here?

FRANK Staying with my father.

PRAED The Roman father?[6]

---

6. Not "Roman Catholic" (he is a Church of England priest) but a father with a Roman sense of duty. The word is used ironically.

FRANK   He's rector here. I'm living with my people this autumn for the sake of economy. Things came to a crisis in July: the Roman father had to pay my debts. He's stony broke in consequence; and so am I. What are you up to in these parts? Do you know the people here?

PRAED   Yes: I'm spending the day with a Miss Warren.

FRANK [*Enthusiastically.*]   What! Do you know Vivie? Isnt she a jolly girl? I'm teaching her to shoot with this. [*Putting down the rifle.*] I'm so glad she knows you: youre just the sort of fellow she ought to know. [*He smiles, and raises the charming voice almost to a singing tone as he exclaims*] It's e v e r so jolly to find you here, Praed.

PRAED   I'm an old friend of her mother. Mrs Warren brought me over to make her daughter's acquaintance.

FRANK   The mother! Is s h e here?

PRAED   Yes: inside, at tea.

MRS WARREN [*Calling from within.*]   Prad-dee-ee-ee-eee! The tea-cake'll be cold.

PRAED [*Calling.*]   Yes, Mrs Warren. In a moment. Ive just met a friend here.

MRS WARREN   A what?

PRAED [*Louder.*]   A friend.

MRS WARREN   Bring him in.

PRAED   All right. [*to* FRANK] Will you accept the invitation?

FRANK [*Incredulous, but immensely amused.*]   Is that Vivie's mother?

PRAED   Yes.

FRANK   By jove! What a lark! Do you think she'll like me?

PRAED   Ive no doubt youll make yourself popular, as usual. Come in and try. [*Moving towards the house.*]

FRANK   Stop a bit. [*Seriously.*] I want to take you into my confidence.

PRAED   Pray dont. It's only some fresh folly, like the barmaid at Redhill.

FRANK   It's ever so much more serious than that. You say youve only just met Vivie for the first time?

PRAED   Yes.

FRANK [*Rhapsodically.*]   Then you can have no idea what a girl she is. Such character! Such sense! And her cleverness! Oh, my eye, Praed, but I can tell you she is clever! And—need I add?—she loves me.

CROFTS [*Putting his head out of the window.*]   I say, Praed: what are you about? D o come along. [*He disappears.*]

FRANK   Hallo! Sort of chap that would take a prize at a dog show, aint he? Who's he?

PRAED   Sir George Crofts, an old friend of Mrs Warren's. I think we had better come in.

[*On their way to the porch they are interrupted by a call from the gate. Turning, they see an elderly clergyman looking over it.*]

THE CLERGYMAN [*Calling.*]   Frank!

FRANK   Hallo! [*To* PRAED.] The Roman father. [*To the clergyman.*] Yes, gov'nor: all right: presently. [*To* PRAED.] Look here, Praed: youd better go in to tea. I'll join you directly.

PRAED   Very good. [*He goes into the cottage.*]

[*The clergyman remains outside the gate, with his hands on the top of it. The* REV. SAMUEL GARDNER, *a beneficed clergyman of the Established*]

Church, is over 50. Externally he is pretentious, booming, noisy, important. Really he is that obsolescent social phenomenon the fool of the family dumped on the Church by his father, the patron, clamorously asserting himself as father and clergyman without being able to command respect in either capacity.]

REV. SAMUEL   Well, sir. Who are your friends here, if I may ask?

FRANK   Oh, it's all right, gov'nor! Come in.

REV. SAMUEL   No sir; not until I know whose garden I am entering.

FRANK   It's all right. It's Miss Warren's.

REV. SAMUEL   I have not seen her at church since she came.

FRANK   Of course not: she's a third wrangler. Ever so intellectual. Took a higher degree than you did; so why should she go to hear you preach?

REV. SAMUEL   Dont be disrespectful, sir.

FRANK   Oh, it dont matter: nobody hears us. Come in. [*He opens the gate, unceremoniously pulling his father with it into the garden.*] I want to introduce you to her. Do you remember the advice you gave me last July, gov'nor?

REV. SAMUEL   [*Severely.*]   Yes, I advised you to conquer your idleness and flippancy, and to work your way into an honorable profession and live on it and not upon me.

FRANK   No; thats what you thought of afterwards. What you actually said was that since I had neither brains nor money, I'd better turn my good looks to account by marrying somebody with both. Well, look here. Miss Warren has brains: you cant deny that.

REV. SAMUEL   Brains are not everything.

FRANK   No, of course not: theres the money—

REV. SAMUEL   [*Interrupting him austerely.*]   I was not thinking of money, sir. I was speaking of higher things. Social position, for instance.

FRANK   I dont care a rap about that.

REV. SAMUEL   But I do, sir.

FRANK   Well, nobody wants you to marry her. Anyhow, she has what amounts to a high Cambridge degree; and she seems to have as much money as she wants.

REV. SAMUEL   [*Sinking into a feeble vein of humor.*]   I greatly doubt whether she has as much money as y o u will want.

FRANK   Oh, come; I havnt been so very extravagant. I live ever so quietly; I dont drink; I dont bet much; and I never go regularly on the razzle-dazzle as you did when you were my age.

REV. SAMUEL   [*Booming hollowly.*]   Silence, sir.

FRANK   Well, you told me yourself, when I was making ever such an ass of myself about the barmaid at Redhill, that you once offered a woman £50 for the letters you wrote to her when—

REV. SAMUEL   [*Terrified.*]   Sh-sh-sh, Frank, for heaven's sake! [*He looks round apprehensively. Seeing no one within earshot he plucks up courage to boom again, but more subduedly.*] You are taking an ungentlemanly advantage of what I confided to you for your own good, to save you from an error you would have repented all your life long. Take warning by your father's follies, sir; and dont make them an excuse for your own.

FRANK   Did you ever hear the story of the Duke of Wellington and his letters?

REV. SAMUEL   No, sir; and I dont want to hear it.

FRANK   The old Iron Duke didnt throw away £50: not he. He just wrote: "Dear Jenny: publish and be damned! Yours affectionately, Wellington." Thats what you should have done.

REV. SAMUEL [*Piteously.*]   Frank, my boy: when I wrote those letters I put myself into that woman's power. When I told you about them I put myself, to some extent, I am sorry to say, in your power. She refused my money with these words, which I shall never forget. "Knowledge is power" she said; "and I never sell power." Thats more than twenty years ago; and she has never made use of her power or caused me a moment's uneasiness. You are behaving worse to me than she did, Frank.

FRANK   Oh yes I dare say! Did you ever preach at her the way you preach at me every day?

REV. SAMUEL [*Wounded almost to tears.*]   I leave you sir. You are incorrigible. [*He turns towards the gate.*]

FRANK [*Utterly unmoved.*]   Tell them I shant be home to tea, will you, gov'nor, like a good fellow? [*He moves towards the cottage door and is met by* PRAED *and* VIVIE *coming out.*]

VIVIE. [*To* FRANK.] Is that your father, Frank? I do so want to meet him.

FRANK   Certainly. [*Calling after his father.*] Gov'nor. Youre wanted. [*The parson turns at the gate, fumbling nervously at his hat.* PRAED *crosses the garden to the opposite side, beaming in anticipation of civilities.*] My father: Miss Warren.

VIVIE [*Going to the clergyman and shaking his hand.*]   Very glad to see you here, Mr Gardner. [*Calling to the cottage.*] Mother: come along: youre wanted.

[MRS WARREN *appears on the threshold, and is immediately transfixed recognizing the clergyman.*]

VIVIE [*Continuing.*]   Let me introduce—

MRS WARREN [*Swooping on the* REVEREND SAMUEL.]   Why, it's Sam Gardner, gone into the Church! Well, I never! Dont you know us, Sam? This is George Crofts, as large as life and twice as natural. Dont you remember me?

REV. SAMUEL [*Very red.*]   I really—er—

MRS WARREN   Of course you do. Why, I have a whole album of your letters still: I came across them only the other day.

REV. SAMUEL [*Miserably confused.*]   Miss Vavasour, I believe.

MRS WARREN [*Correcting him quickly in a loud whisper.*]   Tch! Nonsense! Mrs Warren: dont you see my daughter there?

Act 2

Inside the cottage after nightfall. Looking eastward from within instead of westward from without, the latticed window, with its curtains drawn, is now seen in the middle of the front wall of the cottage, with the porch door to the left of it. In the left-hand side wall is the door leading to the kitchen. Farther back against the same wall is a dresser with a candle and matches on it, and FRANK's *rifle standing beside them, with the barrel resting in the plate-rack. In the centre a table stands with a lighted lamp on it.* VIVIE's *books and writing materials are on a table to the right of the window, against the wall. The fireplace is on the right, with a settle: there is no fire. Two of the chairs are set right and left of the table. The cottage door opens, shewing a fine starlit night without; and* MRS WARREN, *her shoulders wrapped in a shawl borrowed from* VIVIE, *enters, followed by* FRANK, *who throws his cap on the window seat. She has had enough of walking, and gives a gasp of relief as she unpins her hat; takes it off; sticks the pin through the crown; and puts it on the table.*

MRS WARREN O Lord! I dont know which is the worst of the country, the walking or the sitting at home with nothing to do. I could do with a whisky and soda now very well, if only they had such a thing in this place.

FRANK Perhaps Vivie's got some.

MRS WARREN Nonsense! What would a young girl like her be doing with such things! Never mind: it dont matter. I wonder how she passes her time here! I'd a good deal rather be in Vienna.

FRANK Let me take you there. [*He helps her to take off her shawl, gallantly giving her shoulders a very perceptible squeeze as he does so.*]

MRS WARREN Ah! would you? I'm beginning to think youre a chip of the old block.

FRANK Like the gov'nor, eh? [*He hangs the shawl on the nearest chair, and sits down.*]

MRS WARREN Never you mind. What do you know about such things? Youre only a boy. [*She goes to the hearth, to be farther from temptation.*]

FRANK Do come to Vienna with me? It'd be ever such larks.

MRS WARREN No, thank you. Vienna is no place for you—at least not until youre a little older. [*She nods at him to emphasize this piece of advice. He makes a mock-piteous face, belied by his laughing eyes. She looks at him; then comes back to him.*] Now, look here, little boy [*taking his face in her hands and turning it up to her*]; I know you through and through by your likeness to your father, better than you know yourself. Dont you go taking any silly ideas into your head about me. Do you hear?

FRANK [*Gallantly wooing her with his voice.*] Cant help it, my dear Mrs Warren: it runs in the family.

[*She pretends to box his ears; then looks at the pretty laughing upturned face for a moment, tempted. At last she kisses him, and immediately turns away, out of patience with herself.*]

MRS WARREN There! I shouldnt have done that. I am wicked. Never you mind, my dear: it's only a motherly kiss. Go and make love to Vivie.

FRANK So I have.

MRS WARREN [*Turning on him with a sharp note of alarm in her voice.*] What!

FRANK Vivie and I are ever such chums.

MRS WARREN What do you mean? Now see here: I wont have any young scamp tampering with my little girl. Do you hear? I wont have it.

FRANK [*Quite unabashed.*] My dear Mrs Warren: dont you be alarmed. My intentions are honorable: ever so honorable; and your little girl is jolly well able to take care of herself. She dont need looking after half so much as her mother. She aint so handsome, you know.

MRS WARREN [*Taken aback by his assurance.*] Well, you have got a nice healthy two inches thick of cheek all over you. I dont know where you got it. Not from your father, anyhow.

CROFTS [*In the garden.*] The gipsies, I suppose?

REV. SAMUEL [*Replying.*] The broomsquires[7] are far worse.

MRS WARREN [*To* FRANK.] S-sh! Remember! youve had your warning.
[CROFTS *and the* REVEREND SAMUEL *come in from the garden, the clergyman continuing his conversation as he enters.*]

REV. SAMUEL The perjury at the Winchester assizes[8] is deplorable.

MRS WARREN Well? What became of you two? And wheres Praddy and Vivie?

CROFTS [*Putting his hat on the settle and his stick in the chimney corner.*] They went up the hill. We went to the village. I wanted a drink. [*He sits down on the settle, putting his legs up along the seat.*]

MRS WARREN Well, she oughtnt to go off like that without telling me. [*To* FRANK.] Get your father a chair, Frank: where are your manners? [FRANK *springs up and gracefully offers his father his chair; and then takes another from the wall and sits down at the table, in the middle, with his father on his right and* MRS WARREN *on his left.*] George: where are you going to stay to-night? You cant stay here. And whats Praddy going to do?

CROFTS Gardner'll put me up.

MRS WARREN Oh no doubt youve taken care of yourself! But what about Praddy?

CROFTS Dont know. I suppose he can sleep at the inn.

MRS WARREN Havnt you room for him, Sam?

REV. SAMUEL Well—er—you see, as rector here, I am not free to do as I like. Er—what is Mr Praed's social position?

MRS. WARREN Oh, he's all right: he's an architect. What an old stick-in-the-mud you are, Sam!

FRANK Yes, it's all right, gov'nor. He built that place down in Wales for the Duke. Caernarvon Castle they call it. You must have heard of it. [*He winks with lightning smartness at* MRS WARREN, *and regards his father blandly.*]

REV. SAMUEL Oh, in that case, of course we shall only be too happy. I suppose he knows the Duke personally.

FRANK Oh, ever so intimately! We can stick him in Georgina's old room.

MRS WARREN Well, thats settled. Now if those two would only come in and let us have supper. Theyve no right to stay out after dark like this.

CROFTS [*Aggressively.*] What harm are they doing you?

MRS WARREN Well, harm or not, I dont like it.

FRANK Better not wait for them, Mrs Warren. Praed will stay out as long as possible. He has never known before what it is to stray over the heath on a summer night with my Vivie.

CROFTS [*Sitting up in some consternation.*] I say, you know! Come!

REV. SAMUEL [*Rising, startled out of his professional manner into real force and sincerity.*] Frank, once for all, it's out of the question. Mrs Warren will tell you that it's not to be thought of.

CROFTS Of course not.

FRANK [*With enchanting placidity.*] Is that so, Mrs Warren?

---

7. Small country landowners.   8. Law courts.

MRS WARREN [*Reflectively.*]   Well, Sam, I dont know. If the girl wants to get married, no good can come of keeping her unmarried.

REV. SAMUEL [*Astounded.*]   But married to him!—your daughter to my son! Only think: it's impossible.

CROFTS   Of course it's impossible. Dont be a fool, Kitty.

MRS WARREN [*Nettled.*]   Why not? Isnt my daughter good enough for your son?

REV. SAMUEL   But surely, my dear Mrs Warren, you know the reasons—

MRS WARREN [*Defiantly.*]   I know no reasons. If you know any, you can tell them to the lad, or to the girl, or to your congregation, if you like.

REV. SAMUEL [*Collapsing helplessly into his chair.*]   You know very well that I couldnt tell anyone the reasons. But my boy will believe me when I tell him there a r e reasons.

FRANK   Quite right, Dad: he will. But has your boy's conduct ever been influenced by your reasons?

CROFTS   You cant marry her: and thats all about it. [*He gets up and stands on the hearth, with his back to the fireplace, frowning determinedly.*]

MRS WARREN [*Turning on him sharply.*]   What have you got to do with it, pray?

FRANK [*With his prettiest lyrical cadence.*]   Precisely what I was going to ask, myself, in my own graceful fashion.

CROFTS [*To* MRS WARREN.]   I suppose you dont want to marry the girl to a man younger than herself and without either a profession or twopence to keep her on. Ask Sam, if you dont believe me. [*To the parson.*] How much more money are you going to give him?

REV. SAMUEL   Not another penny. He has had his patrimony; and he spent the last of it in July. [MRS WARREN's *face falls.*]

CROFTS [*Watching her.*]   There! I told you. [*He resumes his place on the settle and puts up his legs on the seat again, as if the matter were finally disposed of.*]

FRANK [*Plaintively.*]   This is ever so mercenary. Do you suppose Miss Warren's going to marry for money? If we love one another—

MRS WARREN   Thank you. Your love's a pretty cheap commodity, my lad. If you have no means of keeping a wife, that settles it: you cant have Vivie.

FRANK [*Much amused.*]   What do y o u say, gov'nor, eh?

REV. SAMUEL   I agree with Mrs Warren.

FRANK   And good old Crofts has already expressed his opinion.

CROFTS [*Turning angrily on his elbow.*]   Look here: I want none of y o u r cheek.

FRANK [*Pointedly.*]   I'm ever so sorry to surprise you, Crofts, but you allowed yourself the liberty of speaking to me like a father a moment ago. One father is enough, thank you.

CROFTS [*Contemptuously.*]   Yah! [*He turns away again.*]

FRANK [*Rising.*]   Mrs Warren: I cannot give my Vivie up, even for your sake.

MRS WARREN [*Muttering.*]   Young scamp!

FRANK [*Continuing.*]   And as you no doubt intend to hold out other prospects to her, I shall lose no time in placing my case before her. [*They stare at him; and he begins to declaim gracefully*]

He either fears his fate too much,
Or his deserts are small,
That dares not put it to the touch
To gain or lose it all.[9]

[*The cottage door opens whilst he is reciting; and* VIVIE *and* PRAED *come in. He breaks off.* PRAED *puts his hat on the dresser. There is an immediate improvement in the company's behavior.* CROFTS *takes down his legs from the settle and pulls himself together as* PRAED *joins him at the fireplace.* MRS WARREN *loses her ease of manner and takes refuge in querulousness.*]

MRS WARREN   Wherever have you been, Vivie?

VIVIE [*Taking off her hat and throwing it carelessly on the table.*]   On the hill.

MRS WARREN   Well, you shouldnt go off like that without letting me know. How could I tell what had become of you? And night coming on too!

VIVIE [*Going to the door of the kitchen and opening it, ignoring her mother.*]   Now, about supper? [*All rise except* MRS WARREN.] We shall be rather crowded in here, I'm afraid.

MRS WARREN   Did you hear what I said, Vivie?

VIVIE [*Quietly.*]   Yes, mother. [*Reverting to the supper difficulty.*] How many are we? [*Counting.*] One, two, three, four, five, six. Well, two will have to wait until the rest are done: Mrs Alison has only plates and knives for four.

PRAED   Oh, it doesnt matter about me. I—

VIVIE   You have had a long walk and are hungry, Mr Praed: you shall have your supper at once. I can wait myself. I want one person to wait with me. Frank: are you hungry?

FRANK   Not the least in the world. Completely off my peck, in fact.

MRS WARREN [*To* CROFTS.]   Neither are you, George. You can wait.

CROFTS   Oh, hang it. Ive eaten nothing since tea-time. Cant Sam do it?

FRANK   Would you starve my poor father?

REV. SAMUEL [*Testily.*]   Allow me to speak for myself, sir. I am perfectly willing to wait.

VIVIE [*Decisively.*]   Theres no need. Only two are wanted. [*She opens the door of the kitchen.*] Will you take my mother in, Mr Gardner. [*The parson takes* MRS WARREN; *and they pass into the kitchen.* PRAED *and* CROFTS *follow. All except* PRAED *clearly disapprove of the arrangement, but do not know how to resist it.* VIVIE *stands at the door looking in at them.*] Can you squeeze past to that corner, Mr Praed: it's rather a tight fit. Take care of your coat against the white-wash: thats right. Now, are you all comfortable?

PRAED [*Within.*]   Quite, thank you.

MRS WARREN [*Within.*]   Leave the door open, dearie. [VIVIE *frowns; but* FRANK *checks her with a gesture, and steals to the cottage door, which he softly sets wide open.*] Oh Lor, what a draught! Youd better shut it, dear.
      [VIVIE *shuts it with a slam, and then, noting with disgust that her mother's hat and shawl are lying about, takes them tidily to the window seat, whilst* FRANK *noiselessly shuts the cottage door.*]

9. From the poem *My Dear and Only Love*, by the marquis of Montrose (1612–1650).

FRANK [*Exulting.*]   Aha! Got rid of em. Well, Vivvums: what do you think of my guvernor?

VIVIE [*Preoccupied and serious.*]   Ive hardly spoken to him. He doesnt strike me as being a particularly able person.

FRANK   Well, you know, the old man is not altogether such a fool as he looks. You see, he was shoved into the Church rather; and in trying to live up to it he makes a much bigger ass of himself than he really is. I dont dislike him as much as you might expect. He means well. How do you think youll get on with him?

VIVIE [*Rather grimly.*]   I dont think my future life will be much concerned with him, or with any of that old circle of my mother's, except perhaps Praed. [*She sits down on the settle.*] What do you think of my mother?

FRANK   Really and truly?

VIVIE   Yes, really and truly.

FRANK   Well, she's ever so jolly. But she's rather a caution, isn't she? And Crofts! Oh my eye, Crofts! [*He sits beside her.*]

VIVIE   What a lot, Frank!

FRANK   What a crew!

VIVIE [*With intense contempt for them.*]   If I thought that *I* was like that— that I was going to be a waster, shifting along from one meal to another with no purpose, and no character, and no grit in me, I'd open an artery and bleed to death without one moment's hesitation.

FRANK   Oh no, you wouldnt. Why should they take any grind when they can afford not to? I wish I had their luck. No: what I object to is their form. It isnt the thing: it's slovenly, ever so slovenly.

VIVIE   Do you think your form will be any better when youre as old as Crofts, if you dont work?

FRANK   Of course I do. Ever so much better. Vivvums mustnt lecture: her little boy's incorrigible. [*He attempts to take her face caressingly in his hands.*]

VIVIE [*Striking his hands down sharply.*]   Off with you: Vivvums is not in a humor for petting her little boy this evening. [*She rises and comes forward to the other side of the room.*]

FRANK [*Following her.*]   How unkind!

VIVIE [*Stamping at him.*]   Be serious. I'm serious.

FRANK   Good. Let us talk learnedly. Miss Warren: do you know that all the most advanced thinkers are agreed that half the diseases of modern civilization are due to starvation of the affections in the young. Now, I—

VIVIE [*Cutting him short.*]   You are very tiresome. [*She opens the inner door.*] Have you room for Frank there? He's complaining of starvation.

MRS WARREN [*Within.*]   Of course there is. [*Clatter of knives and glasses as she moves the things on the table.*] Here! theres room now beside me. Come along, Mr Frank.

FRANK   Her little boy will be ever so even with his Vivvums for this. [*He passes into the kitchen.*]

MRS WARREN [*Within.*]   Here, Vivie: come on you too, child. You must be famished. [*She enters, followed by* CROFTS, *who holds the door open for* VIVIE *with marked deference. She goes out without looking at him; and he shuts the door after her.*] Why, George, you cant be done: youve eaten nothing. Is there anything wrong with you?

CROFTS   Oh, all I wanted was a drink. [*He thrusts his hands in his pockets, and begins prowling about the room, restless and sulky.*]

MRS WARREN   Well, I like enough to eat. But a little of that cold beef and cheese and lettuce goes a long way. [*With a sigh of only half repletion she sits down lazily on the settle.*]

CROFTS   What do you go encouraging that young pup for?

MRS WARREN [*On the alert at once.*]   Now see here, George: what are you up to about that girl? Ive been watching your way of looking at her. Remember: I know you and what your looks mean.

CROFTS   Theres no harm in looking at her, is there?

MRS WARREN   I'd put you out and pack you back to London pretty soon if I saw any of your nonsense. My girl's little finger is more to me than your whole body and soul. [CROFTS *receives this with a sneering grin.* MRS WARREN, *flushing a little at her failure to impose on him in the character of a theatrically devoted mother, adds in a lower key*] Make your mind easy: the young pup has no more chance than you have.

CROFTS   Maynt a man take an interest in a girl?

MRS WARREN   Not a man like you.

CROFTS   How old is she?

MRS WARREN   Never you mind how old she is.

CROFTS   Why do you make such a secret of it?

MRS WARREN   Because I choose.

CROFTS   Well, I'm not fifty yet; and my property is as good as ever it was—

MRS WARREN [*Interrupting him.*]   Yes; because youre as stingy as youre vicious.

CROFTS [*Continuing.*]   And a baronet isnt to be picked up every day. No other man in my position would put up with you for a mother-in-law. Why shouldnt she marry me?

MRS WARREN   You!

CROFTS   We three could live together quite comfortably. I'd die before her and leave her a bouncing widow with plenty of money. Why not? It's been growing in my mind all the time Ive been walking with that fool inside there.

MRS WARREN [*Revolted.*]   Yes; it's the sort of thing that would grow in your mind.

[*He halts in his prowling; and the two look at one another, she steadfastly, with a sort of awe behind her contemptuous disgust: he stealthily, with a carnal gleam in his eye and a loose grin.*]

CROFTS [*Suddenly becoming anxious and urgent as he sees no sign of sympathy in her.*]   Look here, Kitty: youre a sensible woman: you neednt put on any moral airs. I'll ask no more questions; and you need answer none. I'll settle the whole property on her; and if you want a cheque for yourself on the wedding day, you can name any figure you like—in reason.

MRS WARREN   So it's come to that with you, George, like all the other worn-out old creatures!

CROFTS [*Savagely.*]   Damn you!

[*Before she can retort the door of the kitchen is opened; and the voices of the others are heard returning.* CROFTS, *unable to recover his presence of mind, hurries out of the cottage. The clergyman appears at the kitchen door.*]

REV. SAMUEL [*Looking around.*]   Where is Sir George?

MRS WARREN   Gone out to have a pipe. [*The clergyman takes his hat from
the table, and joins* MRS WARREN *at the fireside. Meanwhile* VIVIE *comes
in, followed by* FRANK, *who collapses into the nearest chair with an air of
extreme exhaustion.* MRS WARREN *looks round at* VIVIE *and says, with her
affectation of maternal patronage even more forced than usual*] Well,
dearie: have you had a good supper?

VIVIE   You know what Mrs Alison's suppers are. [*She turns to* FRANK *and
pets him.*] Poor Frank! was all the beef gone? did it get nothing but bread
and cheese and ginger beer? [*Seriously, as if she had done quite enough
trifling for one evening.*] Her butter is really awful. I must get some down
from the stores.

FRANK   Do, in heaven's name!

  [VIVIE *goes to the writing-table and makes a memorandum to order the
  butter.* PRAED *comes in from the kitchen, putting up his handkerchief,
  which he has been using as a napkin.*]

REV. SAMUEL   Frank, my boy: it is time for us to be thinking of home. Your
mother does not know yet that we have visitors.

PRAED   I'm afraid we're giving trouble.

FRANK [*Rising.*]   Not the least in the world; my mother will be delighted
to see you. She's a genuinely intellectual artistic woman; and she sees
nobody here from one year's end to another except the gov'nor; so you
can imagine how jolly dull it pans out for her. [*To his father.*] Y o u r e
not intellectual or artistic are you, pater? So take Praed home at once;
and I'll stay here and entertain Mrs Warren. Youll pick up Crofts in the
garden. He'll be excellent company for the bull-pup.

PRAED [*Taking his hat from the dresser, and coming close to* FRANK.]   Come
with us, Frank. Mrs Warren has not seen Miss Vivie for a long time; and
we have prevented them from having a moment together yet.

FRANK [*Quite softened, and looking at* PRAED *with romantic admiration.*]   Of course. I forgot. Ever so thanks for reminding me. Perfect
gentleman, Praddy. Always were. My ideal through life. [*He rises to go,
but pauses a moment between the two older men, and puts his hand on*
PRAED'S *shoulder.*] Ah, if you had only been my father instead of this
unworthy old man! [*He puts his other hand on his father's shoulder.*]

REV. SAMUEL [*Blustering.*]   Silence, sir, silence; you are profane.

MRS WARREN [*Laughing heartily.*]   You should keep him in better order,
Sam. Goodnight. Here: take George his hat and stick with my compliments.

REV. SAMUEL [*Taking them.*]   Goodnight. [*They shake hands. As he passes*
VIVIE *he shakes hands with her also and bids her goodnight. Then, in booming command, to* FRANK.] Come along, sir, at once. [*He goes out.*]

MRS WARREN   Byebye, Praddy.

PRAED   Byebye, Kitty.

  [*They shake hands affectionately and go out together, she accompanying
  him to the garden gate.*]

FRANK [*To* VIVIE.]   Kissums?

VIVIE [*Fiercely.*]   No. I hate you. [*She takes a couple of books and some
paper from the writing-table, and sits down with them at the middle table,
at the end next the fireplace.*]

FRANK [*Grimacing.*]   Sorry. [*He goes for his cap and rifle.* MRS WARREN *returns. He takes her hand.*] Goodnight, d e a r Mrs Warren. [*He kisses her hand. She snatches it away, her lips tightening, and looks more than half disposed to box his ears. He laughs mischievously and runs off, clapping-to the door behind him.*]

MRS WARREN [*Resigning herself to an evening of boredom now that the men are gone.*]   Did you ever in your life hear anyone rattle on so? Isnt he a tease? [*She sits at the table.*] Now that I think of it, dearie, dont you go on encouraging him. I'm sure he's a regular good-for-nothing.

VIVIE [*Rising to fetch more books.*]   I'm afraid so. Poor Frank! I shall have to get rid of him; but I shall feel sorry for him, though he's not worth it. That man Crofts does not seem to me to be good for much either: is he? [*She throws the books on the table rather roughly.*]

MRS WARREN [*Galled by* VIVIE'*s indifference.*]   What do you know of men, child, to talk that way about them? Youll have to make up your mind to see a good deal of Sir George Crofts, as he's a friend of mine.

VIVIE [*Quite unmoved.*]   Why? [*She sits down and opens a book.*] Do you expect that we shall be much together? You and I, I mean?

MRS WARREN [*Staring at her.*]   Of course: until youre married. Youre not going back to college again.

VIVIE   Do you think my way of life would suit you? I doubt it.

MRS WARREN   Y o u r way of life! What do you mean?

VIVIE [*Cutting a page of her book with the paper knife on her chatelaine.*]   Has it really never occurred to you, mother, that I have a way of life like other people?

MRS WARREN   What nonsense is this youre trying to talk? Do you want to shew your independence, now that youre a great little person at school? Dont be a fool, child.

VIVIE [*Indulgently.*]   Thats all you have to say on the subject, is it, mother?

MRS WARREN [*Puzzled, then angry.*]   Dont you keep on asking me questions like that. [*Violently.*] Hold your tongue. [VIVIE *works on, losing no time, and saying nothing.*] You and your way of life, indeed! What next? [*She looks at* VIVIE *again. No reply.*] Your way of life will be what I please, so it will. [*Another pause.*] Ive been noticing these airs in you ever since you got that tripos or whatever you call it. If you think I'm going to put up with them youre mistaken; and the sooner you find it out, the better. [*Muttering.*] All I have to say on the subject, indeed! [*Again raising her voice angrily.*] Do you know who youre speaking to, Miss?

VIVIE [*Looking across at her without raising her head from her book.*]   No. Who are you? What are you?

MRS WARREN [*Rising breathless.*]   You young imp!

VIVIE   Everybody knows my reputation, my social standing, and the profession I intend to pursue. I know nothing about you. What is that way of life which you invite me to share with you and Sir George Crofts, pray?

MRS WARREN   Take care. I shall do something I'll be sorry for after, and you too.

VIVIE [*Putting aside her books with cool decision.*]   Well, let us drop the subject until you are better able to face it. [*Looking critically at her mother.*] You want some good walks and a little lawn tennis to set you up. You are shockingly out of condition: you were not able to manage twenty yards uphill today without stopping to pant; and your wrists are mere rolls of fat. Look at mine. [*She holds out her wrists.*]

MRS WARREN [*After looking at her helplessly, begins to whimper.*]   Vivie—

VIVIE [*Springing up sharply.*]   Now pray dont begin to cry. Anything but that. I really cannot stand whimpering. I will go out of the room if you do.

MRS WARREN [*Piteously.*]   Oh, my darling, how can you be so hard on me? Have I no rights over you as your mother?

VIVIE   Are you my mother?

MRS WARREN [*Appalled.*]   Am I your mother! Oh, Vivie!

VIVIE   Then where are our relatives? my father? our family friends? You claim the rights of a mother: the right to call me fool and child; to speak to me as no woman in authority over me at college dare speak to me; to dictate my way of life; and to force on me the acquaintance of a brute whom anyone can see to be the most vicious sort of London man about town. Before I give myself the trouble to resist such claims, I may as well find out whether they have any real existence.

MRS WARREN [*Distracted, throwing herself on her knees.*]   Oh no, no. Stop, stop. I am your mother: I swear it. Oh, you cant mean to turn on me— my own child! It's not natural. You believe me, dont you? Say you believe me.

VIVIE   Who was my father?

MRS WARREN   You dont know what youre asking. I cant tell you.

VIVIE [*Determinedly.*]   Oh yes you can, if you like. I have a right to know; and you know very well that I have that right. You can refuse to tell me, if you please; but if you do, you will see the last of me tomorrow morning.

MRS WARREN   Oh, it's too horrible to hear you talk like that. You wouldnt—you c o u l d n t leave me.

VIVIE [*Ruthlessly.*]   Yes, without a moment's hesitation, if you trifle with me about this. [*Shivering with disgust.*] How can I feel sure that I may not have the contaminated blood of that brutal waster in my veins?

MRS WARREN   No, no. On my oath it's not he, nor any of the rest that you have ever met. I'm certain of that, at least.

[VIVIE's *eyes fasten sternly on her mother as the significance of this flashes on her.*]

VIVIE [*Slowly.*]   You are certain of that, a t l e a s t. Ah! You mean that that is all you are certain of. [*Thoughtfully.*] I see. [MRS WARREN *buries her face in her hands.*] Dont do that, mother: you know you dont feel it a bit. [MRS WARREN *takes down her hands and looks up deplorably at* VIVIE, *who takes out her watch and says*] Well, that is enough for tonight. At what hour would you like breakfast? Is half-past eight too early for you?

MRS WARREN [*Wildly.*]   My God, what sort of woman are you?

VIVIE [*Coolly.*]   The sort the world is mostly made of, I should hope. Otherwise I dont understand how it gets its business done. Come [*taking her mother by the wrist, and pulling her up pretty resolutely*]: pull yourself together. Thats right.

MRS WARREN [*Querulously.*]   Youre very rough with me, Vivie.

VIVIE   Nonsense. What about bed? It's past ten.

MRS WARREN [*Passionately.*]   Whats the use of my going to bed? Do you think I could sleep?

VIVIE   Why not? I shall.

MRS WARREN   You! youve no heart. [*She suddenly breaks out vehemently in her natural tongue—the dialect of a woman of the people—with all her affectations of maternal authority and conventional manners gone, and an overwhelming inspiration of true conviction and scorn in her.*] Oh, I wont bear it: I wont put up with the injustice of it. What right have you to set yourself up above me like this? You boast of what you are to me—to m e, who gave you the chance of being what you are. What chance had I! Shame on you for a bad daughter and a stuck-up prude!

VIVIE   [*Sitting down with a shrug, no longer confident; for her replies, which have sounded sensible and strong to her so far, now begin to ring rather woodenly and even priggishly against the new tone of her mother.*]   Dont think for a moment I set myself above you in any way. You attacked me with the conventional authority of a mother: I defended myself with the conventional superiority of a respectable woman. Frankly, I am not going to stand any of your nonsense; and when you drop it I shall not expect you to stand any of mine. I shall always respect your right to your own opinions and your own way of life.

MRS WARREN   My own opinions and my own way of life! Listen to her talking! Do you think I was brought up like you? able to pick and choose my own way of life? Do you think I did what I did because I liked it, or thought it right, or wouldnt rather have gone to college and been a lady if I'd had the chance?

VIVIE   Everybody has some choice, mother. The poorest girl alive may not be able to choose between being Queen of England or Principal of Newnham; but she can choose between ragpicking and flower-selling, according to her taste. People are always blaming their circumstances for what they are. I dont believe in circumstances. The people who get on in this world are the people who get up and look for the circumstances they want, and, if they cant find them, make them.

MRS WARREN   Oh, it's easy to talk, very easy, isnt it? Here! would you like to know what my circumstances were?

VIVIE   Yes: you had better tell me. Wont you sit down?

MRS WARREN   Oh, I'll sit down: dont you be afraid. [*She plants her chair farther forward with brazen energy, and sits down.* VIVIE *is impressed in spite of herself.*] D'you know what your gran'mother was?

VIVIE   No.

MRS WARREN   No you dont. I do. She called herself a widow and had a fried-fish shop down by the Mint, and kept herself and four daughters out of it. Two of us were sisters: that was me and Liz; and we were both good-looking and well made. I suppose our father was a well-fed man: mother pretended he was a gentleman; but I dont know. The other two were only half sisters: undersized, ugly, starved looking, hard working, honest poor creatures: Liz and I would have half-murdered them if mother hadnt half-murdered us to keep our hands off them. They were the respectable ones. Well, what did they get by their respectability? I'll tell you. One of them worked in a whitelead factory twelve hours a day for nine shillings a week until she died of lead poisoning. She only expected to get her hands a little paralyzed; but she died. The other was always held up to us as a model because she married a Government laborer in the Deptford victualling yard, and kept his room and the three children neat and tidy on eighteen shillings a week—until he took to drink. That was worth being respectable for, wasnt it?

VIVIE [*Now thoughtfully attentive.*]   Did you and your sister think so?

MRS WARREN   Liz didnt, I can tell you: she had more spirit. We both went to a church school—that was part of the ladylike airs we gave ourselves to be superior to the children that knew nothing and went nowhere—and we stayed there until Liz went out one night and never came back. I know the school-mistress thought I'd soon follow her example; for the clergyman was always warning me that Lizzie'd end by jumping off Waterloo Bridge. Poor fool: that was all he knew about it! But I was more afraid of the whitelead factory than I was of the river; and so would you have been in my place. That clergyman got me a situation as a scullery maid in a temperance restaurant where they sent out for anything you liked. Then I was waitress; and then I went to the bar at Waterloo station: fourteen hours a day serving drinks and washing glasses for four shillings a week and my board. That was considered a great promotion for me. Well, one cold, wretched night, when I was so tired I could hardly keep myself awake, who should come up for a half of Scotch but Lizzie, in a long fur cloak, elegant and comfortable, with a lot of sovereigns in her purse.

VIVIE [*Grimly.*]   My aunt Lizzie!

MRS WARREN. Yes; and a very good aunt to have, too. She's living down at Winchester now, close to the cathedral, one of the most respectable ladies there. Chaperones girls at the county ball, if you please. No river for Liz, thank you! You remind me of Liz a little: she was a first-rate business woman—saved money from the beginning—never let herself look too like what she was—never lost her head or threw away a chance. When she saw I'd grown up good-looking she said to me across the bar "What are you doing there, you little fool? wearing out your health and your appearance for other people's profit!" Liz was saving money then to take a house for herself in Brussels; and she thought we two could save faster than one. So she lent me some money and gave me a start; and I saved steadily and first paid her back, and then went into business with her as her partner. Why shouldnt I have done it? The house in Brussels was real high class: a much better place for a woman to be in than the factory where Anne Jane got poisoned. None of our girls were ever treated as I was treated in the scullery of that temperance place, or at the Waterloo bar, or at home. Would you have had me stay in them and become a worn out old drudge before I was forty?

VIVIE [*Intensely interested by this time.*]   No; but why did you choose that business? Saving money and good management will succeed in any business.

MRS WARREN   Yes, saving money. But where can a woman get the money to save in any other business? Could you save out of four shillings a week and keep yourself dressed as well? Not you. Of course, if youre a plain woman and cant earn anything more; or if you have a turn for music, or the stage, or newspaper writing; thats different. But neither Liz nor I had any turn for such things: all we had was our appearance and our turn for pleasing men. Do you think we were such fools as to let other people trade in our good looks by employing us as shopgirls, or barmaids, or waitresses, when we could trade in them ourselves and get all the profits instead of starvation wages? Not likely.

VIVIE   You were certainly quite justified—from the business point of view.

MRS WARREN   Yes; or any other point of view. What is any respectable girl brought up to do but to catch some rich man's fancy and get the benefit of his money by marrying him?—as if a marriage ceremony could make any difference in the right or wrong of the thing! Oh! the hypocrisy of the world makes me sick! Liz and I had to work and save and calculate just like other people; elseways we should be as poor as any good-for-nothing drunken waster of a woman that thinks her luck will last for ever. [*With great energy.*] I despise such people: theyve no character; and if theres a thing I hate in a woman, it's want of character.

VIVIE   Come now, mother: frankly! Isnt it part of what you call character in a woman that she should greatly dislike such a way of making money?

MRS WARREN   Why, of course. Everybody dislikes having to work and make money; but they have to do it all the same. I'm sure Ive often pitied a poor girl; tired out and in low spirits, having to try to please some man that she doesnt care two straws for—some half-drunken fool that thinks he's making himself agreeable when he's teasing and worrying and disgusting a woman so that hardly any money could pay her for putting up with it. But she has to bear with disagreeables and take the rough with the smooth, just like a nurse in a hospital or anyone else. It's not work that any woman would do for pleasure, goodness knows; though to hear the pious people talk you would suppose it was a bed of roses.

VIVIE   Still, you consider it worth while. It pays.

MRS WARREN   Of course it's worth while to a poor girl, if she can resist temptation and is good-looking and well conducted and sensible. It's far better than any other employment open to her. I always thought that oughtnt to be. It c a n t be right, Vivie, that there shouldnt be better opportunities for women. I stick to that: it's wrong. But it's so, right or wrong; and a girl must make the best of it. But of course it's not worth while for a lady. If you took to it youd be a fool; but I should have been a fool if I'd taken to anything else.

VIVIE [*More and more deeply moved.*]   Mother; suppose we were both as poor as you were in those wretched old days, are you quite sure that you wouldnt advise me to try the Waterloo bar, or marry a laborer, or even go into the factory?

MRS WARREN [*Indignantly.*]   Of course not. What sort of mother do you take me for! How could you keep your self-respect in such starvation and slavery? And whats a woman worth? whats life worth? without self-respect! Why am I independent and able to give my daughter a first-rate education, when other women that had just as good opportunities are in the gutter? Because I always knew how to respect myself and control myself. Why is Liz looked up to in a cathedral town? The same reason. Where would we be now if we'd minded the clergyman's foolishness? Scrubbing floors for one and sixpence a day and nothing to look forward to but the workhouse infirmary. Dont you be led astray by people who dont know the world, my girl. The only way for a woman to provide for herself decently is for her to be good to some man that can afford to be good to her. If she's in his own station of life, let her make him marry her; but if she's far beneath him she cant expect it: why should she? it wouldn't be for her own happiness. Ask any lady in London society that has daughters; and she'll tell you the same, except that I tell you straight and she'll tell you crooked. Thats all the difference.

VIVIE [*Fascinated, gazing at her.*]   My dear mother; you are a wonderful woman: you are stronger than all England. And are you really and truly not one wee bit doubtful—or—or—ashamed?

MRS WARREN   Well, of course, dearie, it's only good manners to be ashamed of it; it's expected from a woman. Women have to pretend to feel a great deal that they dont feel. Liz used to be angry with me for plumping out the truth about it. She used to say that when every woman could learn enough from what was going on in the world before her eyes, there was no need to talk about it to her. But then Liz was such a perfect lady! She had the true instinct of it; while I was always a bit of a vulgarian. I used to be so pleased when you sent me your photos to see that you were growing up like Liz: youve just her ladylike, determined way. But I cant stand saying one thing when everyone knows I mean another. Whats the use in such hypocrisy? If people arrange the world that way for women, theres no good pretending it's arranged the other way. No: I never was a bit ashamed really. I consider I had a right to be proud of how we managed everything so respectably, and never had a word against us, and how the girls were so well taken care of. Some of them did very well: one of them married an ambassador. But of course now I darent talk about such things: whatever would they think of us! [*She yawns.*] Oh dear! I do believe I'm getting sleepy after all. [*She stretches herself lazily, thoroughly relieved by her explosion, and placidly ready for her night's rest.*]

VIVIE   I believe it is I who will not be able to sleep now. [*She goes to the dresser and lights the candle. Then she extinguishes the lamp, darkening the room a good deal.*] Better let in some fresh air before locking up. [*She opens the cottage door, and finds that it is broad moonlight.*] What a beautiful night! Look! [*She draws aside the curtains of the window. The landscape is seen bathed in the radiance of the harvest moon rising over Blackdown.*]

MRS WARREN [*With a perfunctory glance at the scene.*]   Yes, dear; but take care you dont catch your death of cold from the night air.

VIVIE [*Contemptuously.*]   Nonsense.

MRS WARREN [*Querulously.*]   Oh yes: everything I say is nonsense, according to you.

VIVIE [*Turning to her quickly.*]   No: really that is not so, mother. You have got completely the better of me tonight, though I intended it to be the other way. Let us be good friends now.

MRS WARREN [*Shaking her head a little ruefully.*]   So it has been the other way. But I suppose I must give in to it. I always got the worst of it from Liz; and now I suppose it'll be the same with you.

VIVIE   Well, never mind. Come: goodnight, dear old mother. [*She takes her mother in her arms.*]

MRS WARREN [*Fondly.*]   I brought you up well, didnt I, dearie?

VIVIE   You did.

MRS WARREN   And youll be good to your poor old mother for it, wont you?

VIVIE   I will, dear. [*Kissing her.*] Goodnight.

MRS WARREN [*With unction.*]   Blessings on my own dearie darling! a
mother's blessing!

> [*She embraces her daughter protectingly, instinctively looking upward
> for divine sanction.*]

Act 3

*In the Rectory garden next morning, with the sun shining from a cloudless sky.
The garden wall has a five-barred wooden gate, wide enough to admit a carriage,
in the middle. Beside the gate hangs a bell on a coiled spring, communicating
with a pull outside. The carriage drive comes down the middle of the garden and
then swerves to its left, where it ends in a little gravelled circus opposite the
Rectory porch. Beyond the gate is seen the dusty high road, parallel with the wall,
bounded on the farther side by a strip of turf and an unfenced pine wood. On the
lawn, between the house and the drive, is a clipped yew tree, with a garden bench
in its shade. On the opposite side the garden is shut in by a box hedge; and there
is a sundial on the turf, with an iron chair near it. A little path leads off through
the box hedge, behind the sundial.*

*FRANK, seated on the chair near the sundial, on which he has placed the morn-
ing papers, is reading* The Standard. *His father comes from the house, red-eyed
and shivery, and meets* FRANK's *eye with misgiving.*

FRANK [*Looking at his watch.*]   Half-past eleven. Nice hour for a rector to
come down to breakfast!

REV. SAMUEL   Dont mock, Frank: dont mock. I am a little—er—[*Shivering.*]—

FRANK   Off color?

REV. SAMUEL [*Repudiating the expression.*]   No, sir: u n w e l l this morning. Wheres your mother?

FRANK   Dont be alarmed: she's not here. Gone to town by the 11.13 with
Bessie. She left several messages for you. Do you feel equal to receiving
them now, or shall I wait til youve breakfasted?

REV. SAMUEL   I h a v e breakfasted, sir. I am surprised at your mother
going to town when we have people staying with us. Theyll think it very
strange.

FRANK   Possibly she has considered that. At all events, if Crofts is going
to stay here, and you are going to sit up every night with him until four,
recalling the incidents of your fiery youth, it is clearly my mother's duty,
as a prudent housekeeper, to go up to the stores and order a barrel of
whisky and few hundred siphons.

REV. SAMUEL   I did not observe that Sir George drank excessively.

FRANK   You were not in a condition to, gov'nor.

REV. SAMUEL   Do you mean to say that I—?

FRANK [*Calmly.*]   I never saw a beneficed clergyman less sober. The anecdotes you told about your past career were so awful that I really dont
think Praed would have passed the night under your roof if it hadnt been
for the way my mother and he took to one another.

REV. SAMUEL   Nonsense, sir. I am Sir George Crofts' host. I must talk to
him about something; and he has only one subject. Where is Mr Praed
now?

FRANK   He is driving my mother and Bessie to the station.

REV. SAMUEL   Is Crofts up yet?

FRANK   Oh, long ago. He hasnt turned a hair: he's in much better practice than you. Has kept it up ever since, probably. He's taken himself off somewhere to smoke.

> [FRANK *resumes his paper. The parson turns disconsolately towards the gate; then comes back irresolutely.*]

REV. SAMUEL   Er—Frank.

FRANK   Yes.

REV. SAMUEL   Do you think the Warrens will expect to be asked here after yesterday afternoon?

FRANK   Theyve been asked already.

REV. SAMUEL [*Appalled.*]   What!!!

FRANK   Crofts informed us at breakfast that you told him to bring Mrs Warren and Vivie over here today, and to invite them to make this house their home. My mother then found she must go to town by the 11.13 train.

REV. SAMUEL [*With despairing vehemence.*]   I never gave any such invitation. I never thought of such a thing.

FRANK [*Compassionately.*]   How do you know, gov'nor, what you said and thought last night?

PRAED [*Coming in through the hedge.*]   Good morning.

REV. SAMUEL   Good morning. I must apologize for not having met you at breakfast. I have a touch of—of—

FRANK   Clergyman's sore throat, Praed. Fortunately not chronic.

PRAED [*Changing the subject.*]   Well, I must say your house is in a charming spot here. Really most charming.

REV. SAMUEL   Yes: it is indeed. Frank will take you for a walk, Mr Praed, if you like. I'll ask you to excuse me: I must take the opportunity to write my sermon while Mrs Gardner is away and you are all amusing yourselves. You wont mind, will you?

PRAED   Certainly not. Dont stand on the slightest ceremony with me.

REV. SAMUEL   Thank you. I'll—er—er—[*He stammers his way to the porch and vanishes into the house.*]

PRAED   Curious thing it must be writing a sermon every week.

FRANK   Ever so curious, if he did it. He buys em. He's gone for some soda water.

PRAED   My dear boy: I wish you would be more respectful to your father. You know you can be so nice when you like.

FRANK   My dear Praddy: you forget that I have to live with the governor. When two people live together—it doesnt matter whether theyre father and son or husband and wife or brother and sister—they cant keep up the polite humbug thats so easy for ten minutes on an afternoon call. Now the governor, who unites to many admirable domestic qualities the irresoluteness of a sheep and the pompousness and aggressiveness of a jackass—

PRAED   No, pray, pray, my dear Frank, remember! He is your father.

FRANK   I give him due credit for that. [*Rising and flinging down his paper.*] But just imagine his telling Crofts to bring the Warrens over here! He must have been ever so drunk. You know, my dear Praddy, my mother wouldnt stand Mrs Warren for a moment. Vivie mustnt come here until she's gone back to town.

PRAED   But your mother doesnt know anything about Mrs Warren, does she? [*He picks up the paper and sits down to read it.*]

FRANK   I don't know. Her journey to town looks as if she did. Not that my mother would mind in the ordinary way: she has stuck like a brick to lots of women who had got into trouble. But they were all nice women. Thats what makes the real difference. Mrs Warren, no doubt, has her merits; but she's ever so rowdy; and my mother simply wouldnt put up with her. So—hallo! [*This exclamation is provoked by the reappearance of the clergyman, who comes out of the house in haste and dismay.*]

REV. SAMUEL   Frank: Mrs Warren and her daughter are coming across the heath with Crofts: I saw them from the study windows. What am I to say about your mother?

FRANK   Stick on your hat and go out and say how delighted you are to see them; and that Frank's in the garden; and that mother and Bessie have been called to the bedside of a sick relative, and were ever so sorry they couldnt stop; and that you hope Mrs Warren slept well; and—and—say any blessed thing except the truth, and leave the rest to Providence.

REV. SAMUEL   But how are we to get rid of them afterwards?

FRANK   Theres no time to think of that now. Here! [*He bounds into the house.*]

REV. SAMUEL   He's so impetuous. I dont know what to do with him, Mr Praed.

FRANK   [*Returning with clerical felt hat, which he claps on his father's head.*]   Now: off with you. [*Rushing him through the gate.*] Praed and I'll wait here, to give the thing an unpremeditated air. [*The clergyman, dazed but obedient, hurries off.*]

FRANK   We must get the old girl back to town somehow, Praed. Come! Honestly, dear Praddy, do you like seeing them together?

PRAED   Oh, why not?

FRANK   [*His teeth on edge.*]   Dont it make your flesh creep ever so little? that wicked old devil, up to every villainy under the sun, I'll swear, and Vivie—ugh!

PRAED   Hush, pray. Theyre coming.

[*The clergyman and* CROFTS *are seen coming along the road, followed by* MRS WARREN *and* VIVIE *walking affectionately together.*]

FRANK   Look: she actually has her arm round the old woman's waist. It's her right arm: she began it. She's gone sentimental, by God! Ugh! ugh! Now do you feel the creeps? [*The clergyman opens the gate; and* MRS WARREN *and* VIVIE *pass him and stand in the middle of the garden looking at the house.* FRANK, *in an ecstasy of dissimulation, turns gaily to* MRS WARREN, *exclaiming*] Ever so delighted to see you, Mrs Warren. This quiet old rectory garden becomes you perfectly.

MRS WARREN   Well, I never! Did you hear that, George? He says I look well in a quiet old rectory garden.

REV. SAMUEL   [*Still holding the gate for* CROFTS, *who loafs through it, heavily bored.*]   You look well everywhere, Mrs Warren.

FRANK   Bravo, gov'nor! Now look here: lets have a treat before lunch. First lets see the church. Everyone has to do that. It's a regular old thirteenth century church, you know: the gov'nor's ever so fond of it, because he got up a restoration fund and had it completely rebuilt six years ago. Praed will be able to shew its points.

PRAED [*Rising.*] Certainly, if the restoration has left any to shew.

REV. SAMUEL [*Mooning hospitably at them.*] I shall be pleased, I'm sure, if Sir George and Mrs Warren really care about it.

MRS WARREN Oh, come along and get it over.

CROFTS [*Turning back towards the gate.*] Ive no objection.

REV. SAMUEL Not that way. We go through the fields, if you dont mind. Round here. [*He leads the way by the little path through the box hedge.*]

CROFTS Oh, all right. [*He goes with the parson.*]

[PRAED *follows with* MRS WARREN. VIVIE *does not stir: she watches them until they have gone, with all the lines of purpose in her face marking it strongly.*]

FRANK Aint you coming?

VIVIE No. I want to give you a warning, Frank. You were making fun of my mother just now when you said that about the rectory garden. That is barred in future. Please treat my mother with as much respect as you treat your own.

FRANK My dear Viv: she wouldnt appreciate it: the two cases require different treatment. But what on earth has happened to you? Last night we were perfectly agreed as to your mother and her set. This morning I find you attitudinizing sentimentally with your arm round your parent's waist.

VIVIE [*Flushing.*] Attitudinizing!

FRANK That was how it struck me. First time I ever saw you do a second-rate thing.

VIVIE [*Controlling herself.*] Yes, Frank: there has been a change; but I dont think it a change for the worse. Yesterday I was a little prig.

FRANK And today?

VIVIE [*Wincing; then looking at him steadily.*] Today I know my mother better than you do.

FRANK Heaven forbid!

VIVIE What do you mean?

FRANK Viv: theres a freemasonry among thoroughly immoral people that you know nothing of. Youve too much character. T h a t s the bond between your mother and me: thats why I know her better than youll ever know her.

VIVIE You are wrong: you know nothing about her. If you knew the circumstances against which my mother had to struggle—

FRANK [*Adroitly finishing the sentence for her.*] I should know why she is what she is, shouldnt I? What difference would that make? Circumstances or no circumstances, Viv, you wont be able to stand your mother.

VIVIE [*Very angrily.*] Why not?

FRANK Because she's an old wretch, Viv. If you ever put your arm round her waist in my presence again, I'll shoot myself there and then as a protest against an exhibition which revolts me.

VIVIE Must I choose between dropping your acquaintance and dropping my mother's?

FRANK [*Gracefully.*] That would put the old lady at ever such a disadvantage. No, Viv: your infatuated little boy will have to stick to you in any case. But he's all the more anxious that you shouldnt make mistakes. It's no use, Viv: your mother's impossible. She may be a good sort; but she's a bad lot, a very bad lot.

VIVIE [*Hotly.*] Frank—! [*He stands his ground. She turns away and sits down on the bench under the yew tree, struggling to recover her self-command. Then she says*] Is she to be deserted by all the world because she's what you call a bad lot? Has she no right to live?

FRANK No fear of that, Viv: s h e wont ever be deserted. [*He sits on the bench beside her.*]

VIVIE But I am to desert her, I suppose.

FRANK [*Babyishly, lulling her and making love to her with his voice.*] Mustnt go live with her. Little family group of mother and daughter wouldnt be a success. Spoil our little group.

VIVIE [*Falling under the spell.*] What little group?

FRANK The babes in the wood: Vivie and little Frank. [*He nestles against her like a weary child.*] Lets go and get covered up with leaves.

VIVIE [*Rhythmically, rocking him like a nurse.*] Fast asleep, hand in hand, under the trees.

FRANK The wise little girl with her silly little boy.

VIVIE The dear little boy with his dowdy little girl.

FRANK Ever so peaceful, and relieved from the imbecility of the little boy's father and the questionableness of the little girl's—

VIVIE [*Smothering the word against her breast.*] Sh-sh-sh-sh! little girl wants to forget all about her mother. [*They are silent for some moments, rocking one another. Then* VIVIE *wakes up with a shock, exclaiming*] What a pair of fools we are! Come: sit up. Gracious! your hair. [*She smoothes it.*] I wonder do all grown up people play in that childish way when nobody is looking. I never did it when I was a child.

FRANK Neither did I. You are my first playmate. [*He catches her hand to kiss it, but checks himself to look round first. Very unexpectedly, he sees* CROFTS *emerging from the box hedge.*] Oh damn!

VIVIE Why damn, dear?

FRANK [*Whispering.*] Sh! Here's this brute Crofts. [*He sits farther away from her with an unconcerned air.*]

CROFTS. Could I have a few words with you, Miss Vivie?

VIVIE Certainly.

CROFTS [*To* FRANK.] Youll excuse me, Gardner. Theyre waiting for you in the church, if you don't mind.

FRANK [*Rising.*] Anything to oblige you, Crofts—except church. If you should happen to want me, Vivvums, ring the gate bell. [*He goes into the house with unruffled suavity.*]

CROFTS [*Watching him with a crafty air as he disappears, and speaking to* VIVIE *with an assumption of being on privileged terms with her.*] Pleasant young fellow that, Miss Vivie. Pity he has no money, isnt it?

VIVIE Do you think so?

CROFTS Well, whats he to do? No profession. No property. Whats he good for?

VIVIE I realize his disadvantages, Sir George.

CROFTS [*A little taken aback at being so precisely interpreted.*] Oh, it's not that. But while we're in this world we're in it; and money's money. [*Vivie does not answer.*] Nice day, isnt it?

VIVIE [*With scarcely veiled contempt for this effort at conversation.*] Very.

CROFTS [*With brutal good humor, as if he liked her pluck.*] Well, thats not what I came to say. [*Sitting down beside her.*] Now listen, Miss Vivie. I'm quite aware that I'm not a young lady's man.

VIVIE Indeed, Sir George?

CROFTS No; and to tell you the honest truth I dont want to be either. But when I say a thing I mean it; when I feel a sentiment I feel it in earnest; and what I value I pay hard money for. Thats the sort of man I am.

VIVIE It does you great credit, I'm sure.

CROFTS Oh, I dont mean to praise myself. I have my faults, Heaven knows: no man is more sensible of that than I am. I know I'm not perfect: thats one of the disadvantages of being a middle-aged man; for I'm not a young man, and I know it. But my code is a simple one, and, I think, a good one. Honor between man and man; fidelity between man and woman; and no cant about this religion or that religion, but an honest belief that things are making for good on the whole.

VIVIE [*With biting irony.*] "A power, not ourselves, that makes for righteousness," eh?

CROFTS [*Taking her seriously.*] Oh certainly. Not ourselves, of course. You understand what I mean. Well, now as to practical matters. You may have an idea that Ive flung my money about; but I havnt: I'm richer today than when I first came into the property. Ive used my knowledge of the world to invest my money in ways that other men have overlooked; and whatever else I may be, I'm a safe man from the money point of view.

VIVIE It's very kind of you to tell me all this.

CROFTS Oh well, come, Miss Vivie: you neednt pretend you dont see what I'm driving at. I want to settle down with a Lady Crofts. I suppose you think me very blunt, eh?

VIVIE Not at all: I am much obliged to you for being so definite and businesslike. I quite appreciate the offer: the money, the position, L a d y C r o f t s, and so on. But I think I will say no, if you don't mind. I'd rather not. [*She rises, and strolls across to the sundial to get out of his immediate neighborhood.*]

CROFTS [*Not at all discouraged, and taking advantage of the additional room left him on the seat to spread himself comfortably, as if a few preliminary refusals were part of the inevitable routine of courtship.*] I'm in no hurry. It was only just to let you know in case young Gardner should try to trap you. Leave the question open.

VIVIE [*Sharply.*] My no is final. I wont go back from it.

[CROFTS *is not impressed. He grins; leans forward with his elbows on his knees to prod with his stick at some unfortunate insect in the grass; and looks cunningly at her. She turns away impatiently.*]

CROFTS I'm a good deal older than you. Twenty-five years; quarter of a century. I shant live for ever; and I'll take care that you shall be well off when I'm gone.

VIVIE I am proof against even that inducement, Sir George. Dont you think youd better take your answer? There is not the slightest chance of my altering it.

CROFTS [*Rising after a final slash at a daisy, and coming nearer to her.*] Well, no matter. I could tell you some things that would change your mind fast enough; but I wont, because I'd rather win you by honest affection. I was a good friend to your mother: ask her whether I wasnt.

She'd never have made the money that paid for your education if it hadnt been for my advice and help, not to mention the money I advanced her. There are not many men would have stood by her as I have. I put not less than £40,000 into it, from first to last.

VIVIE [*Staring at him.*]   Do you mean to say you were my mother's business partner?

CROFTS   Yes. Now just think of all the trouble and the explanations it would save if we were to keep the whole thing in the family, so to speak. Ask your mother whether she'd like to have to explain all her affairs to a perfect stranger.

VIVIE   I see no difficulty, since I understand that the business is wound up, and the money invested.

CROFTS [*Stopping short, amazed.*]   Wound up! Wind up a business thats paying 35 per cent in the worst years! Not likely. Who told you that?

VIVIE [*Her color quite gone.*]   Do you mean that it is still—? [*She stops abruptly, and puts her hand on the sundial to support herself. Then she gets quickly to the iron chair and sits down.*] What business are you talking about?

CROFTS   Well, the fact is it's not what would be considered exactly a high-class business in my set—the county set, you know—our set it will be if you think better of my offer. Not that theres any mystery about it: dont think that. Of course you know by your mother's being in it that it's perfectly straight and honest. Ive known her for many years; and I can say of her that she'd cut off her hands sooner than touch anything that was not what it ought to be. I'll tell you all about it if you like. I dont know whether youve found in travelling how hard it is to find a really comfortable private hotel.

VIVIE [*Sickened, averting her face.*]   Yes: go on.

CROFTS   Well, thats all it is. Your mother has a genius for managing such things. We've got two in Brussels, one in Ostend, one in Vienna, and two in Budapest. Of course there are others besides ourselves in it; but we hold most of the capital; and your mother's indispensable as managing director. Youve noticed, I daresay, that she travels a good deal. But you see you cant mention such things in society. Once let out the word hotel and everybody says you keep a public-house. You wouldnt like people to say that of your mother, would you? Thats why we're so reserved about it. By the way, youll keep it to yourself, wont you? Since it's been a secret so long, it had better remain so.

VIVIE   And this is the business you invite me to join you in?

CROFTS   Oh, no. My wife shant be troubled with business. Youll not be in it more than youve always been.

VIVIE   I always been! What do you mean?

CROFTS   Only that youve always lived on it. It paid for your education and the dress you have on your back. Dont turn up your nose at business, Miss Vivie: where would your Newnhams and Girtons[1] be without it?

VIVIE [*Rising, almost beside herself.*]   Take care. I know what this business is.

CROFTS [*Staring, with a suppressed oath.*]   Who told you?

---

1. Girton, like Newnham, is a women's college at Cambridge University.

VIVIE Your partner. My mother.

CROFTS [*Black with rage.*] The old—

VIVIE Just so.

[*He swallows the epithet and stands for a moment swearing and raging foully to himself. But he knows that his cue is to be sympathetic. He takes refuge in generous indignation.*]

CROFTS She ought to have had more consideration for you. I'd never have told you.

VIVIE I think you would probably have told me when we were married; it would have been a convenient weapon to break me in with.

CROFTS [*Quite sincerely.*] I never intended that. On my word as a gentleman I didnt.

[VIVIE *wonders at him. Her sense of the irony of his protest cools and braces her. She replies with contemptuous self-possession.*]

VIVIE It does not matter. I suppose you understand that when we leave here today our acquaintance ceases.

CROFTS Why? Is it for helping your mother?

VIVIE My mother was a very poor woman who had no reasonable choice but to do as she did. You were a rich gentleman; and you did the same for the sake of 35 per cent. You are a pretty common sort of scoundrel, I think. That is my opinion of you.

CROFTS [*After a stare: not at all displeased, and much more at ease on these frank terms than on their former ceremonious ones.*] Ha! ha! ha! ha! Go it, little missie, go it: it doesnt hurt me and it amuses you. Why the devil shouldnt I invest my money that way? I take the interest on my capital like other people: I hope you dont think I dirty my own hands with the work. Come! you wouldnt refuse the acquaintance of my mother's cousin the Duke of Belgravia because some of the rents he gets are earned in queer ways. You wouldnt cut the Archbishop of Canterbury, I suppose, because the Ecclesiastical Commissioners have a few publicans and sinners among their tenants. Do you remember your Crofts scholarship at Newnham? Well, that was founded by my brother the M.P.[2] He gets his 22 per cent out of a factory with 600 girls in it, and not one of them getting wages enough to live on. How d'ye suppose they manage when they have no family to fall back on? Ask your mother. And do you expect me to turn my back on 35 per cent when all the rest are pocketing what they can, like sensible men? No such fool! If youre going to pick and choose your acquaintances on moral principles, youd better clear out of this country, unless you want to cut yourself out of all decent society.

VIVIE [*Conscience stricken.*] You might go on to point out that I myself never asked where the money I spent came from. I believe I am just as bad as you.

CROFTS [*Greatly reassured.*] Of course you are; and a very good thing too! What harm does it do after all? [*Rallying her jocularly.*] So you dont think me such a scoundrel now you come to think it over. Eh?

VIVIE I have shared profits with you; and I admitted you just now to the familiarity of knowing what I think of you.

CROFTS [*With serious friendliness.*] To be sure you did. You wont find me

2. Member of Parliament.

a bad sort: I dont go in for being superfine intellectually; but Ive plenty of honest human feeling; and the old Crofts breed comes out in a sort of instinctive hatred of anything low, in which I'm sure youll sympathize with me. Believe me, Miss Vivie, the world isnt such a bad place as the croakers make out. As long as you dont fly openly in the face of society, society doesnt ask any inconvenient questions; and it makes precious short work of the cads who do. There are no secrets better kept than the secrets everybody guesses. In the class of people I can introduce you to, no lady or gentleman would so far forget themselves as to discuss my business affairs or your mother's. No man can offer you a safer position.

VIVIE [*Studying him curiously.*]   I suppose you really think youre getting on famously with me.

CROFTS   Well, I hope I may flatter myself that you think better of me than you did at first.

VIVIE [*Quietly.*]   I hardly find you worth thinking about at all now. When I think of the society that tolerates you, and the laws that protect you! when I think of how helpless nine out of ten young girls would be in the hands of you and my mother! the unmentionable woman and her capitalist bully—

CROFTS [*Livid.*]   Damn you!

VIVIE   You need not. I feel among the damned already.
    [*She raises the latch of the gate to open it and go out. He follows her and puts his hand heavily on the top bar to prevent its opening.*]

CROFTS [*Panting with fury.*]   Do you think I'll put up with this from you, you young devil?

VIVIE [*Unmoved.*]   Be quiet. Some one will answer the bell. [*Without flinching a step she strikes the bell with the back of her hand. It clangs harshly; and he starts back involuntarily. Almost immediately* FRANK *appears at the porch with his rifle.*]

FRANK [*With cheerful politeness.*]   Will you have the rifle, Viv; or shall I operate?

VIVIE   Frank: have you been listening?

FRANK [*Coming down into the garden.*]   Only for the bell, I assure you; so that you shouldn't have to wait. I think I shewed great insight into your character Crofts.

CROFTS   For two pins I'd take that gun from you and break it across your head.

FRANK [*Stalking him cautiously.*]   Pray dont. I'm ever so careless in handling firearms. Sure to be a fatal accident, with a reprimand from the coroner's jury for my negligence.

VIVIE   Put the rifle away, Frank: it's quite unnecessary.

FRANK   Quite right, Viv. Much more sportsmanlike to catch him in a trap. [CROFTS, *understanding the insult, makes a threatening movement.*] Crofts: there are fifteen cartridges in the magazine here; and I am a dead shot at the present distance and at an object of your size.

CROFTS   Oh, you neednt be afraid. I'm not going to touch you.

FRANK   Ever so magnanimous of you under the circumstances! Thank you!

CROFTS   I'll tell you this before I go. It may interest you, since youre so fond of one another. Allow me, Mister Frank, to introduce you to your half-sister, the eldest daughter of the Reverend Samuel Gardner. Miss

Vivie: your half-brother. Good morning. [*He goes out through the gate and along the road.*]

FRANK [*After a pause of stupefaction, raising the rifle.*] Youll testify before the coroner that it's an accident, Viv. [*He takes aim at the retreating figure of* CROFTS. VIVIE *seizes the muzzle and pulls it round against her breast.*]

VIVIE Fire now. You may.

FRANK [*Dropping his end of the rifle hastily.*] Stop! take care. [*She lets go. It falls on the turf.*] Oh, youve given your little boy such a turn. Suppose it had gone off! ugh! [*He sinks on the garden seat, overcome.*]

VIVIE Suppose it had: do you think it would not have been a relief to have some sharp physical pain tearing through me?

FRANK [*Coaxingly.*] Take it ever so easy, dear Viv. Remember; even if the rifle scared that fellow into telling the truth for the first time in his life, that only makes us the babes in the wood in earnest. [*He holds out his arms to her.*] Come and be covered up with leaves again.

VIVIE [*With a cry of disgust.*] Ah, not that, not that. You make all my flesh creep.

FRANK Why, whats the matter?

VIVIE Goodbye. [*She makes for the gate.*]

FRANK [*Jumping up.*] Hallo! Stop! Viv! Viv! [*She turns in the gateway.*] Where are you going to? Where shall we find you?

VIVIE At Honoria Fraser's chambers, 67 Chancery Lane, for the rest of my life. [*She goes off quickly in the opposite direction to that taken by* CROFTS.]

FRANK But I say—wait—dash it! [*He runs after her.*]

Act 4

HONORIA FRASER'*s chambers in Chancery Lane. An office at the top of New Stone Buildings, with a plate-glass window, distempered walls, electric light, and a patent stove. Saturday afternoon. The chimneys of Lincoln's Inn*[3] *and the western sky beyond are seen through the window. There is a double writing table in the middle of the room, with a cigar box, ash pans, and a portable electric reading lamp almost snowed up in heaps of papers and books. This table has knee holes and chairs right and left and is very untidy. The clerk's desk, closed and tidy, with its high stool, is against the wall, near a door communicating with the inner rooms. In the opposite wall is the door leading to the public corridor. Its upper panel is of opaque glass, lettered in black on the outside,* FRASER AND WARREN. *A baize screen hides the corner between this door and the window.*

FRANK, *in a fashionable light-colored coaching suit, with his stick, gloves, and white hat in his hands, is pacing up and down the office. Somebody tries the door with a key.*

FRANK [*Calling.*] Come in. It's not locked.

[VIVIE *comes in, in her hat and jacket. She stops and stares at him.*]

VIVIE [*Sternly.*] What are you doing here?

FRANK Waiting to see you. Ive been here for hours. Is this the way you attend to your business? [*He puts his hat and stick on the table, and*

---

3. One of the four legal societies in London collectively known as the Inns of Court.

*perches himself with a vault on the clerk's stool, looking at her with every
appearance of being in a specially restless, teasing flippant mood.*]

VIVIE   Ive been away exactly twenty minutes for a cup of tea. [*She takes
off her hat and jacket and hangs them up behind the screen.*] How did you
get in?

FRANK   The staff had not left when I arrived. He's gone to play cricket on
Primrose Hill.[4] Why dont you employ a woman, and give your sex a
chance?

VIVIE   What have you come for?

FRANK   [*Springing off the stool and coming close to her.*]   Viv: lets go and
enjoy the Saturday half-holiday somewhere, like the staff. What do you
say to Richmond,[5] and then a music hall, and a jolly supper?

VIVIE   Cant afford it. I shall put in another six hours work before I go to
bed.

FRANK   Cant afford it, cant we? Aha! Look here. [*He takes out a handful
of sovereigns and makes them chink.*] Gold, Viv: gold!

VIVIE   Where did you get it?

FRANK   Gambling, Viv: gambling. Poker.

VIVIE   Pah! It's meaner than stealing it. No: I'm not coming. [*She sits down
to work at the table, with her back to the glass door, and begins turning
over the papers.*]

FRANK   [*Remonstrating piteously.*]   But, my dear Viv, I want to talk to you
ever so seriously.

VIVIE   Very well: sit down in Honoria's chair and talk here. I like ten
minutes chat after tea. [*He murmurs.*] No use groaning: I'm inexorable.
[*He takes the opposite seat disconsolately.*] Pass that cigar box, will you?

FRANK   [*Pushing the cigar box across.*]   Nasty womanly habit. Nice men
dont do it any longer.

VIVIE   Yes: they object to the smell in the office; and weve had to take to
cigarets. See! [*She opens the box and takes out a cigaret, which she lights.
She offers him one; but he shakes his head with a wry face. She settles
herself comfortably in her chair, smoking.*] Go ahead.

FRANK   Well, I want to know what youve done—what arrangements youve
made.

VIVIE   Everything was settled twenty minutes after I arrived here. Honoria
has found the business too much for her this year; and she was on the
point of sending for me and proposing a partnership when I walked in
and told her I hadnt a farthing in the world. So I installed myself and
packed her off for a fortnight's holiday. What happened at Haslemere
when I left?

FRANK   Nothing at all. I said youd gone to town on particular business.

VIVIE   Well?

FRANK   Well, either they were too flabbergasted to say anything, or else
Crofts had prepared your mother. Anyhow, she didnt say anything; and
Crofts didnt say anything; and Praddy only stared. After tea they got up
and went; and Ive not seen them since.

VIVIE   [*Nodding placidly with one eye on a wreath of smoke.*]   Thats all right.

---

4. A park in northwest London.   5. A residential suburb in southwest London.

FRANK [*Looking round disparagingly.*]   Do you intend to stick in this confounded place?

VIVIE [*Blowing the wreath decisively away, and sitting straight up.*]   Yes. These two days have given me back all my strength and self-possession. I will never take a holiday again as long as I live.

FRANK [*With a very wry face.*]   Mps! You look quite happy. And as hard as nails.

VIVIE [*Grimly.*]   Well for me that I am!

FRANK [*Rising.*]   Look here, Viv: we must have an explanation. We parted the other day under a complete misunderstanding. [*He sits on the table, close to her.*]

VIVIE [*Putting away the cigaret.*]   Well: clear it up.

FRANK   You remember what Crofts said?

VIVIE   Yes.

FRANK   That revelation was supposed to bring about a complete change in the nature of our feeling for one another. It placed us on the footing of brother and sister.

VIVIE   Yes.

FRANK   Have you ever had a brother?

VIVIE   No.

FRANK   Then you dont know what being brother and sister feels like? Now I have lots of sisters; and the fraternal feeling is quite familiar to me. I assure you my feeling for you is not the least in the world like it. The girls will go their way; I will go mine; and we shant care if we never see one another again. Thats brother and sister. But as to you, I cant be easy if I have to pass a week without seeing you. Thats not brother and sister. It's exactly what I felt an hour before Crofts made his revelation. In short, dear Viv, it's love's young dream.

VIVIE [*Bitingly.*]   The same feeling, Frank, that brought your father to my mother's feet. Is that it?

FRANK [*So revolted that he slips off the table for a moment.*]   I very strongly object, Viv, to have my feelings compared to any which the Reverend Samuel is capable of harboring; and I object still more to a comparison of you to your mother. [*Resuming his perch.*] Besides, I dont believe the story. I have taxed my father with it, and obtained from him what I consider tantamount to a denial.

VIVIE   What did he say?

FRANK   He said he was sure there must be some mistake.

VIVIE   Do you believe him?

FRANK   I am prepared to take his word as against Crofts'.

VIVIE   Does it make any difference? I mean in your imagination or conscience; for of course it makes no real difference.

FRANK [*Shaking his head.*]   None whatever to m e.

VIVIE   Nor to me.

FRANK [*Staring.*]   But this is ever so surprising! [*He goes back to his chair.*] I thought our whole relations were altered in your imagination and conscience, as you put it, the moment those words were out of the brute's muzzle.

VIVIE   No: it was not that. I didnt believe him. I only wish I could.

FRANK   Eh?

VIVIE   I think brother and sister would be a very suitable relation for us.

FRANK   You really mean that?

VIVIE   Yes. It's the only relation I care for, even if we could afford any other. I mean that.

FRANK [*Raising his eyebrows like one on whom a new light has dawned, and rising with quite an effusion of chivalrous sentiment.*]   My dear Viv: why didnt you say so before? I am ever so sorry for persecuting you. I understand, of course.

VIVIE [*Puzzled.*]   Understand what?

FRANK   Oh, I'm not a fool in the ordinary sense: only in the Scriptural sense of doing all the things the wise man declared to be folly, after trying them himself on the most extensive scale. I see I am no longer Vivvum's little boy. Dont be alarmed: I shall never call you Vivvums again—at least unless you get tired of your new little boy, whoever he may be.

VIVIE   My new little boy!

FRANK [*With conviction.*]   Must be a new little boy. Always happens that way. No other way, in fact.

VIVIE   None that you know of, fortunately for you.

[*Someone knocks at the door.*]

FRANK   My curse upon yon caller, whoe'er he be!

VIVIE   It's Praed. He's going to Italy and wants to say goodbye. I asked him to call this afternoon. Go and let him in.

FRANK   We can continue our conversation after his departure for Italy. I'll stay him out. [*He goes to the door and opens it.*] How are you, Praddy? Delighted to see you. Come in.

[PRAED, *dressed for travelling, comes in, in high spirits.*]

PRAED   How do you do, Miss Warren? [*She presses his hand cordially, though a certain sentimentality in his high spirits jars on her.*] I start in an hour from Holborn Viaduct.[6] I wish I could persuade you to try Italy.

VIVIE   What for?

PRAED   Why, to saturate yourself with beauty and romance, of course.

[VIVIE, *with a shudder, turns her chair to the table, as if the work waiting for her were a support to her.* PRAED *sits opposite to her.* FRANK *places a chair near* VIVIE, *and drops lazily and carelessly into it, talking at her over his shoulder.*]

FRANK   No use, Praddy. Viv is a little Philistine. She is indifferent to my romance, and insensible to my beauty.

VIVIE   Mr Praed: once for all, there is no beauty and no romance in life for me. Life is what it is; and I am prepared to take it as it is.

PRAED [*Enthusiastically.*]   You will not say that if you come with me to Verona and on to Venice. You will cry with delight at living in such a beautiful world.

FRANK   This is most eloquent, Praddy. Keep it up.

PRAED   Oh, I assure you I have cried—I shall cry again, I hope—at fifty! At your age, Miss Warren, you would not need to go so far as Verona. Your spirits would absolutely fly up at the mere sight of Ostend. You would be charmed with the gaiety, the vivacity, the happy air of Brussels.

VIVIE [*Springing up with an exclamation of loathing.*]   Agh!

6. A road bridge in the City of London.

PRAED [*Rising.*]   Whats the matter?

FRANK [*Rising.*]   Hallo, Viv!

VIVIE [*To* PRAED, *with deep reproach.*]   Can you find no better example of your beauty and romance than Brussels to talk to me about?

PRAED [*Puzzled.*]   Of course it's very different from Verona. I dont suggest for a moment that—

VIVIE [*Bitterly.*]   Probably the beauty and romance come to much the same in both places.

PRAED [*Completely sobered and much concerned.*]   My dear Miss Warren: I—[*Looking inquiringly at* FRANK.] Is anything the matter?

FRANK   She thinks your enthusiasm frivolous, Praddy. She's had ever such a serious call.

VIVIE [*Sharply.*]   Hold your tongue, Frank. Dont be silly.

FRANK [*Sitting down.*]   Do you call this good manners, Praed?

PRAED [*Anxious and considerate.*]   Shall I take him away, Miss Warren? I feel sure we have disturbed you at your work.

VIVIE   Sit down: I'm not ready to go back to work yet. [PRAED *sits.*] You both think I have an attack of nerves. Not a bit of it. But there are two subjects I want dropped, if you dont mind. One of them [*To* FRANK.] is love's young dream in any shape or form: the other [*To* PRAED.] is the romance and beauty of life, especially Ostend and the gaiety of Brussels. You are welcome to any illusions you may have left on these subjects: I have none. If we three are to remain friends, I must be treated as a woman of business, permanently single [*To* FRANK.] and permanently unromantic [*to* PRAED].

FRANK   I also shall remain permanently single until you change your mind. Praddy: change the subject. Be eloquent about something else.

PRAED [*Diffidently.*]   I'm afraid theres nothing else in the world that I c a n talk about. The Gospel of Art is the only one I can preach. I know Miss Warren is a great devotee of the Gospel of Getting On; but we cant discuss that without hurting your feelings, Frank, since you are determined not to get on.

FRANK   Oh, dont mind my feelings. Give me some improving advice by all means: it does me ever so much good. Have another try to make a successful man of me, Viv. Come; lets have it all: energy, thrift, foresight, self-respect, character. Dont you hate people who have no character, Viv?

VIVIE [*Wincing.*]   Oh, stop, stop: let us have no more of that horrible cant. Mr Praed: if there are really only those two gospels in the world, we had better all kill ourselves; for the same taint is in both, through and through.

FRANK [*Looking critically at her.*]   There is a touch of poetry about you today, Viv, which has hitherto been lacking.

PRAED [*Remonstrating.*]   My dear Frank: arnt you a little unsympathetic?

VIVIE [*Merciless to herself.*]   No: it's good for me. It keeps me from being sentimental.

FRANK [*Bantering her.*]   Checks your strong natural propensity that way, dont it?

VIVIE [*Almost hysterically.*]   Oh yes; go on: dont spare me. I was sentimental for one moment in my life—beautifully sentimental—by moonlight; and now—

FRANK [*Quickly.*] I say, Viv: take care. Dont give yourself away.

VIVIE Oh, do you think Mr Praed does not know all about my mother? [*Turning on* PRAED.] You had better have told me that morning, Mr Praed. You are very old fashioned in your delicacies, after all.

PRAED Surely it is you who are a little old fashioned in your prejudices, Miss Warren, I feel bound to tell you, speaking as an artist, and believing that the most intimate human relationships are far beyond and above the scope of the law, that though I know that your mother is an unmarried woman, I do not respect her the less on that account. I respect her more.

FRANK [*Airily.*] Hear! Hear!

VIVIE [*Staring at him.*] Is that a l l you know?

PRAED Certainly that is all.

VIVIE Then you neither of you know anything. Your guesses are innocence itself compared to the truth.

PRAED [*Rising, startled and indignant, and preserving his politeness with an effort.*] I hope not. [*More emphatically.*] I hope not, Miss Warren.

FRANK [*Whistles.*] Whew!

VIVIE You are not making it easy for me to tell you, Mr Praed.

PRAED [*His chivalry drooping before their conviction.*] If there is anything worse—that is, anything else—are you sure you are right to tell us, Miss Warren?

VIVIE I am sure that if I had the courage I should spend the rest of my life in telling everybody—stamping and branding it into them until they all felt their part in its abomination as I feel mine. There is nothing I despise more than the wicked convention that protects these things by forbidding a woman to mention them. And yet I cant tell you. The two infamous words that describe what my mother is are ringing in my ears and struggling on my tongue; but I cant utter them: the shame of them is too horrible for me. [*She buries her face in her hands. The two men, astonished, stare at one another and then at her. She raises her head again desperately and snatches a sheet of paper and a pen.*] Here: let me draft you a prospectus.

FRANK Oh, she's mad. Do you hear, Viv? mad. Come! pull yourself together.

VIVIE You shall see. [*She writes.*] "Paid up capital: not less than £40,000 standing in the name of Sir George Crofts, Baronet, the chief shareholder. Premises at Brussels, Ostend, Vienna and Budapest. Managing director: Mrs Warren"; and now dont let us forget her qualifications: the two words. [*She writes the words and pushes the paper to them.*] There! Oh no: dont read it: dont! [*She snatches it back and tears it to pieces; then seizes her head in her hands and hides her face on the table.*]

[FRANK, *who has watched the writing over his shoulder, and opened his eyes very widely at it, takes a card from his pocket; scribbles the two words on it; and silently hands it to* PRAED, *who reads it with amazement, and hides it hastily in his pocket.*]

FRANK [*Whispering tenderly.*] Viv, dear: thats all right. I read what you wrote: so did Praddy. We understand. And we remain, as this leaves us at present, yours ever so devotedly.

PRAED We do indeed, Miss Warren. I declare you are the most splendidly courageous woman I ever met.

[*This sentimental compliment braces* VIVIE. *She throws it away from her with an impatient shake, and forces herself to stand up, though not without some support from the table.*]

FRANK Dont stir, Viv, if you dont want to. Take it easy.

VIVIE Thank you. You can always depend on me for two things: not to cry and not to faint. [*She moves a few steps towards the door of the inner room, and stops close to* PRAED *to say.*] I shall need much more courage than that when I tell my mother that we have come to the parting of the ways. Now I must go into the next room for a moment to make myself neat again, if you dont mind.

PRAED Shall we go away?

VIVIE No; I shall be back presently. Only for a moment. [*She goes into the other room,* PRAED *opening the door for her.*]

PRAED What an amazing revelation! I'm extremely disappointed in Crofts: I am indeed.

FRANK I'm not in the least. I feel he's perfectly accounted for at last. But what a facer for me, Praddy! I cant marry her now.

PRAED [*Sternly.*] Frank! [*The two look at one another,* FRANK *unruffled,* PRAED *deeply indignant.*] Let me tell you, Gardner, that if you desert her now you will behave very despicably.

FRANK Good old Praddy! Ever chivalrous! But you mistake: it's not the moral aspect of the case: it's the money aspect. I really cant bring myself to touch the old woman's money now.

PRAED And was that what you were going to marry on?

FRANK What else? *I* havnt any money, nor the smallest turn for making it. If I married Viv now she would have to support me; and I should cost her more than I am worth.

PRAED But surely a clever bright fellow like you can make something by your own brains.

FRANK Oh yes, a little. [*He takes out his money again.*] I made all that yesterday in an hour and a half. But I made it in a highly speculative business. No, dear Praddy: even if Bessie and Georgina marry millionaires and the governor dies after cutting them off with a shilling, I shall have only four hundred a year. And he wont die until he's three score and ten: he hasnt originality enough. I shall be on short allowance for the next twenty years. No short allowance for Viv, if I can help it. I withdraw gracefully and leave the field to the gilded youth of England. So thats settled. I shant worry her about it: I'll just send her a little note after we're gone. She'll understand.

PRAED [*Grasping his hand.*] Good fellow, Frank! I heartily beg your pardon. But must you never see her again?

FRANK Never see her again! Hang it all, be reasonable. I shall come along as often as possible, and be her brother. I can n o t understand the absurd consequences you romantic people expect from the most ordinary transactions. [*A knock at the door.*] I wonder who this is. Would you mind opening the door? If it's a client it will look more respectable than if I appeared.

PRAED Certainly. [*He goes to the door and opens it.* FRANK *sits down in* VIVIE's *chair to scribble a note.*] My dear Kitty: come in: come in.

[MRS WARREN *comes in, looking apprehensively round for* VIVIE. *She has done her best to make herself matronly and dignified. The brilliant hat is replaced by a sober bonnet, and the gay blouse covered by a costly black silk mantle. She is pitiably anxious and ill at ease: evidently panic-stricken.*]

MRS WARREN [*To* FRANK.] What! Y o u r e here, are you?

FRANK [*Turning in his chair from his writing, but not rising.*] Here, and charmed to see you. You come like a breath of spring.

MRS WARREN Oh, get out with your nonsense. [*In a low voice.*] Wheres Vivie?

[FRANK *points expressively to the door of the inner room, but says nothing.*]

MRS WARREN [*Sitting down suddenly and almost beginning to cry.*] Praddy: wont she see me, dont you think?

PRAED My dear Kitty: dont distress yourself. Why should she not?

MRS WARREN Oh, you never can see why not: youre too innocent. Mr Frank: did she say anything to you?

FRANK [*Folding his note.*] She m u s t see you, if [*very expressively*] you wait til she comes in.

MRS WARREN [*Frightened.*] Why shouldnt I wait?

[FRANK *looks quizzically at her; puts his note carefully on the inkbottle, so that* VIVIE *cannot fail to find it when next she dips her pen; then rises and devotes his attention entirely to her.*]

FRANK My dear Mrs Warren: suppose you were a sparrow—ever so tiny and pretty a sparrow hopping in the roadway—and you saw a steam roller coming in your direction, would you wait for it?

MRS WARREN Oh, dont bother me with your sparrows. What did she run away from Haslemere like that for?

FRANK I'm afraid she'll tell you if you rashly await her return.

MRS WARREN Do you want me to go away?

FRANK No: I always want you to stay. But I a d v i s e you to go away.

MRS WARREN What! and never see her again!

FRANK Precisely.

MRS WARREN [*Crying again.*] Praddy: dont let him be cruel to me. [*She hastily checks her tears and wipes her eyes.*] She'll be so angry if she sees Ive been crying.

FRANK [*With a touch of real compassion in his airy tenderness.*] You know that Praddy is the soul of kindness, Mrs Warren. Praddy: what do y o u say? Go or stay?

PRAED [*To* MRS WARREN.] I really should be very sorry to cause you unnecessary pain; but I think perhaps you had better not wait. The fact is—[VIVIE *is heard at the inner door.*]

FRANK Sh! Too late. She's coming.

MRS WARREN Dont tell her I was crying. [VIVIE *comes in. She stops gravely on seeing* MRS WARREN, *who greets her with hysterical cheerfulness.*] Well, dearie. So here you are at last.

VIVIE I am glad you have come: I want to speak to you. You said you were going, Frank, I think.

FRANK Yes. Will you come with me, Mrs Warren? What do you say to a trip to Richmond, and the theatre in the evening? There is safety in Richmond. No steam roller there.

VIVIE   Nonsense, Frank. My mother will stay here.

MRS WARREN [*Scared.*]   I dont know: perhaps I'd better go. We're disturbing you at your work.

VIVIE [*With quiet decision.*]   Mr. Praed: please take Frank away. Sit down, mother. [MRS WARREN *obeys helplessly.*]

PRAED   Come, Frank. Goodbye, Miss Vivie.

VIVIE [*Shaking hands.*]   Goodbye. A pleasant trip.

PRAED   Thank you: thank you. I hope so.

FRANK [*To* MRS WARREN.]   Goodbye: youd ever so much better have taken my advice. [*He shakes hands with her. Then airily to* VIVIE] Byebye, Viv.

VIVIE   Goodbye. [*He goes out gaily without shaking hands with her.*]

PRAED [*Sadly.*]   Goodbye, Kitty.

MRS WARREN [*Sniveling.*]   —oobye!

> [PRAED *goes.* VIVIE, *composed and extremely grave, sits down in Honoria's chair, and waits for her mother to speak.* MRS WARREN, *dreading a pause, loses no time in beginning.*]

MRS WARREN   Well, Vivie, what did you go away like that for without saying a word to me? How could you do such a thing! And what have you done to poor George? I wanted him to come with me; but he shuffled out of it. I could see that he was quite afraid of you. Only fancy: he wanted me not to come. As if [*Trembling.*] I should be afraid of you, dearie. [VIVIE's *gravity deepens.*] But of course I told him it was all settled and comfortable between us, and that we were on the best of terms. [*She breaks down.*] Vivie: whats the meaning of this? [*She produces a commercial envelope, and fumbles at the enclosure with trembling fingers.*] I got it from the bank this morning.

VIVIE   It is my month's allowance. They sent it to me as usual the other day. I simply sent it back to be placed to your credit, and asked them to send you the lodgment receipt. In future I shall support myself.

MRS WARREN [*Not daring to understand.*]   Wasnt it enough? Why didnt you tell me? [*With a cunning gleam in her eye.*] I'll double it: I was intending to double it. Only let me know how much you want.

VIVIE   You know very well that that has nothing to do with it. From this time I go my own way in my own business and among my own friends. And you will go yours. [*She rises.*] Goodbye.

MRS WARREN [*Rising, appalled.*]   Goodbye?

VIVIE   Yes: Goodbye. Come: dont let us make a useless scene: you understand perfectly well. Sir George Crofts has told me the whole business.

MRS WARREN [*Angrily.*]   Silly old— [*She swallows an epithet, and turns white at the narrowness of her escape from uttering it.*]

VIVIE   Just so.

MRS WARREN   He ought to have his tongue cut out. But I thought it was ended: you said you didnt mind.

VIVIE [*Steadfastly.*]   Excuse me: I d o mind.

MRS WARREN   But I explained—

VIVIE   You explained how it came about. You did not tell me that it is still going on. [*She sits.*]

> [MRS WARREN, *silenced for a moment, looks forlornly at* VIVIE, *who waits, secretly hoping that the combat is over. But the cunning expression comes back into* MRS WARREN's *face; and she bends across the table, sly and urgent, half whispering.*]

MRS WARREN   Vivie: do you know how rich I am?

VIVIE   I have no doubt you are very rich.

MRS WARREN   But you dont know all that that means: youre too young. It means a new dress every day; it means theatres and balls every night; it means having the pick of all the gentlemen in Europe at your feet; it means a lovely house and plenty of servants; it means the choicest of eating and drinking; it means everything you like, everything you want, everything you can think of. And what are you here? A mere drudge, toiling and moiling early and late for your bare living and two cheap dresses a year. Think over it. [*Soothingly.*] Youre shocked, I know. I can enter into your feelings; and I think they do you credit; but trust me, nobody will blame you: you may take my word for that. I know what young girls are; and I know youll think better of it when youve turned it over in your mind.

VIVIE   So thats how it's done, is it? You must have said all that to many a woman, mother, to have it so pat.

MRS WARREN [*Passionately.*]   What harm am I asking you to do? [VIVIE *turns away contemptuously.* MRS WARREN *continues desperately.*] Vivie: listen to me: you dont understand: youve been taught wrong on purpose: you dont know what the world is really like.

VIVIE [*Arrested.*]   Taught wrong on purpose! What do you mean?

MRS WARREN   I mean that youre throwing away all your chances for nothing. You think that people are what they pretend to be: that the way you were taught at school and college to think right and proper is the way things really are. But it's not: it's all only a pretence, to keep the cowardly slavish common run of people quiet. Do you want to find that out, like other women, at forty, when youve thrown yourself away and lost your chances; or wont you take it in good time now from your own mother, that loves you and swears to you that it's truth: gospel truth? [*urgently*] Vivie: the big people, the clever people, the managing people, all know it. They do as I do, and think what I think. I know plenty of them. I know them to speak to, to introduce you to, to make friends of for you. I dont mean anything wrong; thats what you dont understand: your head is full of ignorant ideas about me. What do the people that taught you know about life or about people like me? When did they ever meet me, or speak to me, or let anyone tell them about me? the fools! Would they ever have done anything for you if I hadnt paid them? Havnt I told you that I want you to be respectable? Havnt I brought you up to be respectable? And how can you keep it up without my money and my influence and Lizzie's friends? Cant you see that youre cutting your own throat as well as breaking my heart in turning your back on me?

VIVIE   I recognize the Crofts philosophy of life, mother. I heard it all from him that day at the Gardners'.

MRS WARREN   You think I want to force that played-out old sot on you! I dont, Vivie: on my oath I dont.

VIVIE   It would not matter if you did: you would not succeed. [MRS WARREN *winces, deeply hurt by the implied indifference towards her affectionate intention.* VIVIE, *neither understanding this nor concerning herself about it, goes on calmly.*] Mother: you dont at all know the sort of person I am. I dont object to Crofts more than to any other coarsely built man of his class. To tell you the truth, I rather admire him for being strong-minded enough to enjoy himself in his own way and make plenty of money instead of living the usual shooting, hunting, dining-out, tailoring, loafing life of his set merely because all the rest do it. And I'm perfectly aware that if I'd been in the same circumstances as my aunt Liz, I'd have done exactly what she did. I dont think I'm more prejudiced or straitlaced than you: I think I'm less. I'm certain I'm less sentimental. I know very well that fashionable morality is all a pretence, and that if I took your money and devoted the rest of my life to spending it fashionably, I might be as worthless and vicious as the silliest woman could possibly want to be without having a word said to me about it. But I dont want to be worthless. I shouldnt enjoy trotting about the park to advertize my dressmaker and carriage builder, or being bored at the opera to shew off a shopwindowful of diamonds.

MRS WARREN [*Bewildered.*]   But—

VIVIE   Wait a moment: Ive not done. Tell me why you continue your business now that you are independent of it. Your sister, you told me, has left all that behind her. Why dont you do the same?

MRS WARREN   Oh, it's all very easy for Liz: she likes good society, and has the air of being a lady. Imagine me in a cathedral town! Why, the very rooks in the trees would find me out even if I could stand the dulness of it. I must have work and excitement, or I should go melancholy mad. And what else is there for me to do? The life suits me: I'm fit for it and not for anything else. If I didnt do it somebody else would; so I dont do any real harm by it. And then it brings in money; and I like making money. No; it's no use: I cant give it up—not for anybody. But what need you know about it? I'll never mention it. I'll keep Crofts away. I'll not trouble you much: you see I have to be constantly running about from one place to another. Youll be quit of me altogether when I die.

VIVIE   No: I am my mother's daughter. I am like you: I must have work, and must make more money than I spend. But my work is not your work, and my way not your way. We must part. It will not make much difference to us: instead of meeting one another for perhaps a few months in twenty years we shall never meet: thats all.

MRS WARREN [*Her voice stifled in tears.*]   Vivie: I meant to have been more with you: I did indeed.

VIVIE   It's no use, mother: I am not to be changed by a few cheap tears and entreaties any more than you are, I daresay.

MRS WARREN [*Wildly.*]   Oh, you call a mother's tears cheap.

VIVIE   They cost you nothing; and you ask me to give you the peace and quietness of my whole life in exchange for them. What use would my company be to you if you could get it? What have we two in common that could make either of us happy together?

MRS WARREN [*Lapsing recklessly into her dialect.*]   We're mother and daughter. I want my daughter. Ive a right to you. Who is to care for me when I'm old? Plenty of girls have taken to me like daughters and cried at leaving me; but I let them all go because I had you to look forward to. I kept myself lonely for you. Youve no right to turn on me now and refuse to do your duty as a daughter.

VIVIE [*Jarred and antagonized by the echo of the slums in her mother's voice.*]   My duty as a daughter! I thought we should come to that presently. Now once for all, mother, you want a daughter and Frank wants a wife. I dont want a mother; and I dont want a husband. I have spared neither Frank nor myself in sending him about his business. Do you think I will spare y o u ?

MRS WARREN [*Violently.*]   Oh, I know the sort you are: no mercy for yourself or anyone else. *I* know. My experience has done that for me anyhow: I can tell the pious, canting, hard, selfish woman when I meet her. Well, keep yourself to yourself: *I* dont want you. But listen to this. Do you know what I would do with you if you were a baby again? aye, as sure as there's a Heaven above us.

VIVIE   Strangle me, perhaps.

MRS WARREN   No: I'd bring you up to be a real daughter to me, and not what you are now, with your pride and your prejudices and the college education you stole from me: yes, stole: deny it if you can: what was it but stealing? I'd bring you up in my own house, I would.

VIVIE [*Quietly.*]   In one of your own houses.

MRS WARREN [*Screaming.*]   Listen to her! listen to how she spits on her mother's grey hairs! Oh, may you live to have your own daughter tear and trample on you as you have trampled on me. And you will: you will. No woman ever had luck with a mother's curse on her.

VIVIE   I wish you wouldnt rant, mother. It only hardens me. Come: I suppose I am the only young woman you ever had in your power that you did good to. Dont spoil it all now.

MRS WARREN   Yes, Heaven forgive me, it's true; and you are the only one that ever turned on me. Oh, the injustice of it! the injustice! the injustice! I always wanted to be a good woman. I tried honest work; and I was slave-driven until I cursed the day I ever heard of honest work. I was a good mother; and because I made my daughter a good woman she turns me out as if I was a leper. Oh, if I only had my life to live over again! I'd talk to that lying clergyman in the school. From this time forth, so help me Heaven in my last hour, I'll do wrong and nothing but wrong. And I'll prosper on it.

VIVIE   Yes: it's better to choose your line and go through with it. If I had been you, mother, I might have done as you did; but I should not have lived one life and believed in another. You are a conventional woman at heart. That is why I am bidding you goodbye now. I am right, am I not?

MRS WARREN [*Taken aback.*]   Right to throw away all my money?

VIVIE   No: right to get rid of you? I should be a fool not to! Isnt that so?

MRS WARREN [*Sulkily.*]   Oh well, yes, if you come to that, I suppose you are. But Lord help the world if everybody took to doing the right thing! And now I'd better go than stay where I'm not wanted. [*She turns to the door.*]

VIVIE [*Kindly.*]   Wont you shake hands?

MRS WARREN [*After looking at her fiercely for a moment with a savage impulse to strike her.*]   No, thank you. Goodbye.

VIVIE [*Matter-of-factly.*]   Goodbye. [MRS WARREN *goes out, slamming the door behind her. The strain on* VIVIE's *face relaxes; her grave expression breaks up into one of joyous content; her breath goes out in a half sob, half laugh of intense relief. She goes buoyantly to her place at the writing-table; pushes the electric lamp out of the way; pulls over a great sheaf of papers;*

and is in the act of dipping her pen in the ink when she finds FRANK's *note. She opens it unconcernedly and reads it quickly, giving a little laugh at some quaint turn of expression in it.*] And goodbye, Frank. [*She tears the note up and tosses the pieces into the wastepaper basket without a second thought. Then she goes at her work with a plunge, and soon becomes absorbed in its figures.*]

1893   1898

FRANCIS THOMPSON
1859–1907

Much of the poetry of the 1890s was written by members of groups such as The Rhymers' Club, of which Ernest Dowson and the young Yeats were members. Henley, too, had a band of writers associated with him who shared his views on life and poetry. Although Francis Thompson preferred to work more independently (he declined an invitation to join The Rhymers'), his poetry does have affinities with the writings of other poets of the time, in particular because of his Roman Catholicism, a religion that had attracted several converts during the nineties, including Dowson, Lionel Johnson (1867–1902), and the artist Aubrey Beardsley (1872–1898).

Thompson's career seems like a tale from one of the novels of Graham Greene. The son of Roman Catholic converts, he was anxious to enter the priesthood but was not considered an eligible candidate. Later, after an unsuccessful attempt to complete medical school, he moved to London. Here he lived for several years as a tramp, suffering painfully not only from poverty but from an addiction to opium: when in his poems Thompson speaks of being an outcast, he speaks with the authority of experience. In 1888 he was rescued by magazine editor Wilfred Meynell, who recognized his literary talents and encouraged him to publish his poems. Owing to shattered health and to a marked streak of indolence, Thompson's output in poetry was not extensive; but in his few best poems his achievement is impressive and distinctive. As his friend Coventry Patmore noted, *The Hound of Heaven* is one of the finest odes in English literature. In its fast-paced passages it reminds us of the odes of Shelley, about whom Thompson wrote an appreciative essay. An even more important influence than Shelley on Thompson was that of the seventeenth-century Metaphysical poets, particularly the Roman Catholic poet Richard Crashaw. The Crashaw-like blending of religious fervor and striking conceits (such as "traitorous trueness"), evident in the very title of *The Hound of Heaven,* seemed merely fantastic to some of Thompson's readers in the 1890s. To later readers, accustomed to the metaphysical devices of much twentieth-century poetry, it has seemed less bizarre. Interesting comparisons may also be made between Thompson and Gerard Manley Hopkins, another Roman Catholic writer who likewise demonstrated, as the nineteenth century drew to its close, the remarkable variety in the poetry of the Victorian age.

The Hound of Heaven

I fled Him,[1] down the nights and down the days;
I fled Him, down the arches of the years;
I fled Him, down the labyrinthine ways
Of my own mind; and in the mist of tears
5   I hid from Him, and under running laughter.
             Up vistaed hopes I sped;
             And shot, precipitated,
Adown Titanic glooms of chasmed fears,
  From those strong Feet that followed, followed after.
10   But with unhurrying chase,
          And unperturbèd pace,
     Deliberate speed, majestic instancy,°   *urgency*
        They beat—and a Voice beat
         More instant than the Feet—
15   "All things betray thee, who betrayest Me."

        I pleaded, outlaw-wise,
By many a hearted casement, curtained red,
  Trellised with intertwining charities
(For, though I knew His love Who followed,
20   Yet was I sore adread
Lest, having Him, I must have naught beside);[2]
But, if one little casement parted wide,
  The gust of His approach would clash it to.
  Fear wist not to evade, as Love wist to pursue.[3]
25 Across the margent° of the world I fled,   *boundary*
  And troubled the gold gateways of the stars,
  Smiting for shelter on their clangèd bars;
        Fretted to dulcet jars
And silvern chatter the pale ports o' the moon.[4]
30 I said to dawn, Be sudden; to eve, Be soon;
  With thy young skyey blossoms heap me over
        From this tremendous Lover!
Float thy vague veil about me, lest He see!
  I tempted all His servitors, but to find
35 My own betrayal in their constancy,
In faith to Him their fickleness to me,
  Their traitorous trueness, and their loyal deceit.
To all swift things for swiftness did I sue;
  Clung to the whistling mane of every wind.
40   But whether they swept, smoothly fleet,
    The long savannahs° of the blue;   *plains*

1. Cf. Saint Augustine's *Confessions* 4.4.7: "And lo, Thou wert close on the heels of those fleeing from Thee, God of vengeance and fountain of mercies, both at the same time, who turnest us to Thyself by most wonderful means."
2. The speaker, afraid that love of God will exclude other kinds of love, is seeking shelter in one of the warm dwellings associated with human love. But his pursuer cuts off his escape, forcing him to remain outside, an outcast (lines 22–23).
3. This line apparently means that Fear did not know how to escape so effectively as Love knew how to pursue.
4. I.e., shook the gates of the moon until they gave forth soft and silvery sounds.

Or whether, Thunder-driven,
They clanged his chariot 'thwart a heaven
Plashy with flying lightnings round the spurn o' their feet—
45   Fear wist not to evade as Love wist to pursue.
Still with unhurrying chase,
And unperturbèd pace,
Deliberate speed, majestic instancy,
Came on the following Feet,
50   And a Voice above their beat—
"Naught shelters thee, who wilt not shelter Me."

I sought no more that after which I strayed
In face of man or maid;
But still within the little children's eyes
55   Seems something, something that replies;
They at least are for me, surely for me!
I turned me to them very wistfully;
But, just as their young eyes grew sudden fair
With dawning answers there,
60   Their angel plucked them from me by the hair.
"Come then, ye other children, Nature's—share
With me," said I, "your delicate fellowship;
Let me greet you lip to lip,
Let me twine with you caresses,
65   Wantoning
With our Lady-Mother's⁵ vagrant tresses,
Banqueting
With her in her wind-walled palace,
Underneath her azured daïs,⁶
70   Quaffing, as your taintless way is,
From a chalice
Lucent-weeping out of the dayspring."⁷
So it was done;
I in their delicate fellowship was one—
75   Drew the bolt of Nature's secrecies.
I knew all the swift importings°   *meanings*
On the willful face of skies;
I knew how the clouds arise
Spumèd of the wild sea-snortings;
80   All that's born or dies
Rose and drooped with—made them shapers
Of mine own moods, or wailful or divine—
With them joyed and was bereaven.
I was heavy with the even,
85   When she lit her glimmering tapers
Round the day's dead sanctities.
I laughed in the morning's eyes.
I triumphed and I saddened with all weather,
Heaven and I wept together,
90   And its sweet tears were salt with mortal mine;
Against the red throb of its sunset-heart

5. I.e., Mother Nature's.
6. Blue canopy of the sky.

7. Overflowing with shining light from the sun
(i.e., the children of Nature drink the sunshine).

I laid my own to beat,
And share commingling heat;
But not by that, by that, was eased my human smart.
95 In vain my tears were wet on Heaven's gray cheek.
For ah! we know not what each other says,
These things and I; in sound *I* speak—
Their sound is but their stir, they speak by silences.
Nature, poor stepdame, cannot slake my drouth;
100 Let her, if she would owe° me,   *own*
Drop yon blue bosom-veil of sky, and show me
The breasts o' her tenderness;
Never did any milk of hers once bless
My thirsting mouth.
105 Nigh and nigh draws the chase,
With unperturbèd pace,
Deliberate speed, majestic instancy;
And past those noisèd Feet
A voice comes yet more fleet—
110 "Lo naught contents thee, who content'st not Me."

Naked I wait Thy love's uplifted stroke!
My harness° piece by piece Thou hast hewn from me,   *armor*
And smitten me to my knee;
I am defenseless utterly.
115 I slept, methinks, and woke,
And, slowly gazing, find me stripped in sleep.
In the rash lustihead of my young powers,
I shook the pillaring hours
And pulled my life upon me;⁸ grimed with smears,
120 I stand amid the dust o' the mounded years—
My mangled youth lies dead beneath the heap.
My days have crackled and gone up in smoke,
Have puffed and burst as sun-starts° on a stream.   *bubbles*
Yea, faileth now even dream
125 The dreamer, and the lute the lutanist;
Even the linked fantasies, in whose blossomy twist
I swung the earth a trinket at my wrist,
Are yielding;⁹ cords of all too weak account
For earth with heavy griefs so overplussed.
130 Ah! is Thy love indeed
A weed, albeit an amaranthine¹ weed,
Suffering no flowers except its own to mount?
Ah! must—
Designer infinite!—
135 Ah! must Thou char the wood ere Thou canst limn² with it?
My freshness spent its wavering shower i' the dust;
And now my heart is as a broken fount,
Wherein tear-drippings stagnate, spilt down ever
From the dank thoughts that shiver

8. Like Samson when he shook the pillars of the temple of Dagon and pulled down the roof on his head (Judges 16).
9. I.e., even his power of creating an imaginary world by poetry and song ("linked fantasies") is now inadequate.
1. Unfading and immortal.
2. Draw, as with charcoal.

140   Upon the sightful branches of my mind.
               Such is; what is to be?
    The pulp so bitter, how shall taste the rind?
    I dimly guess what Time in mists confounds;
    Yet ever and anon a trumpet sounds
145   From the hid battlements of Eternity;
    Those shaken mists a space unsettle, then
    Round the half-glimpsèd turrets slowly wash again.
           But not ere him who summoneth
           I first have seen, enwound
150   With blooming robes, purpureal, cypress-crowned;
    His name I know, and what his trumpet saith.
    Whether man's heart or life it be which yields
           Thee harvest, must Thy harvest fields
           Be dunged with rotten death?

155   Now of that long pursuit
           Comes on at hand the bruit;°   *noise*
           That Voice is round me like a bursting sea:
           "And is thy earth so marred,
           Shattered in shard[3] on shard?
160   Lo, all things fly thee, for thou fliest Me!
           Strange, piteous, futile thing,
    Wherefore should any set thee love apart?
    Seeing none but I makes much of naught," He said,
    "And human love needs human meriting,
165   How hast thou merited—
    Of all man's clotted clay the dingiest clot?
           Alack, thou knowest not
    How little worthy of any love thou art!
    Whom wilt thou find to love ignoble thee
170   Save Me, save only Me?
    All which I took from thee I did but take,
           Not for thy harms,
    But just that thou might'st seek it in My arms.
           All which thy child's mistake
175   Fancies as lost, I have stored for thee at home;
           Rise, clasp My hand, and come!"

        Halts by me that footfall;
        Is my gloom, after all,
    Shade of His hand, outstretched caressingly?
180   "Ah, fondest,° blindest, weakest,   *most foolish*
    I am He Whom thou seekest!
    Thou dravest love from thee, who dravest Me."

1890–92   1893

3. Fragment, as of broken pottery.

MARY ELIZABETH COLERIDGE
1861–1907

The great-great niece of Samuel Taylor Coleridge, Mary Elizabeth Coleridge once wrote, "I have no fairy god-mother, but lay claim to a fairy great-great uncle, which is perhaps the reason that I am condemned to wander restlessly around the Gates of Fairyland, although I have never yet passed them." Born in London to a literary and musical family that regularly entertained guests such as Tennyson and Browning, Coleridge lived her whole life at home with her parents and one sister. She was unusually well educated, under the supervision of a tutor, William Cory, a scholar and poet, who had been forced by scandal to leave his teaching position at Eton. Mary Coleridge thus received an education usually reserved for boys. She knew six languages, including Greek, and she studied philosophy. In the 1890s she began giving lessons in English literature to working girls; in 1895, she started to teach at the Working Woman's College, an activity she continued for the rest of her life. She died suddenly of appendicitis at the age of forty-six.

Mary Coleridge's tutor, Cory, encouraged her to write poetry and short stories. When Henry Newbolt, a poet and family friend, joined her reading group of women friends, The Quintette, he urged her to publish her first two novels. She later published three more, in addition to a number of stories and essays. Although she wrote poetry continuously, she published little of it during her life. When a manuscript of her poems was given to Robert Bridges, a family friend who was also a friend of Gerard Manley Hopkins and responsible for the posthumous publication of Hopkins's poetry, Bridges recognized her talent. He made suggestions for revisions and encouraged her to publish a volume. She allowed two small volumes to be privately printed in the nineties, under the pseudonym *Anodos*, or the wanderer; most of her poetry was published after her death.

Although Mary Coleridge did not participate in the feminist debates of her time, her poems contain a subversive sense of anarchic feminine energy. She believed women had a spiritual identity distinct from men's; she wrote, "I don't think we are separate only in body and in mind, I think we are separate in soul too." Some of her poems rewrite earlier texts. Sandra Gilbert and Susan Gubar have speculated that *The Other Side of a Mirror* portrays the mad Bertha Mason from Charlotte Brontë's *Jane Eyre*; Angela Leighton and Margaret Reynolds have argued that *The Witch* reimagines Samuel Taylor Coleridge's visionary poem *Christabel*. Both of these poems demonstrate another characteristic of her writing—presentation of a luminous narrative fragment with little sense of surrounding context. The effect in the words of Henry Newbolt, the first friend who had encouraged her to publish, is one of "very deep shadows filled with strange shapes."

The Other Side of a Mirror

I sat before my glass one day,
    And conjured up a vision bare,
Unlike the aspects glad and gay,
    That erst were found reflected there—
5   The vision of a woman, wild
    With more than womanly despair.

Her hair stood back on either side
A face bereft of loveliness.

It had no envy now to hide
10   What once no man on earth could guess.
It formed the thorny aureole
     Of hard unsanctified distress.

Her lips were open—not a sound
     Came through the parted lines of red.
15   Whate'er it was, the hideous wound
     In silence and in secret bled.
No sigh relieved her speechless woe,
     She had no voice to speak her dread.

And in her lurid eyes there shone
20   The dying flame of life's desire,
Made mad because its hope was gone,
     And kindled at the leaping fire
Of jealousy, and fierce revenge,
     And strength that could not change nor tire.

25   Shade of a shadow in the glass,
     O set the crystal surface free!
Pass—as the fairer visions pass—
     Nor ever more return, to be
The ghost of a distracted hour,
30   That heard me whisper, "I am she!"

1882   1896

The Witch

I have walked a great while over the snow,
And I am not tall nor strong.
My clothes are wet, and my teeth are set,
And the way was hard and long.
5   I have wandered over the fruitful earth,
But I never came here before.
Oh, lift me over the threshold, and let me in at the door!

The cutting wind is a cruel foe.
I dare not stand in the blast.
10   My hands are stone, and my voice a groan,
And the worst of death is past.
I am but a little maiden still,
My little white feet are sore.
Oh, lift me over the threshold, and let me in at the door!

15   Her voice was the voice that women have,
Who plead for their heart's desire.
She came—she came—and the quivering flame
Sank and died in the fire.
It never was lit again on my hearth

20   Since I hurried across the floor,
     To lift her over the threshold, and let her in at the door.

1892   1907

RUDYARD KIPLING
1865–1936

Rudyard Kipling shares with an earlier Victorian, William Makepeace Thackeray, the distinction of having been born in India and, at the age of six, having been sent home to England for his education. For his first six years in England, he was desperately unhappy; his parents had made the disastrous choice of a rigidly Calvinistic foster home in which to board him, where he was treated with considerable cruelty. His parents finally removed him from the home when he was twelve and sent him to a private school, where his experience was far better. His views in later life were deeply affected by the English schoolboy code of honor and duty, especially when it involved loyalty to a group or team. At seventeen he rejoined his parents in India, where his father was a teacher of sculpture at the Bombay School of Art. For seven years he worked in India as a newspaper reporter and a part-time writer before returning to England, where his poems and stories (published while he was abroad) had brought him early fame. In 1892, after his marriage to an American woman, he lived for a five-year interval in Brattleboro, Vermont, until driven out in consequence of a quarrel with his wife's relatives. So violent was the quarrel that in later trips to North America, the Kiplings restricted their travels to Canada. Upon returning to England from Vermont, Kipling settled on a country estate and purchased, at the turn of the century, an expensive early-model automobile. He seems to have been the first English author to own an automobile, which was appropriate because of his keen interest in all kinds of machinery and feats of engineering—one of many tastes in which he differed markedly from his contemporaries in the nineties, the aesthetes. He was also the first English author to receive the Nobel Prize for Literature (1907).

In the final decades of the nineteenth century, India was the most important colony of Britain's empire. English people were consequently curious about the world of India, a world that Kipling's stories and poems helped them to envision. Indeed, Leonard Woolf, Virginia Woolf's husband, wrote the following about his experience in India in the early years of this century: "I could never make up my mind whether Kipling had molded his characters accurately in the image of Anglo-Indian society or whether we were molding our characters accurately in the image of a Kipling story." During his seven years in India in the 1880s, Kipling gained a rich experience of colonial life, which he presented in his stories and poems. His first volume of stories, *Plain Tales from the Hills* (1888), explores some of the psychological and moral problems of the Anglo-Indians and their relationship with the people they had colonized. In his two *Jungle Books* (1894, 1895) he ingeniously draws on the Indian scene to create a world of jungle animals. And although Kipling never professed to fully understand the way of life of the Indians themselves, or their religions, he was fascinated by them and tried to portray them with understanding. This effort is especially evident in his narrative *Kim* (1901), in which the contemplative and religious way of life of Indians is treated with no less sympathy than the active and worldly way of life of the Victorian English governing classes. It is usually said that Kipling, one of the great masters of the short story, and a superb craftsman, was not as a rule successful with long narratives, but *Kim* disproves the rule.

In his poems, Kipling also draws on the Indian scene, most commonly as it is viewed through the eyes of private soldiers of the regular army, men who had been sent out from England to garrison the country and fight off invaders on the northwest frontiers. Kipling is usually thought of as the poet of British imperialism, as indeed he often was, but in these poems about ordinary British soldiers in India, there is little by way of flag-waving celebrations of the triumph of empire. The soldier who speaks in *The Widow at Windsor* is simply bewildered by the events in which he has taken part. As one of the soldiers of the queen (one of "Missis Victorier's sons"), he has done his duty, but he does not see the course of the empire as a divine design to which he has been a contributor. In presenting India through the eyes of the common soldier, Kipling frequently reflects racist attitudes, such as those in *The Ladies*, which readers today may find offensive. Nonetheless, Kipling can be credited with developing a new subject in the working-class soldier, which proved an effective way to portray modern social experience.

This fresh perspective of the common individual on events, expressed in the accent of the London cockney, was one of the qualities that gained Kipling an immediate audience for his *Barrack-Room Ballads* (1890, 1892). For many years Kipling was exceedingly popular. What attracted his vast audience was not just the freshness of his subjects but his mastery of swinging verse rhythms. Aside from his genius, Kipling's literary ancestry helps explain his success. In part he learned his craft as a poet from traditional sources. He was not unsophisticated or unlearned; in his own family he had connections with the Pre-Raphaelites, and he was considerably influenced by such immediate literary predecessors as Swinburne and Browning. But the special influences on his style and rhythms were not traditional. One was the Protestant hymn. Both of his parents were children of Methodist clergymen, and hymn singing, as well as preaching, affected him profoundly: "Three generations of Wesleyan ministers . . . lie behind me," he noted. The second influence came from what seems an antithetical secular quarter, the songs of the music hall. As a teenager in London, Kipling had enjoyed music-hall entertainments, which were to reach their peak of popularity in the 1890s. According to his biographer Sir Angus Wilson, even though Kipling was, like Tennyson, the "most unmusical" of writers, he knew how to make poems that call to be set to music, such as *The Road to Mandalay* or *Gentlemen Rankers,* with its memorable refrain (still popular in America): "We're poor little lambs who've lost our way, Baa! Baa! Baa!" Such a poem as *The Ladies* is ideal fare for a music-hall number and gains immeasurably by being sung.

Today Kipling's stories are more valued than his poems. In his portrayal of the British community in India and their relationship with the people they ruled, Kipling created a rich and various fictional world that reflects profoundly upon England's imperialism as lived in all its peculiar social relationships by the officers of the empire. After returning from India, he gradually turned to English subjects in his short stories, which he continued to write until his death in 1936. In their representation of new subjects, their wonderful ear for dialect, their economy of style, and their complex irony, Kipling's short stories provide some of the best examples of the genre.

The Man Who Would Be King[1]

"Brother to a Prince and fellow to a beggar if he be found worthy."[2]

The law, as quoted, lays down a fair conduct of life, and one not easy to follow. I have been fellow to a beggar again and again under circumstances which prevented either of us finding out whether the other was worthy. I have still to be brother to a Prince, though I once came near to kinship with what might have been a veritable King and was promised the reversion of a Kingdom—army, law-courts, revenue and policy all complete. But, to-day, I greatly fear that my King is dead, and if I want a crown I must go and hunt it for myself.

The beginning of everything was in a railway train upon the road to Mhow from Ajmir. There had been a Deficit in the Budget, which necessitated traveling, not Second-class, which is only half as dear as First-class, but by Intermediate, which is very awful indeed. There are no cushions in the Intermediate class, and the population are either Intermediate, which is Eurasian, or native, which for a long night journey is nasty, or Loafer,[3] which is amusing though intoxicated. Intermediates do not patronize refreshment-rooms. They carry their food in bundles and pots, and buy sweets from the native sweetmeat-sellers, and drink the roadside water. That is why in the hot weather Intermediates are taken out of the carriages dead, and in all weathers are most properly looked down upon.

My particular Intermediate happened to be empty till I reached Nasirabad, when a huge gentleman in shirt-sleeves entered, and, following the custom of Intermediates, passed the time of day. He was a wanderer and a vagabond like myself, but with an educated taste for whiskey. He told tales of things he had seen and done, of out-of-the-way corners of the Empire into which he had penetrated, and of adventures in which he risked his life for a few days' food. "If India was filled with men like you and me, not knowing more than the crows where they'd get their next day's rations, it isn't seventy millions of revenue the land would be paying—it's seven hundred millions," said he; and as I looked at his mouth and chin I was disposed to agree with him. We talked politics—the politics of Loaferdom that sees things from the underside where the lath and plaster is not smoothed off—and we talked postal arrangements because my friend wanted to send a telegram back from the next station to Ajmir, which is the turning-off place from the Bombay to the Mhow line as you travel westward. My friend had no money beyond eight annas which he wanted for dinner, and I had no money at all, owing to the hitch in the Budget before mentioned. Further, I was going into a wilderness where, though I should resume touch with the Treasury, there were no telegraph offices. I was, therefore, unable to help him in any way.

"We might threaten a Station-master, and make him send a wire on tick,"[4] said my friend, "but that'd mean inquiries for you and for me, and I've got

1. Originally published in December 1888.
2. Meant to suggest the principles of Freemasonry, a secret fraternal society that developed from the masons' guild in medieval Britain. By Victorian times it had grown to a prominent national organization, whose members were bound to help each other in times of distress. The places mentioned in the beginning of the story are in northern India.
3. A European in India with no official attachment or position.
4. On credit.

my hands full these days. Did you say you are traveling back along this line within any days?"

"Within ten," I said.

"Can't you make it eight?" said he. "Mine is rather urgent business."

"I can send your telegram within ten days if that will serve you," I said.

"I couldn't trust the wire to fetch him now I think of it. It's this way. He leaves Delhi on the 23d for Bombay. That means he'll be running through Ajmir about the night of the 23d."

"But I'm going into the Indian Desert," I explained.

"Well *and* good," said he. "You'll be changing at Marwar Junction to get into Jodhpore territory—you must do that—and he'll be coming through Marwar Junction in the early morning of the 24th by the Bombay Mail. Can you be at Marwar Junction on that time? 'Twon't be inconveniencing you because I know that there's precious few pickings to be got out of these Central India States—even though you pretend to be correspondent of the *Backwoodsman*."[5]

"Have you ever tried that trick?" I asked.

"Again and again, but the Residents[6] find you out, and then you get escorted to the Border before you've time to get your knife into them. But about my friend here. I *must* give him a word o' mouth to tell him what's come to me or else he won't know where to go. I would take it more than kind of you if you was to come out of Central India in time to catch him at Marwar Junction, and say to him:—'He has gone South for the week.' He'll know what that means. He's a big man with a red beard, and a great swell[7] he is. You'll find him sleeping like a gentleman with all his luggage round him in a Second-class compartment. But don't you be afraid. Slip down the window, and say:—'He has gone South for the week,' and he'll tumble.[8] It's only cutting your time of stay in those parts by two days. I ask you as a stranger—going to the West,"[9] he said, with emphasis.

"Where have *you* come from?" said I.

"From the East," said he, "and I am hoping that you will give him the message on the Square[1]—for the sake of my Mother as well as your own."

Englishmen are not usually softened by appeals to the memory of their mothers, but for certain reasons, which will be fully apparent, I saw fit to agree.

"It's more than a little matter," said he, "and that's why I ask you to do it— and now I know that I can depend on you doing it. A Second-class carriage at Marwar Junction, and a red-haired man asleep in it. You'll be sure to remember. I get out at the next station, and I must hold on there till he comes or sends me what I want."

"I'll give the message if I catch him," I said, "and for the sake of your Mother as well as mine I'll give you a word of advice. Don't try to run the Central India States just now as the correspondent of the *Backwoodsman*. There's a real one knocking about here, and it might lead to trouble."

"Thank you," said he, simply, "and when will the swine be gone? I can't

---

5. The Allahabad *Pioneer*, which employed Kipling as a roving correspondent.
6. British political officers appointed to oversee doings at the court of one of the quasi-independent Native States.

7. Fashionable fellow.
8. Catch on, understand.
9. This, and the following phrase, are from the code of the Freemasons.
1. Honestly.

starve because he's ruining my work. I wanted to get hold of the Degumber Rajah down here about his father's widow, and give him a jump."

"What did he do to his father's widow, then?"

"Filled her up with red pepper and slippered her to death as she hung from a beam. I found that out myself, and I'm the only man that would dare going into the State to get hush-money for it. They'll try to poison me, same as they did in Chortumna when I went on the loot there. But you'll give the man at Marwar Junction my message?"

He got out at a little roadside station, and I reflected. I had heard, more than once, of men personating correspondents of newspapers and bleeding small Native States with threats of exposure, but I had never met any of the caste before. They lead a hard life, and generally die with great suddenness. The Native States have a wholesome horror of English newspapers, which may throw light on their peculiar methods of government, and do their best to choke correspondents with champagne, or drive them out of their mind with four-in-hand barouches.[2] They do not understand that nobody cares a straw for the internal administration of Native States so long as oppression and crime are kept within decent limits, and the ruler is not drugged, drunk, or diseased from one end of the year to the other. Native States were created by Providence in order to supply picturesque scenery, tigers, and tall-writing. They are the dark places of the earth, full of unimaginable cruelty, touching the Railway and the Telegraph on one side, and, on the other, the days of Harun-al-Raschid.[3] When I left the train I did business with divers Kings, and in eight days passed through many changes of life. Sometimes I wore dress-clothes and consorted with Princes and Politicals,[4] drinking from crystal and eating from silver. Sometimes I lay out upon the ground and devoured what I could get, from a plate made of a flapjack, and drank the running water, and slept under the same rug as my servant. It was all in the day's work.

Then I headed for the Great Indian Desert upon the proper date, as I had promised, and the night Mail set me down at Marwar Junction, where a funny little, happy-go-lucky, native-managed railway runs to Jodhpore. The Bombay Mail from Delhi makes a short halt at Marwar. She arrived as I got in, and I had just time to hurry to her platform and go down the carriages. There was only one Second-class on the train. I slipped the window, and looked down upon a flaming red beard, half covered by a railway rug. That was my man, fast asleep, and I dug him gently in the ribs. He woke with a grunt, and I saw his face in the light of the lamps. It was a great and shining face.

"Tickets again?" said he.

"No," said I. "I am to tell you that he is gone South for the week. He is gone South for the week!"

The train had begun to move out. The red man rubbed his eyes. "He has gone South for the week," he repeated. "Now that's just like his impidence. Did he say that I was to give you anything?—'Cause I won't."

"He didn't," I said, and dropped away, and watched the red lights die out in the dark. It was horribly cold, because the wind was blowing off the sands.

---

2. Fashionable four-wheeled carriages.
3. Caliph of Baghdad (763–809), who figures in

many tales of the *Arabian Nights*.
4. I.e., residents.

I climbed into my own train—not an Intermediate Carriage this time—and went to sleep.

If the man with the beard had given me a rupee I should have kept it as a memento of a rather curious affair. But the consciousness of having done my duty was my only reward.

Later on I reflected that two gentlemen like my friends could not do any good if they foregathered and personated correspondents of newspapers, and might, if they "stuck up"[5] one of the little rat-trap states of Central India or Southern Rajputana, get themselves into serious difficulties. I therefore took some trouble to describe them as accurately as I could remember to people who would be interested in deporting them; and succeeded, so I was later informed, in having them headed back from Degumber borders.

Then I became respectable, and returned to an Office where there were no Kings and no incidents except the daily manufacture of a newspaper. A newspaper office seems to attract every conceivable sort of person, to the prejudice of discipline. Zenana-mission ladies[6] arrive, and beg that the Editor will instantly abandon all his duties to describe a Christian prize-giving in a back-slum of a perfectly inaccessible village; Colonels who have been over-passed for commands sit down and sketch the outline of a series of ten, twelve, or twenty-four leading articles on Seniority *versus* Selection; missionaries wish to know why they have not been permitted to escape from their regular vehicles of abuse and swear at a brother missionary under special patronage of the editorial We; stranded theatrical companies troop up to explain that they cannot pay for their advertisements, but on their return from New Zealand or Tahiti will do so with interest; inventors of patent punkah[7]-pulling machines, carriage couplings and unbreakable swords and axle-trees call with specifications in their pockets and hours at their disposal; tea-companies enter and elaborate their prospectuses with the office pens; secretaries of ball-committees clamor to have the glories of their last dance more fully expounded; strange ladies rustle in and say:—"I want a hundred lady's cards printed *at once*, please," which is manifestly part of an Editor's duty; and every dissolute ruffian that ever tramped the Grand Trunk Road makes it his business to ask for employment as a proof-reader. And, all the time, the telephone-bell is ringing madly, and Kings are being killed on the Continent, and Empires are saying—"You're another," and Mister Gladstone[8] is calling down brimstone upon the British Dominions, and the little black copy-boys are whining, *"kaa-pi chay-ha-yeh"* (copy wanted) like tired bees, and most of the paper is as blank as Modred's shield.[9]

But that is the amusing part of the year. There are other six months wherein none ever come to call, and the thermometer walks inch by inch up to the top of the glass, and the office is darkened to just above reading-light, and the press machines are red-hot of touch, and nobody writes anything but accounts of amusements in the Hill-stations[1] or obituary notices. Then the telephone becomes a tinkling terror, because it tells you of the sudden deaths of men and women that you knew intimately, and the prickly-heat

5. Fraudulently extorted money from. "Foregathered": met.
6. Female missionaries doing work among Indian women.
7. Large swinging fan, usually worked by hand.
8. William Ewart Gladstone (1809–1898), leader of the Liberal Party from 1868 to 1875 and 1880 to 1894, opposed to overseas expansion.
9. The shield of King Arthur's traitorous nephew was blank because he had done no deeds of valor.
1. Official outposts in the northern hills.

covers you as with a garment, and you sit down and write:—"A slight increase of sickness is reported from the Khuda Janta Khan[2] District. The outbreak is purely sporadic in its nature, and, thanks to the energetic efforts of the District authorities, is now almost at an end. It is, however, with deep regret we record the death, etc."

Then the sickness really breaks out, and the less recording and reporting the better for the peace of the subscribers. But the Empires and the Kings continue to divert themselves as selfishly as before, and the Foreman thinks that a daily paper really ought to come out once in twenty-four hours, and all the people at the Hill-stations in the middle of their amusements say:— "Good gracious! Why can't the paper be sparkling? I'm sure there's plenty going on up here."

That is the dark half of the moon, and, as the advertisements say, "must be experienced to be appreciated."

It was in that season, and a remarkably evil season, that the paper began running the last issue of the week on Saturday night, which is to say, Sunday morning, after the custom of a London paper. This was a great convenience, for immediately after the paper was put to bed, the dawn would lower the thermometer from 96° to almost 84° for half an hour, and in that chill—you have no idea how cold is 84° on the grass until you begin to pray for it—a very tired man could set off to sleep ere the heat roused him.

One Saturday night it was my pleasant duty to put the paper to bed alone. A King or courtier or a courtesan or a community was going to die or get a new Constitution, or do something that was important on the other side of the world, and the paper was to be held open till the latest possible minute in order to catch the telegram. It was a pitchy black night, as stifling as a June night can be, and the *loo*, the red-hot wind from the westward, was booming among the tinder-dry trees and pretending that the rain was on its heels. Now and again a spot of almost boiling water would fall on the dust with the flop of a frog, but all our weary world knew that was only pretence. It was a shade cooler in the press-room than the office, so I sat there, while the type clicked and clicked and the night-jars hooted at the windows, and the all but naked compositors wiped the sweat from their foreheads and called for water. The thing that was keeping us back, whatever it was, would not come off, though the *loo* dropped and the last type was set, and the whole round earth stood still in the choking heat, with its finger on its lip, to wait the event. I drowsed, and wondered whether the telegraph was a blessing, and whether this dying man, or struggling people, was aware of the inconvenience the delay was causing. There was no special reason beyond the heat and worry to make tension, but, as the clock hands crept up to three o'clock and the machines spun their fly-wheels two and three times to see that all was in order, before I said the word that would set them off, I could have shrieked aloud.

Then the roar and rattle of the wheels shivered the quiet into little bits. I rose to go away, but two men in white clothes stood in front of me. The first one said:—"It's him!" The second said:—"So it is!" And they both laughed almost as loudly as the machinery roared, and mopped their foreheads. "We see there was a light burning across the road and we were sleeping in that

2. God knows town; i.e., nowheresville.

ditch there for coolness, and I said to my friend here, 'The office is open. Let's come along and speak to him as turned us back from the Degumber State,' " said the smaller of the two. He was the man I had met in the Mhow train, and his fellow was the red-bearded man of Marwar Junction. There was no mistaking the eyebrows of the one or the beard of the other.

I was not pleased, because I wished to go to sleep, not to squabble with loafers. "What do you want?" I asked.

"Half an hour's talk with you cool and comfortable, in the office," said the red-bearded man. "We'd *like* some drink—the Contrack doesn't begin yet, Peachey, so you needn't look—but what we really want is advice. We don't want money. We ask you as a favor, because you did us a bad turn about Degumber."

I led from the press-room to the stifling office with the maps on the walls, and the red-haired man rubbed his hands. "That's something like," said he. "This was the proper shop to come to. Now, Sir, let me introduce to you Brother[3] Peachey Carnehan, that's him, and Brother Daniel Dravot, that is *me*, and the less said about our professions the better, for we have been most things in our time. Soldier, sailor, compositor, photographer, proof-reader, street-preacher, and correspondents of the *Backwoodsman* when we thought the paper wanted one. Carnehan is sober, and so am I. Look at us first and see that's sure. It will save you cutting into my talk. We'll take one of your cigars apiece, and you shall see us light."

I watched the test. The men were absolutely sober, so I gave them each a tepid peg.[4]

"Well *and* good," said Carnehan of the eyebrows, wiping the froth from his moustache. "Let me talk now, Dan. We have been all over India, mostly on foot. We have been boiler-fitters, engine-drivers, petty contractors, and all that, and we have decided that India isn't big enough for such as us."

They certainly were too big for the office. Dravot's beard seemed to fill half the room and Carnehan's shoulders the other half, as they sat on the big table. Carnehan continued: "The country isn't half worked out because they that governs it won't let you touch it. They spend all their blessed time in governing it, and you can't lift a spade, nor chip a rock, nor look for oil, nor anything like that without all the Government saying—'Leave it alone and let us govern.' Therefore, such as it is, we will let it alone, and go away to some other place where a man isn't crowded and can come to his own. We are not little men, and there is nothing that we are afraid of except Drink, and we have signed a Contrack on that. *Therefore*, we are going away to be Kings."

"Kings in our own right," muttered Dravot.

"Yes, of course," I said. "You've been tramping in the sun, and it's a very warm night, and hadn't you better sleep over the notion? Come to-morrow."

"Neither drunk nor sunstruck," said Dravot. "We have slept over the notion half a year, and require to see Books and Atlases, and we have decided that there is only one place now in the world that two strong men can Sar-a-*whack*.[5] They call it Kafiristan. By my reckoning it's the top right-hand

---

3. Meant to recall the Freemason connection.
4. A drink.
5. A reference to Sir James Brooke (1803–1868), "the White Rajah of Sarawak," who in return for helping the raja of Sarawak, in Borneo, put down a rebellion, succeeded him after his death and established a dynasty.

corner of Afghanistan, not more than three hundred miles from Pesha-wur. They have two and thirty heathen idols there, and we'll be the thirty-third. It's a mountainous country, and the women of those parts are very beautiful."

"But that is provided against in the Contrack," said Carnehan. "Neither Women nor Liquor, Daniel."

"And that's all we know, except that no one has gone there, and they fight, and in any place where they fight, a man who knows how to drill men can always be a King. We shall go to those parts and say to any King we find— 'D'you want to vanquish your foes?' and we will show him how to drill men; for that we know better than anything else. Then we will subvert that King and seize his Throne and establish a Dy-nasty."

"You'll be cut to pieces before you're fifty miles across the Border," I said. "You have to travel through Afghanistan to get to that country. It's one mass of mountains and peaks and glaciers, and no Englishman has been through it. The people are utter brutes, and even if you reached them you couldn't do anything."

"That's more like," said Carnehan: "If you could think us a little more mad we would be more pleased. We have come to you to know about this country, to read a book about it, and to be shown maps. We want you to tell us that we are fools and to show us your books." He turned to the bookcases.

"Are you at all in earnest?" I said.

"A little," said Dravot, sweetly. "As big a map as you have got, even if it's all blank where Kafiristan is, and any books you've got. We can read, though we aren't very educated."

I uncased the big thirty-two-miles-to-the-inch map of India, and two smaller Frontier maps, hauled down volume INF-KAN of the *Encyclopaedia Britannica*, and the men consulted them.

"See here!" said Dravot, his thumb on the map. "Up to Jagdallak, Peachey and me know the road. We was there with Roberts's Army.[6] We'll have to turn off to the right at Jagdallak through Laghmann territory. Then we get among the hills—fourteen thousand feet—fifteen thousand—it will be cold work there, but it don't look very far on the map."

I handed him Wood on the *Sources of the Oxus*.[7] Carnehan was deep in the *Encyclopaedia*.

"They're a mixed lot," said Dravot, reflectively; "and it won't help us to know the names of their tribes. The more tribes the more they'll fight, and the better for us. From Jagdallak to Ashang. H'mm!"

"But all the information about the country is as sketchy and inaccurate as can be," I protested. "No one knows anything about it really. Here's the file of the *United Services' Institute*. Read what Bellew says."

"Blow Bellew!" said Carnehan. "Dan, they're an all-fired lot of heathens, but this book here says they think they're related to us English."

I smoked while the men pored over *Raverty, Wood*, the maps, and the *Encyclopaedia*.

"There is no use your waiting," said Dravot, politely. "It's about four o'clock now. We'll go before six o'clock if you want to sleep, and we won't steal any

---

6. In the Second Afghan War (1878–80), a force under the command of General Frederick Roberts made a three-hundred-mile forced march through the area.

7. The Oxus is a river whose sources are in the area.

of the papers. Don't you sit up. We're two harmless lunatics and if you come, to-morrow evening, down to the Serai[8] we'll say good-bye to you."

"You *are* two fools," I answered. "You'll be turned back at the Frontier or cut up the minute you set foot in Afghanistan. Do you want any money or a recommendation downcountry? I can help you to the chance of work next week."

"Next week we shall be hard at work ourselves, thank you," said Dravot. "It isn't so easy being a King as it looks. When we've got our Kingdom in going order we'll let you know, and you can come up and help us to govern it."

"Would two lunatics make a Contrack like that?" said Carnehan, with subdued pride, showing me a greasy half-sheet of note-paper on which was written the following. I copied it, then and there, as a curiosity:

This Contract between me and you persuing witnesseth in the name of God—Amen and so forth.

(One)   That me and you will settle this matter together: i. e., to be Kings of Kafiristan.

(Two)   That you and me will not, while this matter is being settled, look at any Liquor, nor any Woman, black, white or brown, so as to get mixed up with one or the other harmful.

(Three)   That we conduct ourselves with dignity and discretion and if one of us gets into trouble the other will stay by him.

Signed by you and me this day.
Peachey Taliaferro Carnehan.
Daniel Dravot.
Both Gentlemen at Large.

"There was no need for the last article," said Carnehan, blushing modestly; "but it looks regular. Now you know the sort of men that loafers are—we *are* loafers, Dan, until we get out of India—and *do* you think that we would sign a Contrack like that unless we was in earnest? We have kept away from the two things that make life worth having."

"You won't enjoy your lives much longer if you are going to try this idiotic adventure. Don't set the office on fire," I said, "and go away before nine o'clock."

I left them still poring over the maps and making notes on the back of the "Contrack." "Be sure to come down to the Serai to-morrow," were their parting words.

The Kumharsen Serai is the great foursquare sink of humanity where the strings of camels and horses from the North load and unload. All the nationalities of Central Asia may be found there, and most of the folk of India proper. Balkh and Bokhara there meet Bengal and Bombay, and try to draw eye-teeth. You can buy ponies, turquoises, Persian pussy-cats, saddle-bags, fat-tailed sheep and musk in the Kumharsen Serai, and get many strange things for nothing. In the afternoon I went down there to see whether my friends intended to keep their word or were lying about drunk.

A priest attired in fragments of ribbons and rags stalked up to me, gravely twisting a child's paper whirligig.[9] Behind was his servant bending under the

---

8. Place or building for the accommodation of travelers and their pack animals.

9. Pinwheel.

load of a crate of mud toys. The two were loading up two camels, and the inhabitants of the Serai watched them with shrieks of laughter.

"The priest is mad," said a horse-dealer to me. "He is going up to Kabul to sell toys to the Amir.[1] He will either be raised to honor or have his head cut off. He came in here this morning and has been behaving madly ever since."

"The witless are under the protection of God," stammered a flat-cheeked Usbeg[2] in broken Hindi. "They foretell future events."

"Would they could have foretold that my caravan would have been cut up by the Shinwaris almost within shadow of the Pass!" grunted the Eusufzai agent of a Rajputana trading-house whose goods had been feloniously diverted into the hands of other robbers just across the Border, and whose misfortunes were the laughing-stock of the bazar. "Ohé, priest, whence come you and whither do you go?"

"From Roum[3] have I come," shouted the priest, waving his whirligig; "from Roum, blown by the breath of a hundred devils across the sea! O thieves, robbers, liars, the blessing of Pir Khan on pigs, dogs, and perjurers! Who will take the Protected of God to the North to sell charms that are never still to the Amir? The camels shall not gall,[4] the sons shall not fall sick, and the wives shall remain faithful while they are away, of the men who give me place in their caravan. Who will assist me to slipper the King of the Roos[5] with a golden slipper with a silver heel? The protection of Pir Khan be upon his labors!" He spread out the skirts of his gaberdine and pirouetted between the lines of tethered horses.

"There starts a caravan from Peshawur to Kabul in twenty days, *Huzrut*,[6]" said the Eusufzai trader. "My camels go therewith. Do thou also go and bring us good-luck."

"I will go even now!" shouted the priest. "I will depart upon my winged camels, and be at Peshawur in a day! Ho! Hazar[7] Mir Khan," he yelled to his servant, "drive out the camels, but let me first mount my own."

He leaped on the back of his beast as it knelt, and, turning round to me, cried:—"Come thou also, Sahib, a little along the road, and I will sell thee a charm—an amulet that shall make thee King of Kafiristan."

Then the light broke upon me, and I followed the two camels out of the Serai till we reached open road and the priest halted.

"What d' you think o' that?" said he in English. "Carnehan can't talk their patter, so I've made him my servant. He makes a handsome servant. 'Tisn't for nothing that I've been knocking about the country for fourteen years. Didn't I do that talk neat? We'll hitch on to a caravan at Peshawur till we get to Jagdallak, and then we'll see if we can get donkeys for our camels, and strike into Kafiristan. Whirligigs for the Amir, O Lor! Put your hand under the camel-bags and tell me what you feel."

I felt the butt of a Martini,[8] and another and another.

"Twenty of 'em," said Dravot, placidly. "Twenty of 'em, and ammunition to correspond, under the whirligigs and the mud dolls."

---

1. The ruler of Afghanistan. Kabul is in Afghanistan.
2. Person from Uzbekistan.
3. Turkey.
4. Become sore.

5. Czar of Russia.
6. Presence; an honorary form of address.
7. Get ready.
8. Rifle issued to British infantry.

"Heaven help you if you are caught with those things!" I said. "A Martini is worth her weight in silver among the Pathans."[9]

"Fifteen hundred rupees of capital—every rupee we could beg, borrow, or steal—are invested on these two camels," said Dravot. "We won't get caught. We're going through the Khaiber with a regular caravan. Who'd touch a poor mad priest?"

"Have you got everything you want?" I asked, overcome with astonishment.

"Not yet, but we shall soon. Give us a memento of your kindness, *Brother*. You did me a service yesterday, and that time in Marwar. Half my Kingdom shall you have, as the saying is." I slipped a small charm compass from my watch-chain and handed it up to the priest.

"Good-bye," said Dravot, giving me hand cautiously. "It's the last time we'll shake hands with an Englishman these many days. Shake hands with him, Carnehan," he cried, as the second camel passed me.

Carnehan leaned down and shook hands. Then the camels passed away along the dusty road, and I was left alone to wonder. My eye could detect no failure in the disguises. The scene in Serai attested that they were complete to the native mind. There was just the chance, therefore, that Carnehan and Dravot would be able to wander through Afghanistan without detection. But, beyond, they would find death, certain and awful death.

Ten days later a native friend of mine, giving me the news of the day from Peshawur, wound up his letter with:—"There has been much laughter here on account of a certain mad priest who is going in his estimation to sell petty gauds and insignificant trinkets which he ascribes as great charms to H. H. the Amir of Bokhara. He passed through Peshawur and associated himself to the Second Summer caravan that goes to Kabul. The merchants are pleased, because through superstition they imagine that such mad fellows bring good-fortune."

The two, then, were beyond the Border. I would have prayed for them, but, that night, a real King died in Europe, and demanded an obituary notice.

The wheel of the world swings through the same phases again and again. Summer passed and winter thereafter, and came and passed again. The daily paper continued and I with it, and upon the third summer there fell a hot night, a night-issue, and a strained waiting for something to be telegraphed from the other side of the world, exactly as had happened before. A few great men had died in the past two years, the machines worked with more clatter, and some of the trees in the Office garden were a few feet taller. But that was all the difference.

I passed over to the press-room, and went through just such a scene as I have already described. The nervous tension was stronger than it had been two years before, and I felt the heat more acutely. At three o'clock I cried, "Print off," and turned to go, when there crept to my chair what was left of a man. He was bent into a circle, his head was sunk between his shoulders, and he moved his feet one over the other like a bear. I could hardly see whether he walked or crawled—this rag-wrapped, whining cripple who addressed me by name, crying that he was come back. "Can you give me a drink?" he whimpered. "For the Lord's sake, give me a drink!"

9. The principal tribe in Afghanistan.

I went back to the office, the man following with groans of pain, and I turned up the lamp.

"Don't you know me?" he gasped, dropping into a chair, and he turned his drawn face, surmounted by a shock of grey hair, to the light.

I looked at him intently. Once before had I seen eyebrows that met over the nose in an inch-broad black band, but for the life of me I could not tell where.

"I don't know you," I said, handing him the whiskey. "What can I do for you?"

He took a gulp of the spirit raw, and shivered in spite of the suffocating heat.

"I've come back," he repeated; "and I was the King of Kafiristan—me and Dravot—crowned Kings we was! In this office we settled it—you setting there and giving us the books. I am Peachey—Peachey Taliaferro Carnehan, and you've been setting here ever since—O Lord!"

I was more than a little astonished, and expressed my feelings accordingly.

"It's true," said Carnehan, with a dry cackle, nursing his feet, which were wrapped in rags. "True as gospel. Kings we were, with crowns upon our heads—me and Dravot—poor Dan—oh, poor, poor Dan, that would never take advice, not though I begged of him!"

"Take the whiskey," I said, "and take your own time. Tell me all you can recollect of everything from beginning to end. You got across the border on your camels, Dravot dressed as a mad priest and you his servant. Do you remember that?"

"I ain't mad—yet, but I shall be that way soon. Of course I remember. Keep looking at me, or maybe my words will go all to pieces. Keep looking at me in my eyes and don't say anything."

I leaned forward and looked into his face as steadily as I could. He dropped one hand upon the table and I grasped it by the wrist. It was twisted like a bird's claw, and upon the back was a ragged, red, diamond-shaped scar.

"No, don't look there. Look at *me*," said Carnehan.

"That comes afterward, but for the Lord's sake don't distrack me. We left with that caravan, me and Dravot playing all sorts of antics to amuse the people we were with. Dravot used to make us laugh in the evenings when all the people was cooking their dinners—cooking their dinners, and . . . what did they do then? They lit little fires with sparks that went into Dravot's beard, and we all laughed—fit to die. Little red fires they was, going into Dravot's big red beard—so funny." His eyes left mine and he smiled foolishly.

"You went as far as Jagdallak with that caravan," I said, at a venture, "after you had lit those fires. To Jagdallak, where you turned off to try to get into Kafiristan."

"No, we didn't neither. What are you talking about? We turned off before Jagdallak, because we heard the roads was good. But they wasn't good enough for our two camels—mine and Dravot's. When we left the caravan, Dravot took off all his clothes and mine too, and said we would be heathen, because the Kafirs[1] didn't allow Mohammedans to talk to them. So we dressed betwixt and between, and such a sight as Daniel Dravot I never saw yet nor expect to see again. He burned half his beard, and slung a sheep-

_____
1. Non-Muslims.

skin over his shoulder, and shaved his head into patterns. He shaved mine, too, and made me wear outrageous things to look like a heathen. That was in a most mountaineous country, and our camels couldn't go along any more because of the mountains. They were tall and black, and coming home I saw them fight like wild goats—there are lots of goats in Kafiristan. And these mountains, they never keep still, no more than goats. Always fighting they are, and don't let you sleep at night."

"Take some more whiskey," I said, very slowly. "What did you and Daniel Dravot do when the camels could go no further because of the rough roads that led into Kafiristan?"

"What did which do? There was a party called Peachey Taliaferro Carnehan that was with Dravot. Shall I tell you about him? He died out there in the cold. Slap from the bridge fell old Peachey, turning and twisting in the air like a penny whirligig that you can sell to the Amir—No; they was two for three ha'pence, those whirligigs, or I am much mistaken and woful sore. And then these camels were no use, and Peachey said to Dravot—'For the Lord's sake, let's get out of this before our heads are chopped off,' and with that they killed the camels all among the mountains, not having anything in particular to eat, but first they took off the boxes with the guns and the ammunition, till two men came along driving four mules. Dravot up and dances in front of them, singing,—'Sell me four mules.' Says the first man,— 'If you are rich enough to buy, you are rich enough to rob;' but before ever he could put his hand to his knife, Dravot breaks his neck over his knee, and the other party runs away. So Carnehan loaded the mules with the rifles that was taken off the camels, and together we starts forward into those bitter cold mountaineous parts, and never a road broader than the back of your hand."

He paused for a moment, while I asked him if he could remember the nature of the country through which he had journeyed.

"I am telling you as straight as I can, but my head isn't as good as it might be. They drove nails through it to make me hear better how Dravot died. The country was mountaineous and the mules were most contrary, and the inhabitants was dispersed and solitary. They went up and up, and down and down, and that other party, Carnehan, was imploring of Dravot not to sing and whistle so loud, for fear of bringing down the tremenjus avalanches. But Dravot says that if a King couldn't sing it wasn't worth being King, and whacked the mules over the rump, and never took no heed for ten cold days. We came to a big level valley all among the mountains, and the mules were near dead, so we killed them, not having anything in special for them or us to eat. We sat upon the boxes, and played odd and even with the cartridges that was jolted out.

"Then ten men with bows and arrows ran down that valley, chasing twenty men with bows and arrows, and the row was tremenjus. They was fair men— fairer than you or me—with yellow hair and remarkable well built.[2] Says Dravot, unpacking the guns—'This is the beginning of the business. We'll fight for the ten men,' and with that he fires two rifles at the twenty men, and drops one of them at two hundred yards from the rock where we was sitting. The other men began to run, but Carnehan and Dravot sits on the

2. There was a legend that Alexander the Great left a Greek colony in the area.

boxes picking them off at all ranges, up and down the valley. Then we goes up to the ten men that had run across the snow too, and they fires a footy little arrow at us. Dravot he shoots above their heads and they all falls down flat. Then he walks over and kicks them, and then he lifts them up and shakes hands all round to make them friendly like. He calls them and gives them the boxes to carry, and waves his hand for all the world as though he was King already. They takes the boxes and him across the valley and up the hill into a pine wood on the top, where there was half a dozen big stone idols. Dravot he goes to the biggest—a fellow they call Imbra—and lays a rifle and a cartridge at his feet, rubbing his nose respectful with his own nose, patting him on the head, and saluting in front of it. He turns round to the men and nods his head, and says,—'That's all right. I'm in the know too, and all these old jim-jams are my friends.' Then he opens his mouth and points down it, and when the first man brings him food, he says—'No;' and when the second man brings him food, he says—'No;' but when one of the old priests and the boss of the village brings him food, he says—'Yes;' very haughty, and eats it slow. That was how we came to our first village, without any trouble, just as though we had tumbled from the skies. But we tumbled from one of those damned rope-bridges, you see, and you couldn't expect a man to laugh much after that."

"Take some more whiskey and go on," I said. "That was the first village you came into. How did you get to be King?"

"I wasn't King," said Carnehan. "Dravot he was the King, and a handsome man he looked with the gold crown on his head and all. Him and the other party stayed in that village, and every morning Dravot sat by the side of old Imbra, and the people came and worshipped. That was Dravot's order. Then a lot of men came into the valley, and Carnehan and Dravot picks them off with the rifles before they knew where they was, and runs down into the valley and up again the other side, and finds another village, same as the first one, and the people all falls down flat on their faces, and Dravot says,—'Now what is the trouble between you two villages?' and the people points to a woman, as fair as you or me, that was carried off, and Dravot takes her back to the first village and counts up the dead—eight there was. For each dead man Dravot pours a little milk on the ground and waves his arms like a whirligig and 'That's all right,' says he. Then he and Carnehan takes the big boss of each village by the arm and walks them down into the valley, and shows them how to scratch a line with a spear right down the valley, and gives each a sod of turf from both sides o' the line. Then all the people comes down and shouts like the devil and all, and Dravot says,—'Go and dig the land, and be fruitful and multiply,'[3] which they did, though they didn't understand. Then we asks the names of things in their lingo—bread and water and fire and idols and such, and Dravot leads the priest of each village up to the idol, and says he must sit there and judge the people, and if anything goes wrong he is to be shot.

"Next week they was all turning up the land in the valley as quiet as bees and much prettier, and the priests heard all the complaints and told Dravot in dumb show what it was about. 'That's just the beginning,' says Dravot. 'They think we're Gods.' He and Carnehan picks out twenty good men and

3. God's command to Adam and Eve (Genesis 1.28).

shows them how to click off a rifle, and form fours, and advance in line, and they was very pleased to do so, and clever to see the hang of it. Then he takes out his pipe and his baccy-pouch and leaves one at one village and one at the other, and off we two goes to see what was to be done in the next valley. That was all rock, and there was a little village there, and Carnehan says,— 'Send 'em to the old valley to plant,' and takes 'em there and gives 'em some land that wasn't took before. They were a poor lot, and we blooded 'em with a kid[4] before letting 'em into the new Kingdom. That was to impress the people, and then they settled down quiet, and Carnehan went back to Dravot, who had got into another valley, all snow and ice and most mountaineous. There was no people there, and the Army got afraid, so Dravot shoots one of them, and goes on till he finds some people in a village, and the Army explains that unless the people wants to be killed they had better not shoot their little matchlocks;[5] for they had matchlocks. We makes friends with the priest and I stays there alone with two of the Army, teaching the men how to drill, and a thundering big Chief comes across the snow with kettle-drums and horns twanging, because he heard there was a new God kicking about. Carnehan sights for the brown[6] of the men half a mile across the snow and wings one of them. Then he sends a message to the Chief that, unless he wished to be killed, he must come and shake hands with me and leave his arms behind. The Chief comes alone first, and Carnehan shakes hands with him and whirls his arms about, same as Dravot used, and very much surprised that Chief was, and strokes my eyebrows. Then Carnehan goes alone to the Chief, and asks him in dumb show if he had an enemy he hated. 'I have,' says the Chief. So Carnehan weeds out the pick of his men, and sets the two of the Army to show them drill, and at the end of two weeks the men can manoeuvre about as well as Volunteers. So he marches with the Chief to a great big plain on the top of a mountain, and the Chief's men rushes into a village and takes it; we three Martinis firing into the brown of the enemy. So we took that village too, and I gives the Chief a rag from my coat and says, 'Occupy till I come;'[7] which was scriptural. By way of a reminder, when me and the Army was eighteen hundred yards away, I drops a bullet near him standing on the snow, and all the people falls flat on their faces. Then I sends a letter to Dravot, wherever he be by land or by sea."

At the risk of throwing the creature out of train I interrupted,—"How could you write a letter up yonder?"

"The letter?—Oh!—The letter! Keep looking at me between the eyes, please. It was a string-talk letter, that we'd learned the way of it from a blind beggar in the Punjab."

I remember that there had once come to the office a blind man with a knotted twig and a piece of string which he wound round the twig according to some cipher of his own. He could, after the lapse of days or hours, repeat the sentence which he had reeled up. He had reduced the alphabet to eleven primitive sounds; and tried to teach me his method, but failed.

"I sent that letter to Dravot," said Carnehan; "and told him to come back because this Kingdom was growing too big for me to handle, and then I struck

---

4. I.e., a kid goat, a fake religious ritual.
5. Primitive kind of musket.
6. Fires into the middle of a group of game birds rather than aiming at a particular one (a hunting term).
7. In Jesus' parable of the talents, a nobleman gives each of his servants a coin to invest with those instructions (Luke 19.13).

for the first valley, to see how the priests were working. They called the village we took along with the Chief, Bashkai, and the first village we took, Er-Heb. The priests at Er-Heb was doing all right, but they had a lot of pending cases about land to show me, and some men from another village had been firing arrows at night. I went out and looked for that village and fired four rounds at it from a thousand yards. That used all the cartridges I cared to spend, and I waited for Dravot, who had been away two or three months, and I kept my people quiet.

"One morning I heard the devil's own noise of drums and horns, and Dan Dravot marches down the hill with his Army and a tail of hundreds of men, and, which was the most amazing—a great gold crown on his head. 'My Gord, Carnehan,' says Daniel, 'this is a tremenjus business, and we've got the whole country as far as it's worth having. I am the son of Alexander by Queen Semiramis,[8] and you're my younger brother and a God too! It's the biggest thing we've ever seen. I've been marching and fighting for six weeks with the Army, and every footy little village for fifty miles has come in rejoiceful; and more than that, I've got the key of the whole show, as you'll see, and I've got a crown for you! I told 'em to make two of 'em at a place called Shu, where the gold lies in the rock like suet in mutton. Gold I've seen, and turquoise I've kicked out of the cliffs, and there's garnets in the sands of the river, and here's a chunk of amber that a man brought me. Call up all the priests and, here, take your crown.'

"One of the men opens a black hair bag and I slips the crown on. It was too small and too heavy, but I wore it for the glory. Hammered gold it was— five pound weight, like a hoop of a barrel.

" 'Peachey,' says Dravot, 'we don't want to fight no more. The Craft's[9] the trick, so help me!' and he brings forward that same Chief that I left at Bash kai—Billy Fish we called him afterward, because he was so like Billy Fish that drove the big tank-engine at Mach on the Bolan in the old days. 'Shake hands with him,' says Dravot, and I shook hands and nearly dropped, for Billy Fish gave me the Grip.[1] I said nothing, but tried him with the Fellow Craft Grip. He answers, all right, and I tried the Master's Grip, but that was a slip. 'A Fellow Craft he is!' I says to Dan. 'Does he know the word?' 'He does,' says Dan, 'and all the priests know. It's a miracle! The Chiefs and the priests can work a Fellow Craft Lodge in a way that's very like ours, and they've cut the marks on the rocks, but they don't know the Third Degree, and they've come to find out. It's Gord's Truth. I've known these long years that the Afghans knew up to the Fellow Craft Degree, but this is a miracle. A God and a Grand-Master of the Craft am I, and a Lodge in the Third Degree I will open, and we'll raise the head priests and the Chiefs of the villages.'

" 'It's against all the law,' I says, 'holding a Lodge without warrant from any one; and we never held office in any Lodge.'

" 'It's a master-stroke of policy,' says Dravot. 'It means running the country as easy as a four-wheeled bogy[2] on a down grade. We can't stop to inquire now, or they'll turn against us. I've forty Chiefs at my heel, and passed and raised according to their merit they shall be. Billet these men on the villages

---

8. Legendary Assyrian queen.
9. Freemasonry.

1. Freemason handshake.
2. Railway truck.

and see that we run up a Lodge of some kind. The temple of Imbra will do for the Lodge-room. The women must make aprons as you show them. I'll hold a levee[3] of Chiefs to-night and Lodge to-morrow.'

"I was fair run off my legs, but I wasn't such a fool as not to see what a pull this Craft business gave us. I showed the priests' families how to make aprons of the degrees, but for Dravot's apron the blue border and marks was made of turquoise lumps on white hide, not cloth. We took a great square stone in the temple for the Master's chair, and little stones for the officers' chairs, and painted the black pavement with white squares, and did what we could to make things regular.

"At the levee which was held that night on the hillside with big bonfires, Dravot gives out that him and me were Gods and sons of Alexander, and Past Grand-Masters in the Craft, and was come to make Kafiristan a country where every man should eat in peace and drink in quiet, and specially obey us. Then the Chiefs come round to shake hands, and they was so hairy and white and fair it was just shaking hands with old friends. We gave them names according as they was like men we had known in India—Billy Fish, Holly Wilworth, Pikky Kergan that was Bazar-master when I was at Mhow, and so on and so on.

"*The* most amazing miracle was at Lodge next night. One of the old priests was watching us continuous, and I felt uneasy, for I knew we'd have to fudge the Ritual, and I didn't know what the men knew. The old priest was a stranger come in from beyond the village of Bashkai. The minute Dravot puts on the Master's apron that the girls had made for him, the priest fetches a whoop and a howl, and tries to overturn the stone that Dravot was sitting on. 'It's all up now,' I says. 'That comes of meddling with the Craft without warrant!' Dravot never winked an eye, not when ten priests took and tilted over the Grand-Master's chair—which was to say the stone of Imbra. The priest begins rubbing the bottom end of it to clear away the black dirt, and presently he shows all the other priests the Master's Mark, same as was on Dravot's apron, cut into the stone. Not even the priests of the temple of Imbra knew it was there. The old chap falls flat on his face at Dravot's feet and kisses 'em. 'Luck again,' says Dravot, across the Lodge to me, 'they say it's the missing Mark that no one could understand the why of. We're more than safe now.' Then he bangs the butt of his gun for a gavel and says:—'By virtue of the authority vested in me by my own right hand and the help of Peachey, I declare myself Grand-Master of all Freemasonry in Kafiristan in this the Mother Lodge o' the country, and King of Kafiristan equally with Peachey!' At that he puts on his crown and I puts on mine—I was doing Senior Warden—and we opens the Lodge in most ample form. It was a amazing miracle! The priests moved in Lodge through the first two degrees almost without telling, as if the memory was coming back to them. After that, Peachey and Dravot raised such as was worthy—high priests and Chiefs of far-off villages. Billy Fish was the first, and I can tell you we scared the soul out of him. It was not in any way according to Ritual, but it served our turn. We didn't raise more than ten of the biggest men, because we didn't want to make the Degree common. And they was clamoring to be raised.

" 'In another six months,' says Dravot, 'we'll hold another Communication

3. Gathering.

and see how you are working.' Then he asks them about their villages, and learns that they was fighting one against the other and were fair sick and tired of it. And when they wasn't doing that they was fighting with the Mohammedans. 'You can fight those when they come into our country,' says Dravot. 'Tell off every tenth man of your tribes for a Frontier guard, and send two hundred at a time to this valley to be drilled. Nobody is going to be shot or speared any more so long as he does well, and I know that you won't cheat me because you're white people—sons of Alexander—and not like common, black Mohammedans. You are *my* people and by God,' says he, running off into English at the end—'I'll make a damned fine Nation of you, or I'll die in the making!'

"I can't tell all we did for the next six months because Dravot did a lot I couldn't see the hang off, and he learned their lingo in a way I never could. My work was to help the people plough, and now and again go out with some of the Army and see what the other villages were doing, and make 'em throw rope-bridges across the ravines which cut up the country horrid. Dravot was very kind to me, but when he walked up and down in the pine wood pulling that bloody red beard of his with both fists I knew he was thinking plans I could not advise him about, and I just waited for orders.

"But Dravot never showed me disrespect before the people. They were afraid of me and the Army, but they loved Dan. He was the best of friends with the priests and the Chiefs; but any one could come across the hills with a complaint and Dravot would hear him out fair, and call four priests together and say what was to be done. He used to call in Billy Fish from Bashkai, and Pikky Kergan from Shu, and an old Chief we called Kafuzelum—it was like enough to his real name—and hold councils with 'em when there was any fighting to be done in small villages. That was his Council of War, and the four priests of Bashkai, Shu, Khawak, and Madora was his Privy Council. Between the lot of 'em they sent me, with forty men and twenty rifles, and sixty men carrying turquoises, into the Ghorband country to buy those hand-made Martini rifles, that come out of the Amir's workshops at Kabul, from one of the Amir's Herati regiments that would have sold the very teeth out of their mouths for turquoises.

"I stayed in Ghorband a month, and gave the Governor there the pick of my baskets for hush-money, and bribed the Colonel of the regiment some more, and, between the two and the tribes-people, we got more than a hundred hand-made Martinis, a hundred good Kohat Jezails[4] that'll throw to six hundred yards, and forty man-loads of very bad ammunition for the rifles. I came back with what I had, and distributed 'em among the men that the Chiefs sent to me to drill. Dravot was too busy to attend to those things, but the old Army that we first made helped me, and we turned out five hundred men that could drill, and two hundred that knew how to hold arms pretty straight. Even those cork-screwed, hand-made guns was a miracle to them. Dravot talked big about powder-shops and factories, walking up and down in the pine wood when the winter was coming on.

" 'I won't make a Nation,' says he. 'I'll make an Empire! These men aren't niggers; they're English! Look at their eyes—look at their mouths. Look at the way they stand up. They sit, on chairs in their own houses. They're the

---

4. Afghan muskets.

Lost Tribes, or something like it, and they've grown to be English. I'll take a census in the spring if the priests don't get frightened. There must be a fair two million of 'em in these hills. The villages are full o' little children. Two million people—two hundred and fifty thousand fighting men—and all English! They only want the rifles and a little drilling. Two hundred and fifty thousand men, ready to cut in on Russia's right flank when she tries for India! Peachey, man,' he says, chewing his beard in great hunks, 'we shall be Emperors—Emperors of the Earth! Rajah Brooke[5] will be a suckling to us. I'll treat with the Viceroy on equal terms. I'll ask him to send me twelve picked English—twelve that I know of—to help us govern a bit. There's Mackray, Sergeant-pensioner at Segowli—many's the good dinner he's given me, and his wife a pair of trousers. There's Donkin, the Warder of Tounghoo Jail; there's hundreds that I could lay my hand on if I was in India. The Viceroy shall do it for me. I'll send a man through in the spring for those men, and I'll write for a dispensation from the Grand-Lodge for what I've done as Grand-Master. That—and all the Sniders[6] that'll be thrown out when the native troops in India take up the Martini. They'll be worn smooth, but they'll do for fighting in these hills. Twelve English, a hundred thousand Sniders run through the Amir's country in driblets—I'd be content with twenty thousand in one year—and we'd be an Empire. When everything was shipshape, I'd hand over the crown—this crown I'm wearing now—to Queen Victoria on my knees, and she'd say: "Rise up, Sir Daniel Dravot." Oh, it's big! It's big, I tell you! But there's so much to be done in every place—Bashkai, Khawak, Shu, and everywhere else.'

" 'What is it?' I says. 'There are no more men coming in to be drilled this autumn. Look at those fat, black clouds. They're bringing the snow.'

" 'It isn't that,' says Daniel, putting his hand very hard on my shoulder; 'and I don't wish to say anything that's against you, for no other living man would have followed me and made me what I am as you have done. You're a first-class Commander-in-Chief, and the people know you; but—it's a big country, and somehow you can't help me, Peachey, in the way I want to be helped.'

" 'Go to your blasted priests, then!' I said, and I was sorry when I made that remark, but it did hurt me sore to find Daniel talking so superior when I'd drilled all the men, and done all he told me.

" 'Don't let's quarrel, Peachey,' says Daniel, without cursing. 'You're a King, too, and the half of this Kingdom is yours; but can't you see, Peachey, we want cleverer men than us now—three or four of 'em, that we can scatter about for our Deputies. It's a hugeous great State, and I can't always tell the right thing to do, and I haven't time for all I want to do, and here's the winter coming on and all.' He put half his beard into his mouth, and it was as red as the gold of his crown.

" 'I'm sorry, Daniel,' says I. 'I've done all I could. I've drilled the men and shown the people how to stack their oats better; and I've brought in those tinware rifles from Ghorband—but I know what you're driving at. I take it Kings always feel oppressed that way.'

" 'There's another thing too,' says Dravot, walking up and down. 'The winter's coming and these people won't be giving much trouble and if they do we can't move about. I want a wife.'

---

5. See n. 5, p. 1870.

6. Older rifles being replaced by Martinis.

" 'For Gord's sake leave the women alone!' I says. 'We've both got all the work we can, though I *am* a fool. Remember the Contrack, and keep clear o' women.'

" 'The Contrack only lasted till such time as we was Kings; and Kings we have been these months past,' says Dravot, weighing his crown in his hand. 'You go get a wife too, Peachey—a nice, strappin', plump girl that'll keep you warm in the winter. They're prettier than English girls, and we can take the pick of 'em. Boil 'em once or twice in hot water, and they'll come as fair as chicken and ham.'

" 'Don't tempt me!' I says. 'I will not have any dealings with a woman not till we are a dam' side more settled than we are now. I've been doing the work o' two men, and you've been doing the work o' three. Let's lie off a bit, and see if we can get some better tobacco from Afghan country and run in some good liquor; but no women.'

" 'Who's talking o' *women?*' says Dravot. 'I said *wife*—a Queen to breed a King's son for the King. A Queen out of the strongest tribe, that'll make them your blood-brothers, and that'll lie by your side and tell you all the people thinks about you and their own affairs. That's what I want.'

" 'Do you remember that Bengali woman I kept at Mogul Serai when I was a plate-layer?'[7] says I. 'A fat lot o' good she was to me. She taught me the lingo and one or two other things; but what happened? She ran away with the Station-master's servant and half my month's pay. Then she turned up at Dadur Junction in tow of a half-caste, and had the impidence to say I was her husband—all among the drivers in the running-shed!'

" 'We've done with that,' says Dravot. 'These women are whiter than you or me, and a Queen I will have for the winter months.'

" 'For the last time o' asking, Dan, do *not*,' I says. 'It'll only bring us harm. The Bible says that Kings ain't to waste their strength on women, 'specially when they've got a new raw Kingdom to work over.'[8]

" 'For the last time of answering, I will,' said Dravot, and he went away through the pine-trees looking like a big red devil. The low sun hit his crown and beard on one side and the two blazed like hot coals.

"But getting a wife was not as easy as Dan thought. He put it before the Council, and there was no answer till Billy Fish said that he'd better ask the girls. Dravot damned them all round. 'What's wrong with me?' he shouts, standing by the idol Imbra. 'Am I a dog or am I not enough of a man for your wenches? Haven't I put the shadow of my hand over this country? Who stopped the last Afghan raid?' It was me really, but Dravot was too angry to remember. 'Who brought your guns? Who repaired the bridges? Who's the Grand-Master of the sign cut in the stone?' and he thumped his hand on the block that he used to sit on in Lodge, and at Council, which opened like Lodge always. Billy Fish said nothing, and no more did the others. 'Keep your hair on, Dan,' said I; 'and ask the girls. That's how it's done at Home, and these people are quite English.'

" 'The marriage of the King is a matter of State,' says Dan, in a white-hot rage, for he could feel, I hope, that he was going against his better mind. He walked out of the Council-room, and the others sat still, looking at the ground.

---

7. Layer of railway track.
8. "Give not thy strength unto women, nor thy ways to that which destroyeth kings" (Proverbs 31.3).

" 'Billy Fish,' says I to the Chief of Bashkai, 'what's the difficulty here? A straight answer to a true friend,' 'You know,' says Billy Fish. 'How should a man tell you who know everything? How can daughters of men marry Gods or Devils? It's not proper.'

"I remembered something like that in the Bible;[9] but if, after seeing us as long as they had, they still believed we were Gods, it wasn't for me to unde- ceive them.

" 'A God can do anything,' says I. 'If the King is fond of a girl he'll not let her die.' 'She'll have to,' said Billy Fish. 'There are all sorts of Gods and Devils in these mountains, and now and again a girl marries one of them and isn't seen any more. Besides, you two know the Mark cut in the stone. Only the Gods know that. We thought you were men till you showed the sign of the Master.'

"I wished then that we had explained about the loss of the genuine secrets of a Master-Mason at the first go-off; but I said nothing. All that night there was a blowing of horns in a little dark temple half-way down the hill, and I heard a girl crying fit to die. One of the priests told us that she was being prepared to marry the King.

" 'I'll have no nonsense of that kind,' says Dan. 'I don't want to interfere with your customs, but I'll take my own wife.' 'The girl's a little bit afraid,' says the priest. 'She thinks she's going to die, and they are a-heartening of her up down in the temple.'

" 'Hearten her very tender, then,' says Dravot, 'or I'll hearten you with the butt of a gun so that you'll never want to be heartened again.' He licked his lips, did Dan, and stayed up walking about more than half the night, thinking of the wife that he was going to get in the morning. I wasn't any means comfortable, for I knew that dealings with a woman in foreign parts, though you was a crowned King twenty times over, could not but be risky. I got up very early in the morning while Dravot was asleep, and I saw the priests talking together in whispers, and the Chiefs talking together too, and they looked at me out of the corners of their eyes.

" 'What is up, Fish?' I says to the Bashkai man, who was wrapped up in his furs and looking splendid to behold.

" 'I can't rightly say,' says he; 'but if you can induce the King to drop all this nonsense about marriage, you'll be doing him and me and yourself a great service.'

" 'That I do believe,' says I. 'But sure, you know, Billy, as well as me, having fought against and for us, that the King and me are nothing more than two of the finest men that God Almighty ever made. Nothing more, I do assure you.'

" 'That may be,' says Billy Fish, 'and yet I should be sorry if it was.' He sinks his head upon his great fur cloak for a minute and thinks. 'King,' says he, 'be you man or God or Devil, I'll stick by you to-day. I have twenty of my men with me, and they will follow me. We'll go to Bashkai until the storm blows over.'

"A little snow had fallen in the night, and everything was white except the greasy fat clouds that blew down and down from the north. Dravot came out

9. "That the sons of God saw the daughters of men that they were fair; and they took them wives of all which they chose" (Genesis 6.2).

with his crown on his head, swinging his arms and stamping his feet, and looking more pleased than Punch.

" 'For the last time, drop it, Dan,' says I, in a whisper. 'Billy Fish here says that there will be a row.'

" 'A row among my people!' says Dravot. 'Not much. Peachey, you're a fool not to get a wife too. Where's the girl?' says he, with a voice as loud as the braying of a jackass. 'Call up all the Chiefs and priests, and let the Emperor see if his wife suits him.'

"There was no need to call any one. They were all there leaning on their guns and spears round the clearing in the centre of the pine wood. A deputation of priests went down to the little temple to bring up the girl, and the horns blew up fit to wake the dead. Billy Fish saunters round and gets as close to Daniel as he could, and behind him stood his twenty men with matchlocks. Not a man of them under six feet. I was next to Dravot, and behind me was twenty men of the regular Army. Up comes the girl, and a strapping wench she was, covered with silver and turquoises, but white as death, and looking back every minute at the priests.

" 'She'll do,' said Dan, looking her over. 'What's to be afraid of, lass? Come and kiss me.' He puts his arm round her. She shuts her eyes, gives a bit of a squeak, and down goes her face in the side of Dan's flaming red beard.

" 'The slut's bitten me!' says he, clapping his hand to his neck, and, sure enough, his hand was red with blood. Billy Fish and two of his matchlock-men catches hold of Dan by the shoulders and drags him into the Bashkai lot, while the priests howl in their lingo,—'Neither God nor Devil, but a man!' I was all taken aback, for a priest cut at me in front, and the Army behind began firing into the Bashkai men.

" 'God A-mighty!' says Dan. 'What is the meaning o' this?'

" 'Come back! Come away!' says Billy Fish. 'Ruin and Mutiny is the matter. We'll break for Bashkai if we can.'

"I tried to give some sort of orders to my men—the men o' the regular Army—but it was no use, so I fired into the brown of 'em with an English Martini and drilled three beggars in a line. The valley was full of shouting, howling creatures, and every soul was shrieking, 'Not a God nor a Devil, but only a man!' The Bashkai troops stuck to Billy Fish all they were worth, but their matchlocks wasn't half as good as the Kabul breech-loaders, and four of them dropped. Dan was bellowing like a bull, for he was very wrathy; and Billy Fish had a hard job to prevent him running out at the crowd.

" 'We can't stand,' says Billy Fish. 'Make a run for it down the valley! The whole place is against us.' The matchlock-men ran, and we went down the valley in spite of Dravot's protestations. He was swearing horribly and crying out that he was a King. The priests rolled great stones on us, and the regular Army fired hard, and there wasn't more than six men, not counting Dan, Billy Fish, and Me, that came down to the bottom of the valley alive.

"Then they stopped firing and the horns in the temple blew again. 'Come away—for Gord's sake come away!' says Billy Fish. 'They'll send runners out to all the villages before ever we get to Bashkai. I can protect you there, but I can't do anything now.'

"My own notion is that Dan began to go mad in his head from that hour. He stared up and down like a stuck pig. Then he was all for walking back alone and killing the priests with his bare hands; which he could have done.

'An Emperor am I,' says Daniel, 'and next year I shall be a Knight of the Queen.'

" 'All right, Dan,' says I; 'but come along now while there's time.'

" 'It's your fault,' says he, 'for not looking after your Army better. There was mutiny in the midst and you didn't know—you damned engine-driving, plate-laying, missionary's-pass-hunting hound!' He sat upon a rock and called me every foul name he could lay tongue to. I was too heart-sick to care, though it was all his foolishness that brought the smash.

" 'I'm sorry, Dan,' says I, 'but there's no accounting for natives. This business is our Fifty-Seven.[1] Maybe we'll make something out of it yet, when we've got to Bashkai.'

" 'Let's get to Bashkai, then,' says Dan, 'and, by God, when I come back here again I'll sweep the valley so there isn't a bug in a blanket left!'

"We walked all that day, and all that night Dan was stumping up and down on the snow, chewing his beard and muttering to himself.

" 'There's no hope o' getting clear,' said Billy Fish. 'The priests will have sent runners to the villages to say that you are only men. Why didn't you stick on as Gods till things was more settled? I'm a dead man,' says Billy Fish, and he throws himself down on the snow and begins to pray to his Gods.

"Next morning we was in a cruel bad country—all up and down, no level ground at all, and no food either. The six Bashkai men looked at Billy Fish hungry-wise as if they wanted to ask something, but they said never a word. At noon we came to the top of a flat mountain all covered with snow, and when we climbed up into it, behold, there was an Army in position waiting in the middle!

" 'The runners have been very quick,' says Billy Fish, with a little bit of a laugh. 'They are waiting for us.'

"Three or four men began to fire from the enemy's side, and a chance shot took Daniel in the calf of the leg. That brought him to his senses. He looks across the snow at the Army, and sees the rifles that we had brought into the country.

" 'We're done for,' says he. 'They are Englishmen, these people,—and it's my blasted nonsense that has brought you to this. Get back, Billy Fish, and take your men away; you've done what you could, and now cut for it. Carnehan,' says he, 'shake hands with me and go along with Billy. Maybe they won't kill you. I'll go and meet 'em alone. It's me that did it. Me, the King!'

" 'Go!' says I. 'Go to Hell, Dan. I'm with you here. Billy Fish, you clear out, and we two will meet those folk.'

" 'I'm a Chief,' says Billy Fish, quite quiet. 'I stay with you. My men can go.'

"The Bashkai fellows didn't wait for a second word, but ran off, and Dan and me and Billy Fish walked across to where the drums were drumming and the horns were horning. It was cold—awful cold. I've got that cold in the back of my head now. There's a lump of it there."

The punkah-coolies had gone to sleep. Two kerosene lamps were blazing in the office, and the perspiration poured down my face and splashed on the blotter as I leaned forward. Carnehan was shivering, and I feared that his

---

1. Mutiny of 1857, when the Bengal Army rebelled against their British officers.

mind might go. I wiped my face, took a fresh grip of the piteously mangled hands, and said: "What happened after that?"

The momentary shift of my eyes had broken the clear current.

"What was you pleased to say?" whined Carnehan. "They took them without any sound. Not a little whisper all along the snow, not though the King knocked down the first man that set hand on him—not though old Peachey fired his last cartridge into the brown of 'em. Not a single solitary sound did those swines make. They just closed up tight, and I tell you their furs stunk. There was a man called Billy Fish, a good friend of us all, and they cut his throat, Sir, then and there, like a pig; and the King kicks up the bloody snow and says:—'We've had a dashed fine run for our money. What's coming next?' But Peachey, Peachey Taliaferro, I tell you, Sir, in confidence as betwixt two friends, he lost his head, Sir. No, he didn't neither. The King lost his head, so he did, all along o' one of those cunning rope-bridges. Kindly let me have the paper-cutter, Sir. It tilted this way. They marched him a mile across that snow to a rope-bridge over a ravine with a river at the bottom. You may have seen such. They prodded him behind like an ox. 'Damn your eyes!' says the King. 'D'you suppose I can't die like a gentleman?' He turns to Peachey—Peachey that was crying like a child. 'I've brought you to this, Peachey,' says he. 'Brought you out of your happy life to be killed in Kafiristan, where you was late Commander-in-Chief of the Emperor's forces. Say you forgive me, Peachey.' 'I do,' says Peachey. 'Fully and freely do I forgive you, Dan.' 'Shake hands, Peachey,' says he. 'I'm going now. Out he goes, looking neither right nor left, and when he was plumb in the middle of those dizzy dancing ropes, 'Cut, you beggars,' he shouts; and they cut, and old Dan fell, turning round and round and round twenty thousand miles, for he took half an hour to fall till he struck the water, and I could see his body caught on a rock with the gold crown close beside.

"But do you know what they did to Peachey between two pine trees? They crucified him, Sir, as Peachey's hand will show. They used wooden pegs for his hands and his feet; and he didn't die. He hung there and screamed, and they took him down next day, and said it was a miracle that he wasn't dead. They took him down—poor old Peachey that hadn't done them any harm—that hadn't done them any . . . "

He rocked to and fro and wept bitterly, wiping his eyes with the back of his scarred hands and moaning like a child for some ten minutes.

"They was cruel enough to feed him up in the temple, because they said he was more of a God than old Daniel that was a man. Then they turned him out on the snow, and told him to go home, and Peachey came home in about a year, begging along the roads quite safe; for Daniel Dravot he walked before and said:—'Come along, Peachey. It's a big thing we're doing.' The mountains they danced at night, and the mountains they tried to fall on Peachey's head, but Dan he held up his hand, and Peachey came along bent double. He never let go of Dan's hand, and he never let go of Dan's head. They gave it to him as a present in the temple, to remind him not to come again, and though the crown was pure gold, and Peachey was starving, never would Peachey sell the same. You knew Dravot, Sir! You knew Right Worshipful Brother Dravot! Look at him now!"

He fumbled in the mass of rags round his bent waist; brought out a black horsehair bag embroidered with silver thread; and shook therefrom on to my table—the dried, withered head of Daniel Dravot! The morning sun that had long been paling the lamps struck the red beard and blind, sunken eyes; struck, too, a heavy circlet of gold studded with raw turquoises, that Carnehan placed tenderly on the battered temples.

"You behold now," said Carnehan, "the Emperor in his habit as he lived[2]—the King of Kafiristan with his crown upon his head. Poor old Daniel that was a monarch once!"

I shuddered, for, in spite of defacements manifold, I recognized the head of the man of Marwar Junction. Carnehan rose to go. I attempted to stop him. He was not fit to walk abroad. "Let me take away the whiskey, and give me a little money," he gasped. "I was a King once. I'll go to the Deputy Commissioner and ask to set in the Poorhouse till I get my health. No, thank you, I can't wait till you get a carriage for me. I've urgent private affairs—in the south—at Marwar."

He shambled out of the office and departed in the direction of the Deputy Commissioner's house. That day at noon I had occasion to go down the blinding hot Mall, and I saw a crooked man crawling along the white dust of the roadside, his hat in his hand, quavering dolorously after the fashion of street-singers at Home. There was not a soul in sight, and he was out of all possible earshot of the houses. And he sang through his nose, turning his head from right to left:

> "The Son of Man goes forth to war,
>   A golden crown to gain;
> His blood-red banner streams afar—
>   Who follows in his train?"[3]

I waited to hear no more, but put the poor wretch into my carriage and drove him off to the nearest missionary for eventual transfer to the Asylum. He repeated the hymn twice while he was with me, whom he did not in the least recognize, and I left him singing it to the missionary.

Two days later I inquired after his welfare of the Superintendent of the Asylum.

"He was admitted suffering from sunstroke. He died early yesterday morning," said the Superintendent. "Is it true that he was half an hour bareheaded in the sun at midday?"

"Yes," said I, "but do you happen to know if he had anything upon him by any chance when he died?"

"Not to my knowledge," said the Superintendent.

And there the matter rests.

1888

Danny Deever

"What are the bugles blowin' for?" said Files-on-Parade.°   *army private*
"To turn you out, to turn you out," the Color-Sergeant[1] said.

---

2. Allusion to Hamlet's description of his father's ghost, "My father, in his habit as he lived" (*Hamlet* 3.4.135).
3. A well-known hymn, corrected in later editions

to the actual words of the first line: "The Son of God goes forth to war."
1. High-ranking noncommissioned officer.

"What makes you look so white, so white?" said Files-on-Parade.
"I'm dreadin' what I've got to watch," the Color-Sergeant said.
5   For they're hangin' Danny Deever, you can hear the Dead March play,
The regiment's in 'ollow square[2]—they're hangin' him today;
They've taken of his buttons off an' cut his stripes[3] away,
An they're hangin' Danny Deever in the mornin'.

"What makes the rear rank breathe so 'ard?" said Files-on-Parade.
10 "It's bitter cold, it's bitter cold," the Color-Sergeant said.
"What makes that front-rank man fall down?" said Files-on-Parade.
"A touch o' sun, a touch o' sun," the Color-Sergeant said.
    They are hangin' Danny Deever, they are marchin' of 'im round,
They 'ave 'alted Danny Deever by 'is coffin on the ground;
15 An' 'e'll swing in 'arf a minute for a sneakin' shootin' hound—
O they're hangin' Danny Deever in the mornin'!

" 'Is cot was right-'and cot to mine," said Files-on-Parade.
" 'E's sleepin' out an' far tonight," the Color-Sergeant said.
"I've drunk 'is beer a score o' times," said Files-on-Parade.
20 " 'E's drinkin bitter beer[4] alone," the Color-Sergeant said.
    They are hangin' Danny Deever, you must mark 'im to 'is place,
For 'e shot a comrade sleepin'—you must look 'im in the face;
Nine 'undred of 'is county[5] an' the Regiment's disgrace,
While they're hangin' Danny Deever in the mornin'.

25 "What's that so black agin the sun?" said Files-on-Parade.
"It's Danny fightin' 'ard for life," the Color-Sergeant said.
"What's that that whimpers over'ead?" said Files-on-Parade.
"It's Danny's soul that's passin' now," the Color-Sergeant said.
    For they're done with Danny Deever, you can 'ear the quickstep play,
30 The regiment's in column, an' they're marchin' us away;
Ho! the young recruits are shakin', an' they'll want their beer today,
After hangin' Danny Deever in the mornin'.

1890

The Widow at Windsor

    'Ave you 'eard o' the Widow at Windsor
      With a hairy gold crown on 'er 'ead?
    She 'as ships on the foam—she 'as millions at 'ome,
      An' she pays us poor beggars in red.
5   (Ow, poor beggars in red!)
    There's 'er nick[1] on the cavalry 'orses,
      There's 'er mark[2] on the medical stores—

2. Ceremonial formation: the troops line four sides of a parade square, facing inward.
3. Chevrons denoting rank, worn by corporals and sergeants on the sleeves of their tunics.
4. Or simply "bitter," a favorite variety of beer drunk in English pubs. The word *bitter* thus becomes a grim pun.

5. English regiments often bear the name of a particular county from which most of its men have been recruited (e.g., the Lancashire Fusiliers).
1. A nick on one of their hoofs identified army horses as property of the Crown.
2. The queen's mark: "V.R.I." (*Victoria Regina et Imperatrix*, "Victoria Queen and Empress").

An' 'er troopers° you'll find with a fair wind be'ind　　　　*troopships*
　　That takes us to various wars.
10　　　　(Poor beggars!—barbarious wars!)
　　　　　Then 'ere's to the Widow at Windsor,
　　　　　　An' 'ere's to the stores an' the guns,
　　　　　The men an' the 'orses what makes up the forces
　　　　　　O' Missis Victorier's sons.
15　　　　(Poor beggars! Victorier's sons!)

Walk wide o' the Widow at Windsor,
　　For 'alf o' Creation she owns:
We 'ave bought 'er the same with the sword an' the flame,
　　An' we've salted it down with our bones.
20　　　(Poor beggars!—it's blue with our bones!)
Hands off o' the sons o' the widow,
　　Hands off o' the goods in 'er shop,
For the kings must come down an' the emperors frown
　　When the Widow at Windsor says "Stop!"
25　　　(Poor beggars!—we're sent to say "Stop!")
　　　　　Then 'ere's to the Lodge o' the Widow,³
　　　　　　From the Pole to the Tropics it runs—
　　　　　To the Lodge that we tile with the rank an' the file,
　　　　　　An' open in form with the guns.
30　　　(Poor beggars!—it's always they guns!)

We 'ave 'eard o' the Widow at Windsor,
　　It's safest to leave 'er alone:
For 'er sentries we stand by the sea an' the land
　　Wherever the bugles are blown.
35　　　(Poor beggars!—an' don't we get blown!)
Take 'old o' the Wings o' the Mornin',
　　An' flop round the earth till you're dead;
But you won't get away from the tune that they play
　　To the bloomin' old rag over'ead.
40　　　(Poor beggars!—it's 'ot over'ead!)
　　　　　Then 'ere's to the sons o' the Widow,
　　　　　　Wherever, 'owever they roam.
　　　　　'Ere's all they desire, an' if they require
　　　　　　A speedy return to their 'ome.
45　　　(Poor beggars!—they'll never see 'ome!)

　　　　　　　　　　　　　　　　　　　　　　　　　1892

The Ladies

I've taken my fun where I've found it;
　　I've rogued an' I've ranged in my time;
I've 'ad my pickin' o' sweethearts,
　　An' four o' the lot was prime.

---

3. One of the lodges in the forest surrounding Windsor Castle where the queen and her family could relax in seclusion.

5   One was an 'arf-caste widow,
     One was a woman at Prome,[1]
  One was the wife of a *jemadar-sais,*°   *head groom*
     An' one is a girl at 'ome.

Now I aren't no 'and with the ladies,
10   *For, takin' 'em all along,*
You never can say till you've tried 'em,
     An' then you are like to be wrong.
There's times when you'll think that you mightn't,
     There's times when you'll know that you might;
15 *But the things you will learn from the Yellow an' Brown,*
     They'll 'elp you a lot with the White!

I was a young un at 'Oogli,[2]
     Shy as a girl to begin;
Aggie de Castrer she made me,
20   An' Aggie was clever as sin;
Older than me, but my first un—
     More like a mother she were—
Showed me the way to promotion an' pay,
     An' I learned about women from 'er!

25 Then I was ordered to Burma,
     Actin' in charge o' Bazar,[3]
An' I got me a tiddy° live 'eathen   *tiny*
     Through buyin' supplies off 'er pa.
Funny an' yellow an' faithful—
30   Doll in a teacup she were—
But we lived on the square, like a true-married pair,
     An' I learned about women from 'er!

Then we was shifted to Neemuch[4]
     (Or I might ha' been keepin' 'er now),
35 An' I took with a shiny she-devil,
     The wife of a nigger at Mhow;
'Taught me the gypsy-folks' *bolee;*[5]
     Kind o' volcano she were,
For she knifed me one night 'cause I wished she was white,
40   And I learned about women from 'er!

Then I come 'ome in a trooper,
     'Long of a kid o' sixteen—
'Girl from a convent at Meerut,
     The straightest I ever 'ave seen.
45 Love at first sight was 'er trouble,
     She didn't know what it were;
An' I wouldn't do such, 'cause I liked 'er too much,
     But—I learned about women from 'er!

1. Town in Burma.
2. Hoogli, a town near Calcutta.
3. Shop selling provisions to troops.

4. Nimach, Mhow (line 36), and Meerut (line 43) are towns in India.
5. Slang.

I've taken my fun where I've found it,
50   An' now I must pay for my fun,
For the more you 'ave known o' the others
    The less will you settle to one;
An' the end of it's sittin' and thinkin',
    An' dreamin' Hell-fires to see;
55 So be warned by my lot (which I know you will not),
    An' learn about women from me!

What did the Colonel's Lady think?
    Nobody never knew.
Somebody asked the Sergeant's Wife,
60   *An' she told 'em true!*
When you get to a man in the case,
    They're like as a row of pins—
For the Colonel's Lady an' Judy O'Grady
    Are sisters under their skins!

1896

Recessional[1]

1897

God of our fathers, known of old—
    Lord of our far-flung battle-line—
Beneath whose awful Hand we hold
    Dominion over palm and pine—
5   Lord God of Hosts, be with us yet
Lest we forget—lest we forget!

The tumult and the shouting dies—
    The Captains and the Kings depart—
Still stands Thine ancient Sacrifice,
10   An humble and a contrite heart.[2]
Lord God of Hosts, be with us yet,
Lest we forget—lest we forget!

Far-called, our navies melt away—
    On dune and headland sinks the fire[3]—
15 Lo, all our pomp of yesterday
    Is one with Nineveh and Tyre![4]
Judge of the Nations, spare us yet,
Lest we forget—lest we forget!

1. A hymn sung as the clergy and choir leave a church in procession at the end of a service. Kipling's hymn was written on the occasion of the Jubilee celebrations honoring the sixtieth anniversary of Queen Victoria's reign, celebrations that had prompted a good deal of boasting in the press about the greatness of her empire. *Recessional* was first published in the *Times,* and Kipling refused to accept any payment for its publication, then or later.

2. Cf. Psalm 51.17: "The sacrifices of God are a broken spirit: a broken and a contrite heart, O God, thou wilt not despise."
3. Bonfires were lit on high ground all over Britain on the night of the Jubilee.
4. Once capitals of great empires. The ruins of Nineveh, in Assyria, were discovered buried in desert sands by British archaeologists in the 1850s. Tyre, in Phoenicia, had dwindled into a small Lebanese town.

If, drunk with sight of power, we loose
20   Wild tongues that have not Thee in awe—
Such boasting as the Gentiles use
   Or lesser breeds without the Law[5]—
Lord God of Hosts, be with us yet,
Lest we forget—lest we forget!

25 For heathen heart that puts her trust
   In reeking tube and iron shard—
All valiant dust that builds on dust,
   And guarding calls not Thee to guard—
For frantic boast and foolish word,
30 Thy mercy on Thy People, Lord!

1897   1897, 1899

The Hyenas

After the burial-parties leave
   And the baffled kites[1] have fled;
The wise hyenas come out at eve
   To take account of our dead.

5 How he died and why he died
   Troubles them not a whit.
They snout the bushes and stones aside
   And dig till they come to it.

They are only resolute they shall eat
10   That they and their mates may thrive,
And they know that the dead are safer meat
   Than the weakest thing alive.

(For a goat may butt, and a worm may sting,
   And a child will sometimes stand;
15 But a poor dead soldier of the king
   Can never lift a hand.)

They whoop and halloo and scatter the dirt
   Until their tushes° white   *canine teeth*
Take good hold in the army shirt,
20   And tug the corpse to light,

And the pitiful face is shown again
   For an instant ere they close;
But it is not discovered to living men—
   Only to God and to those

5. Cf. Romans 2.14: "For when the Gentiles, which have not the law, do by nature the things contained in the law, these, having not the law, are a law unto themselves."
1. Birds of prey that feed on dead bodies.

25 Who, being soulless, are free from shame,
Whatever meat they may find.
Nor do they defile the dead man's name—
That is reserved for his kind.

1918, 1919

ERNEST DOWSON
1867–1900

Ernest Christopher Dowson spent much of his childhood traveling with his father on the Continent, mostly in France. His education was thus irregular and informal, but he acquired a thorough knowledge of French and of his favorite French writers—Gustave Flaubert, Honoré de Balzac, and Paul Verlaine—and a good knowledge of Latin poetry, especially Catullus, Propertius, and Horace. Dowson went to Oxford in 1886, but he did not take to regular academic instruction and left after a year. Though nominally assisting his father to manage a dock in the London district of Limehouse, Dowson spent most of his time writing poetry, stories, and essays and talking with Lionel Johnson, W. B. Yeats, and other members of The Rhymers' Club, in which he played a prominent part. Between 1890 and 1894 Dowson, though leading the irregular life of so many of the nineties poets, produced his best work, and his volume *Verses* came out in 1896. Late nights and excessive drinking impaired a constitution already threatened by tuberculosis. He moved to France in 1894, making a living by translating from the French for an English publisher but growing steadily worse in health. After his return to England, he was discovered in a dying condition by a friend, who took him to his home and nursed him until his death six weeks later.

Dowson was a member of what Yeats called "the tragic generation" of poets in the nineties who seemed to be driven by their own restless energies to dissipation and premature death. As a poet, he was considerably influenced by Swinburne (whose feverish emotional tone he often captures very skillfully). He experimented with a variety of meters, and in *Cynara* used the alexandrine as the normal line of a six-line stanza in a manner more common in French than in English poetry. He was also especially interested in the work of the French symbolist poets and in their theories of verbal suggestiveness and of poetry as incantation: he believed (as he once wrote in a letter) that a finer poetry could sometimes be achieved by "mere sound and music, with just a suggestion of sense."

Cynara

Non sum qualis eram bonae sub regno Cynarae[1]

Last night, ah, yesternight, betwixt her lips and mine
There fell thy shadow, Cynara! thy breath was shed

---

1. I am not as I was under the reign of the good Cynara (Latin). This is the third line and part of the fourth of an ode of Horace (4.1) in which the poet pleads with Venus to stop tormenting him with love, since he is growing old and is no longer what he was when under the sway of Cynara (*Sin-ah-rah*), the girl he used to love. Of Dowson's

"Cynara" Yeats later wrote: "Dowson, who seemed to drink so little and had so much dignity and reserve, was breaking his heart for the daughter of the keeper of an Italian eating house, in dissipation and drink." Dowson's "Cynara" was, in fact, a Polish woman by the name of Adelaide Foltino-wicz.

Upon my soul between the kisses and the wine;
And I was desolate and sick of an old passion,
5   Yea, I was desolate and bowed my head:
I have been faithful to thee, Cynara! in my fashion.

All night upon mine heart I felt her warm heart beat,
Night-long within mine arms in love and sleep she lay;
Surely the kisses of her bought red mouth were sweet;
10   But I was desolate and sick of an old passion,
         When I awoke and found the dawn was gray:
I have been faithful to thee, Cynara! in my fashion.

I have forgot much, Cynara! gone with the wind,
Flung roses, roses riotously with the throng,
15   Dancing, to put thy pale, lost lilies out of mind;
But I was desolate and sick of an old passion,
         Yea, all the time, because the dance was long:
I have been faithful to thee, Cynara! in my fashion.

I cried for madder music and for stronger wine,
20   But when the feast is finished and the lamps expire,
Then falls thy shadow, Cynara! the night is thine;
And I am desolate and sick of an old passion,
         Yea, hungry for the lips of my desire:
I have been faithful to thee, Cynara! in my fashion.

                                                      1891, 1896

They Are Not Long

Vitae summa brevis spem nos vetat incohare longam.[1]

They are not long, the weeping and the laughter,
         Love and desire and hate:
I think they have no portion in us after
         We pass the gate.

5   They are not long, the days of wine and roses:
         Out of a misty dream
Our path emerges for a while, then closes
         Within a dream.

                                                      1896

Carthusians[1]

Through what long heaviness, assayed in what strange fire,
      Have these white monks been brought into the way of peace,

1. The shortness of life prevents us from entertaining far-off hopes (Latin; Horace, *Odes* 1.4).
1. A monastic order founded in 1084 at Chartreuse in the French Alps. The Carthusian regimen
is stringently ascetic; each white-robed monk is a
silent solitary except when participating in services
of worship. Cf. Arnold, *Stanzas from the Grande
Chartreuse* (p. 1493).

Despising the world's wisdom and the world's desire,
  Which from the body of this death bring no release?

5 Within their austere walls no voices penetrate;
  A sacred silence only, as of death, obtains;
Nothing finds entry here of loud or passionate;
  This quiet is the exceeding profit of their pains.

From many lands they came, in divers fiery ways;
10   Each knew at last the vanity of earthly joys;
And one was crowned with thorns, and one was crowned with bays,[2]
  And each was tired at last of the world's foolish noise.

It was not theirs with Dominic to preach Gôd's holy wrath,
  They were too stern to bear sweet Francis'[3] gentle sway;
15 Theirs was a higher calling and a steeper path,
  To dwell alone with Christ, to meditate and pray.

A cloistered company, they are companionless,
  None knoweth here the secret of his brother's heart:
They are but come together for more loneliness,
20   Whose bond is solitude and silence all their part.

O beatific life! Who is there shall gainsay,
  Your great refusal's victory, your little loss,
Deserting vanity for the more perfect way,
  The sweeter service of the most dolorous Cross.

25 Ye shall prevail at last! Surely ye shall prevail!
  Your silence and austerity shall win at last:
Desire and mirth, the world's ephemeral lights shall fail,
  The sweet star of your queen is never overcast.

We fling up flowers and laugh, we laugh across the wine;
30   With wine we dull our souls and careful strains of art;
Our cups are polished skulls round which the roses twine:
  None dares to look at Death who leers and lurks apart.

Move on, white company, whom that has not sufficed!
  Our viols cease, our wine is death, our roses fail:
35 Pray for our heedlessness, O dwellers with the Christ!
  Though the world fall apart, surely ye shall prevail.

1891   1899

<hr />

2. A crown of bay leaves (or laurel) was awarded
to poets whose work was admired.
3. Saint Francis of Assisi, founder of the Franciscan order of friars in 1209, was a gentle and
tender-spirited leader who worked and preached
among the poor. Saint Dominic, founder of the
Dominican order of friars (1215), whose preaching
was especially directed to converting heathens to
Christianity.

Poems in Process

In all ages, some poets have claimed that their poems were not willed but were inspired, whether by a muse, by divine visitation, or by sudden emergence from the author's subconscious mind. But as the poet Richard Aldington has remarked, "genius is not enough; one must also work." The working manuscripts of the greatest writers show that, however involuntary the origin of a poem, vision was usually followed by laborious revision before the work achieved the seeming inevitability of its final form.

Although some earlier poetic manuscripts have survived, it was not until the nineteenth century that the working drafts of poets began to be widely preserved, and so remain abundantly available. The examples from major poets that are transcribed here represent various stages in the composition of a poem, and a variety of procedures by individual poets. The selections from Blake, Byron, Shelley, and Keats are drafts that were written, emended, crossed out, and rewritten in the heat of first invention; while poems by Wordsworth, Hopkins, and Yeats are shown in successive stages of revision over an extended period of time. Shelley's *O World, O Life, O Time* originated in a few key nouns, together with an abstract rhythmic pattern that was only later fleshed out with words, while Yeats's *After Long Silence* began as a prose sketch that gradually and laboriously was reshaped into a metric and stanzaic form. Still other poems—Tennyson's *The Lady of Shalott*, Yeats's *The Sorrow of Love*—were subjected to radical revision long after the initial versions had been committed to print. In all these examples we look on as poets, no matter how rapidly they achieve a result they are willing to let stand, carry on their inevitably tentative efforts to meet the multiple requirements of meaning, syntax, meter, sound pattern, and the constraints imposed by a chosen stanza. And because these are all very good poets, the seeming conflict between the necessities of significance and form results not in the distortion but in the perfecting of the poetic statement.

Our transcriptions from the poets' drafts attempt to reproduce, as accurately as the change from script to print will allow, the appearance of the original manuscript page. A poet's first attempt at a line or phrase is reproduced in larger type, the emendations in smaller type. The line numbers in the headings that identify an excerpt are those of the final form of the complete poem.

SELECTED BIBLIOGRAPHY

Autograph Poetry in the English Language, 2 vols., 1973, compiled by P. J. Croft, reproduces and transcribes one or more pages of manuscript in the poet's own hand, from the 14th century to the late twentieth century. Volume 1 includes Blake and Burns; volume 2 includes many of the other poets represented in this volume of *The Norton Anthology of English Literature*, from Wordsworth to Dylan Thomas. Books that discuss the process of composition and revision, with examples from the manuscripts and printed versions of poems, are Charles D. Abbott, ed., *Poets at Work*, 1948; Phyllis Bartlett, *Poems in Process*, 1951; A. F. Scott, *The Poet's Craft*, 1957; George Bornstein, *Poetic Remaking: The Art of Browning, Yeats, and Pound*, 1988. In

Word for Word: A Study of Authors' Alterations, 1965, Wallace Hildick analyzes the composition of prose fiction as well as poems; a shorter version, Word for Word: The Rewriting of Fiction, 1965, discusses the revision of novels by George Eliot, Samuel Butler, Hardy, Lawrence, James, and Woolf. Byron's "Don Juan," ed. T. G. Steffan and W. W. Pratt, 4 vols., 1957, transcribes the manuscript drafts; the Cornell Wordsworth, in process, reproduces, transcribes, and discusses various versions of Wordsworth's poems from the first manuscript drafts to the final publication in his lifetime, and the Cornell Yeats, also in process, does the same for Yeats. For facsim-

iles and transcripts of Keats's poems, see John Keats: Poetry Manuscripts at Harvard, ed. Jack Stillinger, 1990. Jon Stallworthy, Between the Lines: Yeats's Poetry in the Making, 1963, reproduces and analyzes the sequential drafts of a number of Yeats's major poems. Valerie Eliot has edited T. S. Eliot's The Waste Land: A Facsimile and Transcript of the Original Drafts Including the Annotations of Ezra Pound, 1971, while Dame Helen Gardner has transcribed and analyzed the manuscript drafts of Eliot's Four Quartets in The Composition of Four Quartets, 1978.

WILLIAM BLAKE
The Tyger[1]

[First Draft]

The Tyger

1   Tyger Tyger burning bright
In the forests of the night
What immortal hand or eye
~~Dare~~ Could frame thy fearful symmetry

       Burnt in
2   ~~In what~~ distant deeps or skies
~~The cruel Burnt the~~ fire of thine eyes
On what wings dare he aspire
What the hand dare sieze the fire

3   And what shoulder & what art
Could twist the sinews of thy heart
And when thy heart began to beat
What dread hand & what dread feet

~~Could fetch it from the furnace deep~~
~~And in thy horrid ribs dare steep~~
~~In the well of sanguine woe~~
~~In what clay & what mould~~
~~Were thy eyes of fury rolld~~

    ~~Where~~   ~~where~~
4   ~~What~~ the hammer ~~what~~ the chain
In what furnace was thy brain

1. These drafts have been taken from a notebook used by William Blake, called the Rossetti MS because it was once owned by Dante Gabriel Rossetti, the Victorian poet and painter; David V. Erd-man's edition of The Notebook of William Blake (1973) contains a photographic facsimile. The stanza and line numbers were written by Blake in the manuscript.

dread grasp

What the anvil what the ~~arm arm~~ ~~grasp~~ ~~clasp~~

Dare ~~Could~~ its deadly terrors ~~clasp~~ ~~grasp~~ clasp

6 Tyger Tyger burning bright
In the forests of the night
What immortal hand & eye
frame
Dare ~~form~~ thy fearful symmetry

[*Trial Stanzas*]

Burnt in distant deeps of skies
The cruel fire of thine eye,
Could heart descend or wings aspire
What the hand dare sieze the fire

dare he ~~smile laugh~~
5 3 And ~~did he laugh~~ his work to see

ankle
~~What the shoulder what the knee~~

Dare
4 ~~Did~~ he who made the lamb make thee
1 When the stars threw down their spears
2 And waterd heaven with their tears

[*Second Full Draft*]

Tyger Tyger burning bright
In the forests of the night
What Immortal hand & eye
Dare frame thy fearful symmetry

And what shoulder & what art
Could twist the sinews of thy heart
And when thy heart began to beat
What dread hand & what dread feet

When the stars threw down their spears
And waterd heaven with their tears
Did he smile his work to see
Did he who made the lamb make thee

Tyger Tyger burning bright
In the forests of the night
What immortal hand & eye
Dare frame thy fearful symmetry

[*Final Version, 1794*][2]

The Tyger

Tyger Tyger, burning bright,
In the forests of the night;
What immortal hand or eye,
Could frame thy fearful symmetry?

In what distant deeps or skies
Burnt the fire of thine eyes!
On what wings dare he aspire?
What the hand, dare sieze the fire?

And what shoulder, & what art,
Could twist the sinews of thy heart?
And when thy heart began to beat,
What dread hand? & what dread feet?

What the hammer? what the chain,
In what furnace was thy brain?
What the anvil? what dread grasp,
Dare its deadly terrors clasp?

When the stars threw down their spears
And water'd heaven with their tears:
Did he smile his work to see?
Did he who made the Lamb make thee?

Tyger, Tyger burning bright,
In the forests of the night:
What immortal hand or eye,
Dare frame thy fearful symmetry?

WILLIAM WORDSWORTH
She dwelt among the untrodden ways

[*Version in a Letter to Coleridge,
December 1798 or January 1799*][1]

My hope was one, from cities far
Nursed on a lonesome heath:
Her lips were red as roses are,
Her hair a woodbine wreath.

She lived among the untrodden ways
Beside the springs of Dove,

2. As published in *Songs of Experience*.
1. Printed in Ernest de Selincourt's *Early Letters
of William and Dorothy Wordsworth* (1935). By
deleting two stanzas, and making a few verbal
changes, Wordsworth achieved the terse published
form of his great dirge.

A maid whom there were none to praise,
   And very few to love;

A violet by a mossy stone
   Half-hidden from the eye!
Fair as a star when only one
   Is shining in the sky!

And she was graceful as the broom
   That flowers by Carron's side;[2]
But slow distemper checked her bloom,
   And on the Heath she died.

Long time before her head lay low
   Dead to the world was she:
But now she's in her grave, and Oh!
   The difference to me!

[*Final Version, 1800*][3]

Song

She dwelt among th' untrodden ways
   Beside the springs of Dove,
A Maid whom there were none to praise
   And very few to love.

A Violet by a mossy stone
   Half-hidden from the Eye!
—Fair, as a star when only one
   Is shining in the sky!

She *liv'd* unknown, and few could know
   When Lucy ceas'd to be;
But she is in her Grave, and Oh!
   The difference to me.

LORD BYRON
From Don Juan[1]

[*First Draft: Canto 3, Stanza 9*]

~~Life is a play and men~~
All tragedies are finished by a death,
All Comedies are ended by a marriage,
~~For Life can go no further.~~

2. The Carron is a river in northwestern Scotland. "Broom" (preceding line) is a shrub with long slender branches and yellow flowers.
3. As published in the second edition of *Lyrical Ballads*.

1. Reproduced from transcripts made of Byron's manuscripts in T. G. Steffan and W. W. Pratt, *Byron's "Don Juan"* (1957). The stanzas were published by Byron in their emended form.

~~These two form the last gasp of Passion's breath~~
~~All further is a blank—I won't disparage~~
~~That holy state—but certainly beneath~~
~~The Sun—of human things~~
~~These two are levellers, and human breath~~
~~So~~ ~~These point the epigram of human breath;~~
~~Or any~~ The future states of both are left to faith,
~~Though Life and love I like not to disparage~~
~~The~~ For authors ~~think~~ description might disparage
        fear
~~'Tis strange that poets never try to wreathe~~ [sic?]
~~With cith~~ ~~'Tis strange that poets of the Catholic faith~~
~~Neer go beyond—and—but seem to dread miscarriage~~
~~So dramas close with death or settlement for life~~
~~Veiling~~ ~~Leaving the future states of Love and Life~~
~~The paradise beyond like that of life~~
~~And neer describing either~~
~~To more conjecture of a devil~~ ~~and~~ ~~or wife~~
~~And don't say much of paradise or wife~~
The worlds to come of both—~~&~~ or fall beneath,
And ~~all~~ ~~both the worlds would blame them for miscarriage~~
And then both worlds would punish their miscarriage—
~~So leaving both with priest & prayerbook ready~~
So leaving ~~clerg both a~~ each their Priest and prayerbook ready,
They say no more of death or of the Lady.

[*First Draft: Canto 14, Stanza 95*]

        quote   seldom
Alas! ~~I speak by~~ Experience—~~never~~ yet
~~I had a paramour—and I've had many—~~
             ~~some small~~
~~To whom I did not cause a deep~~ regret—
~~Whom I had not some reason to~~ regret
~~For Whom—I did not feel myself~~ a Zany—
Alas! by all experience, seldom yet
(I merely quote what I have heard from many)
Had lovers not some reason to regret
The passion which made Solomon a Zany.
~~I also had a wife—~~not to forget—
I've also seen some wives—not to forget—
The marriage state—the best or worst of any—
    were   paragons
Who ~~was~~ the very ~~paragon~~ of wives,
Yet made the misery of ~~both our~~ lives.
        ~~many~~
        ~~several~~
        ~~of~~ at least two

PERCY BYSSHE SHELLEY

The three stages of this poem labeled "First Draft" are scattered through one of Shelley's notebooks, now in the Huntington Library, San Marino, California; these drafts have been transcribed and analyzed by Bennett Weaver, "Shelley Works Out the Rhythm of *A Lament*," *PMLA* 47 (1932): 570–76. They show Shelley working with fragmentary words and phrases, and simultaneously with a wordless pattern of pulses that marked out the meter of the single lines and the shape of the lyric stanzas. Shelley left this draft unfinished.

Apparently at some later time, Shelley returned to the poem and wrote what is here called the "Second Draft"; from this he then made, on a second page, a revised fair copy that provided the text that Mary Shelley published in 1824, after the poet's death. These two manuscript pages are now in the Bodleian Library, Oxford; the first page is photographically reproduced and discussed by John Carter and John Sparrow, "Shelley, Swinburne, and Housman," *Times Literary Supplement*, November 21, 1968, pp. 1318–19.

O World, O Life, O Time

[*First Draft, Stage 1*]

Ah time, oh night, oh day
~~Ni nal ni na, na ni~~
~~Ni na ni na, ni na~~
Oh life O death, O time
    Time a di
~~Never Time~~
Ah time, a time O-time
    ~~Time!~~

[*First Draft, Stage 2*]

Oh time, oh night oh day
~~O day oh night, alas~~
  ~~O~~ Death time night ~~oh~~
Oh, Time
Oh time o night oh day

[*First Draft, Stage 3*]

Na na, na na ná na
Nă nă na na na—nă nă
  Nă nă nă nă nā nā
Na na nă nă nâ ă na

Na na na—nă nă—na na
  Na na na na—na na na na na
Na na na na na.
    Na na
Na na na na na
    Na na
Na na na na na ˇ na!

Oh time, oh night, o day

       alas
  O day ~~serenest,~~ o day
  O day alas the day
That thou shouldst sleep when we awake to say

O time time—o death—o day
                for
O day, o death life is far from thee
O thou wert never free
For death is now with thee
~~And life is far from~~
O death, o day for life is far from thee

[*Second Draft*][1]

Out of the day & night   I am
A joy has taken flight   despair
Fresh spring & summer   & winter hoar
Fill my faint heart with grief, but with
                                            delight
        No more—o never more!

~~Wo~~
        O World, o life, o time
        ~~Will ye~~   On whose last steps I climb
Trembling at those which I have trod[2] before
When will return the glory of yr prime
        No more   Oh never more

        Out of the day & night
        A joy has taken flight—
                        autumn
~~From~~ Green spring, & ~~summer gra~~[3] & winter hoar

[FAIR COPY]

O World   o Life   o Time
On whose last steps I climb
Trembling at that where I had stood before
When will return the glory of yr prime?
        No more, o never more

                    2
        Out of the day & night
        A joy has taken flight
Fresh spring & summer   [4] & winter hoar

1. Shelley apparently wrote the first stanza of this draft low down on the page, and ran out of space after crowding in the third line of the second stanza; he then, in a lighter ink, wrote a revised form of the whole of the second stanza at the top of the page. In this revision, he left a space after "summer" in line 3, indicating that he planned an insertion that would fill out the four-foot meter of this line, and so make it match the five feet in the corresponding line of the first stanza.

In the upper right-hand corner of this manuscript page Shelley wrote "I am despair"—seemingly to express his bleak mood at the time he wrote the poem.

For this draft and information, and for the transcript of the fair copy that follows, the editors are indebted to Donald H. Reiman.

2. Shelley at first wrote "trod," then overwrote that with "stood." In the following line, Shelley at first wrote "yr," then overwrote "thy."
3. Not clearly legible; it is either "gra" or "gre." A difference in the ink from the rest of the line indicates that Shelley, having left a blank space, later started to fill it in, but thought better of it and crossed out the fragmentary insertion.
4. This fair copy of the second draft retains, and even enlarges, the blank space, indicating that Shelley still hasn't made up his mind what to insert after the word "summer." We may speculate, by reference to the fragmentary version of this stanza in the second draft, that he had in mind as possibilities either an adjective, "gray" or "green," or else the noun "autumn." Mary Shelley closed up this space when she published the poem in 1824, with

Move my faint heart with grief but with delight
No more, o, never more

JOHN KEATS
From The Eve of St. Agnes[1]

[*Stanza 26*]

But soon his heart revives—her prayers said
She lays aside her neck   pearled
                strips her hair of all its ∧ wreathes pearl
Unclasps her bosom jewels
And twist it in one knot upon her head

                                soon
But soon his heart revives—her praying done,
Of all its wreathed pearl she strips her hair
Unclasps her warmed jewels one by one

              her bursting
Loosens the boddice from her
              her Boddice lace string
              her Boddice and her bosom bar
              her

[HERE KEATS BEGINS A NEW SHEET]

Loosens her fragrant boddice and doth bare
Her

26

Anon
But soon his heart revives—her praying done,
                          frees:
Of all its wreathe'd pearl her hair she strips
Unclasps her warmed jewels one by one

                          by degrees
                    to her knees
Loosens her fragrant boddice: and down slips
Her sweet attire falls light creeps down by

          creeps rusteling to her knees
          Mermaid   in sea weed
Half hidden like a Syren of the Sea
And more melodious

              dreaming
She stands awhile in ∧ thought; and sees

                  on
In fancy fair Saint Agnes in her bed
But dares not look behind or all the charm is fl dead

the result that editors, following her version, have until very recently printed this line as though Shelley had intended it to be one metric foot shorter than the corresponding line of stanza 1.

1. Transcribed from what is probably the best known of all manuscripts, that which contains Keats's first draft of all but the first seven stanzas of *The Eve of St. Agnes;* it is now in the Houghton Library, Harvard University. Keats's published version of the poem, above, contains some further changes in wording.

[*Stanza 30*]

But
~~And still she slept.~~

And still she slept an azure-lidded sleep
In blanched linen, smooth and lavender'd
While he from frorth the closet brough a heap

fruits
Of candied ~~sweets~~ ~~sweets, with~~

apple Quince and plumb and gourd
creamed
With jellies soother than the ~~dairy~~ curd
tinct
And lucent syrups ~~smooth~~ with ciannamon
~~And sugar'd dates from that oer Euphrates fard~~

in Brigantine transferred
Manna and daites in ~~Brigantine transferd~~

and manna wild transferd
~~And Manna wild and Bragantine~~

sugar'd dates transferred
~~In Brigantine from Fez~~
From fez—and spiced danties every one

glazed
From ~~wealthy~~ Samarchand to cedard lebanon
silken

argosy

To Autumn[2]

Season of Mists and mellow fruitfulness
Close bosom friend of the naturring sun;
Conspiring with him how to load and bless
The Vines with fruit that round the thatch eves run
To bend with apples the moss'd Cottage trees
And fill all furuits with sweeness to the core
To swell the gourd, and plump the hazle shells
With a white kernel; to set budding more
And still more later flowers for the bees
Until they think wam days with never cease
For Summer has o'erbrimm'd their clammy cells—

oft amid thy stores?
Who hath not seen thee? ~~for thy haunts are many~~
abroad
Sometimes whoever seeks ~~for thee~~ may find
Thee sitting careless on a granary floorr
Thy hair soft lifted by the winnowing wind

husky
~~While bright the Sun slants through the ∧ barn,—~~
or on a half reap'd furrow sound asleep
~~Or sound asleep in a half reaped field~~

---

2. From an untitled manuscript—apparently Keats's first draft of the poem—in the Houghton Library, Harvard University. The many pen-slips and errors in spelling indicate that Keats wrote rapidly, in a state of creative excitement. Keats made a few further changes before publishing the poem in the form included in the selections above.

~~Dos'd with read poppies, while thy reeping hook~~
~~Spares form Some slumbrous~~
~~minutes while warm slumpers creep~~
Or on a half reap'd furrow sound asleep
Dos'd with the fume of poppies, while thy hook
Spares the next swath and all its twined flowers
~~Spares for some slumbrous minutes the next swath;~~
And sometimes like a gleans thost dost keep
Steady thy laden head across the brook;
Or by a Cyder-press with patent look
Thou watchest the last oozing hours by hours

Where are the songs of Sping? Aye where are they?
Think not of them thou hast thy music too—
barred   bloom
While ~~a gold~~ clouds ~~gilds~~ the soft-dying day
And   with
~~And~~ Touch~~ing the~~ the stibble plains ∧ rosy hue—
Then in a waiful quire the small gnats mourn
Among the river sallows, ~~on the~~ borne afots
Or sinking as the light wind lives and dies;
And full grown Lambs loud bleat from hilly bourn,
Hedge crickets sing, and now again full soft
The Redbreast whistles from a garden croft:
~~And now flock still~~
And Gather'd Swallows twiter in the Skies—

ALFRED, LORD TENNYSON
From The Lady of Shalott[1]

[*Version of 1832*]

PART THE FIRST.

On either side the river lie
Long fields of barley and of rye,
That clothe the wold, and meet the sky.
And thro' the field the road runs by
        To manytowered Camelot.
The yellowleavèd waterlily,
The greensheathèd daffodilly,
Tremble in the water chilly,
        Round about Shalott.

Willows whiten, aspens shiver,
The sunbeam-showers break and quiver

---

1. First published in Tennyson's *Poems* of 1832 (dated 1833 on the title page). The volume was severely criticized by some reviewers; partly in response to this criticism, Tennyson radically revised a number of the poems, including *The Lady of Shalott*, before reprinting them in his *Poems* (1842).

Parts 1 and 4 are reproduced here in the version of 1832. The final form of the poem reprinted in the selections from Tennyson, above, differs from the revised version that Tennyson published in 1842 only in line 157, which in 1842 read: "A corse between the houses high"; Tennyson changed the line to "Dead-pale between the houses high" in 1855.

In the stream that runneth ever
By the island in the river,
        Flowing down to Camelot.
Four gray walls and four gray towers
Overlook a space of flowers,
And the silent isle imbowers
        The Lady of Shallot.

Underneath the bearded barley,
The reaper, reaping late and early,
Hears her ever chanting cheerly,
Like an angel, singing clearly,
        O'er the stream of Camelot.
Piling the sheaves in furrows airy,
Beneath the moon, the reaper weary
Listening whispers, " 'tis the fairy
        Lady of Shalott."

The little isle is all inrailed
With a rose-fence, and overtrailed
With roses: by the marge unhailed
The shallop flitteth silkensailed,
        Skimming down to Camelot.
A pearlgarland winds her head:
She leaneth on a velvet bed,
Full royally apparellèd,
        The Lady of Shalott.

* * *

PART THE FOURTH.

In the stormy eastwind straining
The pale-yellow woods were waning,
The broad stream in his banks complaining,
Heavily the low sky raining
        Over towered Camelot:
Outside the isle a shallow boat
Beneath a willow lay afloat,
Below the carven stern she wrote,
        THE LADY OF SHALOTT.

A cloudwhite crown of pearl she dight.
All raimented in snowy white
That loosely flew, (her zone in sight,
Clasped with one blinding diamond bright,)
        Her wide eyes fixed on Camelot,
Though the squally eastwind keenly
Blew, with folded arms serenely
By the water stood the queenly
        Lady of Shalott.

With a steady, stony glance—
Like some bold seer in a trance,
Beholding all his own mischance,
Mute, with a glassy countenance—
        She looked down to Camelot.
It was the closing of the day,
She loosed the chain, and down she lay,
The broad stream bore her far away,
        The Lady of Shalott.

As when to sailors while they roam,
By creeks and outfalls far from home,
Rising and dropping with the foam,
From dying swans wild warblings come,
        Blown shoreward; so to Camelot
Still as the boathead wound along
The willowy hills and fields among,
They heard her chanting her deathsong,
        The Lady of Shalott.

A longdrawn carol, mournful, holy,
She chanted loudly, chanted lowly,
Till her eyes were darkened wholly,
And her smooth face sharpened slowly
        Turned to towered Camelot:
For ere she reached upon the tide
The first house by the waterside,
Singing in her song she died,
        The Lady of Shalott.

Under tower and balcony,
By gardenwall and gallery,
A pale, pale corpse she floated by,
Deadcold, between the houses high.
        Dead into towered Camelot.
Knight and burgher, lord and dame,
To the plankèd wharfage came:
Below the stern they read her name,
        "The Lady of Shalott."

They crossed themselves, their stars they blest,
Knight, ministrel, abbot, squire and guest.
There lay a parchment on her breast,
That puzzled more than all the rest,
        The wellfed wits at Camelot.
"The web was woven curiously
The charm is broken utterly,
Draw near and fear not—this is I,
        The Lady of Shalott."

From Tithonus[2]

[*Lines 1–10*]

[TRINITY COLLEGE MANUSCRIPT]

Ay me! Ay me! the woods decay & fall

~~The stars blaze out & never rise again~~.

the

The vapours weep their substance to ground
Man‸ comes & tills the earth & lies beneath
And after many summers dies the ~~rose~~ swan
Me only fatal immortality
Consumes: I wither slowly in thine arms:
Here at the quiet limit of the world

e   yet

A white-haired shad~~ow~~‸roaming like a dream
The ever-silent spaces ‸of the East
Far-folded mists & gleaming halls of morn.

[HEATH MANUSCRIPT]

Tithon

Ay me! ay me! the woods decay and fall,
The vapours weep their substance to the ground,
Man comes and tills the earth and lies beneath,
And after many summers dies the rose.
Me only fatal immortality
Consumes: I wither slowly in thine arms,
Here at the quiet limit of the world,
A white-haired shadow roaming like a dream
The ever-silent spaces of the East,
Far-folded mists, and gleaming halls of morn.

[AS PRINTED IN 1864]

Tithonus

The woods decay, the woods decay and fall,
The vapours weep their burthen to the ground,
Man comes and tills the field and lies beneath,
And after many a summer dies the swan.
Me only cruel immortality
Consumes: I wither slowly in thine arms,
Here at the quiet limit of the world,
A white-haired shadow roaming like a dream

2. Three manuscript drafts of *Tithonus* are extant. Two are in Tennyson's Notebooks Nos. 20 and 21, at Trinity College, Cambridge; a third one, written 1833, is in the Commonplace Book compiled by Tennyson's friend J. M. Heath, which is in the Fitzwilliam Museum at Cambridge University. According to Tennyson's editor, Christopher Ricks, the Heath version is later than those in the Trinity Manuscripts. The transcriptions here of Tennyson's opening lines are from the first draft (Trinity College manuscript, Notebook 20), and from the Heath manuscript, where the poem is titled "Tithon." These are followed by the final version of *Tithonus* that Tennyson published in 1864. As late as in the edition of 1860, the opening words had remained "Ay me! ay me!" and "field" (line 3) had remained "earth."

The ever-silent spaces of the East,
Far-folded mists, and gleaming halls of morn.

GERARD MANLEY HOPKINS
Thou art indeed just, Lord[1]

*Justus quidem tu es, Domine, si disputem tecum; verumtamen
justa loquar ad te: quare via impiorum prosperatur?* etc.
—Jer. xii 1.

March 17 1889

Lord, if I
Thou art indeed just, ~~were I to~~ contend

sir,   plead
With thee; but, ~~Lord~~, so what I ~~speak~~ is just.

Why do sinners' ways prosper? and why must

Disappointment all I endeavour end?
Wert thou my enemy, O thou my friend,
How wouldst thou worse, I wonder, than thou dost

O the sots and   of
Defeat, thwart me? ~~Ah! sots, revellers,~~ thralls ^ lust
Do in   that
In spare hours ~~do~~ more thrive than I ~~who~~ spend,

great   See,
Sir, ~~my~~ life on thy^cause. ~~Look~~, banks and brakes
Now, leavèd   lacèd they are
~~Leaved~~ how thick! ~~broidered all~~ again

look
With fretty chervil, ~~now~~, and fresh wind shakes
Them; birds build—but not I build; no, but strain,
Time's eunuch, and not breed one work that wakes.
Mine, O   send my
~~Then send~~, thou lord of life, ~~these~~ roots ^ ~~their~~ rain.

WILLIAM BUTLER YEATS

Yeats usually composed very slowly and with painful effort. He tells us in his *Auto-biography* that "five or six lines in two or three laborious hours were a day's work, and I longed for somebody to interrupt me." His manuscripts show the slow evolution of his best poems, which sometimes began with a prose sketch, were then versified, and

1. From a manuscript in the Bodleian Library, Oxford University; it is a clean copy, made after earlier drafts, which Hopkins goes on to revise further. Differences in the ink show that the emendation "lacèd they are" (line 10) was made during the first writing, but that the other verbal changes were made later. The interlinear markings are Hopkins's metrical indicators; he explains their sig-nificance in the "Author's Preface," included in *Poems of Gerard Manley Hopkins* (1970), ed. W. H. Gardner and N. H. MacKenzie.

The epigraph is from the Vulgate translation of Jeremiah 12.1; a literal translation of the Latin is "Thou art indeed just, Lord, [even] if I plead with Thee; nevertheless I will speak what is just to Thee: Why does the way of the wicked prosper? etc."

underwent numerous revisions. In many instances, even after the poems had been published, Yeats continued to revise them, sometimes drastically, in later printings.

The Sorrow of Love[1]

[Manuscript, 1891][2]

The quarrel of the sparrows in the eaves,
The full round moon and the star-laden sky,
The song of the ever-singing leaves,
Had hushed away earth's old and weary cry.

And then you came with those red mournful lips,
And with you came the whole of the world's tears,
And all the sorrows of her labouring ships,
And all the burden of her million years.

And now the angry sparrows in the eaves,
The withered moon, the white stars in the sky,
The wearisome loud chanting of the leaves,
Are shaken with earth's old and weary cry.

[First Printed Version, 1892][3]

The quarrel of the sparrows in the eaves,
   The full round moon and the star-laden sky,
And the loud song of the ever-singing leaves
   Had hid away earth's old and weary cry.

And then you came with those red mournful lips,
   And with you came the whole of the world's tears,
And all the sorrows of her labouring ships,
   And all burden of her myriad years.

And now the sparrows warring in the eaves,
   The crumbling moon, the white stars in the sky,
And the loud chanting of the unquiet leaves,
   Are shaken with earth's old and weary cry.

[Final Printed Version, 1925][4]

The brawling of a sparrow in the eaves,
   The brilliant moon and all the milky sky,

---

1. Originally composed in Yeats's Pre-Raphaelite mode of the early 1890s, *The Sorrow of Love* was one of his most popular poems. Nonetheless, some thirty years after publication, Yeats rewrote the lyric to give it the greater precision and the colloquial vigor of his poetic style in the 1920s.
2. Manuscript version composed in October 1891, as transcribed by Jon Stallworthy, *Between the Lines: Yeats's Poetry in the Making* (Oxford University Press, 1963), pp. 47–48.
3. From Yeats's *The Countess Kathleen and Various Legends and Lyrics* (1892). In a corrected page proof for this printing, now in the Garvan Collection of the Yale University Library, lines 7–8 originally read: "And all the sorrows of his labouring ships, / And all the burden of his married years." Also, in lines 4 and 12, the adjective was "bitter"

instead of "weary." In his *Poems* (1895), Yeats inserted the missing "the" in line 8, and changed "sorrows" (line 7) to "trouble"; "burden" (line 8) to "trouble"; and "crumbling moon" (line 10) to "curd-pale moon."
4. From *Early Poems and Stories* (1925). Yeats wrote in his *Autobiography* (New York, 1938), p. 371, that "in later years" he had "learnt that occasional prosaic words gave the impression of an active man speaking," so that "certain words must be dull and numb. Here and there in correcting my early poems I have introduced such numbness and dullness, turned, for instance, 'the curd-pale moon' into the 'brilliant moon,' that all might seem, as it were, remembered with indifference, except some one vivid image." Yeats, however, did not recall his emendations accurately. He had in 1925 altered

And all that famous harmony of leaves,
Had blotted out man's image and his cry.

A girl arose that had red mournful lips
And seemed the greatness of the world in tears,
Doomed like Odysseus and the labouring ships
And proud as Priam murdered with his peers;

Arose, and on the instant clamorous eaves,
A climbing moon upon an empty sky,
And all that lamentation of the leaves,
Could but compose man's image and his cry.

Leda and the Swan[5]

[First Version]

Annunciation

Now can the swooping Godhead have his will
Yet hovers, though her helpless thighs are pressed
By the webbed toes; and that all powerful bill
Has suddenly bowed her face upon his breast.
How can those terrified vague fingers push
The feathered glory from her loosening thighs?
All the stretched body's laid on that white rush

       strange
And feels the ~~strong~~ heart beating where it lies
A shudder in the loins engenders there
The broken wall, the burning roof and tower
And Agamemnon dead. . . .
                Being so caught up
Did nothing pass before her in the air?
Did she put on his knowledge with his power
Before the indifferent beak could let her drop
           Sept 18 1923

    swooping
The ~~trembl~~ godhead is half hovering still,
    climbs
Yet ~~climbs~~ upon her trembling body pressed
    webbed
By the toes; & ~~through~~ that all powerful bill
        ~~drown~~ bowed
Has suddenly ~~bowed~~ her face upon his breast.

"the full round moon" (line 2) to "the brilliant moon," and "the curd-pale moon" (line 10, version of 1895) to "a climbing moon."
5. From Yeats's manuscript *Journal*, Sections 248 and 250. This *Journal*, including facsimiles and transcriptions of the drafts of *Leda and the Swan*, has been published in W. B. Yeats, *Memoirs*, ed. Denis Donoghue (Macmillan, London, 1972).
    The first version, entitled *Annunciation*, seems to be a clean copy of earlier drafts; Yeats went on to revise it further, especially the opening octave.

Neither of the other two complete drafts, each of which Yeats labeled "Final Version," was in fact final. Yeats himself crossed out the first draft. The second, although Yeats published it in 1924, was subjected to further revision before he published the poem in *The Tower* (1928), in the final form reprinted in the selections from Yeats, above.
    Yeats's handwriting is hasty and very difficult to decipher. The readings of some words, in the manuscripts both of this poem and of *After Long Silence*, below, are uncertain.

How can those terrified vague fingers push
The feathered glory from her loosening thighs

laid
All the stretched body ~~leans~~ on that white rush

or

~~Her falling body thrown on the white~~ white rush

Can feel etc
or   Her body can but lean on the white rush

But mounts until her trembling thighs are pressed[6]
~~B~~
By the webbed toes; & that all powerful bill
Has suddenly bowed her head on his breast

Final Version

Annunciation

Can hold

The swooping godhead is half hovering still
But mounts, until her trembling thighs are pressed
By the webbed toes, & that all powerful bill
~~Has hung~~ her helpless body
~~Has suddenly bowed her head up~~on his breast.
How can those terrified vague fingers push
The feathered glory from her loosening thighs?
~~How   now its body leans on~~
~~With her body laid on the white rush~~
          all the stretched body laid on the white rush
and ~~Can~~ feel the strange heart beating where it lies?
A shudder in the loins engenders there
The broken wall, the burning roof & tower
And Agamemnon dead . . .
                              Being mastered so
                              ~~Being so caught up~~

So
~~And~~ mastered by the brute blood of the air
                              ~~Being mastered so~~
~~Did nothing pass before her in the air?~~
Did she put on his knowledge with his power
Before the indifferent beak could let her drop.
                              WBY. Sept 18 1923

swoop
A ~~rush~~ upon great wings & hovering still
~~He sinks until~~
~~He has sunk on her down, & her hair~~
~~The great bird sinks, till~~
The bird descends, & her frail ~~thigh~~ thighs are pressed
By the webbed toes, & that all

---

6. This passage is written across the blank page opposite the first version; Yeats drew a line indicating that it was to replace the revised lines 2–4, which he had written below the first version.

that
Now ~~all~~ her body's laid on that white rush[7]
~~All the stretched body, laid on~~ that white rush
~~Now that whole~~
Now ~~that her body on the white~~ rush
Can fee

Final Version

Leda & the Swan

A rush, a sudden wheel and
~~A swoop upon great wings &~~ hovering still
  sinks down   bare frail
stet The bird ~~descends~~ & her ~~frail~~ thighs are pressed
By the ~~toes~~ webbed toes, & that all powerful bill
      laid
Has ~~driven~~ her helpless face upon his breast.
How can those terrified vague fingers push
The feathered glory from her loosening thighs?
              s laid
All the stretched body ~~laid~~ on that white rush
And ~~feel~~ feels the strange heart beating where it lies.
A shudder in the loins engenders there
The broken wall, the burning roof & tower
And Agamemnon dead.
                    Being so caught up
So mastered by the ~~br~~ brute blood of the air
Did she put on his knowledge with his power
Before the indifferent beak could let her drop.

After Long Silence[8]

[Draft 1]

Subject

Your hair is white
My hair is white
Come let us talk of love
What other theme do we know
When we were young

7. Written on the blank page across from the complete version, with an arrow indicating that it was a revision of the seventh line.
8. The drafts of *After Long Silence* are interspersed with other materials on seven pages of a manuscript book, begun in 1928, which includes a number of additional poems that were published in *The Winding Stair and Other Poems* (1933). It begins, like many of Yeats's poems, with a prose sketch, and is labeled simply "Subject." It then passes through a tentative versified stage (Draft 2) in which Yeats sets down four complete lines and a set of possible rhyme words; is subjected to various drafts and revisions; and concludes with the final text that Yeats published in 1933. Yeats did not add the title *After Long Silence* until he wrote out a fair copy for his typist at some time after August 14, 1931.

David R. Clark, "After 'Silence,' The 'Supreme Theme': Eight Lines of Yeats," includes photocopies and transcripts of the drafts of this poem, together with a discussion of its biographical occasion and its interpretation (in *Myth and Reality in Irish Literature*, ed. Joseph Ronsley [Waterloo, Canada, 1977], pp. 149–73).

We were in love with one another
~~A O~~ And therefore ignorant

[*Draft 2*]

Those
                s
~~Your~~ other lover being dead & gone

                                                     friendly light
                                                     hair is white
                       ~~on love descant~~   descant
Upon the ~~sole theme~~ supreme theme of art &   song
Wherein there's theme so fitting for the aged. ;young
We loved each other & were ignorant

[*Draft 3*]

~~It~~
Once more I have kissed your hand & it is right—
All other ~~lovers being estranged~~ or dead
~~The heavy curtain drawn~~ the candle light
~~Waging a doubtful battle~~ with the shade
                                       discant,
~~We call our wisdom up upon our wisdom & descant~~
~~Upon the supreme theme of art & song.~~
Decrepitude increases wisdom—young
We loved each other & were ~~ignorant ignor~~   ignorant

[*Draft 4*]

Un
~~The~~ friendly lamplight hidden by its shade
~~And shutters clapped upon the deepening night—~~
~~The candle hidden by its friendly shade~~
Those curtains drawn upon the deepening night—

~~The curtains drawn on the unfriendly night—~~
That we descant & yet again descant
               supreme theme
Upon the ~~supreme theme~~ of ~~art & song~~ art & song—
Bodily decrepitude is wisdom—young

[*Final MS Version*]

Speech after long silence; ~~&~~ it is right—

                                      or
All other lovers being estranged ~~&~~ dead,

                              hid
Unfriendly lamp-light ~~hid~~ under its shade,

                       upon
The curtain's drawn ~~upon~~ unfriendly night—
That we descant & yet again descant
Upon the supreme theme of art & song,

Bodily decrepitude is wisdom~~M~~; young
We loved each other & were ignorant

Nov
~~Oct~~ 1929

D. H. LAWRENCE
The Piano[1]

Somewhere beneath that piano's superb sleek black
Must hide my mother's piano, little and brown, with
    the back
       stood close to
That ~~was against~~ the wall, and the front's faded silk, both torn
And the keys with little hollows, that my mother's fingers
    had worn.

Softly, in the shadows, a woman is singing to me
Quietly, through the years I have crept back to see
A child sitting under the piano, in the boom of the
    shaking ~~tingling~~ strings
Pressing the little poised feet of the mother who smiles
    as she sings

The full throated woman has chosen a winning, living[2]
    song
And surely the heart that is in me must belong
To the old Sunday evenings, when darkness wandered
    outside
And hymns gleamed on our warm lips, as we watched
    mother's fingers glide
       is
Or is this‸my sister at home in the old front room
Singing love's first surprised gladness, alone in
    the gloom.
She will start when she sees me, and blushing,
    spread out her hands
To cover my mouth's raillery, till I'm bound in
       heart-spun
    her shame's ~~pleading~~ bands.

1. Transcribed from a notebook in which Lawrence at first entered various academic assignments while he was a student at the University College of Nottingham, 1906–8, but then used to write drafts of some of his early poems. These were probably composed in the period from 1906 to 1910. The text reproduced here was revised and published with the title *Piano* in Lawrence's *New Poems,* 1918. A comparison of this draft with *Piano,* reprinted above, will show that Lawrence eliminated the first and fourth stanzas (as well as the last two lines of the third stanza); revised the remaining three stanzas, sometimes radically; and most surprisingly, reversed his original conclusion.

As Lawrence himself explained his revisions of some of his early poems, they "had to be altered, where sometimes the hand of commonplace youth had been laid on the mouth of the demon. It is not for technique that these poems are altered: it is to say the real say."

For transcriptions and discussions of this and other poems in Lawrence's early notebook, see Vivian de Sola Pinto, "D.H. Lawrence: Letter-Writer and Craftsman in Verse," in *Renaissance and Modern Studies* 1 (1957): 5–34.

2. A conjectural reading; the word is not clearly legible.

A woman is singing me a wild Hungarian
    air
And her arms, and her bosom and the whole
    of her soul is bare
And the great black piano is clamouring as my
    mother's never could clamour

      my mother's [   ]³ tunes are
And ~~the tunes of the past is~~ devoured of this music's
    ravaging glamour.

---

3. An undecipherable word is crossed out here.

Selected Bibliographies

The Selected Bibliographies consist of a list of Suggested General Readings on English literature, followed by bibliographies for each of the literary periods in this volume. For ease of reference, the authors within each period are arranged in alphabetical order. Entries for certain classes of writings (e.g., "The Rise and Fall of Empire") are included, in alphabetical order, within the listings for individual authors.

SUGGESTED GENERAL READINGS

Histories of England and of English Literature

New research and new perspectives have made even the most distinguished of the comprehensive, general histories written in past generations seem outmoded. Innovative research in social, cultural, and political history has made it difficult to write a single, coherent account of England from the Middle Ages to the present, let alone to accommodate in a unified narrative the complex histories of Scotland, Ireland, and Wales. Readers who wish to explore the historical matrix out of which the works of literature collected in this anthology emerged are advised to consult the studies of particular periods listed in the appropriate sections of this bibliography. The multivolume *Oxford History of England* is useful, as are the three-volume *Peoples of the British Isles: A New History*, ed. Stanford Lehmberg, 1992, and the nine-volume *Cambridge Cultural History of Britain*, ed. Boris Ford, 1992. Albert Baugh et al., *A Literary History of England*, rev. 1967, remains a convenient source of factual materials about authors, works, and chronology. Given the cultural centrality of London, readers may find Roy Porter's *London: A Social History*, 1994, valuable. Similar observations may be made about literary history. In the light of such initiatives as women's studies, new historicism, and postcolonialism, the range of authors deemed most significant has expanded in recent years, along with the geographical and conceptual boundaries of literature in English. Attempts to capture in a unified account the great sweep of literature from *Beowulf* to late last night have largely given way to studies of individual genres, carefully delimited time periods, and specific authors. For these more focused accounts, see the listings by period.

Among the large-scale literary surveys, *The Cambridge Guide to Literature in English*, 1993, is useful, as is *The Penguin History of Literature*.

The Feminist Companion to Literature in English, ed. Virginia Blain, Isobel Grundy, and Patricia Clements, 1990, is an important resource, and the editorial materials in *The Norton Anthology of Literature by Women* 2nd ed., 1996, ed. Sandra M. Gilbert and Susan Gubar, constitute a concise history and set of biographies of women authors since the Middle Ages. *Annals of English Literature, 1475–1950*, rev. 1961, lists important publications year by year, together with the significant literary events for each year. David Daiches, *A Critical History of English Literature*, 2 vols., rev. 1970, provides a running literary appreciation.

Helpful treatments and surveys of English meter, rhyme, and stanza forms are Paul Fussell Jr., *Poetic Meter and Poetic Form*, rev. 1979; Donald Wesling, *The Chances of Rhyme: Device and Modernity*, 1980; Derek Attridge, *The Rhythms of English Poetry*, 1982; Charles O. Hartman, *Free Verse: An Essay in Prosody*, 1983; John Hollander, *Vision and Resonance: Two Senses of Poetic Form*, rev. 1985; and Robert Pinsky, *The Sounds of Poetry: A Brief Guide*, 1998.

On the development of the novel as a form, see Ian Watt, *The Rise of the Novel*, 1957; *The Columbia History of the British Novel*, ed. John Richetti, 1994; and Margaret Doody, *The True Story of the Novel*, 1996. On women novelists and readers, see Nancy Armstrong, *Desire and Domestic Fiction: A Political History of the Novel*, 1987; and Catherine Gallagher, *Nobody's Story: The Vanishing Acts of Women Writers in the Marketplace, 1670–1820*, 1994.

On the history of playhouse design, see Richard Leacroft, *The Development of the English Playhouse: An Illustrated Survey of Theatre Building in England from Medieval to Modern Times*, 1988. For a survey of the plays that have appeared on these and other stages, see Allardyce Nicoll, *British Drama*, rev. 1962, and the eight-volume *Revels His-*

tory of Drama in English, gen. eds. Clifford Leech and T. W. Craik, 1975–83.

On some of the key intellectual currents that are at once reflected in and shaped by English literature, Arthur T. Lovejoy's classic studies *The Great Chain of Being*, 1936, and *Essays in the History of Ideas*, 1948, remain valuable, along with such works as Lovejoy and George Boas, *Primitivism and Related Ideas in Antiquity*, 1935; Ernst Kantowicz, *The King's Two Bodies: A Study in Medieval Political Theology*, 1957, new ed. 1997; Richard Popkin, *The History of Skepticism from Erasmus to Descartes*, 1960; M. H. Abrams, *Natural Supernaturalism: Tradition and Revolution in Romantic Literature*, 1971; and Michel Foucault, *Madness and Civilization: A History of Insanity in the Age of Reason*, Eng. trans. 1965, and *The Order of Things: An Archaeology of the Human Sciences*, Eng. trans. 1970.

Reference Works

The single most important tool for the study of literature in English is the *Oxford English Dictionary*, 2nd ed., 1989, also available on CD-ROM. The *OED* is written on historical principles: that is, it attempts not only to describe current word use but also to record the history and development of the language from its origins before the Norman conquest to the present. It thus provides, for familiar as well as archaic and obscure words, the widest possible range of meanings and uses, organized chronologically and illustrated with quotations. Beyond the *OED* there are many other valuable dictionaries, such as *The American Heritage Dictionary*, *The Oxford Dictionary of Etymology*, and an array of reference works from *The Cambridge Encyclopedia of the English Language*, ed. David Crystal, 1995, to guides to specialized vocabularies, slang, regional dialects, and the like.

There is a steady flow of new editions of most major and many minor writers in English, along with a ceaseless outpouring of critical appraisals and scholarship. The *MLA International Bibliography* (also on line) is the best way to keep abreast of the most recent work and to conduct bibliographic searches. *The New Cambridge Bibliography of English Literature* ed. George Watson, 1969–77, updated shorter ed. 1981, is a valuable guide to the huge body of earlier literary criticism and scholarship. *A Guide to English and American Literature*, ed. F. W. Bateson and Harrison Meserole, rev. 1976, is a selected list of editions, as well as scholarly and critical treatments. Further bibliographical aids are described in Arthur G. Kennedy, *A Concise Bibliography for Students of English*, rev. 1972; Richard D. Altick and Andrew Wright, *Selective Bibliography for the Study of English and American Literature* rev. 1979, and James L. Harner, *Literary Research Guide*, rev. 1998.

For compact biographies of English authors, see the multivolume *Dictionary of National Biography*, ed. Leslie Stephen and Sidney Lee, 1885–1900, with supplements that carry the work to 1980; condensed biographies will be found in the *Concise Dictionary of National Biography*, 2 parts (1920, 1988). Handy reference books of authors, works, and various literary terms and allusions are *The Oxford Companion to the Theatre*, Phyllis Hartnoll, rev. 1990; *Princeton Encyclopedia of Poetry and Poetics*, ed. Alex Preminger and others, rev. 1993; and *The Oxford Companion to English Literature*, ed. Margaret Drabble, rev. 1998. Low-priced handbooks that define and illustrate literary concepts and terms are *The Penguin Dictionary of Literary Terms and Literary Theory*, ed. J. A. Cuddon, 1991; W. F. Thrall and Addison Hibbard, *A Handbook to Literature*, ed. C. Hugh Holman, rev. 1992; *Critical Terms for Literary Study*, ed. Frank Lentricchia and Thomas McLaughlin, rev. 1995; and M. H. Abrams, *A Glossary of Literary Terms*, rev. 1992. On Greek and Roman background, see G. M. Kirkwood, *A Short Guide to Classical Mythology*, 1959; *The Oxford Classical Dictionary*, rev. 1996; and *The Oxford Companion to Classical Literature*, ed. M. C. Howatson and Ian Chilvers, rev. 1993.

Literary Criticism and Theory

Three volumes of the *Cambridge History of Literary Criticism* have been published, 1989–: *Classical Criticism*, ed. George A. Kennedy; *The Eighteenth Century*, ed. H. B. Nisbet and Claude Rawson, and *From Formalism to Poststructuralism*, ed. Raman Selden. See also M. H. Abrams, *The Mirror and the Lamp: Romantic Theory and the Critical Tradition*, 1953; William K. Wimsatt and Cleanth Brooks, *Literary Criticism: A Short History*, 1957; George Watson, *The Literary Critics*, 1962; René Wellek, *A History of Modern Criticism: 1750–1950*, 9 vols., 1955–1993; Frank Lentricchia, *After the New Criticism*, 1980; and *Redrawing the Boundaries: The Transformation of English and American Literary Studies*, ed. Stephen Greenblatt and Giles Gunn, 1992. Raman Selden, Peter Widdowson, and Peter Brooker have written *A Reader's Guide to Contemporary Literary Theory*, 1997.

The following is a selection of books in literary criticism that have been notably influential in shaping modern approaches to English literature and literary forms: Lionel Trilling, *The Liberal Imagination*, 1950; T. S. Eliot, *Selected Essays*, 3rd ed. 1951, and *On Poetry and Poets*, 1957; Erich Auerbach, *Mimesis: The Representation of Reality in Western Literature*, 1953; William Empson, *Seven Types of Ambiguity*, 3rd ed., 1953; William K. Wimsalt, *The Verbal Icon*, 1954; Northrop Frye, *Anatomy of Criticism*, 1957; Wayne C. Booth, *The Rhetoric of Fiction*, 1961, rev. ed. 1983; W. J. Bate, *The Burden of the Past and the English Poet*, 1970; Harold Bloom, *The Anxiety of Influence*, 1973; and Paul de Man, *Allegories of Reading*, 1979.

René Wellek and Austin Warren, *Theory of Literature*, rev. 1970, is a useful introduction to the variety of scholarly and critical approaches to literature up to the time of its publication. Jonathan Culler's *Literary Theory: A Very Short Introduction*, 1997, discusses recurrent issues and debates. Modern feminist literary criticism was fashioned by such works as Particia Meyers Spacks, *The Female Imagination*, 1975; Ellen Moers, *Literary Women*, 1976; Elaine Showalter, *A Literature of Their Own*, 1977; and Sandra Gilbert and Susan Gubar, *The Madwoman in the Attic*, 1979. More recent studies include Jane Gallop, *The Daughter's Seduction: Feminism and Psychoanalysis*, 1982; Gayatri Chakravorty Spivak, *In Other Worlds: Essays in Cultural Politics*, 1987; Sandra Gilbert and Susan Gubar, *No Man's Land: The Place of the Woman Writer in the Twentieth Century*, 2 vols., 1988–89; Barbara Johnson, *A World of Difference*, 1989; Judith Butler, *Gender Trouble*, 1990; and the critical views sampled in Elaine Showalter, *The New Feminist Criticism*, 1985; *Feminist Literary Theory: A Reader*, ed. Mary Eagleton, 2nd ed., 1995; and *Feminisms: An Anthology of Literary Theory and Criticism*, ed. Robyn R. Warhol and Diane Price Herndl, 2nd ed. 1997. Gay and lesbian studies and criticism are represented in *The Lesbian and Gay Studies Reader*, ed. Henry Abelove, Michele Barale, and David Halperin, 1993, and by such books as Eve Sedgwick, *Between Men: English Literature and Male Homosocial Desire*, 1985, and *Epistemology of the Closet*, 1990; Diana Fuss, *Essentially Speaking: Feminism, Nature, and Difference*, 1989; and Gregory Woods, *A History of Gay Literature: The Male Tradition*, 1998. Convenient introductions to structuralist literary criticism include Robert Scholes, *Structuralism in Literature: An Introduction*, 1974, and Jonathan Culler, *Structuralist Poetics*, 1975. The poststructuralist challenges to this approach are discussed in Jonathan Culler, *On Deconstruction*, 1982; Fredric Jameson, *Poststructuralism; or the Cultural Logic of Late Capitalism*, 1991; John McGowan, *Postmodernism and Its Critics*, 1991; and *Beyond Structuralism*, ed. Wendell Harris, 1996. New historicism is represented in Stephen Greenblatt, *Learning to Curse*, 1990, and in the essays collected in *The New Historicism*, ed. Harold Veeser, 1989, and *New Historical Literary Study: Essays on Reproducing Texts, Representing History*, ed. Jeffrey N. Cox and Larry J. Reynolds, 1993. The related social and historical dimension of texts is discussed in Jerome McGann, *Critique of Modern Textual Criticism*, 1983, and D. F. McKenzie, *Bibliography and Sociology of Texts*, 1986. Characteristic of new historicism is an expansion of the field of literary interpretation extended still further in cultural studies; for a broad sampling of the range of interests, see *The Cultural Studies Reader*, ed. Simon During, 1993, and *A Cultural Studies Reader: History, Theory, Practice*, ed. Jessica Munns and Gita Rajan, 1997. This expansion of the field is similarly reflected in postcolonial studies: see *The Post-Colonial Studies Reader*, ed. Bill Ashcroft, Gareth Griffiths, and Helen Tiffin, 1995, and such influential books as Ranajit Guha and Gayatri Chakravorti Spivak, *Selected Subaltern Studies*, 1988; Edward Said, *Culture and Imperialism*, 1993; and Homi Bhabha, *The Location of Culture*, 1994.

Anthologies representing a range of recent approaches include *Modern Criticism and Theory*, ed. David Lodge, 1988, and *Contemporary Literary Criticism*, ed. Robert Con Davis and Ronald Schlieffer, rev. 1998.

THE VICTORIAN AGE

Studies of the Victorian age and its point of view include Richard D. Altick, *Victorian People and Ideas: A Companion for the Modern Reader of Victorian Literature*, 1973; Patrick Brantlinger, *Rule of Darkness: British Literature and Imperialism, 1830–1914*, 1988; Asa Briggs, *The Age of Improvement*, 1962; W. L. Burn, *The Age of Equipoise: A Study of the Mid-Victorian Generation*, 1964; Jerome Buckley, *The Victorian Temper*, 1951; David Cannadine, *The Decline and Fall of the British Aristocracy*, 1990; A. Dwight Culler, *The Victorian Mirror of History*, 1986; Robin Gilmour, *The Victorian Period: The Intellectual and Cultural Context of Victorian Literature, 1830–1890*, 1993; Walter E. Houghton, *The Victorian Frame of Mind, 1830–1870*, 1957; *Victorian Britain: An Encyclopedia*, ed. Sally Mitchell, 1988; David Newsome, *The Victorian World Picture: Perceptions and Introspections in a World of Change*, 1997; Mary Poovey, *Making a Social Body: British Cultural Formation, 1830–1864*, 1995; Richard L. Stein, *Victoria's Year: English Literature and Culture, 1837–38*, 1988; F. M. L. Thompson, *The Rise of Respectable Society: A Social History of Victorian Britain, 1830–1900*, 1988; and G. M. Young, *Victorian England: Portrait of an Age*, 1936 (republished in 1977 with 215 pages of explanatory notes by George Kitson Clark). Young's essay is a brilliant synthesis, but it can be incomprehensible to readers who are not yet adequately familiar with the history of the age. Such readers should consult David Thomson's *England in the Nineteenth Century*, 1950, or Derek Beales, *From Castlereagh to Gladstone: 1815–1885*, 1970.

Studies of special aspects of the age include James Eli Adams, *Dandies and Desert Saints: Styles of Victorian Masculinity*, 1995; Richard Altick, *The English Common Reader*, 1957; Asa Briggs, *Victorian Things*, 1989; Jerome Buckley, *The Triumph of Time*, 1966; Peter Gay, *The Bourgeois Experience: From Victoria to Freud*, 2 vols., 1984–86; Mark Girouard, *The Return to Camelot*, 1981; Bruce Haley, *The Healthy Body and Victorian Culture*, 1978; Steven Marcus, *The Other Victorians: A Study of Sexuality and Pornography in Mid-Nineteenth-Century England*, 1964; Herbert Sussman, *Victorians and the Machine*, 1968; E. P. Thompson, *The Making of the English Working Class*, 1963; Frank M. Turner, *The Greek Heritage* in *Victorian Britain*, 1981; *The Victorian City*, ed. H. J. Dyos and Michael Wolff, 2 vols., 1973; Jeffrey Weeks, *Sex, Politics and Society: The Regulation of Sexuality Since 1800*, 1981; and Michael Wheeler, *Death and the Future Life in Victorian Literature and Theology*, 1991. For pictures and paintings of the Victorian scene, see Jeremy Maas, *Victorian Painters*, 1969. Also revealing are the illustrations for Henry Mayhew, *London Labour and London Poor*, originally published 1851, reprinted 1967, and Gustav Doré, *London: A Pilgrimage*, originally published 1872 and reprinted 1970. *Nature and the Victorian Imagination*, ed. U. C. Knoepflmacher and G. B. Tennyson, 1977; *Victorian Types, Victorian Shadows: Biblical Typology in Victorian Literature, Art, and Thought*, George Landow, 1980; and *Victorian Literature and the Victorian Visual Imagination*, ed. Carol T. Christ and John O. Jordan, 1995, feature valuable treatments of literature and the visual arts.

Studies of Victorian literature include Isobel Armstrong, *Victorian Poetry: Poetry, Poetics, and Politics*, 1993; Harold Bloom, *The Ringers in the Tower*, 1971; William E. Buckler, *The Victorian Imagination*, 1980; Douglas Bush, *Mythology and the Romantic Tradition*, 1937; Raymond Chapman, *The Sense of the Past in Victorian Literature*, 1986; Carol T. Christ, *The Finer Optic: The Aesthetic of Particularity in Victorian Poetry*, 1975, and *Victorian and Modern Poetics*, 1984; Peter Allan Dale, *The Victorian Critic and the Idea of History*, 1977; Oliver Elton, *A Survey of English Literature*, 1920, vols. 3 and 4; Avrom Fleischman, *Figures of Autobiography: The Language of Self in Victorian and Modern England*, 1983; Pauline Fletcher, *Gardens and Grim Ravines . . . Landscape in Victorian Poetry*, 1983; George Ford, *Keats and the Victorians*, 1944; Hilary Fraser with David Brown, *English Prose of the Nineteenth Century*, 1997; E. D. H. Johnson, *The Alien Vision of Victorian Poetry*, 1952; Robert Langbaum, *The Poetry of Experience*, 1957; John P. McGowan, *Representation and Revelation: Victorian Realism from Carlyle to Yeats*, 1986; Dorothy Mermin, *The Audience in the Poem*, 1983; J. Hillis Miller, *The Disappearance of God: Five Nineteenth-Century Writers*, 1963; John R. Reed, *Victorian Conventions*, 1975; W. David Shaw, *The Lucid Veil: Poetic Truth in the Victorian Age*, 1987; René Wellek, *A History of Modern Criticism*, vol. 4, 1965. Helpful collections of critical essays have been compiled by Robert Preyer in his *Victorian Literature: Selected Essays*, 1965; Isobel Armstrong, *The Major Victorian Poets: Reconsiderations*, 1969; and by Michael Timko in *Victorian Poetry*, Spring 1978. Especially noteworthy is *The Art of Victorian Prose*, ed. George Levine and William Madden, 1968.

For the status of women in Victorian life and literature, see Nina Auerbach, *Woman and the Demon*, 1982, and *Romantic Imprisonment*, 1985; Deirdre David, *Rule Britannia: Women, Empire, and Victorian Writing*, 1996; Sandra Gilbert and Susan Gubar, *The Madwoman in the Attic*, 1979;

Elizabeth Helsinger, Robin Lauterbach Sheets, and William Veeder, *The Woman Question*, 3 vols., 1980; Margaret Homans, *Bearing the Word: Language and Female Experience in Nineteenth-Century Women's Writing*, 1986; Elizabeth Langland, *Nobody's Angels: Middle Class Women and Domestic Ideology in Victorian Culture*, 1995; Angela Leighton, *Victorian Women Poets: Writing against the Heart*, 1992; Dorothy Mermin, *Godiva's Ride: Women of Letters in England, 1830–1880*, 1993; Ellen Moers, *Literary Women*, 1976; Mary Poovey, *Uneven Developments: The Ideological Work of Gender in Mid-Victorian England*, 1988; Eve Kosofsky Sedgwick, *Between Men: English Literature and Male Homosexual Desire*. 1985; Elaine Showalter, *A Literature of Their Own*, 1977; and Martha Vicinus, ed., *Suffer and Be Still*, 1972, *A Widening Sphere*, 1977, and *Ever Yours, Florence Nightingale, Selected Letters* (with Bea Nergaard), 1989.

For classified or annotated lists of other books and articles, see *The Victorian Poets: A Guide to Research*, ed. F. E. Faverty, rev. 1968; *Victorian Fiction: A Guide to Research*, ed. Lionel Stevenson, 1964; *Victorian Fiction: A Second Guide to Research*, ed. George H. Ford, 1978; *Victorian Prose: A Guide to Research*, ed. David J. DeLaura, 1973; Sharon W. Propas, *Victorian Studies: A Research Guide*, 1992; and Laurence W. Mazzeno, *Victorian Poetry: An Annotated Bibliography*, 1995.

For developments in prose fiction during the period, see Lionel Stevenson, *The English Novel: A Panorama*, 1960, and for introductions to individual novelists, see *Victorian Novelists before 1885*, ed. Ira Nadel and William Fredeman, *Dictionary of Literary Biography*, vol. 21, 1983. For special critical issues, see Peter Brooks, *Reading for the Plot: Design and Intention in Narrative*, 1984; Joseph W. Childers, *Novel Possibilities: Fiction and the Formation of Early Victorian Culture*, 1995; Catherine Gallagher, *The Industrial Reformation of English Fiction: Social Discourse and Narrative Form, 1832–1867*, 1985; Peter Garrett, *The Victorian Multiplot Novel*, 1980; George Levine, *The Realistic Imagination*, 1981; D. A. Miller, *The Novel and the Police*, 1988; J. Hillis Miller, *The Form of Victorian Fiction*, 1968; Robert M. Polhemus, *Erotic Faith*, 1990; and Donald Stone, *The Romantic Impulse in Victorian Fiction*, 1980.

Matthew Arnold

The standard edition of Arnold's poetry is the elaborately annotated *Poems of Arnold*, ed. Miriam Allott, 1979. Cecil Lang is editing *The Letters of Matthew Arnold*, 1996–. H. F. Lowry has edited *The Letters of Arnold to . . . Clough*, 1932. R. H. Super has produced an authoritative edition of *The Complete Prose Works*, 11 vols., 1960–77. For a study of those prose works, see William Robbins's *The Ethical Idealism of Matthew Arnold*, 1959, and Joseph Carroll's *The Cultural Theory of Matthew Arnold*, 1982.

The most satisfactory biography is Park Honan's

Matthew Arnold: A Life, 1981, but see also Nicholas Murray, *A Life of Matthew Arnold*, 1996. Lionel Trilling's excellent *Matthew Arnold*, 1949, remains a standard critical and biographical study, but see also Dwight Culler's *Imaginative Reason*, 1966, and G. Robert Stange's *The Poet as Humanist*, 1967. For two centenary assessments, see Stefan Collini, *Arnold*, 1988, and David G. Riede, *Matthew Arnold and the Betrayal of Language*, 1988. Two investigations of Arnold's literary and intellectual background are Leon Gottfried, *Matthew Arnold and the Romantics*, 1983, and Ruth apRoberts, *Arnold and God*, 1983. See also Kenneth Allott, *Matthew Arnold*, 1975, and the selection of essays edited by Harold Bloom, *Matthew Arnold*, 1987.

Emily Brontë
The Complete Poems were first edited by C. W. Hatfield in 1941. A more recent edition is *The Poems of Emily Bronte*, ed. Derek Roper and Edward Chitham, 1995. Information about the Gondal narrative is supplied by Fannie R. Ratchford's *The Brontës' Web of Childhood*, 1941, and *Gondal's Queen, A Novel in Verse*, 1955. The most satisfactory biography is Edward Chitham, *A Life of Emily Brontë*, 1988. Several of the essays in *The Art of Emily Brontë*, ed. Anne Smith, 1977, and in Thomas John Winnifrith, *Critical Essays on Emily Bronte*, 1997, are devoted to the poetry, as is Margaret Homans, *Women Writers and Poetic Identity*, 1980. Also see Irene Taylor, *Holy Ghosts: The Male Muses of Emily and Charlotte Brontë*, 1990. William M. Sale, Jr., and Richard J. Dunn have edited the Norton Critical Edition of *Wuthering Heights*, 3rd ed., 1990.

Elizabeth Barrett Browning
The standard *Complete Works* were edited by Charlotte Porter and Helen Clarke, 6 vols., 1900. Margaret Reynolds has edited a Norton Critical Edition of *Aurora Leigh*, 1996, and Julia Markus had edited *Casa Guidi Windows*, 1977. Of a projected forty-volume collection, *The Brownings' Correspondence*, ed. Philip Kelley and Ronald Hudson (1984–), fourteen volumes have been published. The best critical biography is Dorothy Mermin's *Elizabeth Barrett Browning: The Origins of a New Poetry*, 1989. See also Angela Leighton, *Elizabeth Barrett Browning*, 1986. Interesting recent discussions of Barrett Browning can be found in Ellen Moers, *Literary Women*, 1976; Sandra Gilbert and Susan Gubar, *The Madwoman in the Attic*, 1979; Deirdre David, *Intellectual Women and Victorian Patriarchy*, 1987; Helen Cooper, *Elizabeth Barrett Browning, Woman and Artist*, 1988; and Marjorie Stone, *Elizabeth Barrett Browning*, 1995.

Robert Browning
A standard edition is *The Complete Works of Robert Browning, with Variant Readings and Annotations*, ed. Roma A. King Jr., et al., 9 vols., 1969–89. Five volumes of a projected seven-volume annotated edition of the poetry only, *The Poetical Works of Robert Browning*, have appeared, edited by Ian Jack, Margaret Smith, and Robert Inglesfield, 1983–95. John

Woolford and Daniel Karlin have also edited *The Poems of Browning*, 1991, two volumes of which have appeared. A convenient two-volume collection of the poems edited by John Pettigrew and Thomas J. Collins was published in 1981. For the Brownings' correspondence, see entry under **Elizabeth Barrett Browning**. The standard biography is *The Book, the Ring, and the Poet*, William Irvine and Park Honan, 1974; also see Clyde de L. Ryals, *The Life of Robert Browning: A Critical Biography*. Gertrude Reese Hudson provides a study of his critical reception in *Robert Browning's Literary Life*, 1993. W. C. DeVane's *A Browning Handbook*, rev. 1955, is a compilation of factual data concerning each of Browning's poems: sources, composition, and reputation. Further information is supplied by Norman B. Crowell, *A Reader's Guide to Robert Browning*, 1972, which also offers simplified summaries of critical discussions for twenty-three monologues.

The critical assessments in G. K. Chesterton's *Robert Browning*, 1903, are colorfully expressed and often shrewd. Robert Langbaum's *The Poetry of Experience* relates Browning's monologues to some of the main developments in modern literature. See also Roma A. King Jr., *The Bow and the Lyre*, 1957; W. O. Raymond, *The Infinite Moment*, 1965; Donald Hair, *Browning's Experiments with Genre*; 1972; Ian Jack, *Browning's Major Poetry*, 1973; Herbert Tucker, *Browning's Beginnings*, 1980; Loy Martin, *Browning's Dramatic Monologues and the Post-Romantic Subject*, 1985; and Joseph Bristow, *Robert Browning*, 1991. Useful collections of essays include *The Browning Critics*, ed. Boyd Litzinger and K. L. Knickerbocker, 1965; *Robert Browning: A Collection of Critical Essays*, ed. Philip Drew, 1966; *Browning: The Critical Heritage*, ed. Boyd Litzinger and Donald Smalley, 1970; *Robert Browning*, Isobel Armstrong, 1974; *Robert Browning: A Collection of Critical Essays*, ed. Harold Bloom and Adrienne Munich, 1979; and *Critical Essays on Robert Browning*, ed. Mary Ellis Gibson, 1992.

Thomas Carlyle
The *Works* have been edited by H. D. Traill, 30 vols., 1898–1901. Twenty-one volumes of the *Collected Letters*, projected to extend to thirty volumes, have been published since 1971 (ed. by C. R. Sanders et al.). C. F. Harrold's edition of *Sartor Resartus*, 1937, is helpful concerning Carlyle's debt to German literature, as is Louis Cazamian's *Carlyle*, 1932, concerning his religious background. J. A. Froude, *Thomas Carlyle*, 1882–84, for years the standard biography, has been replaced by Fred Kaplan, *Thomas Carlyle*, 1983. Recommended as studies of Carlyle's thought are Emery Neff, *Carlyle and Mill*, 1926; Philip Rosenberg, *The Seventh Hero: Thomas Carlyle and the Theory of Radical Activism*, 1974; Ruth apRoberts, *The Ancient Dialect: Thomas Carlyle and Comparative Religion*, 1988; and Chris Vanden Bossche, *Carlyle and the Search for Authority*, 1991. That he has affinities with twentieth-century "mythmakers" such as D. H. Lawrence is argued by Albert J. LaValley in *Carlyle*

and the Idea of the Modern, 1968. John Holloway's *The Victorian Sage*, 1953, includes a chapter analyzing Carlyle's rhetoric. George B. Tennyson, *Sartor Called Resartus*, 1965, is an important critical study. See also George Levine, *The Boundaries of Fiction*, 1968, on Carlyle, Macaulay, and Newman, and the collection of essays edited by K. J. Fielding and Rodger L. Tarr, *Carlyle Past and Present*, 1976. Tarr has also compiled *Thomas Carlyle: A Descriptive Bibliography*, 1990.

Lewis Carroll

The standard edition is *The Complete Writings of Lewis Carroll*, 1939. A highly recommended selection is *Alice in Wonderland*, a Norton Critical Edition, ed. Donald J. Gray, 2nd ed., 1992. For his life see Morton N. Cohen, *Lewis Carroll: A Biography*, 1995. See also William Empson. *Some Versions of Pastoral*, 1935. For a variety of recent critical views, see *Soaring with the Dodo: Essays on Lewis Carroll's Life and Art*, ed. Edward Giuliano and James R. Kincaid, 1982, and *Lewis Carroll*, ed. Harold Bloom, 1987. Francis Huxley's *The Raven and the Writing Desk*, 1976, is a brilliant and idiosyncratic discussion of Carroll's work.

Arthur Hugh Clough

The Poems were edited by H. F. Lowry, A. L. F. Norrington, and F. L. Mulhauser, 1951. In 1974 Mulhauser edited a revised edition, with some poems previously omitted. Mulhauser was also editor of *The Correspondence*, 1957. See also *The Oxford Diaries*, ed. Anthony Kenny, 1990. *A. H. Clough: The Uncommitted Mind*, Katherine Chorley, 1962, is a lively but frequently misleading study. *The Poetry of Clough*, Walter Houghton, 1963, contends that Clough is a major satirical poet. On Clough's religious and intellectual background, see Anthony Kenny, *God and Two Poets: Arthur Hugh Clough and Gerard Manley Hopkins*, 1988, and Paul Veyriras, *A. H. Clough*, 1965 (in French). See also the judicious study by Robindra Biswas, *Arthur Hugh Clough: Towards a Reconsideration*, 1972.

Mary Elizabeth Coleridge

The only edition of Coleridge's poetry is *Collected Poems.*, ed. Theresa Whistler, 1954. A posthumous collection of selections from her stories and journals is contained in *Gathered Leaves from the Prose of Mary E. Coleridge*, with a memoir by Edith Sichel, 1910. Sandra M. Gilbert and Susan Gubar, *The Madwoman in the Attic*, 1979, contains a discussion of *The Other Side of a Mirror*.

Charles Dickens

The standard modern edition of Dickens's works is The Clarendon Edition, 1966–. Norton Critical Editions exist for *Bleak House*, ed. George Ford and Sylvere Monod, 1977; *David Copperfield*, ed. Jerome H. Buckley, 1990; *Great Expectations*, ed. Edgar Rosenberg, 1999; *Hard Times*, ed. George Ford and Sylvere Monod, 1990; and *Oliver Twist*, ed. Fred Kaplan, 1993. A modern edition of *The Letters of Charles Dickens*, ed. Madeline House et al., 1965–, is in progress.

Two classic biographies are John Forster, *The Life of Charles Dickens*, 2 vols., 1876, and Edward Johnson, *Charles Dickens*, 2 vols., 1952. For modern biographies, see Fred Kaplan, *Dickens: A Biography*, 1988, and Peter Ackroyd, *Dickens*, 1990. *Dickens: Interviews and Recollections*, 2 vols., Philip Collins, ed., 1981, is another biographical source.

Classic early studies include George Gissing, *Charles Dickens: A Critical Study*, 1903; G. K. Chesterton, *Charles Dickens*, 1906; Edmund Wilson, "Dickens: The Two Scrooges," in his *The Wound and the Bow*, 1952; and George Orwell, "Charles Dickens," in his *A Collection of Essays*, 1954. For modern critical studies see John Carey, *Here Comes Dickens*, 1974; Philip Collins, *Dickens and Crime*, 1962; George H. Ford, *Dickens and His Readers*, 1955; Robert Garis, *The Dickens Theatre*, 1965; Steven Marcus, *Dickens: From Pickwick to Dombey*, 1965; J. Hillis Miller, *Charles Dickens: The World of His Novels*, 1958; Alexander Welsh, *The City of Dickens*, 1971; Angus Wilson, *The World of Charles Dickens*, 1970. Critical responses to Dickens are collected in *Dickens: The Critical Heritage*, ed. Philip Collins, 1971, and *Charles Dickens*, ed. Stephen Wall, 1970. For a collection of modern essays, see *Charles Dickens*, ed. Harold Bloom, 1987.

Ernest Dowson

The standard modern edition of Dowson's poems is *The Poetry of Ernest Dowson*, ed. Desmond Flower, 1st American ed., 1970. Much lively and illuminating comment on Dowson will be found in W. B. Yeats's *Autobiography*, 1955. *Ernest Dowson*, by J. M. Longaker, 1944, and *Ernest Dowson*, by T. B. Swann, 1965, are critical biographies; a short chapter on Dowson in *Essays in Criticism and Research*, by Geoffrey Tillotson, 1967, assesses his relationship with other poets. See also *Letters of Ernest Dowson*, ed. Desmond Flower and Henry Maas, 1967.

See also entries under **The Nineties.**

George Eliot

There is no twentieth-century standard edition of Eliot's complete works. The collected edition of the works, corrected by Eliot, is the Cabinet Edition, 20 vols., 1878–80. Of modern editions, the *Essays* are edited by Thomas Pinney, 1963, and *The George Eliot Letters* are edited by Gordon S. Haight, 9 vols., 1954–78. Margaret Harris and Judith Johnston have edited *The Journals of George Eliot*, 1999. Five of the eight novels have been published in annotated Clarendon editions. Bert G. Hornback has edited the Norton Critical Edition of *Middlemarch*, 1977, and Carol Christ has edited *The Mill on the Floss* for the same series. The best critical biography is Ruby V. Redinger, *George Eliot: The Emergent Self*, 1975; Gordon Haight's *George Eliot: A Biography*, 1968, remains the most exhaustive account of her life. See also Rosemary Ashton, *George Eliot: A Life*, 1997; Rosemarie Bodenheimer, *The Real Life of Mary Ann Evans: George Eliot, Her Letters and Fiction*, 1994; and Frederick R. Karl, *George Eliot, Voice of a Century: A Biography*, 1995.

Good introductions to Eliot's fiction are Joan

Bennett, *George Eliot: Her Mind and Her Art*, 1948, and Joseph Wiesenfarth's essay in *Victorian Novelists before 1885*, ed. Ira Nadel and William Frederman, *Dictionary of Literary Biography*, vol. 21, 1983. F. R. Leavis's influential discussion of Eliot in *The Great Tradition*, 1948, revived critical interest in Eliot's work in this century. See also Dorothea Barrett, *Vocation and Desire: George Eliot's Heroines*, 1989; Gillian Beer, *George Eliot*, 1986; David Carroll, *George Eliot and the Conflict of Interpretations: A Reading of the Novels*, 1992; Deirdre David, *Intellectual Women and Victorian Patriarchy: Harriet Martineau, Elizabeth Barrett Browning, George Eliot*, 1987; W. J. Harvey, *The Art of George Eliot*, 1962; U. C. Knoepflmacher, *George Eliot's Early Novels: The Limits of Realism*, 1968; Alexander Welsh, *George Eliot and Blackmail*, 1985. Barbara Hardy, *Novels of George Eliot: A Study in Form*, 1959, and two collections of essays, *Critical Essays on George Eliot*, 1970, and *Particularities: Readings in George Eliot*, 1982, are standard critical works. Other collections include *George Eliot: The Critical Heritage*, ed. David Carroll, 1971; a special issue of *Nineteenth Century Fiction*, "George Eliot 1880–1980," ed. U. C. Knoepflmacher and George Levine, 1980; and *George Eliot*, ed. Harold Bloom, 1986. An especially useful reference work is George Levine, *An Annotated Critical Bibliography of George Eliot*, 1988.

Michael Field

Michael Field's poetry has not been collected. Individual volumes are titled *Long Ago*, 1889; *Sight and Song*, 1892; *Underneath the Bough, A Book of Verses*, 1893; *Wild Honey From Various Thyme*, 1908; *Mystic Trees*, 1913; *Dedicated: An Early Work of Michael Field*, 1914; *Whym Chow: Flame of Love*, 1914; *The Wattlefold: Unpublished Poems*, 1930. *Works and Days: From the Journal of Michael Field*, ed. T. and D. C. Sturge Moore, 1933, contains selections from the diaries. For critical commentary, see Angela Leighton, *Victorian Women Poets*, 1992, and a special issue of *Victorian Poetry*, *Women Poets 1830–1894*.

Edward FitzGerald

George Bentham edited *The Variorum Edition of the . . . Writings of Edward FitzGerald*, 7 vols., 1902; a critical edition of the *Rubaiyat* has been edited by Christopher Decker, 1997. See also the *Letters*, ed. A. McKinley Terhune, 4 vols., 1980. The biography, by Robert Bernard Martin, is *With Friends Possessed: A Life of Edward FitzGerald*, 1985.

Elizabeth Gaskell

The standard edition of Gaskell's fiction is the Knutsford Edition, ed. A. W. Ward, 8 vols, 1906–20; the best modern editions are by Penguin. A modern edition exists of *The Letters of Mrs. Gaskell*, ed. J. A. V. Chapple and Arthur Pollard, rev. 1997. Biographies include Winifred Gerin, *Elizabeth Gaskell*, 1980, and Jenny Uglow, *Elizabeth Gaskell: A Habit of Stories*, 1993. For critical studies see W. A. Craik, *Elizabeth Gaskell and the English Provincial Novel*, 1975; Angus Easson, *Elizabeth Gaskell*, 1979; Angus Easson, ed., *Elizabeth Gaskell: The Critical Heritage*, 1991; Hilary M. Schor, *Scheherezade in the Marketplace: Elizabeth Gaskell and the Victorian Novel*, 1992; and Patsy Stoneman, *Elizabeth Gaskell*, 1987.

W. S. Gilbert

Gilbert's librettos for Sullivan in their finally revised form comprise *The Complete Plays of Gilbert and Sullivan*, 1976. The earliest published versions, often substantially different from those performed today, are reprinted in Reginald Allen, *The First Night Gilbert and Sullivan*, 1958. Earlier works by Gilbert include *The Bab Ballads*, ed. James Ellis, 1970, and *Gilbert Before Sullivan: Six Comic Plays*, 1967, ed. Jane W. Stedman, 1967. Hesketh Pearson's *Gilbert: His Life and Strife*, 1957, is the best modern biography. A sampling of Gilbert criticism is offered by John B. Hones in *W. S. Gilbert: A Century of Scholarship and Commentary*, 1970. See also Alan Fischler, *Modified Rapture: Comedy in W. S. Gilbert's Savoy Operas*, 1991.

William Ernest Henley

The standard edition, which includes essays and plays as well as poetry, is *The Works of William Ernest Henley*, 7 vols., 1970 (reprint of 1908 edition). See B. Ifor Evans, *English Poetry in the Later Nineteenth Century*, 1933, chapter 12, and Jerome H. Buckley, *William Ernest Henley: A Study of the "Counter-Decadence" of the Nineties*, 1945. Also useful on Henley as a figure of the Nineties is a study by André Guillaume, *William Ernest Henley et son groupe*, 1973.

See also entries under **The Nineties.**

Gerard Manley Hopkins

Robert Bridges edited the first (posthumous) edition of Hopkins's poems in 1918, which has been the nucleus of all subsequent editions. The most recent is *The Poetical Works of Gerard Manley Hopkins*, ed. Norman H. MacKenzie, 1990. In addition to the poems, Hopkins's letters and parts of his notebooks have been published: *The Letters of Gerard Manley Hopkins to Robert Bridges* and *The Correspondence of G. M. Hopkins and Richard Watson Dixon*, ed. C. C. Abbot, 2 vols., 1935; *Further Letters of Gerard Manley Hopkins*, ed. C. C. Abbott, 1938, rev. 1956; *The Journals and Papers of Gerard Manley Hopkins*, ed. Humphry House and Graham Storey, 1969; and *The Sermons and Devotional Writings of Gerard Manley Hopkins*, ed. Christopher Devlin, 1959. A helpful introduction to these works is Norman H. MacKenzie, *A Reader's Guide to Gerard Manley Hopkins*, 1981.

The two best biographies are Robert Bernard Martin, *Gerard Manley Hopkins: A Very Private Life*, 1991, and Norman White, *Hopkins: A Literary Biography*, 1992. Some useful critical studies are W. H. Gardner, *G. M. Hopkins: A Study of Poetic Idiosyncrasy in Relation to Poetic Tradition*, 2 vols., 1944, 1949; Paul L. Mariani, *A Commentary on the Complete Poems of Gerard Manley Hopkins*, 1970; Alison Sulloway, *Gerard Manley Hopkins and the Victorian*

Temper, 1972; Daniel Harris, *Inspirations Unbidden: The "Terrible Sonnets" of Gerard Manley Hopkins*, 1982; Walter J. Ong, *Hopkins, the Self, and God*, 1986; and Virginia Ridley Ellis, *Gerard Manley Hopkins and the Language of Mystery*, 1991. Two good collections of critical essays are *Hopkins*, ed. Geoffrey Hartmann, 1966, and *Hopkins Among the Poets: Studies in Modern Responses to Gerard Manley Hopkins*, ed. Richard F. Giles, 1985.

Thomas Henry Huxley
The Life and Letters of Thomas Henry Huxley, Leonard Huxley, 2 vols., 1900, is the standard biography. William Irvine, *Apes, Angels, and Victorians*, 1955, is lively and informative. See also Harold Cyril Bibby, *Scientist Extraordinary: The Life and Scientific Work of Thomas Henry Huxley*, 1972.

Rudyard Kipling
The Sussex Edition of the complete works, 35 vols., 1937–39, is the standard complete edition. *Rudyard Kipling's Verse: Definitive Edition*, 1940, must now be supplemented by *Early Verse by Rudyard Kipling, 1879–1889: Unpublished, Uncollated and Rarely Collected Poems*, ed. Andrew Rutherford, 1986. T. S. Eliot has edited, with an appreciative and discerning introduction, *A Choice of Kipling's Verse*, 1941. Thomas Pinney edited *The Letters of Rudyard Kipling (1872–99)*, 3 vols., 1988–96. Charles E. Carrington's *Rudyard Kipling*, 1955, is the official biography, but three others are worthy of note: J. I. M. Stewart, *Rudyard Kipling*, 1966; Philip Mason, *Kipling: The Glass, the Shadow, and the Fire*, 1975, an informative account of Kipling's complex relationship with India; and Angus Wilson, *The Strange Ride of Rudyard Kipling*, 1978, a judicious and readable interpretation of Kipling's life and attitudes. Three important midcentury critics have written interesting essays on Kipling: Edmund Wilson in *The Wound and the Bow*, 1941; George Orwell in *Critical Essays*, 1946; and Lionel Trilling in *The Liberal Imagination*, 1950. Studies of his fiction include Helen Pike Bauer, *Rudyard Kipling: A Study of the Short Fiction*, 1994; Elliot L. Gilbert, *The Good Kipling: Studies in the Short Story*, 1971; Sandra Kemp, *Kipling's Hidden Narratives*, 1987; Mark Paffard, *Kipling's Indian Fiction*, 1989; and Zohreh T. Sullivan, *Narratives of Empire: Fictions of Rudyard Kipling*, 1992. Peter Keating has written a study of his poetry, *Kipling the Poet*, 1994. There are a number of useful collections of critical essays: *Kipling's Mind and Art*, ed. Andrew Rutherford, 1964; *Kipling and the Critics*, ed. E. L. Gilbert, 1965; Roger Lancelyn Green, *Kipling: The Critical Heritage*, 1971; *Rudyard Kipling*, ed. John Gross, 1972 and *Critical Essays on Rudyard Kipling*, ed. Harold Orel, 1989.
See also entries under **The Nineties**.

Edward Lear
The Complete Nonsense, ed. Holbrook Jackson, 1947; Ina Rae Hark, *Edward Lear*, 1982; Elizabeth Sewell, *The Field of Nonsense*, 1952. Edward Gorey's *Gorey x 3*, 1976, provides delightful illustrations for Lear's verse-narratives. See also Thomas Byrom, *Nonsense and Wonder: The Poems and Cartoons of Edward Lear*, 1978.

Light Verse
Interesting collections of light verse include *Parodies: An Anthology from Chaucer to Beerbohm*, ed. Dwight Macdonald, 1969; *The Oxford Book of Light Verse*, ed. W. H. Auden, 1938; and *The New Oxford Book of Light Verse*, ed. Kingsley Amis, 1978.
See also entries under **Lewis Carroll, W. S. Gilbert**, and **Edward Lear.**

George Meredith
Phyllis Bartlett's edition of the *Poems*, 1978, supersedes G. M. Trevelyan's edition of 1928. *The Letters*, ed., C. L. Cline, were published in three volumes in 1970. See Lionel Stevenson, *The Ordeal of George Meredith*, 1953; C. Day Lewis, *Introduction to Modern Love*, 1948; and Norman Kelvin, *A Troubled Eden*, 1961. A Norton Critical Edition of his novel, *The Egoist*, was edited by Robert M. Adams in 1979.

John Stuart Mill
The *Collected Works*, ed. John Robson et al., were published in twenty-seven volumes, 1963–90. *Mill: The Spirit of the Age, On Liberty, The Subjection of Women* has been edited by Alan Ryan in the Norton Critical Editions, 1998. Ann P. Robson and John M. Robson have edited *Sexual Equality: Writings by John Stuart Mill, Harriet Taylor Mill, and Helen Taylor*, 1994. *The Life of J. S. Mill* by M. St. J. Packe, 1954, is the standard biography. Studies include A. W. Benn, *The History of English Rationalism in the Nineteenth Century*, 2 vols., 1906; Janice Carlisle, *John Stuart Mill and the Writing of Character*, 1991; Maurice Cowling, *Mill and Liberalism*, 1963; *J. S. Mill: On Liberty in Focus*, ed. John Gray and G. W. Smith, 1991; *A Cultivated Mind: Essays on J. S. Mill Presented to John M. Robson*, ed. Michael Laine, 1991; Emery Neff, *Carlyle and Mill*, 1926; John Robson, *The Improvement of Mankind*, 1968; Alan Ryan, *John Stuart Mill*, 1970; and *Mill: A Collection of Critical Essays*, ed. J. B. Schneewind, 1968.

William Morris
Collected Works, 24 vols., 1910–15; *The Collected Letters of William Morris*, ed. Norman Kelvin, 4 vols., 1984–96; Biographies include J. W. Mackail, *The Life of William Morris*, 2 vols, 1899; Philip Henderson, *William Morris, His Life, Work and Friends*, 1967; and Fiona MacCarthy, *William Morris: A Life for Our Time*, 1995. Also see George Bernard Shaw, *William Morris, As I Knew Him*, 1936; *William Morris: The Critical Heritage*, ed. Peter Faulkner, 1973; Jerome McGann, *Black Riders: The Visible Language of Modernism*, 1993; and Carole Silver, *The Romance of William Morris*, 1982. E. P. Thompson's Marxist approach in *William Morris: Romantic to Revolutionary*, 1977, offers the best study of Morris's politics.

John Henry Cardinal Newman
The forty-one volumes of Newman's works were published over a period of years, but no standard

edition has as yet appeared. His *Letters and Diaries,* on the other hand, have been collected and edited by C. S. Dessain et al., 31 vols., 1961–84. For a useful text, with criticism, of *Apologia pro Vita Sua,* see David J. DeLaura, Norton Critical Edition, 1968. For Newman's religious background and development, see Charles F. Harold, *John Henry Newman,* 1945, and for a comprehensive study see Sheridan Gilley, *Newman and His Age,* 1990. His literary skill is analyzed in John Holloway, *The Victorian Sage,* 1953, chapter 6, and Walter E. Houghton, *The Art of Newman's "Apologia,"* 1945. Especially recommended is Dwight Culler, *The Imperial Intellect,* 1955. William Robbins, *The Newman Brothers,* 1966, develops an interesting contrast between Newman and his free-thinking brother, Francis Newman.

The Nineties

On the special qualities of the literature of the 1890s, see *Edwardians and Late Victorians,* ed. Richard Ellmann, 1960. See also Holbrook Jackson, *The Eighteen Nineties,* 1913, rev. 1976; Graham Hough, *The Last Romantics,* 1947; R. K. R. Thornton, *The Decadent Dilemma,* 1983; John R. Reed, *Decadent Style,* 1985; Linda C. Dowling, *Language and Decadence in the Victorian Fin de Siecle,* 1986; Richard Dellamora, *Masculine Desire: The Sexual Politics of Victorian Aestheticism,* 1990; Elaine Showalter, *Sexual Anarchy: Gender and Culture at the Fin de Siecle,* 1990; Karl Beckson, *London in the 1890's: A Cultural History,* 1992; *The 1890's: An Encyclopedia of British Literature, Art, and Culture,* ed. G. A. Cevasco, 1993; and Rhonda K. Garelick, *Rising Star: Dandyism, Gender, and Performance in the Fin de Siecle,* 1998. Three useful anthologies are *An Anthology of "Nineties" Verse,* ed. A. J. A. Symons, 1928; *Aesthetes and Decadents of the 1890's: An Anthology of British Poetry and Prose,* ed. K. Beckson, 1966; and *Poetry of the Nineties,* ed. R. K. R. Thornton, 1971.

See also entries under **Ernest Dowson, William Ernest Henley, Rudyard Kipling, Walter Pater, Francis Thompson,** and **Oscar Wilde.**

Walter Pater

Works, 10 vols., 1910, and see also Donald Hill's annotated edition of *The Renaissance,* 1980. Thomas Wright, *The Life of Walter Pater,* 2 vols., 1907, is a standard but unreliable source. More satisfactory is Michael Levey, *The Case of Walter Pater,* 1978. A book-length study of Pater by Wolfgang Iser was published in Germany in 1960 and translated in 1987 as *Walter Pater: The Aesthetic Moment.* Critical essays include T. S. Eliot's "Arnold and Pater" in *Selected Essays 1917–32,* 1932; U. C. Knoepflmacher, *Religious Humanism and the Victorian Novel,* 1965; David J. DeLaura, *Hebrew and Hellene in Victorian England: Newman, Arnold, and Pater,* 1969; Carolyn Williams, *Transfigured World: Walter Pater's Aesthetic Historicism,* 1989; and Denis Donoghue, *Walter Pater: Lover of Strange Souls,* 1995. A collection of essays is *Walter Pater: Modern Critical Views,* ed. Harold Bloom, 1985. Highly recommended is Laurence

Evans's chapter on Pater in *Victorian Prose: A Guide to Research,* ed. David J. DeLaura, 1973.

See also entries under **The Nineties.**

Christina Rossetti

The standard variorum edition is *The Complete Poems of Christina Rossetti,* ed. R. W. Crump, 3 vols., 1979–90. The first volume of *The Letters of Christina Rossetti,* ed. Anthony H. Harrison, 1997, has been published. See also *Selected Prose of Christina Rossetti,* ed. David A. Kent and P. G. Stanwood, 1998. Two recent biographies are Kathleen Jones, *Learning Not to Be First: The Life of Christina Rossetti,* 1991, and Jan Marsh, *Christina Rossetti: A Writer's Life,* 1995. Virginia Woolf's *Second Common Reader,* 1932, contains an essay on the poet. Dolores Rosenblum's *Christina Rossetti: The Poetry of Endurance,* 1986, and Antony H. Harrison's *Christina Rossetti in Context,* 1988, are good book-length studies of the poetry. David Kent has edited a collection of critical essays, *The Achievement of Christina Rossetti,* 1987.

Dante Gabriel Rossetti

Rossetti's *Works* were edited by W. M. Rossetti, 1911, and *The Letters* by Oswald Doughty and J. R. Wahl, 4 vols., 1965–67 (an incomplete collection). See Oswald Doughty, *D. G. Rossetti: A Victorian Romantic,* 1960, and Lionel Stevenson, *The Pre-Raphaelite Poets,* 1973. Also recommended are Joan Rees, *The Poetry of Dante Gabriel Rossetti,* 1981; and David Riede, *Dante Gabriel Rossetti and the Limits of Victorian Vision,* 1983, and *Dante Gabriel Rossetti Revisited,* 1992. *The Rossetti Archieve,* ed. Jerome McGann, is an on-line edition currently in progress (jefferson.village.edu/rossetti/rossetti. html).

John Ruskin

The Works were edited by E. T. Cook and Alexander Wedderburn, 39 vols., 1903–12. Cook's early biography of Ruskin, 1911, has been superseded by John Dixon Hunt, *The Wider Sea: A Life of John Ruskin,* 1982, and by Tim Hilton, *John Ruskin: The Early Years,* 1985, the first of two projected volumes. An interesting digest of his aesthetic theories was compiled by Joan Evans in *The Lamp of Beauty: Writings on Art by John Ruskin,* 1958. Also recommended are R. H. Wilenski, *John Ruskin,* 1933; John D. Rosenberg, *The Darkening Glass,* 1961; George P. Landow, *The Aesthetic and Critical Theories of John Ruskin,* 1971; Elizabeth Helsinger, *Ruskin and the Art of the Beholder,* 1982; and Linda M. Austin, *The Practical Ruskin: Economics and Audience in the Late Work,* 1991. See also Robert Hewison, ed., *New Approaches to Ruskin,* 1981.

Bernard Shaw

The first volume of *The Collected Works of Bernard Shaw,* in the Ayot St. Lawrence Edition, 30 vols., appeared in 1930. *Collected Plays with Their Prefaces,* 7 vols., 1975, contains the fully revised texts of all the published plays, together with historical data and miscellaneous Shavian pronouncements on each play. There is a Norton Critical Edition, *Bernard Shaw's Plays,* ed. Warren Sylvester Smith,

1970. Selections of prose include *Bernard Shaw, Selected Prose*, ed. Diarmuid Russell, 1952; *Plays and Players*, ed. A. C. Ward, 1952; *The Nondramatic Literary Criticism of Bernard Shaw*, ed. Stanley Weintraub, 1972; *Shaw on Music*, ed. Eric Bentley, 1972; and *Bernard Shaw on Language*, ed. Abraham Tauber, 1963. The *Collected Letters of Bernard Shaw*, ed. Dan H. Laurence, 1965–, collects his voluminous correspondence.

The standard biography is Michael Holroyd, *Bernard Shaw*, 4 vols, 1988–93. Also of interest is Hesketh Pearson, *George Bernard Shaw: His Life and Personality*, 1963. Other biographical sources are *Shaw: An Autobiography, Selected from His Writings*, 2 vols., ed. Stanley Weintraub, 1969–70, and *Shaw: Interviews and Recollections*, ed. A. M. Gibbs, 1990.

Critical studies include Eric Bentley, *Bernard Shaw: A Reconsideration*, 1947; Charles A. Carpenter, *Bernard Shaw and the Art of Destroying Ideals*, 1969; Louis Crompton, *Shaw the Dramatist*, 1969; *Shaw and Politics*, ed. T. F. Evans, 1991; J. Ellen Gainor, *Shaw's Daughters: Dramatic and Narrative Constructions of Gender*, 1991; Gareth Griffith, *Socialism and Superior Brains: The Political Thought of Bernard Shaw*, 1992; and Sally Peters, *Bernard Shaw: The Ascent of the Superman*, 1996. Two useful collections of essays are *George Bernard Shaw*, ed. Harold Bloom, 1987, and *Critical Essays on George Bernard Shaw*, ed. Elsie B. Adams, 1991.

Algernon Charles Swinburne

Complete Works, ed. E. W. Gosse and T. J. Wise, 20 vols., 1925–27, and *The Swinburne Letters*, ed. Cecil Y. Lang, 6 vols., 1959–62. Rikky Rooksby, *A. C. Swinburne: A Poet's Life*, 1997, is the best biography. For an attack on Swinburne's shortcomings as a poet, see A. E. Housman's essay of 1910, first published in *American Scholar*, Winter 1969–70. For more sympathetic readings see the special Swinburne issue of *Victorian Poetry*, Spring-Summer 1971, and also see Jerome J. McGann, *Swinburne: An Experiment in Criticism*, 1972; David Riede, *Swinburne: A Study of Romantic Mythmaking*, 1978; Margot K. Louis, *Swinburne and His Gods: The Roots and Growth of an Agnostic Poetry*, 1990; the chapter on Swinburne in Camille Paglia, *Sexual Personae*, 1990; and *The Whole Music of Passion: New Essays on Swinburne*, ed. Rikky Rooksby and Nicholas Shrimpton, 1993.

Alfred, Lord Tennyson

Tennyson's *Works* were edited by his son Hallam, Lord Tennyson, in 9 vols., 1907–8. The *Poems* in one volume were edited by Christopher Ricks in 1969 and extensively revised in three volumes in 1988. Norton Critical Editions of Tennyson's work are *Tennyson's Poetry*, ed. Robert W. Hill, Jr., 1972, and *In Memoriam*, ed. Robert H. Ross, 1974. *In Memoriam* has been edited by Susan Shatto and Marion Shaw, 1982. Three volumes of *The Letters of Alfred, Lord Tennyson*, to 1870, were edited by Cecil Y. Lang and Edgar F. Shannon, 1981–90.

Hallam Tennyson's *Alfred, Lord Tennyson: A Memoir*, 2 vols., 1897, is a mine of anecdotes and valuable information. *The Tennyson Archive*, ed. Christopher Ricks and Aidan Day, 23 vols., 1987–89, is a monumental production concerning the manuscripts. The standard biography is Robert Martin, *Tennyson*, 1980. Sir Harold Nicolson, *Tennyson*, 1923, a critical study more than a biography, gives a lively but distorted assessment of Tennyson's achievement. A number of critical studies have successively corrected Nicolson's oversights and have variously demonstrated that Tennyson is one of the finest of poets. These include Jerome H. Buckley, *Tennyson: The Growth of a Poet*, 1961; Christopher Ricks, *Tennyson*, 1972; F. E. L. Priestley, *Language and Structure in Tennyson's Poetry*, 1973; James R. Kincaid, *Tennyson's Major Poems: The Comic and Ironic Patterns*, 1975; W. David Shaw, *Tennyson's Style*, 1976; and, most especially to be recommended, A. Dwight Culler, *The Poetry of Tennyson* 1977. See also Daniel Albright, *Tennyson: The Muses' Tug-of-War*, 1986; Alan Sinfield, *Alfred Tennyson*, 1986; Herbert F. Tucker, *Tennyson and the Doom of Romanticism*, 1988; Donald S. Hair, *Tennyson's Language*, 1991; and Gerhard Joseph, *Tennyson and the Text: The Weaver's Shuttle*. 1992.

Some of the most interesting discussions are in introductory essays to Tennyson's poems by T. S. Eliot, 1936; W. H. Auden, 1944; H. Marshall McLuhan, 1956; Jerome Buckley, 1958; and George MacBeth, 1971. Also useful are A. C. Bradley, *A Commentary on Tennyson's "In Memoriam,"* 1901; E. D. H. Johnson, *The Alien Vision of Victorian Poetry*, 1952; *Critical Essays on the Poetry of Tennyson*, ed. John Killham, 1960; and Herbert F. Tucker, *Critical Essays on Alfred Lord Tennyson*, 1993. Book-length studies of the *Idylls* have been published by Clyde de L. Ryals, 1967, John R. Reed, 1969, and John D. Rosenberg, 1973. A collection of critical essays on *In Memoriam* was edited by John Dixon Hunt, 1970; and Timothy Peltason has published a study of the poem, *Reading In Memoriam*, 1985.

Francis Thompson

Complete Poetical Works was edited by Wilfred Meynell, 3 vols., 1913. Biographies are Paul van K. Thompson, *Francis Thompson*, 1961, and Brigid M. Boardman, *Between Heaven and Charing Cross: The Life of Francis Thompson*, 1988. For a general introduction, see Beverly Taylor, *Francis Thompson*, 1987.

See also entries under **The Nineties**.

Oscar Wilde

There is no standard complete edition, but a convenient one-volume collection is *The Complete Works of Oscar Wilde*, 1989. Rupert Hart-Davis has edited the *Letters*, 1962, and its supplement, *More Letters*, 1985. The standard biography is Richard Ellmann, *Oscar Wilde*, 1988. See also the psychoanalytic biography by Melissa Knox, *Oscar Wilde: A Long and Lovely Suicide*, 1994. Earlier biographies include Hesketh Pearson, *The Life of Oscar Wilde:*

His *Life and Wit*, 1946, and H. Montgomery Hyde, *Oscar Wilde: A Biography*, 1975. *Oscar Wilde, a Pictorial Biography*, by Wilde's son, Vyvyan Holland, 1960, has splendid photographs of Wilde and his contemporaries and also provides a concise factual account of his life. The essays by Ian Fletcher and John Stokes in *Anglo-Irish Literature: A Review of Research*, 1976, and *Recent Research on Anglo-Irish Writers*, 1983 (both ed. Richard J. Finneran), provide a full-scale guide to editions of Wilde and studies of his life and work.

Oscar Wilde: A Collection of Critical Essays, ed. Richard Ellmann, 1969, is valuable for its coverage of responses to Wilde by other writers such as Yeats and Shaw. *Oscar Wilde: The Critical Heritage*, ed. Karl Beckson, 1970, is especially helpful with regard to the plays; it covers the period 1881–1927.

For an account of the contemporary reception of Wilde, see Regina Gagnier, *Idylls of the Marketplace: Oscar Wilde and the Victorian Public*, 1986. See also Camille Paglia, *Sexual Personae*, 1990; *Critical Essays on Oscar Wilde*, ed. Regina Gagnier, 1991; Ed Cohen, *Talk on the Wilde Side: Toward a Genealogy of Discourse on Male Sexualities*, 1993; Gary Schmidgall, *The Stranger Wilde: Interpreting Oscar*, 1994; Lawrence Damson, *Wilde's Intentions: The Artist in His Criticism*, 1997; *The Cambridge Companion to Oscar Wilde*, ed. Peter Raby, 1997; and Karl Beckson, *The Oscar Wilde Encyclopedia*, 1998. Harold Bloom has edited two anthologies of critical essays: *Oscar Wilde: Modern Critical Views*, 1985, and *Oscar Wilde's The Importance of Being Earnest: Modern Critical Interpretations*, 1988.

See also entries under **The Nineties.**

Geographic Nomenclature: England, Great Britain, The United Kingdom

The **British Isles** refers to the prominent group of islands off the northwest coast of Europe, especially to the two largest, **Great Britain** and **Ireland**. At present these comprise two sovereign states: **The Republic of Ireland**, or **Eire**, and **The United Kingdom of Great Britain and Northern Ireland**—known for short as **The United Kingdom** or **The U.K.** Most of the smaller islands are part of **The U.K.** but a few, like the **Isle of Man** and the tiny **Channel Islands**, are very largely independent. **The U.K.** is often loosely referred to as "**Britain**" or "**Great Britain**" and is sometimes simply called "**England.**" The latter usage, though technically inaccurate and occasionally confusing, is common among Englishmen as well as foreigners, though, for obvious reasons, it is rarely heard among the inhabitants of the other countries of **The U.K.**—**Scotland**, **Wales**, and **Northern Ireland** (sometimes called **Ulster**). England is by far the most populous part of the kingdom, as well as the seat of its capital, London.

From the first to the fifth century C.E. most of what is now **England** and **Wales** was a province of the Roman Empire called **Britain** (in Latin, **Britannia**). After the fall of Rome, much of the island was invaded and settled by peoples from northern Germany and Denmark speaking what we now call Old English. They are collectively known as the Anglo-Saxons, and the word **England** is related to the first element of their name. By the time of the Norman Conquest (1066) most of the kingdoms founded by the Anglo-Saxons and subsequent Viking invaders had coalesced into the kingdom of **England**, which, in the latter Middle Ages, conquered and largely absorbed the neighboring Celtic kingdom of **Wales**. In 1603 James VI of **Scotland** inherited the island's other throne as James I of **England**, and for the next hundred years—except for the brief period of Puritan rule—**Scotland** and **England** (with **Wales**) were two kingdoms under a single king. In 1707 the Act of Union welded them together as **The United Kingdom of Great Britain**, which, upon the incorporation of **Ireland** in 1801, became **The United Kingdom of Great Britain and Ireland**. With the division of Ireland and the establishment of **The Irish Free State** after World War I, this name was modified to its present form. In 1949 **The Irish Free State** became **The Republic of Ireland**; and in 1997 **Scotland** voted to restore the separate parliament it had relinquished in 1707, without, however, ceasing to be part of **The United Kingdom**.

The **British Isles** are further divided into counties, which in **Great Britain** are also known as shires. This word, with its vowel shortened in pronunciation, forms the suffix in the names of many counties, such as **Yorkshire, Wiltshire, Somersetshire**.

The Latin names **Britannia (Britain), Caledonia (Scotland)**, and **Hibernia (Ireland)** are sometimes used in poetic diction; so too is **Britain**'s ancient Celtic name, **Albion**. Because of its accidental resemblance to *albus* (Latin for "white"), **Albion** is especially associated with the chalk cliffs which seem to gird much of the English coast like defensive walls.

The **British Empire** took its name from **The British Isles** because it was created not only by the **English** but by the **Irish, Scots**, and **Welsh**, as well as by civilians and servicemen from other constituent countries of the Empire.

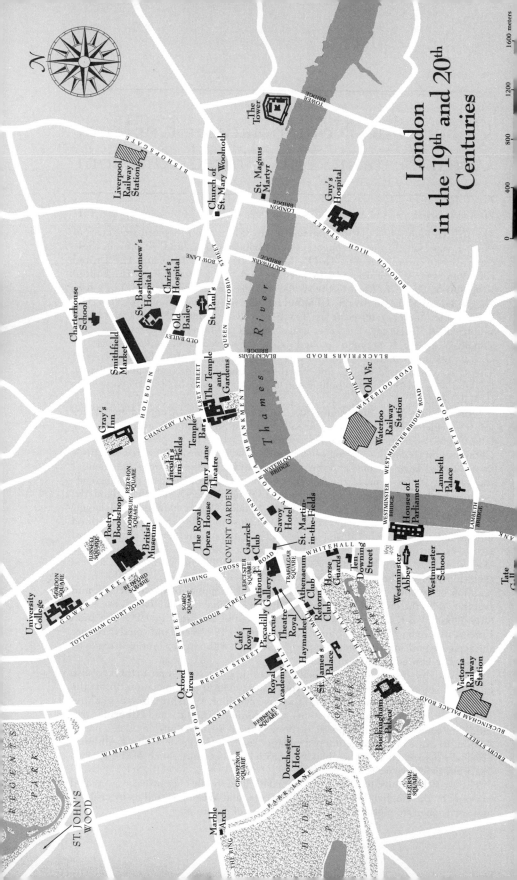

London
in the 19th and 20th
Centuries

British Money

Since 1971, British money has been calculated on the decimal system, with 100 pence to the pound; the pound has fluctuated from a bit more than 2 American dollars to virtual parity—whatever dollars may be worth. Before 1971, the pound consisted of 20 shillings, each containing 12 pence, making 240 pence to the pound. In paper money the change has not been great; 5- and 10-pound notes constitute the mass of bills under both the old and the new systems; nowadays, in addition, 20- and 50-pound notes have been added. But in the smaller coinage the change has been considerable and the simplification remarkable. Most notable is the abolition of the shilling, which goes into retirement now with the mark (worth in its day two-thirds of a pound or 13 shillings 4 pence) and the angel (once 10 shillings but replaced by the 10-shilling note, now in its turn abolished). The guinea, an oddity of the old currency, amounted to a pound and a shilling; though it has not been minted since 1813, a very few quality items or prestige awards (like horse races) may still be quoted in guineas. Colloquially, a pound was (and is) called a quid; a shilling a bob; sixpence a tanner; a penny, half-penny, or farthing, a copper. The common signs were £ for pound, s. for shilling, d. for a penny (from Latin *denarius*). A sum would normally be written £2.19.3, i.e., 2 pounds, 19 shillings, 3 pence. In Joyce's *Ulysses*, that is Leopold Bloom's budget for June 16, 1904. In new currency, it would be about £2.96.

Old	New
1 pound note	1 pound coin (or note in Scotland)
10 shilling (half-pound note)	50 pence
5 shilling (crown)	
	20 pence
2½ shilling (half crown)	
2 shilling (florin)	10 pence
1 shilling	5 pence
6 pence	
2½ pence	1 penny
2 pence	
1 penny	
½ penny	
¼ penny (farthing)	

What the pound was worth at any point in history is ever easy to state. In the first part of the twentieth century, 1 pound equaled about 5 American dollars; but those dollars bought three or four times what they would today. Historians sometimes attempt to calculate the value of the pound in terms of the goods and services it would purchase, but these too vary radically with special circumstances such as wars and poor harvests. Nevertheless, it is clear that money used to be worth much more than it is now. In the early sixteenth century, according to Hugh Latimer, people would say, "Oh, he's a rich man, he's worth £500." Four centuries later, Virginia Woolf argued that £500 a year (along with a room of one's own) was the bare minimum necessary for a woman to be able to write. Whatever Latimer meant by "rich," or Woolf by "necessary," it is clear that the value of the pound had declined drastically over this period, as it has continued to do in the course of the twentieth century. In Britain today, a worker on minimum wage earns more than £500 a month, an income associated with severe poverty.

In the Anglo-Saxon period, the silver penny was the biggest coin in general circulation; 4 of them would buy a sheep. Peasants and craftsmen before the Black Death of the fourteenth century made at most 2 or 3 pence a day—an annual income of £3 or £4; after the onset of the plague, wages nearly doubled, due to the shortage of laborers. Throughout the medieval period, kings and commoners worried less about inflation than about the debasement of the silver currency. In 1124, dozens of mintmasters had their right hands chopped off on Christmas Day for issuing inferior coinage. In the early sixteenth century, under Henry VIII and his son Edward VI, the silver content of coins fell as low as 25 percent. Elizabeth I considered the revaluation of the silver coinage to be one of her greatest achievements as queen. Nevertheless, her reign was marked by sustained inflation of prices, caused in part by the influx of gold and silver from the New World, and in part by the rising population.

In the Elizabethan era, admission to the public theaters cost a penny for those who stood throughout the performance. Playwrights were paid about £6 for each play, so to make a living a writer had to be prolific (or, like Shakespeare, own shares in the theater company). In the same period, 40 pounds a year in independent income (generally rent from lands) was the minimum requirement for a justice of the peace; it marked the threshold of gentry status and was also the sum fixed by King James I at which a man could be forced to accept knighthood (paying a fee to the crown). In 1661, following further inflation, Samuel Pepys calculated his worth at a modest £650 just after he had begun working for the navy; five years later, that good bourgeois was worth more than £6000, and his annual income was about £3000. Of course, he was working for most of this income. Pepys was a rising official and would become a very important one; but he never achieved a title or even knighthood because the smell of commerce had never been washed from his money by possession of land.

Various writers provide examples of the incomes of rich and poor in the eighteenth and nineteenth centuries. Joseph Andrews (in Fielding's novel, published 1742) worked as a footman in the house of Lady Booby for £8 a year; in addition, he got his room, board, and livery, plus the occasional tip. Among the comfortable classes, Mr. Bennet of Jane Austen's *Price and Prejudice* (1813) enjoyed an income of £2000 a year (with a family of five nonearning females to support), while Mr. Darcy had close to £10,000, nearing the level of the aristocracy. In his deepest degradation David Copperfield (of Dickens's 1850 novel) worked in the warehouse of Murdstone & Grinby for 6 or 7 shillings a week (£15 to £18 a year). Mr. Murdstone paid extra for his lodging and laundry, but even so the boy was bitterly impoverished, though he had only himself to feed. When his father died, his mother was thought to be pretty well taken care of with £105 a year, less than £9 per month. Even in 1888, Annie Besant reports workers in Bryant and May's match factory made 4 to 9 shillings a week and paid for their own lodging—this, in the words of Ada Nield Chew, was not a living wage, but "a lingering, dying wage." Far removed from this world is Jack Worthing in Wilde's comedy *The Importance of Being Earnest* (1895), who receives £7000 or £8000 a year from investments and has a country house with about fifteen hundred acres attached to it, though it yields no income worth talking about.

While incomes have risen enormously over the centuries, and the value of the pound declined accordingly, the gap between rich and poor has remained. So too has the gap between the country and the city: London has always been very expensive, and elsewhere a small income goes further. To a large extent, one's position in terms of class and geography determines not only what money can buy but what it means.

We have only to contrast Jack Worthing's vague estimate of his income with the factory workers' exact sense of the value of a shilling. As Woolf acknowledged, having a purse with the power "to breed ten-shilling notes automatically," changes one's view of money and of the world. Perhaps it is because British currency has been so important in shaping people's views of themselves and their society that many Britons are reluctant to let it go. The question of whether the United Kingdom should relinquish the pound and the penny to join the single European currency (the Euro) is a matter of fierce and prolonged debate. For some, the pound, far more than the flag, is an enduring symbol of the nation. Whether or not one holds this view, it can at least be said that over the centuries the pound has undergone as many crises and transformations as the nation itself.

The British Baronage

The English monarchy is in principle hereditary, though at times during the Middle Ages the rules were subject to dispute. In general, authority passes from father to eldest surviving son, from daughters in order of seniority if there is no son, to a brother if there are no children, and in default of direct descendants to collateral lines (cousins, nephews, nieces) in order of closeness. There have been breaks in the order of succession (1066, 1399, 1688), but so far as possible the usurpers have always sought to paper over the break with a legitimate, i.e., a hereditary claim. When a queen succeeds to the throne and takes a husband, he does not become king unless he is in the line of blood succession; rather, he is named prince consort, as Albert was to Victoria. He may father kings, but is not one himself.

The original Saxon nobles were the king's thanes, ealdormen, or earls, who provided the king with military service and counsel in return for booty, gifts, or landed estates. William the Conqueror, arriving from France, where feudalism was fully developed, considerably expanded this group. In addition, as the king distributed the lands of his new kingdom, he also distributed dignities to men who became known collectively as "the baronage." "Baron" in its root meaning signifies simply "man," and barons were the king's men. As the title was common, a distinction was early made between greater and lesser barons, the former gradually assuming loftier and more impressive titles. The first English "duke" was created in 1337; the title of "marquess," or "marquis" (pronounced "markwis"), followed in 1385, and "viscount" ("vyekount") in 1440. Though "earl" is the oldest title of all, it now comes between a marquess and a viscount in order of dignity and precedence, and the old term "baron" now designates a rank just below viscount. "Baronets" were created in 1611 as a means of raising revenue for the crown (the title could be purchased for about £1000); they are marginal nobility and do not sit in the House of Lords.

Kings and queens are addressed as "Your Majesty," princes and princesses as "Your Highness," the other hereditary nobility as "My Lord" or "Your Lordship." Peers receive their titles either by inheritance (like Lord Byron, the sixth baron of that line) or from the monarch (like Alfred Lord Tennyson, created first Baron Tennyson by Victoria). The children, even of a duke, are commoners unless they are specifically granted some other title or inherit their father's title from him. A peerage can be forfeited by act of attainder, as for example when a lord is convicted of treason; and, when forfeited, or lapsed for lack of a successor, can be bestowed on another family. Thus Robert Cecil was made in 1605 first earl of Salisbury in the third creation, the first creation dating from 1149, the second from 1337, the title having been in abeyance since 1539. Titles descend by right of succession and do not depend on tenure of land; thus, a title does not always indicate where a lord dwells or holds power. Indeed, noble titles do not always refer to a real place at all. At Prince Edward's marriage in 1999, the queen created him earl of Wessex, although the old kingdom of Wessex has had no political existence since the Anglo-Saxon period, and the name was all but forgotten until it was resurrected by Thomas Hardy as the setting of his novels. (This is perhaps but one of many ways in which the world of the aristocracy increasingly resembles the realm of literature.)

The king and queen Prince and princess	(These are all of the royal line.)
Duke and duchess Marquess and marchioness Earl and countess Viscount and viscountess Baron and baroness Baronet and lady	(These may or may not be of the royal line, but are ordinarily remote from the succession.)

Scottish peers sat in the parliament of Scotland, as English peers did in the parliament of England, till at the Act of Union (1707) Scots peers were granted sixteen seats in the English House of Lords, to be filled by election. Similarly, Irish peers, when the Irish parliament was abolished in 1801, were granted the right to elect twenty-eight of their number to the House of Lords in Westminster. (Now that the Republic of Ireland is a separate nation, of course, this no longer applies.) The House of Lords still retains some power to influence or delay legislation. But this upper house is now being reformed. All or most of the hereditary peers are to be expelled, while recipients of nonhereditary Life Peerages will remain and vote as before.

Below the peerage the chief title of honor is "knight." Knighthood, which is not hereditary, is generally a reward for services rendered. A knight (Sir John Black) is addressed, using his first name, as "Sir John"; his wife, using the last name, is "Lady Black"—unless she is the daughter of an earl or nobleman of higher rank, in which case she will be "Lady Arabella." The female equivalent of a knight bears the title of "Dame."

Though the word itself comes from the Anglo-Saxon *cniht*, there seems to be some doubt as to whether knighthood amounted to much before the arrival of the Normans. The feudal system required military service as a condition of land tenure, and a man who came to serve his king at the head of an army of tenants required a title of authority and badges of identity—hence the title of knighthood and the coat of arms. During the Crusades, when men were far removed from their land (or had even sold it in order to go on crusade), more elaborate forms of fealty sprang up that soon expanded into orders of knighthood. The Templars, Hospitallers, Knights of the Teutonic Order, Knights of Malta, and Knights of the Golden Fleece were but a few of these companionships; not all of them were available at all times in England.

Gradually, with the rise of centralized government and the decline of feudal tenures, military knighthood became obsolete, and the rank largely honorific; sometimes, as under James I, it degenerated into a scheme of the royal government for making money. For hundreds of years after its establishment in the fourteenth century, the Order of the Garter was the only English order of knighthood, an exclusive courtly companionship. Then, during the late seventeenth, the eighteenth, and the nineteenth centuries, a number of additional orders were created, with names such as the Thistle, Saint Patrick, the Bath, Saint Michael and Saint George, plus a number of special Victorian and Indian orders. They retain the terminology, ceremony, and dignity of knighthood, but the military implications are vestigial.

Although the British Empire now belongs to history, appointments to the Order of the British Empire continue to be conferred for services to that empire at home or abroad. Such honors (commonly referred to as "gongs") are granted by the monarch in her New Year's and Birthday lists, but the decisions are now made by the government in power. In recent years there have been efforts to popularize and democratize the dispensation of honors, with recipients including rock stars and actors. But this does not prevent large sectors of British society from regarding both knighthood and the peerage as largely irrelevant to modern life.

The Royal Lines of England and Great Britain

England

SAXONS AND DANES

Egbert, king of Wessex	802–839
Ethelwulf, son of Egbert	839–858
Ethelbald, son of Ethelwulf	858–860
Ethelbert, second son of Ethelwulf	860–866
Ethelred I, third son of Ethelwulf	866–871
Alfred the Great, fourth son of Ethelwulf	871–899
Edward the Elder, son of Alfred	899–924
Athelstan the Glorious, son of Edward	924–940
Edmund I, third son of Edward	940–946
Edred, fourth son of Edward	946–955
Edwy the Fair, son of Edmund	955–959
Edgar the Peaceful, second son of Edmund	959–975
Edward the Martyr, son of Edgar	975–978 (murdered)
Ethelred II, the Unready, second son of Edgar	978–1016
Edmund II, Ironside, son of Ethelred II	1016–1016
Canute the Dane	1016–1035
Harold I, Harefoot, natural son of Canute	1035–1040
Hardecanute, son of Canute	1040–1042
Edward the Confessor, son of Ethelred II	1042–1066
Harold II, brother-in-law of Edward	1066–1066 (died in battle)

HOUSE OF NORMANDY

William I the Conqueror	1066–1087
William II, Rufus, third son of William I	1087–1100 (shot from ambush)
Henry I, Beauclerc, youngest son of William I	1100–1135

HOUSE OF BLOIS

Stephen, son of Adela, daughter of William I	1135–1154

HOUSE OF PLANTAGENET

Henry II, son of Geoffrey Plantagenet by Matilda, daughter of Henry I	1154–1189
Richard I, Coeur de Lion, son of Henry II	1189–1199
John Lackland, son of Henry II	1199–1216
Henry III, son of John	1216–1272
Edward I, Longshanks, son of Henry III	1272–1307
Edward II, son of Edward I	1307–1327
Edward III of Windsor, son of Edward II	1327–1377
Richard II, grandson of Edward III	1377–1400

HOUSE OF LANCASTER

Henry IV, son of John of Gaunt, son of
Edward III   1399–1413
Henry V, Prince Hal, son of Henry IV   1413–1422
Henry VI, son of Henry V   1422–1471 (deposed)

HOUSE OF YORK

Edward IV, great-great-grandson of
Edward III   1461–1483
Edward V, son of Edward IV   1483–1483 (murdered)
Richard III, Crookback   1483–1485 (died in battle)

HOUSE OF TUDOR

Henry VII, married daughter of
Edward IV   1485–1509
Henry VIII, son of Henry VII   1509–1547
Edward VI, son of Henry VIII   1547–1553
Mary I, "Bloody," daughter of Henry VIII   1553–1558
Elizabeth I, daughter of Henry VIII   1558–1603

HOUSE OF STUART

James I (James VI of Scotland)   1603–1625
Charles I, son of James I   1625–1649 (executed)

COMMONWEALTH & PROTECTORATE

Council of State   1649–1653
Oliver Cromwell, Lord Protector   1653–1658
Richard Cromwell, son of Oliver   1658–1660 (resigned)

HOUSE OF STUART (RESTORED)

Charles II, son of Charles I   1660–1685
James II, second son of Charles I   1685–1688

(INTERREGNUM, 11 DECEMBER 1688 TO 13 FEBRUARY 1689)

William III of Orange, by Mary,
daughter of Charles I   1685–1701
and Mary II, daughter of James II   –1694
Anne, second daughter of James II   1702–1714

Great Britain

HOUSE OF HANOVER

George I, son of Elector of Hanover and
Sophia, granddaughter of James I   1714–1727
George II, son of George I   1727–1760
George III, grandson of George II   1760–1820
George IV, son of George III   1820–1830

William IV, third son of George III   1830–1837
Victoria, daughter of Edward, fourth son
  of George III   1837–1901

HOUSE OF SAXE-COBURG AND GOTHA

Edward VII, son of Victoria   1901–1910

HOUSE OF WINDSOR (NAME ADOPTED 17 JULY 1917)

George V, second son of Edward VII   1910–1936
Edward VIII, eldest son of George V   1936–1936 (abdicated)
George VI, second son of George V   1936–1952
Elizabeth II, daughter of George VI   1952–

Religions in England

Religious distinctions and denominations are important in British social history, hence deeply woven into the nation's literature. The numerous (over three hundred) British churches and sects divide along a scale from high to low, depending on the amount of authority they give to the church or the amount of liberty they concede to the individual conscience. At one end of the scale is the Roman Catholic Church, asserting papal infallibility, universal jurisdiction, and the supreme importance of hierarchy as guide and intercessor. For political and social reasons, Catholicism struck deep roots in Ireland but in England was the object of prolonged, bitter hatred on the part of Protestants from the Reformation through the nineteenth century. The Established English (Anglican) Episcopal church has been the official national church since the sixteenth century; it enjoys the support (once direct and exclusive, now indirect and peripheral) of the national government. Its creed is defined by Thirty-Nine Articles, but these are intentionally vague, so there are numerous ways of adhering to the Church of England. Roughly and intermittently, the chief classes of Anglicans have been known as High Church (with its highest portion calling itself Anglo-Catholic); Broad Church, or Latitudinarian (when they get so broad that they admit anyone believing in God, they may be known as Deists, or some may leave the church altogether and be known as Unitarians); and Low Church, whose adherents may stay in the English church and yet come close to shaking hands with Presbyterians or Methodists. These various groups may be arranged, from the High down to the Low Church, in direct relation to the amount of ritual each prefers and in the degree of authority conceded to the upper clergy—and in inverse relation to the importance ascribed to a saving faith directly infused by God into an individual conscience.

All English Protestants who decline to subscribe to the English established church are classed as Dissenters or Nonconformists; for a time in the sixteenth and seventeenth centuries, they were also known as Puritans. (Nowadays, though Puritanism has less distinct theological meaning, it marks a distinct character type; because of his passionate emphasis on individual conscience and moral economy, Bernard Shaw was a prototypical Puritan.) The Presbyterians model their church government on that established by John Calvin in the Swiss city of Geneva. It has no bishops, and therefore is more democratic for the clergy; but it gains energy by associating lay elders with clergymen in matters of social discipline and tends to be strict with the ungodly. From its first reformation the Scottish Kirk was fixed on the Presbyterian model. During the civil wars of the seventeenth century, a great many sects sprang up on the left wing of the Presbyterians, most of them touched by Calvinism but some rebelling against it; a few of these still survive. The Independents became our modern Congregationalists; the Quakers are still Quakers, as Baptists are still Baptists, though multiply divided. But many of the sects flourished and perished within the space of a few years. Among these now vanished groups were the Shakers (though a few groups still exist in America), the Seekers, the Ranters, the Anabaptists, the Muggletonians, the Fifth Monarchy Men, the Family of Love, the Sweet Singers of Israel, and many others, forgotten by all except scholars. During the eighteenth and nineteenth centuries, new sects arose, supplanting old ones; the Methodists, under John and Charles Wesley, became numerous and important, taking root particularly in Wales. (The three "subject" nationalities, Ireland, Scotland, and Wales, thus turned three different ways to avoid the Anglican church.) With the passage of time a small number of Swedenborgians sprang up, followers of the Swedish mystic Emanuel Swedenborg—to be followed by the Plymouth Brethren, Christian Scientists, Jehovah's Witnesses, and countless other nineteenth-century groups. All these sects constantly grow, shrink, split, and occasionally disappear as they succeed or fail in attracting new converts.

Within the various churches and sects, independent of them all but amazingly persistent, there has always survived a stream of esoteric or hermetic thought—a belief in occult powers, and sometimes in magic also, exemplified by the pseudo-sciences of astrology and alchemy but taking many other forms as well. From the mythical Egyptian seer Hermes Trismegistus through Paracelsus, Cornelius Agrippa, Giordano Bruno, Jakob Boehme, the society of Rosicrucians, and a hundred other shadowy figures, the line can be traced to William Blake and William Butler Yeats, who both in their different ways brought hermetic Protestantism close to its ultimate goal, a mystic church of a single consciousness, poised within its mind-elaborated cosmos.

Christianity is not, of course, the only religion present on the British Isles. The few Jews in medieval England were regarded as resident aliens, as were those in other European countries. In 1290 all English Jews who refused baptism were expelled from the kingdom, and officially, there were no Jews living in England between that time and the mid-1650s, when Cromwell encouraged Jewish merchants to settle in London. A considerable number of east European Jews emigrated to England in the first half of the twentieth century (many as refugees), but the country's Jewish population as a whole remains quite small (less than half a million). Hardly any Muslims or Hindus lived in the U.K. before the dissolution of the Empire shortly after World War II. Today both religions have a large and growing representation among ex-colonial immigrants and their children.

Poetic Forms and
Literary Terminology

Systematic literary theory and criticism in English began in the sixteenth century, at a time when the standard education for upper-class students emphasized the study of the classical languages and literatures. As a consequence, the English words that were introduced to describe meter, figures of speech, and literary genres often derive from Latin and Greek roots.

RHYTHM AND METER

Verse is generally distinguished from prose as a more compressed and more regularly rhythmic form of statement. This approximate truth underlines the importance of **meter** in poetry, as the means by which rhythm is measured and described.

In Latin and Greek, meter was established on a **quantitative** basis, by the regular alternation of long and short syllables (that is, syllables classified according to the time taken to pronounce them). Outside of a few experiments (and the songs of Thomas Campion), this system has never proved congenial to Germanic languages such as English, which distinguish, instead, between **stressed** and **unstressed,** or accented and unaccented syllables. Two varieties of accented stress may be distinguished. On the one hand, there is the natural stress pattern of words themselves; *sýllable* is accented on the first syllable, *deplórable* on the second, and so on. Then there is the sort of stress that indicates rhetorical emphasis. If the sentence "You went to Greece?" is given a pronounced accent on the last word, it implies "Greece (of all places)?" If the accent falls on the first word, it implies "you (of all people)?" The meter of poetry—that is, its rhythm—is ordinarily built up out of a regular recurrence of accents, whether established as **word accents** or **rhetorical accents;** once started, it has (like all rhythm) a tendency to persist in the reader's mind.

The unit that is repeated to give steady rhythm to a poem is called a **foot;** in English it usually consists of accented and unaccented syllables in one of five fairly simple patterns:

The **iambic foot** (or **iamb**) consists of an unstressed followed by a stressed syllable, as in *uníte, repeát,* or *insíst.* Most English verse falls naturally into the iambic pattern.

The **trochaic foot** (**trochee**) inverts this order; it is a stressed followed by an unstressed syllable—for example, *únit, reáper,* or *ínstant.*

A-47

The **anapestic foot** (**anapest**) consists of two unstressed syllables followed by a stressed syllable, as in *intercéde, disarránged,* or *Cameróon.*

The **dactylic foot** (**dactyl**) consists of a stressed syllable followed by two unstressed syllables, as in *Wáshington, Écuador,* or *ápplejack.*

The **spondaic foot** (**spondee**) consists of two successive stressed syllables, as in *heartbreak, headline,* or *Kashmir.*

In all the examples above, word accent and the quality of the metrical foot coincide exactly. But the metrical foot may well consist of several words, or, on the other hand, one word may well consist of several metrical feet. *Phótolithógraphy* consists of two dactyls in a single word; *dárk and with spóts on it,* though it consists of six words rather than one, is also two dactyls. When we read a piece of poetry with the intention of discovering its underlying metrical pattern, we are said to **scan** it—that is, we go through it line by line, indicating by conventional signs which are the accented and which the unaccented syllables within the feet. We also count the number of feet in each line; a line is, formally, also called a **verse** (from Latin *versus,* which means one "row" of metrical feet). Verse lengths are conventionally described in terms derived from the Greek:

Monometer: one foot (of rare occurrence)
Dimeter: two feet (also rare)
Trimeter: three feet
Tetrameter: four feet
Pentameter: five feet
Hexameter: six feet (six iambic feet make what is called an **Alexandrine**)
Heptameter: seven feet (also rare)

Samuel Johnson wrote a little parody of simpleminded poets which can be scanned this way:

> Ĭ pút m̆y hát ŭpón m̆y héad
> Ănd wálked ĭntó thĕ Stránd
> Ănd thére Ĭ mét ănóthĕr mán
> Whŏse hát wăs ín hĭs hánd.

The poem is iambic in rhythm, alternating tetrameter and trimeter in the length of the verse-lines. The fact that it scans so nicely is, however, no proof that it is good poetry. Quite the contrary. Many of poetry's most subtle effects are achieved by establishing an underlying rhythm and then varying it by means of a whole series of devices, some dramatic and expressive, others designed simply to lend variety and interest to the verse. A well-known sonnet of Shakespeare's (*116*) begins,

> Let me not to the marriage of true minds
> Admit impediments. Love is not love
> Which alters when it alteration finds,
> Or bends with the remover to remove.

It is possible to read the first line of this poem as mechanical iambic pentameter:

Lĕt mé nŏt tó thĕ márriăge óf trŭe mińds

But of course nobody ever reads it that way, except to make a point; read with normal English accent and some sense of what it is saying, the line would form a pattern something like this:

Lét mĕ nŏt tŏ thĕ márriăge ŏf trúe mińds

which is neither pentameter nor in any way iambic. The second line is a little more iambic, but, read expressively also falls short of pentameter:

Ădmít ĭmpédĭmeñts. Lóve ĭs nŏt lóve

Only in the third and fourth lines of the sonnet do we get verses that read as five iambic feet.

The fact is that perfectly regular metrical verse is easy to write and dull to read. Among the devices in common use for varying too regular a pattern are the insertion of a trochaic foot among iambics, especially at the opening of a line, where the soft first syllable of the iambic foot often needs stiffening (see line 1 of the sonnet above); the more or less free addition of extra unaccented syllables; and the use of **caesura,** or strong grammatical pause within a line (conventionally indicated, in scanning, by the sign ‖). The second line of the sonnet above is a good example of caesura:

Admit impediments. ‖ Love is not love

The strength of the caesura, and its placing in the line, may be varied to produce striking variations of effect. More broadly, the whole relation between the poem's sound and rhythm-patterns and its pattern as a sequence of assertions (phrases, clauses, sentences) may be manipulated by the poet. Sometimes the statements fit neatly within the lines, so that each line ends with a strong mark of punctuation; they are then known as **end-stopped lines.** Sometimes the sense flows over the ends of the lines, creating **run-on lines;** this process is also known, from the French, as **enjambment** (literally, "straddling").

End-stopped lines (Marlowe, *Hero and Leander*, lines 45–48):

> So lovely fair was Hero, Venus' nun,
> As Nature wept, thinking she was undone,
> Because she took more from her than she left
> And of such wondrous beauty her bereft.

Run-on lines (Keats, *Endymion* 1.89–93):

> Full in the middle of this pleasantness
> There stood a marble altar, with a tress
> Of flowers budded newly; and the dew
> Had taken fairy fantasies to strew
> Daisies upon the sacred sward, . . .

Following the example of such poets as Blake, Rimbaud, and Whitman, many twentieth-century poets have undertaken to write what is called **free** verse—that is, verse which has neither a fixed metrical foot nor (consequently) a fixed number of feet in its lines, but which depends for its rhythm on a pattern of cadences, or the rise and fall of the voice in utterance, or the pattern indicated to the reader's eye by the breaks between the verse lines. As in traditional versification, free verse is printed in short lines instead of with the continuity of prose; it differs from such versification, however, by the fact that its stressed syllables are not organized into a regular metric sequence.

SENSE AND SOUND

The words of which poetic lines—whether free or traditional—are composed cause them to have different sounds and produce different effects. Polysyllables, being pronounced fast, often cause a line to move swiftly; monosyllables, especially when heavy and requiring distinct accents, may cause it to move heavily, as in Milton's famous line (*Paradise Lost* 2.621):

> Rocks, caves, lakes, fens, bogs, dens, and shades of death

Poetic assertions are often dramatized and reinforced by means of **alliteration**—that is, the use of several nearby words or stressed syllables beginning with the same consonant. When Shakespeare writes (*Sonnet 64*),

> Ruin hath taught me thus to ruminate
> That Time will come and take my love away,

the alliterative *r*'s and rich internal echoes of the first line contrast with the sharp anxiety and directness of the alliterative *t*'s in the second. When Dryden starts *Absalom and Achitophel* with the couplet,

> In pious times, ere priestcraft did begin,
> Before polygamy was made a sin,

the satiric undercutting is strongly reinforced by the triple alliteration that links *"pious"* with *"priestcraft"* and *"polygamy."*

Assonance, or repetition of the same or similar vowel sounds within a passage (usually in accented syllables), also serves to enrich it, as in two lines from Keats's *Ode on Melancholy*:

> For shade to shade will come too drowsily,
> And drown the wakeful anguish of the soul.

It is clear that the round, hollow tones of "drowsily," repeated in "drown" and darkening to the full *o*-sound of "soul," have much to do with the effect of the passage. A related device is **consonance**, or the repetition of a pattern of consonants with changes in the intervening vowels—for example: *linger, longer, languor; rider, reader, raider, ruder.*

The use of words that seem to reproduce the sounds they designate (known as **onomatopoeia**) has been much attempted, from Virgil's galloping horse—

Quadrupedante putrem sonitu quatit ungula campum—

through Tennyson's account, in *The Princess*, of

> The moan of doves in immemorial elms,
> And murmuring of innumerable bees—

to many poems in the present day.

RHYME AND STANZA

Rhyme consists of a repetition of accented sounds in words, usually those falling at the end of verse lines. If the rhyme sound is the very last syllable of the line (*rebound, sound*), the rhyme is called **masculine;** if the accented syllable is followed by an unaccented syllable (*hounding, bounding*), the rhyme is called **feminine.** Rhymes amounting to three or more syllables, like forced rhymes, generally have a comic effect in English, and have been freely used for this purpose, e.g., by Byron (*intellectual, henpecked-you-all*). Rhymes occurring within a single line are called **internal;** for instance, the Mother Goose rhyme "Mary, Mary, quite contrary," or from Coleridge's *Ancient Mariner* ("We were the first that ever burst / Into that silent sea"). **Eye rhymes** are words used as rhymes that look alike but actually sound different (for example, *alone, done; remove, love*); **off rhymes** (sometimes called **partial, imperfect,** or **slant rhymes**) are occasionally the result of pressing exigencies or lack of skill, but are also, at times, used deliberately by modern poets for special effects. For instance, a poem by Wilfred Owen (*Strange Meeting*) contains such paired words (which Owen called "pararhymes") as *years / yours* or *tigress / progress.*

Blank verse is unrhymed iambic pentameter; until the recent advent of free verse, it was the only unrhymed measure to achieve general popularity in English. Though first used by the earl of Surrey in translating Virgil's *Aeneid*, blank verse was during the sixteenth century employed primarily in plays; *Paradise Lost* was one of the first nondramatic poems in English to use it. But Milton's authority and his success were so great that during the eighteenth and nineteenth centuries blank verse came to be used for a great variety of discursive, descriptive, and philosophical poems—besides remaining the standard metrical form for epics. Thomson's *Seasons*, Cowper's *Task*, Wordsworth's *Prelude*, and Tennyson's *Idylls of the King* were all written in blank verse.

A **stanza** is a recurring unit of a poem, consisting of a number of verses. Certain poems (for example, Dryden's *Alexander's Feast*) have stanzas comprising a variable number of verses, of varying lengths. Others are more regular, and are identified by particular names.

The simplest form of stanza is the **couplet;** it is two lines rhyming together. A single couplet considered in isolation is sometimes called a **distich;** when it expresses a complete thought, ending with a terminal mark of punctuation such as a semicolon or period, it is called a **closed couplet.** The development of very regular end-stopped couplets, their use in so-called heroic tragedies, and their consequent acquisition of the name **heroic couplets** took place for the most part during the mid-seventeenth century. The heroic couplet was the principal form in English neoclassical poems.

Another traditional and challenging form of couplet is the **tetrameter, or four-beat couplet.** All rhymed couplets are hard to manage without monotony; and since, in addition, a four-beat line is hard to divide by caesura without splitting it into two tick-tock dimeters, tetrameter couplets have posed a perpetual challenge to poets, and still provide an admirable finger-exercise for aspiring versifiers. An instance of tetrameter couplets managed with marvelous variety, complexity, and expressiveness is Marvell's *To His Coy Mistress*:

> Thou by the Indian Ganges' side
> Shouldst rubies find; I by the tide
> Of Humber would complain. I would
> Love you ten years before the Flood,
> And you should, if you please, refuse
> Till the conversion of the Jews.

English has not done much with rhymes grouped in threes, but has borrowed from Italian the form known as **terza rima,** in which Dante composed his *Divine Comedy*. This form consists of linked groups of three rhymes according to the following pattern: *aba bcb cdc ded*, etc. Shelley's *Ode to the West Wind* is composed in stanzas of *terza rima*, the poem as a whole ending with a couplet.

Quatrains are stanzas of four lines; the lines usually rhyme alternately, *abab*, or in the second and fourth lines, *abcb*. When they alternate tetrameter and trimeter lines, as in Johnson's little poem about men in hats (above), or as in *Sir Patrick Spens*, they are called **ballad stanza.** Dryden's *Annus Mirabilis* and Gray's *Elegy Written in a Country Churchyard* are in **heroic quatrains;** these rhyme alternately *abab*, and employ five-stress iambic verse throughout. Tennyson used for *In Memoriam* a tetrameter quatrain rhymed *abba*, and FitzGerald translated *The Rubáiyát of Omar Khayyám* into a pentameter quatrain rhymed *aaba*; but these forms have not been widely adopted.

Chaucer's *Troilus and Criseide* is the premier example in English of **rhyme royal,** a seven-line iambic pentameter stanza consisting essentially of a quatrain dovetailed onto two couplets, according to the rhyme scheme *ababbcc* (the fourth line serves both as the final line of the quatrain and as the first line of the first couplet). Closely akin to rhyme royal, but differentiated by an extra *a*-rhyme between the two *b*-rhymes, is **ottava rima,** that is, an eight-line stanza rhyming *abababcc*. As its name suggests, ottava rima is of Italian origin; it was first used in English by Wyatt. Its final couplet, being less prepared for than in rhyme royal, and usually set off as a separate verbal unit, is capable of manifesting a witty snap, for which Byron found good use in *Don Juan*.

The longest and most intricate stanza generally used for narrative purposes in English is that devised by Edmund Spenser for *The Faerie Queene*. The **Spenserian stanza** has nine lines rhyming *ababbcbcc*; the first eight lines are pentameter, the last line an Alexandrine. Slow-moving, intricate of pattern, and very demanding in its rhyme scheme (the *b*-sound recurs four times, the *c*-sound three), the Spenserian stanza has nonetheless appealed widely to poets who seek a rich and complicated metrical form. Keats's *Eve of St. Agnes* and Shelley's *Adonais* are brilliantly successful nineteenth-century examples of its use.

The **sonnet**, originally a stanza of Italian origin that has developed into an independent lyric form, is usually defined nowadays as fourteen lines of iambic pentameter. None of the elements in this definition is absolute and in earlier centuries there were sonnets in hexameters (the first of Sidney's *Astrophil and Stella*), and sonnets of as many as twenty lines (Milton's *On the New Forcers of Conscience*). Most, however, approximate the definition. Most Elizabethan sonnets dealt with love; and some poets, like Sidney, Spenser, and Shakespeare, imitated Petrarch in grouping together their sonnets dealing with a particular lady or situation. The term for these gatherings is **sonnet sequences**; the extent to which they tell a sequential story, and the extent to which such stories are autobiographical, vary greatly. Since Elizabethan times, the sonnet has been applied to a wide range of subject matters—religious, political, satiric, moral, and philosophic.

In blank verse or irregularly rhymed verse, where stanzaic divisions do not exist or are indistinct, the poetry sometimes falls into **verse paragraphs**, which are in effect divisions of sense like prose paragraphs. This division can be clearly seen in Milton's *Lycidas* and *Paradise Lost*. An intermediate form, clearly stanzaic but with stanzas of varying patterns of line-length and rhyme, is illustrated by Spenser's *Epithalamion*; in this instance, the division into stanzas is reinforced by a **refrain**, which is simply a line repeated at the end of each stanza. Ballads also customarily have refrains; for example, the refrain of *Lord Randall* is

> mother, make my bed soon,
> For I'm weary wi' hunting, and fain wald lie down.

FIGURATIVE LANGUAGE

The act of bringing words together into rich and vigorous poetic lines is complex and demanding, chiefly because so many variables require control. There is the "thought" of the lines, their verbal texture, their emotional resonance, the developing perspective of the reader—all these to be managed at once. One of the poet's chief resources toward this end is figurative language. Here, as in matters of meter, one may distinguish a great variety of devices, some of which we use in everyday speech without special awareness of their names and natures. When we say someone eats "like a horse" or "like a bird," we are using a **simile**, that is, a comparison marked out by a specific word of likening—"like" or "as." When we omit the word of comparison but imply a likeness—as in the sentence "That hog has guzzled all the champagne"—we are making use of **metaphor**. The **epic simile**, frequent in epic poetry, is an extended simile in which the thing compared is described as an object in its own right, beyond its point of likeness with the main subject. Milton starts to compare Satan to Leviathan, but concludes his simile with the story of a sailor who moored his ship by mistake, one night, to a whale (*Paradise Lost* 1.200–208). Metaphors and similes have been distinguished according to their special effects; they may be, for instance, violent, comic, degrading, decorative, or ennobling.

When we speak of "forty head of cattle" or ask someone to "lend a hand" with a job, we are using **synecdoche**, a figure that substitutes the part for the whole. When we speak of a statement coming "from the White House," or a man much interested in "the turf," (that is, the race-course), we are using **metonymy**, or the substitution of one term for another with which it is closely associated. **Antithesis** is a device for placing opposing ideas in grammatical parallel, as, for example, in the following passage from Alexander Pope's *Rape of the Lock* (5.25–30), where there are more examples of antithesis than there are lines:

> But since, alas! frail beauty must decay,
> Curled or uncurled, since locks will turn to gray;
> Since painted, or not painted, all shall fade,
> And she who scorns a man must die a maid;
> What then remains but well our power to use,
> And keep good humor still whate'er we lose?

Irony is a verbal device that implies an attitude quite different from (and often opposite to) that which is literally expressed. In Pope's *The Rape of the Lock* (4.131–32), after poor Sir Plume has stammered an incoherent request to return the stolen lock of hair, the Baron answers ironically:

> "It grieves me much," replied the Peer again,
> "Who speaks so well should ever speak in vain."

And when Donne "proves," in *The Canonization*, that he and his mistress are going to found a new religion of love, he seems to be inviting us to take a subtly ironic attitude toward religion as well as love.

Because it is easy to see through, **hyperbole**, or willful exaggeration, is a favorite device of irony—which is not to say that it may not be "serious" as well. When she hears that a young man is "dying for love" of her, a sensible young woman does not accept this statement literally, but it may convey a serious meaning to her nonetheless. The **pun**, or play on words (known to the learned, sometimes, as **paronomasia**), may also be serious or comic in intent; witness, for example, the famous series of puns on Donne's name in his *Hymn to God the Father*. **Oxymoron** is a conjunction of two terms that in ordinary use are contraries or incompatible—for instance, Milton's famous description of hell as containing "darkness visible" (*Paradise Lost* 1.63). A **paradox** is a statement that seems absurd but turns out to have rational meaning after all, usually in some unexpected sense; Donne speaks of fear being great courage and high valor (*Satire* 3, line 16), and turns out to mean that fear of God is greater courage than any earthly bravery. A **conceit** is a far-fetched and unusually elaborate comparison. Writing in the fourteenth century, the Italian poet Petrarch popularized a great number of conceits handy for use in love poetry, and readily adapted by his English imitators. Wyatt, for example, is using **Petrarchan conceits** when he compares love to a warrior, or the lover's state to that of a storm-tossed ship; and a hundred other sonneteers developed the themes of the lady's stony heart, incendiary glances, and so forth. On the other hand, the **metaphysical conceit** was a more intellectualized, many-leveled comparison, giving a strong sense of the poet's ingenuity in overcoming obstacles—for instance, Donne's comparison of separated lovers to the legs of a compass (A *Valediction: Forbidding Mourning*) or Herbert's comparison of devotion to a pulley, in the poem of that name.

Personification (or in the term derived from Latin **prosopopoeia**) is the attribution of human qualities to an inanimate object (for example, the Sea) or an abstract concept (Freedom); a special variety of it is called (in a term of John Ruskin's invention) the **pathetic fallacy.** When we speak of leaves "dancing" or a lake "smiling," we attribute human traits to nonhuman objects. Ruskin thought this was false and therefore "morbid"; modern criticism tends to view the practice as artistically and morally neutral. A more formal and abstract variety of personification is **allegory,** in which a narrative (such as *Pilgrim's Progress*) is constructed by representing general concepts (Faithfulness, Sin, Despair) as persons who act out the plot. A **fable** (like Chaucer's *The Nun's Priest's Tale*) represents beasts behaving like humans; a **parable** is a brief story, or simply an observation, with strong moral application; and an **exemplum** is a story told to illustrate a point in a sermon.

A special series of devices, nearly obsolete today, used to be available to poets who could count on readers trained in the classics. These were the devices of **classical allusion**—that is, reference to the mythology (stories about the actions of gods and other supernatural beings) of the Greeks and Romans. In their simplest form, the classic **myths** used to provide a repertoire of agreeable stage properties, and a convenient shorthand for expressing emotional attitudes. Picturesque creatures like centaurs, satyrs, and sphinxes, heroes and heroines like Hector and Helen, and the whole pantheon of Olympic deities could be used to make ready reference to a great many aspects of human nature. One does not have to explain the problems of a man who is "cleaning the Augean stables"; if he is afflicted with an "Achilles' heel," or is assailing "Hydra-headed difficulties," his state is clear. These descriptive phrases, making **allusion** to mythological stories, suggest in a phrase situations that would normally require cumbersome explanations. But because it used to be taken for granted that the classical mythology was the common possession of all educated readers, the classic myths entered into English literature as early as Chaucer. In poets like Spenser and Milton, classical allusion becomes a kind of enormously learned game, in which the poet seeks to make his points as indirectly as possible. For instance, Spenser writes in the *Epithalamion*, lines 328–29:

> Lyke as when Jove with fayre Alcmena lay,
> When he begot the great Tirynthian groome.

The mere mention of Alcmena in the first line suggests, to the informed reader, Hercules, the son of Jupiter (Jove) by Alcmena. Spenser's problem in the second line is to find a way of referring to him that is neither redundant nor heavy-handed. "Tirynthian" reminds the reader of Hercules' long connection with the city of Tiryns, stretching our minds (as it were) across his whole career; and "groome" compresses references to a man-child, a servant, and a bridegroom, all of which apply to different aspects of Hercules' history. Thus, far from simply avoiding redundancy, Spenser has enriched, for the reader who possesses the classical information, the whole texture of his verse, thought, and feeling.

SCHOOLS

Literary scholars and critics often group together in **schools** writers who share stylistic traits or thematic concerns. Whether they considered themselves a group doesn't much matter; although in some cases—for example, the Imagists or the Beat poets—the writers themselves have identified themselves as belonging to a group. None of the **Romantic poets** knew they were being romantic, although Hazlitt, Shelley, and other writers of the time recognized shared features that they called "the spirit of the age." The followers of Spenser are known as **Spenserians;** they knew they admired and to some extent wrote like Spenser, but didn't realize that made them a group. **Cavalier** poets are set decisively apart from **Metaphysical** poets, though pretty surely none of the two-dozen-odd men involved knew that was what they were. And so with the **Gothic novelists,** and the so-called **Graveyard School** of the eighteenth century; these schools are generally grouped, defined, and named by scholars and critics after the event.

Intellectual affinities have led some writers to be classified under the names of the philosophical schools of Greece and Rome. These are chiefly the **Epicureans,** who specify that the aim of life and the source of value is pleasure; the **Stoics,** who emphasize stern virtue and the dignified endurance of what cannot be avoided; and the **Skeptics,** who doubt that anything can be known for certain. These categories are useful as capsule descriptions, but they aren't very tidy, as they are omissive, overlap one another, and cut across other categories. Dryden is an author strongly tinged with skepticism, but many of his poems suggest an unabashed epicureanism. *The Vanity of Human Wishes,* by Samuel Johnson, is the classic poem in English of stoic philosophy, but it also expresses a particularly strong coloring of Christian humanism.

TERMS OF LITERARY ART

The following section defines frequently used literary terms, especially frequently used terms that are closely related or tend to be mistaken for each other.

Allegory, Symbol, Emblem, Type. Allegory is a narrative in which the agents, and sometimes also the setting, are personified concepts or character-types, and the plot represents a doctrine or thesis. John Bunyan's *Pilgrim's Progress,* for example, allegorizes the Christian doctrine of salvation by narrating how the character named Christian, warned by Evangelist, flees the City of Destruction and makes his laborious way to the Celestial City; en route he meets such characters as Faithful and the Giant Despair, and passes through places like the Slough of Despond and Vanity Fair. A literary **symbol** is the representation of an object or event which has a further range of reference beyond itself. Examples of sustainedly symbolic poems are William Blake's *The Sick Rose* and William Butler Yeats's *Sailing to Byzantium.* In the sixteenth and seventeenth centuries, an **emblem** was an enigmatic picture of a physical object, to which was attached a motto and a verse explaining its significance. In present-day usage, an emblem is any object which is widely understood to signify an abstract concept; thus a dove is an emblem of peace, and a cross, of Christianity. In what was once a widespread Christian mode of biblical interpretation, a **type** was a person or event in the Old Testament which was regarded as historically real, but also as "prefiguring" a person or event in the New Testament. Thus Adam was often said to be a type of Christ, and the act of Moses in liberating the children of Israel was said to prefigure Christ in freeing men from Satan.

Baroque and **Mannerist** are terms imported into literary study from the history of art, and applied by analogy. Michelangelo is a **baroque** artist; he holds great masses in powerful dynamic tension, his style is heavily ornamented and restless. In these respects he is sometimes compared to Milton. El Greco is a **mannerist,** whose gaunt and distorted figures often seem to be laboring under great spiritual stress, whose light seems to be focused in spots against a dark background. He has been compared to Donne. Analogies of this sort are occasionally suggestive, but can readily deteriorate into parallels that are forced and nominal rather than substantial.

Bathos. See **Pathos,** the **Sublime,** and **Bathos.**

Burlesque and **Mock Heroic** differ in that the former makes its subject ludicrous by directly cutting it down, the latter by inflating it. In Pope's mock-heroic *Dunciad,* the figure of Dulness (Colley Cibber) is given inappropriately heroic dimensions; in Butler's burlesque *Hudibras,* the knightly hero is characterized by low and vulgar attributes, and persistently engages in inappropriately low behavior. Burlesque contributed to the development of the English novel; and during the nineteenth century, when formal drama tended to be stagy and melodramatic, a vigorous burlesque stage flourished in England, making fun of the classics. See **Imitation** and **Parody.**

Catastrophe and **Catharsis.** The **catastrophe** is the conclusion of a play; the word means "down-turning," and is usually applied only to tragedies, in which a frequent kind of catastrophe is the death of the protagonist. (A term for the precipitating final scene that applies both to tragedy and to comedy is **denouement,** which in French means "unknotting.") **Catharsis** in Greek signifies "purgation" or "purification." In Aristotle's *Poetics,* the special effect of tragedy is the "catharsis" of the "emotions of pity and fear" that have been aroused in the audience by the events of the drama.

Chiasmus and **Zeugma.** **Chiasmus** is an inversion of the word order in two parallel phrases, as in John Denham's *Cooper's Hill*: "Strong without rage, without o'erflowing full." **Zeugma** is the use of a single verb or adjective to control two nouns, as in Pope's *The Rape of the Lock*: "Or stain her honor, or her new brocade."

Classic and **Neoclassic.** See **Gothic, Classic, Neoclassic.**

Convention and **Tradition.** **Conventions** are agreed-upon artistic procedures peculiar to an art form. None of Shakespeare's contemporaries spoke blank verse in everyday life, but characters in his plays do, and the audience accepts it—as the audience at an opera accepts that characters will sing arias to express their feelings. A **tradition** consists of beliefs, attitudes, and ways of representing things that is widely shared by writers over a span of time; it generally includes a number of conventions.

Didactic poetry is designed to teach a branch of knowledge, or to embody in fictional form a moral, religious, or philosophical doctrine. The term is not derogatory. John Milton's *Paradise Lost*, for example, can be called didactic, insofar as it is organized, as Milton claimed in his invocation, to "assert Eternal Providence / And justify the ways of God to men." In the eighteenth century, a number of poets wrote didactic poems called **georgics** (modeled on the Roman Virgil's *Georgics* on rural life and farming), which described such applied arts as making cider or running a sugar plantation.

Dramatic irony and **Dramatic monologue** are quite different literary modes. In **dramatic irony** a stage character says something that has one meaning for him, but quite another for the audience who possesses relevant knowledge that the speaker lacks. The **dramatic monologue** is a form that was perfected by Robert Browning in such poems as *My Last Duchess* and *The Bishop Orders His Tomb*. In it, the poetic speaker unintentionally reveals to the reader his character and temperament by what he says, usually to another person whose presence we infer from the utterance of the speaker.

Eclogue. See Pastorals.

Emblem. See Allegory, Symbol, Emblem, Type.

Epigram, Epigraph, Epitaph. An **epigram** is a short, witty statement in verse or prose. One of Oscar Wilde's characters remarks, "I can resist everything, except temptation." An **epigraph** is an apposite quotation placed at the beginning of a book or a section of it. An **epitaph** is a brief statement about someone who has died; usually, it is intended to be inscribed on a tombstone.

Eulogy and **Elegy.** The **eulogy** is a work of praise, in prose or poetry, for a person either very distinguished or recently dead. In its usual modern sense, an **elegy** is a formal, and usually long, poetic lament for someone who has died. In an extended sense, the term is also used to designate poems on the transience of earthly things (such as the Old English *The Seafarer*) or poetic meditations on mortality (such as Thomas Gray's *Elegy Written in a Country Churchyard*).

Euphemism and **Euphuism. Euphemism,** or "fine speech," is a verbal device for avoiding an unpleasant concept or expression, as when, instead of saying a person "died," we say he "passed away." Euphues was the hero of a prose romance (published 1579–80) by John Lyly; his adventures are recounted in a mannered style full of puns, alliteration, and antithetical "points." Under the name of **Euphuism** this courtly style enjoyed a brief vogue in the Elizabethan era.

Fancy and **Imagination.** The distinction between these two mental powers was central to the literary theory of S. T. Coleridge. **Fancy** (a word directly derived by contraction from "fantasy") was defined by Coleridge as the power of combining several known properties into new combinations; **imagination,** on the other hand, was the faculty of using such properties to create an integral whole that is entirely new.

Folios, Quartos, etc., are terms used to specify the size of book pages. To make a **folio,** a sheet of paper (14" × 20" or larger) is folded just once (producing thereby four pages); **quartos** are folded twice (producing eight pages). Shakespeare's plays were first printed in quartos (often in several different editions), but when they were collected together, in 1623, they appeared as the First Folio edition.

Genre, Decorum. A **genre** is an established literary form or type, such as stage comedy, the picaresque novel, the epic, the sonnet. Works belonging to a certain genre tend to represent certain characters and events, and to seek a similar effect. **Decorum,** in literary criticism—where it was a central concept from the Renaissance through the eighteenth century—designates the requirement that there should be a propriety, or fitness, in the way that the character, actions, and style are matched to each other in a particular genre. Low characters, actions, and style, for example, were thought appropriate for satire, while epic demanded characters of high estate, engaged in great actions, and speaking in an appropriately high style.

Gothic, Classic, Neoclassic. These terms are used to distinguish prominent tendencies in literature and the other arts. The term **Gothic** originally referred to the Goths, an early Germanic tribe, then came to signify "medieval." In the eighteenth century "Gothic" connoted primitive and irregular work, possessing the qualities of the relatively barbaric North. **Gothic novels** were a very popular type of prose fiction, inaugurated by Horace Walpole's *Castle of Otranto* (1764), usually set in a medieval castle, which aimed to evoke chilling terror from their readers. **Classic** implies lucid, rational, and orderly works, such as are usually attributed to the writers and thinkers in the classic era of the Greeks and Romans. **Neoclassic**— a term often applied to the period in England from 1660 through most of the eighteenth century—implies an ideal of life, art, and thought deliberately modeled on Greek and Roman examples.

Heroic poems, Heroic drama, Heroic couplets. Because they concentrate on the figure of a typical hero (Achilles, Aeneas), epic poems were frequently called "**heroic.**" Trying to transfer epic grandeur to the stage, playwrights of the Restoration period wrote what was called **heroic drama,** but usually achieved only grandiosity. The stately iambic pentameter couplets in which they made their characters speak became known as **heroic couplets.**

Humor. See **Wit** and **Humor.**

Humors and **Temperaments** are psychological terms used by Renaissance writers. It was believed that every person's constitution contained four basic humors: the **choleric** (bile), the **sanguine** (blood), the **phlegmatic** (phlegm), and the **melancholy** (black bile). The **temperament,** or mixture, of these four humors was held to determine both a person's physical condition and a person's type of character. When a particular humor predominated, it pushed the character in that direction: choler = anger; sanguine = geniality; phlegm = cold torpor; and melancholy = gloomy self-absorption.

Imagination. See **Fancy** and **Imagination.**

Imitation and **Parody** are forms in which a literary work refers back to a predecessor. In the eighteenth century, an "imitation" was a poem that deliberately echoed an older work, but adapted it to subject matter in the writer's own era, usually with a satirical aim directed against that subject matter; Alexander Pope, for example, wrote a number of satires on contemporary life that he entitled *Imitations of Horace*. A **parody** imitates the characteristic style and other features of a particular literary work—or else of a particular literary type—but in such a way as to satirize that work, by making it either amusing or ridiculous. *Northanger Abbey* (1818) by Jane Austen was a good-humored parody of the popular horror-narratives known as gothic novels. (See **Burlesque** and **Gothic**.)

Irony, Sarcasm. **Irony** and **sarcasm** are both ways of saying one thing but implying something sharply different, often opposite; they differ, however, in the way they go about doing so. **Sarcasm** is a broad and taunting form of using apparent praise in order in fact to denigrate. The patriarch Job is bitterly sarcastic when he replies to his would-be comforters (12.2), "No doubt but ye are the people, and wisdom shall die with you." On the other hand, Jane Austen, in the first sentence of *Pride and Prejudice*, overstates the case just enough to make it drily **ironic** when she writes, "It is a truth universally acknowledged, that a single man in possession of a good fortune, must be in want of a wife." (See **Irony**, in the section "Figurative Language," above.)

Legend. See **Myth** and **Legend**.

Logic. See **Rhetoric** and **Logic**.

Masque. The **Masque**, which flourished during the reigns of Elizabeth I, James I, and Charles I, was an elaborate court entertainment that combined poetic drama, music, song, dance, and splendid costumes and settings. For a discussion of the English masque, see the introduction to Jonson's *Pleasure Reconciled to Virtue*.

Myth and **Legend.** **Myths** are hereditary narratives that purport to account, in supernatural terms, for why the world is as it is, and why people act as they do; they also often provide the rules by which people conduct their lives. Myths often spring up to explain rituals, the original meanings of which have been forgotten. A system of related myths is called a **mythology**—a body of supernatural narratives believed to be true by a particular cultural group. The term "myth" is frequently extended to a set of supernatural narratives that are developed by individual poets such as William Blake and W. B. Yeats. Three great mythologies that have been exploited by poets long after they ceased to be believed are the classical (Greek and Roman), the Celtic, and the Germanic. A **legend** is an old and popularly repeated story, of which the protagonist is not supernatural, but a human being. If a hereditary story concerns supernatural beings who are not gods, and the story is not part of a systematic mythology, it is usually classified as a **folktale**.

Naturalism. See **Realism** and **Naturalism**.

Neo-Classic. See **Gothic, Classic, Neoclassic**.

Novel. See **Romance, Novel**.

Ode. A long lyric poem serious in subject and treatment, written in an elevated style and, usually, in an elaborate stanza. See the discussion of English odes in the headnote to Jonson's *Ode on Cary and Morison*.

Pastoral, Eclogue, and **Pastoral Elegy. Pastorals** (from the Latin word for "shepherd") are deliberately conventional poems that project a cultivated poet's nostalgic image of the peace and simplicity of the life of shepherds and other rural folk in an idealized natural setting. The form was established by the Greek poet Theocritus in the third century B.C.E.; it is sometimes also called an **eclogue,** which was the title that the Roman poet Virgil gave to his collection of pastorals. The pastorals by Theocritus and later classical poets often included a poem in which a shepherd mourns the death of a fellow shepherd; from these poems developed the highly conventional **pastoral elegy,** a type that includes such great laments as Milton's *Lycidas* and Shelley's *Adonais. Lycidas* is also an example of the extension of the classical pastoral to a Christian range of reference, by way of the use of the term "pastor" (shepherd) for a parish priest or minister and the frequent representation of Christ as "the Good Shepherd."

Pathos, the Sublime, and Bathos. In Greek, **pathos** signified deep feeling, especially suffering; in modern criticism, it is used in a more limited way to signify a scene or passage designed to evoke the feelings of pity or sympathetic sorrow from an audience. An example is the passage in which King Lear is briefly reunited with his daughter Cordelia, beginning

> Pray, do not mock me.
> I am a very foolish fond old man . . .

In the first century the Greek rhetorician Longinus wrote a treatise *On the Sublime,* in which he proposed that sublimity ("loftiness") is the greatest of stylistic qualities in literature; the effect of the sublime on the reader is *elestasis* ("transport"). In 1757 Edmund Burke published a highly influential treatise on *The Sublime and Beautiful,* in which he distinguished the sublime from the beautiful, not as a stylistic quality, but as the representation of objects that are vast, obscure, and powerful, which evoke from the reader a "delightful horror" that combines pleasure and terror. **Bathos** (Greek for "depth") was used by Pope, in a parodic parallel to Longinus' "sublime," to signify an unintentional descent in literature, when an author, straining to be passionate or elevated, overshoots the mark and falls into the trivial or the ridiculous.

Poetic diction, Poetic license, Poetic justice. Poetic diction denotes a distinctive language used by a poet which is not current in the discourse of the age; an example is the deliberately archaic language of Spenser's *The Faerie Queene.* In modern critical discussion, the term is applied especially to the style of eighteenth-century poets who, according to the reigning principle of decorum (see **Decorum**), believed that a poet must adapt the level of his diction to the dignity of the high genres of epic, tragedy, and ode. The results were such phrases as "the finny tribe" for "fish" and "the bleating kind" for "sheep." **Poetic license** designates the freedom of a poet or other literary writer to depart, for special effects, from the norms of common discourse and of literal or historical truth. Examples: the use of archaic words, meter, and rhyme, and the use of other literary conventions. (See **Convention.**) **Poetic justice** was coined by Thomas Rymer, in the later seventeenth century, to denote his claim that a narrative or drama should, at the end, distribute rewards and punishments in proportion to the virtues and vices of each character. No important critic since Rymer has adopted this doctrine, except in a highly qualified way.

Quarto. See **Folios, Quartos.**

Realism and **Naturalism** are both terms applied to prose fictions that aim at a faithful representation of actual existence; they differ, however, in the aspects of that existence that they represent and in the manner in which they represent them. The realistic novel attempts to give the effect of representing ordinary life as it commonly occurs. Realistic novelists such as George Eliot in England and William Dean Howells in America present everyday characters experiencing ordinary events, rendered in great detail. **Naturalism,** which the French novelist Émile Zola developed in the 1870s and later, is based on the philosophy that a human being is merely a higher-order animal, whose character and behavior are determined by heredity and environment. Zola, followed by such later naturalistic novelists as the Americans Frank Norris and Theodore Dreiser, typically represents characters who inherit such compulsive instincts as greed and the sexual drive and are shaped by the social and economic forces of family, class, and the milieu into which they are born. Naturalistic novelists also often display an almost medical candor in describing human activities and bodily functions largely unmentioned in earlier fiction.

Rhetoric and **Logic.** **Rhetoric** was developed by Greek and Roman theorists as the art of using all available means of persuading an audience, either by speech or in writing; it had a great influence on literary criticism in the Renaissance and through the eighteenth century. Rhetorical theorists developed a detailed analysis of figures of speech, largely as effective means to the overall aim of persuasion. In the present century, however, the analysis of such figures has been excerpted from this rhetorical context and made an independent and central concern of language theorists and literary critics. See **Figurative language. Logic** is the study of the principles of reasoning. Logic may be used to persuade an audience, but it does not, like rhetoric, avail itself of all means of persuasion, emotional as well as rational; instead, logic limits itself to a concern with the formal procedures of reasoning from sound premises to valid conclusions.

Romance and **Novel.** Medieval **romances** were verse narratives of adventure, usually about a knightly hero on a quest to gain a lady's favor, who encounters both natural tribulations and supernatural marvels. The term "romance" has since come to be opposed to realism (see **Realism** and **Naturalism**) and is applied to prose fictions that represent characters and events which are more picturesque, fantastic, adventurous, or heroic than one encounters in ordinary life. The **novel,** as distinguished from the prose romance, undertakes to be a more realistic representation of common life and social relationships and tends to avoid the fantastic, the fabulous, and the realm of high derring-do. (See **Realism.**)

Sarcasm. See **Irony, Sarcasm.**

Satire designates literary forms which diminish or derogate a subject by making it ridiculous and by evoking toward it amusement, or scorn, or indignation. In **formal satire,** such as Alexander Pope's *Moral Essays*, the satire is accomplished in a direct, first-person address, either to the audience or to a listener within the work. **Indirect satire** is not a direct address, but is cast in the form of a fictional narrative, as in Swift's *Gulliver's Travels* or Byron's *Don Juan*. For a discussion of the backgrounds of English satire, see the introduction to Donne's *Satire 3*.

Sublime. See **Pathos, the Sublime,** and **Bathos.**

Symbol. See **Allegory, Symbol, Emblem, Type.**

Tradition. See **Convention** and **Tradition.**

Type. See **Allegory, Symbol, Emblem, Type.**

Wit and **Humor,** in their present use, designate elements in a literary work which are designed to amuse or to excite mirth in the reader or audience. **Wit,** through the seventeenth century, had a broad range of meanings, including general intelligence, mental acuity, and ingenuity in literary invention, especially in a brilliant and paradoxical style. From this last application there derived the most common present use of "wit" to denote a kind of verbal expression that is brief, deft, and contrived to produce a shock of comic surprise; a characteristic form of wit, in this sense, is the epigram. (See **Epigram.**) **Humor** goes back to the ancient theory of the four humors and the application of the term "humorous" to a comically eccentric character who has an imbalance of the humors in his or her temperament. (See **Humors** and **Temperament.**) As we now use the word, **humor** is ascribed both to a comic utterance and to the comic appearance or behavior of a literary character. A humorous utterance, unlike a witty utterance, need not be intended to be comic by the speaker, and is not cast in the neat epigrammatic form of a witty saying. In Shakespeare's *Twelfth Night,* for example, Malvolio's utterances, as well as his appearance and behavior, are all found humorous by the audience, but his utterances are never witty and are humorous despite his own very solemn intentions.

Zeugma. See **Chiasmus** and **Zeugma.**

PERMISSIONS ACKNOWLEDGMENTS

Index

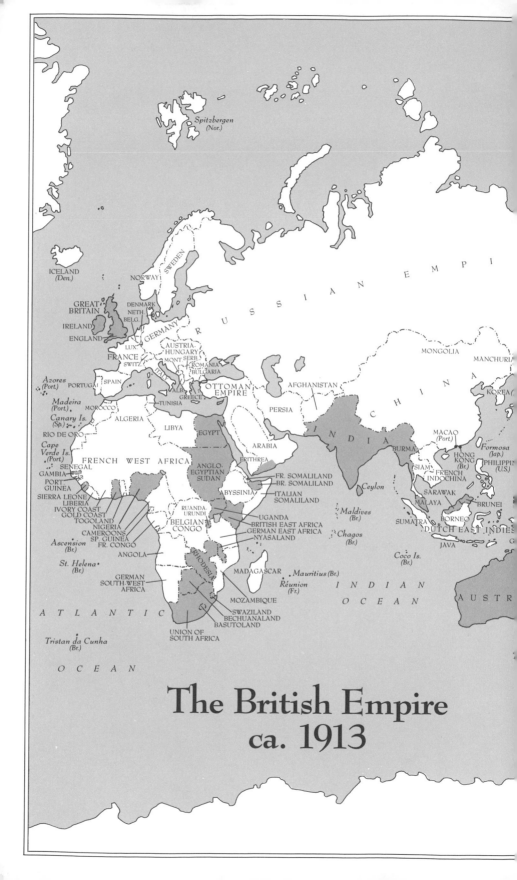

The British Empire ca. 1913

GREENLAND
(Den.)

ALASKA
(U.S.)

C A N A D A

U N I T E D
S T A T E S

A T L A N T I C
O C E A N

Bermuda
(Br.)

Bahamas (Br.)

HAITI
DOMINICAN REPUBLIC
Puerto Rico (U.S.)

MEXICO

BR.
HONDURAS

CUBA

Guadeloupe (Fr.)
Martinique (Fr.)

JAMAICA

Grenada
(Br.)

Barbados (Br.)
Trinidad (Br.)

GUATEMALA
EL SALVADOR
HONDURAS
NICARAGUA
COSTA RICA

PANAMA

VENEZUELA

BR. GUIANA
DUTCH GUIANA
FR. GUIANA

COLOMBIA

Galapagos Is.

ECUADOR

B R A Z I L

PERU

BOLIVIA

PARAGUAY

CHILE

ARGENTINA

URUGUAY

Falkland Is.
(Br.)

P A C I F I C

O C E A N

Hawaiian Islands
(U.S.)

I F I C

E A N

hall Is.

go

mon Is. (Br.)

e Hebrides
(Br. & Fr.)

edonia

NEW
ALAND

Marquesas Is.

French Polynesia

Tahiti

Chazaud